Monster Collection

Introduction by Scare Street
Written by Ron Ripley, David Longhorn,
Sara Clancy and A.I. Nasser

Edited by Emma Salam

Thank You and Bonus Novel!

We'd like to take a moment to thank you for your ongoing support. You make this all possible! To really show you our appreciation for purchasing this book, we're giving away one of our full length horror novels. **We'd love to send you a full length horror novel in 3 formats (MOBI, EPUB and PDF) absolutely free!** This will surely make chills run down your spine!

Download your full length horror novel, get free short stories, and receive future discounts by visiting **www.ScareStreet.com**

See you in the shadows,
Team Scare Street

Pound of Flesh

Wrath and Vengeance Book 1

Written by Sara Clancy

Chapter 1

The night stained the red desert sand a deep, purplish hue. There were no town lights around to compete against the stars for mastery of the sky. So they choked it, slashing across the ebony backdrop in almost solid bars. The air had become uncomfortably cold, but the sand still clung to the blistering heat of the day. With every step, it seeped through the soles of Aleksandr's boots and made his feet sweat.

Aleksandr tried to hide his pained limp as he made his way to the back of his car. He made sure to train his eyes on the ground as the driver's door opened. Since the high beams were on and the keys still in the ignition, the car began an annoying repetitive 'ding' that made Aleksandr's head throb. His father didn't come to the back to help him but instead headed forward towards the edge of the ravine. The canyon, gouged too deep into the earth for the lights to reach, weaved out to the horizon like squirming snakes.

Desert nights were rarely as dark as believed. Under the uninterrupted moonlight, the world was blue and purple with only patches of black. Normally, Aleksandr loved this time of the day. He sought solace in the cold and protection in the darkness. But those comforts were lost on the nights when he was forced to deal with a corpse.

The trunk wrenched open with a protesting squeal of rust, and a small light flickered to life. It was barely strong enough to fight the shadows away from the wrinkles in the plastic sheeting. Without hesitation, Aleksandr reached in to grab the wrapped body. Rigor mortis hadn't set in yet, but it still wasn't an easy task to pull out so many pounds of dead weight. All the tugging and yanking worked the plastic sheeting out of place, making it crackle loudly in the silence of the night around them. Blood bubbled free from the new gaps. It dripped to the earth and sunk into Aleksandr's shirt. He'd stink of it for days.

If it had been up to him, Aleksandr would have opted for dismemberment. Just like they did with all the others. Of course, that option was more time consuming and far messier, but it also spared his now beaten body from any heavy lifting. This man hadn't died easy. He had fought like hell and inflicted as much damage as he possibly could before Aleksandr had managed to crush his skull. The second he had died was the second his father had stopped being amused. He wanted the body out of his sight immediately. He hadn't even given Aleksandr enough time to stop his sliced-up knuckles from bleeding before demanding that he carry the corpse to the car. The drive hadn't helped. His body trembled, each shake provoking fresh waves of pain. His head felt like it was about to explode, and his right eye was already starting to swell. Chopping the body up would always be Aleksandr's choice of disposal. Not that he could ever say it. His parents were only too keen to enforce their laws. And this one they held almost sacred. Only women were dismembered and scattered like scraps. Men remained intact.

Clenching his teeth, he turned his pained scream into a low grunt as he finally succeeded in tossing the body over his shoulder. The soft sand shifted under his boots as he staggered his way to the edge of the sheer drop. Only a few feet separated the trunk from the canyon, but he might as well have been scaling Everest. His legs wobbled, his shoulder screamed, his ribs threatened to snap.

Still, he kept putting one foot in front of the other. Aleksandr hadn't survived nineteen years with his family by showing weakness. Sitting on the hood of the car, his father gave no impression of paying any attention to what was happening. Aleksandr felt the weight of his eyes all the same.

With sharp jerks, Aleksandr tried to work his long, matted fringe out of his eyes. The high beams had destroyed his night vision. One wrong step and he would topple over the edge along with the corpse. Bracing his feet wide, he lurched forward and threw the body off his shoulder. It was a bad toss. Instead of dropping over the edge, the dead weight slammed solidly against the minimal patch of earth that still separated Aleksandr from the edge. Dust stirred at the impact. The barely there wind caught the particles and helped them spread into a weak cloud. It coated Aleksandr's throat and forced him to cough. It took so much effort not to scream in agony that he almost missed that the body at his feet was moaning. For one, heart-rending moment, Aleksandr wanted to drop down and hurriedly tell the man to remain silent. But before he could fully form the thought, his father had started laughing.

"He's still alive?" His pleased tone chilled Aleksandr's skin. Nothing good had ever followed that tone. "Think he's got it in him to go another round?"

Aleksandr looked down at the bloodied and broken form that half stuck out of the plastic wrapping. It barely looked human anymore. The gargled groans it released certainly didn't sound like one, either.

"Aleksandr?" his father snapped. He wanted an answer.

"I think it was just a death rattle."

That made his father snort, a sound of pure disgust. There were few things Petya Sokolovsky detested more than weakness. It didn't matter what form it came in, or how deserved it was, or even if it actually existed. If Petya decided it was there, the person was no longer human. They were little more than a toy. And all of his games were cruel.

Aleksandr closed his eyes as the man at his feet began to twitch. Small moans rattled from his chest. He was still alive. Aleksandr raised his foot up but he was too slow. Petya had noticed. He was sliding off the hood of the car, calling out for Aleksandr to stop. Kicking the man over the edge would be direct defiance of his father. Not something he could risk in his current condition.

"That's not a death rattle. He's alive."

"Not for long," Aleksandr barely raised his voice and kept his face down, hiding behind his hair.

"What's wrong with you?" Petya said as he stalked closer. "Here you have the gift of playing a little longer and you give it up? I sometimes wonder if you're my son at all."

"I'm hungry." Knowing that wouldn't satisfy his father, Aleksandr shrugged his shoulders and chanced a look at him. "And he's not much of a challenge like this."

Petya paused. Watching his father contemplate that, Aleksandr's heart began to throb painfully. Blood rushed through his ears like a surging tide. It left him barely able to hear the man's low mutterings. *Just let him die*, Aleksandr silently pleaded. *Let me finish it.*

"What are you waiting for?" Petya snapped, his Russian accent thickening the words. "No point wasting your energy on him. Just toss him over the edge already."

Aleksandr caught himself as he slumped with relief, making his fall look more like eagerness to obey. The moonlight glistened off of the man's wide eyes and turned his blood a rich, almost tar-like black. As he twisted his hands in the plastic, Aleksandr watched fresh blood oozing from the corner of moving lips. He wanted to reassure the man that it would be over soon enough. One drop. One more hit. The fall would be enough. As the plastic crackled between his fingers, he realized that the man wasn't just moaning. There was a method to the pattern. He was trying to talk. Aleksandr's stomach churned. The begging was always the worst part.

"Hurry up or I'm coming over there," Petya snarled.

Aleksandr looked down at the man's pleading eyes. There would be a lot more bloodshed if Petya came over. *He's suffered enough.* Aleksandr began to pull, but the man's hand snapped out, and with the last of his strength, latched onto Aleksandr's forearm. The hold was loose enough to pry off, but the shock of the touch froze him in place.

"They'll come for you." The man's words were barely more than broken gasps. But he repeated it until Aleksandr was sure that he had heard it right. "They'll come."

It wasn't the first time he had heard such threats. Victims liked to cling to the idea that there would be some divine retribution. That Aleksandr and his family would be forced to pay for all the evils they had inflicted upon the world. That someday, somehow, they'd get their revenge. Aleksandr didn't have the heart to tell them that it was a fool's dream. The truly wicked never had to pay.

"Alek!" Petya snapped.

Following his father's command, he began to lift. The man's nails dug into Aleksandr's skin. Even then, the grip was flimsy and weak, but they found some of the raw wounds and opened them again. Fresh blood seeped between the man's fingers and trickled down Aleksandr's arm. The two streams of black blood merged into one grotesque puddle against the plastic.

"They'll come for you," the man jerked as he choked on his blood. His fingers trembled as he squeezed. Each word made was a desperate struggle. "I unleash the Furies on you. They'll kill you all."

Aleksandr furrowed his brow. He was sure that he had heard the words right, but it was gibberish. Nonsense. But an alluring thought all the same. The man surged on, fueled by fury to voice his last words.

"They'll grow strong on your terror," he sputtered. "Show you hell before they drag you down into it."

Aleksandr silently watched the man drown on his own blood. People promised wrath and vengeance, but at the end of the day, Petya and Olga were always the ones left standing.

"Nature itself fears the sisters," the man whimpered.

"I'm getting bored!" Petya yelled, barely interested in the words he was saying.

Enough. Get rid of him already, a voice hissed in Aleksandr's head. Pure disgust filled the man's eyes as Aleksandr reached down towards him.

"You'll all die," the man whispered. "Screaming."

Leaning closer, Aleksandr flicked his gaze to his father, making sure that he wouldn't hear the response.

"I hope so."

And with that, Aleksandr yanked. One hard movement that made his muscles ache and the wounds on his back rip open again. The plastic unraveled and hurled the man over the edge and into the abyss. He didn't make a sound. Not even one little gasp to break the silence. Only the soft thud signified the end of his life. It always seemed like there should be something more significant to the moment, but there never was.

Lifting his hand up, Aleksandr studied the blood that coated his arm. Black tar. Like his blood had rotted within his veins. It should smell more putrid. There was no way that their blood hadn't mingled.

Aleksandr slowly lowered his arm as his father walked lazily to the edge. It would be impossible to see all the way to the bottom of the pit at this time of night. And even if he could, the rocky, uneven ground would hide the body from sight. Those facts didn't stop his father from peering over the rim and releasing a low whistle.

"Well, he went harder than most," Petya laughed. Looking over his shoulder, he cocked his head to the side. "What are you sulking about now?"

"Nothing," he said. "Our blood mixed. I'm going to have to get tested again. In case he was sick."

Petya dismissed his concern with a wave.

"He looked healthy enough."

Aleksandr let the subject drop. The health of Petya's children had never been a top priority. Blood dripped down sinking into the sand, each drop pulsing in time with Aleksandr's slowing heartbeat.

"I'm bored," Petya declared. He smacked a hand against Aleksandr's shoulder as he headed back to the car. The blow found a wound with expert precision. "Don't worry. I've already picked out the next one for you. Won't take me long to snatch them up."

Aleksandr hunched his shoulders and lowered his head. "There's no rush."

"Good God boy. Where is your appetite?"

"I don't want to bring attention to the family."

Petya was silent for a moment. The seconds pressed down on Aleksandr. All he could do was wait to see if his father would accept the excuse or drive a knife into his back.

Finally, his father smiled and hit his shoulder again. "For your birthday, we'll take the risk. It's a special occasion, right?"

"Right," Aleksandr mumbled.

"They're perfect, Alek," he laughed, low and dark and promising all sorts of horrors. "They'll give you a real challenge."

Chapter 2

"Evelyn!"

Hearing her coach's shout over the noise and clatter of the gym, she furled herself until her back pressed against the punching bag. Heavy bag sit-ups weren't new to her exercise routine, but she still couldn't grow to the disorientation of hanging upside down. More precisely, seeing the flipped version of the gym while blood rushed to her head as the punching bag she was latched onto swung slightly. Her thigh muscles trembled as she forced them to squeeze the bag a little harder. There was still the threat that they'd give out and drop her onto the padded flooring. Still, it was a nice rest for her aching stomach muscles.

Her coach waved an arm over his head to grab her attention. "You're up," he called. "Show some hustle!"

Contracting her abs, she hurled herself against gravity to grab the top straps of the punching bag. The chain rattled as she gripped it, released her legs, and dropped to the mat. It was strange to be upright again. Even stranger to walk. She was halfway across the gym before she had worked the wobbly feeling from her legs. She relished the sensations. The pull and throb and twitch of well-worked muscles. It was proof that she was pushing herself.

Like the others who would be sparring today, her kit was set out on a folding table near the boxing ring. Ankle brace, headgear, mouth guard, and gloves. She strapped them all into place with practiced ease. Even so, her coach wasn't above looking put out and annoyed by the time she was set. There was no real anger in it. Coach Wallace kept his praise rare but heartfelt. No shallow appreciation or coddling. Evelyn liked that about him.

Coach Wallace pulled up one of the middle ropes as he stomped down on the other, giving her enough room to sweep inside the ring. The mat gave a little under her feet. A slight, passive resistance that was familiar and welcoming and always enticed her to bounce on her toes. Her opponent for the night was already inside. Evelyn and Judy shared a smile that was all excitement and anticipation. There were a good few women who worked with Coach Wallace, but not many wanted to turn kickboxing into their profession. So, even though Evelyn and Judy were dancing on the edges of different weight classes, they were often put together for training. That was fine by Evelyn. Judy was always fun. She was fast, dedicated, and fierce.

"Tired?" Judy teased.

"I can still take you down."

"Prove it."

"You know, we really need to get better at trash talk," Evelyn said.

Judy chuckled and turned to Coach Wallace. "Yeah. Aren't you supposed to teach us that or something?"

"You're both idiots," Coach Wallace dismissed. All he needed was a wave of his arm to get the women to focus.

They exchanged a smile, tapped their gloves, and waited for the bell. Evelyn loved this part. When adrenaline heightened the anticipation. When her muscles twitched with the barely contained desire to throw itself into the fight. Before the ding had faded, Judy was already taking advantage of her extra height. Her roundhouse kick snapped straight towards Evelyn's head. There was a little time to block the blow, but the impact still hurt. It made Evelyn stagger to the side, but she quickly regained her footing enough to jab at Judy's exposed inner thigh. That got her to back up a little bit. They danced around the ring, exchanging strike for strike, both reveling in the contest. The pain and motion and the way their bodies came alive. It was addictive.

Crouching to avoid a right hook, Evelyn spun on her toes and slipped behind Judy. The world passed by in a blur, but one figure caught her attention. A man she had never seen before stood by the far wall. Spending most of her time at the gym, she knew everybody by sight at least. But she'd never seen this man before. Stranger still, he was dressed in a crisp button-down shirt and slacks instead of workout gear. What stuck out the most was that he was staring at her. Unwavering. Unblinking. A smile slowly curled his lips, provoking a chill to creep down her spine.

Judy's fist crashed into Evelyn's temple. Hard enough to make her brain slosh and stagger her vision with a flash of white. Muscle memory took over, and Evelyn surged up, her arms braced before her to shield her head. It took a flurry of blows for Judy to tire enough for Evelyn to counter strike and force her back. As the fight raged on, her mind flooded with adrenaline. Everything that didn't exist within the ring faded into the background. The score. The stranger. The weird feeling that he had provoked. None of it mattered more than landing the perfect punch. There was a serenity in the chaos. Time passed in a blur and it wasn't until Coach Wallace marked the end that she realized how exhausted she was. Bracing her hands behind her head, she sucked in deep breaths. She felt accomplished. Proud even. And that dulled the pain.

Yanking off her headgear dislodged her band, and allowed a cascade of sweaty crinkly hair to drop around her face. Evelyn puffed out her cheeks with annoyance. It was hard to get it all back in order with gloves on, even if they were fingerless. Struggling with the task, she listened to Coach Wallace's breakdown of the bout. He never sugar-coated anything, and one slip up was enough to earn a girl another hour of fundamentals. She had hoped that he hadn't noticed her moment of distraction. Of course he had, and then shackled her with another round of burpees as punishment. Her arms wobbled at the thought of the pushups, although the jump that followed wasn't going to be a picnic.

Judy got the same punishment for her weak footwork and they ended up side by side on the mats in the corner. Before they performed the first one, Evelyn knew that it was going to evolve into a contest. One that only ended when someone collapsed. Evelyn hit the mat first.

"Have my arms fallen off," she asked as she flopped her limbs wide.

"No." Judy was breathing too hard to laugh properly.

The mat wasn't comfortable, but she pressed her cheek against it anyway. "Are you sure? I can't feel them anymore."

"Wait until tomorrow."

Evelyn groaned at the prospect. Closing her eyes, she melted against the ground and wondered if it was weird that she had grown to love the scent of clean sweat and plastic.

"Hey," Judy said as she thumped her back. "Come on. Coach is saying to hit the showers."

After a halfhearted attempt to get up, she groaned. "Nope. I live here now. Bring food and a blanket."

"I can get you a sweat towel and your water."

"Food," she pleaded. "Hungry."

"Well, I guess you'll have to suck it up."

With a pained groan, Judy lurched to her feet, leaving Evelyn to reluctantly follow.

Standing still long enough to have a shower helped settle her overworked muscles. That didn't mean that she wasn't utterly exhausted as she struggled to get into a pair of denim jeans and a crop top. It was convenient that she lived in such a warm climate. Having worked so hard to create her visible six-pack, she wasn't likely to let a bit of cold weather keep her from showing them off.

It wasn't an easy walk out of the gym, harder still to lift her hand to wave goodbye, but it was important to maintain certain standards. So she suffered through her farewells, and she headed out into the night. After hours in the gym's air conditioning, the heat of the summer night was stifling. Like a swamp turned airborne. She pulled the strap of her gym bag higher onto her shoulder as she cut across the parking lot.

Take out, she decided. *Take out is a necessity.* There should still be time to grab something decent before all the restaurants closed. But she would have to hurry. Pulling her phone out of the bag's outer pocket, she hit the speed dial. Her dad answered before she had time to get it to her ear.

"Hey, princess. How was training?"

"Excruciating in the best possible way," she grinned. "I'm starving and plan to gorge myself on burgers and fries. You in?"

"Are the fries curly?"

"Are there other types of fries?" she replied with a scoff.

"I have never been so proud of you." The line crackled as he laughed. She was yet to have a phone that could handle his hyena cackle. "I'm in. Extra pickles on the burger."

Her brow furrowed as she approached her car and noticed a small mass gathered in the shadows around one of her rear wheels. A few more cautious steps and the lump took form. *A child?* Curled into a ball, face pressed against its knees and arms wrapped around its legs, Evelyn couldn't see a hint of its face. Not that she would have recognized them anyway. Evelyn was an only child and never had a reason to come into contact with kids. Another step and she could see that its slight shoulders were shaking as it sobbed.

"Dad, I think there's a lost kid here."

"What?" he asked. "Where is 'here'?"

"The gym parking lot." She looked around. Cars filled the parking lot; their crooked rows lined up enough for the windshields to reflect the glow of the lamp posts. Beside the child, it looked like she was alone. "I can't see their parents."

"Wait, 'their'? I thought you said that there was only one child."

"There is." She lowered her voice to a whisper to add, "I just can't tell if they're a boy or a girl."

The whole situation was sending up warning flags in her mind. So it didn't surprise her when her father asked, "Is anyone with you?"

She looked again. While she could spot some people in the windows of the gym, none of them approached the lot.

"No."

"Princess," he said, his voice thick with warning.

It was enough to have her take a small step backwards, but she couldn't bring herself to just straight up abandon the child.

"Hey, kid." She called out louder than she should, given the small distance remaining between them. The child didn't respond. It just kept sobbing. "Are you alright?"

The sounds turned into a mix of squeaks and little gulps of air. Listening for a moment, she was reasonably sure that the child was actually trying to say something.

"I can't understand you," Evelyn said.

"What's going on?" her dad asked.

"The kid is crying."

"Maybe their parents are inside."

Evelyn was sure that her father didn't exactly believe that. He was paranoid by nature and there was enough in this cocktail of events to make them both hesitate. She looked over her shoulder at the gym door and called out for Coach Wallace.

"He's nice," she assured the child. "And I'm sure he'll be able to fix this all up. Come on, let's go to the light. They have air conditioning."

Her soft words didn't offer any solace. If anything, the child only dug deeper into a ball and wailed louder.

"Oh, no. Don't cry. It's all going to be okay," she said hurriedly. "Just take a deep breath. Stay here. I'll be right back."

"Evelyn?" her father asked over the line.

"I'm going to head back in and get Coach Wallace," she told him.

"Keep me on the line."

"Sure."

As she searched the serene parking lot again, the pit of her gut gave a sharp twist. It was a familiar sensation. A warning that something wasn't quite right. Hard experience had taught Evelyn to listen to what her body told her, and she wasn't about to start ignoring it now.

"I'll be right back," she told the child and turned, intent on jogging back to the open gym door.

Before she could take a step, however, a small voice mingled with the sobs. It was inaudible at first, but definitely there, and full of pleading. Evelyn took another look around, hoping to spot someone else. Preferably someone who was better with children. Evelyn hadn't interacted with kids since she was one. But the parking lot was still empty. Quiet.

"I'm sorry, I still can't understand. What are you saying?" she asked the child.

The mumbled squeaks grew louder but still didn't make much sense.

"I'm just going to go find a responsible adult, okay?"

"No!" the child suddenly wailed.

"Look, kid, I'm only a teenager myself. What we need is an adult." She tried to make it sound light, hoping that it might get the kid to calm down a bit.

It didn't stop the little hiccupped sobs that shook the kid's shoulders, but at least the child lifted its head. Evelyn forced a small smile as she studied the child's face, hoping that she might recall the features. A few people here had kids. She might have seen them in passing. No older than nine years old, the child still had some baby fat to round out their cheeks, making their chin appear a little more pointed. Seeing their face didn't help her to decide if the child was a boy or a girl. Everything about them seemed to have been carefully crafted to hover in a non-committal middle ground. In the dark, it was hard to tell what color the eyes were, but they were naturally wide and large, making the child's neutral expression look doe-eyed and pleading. They also made it easy to see that there weren't any tears. All that crying and they hadn't shed a single tear.

Evelyn took a step backwards. "What's your name?"

The child didn't answer. Only stared. The unblinking expression instantly reminded her of the man in the gym. The skin on the back of Evelyn's neck chilled.

"Well, kiddo, I'm going to go get help."

"Don't leave," the child said. Their voice was light, almost breathless, and gave their words a Russian accent.

"I think I saw your father inside. I'll be right back."

"Don't leave."

"Would you like to come with me?" She kept the phone to her ear with one hand and reached out to the child with the other.

The child locked their eyes onto Evelyn's offered hand like it was trick.

"Come on," Evelyn said, trying to keep her growing concern out of her voice. "It's okay."

Timidly, the child lifted their hand.

"That's it," she encouraged.

The little fingers curled as the hand hovered in the air. It would be impossible for the child to reach Evelyn without getting up, but that seemed to be a line that they weren't keen on crossing.

"I just want to help you," Evelyn said.

A wild, shrill scream severed the silence. Evelyn barely had time to snap her head up before the creature rushed towards her from the shadows. It had a human form but didn't move like one. Sharp jolts and twitches rattled the body as it approached with incredible speed.

The light only hit its face for a fraction of a second. It was still enough to sear the image into Evelyn's mind. Grotesque, mangled, bloated with rot and twisted into an expression of pure fury. Its eyes were gone, the surrounded skin shredded as if they had been savagely gouged out.

Evelyn's arms instantly snapped, her feet slipped into a fighter's stance, and her hand painfully squeezed the phone as it tried to ball into a fist. But the impact didn't come from the monster charging towards her. The back of her skull exploded with searing pain. A blinding white light consumed her vision, returning only as a blur when she collapsed to the hot asphalt. Another blow came before she could gather her senses. A storm continued within her skull, slushing her brain about, leaking blood out into her hair, forcing her eyes to roll every time she tried to focus.

"Evelyn?" Her father's frantic voice pulled her from delirium.

The ground lurched and swayed.

"Evelyn?!"

Her vision cleared enough to see her phone a few inches beyond her fingertips. The screen lit up with an almost ethereal glow as her father called her again.

"Dad." She couldn't get her voice to work. Every muscle shook as she reached towards the mobile. It was kicked away by the tip of a polished shoe. Evelyn lifted her head to try and see where it ended, but even that small movement almost made her vomit. Blood dripped down the sides of her neck in steady streams. She barely had time to acknowledge that sensation before rough hands gripped her wrists and yanked them behind her back. A click and slide, and restraints bit savagely into her skin.

"Open the door," a man with a thick, Russian accent hissed.

"Evelyn, who is that?" her dad screamed. "Princess, answer me! What's happening?"

"Dad," she croaked.

Swallowing thickly, she filled her lungs, but her scream faltered as she was hurled to her feet and shoved into the back seat of her car. The seats felt strange against her cheek. A dozen items she hadn't cleaned out jabbed painfully into her at all angles. Every heartbeat pulsed behind her eyes and brought a fresh wave of pain. Vaguely, she realized that she was losing consciousness. Nothingness dragged her down like an undercurrent. It became an unbeatable battle to keep her eyes open. Even the sudden roar of the engine and the rumble of the moving car couldn't draw her back to the surface. Lights flashed against her eyelids over and over. *Streetlights. The highway.* The words bubbled up through the thick haze of her mind. *Dad.*

"Good job, Ivan. I'm proud of you." The voice was deeper than the child's. A man. But held the same strong accent.

"She's still talking," the child said.

"She'll pass out soon enough." The man sounded pleased. Entertained. "Hopefully she'll show a little more fight for Aleksandr."

The child didn't respond to that and the man began to play with the radio. *Dad.* Evelyn hadn't known that the word had passed her lips until she heard the man laughing. The sound made her stomach roll as it chased her into the darkness.

Chapter 3

Aleksandr jerked awake. Before he had even opened his eyes, he had grabbed his hunting knife, the end of the hilt pressed hard against his sternum. With the solid doors closed tight, the air inside the walk-in cupboard had become humid and thick. The unbearable heat carried the stench of his sweat and made more sweat bead across his skin. Lying in complete darkness, he held his breath and strained to hear any trace of movement.

His parents didn't take well to any attempt to keep them from doing what they wanted. But they cared very little if their children lived in squalor. Aleksandr had taken full advantage of that to conceal his alarm system. Beer cans and other debris covered his floor; enough that it was nearly impossible to move about his room without making some noise. The next sound made his hand clench the knife. Sweat seeped between his fingers as he tried to trace the path of the noise. The floorboards creaked softly, telling him that the intruder was creeping towards his bed.

The following silence crushed Aleksandr as he waited. It didn't matter that he had anticipated the sound. The next clatter still made him flinch. It was closer to the wardrobe than the first.

"Alek?"

The small whisper made the air rush from Aleksandr's lungs. The knife slipped from his hand as he sagged with relief and the sweat-soaked hair of his fringe tickled the bridge of his nose. Stretching out, he tapped the door with the tip of his boot. It didn't take long for the door to crack open slightly.

The thin slip of moonlight might as well have been a spotlight. Squinting against the glare, he peered up to see his younger sibling lean into the gap. It wasn't easy to tell Nadya and Ivan apart in the best of conditions, let alone in the dark. The twins had perfected their charades to the point that they could possibly live their entire life as the other and their parents would never notice. *Not never*, a voice in the back of Aleksandr's head whispered. *They'll hit puberty soon enough.*

The thought terrified him. Being a biological relative had never protected anyone from Olga and Petya Sokolovsky's appetites. People like them couldn't be without playthings. And there wasn't a level of depravity that they didn't take as a personal challenge. The idea that they could someday be without a victim when little Nadya looked like a woman chilled Aleksandr to his core. She wouldn't be off limits. No one ever was.

He shoved the thought aside, turning his attention back to the moment and the child standing nervously before him. Shoulders hunched, fists balled into their pajama pants, head hung low.

"Nadya," he said with a sleepy smile. The jacket he had been sleeping on shifted under his hand as he pushed himself into a sitting position. "What are you doing up?"

"I had a nightmare."

He nodded. Years had forged the word into a code. Like a few of the Sokolovsky children before her, Nadya hadn't outgrown her bedwetting stage. From what Aleksandr had read, it was common enough reaction for children facing trauma. It was probably one of the healthier responses, all things considered. Smiling, he lurched to his feet.

"Have you showered yet?"

"No. I was worried mother would hear the running water."

Aleksandr grunted at that, hoping that the sound would cover his relief that he wouldn't have to go anywhere near the upstairs bathroom. If Nadya and Ivan had noticed his disgust for that room, or bathrooms in general, they had never mentioned it. Aleksandr preferred it that way. Having been born long after Timofey's death, all the twins knew about him was what Aleksandr had told them. His crooked smile. His easy nature and love of building sand castles. That's how Aleksandr believed the twins should know him, and all he wanted to remember. They never needed to know how he had been murdered. Or where he had taken his last breath.

"We'll take the sheets to another house. Wash them there," he whispered as he slipped his hunting knife into its sheath.

Nadya waited for him to attach it to the waistband of his jeans before she said, "Mother will notice."

"We'll put mine and Ivan's in with it. If she says anything, we say that I couldn't sleep so I did some laundry."

She nodded once. It wasn't a motion of agreement, but more like she was just filing away the lie. Her hands tightened in the front of her soiled pajamas.

"I'm sorry to wake you," she said.

Crouching down in front of her, Aleksandr gently flicked her downturned forehead.

"What a stupid thing to say," he said.

Using the back of her hand, she rubbed her forehead, a small smile curling her lips. Hooking his hands under her arms, he lifted her up and sat her on his hip. Partly because he didn't want to risk her waking up mother by hitting any more cans on their way out, but mostly because she needed the hug.

The damp material of her pants pressed against his side, but he didn't pay it any mind. The only thing that bothered him was the pain that still strummed through him. A few days had passed since his last fight, and most of the swelling had gone down, but it still hurt.

As silent as ghosts, they moved down the hallway and slipped into the twins' room. There wasn't anything that distinguished the two bunks. Identical sheets. Identical toys. Sitting his sister on the railing, he picked up the nearest teddy bear and passed it to her.

"Hold Teddy for me."

She clutched the toy to her chest with both arms.

"I had a nightmare," she said meekly.

They both knew that wasn't the real course. All things considered, delayed bedwetting wasn't the worst way mental trauma could manifest itself. He'd take it over self-harm or suicidal tendencies any day. For a nine-year-old, however, it was mortifying. So, they lied. She blamed her dreams, he pretended to believe her, and they carried on like it had never happened.

"Zombies again?" he asked.

She nodded.

"They aren't real."

"Ivan has a book that says they're real in Haiti."

"Haiti's a long way off."

"But if it can happen there, it can happen anywhere," she insisted, tugging restlessly on the teddy bear's arm. "We have a lot of dead bodies just lying around."

Aleksandr crouched down in front of his sister, resting his forearms on his thighs.

"They aren't real, Nadya."

She opened her mouth, but he cut off her protests.

"Even if they were, they won't be able to get you. Scavengers would get them before they could cross the desert."

"The girls are kept closer," she pouted.

"They're all cut into pieces," he said with a smile. "What's a shin going to do? Or is it the elbows that I need to look out for?"

A small giggle bubbled up out of her even as she continued to clutch her bear tight.

"Do you think the severed feet hop?" he asked. "Or do they move forward by wiggling their toes?"

Scowling playfully, she smacked him with the teddy. Smiling at her, he reeled back at the blow, arms held up as if to fend off the attack. The reaction earned him another giggle and he decided it was time to get back to work. He didn't get far in stripping the bed before she chastised him.

"I'm old enough to help, Alek."

The reminder of her age made him slightly ill. "Alright. Go and get some clean sheets."

Carefully and quietly, she slipped off of the ladder and left the room. He had both beds stripped by the time she got back and, between them, the sheets were changed in record time. They didn't need to discuss it to know that they would work by moonlight alone. As Aleksandr rolled the items into one giant ball, Nadya flopped down on the sheets to squirm and kick, working in as many wrinkles as possible. By the time they finished, it was as if nothing had happened.

"Do you think Petya and Olga know?" Nadya asked.

He knew she wasn't talking about her nightly accidents.

"No. They'd already be using it against you." He placed a hand on the back of her head. "There's nothing to be ashamed of, Nadya. We're all afraid of something."

"They're not," she said softly.

"Wait until you see Petya around a snake."

She blinked up at him. "Snakes? Really?"

Aleksandr nodded.

"But ... he's a killer. He can't be afraid of snakes."

"Fear doesn't have much to do with logic," he said.

Contemplating that for a moment, she asked, "Is Olga afraid of snakes?"

"No. But she'd flay herself before she'd set foot on the thirteenth floor. And no, I don't know why, she's never shared that. I just know she's paranoid of the number thirteen."

Nadya, having apparently gotten what she needed from the conversation, deemed it over. She snatched up a change of clothes and they left the room. Once again, Aleksandr carried her. It was better to keep it down to one set of footsteps. He barely dared to breathe as he crept down the staircase. Nadya's tight grip on his shoulders tightened with every step, and she never stopped looking around.

The house was dark, but he knew the path well. Years of hunting had made it second nature for him to move silently. Although, at this point, it wasn't just noise that was the threat. Every shadow was thick enough to hide their dark-haired mother. He went straight to the front door. The little click of the turning door handle sounded like a cocking gun in the tense silence. Nadya flinched at the sound and pressed her face against her brother's shoulder.

Gathering his courage, Aleksandr opened the door and slipped outside. The night air was just as oppressive as it was inside. Living off of generators made the concept of air-conditioning a luxury. The first step onto the sand made him lose balance slightly. Nadya's nails found some cuts on his arm and reopened them as she scrambled. Blood oozed out.

"Let go," he whispered hurriedly.

She obeyed and leaned back enough to level him with a hurt look. "I'm sorry."

"Show me your hand," he said.

There were a few smears of blood on her fingertips.

"I didn't mean to," she said.

"Shh, I'm not mad. Do you have any open cuts?" Realizing that she wasn't following, he added. "Father still hasn't given me the money to get tested yet."

"You think that the man was sick?" she asked as he started walking again.

He shrugged. There wasn't much need for any more discussion. Nadya had been through this enough times to understand. Until he was sure that he was healthy, they were to be careful. It wasn't an easy task to keep their blood from mixing given their family lifestyle. All they could do was try.

Getting across the shifting sands was harder with Nadya in his arms, her weight throwing him off balance. She was still clinging to his neck, her small arms starting to shake with fear as well as the cold, but he didn't have the heart to put her down. Having grown accustomed to the heat that remained within the walls, and the wardrobes specifically, Aleksandr felt the chilly wind all the more. It might have been smarter to grab a jacket.

Navigating by the moonlight, he made his way to the back of the house and further off to a neighboring building. Years had passed since the last of the residents had left the town, leaving the land for the desert to reclaim. It had done so with a vengeance. Rolling dunes had invaded the homes through open doors and broken windows. The wind had eroded some structures down to their foundations, while others had sandy hills that reached to the rooftops. The why and how of the evacuations was a mystery he couldn't be bothered looking into. Drought. Famine. Mine closure or disease. It all ended up the same. No one cared about the town anymore. People had forgotten about it. And, in doing so, had created the perfect killing field. A whole town entirely under their control. A place removed from the rest of the world by impassable wastelands. They could do whatever they wanted here. And when they had turned their home into a grotesque slaughterhouse that no amount of bleach could clean, they could simply move to another building and start again.

It even had running water and electricity, although both were sporadic and unreliable. The original plan must have been for self-reliance. Their water came from underground lakes that filled during the short rainy season, and their power from an industrial generator. Their father had succeeded in getting the engine to run, but there was no saving the wires. Time and weather had ravaged them beyond repair. Flicking on a light switch came with the potential of electrocution. Exhausted and sore, Aleksandr was glad that one of the few functioning buildings was nearby.

In a relatively short time, the load of laundry was on and they were trudging back up the hill. He would deal with the rest in the morning. Uphill was much harder. Shifting Nadya so that she was clinging to his back, he hunched forward and kept moving. The sand kept slipping them back down. So it took three steps to go the distance of one.

"Alek?" Nadya whispered.

He lifted his head and his stomach plummeted. Headlights severed the darkness with razor precision. The car twisted around the winding roads but was unmistakably coming closer. *Father's home.*

"Alek."

She filled the world with every ounce of her fear.

"It's okay," he replied as he lowered onto one knee.

Without further prompting, she crawled off of his back and lay down on the sand beside him. Keeping low, the sand and darkness worked in their favor.

"We'll wait until he's inside and then sneak back to your room," he told his sister.

"What if he sees us?"

He swallowed thickly. "Then I'll distract him and you run. You were never out here. Got it?"

She nodded. Lights flashed across the dune and they both plastered themselves to the sand. Aleksandr didn't recognize the sound of the engine. *A new car*, he figured. His fingertips twitched with the urge to reach for his weapon, but moving right now wasn't a smart option. Slowly, Nadya's fragile hand pushed across the sand to wrap around one of his fingers. She was big enough to grab more but didn't try to. The engine stopped and the sound of car doors opening and closing cut the following silence. Aleksandr's heart slammed against his ribs as he waited. A new car meant a new plaything. They went in the shed. This routine promised a window of opportunity for Aleksandr to get Nadya back into the house unseen.

Then he heard the front door open. They'd need a new plan. Their mother was awake. Nadya's fingers tightened to the brink of pain as they listened to their parents greeting each other with an exuberant passion. Olga and Petya were creatures of the same nature. They wallowed in their obsession with each other. Feeding and validating the other's darkest desires, urging them to 'greatness', both demonically liberating and deadly possessive at once.

Petya had been a brutal and cruel man since birth. The kind of abomination that people wouldn't be surprised to hear was a serial killer. Impulsive, reckless, bored with the clean-up; it hadn't taken long for police to start closing in. Petya had intended Olga to be his last thrill. He had decided to die by a hailstorm of police-issued bullets rather than submit to capture. Olga was stunning and alluring and *there*. In his haste to have his fun before the law caught up with him, he hadn't done his research. The night he had come for her, Petya had no idea that Olga's body count and twisted appetite dwarfed his own.

Eerily beautiful, with long midnight hair, framing sharp bone structure and enormous dark eyes, Olga looked about as frail and delicate as a bird. It was all a trap. A lure. She had the looks to draw people in and the fake charm to put them at ease. Petya was a firestorm. All heat and fury. Olga was a tornado. Unpredictable and far-reaching. Both were deadly in their own right. Combined, they were devastating. And Ivan was alone with them. Ivan, and a new victim that would be whipping them into a bloodlust.

Nadya's hand tightened on Aleksandr's finger again. He barely turned his head, just enough to meet her gaze out of the corner of his eyes and nodded once. *I'll get him out of there*, the motion promised. Her grip loosened, and a slight pain filled Aleksandr's chest. Soon she'd be old enough to know he wasn't as infallible as she assumed. *But not tonight*, he told himself. *Tonight, keep them safe.*

They waited in tense silence, the air freezing their backs. Barely daring to breathe, they listened until their parents' declarations of devotion switched to Russian. That was a sign that they'd be too wrapped up in each other to notice anything else.

Finally, the switch happened. Aleksandr's muscles tensed as he waited to hear each of his parents' voices. The second he did, he was on his feet and hurling Nadya into his arms. He bolted towards the back door of the house. The hill of sand wasn't any easier to maneuver at speed. But time didn't allow him to stop or slow down. As he neared the top, he found himself thankful that his father had claimed another victim. There were limited areas in town that the average car could surmount without getting bogged. If he had been using his own, he could have parked in the back, unknowingly stranding them. Their victim, however, seemed to have one that needed to stick to the wind-cleared road out front. It gave them a chance.

The car's high beams looked as bright as a prison spotlight. Its range, however, was limited, leaving the bulk of the building to the shadows. Aleksandr made sure that every step he took kept him within the darkness and the safety it provided. Panting hard, he reached the back door and pressed his back against the stable wall. The weathered paint cracked off at the slight touch. Set upon stilts, the house had a narrow crawlspace and a few stone steps that led to the door. Both offered hiding places for a child as small as Nadya.

Coaxing her to crouch down on the far side of the stairs, away from the intruding light, he caught her eyes and pressed one finger to his lips. She didn't really need the reminder to be silent. The gesture was a sign to stay put and that he'd bring Ivan to her. She nodded and crawled deeper into the shadows under the house, slipping into them until he could barely see her.

Aleksandr waited until she was settled, even though every second of hesitation made his chest hurt a little more. *Make sure she's safe,* he told himself. *You can't lose them both.* It took everything he had to keep his expression neutral as images of Dimitry and Tanya flashed across his mind. The twins that had come before. The ones Aleksandr had utterly failed. Dimitry had been alone with their mother when she was bored. Olga had her fun, and Dimitry had ended up buried under the back porch.

His nails dug painfully into his palms as he clenched his fists. It wasn't enough to keep the memory away. Tanya, cold and broken on the floor. Her face twisted in a silent scream, eyes wide and accusing as they started to rot, the air exposure staining the whites a murky brown. Aleksandr flinched at the memory of their father patting his shoulder. *She had to die, Alek,* the ghostly voice whispered in the back of his head. It was still light with laughter. *I didn't want to break up the set.*

It was perhaps one of the greatest cruelties of life that, while so many good people struggled to have kids, Olga and Petya Sokolovsky kept churning out twins. Dimitry and Tanya didn't need to die, but Aleksandr had learned from it. There was no safe place around their parents. *Never draw attention to yourself,* he had taught them long before they were old enough to understand. *Be quiet. Be still. Be obedient. I'll come and get you the first second I can.*

Nadya finally stilled. Aleksandr instantly turned and started across the back of the house. The sand helped to quieten Aleksandr's steps as he crept around the side. Pressed against the building, he was once again grateful for his limited height. Malnourishment had a way of stunting growth. Most surviving Sokolovsky children rarely broke five feet. Aleksandr had made it to five-foot-five and thankfully stopped there. The taller he was, the harder it would have been to hide.

A windstorm last night had worked the sand into a sharper slope than usual. It left the crawl space exposed at the back of the house and smothered it at the front. So when he reached the front edge of the building, he didn't have to worry about anyone spotting his legs.

Crouching down, he peeked around the corner. Olga and Petya were mauling each other, half leaning against the hood of an old VW Bug. They had already discarded numerous items of clothing, a few of which had landed on the crumpled body at their feet. Aleksandr spared the woman a glance. It was hard to tell if she was alive. Dumped at an awkward angle and with her dark skin that mixed with the shadows, he couldn't be sure if she was breathing. He couldn't trust a hysterical fit to work as a distraction.

Ivan obediently stood where Petya would have ordered him to. By the front of the car. Dead center of one of the high beams. Desperate not to look at his parents or the woman, he stood with his gaze locked straight ahead. His thumbs were digging into the sides of his index fingers, hard enough to already draw blood. Aleksandr watched as his younger brother struggled to stop the nervous habit. It was never safe to bleed around Petya and Olga. Especially now. Sadists didn't have much use for an unconscious victim. Until their newest conquest opened her eyes, they had all the desire to torture and no outlet. Getting their attention while they were in this state would be the same as thrashing about in shark-infested waters.

Aleksandr's breathing evened out as he lingered in his hiding place. His heart, however, continued to pound against his ribs like a panicked bird. Ivan was utterly exposed. Checking that all other parties remained occupied, Aleksandr wiped his sweaty palms off on his shirt. There was no getting rid of the layer of sand. It was irritatingly grainy against his skin as he curled his now dry hand around the hilt of his knife. Pulling it free of its sheath created barely more than a soft rasp. At that moment, it seemed as loud as a scream.

Shifting back on his heels, he reached up to scratch the sharp edge against the side of the house. The brittle paint cracked off quickly, the specks dancing in the gentle breeze like falling snow. It didn't seem to move out from around the corner far enough, so he pushed them further with a few steady breaths. He was getting lightheaded by the time he succeeded to get the flurries into the ring of light.

Come on, Ivan, Aleksandr silently encouraged as he continued the process for a few moments more. The flakes were tiny but didn't look like sand. If luck were on their side, his brother would see the difference. When almost a minute had passed, Aleksandr crouched, lowered his hand, and rocked forward again, peeking around the edge. Ivan still faced straight ahead. *You can do it*, Aleksandr thought. *See.*

A small furrow flashed across Ivan's face, leaving just as fast as it had come. He stood solid as his eyes flicked towards the house corner. Aleksandr lifted his chin, needed a sign that his brother saw him and not just the shadows. The tension in his chest eased slightly as he watched Ivan cross the fingers of his right hand. They could fill a dictionary with their secret language. *I see you. I know you're there. I don't know where Nadya is.*

That's my boy, Aleksandr thought. A small smile tipped his lips as he nodded to his brother. *I've got her. I'm here for you.* Checking that the coast was still clear, he lifted his hand, not drawing it into the light but high enough to coax Ivan forward. A fine tremor ran the length of Ivan's body as he turned his head towards Olga and Petya then back again. Aleksandr kept his hand up. Not demanding. Waiting.

Eyes locked onto Aleksandr's face, Ivan took his first tentative step. A solid slap of metal made the brothers jump. Neither breathed as Olga pulled away from her husband, her eyes passing right over Ivan as she tossed her hair back. Then their captive moaned and released a sudden groan. The night filled with sound. Cackling laughter, pained moans, and the solid thump of Olga stomping and kicking the unconscious girl.

Ivan refused to look, but his eyes widened, his body tensed. He was preparing to get caught up in the attack. They hadn't remembered him yet. This was their chance. The best one they'd get. Aleksandr motioned him forward, and Ivan broke into a sprint. His little arms pumped wildly as his feet tripped over the uneven sand, threatening to bring him to the ground.

The instant he was close enough, Aleksandr lunged forward. In one smooth motion, he snatched Ivan up, spun, and raced back down the slope. Aleksandr held his brother just a little too tight. Enough that they both had a little trouble breathing. With one arm wrapped around his bony waist and the other cupping his head, Aleksandr tightened his grip until Ivan didn't need to hold on.

Skidding to a stop by the back stairs, he forced himself to put Ivan down, taking care not to nick him with the knife. Cupping his brother's cheek with his free hand, he quickly looked him over. There wasn't any visible damage.

"Did he hurt you?" Aleksandr asked a little breathlessly.

Ivan shook his head. "Nadya?"

Right on cue, she slithered out from under the house and gathered her twin in a bone-crushing hug. It was clear that they needed the moment, the reassurance. Even if they had no time for it.

"Come on," Aleksandr coaxed. "We're supposed to be asleep."

Parting to stand side by side, the twins blindly reached out and found the other's hand. They clutched at each other tight enough to hurt. Neither so much as winced. Holding hands was a coping mechanism, one they had developed around the time they realized that their hands were attached to their arms. Back then, their parents had found it adorable. Then amusing. But now that they were approaching their tenth birthday, Aleksandr just hoped that they wouldn't start reading something more sinister in the gesture.

He studied their identical expressions. Terrified but ready. It was all he could ask for right now. As he grabbed the door handle, the kids cupped their free hands over their noses. He opened the door and a putrid stench wafted out over them. It hadn't smelt like a bed of roses before, but the closed door had been keeping most of it contained. Holding the knife at the ready, Aleksandr crept forward. There were numerous reasons why the kitchen was a horrible and dangerous place. Tonight, the worst of it was the rotting corpses set up at the kitchen table. Olga had become lonely while cooking one day so had decided to set a few of them up. After losing interest, she had just left them. The desert heat had accelerated their decomposition and the stench had drawn all manner of insects. It was getting impossible to make it across the room without standing in melted flesh and fat.

The twins were still close behind him as they slipped out the kitchen door and into a hallway. Silence encased them. The stench stayed. Fat did that. It went airborne, ready to latch onto skin and hair as you pass. The same reason he had always smelled like French fries at the fast food job he had held down for a month. Aleksandr led the way across the living room and foyer. The silence around them set him on edge. His parents could have easily come in while they had been moving around. Holding up a hand to keep the kids back, he hurried forward and pressed his shoulder against the front door, keeping it closed. The moment he was in place, the twins ran past him and up the stairs. He waited for them to be out of sight before he followed.

Aleksandr couldn't relax until they were all inside the twins' room. Ivan checked under the bed. Nadya checked the closest. Watching them, Aleksandr couldn't help wonder how many other kids checked to see if their parents were lurking in their rooms.

Somewhere along the way, Nadya had lost her fresh change of clothes. By the way they moved, he could see that both of the twins were anxious to have a bath. To get the stench off of them. That was out of the question for tonight. They'd have to settle for Aleksandr's preferred method. Olga and Petya were firm believers of 'go-bags' and it was perhaps the only useful habit they had given their children. They all hid bags, with everything they needed, all over the place. The twins' room wasn't any different. Dousing the children with lemon juice to kill the smell, he let them hurriedly wash off with a few bottles of water and some clean rags. They were well-skilled with the task and were impressively clean by the end.

They both opted for sleeping on the bottom bunk, pressed tight together even though there was extra space. The screaming started as he tucked them in. Even with the windows closed, the tortured girl sounded like she was inside the room with them. Both kids squirmed down in the sheets.

"That's not the new one," Nadya noted meekly.

"I guess she's still unconscious," Aleksandr said as he pulled a small box out from under the bed. "It doesn't matter to us."

Ivan stared up at him with wide, pleading eyes. "I don't like it when they scream."

Aleksandr smiled slightly as he rolled a bit of marijuana into possibly the world's smallest joint. They were small themselves. They didn't need much. He gave it and the lighter to Ivan first. He needed it more. The twins took their medicine as he readied their IPods and noise-canceling headphones. Each time they inhaled, one of those old anti-drug ads played in his head. He wondered how some of them would see the usage if they were in his position. The sole caregiver of two children too traumatized to sleep. What would they do when a serial killer insisted that they eat in front of corpses? Or worse still, when the corpses *were* the meals. How would they get them to eat? And smile afterwards? And feel anything beyond the constant looming threat of death?

Soon enough, they were done. The screaming wasn't. The blood curdling cries fought against their high to make them whimper. Aleksandr leaned forward and handed out the IPods and headphones. Before they could put them in place, he smiled.

"Can I tell you both a secret?" he asked.

They both nodded.

"I hate it when they scream, too."

They had small smiles as they tugged on the headphones and turned the music on. Both had it set loud enough that Aleksandr could hear the rhythmic beats and muffled singing. He wasn't the biggest fan of opera, but it was the best for drowning the world out. It didn't take long for the drug to work through their system, and they settled, toppling into sleep soon after.

Aleksandr leaned back against the foot of their bed, his knife ready on his lap, and waited for dawn. As the screams and begging and sobs wafted in from outside, he pulled up his legs and balled his hands into fists. It had been days since the guy he had tossed into the canyon had promised him this all would end, and nothing had changed.

Nothing would ever change.

Monsters couldn't be killed.

Chapter 4

A searing pain shoved Evelyn back into the waking world. It felt like razor blades had replaced her bones. A light flickered against her eyelids, each burst driving into her brain like an icepick. She tried to flinch away from it, but that only brought more pain. Every attempt to move, no matter how small, revealed some new damage that she hadn't known was there. From head to toe, she could feel the bruises welling up. Grinding her teeth, she whimpered through the pain and tried to think back, to pinpoint what had happened. It was as if her mind had sunk deep into a thick, static swamp. No matter how hard she dug, she couldn't reach it. She couldn't remember.

When she stayed still enough, the pain ebbed away, and she was able to process other sensations. Thin, hard rows dug into her side, uncomfortable and unrelenting as she lay on them. Carefully, she tried to wiggle away. The process was slow and excruciating. She had barely moved half an inch before her back pressed against a wall. Preparing for the agony, she forced her eyes open and looked around.

She didn't recognize the room. But then she could barely make out the floor. It appeared to be one uninterrupted slab of concrete. The air was hot and tainted with the scent of blood. Before her, an old box TV sat on a chair a few feet away, the black and white images creating the light that had flashed against her eyelids. It seemed like existence ended beyond the TV set. Blinking a few times, it occurred to her that this wasn't possible. It was just dark. Like a bottomless pit. Small gleams drew her attention. She squinted, focused on them, and realized that it was the light of the TV reflected in metal. Rows of metal.

A cage, she realized with a growing sense of dread. *I'm in a cage.* Wanting to sit up but not having the strength to do it, she settled for lifting her head. The new position set waves of crackling agony through her without giving her anything more for the trouble. There was nothing else to see. Unable to withstand the pain, she lowered her head back down, clenched her teeth, and struggled through each breath. Her eyes squeezed shut.

Ear-splitting screams shattered the silence. She bolted upright, her head scraping the top of the cage, and twisted around, desperately seeking out the source. It came from everywhere at once. Echoing. Her brain bashed against her skull. She couldn't see. The shrieks grew louder. Each one contained more horror and pain than Evelyn had ever known was possible. Latching onto the side of the cage with trembling hands, it took the last of her strength to keep from crumbling. The shrieks bombarded her ears and reduced her brain to slush. There was more than one voice. Three, maybe four, she couldn't tell. But they were close. So close.

"Where are you?!" she bellowed, unable to hear her own voice over the tormented cries.

Her vision focused enough for her to make out the images on the TV. The quartered screen displayed four different movies at once. Evelyn peered at it and realized it wasn't a movie. By the quality and rounded edges, she was sure that they were security camera footage. Each one seemed to have been from the same camera at different times. They all showed the same room from identical angles. There was little more than a table with a woman strapped to it. Each screen flickered through a collection of their own. For a moment, she couldn't make out what was happening. Her brain revolted against it. But the safety of her denial didn't last. Bile rushed into her throat when she realized what the standing couple was doing to the girls. That they were the reasons for the screams. Them and their knives, their branding irons, their pliers, their hammers and nails. It was a mercy when tears filled Evelyn's eyes and reduced her vision again. Her whole body shook violently. She couldn't breathe. Hell played out across the screen and rang in her ears.

A violent sob broke Evelyn in half. Hitting the front of the cage hard, she lost her grip on the rails and crumbled to the ground. She pulled herself into a tight ball as hot tears ran free. The screaming didn't stop. She clawed at her ears, either to smother the sound or rip them off, she didn't care. Her only thought was to make it stop. It didn't. It never would. Those screams would still be echoing in her ears until her dying day.

The sound clicked off. A shrill whine pierced her ears, broken only by her weeping and the choked whimpers for her father. She hadn't even known that she was calling for him. Each attempt to stop herself only made her voice lower and more desperate. Her lips never stopped moving.

Tinkling laughter drifted out from somewhere behind the TV. Unable to lift her head, Evelyn flopped onto her side and searched the shadows. She couldn't see anyone.

"Baby talk? Already? We haven't even touched you yet," an almost sweet voice taunted. It was a woman's voice. Evelyn searched the fractured remains of her mind but couldn't recall ever having heard it before.

Lowering her hands from her ears, Evelyn waited to hear it again, not sure if it was her imagination.

"Nothing else to say?" the voice asked.

Another Russian accent, Evelyn thought. It dredged up a foggy memory and she clung to it in an attempt to make it clear. *A boy. Or was it a girl?* The confusion sent her thoughts spiraling. She clenched her hands around the metal and forced herself to focus.

"Who's there?"

"Who's there?" the voice parroted in a high tone. "Where am I? Why are you doing this to me? It's always the same insipid questions. Can't any of you show the slightest bit of creativity?" A soft huff broke the following silence and then she continued. "I'm here, the last woman you will ever lay eyes on. You're somewhere no one will ever find you. And I'm doing this because it makes me feel good."

The muscles of Evelyn's arms vibrated with the effort of dragging herself back up into a sitting position. When she achieved it, she flopped backwards, letting the wall of the cage keep her upright. The screen still flickered. Even as she purposely avoided looking at it again, she couldn't get her eyes to adjust enough to pick the woman out from the shadows. There was nothing. As if she were suspended in the middle of a black hole.

"I don't understand," she choked out.

"Of course, you don't," the women said. "Girls like you never could. You lack the intelligence. The creativity. The vision. If you could ever understand me, you wouldn't be in the cage right now."

Evelyn kept her voice soft. "I can understand. I'm sure I can if you just explain it."

The woman laughed. "Oh, the easiest way is to show you. Shall I turn the sound on again?"

"No!" Evelyn cried before falling into a string of pleas.

It only made the woman laugh again.

"All that effort to look like a man and you're still such a simple, pathetic creature. Scared of a video. You don't know what real fear is, but you will. I promise you that."

Evelyn couldn't tell if it were the words themselves or the blow she had taken to the head. Either way, she couldn't follow. The words sounded right, but their meaning, the situation, the woman herself – none of it made sense. She rattled the cage. It didn't open. Feeling the resistance helped to clear her mind enough for some sobering facts to sink in. *I'm trapped. She isn't going to let me out. I've been kidnapped.* Her mind wanted to balk at the thought. It was too strange. Too unbelievable. This was the sort of thing she heard about on the news while safe on her living room couch. Something that was in the back of her mind but never considered an actual possibility. She walked to her car with her keys in her hand and kept her house locked up when she was alone. It was something she guarded against just to laugh off as paranoia. It couldn't really happen to her.

Desperation took hold and she slammed her hands against the side of the cage. Thrashed and kicked. Threw herself at the sides until the cage almost tipped over. The walls held strong. The woman laughed.

"Finally catching on, are you? Well done."

Evelyn leaned back and stomped both of her feet against the side. "Let me out!"

The TV was unmuted. Screams covered her frantic demands. She pressed the palm of her hands onto her ears until she was sure that her head was about to crack open like an egg. Tears burned her eyes like coals. Each movement felt like her skin would rip open. Blood seeped from the back of her head to drip down her spine. She couldn't breathe. The screams of the woman who came before her broke something inside of her. Something she didn't know was there before this moment, but now understood to be incredibly fragile. It was something that would never be whole again. She fought until her body couldn't anymore. There was nothing to show for her efforts but the blood on her palms and the pain in her legs. She pulled her knees to her chest, curling into the tightest ball she could, and wept. The sound clicked off.

"Giving up already?" the woman asked. "And here I thought you'd be a challenge for him."

Evelyn sucked in a stammered breath. "For who?"

"My boy. You're going to make him a man."

Every battered muscle in her body tensed at once.

"No, he's not going to rape you," she scoffed bitterly. "He shows no interest in such things. I sometimes worry that he doesn't have the inclination. How do people put it? Swings the other way? He always demands men, you see. Now that you mention it, it might actually be quite good for correcting that behavior. With all those muscles, you look very masculine. But no, that isn't what you're here for.

He won't touch you like that."

As the woman talked, Evelyn collected what remained of her courage. She lifted her head and focused her gaze beyond the TV.

"Then what will he do to me?" she asked.

The woman was silent for a long moment. "Would you like to see?"

Evelyn clasped her hands over her ears, preparing for the TV to be unmuted again. Instead, the room echoed with the click of the woman's shoes. Hearing them approach made Evelyn scatter back. But there was nowhere to go. The shadows congealed to create a slender frame. Caught between wanting to hide and a fierce need to put a face to this monster, her eyes flicked to the woman and away. There wasn't much to see. The woman seemed to be made from the shadows themselves. Her body was just an empty darkness impressed on the other shadows.

A sharp jerk tossed Evelyn to the side. She hadn't known the cage had wheels. Now they squeaked like nails on a chalkboard. The cage vibrated as it was rolled over on the raw, unsmoothed concrete floor. The woman pushed her around the TV and into the abyss. Evelyn couldn't understand how the woman could see where she was going. Another sharp jolt and they stopped. There was no way to tell where the woman was now. The inability to see anything let Evelyn's mind run wild. She kept imagining that her kidnapper was standing right beside her. Or crouching down, her face barely an inch from her own. The thoughts wracked her nerves until she restlessly shifted from one side of the cage to the other and back again.

Before her, a latch popped. There was a slight whoosh and the stench of blood assaulted her nose anew. She gagged on the coppery smell. If there had been anything in her stomach, it would have ended up on her lap. A soft, electrical hum cut the pregnant silence. Clicking and sputtering, long fluorescent lights flooded the area with a stark, white light. Each flash blinded her. Seared her brain until the image of the room burned onto the back of her eyes. She saw it in the darkness. A concrete room. Gray stone stained with different shades of black. Finally, the light remained on and she found that she had been mistaken. It wasn't black. It was red. Blood.

Streaks and splotches covered the walls and drenched the floor. An overlapping puddle that ranged from fresh crimson to old, deep maroon. There was no doubt that the room had been used for something grotesque. And used quite a bit. Evelyn couldn't turn away from it even as the woman stepped into the lit room. Lithe and graceful, the long black dress clung to her like a second skin. Her long heels clicked with every step as she stalked to the center of the room. Then, with her arms held up like a game show model, she sprung back around to face Evelyn.

"So, what do you think? Do you know how lucky you are? Not everyone gets to know the exact room they're going to die in."

Evelyn swallowed thickly. She didn't know what to say, or think. Every attempt to form an escape plan left her head feeling like a hollow shell.

"He's going to beat you to death," the woman continued gleefully. "Crush that little head of yours against the stones like rotten fruit. Break your bones. Turn all your organs into a stew. How long do you think you'll last? Oh, do make it fun for us."

"Your son?" she breathed heavily. The image of a big-eyed boy sitting by the wheel of her car flashed across her mind. "He's just a child!"

The woman dismissed her with an amused wave of her hand. "Not Ivan, you fool. Aleksandr. You haven't met him. Yet. It was Ivan and my husband who got you for Alek. You're a birthday present. Be sure to make it enjoyable for him."

All the words drifted to the back of Evelyn's mind as an image, a memory, surged forward. The creature that had attacked her. The horrible, nightmarish being that had hurled itself from the shadows.

"That monster is your husband?"

Fury twisted up the woman's doll like features. She stalked towards the cage. Evelyn watched the woman reach into the shadows an instant before a strong current coursed through her veins and seized her muscles. As Evelyn thrashed, her jaw squeezing tight as the pain increased and fire replaced her blood, a single word came to her. Taser.

The crackle of electricity finally stopped and the woman grabbed the top of the cage. Instead of a Taser, the woman held a cattle prod in her hand. It clashed against the metal as she shook the cage. Every so often, the button would be pressed, and a dancing stream of blue light would zip between the prongs.

"How dare you," the woman hissed, eyes blazing with rage. "My Petya is the greatest man on this earth. He is glorious. Your pathetic brain can't contemplate his magnificence!"

She stabbed the prod through the bars. Driving it into Evelyn's bare stomach. Agony held her solid. Helpless. The scent of cooking flesh and burnt hair struck her nose. Working herself into a frenzy, the woman alternated between spitting Russian words at her and sticking the cattle prod in harder. The pain built. Combining and pushing her to the brink of consciousness. Evelyn longed to topple over the edge. To fall into oblivion and leave this behind. The pain kept her in place. Locked her to reality.

"Olga?"

The fresh waves of pain stopped, but there was no real release. Electricity seemed to spark between each of her cells. Locking her joints into place. Leaving her jerking against the bottom of the cage like a fish on dry land. A male voice laughed and spoke with benevolent reprimand.

"I can't leave you alone for a moment. Didn't the other one satisfy you?"

In the corner of her eyes and edge of consciousness, Evelyn saw the woman point at her with the cattle prod. Mercifully, it didn't make contact. The bars of electricity sparked a hair's width from her eye.

"She insulted you, my love. I couldn't let that stand."

"Now, now, sticks and stones, dearest," the man chuckled.

"But–" her words cut short and the man clicked his tongue.

"We agreed. She's for Aleksandr."

The woman scowled. "I'll keep her alive."

"Alive and ready to fight are two different things. She'll be his first real kill. We want it to be a special memory for him."

There was a moment of silence before the cattle prod was left atop the cage. Evelyn longed to reach for it. To take the weapon. But she couldn't move. Tears dripped from the edges of her eyes as she helplessly stared up at it.

"Do you remember *our* first?" the woman, Olga, asked with a sultry tone.

The smile was evident in the man's voice as he replied, "You had her squealing like a pig."

The rest of the conversation faded away as Evelyn saw the shadows above her begin to swirl. They clustered and heaved like a churning ocean. Like oil and tar. Creating a colossal drop that slowly swelled and lowered down towards her. *Can't they see it? Can't they see?* If the madmen were aware of what was happening above their heads, they made no sign of it. Her screams lodged in her paralyzed throat as a needle thin nail pierced the bubble. Moving as smoothly as a scalpel, they dragged down along the curve of the droplet, splitting it in two. The creature that emerged was only vaguely human in shape. With nails as long as Evelyn's arm, it crawled free. Its bones stood stark against its skin. The sharp curve of the spine kept it forever hunched over. It scurried across the ceiling on the tips of its nails and the toes of its disjointed legs.

Look up! Look up! She screamed the words in her head over and over but couldn't get it to pass her lips. Directly above Evelyn now, the monster rotated its head. Twisting until she was forced to stare into the shiny silver disks of its tiny pupils. A smile spread across its face, rippling the skin like curtains being drawn back. Broken fangs glowed with the same ferocity of its eyes. *See it! Please, God, see it!* The couple continued to chat between them, their Russian words drenched with love and lust, completely unaware. Helpless sobs turned to whimpers in her throat as slowly, lazily, a serpentine tongue slipped out of the creature's mouth and coiled about. Her mind was still screaming as the lack of oxygen tainted the edges of her vision. The burning pupils followed her into the darkness as her eyes rolled back in her head, and she fell back, unconscious.

Chapter 5

The videos played on an endless loop. Static periodically washed across the screen of the old, clunky television set, but the sound was perfect. They had apparently rigged the room for the singular purpose of blasting the bloodied screams, pleas, and feeble babbling of the women. Their victims. And they had succeeded. Evelyn longed to cup her hands over her ears, make some attempt to dampen the ear-splitting noise, but she didn't dare move.

The noise crawled over the inside of her skull like a swarm of insects, burrowing into her brain to keep her from latching onto any constructive thought. She knew what she had to do. *Think it over. Break it into tasks. Have a plan.*

The lingering traces of electricity had already left her body. Knowing that didn't stop her hands from twitching. Each time they did, a fresh wave of fear crashed down upon her. *Stay still. Don't draw that thing's attention.*

That panicked thought made the pecking order clear. The monster that had slithered from the ceiling had beat out the serial killers. It had long since dragged itself out of her limited line of sight and escaped into the shadows.

Gathering every last ounce of her reckless bravery, she shifted her gaze. Only the flickering light of the TV pushed back against the endless pool of shadows. Pain pulsed in her eyeballs as she strained to look at every inch of the ceiling. The unfinished surface of the concrete slab offered hiding places for the darkness to remain. It tricked her more than once into thinking that she had spotted the monster, and her heart stammered every time. But there was nothing.

There was no comfort in that.

The wound on the back of her head ground against the bars of the cage as she pushed her head back. Not secure enough to get up just yet but desperate to catch sight of the monster again. *It was real.* She hurled the thought to the universe at large. A demand rather than a plea. *It was real. It had to be.* The other option was too horrific to consider. *Not now. It can't start now.*

Evelyn had learned about the giant, genetic clock ticking against her that said her mother had abducted her. Her mother had ranted that they were being hunted. That demons were snatching people and replacing them with fakes. But '*Mommy* can see them'. Evelyn shuddered as she recalled the statements that were repeated over and over again. She knew what they were doing. She wasn't going to let them get her daughter.

The psychotic episode hadn't lasted, but it had done enough. From then on, Evelyn knew her parents were lying when they told her, 'mommy's just not feeling well. She'll get better soon'. It wasn't the flu or some random bug. There was a wound in her mother's brain, or something psychic that would never fully heal. Years of soul training tests and medicinal cocktails, therapists, and crushing, accumulating debt; it had all boiled down to endurance. The three of them had lived on a tightrope, trying to be happy while knowing that a gentle breeze could ruin it all. There was no cure. And Evelyn was her mother's child. They had the same wild hair, dark eyes, and full lips. They shared a taste for spicy food and both had double jointed fingers. It wasn't out of the question that these similarities were the complete inventory of what she had inherited.

Despite this, she had hoped for a few more good years. Her mother hadn't shown any warning signs until she was in her twenties. But then, her mother hadn't been in a situation like this. Stress had a way of forcing things like this to the surface. Evelyn couldn't stomach that option right now. The monstrous deformity had to be real.

A sudden move banged her head against the bars. Pain exploded out from the wound on her skull and her vision blurred for a moment. It was oddly comforting. *A head injury. Stress. Fear.* She rattled them off and clutched them close. Any of these could result in hallucinations. Blinking rapidly, she sucked in a deep breath, feeling a fantastic sense of accomplishment when her lungs swelled. The shackles of fear weren't holding her as tightly as they had before. Taking advantage of her recklessness, she rolled onto her side and pushed up onto one forearm.

Carefully, she avoided looking at the TV screen and used its flickering light to search the room. The glow wasn't as effective against the dense shadows as she had hoped. It took a moment for her eyes to adjust and allow her to make out a few shapes, objects, and what she assumed were the walls. It was almost an afterthought to look for the couple. *The real threat*, she reminded herself.

That was a concept she had a harder time wrapping her head around. Taken by serial killers. It just didn't seem real. A vague memory of watching scary movies with her dad played in the back of her mind. She could almost hear herself bragging about all the things she would have done differently to stay alive. Cocksure and laughing. Safe in her own home. Then, she hadn't doubted that she could survive where all the characters had failed. It was a lot harder to be that confident now.

Shoving the thoughts away, she grounded herself in the moment and tried to do something useful. The room appeared to be empty. At least nothing moved within her limited field of vision. She hated not being able to hear anything beyond the recorded screams. The bare concrete ground would whisper even the slightest movement. She scanned the area restlessly until she was satisfied. No couple. No monster. No other living victims. She was utterly alone.

A sudden convulsion caught her off guard. Unprepared, she lurched to the side, her knees slamming into the bars of her narrow cage as she curled in on herself. Sparks of pain sizzled along her nerves at the impact. It took her breath away even as it cleared her mind. Nausea rolled the pit of her stomach. She dry-heaved until her stomach ached. All that came up was spit and bile. *Nothing in my stomach.* She clung to the realization and tried to think. *It takes two hours for food to work through your stomach. I ate just before training. Training took an hour. So these freaks must have had me for at least one hour.*

Pressing her lips tight, she tried to recall a map of the city. Maybe calculate where they could have taken her in that time. It was all for nothing. For all she knew, she could have been staring at the walls for two hours already. And there was no way to tell how long she had been unconscious.

Humidity thickened the air. Combined with the stale heat and the persistent, coppery stench of old blood, breathing became a forced act. One that she put off for as long as possible. Sweat drenched her workout gear. She spared a moment to account for everything. Crop top, sports bra, shorts. Only her sneakers were missing. If she tried hard enough, Evelyn could believe that they hadn't touched her.

Water dripped from the compact waves of her hair as she pushed it off her forehead. The damp tendril flopped back down to obscure her vision again. Without any other distraction, the television pulled her eyes back to the screen. The footage never faltered. All she could do was stare. Tears welled, the salt burning her eyes. They fell, as hard trembles wracked her body. She stared. Barely able to breathe past her choking sobs, Evelyn's shock held her in place, forcing her to watch the endless parade of women. *There's so many of them*, she thought as the figures writhed and screamed, begging for death as the couple gleefully cackled. *None of them survived.* The ultimate truth of that cut into the depths of her soul. *They all died. And I will, too.*

The knowledge struck her and created a bottomless, icy void within her ribs. It spread quickly, chilling her bone marrow and shattering something inside her that she hadn't even known could be damaged. The images on the screen took on a new meaning. It wasn't something that she could step back from. Something that just happened to others, not her, not in real life. She watched the horror with the certainty that she would face the same fate.

"I'm going to die here."

The recorded screams drowned out the words, but feeling her lips move was enough. Gasping for air, Evelyn glanced at the door beside her. The one that the woman had shown her. The opening to the blood-stained room. It was barely visible in the gloom. That didn't dampen the physical effect of it. Her stomach heaved, her throat constricted, every inch of her body burned with the consuming desire to topple into hysterics.

Clutching the bars of her cage until her knuckles ached, she forced herself not to look away. She needed to see it, to endure the rising, crushing panic, or she'd never accept the reality.

"They're going to kill me."

With those words, the last of her warmth faded. Her feral hysteria fell silent. There was nothing left inside her skin but the numbing cold. Barely feeling her body anymore, she slumped back against the bars and watched the television with an unblinking stare. Despair made it easier to stomach the video.

I'm going to die here. She repeated the thought until the words no longer made her flinch or whimper. Blistering tears carved paths through the sweat, blood, and grime that smeared her face. It was the only thing she felt anymore. Everything else was just gone.

There was no way for her to tell just how long shock had kept her cocooned within oblivion. But there was a benefit to it. With her mind finally silent, she was able to step back and properly assess her options. There was a choice before her. One that she had to make now, while she had the limited freedom to do so. *Should I fight? Or should I just get it over with?*

Before the question had even formed, she knew which one she was going to pick. In essence, she had decided before she had hit puberty. As she watched her mother struggle to keep her identity, her freedom, her tenuous mastery of her own mind, she'd vowed that she'd never follow. It was a battle she didn't see any value in fighting.

For some, the promise of one more minute, one more second, one more breath of life was enough to hold on to. The flicker of hope. That's what kept her mother going. Hope that someday it would get better. Hope that she could come home. Hope that they'd be a family again. But for Evelyn, the cost was too high. The terror of deterioration too great. Every woman that flicked across the screen was in the same state as the others. Utter devastation. Not just physically, but emotionally, mentally. There was nothing left. No going back. An integral part of themselves had been broken. *They had all fought so hard to live, gave up everything for it, and what did they get in return?* Even if they had survived, the best they could look forward to was what Evelyn's mother had now. A safe place. Watchful eyes. And a world of drugs to numb the pain. The remainder of their lives would pass in a functional but meaningless haze. Where nothing mattered and emotion was a concept that could be understood but never felt. No fate could have ever terrified Evelyn more. Not torture. Certainly not death.

Conviction alone wasn't enough to stifle survival instinct. It reared up in the back of her mind, continually whispering promises it couldn't keep. *Hold on. Look for an escape. Do what you have to do. There will be a chance. You can run. You can get out of this.* The siren song continued, as strong and persistent as the women's screams. They were glorious thoughts, but Evelyn knew she wouldn't listen. The proof of it was playing out before her eyes. She didn't have it in her. She couldn't do what these women did. Bring on her last breath. She'd take it now.

That didn't make the decision any less bitter. Squeezing her eyes shut, she tried to drown out the sounds of Hell and the alluring whispers. *It will hurt. Think about the pain. What if someone finds your body? What if they tell dad what happened to you?* Instead of breaking her will, that last thought strengthened it. *He'll understand. It'll be a small comfort knowing that I suffered for only days instead of months, or years, which will help him on the long run.*

Lifting her chin and steeling her spine, Evelyn forced her eyes open and stared down the screen. She'd never gone into a fight unprepared and she wasn't about to start now. Her one, brief encounter with the couple had made two things clear. The man called the shots, but the woman was the one with a hairline trigger. If Evelyn could push her hard enough, fast enough, she might lose her temper and kill her quickly. So Evelyn wanted to know exactly where those buttons were. The tapes were a golden resource. It showed both of them in their element.

Like a boxing tape, she told herself. *You've done this before, do it again. Observe. Think. How do they move? What do they think? Look for a weakness. Search for a pattern.* Being resigned to death didn't mean she was going to go easily. If she could, she'd give them hell, and take at least one of them down with her.

***

The sun seared Aleksandr's back like burning embers. Sweat had long since turned his thin shirt damp, but it didn't offer any relief. It only added to the stifling humidity that hovered over the smoldering sand. He could feel his exposed shoulders cooking in the heat and spared a moment to rub a bit more dirt onto his skin. The particles clung to his beading sweat, creating a thin layer of protection. All the while, he continued to keep his eyes on the cougar in the distance. It continued to ignore him and prowl further along the edge of the canyon.

Straightening once again, Aleksandr followed the animal, careful with his steps. Small clusters of rocks rose up from the loose sand here and there, creating a broken barrier between him and the drop-off. Each footstep disturbed the sand, and when the wall wasn't there to stop it, the grains washed over the rim and dusted down the canyon. Aleksandr could barely pick up on the sound himself, but it put the cougar on edge. There was nothing but open desert between him and the animal he had been tracking for the past few miles. It seemed fine with Aleksandr keeping it company so long as he didn't bother it.

With a vast distance between them, they had walked together into the wasteland of sand. Aleksandr had just been buying his time. Not for the shot. He'd had that for a while. This whole process was just about drawing out the experience, having an excuse to stray from the house, to keep away for a little longer.

Avoiding his parents was a dangerous game. The majority of the time, it was a matter of 'out of sight, out of mind'. But then there were other days, when they felt restless, unfocused, or threatened. On those days, getting out of their way without raising attention was a matter of survival. That didn't make it any easier. Proper preparation and dumb luck were both needed to escape punishment. Hunting was one of the few things they allowed. For the twins, it was schoolwork. Aleksandr didn't believe for a second that either of them cared about the twins' education. They found the whole process tedious and left it for Aleksandr to deal with. Today was special. An opening that only came once a year. Today was his and Radmiar's birthday. They were twenty.

Aleksandr held an extraordinary hatred for his twin. From the moment they were born, Radmiar had strived to live up to the Sokolovsky family morals. He had been their parents' most studious pupil and had graduated their hellish school with honors. To the point that their parents had unleashed him upon the world on his fifteenth birthday. Radmiar had left with a gleeful smile and a shiny knife, and had thrived. Aleksandr knew that it was a horrible situation for the general public, but he was just grateful that his demonic sibling was away from the twins. And he did serve his purpose. This day was devoted to Radmiar, and their dedication gave Aleksandr and the twins the perfect opportunity to slip away for the day.

Ivan and Nadya had been carefully squirreled away, hidden amongst the field of abandoned buildings, far enough that their parents would lose interest before they ever found them. There, they could safely catch up on the mountain of schoolwork they were behind on. Aleksandr was hoping that they would put it off for a while and take the opportunity to play, as children should. They had both been snickering as he had left their hiding place. So there was a decent chance that they were planning on putting their work aside for a while. A small smile played across his lips as he thought about it. His birthday had become the best day of the year. His parents were distracted, the twins could exercise a bit of independence, and he could catch his breath.

Wandering the desert helped to clear his mind. There was nothing out there to disturb the blanket of sand or mar the peaks and valleys of crimson stone. The utter isolation allowed him to indulge in one of his favorite fantasies. When he was younger, he had read a novel about aliens and far off planets. No matter how many times he wracked his brain, he couldn't recall the title, but the adventure had remained lodged firmly in his mind. And with it, the idea of being alone on a vast, desolate planet. Just him and the sheer nothingness of space. Alone in oblivion. There was such delightful, blissful comfort in that.

Stalking along the rim of the canyon, he noticed that the massive cat had gained a greater distance than he had anticipated. He crouched low and lifted his rifle, lining the cougar up in the scope. Olga had a fixation with firearms. Even at the age of eight, he hadn't been surprised that his request for a hunting rifle had resulted in him receiving an AK 47 Kalashnikov. She didn't care that the military-grade weapon was ridiculously ill-suited to the task. She liked her toys, so he had to make do.

His tight grip held the rifle as still as stone, tracking the cougar through its mounted scope. The brilliant colors of the desert made him wonder if he could get the twins interested in the games he used to play. The sunburnt red sands would be perfect for pretending that they were on Mars, Pluto, when the night came, and the temperature dropped. Or maybe they were still young enough to come up with an alien planet all on their own.

The twins hadn't taken to his first attempts to draw them into the world of make-believe. Logically, he didn't know what he had been expecting. They had their own games and tricks to serve as their coping mechanisms. Nadya adored the sea. Sharks, sunken ships, mermaids, and all of the mysteries that remained hidden in its depths. Ivan took more interest in ghosts and myths. Naturally, the Bermuda Triangle had become their common ground. Still, he couldn't entirely give up the hope that he could pass on something of value to them.

So far, his greatest success had been camping. Tonight, with their parents distracted by their traditional prolonged phone call with Radmiar, was the perfect chance for them to slip away. They'd be able to push further out. Find a place where no one else had ever been. Open fire cooking, Ivan's ghost stories, and falling asleep under the stars. Aleksandr couldn't think of a better way to spend the first night of his twentieth year.

Something caught the cougar's attention and instead of heading into the canyon, it began to turn in tight, restless circles. The motion quickly shifted from disturbed to distress. Aleksandr looked around them both with the scope and without, but he couldn't find anything that would be terrifying to the predator. By the time he focused back on the cougar, its rapid movements had kicked up enough dust that it obscured his vision.

The canyon was full of carnivores. Not by natural design. They were attracted to the dumping ground and now the regular supply of corpses. An overabundance of predators made territorial disputes common, and Aleksandr assumed that he just couldn't see the second animal in the fight.

Deciding to keep his distance until this battle ran its course, he held the rifle's scope level again and slowly sunk down onto one knee. Maybe this would spare him a bullet. He just hoped they didn't fall over the edge. Since he didn't have a car, getting the animal back to town was already going to be a nightmare. But dragging a few hundred pounds of dead muscle up a broke sheer mountain face was not how he wanted to spend the vast majority of his day.

Aleksandr aimed at the sights on the dust pile and curled his finger around the trigger. He didn't fire. Not yet. Deepening his breathing, he adjusted his grip, preparing his body to take the recoil. The ball of sand and fur drifted back and forth a few feet. Aleksandr twisted his torso to follow it with the barrel. He was approaching an uncomfortable angle when he heard it. A dry, bony rattling.

Freezing in place, he looked out of the corner of his eyes, searching the exposed piles of rock and rumble beside him. The trail caught his attention first. *Shit*, he thought sharply. Although, as a part of his mind mentioned, it was probably a situation deserving of stronger language than 'shit'. Still, the word repeated in his mind, both in Russian and English. He couldn't berate himself enough for missing the snake trail. The soft sand had left a perfect indent of the slithering path. All the while, the rattling continued without pause, drawing his eyes to a deep, shadowy cave formed by two piled slabs of stone. The rattlesnake's forked tongue flicked out, tasting the air just a few inches off of Aleksandr's elbow. *Well within striking distance*, Aleksandr noted.

There was barely room for it to move within the tight confines of its hiding place. Still, its stony brown body curled relentlessly over itself. Aleksandr recognized its intent instantly. It was working itself into a better position, gearing up to strike. Aleksandr locked his arms, his joints, clenched every muscle in an attempt to remain perfectly still. *Not fast enough to bring the barrel around*, he thought, forcing his breathing to remain long and even, his heartbeat slow. *Nothing to block it with.*

His hunting knife felt heavy and useless against his hip. Close at hand but still too far to be of any use to him. It would strike before he could even brush his fingers against the hilt. As if sensing his thoughts, the rattlesnake shook its tail with renewed ferocity. Every other sound fell away until the clatter of bone-like scales became the only sound left in existence. Aleksandr glanced down at the bare skin of his arm. In a stained and torn singlet, there was nothing to stop the snake's fangs. Nothing to protect his dust smeared skin or the veins underneath. *The venom will reach your heart long before you get back*, a voice whispered in the back of his head. Careful not to move his head, Aleksandr looked around at the sun-drenched land. Sand and stone stretched out to the horizon. The sky was a brilliant, cloudless blue, disturbed only by the lazy swirls of a bird. *All things considered, this isn't that bad of a place to die.*

Acceptance or not, Aleksandr wasn't going to do anything to hurry the snake's decision. There was still a chance that it would choose to let him be. Their stalemate stretched out until his joints began to protest the unnatural position. His legs steadily grew numb and filled with rolling currents of pins and needles. The Kalashnikov became a crushing lead weight. As time passed, it became impossible to stop the fine tremors from working their way along his arms. The movement was tiny. The rattlesnake spotted them instantly.

It moved faster, head weaving from side to side, tail rattling harder. Aleksandr clenched his jaw and held his breath, trying to master his body again. But his screaming muscles longed to be released. His vision narrowed down to only the snake. Death was looming ever closer, and it became harder to silence the part of him that relished the idea of leaving this life behind. Rattlesnake venom wasn't a pleasant way to go. But not the worst by far. He knew that from experience.

Six hours if the snake is mature and its bite true, he thought. If it's not, the death time could take up to two days. That soured the thought. Not so much as the mental image of the twins. Whatever siren call death held for him, he knew that the end-result would always be the same. He would do whatever was necessary to stay alive. Because he couldn't leave them alone. Not yet. Not when they were so unprepared to survive on their own.

None of that mattered. The decision wasn't his. It belonged to the little reptile with unblinking eyes and a tiny curl in its scales that looked like a mocking smile. Its tongue flicked out. The rattling sounded inside and outside of Aleksandr's head. Sweat rolled down his spine. Fire burned within his limbs. Suddenly, there was a crushing, consuming silence.

Aleksandr closed his eyes and prepared himself for the fangs to plunge into his skin. He waited. The pain didn't come. Releasing a long breath, he assessed his body, sure that his mind was just trying to protect him. Nothing.

The silence persisted, so he opened his eyes. Careful not to move, he flicked his gaze back to the little cave by his left side. Finding it empty left him brave enough to turn his head slightly. The snake was gone. He searched, not wanting to move if it had decided to curl a path around his legs. There was no retreating line in the sand. So it had to have gone over the solid stones. He looked back to the top of the tiny cave just in time to spot the upturned tip of its tail drop over the edge. It was the shortest path to the canyon but also a sheer drop for a decent distance. High enough to cause some damage.

Shocked, Aleksandr lunged for the edge. Blood swiftly flooded back through his legs, the sudden surge making him stumble. He scrambled up the cluster of rocks, flattening himself onto his stomach, and peered over the edge. The snake had landed on the nearest ledge, about half a mile down, its body easy to spot on the bright yellow stone. Its injuries robbed it of its grace, leaving it to move in jerks and twitches. Whatever pain it felt, it wasn't enough to stop it from rushing to the edge of the ledge and throwing itself off that one too. Aleksandr waited and caught sight of it, barely more than a little slip of a shadow, doing the same again. It propelled itself down the cliff side until it was too small to keep track of.

A clatter of stone snapped Aleksandr out of his shock. Instinct kicked in. He pushed up onto his knees, snatched up his Kalashnikov, and was ready to fire in an instant. It took another rumble of stone for him to think of looking down. The cougar he had been tracking had thrown itself into the open air. It landed on a far-off ledge with a solid thud. Crawling to the edge left a smear of blood on the stone. But, just as with the snake, it wasn't deterred by its injuries. With unbridled determination, it crawled itself to the edge and hurled off again.

What the hell? The thought echoed in his mind as he looked out over the massive canyon.

Dozens, hundreds of shadowy figures were completing the same suicidal leap. Animals of all species desperately throwing themselves into the canyon, sacrificing their bodies to get into the recesses of the earth as quickly as possible. Disbelief left him numb.

Nature itself fears the sisters.

The man's warning pressed to the forefront of his mind like a branding iron. *Stop it,* he commanded himself. *You cracked his skull open like an egg. He wouldn't have known what he was saying. It was gibberish.* All of his logic didn't change what he had just witness. He knew what he had seen. *They would rather die than face the Furies.* Angry at his roaming thoughts, he lumbered to his feet, barely able to keep his grip on the rifle as his arms slackened and watched it all unfold.

A tarantula scurried over his boot. Snakes he could handle. Spiders, however, made his skin crawl. Sharply kicking it off made his body twist, the motion moving him just out of the way of a charging desert ram. The very tip of its curled horn hooked onto one of the holes of Aleksandr's shirt. One hundred and thirty odd pounds of compact muscle wasn't a match for the crazed ram. The momentum alone knocked Aleksandr off of his feet, and he would have been dragged right over the edge if the old threadbare material hadn't ripped.

He hit the ground hard and rolled, the rifle clashing against his chest as dust filled his lungs. The ram leapt over the edge and Aleksandr felt that he was about to follow. One hand clutched his rifle while the other snapped out in search for a handhold. Finally, his desperate fingers latched onto the cave the snake had occupied.

Pain exploded within his shoulder joint as his grip wrenched him into a sudden stop. His legs flung around until everything below his hips dangled over the edge. Hooking one leg up onto the solid stone and shifting his weight was enough to make sure he didn't fall to his death. Huffing out a sigh of relief, he dropped his forehead to the ground. His military style desert sunglasses dug into the bridge of his nose and the hard body of the Kalashnikov was now painfully trapped between his arm and his stomach. His arm, in turn, wasn't doing so well with his body weight grinding it into the uneven stone. In all, he was uncomfortable, sore, and still unwilling to release his grip on the tiny cave that had saved his life.

His relief died the moment of the first traces of vibration. Small pebbles trembled across the ground, and a fine sheen of dust rose up to create an artificial fog around him. Aleksandr snapped his head up then instantly shoved his head back down. He barely had enough time to release his grip on his rifle and pull it free from under his body before the first of the razor-sharp hooves crashed down around him. The wild desert sheep stampeded around him like a storm. Not a single one of them hesitated to perform their deathly leap. The ground rumbled underneath him as smaller animals crawled over his back.

Then, just as suddenly as it had begun, it was over. The final, agonizing cries of the animals faded. The last dull thuds of impact shook the ground.

And it was done.

Choking on the dust that still hovered in the air, Aleksandr scrambled across the small clustering of stones, not stopping until the burning sand was under him. There, he braced his right foot, rose up onto his left shin, and snapped his rifle to the ready.

Russian born and raised, Petya had completed his mandatory military service. He had been a horrible soldier but an excellent drill sergeant and had taught all of his children well. So much so that taking the shooting position and carefully scanning the impromptu sandstorm was a task Aleksandr completed without thought. The dark, curved lenses of his sunglasses protected his eyes from most of the floating debris. For the first time, he was grateful for his parents' love of army supplies. Specially designed to endure sandstorms, the sunglasses gripped his face, clutching like a second skin and enduring the rough treatment without a scratch. The lenses muted the colors around him, turning the bright crimson sand cloud into a murky blood red. Here and there, he thought he spotted shadows. Something shifting through the churning haze. But he never got a clear sight. Whatever provoked the animals into a suicidal rampage kept itself out of sight.

The particles of sand invaded his lungs on every breath. His heartbeat filled his ear. There was little else to compete against the noise. It was quiet enough that Aleksandr could swear he caught the soft, almost chime-like sound of the sand returning to the earth. It settled over him, leaving a thin layer over the top of his weapon. A few of the tiny particles toppled off of the barrel as he panned it back and forth across the desert mist.

Steadily, one sound emerged from the haze. A hard, steady beating that he, at first, mistook for his own heart. But with each repetition, the noise grew louder until there could be no mistake. It was the sound of beating wings. Colossal wings. Ones without the rustle of feathers. Something bat-like. The settling sand stirred once more, this time scattering from his rifle in all directions at once.

It's above me.

His rapid heartbeat was like thunder in his chest. An icy chill rolled down his spine even as his hands began to sweat. Steadying himself, he tipped his face up. One powerful whoosh and the sand dispersed, clearing a small patch of the sky allowing him to catch sight of the creature that hovered above him. Aleksandr's eyes widened. *That's not possible.*

The creature's body was hunched and disjointed, easily kept aloft by the slow beat of its enormous, leathery wings. Its torso was somehow both gaunt and muscular at once, covered in a thin layer of what looked to be toughened sheepskin, exposing every jut of bone and curve of muscle. Its arms resembled something human, but mummified and tipped with claws, and it kept them close to its bulbous chest. Aleksandr trailed his eyes from its horned face to its cloven feet but couldn't believe that any of it was real. The fangs, however, his brain had no trouble processing. Without them, the monster's face would have almost resembled a horse. Saliva dripped from them as it locked its tiny, glowing red eyes onto Aleksandr and swooped.

Jarred from his shock, Aleksandr threw himself away from its outstretched claws, only remembering the cliff when he fell over it. He clawed at the side of the cliff as he fell, the rock crumbling and slipping past his fingertips. His forgotten Kalashnikov swung out wide until the strap snapped and began to choke him. Broken stone sliced open his hand, making blood slick his tenuous grip. His feet crunched each ledge they found, adding to the rainstorm of rubble that washed out around him.

Entirely unprepared to discover a decent handhold, he almost fell from his small perch in surprise. The ledge was barely wider than the width of a belt, but the security it offered left Aleksandr deliriously happy. Each heaved breath threatened to dislodge him, but he pressed tighter still. Close enough that the rough stone scratched the side of his face as he looked back up.

The dust settled once again, leaving nothing to block or distort his vision of the monster that now crouched on the rim. The monstrosity watched him with unblinking eyes that glowed like smoldering embers. Trapped in place, he could only watch as it slowly pulled its lips back in a snarl, exposing rows of splintered fangs. The sound it made was a grotesque mix of a growl and a purr. It enjoyed his fear. Delighted in his helplessness.

Tipping forward, it stretched its bony arms out towards the wall of stone. Barely able to breathe, Aleksandr wrenched one hand free and reached behind him for his dangling rifle. He flinched as each nail clicked against the side of the rock wall. The gun slipped from his reaching grasp. Above him, the creature growled again, sending fresh spirals of panic swirling through his stomach. In his desperation, he threw himself hard and swayed wildly, almost losing his grip. Rubble dropped down on top of him, the debris marking the sound of crunching stone. Still struggling for his weapon, he looked back up. Wide-open jaws consumed his attention. For one gut-wrenching moment, he thought the monster was already on him. But then other meaning slipped back into his awareness. Most notably, the good distance that remained between them. That distance was rapidly diminishing as the monster crawled head first down the wall towards him.

Aleksandr reached behind him again. Sparks of pain crackled through his shoulder joint as he strained. Blood slicked his fingertips, slipped the hilt of the gun out of his grasp every time he managed to touch it. The battle clattered against the wall. His feet struggled to keep their position as he threw himself harder into his desperate grab. Hot spit dripped onto his face as the monster rapidly closed the remaining distance between them.

Grabbing the strap, he yanked hard to slide the rifle around. Seconds felt like hours as he fumbled to get the butt of the gun in his hands. With one last surge, he managed to get it in his palm and swing it around as best he could while the strap still choked him. It was an awkward angle that made it almost impossible to properly brace for the recoil.

He fired off a shot.

The sudden kickback knocked him loose, and he slid for a short distance before managing to find another hold. All that effort had been a waste. The bullet had gone wide. Not even nicking the monstrosity. His finger trembled as he squeezed the trigger again. Again, it slid across the stone wall, barely losing any speed as it avoided pathetic shots. Its jaws stretched wide as it consumed the last distance separating them. Rancid breath assaulted Aleksandr's nose even as he tucked his head to his chin, a pitiful attempt to protect himself. One last shot and there was nothing left to do but brace for the inevitable bite.

Chapter 6

Aleksandr clutched at the wall, suspended in that torturous moment of anticipation, feeling every second as it ticked away. His blind panic couldn't last forever. Gradually, it faded. His heartbeat kept its furious pace, but he could at least think again. It dawned on him that it wasn't just a trick of perception. His surge of adrenaline wasn't playing with his concept of time. A few minutes had passed, and the monster had yet to strike.

Taking a few sobering breaths, he gathered his courage and forced himself to look up. A part of him expected to see the hideous deformity an inch from his face. Waiting him out. Wanting to see his facial expression as it tore his skin apart. But there was nothing to block the blazing sun, and he was left to squint against its glare.

A long, uneven stretch of stone rose up before him to push against the clear blue sky. Blood seeped from his fingertips as his hands shook. While it greased his already tenuous grip on the rifle, he managed to keep it pressed tight against his skin as he glanced around, searching for any sign of the beast. Nothing. Everything was in place and order. No more suicidal animals. No disgusting growls. No stirred dust or steady beat of wings. Just the glaring sun and the oppressive heat.

Aleksandr released a disbelieving, near delirious huff. Not exactly a laugh but close. He could have believed that it had all been in his head if it wasn't for the single drop of saliva that oozed through the cold sweat on his forehead. That one bit of proof grounded him. *It was real*, a voice whispered in his head. *So where did it go?*

Tightening his grip, he looked around again, this time making sure to check the ground far below. The deadly drop didn't bother him at that moment. Nor did the dozens of animals and smears of blood that marred the stone slab. What turned his flesh to ice was the distinct lack of anything that resembled the monster he had seen. If one of his stray bullets had managed to find their target, it hadn't been a kill shot. *Where the hell is it?*

While the monster remained hidden, something took his notice. Thin shadows gathered in a series of holes that worked their way up the side of the cliff. A rhythmic pattern of holes that started at the rim and stopped a few inches from his weak handholds. It took a moment for his muddled brain to figure out what he was seeing. More proof. The creature's claws had gouged chunks out of the stone and, if he reached far enough, he could touch them. The discovery made his head snap up with enough haste that he almost dislodged himself from his ledge. This time, he focused his attention on the sky. *It's the only place it could have gone*, he reasoned to himself.

"Alek!"

A jolt ran through him at the sudden bellow of his name. His hands squeezed, pulling the trigger. The bullet pinged off the canyon wall, and the recoil slammed into his hip. Unprepared, it knocked him from his perch. A sharp whine filled his ears as he scrambled to steady himself. Finally, he managed to press himself back against the stone. It burned against his cheek as his heartbeat ricocheted within his skin. As the sensations faded, he noticed the booming cackling laughter that echoed off the canyon walls.

"A little jumpy today," Petya called down to him with mirth.

Not daring to peel his body off of the stone just yet, Aleksandr slid his face up, letting his eyes do most of the work to bring the canyon rim into view. A moment later, his father's head poked out over the edge. Aleksandr could only stare at him. *Is he real?*

A familiar taunting smile stretched Petya's face, still visible despite the distance.

"What kind of idiot falls over the edge?" he bellowed down. With an edge of excitement, he added quickly, "Is there blood? An exposed bone?"

Aleksandr took a sobering breath. Or at least tried to. The swell of his chest almost pushed him free. He still didn't know if his father was real or a phantom. Either way, he reasoned that it was worth the effort of talking to 'it'.

"I'm fine."

"Shame," Petya chuckled.

Readjusting his grip, Aleksandr pushed his face up just a little more, ensuring that his voice would be clear when he asked, "Is it up there?"

The trigger was smooth and cool under his skin. It wasn't gun safety, he knew, but he wasn't removing his finger until he was entirely sure that it was gone.

"Who?" Petya shouted.

A fresh spike of fear almost dislodged him. *Who*. Not *what*. That word opened up options Aleksandr didn't want to contemplate.

"Are the twins with you? Did you bring them out here?"

If there was a benevolent spirit that gave a damn about humanity, Aleksandr knew it wouldn't listen to someone like him, but he still prayed, just in case. *Please, let them be safe. Don't let them be up there.*

"Why?" The tip in his tone was blatantly teasing.

Aleksandr clenched his teeth. A sharp snarl cut through every word as he screamed at his father, "Are they up there?!"

Any other time in his life, fear would have instantly broken Aleksandr's bravado. Today, however, fear let him clutch his rage close. Petya's voice was like an arctic breeze as he replied.

"No."

Aleksandr sagged with relief. At least, as much as he could, given his current situation.

"You better have a damn good reason for talking to me like that, boy," Petya added.

Now, his courage chose to leave him, and he was left to grapple for an excuse. Something his father would believe. He had the notion of coming up with some grand explanation, but what came out of his mouth was simply, "There was something up there! A monster!"

A long moment of silence followed.

"What the hell are you talking about?" Petya laughed.

"I saw something," Aleksandr insisted.

Petya's laughter grew louder, filling the canyon and sky. "What drugs are you on?"

"Nothing."

"Peyote and roaming the desert is a little Mason Family, don't you think? I raised you to have some higher standards."

Aleksandr released a long sigh. If Petya felt comfortable enough to mock him, then the demonic creature couldn't be anywhere within sight. And that left him with another problem. His arm was throbbing, and his fingers were going numb. If he didn't get to the rim soon, his only option was going to be down, and even that wouldn't be easy.

The moment he released his grip, the rifle swung around to tap against his spine. With near expert precision, the long, still-heated metal found the holes in his ragged cargo pants and seared his skin. He clenched his jaw and tried his best to ignore the pain. Studying his situation again didn't reveal any good options.

Waving one hand to regain Petya's attention, he shouted, "Throw down a rope?"

A wave of dust and rubble toppled down on his head as Petya shifted around for a better look.

"You got down there. You can get back up yourself."

Separation and the shield of his sunglasses left Aleksandr feeling safe enough to roll his eyes. *Right. Stupid to even ask.* Readjusting his grip, he eyed the deep grooves carved into the stone nearest his hand. If they were stable enough, the claw marks would work as a ladder. A small mercy. That's where his luck ended, however. There wasn't much that could serve as decent footholds, so for the vast majority of his trip, his arms would be doing all of the work. Licking his lips and rolling his shoulders, he mentally prepared himself for the climb. Years of hunting, boxing, and carrying dead bodies had left him top heavy. All of his strength was located in his arms. The rest of him was slim and, given that he was on the shorter side, it was easy enough for him to pull himself up in a dead lift. Aleksandr knew he could trust his body. In situations like these, the mind was what gave out first. Determination was a powerful but fragile thing. And integral to survival.

One last, soothing breath and he committed himself to the task. He rolled his shoulders, tightened his grip, and locked his eyes onto his target. Jumping as hard as he could and stretching his short body to the point of breaking, he desperately worked his fingers into the gaps. It wasn't the best grip but enough for him to launch up and surge towards the next.

It didn't take long for fire to crackle alight behind his ribs. The inferno spread quickly, striving to consume every muscle above his torso. Sweat dripped from his skin. Soaked through, his shirt plastered to his skin and trapped in increasing body heat. He blocked out the pain, the quiver in his arms and the fear that brimmed inside him every time he recalled that there was nothing beyond his dangling feet. All that existed was the next handhold. Then the next. It felt like his body was shaking apart by the time his bloody, questing hand wrapped around the rim.

All of the pain to get there couldn't compete with the agony of those last few inches. Petya gave a bored huff as he watched the odds of his son plummeting to his death steadily dwindling. Aleksandr hooked his leg over the edge and Petya decided that his parenting skills deserved a little appreciation. He idly bragged about setting motivational challenges and aiding in character development. Sprawled out, body on the uneven stones and face smothered in sand, Aleksandr let all of the words fade into a white noise. Delighted as he was to be alive, he couldn't enjoy it. As his adrenaline faded, memories of his encounter rose up from the depths of his mind. Flopping onto his back, he sucked in deep, heavy breaths, and tried to make some sense of it all. Both his euphoria and horror at the mysteries of it were snuffed out the instant Petya's grinning face filled his vision. He blocked out the sun as he loomed over him.

"Don't suppose you have any more of that peyote with you," Petya said.

Aleksandr didn't bother to argue that he was sober. Instead, he just shook his head, feeling the sand stick to every inch of his sweat drenched skin.

"Selfish," Petya scoffed under his breath. "I was looking forward to an interesting afternoon."

"Sorry."

Petya waved him off and retreated into Aleksandr's peripheral vision. Sitting up was awkward. Each muscle had taken advantage of his momentary inactivity to clench up and turn to stone. Exhausted by the time he got up, he rested his forearms on his bent knees and lowered his head. Questions bubbled up from the haze of his mind. None of it made any sense, however, until he unhooked his canteen from his belt and guzzled down a few mouthfuls of water. Wiping his face with his arm just exchanged sweat rather than cleaned any of it away.

"What are you doing here?" Aleksandr asked.

He was happy about his sunglasses as he glanced at Petya's face. It felt like some small measure of protection. His father's smile grew as he held his hands out wide. For all his showmanship, he was admiring the view, not looking at his son.

"I was looking for you. Why else would I be out here?"

That question could never have an unsettling answer. Instead of answering, Aleksandr decided to ask another of his own.

"How did you find me?"

The moment he had voiced the question, he realized how desperate he was to hear his father acknowledge that something was wrong. That he had seen the monster. That the only reason he found him was because the monstrosity had drawn his attention. Something. Anything.

"I was young once, too," Petya laughed. "I know the desire to revisit your kills. Although, I must admit, the gunfire did help a bit."

Aleksandr let his head slump back down, attempting to make the gesture look like one of exhaustion. In truth, he just wanted to hide his disgust at the thought of seeing the mound of corpses that would now be rolling into each other under the summer heat. Swallowing thickly, he asked if Petya had noticed the animal displaying any odd behavior. The older man laughed.

"Are you still going on about this? You're high. Just enjoy the ride."

Aleksandr nodded and choked down some more water. As the cool liquid trailed down his throat, it occurred to him that perhaps he was. When boredom and opportunity lined up, Olga liked to experiment. Mostly, she would just spike his food with different things to see what happened when he ingested them. He hoped she had gotten tired of the habit, especially since he had learned to keep a secret stash of pre-packaged food and sealed drinks. *Had she found the stockpile?* His gut twisted at the thought. There was comfort in knowing that he had planned for such an event. He always kept the twins' food separate from his own. Still, he made a mental note to ask them if they had experienced any ill effects.

Feeling sturdier, he got to his feet. Pain sizzled across his skin and he noticed just how much damage his fall had caused. Part of his shirt was shredded. A thick layer of dirt changed the color of the material, with bloodstains poking out from the mess. His chest was cut up, but with a bit of prodding, he found none of the damage was all that deep. Nothing that couldn't be ignored for a while. Despite his best efforts, a pained groan escaped him as he straightened.

"You look like hell," Petya commented.

Aleksandr didn't reply and Petya didn't expect him to.

The heat had made the canteen water unpleasantly warm, but Aleksandr forced down a few mouthfuls before he finally looked around. Petya had brought the off-road vehicle with him. A high set jeep designed to bounce right over the sand dunes. It was parked a safe distance from the rim but definitely close enough that he should have heard the engine. He hadn't heard a thing.

"You better hurry up, son," Petya declared as he smacked a heavy hand down on Aleksandr's shoulder. "You know how your mother gets when we keep her waiting."

"Waiting for what?"

Petya headed towards the vehicle without ever glancing behind. Warning alarms were blaring inside Aleksandr's head, but not much could be done about it. He had to follow. Each staggered step helped him discover a new cut or bruise. At least nothing seemed to be broken.

He had barely crawled up onto the front passenger seat before his father patted his knee. The touch made Aleksandr's stomach drop. Petya looked far too pleased with himself. Too excited. Nothing good had ever caused or followed that smile.

"Is Radmiar here?" he asked before trying to ease his stomach with a few mouthfuls of water. It briefly occurred to him that Olga may have spiked his canteen, but he was too thirsty to worry about that right now.

"What?" Petya looked at him as if he had lost his mind. "No. Of course not. We gave him a holiday for his birthday, remember?"

"Right," Aleksandr said. *God help anyone in the Philippines right now.*

Despite knowing that he hadn't, Aleksandr still tried to recall if he had been forced to buy or hang party supplies recently. Olga and Petya were very festive when their 'good' children came home. Balloons, streamers, party poppers; all Aleksandr needed was a glimpse of these items for him to break out in a cold sweat.

The engine roared and crisp, cool air gushed out of the vents. It ravaged the sweat on Aleksandr's body and he shivered with delight. Finishing the last of his water, he reattached the canteen to his hip and set the rifle across his lap. The journey didn't help to ease the anxiety clawing in the pit of his stomach. Petya was keeping his silence and that same, self-satisfied smile seemed permanently fixed on his face. As the sensation grew, he began to stroke his bloodied fingers over the body of his rifle.

A notion played around the edge of his awareness. A thought he tried to ignore but only grew stronger. He wished that he could use it. It wasn't the first time he had thought about killing his father. If anything, he had an ever-increasing array of fantasies of how he would do it. That was a dangerous game. It was all too easy for fantasies to become obsessions. And when that change happened, the lines between right and wrong, justice and cruelty, all blurred together. Living with his family, he had learned how integral fantasy was to their 'games'. They were the starting point and the driving force. And it left Aleksandr very weary of holding any daydream too close.

Still, he couldn't help the indulgence. The whole trip back to the ghost town, he allowed fantasies to take over his mind. *One shot to the temple would do* it, he thought, imagining the way Petya's head would explode like a ripe melon. Images flashed across his mind's eye, each one of how he might be able to get to Olga while the element of surprise was still on his side. Of course, it was just fantasies. Even if he and the twins escaped their parents, there would still be all of his older siblings to deal with. Killing them was only trading two serial killers for four. Sliding his fingers over the hard metal, he found the safety and flicked it on.

With a final lurch and a grunted roar from the engine, the jeep bounced over the last of the dunes and the houses came into sight. It made it very clear to Aleksandr just how long he had been contemplating the issue. He was spending an increasing amount of time debating the thought and that, in itself, was dangerous. If he was going to get the twins out, he needed to be smart about it. *Have a plan. Bide your time.* He repeated those words a few times until he felt like it had finally sunk in. Impulsiveness led to death. He had seen that lesson in action.

These familiar thoughts had consumed his mind, shoving everything else aside. A monster of his imagination didn't seem like much of a threat when there was one of blood and flesh sitting next to him. Odds were that it was a combination of dehydration and lack of sleep. Both things that could be easily rectified. But not right now. Not as they were weaving their way through the houses.

Keeping his face down, he glanced up through the mattered tangles of his fringe. Petya was keeping to the roads. Two streets down was the safe house he had left the twins playing in. His heartbeat grew faster as Petya drove past one intersection and kept going. Carefully keeping all reactions from his face, Aleksandr's fingers tightened around the rifle's grip. The house was now only five buildings away. Studying Petya out of the corner of his eyes, Aleksandr couldn't decide if he should be concerned or not.

Three buildings down. *Did he find them alone? Did they mouth off?* Two buildings. *Did he finally notice that Nadya was developing?* The last house passed by and they were in front of the hiding place. Petya slowed the jeep and Aleksandr clicked the safety off. Broken shards of glass still hung in the window frames like rotten teeth. What remained reflected the sunlight like mirrors. It was a slight distraction but not enough to keep anyone from seeing inside. Hoping that his desert sunglasses hid his eyes as well as they battled against the glare, Aleksandr risked a look to the house more than once. He checked every window for a sign of movement. Silently willed his twins to hide well. Petya slowed the car again and Aleksandr slipped a finger under the safe guard to wrap it around the trigger.

The jeep's wheel hit the curb as Petya cut the corner and continued down the road. He watched the safe house dwindle away in the rear view mirror before drawing in a breath again. The hairs on the back of his neck bristled as he felt the weight of Petya's evaluating stare. Hoping to look sufficiently bored, he began to toy with the safety, flicking it on and off at random. It was a habit that Petya himself had and with any luck, he would decide that there had been no threat behind the movement. He didn't dare look if the rouse worked. Just kept his head down and continued to flick the switch.

Petya abruptly hit the brakes. Aleksandr's hand shot out to brace against the dashboard as his head shot up. Instantly, he was on edge and alert. Petya had brought him to the newest 'boxing ring'. *It's too soon,* Aleksandr tried to tell himself. He was still busted up from the last fight. Olga didn't mind the game being rigged one way or another. Petya, however, insisted that it cheapened the sport.

Holding his rifle tight against his chest, Aleksandr looped one arm around the barrel to nip at his thumbnail. The taint of dirt and gunmetal assaulted his tongue. The vile taste wasn't enough to keep him from chewing on the nail as he slowly followed his father to the building. The weather-beaten walls hadn't been enough to keep the desert at bay. It had crept in through the gaps and cracks, covering the floor and leaving little difference between the inside and out. The few clusters of thin shadows didn't bring any relief to the stifling heat. Aleksandr lingered a few steps behind his father, as far back as Petya would allow, and slipped off his sunglasses.

Repeated use had carved a pathway through the sand of the hallway. Each doorway of the lesser used rooms was all but blocked off by the mounds of red sand. Fine top layers flaked off with the slightest breeze to dance in the air, giving it a strange hue. Aleksandr hated the distortion. It almost looked like the place was full of steam. Each time he was led into this house, he found himself glad that he didn't share his younger brother's imagination. Even without being prone to flights of fancy, Aleksandr couldn't get it out of his head that they were walking down into Hell. Or Hades. Or whatever nightmarish landscape was probably waiting for all of them when they finally get to die. *The twins will go somewhere better,* he corrected himself as he chewed his nail. That thought made him smile slightly. Just the slightest twitch of his lips. Even that died the moment they turned the corner into the kitchen. Olga stood by the basement door.

"What's going on?" Aleksandr asked around his nail.

"We've got a surprise for you," Olga said with a glorious smile.

"Why?" he asked.

Petya barked a laugh before he opened the basement door with a flourish, the motion sending a fresh gust of sand into the air. Aleksandr regretted taking his sunglasses off as the particles ground against his eyes.

"Do you really think that we'd forget your birthday?" Petya asked.

Olga beckoned him closer with a wave of her hand and that unmovable smile of hers. Obeying made his skin crawl, but he managed to pull it off. And even succeeded in hiding his cringe when she placed a hand on his shoulder.

"You did remember to get something for Radmiar, right?" she asked.

"Yes. Couldn't forget my twin's birthday."

Apparently wanting to keep their surprise to themselves, neither of his parents turned on the basement light. It left everything as a deep, all-consuming pit. They let him lead the way, which wasn't a task that he particularly relished. He didn't need to know what the surprise was to know that he didn't want any part of it. As the stairs creaked, the sounds rolled over the wall and echoed back to them. Nothing stirred. *Is that a good sign or a bad one?* He decided that it didn't really matter. The conclusion would be the same in the end.

The battered wood of the stairs gave way to the bare concrete of the basement floor. It was perhaps the only place in the entire town that was not coated with sand. Stale blood and stifling humidity made it hard to breathe. Swallowing thickly a few times helped to suppress the impulse to gag. His eyes struggled to adjust to the darkness, leaving him to move by memory alone to stand in the middle of the room. He had never really had a security blanket as a child but was aware of the concept. Now, he clutched at the rifle as if it were a cherished teddy bear.

Straining to hear everything around him, Aleksandr noticed the creak and shuffle of his parents moving about the space. Under it all, there was something else. The faintest trace of a third person's heavier breathing. Whomever his parents had down here, they had been here for a while. The heat alone made it hard to stay in this room for any extended period of time. Blind, sweating, and quickly wearing his nail down to the flesh, Aleksandr could only wait for what was to come next. Tension twisted up his stomach and squeezed his chest.

Surrounded by darkness, it was easy for his mind to convince him that the monster was in the room now. A soft sobbing broke the stillness. That wasn't out of the ordinary. Thin traces of blood joined the grimy tastes assaulting his tongue. It didn't stop him from chewing on the quickly depleting nail. The crying grew louder. *Turn the light on, already.* He sent the thought out as a shout. The crying had turned into a wail, shrill and hopeless, and far harder to ignore. Few things twisted up his nerves like that special brand of desperate bawling. Hooking his tooth around the edge of his broken nail, he bit down. Perhaps it was the pain of peeling skin, but he didn't notice the shift at first. Whoever was crying, was moving. Coming closer. *Didn't they lock him up?* His heart skipped a beat as it hit him that this could be the change they were so excited about. Perhaps the fight was no longer contained within the concrete room. *They let you keep your gun. No sport in that. So, what did they give him?*

Snapping his hand down from his mouth, he grabbed his gun and flicked off the safety. Controlling his breathing, he strained to catch the slightest traces of movement. Any shuffle of feet was lost under the now howling wails. The walls rang with the sound, making it impossible to tell where it was coming from. All he knew was that it was approaching. Slowly but steadily. As swift as a phantom. Aleksandr didn't know if he should inch back or move forward. The crying was desperate but filled with a rage that cut him to the core and held him solid. A spike of fear coursed down his spine and he couldn't keep his thoughts clear anymore. Everything was devoted to the demonic creature in the desert. Its deformed, feral face. Claws and fangs. Wings that dominated the sky. The crying was closer now and no longer sounded human. He couldn't pinpoint what was off about it. But he knew. He could feel it. Whatever was creeping closer to him, wailing and raging, had no trace of humanity. It could try and mimic one, but it wasn't. It was old. Powerful. Full or unrelenting, unbridled hatred. With a strong thud and the crackling hum of electricity, the overhead lights flickered on. A glaring white light flooded the room, driving into his eyes like a thousand needles and he knew. The monster was right beside him.

Chapter 7

Aleksandr whipped around, breathing heavy and rifle lifted at the ready. His ears rung as the crying came to an abrupt end, but there was enough for him to still hear his parents both yell 'ta-da'. They weren't exactly in unison, but there was a solid attempt, and that was a warning sign in itself. Using his long fringe as a shield against the glare, it allowed his eyes to adjust quickly. Still, he squinted hard, making shapes out of the blinding light. His parents came into view and neither of them was disturbed by his raised rifle. Their laughter was harsh and loud, as well as their insults, but Aleksandr didn't pay much attention to either. His focus was on catching sight of the monster. There was nothing beside him. Nothing on the ceiling or walls. It wasn't until he had assured himself that it had all been in his head that he noticed his 'present'.

His gut gave a hard twist when he noticed a woman in the cage. Not a man. Hindsight told him that he should have seen this coming. He had vague memories of her being tossed onto the ground last night. But his focus had been on Ivan then and he hadn't spared her much thought. Also, there was one glaring reason that this had blindsided him.

"I don't understand," Alek said in a soft voice. Loud enough to be heard but not enough to seem like a challenge.

"Alek," Olga sighed as she crossed the floor. One of her hands made the way to the back of his neck while the other rubbed his chest. Both points of contact made him equally uncomfortable. "I think you'll agree that we have been very accepting of this little phase you've been going through. But enough is enough. You're going to be twenty. That's far too old for such childishness."

The woman in the cage couldn't have been out of her teens yet. Close, but not fully. Beyond age and gender, there wasn't much to her that would spark his parents' attention. She was too solid, too strong. They preferred willowy beauties. This girl's arms rolled with thick but compact muscle. Her legs were short but strong and well defined. Even hunched as she was to fit into the tight confines of the pet cage, the muscles of her stomach pressed right against the smooth skin of her exposed abdomen. She was anything but lithe. If it weren't for his own well-worked shoulders and arms, there wouldn't have been a part of Aleksandr's body that she didn't have beat.

Petya strolled across the room toward the cage. The woman's dark eyes watched his every step with a keen focus. She might have been prepared for him to smack his hand down against the top of the metal, but it didn't stop her from flinching. A deep scowl twisted her lips and her eyes narrowed. To her credit, she didn't cower.

"Look at her, Aleksandr," he boasted. "Those arms, those legs, that stomach. She can pass for a man."

"So, I'm a gateway murder?"

A stony silence settled over the room. It wasn't uncommon for the victims to talk. Mostly screaming and begging and desperate wails. Sass was new. And something that no one seemed to know how to respond to. Biting down hard on his nail, Aleksandr watched his father intensely, waiting for a cue on how to respond. After a stunned blink, Petya let out a booming laugh and slapped the top of the cage again. It rattled on its wheels and the girl braced herself.

"Yes, you are. Consider yourself lucky. You're going to make my boy a man."

The muscles of the girl's neck twitched as she clenched her jaw tightly.

"She's still a woman," Aleksandr said softly.

Stealing glances at Petya, Aleksandr silently begged the man to take the excuse. To let him continue to exploit the loophole.

"Alek," Olga purred.

He flinched. "I just don't like killing women."

"That's a bit sexist," the woman noted.

Again, she gained everyone's attention instantly. Tension was in her muscles, her pose, the way she hunched like a cornered animal. But none of it reached her voice. There were no tears or sobs. Every word was carefully constructed to sound almost like a casual conversation. Olga and Petya shared a quick, amused glance. Aleksandr lowered his gaze to the floor by his feet. It didn't stop the memories of the glee his parents took in breaking the strong, or even just those who pretended to be, from flashing across his mind's eye. *She's going to regret this,* he thought.

"Why yes, my dear." Petya's attempt to sound like a game show host thickened his accent. "It is. I do apologize, we did not intend to raise him that way. He's a little slow. Although I think you could guess that yourself with just a glance."

Looking up right then would have been a very stupid decision. Petya only used such vague and limited insults when his attention was fractured. No need to give him any reason to sharpen it.

"But you're going to help him rectify that," Petya continued. He crouched down and wiggled his finger in front of the bars of the cage. "Once he kills you, all will be right."

Out of the corner of his eyes, Aleksandr watched in confusion and horror as the girl mockingly mimicked Petya's movements and chirp, "Goodie."

A deep growl rumbled in Olga's chest, but whatever she was about to say was lost under Petya's amused laughter. Still, her hand became a claw upon the back of Aleksandr's neck, her sharpened nails cutting into tender skin. Aleksandr suppressed his wince and went back to chewing his nail.

"Aleksandr!"

He snapped his head up to his father's disapproving cry. Standing straight, his arms wide, his father tipped his head to the side.

"You don't seem excited," Petya said.

Aleksandr decided it was best not to answer. His mother, however, was of a different mind. Rubbing a hand across the expanse of Aleksandr's chest, she pressed closer to his side. Aleksandr hid his discomfort as best as he could. It was all a grotesque deformity of affection. The motions were off. Too much, too little. An attempt to replicate a concept she could never truly understand.

"Yes, Aleksandr, show some apprehension," she purred. "Don't you know how much trouble your father went to give you a good birthday? It took so long to find a girl who would deform herself to such a state. He hunted her for days."

"Hunted?" The girl's abrupt laughter took everyone by surprise.

Fury radiated from Olga as she watched her husband smile in bemusement down at the woman in the cage. Still laughing, she craned her neck, so she could look Petya dead in the eyes.

"You're the kind of guy that throws dynamite into a lake and calls it fishing, aren't you?" Scoffing over Petya's reply, she turned to Aleksandr. Every joint of his body locked up at the attention, but she seemed utterly at ease. "He distracted me with a kid and hit me over the head. Truly, it was a battle of wits."

"You need to watch your mouth," Olga hissed.

"Or what?" the girl challenged. "You'll kill me?"

Olga's pretty features twisted in disgust and murderous anger. The points of her nails pierced Aleksandr's skin, releasing droplets of blood that trickled down the back of his neck.

"You have no idea what I'll do to you." Olga sounded more animal than human and Aleksandr knew better than to move.

The teen didn't care. She smirked and gestured loosely to the TV set. "I've just spent God knows how long watching your home movies. I know exactly what you're capable of. You're not all that impressive. Sick, twisted, admittedly creative, sure. But impressive? Nah."

Olga laughed, low but shrill. Close to the manic laughter Aleksandr had heard in the darkness, but not an exact replica. Shivers worked their way down his spine as she tightened her grip.

"Do you know how many pathetic little girls like you I've murdered?"

The girl wiggled her fingers and released a long, droning 'o'. "Murder. That's new. No one has ever done something like that before. Should I also be impressed that you can tie your shoes? Brush your hair? Oh, have you managed to color inside the lines, too?"

Aleksandr stood in stunned silence as the girl continued to taunt his mother. Delighted by this sudden change of the routine, Petya didn't do anything to intervene. Olga, however, snapped under the taunting. Pushing Aleksandr aside, she raced across the room to snatch the cattle prod off of its hook on the wall.

Electricity crackled between the exposed barbs. The little stream glowed even within the stark light that flooded the room. A cruel, gleeful expression settled onto Olga's expression as she neared the captive teen. A sudden gab through the bars and the prongs found flesh. Bravado or not, the girl screamed as the current pulsed into her skin. Her cry made both of his parents chuckle. Aleksandr lowered his head to ensure that his fringe covered his face and the twist of disgust he knew had crossed it. Olga stabbed at their victim again. And again. The sickening scent of burning hair and meat began to rise in the humidity.

Laughing with delight, Olga plunged forward. Ready for it this time, the girl twisted her torso, pushing up against the far side of the cage. There wasn't room to avoid the blow but her efforts made her skim the bare skin of her stomach instead of pressing hard against it. The little slip of electricity was still close enough to hurt. Clenching her teeth against the pain, the girl latched onto the long metal shaft of the prod. Instead of pushing it away, the girl pulled. It all happened in an instant.

Caught off guard, Olga stumbled forward. The barbs skipped across the girl's skin and nestled against her side, drawing Olga's slender hand between the barbs. The cage rattled as the girl flung herself forward, and with all the strength she could muster within the confided space, slammed her fist against Olga's trapped hand. The unrelenting bars kept Olga's forearm in place as the blow forced her hand back and there was a loud, sickening crack.

A feral scream ripped out of Olga's throat and she yanked back. The prod still buzzed, the contact was still made, but the girl refused to release her grip. She took the pain to keep the opportunity to strike at Olga's broken wrist again. Petya surged towards the door of the cage. The metal rattled as the woman struggled, the motion making Petya fumble with the lock. One more blow and Olga pulled away. She clutched her wounded hand to her chest, watching with vindictive, righteous glee as Petya wrenched the cage door open.

The girl was ready. Exploiting her smaller size, she drew her legs up to her chest and kicked them out as Petya reached in. With practiced precision, she crunched her left foot into his face, her heel finding his nose. The blow forced his head back and her other foot, following a split second behind, took advantage of that. Twisted into a slight angle, her tiny foot slipped under his now raised chin to hit Petya's exposed throat. *A trained fighter.* There was barely time for the thought to pass though his mind. She was quick. And had already tossed herself at Petya before he had time to stagger back.

Her fist slammed down against Petya's face as she straddled him. Olga lunged forward and kicked at the girl. She rolled out of the way and landed in a crouch. Precision met blind animal instinct as Olga raced forward with a wild scream. The girl laced her fingers together and brought them down onto Olga's back as she attempted to tackle her to the floor. She was able to keep the serial killer from pinning her down but couldn't force Olga back completely. Petya peeled himself from the floor, blood gushing from his broken nose and each breath a strangled wheeze. Caught between astonishment at the sudden turn of events, and the satisfaction of seeing his parents suffer, Aleksandr held his ground and watched it unfold.

The girl had an impressive right hook and didn't shy away from pressing her advantage. Every time it seemed like Olga would regain the upper hand, the girl would latch onto Olga's broken wrist with her hands or legs and squeeze. It was hard to tell through all the screams and chaos, but Aleksandr thought he heard something crunch during one of those counterattacks. Petya stormed to the wall to grab the tool for his favorite form of mental torture. A revolver. Nothing could shatter someone's composure as quickly as a game of Russian Roulette. It was pre-loaded with only one bullet, but the girl had no way to know that the odds were, at least statistically, on her side.

It was a brief distraction, but when Aleksandr looked back to the struggling woman, he saw that the girl was on her back and Olga knelt beside her, choking her, bearing down with her bodyweight. Consumed with savage ecstasy and adrenaline, the pain of the broken wrist no longer bothered her. A twisted smile peeled back Olga's lips and her eyes almost bulged out of her head as she watched the girl twist.

"I'm going to kill you slowly," Olga promised. "Snap every bone in your body. Grind them into dust! Peel your face off! You'll be here forever!"

The girl grabbed at Olga's wrist. Instead of squeezing, she rolled her body. Pulling her knees up in a flawless glide. One knee slipped between Olga's locked elbows. In the same second and with just as much grace, the girl looped her other leg around Olga's neck. A pop of hips. A push of powerful thighs. Only a second and the girl rolled up, forcing Olga, head first, into the concrete. The older woman screamed and thrashed, but leverage and strength kept her locked between the girl's thighs. Flat on her back. Since the girl hadn't relinquished her hold, Olga's injured arm was now pulled straight. Every attempt to free herself failed with a simple rise of the girl's hips. The position didn't just put pressure on the wrist, but threatened to break the elbow, pop the shoulder from its joint, and she squeezed Olga's throat between her thighs.

Aleksandr only realized how quick the motion had been when Petya leveled the gun at the girl's head. Looking up at him meant staring at the blazing fluorescent lights. Squinting, however, didn't take away the complete rebellion on the woman's face.

"Let her go," Petya said slowly, unable to keep the slight smile from his lips.

"No."

Half laughing, half choking, Olga clawed uselessly at the girl's leg. "Shoot her, honey. Right between the eyes!"

Petya cocked the gun, the solid, metallic click was loud even given the competing noises. Taking another bite of his nail, Aleksandr tried not to be too disappointed. It had been fun while it lasted. And, if he nurtured it carefully enough, he might even be able to hold onto the memory of this day. Petya bleeding. Olga smothering sobs of pain. Not a bad day at all.

"Ever played Russian Roulette?" Petya asked as he braced his feet.

The wide, toothy grin that marked his bloodlust slowly spread across Petya's lips. It made Olga cackle and she released her grip on the woman's thigh. She didn't want her freedom anymore. She just wanted to watch.

The girl's chest was heaving but her voice remained solid and strong, "I know you have to actually pull the trigger."

"Let her go, or I will."

Tipping her head, the girl smirked, making it clear that Petya had already played his hand. His parents had already laid it all out. Not just that she was supposed to be Aleksandr's victim, but also how important it was to them that he was the one to kill her. She was brought here for a purpose, something significant, not to die on the concrete floor from a gunshot. Aleksandr dipped his head lower but kept his eyes locked on the unfolding situation. As he searched the girl's face, he knew. He saw it because it was something he spotted every time he caught a glimpse of his reflection. *She's willing to die.* Staring down the barrel as best she could, she violently wrenched Olga's arm.

"Oh, just pull the trigger already!"

Surprised by the sudden scream, Petya flinched. His finger tensed. The little metallic click resounded throughout the room. Despite all of her best efforts, the girl's bravado broke. In that split second, Aleksandr saw a dozen emotions, each passing so quickly that it was hard to catch sight of them all. Amongst them, he spotted terror, regret, and helplessness. *Willing to die but not wanting to,* Aleksandr reasoned.

The break hadn't slipped Petya's attention. Throwing his head back, he released a bout of booming, mocking laughter to the ceiling. Bile burned the back of Aleksandr's throat and his stomach heaved. The power dynamic had shifted once again, moving back to more familiar ground. Reckless or not, the girl was trapped here, helpless and afraid. None of them was prepared for the sudden crack. Or the blood-curdling scream that followed.

While Petya had been gloating, the girl had thrust her hips up. A strained, high-pitched squeal escaped Olga as her eyes rolled in their sockets. A new bulge moved around her shoulder like there was something living under the skin. Shaking off his shock, Aleksandr realized that it was the end of her arm bone. The girl had popped it from the socket.

Petya rushed forward with a bellow of rage. The girl tried to move, but was too tangled up in Olga. Petya swung his foot down as if he intended to kick the girl's head clean off of her shoulders. A wave of blood spewed from her mouth as her head snapped to the side. Dazed, she struggled to get up as Olga slithered free of her now lax thighs. The moment she was free, she twisted around and threw herself at the still stunned victim. Petya pulled her back.

"I want her dead!" Olga screamed.

"And she will be," Petya said. "I promise you that."

Shoving his wife behind him, Petya reached down, grabbed a handful of the girl's hair, and yanked hard on the thick mass. Thick clumps of the thick tresses almost tore out of her scalp as Petya forced her up.

"Get the door," he commanded Olga in a low grunt.

Choking on her rage, Olga moved to the heavy metal door of the cement room. Far taller than the girl, Petya almost had her off of her feet, dangling by her now bloody hair as they crossed the short distance. Putting his whole body into the motion, he managed to toss the small girl into the room. She bounced twice before she smacked into the solid back door.

"Well, you're going to give our boy a decent fight." Petya's bulk filled the doorframe, blocking Aleksandr's view. "Aren't you a feisty little Dominican princess?"

"I'm Puerto Rican, you ass!"

She must have charged at him, because a jolt of surprise once again pulsed through Petya's body. Hurriedly leaping back, he slammed the door shut. Instantly, the girl was beating against the other side of the metal, throwing herself against it, forcing it open a few inches with each assault. After a moment of struggling, Petya managed to keep it closed long enough to push the lock into place. It didn't end the girl's attack. The whole time, she ranted and raved in what Aleksandr assumed was Spanish.

Once again, feeling like the undisputed master of the situation, Petya broke into fits of laughter, his whole body shaking with the force and tears prickling in the corners of his eyes.

"That was exciting," he grinned.

Olga stood next to him, clutching her wounded arm to her side, her chin up in defiance. "I want her dead, Petya."

He cupped her cheeks and gave her a sweet kiss. "Whatever you want, my darling, but let's do this right."

"Right, nothing. Shoot her. Right now! If you love me, you'd do it."

Again a kiss. "It's because I love you, that I'm doing what's best for you. One bullet and it's all over. Would that really satisfy you? No, my love. Your bloodlust would only be satisfied when you see Alek beat the life out of her. One punch at a time."

Pain still simmered across her face, but she was smiling again. Too cheerfully. Too bright. "I want to watch."

"Of course. Now, let's fix you up first."

"No." Now that the heat of the moment had begun to ebb away, Petya did not take the direct refusal well. Olga noticed the shift instantly and pushed her lips out in a playfully sulking pout. "I want to see her bleed, first."

"You're in pain," he chided.

Using her good hand, she toyed with the buttons of his shirt and stepped closer. "Please. It will make me feel better."

Petya watched her for a long moment before he heaved a sigh. "I can never refuse you."

The indulgent smile on his face faded into anger the moment he turned his attention to Aleksandr. Reaching out with one hand, he ordered his son to hand over the rifle without using a word. Reluctantly, Aleksandr shuffled forward, subtly putting on the safety before handing it over. The instant the metal left his fingers, the revolver barrel was pressed firmly between his eyes. Aleksandr's heart hammered against his ribs. Kicking into high gear, his self-preservation instinct begged him to move, to cringe away, to run. Aleksandr locked his knees and forced himself to hold his ground.

"Didn't it occur to you to help?" Petya asked.

Aleksandr stared straight ahead and took a deep breath. The barrel was too close for him to see if the chamber was loaded. A part of him wished it was. Still, he remained frozen. Kept his silence.

"You have nothing to say?" Petya demanded. "Speak!"

Aleksandr swallowed and said the first thing that came to mind, "No one ordered me to intervene. I thought you didn't want me to."

A smile flicked across Petya's face. Looking at Olga, he shrugged, and lowered the gun. Without warning, Petya snapped his hand back up. The tip of the barrel smacked against Aleksandr's skull. The trigger clicked. It took a moment for Aleksandr's mind to understand that the chamber had been empty. He was still alive. A fine tremble shook his head, and his ribs ached from his rapid heartbeat. Thin trails of laughter bubbled from both Petya and Olga. They giggled as Petya once again brought the gun down and shrugged.

"The look on your face," Petya grinned.

"I really thought that was going to be the end of him," Olga commented. She sounded slightly disappointed.

Tightening his fist, Aleksandr took a deep, sobering breath as subtly as he could. Blood rushed through his ears, creating a deafening roar. It made it slightly easier to ignore his parents. That was until Petya roughly smacked his arm.

"In you go," his tone left no room for argument.

Aleksandr took a step towards the door. Before he could touch the handle, Olga tugged his hunting knife free of its sheath. Pushing up onto her toes, she whispered in Aleksandr's ear.

"Make sure she hurts."

Chapter 8

The buzz of fluorescent lights filled the concrete box. The room looked smaller on the inside. Completely bare, there were no shadows or hidden corners. Blood had worked its way deep into the stone, creating a mosaic of rusted red and rotten brown. Evelyn barely needed to turn her head to take in the whole space. No windows. No vents. Nothing to disperse the nauseating stench of bleach.

Holding her hands close to her chest, she backed up to the far wall. The door was the only way in or out. Besides that, there was just one gap in the concrete slabs that made up the walls. A small rectangle, barely wider than her arm, with a single, red dot glowing from the darkness beyond. *A camera light*, she reasoned. *They're filming.*

Whatever happened here, she was still going to end up in their video collection. She didn't know how to process that sickening thought.

A heavy clack made her flinch. She focused on the door, watching it open. The family had perfected this maneuver. As small as the room was, there wasn't enough time for her to charge at the door before it closed again. The lock slammed back into place, but neither she nor the new addition paid it any attention. Evelyn's focus was on sizing up her opponent. She knew he was doing the same. It was impossible to see his eyes through the limp, black hair that covered half of his face, but she felt his gaze. Direct and piercing. Causing the hairs on her arms stand on end.

The man didn't move from his position by the door. Evelyn had prepared herself for something like his parents. She wasn't ready for silence. He was like the world's worst statue. It unnerved her, but not enough to waste the opportunity to get a decent look at him.

The first word that popped into her head was 'disgusting'. This man didn't focus on hygiene. It would take a month to scrub all of the encrusted dirt off of his skin, and the stench of his sweat was stronger than the bleach. The second word, and far more important from a fighter's perspective, was 'Frankenstein'. Every part of him just didn't seem to belong with the others. He was barely taller than Evelyn was, putting him at about five-foot-five at the most, leaving his hands outsized by his frame. The effect was made worse as each of his knuckles were deformed, engorged by untreated breaks and scar tissue.

His legs were stumpy and lean. From the way he had walked, there didn't seem to be much flexibility in his hip joints. *A runner, maybe. Used to squatting. Forward and back motion*, she reasoned. *Attack from the side, low and quick. He's not a kicker.* She trailed her eyes up his short torso. Through the scattered holes of his shirt, she could see that he walked a fine line between lithe muscle and malnutrition. Then, bolted onto the sides of this rickety frame, were the arms of a boxer. Solid and thick. Not defined for the sake of vanity muscle. Nor swollen enough to slow him down. Those arms were built to move hard and fast. And that was a problem. *You're quicker on your feet*, she told herself. *Keep behind him. Strike low. Kick high.*

Suddenly, he moved, cutting her evaluation short. Instead of closing the distance between them, however, he lifted his hand and began to chew on his thumbnail. Barely a second passed before he forced his hand back down, but

Evelyn had seen it and knew it for what it was. A nervous twitch.

The conversations from before played over in her mind. He had never killed a woman before. With him standing there, hiding his eyes, and struggling not to chew on his fingernails, Evelyn doubted he had much experience even speaking to women. At least ones that weren't genetically related to him. Nervous, unfocused, reluctant; she could work with that.

"I should probably say it now before I forget," Evelyn chirped in the cheeriest tone she could muster. "Happy birthday, Aleksandr."

He instantly resumed his impersonation of a statue. As if everything else was put on hold until he could properly process what was happening. Using her advantage, Evelyn beamed at him.

"It is Aleksandr, right? A lot was going on out there, I might have messed it up."

Just when she was sure he wasn't going to respond, he nodded. Once. If it weren't for the sway of his dirty hair, she might have missed it. Intent on keeping him off balance, she winked and pointed at him with finger guns.

"Yeah, I'm a clever one," she boasted.

Her bluff worked. After staring at her for a long moment, he turned his head slightly to the door. Like he was looking for guidance on how to react.

"Hey, we haven't been properly introduced yet, have we? I'm Evelyn Figueroa."

His hand twitched at his side. A fraction of a movement that spoke volumes. Stress was mounting up in Aleksandr. He was aching to give into his coping strategy. A few harder shoves and he'll snap. She knew it.

"I know," she chuckled, waving her arms out to gesture at nothing in particular. "You probably don't want to know stuff like that. My mom used to take me to pet stores to look at the dogs. She'd tell me, don't name them, because then you'll become attached and you'll want to keep them. Is that how it is for you?"

Again, he looked at the door. Still silent. Hand now shaking as he balled it into a fist.

"But what can I say?" she continued. "I'm an old-fashion girl. I think if you're going to kill someone, you should at least know their name. And, from what I picked up, I'm your first. We should make sure that it's special. Maybe some candle light. Soft music. One of us promising to be gentle with the other."

He lowered his head a little more, hiding behind his hair as it fell forward. *Hit a nerve with that one*, she thought.

"Can I ask you a personal question, Alek? Why are you doing this? I mean, I get the urge to kill and all." She motioned her hands before her, grabbing her chest. What she had was minimal, but hopefully, it would be enough to get the job done. "But I'm not exactly your type, am I?"

Aleksandr hunched forward, his face locked onto the floor and his body stone-still. She couldn't see his face anymore, but she didn't have to. Under all the dirt and grime, red splotches had begun to stain his neck. *Blushing or enraged?* she wondered. *Only one way to find out.*

"Is it your parents?" Evelyn asked. "You know what I don't get? How can you be old enough to kill women, but not old enough to make your own decisions?"

"It's not personal." His voice was soft but rough, as if he hadn't spoken more than five words in all his life.

"Not personal?" she repeated. "I gotta say, Alek, I'm taking it pretty damn personally."

He shrugged one shoulder. "You don't matter."

"Well, that's inconvenient."

Not being able to see his eyes didn't dampen their focus. She could feel them gouging into her. Still, it was hard to tell which side of the pendulum he was on. She supposed it didn't matter. Disgust and sexually repressed mortification would have the same result. He'd follow his parents' example and kill whatever's making him uncomfortable. *Taunt him until he snaps.*

"Are you deranged?" he asked.

A burst of hysterical laughter escaped her. "Can't I just be happy I'm out of the cage?"

Aleksandr paused as if to sort out his thoughts. "Is that really what you want your last words to be?"

Evelyn hummed pensively. "You know what? Yes, I do. They have a deep, emotional significance to me. Besides, everything else is just going to be cursing you out in Spanish, and I don't think you can do that justice."

He made a sound, possibly a grunt, or a laugh; she couldn't be sure. A thunderous pounding against the door made them both snap around.

"I guess your folks are getting impatient," Evelyn said. "Can't say that I blame them. You have been slacking."

He took a step closer. That was all it took to shift the energy within the room. All tentative humor and awkwardness shattered, thrusting Evelyn into a boxing ring.

"Sorry," Aleksandr whispered as he balled his fists.

She dropped into her fighting stance and bounced on the balls of her feet. "Yeah, me too. Nothing personal."

There was no hesitation in his first punch. The right hook went straight for her head. Thrusting her arm up, she deflected the blow. Twisted her hips, she snapped her leg up, driving a kick into his side, just above his hip. It was the first time she had kicked someone without padding on and she wasn't prepared for the throbbing pain of bone crunching against bone.

She staggered as the pain rippled up along her leg. Aleksandr grunted, the blow knocking him off balance. It didn't stop him from slamming his fist against her side, the strike was as fast and hard as she had anticipated. Taking the pain, she dropped down to one knee and stomped out in a side-kick. The blow would have shattered his kneecap if he hadn't lunged towards her at the last moment. His weight hit her like a boulder. She couldn't keep them up.

The moment they hit the floor, their battle of precisely thought-out strikes devolved into a bar brawl. Hitting, kicking, scrounging for the upper hand. They might have been equal in height, but Aleksandr had a good few pounds on her. He used each one of them to his advantage, wearing her out until she couldn't keep him from scrambling on top of her, trapping her against the concrete floor. There, they reached a stalemate.

Every time he moved, attempting to deliver a punch or smack her head against the ground, his weight would lift. She never let the opportunity go to waste. He expected her to try and throw him off, not to attack from where she was. An elbow to his temple, a punch to his kidneys. He had to choose between keeping her in place, or inflicting pain himself. Their battle of body and wills consumed them, leaving them oblivious to the trembling until the room was bucking like an enraged bull.

They froze as a feral scream rose up like a coming storm. It started as background noise, barely heard over the earthquake, but soon became a deafening roar. The fluorescent light flickered and rattled within its sockets. Evelyn looked up just as it exploded. Burning sparks and fractured glass rained down on them. She screamed and pressed her face against the heaving floor just as Aleksandr flattened himself upon her, becoming a heavy blanket that crushed the breath from her lungs.

It wasn't until the rumbling stopped that she noticed the room had plunged into darkness. Nothing stirred. Neither of them dared to breathe. The moment remained suspended within a state of shock where they were each waiting for what was still to come. As the ringing left her ears and her surprise began to fade, a new terror surged forward to fill the void. There was no proof. No real reason for her to think it. But every instinct was telling her that something was deeply wrong. It was the same icy, sickening sensation she had felt as she watched the monster claw its way from the ceiling. *Is it back?*

She flinched as Aleksandr placed a gentle hand on her shoulder. A slight tap of reassurance. Evelyn froze, not waiting to remind him that she wasn't whomever he was imagining. The touch was an impulse honed into him after years of necessity. *Who is he normally protecting?* Despite her best efforts, he figured it out on his own and jerked his hand back.

"What was that?" he whispered.

Blinking into the pitch black, she shook her head. "How the hell am I supposed to know? This is your family's freak show."

As the words left her mouth, the realization sunk in. *This isn't the norm. He doesn't know what's going on and he's scared.* It wasn't a comforting thought. *What puts fear into a serial killer?* There were very few answers that would lead to a good ending. And this didn't seem like standard issue police procedure.

Slowly, carefully, Aleksandr's weight lifted off of her. She rolled away from him the first second she got, wanting to put some distance between them, sure that this had to be some kind of trick. A sick mind game.

"Olga?" Aleksandr called.

Evelyn couldn't so much as make out his silhouette in the darkness. Keeping the wall to her back, she climbed to her feet, trying to use the sound of his voice to keep track of him.

"Petya?"

His bellow was met with silence. It seemed to agitate him, his voice becoming harsher with each repetitive call. The silence became palpable. Smothering. Combining with the stifling heat to choke her. Struggling to breathe, Evelyn peeled herself off the wall just far enough to look in the general direction of the gap.

"The camera's off," she mumbled.

"What?" Aleksandr snapped as he shuffled about. "Not possible. They record everything."

She didn't know why she pointed. It wasn't like he could see her, but it felt like the natural thing to do.

"Well, the red light's out."

Once more, his shoes scuffed the floor. "What the hell?"

"Again, this isn't my game," Evelyn said.

The silence beyond the door bled in to fill the room. Aleksandr stopped moving, Evelyn's breathing eased, and everything just faded away. Without sight or sound, she felt like she was lost in the deepest recesses of space. Aimless and alone. It was strange to know that she wasn't. The man who had just been trying to kill her was lurking somewhere beyond her sight. And in this moment, he wasn't the biggest threat anymore. It was the unknown that scared her.

A scream erupted. She lurched away from the wall, spinning around as she tried to pinpoint where it was coming from. It seemed to bounce off of the walls and rise up from beneath her feet. The disorientation didn't last long, and she realized that the scream originated from the other side of the door. But it wasn't like the one that had come with the ground-shaking boom. This was higher pitched without being shrill. And painfully human. Childlike.

"Ivan?" Aleksandr said in a low voice. A split second later, he was beating against the door, screaming at the top of his lungs. "Ivan! Olga, Petya, stop! Don't hurt him!"

In response to his cries, the screams grew desperate. From her time in the cage, Evelyn had learned exactly what the sounds of torture were. She heard them now.

"Mother!"

Aleksandr tossed the word out like a placation. A submission. It wasn't enough to stop the screaming.

"Father, please!"

The child's wails morphed into words. A name. They cried out for Aleksandr, begged for his help. Each word was like a knife to her gut and she didn't even know the kid. Metallic clashes covered the words, the strikes repetitive and even, and it took her a moment before she could decipher it all. *Alek's throwing himself at the door.*

"Stop!" he pleaded and commanded at once, his voice frenzied and wild.

She had only known him for a moment, barely any time at all, but it still set Evelyn on edge to hear him so frantic. Like he was hanging on the very edge of madness. The terrified screams continued, gained strength, provoking Aleksandr to slam himself against the door again and again. It rattled and groaned on its hinges but remained in place.

"Ivan, hold on! I'm right here!"

Aleksandr's words blurred together as he sped up his assault. Hearing it all play out, Evelyn's mind finally caught up with what was happening. The child was who Petya had used to lure her in. That fragile, tiny little thing was now alone with two serial killers.

Her time in the cage had burned the videos into the back of her mind. They still played out there, repeating over and over, and she suspected they'd never stop. As the chaos grew around her, the images in her mind distorted. The child from the parking lot took the place of the women on the tables. She couldn't take it. Bursting forward, she held out one hand and searched for Aleksandr. Her fingertips had barely brushed his arm before he shoved her away.

"Back off!" he roared.

"You can't bust down that door by yourself," Evelyn snapped. "You need help."

"You'd help us? Why?"

"Because he's a child and I'm not a psychopath!"

The desperate cries pushed Aleksandr's hand. Not a word of cooperation passed their lips, but they fell into stride together, their shoulders bumping to keep track of each other as they found the door. Some prodding and shuffling, and they managed to center themselves within the frame; that way both of their shoulders would do most of the damage. Four steps back. One deep breath. Evelyn bounced on her toes as she tried to focus. *This is going to hurt.* Voicing it, even if it was only in her own head, helped her to make her peace with it. When Aleksandr tapped a finger against her wrist, she was ready.

They charged forward. The door rattled but didn't open on the first strike. Or the second. Or the third. Stopping wasn't an option, though. Not when the child continued to plead for their help. Two more attacks and the hinges finally snapped. The door slammed open and they staggered out into a blinding light. Something popped right by her ear. Shadows whipped around her like snow. A thousand things touched her skin and she threw herself back in an attempt to avoid them. Her retreat bumped her into Aleksandr. He didn't shove her away this time. At last, her eyes adjusted, and the world took shape. The room was gone, lost within the drifting confetti, unfurling streamers, and bobbing balloons.

"What is happening?" The sudden silence made her panted breaths sound like shouts.

The colorful slips of paper felt like ice as they built up against her skin. It made her stomach churn, but it was impossible to keep them off of her. There were too many falling too fast. She squinted through the vivid rain, trying to catch a glimpse of the wall, the cage, anything or anyone. It was impossible to see beyond the wall of floating decorations. Streamers hung down like coiled snakes, seemingly attached to nothing. There wasn't an inch of the ceiling that wasn't on display. The few gaps between the balloons were filled by the constantly falling confetti. *Where is it coming from?* she wondered. *It can't just materialize out of nowhere.*

Aleksandr tapped her arm again. One finger, barely making contact.

"Yeah," she replied to the unspoken question as she studied the room. There was almost a foot between them and the wall of twirling balloons. "I'm seeing it too. Don't suppose there's any chance that your parents did this."

"No," he whispered.

She didn't like how closer to a whimper the single word sounded. "It's your birthday, isn't it? Maybe it's a present?"

"Radmiar isn't here," he said, his words and breathing coming fast and sharp. "None of them are here. They shouldn't be here."

"I get it."

She didn't, of course. But she needed Aleksandr calm, and figured that agreeing with him would somewhat soothe him. It worked, and he forced himself to take a deep, slow breath.

Besides the impossibility of the self-regenerating confetti, and the unlikelihood that they could fill the room so swiftly, there were other pressing questions. *Were they still here? Where did the boy go? And why would they do any of it during an earthquake?*

"What do you think made the noise?" Evelyn asked.

At the same time, Aleksandr noted that the lights weren't on. Evelyn's brow furrowed. There were no windows in this room. Without them, it should be as dark as it was in the cell. It took a moment to see what he meant. It was the layer of balloons that clustered above them. They were glowing. She stared at them, trying to understand. A dark shadow raced across her vision. It raced under the glowing layer, making the inflated plastic orbs bounce and shift. Her eyes widened, but before she could say anything, Aleksandr bellowed.

"Ivan?"

The balloons before them bobbed and twisted, drifting about on a breeze that didn't exist. Like they were responding to him. Turning to face them. And just like that, Evelyn felt a thousand eyes upon her. The air felt thicker. Heavy and humid. The shift came with the inescapable knowledge that she was being hunted.

"Do you feel that?" she whispered.

"Yes."

"Is this how these things normally go?"

"No."

She pushed the mounting confetti off of her shoulders. "I don't want to touch any of this."

"Likewise."

"But we're going to, aren't we?"

"You can stay here if you want," he replied absently. "But I'm finding my brother."

She looked at him from the corner of her eyes. "Then what?"

Aleksandr's shoulders tensed up and she knew she had his attention. A part of her longed to keep the conversation going. She needed it. As crazy as it was to have a casual conversation with a killer, in this moment, it was the closest thing she had to sanity. Aleksandr took a step forward. She reached out to stop him, but her hand never made contact. As if not wanting to risk the touch, he stopped dead in his tracks.

"I want my knife," he said.

"How about that big gun you had before? That might be nice, too."

He shrugged, the motion making the piled-up confetti topple off of his shoulder. "I'd prefer my knife."

"Okay." Her stomach twisted into a hard, cold knot as she readied herself for what she was about to do. She didn't want to go in. But she was going to anyway. "I'll get the gun."

Chapter 9

Before this day, Aleksandr thought he knew every level of fear intimately. This one was new. He told himself that they were just decorations. Nothing to worry about. And that was also a first. He'd never actively tried to lie to himself. Comfort with thin promises or distractions with kinder, alternative scenarios. But he had never crossed the line into actually forcing himself to believe it.

Movement seen from the corner of his eye made him flinch. He couldn't understand why Evelyn was still here. He had thought she'd make a break for the door the second they got out. Now she was standing far too close to him, pouncing on her toes, and rolling her shoulders. *People stick to the lesser of two evils*, he thought.

"Ivan?"

"Alek." The weak whimper drifted from beyond the wall of colors.

He sprinted forward, smashing through the barrier of decorations. It was like diving into a kaleidoscopic ocean. Smudges of light consumed him, flooding his vision until it was impossible to see where he was going or where he had been. Shadows circled him, moving too fast to be anything more than a flickering stain across the balloons.

"Ivan!"

Aleksandr's heart became a crushing force in his chest. His breaths turned into broken pants and his vision blurred. A few feet was all it took for him to lose his bearings. The basement wasn't a massive space. He should have hit a wall by now.

"Ivan!"

"Alek, help me."

The sobbed words ripped him apart. Every turn came with an element of pain, his body protesting its treatment over the last few days. The decorations caught on his blood and sweat. Heat pulsated around him like a furnace. Everything seemed to melt and blur together.

"Alek!" Ivan wailed. "Where are you? Help me!"

The voice propelled him forward even as a new voice tried to draw him back.

"Wait! This is obviously a trick!"

Aleksandr ignored Evelyn as he pushed himself deeper into the crush. Odds were that he was running headfirst towards his own death. *So be it!* Because there was the slightest chance that it was his brother, and that was enough. *I won't lose another one.*

Shoving through the pliable wall of adornments, he finally lumbered into a tiny clearing. It was barely wide enough to accommodate his shoulders and stretched out in front of him for only a few feet. Ivan stood at the far end, still and emotionless, like he had been waiting for him. Dark shadows swarmed around Ivan's thin body. Aleksandr caught sight of the ebony smears a dozen times, but they moved too fast through the balloons for him to ever get a decent look at them. Aleksandr didn't care what they were. All that mattered was getting his brother out of this hellhole. Ivan stood still as Aleksandr stalked towards him, dropped down to one knee, and engulfed his brother in a tight hug.

"Are you hurt?" Aleksandr whispered.

The words died in his throat. Something was off. These moments of fearful reunion had become commonplace in their lives. They had a ritual to them. A process that they went through without thought or comment. Ivan would always hug him back, his small hands clutching his shirt, arms shaking slightly with both desperation and relief. All of that raw need was missing now. Slowly, Ivan reached up and loosely looped his arms around Aleksandr's neck. The touch was light, barely there, and made his skin crawl.

Aleksandr pulled back to stare into Ivan's eyes. He *knew* his little brother. He could recognize him on a level that he didn't even apply to himself. The thing in his arms was a perfect replica, but it wasn't his brother. Instinct rose up inside his chest, hissing and snarling like a startled animal, raging against logic and sanity to prove one simple fact. Whatever he was holding wasn't human.

"What's wrong, Alek?" Its voice was Ivan's, but somehow both flat and taunting at once.

Aleksandr shook his head, "What are you?"

Little giggles gurgled out of the boy. They started soft but snowballed and distorted into a shrill cackle. Aleksandr lurched back. The boy's hands gripped harder, nails growing as they slid down Aleksandr's shoulders, drawing blood until they managed to get a firm grip on his arms. With a strength that the tiny hands shouldn't rightfully possess, the boy held him in place. Struggling only forced Aleksandr off of his feet. The monster dragged him closer as its head flipped back, laughing at the ceiling. Its laughter was wild and unhinged, as the top of its head peeled back from its lower jaw, widening until the skin started to rip. Blood oozed from the tears at the edges of its mouth. One wet, thick crack, and its head broke in two like an open bear trap.

Aleksandr's eyes bulged from his skull when he saw thin, deformed arms emerge from its throat. They squirmed and thrashed as they stretched up towards the ceiling. As he watched in horror, spikes pushed free from the leathery skin. All the while, the laughter continued. Loud and manic and still with an undercurrent of his brother's voice.

Aleksandr threw himself back, barely noticing the pain as the clawed fingers shredded his skin. His feet skidded over the concrete as he twisted sharply, but he couldn't shake the grip. Each of the tentacles arched and swayed, like rattlesnakes preparing to strike. Their focus solely on him.

The first strike was just a blur. Flinching back, Aleksandr readied himself for the spike of pain. It came from his arms, but nowhere else. It took a second for his brain to catch up. The attack hadn't come from Ivan's imposter, but from the teen standing beside him. Her first kick had snapped against the boy's neck. The second collided with the junction of the dislocated mouth. Fresh blood spurted free, and the serpentine limbs whipped around. They cracked like whips, forcing Evelyn back. Quick and agile, she barely managed to avoid the attacks and hit at it again, making it reel back.

The laughter grew louder, breathless, as Evelyn grabbed Aleksandr's arm and wrenched him from the boy's grip. Not hesitating when fresh blood rushed free of the wounds. Not caring about the damage.

"Get up!" Evelyn screamed.

Her command broke him free of his shock. His feet were back under him before he knew what he was doing. They ran. The decorations clustered together, blocking their path, melting into each other to create a firmer wall. It smelled like rot and fell apart under his fingers like decaying flesh. Glancing over his shoulder, he couldn't see the monster through the crush.

But the laughter remained. Gleeful. Mocking. Crazed.

Even when he collided with the edge of the staircase, all that met his eyes was decomposing rubber and tousling paper. Air rushed from his lungs at the blow, and he hunched forward with a pained grunt. Fear kept him moving. Evelyn was little more than tuffs of dark, crinkly hair in the gaudy haze. He followed her up the staircase, pushing her back, coaxing her to go faster and clear the way.

Over the unstable, tittering laughter, Aleksandr caught a new sound. Footsteps. Light and fast and closing in behind them. The sound of a child running.

"Go!" Aleksandr bellowed as he shoved Evelyn forcefully.

He wanted to pick her up and toss her, needing her to move faster, to get to the top of the stairs before the monster closed in from behind. They burst through the threshold and were abruptly hurled back into reality. Everything was bright. Normal. Mounds of sand and harsh, glaring sunlight. The rapid shift was nauseating. He stumbled, knocking Evelyn to the ground but managing to keep his footing. Awkwardly, he twisted, grabbed the door, and slammed it shut. Instantly, the handle turned. Aleksandr pressed his shoulder against the door, braced his feet, and pushed with everything he had.

It wasn't enough.

The laughing monstrosity smacked against the other side of the wood. Over and over. Every impact widening the gap a little more. Balloons and confetti spewed out through the crack as the spiked tendrils scraped against the wood. Struggling to keep the pressure, his free hand fumbled with the locks. For all his efforts, the door was only ever flush in the frame for a few seconds at a time. He was never quick enough to engage the bolts. Sweat dripped from his forehead. His muscles burned. Blood smeared across the wood. All the while, the monster kept laughing. Aleksandr knew it was a trick, something to twist him up and lure him in. That knowledge didn't dampen his natural instinct. It raged and screamed against his logical mind. *Get Ivan! Save him! Help him!*

"Shift your leg!"

He looked down to see Evelyn on her back where she had fallen, propped up on her elbows, knees pulled to her chest. There was barely time to move his leg before her feet stomped down against the edge of the door. The blow was sharp and well-timed, landing a split second after the creature's attack. The door crashed back into the frame and Aleksandr rushed to slide the locks into place. One after the other. The door rattled and shook. Laughter grew. Nails scraped frantically against the wood. For one, terrifying moment, Aleksandr was sure it would claw its way through. The last lock clicked into place. Then everything stopped.

The world was silent. Calm.

Relief, shock, and pain pulsed through Aleksandr's veins, leaving him dizzy. Between one blink to the next, he crumpled to the floor like a marionette with its strings cut. Chest heaving, he thumped the back of his head to the floor and tried to catch his breath. It took longer than it should for him to remember that he wasn't alone. Considering recent events, a loose victim didn't seem all that important.

Using the back of his hand, he wiped the sweat from his forehead. It came away with a layer of festering, confetti-speckled sludge. He stared at his arm, at the proof that coated it. This wasn't a moment of madness or an illusion in the desert. It was real. Some part of him knew that this revelation should have affected him more. Cut deeper. Made him suspect that he was honestly losing his mind. But every time he reached for that panic, the only reaction he could muster was a sense of inevitability. His parents boasted that they were the apex predators. Aleksandr had never truly believed it. There was always something worse. And now it was *here*.

They'll come for you. I unleash the Furies upon you. They'll kill you all. You'll die screaming. His last victim's words echoed in his head as he stared at the brownish muck. At the time, it had seemed like a dim fantasy. One that he had longed for. *How is this possible?* he thought. *What the hell are Furies?*

"Do you think your parents are still down there?" Evelyn asked.

"No."

"Are you sure?"

He spared a few moments to catch his breath before bothering to reply. "None of these buildings are structurally sound."

"So what?" She pushed her hair back off of her furrowed brows. "The earthquake hits, they think the building's going to fall, and they run off instead of saving their son?"

"Yes."

"You're kidding?"

"The footage backs up to the cloud. They'd have no reason to stay."

"What about their son?"

Deciding that she wasn't ever going to grasp the concept, he couldn't see any reason to keep the conversation going. In the following silence, his brain quietened, and he finally noticed what had slipped his attention.

"It's not trying to get out," he muttered numbly.

It wasn't more than a passing thought that made it to his lips. In his experience, trapped things tended to fight against their confinement for longer than that.

"It's probably out already," Evelyn hurled herself up to rest her forearms on her knees.

She was still catching her breath, and while she looked at the goo on her arms with disgust, she didn't seem to have enough energy to try and slop it off.

"There's no other exit," Aleksandr said.

"That *thing* is just messing with us. I saw it birth itself from the ceiling. I doubt it has a lot of trouble with walls." She glanced at him and rolled her eyes. "Don't look at me like that. We're both long past any argument that this isn't real."

Aleksandr swallowed thickly. *If it's free, it can get to the twins.* He lunged up onto his feet, tripping over the uneven sand that had gathered by the walls.

"Where are you going?" Evelyn was on her feet and following him before he fully got past her.

"To get my twins."

"By just running out there?"

"Yes."

A few quick steps and she jumped in front of him, shoving one arm out. He jerked to a halt just before she could make contact with his stomach. A snarl rattled in his chest as he glared at her outstretched limb.

"Not touching," she assured. While she put both of her hands up like a hostage, she drifted to stand between him and the door. "Not touching. But I think we should think for a second."

"Are you going to follow me everywhere?"

"Follow? There was no follow. I came *back* for you. I was already at the top of the stairs before you found ... whatever that was."

Aleksandr took one, slow step backwards, his brow furrowed. "Why would you do that?"

"Because I felt a deep emotional bond with you and couldn't leave without getting your number."

Before Aleksandr could even begin to understand what was going on, she gestured behind her to the door.

"Why do you think? I realized that I have no idea where I am. Don't know if you have a car. And, if you do, I have no clue where it is or where you keep the keys. So, my choices were either to run around aimlessly with monsters – which are apparently real now – and two serial killers who could have very big guns. Or, come back and ask you. One of those seemed smarter than the other."

Each word shot out of her mouth at a rapid pace. A verbal tornado. She was able to put an entire conversation into the space of a sentence and it left Aleksandr off-center and grappling to keep up.

"There's one road out," he said at last. "Car's in the shed. Out that door, to the right. Petya always keeps the keys on him so you'll have to hotwire it."

"Hotwire? Because that's a thing most people know how to do."

Isn't it? Aleksandr decided not to voice the question. His education wasn't exactly mainstream. When he tried to side-step her, she cut him off, arm still high. Now, only an inch separated her palm from his stomach. The proximity made him sick, and being essentially the same height, it was hard to avoid making eye contact. It took a concerted effort to keep himself from backing up.

"Quick question," she said, still speaking with that disturbingly fast pace. "What is your plan here?"

"To get my twins."

"Great. Solid plan. Not knocking it. But then what?"

He shook his head, trying to catch up with the jumble of words. "What?"

"Step one; get kids. What's step two? Because that's important. Without step two, you've got two kids in the middle of a barren wasteland with, as mentioned earlier, monsters and serial killers. Seems like your end game is to prolong their agonizing deaths. If that's not what you're going for, maybe we should spitball a few other ideas."

Aleksandr clenched his teeth and rolled his shoulders, showing every sign that he was ready to rip her apart. She wiggled her hands, drawing his attention back to the fact that she was in a submissive posture.

"I'm getting them out of here," he hissed gruffly.

"And, why haven't you done that before now?"

"Because it was safer to stay. That's changed."

"Very true. One thing though; if you didn't stand a chance against your parents, how do you think you'll go with parents *and* monsters?"

"I will hurt you."

"Or," she said, completely unconcerned. "We work together. Hear me out, we both want to leave and get the kids out–"

He pushed forward, spurred on by the heat of rage, "Why would you care about my twins?"

"Because you don't blame kids for their parents." For that one sentence, her easy, nonchalant charade slipped, and he caught sight of the pure core of her anger rearing up to meet his own. Just a glimpse, that was all he got before a small, carefree smile crept back onto her lips. "My plan? We go and get the car, pick up the kids, get the hell out of here, kill whatever tries to stop us."

His brow furrowed. "Then what?"

"You drop me off at the nearest town, and we'll never see each other again."

A simple plan with one glaring problem.

"I have other siblings," he said. "They love our parents. If they find out I helped you ..."

"I'll keep you and the twins out of my police statements. I never saw you. You don't exist."

"We get two days head start before you call anyone."

"I can't do that to my dad."

Aleksandr went to step around her. When she cut him off again, he raised his fist. She raised hers, the other hand still outstretched to keep him at a distance. The gesture might have been threatening if he wasn't distracted by her footwork. Backing up over the uneven sand that smoothly took some skill.

"Counter offer. I call my dad but don't make any police reports for two days."

"You can pull that off?"

She scoffed. "I went through a traumatic event. No one would blame me for needing a few days of hysterical fits mixed in with a few bounds of catatonic staring."

Aleksandr studied her carefully. "How can I trust you?"

"Says the serial killer," she sneered. "How am *I* the suspicious one here? Besides, you don't have a choice. You can't do this on your own and I don't see any other kidnap victims offering assistance."

With practicality warring with suspicion, he considered the offer. Seconds ticked by, each one pressing down on him with a crushing weight.

"If you betray us," he said at last, forcing himself to meet her gaze as he finished, "I will kill you."

"Seems fair," she shrugged.

Bewildered by her casual agreement, he wasn't sure what he was supposed to do next. As he struggled to regain his bearings, she continued.

"But I need to know that you're willing to kill your parents if it comes to it."

"It's a dream come true."

"That's both disturbing and reassuring." Lowering her fist, she twisted her outstretched hand so it wasn't blocking his path anymore, but instead held vertically with her thumb up.

He stared at her hand, puzzled.

"Okay." It was the slowest she had ever said a word. "I guess you're not a 'shake on an agreement' kind of guy. How about a 'fist bump of collusion'?"

Keeping her hand where it was, she curled it into a fist and waited. Thinking that this moment was perhaps the weirdest thing that had ever happened to him, Aleksandr tapped his knuckles against hers. She beamed at him.

"Okay. First things first. Let's get that car."

Aleksandr shook his head. This time, she let him go around her. "We're getting my knife first."

Chapter 10

Evelyn had never experienced anything quite as liberating as reconciling with the fact that she was going to die. It didn't extinguish all of her fear. She could feel it crawling around her organs and drenching her mind. But she could fight against it, crush it under the weight of indifference, and keep it from taking control. Indifference and ridiculing psychopaths. It was a powerful rush. A thrill unlike anything else. She had looked into Olga's eyes and taunted her. Dismissed Petya while he held a loaded gun to her head. She had never felt so powerful. Reality lingered in her thoughts, telling her that it was all just an illusion. She had been, and still was, their victim. Luck and timing had spared her. Simple as that.

But it was a marvelous delusion and she clung to it as she followed Aleksandr out of the building. After so long in darkness and artificial light, the sun was blinding. Muggy heat ravaged her skin and boiled her lungs. Both, she could ignore. The sand, however, was torture. Every step burned like molten gold, the particles sinking into the dozens of cuts that covered her feet. Adrenaline had kept her from noticing the damage earlier. Now, her body was running low on that precious, pain-reducing hormone and the muted sensations were becoming sharp. Smothering her whimpers of pain, she kept moving, forcing herself to keep up with Aleksandr's pace.

In theory, it shouldn't have been a hard task. He was covered in blood and gunk, ripped to shreds, and looked about a second from death. Still, he practically ghosted over the sand. Crouched low, he took the slope in wide, silent steps. Constantly vigilant. Breathing deep and even. Watching him, it was impossible for Evelyn to ignore the fact that she wasn't in her element. This wasn't the ring. Or her home. Or anywhere else that tipped the odds in her favor. They were on his family's home turf, where these killers had grown and adapted. They had the advantage here. *So, adapt as well,* she told herself. *Or burn this place down.*

Aleksandr helped her get up to the house on the hill, but the strain left her breathless and weak. The heat was crushing. It hadn't occurred to her how much cooler it was underground. In reality, it could only be a few degrees difference, but it changed everything. She could almost feel her blood evaporating in her veins. Finally, they reached the shadow of the house. The temperature didn't change, but getting out of the sun felt like stepping onto the dark side of the moon. Aleksandr had his hand on the back door before he seemed to recall that she was there.

"You probably don't want to come inside," he whispered.

"I need water," Evelyn replied. "And I want a knife of my own."

"The kitchen's a mess."

She took in a deep breath, reminded herself not to hit him, and carefully stated that there was no chance in hell he was leaving her outside. Glancing around, he seemed to decide that the argument wasn't worth the risk of exposure.

"Breathe through your mouth," he said.

The fly screen clicked but opened with barely more than a whisper. A gust of putrid air rolled out of the house and she clamped a hand over her mouth and nose. It didn't help. She could feel the bile rising up her throat. It didn't bother Aleksandr. With well-practiced ease, he slipped his head just far enough into the kitchen to check if the coast was clear. The silence was dense, unrelenting. It put

Evelyn on edge. Restlessly, she constantly scanned the area, searching for any sign that the monsters had found them. Not that she fully believed they were gone. Even now, she could feel that something was watching her. Waiting. And that was worse. Being attacked by a malevolent unknown force was one thing. Terror and adrenaline could push her through it. But this wasn't an attack. This was messing with her. Taunting her.

"Keep quiet," Aleksandr whispered.

Evelyn snapped around. She wasn't able to see the majority of his face, but his mouth was visible and his scowl spoke volumes.

"I'm fine," she assured him softly. "I've got this."

While it wasn't exactly convincing, it worked, and Aleksandr slipped silently in to the shadows of the house. Evelyn followed. Nothing of what she had smelled outside prepared her for the overwhelming stench waiting for her inside the kitchen. She gagged, dry heaving against the backs of her teeth even as she tried to swallow it down. One hand pressed against her stomach, the other clutched her mouth. Still, the stench threw her forward, almost rocking her off her feet. Her hand snapped out, looking for anything that could help to keep her upright.

She latched blindly onto the first object her fingers found. A chunky goop oozed up around her fingers. There was a wet crack and she stumbled forward, releasing a new wave of rancid air. Something squirmed against her fingertips as she lifted her head. The scream ripping through her chest didn't have a chance to get out of her throat. She was struggling to pull her hand out of the maggot-filled corpse it had sunken into. It swayed at each of her attempts. Its head lulled back and forth. Jaw slack. The bones rattling together like a cheap imitation of laugher.

Aleksandr grabbed her forearm. One solid push and the corpse toppled to the floor. Her hand slipped out of the broken cavity with a sucking slurp, leaving her hand covered with fresh gunk and squirming, bone-white larvae. Bugs bounced against her face as if trying to find their way into her mouth, her eyes, her nose. She hurled again, her empty stomach straining to find something to throw up. Gripping her around the waist, Aleksandr dragged her to the kitchen sink. One hand on the back of her head, he forced her forward, letting her spit and gasp over the rusted steel.

"I told you," he whispered by her ear.

She wanted to tell him off, but was too busy flipping on the table and frantically scrubbing her hand clean. The little ivory bugs toppled from her skin, squirming with renewed protest before they followed the flow of glugging brown water down the drain. She rubbed until her hands were clean, then kept going. Until her skin was raw and small pinpricks of blood began to well up. The water ran from black to clear. She wouldn't stop even as a red tinge tainted the water.

"You're never going to *feel* clean," Aleksandr whispered.

He placed a kitchen knife beside her elbow and handed her an empty cup. Thirst had been forgotten in her frenzy, but it raced back now. She grabbed the glass filled it under the flowing faucet and drained it all in a few gulps. The first splashes of the tepid water against her gut provoked another, violent heave. Leaning over the rim of the sink, she threw up every last drop. A few more attempts and she was able to keep it down. She drank with a frantic, desperate need. Long after her thirst was quenched. Only stopping when her stomach was on the verge of bursting. Now full, she felt the churn of her stomach on a new level. The rancid air was overpowering.

"For the record," she said as she wrapped shaking fingers around the handle of the knife, "you could have warned me about the bodies."

"I did."

As sick, twisted, and gross as it all was, she almost laughed. Because Aleksandr sounded offended. Childishly offended. And that was just too much to deal with right now. She turned around and stepped into a puddle of goo. A pool of decayed muscle, skin, and fat.

"Oh, God," she whimpered. "It's between my toes."

"What?" Aleksandr stood at the threshold to the next room and turned upon hearing her voice.

For a second, she had thought that the gentle clicks she heard were from him. But they came again as he remained still. Drifted up from the other direction. Aleksandr's mouth furrowed. He heard it too. They both turned, looking across the room to the table. There were four places, all taken. The fifth chair was now empty, its occupant now sprawled in pieces across the floor.

Click. Click. Click.

Aleksandr swallowed. He recognized the sound. Evelyn was sure he did. *Are his parents back?* Torn between running and staying still and silent, she looked to Aleksandr for guidance. His attention drifted to the table. In unison, the four upright corpses jolted in their seats, their bones clicking together within the melted casing of their skin.

"I'm going to need you to tell me what you just saw," Evelyn said in a rush.

"The bodies moved."

"Oh, good," she stammered, trying to maintain her level of sarcasm even as anxiety bubbled up in her gut. "So, it did happen."

In one split second of movement, all four corpses snapped their heads around to face them. Evelyn jumped, the small of her back colliding with the edge of the sink. Aleksandr had frozen in place, one balled fist already raised and ready to strike. The unsteady silence was back. Her heart pounded hard against her ribs as anticipation turned thick and bitter in the back of her mouth. The bodies were still but no longer entirely lifeless. They sat with a rigidity that their rancid muscles couldn't possibly possess. Their lower jaws hung low, creating ghastly smiles. Time had already reduced their eyes to mush. The little that had remained in their sockets sloshed out and drizzled down the exposed bones of their cheeks. It looked like they were crying with laughter.

Click. Click. Click.

Evelyn flicked her eyes around the room, desperately searching for the source of the sound, trying to pinpoint which one of the bodies was moving. They all remained still. Watching. Dead faces distorted in silent laughter.

Click. Click. Click.

Evelyn turned, drawn towards the sound that now distinctly came from behind her.

Bodies crammed themselves against the kitchen window, their bony fingers clacking against the glass as they tried to claw their way in. Behind them, dozens of broken, gnarled corpses, each in a different state of decay, staggered up the slope. The reddish sand flung out in waves as they sprinted towards the house. She threw herself back from the window. Her throat swelled shut, turning her words of warning into a gargled croak.

A blur shot up from under the rickety table. A hand. It latched onto her bare leg, flesh squishing and cartilage snapping. Her bottled scream broke free from her throat. It served as a catalyst, whipping the dead into a frenzy. They slammed against the window, rattled the door, desperate to find a way inside. She leaped back from the table, but the grip was stronger than she had anticipated. It held on. Her retreating steps dragged the shattered, maggot-infested remains she had broken earlier out from under the table. Its jaws snapping ferociously. Hard enough to fracture its teeth and spew the remains over the linoleum.

Evelyn screamed again and pulled back with more force. Still holding on, the corpse slid with her then jerked to a stop, the motion sending a wave of fetid ooze sloshing out of its gaping mouth and hollow eye sockets. Its foul mess pooled under her feet. She slipped and would have fallen helplessly to the floor if Aleksandr hadn't hooked an arm around her shoulders.

Crouching to take her weight, he tossed her back up onto her feet as the bodies hurled themselves from the table. She stomped the writhing mass of bones into mush as he surged past her and kicked the table. It rattled across the linoleum, slamming into the furthest two and keeping them back while he took care of the others. The back door wrenched open and the twitching cadavers swarmed into the room.

"Front door!" Aleksandr bellowed at her over his shoulder.

He retreated out of the room and she moved to follow, the slop under her feet making her slide. That split second was all it took for one of the monsters to close the distance between them. Skeletal fingers seized her arm. Instinctively, she swung her fist, kitchen knife still in her grip. The corpse's skull shattered on impact, releasing a wave of putrid brain matter riddled with insect larva. She was already running before it crumbled. It didn't release its grip. Not even after the arm had popped out of its socket. Evelyn had to break each of the joints to get the fingers off of her.

As she raced past Aleksandr, she tossed the severed limb blindly into the living room. The front door stood before her. It called to her like a beacon, whispering promises of salvation. Her legs struggled to meet the demands of her mind. A quiver rippled along her outstretched arm, her fingers greedily reaching for the doorknob. A few inches still separated them when the worn, metal circle twisted.

The door opened outwards and that seemed to confuse the horde of rotting flesh. It created a bottleneck effect; slowed what could have been a flood of death into a volatile trickle. There was nowhere to go. The living room was a dead end. The exits were a lost cause.

"Upstairs!" Aleksandr commanded.

The stream of death had already filled the small foyer, cutting off the bottom stairs. Evelyn had to jump to grab the top of the staircase banister. With the knife still in her hand, an awkward grip threatened to fail her. Planting one foot on the wall under the stairs, she pushed off, jumped over the railing, and dropped down onto the stairs. Aleksandr did the same, landing a few stairs higher up. Taking them two at a time, she caught up with him and they raced to the top, side-by-side. If either of them had been any bigger, it would have been an impossible maneuver. But the hair's breadth of space allowed them to pull it off.

The rickety house shook and groaned at the sheer number of bodies clambering up the stairs. Plaster cracked off of the walls and sand poured down from the roof. With her heart in her throat, Evelyn prayed that the house stood for just a little longer. It seemed like they were ripping it apart at the seams.

"Twins' room," Aleksandr said as they sprinted down the hallway.

"I don't know your house!" she screamed back.

Abruptly, Aleksandr grabbed the strap of her crop top. When he tossed himself through an open doorway, he yanked her in after him. Instantly, she slammed the door shut and set about barricading with a nearby cabinet. Anger flashed along her veins when she noticed that Aleksandr wasn't helping. Instead, he was dragging the bunk beds from the wall.

"Zombies don't get priority?" she snapped.

Ignoring her, he drove his fist through the wall. A large square of plaster peeled easily from the wall, exposing the building's raw wooden innards.

"You built an escape route in the kids' room?" she asked, back pressed against the cabinet as if she could keep it in place.

"Have you met my family?" he snapped. Retrieving two backpacks from the hiding place, he tossed one over to her. "Are you coming?"

Already pulling the straps onto her shoulders, she bolted across the room. A thin strip of rope was attached to the wall. She couldn't feel the breeze, but one must have been slipping through the gaps to make the rope sway. Needing to hold on with both hands, she bit down on the thin blade of her knife, careful to keep the sharp edge facing out. She gagged as droplets of sludge dripped onto her tongue but grabbed the rope and pushed out into the open space.

It was a tight fit. The uneven blanks of the outer wall scraped her knees while the backpack snagged on inner structure. Aleksandr followed just as the cabinet gave way. The invasion rattled the wall, sending waves of dust and body parts toppling down around them. Hand over hand, Evelyn worked her way down into the gloom. The coarse material scraped along the broken skin of her palms. Heat pulsated around her, making her vision blur and her head swim. A torso hit her, exposed ribs cracking painfully against her wrist bones. The blow loosened her grip. She plummeted down, stomach lurching, rope burning her palms. In one moment of clarity, she tossed the knife away just before she collided with the mound of sand.

It was like falling into a snow drift. Partly accommodating, partly solid. Tucking her arms in, she rolled, helplessly spinning over and over. The sun hit her. Blinding and scorching her at once. Coming to a stop at the base of the hill, she struggled to draw in a deep breath. Every twitch brought a fresh wave of pain. Clenching her teeth, she forced herself up onto her hands and knees and looked back up to the house. A sea of monsters were racing down the hill towards her. Aleksandr was nowhere in sight. Her first thought was to head back up. To find him. Reality sunk in as she got to her feet. In her current state, trying to get back up there was a suicide mission. *Get to the shed,* she told herself. *Get the car. Come back.* How she was going to hotwire it, she didn't know. But the horde was closing in. She needed to move.

Chapter 11

Aleksandr hit the sand hard. Crab crawling, he scuttled out from under the house, holding his knife so the back of the blade was flush along the length of his forearm. The severed limbs squirmed across the sand, trying to follow him as other bodies dropped down around him like boulders. Swooping, he ducked the edge of the building and stepped out into the sun. He straightened up, knife at the ready, and found himself facing a wall. Confused, he twisted around. Orange tiles that time had faded to look like moldy peaches. A thin bathtub. Exposed pipes and a faded overhead light bulb. Hyperventilating, he spun around again. *No. This can't be real.* No matter which way he turned, the walls remained the same. He was back in the house. In the upstairs bathroom.

Panic became acid in his veins. He launched himself at the door, not caring if the dead were waiting for him outside. The lock held. The door refused to budge. *No. No, no, no.* It repeated in his head, faster and faster until it was just a blur. Growing in desperation as the door held. Hot tears welled in his eyes, blurring his vision and he slammed his shoulder against the unrelenting wood.

"Aleksandr."

He froze. Years had passed since he had heard that voice, but he recognized it instantly. Trembling violently, he stared at the door. *Don't look. It's not real. He's not real. Don't look.*

"Aleksandr," the voice came again, weak and sweet.

A child's voice. A perfect replica of his memory. *Remember their trick with Ivan,* he told himself sharply. *Don't fall for it again.*

"Why won't you look at me, Aleksandr?"

He squeezed his eyes shut, forcing the scorching tears to drip free.

"Alek—"

"Stop." It was both a command and plea.

"I'm scared, Aleksandr."

"You're not him." His voice broke into a hard sob. Swallowing thickly, he forced the words out. "I know you're not."

"Aren't you glad to see me?"

"Timofey died many years ago."

Died. It was an easy word to say. A simple word that covered a multitude of sins. That spoke of the main event while sparing him the details.

"I'm here. Aleksandr, I'm cold."

Water sloshed, and Aleksandr hunched in on himself. He fought with everything he had to keep the images from forming in his mind.

"Aleksandr ..."

The plea broke him. He bashed his forehead against the door, choking as he wept.

"You're my big brother. Help me."

Say it! Aleksandr commanded himself. He could feel his grip on reality slipping because the illusion was so much better than the reality. The guilt. The horror. The blood. The lie stood as a comfort he wanted to surrender to. *Say it!* he screamed in his own head. *Admit it! Own what you did!*

"I watched," he snarled. "Petya and Olga forced me to watch as they beat

Timofey into a coma. He wanted to leave."

"Turn around, Alek."

He stabbed the door with his knife, his white knuckled grip helping him endure the words.

"They took him in here after," Aleksandr forced himself to continue, every word like barbed wire in this throat. "They put the cold water on him to wake him up."

"And you watched." The accusation and disgust in Timofey's voice ripped Aleksandr in two.

Not the real Timofey. The truth was like a whisper in a hurricane. Barely heard and of little consequence.

"I watched," he admitted. "I watched when they turned the hot water on instead. They laughed when your skin bristled."

Not really.

"And you watched."

"You didn't wake up. But you were alive. You were breathing."

Water hit the backs of his feet in little waves. The sensation birthed a fresh wave of panic within Aleksandr's mind, the rush dispersing his thoughts like smoke. He knew there was something he needed to remember. Something important.

"You didn't save me." Timofey no longer spoke in the voice of a four-year-old. Instead, the voice sounded dark, furious, and ancient.

"I sat with you," Aleksandr sobbed, blinded by tears and grief. "I held your hand. It was all they'd let me do."

"You left me to rot."

"I wanted to bury you. I swear I did. They wouldn't let me."

The sound of wet footsteps stalked up behind him. Accompanied by the rising water. His eyes snapped up open wide as he felt the tepid water splash against his calves.

Hot breath brushed across his ear as a demonic voice growled, "You bathed with my corpse."

No, the thought spiraled away before Aleksandr could grasp it.

"They made me. I didn't want to," he whimpered.

"For months." The overly sweet scent of decay hit Aleksandr's nose as the water reached his knees. "I lay there for months and you did nothing."

"I'm sorry. I'm so sorry, Timofey."

"Look at me."

Aleksandr shook his head, never lifting it from the door.

"Look what you did. What you allowed to happen!"

Waves lapped against Aleksandr's hips. Horror shot through him like an eclectic blot, igniting every sense that grief had suppressed. *Ivan. Nadya.* The thought seized his lungs. Turning them to ice and freezing his shock. *They need you!*

"I needed you," the voice hissed.

No! The word cracked through the haze of his mind like a bolt of lightning. Staring down at the rising water, he clenched his hand and stabbed the door again. *Nadya and Ivan are alive. They're waiting for me. Go and get them!*

"You can't save them."

Aleksandr narrowed his eyes. "You're not Timofey."

"I've come to take you with me, big brother." The water had reached his ribs as the creature plastered itself to his back. "You, me, and the twins. We're all going to Hell."

Rage exploded under his skin. Throwing his head back, he cracked his skull against the monster. It howled with fury but only retreated a step. It was enough. Aleksandr spun around and brought the knife up, shoving the long blade under the monster's ribs before he even realized what he was looking at. The beast from the desert. It loomed over him, fire blazing in its eye sockets as smoke poured from between its fangs.

His horror, his dread, his guilt and emerging hysteria. Nothing compared to the pure blinding rage that consumed him now. *Not my kids.* He spat the words out in his mind, knowing somehow that the monstrosity before could hear. *Never my kids!*

Its jaws widened, lips rolling back to bare engorged fangs. It lunged forward. Raising one arm up to fend off the strike, Aleksandr yanked the blade free and drove it down into one of its eyes. A roar rattled the room, but it was the water that terrified him. Each movement sent waves crashing into his face. It pushed past his lips and solidified like concrete in his throat.

Ivan and Nadya!

He clutched the thought before him like a shield as he drove the knife down over and over.

Never again! Never them!

Flattening his feet against the door, he pushed off, forcing the monster back, giving him just enough room to swing the knife around. One push. One slice. And the creature's innards spilt out into the water.

Not them!

Hot blood blossomed around him as the water covered his head.

Not them!

One more stab and the floor dropped, leaving him to fall into oblivion.

***

Gripping the metal pole with both hands, Evelyn pulled the shed's sliding door open. She kept her side pressed to the moving door in hopes that it would protect her from whatever might be lurking within the shadows. When nothing came rushing out, she glanced back at the house and froze. The sun was gone. Between one blink and the next, the light that had been scorching her eyes had disappeared from the sky. No sunset. No last final blazes of the day. A blanket of ebony had been laid over the land, without stars or a moon to disrupt the empty abyss. The only light was the soft glow that slipped out from the open shed door. It barely made it a few feet before her, and ended with a razor-sharp edge.

But the world wasn't silent. Little shifts and grunts. Quiet whispers. Footsteps. And the far away sound of laughter. They all echoed towards her, making it impossible for her to turn her back to the darkness. With one hand trailing along the wall, she worked her way to the gap and backed inside. A heavy thud made her turn, the night forgotten as a body dropped from the open door of the car. From her position by the door, she could only see a silky stream of blonde hair and an ever-increasing pool of blood.

"Olga," Petya chastised as he came around the back of the vehicle to survey the damage. "Look what you did."

"She was making eyes at you," Olga dismissed.

"So you gouge her eyes out. You don't kill her. Now what are we going to use as a distraction?"

Evelyn inched backwards as they spoke, trying to slip out into the night before they noticed her presence. She couldn't tear her eyes from the body as she moved. A sharp, short click made her freeze. Lifting her gaze, the first thing she saw was the barrel of the revolver. Petya held it aimed between her eyes, his smile easy. Almost charming.

"Evelyn," he chuckled. "This is a surprise. Isn't life fun sometimes?"

Olga held the frame as she leaned out of the back of the car.

"How did she get out of the cell?"

"I don't know, darling," Petya said. "Why don't we ask her?"

Evelyn glanced between them and the revolver. "Shouldn't you be asking about at least one of your kids?"

Olga pulled further out from the car, curling around her husband's shoulders to whisper into his ear. "Shoot her."

Petya used his free hand to stroke her hair. "Now, now, my love. Let's not be rash. We know how much our guests like live bait."

A column of ice speared Evelyn, cracking through her ribs and stealing her breath. *The twins.* She didn't know. Had only seen one of them while they served as bait. Still, the idea of children being left to face the monsters stalking the desert left her chilled to the bone.

"What did you do?" she whispered.

"It doesn't seem like you really grasp the concept of a gun to your head," Petya noted.

"You don't grasp the concept of parenting. So, it looks like we all have our faults."

"I'm going to peel the skin off of your face," Olga hissed.

"Come over here and do it!" Evelyn snapped. "You think you can scare me? I've had a really hard day!"

Noise rose up behind her. The rim of light had shrunk since she had last looked back. Now, the threshold was the borderline of reality. Nothing existent beyond it. Something paced back and forth in the darkness. Throaty snarls drifted out from the shadows. She backed up a few paces, the fear of what lurked outside far greater than the couple in front of her. At least, that's what she had thought. It was hard to hold onto that conviction when the silence returned.

"We need to go," Olga said. It was strange to hear the notes of fear weaving their way through the woman's words. "Get the girl already."

Petya's arm never wavered. But he didn't take a step towards Evelyn either. His eyes kept flicking from her to the shadows beyond her shoulder. Despite everything, a twisted little smile curled Evelyn's lips.

"How does it feel to be hunted?" she asked.

78

Petya's eyes flared. The tendons in his throat pressed against his skin as he bared his teeth. "Get in the car."

"No."

Taking only one step closer, he made a show of training the gun between her eyes. "Now."

Evelyn lifted her chin. "You want me? Come over here and get me."

Her bravado shattered as the first gunshot boomed. The walls of the shed held the sound, throwing it back on her as she cowered, arms instinctively coming up to protect her head. Panting heavily, it slowly dawned on her that she wasn't injured. Lowering her hands, she saw that neither of the killers was looking at her, their attention was on the rafters. She glanced up to see two shotguns poking over the edge. It took a moment for her eyes to adjust to the dim light and see the tiny forms behind the weapons. Two identical children, their pale faces ghostlike in the shadows.

"Ivan," Petya said slowly. "Did you just shoot at me?"

"No, father. That was all Nadya."

The little figure next to the first waved.

Olga stood up in the doorframe of the car. "Get down here right now."

The second shot punched a hole through the top of the car, a few inches away from the woman's shoulder.

"The next one's in your head," Nadya bellowed as loudly as her cherub like voice could muster.

"Where's Aleksandr?" Ivan demanded.

At this distance, it was hard to keep track of which one of them was talking. Even their voices were on par, almost indistinguishable.

"He's down here," Petya said. "Come down, children. We'll take you to him."

"Stay up there," Evelyn shouted to them.

A few light whispers passed back and forth before one of them said, "We don't know you."

"I'm Evelyn," she replied. "And I promised Aleksandr that I'd help get you out of here."

Olga snapped her head around, her face twisted with disgust. "You and Alek? He betrayed us?"

"How does any of that surprise you?"

"I'm getting tired of your mouth," Olga emerged fully from the vehicle.

Without concern for the children above or the monsters outside, the older woman stalked towards Evelyn with a singular, predatory purpose. Evelyn shifted one foot back, raising her hands, fists balled and ready to fight.

"I've been looking forward to this," Evelyn said.

The side of the shed suddenly exploded, raining down like shrapnel. Evelyn sprinted to the side, rushing towards the children as she sought shelter from the shards. The building groaned as it swayed, the pillars toppling as the roof came down in fragments. Screams splintered the night. Some from the couple, some from the twins as their perch started to give way, and some of the more frantic ones that Evelyn knew were her own.

Her breath turned into a solid lump in her throat as two colossal serpents smashed through the remaining parts of the walls. Their fangs alone were as long as her body. Their bodies curled and swiped, reaping greater destruction with every move. Covering her head with her arms, she ran, searching the space above her head as she moved. She hadn't yet figured out where the meek light was coming from, but it remained even as the shed toppled. As if they wanted to ensure that they could see the monstrous reptiles that were coming for them now.

"Nadya! Ivan!" she screamed.

Both snakes reared, tracking her movement with onyx eyes and flicking tongues. A pillar crashed down between her and the animals. They lashed out, striking at the moving wood as she ran past. It was getting harder to move. The debris that fell upon her steadily growing larger. Gunfire boomed as Petya faced off with the animals. Out of the corner of her eyes, Evelyn noticed Olga joining the fight. But her attention wasn't on them, or the snakes, or the shed. She had finally spotted the twins. Both of them were hanging from a rafter, their small arms struggling to hold on as it rattled and quaked.

"It's okay!" she screamed up to them, flinching away as one of the serpents struck beside her.

The blow wasn't aimed at her. It didn't even notice her as its massive body rolled above her, making her drop. With a thunderous crush, it destroyed the last of the shed that had been keeping up the children's hiding place. Like a severed tree, it began to fall. Slowly at first. Quickly gaining strength. Evelyn sprinted alongside it.

"One of you, drop!" she commanded. "I'll catch you."

Neither seemed inclined to take her up on the offer, but gravity pulled one down. She caught them, the collision painful and knocking them both to the ground.

"Nadya!" the boy screamed up to his still hanging sister.

He stomped on Evelyn's chest in his hurry to get up, his fragile body feeling a thousand pounds as it drove into her stomach. The small girl above them had scrambled up onto a pillar and thrown herself. Evelyn shot up, already knowing that she wasn't going to get there fast enough. But the small girl had jumped for her. She landed on the back of the snake as it slithered past. The giant reptile reared and hissed, lashing out with gaping jaws to try and swallow the girl. But Nadya was fast and fearless. She slipped around the snake's rapidly coiling body, ensuring that there was always a layer of its own flesh between her and the fangs.

"Where's the gun?" Ivan demanded as he searched through the rubble. He wasn't strong enough to lift most of it.

In one smooth move, Evelyn pulled off the backpack and forced the straps over the boy's arms. While she hadn't had a chance to look inside it yet, she doubted Aleksandr would have given her dead weight to carry. Whatever was in it would be critical for survival. Ivan whipped around to face her, his eyes screaming in panic while his face remained impassive.

"Can you hot wire a car?" she asked.

"Who cares about the car?" he snapped.

"You and Alek," Evelyn hissed as she hurled the boy up into her arms. He squirmed and thrashed but it was easy enough to keep her hold. "Get the car started. I'll get your sister. We gotta get Alek."

Not bothering to give a sign of agreement, Ivan just focused his gaze on the vehicle in question. They charged through the battle zone. Gunshots booming. Wood cracking. Snakes thrashing wildly in their desperate attempt to sink their fangs into flesh. Even with the walls and roof reduced to rubble, the glowing light remained in the same dimensions as before. A sharp-edged box cut out of the surrounding darkness.

Nearing the vehicle, she crouched low to drop Ivan off. He jumped from her arms and was already running before he hit the ground. Adrenaline pushed her to the brink of insanity. That was all she could think to explain why she picked up a piece of twisted metal and drove it deep into the nearest snake's side. It thrashed, its huge body slamming against the ground hard enough to make it tremble. The unstable remains she stood upon slid and she fell, smacking into Olga before she hit the ground. Ignoring everything that was going on around her, the woman clawed her way on top of Evelyn, pressing her down with one hand as the other retrieved the nearest debris.

Evelyn drove the point of her elbow down into the soft hollow between Olga's collarbones. The woman snarled like a wild animal, taking the pain and attempting to strike again. Evelyn snapped her fist up, her knuckles slicing open on the crazed woman's teeth. Blood dripped from Olga's mouth, some her own, and some of Evelyn's. Olga clawed and ripped at every patch of vulnerable skin she could find. Evelyn screamed in agony as the nails sunk into her flesh.

Caught in her frenzied bloodlust, Olga abandoned her wild strikes in favor of her teeth. Flopping down upon Evelyn, using her larger bulk to pin the teen's wrists to the ground, the serial killer latched onto Evelyn's neck. There was a moment of intense, burning pressure before Evelyn felt her skin pop like a ripe tomato. Olga's teeth sunk deep. Blood spurted free. Drenching her skin and gushing into Olga's mouth. The taste seemed to feed her madness and she began to shake her head like a dog, widening the wound. Evelyn bucked, trying to shake the woman off, all of her attempts only increasing the damage. Even the serpent's body winding inches above them didn't deter the attack.

Suddenly, Olga lurched back. There was a flash of metal. A short scream and a quick jerk. Evelyn looked up to find that she no longer had the mad woman's attention. Aleksandr stood behind his mother, one arm wrapped around as if in an embrace. It took a split second to realize that Aleksandr had pulled his mother back by her hair. And that his loving hug actually ended with a knife plunged into the woman's gut. Olga twitched. Blood oozed from her slack mouth as she turned to look at her son.

"Alek," she whispered.

His face remained an expressionless mask as Aleksandr pulled the knife from its fleshy sheath. He yanked Olga's head back and swiped the blade across the exposed throat. A wave of blood washed out over Evelyn as the woman gargled and groaned.

"Move," Alek demanded as he reared up, dragging the bleeding woman up with him.

Evelyn rolled onto her stomach, pushed up onto all fours, and twisted to look at him. "Nadya?"

"Car."

As if to add substance to his single word, the engine roared to life. It drew everyone's attention.

"Go!" Aleksandr ordered.

The word was barely heard over Petya's agonized scream. *He's seen his wife,* Evelyn realized. A new layer of hell and vengeance was charging towards them and she didn't want to be around when it struck. The ground bucked like a living beast as the snakes snapped around, torn between blocking the vehicle and attacking those still out in the open. As she ran over the debris, she caught sight of the vehicle. One of the twins was behind the wheel, barely able to see over the dash as they sunk into their seat to touch the pedals. The other had found their shotgun. As she neared, Evelyn realized that the backpack must have had some ammo, because they reached into the pockets each time they needed to reload.

The vehicle lurched forward for a few feet before the snake slammed its body down to block its path. Then the shooter would pop, fire at it to get it moving, and the process would begin again. Putting everything she had left into her sprint, she raced to the vehicle and threw herself in through and open back window. The shooter whipped around. There wasn't much room to move the gun and Evelyn was easily able to grab the barrel.

"Don't shoot me," she hissed.

She wasn't sure which one she was talking to, Ivan or Nadya, but it didn't matter. The driver slammed their foot down and the vehicle lurched forward. Built for rough terrain, the wheels rocked over the remains of the shed, weaving, tossing the occupants one way then the next. They plunged out into the night just as something solid slammed down upon the roof. Evelyn had to flatten herself against the seat so the child could whip the gun around. The shot never came. Aleksandr threaded himself through the driver's side window, seamlessly taking over for the child driver as they scrambled out of the way.

"Father?" the shooter asked.

"Alive," Aleksandr said.

"Why would you do that?" the driver whined.

"Because," he said as he forced the car faster into the bottomless night. "Live bait is a better distraction."

Chapter 12

They had to drive for forty-five minutes for the stars to return to the sky. Further still for any recognizable landmarks to appear through the car's high beams. Evelyn hadn't noticed how strange the world had become until the real world began to emerge from the fake one. Clicking into place as they left the monsters behind. During this time, Nadya had been in the back, helping a very confused Evelyn tend to her wounds. It was almost comical, catching the teen's expressions in the rearview mirror when the ten-year-old informed her she needed stitches. As the twins had pointed out to her, a proper serial killer needs to know how to tend to their own injuries, and the Sokolovsky children had been taught well. That didn't mean that Evelyn was too excited about the idea of a pre-teen jabbing her neck repeatedly in the back of a moving car. The humor wore off the instant the needle sunk in for the first stitch. All the essentials were in their emergency evacuation bags, but any good quality painkiller wouldn't have lasted, stored in such conditions. Evelyn had to endure with aspirin and a few small bottles of vodka.

Driving flat out the entire way, they neared the small rural town earlier than anticipated. The agreement had been that they would stop, but none of them had felt safe enough to do so. It barely took a second to speed down the empty main road and join the highway. Once streetlights and other cars became a common enough sight, Aleksandr passed the driving over to the twins. They had done it enough times for him to have faith in their abilities. Working in tandem, one working the wheel and the other the pedals, they actually added up to be a decent driver.

Slipping into the back seat, he landed with a pained grunt and started to rummage around for any first-aid supplies that hadn't been used. There was a bit of damage that would need looking after properly, and one of his fingers was most certainty broken, but nothing seemed life threatening.

"Are they okay driving?" Evelyn asked as she stared at the children.

He wondered if it was pain, exhaustion, or shock that had put her in such an apathetic state. In any case, her words had steadily slowed and decreased. Now, the brief conversation that did take place mostly revolved around checking for injuries and tending to the wounds mentioned. No one had approached the topic of what had happened yet. For his part, Aleksandr had avoided it out of superstition. A fear that, if he addressed it, the monsters would appear again.

"They're fine," Aleksandr assured as he lightly tapped the back of the driver's seat with his foot. "You are doing the speed limit, right?"

"Yep," they chirped in unison.

"Because speeding will draw attention and get us pulled over."

The car slowed a little and he shook his head.

"Okay," Evelyn said suddenly. "I can't take it anymore. What the fu–"

"Hey," Aleksandr cut her off with a snarl.

In the rhythmic glow of the passing street lights, he met her gaze and jerked his head towards the twins.

"Seriously? They just faced off with giant snakes, serial killers, zombies, and whatever else happened to them out there, but you're concerned about them hearing mild swear words?"

"You have to have some boundaries," he noted as he began to wash out the cuts on his arms with bottled water.

She gaped at him for a long moment. "Fine. What the *frick-frack* happened out there?"

"Furies," Ivan chirped. "I told you they were real. No one ever listens to me."

"That's because you're boring," Nadya noted.

By the sound of it, she earned a playful smack for her trouble. Aleksandr sunk deeper into the seat, eyes drifting closed and a smile growing on his face as he listened to them squabble. *Alive. Safe. And as sane as can be expected.*

"What is a fury?" Evelyn cut in.

"Oh," Ivan sounded surprised for the follow up question and took a moment to organize his thoughts.

Aleksandr had to admit that, at this point in time, he didn't care what they were. All that mattered was that they were free. Finally, free. At least for now. Everything else was a problem for another day.

"It's ancient Greek mythology," Ivan said, quickly muttering an 'I think' before raising his voice again. "They're like, three demonic sisters or something. In the stories, when people want revenge on evil people, they ask the sisters to do it for them."

"Why not just do it themselves?" Nadya said, honestly perplexed.

"I don't know. Weak stomachs?" Ivan replied.

Aleksandr didn't interrupt. He knew the kids had seen something, horrors on a far greater scale than what they were prepared for, but he wasn't about to open those wounds while they were in a moving car. That was a conversation to be had when they were safe, clean, and had a full stomach. In their need to flee, he still hadn't been able to give them hugs. His arms ached for it and a part of his soul screamed in protest at the separation, but this too had to wait. Because he knew, once he had them close, he wasn't about to let go for a while. They needed to put some distance behind them first.

"One of my victims cursed us," he mumbled. "I hadn't thought it was real."

"That's because you didn't listen to me," Ivan said, his haughty tone making Aleksandr smile.

"So, according to these stories, the Furies just get called in to murder people? There has to be a simpler way to do that," Evelyn said.

Ivan hummed thoughtfully. "No, I think they're supposed to drive people crazy first. Then kill them."

"Okay, genius," Nadya said. "Why did they keep stopping all the time?"

Letting his head flop back against the seat, Aleksandr stared up at the ceiling of the vehicle. The passing streetlights flashed against the worn material above him in a rhythmic pulse. Maybe it was the head injury or the increasing blood loss, but he found the light fascinating.

"Because we weren't afraid enough," Aleksandr said.

"What?" Nadya asked.

"One of the illusions," he mumbled, realizing a heartbeat later that he still needed to elaborate. "It felt like it needed me to be afraid of it. That my fear made it stronger. When I got angry instead, it got weaker."

"Well, I guess we aren't exactly its normal victims," Nadya mumbled.

"Like we have a higher tolerance level," Ivan happily continued the thought. "We've spent every day with murderous crazy. That has to make us ... what's the word?"

"Immune?" Nadya said.

"No, not that."

"Adapted," Evelyn said. "You all know how to cope with it and can keep going."

"Yeah, that." Ivan said. "But, I don't know why they didn't get you."

"Because I don't give a ... frick-frack," she hissed the last words and Aleksandr chuckled. "Plus, I'm not exactly a stranger to crazy. It's a far different breed to yours, but still ..."

She let the thought drop and no one was inclined to pick it up again.

"Alek?" Ivan suddenly sounded so much like the child he was, scared and vulnerable, that Aleksandr instantly sat up.

He leaned forward, pushing himself between the two front seats to properly see his brother.

"Yes?"

"Do you think mother and father are really dead?"

"Yes, I do."

Ivan kept his silence, trusting Nadya to carry the thought on from there.

"The others aren't going to be happy. They'll come for us."

"They won't find us," he promised. "We're going someplace far away. Someplace safe. Where we'll live new and boring lives. Where we'll be happy."

"What if they find us?" Ivan asked, his wide eyes focused on the road, as if he could will himself to be older and braver than his years.

"Then we'll kill them," Aleksandr said simply.

"What if the monsters find us?" Nadya asked.

"We'll kill them, too." Forcing a smile, Aleksandr twisted his arms around so he could place a hand on each of their heads. "For now, let's just say that the plan is to slaughter anything that messes with us. Okay?"

"Okay," they both said in unison.

"Good. Now, let's just get as far as we can with this car and we'll reassess from there."

They both nodded their agreement and for a moment seemed satisfied.

"What about her?" Nadya asked.

There was no need to specify who 'her' was. There was only one person in the car who didn't belong.

"Yeah," Ivan chirped. "Are we killing her?"

"And waste all the stitches Nadya put in my neck?" Evelyn said.

At the mention of her work, Nadya was suddenly all in favor of keeping their guest alive. It sparked a fast-paced conversation between the twins that only stopped when Aleksandr returned his hands to their heads.

"We're getting her to the city," Aleksandr said. "And then we're going our separate ways. Never to see each other again."

Ivan snuck a glance at him. "She's not coming with us?"

"It's just us three now. She's not a part of this," Aleksandr said.

"Okay," Nadya said softly. "But, what if the Furies don't see it that way? What if they come after her, too?"

Aleksandr hadn't considered the thought and, when he looked back to meet Evelyn's gaze, he realized she hadn't either. There was every chance in this world that they would never see the Furies again. Olga and Petya and been the cause of it all. The human plague that had spread nothing but misery and death. The twins, himself, Evelyn, it was possible that they had just been caught in the crossfire. Now that they had claimed their prize, the Furies might be satisfied to let them go. At the very least, Evelyn should be spared. Her hands were clean.

As much as Aleksandr searched the corners of his mind, he knew that he wouldn't find an answer. The world he had known was gone. A few shadows remained, but none of them meant what they had only a few days ago. He had no idea what was to come. Or what would follow. All that he knew for sure was that their liberation had come at a cost. There was a tether now that existed between them and Evelyn. A debt that he couldn't turn his back on.

"I'd have to help her," he told Nadya.

Neither of the twins appeared completely satisfied with this, but they lapsed into silence, storing their questions for another day and focusing on the road ahead. As Aleksandr watched them, still unable to believe that they were here with him, partly believing that he was still back in that room with the monster breathing on his neck, he heard Evelyn mutter.

"So much for a clean break."

No one spoke again. There was nothing more to say for tonight. They each just stared out into the night, waiting impatiently for the rising sun.

* * *

Devil's Playground
Wrath and Vengeance Series
Book 2
Written by Sara Clancy

Chapter 1

Aleksandr smiled while tightening his grip on the knife. The edge of the table kept the cooing elderly ladies blissfully unaware of the danger they were in. So they remained standing where they were, blocking Aleksandr's exit and praising the twins who sat opposite him. In Las Vegas, buffets were big business, and it wasn't any different at the Flamingo Casino and Hotel. Hundreds of people bustled around them, running the spectrum of humanity. Happy families, retired locals, gambling addicts and the obviously hung over who had barely managed to peel themselves out of bed. It would be insane or reckless for the couple to try anything in such a public place. Aleksandr marveled at how many people found that idea comforting instead of terrifying. As if insane, reckless people didn't exist.

"My, how clever you are," one of the women said before leaning closer.

Aleksandr calculated how long it would take him and his siblings to jump over the woman's corpse and get to an exit. If they cut across the courtyard, they'd be on the crowded Strip before security organized themselves. Surveillance cameras would be a problem.

"How old are you two sweethearts?" one of the women asked.

"Six," Nadya declared the lie cheerfully, believably, bouncing slightly in her seat.

As the couple prattled on about how intelligent the twins were for their age, Aleksandr arched an eyebrow at his sister. She shrugged, unapologetic. A lifetime with serial killers had taken its toll on the Sokolovsky siblings. Malnutrition and squalor had left all three of them smaller than average. Hard labor in the burning desert sun and countless, bloody fights had aged Aleksandr. The twins, however, still had an angelic, innocent appearance. Thin, frail, with large doe-like eyes, and childishly soft voices, they could pass for nearly half their age, which was something they exploited ruthlessly. For fun and to pander to their egos. Aleksandr generally didn't mind. Kids' rates made family days out a lot cheaper.

Aleksandr struggled to keep his polite smile in place as the woman switched to gushing about how sweet the twins were. Watching them perform for the women, Aleksandr had to admit that his siblings were, by nature, very kindhearted. But nature only goes so far when nurture gets involved. Petya and Olga Sokolovsky had intended for all the children to follow in their footsteps. He wondered if the women would still think them 'sweet' if they were aware that the twins knew precisely how to skin someone alive.

The woman closest to him fixed him with a warm smile. "You must be so proud of your little sisters."

Ivan almost cackled with glee. The twins were masters of perceptive manipulation. Ivan and Nadya could be either boys or girls, pass as each other, or mentally meld into a singular person. It was impossible to catch them in a lie or trick them into revealing themselves. The only way anyone would ever know the truth is if they decided to let them in on the secret.

"My kids," Aleksandr corrected.

He swiped the index finger of his free hand across the tabletop. The tiny movement went unnoticed by the perplexed woman but carried an explicit message to the children before him. *You've had your fun. I want them gone.*

"I'm sorry, dear," one of the women said as she placed a hand on his tensed shoulder. "What do you mean?"

"They're mine. Not my siblings."

Ivan looked up at the woman standing next to him as she released a nervous laugh, excited to see how she responded. Nadya was losing interest, and Aleksandr was growing impatient.

"You're trying to trick us," the woman beside Aleksandr said at last. She squeezed his shoulder as if it would somehow prove her point. "You're far too young."

"I'm twenty-two," he said coolly. There was no reason to lie about his own age. People always paid more attention to children. "They're mine."

The energy around the table shifted the instant the women did the math. Looking a little flustered, they managed to hold their smiles through their farewells, but barely got three steps away before they started whispering amongst themselves.

"We work so hard to manipulate people," Ivan sulked. "And all you have to do is mention teen pregnancy. It's not fair."

"Yeah, but he can only trick people into going away," Nadya noted.

Without their distraction, the twins went back to their separate activities. Nadya was fascinated by the live flamingos that filled the little oasis beyond the glass wall while Ivan had his *Real World News* magazine. The publication insisted on calling itself a newspaper. In truth, they were a trash tabloid full of stories about Bigfoot, conspiracy theories, aliens, and monsters recently found in local swimming pools. Ever since their encounter in the desert, Ivan's interest in the paranormal had become an obsession.

Enraptured with his reading, Ivan blindly reached out towards his plate. Aleksandr watched silently as his brother placed some strips of bacon on a syrup-drenched pancake, rolled it all up, and proceeded to eat the cylinder one-handed. Nadya was quick to follow suit, preferring to stare at the birds rather than use cutlery. Seeing his siblings mindlessly devouring their second helpings always made Aleksandr smile. Two years ago, they had struggled to finish a snack unless they were high. It was hard for any of them to stomach a meal while their parents would randomly go through cannibalistic phases. Aleksandr had never experienced a greater triumph than seeing his siblings at last put on a bit of fat.

Munching on a strawberry, he let the kids do as they pleased and subtly checked the crowd. The hot desert sun pulsed against the tainted glass, pushing back against the arctic chill of the industrial air-conditioning. Outside, tourists milled about, heading for the hotel pools or observing the flock of flamingos. The rush of the small waterfalls was barely audible over the crush of people inside. There were a few recognizable faces, mostly the serving staff and slot jockeys. No one was paying them any undue attention, although there were a few people sneaking glances at their table, offering weak smiles of acknowledgement when Aleksandr caught their eyes.

Only after they had gone on the run did he notice how fascinated people were with twins. Sometimes it was nothing more than a curious double-take, like they were merely checking they weren't seeing things. Others, like their most recent visitors, felt compelled to point out how cute the twins were, either to Aleksandr himself or their own companions. For some reason that Aleksandr couldn't fathom, the general public was more amused by female twins, or perhaps just considered it socially acceptable to point them out. Whatever the case, the days they decided to be girls always drew more attention. Still perusing the continually shifting crowd, he heard Ivan choke and rapidly tap the tabletop.

"You speak two languages," Nadya said, remembering to cover up her Russian accent halfway through the sentence. "Pick one."

Ivan gulped and croaked. "They're taking a psychic to the ghost town."

A pulse of anxiety coursed through Aleksandr's veins like melted iron, but he kept it from showing on his face. Just the mention of that hellhole was enough to cast him back into a maze of nightmarish memories. A cluster of abandoned buildings, separated from the rest of the world by miles of scorched desert had been the perfect place for Olga and Petya Sokolovsky to play out their darkest desires. Nothing was too depraved. Nothing was off limits. Each time he blinked, he could still see the small concrete room hidden under the sand. The crippling humidity. The stench of blood assaulted his nose. He could feel bones cracking against his knuckles.

None of that scared him now. For all their cruelty, his parents weren't the only monsters out there. He had witnessed the Furies. It was a daily struggle to make peace with the knowledge that creatures from ancient Greek mythology had killed their parents. At least in part. Aleksandr had helped the cause along. The worst part was the uncertainty. *Where had they gone? Where were they now? And what else was out there?*

Shaking away his thoughts, Aleksandr shrugged and popped another piece of fruit into his mouth. But having something to keep his teeth busy didn't quell the need to chew on his thumbnail.

"Oh, yeah?" he asked as casually as he could.

The twins fought over the magazine until they settled for spreading it out on the table between them. Education hadn't been a top priority for their parents. None of them could read without moving their lips slightly, and Nadya still needed to keep her place with her finger.

"It is hoped," she read aloud, exaggerating every syllable, "that the psychic will be able to make contact with the lingering spirits of the victims. This could bring new energy to investigators, who are still searching the property for human remains."

"Just throw a stick. You'll find one," Ivan muttered.

Nadya hunched her shoulders and lowered her voice to a hurried whisper, "Right? It's not like Olga and Petya put any effort into hiding them."

The twins shared a silent look before turning in unison to stare at their older brother.

"How many victims were there?" they asked in a synchronized whisper.

Aleksandr could only shrug. He had stopped counting long before the twins were born.

"Wait, what?" Nadya mumbled as she pressed closer to the page, eyes squinted as she read and reread the passage. Her head shot up. "They want to talk to our parents, too."

"Our parents are dead," Aleksandr said.

That got him a couple of dirty looks.

Ivan rolled his eyes and heaved a long-suffering sigh. "They want the psychic to make contact with them."

Biting back a smile, he mumbled, "Right."

"Can they do that?" Nadya battled to keep the panic out of her voice.

"Not unless they can tap into hell," Aleksandr dismissed.

Ivan, however, hummed thoughtfully. After a brief glance around to make sure that no one was listening in, he continued, "They did die violent deaths. They could be ghosts."

Nadya bit her lips. "What do we do?"

"Nothing," Aleksandr said.

"But," she stammered. "They could tell the psychic about us."

Still chewing on his nail, Aleksandr offered his sister a reassuring smile. "No one will believe them."

"Yeah," Ivan said, although he didn't sound convincing. "Besides, they were sucky parents. It wouldn't occur to them to mention us."

"Do you remember what Alek did to Olga?" Nadya said in a low whisper.

Aleksandr remembered. Slicing his mother's throat was the only time he had ever enjoyed violence. It had come with an intoxicating rush of righteousness.

"Yeah, that," Nadya said, attention darting between her brothers. "Also, we left them behind. You know they're going to be mad about that."

Aleksandr chewed harder on his nail, tasting fruit juice and soap. "Let them be," he dismissed.

Frustrated by their lack of concern, she folded her little arms on the table and leaned in.

"What if this psychic stirs up the Furies?" she asked.

An uneasy silence fell over the table, each of the three refusing to show just how deeply the thought terrorized them. The Furies had been the whole reason they had decided to settle in a larger city instead of a small, off-the-map town. In their heart, they were serial killers, and Aleksandr knew that beast well. Death wasn't always as important as fulfilling the core needs. And the Furies needed to torture their prey before killing them. They wielded madness like a blade, creating images and situations designed to feed off of their victims' fear. Last time, they had conjured a zombie horde and a colossal snake. They would need privacy for that or everyone would know they existed. Las Vegas had, among other things, a lot of witnesses.

Aleksandr forced a smile and looked at each of his siblings in turn.

"No matter what happens, we'll face it together. Just like we always do."

Seemingly comforted by that, Ivan and Nadya proceeded to read through the entire article. It took them a while.

Ivan made a surprised grunt. "It seems like Evelyn's keeping her mouth shut."

"I told you she would," Nadya boasted.

Aleksandr hadn't shared his sister's confidence. Silence was a lot to ask of someone you almost murdered. Neither of Aleksandr's parents had approved of his insistence that he only wanted to kill men. It had just been a ploy to hold off on murdering anyone, but they had called his bluff, forcing him to fight random men they had plucked off the street. Eventually, even this had run thin. Petya had believed that, since she was a kick-boxer with a solid build, Evelyn was manly enough to 'ease' his son into murdering women.

The arrival of the Furies had forced her to work with him to survive, but he hadn't expected their truce to last once the threat was gone. There was no reason for her to put in the prolonged effort of protecting them. Even if she wanted to, it would be near impossible for her to keep her story straight on the long run. Not with the police, reporters, and the FBI all scrambling for every scrap of information she might have.

A sharp thud sliced through the chatter that filled the room, reducing it to an awkward, confused muttering. Everyone looked around, searching for the source of the abrupt noise. The second blow stilled the room. Fine lines slithered out across the glass with the sound of cracking ice. Aleksandr turned to the window just as a blur of pink rushed towards him. It slammed into the glass with a heavy thud, breaking the glass even as the protective coating kept it from shattering. Nadya yelped with surprise, the noise lost under the sudden burst of chaos. The now constant attack of the glass whipped the crowd into a frenzy. Everyone ran in all directions, pushing people over and toppling tables.

In one smooth motion, she snatched up her backpack that had been hanging on the back of her seat and leaped onto the table. Three quick strides and she threw herself off the edge, right into Aleksandr's waiting arms. The crashing continued as they ducked down under the table. There was more than enough space for both of the tiny children, and Aleksandr used his body to shelter them from the people stampeding through the pathways.

He didn't need to tell them to put their backpacks on. In practiced, synchronized movements, they clicked the harness straps into place – one around their narrow chests, the other around their waists, and balled themselves up tightly, their puny frames easily fitting behind the shield of the packs. Aleksandr reached up to grab the knife off the table, his eyes continually scanning the courtyard outside the window. The thuds had increased. Growing louder. Stronger. It sounded like the sky was falling. Cracks formed cobwebs across the glass, distorting his vision, making it a jumbled mess of fractured colors. Blurs shifted beyond it. The frothing waterfall. Green grass. Blazing pink flamingos. A few more strikes and the glass gave way, raining down in sharp chunks, allowing crazed, injured flamingos to fall sprawling into the room. Aleksandr pulled his siblings closer, making sure the table protected them from the jagged shrapnel.

The birds looked considerably larger as they frantically flapped across the tables and floors, their strong legs snapping out and massive beaks clashing. Ducking his head, Aleksandr hunched over the twins, careful to keep the knife in his hand from finding their skin.

Pandemonium surrounded them; demolished glass, screaming tourists, pounding feet and the dying, frantic screams of the flamingos. The three of them remained where they were until the evacuation finished. It took longer for the kamikaze birds to either die or settle. Then there were only soft sobs and the crunch of broken glass underfoot. Aleksandr lifted his head and peeked up over the table. The windows were now gaping wounds in the side of the building, opening up to the shredded courtyard littered with dying wildlife and injured tourists. There were a few other people still left in the restaurant with them, staggering about in a daze, looking over the damage with wide eyes.

Aleksandr realized how lucky he was for feeling the cold when he straightened. Shards and fragments that hadn't managed to cut through his long-sleeved shirt toppled off of his back, sounding like chimes as they clashed together. An exotic bird was flopped over the table, still twitching in its death throes.

"Okay," Aleksandr said as he coaxed the twins up. "It's over. Be careful around the glass."

He held their hands, supplying something for them to push off of as they climbed up onto their feet, sparing them from touching the ground. There was no reason to insist that they not look at the carnage. They had each seen far worse. That said, both of the boys were compelled to give their sister a sympathetic pat on the shoulder.

"Sorry about your birds," Ivan said.

Nadya made a soft, sad little noise and looked up to Aleksandr. "What just happened?"

Aleksandr's stomach filled with the burning, bitter taste of bile as he looked around them again. "Nature itself fears the Furies."

He hadn't known that he had spoken the words until he shook himself from his surprise and glanced down at the twins.

"They're back, aren't they?" they asked in unison.

"Yeah," he nodded.

"So," Nadya said softly, looking down at the closest, lifeless birds. "What do we do now?"

"Right now, we need to get out of here before people start asking questions," Aleksandr said.

He took a step before the twins grabbed his hands and squeezed.

"Don't forget to tip," Nadya said.

"Seriously," Aleksandr replied through clenched teeth.

Ivan shrugged. "I think they're having a bad day."

Chapter 2

Evelyn looked up as she heard someone call her name. From the corner of her eye, she could see her father shifting about, moving back and forth as if he just needed the right angle to see the edge of the phone screen. All this time and he still couldn't understand the limitations of video calls.

"Who's that, sweetie?" he asked, failing to cover his growing frustration.

Evelyn chuckled, flipped her phone in her hand, and held it up so he could see her approaching friend.

"Dad, you remember Judy."

"Oh, right." He was instantly at ease again, his voice rich and warm. "How are you, Judy?"

Judy waved somewhat apologetically, ducking lower to meet his eyes. She had to because Evelyn wasn't about to stand on her toes to cover the distance.

"Hi, Mr. Figueroa."

"Don't leave me in suspense," her father said. "What's the comp like?"

Judy smiled. "It's been really fun. Although I didn't place as well as your daughter."

Evelyn turned the screen back to herself. One great thing about video calls was that it was easy to direct the conversation. "We're in different weight divisions."

"We won't be for much longer if you keep putting on muscle like you have been," Judy interrupted.

Evelyn ignored her. "There are stronger competitors in her division."

"Ah," her father performed his best impersonation of a wise old man.

Judy leaned onto a sharp angle, managing to hover her head over Evelyn's shoulder and reenter the shot.

"I hope she told you that she won her division. She's a kickboxing champion now."

Holding the phone steady, Evelyn lifted up her duffle bag and shook it. "I've already shown him my new shiny trophy."

"And I'm deciding where to put the new shelf," her father added. "She's filled up the one above the fireplace."

"Well, maybe you can take my kindergarten penmanship award off of it and clear up some room," Evelyn teased.

She laughed as her father let out a horrified gasp. "But your l's were so loopy."

"Maybe you can convince her to stay for the presentation, Mr. Figueroa," Judy cut in.

Evelyn shook her head. "Not happening."

"Come on, Eve," Judy protested. "You just won a championship. You should be really proud."

"I am."

"So, get your photo taken. Shake hands. There are reporters in there waiting to hear from you."

"Reporters?" her father asked. "Sorry to tell you Judy, but you haven't got a chance. Reporters and my girl don't get along."

Judy paused as if it had all just clicked into place in her head.

"They're not here for that," she said, less to convince Evelyn and more to reassure her.

Evelyn chuckled bitterly. "Maybe they'll toss me a few relevant questions at first, but they wouldn't be able to help themselves. Eventually, it'll all be about the Sokolovskys."

Judy flinched. "It's been two years, Eve."

"Right. Because that matters. I mean, no one talks about Jack the Ripper anymore."

Being kidnapped by serial killers, and everything that had happened after that had affected Evelyn in ways she hadn't anticipated. Most of her friendships had withered and died. But Judy remained. They had actually grown closer, in no small part because unlike so many other people, she knew when to be quiet. She used that skill now and let Evelyn and her father finish their conversation. Mostly, it was the ritual Evelyn referred to as the 'game plan'.

She confirmed that they were going straight to the hotel. Assured him that they knew the way and would keep to well-trafficked streets. They set a time for their next call and promised to stick together. Finally, her father was satisfied.

"Love you, dad," she smiled.

"Love you, too."

While he didn't try to prolong the call by continually bringing up random topics of conversation, Evelyn knew he was reluctant to end the call. They had been talking when Petya Sokolovsky had abducted her. One substantial blow to the back of her head had spared Evelyn from the details of that encounter. Her father hadn't been so lucky. He had been forced to listen to it all. Most of the time he could put on a brave face and play down how much that had traumatized him. When it came to ending these calls, however, there was no place for him to hide. Evelyn heard it clearly in his voice every time. There was a part of him that truly believed this was the last time he would ever talk to his daughter.

"I'll send you a picture from the hotel," she said, trying to lighten the mood. "I'm victorious, and as such, I deserve my body weight in French fries. I need you to be jealous of that."

Hearing his light chuckle caused unshed tears to burn the back of her eyes.

"Oh, I'm jealous. And bitter. I'm going to have to send you a picture of me with a pizza just to even the score," he said.

One more farewell and she ended the call quickly, trying to make sure he was still in a good mood. There were still a few hours left until sunset. Even if they crawled, there was plenty of time for them to get to their hotel before the last rays died. Still, Evelyn kept a quick pace. Being out after dark made her skin crawl. Just like parking lots, children without supervision, and any stranger that looked at her for too long. All of these had played a part that night. And they were the emotional triggers that everyone seemed okay with handling. But there were a lot of other issues under the surface. Darker ones. The real ones that made her wake up screaming.

The Furies.

She'd seen their power. Their viciousness. Those demonic creatures were out in the world somewhere, and she couldn't believe that they would let her go. There was no doubt that the creatures were intelligent. Enough to use traps and wield their victims' deepest fears as weapons. But they hadn't been merciful. One had seen Petya take her. Another had tormented her while she was held captive in Olga's cage. They must have known she was a victim. But that wasn't enough to secure a reprieve from the Furies. Sometimes, when Evelyn needed the reassurance, she'd tell herself that she had simply been collateral damage. Wrong place, wrong time. The thought helped her sleep, but nothing could keep her instincts from awakening again the next day. She knew, without a doubt or reason, that they would eventually come back for her. Demand her life as payment for supposed sins. And there was nothing she could do about it. These fears were ones that no one wanted to deal with. She couldn't even discuss them in therapy. Everyone would think she was mad. Just like her mother.

Moving with purpose, they crossed the road and continued on their way, heading into the blinding light of the sun. Judy tried to pull Evelyn from her thoughts a few times. After failing, the taller woman decided to carry on the conversation herself. Evelyn was too amused by the stream of consciousness leaving her friend's mouth to feel guilty about her silence.

The streets weren't bare. People clustered in small groups on the street corners or outside of storefronts. Evelyn rolled her shoulders, trying to work the tension out. The day was pleasantly warm. The sky a clear blue about an hour away from being painted with the colors of the sunset. It was a beautiful, peaceful moment, and she reminded herself that it was important to notice these sorts of things. Some of her muscles gave a painful twinge. A few of her competitors had landed some impressive blows. She was going to be feeling them for the next few days.

"Does our hotel have a sauna?" she asked.

"I knew you weren't paying attention," Judy teased.

"You mentioned a sauna?"

"No."

Evelyn turned to her friend before realizing that Judy was just messing with her.

"Yeah, it does," Judy said with a wide smile. "We should hit it up."

The hotel was coming into sight on the horizon when they approached a group of three men. Evelyn had noticed them early on, mostly because of the effects they were having on the people around them. Older than teens but not out of their twenties, the men routinely showed an aggressive amount of interest in the women that passed them. Evelyn was too far away to hear what the men were saying. Whatever it was, it left the women they encountered very uncomfortable. Anger pushed into her stomach like thorns as she watched the trio laughing and congratulating each other. It was a game for them. One they played with the unwilling people that passed them. Apparently, the whole objective was to cause discomfort and disgust.

"Great," Judy heaved a sigh as she straightened her spine and fixed her eyes straight ahead.

Evelyn glanced over each of the men in turn. It didn't seem like they were armed. She checked the street. No vans or waiting cars. The men were willing to follow women for a few steps but kept close to the chosen outpost. It was easy to spot the moment the men saw them. That was when the laughter began.

"Damn," a man with dark hair called after them as they passed. "You girls need to lay off the weights!"

"Dude," the blonde one cut it, "those are guys."

Judy rolled her eyes, lamenting their lack of creativity. All the while, Evelyn's spikes of anger had grown into a burning blistering heat. It felt like fire was lapping down her limbs. The sensation grew as one with a ratty goatee fell into step beside them.

"Don't you listen to them, sweethearts. You girls are beautiful!"

"Just keep walking," Judy whispered as Evelyn grinded her teeth.

They barely made it a few steps before the 'white knight' took offence to their silence.

"Hey, I just gave you a compliment! Least you could do is give me a little 'thank you!'"

"Go away," Evelyn hissed through her teeth.

"Damn, no need to be rude."

The man fell back, rejoining his friends. Their laughter grew louder. They kept moving without looking back.

"Bitch!" The one with the goatee shouted.

Evelyn stopped dead in her tracks and shoved her duffle bag into Judy's stomach.

"Hold my bag," she said as she whipped around.

"Eve, no!"

Evelyn heard her friend's continued protests, but none of it really reached her. It all faded away under the white noise filling her head. The blonde man noticed her first and quickly informed the others of her approach. A smug smirk tipped the lips of the man with the goatee as he stalked forward to meet her, his hands relentlessly slicking back his already gelled hair.

"Oh, she looks mad," he called back to his friends before grinning at Evelyn. "Don't worry, honey. I've got something right here that can help you with that."

He grabbed his crotch. Evelyn slammed her fist into his gut. Releasing a wheezing gasp, he doubled forward, eyes bulging out of his skull. Not giving him a chance to process what was happening, she cupped the back of his head and drove her knee into his face. There was a solid crunch and a satisfying spurt of blood. His friends' cries of outrage drifted across the edges of her awareness, noted but dismissed. One hard yank sprawled the injured man out over the pavement. Judy was at Evelyn's back before goatee's friends could upgrade from protest to action. Even while Judy kept her hands up in a placating manner, the set of her feet and shoulders said she was ready for a fight.

"We're both trained fighters." Judy kept her voice smooth and calm, but the threat was there. "Let's not let this get violent, boys."

The men lingered back, their eyes darting between the women and their injured friend. It seemed that they were considering for the first time that the girls' muscles might not just be for show. Their indecision was most likely aided by the fact that Evelyn had used the distraction to kick the man onto his back and now had her foot pressing down on his neck. He wheezed and jerked and clawed at her ankle. All she had to do was apply a bit more pressure and threaten to crush his throat to get him to give up.

"Get the hell off of him!" one of them snarled at her.

Evelyn didn't care which one it was. Blinded by fury, she pushed down, making the man at her feet choke.

"We're going to kick your ass!" the other promised.

The threat made Evelyn laugh, bitter and wild. "Really? Oh, that would be fun to see."

Judy dropped into a fighter's stance as the man's friends surged forward a step. That was it, though. As boastful as they were, none of them were inclined to pit themselves against women who had bigger biceps than them.

"What we have here," Evelyn snarled, each word sharp and short, "is a conflict of ideology. Oh, no, don't talk. Let me guess. You all believe that, because he didn't lay a hand on me, I'm overreacting?"

"He just gave you a compliment!"

She didn't care which one of them had said it, her reaction was the same. She squeezed the man's throat with her heel.

"You mispronounced 'harassment'," she laughed. "What? Do you all think he has a right to harass women without repercussion? That about cover it? Yeah, I thought so."

"Evelyn," Judy pleaded in a whisper, "this is assault."

Evelyn snorted and ignored the warning. "Now let me tell you my ideology. I'm of the opinion that I'm not going to get murdered so you can feel like a big man."

"We didn't touch you!" one at the back of the pack bellowed.

White hot rage pulsed through her veins and flared in her eyes. "You think rapists just woke up one day and decided to give it a go? No! They start small. Test the waters. See how much they can get away with. And when dumb-shits like you don't call them on it, they push further. Then further."

"You're insane!" someone accused.

"No, I'm pissed!" she corrected. "I'm mad as hell that I have to remind idiots like you that I'm not your toy. I'm not here for your amusement. You don't have rights to me or my body!"

"Evelyn," Judy whispered before turning back to the men. "Look, she's having a hard time–"

"Don't apologize for me!" Evelyn snapped.

"You should listen to your friend," the blonde said. "Because she's right. This is assault. Do you wanna see what the cops think of this?"

"Honey, you're not paying attention. I see this as a fight for my goddamn humanity! I'm willing to fight, kill, and die for it! The question is," she pushed her foot down harder to make sure that she had their attention, "how far are you ready to go to support him treating women like shit?"

A part of her hoped that they wouldn't believe her. That they'd give her an excuse to unleash some of the anger that was boiling her alive. She doubted it was her argument that convinced them to take a step back. Perhaps it was her chilling glare, or the predatory stance of her body, or the sheer fact that she meant every word she said. *Pity,* Evelyn thought as she looked down at the man sprawled across the pavement. He was gasping for breath. A blue hue tinged his lips. And his eyes were so wide and unblinking that it was hard not to find him pitiful.

"The next time you have the urge to torment a woman, I want you to remember this moment," she hissed.

Judy smiled weakly. "Well, we'll just be on our way then. Right, Eve?"

"Fine," Evelyn hissed begrudgingly. She squeezed her foot down a bit, just enough to make sure she had the man's attention. "I'm going to let you up. If you do anything stupid, and that includes telling me that I need to 'calm down' or questioning my menstrual cycle, I swear on everything holy in this world, I will curve-stomp your scrawny hide. Understood?"

He made a gargled noise that she took as agreement, and she slowly pulled her foot back. Instantly, he rolled onto his side, hacking and wheezing, coughing hard in an attempt to force his airways back into shape. Judy grabbed her arm, anxiously pulling her back from the men. Blinking through the haze of her receding anger, Evelyn noticed that they had drawn a small crowd of spectators. The dozen or so people stared at them with wide eyes, some scowling while others chuckled. A lot of them had their phones out recording the scene, but Evelyn couldn't spot a single person who was actually calling the police. A part of her wondered if that meant they had some degree of support for her, but she couldn't follow the thought very far. She was suddenly, utterly, exhausted. Mentally and physically.

Given their limited numbers, the gathering of spectators had a few big gaps. No one made an attempt to intercept the girls as they walked away. Judy had left the duffle bag a few feet from where they had started, and Evelyn collected it without breaking stride, looping the short straps over her shoulders. It didn't take long for them to leave the onlookers behind and once again be relatively alone on the street.

The walk to the hotel was done in silence. While Judy kept close to her side, there was no mistaking the sidelong glares she kept tossing in her friend's direction. Finally, they were in the hotel lobby and Evelyn released a long, tired sigh.

"Thanks for having my back," she said as they joined the queue for check in.

"For the record," Judy said in a low voice. "I did not enjoy that."

"Well, you weren't really supposed to," Evelyn said. "Street harassment isn't exactly known for being enjoyable."

Judy turned to face her fully, her eyebrows knitting together as she stared down at Evelyn.

"Did *you* enjoy that?"

Evelyn tried to dismiss it with a grunt, but her friend wouldn't be deterred. "Enjoy is a strong word."

"Then what?"

She puffed her cheeks, trying to find a way of saying 'righteous' that wouldn't lead to a lecture. All of her stalling worked, and Judy was called up to the counter before Evelyn was forced to answer. There was no time to discuss anything as they checked in. By the time they met up at the elevators, most of the anger had faded away, leaving only a slight but sharp irritation.

Judy slammed the call button with far more force than necessary. "You were out of line, Eve."

"That's a matter of opinion," she dismissed.

"No, it's really not and–" Judy cut herself off as she glanced around. "Do you hear a church bell?"

"Oh, that's my ringtone."

Evelyn dug through the outer pocket of her duffle bag. She still noticed Judy rolling her eyes.

"AC/DC rock and *Hell's Bells* is a classic," Evelyn snapped as she finally grasped her phone.

Instead of responding, the taller woman stared straight ahead, waiting for the elevator doors to open. She thought she had missed the call when the sound suddenly clicked off. Fumbling with the buttons, she lit up the screen to display a text message. A spike of fear coursed through her, as cold as an arctic chill. She whipped around, scanning the lobby. Checking every face. Every corner. Every possible hiding place where someone could be lurking. Watching.

"Eve?" Judy asked.

Evelyn barely heard her over the blood rushing through her ears.

"Eve, what's wrong?" Concern weaved around each word.

A frigid hand reached through Evelyn's ribcage to crush her lungs. She couldn't breathe. The room spun, becoming a blur of strange faces and fuzzy colors. People gathered in around them, pressing in close as they waited for the elevator. Too close. All within arm's reach. All looming over her, their eyes dark and brimming with the threat of violence. Staring at her. There was no air.

"Eve," Judy placed a hand on Evelyn's shoulder. "Talk to me. What's happening?"

You have no idea what they look like, a voice whispered in the back of Evelyn's head. *Any one of them can be the Sokolovsky siblings you've never met. And they're all close enough to kill you.*

The elevator gave a musical ping as the doors whooshed opened.

"We'll take the next one," Evelyn declared.

Grabbing Judy's arm, Evelyn hurled her friend out of the moving stream of the people, shoving and dragging her until they were on the far side of the lobby.

Judy frowned. "Okay. I'm trying to be supportive, but I'm getting a little scared."

After checking the lobby once more, Evelyn finally met her friend's eyes once more.

"Everything's fine. But you might want to alert security if you're staying. Maybe think about heading home early."

"What?"

"I'm probably just being paranoid," Evelyn said, forcing a smile. "It's just that I've got to head off early and I don't like to think of you all alone here."

"Where are you going?"

She gave her friend a tight hug, hoping that it would placate her a bit.

"I'm fine. I just got a frantic text from an old friend and I really need to go see them. So, I'm going to head to the airport. Now. I'm going to call a cab."

Judy watched her for a long moment before casting a cautious glance around the lobby. "I'm going with you to the airport."

"Great, that's probably for the best. Check out for me?"

Evelyn passed Judy the room key she had just been given and pulled her duffle bag higher over her shoulder. As she lifted her mobile to call a taxi, she accidently reread the text message she had received from an unlisted number. She flinched.

Ready or not, here we come.

Chapter 3

After a series of harmonious bells, a voice came over the speaker system, reminding all the patrons that Shark Reef would be closing in an hour. It had surprised her how quickly Aleksandr had replied to the message she had left on a stop light enthusiasts' website. They had picked the random little site as their meeting point should anything go wrong, but she hadn't assumed he would be checking every minute. It left her with a gnawing sensation in the pit of her stomach. *What had happened on his end?*

By the time she had finished the mad dash to the airport, she knew where she was going. Las Vegas. Not exactly where she thought he would be heading. Close to three hours of travel time and a tense taxi ride later, she had slipped into Mandalay Bay Casino and Hotel. It was just before nine, making her one of the last admissions to Shark Reef for the day. All things considered, she probably shouldn't have been annoyed that she had to pay $25 dollars to get in. Travelling from Florida to Vegas last minute had obviously cost a lot more. But it was the principle of the thing. *Couldn't Aleksandr have picked one of the thousands of other heavily populated places that had free admission?*

A chill lingered in the air as she made her way through the submerged tunnels. Colorful reefs were built up on either side of her, brimming with tropical fish and eels. Spotlights were set over the water above her. It turned the water a clear, crystal blue. An unsettlingly large shark swam lazily towards the glass. At the last moment, it changed course, skirting over the top of the dome and casting a dark shadow over her as it passed. The bottom tip of its tail skimmed across the thick glass, stirring up the water and making it swirl down the hallway.

Goosebumps rose up on her skin as she wandered down the dim corridors. She had a jacket in the duffle bag strapped to her back, but she didn't make a move to get it out. At five foot tall, she wasn't intimidating. All she had to deter an attack was her hard-earned bulk. Since it was almost closing time, the crowds that would normally be cluttering the passageways had thinned, leaving only a few stragglers. Without the people, it was easier to hear the soft tune playing over the loudspeakers. It was barely more than a mumble and offered little competition to the echo of the footsteps. The clipped thuds rolled towards her long before she saw who was making them. And since she was nearing a junction that branched out into numerous hallways, it was hard to pinpoint where anyone was. *At least it's impossible for someone to creep up on me.*

From the moment she had received the text, she hadn't been able to silence the voice that repeated the same warning in the back of her head. *I don't know what they look like. They could be anyone.* She was well aware that there were some Sokolovsky kids whom she was yet to meet. And she knew that they took after their parents. Highly trained, motivated, gleeful killers. *They know me,* the voice continued when she couldn't silence it. *They know my number. They probably know what I look like. They could have followed me here.*

A pair of teenagers ran past, shrieking playfully as they chased each other through the halls, neither one taking special care to avoid hitting anything. Evelyn moved out of the way, heart lurching into her throat, her hands instantly balling into fists. She barely managed to keep herself from striking out as her shoulder smacked against the glass. It felt like a slab of ice against her bare skin, the shock jerking her from her budding panic. *Get your act together, Eve,* she hissed to herself as she followed the teens with her eyes. They entered the bulbous room at the end of the hallway and disappeared from sight. It was then that she noticed the man. The bright yellow light that illuminated the room hit him from behind, letting shadows streak across his face. They didn't hide his face, but distorted it, sharpening his features, and leaving his eyes as dark discs. He was barely visible around the corner, but she knew he was watching her.

Pushing off from the wall, Evelyn held his gaze and squared her shoulders, wanting him to know that he was on her radar. He watched her for a moment longer. Silent. Still. Her heart pounded against her ribs and she clenched her jaw, determined not to let it show. Slowly, he turned and disappeared down another passageway.

Her breath released in one sudden rush. Strong enough that she had to brace a hand against the glass wall to keep from doubling over. She hated herself in that moment. She felt weak, useless, and pathetic. She detested it all. Rolling her shoulders, she tilted her head from side to side, determined to get her body back under control. That turned out to be the easy part. It was far harder to get her mind on board. She couldn't chase off the thought that all anyone really needed was one decent shot. One second. It all played out in her mind's eye. A meaningless bump as they passed in the street. Slide a knife between her ribs. Fade back into the crowd and disappear before anyone knew what happened. She could bleed to death in the gutter without ever seeing who had ended her life.

Growling in frustration, she pushed her hands through the tight crinkles of her hair. She had cut it short for the competition and was still getting used to how the ends abruptly gave way to the skin of her neck. What had started as exploring the strange new sensation had become a habit. She ran her hands over her hair a few more times before rubbing at the tense muscles of her neck. *Dad's not going to like this.* She knew it as a fact. It was just a matter of time. Judy had, in the end, accepted her original story of a friend in distress at face value. That didn't mean she hadn't pressed for more information. For now, Judy had agreed to head home. But Evelyn knew it was only a matter of time before she started comparing notes with her father. And that could cause problems down the line.

For now, her father gave every appearance of being onboard. Perhaps it was just because their conversation had been interrupted by the alarm. Being a devoted father and a decorated firefighter didn't always go hand in hand. Sometimes, he had to focus on one thing and let the other slide. Since his daughter was safe, he had turned his attention to the apartment complex that was currently alight.

Unable to dwell on his paranoia, he could only focus on the facts she had presented. Simply, that she was meeting up with an old friend in a fun town. It told her how introverted she had been lately, that he was excited by the idea of her socializing in a way that didn't involve hitting someone in the face. Besides that, it was Vegas. Well-lit, heavily populated, and surveillance everywhere. In his enthusiasm, he had insisted on paying for her room. That worked out surprisingly well. Aleksandr now worked at the Polaris, a grand new hotel with a galactic theme. It was right in the middle of The Strip. Perfect placement to make her father feel his little girl was safe and secure.

The sound of thundering feet raced towards her and made her jump. Evelyn whipped around, arms instinctively rising up into a boxer's defensive stance. Her flash of panic got a bit confusing as she spotted two small children barreling towards her. They were miniature tornados, shrieking and laughing and flailing their arms about. Their novelty hoodies were far too large. The hoods were supposed to make them look like their faces were coming out of a shark's mouth. For these two, the hoods flopped down and covered half of their faces like masks. The combination of too long sleeves and hyped-up movement made them look like the flailing tube men Evelyn had spotted outside of car dealerships. A smile curled her lips until she noticed they were coming right towards her. Her fingers clenched into a fist, and she wondered if she should take a swing at a child.

"Eve!" a familiar chorus of voices cried.

She had barely known them for a day, but their voices were forever burned into the back of her mind. *Ivan and Nadya.*

"Hey, guys," she lowered her arms and stretched her hands out, figuring that their excitement probably meant they were going to get a high-five. They had been strangely persistent about giving her one when they had parted.

It hadn't even occurred to her that they would lock onto her legs. Their thin arms held a surprising amount of strength as they wrapped around her thighs. They felt like boa constrictors, squeezing until she could feel her heartbeat pulsing in her compressed limbs.

"Hey," she stammered.

The whole scenario got stranger when they popped their heads up to grin at her, faces still hidden under a goofy shark face. How they could see through the gray material was beyond her. Admittedly, it was the only time they had really looked like Aleksandr. She flipped the hoods back and studied their faces. *How are they still so similar?* It seemed to go against nature and hormones for them to be so identical at their age. The points of their chins dug into her hipbones as they grinned up at her.

"So, which one's which?" she asked with a smile of her own.

They chirped their names. There was a decent chance that they were lying.

"How have you guys been?" Evelyn asked.

They said 'good' in unison, sounding so much like normal little kids. Albeit, kids far younger than they actually were. If she remembered correctly, these two were eleven, quickly approaching their teen years. This was quickly getting disorientating.

"Where's Aleksandr?"

"He's behind us," the one that had identified himself as Ivan said.

"He's always slow when we come here," Nadya added.

Evelyn nodded. Having had a lot of time to obsess over every detail of her encounter, Evelyn had developed a theory about Aleksandr. Mostly that he just didn't like water. Everyone else in his family had kept themselves relatively clean and presentable. As much as they could be while running around in the desert. Meanwhile, Aleksandr had looked like he had just crawled his way out of a grave. Dirt smeared skin, hair matted into clumps, and carrying with him the ever-present scent of sweat and blood. At the time, she thought he just didn't see hygiene as a priority. *God knows he had more pressing problems,* she thought. But the more she thought about it, the more she wondered if there had been another reason.

"There he is," Nadya said.

Evelyn looked up to see a couple of men at the end of the corridor. At first, she was a little confused as to why she couldn't pick him out of the limited crowd. Then it hit her; this was the first time she had ever seen most of his face. The entire time they had been in the ghost town, Aleksandr had worn his grimy hair like a shield. It had covered his face down to the tip of his nose, leaving only his jawline and mouth exposed. She had never even seen his eyes. They had almost died together, almost killed each other, and she had no idea what the hell he really looked like.

Facial recognition or not, she remembered his body. For a moment, she had been sure her life depended on being able to beat him to death. She had sized him up very carefully for a fight and wasn't about to forget that. His height, strong arms, broad shoulders atop a rickety frame. Like a Frankenstein monster, it didn't seem like any of his body parts belonged with the others. She craned her neck and spotted Aleksandr stalking towards them, shoulders hunched, and jaw clenched.

Evelyn wasn't prepared for how comforting it would be to come face to face with Aleksandr for the first time since they had gone their separate ways. He hadn't completely abandoned his habit of hiding behind his hair. His sweeping fringe covered one eye, the hair lighter and softer now that it was actually clean. A scruffy half-hearted attempt at a beard covered his jaw and enclosed his mouth. It was the kind of facial hair that could suggest either a 'struggling artist' type or one too lazy to shave each morning. His cheekbones were as sharp and straight as his nose, elongating his face, with no fat to fill it out. Unlike his siblings, his eyes were narrow, and shielded under a strong brow bone. It gave him a direct, uncomfortably piercing gaze and turned his eyes into black discs. Shark-like. His stare threw her so much that she almost missed the fact that he was clean. Head to toe. There wasn't even a single stain or tear on his well-fitted shirt. And that was just strange. Like he was wearing a costume. He grunted to them as he got closer, passing by them without breaking stride.

"I guess we're moving," Evelyn muttered to the kids.

The twins each grabbed one of her hands. An innocent act that left Evelyn with an ominous twist in her gut. Still, she didn't let go, walking along with them as if it were the most normal thing in the world. Like they had done it a thousand times before. Turtles and stingrays swept past them. Their footsteps beat against the floor like the pounding of a drum. It didn't take long to catch up with Aleksandr, but no one seemed inclined to talk. At least, not about anything relevant. The twins would sporadically gush about a shark or a particularly bright fish.

Just as Evelyn began to think he was stalling, she realized that they had done a loop around the exhibit and were now back in the bulbous, yellow junction room. That's when it clicked. Since Mandalay Bay had stopped admittance for the day, the loop had allowed Aleksandr to take stock of everyone who was left in the exhibit. Apparently, there was no one he was worried about because he picked a spot halfway down one of the hallways, where it would be impossible for anyone to creep up on them unseen. He crossed his arms over his chest, leaned back against the dome wall and turned his sharp gaze onto Evelyn. The twins still had her hands in surprisingly strong grips. *So, I can't do a surprise attack,* Evelyn realized.

Forcing a smile, she gestured to Aleksandr with her chin. "You look good."

Nadya tugged her hand sharply. "Don't objectify him."

The teasing glint in her eye was hard to miss, but Evelyn wasn't ready to rise to the bait.

"I just meant that he's put on weight."

"So now you're body shaming?" Ivan demanded, face scrunching up in mock mortification.

Their matching scowls weren't enough to hide the mirth in their eyes. It was clear that she was the butt of their joke.

"You know," Evelyn said with a put-upon sigh, "if you're going to make me play your games, at least let me in on the rules."

"We're not playing a game," Ivan said, the picture of innocence.

"So, you're just annoying?" Evelyn teased.

"I blame TV."

There was a roughness to Aleksandr's voice that normally only came from disuse. Or smoke inhalation. He spoke as if he resented each syllable passing his lips and was the only one that still had his Russian accent.

"So," Evelyn clicked her tongue and decided it was time to get to the point. "I got a text."

Ivan warily released her hand and let her retrieve her phone from her pocket. She unlocked it and handed it over to the elder Sokolovsky. Years of bare-knuckle boxing had twisted up the joints of Aleksandr's hands. Each knuckle pushed against his scarred skin at strange angles as he took the phone.

"Don't suppose you recognize the number," she asked.

Ivan latched back onto Evelyn's hand as he and Nadya pushed up onto their toes, lifting their chins to catch a glimpse of the screen.

Aleksandr read the short message, barely managing to keep himself from swearing aloud.

"Vera and Vlas."

The twins stiffened, their little hands squeezing her fingers. Evelyn nodded once, waiting for Aleksandr to continue. He didn't.

"I'm guessing they're your siblings?" she prompted.

"This is their version of *Hide and Seek*. They'll kill you when they find you," Aleksandr replied. He reread the message and arched a brow. "You received this a few hours ago?"

"Yeah. I was in Tampa checking into a hotel. Came right here after."

The skin around his eyes pulled tight. "You didn't go home?"

"And risk leading them back to my dad? No, of course not!"

"But it's fine to lead them here to us?" Nadya asked.

"Yeah, I'm not buying this innocent act," she said. "You are one creepy, dangerous little kid. And for the record, I didn't suggest bringing you guys to this little meeting. That was *him*." She jerked her chin to indicate Aleksandr. No one seemed to care.

"Why were you in Tampa?" Aleksandr asked.

"I went there for a kickboxing competition. I suppose that's how they found me. I had to register months in advance. Thing is, I never gave the organizers my number, just an email address. I still haven't figured out how they got it."

"Why didn't you go to the cops?" Ivan asked.

"Mostly because of the current state of stalking laws," Evelyn replied, the words tasting bitter on her tongue.

The twins looked to Aleksandr. He was clicking around on Evelyn's phone but felt their question.

"They didn't do anything illegal."

Ivan checked with his sister before saying, "Aren't they stalking her?"

Nadya nodded in agreement.

"The text doesn't prove that," Aleksandr explained as he passed the mobile back to Evelyn. This time, Nadya released her grip to allow Evelyn to move. "For it to legally count as harassment or stalking, there has to be a clear threat of violence or death. This text isn't illegal. I'm sure the police would believe her, but their hands would be tied. Besides, she doesn't want Vera and Vlas in jail." Meeting Evelyn's gaze, he crossed his arms over his chest again. He wanted her to be the one to say it.

"I want you to kill them."

He smiled for a moment, more surprised than pleased. "You didn't even hesitate."

"Should I have?" Evelyn asked.

Aleksandr stared at her for a heartbeat. Suddenly, he crouched down, all smiles and thick Texan drawl, excitedly pointing out the fish to the now hyper twins. The performance only made sense once Evelyn spotted the small family coming towards them. She had been so caught up in the conversation that she hadn't even noticed them. The second the strangers had passed by, Aleksandr straightened, and the kids settled.

"We have bigger problems," he said, as if they had never been interrupted.

"Bigger than murderous siblings?" Evelyn's smirk fell the moment the words were out of her mouth. "The Furies."

"They dropped by this morning," Ivan mumbled.

"They killed my birds," Nadya said in the same tone.

"That's why you were so quick to reply. You were already trying to contact me," Evelyn shook her head. *How hadn't that occurred to me?* "Why are you still here? Shouldn't you be running for the hills?"

"I don't want to risk them catching us in a desert again," Aleksandr answered.

The screaming teenagers that had startled Evelyn before came roaring towards them, backtracking their way to the exit. Shifting closer to the wall, Evelyn waited impatiently for them to get out of earshot. She almost screamed when the teens felt the sudden need to stop and have a discussion only a few feet away, unintentionally trapping Evelyn and the Sokolovsky siblings in an uncomfortable silence. It gave Evelyn time to think. To weigh her options against her conscience. After what seemed like an eternity, the teens set off running again.

"Would ... um ..." Evelyn clicked her fingers.

"Vera and Vlas," Ivan whispered.

"Yeah, them. Would they have followed me here?"

Aleksandr tipped his head to the side. "If they found you once, they'll find you again. So, you might need to get going soon."

"I thought we wanted her help with the Furies," Nadya protested.

"That was before I knew Vera and Vlas had set up their game," he said. Tossing the siblings a meaningful look, he prodded, "They picked her. What does that tell you?"

Both of the twins let go of Evelyn's hands.

"A family game," they said in unison.

Evelyn looked between them. "I don't know what that means."

"It means Radmiar is playing too," Ivan said.

Biting back her frustration, she looked between them. "Who?"

"My twin," Aleksandr said.

Another one? "How many pairs of twins did your parents churn out?" she snapped in frustration.

"Four," Ivan and Nadya answered swiftly.

Aleksandr snapped his fingers and pointed at Evelyn. "She's right. We need to run."

"What happened to Las Vegas being a better battlefield than the desert?" Evelyn protested.

"It's too much," he hissed. "We can't fight our siblings *and* the Furies."

"So, we don't," she cut in.

"That's not an option," Aleksandr spat.

Unsure of how much they would like her idea, Evelyn forced herself to hold Aleksandr's fierce gaze, struggling to think of a way to make it sound convincing. "Your siblings don't know about the Furies, right?"

Lines formed between Aleksandr's eyebrows, but he nodded once.

"Just over two years ago, the Furies took your parents," she said.

"I remember." The words were barely audible.

"That's a year of peace for each."

Aleksandr's eyes narrowed into slits as he caught onto her thinking. "You want to pit my siblings and the Furies against each other?"

"It's our best shot."

"You're trying to bleed a hog in a snowstorm," he snarled.

"What does that even mean?"

Ivan tugged her hand. "The hog would freeze in icy conditions."

"Basically," Nadya continued, "he's saying it's a stupid idea doomed to fail."

Evelyn swept her hands out in an exaggerated shrug. "Fine. What's your master plan? Run? See which one can hunt you down first? How's that a better idea?"

"Your problem is that you think you're in control," Aleksandr said.

"No, I'm thinking strategically," she argued. "You know the layout around here. Your killer siblings don't. And they'll be under pressure. Anything brazen will have a heap of tourists calling the police. Hell, all of these casinos would have their own security with pretty good response time. And we have the element of surprise. They don't know about the Furies. Logically, those demonic chicks would love to get their hands on anyone in your family. Vengeance is vengeance. So, let's set them up against each other and pick off the wounded survivors."

Aleksandr glanced around and stepped closer.

"You're worried about being overheard?" She balled her hands in frustration. "We've counted everyone. We're alone. And I don't think those security cameras are rigged for sound."

He glared at her. "We survive because we're careful."

"Right."

"You realize what you're suggesting, right? This would be *murder*."

Is he kidding me? "So?"

"You've never killed anyone. Do you really think you can stomach it?"

Evelyn looked Aleksandr dead in the eye. "Hell, yes."

"Simple as that?"

"It's a simple question. Do I value my life more than theirs? Yeah, I do."

"The actuality is different," he dismissed.

"I didn't ask for any of this. They want to use me, I'll shove these games down their throat."

Aleksandr blew a hard breath out through his nose. He looked off to the side as he thought before he turned to each of the twins in turn.

"I'm in," Nadya chirped. "Think about it, Alek. We're not going to get another chance like this. We could get rid of them all in one go. Let's not waste it!"

They all turned to Ivan. It didn't sit well with Evelyn knowing that all of this rested on a child's shoulders. Guilt or not, she wasn't about to intervene. She needed this to end.

"I've always wanted to beat them at their own game," the little boy said with a smile and a shrug.

"And you guys realize that we could die?" Aleksandr said carefully.

Instantly, both twins rolled their eyes and threw their hands in the air. "No, really? How new and different. Never been in *that* situation before."

"Okay, shut up," Aleksandr muttered, fighting back a smile. "Guess it's settled." He extended a hand towards Evelyn. "Kill them all or die trying."

A storm of relief and fear raged within Evelyn's skin, but she smiled anyway, shook his hand, and sealed the deal.

That's when the fish scattered.

Chapter 4

An icy chill rolled down Aleksandr's spine. He froze, every joint locking into place. Clear water filled his peripheral vision. The once teeming wildlife was now barely more than little specks, disappearing into the deeper, murkier recesses of the massive tank.

"Alek," Nadya asked.

She sounded small and weak and so utterly fragile that his chest tightened.

"They're here." Ivan muttered the words as if he hadn't intended anyone to hear.

The light around them shifted and dulled. Aleksandr's first thought was that the staff was closing up, intending for the dimming light to force the guests out. The notion died as he watched Evelyn look up. Shock twisted her features as a deep crimson glow washed out to cover her skin. He didn't have to look up. Blood. It didn't move through the water like a liquid. Instead, it rushed down to cover the dome-like crackling flames. Within an instant, the world was reduced to shades of black and red. They crouched low, gathering into the middle of the hallway.

"Alek," Ivan said softly.

Twisting around, Aleksandr snatched up his brother, holding him close with one arm while reaching for sister. Evelyn had already collected the little girl and straightened.

"I've got her," Evelyn said in a rush. "Let's go."

Aleksandr broke into a run, Evelyn close to his side. They had barely started when the ground shook violently. It was just a short burst but almost threw them all to the ground. The familiar sound of cracking glass turned his blood cold.

"Run!" he commanded.

The cry pulled them all out of the horrified shock, and they sprinted down the crimson hallway. The overhead speakers crackled and screamed, releasing a shrill cry that drove into Aleksandr's ears like ice picks. Time between the tremors dwindled until it seemed that every passing second was punctuated with a shudder. Side by side, Aleksandr and Evelyn burst into one of the circular junction rooms, the children clutched protectively to their chests.

"Which way? Which way?" Evelyn shot the words out with the speed of a Gatling gun.

Aleksandr took the lead, heading directly to the passage on the right. The glass dome behind them shattered. Water as red and hot as blood gushed into the hallway, creating a small wave that chased them down and knocked them off their feet. Aleksandr balled himself tight, curling protectively around Ivan as the rush of blood drove them into a wall. He gagged, blood running down his throat. Panic exploded inside of Aleksandr as the liquid sloshed over his head. Scrambling and stumbling, he got to his feet, gulping down a deep breath as his head and shoulders broke free of the rising water line.

"Are you okay?" Aleksandr asked, cupping his brother's cheek.

Ivan was choking, but nodded.

"Nadya!"

No sooner had he bellowed the word than Evelyn burst up from the coursing water, her arms wrapped tight around Nadya's slender waist. The blood and dim light made it impossible to tell if she was injured. Before he could ask, her hand shot up, pointing back down the hallway as she started to scream. Aleksandr followed her gaze. A shark, far bigger than any of what they actually had in the tank, was now lodged halfway through the dome wall. Its skin was rotten, flying off in chunks as it thrashed for freedom. Each movement broke the glass a little more. Blood gushed inside. The tide grew higher as more sharks slammed into the dome, a flash of teeth before receding back into the depths.

"Go!"

Aleksandr's command wasn't needed. The dual threat of drowning or being eaten alive had spurred Evelyn out of her shock, and she was already racing for the door. The blood lapped at Aleksandr's thighs, high enough to make every step a battle. In seconds, the hot liquid was pushing at his hips. It made it harder to keep his footing each time the sharks attempted to get inside.

"Right!" Aleksandr bellowed as they reached the end of the hallway.

From here, it was a series of twists and turns, the walls filled with small tanks of jellyfish and crabs. The overhead lights flicked off, casting the world into an inky darkness. They kept running. The water pushed at his spine. Somewhere behind them, the glass released one last cry and then the world was filled with the rumbling roar of an approaching wave. Ivan clutched his fingers into Aleksandr's shirt, holding onto him for dear life. Pressed this close, Aleksandr could hear his brother's mumbled words over the rest of the chaotic noises.

"It's not real. It's not real. It's not real."

Aleksandr began to repeat the noises in his head, but that didn't stop him from pushing forward. The wave hit him like a punch to his spine. Thrown off his feet, he burst out into a blinding light, his shoulder smacking down against the tiled floor. Panting heavily and still clutching his brother tight, Aleksandr surged up onto his feet. But there was no pressure from the building liquid now and he over-sold his movements, causing him to stagger and trip. If it weren't for the wall he smacked blindly into, he would have fallen again.

"Sir, are you alright?"

On the verge of hyperventilating, Aleksandr could only blink into the array of bright, colorful lights. Faces faded into the haze. Each one staring at him with wide eyes, creeping closer as they murmured amongst themselves.

"Hey, kid, you okay?"

Aleksandr couldn't pinpoint who had spoken. Could barely even see them. But he knew without a doubt that someone was reaching towards Ivan. *Trying to take him away!* The thought rushed burning hot into his mind and Aleksandr stumbled back, twisting his body to shield his brother, his teeth bared in a feral growl.

"What the hell, man? Let the kid go!"

"He's claustrophobic," Evelyn's voice broke into the haze of Aleksandr's panic. "It's okay, I'm so sorry we worried you. We thought he'd be fine."

"We didn't know it was underwater," Aleksandr whipped around, seeking out Nadya's voice.

She was at his side before he could clear his vision, her arms wrapped around his leg. The reassurance of the touch pushed aside his confusion and dread. Still, fine tremors pulsed through his hands as he crouched down and drew his sister into a tight hug.

What followed was a familiar activity. Checking for battle wounds. The twins insisted that they weren't hurt and offered little smiles that did more to calm him than anything else could have. All the while, he was vaguely aware of Evelyn standing a few feet off to the side. She was still prattling on, talking about panic attacks and getting lost, and a flickering light that had, apparently, been very scary.

He ignored it for the most part until he was sure his siblings were okay. They were still trembling as he gathered them into a group hug. He kissed the crowns of their heads in turn and released a long sigh.

"It's okay," he said.

When the assurances didn't appease them, he tightened his grip.

"Who wants pizza?"

That earned him a chuckle and they patted his back, signaling that they were okay. At least for now. Pulling back, he cupped their cheeks, gave them a smile, and finally turned, preparing himself to deal with the gathering crowd. Instead, Evelyn came up beside him and began to insistently shove him.

"Thanks again. It's really cool so many people care. He'll be fine," she spoke swiftly, the words broken by awkward laughter and random waves of her arm.

Once she got him and the twins moving, the remaining crowd began to disperse and went back to what they had been doing. It only took a few quick glances for Aleksandr to realize that they were in the aquarium's gift shop. Keeping the twins close to his sides, they weaved around the array of souvenirs. For once, they didn't seem interested in anything. It was the quickest they had ever crossed the shop, and soon enough, they were out into the main hallways of the casino.

"Okay, I don't think anyone still cares," Evelyn said quickly as she came up beside them, still glancing around. "Are you guys okay? No one hurt?"

"We're fine," Nadya nodded.

"What about you?" Ivan asked.

Aleksandr blinked, feeling a little more himself and realizing that he probably should have asked that earlier. One of her hands restlessly twisted in the strap of her duffle bag as she assured them that she was fine. It didn't stop them from picking up their pace. They had crossed the entire casino before his heartbeat had settled back into a normal rhythm.

"So, where are we going?" Evelyn asked at last.

"For pizza," Ivan said.

Her stride stumbled. "You're getting pizza right now?"

Nadya tossed her a confused look. "When is it a bad time for pizza?"

"Right," Evelyn said.

It was clear she had a lot more to say about the situation but managed to keep her silence until they were on the monorail platform. Ivan explained how the small tram line linked Mandalay Bay to The Luxor, and that the maps of Las Vegas were deceptive. Everything was so big that walking times took far longer than people expected. The chatter seemed to ease her nerves, and in the end, she was even smiling down at the small boy.

Night had fallen while they had been inside. That said, darkness never really got a tight grip in this town. Neon lights fought it back and kept everything in a perpetual state of midday brightness. The nighttime crowds were starting to gather. People in search of entertainment or shuffling out from one bar to another. Evelyn was bouncing restlessly on the balls of her feet by the time they got on the monorail. It was a short trip, but she deteriorated enough that she was jumping slightly and making clicking sounds with her tongue. *Adrenaline or shock?* Aleksandr couldn't decide which one it was, but figured getting some food into her stomach was a good idea.

She was ready the moment the monorail pulled up in front of the Egyptian-themed hotel. The sky was dark enough now that the beam of light shooting from the tip of the onyx pyramid was visible for miles. People milled around the replica statues that guarded the area into the building itself, smaller versions of the sphinx and the like. The desert air felt uncomfortably hot after the air-conditioning, but it was fresh and flowing, and Aleksandr took in a few greedy breaths. The platform thinned quickly, and Evelyn took to pacing back and forth a few feet, her hands on her hips and her chest heaving as she sucked in deep breaths. Once she was sure that no one would overhear, she turned abruptly to them.

"So, this changes things, huh?" Evelyn said, puffing out her cheeks like she had just run a marathon.

"We knew the Furies were here."

"Yeah, yeah, I got that part," she said, pacing again. "It's just ... I always thought that they were real, you know? This is new. New and not exactly good."

"What do you mean?" Ivan asked.

Nadya scrunched up her face. "We don't have time to deal with you going into denial."

"Oh, I'm not. Though I am freaking out that you guys aren't freaking out," she said. "Take the flamingos. You said that the Furies messed them up, right?"

"Yes," Aleksandr said, his stomach churning as he realized there was something he was missing.

"Other people saw that, right?" she pressed. "There were witnesses? Tangible evidence left behind?"

"So?" Nadya asked.

"So?" Evelyn laughed. "So, we're not covered in blood. I'm bone dry, how about you guys? Yeah, that's what I mean. No one else saw that. You might not have noticed while you got settled, but even the people coming out of the aquarium behind us kept giving us weird looks. Unless torrents of blood are a normal occurrence and they've just gotten bored with it all, we were the only ones who saw that. None of it was real. *All* of it was in our heads. And that, my friends, might cause a few issues down the line."

Dread opened up in the pit of Aleksandr's stomach. "Oh."

"Yeah. Oh." Evelyn laced her fingers together and placed the tangled digits on the back of her head, dragging in a few deep breaths as she jumped from one foot to another. It seemed to do the trick and she was able to calm down at last.

"Maybe this is a good sign," Nadya said.

"Oh?" Evelyn asked, almost as if she were mimicking Aleksandr's earlier comment.

"Last time, it seemed like all three of the Furies needed to be present for things to get really bad," Ivan agreed. "Maybe this means that only one has found us. We still have time."

The rhythmic sound of bells cut into the conversation and she pulled it out from the cup of her bra. Aleksandr hadn't seen her put it in there and was wondering why she didn't use her pockets. He was still contemplating it as Evelyn read over the text message. With an annoyed huff, she smiled bitterly and tossed Aleksandr the phone.

"Not as much time as you think. Family's coming."

Aleksandr looked down at a picture of a plane ticket, the location of departure blanked out but the arrival point clear. It was a one-way ticket to Las Vegas.

Chapter 5

Las Vegas made Evelyn feel small. The Strip was a broad, straight stretch of concrete, parting the colossal buildings like an obsidian river through a canyon. Working together, the towering summits of the buildings held up the night sky like it was a thick, dense blanket. The darkness drooped slightly around the tips but was unable to penetrate the glittering, dazzling array of lights.

Spacious walkways braced The Strip, nestled between the road and the casino grounds. Periodically, long staircases rose up at least two stories high to join a network of bridges that connected the hotels and tourist attractions.

They seemed to be the only way to navigate.

Unlike what the movies had promised her, The Strip wasn't an open, flowing stretch of road that served as the perfect vantage point to take it all in. Not only did a waist-high fence block anyone from crossing, the traffic was horrible. The sheer number of vehicles had reduced both directions to a crawl. Four miles of blocked roads with surprisingly patient people. No one honked or yelled. They all just inched forward when they could, Porsches and Lamborghinis bumper to bumper with minivans and rusted wrecks.

The twins led the way, swinging their joined hands as they weaved through the crowd and took bites of their ice-cream cones in near perfect, mindless unison. They straddled the line between creepy and adorable, which seemed to be their preference. Evelyn nibbled on her cone with far more reluctance. The twins had been the first ones to shake off their shock and point out that their only real defense against the Furies was to starve them. They fed off fear. Their fear. So, the calmer they remained, the better they would fair in the long run. Comfort food, as they had reasoned while staring up at their brother with imploring eyes, was the perfect way to relax. Aleksandr hadn't put up much of a fight. A quick pizza dinner and ice-cream for the walk back.

Daytime heat lingered in the air, quickly melting Evelyn's ice-cream, turning it into liquid trails that pooled against her fingers. Food wasn't enough of a distraction to clear Evelyn's mind like it did the twins. But her first real sight of Las Vegas in all its glory made up for that. Without a glance behind, the twins trotted up a flight of stairs, working against the tide of the crowd to reach the bridge. It seemed like every inch of space was taken up by someone. And there was never any theme within them. Evelyn found herself just as likely to pass someone heading for a club as she was to spot someone in their pajamas. Costumes, gym gear, designer brands and souvenir shirts. Anything and everything. All she had to do was look long enough to spot it. Nothing was uncommon. Nothing was strange. There was no point of reference, and without it, everything around her felt artificial. A staged production designed for entertainment. A play that would render it impossible to notice what didn't belong until it was right next to her. It put her on edge, and she shifted a little closer to Aleksandr, closing ranks.

The entrance of the Polaris Casino reared up before them, and she was captivated once again. Even in the blazing chaos of The Strip, the glistening cobalt of Polaris stood out. It was laced with rockets and planets and topped with a stark white star that, in the night, seemed to hover above the building.

The industrial air conditioner droned, a constant hum that grew louder as they added to the stream of people funneling through the enormous doors. Synthetic, chilly air blasted them from all directions the moment they crossed the threshold, freezing the sweat on Evelyn's skin and making her shiver. She flinched at the sensation. A second of hesitation that earned her a gentle shove. Apparently, the stranger behind her hadn't anticipated the sudden stop and had kept walking. Both muttered an apology, but neither of them could keep the irritation from their voice.

The gambling floor was directly in front of the entrance. An electronic sea of flashing lights, clashing melodies, and the constant chatter of coins against metal. White lattice-work and computer screens covered the domed roof, creating the illusion of a spaceship's window, with rainbow nebulas and swirling galaxies passing by at a lazy pace. If Aleksandr's shoulder hadn't nudged her, she probably would have stopped walking again and stared at the display.

Circling the edges of the poker machine pit, they passed by a long series of glass doors and a small bar that sold novelty shaped cups filled with neon-colored daiquiris. The check-in counter lay a bit deeper into the structure, away from all the windows and sheltered from the sunlight. The manufactured darkness made the array of decorative lights far more impressive. A dozen people worked the front desk, but they couldn't keep up with demand. The people waiting to check in created a long, winding snake that coiled back and forth on itself, filling up the waiting room. She joined the end of the line, a little surprised when the Sokolovsky siblings joined her.

Since the single queue only splintered towards the end, it was impossible to choose their server. Evelyn didn't know that this was a problem until her small group was heading towards a woman at the far end of the counter. The kids groaned, and Aleksandr grunted as if in physical discomfort.

"What am I missing?" she whispered.

"Carrie doesn't like us," Nadya said.

"That's not true," Aleksandr said, carefully covering up his Russian accent as they approached the table. "She doesn't like how I'm raising you."

There wasn't time to ask any further questions. Carrie looked them over as they came up and forced a smile.

"Alex." There was a sharp edge to her voice as her eyes lingered on the twins. "I'm afraid you'll have to wait. We're a little busy right now. As I'm sure you can see."

Evelyn gripped her bag tightly to suppress her need to whip around when Aleksandr replied, his voice now drenched with a heavy Southern drawl.

"Oh, I don't need anything. This here's my friend Eve. She's checking in."

"Of course," Carrie said.

Evelyn handed over her identification and a credit card, receiving a sheet of paperwork in return. As she filled it in, she snuck glances at the front desk worker. At the same time, Carrie was watching the children.

"So," Carrie leaned against the counter and spoke with an overly sweet tone. "Don't you two look pretty today?"

"Thank you," they said in unison.

"But, well, I can't tell who's who. Which one of you is Ian?"

Evelyn refocused on her paperwork, trying not to look surprised by the alias.

The children didn't hesitate, each rattling off the fake names as if they were the only things they have ever gone by.

"It's so hard to tell when you're both dressed up like that." Carrie looked purposefully at Aleksandr as she added, "You know, you can choose different outfits."

Evelyn looked over just in time to see Aleksandr glare at the woman.

"They wear what they want," Aleksandr said, his voice sharp.

"Well, kids don't always know what's good for them. That's why parents make the decisions. What they wear. What they do. Where they're raised."

"We like Vegas," Ivan chirped.

"I'm sure you do," Carrie said with that same sickly-sweet tone.

Evelyn hurried through the process of checking in.

"How was school today?" Carrie asked.

Aleksandr's eyes narrowed at the question.

"Oh, right, you're not enrolled yet."

"Yes, we are," Ivan said.

A small pit of fire began to crackle in the depths of Nadya's eyes. "We're homeschooled."

"Of course, I forgot."

"Wow," Evelyn couldn't help but mutter.

She had no idea that someone could fit that much disgust in only four words.

With the paperwork finished, Carrie didn't have time for further comments. Swiftly, she checked Evelyn in, slid a few items over the polished marble countertop, and called for the next person in line.

Along with a key card, there was a map, a pamphlet, and a few coupons for different attractions within the casino. Evelyn studied the floor plans carefully as she shoved everything else into the outer pocket of her duffle bag. The layout of the casino was a strange mix of straightforward and overly complicated. Large areas filled the map with blocks of color, but there seemed to be an endless array of pathways that weaved around all of them.

The twins didn't hesitate, entirely at home amongst the chaos, leading the way past a small convenience store and what seemed to be the entrance to a fun zone. Kids swarmed the area, shrieking with delight as they raced around, their cries accompanied by the whirl of electronic games and the tell-tale 'pew' that the universe had reserved as the only authentic sound for lasers. The air was full of scents. Popcorn and hotdogs and spilt soda pop. Individuals in stylized astronaut costumes wandered around the swirling mass of people, selling large, soft tuffs of cotton candy wrapped around glowing sticks. As they passed the threshold, Evelyn noticed that there was what looked to be a downed alien craft nestled in the back of the long room. A sign taped to the front boasted that it was the largest laser tag arena in the world.

The twins didn't so much as glance at the other kids or the playground as they passed. On the other side of the door, they cut off to the side, swiped a small plastic disc across a nondescript part of the wall, and popped open a concealed door. Its camouflage was far from perfect. But, with all of her senses assaulted at once, Evelyn knew she would have missed it.

Having lost track of which twin was which, she couldn't say who held the door open for her, but she was ushered through into a brightly lit hallway. Once again, her mind screamed 'wrong'. The stark contrast was jarring. Gone was the beautifully decorated halls, the attention to detail, the color and glee and all the trappings of the facade. The corridor before her was long and barren. Just block stone walls thick with layers of white paint. The sick feeling of claustrophobia began to seep into her chest. Compared to the vastness they had just passed through, the walls felt like they were squeezing in on her. The heavy door clicked shut behind them, and Evelyn flinched.

"Staff entrance," Aleksandr said, his voice booming in the sudden silence.

She nodded as if she wasn't concerned, as if the constant hum of the fluorescent lights above them weren't grating on her nerves.

Their footsteps echoed out behind them and before them, making it sound as if they weren't alone. Finishing the last bites of her ice-cream, Evelyn wiped her hand off on the loose material of her dress. For some reason, the sweet, milky scent of the treat only hit her now. It lingered as she moved, and she made a mental note to wash out her clothes when she got to her room.

They reached a set of three elevators. Unlike the hallway, no attempt had been made to hide the receiving pad. It was an ugly black slab mounted on the wall that released a series of flashes when one of the twins swiped the small plastic disc across it. Only once it was activated, did the elevator's call button light up. It hit Evelyn then. Her room was on the thirteenth floor. This elevator just went down.

"Where are we going?" she asked, subconsciously balling her fists by her sides.

"Our room," one of the twins said.

"I want them settled before I go to work," Aleksandr said.

Evelyn glanced around quickly, making sure the hallway was empty before asking, "You're going to work *now*?"

"I've got a bit of time," he said before he caught her point. "This is staff accommodation. If I get fired, we're homeless."

Evelyn was about to ask why they would even care about that, given that their parents had surely taught them how to survive with far less, when it hit her. They weren't even near their floor and they've had to use a specialized key twice. There were laws that forbade hotels from giving out guest room numbers. That had to hold true for staff as well. And, as she looked around, she spotted exposed surveillance cameras monitoring every inch of the corridor. A few people passed, greeting the Sokolovskys with a smile before jerking their heads towards Evelyn. They only picked up their pace again after Aleksandr had made the introduction, still referring to her as Eve with that flawless Southern accent. Every person reminded him to '*make sure the boss doesn't see her*'. *Security*, she decided. That's what the hotel offered. *No apartment complex or doorman could compare.*

The elevator doors finally opened, allowing a few people in a variety of uniforms to shuffle out. All of them noticed Evelyn, mostly nothing more than a frown to recognize that she didn't belong. Some, however, lingered and questioned, refusing to move on until Aleksandr had reassured them that it was all okay. The conversations all ended the same, with his co-workers warning him about the bosses catching him with a guest in his room.

The elevator carriage itself was small and just like the corridor they had left, devoid of all luxuries. No decorations or attempts to cover the bare steel walls.

There was nothing that made Evelyn question the reliability of the machine, but after seeing the guest areas, it felt sterile and cold. The ride was smooth, but it made a weird, rattling noise. That's when she was able to pinpoint what felt off.

No music. It hadn't occurred to her how odd it was not to have music playing through the speaker system. It added an alien feel to a normal situation, and she found herself grateful for the twins' endless chatter. Since they were the only people riding, the kids didn't bother to keep up the English pretense and spoke amongst themselves in Russian. Every so often, Aleksandr would add something, but he spent most of the ride chewing on his thumbnail. Evelyn didn't bother asking what they were discussing. Her attention was fixed on the levels clicking off. Each one was displayed on a small screen above the buttons. She had never known a building could have six basements. They stopped on 'basement five' and exited onto a narrow hallway.

It was half the width of the ones above, the walls close enough that Evelyn could shove out her elbows and touch both sides at once. If two regular-sized people were to pass, they'd have to twist and shuffle awkwardly. It made her grateful to be short. Otherwise, the walls would have been stifling. She didn't even have to duck under the globes attached rather low on the walls. Everything was a perfect white. Walls, floor, carpets, and doors. There were no twist and turns in the hallway. Just one long, thin corridor that stretched out to the horizons, each coming to an abrupt stop with a bright crimson door.

In a sudden burst of excitement, the twins sprinted forward, Russian words spilling from their mouths as they shoved at each other, trying to get ahead. The fight only increased as they reached their room, both battling to use their key cards to open the door while simultaneously pushing the other one away. Evelyn laughed at the sight, a warm flush filling her chest. *After all they've seen, they're still just kids.* Her smile faded when she realized that Aleksandr might need to intervene soon. He had been the last to exit the elevator, leaving him trapped behind Evelyn. She cast a glance over her shoulder, catching a flicker of a smile before Aleksandr was able to hide it.

"Should they be speaking Russian?" she asked. "What if someone overhears them?"

"Plenty of people are bilingual," he mumbled.

During the trip down, he had finished with his thumbnail and was now chewing on his middle finger. Evelyn missed which one of the twins won the battle, but the door snapped open, clashing against something with a loud crack. They rushed in, Aleksandr and Evelyn only a step behind. He had to scoot in around her when she suddenly stopped at the threshold. She had never had a problem with tight spaces before, but she was starting to now.

The room itself was as thick as the hallway and looked oddly like a train carriage. With the door pushed all the way back, she could only see the foot of the bunk beds the kids were now crawling all over. A high set, built-in wardrobe was on her left, the sliding doors taking up the majority of the limited wall space. There was just enough space left over at the end of the room for a single, tiny sink and a small bar fridge. Drawn curtains hung on the wall directly opposite from the door, the same vibrant blue as the blankets tucked neatly around the single beds.

"Why are there curtains?" She didn't know why it was the first question that entered her mind, but she didn't regret it. "Aren't we underground?"

She jumped slightly when one of the twins blurred past her face. Having hooked their legs over the safety rail of the top bunk, they swung upside down and smiled up at her.

"Ivan," they clarified before continuing, "they're fake. They didn't even put anything interesting on the other side. How lazy is that? I want to put up a poster, but we can't damage the walls."

"It's to stop us from getting cabin fever," Nadya added.

Still standing in the doorway, Evelyn couldn't see what the girl was doing, but judging by the sound, she was rummaging through something. Possibly a cubby set into the wall by the bottom bunk.

"Isn't that when people stuck together for a while end up killing each other?" Ivan asked. He didn't attempt to sit up right even as blood began to pool in his head.

"Yeah," Nadya said distractedly.

Ivan turned his head to his sister as he let his arms drop. "How would a window stop that? Cabins have windows."

Nadya's response came in Russian, and they started to bicker again. Still uneasy about anyone overhearing them, Evelyn finally stepped into the room. She was standing halfway along the bed before she was able to close the door.

"Are all the staff rooms this small?" she asked.

"They don't normally let families stay on site." Aleksandr was more focused on hanging up the kids' backpacks than the conversation itself. "This is the only room with two beds. And I like having them close."

As Evelyn began to contemplate where Aleksandr had been sleeping for the last two years, he slid back one of the wardrobe doors to retrieve his uniform. Since the bottom of the cupboard was set a few feet off the ground, Evelyn easily noticed the blankets and pillows gathered into a makeshift nest.

Trauma or convenience? The question rolled around her head as she glanced around, trying to imagine what it would be like to live in such limited space with two other people. *Awkward.* It wasn't an imaginative answer but it was all she had. As an only child, she didn't know if sibling dynamics would make it any easier.

Aleksandr is more than their brother, though. She had only seen them interacting with Olga and Petya for a few moments. That was enough. Aleksandr was the only real parent the twins had ever known. Whether or not that helped in this situation, she had no idea. Either way, it worked. All of them appeared completely content with their living situation. Moving around each other as if they had all the space they could ever need. Each instinctively aware of the others. Completing little tasks without ever bumping into each other. Evelyn flinched as Nadya tossed something to Ivan, without a word of warning or a shared look. Ivan caught it while he was climbing back up onto the top bunk.

How much time would you have to spend with someone to get in sync like that? The question had barely passed her mind before it was chased out by another. Looking at all three of them in turn, she wondered. *What did they survive together to build this close of a bond?* Standing in the far corner, Aleksandr pulled his long-sleeved shirt off, revealing a sleeveless undershirt, the snug material pulling tight across the scarred flesh it concealed. He didn't bother to take the undershirt off as he wiped his exposed skin down with wet wipes.

"Okay," Nadya declared, a giddy little edge to her voice. "Slides are ready. Take your seats."

Aleksandr looked over to them with an arched eyebrow. When it was Evelyn's turn to cast a similar look to the kids, they both lunged forward. Clutching her duffle bag kept her from hitting either of them on reflex. The urge didn't leave her entirely as the twins dangled from the safety rail, giggling at her expense.

"She's going to stab you if you keep that up."

Aleksandr gave the warning in a bored, disinterested tone. It was enough to make them stifle their laughter, even though they didn't look at all sorry.

"What slides?" Evelyn asked.

"We knew that this was coming sooner or later," Ivan said, letting Nadya finish off the rest of the thought.

"So, we organized a crash course in Sokolovsky sibling history."

"Convenient," Evelyn said.

"So, sit down already," they declared as one, their excitement making her smile.

Placing her duffle bag down on the floor, she glanced around. There weren't any seats. Not even extra space for one. Settling down onto the carpet, she rested her back against the door. It had felt like the best place to sit until the paranoid part of her mind worked up. Her head filled with images of knives slipping under the gap of the door, slicing into her flesh before she even knew that she was under attack. She shuffled forward a few feet and leaned a shoulder against the wooden base of Aleksandr's wardrobe. Aleksandr loomed above her, reaching into the cupboard and grasping the hanging rail. In one smooth leap, he swung himself inside, peeking his head out a second later. He looked like a perching bird.

The lights flicked off, plunging the room into darkness, with only the smallest slip of light creeping in from under the door. Evelyn's chest tightened, and her muscles clenched. With a slight click, a bright light projected onto the curtains, displaying the main screen of a smartphone.

"Lady and my other brother," Nadya declared as if she were a circus ringleader. "We welcome you to Serial Killer 101."

Chapter 6

Evelyn squirmed, trying to get comfortable on the thin carpet. Each time she shuffled, she could pick up the scent of the rug shampoo. A clean, soapy smell that mixed with the lingering traces of the wooden furniture and fabric softener. She took a curious, discreet sniff. No rot, blood, or sweat. It was a level of cleanliness that she hadn't expected Aleksandr capable of when they had first met. He had reeked, then. The whole house had. Evelyn had seen the corpses that had been set up around the kitchen table and had always believed there were more. Perhaps put on display. Maybe hidden under the floorboards or piled in a forgotten room.

Nadya started to speak, her small but firm voice snapping Evelyn out of her thoughts.

"As you know, our little family started off with Petya and Olga."

She clicked a button, and a photograph filled the projection, the image warped by the folds of the curtains. Seeing the couple made Evelyn's stomach cramp, the edge of her panic dulled only by repetition. She knew those pictures. Every tabloid magazine and news outlet had been plastered with them for months after the news had broken. As if it were impossible for them to find another shot of the couple. Or perhaps they just liked the contrast. Beautiful, beaming newlyweds above descriptions of brutality and madness. The photograph had been taken a few years before Evelyn had encountered them. Not much had changed.

"I never get over how pretty they are," Evelyn muttered, the words mindlessly slipping past her lips. "It doesn't seem right. I know, I know, that's not how it works. You can't always see someone in a crowd and go, 'them, they're psychos, but ... they're both just really pretty."

"Her hair always smelled like coconuts," Ivan said in a soft voice. A single second was all it took for whatever nostalgia the small boy felt to wither in disgust. His nose scrunched up. "I hate coconuts."

"You're allergic to them," Aleksandr noted.

"That's why I hate them. They're trying to kill me."

"Anyway," Nadya said loudly, regaining everyone's attention. "What Evelyn might not know is that not only were they both serial killers long before they met, but they really liked to reproduce. In total, they had eleven kids. Seven of us are still alive."

"Wait. What happened to the others?" Evelyn asked.

The Sokolovsky siblings had never seemed more alike than when they fixed Evelyn with the same baffled expression. They each stared at her for a long moment before looking at each other. Apparently, Ivan was the one nominated to speak.

"Have you repressed everything you've ever learned about our parents?"

"They killed their own children?" An icy pit opened up inside of Evelyn's skin as she said the words.

"Duh," Ivan said. "Didn't you know that?"

Four. They killed four of their children. She didn't know why it surprised her, rattled her, but it did. Olga and Petya had been both narcissistic and obsessed with each other. *Shouldn't that have given some protection to their kids? At the very least, shouldn't they have taken some pride in what they created together?*

"I can't wrap my head around it," she admitted.

"Alek," Nadya whined. "We didn't plan on her being this behind. She's ruining our lecture."

Aleksandr grunted but didn't say anything, leaving Evelyn to assure the kids that it was fine. She'll keep up.

"Now, there's obviously us three," Nadya said. "So, we're down to four."

"Three if you're counting Dima," Evelyn said.

They all turned to her again.

"Olga and Petya had two documented children," Evelyn began, deciding that it would be easier to lay out what she knew and let the twins fill in the blanks. "Zoya; who died at three months due to SIDS. Though, I guess that was a misdiagnosis. And Dima, a black widow. Basically, the vast majority of people she dated went missing. They suspect her of dozens of murders in numerous countries but only had enough evidence to convict her of three. She was arrested in Mexico five years ago. She's still down there. I hear she's married a guard. They fired him, of course, but they still got married."

"And we weren't invited," Nadya mumbled.

"How do you know all that?" Aleksandr asked.

Shrugging one shoulder, Evelyn smiled. "A friend in the FBI told me."

"What?" all three of them asked at once.

"What?" she parroted back, her words coming faster as she continued. "Our story was that I single-handedly escaped the most prolific serial killers since Elizabeth Bathory. You didn't think that anyone in law enforcement might have a few questions? That some criminal profilers might see this as a learning opportunity? Yeah, I made a friend in the FBI, and to put me at ease, they answered some of my questions."

"And you asked about Olga and Petya?" one of the twins asked. She didn't catch which one.

"Wouldn't you?" she asked.

"And we're not going to this friend because ..." Aleksandr prompted.

"They're not crooked. Look, I'm new to all of this, so stop me if I'm wrong, but isn't it harder to get away with killing people when cops are around? Unless you were angling to get into witness protection."

In the dim light, Evelyn couldn't see Aleksandr's eyes. She felt them narrow on her, though. Sharp and angry.

"Is witness protection an option? That doesn't sound too bad," Nadya noted.

"They'd never let me keep custody of you," Aleksandr said.

"Can't we explain that you're not like them?"

"I killed people, Nadya. As a legal adult, I beat men to death with my bare fists and helped get rid of bodies."

"Olga and Petya made you," Ivan protested and comforted at once.

"For some people, that won't matter. I was an adult. In their heads, it's a simple matter. I could have gone to the police and I didn't. Best case scenario; you two will be kept together and I'll be put in a cell somewhere. Worst; they'll separate all of us, most likely somewhere the others will find you, and I'll be tried in a state that still has the death penalty."

"We're not going to the cops," Nadya said with conviction.

"Appreciate it." A small smile played in Aleksandr's words.

An uneasy silence followed, broken by Nadya clearing her throat.

"So, like I was saying. We don't have to worry about Dima right now." She clicked past the next photograph too quickly to get a decent look at the picture. "That leaves three."

Another soft click and two faces splashed across the curtains. A male and a female, both looking around twenty-four years old. Evelyn cringed, at first not knowing why. Then it clicked. Their coal black eyes. Thin, straight noses. Full lips that carried a natural pout. They looked like their mother. Evelyn clenched her teeth as the memories she had been struggling to fight off seeped into her mind. Olga. A cage in a heated, dirty basement. The crackle of a cattle prod. Searing pain and unbridled fear and the screams she could still hear every time she tried to sleep.

"These are Vera and Vlas," Ivan's voice invaded Evelyn's thoughts and dragged her back to the present.

She felt like she had been pulled out of the ocean depths and gulped down a lungful of air. It was a relief to hear Aleksandr cut in with a question of his own, allowing her a few extra moments to pull herself together.

"Where did you get this picture?" Aleksandr asked.

"Their Facebook page," one of the twins chirped.

Evelyn blinked in confusion, needed to say the words aloud to believe them. "Serial killers have Facebook pages."

"Well, yeah, but they don't advertise the murder stuff on them," Ivan said.

"It's for their business," Nadya added. "They're wildness tour guides. And hunters."

"I will give you candy if you promise me right now that you mean scavenger hunters," Evelyn said.

"They hunt people," Ivan said.

"You just missed out on Twizzlers," Evelyn said.

The light giggle she provoked from the children helped to ease the tension in her chest. And she was almost certain that she heard Aleksandr give a short, breathy chuckle. It was a strange sort of achievement to make Aleksandr show any sign of amusement.

Nadya cleared her throat again, her scowl visible by the reflected light.

"If everyone could agree to hold their questions to the end." She didn't wait for a reply before continuing, "These are Vera and Vlas. If it's not obvious, they're twins."

"Only there isn't a good one," Ivan cut in, wiggling his fingers and wavering his voice as if he were telling a ghost story. "They're both the evil twin. Mwahaha!"

While Evelyn didn't see Nadya thump her brother, she heard it.

"Anyway," Nadya stressed the word. "Like Petya and Olga, they worked as a team to capture their prey and take them somewhere isolated. The difference is, they'll give their prey a head start and then hunt them down."

Evelyn stared at the faces, trying to memorize each detail. It unsettled her how approachable they looked. Like the people you see in brochures for international tour companies. Idealistic, relaxed, adventure seekers. Fear gathered within her like a brewing storm as she stared at the picture. Her skin prickled, a slight sensation, barely there but enough to remind her that terror wasn't an option. Not with the Furies lurking so close. Remembering them jolted everything back into perspective. Vera and Vlas threatened death. The Furies madness. Evelyn would take the grave over a padded cell every time.

"Trained hunters," she said. "Great."

"It works in our favor," Aleksandr said around a nail.

She threw him a questioning look before remembering that they couldn't see each other in the dark. "Please explain how."

"They are territorial predators exclusive to rural environments," he said, as if it were obvious.

"Yeah. That sounds important," she said. "Counter point; they hunt people. We're people. So ..."

He huffed, the sound barely audible, not enough to know if it was amusement or annoyance. "Their M.O. is simple and they keep to it," he said.

"M.O. is modus operandi," one of the twins stage-whispered to Evelyn. "It means how they do something."

"I knew that one," she whispered back with a smile.

The other twin scoffed. "Yeah, because you cheated and asked a cop."

Aleksandr didn't stop his explanation to accommodate their whispered conversation. It was the longest Evelyn had ever heard him talk and play tricks with his voice. His accent thickened around his words. His voice rough like crunching gravel. Low and steady like static.

"They keep to stalking grounds and victims they're familiar with. Prostitutes or homeless people only. Someone easily lured, whose absence won't be missed straight away. Never any high-risk targets."

"Aren't those people the definition of 'high-risk'?" Evelyn asked.

All three of them chuckled.

"You can't be a hunter if you're still thinking like prey," Aleksandr said. "Non-transient people with wide social networks are high-risk for *us*. Vera and Vlas don't like attention or press coverage. Sure as hell can't hold their own against a taskforce. Don't have the skill set or required ego. So, they stick religiously to people that the mass population don't care about. The stray sheep on the edges of the herd."

"Right," Evelyn mumbled.

"Once they've got their target, they instantly retreat with them back into the wilderness. A place they know well. Somewhere isolated where they can have complete control. The hunt, kill, and disposal will all take place there. Privacy is essential."

"So," Evelyn said, "you're saying that killing in a place like Las Vegas is way out of their comfort zones?"

"Witnesses, security cameras, police, numerous victims at once," Ivan rattled off.

Evelyn refocused on the projected smiling faces as Aleksandr continued.

"Most people like us, the ones that don't get caught, are creatures of habit. We find something we like, and we stick with it," Aleksandr said. "Lure. Isolate. Control. Any reminder that they don't have the upper hand will make them hesitate."

"And never go with them to a second location," Nadya added.

Evelyn nodded even though no one could see her. "Can you send me that photo? I want to make sure that I remember them. Ah, right, my number."

Evelyn's phone beeped, buzzing against her chest with an incoming call before she could finish the sentence. Resenting the distinct lack of woman's clothing that had decent sized pockets, she pulled her phone out of her bra. Something about having the phone in the palm of her hand made her remember Aleksandr's fumbling on the device earlier. *He texted the twins*, she realized as a message alert illuminated the screen. *Damn it, Alek. Couldn't you have gone for the less creepy way of giving them my number?*

"Right. Thanks. So, does anyone have any other suggestions on how to deal with these guys? I mean, apart from 'don't get in the car'?"

"Look for a Mohawk braid," one of the twins said.

Evelyn's brow furrowed. "I don't know what that is."

"It's a braid that looks like a Mohawk. Duh," Ivan said.

"Vera has thick hair and braids along the top of her head for a kill," Aleksandr explained.

"She thinks it makes her look like a Viking," Nadya added.

Aleksandr snorted but continued, "It'll be multicolored and rather noticeable."

"I'm sorry," Evelyn cut in. "I can accept that ancient Greek monsters are real, but a serial killer with rainbow hair is just too much."

"It's not rainbow," the kids corrected as one.

"They both loved their trophies," Aleksandr said. "Vlas goes the traditional route and takes photos with the corpses. He'd keep them in a hunting cabin or lockbox somewhere. Vera's the dramatic one. She takes a lock of hair from each victim and braids them into her own. Hence, multicolored braid."

"How many victims are we talking about?" Evelyn asked.

She heard a shuffle of material and assumed Aleksandr had shrugged.

"It's hard to tell since we've been in hiding. If they've kept their pace, I'd say their death count would be around forty-three by now."

"Forty-three? Vera and Vlas have killed *forty-three* people?" Evelyn asked.

No one responded, but they didn't have to. The information couldn't be taken back now. It was lodged in her brain like a hot fire poker. *No fear*, she commanded herself. *Remember the Furies.*

"Okay," Evelyn said slowly. "So, who's the third one?"

"Radmiar."

She didn't know which one of the kids had spoken before the picture changed and she was momentarily blinded. Squinting to refocus, Evelyn found herself staring at a photograph of Aleksandr. Only with short cropped hair and a radiating smile. It was strange to see him so casual. So relaxed. Especially with Petya's arm slung over his shoulders.

"Radmiar's your *identical* twin," she said numbly.

Aleksandr grunted but didn't say anything. Tension filled the room, making the air dense.

"So," Evelyn said as she shifted around again. "What's he like?"

The question made Aleksandr snarl. Each word that left his mouth was razor sharp and filled with hatred. "He thinks he's the love child of Richard Ramirez,

Ted Bundy, and Hannibal Lector. A gentleman killer."

"Richard Ramirez," Evelyn said. "That sounds familiar."

"The Night Stalker," he said. "San Francisco, 1984 to 85. Home invader and sadist. Chose places at random. Broke in, raped, tortured, and murdered the occupants. No victim preference. He was happy as long as he got to kill someone."

"Wait, how does that add up with Bundy? I mean, they were both rapists," she cringed, feeling weird talking about such things in front of the twins. "But Bundy used charm, didn't he? Tricks to get women close?"

"Radmiar likes to alternate," Aleksandr said. "He's going to be the bigger threat. This is his perfect hunting ground, and he will hate you."

Evelyn looked at the photograph again. If she had been ignorant about who they were, she would have considered it a beautiful family photo.

"It does look like he's fond of his parents," she said. "Does he really blame me for their deaths?"

The twins snickered, and she looked around.

"What?" she asked.

"Radmiar has an issue with women," Aleksandr clarified.

"He only listened to Olga because he was terrified of her," Nadya added. "The rest of us weren't so lucky."

"Hey, at least we don't have to worry about all three of them joining forces," Ivan said. "Even avenging our parents wouldn't be enough to keep them from each other's throats for long. Vera despises him."

"Your mouth is going to set him off." There was a hint of amusement in Aleksandr's voice, as if he were eager to witness the fallout.

"Is that something I should aim for?" she asked.

"It would throw him off his game," Aleksandr replied. "He's like Petya. The kill for him is a sideshow. The main event is the fear he causes. The more you backchat, the more he'll want to destroy you–"

A sharp knock on the door cut off their conversation.

Chapter 7

Frozen in place, no one dared to breathe as they waited. The few seconds of silence were enough for the anticipation to burn against Evelyn's nerve endings. Another series of knocks. Nothing to tell them what threat stood on the other side of the wood. She balled her fists. Rolled her shoulders.

"Alex?" a woman's voice called through the door.

"Damn it," Aleksandr hissed under his breath.

The siblings broke into a flurry of movement. The projector shut off as the overhead lights flicked on. Aleksandr swung down, hopping over Evelyn's lap and pressing himself against the door, one arm on the handle while he checked the peephole.

"Alex, are you in here?"

"Yeah, Alison," he called out with his Southern drawl. "Just give me a second."

The twins crawled along the side of the bunk bed, moving from the bottom to perch on the top. Side-by-side, they looked sweet and innocent. As she stood up, her feet a little numb, Evelyn caught a flash of metal before they hid whatever they had under a pillow. *A knife*, she figured. Aleksandr glanced at the twins. They nodded and all three of them broke into wide smiles. Evelyn didn't have time to deal with how unsettling she found that before Aleksandr unlocked the door and pulled it open.

"Hey, Alison," Aleksandr sounded delighted to see her. "What can I do for you?"

"Hi, I'm sorry to bother you."

"Nah, come on. You're always welcome. You know that."

Even as he said the words, Aleksandr made sure that his broad shoulders covered the gap, essentially blocking her from entering. There was no stopping the woman's view, however. She had a good few inches on Aleksandr and could easily look over his head. Alison pushed her wavy brown hair over her shoulder as she smiled up at the twins.

"Hey there, cutie pies," she beamed. "How are you two today?"

"Good," they said playfully before giggling, like shy little kids ready to hide behind their mother's skirt.

Alison's easy smile faltered when she caught sight of Evelyn. Recovering quickly, she raked her gaze over Evelyn once before refocusing on Aleksandr.

"Oh, I didn't know that you had company."

Evelyn waved sheepishly. The gesture wasn't noticed or acknowledged.

"She's an old friend," Aleksandr said. "Just in town for a few days. She's checked in upstairs."

"Alex," Alison spoke the name with both indulgence and warning.

"Yeah, I know. But the kids really wanted to show her some stuff and they were so excited. Could you tell those little faces 'no'? She'll be heading back up in a second." Tilting his head, he chuckled softly. "Sorry, I've completely forgotten. Why did you say you were here?"

Alison gave a little laugh, one that showed she was more distracted than she wanted to seem. "There's been a mix up with the rosters. Jim didn't put any guys on and we've got some orange flags."

"Orange flags?" Evelyn asked.

"It's a room service thing. If someone's been ..." Alison's gaze skirted to the twins as she tried to think up a child appropriate code word. "*Mean* to a female server, they're marked as orange in the system, so we know not to send any more women up on their own. If they ... bully a man, they're marked as yellow. If they're just all round horrible, they're red."

Evelyn struggled to smother her laughter as she nodded along. It was surreal. *I was worried about mentioning 'rape,' while she's worried about the word 'jerk'.* Evelyn resisted the urge to shake her head. *This is just a world of wrong.*

Evelyn wasn't sure what to say. Or even if she could without a burst of manic laughter passing her lips. Mercifully, Alison was satisfied with a smile and refocused on Aleksandr, holding his gaze with a beseeching smile.

"Is there any chance you could come in early?"

"I thought Dan was on shift."

Alison snorted. "Yeah, Jim put him as administration supervisor. So ..."

"Right," Aleksandr matched her frustrated laughter and continued in what had to be a poor imitation of Jim's voice. "The A.S. answers the phones and takes the orders. Can they do that from the floor?"

"Okay, that's way too close to accurate. You're creeping me out," Alison said with a smile. "So? Please, Alex. I'm sure room 3622 is going to call in again and I don't want to have to go up there."

"Is he a meanie?" Nadya asked, softening her voice and widening her eyes, a picture of untarnished purity.

Ivan quickly followed suit, adopting the same expression as he asked, "What did he do, Alley?"

Watching Alison's discomfort increase, Evelyn found herself wondering how often the little brats had messed with her like that. They seemed to like this game a lot.

Aleksandr turned to the kids, the angle just enough to hide his sneer from the visitor.

"He never learned his manners." His voice remained light while his expression left no room for argument.

They nodded, their game over.

"Please, Alex," Alison said. "Dan said that you'll be able to leave early. As soon as the morning shift starts."

Aleksandr looked at the twins again. It was barely more than a glance, but Evelyn felt like she was on the outskirts of an entire conversation. In the end, Aleksandr turned back to Alison and shrugged.

"Sure thing. I'll be right up."

"Thank you, thank you, thank you!" Alison beamed. "You know, I can wait if you want some walking company."

"You need me to start right now," Aleksandr said.

"There's also that," Alison winced. "Did I mention, thank you?"

Aleksandr heaved a sigh. "Let me just grab my stuff. I'll get changed in the bathroom."

Evelyn glanced around, noticing for the first time that the room didn't have an attached en-suite.

"It's dorm room style," one of the twins whispered, as if picking up on Evelyn's thoughts. "Restrooms are those red doors down the hallway."

Evelyn meant to thank them for the information, but Aleksandr side-swiped her, maneuvering past her to get to the wardrobe, and she forgot.

He hid his discomfort well, careful never to let Alison see how much he hated the brief, unavoidable moments of physical contact. Evelyn slipped onto the bottom bunk at the first opportunity, trying to make it easier on him. Unfortunately, it left her awkwardly close to Alison. Neither of the women were inclined to acknowledge the other and the resulting silence was tense.

"Oh, hey," Alison stammered. "Did you guys hear about what happened at the Flamingo?"

The noise Aleksandr made was a perfect expression of good-natured indifference. "Nah. We don't really go around there."

"Well, you know that flock of real flamingos they have on display, right?"

He nodded.

"They went crazy!"

Aleksandr finally turned around to face her. "They're pink puffballs on sticks. What exactly would their going 'crazy' look like?"

"Apparently, it involved a lot of property damage. I was talking to my friend who works the front desk. She wasn't actually there when it happened, but she said the whole habitat was just destroyed. They even smashed into the buffet area."

Evelyn watched in awe as Aleksandr morphed his face into shock and horror. It had never occurred to her that he could be a good actor.

"Was anyone hurt?"

"A couple of people are in the hospital," Alison said. "Apparently, more were injured in the stampede rather than by the birds themselves."

"I'll never understand that," Aleksandr said with a frown. "How could someone just ... run over another human being?"

Alison shrugged. "People act weird when they're scared."

"Yeah, maybe."

Evelyn rubbed the knuckles of one hand over her mouth, trying to hide her reactions. It was like being in a parallel universe. Sitting there, watching Aleksandr Sokolovsky talk about the goodness of humanity, all the time using a Southern accent and showing social skills. She couldn't decide if she found it creepy or hilarious.

"Anyway, it's becoming a whole big thing. Reporters have been swarming the place all day and animal rights groups are up in arms. But this is the scariest bit. My friend, the one who works there, overheard some cops talking. And they think it could be a terrorist attack. Like someone poisoned the birds to have them act like that."

Aleksandr nodded and shrugged at the same time. Like he didn't agree but was too nice to say as much.

"Yeah, I know," Alison said. "It sounds like a bad conspiracy theory, but you can't be too careful these days."

"We'll have to keep an eye on the news updates," Aleksandr said.

With that, the conversation was over. A tense silence returned when the two women tried to avoid eye contact. It didn't last, and they shared the compulsory polite smile when that inevitably happened.

Alison looked to be around the same age as Evelyn, close to her twenties but not there yet. While she was trying to suppress the urge, Alison couldn't keep from sneaking glances at Evelyn. A few years ago, she might not have noticed the quick flick of eyes. Now, each glance felt like ice water sloshing over bare skin. Not able to stand it for long, Evelyn deliberately met the girl's eyes again. Surprise flashed over Alison's face before she was able to cover it with a tight smile.

"I'm Alison, by the way."

"Eve. Nice to meet you."

While she didn't have any experience with using an actual alias, Evelyn had been using her name to sort people out for years. When she was a kid, she had the facial recognition skills of a goldfish. It would take a few meetings for her to remember anyone. Not recalling someone's name was awkward. Forgetting who she didn't like was worse. The process was simple. She was 'Eve' for the irritating people, 'Evelyn' for others. Today, it was Evelyn to people she knew wouldn't try to kill her, Eve for the rest, and that churned her stomach.

"Know him for long?" Alison asked.

"Feels like it."

Alison's shoulders tensed up before she mumbled, "You have wonderful kids. You should know that."

Rattled by a rush of confusion, Evelyn barked a laugh. "What? Hold up. They're not mine."

"Oh," Alison stammered. "I just thought ... well, you know what a stickler for the rules Alex is. Two years and he's never even taken an extra coffee sweetener without permission."

"Yeah, he's a good ol' boy," Evelyn said.

Soft giggles drifted down from the top bunk, but Aleksandr kept his silence, gathering his uniform and snatching up the key. It seemed like he was yearning for his longer fringe right now, because he kept ducking his head, trying to hide his face behind his hair.

"Have you met their mother?" Alison asked.

Evelyn quickly thought back but couldn't recall him mentioning what lie he used. So, she decided to keep her mouth shut and smiled.

"It's a private matter," Aleksandr said, his abrupt tone enough to have Alison flush. He ignored her discomfort, focused only on the twins. "You guys know the drill. Lock the doors. Early to bed."

"We'll be good," they nodded.

Evelyn wondered just how far their version differed from the norm. As subtly as she could, she rechecked the room, this time looking for anything that could double as a booby-trap. She didn't see anything. The twins leaned over the edge of the bunk for a farewell hug. Given how short Aleksandr was, it was a bit of a trust fall, but they never hesitated. Each picked a shoulder, and they clung to him like he was leaving for years. *Like they'll never see him again*, Evelyn thought.

Murmured whispers passed between them before Aleksandr tried to push them back up. They refused to go, clutching onto him until he pulled them entirely from the top bunks. A few more whispers and what could have been a sniff, they let him put them down.

"Listen to Eve." His voice was thick, and he swallowed hard to get rid of it. Quickly, he hooked his fingers under each of the kids' chins and tipped their heads up. "Unless she says something stupid, then you guys are in charge."

They nodded.

He turned to leave, seemingly surprised to find Alison blocking the doorway.

"The boss is doing rounds tonight," she said weakly.

"Shit," he hissed under his breath, the hint of his Russian accent slipping out. Catching himself, he looked over his shoulder to Evelyn. "I could be fired if they found you down here."

Evelyn scooted off of the bed and grabbed her duffle bag.

"That's okay. I should check in with my dad and I need a shower." The idea of being alone made bile rise up from her stomach. She fought hard to keep it from showing on her face. It was a losing battle, so she twisted and busied herself by searching through her duffle bag's pocket, plucking the two room keys free. She handed one of them over to the nearest twin. "If you guys need anything."

Obviously, she wasn't as good as them at having silent conversations, but she thought she got the main points across. *Call me as soon as the boss leaves.*

They nodded in unison. Either they understood already, or texted her all the questions they couldn't ask now. Either way, she couldn't risk saying more knowing Alison was within earshot. They stood there, looking small and frail. No matter how hard they tried to hide it behind an expression of prepared conviction, they couldn't keep the traces of fear from inching into their wide eyes. Evelyn's arms twitched with the sudden urge to hug them. It was hard to leave.

"Be happy," one of them said with a smile.

Evelyn grinned. "You too."

There wasn't anything left to say. Nothing to stall with. Aleksandr shuffled behind her, impatient to get moving, feeling the looming threat of the soon approaching boss. The last thing they needed right now was to lose the safe hiding place the staff accommodation supplied. She almost laughed when the thought popped into her head. *This was a lot easier when we only had to worry about demonic beings.* Juggling responsibilities and authority figures messed things up.

Aleksandr's resolve to leave quickly snapped when the opportunity presented itself. As Evelyn slipped into the hall, he rushed back in and said another farewell, again keeping his voice low. At length, he stepped outside to join the two women. The door instantly slammed shut behind him, and there was a series of clicks. A half a dozen locks that probably weren't supposed to be there.

"Is something wrong?" Alison asked.

"It's just been a hard day," he dismissed.

Refraining from further questions, Alison took to trying to distract Aleksandr with constant, light-hearted chatter. It allowed him to walk in silence for the greater part of the hallway. It also gave Evelyn the ability to glance back to the room door without being caught. *They're safer right now than you are*, the voice of reason whispered in her head. At the elevator, Aleksandr once again hesitated.

Forty-three victims. Bundy. Sadist. Hunters. The words crowded into her head, each one carrying a crippling weight. She didn't want to go. Alison's brow furrowed in confusion as she eyed them each carefully.

"You need to swipe for this elevator," she said with a weak smile. No one moved. "Don't worry, I'll get it."

She reached out, swiped and called the elevator down. Evelyn tried not to flinch at the little beep.

"Just," Evelyn shrugged helplessly, "be happy. Or busy." *Be anything but afraid.*

A small smile twitched the corner of his lips. "You too. I'll text you if I get off early. My shift's scheduled to finish at 3 a.m."

"I'll be ready," she promised.

Aleksandr held out his hand, and Evelyn could only gape at it, knitting her brows. It was oddly reminiscent of their first encounter, only with the roles reversed. When they had agreed to work together to save the twins from the Furies. He had looked at her outstretched hand like it was an alien artifact. They had only parted ways with a handshake after his parents were dead, and they had managed to flee. If the world were fair, that would have been the last time they would have ever seen each other. Now, the same simple gesture held a new meaning. An acknowledgement that they both didn't want the other to die. Evelyn suspected that he hadn't made the offer to many other people in his life. She took the battered hand, wrapped her fingers around knuckles that had been shattered a dozen times over, and shook it. *He thinks one of us is going to be dead by 3 a.m.*

"It's only a few hours," Alison said with a nervous giggle.

Neither of them acknowledged her. With a sharp ping, the elevator doors opened. The carriage was empty and as Evelyn got inside, she felt every square inch of the open space pressing against her like a crowd of people. She couldn't pinpoint the moment when being alone had started to feel like a threat.

Aleksandr watched her until the doors closed and Evelyn was left staring at her own reflection distorted in the dull metal. Then there was the whirl of the machines, and the unsettling absence of elevator music.

It was almost a relief when she was back on the ground floor. She hurried out into the corridor, ignoring the odd looks her presence drew. Head high, shoulders back, she retraced her steps until she was once again in the organized chaos of the hotel lobby. It was a simple test of how much of the map information about the layout she had managed to retain. She weaved through the crowd, her head already pounding with the sudden onslaught of noise and flashing lights.

Once she was back at the front desk, she cut to the right and entered into the gambling pit. The guest elevators closest to her room were situated on the far side. Lighted pathways cut through the forest of metal and neon. The noise was deafening. Every other breath had the taint of either alcohol or cigarette smoke. Her eyes darted about, trying to keep track of all the people around her. It was an impossible task. There was barely a single machine free. Waitresses, dressed in green and covered in glow-in-the-dark jewelry, slipped through the masses, effortlessly carrying an array of glasses. Groups passed her, laughing and filling the space, causing her to sidestep them. Her skin crawled as faceless multitudes passed; close enough that she could feel the air stirring against her bare arms.

The edges of the key card dug uncomfortably into Evelyn's fingers as she tightened her grip on it. Only relenting when she felt that the thin slip of plastic was about to snap. Picking up her pace, she emerged out of the gambling area and onto a wide marble floor. Before her, a short hallway dedicated to guest elevators brimmed over with people. In keeping with the casino's theme, each of the sliding doors was refurbished to look like airlocks on a spaceship. The doors opened randomly, allowing groups of excited people to flow out and into the casino itself. Far fewer people were waiting to go up. Keeping to the fringes, she tried to be subtle about her surveillance of the crowd. It was easier to pick up little snippets of conversation than it was to keep track of the faces around her.

With everyone eager to get on with their nights, the hallway experienced vast ebbs and flows, filling rapidly when the door opened and emptying just as quickly. Evelyn didn't have to wait long for her turn, but she lingered, ensuring she was the last one to enter her carriage. As the shortest person in the elevator, she couldn't tell how many people were in there with her. So she pushed closer to a group of already tipsy women that, among other things, babbled about the phones they had forgotten in their rooms.

Food and entertainment venues filled the first three floors and the elevator stopped on each of them. Cramming to capacity, Evelyn was forced back against the wall, barely able to hold onto her rising panic as strangers crowded into her personal space. The situation improved once they passed the three floors. A few people got off on the sixth floor. A woman on the eighth. Another couple on the ninth. Bit by bit, their numbers eroded. When there was only a handful left, Evelyn looked around, taking stock. A couple that wasn't afraid of public displays of affection. An overworked woman scrolling through the messages on her phone. Three men that favored the word 'dude'. She almost missed the man in the back corner. He kept to her peripheral vision, his hands in his pockets and a baseball cap pulled down to cover his face.

She watched him for a moment. He didn't look up. Not even for a second. Didn't move. It left a bitter taste in the back of her mouth. At the next stop, the 'dude' men got out. Evelyn took the opportunity to switch to the opposite corner, shuffling around those that remained until she could press her back against the side wall. The new position should have given her a clear view of the man's profile wearing the baseball cap. But, when chanced a casual glace, the back corner was empty. A spike of fear speared her when she caught sight of him in the corner of her eyes. He had switched with her, moving to keep himself, his face, out of sight.

The working woman got off next and the man stood still. Then the couple. The man remained a dark pillar in the back of the carriage. Anxiety squeezed her chest, the sensation growing when she glanced at the series of call buttons and found them all dark. She had deliberately kept from pressing her floor. He hadn't picked one either. The realization settled in the pit of her stomach like a lump of ice as the doors slid closed. Without the next destination selected, the elevator sat where it was, the soft notes of piano music drifting through the speakers. The man remained where he was. A dark shadow on the edge of her vision. She took a deep, calming breath and glanced up at the display. *Ninth floor*, she thought. The idea of making a run for it when the doors opened again crossed her mind.

What if he follows? What if he had picked this floor and it's an ambush? In an attempt to maintain her composure, she reminded herself that she didn't know for sure the man was Vlas. Or Radmiar. The notion felt hollow since he was still hiding his face. From her, and undoubtedly, from the security cameras.

Time stretched and Evelyn began to pray that someone in the lobby would hit the call button. It almost felt like a physical blow when there was a beep and the doors opened again, still on the ninth floor. The man still didn't move. Evelyn didn't know if she should run. *He's waiting for me to choose.* Trying to be casual, she pretended like she had only just realized she had forgotten to hit the floor and glanced over to him.

"Which one do you need?" she asked him, struggling to keep her nerves from entering her voice.

She threw in a smile for good measure. Seconds ticked by and the man said nothing. *Just go,* she commanded herself. No sooner had her mind settled on the decision than the doors slid closed again. They sealed with a whispered gasp. Her hands clutched the strap of her duffle bag as the man took his first step forward. There was a stagger in his stride as he moved forward. The stench of alcohol followed him in a cloud. For half a heartbeat, she believed the lie, willing to dismiss him as a man too drunk to pay attention. Then she noticed that, despite all his stumbling, his face was always perfectly hidden behind the bill of the baseball cap. And his hands never left his pockets to help with his balance.

With a seemingly drunken swipe, he dragged his hand down the rows of buttons, illuminating half a dozen. Like he didn't have the coordination left to select a single floor. Evelyn's stomach tensed as the last of her doubt died. Repositioning herself to keep some distance between them, she was forced deeper into the carriage. Her eyes never left the man as she slipped the strap of her duffle bag over her shoulders, nestling the bulk of the bag against her back and freeing her hands.

The elevator lurched. Music continued to play, filling the silence as the elevator rose. All the while, the man stood before the doors. Right in the center, stone still, blocking her path with his head low and his hands shoved into his pockets. He wasn't wavering anymore. The lights above the door clicked off. Evelyn silently bounced on her toes, rolling her shoulders as she tried to think. To plan. She had just enough sense left to shove her room key into the side of her bra, safely nestling it against her phone. It didn't have her room number on it but she wasn't about to risk the man getting it. *Vlas or Radmiar?* she wondered. They approached the next floor. *Planned exit or coincidence?* It didn't matter. It was her only chance out and she was taking it. She drew in a deep breath, letting it out slowly as she waited for the bell.

With a metallic ding, the doors opened. Evelyn crouched low, rendering the man a human shield against any attack. Keeping her weight on one foot, she kicked, stomping her heel against the back of the man's knee. A startled gasp left him as he buckled. He dropped to one knee, giving her just enough room to leap over him and out into the hallway. One quick glance told her that they were still alone. She whipped around, walking backwards, fists up and ready to strike. The stranger was back on his feet. He charged forward but the doors were already moving again, already only a few inches from closing. A feral snarl left his mouth. He slammed his fist against the metal, making the doors rattle. Distracted by his burst of anger, he failed to get a hand through the gap. In the last second before the doors sealed, Evelyn watched him reach for the buttons.

The elevator rose and she burst to the side. Running up and down the hallway, hitting the call button for every other elevator present. A few of them opened immediately and she reached in, blindly hitting the buttons before moving onto the next. Some she hit high. Some low. Evelyn didn't know if Vera was waiting, if she could see anything from her 'second location', but hoped that all the chaos of the elevators might create some confusion. Buy her some time. Slamming through a heavy metal door, she entered the stairwell.

She longed to head to her room. To flee to the safety it promised with its door and locks and phone to call security. It was so close. One floor up. She was halfway up the first flight of stairs before it hit her. All of the buttons the man had pressed had been for higher floors. *Do they know where my room is? Is that where he was trying to take me?* Spinning on her toes, she started down. *Get to the front desk. Change your room.* The decisions gave her something to focus on. A goal to run towards. Sliding down the safety rails more than touching the actual stairs, Evelyn raced down the floors. Her heart slammed against her ribs, sweat marked her forehead. She kept going, speeding up every time she was forced to pass by one of the doors. It was impossible to shake the images that pushed into her mind. The absolute convictions that they were hiding on the other side of the doors. Waiting on every floor. Like trap door spiders. Just waiting for her to pass. To come close enough to strike.

It didn't feel real when she reached the ground floor. Sweat glistened on her forehead and the burst of activity had left a deep burn in her thighs. The bare, stone walls of the stairwell turned her panted breath into a bellow. She hesitated at the final door. The last chance for her nightmare image to become a reality. *Keep going. Before they catch up. Go!* Exploding onto the hallway of elevators, side-stepping the crowds, always moving forward. The second the crowd thinned, she forced herself into a sprint. Her shoes squeaked across the marble floor until she was back in the gambling area. Years of footwork practice had never seemed more relevant.

She didn't see the man again. *You wouldn't know if you did,* a voice in the back of her head accused. *You never saw his face.* Constantly looking around her, ignoring the strange glances from workers and patrons, she hurried through the pathways. The further she got, the easier it was to believe the voice in her head telling her that she was being paranoid. That didn't stop her from pulling out her phone, resolved to text Aleksandr and the twins. False alarm or not, if felt like she should tell them.

A sharp gasp pulled from her mouth as the phone buzzed in her hand. Swallowing thickly, she looked around, expecting to have to explain her actions away to a few people. She didn't. No one was paying attention. She couldn't spot a single person looking in her direction with more than a few seconds of mild interest. The complete indifference made her feel utterly alone. Like she was right back in that ghost town. Like she could scream and rage and barely draw anyone's interest.

Her heart stammered when she looked back at her phone. A single text message illuminated the screen.

Come out, come out, wherever you are.

Chapter 8

Aleksandr fiddled restlessly with the cuffs of his dress shirt. It was too clean. Too crisp with starch. He felt like he was going to stain it with sweat and dirt the moment it touched his skin. *Alex wouldn't have a problem with it,* he reminded himself. *And you're Alex Cooper from Mooresville, Alabama.* Repeating it helped. Like a little anchor tethering him to a far bigger lie. *Alex Cooper from Mooresville, Alabama. A town too small to bother putting in sidewalks. Couldn't if they wanted to. Whole dang town has historic significance. We keep it the way it was back in 1818.* The longer he thought as 'Alex', the easier it was to nail the accent. It was perhaps the most useful skill his parents had ever taught him. A good alias wasn't just a name you could throw out when questioned. It was a whole identity. Another life you can step into. A disguise that could fool the world.

Olga and Petya had never relinquished their grip on Aleksandr. Not because they viewed him as a threat. Aleksandr was useful. He took care of the kids and lugged bodies about. He was an amusement, someone they could torment when no one else was on hand. And, perhaps most importantly, he submitted and kept his mouth shut. Because of this, Aleksandr never had the opportunity to practice living as someone else like his siblings had. That had been a point of terror when he and his siblings had first set out into the world. He was sure Radmiar would see right through it and show up on their doorstep. For a year, he had waited every second for that fatal tap on his shoulder. Or for his coworkers to grow suspicious and call the police. Now, at last, his fear had become reality and he wasn't sure what to do about it. *Alex Cooper. Mooresville, Alabama. Father of twins. Ian and Natasha. Alex.*

"Cooper!"

Dan's sharp voice made him jolt and he snapped his head up, fingers still playing with his cuffs. The room service office was tiny and on the edges of the kitchen. After all the tables, computers, stock, and files were put in, there was about the length and width of a king-sized bed left over for walking space. For some reason, the architects had put a drive-thru style window in the wall that separated the office from the wide walkway where they kept all the serving trays lined up and ready to go.

Dan was leaning his head through the small gap, far too wide to fit much more of his body through, and clicked his fingers to draw Aleksandr's attention.

"Hey, Alex, over here. Got your attention yet?"

Aleksandr smiled. "Not all of it."

While he rolled his eyes, Dan did look somewhat amused. "Great. Have I got enough of it for you to do what we pay you for?"

"That depends," Aleksandr said as he crossed the distance. "Can I half ass it?"

"Yeah, sure. I don't care."

Leaning one shoulder against the side of the wall, his smile grew. "Right. So, I'm guessing room 3622 called in an order?"

"And demanded that I send my prettiest server," Dan said, looking torn between finding the client disgusting and hilarious. "Remember to bat your eyelashes, Cooper."

Remembering a second later that *Alex* wouldn't take the intended insult, no matter how playful, in silence, he replied, "Is this because I'm short?"

"It's more because you have a resting murder face."

His stomach dropped. "Huh?"

Dan laughed. "You know, like resting bitch face?"

Aleksandr racked his brain but couldn't come up with anything. Growing up without any human contact, beyond his immediate family or the people who were their murder victims, had left Aleksandr with gaps in information. Little things like speech patterns and standard body language. It's why he had picked Mooresville, Alabama for his fake home. All he had to do was mention that the town had a population of under a hundred people and people normally let a lot of weirdness go, deciding that a small country boy was bound to be out of it.

Dan laughed louder and shook his head. "Resting bitch face. It's when someone looks like they're angry even when they aren't doing anything. It's just their face. You, my friend, have a resting murder face. You're a great guy, don't get me wrong, but you always look you want to stab someone."

"How great for me," Aleksandr mumbled.

"Well, it'll hopefully work to get room 3622 to back off. Just go and do that squinty thing with your eyes. Yeah, that thing."

"I'm not doing anything," Aleksandr protested.

Dan's smile turned smug. "Perfect."

Pulling back into the office, he slid the drive-thru window closed and ducked out of sight. Aleksandr released a long, slow sigh and finally read over the sheet. The wait-staff used a special shorthand, which gave him the perfect excuse to ask about any words he didn't know. This was a basic order, however. Something obviously thrown out there as an excuse to get one of the girls to his room. A bottle of champagne and some chocolate dipped strawberries.

All alcoholic drinks had to be accounted for, so he headed to the bar area and handed the sheet over to the night staff rather than try and read out the brand name. While they worked, Aleksandr strummed his hands on the countertop, noticing the bottle opener on the other side of the counter. It was the Swiss army style, with more options than just the corkscrew. Earlier, he had rejected the idea of taking a knife with him. *Too much risk*, he had decided. If the security team found him with it, they wouldn't buy the excuse that he had forgotten it in the small pockets of his vest. *One solid strike and the sharp edge could lodge in my stomach*. But a corkscrew. That would be both useful and plausible for him to have. Casting a quick look around to make sure he didn't have anyone's attention, he jumped up slightly, laying over the countertop as he snatched up the weapon. There was just enough time to shove it into his pocket before the bartender returned.

Neither one of them was big on idle conversation, and so he was able to get away rather quickly. Soon enough, Aleksandr was weaving his way around the hidden staff corridors. It was a maze. With long stretches of barren hallways leaving a few areas marked with doors. There was a distinct absence of windows, signs, or markings that could give a hint of what was on the other side. Time, practice, and dedication had allowed him to get a decent handle on the layout. He walked quickly and made it through the hallways at a rapid pace. Every so often, he checked his phone. The twins sent him texts, mostly bickering about the other one or whatever movie they were watching. It always made him smile.

Soon enough, he was opening the doorway and stepping out onto the 36th floor. Aleksandr paused midstride to look around. Standing at the center of a T-intersection, he was surrounded by three long, empty hallways. Silence. No murmur of TVs. No conversations drifting through the walls. No one came out or was working their way back to the room. Aleksandr knew that it wasn't entirely a strange situation, but he was already on edge and he wasn't quite able to push the sensation aside. He checked the three directions again and found them still empty. A part of him took comfort in that. Even if there were someone waiting around the corner, there would be plenty of time for him to notice them before they were close enough to do anything. However, knowing that anyone could be hiding behind the doors, waiting for him to pass, kept him from relaxing.

Patting his pocket to reassure himself that the corkscrew was still there, he set off to the right. *A full bottle of champagne and a metal tray can do some damage too,* he reminded himself. *Alert, not afraid.* The carpet smothered his footsteps as he moved, reducing them to a whispered shuffle. Overhead lights blazed, chasing off shadows, the straight lines leaving only the rooms to hide in. Still, he couldn't shake the feeling that there was someone there. His skin prickled with the sensation of being watched. He kept to the center of the corridor.

A sharp series of beeps made him jump. He grabbed his phone, both to silence the sound and to check the next text. The phone buzzed in his palm, clearing his mind enough to realize that it was an incoming call. Evelyn.

He didn't have to say anything. She started talking the moment he answered the call, fast enough that he missed a few words in the short amount of time it took to get the phone to his ear. He caught on soon enough.

"You didn't see their face?" he asked, balancing the tray with one hand and clutching his mobile phone with the other.

"Seriously?" The small speaker struggled to keep up with her increasingly rapid pace. "Remember how I know what your brother looks like? If I had positively identified him, don't you think I would have lead with that? I'm not trying to annoy you. This isn't a dramatic reveal. So, no, I didn't see his damn face, *Aleksandr.*"

He paused at the chastising tone, not exactly sure how to respond to it. Not that he needed to. It seemed that, when excited, she lost all need to breathe.

"You need to calm down," he said, not sure that she'd even heard him.

She did. Because she switched to Spanish. He'd only ever heard her do it once before and that was when she was cussing out his parents, trying to prod them into killing her quick.

"I don't know Spanish." He had to remind her a few times before she heard him.

The abrupt silence made his stomach drop. Paranoia twitched along the edges of his mind and he looked around himself once again. The hall was still silent. Abandoned.

"Right," she said, her voice tense but in unmistakable English. "I've switched rooms. I'm going to dump my bag and check in with my dad."

"Are you sure?"

"My dad's going to want to see the room. If he doesn't, he's going to get worried and call the cops. We can't have them interfering yet or your siblings will scatter, and we'll lose our chance. I'm not going to be dumb about it. That's one of the reasons I'm calling. Who do you trust on the security team? I'm going to ask for an escort up. I figured that Vera and Vlas should be deterred by that, yeah?"

"Yeah, that should work." Aleksandr shifted through his thoughts, trying to remember who of the more physically imposing boys were on shift tonight. He gave her a few names to pick from and she repeated them back.

"What do you want me to do with the twins?" she asked.

Aleksandr's brow furrowed. "You didn't call them first?"

"No," she said slowly. "They're kids and I'm not an idiot."

"And they're not delicate," he countered. "But they are on their own."

"Right. Well, it still seems like we should have a plan before we bring them in on it," she said, somewhat defensively.

"There's nowhere safer for them than at ..." his words died off as a door halfway down the corridor popped open.

Without a single sound to compete against it, Aleksandr could distinctly hear the soft whisper of the door sliding against the carpet. His fingers tightened around his phone and his muscles twitched, caught between fight and flight. Evelyn didn't utter a word. There was only silence. Then, soft and sharp, there was the squeak of rubber. Like someone dragging their fingers against a balloon. He took a step backwards, knees trembling slightly as fear rattled his bones. Air pulled out of the room until he couldn't draw a proper breath.

His parents had loved to celebrate things, but even this they couldn't leave untwisted. Every holiday and milestone had been marked with blood and agony. Decorations had become a warning sign. An omen. A threat. The high-pitched squeal of rubber on skin cut through the silence. Louder. Closer. He stepped back, heart rattling around his chest as if it were hollow. Adrenaline flooded his veins as movement entered his vision. Bumping against the ceiling, a single, clear balloon floated out of the room. As if by an invisible hand, it traveled out into the middle of the corridor, dripping blood onto the carpet. Each drop landed with a slight thud that made him flinch.

"The Furies are here," he whispered into the phone.

Her response was instant. "Where are you?"

"Get the twins out of here," he corrected as he backed up, keeping his pace slow and steady, not wanted to provoke the unseen creature.

"I'm on it."

There was a burst of movement on the other end of the phone line, but Aleksandr barely noticed it. His attention was on the balloon. It spun in place, never rising or falling, completely unaffected by the push of the air conditioner. Crimson liquid trailed down the single, silver thread attached to the knot. It remained perfectly straight. *Something's holding it in place,* a voice in his head whispered.

"Alek?"

"They'll know the rendezvous place," he assured, eyes still locked on the single decoration. Childhood fears raged within him as he took a final step back and reentered the intersection. "I'm going to run for my life now."

"Good luck with the cardio," she replied before swearing in Spanish. "Sorry, it's just the 'feeding off fear' thing. I thought a joke–"

"No, I got it," Aleksandr said.

Every muscle in his body tensed as anxiety built inside of him. He didn't want to hang up. Right now, he was on the edge of a storm. It was coming for him. It would have him soon but right now, in this moment, he had some illusion of safety. That it might pass by with only a bitter rain. He knew the Fury was toying with him. Waiting with an anticipation of its own for what was to come. The moment he hung up, the game would start.

"Good luck," she whispered.

"You too."

In one motion, he dropped the tray, grabbing the neck of the champagne bottle as it fell, hung up the phone, and bolted to the side. He was already a few rooms down before the tray clattered against the ground. One sharp crack and then the silence returned. Nothing but his thudding feet and the slosh of the champagne as he pumped his arms. He might not be able to hear it, but he felt it. The air thickened and chilled and there was an unmistakable sensation that there was *something* behind him. Following. Closing in no matter how fast he pushed himself. The hair on the back of his neck rose, and slowing down to wait for the elevator was no longer an option.

Racing past them, he sprinted down the long stretch of empty corridor and almost lost his footing as he rounded a corner. A bit further and the sound of a party pushed onto the edges of his hearing. A ballroom was situated on the far side of the hotel. It had been booked out by a group wanting to give their daughter an extravagant 21st birthday. By the sounds of it, the party was in full swing. The promise of a crowd spurred him on. The air was heavy. Breathing was impossible, and his lungs burned like embers within his chest. He didn't dare look behind him. Didn't want to see what was there.

The double doors came into view, sound pulsing and light flicking through the cracks. Aleksandr didn't slow down to get through. Just slammed his shoulder into the jamb and stumbled slightly as the doors cracked open. Instantly, his senses were bombarded. Flashing lights blinding him as the scent of alcohol and sweat filled his nose. The air-conditioner wasn't able to compete against the sheer number of bodies, and sticky humidity that filled the enclosed space. In a flash, he was back in the desert, the ghost town, surrounded by burning sand and rotting corpses. He blinked rapidly, pushing the memories away as he shoved his way into the writhing crowd.

It was impossible to move without bumping into someone. They had to be well beyond fire safety numbers. Every move resulted in a spilt drink, but no one seemed bothered by it, having grown used to the bodies crushing them. Aleksandr set his focus onto the back wall. To the hidden entrance for the staff hallways. *Get out!* The words screamed in his head as he moved, followed closely by another warning. *Keep them distracted until the twins are out!*

Half way across the room, he blinked, and the crush of flesh pressing against him was gone. Thrown off balance by the sudden open space, Aleksandr staggered a few feet, desperately searching everywhere. Confetti fell all around him, gathering on his shoulders and sticking to his hair. They flipped past the flashing lights, creating a tapestry of color and shadows. He squinted through it. The room was empty. Not a single piece of tinsel fell upon another body. There was only him left.

The music continued to pulse, the beat pounding against his sternum like a physical blow. The strike radiated throughout his body. Rattled in his joints. The vibration slowed his steps, reducing his run into a wobbling walk. He spun around trying to see every inch of the huge ballroom at once. The decorations continued to fall, the clutter punctuated by toppling balloons that momentarily blocked out large chunks of his sight. The inflated rubber bounced against his feet as he walked, warping his staggering steps all the more. In the world of vibrant, gleaming color, the white figure stood out like an exposed bone.

Aleksandr locked his gaze onto the far corner of the room, where the shape crouched behind the rainbow rain. It was impossible to see it all at once through the haze. Realization came to him in fractured pieces. It was human in shape. But huge. Larger than a bull. Its face was long and distorted, its mouth gaping open in a silent scream. On all fours, it twisted around to look at him. Aleksandr couldn't see its face in full, but he felt the weight of its gaze. Knew it was staring at him. Felt its rage. Its disgust and fury.

It tilted its head and crawled towards him, moving faster than its limbs should allow, a blur of color amongst the falling confetti. Aleksandr turned and sprinted for the door. Already, the monster was right behind him. He could feel it closing in. The weight of its presence pressing against his back. Its hatred for him filling the air with an eclectic charge. *It's not real. It's not real!* he repeated in his head. *It's only strong if you fear it.*

That knowledge did little to calm the terror rampaging through his body. Hot, rancid air pressed against his back of his neck. Balloons and hunks of plastic whirled around his feet, stirred into a flurry by the huge beast right behind him. Aleksandr threw himself at the double doors, still clinging to the promise in his head that he wasn't afraid. He had braced for the first blow of the doors, but hitting the concrete floor beyond knocked the wind out of him. Curling into a protective ball, he endured the flurry of thuds that battered him. *Don't be afraid!*

Noise snapped him back into reality. A thousand voices joined the bass of the song; conversations and laughter and a name being repeated with increasing demand. Aleksandr flung his eyes open, already scrambling further away from the door as he tried to catch sight of the ivory monstrosity. There was just enough time to glimpse angry, confused faces before the double doors swung shut and cut off his view of the ballroom. They muffled the sound somewhat. Enough that he could hear his panted breaths and the same voice repeating that name.

"Alex!"

He whipped around to find Alison crouched beside him, her hand lifting towards his shoulder.

"Don't touch me," he hissed out.

Whether it was his tone or the demand, he didn't know, but she flinched back as if he had struck her.

"What is wrong with you?" she demanded.

Aleksandr ignored the question as he looked around. There were a few other people in the hallway. Aside from the onlookers, there were a few staff members that were picking him up off the floor, muttering a lot but trying not to swear as they tended to oblivious guests. As the adrenaline faded, he began to feel the pain. Different points that littered his body but mostly centered around his shoulders. It occurred to him then that he had never been alone in the ballroom. And his escape had forced him to barrel through a sizable crowd.

"Alex."

He didn't know how long Alison had been repeating his name but she seemed to be relieved when he finally looked over to her.

"Are you alright?"

"No," he said softly before he got to his feet, mumbled an apology, and started running again.

Chapter 9

"You need to get out now!"

Evelyn gripped her mobile phone, pressing it hard against her ear as she raced through the gambling area. It hadn't been long since she was here, but the crowd had thickened considerably. People in various states of intoxication clogged the pathways, slowing her pace, forcing her to duck and weave around their bodies before she could surge forward again.

"Meet us at the staff entrance," was the only reply she got before the line went dead.

Evelyn had no idea which one of the twins had answered. She reasoned that it didn't matter. Telling one was as good as telling both. Shoving her mobile back into her bra, she ducked deeper into the sea of poker machines, seeking out the path of least resistance. Her bag thumped against her back. It only contained a few hard items, yet all of them had positioned themselves to dig into her spine.

Finally, the area cleared and she burst out onto the polished floor of the lobby. Her shortcut had put her off course, taking her back to the entrance. Skidding to a stop made the contents of her bag shift and threw her off balance. Instead of falling, she dropped willingly and braced her hands on the cold tiled floor. One jump and she had herself organized into a sprinter's stance. Her legs wobbled, desperate for a break. Vaguely, she was aware that she had drawn some attention. It didn't matter. She ignored them all as she darted off to the front desk.

Fewer people milled aimlessly around there. With everyone eager to check in, the general public swiftly joined the lines and got out of her way. She picked up a decent pace as she yanked the strap of her duffle bag off her shoulders. Careful not to hit any of the startled staff, she tossed it over the partition, between the workers and the wall behind them.

"Sorry, in a rush! Reservation under Figueroa! Thanks!"

She was gone before they could ask any questions, resigned to the fact that the bag probably wouldn't be there when she returned. If she returned. After the incident at the Flamingo, there was going to be some paranoia over a random bag being hurled towards them as the owner fled. Some, she reasoned, were going to call the cops. A new time limit pressed down against her shoulders like a weight. *Get the kids out before they get organized.*

Her lungs burned as she ran past the games area, heading straight for the hidden door. The kids came out just as she reached it. Once more, they looked far more prepared than Evelyn felt. Matching black sneakers, jeans, and tops. Only their backpacks would keep them from disappearing entirely into the night.

"Alek?" one asked the second Evelyn was in earshot. It was impossible to tell which one. The child snarled, for an instant looking remarkably like Petya. "I'm Nadya. Where's Alek?"

"He said you'd know where to meet him," she said through panted breaths.

"Okay." Nadya looked at her twin and nodded once.

They set off together.

"Let me take your backpacks," Evelyn said.

They scowled at her.

"We might need to run. I don't want you guys weighed down."

"And I don't want to get stabbed," Ivan said almost conversationally.

They quickened their pace as Evelyn studied them.

"I won't let that happen," she promised.

The twins shared a look before Ivan answered, "We appreciate that. But we're still going to keep the Kevlar inserts. You know, as a backup plan. No offence."

Evelyn pushed closer to keep them from getting separated by a passing family.

"Kevlar?" she asked.

They nodded.

"As in bulletproof?" she asked.

"And stab proof," Nadya added.

"Where would you even get those?"

"Internet," they replied in unison.

"Okay, whatever, let's just get–"

Her words clogged in her throat as goosebumps spread out across her skin and ice lined the pit of her stomach. It was the same sickly sensation she had felt in the elevator. Quickly, she scanned the crowd, easily spotting the only stationary figure. A man in a baseball cap. He no longer made any attempt to hide his face. Vlas stared at them, smiling when he noticed he had Evelyn's attention.

She blindly reached for the twins. "We need to go back."

"That's a dead end," Ivan protested before he caught sight of his brother.

He grabbed his sister's hand and tugged, forcing her faster, leaving Evelyn to hurry behind. The three of them were in front of the games area when they once again jerked to a stop. Vera stood before them in the center of the hall.

"They're herding us back down the hall," Nadya said, the first traces of fear seeping into her voice. "The chapel. No one would be there this time of night."

Evelyn pulled the kids closer, trying to position herself between them and the hunters. But even as they closed in, Vera and Vlas placed themselves with care. Keeping track of one put the other out of sight. They took advantage of the constant flow of people that passed between them. Edging in closer every time Evelyn's view was obstructed.

"There's an emergency exit at the back of the maze," Nadya said. "Red room. Take the ladder up to the catwalk."

"Try and keep up," Ivan said.

Small hands gripped her arms, yanked once, and they were gone. Evelyn spun, running before she was able to catch sight of the twins again. Small as they were, the other guests were willing to give them the right of way, allowing them to pull ahead. She lost them again as they passed through the towering threshold. But the entrance to the maze stood before her, huge and neon, and drawing a crowd.

A ticket taker stood to one side, with a velvet rope stopping anyone from cutting the line. With an amused smile, the man watched the twins slip under the rope.

"Just make sure Alex settles the bill later," he called after the children.

"Promise!" Nadya said.

Ivan ran backwards for a few paces, just long enough to point Evelyn out of the crowd. "She's our babysitter!"

The ticket taker waved Evelyn through with a jerk of his chin.

"Ya better hurry up," he teased. "They'll disappear in there."

Evelyn wondered how many times the twins had done this to leave everyone so accustomed to the action. She hurtled the low hanging rope, tossing back a 'thank you', and ignoring the angry protests of those waiting in line.

A heavy plastic sheet hung down across the entrance, the shredded strips drifting in the air-conditioning. Evelyn pushed through, unprepared for the violet light that assaulted her eyes. Florescent paint covered the pillars that stood at random intervals, glowing in the manufactured darkness. Strangers ran about in contained chaos, their gleeful laughter turning into shrieks as they set off a series of motion sensors. Smoke machines spewed a dense fog from the walls, pressurized air shot out in puffs, and robotic aliens dropped down from the ceiling.

Pushing up onto her toes, Evelyn searched for the twins. A glimpse of their backpacks had her running to her left. Pain exploded across her face as she collided with the mirror. A few people laughed around her, and someone spared her a sympathetic pat on her shoulder as they passed. Biting back curses and tasting blood, she smacked her hand against the polished glass. Having the chilled glass under her palm helped her to judge the angle it was set on. The little tricks that kept her from being able to see her reflection as she approached. The image rippled, and she looked over her shoulder, noticing the curtain that hid another passageway. Guests flooded through the gap in the fabric, making the material sway and allowing her glimpses of the complete darkness that lay beyond.

Fearing that she had completely lost track of the twins, she hurried to follow. The moment she forced her way through the curtains, she froze. She wasn't in the dark. The maze was gone, replaced by a brightly lit hallway. Her blood felt too hot for her veins as she recognized the space. Her old family home. The place she had lived before her father had joined the fire department. When they didn't have the money or health insurance needed to properly care for her mother. Back when it was a constant struggle to afford her mother's medication.

The home was just as she remembered it. Everything was larger than it should have been. Oversized. *It's not bigger*, a voice whispered in the back of her head. *I'm smaller*. All the proportions resembled a child's perspective. The thought hit her like a blow to the gut. She couldn't place her finger on it, or pinpoint the reason behind it, but something on the edges of her awareness whispered that she knew this day. And that she didn't want to remember it. Whatever moment the Furies were going to use against her was better left to the oblivion of early childhood.

She turned to flee back the way she had come, but the curtains were gone. Replaced with the narrow doorway of their rundown apartment. Her mother stood before her. Towered over her. She looked wrong. Her fingers were as long as an arm, each digit withered and bony, resembling her distorted neck. It was the expression that made Evelyn retreat a step. Dark eyes wide with fear. Smile forced and tight.

It's not real. It's not real, she told herself. *I'm in a maze. There are people around. This isn't real*. None of her assertions made any difference. Evelyn was a child again, shrinking under her mother's unblinking gaze.

"Come here, darling," her mother purred. "We have to be quick. They'll stop us if we're not quick."

Evelyn shook her head, her mind slipping. Her conviction of reality crumbling under the weight of her senses. The scent of rose moisturizer wafted around the woman before her. Mixed with the wet, musky smell that seemed to forever cling to the walls of the apartment. Somewhere in the distance, a pot was boiling over, the lid clattering against the base and the hotplate hissing as the water dripped onto it.

"Eve," her mother said, her face still locked in her twisted expression. The floorboards groaned as the woman took a step forward. "It won't hurt. Mommy's going to save you."

Dark shadows rose up from behind this macabre apparition of her mother. A thousand, spindly arms that ran along the wall, growing, thickening, and reaching for Evelyn. She ran. The corridor of the house was large. The world from a child's eyes. Her feet slapped hard against the floor as if she couldn't quite work her aching legs. No matter how fast she pushed herself, her mother's whispering voice was forever in her ear.

"Evelyn. Come to mommy. This is for your own good. I wouldn't let the monsters get you."

Memories swirled in her mind like fog. She couldn't recall exactly what had happened but she knew that she had done this before. Lived this exact moment in time. That she was playing out an event she had fought hard to forget. Hurling herself into her bedroom, she slammed the door shut, pressing the small button on the metal door handle to engage the lock.

Mother has the key. Even the voice in her head had returned to its childish origin. *Hide! Hide! Hide!* There wasn't anywhere to hide. The box bed sat flush against the floor and the windows were sealed by a half-dozen metal bars. Hands trembling and at the point of hyperventilation, Evelyn spotted the closet. A series of shelves created a ladder to the top, where a thin space stored all the winter blankets. It looked as tall as Everest to her. An impossible summit.

"Eve, you open this door right now! You're being very naughty!"

Spurred on by the rattle of the door handle, she hurried to the cupboard and scurried up. Her foot hit a music box and pushed it over the edge. It smashed against the floor, the metallic tune clicking to life.

Swan Lake, her dying adult mind recalled. *The box played Swan Lake.* She felt weak and small as she scurried up the makeshift ladder. Stretching until her joints throbbed, she managed to reach the top. The blankets scratched her palms as she tugged at them. She pushed and shoved, creating enough room for her to crawl inside, burrowing into the layers of soft material. They smothered the light, tainting it with a purple hue, trapping her humid breath against her face. She wiggled and squirmed until she was completely hidden. Until the back of the closet kept her from going any further.

Don't stop! Mom will get you! The thought made her ill. Wiggling and squirming on her stomach, Evelyn worked her way to the corner furthest from the shelves.

"Eve!" the scream was interrupted with the sound of the door crashing into the wall. "Mommy won't hurt you. Mothers don't do things like that!"

It's not real! She gripped tight to the words. Held onto them like a lifeline. A new memory emerged into her awareness, battering against the gnarled shreds of her mind. Her father's voice. The words that he had spoken in reprimand. With fondness. In approval. As a shared joke between them. *Words don't mean a thing if they aren't followed by action.*

"Eve!" the sheets moved against her as her mother tore at the blankets.

It's not real, Evelyn thought as she trembled, struggling to recall her father's words again.

"Come out! Listen to Mother!"

Words don't mean a thing if they aren't followed by action.

"It's not real!" The words ripped from her throat as she bolted upright and threw herself over the edge of the closet, lunging for the monster in a blind panic.

Darkness engulfed her. A small tinkle of laughter met her ears. Not a malicious sound, but one of happiness. Other voices quickly joined the first. Evelyn blinked, looking around to find herself curled up against a wall. One situated in a small dead end that splintered away from the main path of the maze. Slips of color and glowing bands of light passed by the mouth of the offshoot, but none of them stopped. Panting for breath, she realized that her scream, if it had truly passed her lips at all, had gone by unnoticed. The maze was filled with playful shrieks and dramatic cries, all the others followed with peals of laughter.

The air-conditioning ravaged the cold sweat that had soaked into Evelyn's dress, transforming it into a blanket of ice. Brutal shivers wracked her body. Each heaved breath almost split her in two. Her arms quaked as she pushed herself up onto her knees. The second her legs took her full weight, they buckled, and she slumped back against the wall. It was a struggle to get her feet flat on the floor. But it was worth it. Her knees felt like a barrier, protecting her from the people that raced past.

Get up, her mind screamed at her. *Find the twins. Move. Do something!* But her legs were numb and her head was swimming in a churning sea of half-hidden memories, surrounded by delighted screams and raucous laughter that didn't spare her. The tune of the music box remained. Little pings of metal playing out the melody on an endless loop. Evelyn had forgotten the events of that day. Too young at the time for her brain to hold onto the details. But the fear had remained. And remembering it now made a dozen little things snap into place.

The lingering dread she had always felt around her mother. The anxiety that no reassurance could tame. *It's not her fault*, she recalled her father saying. *Mommy's ill. She acts out. But she loves you and would never, ever hurt you.* Tears burned the back of her eyes as she tried to remember how the day had ended. But there was only static. The memory lost to time.

Had she hurt me? Had she tried to kill me? The questions whirled in her mind and she couldn't find an answer. She supposed it didn't matter. The damage was done. Over the years, with proper care and medication, her mother had vastly improved. She was in control. Pleasant, kind, and gentle. But Evelyn could never truly relax around her. She had thought it was because her mother was living proof of what Evelyn's future could be. Only time would tell if she had inherited the genes, the alterations in the brain, the genetic fault that lead to madness. It crushed something fragile inside her to know the truth. *I'm terrified of my mother.*

Evelyn drew in a deep breath and balled her fists, digging her nails into her palm. The small points of physical pain helped. It was a tether to reality. *The Furies are still here. Get out!* That was enough to get her moving. Bracing one hand on the wall, she pushed herself up into a crouch. The light shifted, dulling as a new shadow washed over her.

She jerked her head up to see the outline of a woman. Slender but sturdy, she filled the narrow entrance to the small dead end, leaving only a few feet left between them. The colorful rotating lights flashed over the strange woman in intervals, illuminating the different shades that were carefully woven into her hair. *Don't show fear. She's a coward. Don't let her get comfortable.*

"Oh, great," Evelyn huffed, immensely proud that her voice didn't crack. "You're here. Super."

Vera didn't have Aleksandr's skill at concealing her emotions. Confusion and annoyance had their turns on her features before she replied.

"You know who I am?"

"Yeah, yeah, hold on. Let me get up." Evelyn was grateful for the shadows. It helped to hide just how much she was looking around. "Is there any chance we could postpone this? I *really* need to get out of here. And not-for-nothing, but you should, too."

Vera's shock helped to ease Evelyn's nerves, allowing her to take more information in. The hunter was taller, and while fit, lacked Evelyn's muscle. *A runner's body,* Evelyn reasoned. *A tracker. Not a fighter.*

"You normally use rifles, right?"

"Crossbow," Vera smiled. "Takes longer to bleed out."

"Also lets you keep your distance," Evelyn replied, mimicking the woman's vicious grin.

Vera frowned. "I don't think you understand the situation you're in."

"Oh, no. I've got it. I'm in a heavily-trafficked location that's constantly monitored by night vision cameras and an extensive security team. Simple enough."

If the swiveling lights hadn't hit Vera at just the right moment, Evelyn would have missed the small jolt that ran through her body.

"Wait, did you not know that this place would be swarming with cameras? Seriously? Yeah, sure, why not? Let's just let children and drunken people run around in darkened rooms unattended. That's not a lawsuit waiting to happen."

The constant knowledge that the Furies were close made her muscles twitch. She wanted to run. Needed to move. Being forced to stay put a hint of manic laughter into her words.

"You dumbass," she continued. "When was the last time you came into a city? I mean, not just on the outskirts, preying off of desperate people? Class act, by the way. Not like those people don't have enough problems."

"Are you actually insane?" Vera gaped at her.

Shrugging one shoulder, Evelyn couldn't keep the crazed smile from her face. A demonic force was swirling around her and she was trapped making small talk with a serial killer sporting self-esteem issues.

"There's the looming possibility. Just this genetic thing, doesn't matter right now." Feeling Vera's unease, Evelyn pushed her minimal advantage. "What does matter is that we need to leave. Preferably in separate directions. Oh, come on,

Vera. It's not like you're going to do anything here. Too public, right? You're even running the risk of being overheard right now."

"Did Alek tell you that?" Confidence inched into her smirk. "The game is about quantity, not quality. I can slit your throat right here. Just like you did to our mother."

Evelyn couldn't keep down the bark of laughter. "Yeah, about that … that wasn't us."

"And who was it?"

"You stick around here, you're going to find out. Personally, I'm going to run."

"You're not going anywhere." The lights flashed against the dull slip Vera pulled from the sleeve of her jacket.

Evelyn couldn't tell if the knife was bone or plastic, but she could see it was sharp.

"If it's any comfort, your death will keep Radmiar from winning the game. Which is about as much as your life could offer."

"I'm leaving," Evelyn said with all the authority she could muster. "Get out of the way, or I'm going through you."

Vera hesitated but didn't retreat. She remained in her position, blocking the only exit. Fear swirled like a live animal in the bottom of Evelyn's stomach. Coiled around her spine and squeezed until she wanted to sob. But in a moment of clarity, she realized that her terror had nothing to do with the woman in front of her. The Huntress was a threat. Not the apex predator.

"Look, I'm getting the hell out of here. And if you had any shred of self-preservation, you'd start running too!"

Vera paused. "Do you think I'll fall for that?"

"Did you stop to learn anything about the state they found your parents in? Or the ghost town for that matter?" she countered. "We didn't move all those corpses about or destroy the shed. Something else was there. And, no offence, but you don't seem all that scary in comparison."

"I can change that." She twisted the knife in her hand.

"It's good to have goals." Evelyn shrugged. She ended the dismissive gesture with a sudden, sharp front kick. Unprepared, Vera didn't have time to block the attack. Evelyn's heel snapped up against the hunter's nose with a firm crack. Staggering back a few steps, Vera gripped her nose, a furious roar ripping from her throat. It wasn't a large opening, but it was all Evelyn needed. She threw herself against the taller woman, knocking her further back, increasing the gap wide enough to slip through.

Vera snarled, one hand snapping out to latch onto Evelyn's hair. She missed the short strands, her nails digging deep into the bare skin of Evelyn's neck instead. Blood oozed out of the gouged flesh, spilling down her skin and soaking into the back of her dress. Evelyn didn't stop running. She pushed through the crowd, continually searching for a glimpse of the twins as she tried to disappear. A few of the people she bumped into yelled after her, halfhearted protests that did little more than mark her progress. She swore under her breath as she heard the second wave of annoyance. Vera was pursuing her, and thanks to the crowd, she knew precisely where to go.

The air was stale with the manufactured fog. Strobe lights messed with her depth perception. Illusions and spring traps attacked from all sides. Luminescent paint and glow sticks blurred the lines between people and the walls. The only similarity each room had was that they all hosted a series of hidden passageways. There was no point of reference. Nothing that could help her orientate herself. Within a heartbeat, Evelyn was lost.

"Eve."

A new spike of fear rocked Evelyn to the core. Her mother's voice whispered in her ear again.

"Come to mother."

She whipped around, searching the swirling, cackling masses as she moved. A glimpse of a swollen, perfectly arranged hairstyle had her running again. She squeezed through one of the smaller openings in the wall, trying to ignore the array of alien figures that lurched out at her when she ventured too near. A plastic tube was set into the wall of the next room. Tiny enough that anyone passing through would have to crawl on their stomachs. Smaller than her pursuer, Evelyn pressed her advantage, scurrying through the tight passage at a rapid pace.

The plastic cylinder glowed as it snaked back and forth. The rainbow flowed endlessly, switching from one to the next as she moved. Long before she saw the change, she felt it. The plastic under her hands became brittle and fine, cracking against her skin, flaking off with every shift she made. Steadily, the colors darkened. A final turn and the end of the tube came into sight. A sole point of light set far off in the distance. With an electrical hiss, the walls of the container turned black. That's when she felt it.

Like fingers of ice sliding down her spine. The sensation played upon her most primal instincts, the ones that naturally knew when a predator was nearby. Something was in the tube with her. Behind her. Coming closer. The knowledge settled into her mind as if it had always been there. The creature she couldn't see was ancient. Ferocious. And hunting her down.

Evelyn pushed herself faster, dragging her body through the oppressive darkness. The air steadily thickened. Becoming stale and humid. Coating her throat as she breathed. Broken patches of the tube tore into her dress like claws, searching for the vulnerable skin of her stomach as if it was rusted metal.

"Eve," her mother's voice whispered from just behind her ear.

It's not real, she clung to the words. *Don't give it your fear. Don't feed it.* The tunnel under her rippled and hardened, taking on the texture of a cheese grater. It sliced at her palms and knees. Digging deeper. Driving into her flesh with every push forward. Evelyn refused to slow as blood slicked her skin. The roof closed in. The walls narrowed. Every inch towards the pinpoint of light took a little more of her flesh. She kept moving.

"Eve! Listen to mother!"

Enduring the pain, she clenched her jaw, reaching for something within her that wasn't polluted by terror. She found rage. *How dare it bring my mother into this?* She hurled the thought to the forefront of her mind. *How dare it attack me!* She conjured the frenzied fury she had felt only a few hours ago. The blind, pure, volatile hatred that Petya and Olga had introduced her to.

The unseen creature was at her heels, calling to her over and over, voice alternating between monstrous impersonations of her mother and father. Calling her back. Promising not to hurt her. Evelyn squeezed her eyes shut and focused on the white-hot lead that had filled her chest and scorched her bones. *I didn't do anything wrong! How dare they!*

One last lurch forward and the plastic gave way. She dropped, smacking hard against the padded floor as bright crimson light assaulted her eyes. Heaving short, heavy breaths, she rolled onto her back and grabbed at her stomach. The damage was gone but the agony lingered. The physical sensation of being flayed alive. A phantom pain that returned with every twist of muscle. Her hands trembled. She could still feel the hardened plastic scraping against her bones and her blood rushing free.

Red room, she acknowledged an instant before a noise drew her attention. Something was clambering towards, rattling the tunnel with its rapid pace. Lurching to her feet, Evelyn pulled her phone from her bra. Before she could unlock it, a text alert met her blurring vision.

Got out. Bellagio dancing fountain. Good Luck.

Her rush of relief was short lived. The tube was rattling in place now. A quick glance didn't reveal the ladder the twins had spoken of. Just a square crimson room with padded walls. Every step was agonizing. Each twitch of muscle and skin revived the illusions of pain the Furies had forced her through. Still, she lapped the room, smacking her hand against the padded walls, searching for a hidden exit. The crimson material rippled at her touch as if they were liquid. A patch of the wall pushed in deeper than the others before it. Clawing at the material, she found a gap deep enough to sink her fingers into. With one hard tug, she peeled a section of the padding free.

Handrails were bolted into the brick wall at regular intervals, the lowest starting a few inches beyond her reach. *The twins would have stood on each other's shoulders to reach it*, she reasoned. But there wasn't anything that could provide her with a boost. Evelyn was left to back up a few paces and rush the wall. She planted one foot against the bricks and used it to push up. The metal bar banged across her fingertips before slipping her grip. Muscle memory had her coiling herself up, rolling back over her shoulders and ending in a crouch.

"Eve." Her mother's sing-song voice echoed from the tunnel.

The ladder's real, she told herself. *Whatever else, the ladder's real. Don't mess up again.* Her body longed to charge blindly at the wall. The instinct to flee pushing at her insides. She battled against it. Forced herself to hold still, take a deep breath. Focus. She ran for the wall again, stopped against the stone, pushed herself up. The rail was torture against her sensitive palms, but she locked her fingers around it. The extra pull-ups her coach forced her to do in preparation for the championship paid off now. Pulling herself up was easy, her muscles sore but reliable.

For the first few bars, she had to rely on her arms alone. Her pace picked up once her feet reached the railings, pausing only to kick the padding back into place. The red fabric oozed around her boot. She ignored it. Focused instead on the next rail. Then the next. Simple tasks. Swift progression.

She only looked down when she heard a thunderous clatter. Vera emerged from the tunnel. The floor swallowed her instantly, sloshing back and forth like a pool of liquid. Clinging to the ladder, Evelyn realized that the walls were melting, transforming into a dark sludge that flowed down to cover the floor. Vera broke back through the surface with a harrowing scream. She staggered to her feet, eyes full of rage and knife high.

Evelyn saw the exact moment when the hunter realized that this wasn't another one of the maze's quirks. The fight left her, replaced by confusion as she cupped a hand into the pool that lapped at her waist. Even from her perch on the wall, Evelyn could smell the rot. Instantly recognizing it as the stench of decay.

With a disgusted grunt, Vera wiped her hand over her face, trying to remove the unknown substance. It was at this moment that she spotted Evelyn. Their eyes met. It was strange to see fear starting to affect such a woman, and Evelyn found that she couldn't look away.

The festering liquid swirled as the sharp tip of a shark fin broke through the sludge. It streaked from one side of the room to the other before sinking again. Vera screamed and leaped back. A fine tremble took hold of her body as the fin flashed again. Frozen in fear, Vera's eyes rolled in her skull, trying to see everything at once.

The aquarium, Evelyn recalled. *The water was for Aleksandr. Was the shark a warning for the siblings, a taunt that Vera was on her way, or had it been for her?* Aleksandr had been careful. They had checked the area together. *Security cameras, maybe? That could have been how they found me in the elevators. Had they been there?* Thoughts rushed through her head, each coming at once, passing in an instant. The picture they had sent her of a plane ticket hadn't had a time. She had just believed that they had followed. *They could have sat right behind me the entire flight. I wouldn't have known.*

Again, the shark emerged. Closer to Vera. Lingering longer. The hunter's horrified scream rattled the walls and snapped Evelyn out of her daze. She clambered up the ladder, not daring to look back down. Not as the liquid thrashed and crashed. As Vera released blood-chilling shrieks, Evelyn hurled herself up onto the catwalk, and the noise abruptly stopped. Without hesitation, Evelyn ran to the fire exit, leaving the hunter behind.

Chapter 10

The evening crowd clogged up the staircase, slowing Aleksandr's process to one step every few minutes. Gnashing his teeth, he gripped the railing and hurled himself over the ledge. It was a short drop, but the impact was like electricity sparking in his joints. His knees buckled, and he braced his hands on the concrete sidewalk. But he kept going, sprinting the last distance to the edge of the dancing fountains. The Bellagio casino rose up on his right. The curved, simplistic structure lit with golden and purple light, the reflection dancing across the large, shallow lake that sat at the bottom of the building.

The water stretched out to the sidewalk, enclosed by a decorated viewing area. Already, pedestrians were slowing and clogging the walkways, each one waiting for the next performance. The dancing fountains of Bellagio were a historic crowd pleaser and never failed to draw attention. Aleksandr worked his way along the edge, craning his neck and desperately checking the gaps between bodies. Every passing second crushed him.

A monotone horn blared through hidden speakers. The Bellagio went dark and a series of small water jets broke through the water's surface. The first strings of classical music began to play and the jets shot up thin, towering pillars of water. Stark, white light illuminated the streams as they began to writhe in time with the melody. Everyone stilled, entranced. Aleksandr intended to make the most of it.

Leaping up onto a public bench, he combed the now still bodies. Desperate for even a glimpse of the twins. Two tight spins produced nothing.

"Nadya! Ivan!"

His outburst drew a few harsh looks. One person went so far as to shush him. It didn't stop him from calling out again. Finally, he noticed a shift in the horde and two small figures dashed towards him. Relief broke through him. Every muscle in his body went slack, dropping him from the bench. He landed hard on his knees but didn't feel the pain. Couldn't even feel his arms as he opened them wide and welcomed the twins. They threw their tiny frames against his chest with enough force to push him back. Instead of bracing himself, he clutched onto them, barely remembering not to crush them in his need to have them close. Small fingers clenched his uniform to its tearing point, their thin chests heaving hard as they gasped for air. He kissed their hair in turn and squeezed them tighter.

"Are you okay? Are you hurt?"

Nadya whimpered. A broken sound that escaped her chest as when she would wake up from a nightmare. Or when she would be left alone with Olga and Petya. Ivan kept his silence and trembled.

"I'm here," Aleksandr said, struggling to even out his voice. "I've got you. I'm right here. Are you bleeding? Is anything broken?"

Both of them pushed their faces harder against his shoulders. Eventually, with a little more encouragement, they shook their heads. Aleksandr's eyes closed as he released a deep sigh.

"Where's Evelyn?"

"We left her," Ivan almost sobbed.

"She fell behind," Nadya added, trying and failing to sound emotionless.

"You did the right thing." He pulled back enough to meet their eyes. "Look at me. You did the right thing."

They begrudgingly nodded.

"We saw Vera and Vlas," Nadya said softly. "They chased us. We didn't see where they went."

Aleksandr heard what she was trying to say. *They have her.*

"We shouldn't have left her," Ivan mumbled.

"Better her than you," Aleksandr corrected instantly.

"They're going to find us again," Nadya said.

"Not Vera."

They all tensed and turned to the panting voice, Aleksandr resenting the fact that he hadn't even noticed her approach. Sweat dripped from Evelyn's brow. Deep, heaved breaths rocked her body as she laced her fingers behind her head. After a few failed attempts, she managed to push a word out.

"Dead." She didn't have the energy left to wince and just flicked a hand out towards them. "Sorry. No. Tact."

"You're sure?" Aleksandr asked as he unzipped Ivan's backpack, retrieved a bottle of water, and passed it to her.

She took it with an ecstatic smile. A few hard gulps and she gave up on a verbal answer, settling on a nod instead.

"You killed her?"

The music continued to play. That, the delighted cheers of the audience, and the random throb of the jets efficiently covered their conversation from prying ears.

"Furies," Evelyn choked.

"Did you see her body?" Ivan asked.

Evelyn shook her head and finished off the last of the water.

"Then we can't be sure," Nadya said. "What if she escaped?"

A half-deranged giggle spilt from Evelyn's lips. A hard task since she was still heaving her breaths. "Big ... shark."

"That would do it," Ivan nodded.

Nadya whimpered again. "Radmiar isn't going to like this. Did you see him in the maze?"

"Nah," Evelyn said.

Aleksandr swallowed thickly and forced a smile before he gathered the twins, turning them around to face him. Placing a hand on each of their shoulders, he kept his voice light.

"One down. We should celebrate. Do something to keep the Furies from getting any stronger. So, your choice. Pick something fun. And quick."

Aleksandr watched as the fear seeped from their little faces. He knew they still felt it. It would linger in their bones just as it did his. But they were skilled at hiding their emotions. A fact that Aleksandr found a source of both pride and torment. At last, the kids looked to each other, nodded once, and the decision was made.

"We want chocolate," they said in unison.

The answer pleased him more than it should have. "Then we're getting chocolate. How about we go to that Bellagio chocolate fountain?"

"There's a *fountain* of *chocolate*?" Evelyn said, at last having caught her breath. "And you waited until *now* to tell me?"

Her exaggerated outrage provoked a little giggle from the twins. Working that advantage, she huffed and rolled her eyes, putting on a bit of a performance. For one brief moment, they were just kids. The world felt still.

"Let's get moving before they close," Aleksandr said around a lump that was forming in his throat.

Evelyn subtly closed ranks as they started herding the kids, angling her body to shield them from the crowd. When he was sure that the kids wouldn't see, he caught her eyes and mouthed 'thank you'. She shrugged one shoulder. As if they were old friends. Like these actions weren't deserving of gratitude. Aleksandr didn't know what to make of it. There had never been anyone willing to help him protect the twins, and he knew he couldn't afford to rely on it. Their chance of survival shriveled as he did.

They made their way around the edge of the lake, shifting in and out of the lampposts' glow, unnoticed by the captivated crowd. Rounding the edge, they started up the incline towards the Bellagio. They were halfway to their goal when a familiar face emerged from the masses. Vlas stood before them, chest heaving and arms trembling with rage. That, Aleksandr had expected. The tears that streaked down from his red-rimmed eyes threw him off, though.

"How do they keep doing that?" Evelyn muttered as she tugged Nadya behind her.

Aleksandr mirrored the action with Ivan as Vlas stalked closer. His body twitched with barely contained rage.

"I want her," Vlas hissed, one trembling hand shooting out to jab towards Evelyn. "Hand her over, and the rest of you can leave."

"That's not how the game goes," Aleksandr said.

"Screw the game!" he roared, his voice cracking around each word.

A few people looked over. Most ignored them soon enough, writing the situation off as a drunken dispute that didn't concern them. It allowed Vlas to stalk closer. When there was only a foot left separating them, he stopped in front of Aleksandr and hissed.

"She killed Vera." Vlas allowed one sob to leave him before he straightened his spine and clenched his jaw. "Hand her over, Alek. None of you mean a damn thing to me. Let Radmiar take you. I don't care. But that thing is going to die screaming."

"For what it's worth, I didn't do it," Evelyn cut in.

"Liar!" Fixing his eyes on her with a startling intensity, he continued, "You were the only one in the room with her."

"No, I wasn't."

"Vlas," Aleksandr cut in, hoping to break his attention. "It wasn't her."

"Liar!"

Out of the corner of his eyes, Aleksandr noticed that they had drawn a little attention. Once again, however, there was barely more than a few annoyed glares at the interruption.

"It was the Furies," Ivan said, barely poking his head out from behind Aleksandr's legs.

"What the hell is a Fury?"

"It's what's coming for you," Evelyn said. "All of us, actually. So, Alek, get the kids out of here."

Vlas smiled. Wolfish and dripping with bloodlust. Just like his sister, he wasn't ready for Evelyn to return the gesture with just as much venom.

"I'd love to have a private moment with you, Vlas."

Vlas flicked his eyes towards Aleksandr. "Is she serious?"

"She's a champion kick-boxer that knows you're kind of useless without a long distance weapon in your hand," Aleksandr said. "So yeah, she's serious."

"Alek," Nadya said, her voice small and her hand tugging sharply at his shirt. "Alek."

Unwilling to take his eyes off of Vlas, Aleksandr tipped his head to the side, just enough for his sister to know that he was listening. Instead of talking, she tugged harder at his shirt until the seams began to rip.

"What is it?"

"The lake." She whined the words, her fear drawing everyone's attention to the water.

The spotlights remained trained on the dancing pillars of water. Their glow left the majority of the lake to the shadows, leaving the water dark and inky. It took him a moment to spot what his sister was talking about. The ripples weren't as they should be. There was no uniform fold to the water. As he watched, the distortions deepened and took shape. It was no longer an ebony pool. It was a sheet of onyx silk draped over the mouth of hell. Thousands of bodies writhed before them. Tormented screams and agonized groans rose to cover the music that still pumped through the speakers. A feral hiss cracked over the sound and Aleksandr leapt back, trying to push the twins behind him. Geysers of steam shot up to the night sky, scorching his skin despite the distance between them.

"Aleksandr," Ivan said meekly.

"I see it too," he assured.

The next bellow of steam was a lot closer and they cringed away again. Aleksandr would have retreated onto the side road if a parked car hadn't stopped him. When the steam evaporated, Aleksandr instantly noticed the new object that was bobbing in the middle of the lake. Despite it lingering between two of the spotlights, it was almost completely shrouded in shadows. Still, it was undeniably a human head. All if its features were gone. Except for its eyes. They stood out against the darkness, glowing discs of marble. It was staring at them. Unblinking. The gaze it made robbed him of his breath and turned his blood cold.

"How are you doing this?" Vlas could barely form the words around the tremor in his voice.

"We're not," Nadya said. "That's a Fury."

Despite the fear in her eyes, Evelyn couldn't seem to suppress her smirk as she looked Vlas over. "This is your first time on this side of things, huh? Not so great being the prey, is it?"

Aleksandr didn't dare take his eyes off of the floating head. Even still, it moved progressively closer, traveling a few feet each time he blinked. "Vlas." Aleksandr didn't know why the words came out of his mouth, but he didn't try to stop them. "Run."

"I'm not–" His voice choked off in a ghastly grunt. Aleksandr looked over just in time to see the true horror distorting his brother's features. "Where'd it go?"

Aleksandr whipped back around. His gaze couldn't have strayed for more than a few seconds, but it was enough for the area to now be covered with a thick layer of steam. The swirling white made the dark head stand out like a stain upon the earth. Only the tip of it was visible over the edge of the railing. It rose steadily, slowly, growing from the abyss until its clouded eyes peeked up over the stone.

"Run!" Evelyn snapped, no longer caring if they drew any attention.

Ivan latched onto Aleksandr's arm with a vice grip, making it easy for him to hurl the small boy up. Almost instantly, Aleksandr had Ivan on one hip and was reaching for Nadya. Evelyn had already claimed her.

"I've got her," Evelyn said, already snatching up Nadya and bolting ahead. "Come on!"

Vlas made no move to stop them as they shoved past him. Not that Aleksandr had expected him to. Without Vera, his audience and driving force, the hunter was lost. The creature from the abyss climbing over the railing clarified the matter, though. Vlas spun on his heel, bumping against Aleksandr's back as he fought to keep close.

For the moment, all thoughts of revenge were put aside to embrace the safety of the herd. Vlas wasn't weighed down with a child, but he didn't pull ahead, instead inserting himself between Aleksandr and Evelyn and stubbornly staying there as they sprinted up the remaining bit of pathway to the Bellagio main entrance.

Even though Ivan was tiny for his age, his grip rivalled a boa constrictor. Aleksandr could barely breathe as Ivan's arms squeezed his neck. The small boy's legs threatened to crack Aleksandr's ribs each time they were slightly jostled. Despite this, Aleksandr still clung tightly to his brother, terrified that the child would slip from his grip. They dodged around the cars pulling up into the valet docks. For a moment, he lost sight of Evelyn and Nadya as they rounded the back of a Hummer. He went around the front, with Vlas trying to squeeze between him and the metal of the car.

A black object instantly drew their attention as they were about to leap up onto the sidewalk. Only a few inches separated the wheel from the gutter. The brilliant lights of the entrance illuminated the space. But the ebony head was still there, somehow completely inside the cracks, frosted eyes shining like silver. With a startled cry, Vlas lurched to the side, trying to cut in front of Aleksandr and get some distance. There wasn't enough space. The two collided and they both slammed into the concrete with a bone-rattling thud. Aleksandr twisted, taking as much of the impact as he could. Pain exploded through his knee and hip, radiating out along his nerves. But he kept Ivan off the ground. Blinking back tears, he saw that Ivan hadn't fared much better.

"Go," Aleksandr said as he shoved Ivan out of his arms. "Eve!"

Evelyn was already at the glass doors of the entrance. She almost ran into them as she skidded to a stop. One glance and she knew what he was asking. Holding out one hand, she waited for Ivan to catch up.

A small group had formed around them. Mostly made up of people checking if they were okay, with a few onlookers lingering on the fringes. Aleksandr took the nearest hand and let them hurl him to his feet. His scream of pain turned into a strangled hiss as he clenched his teeth.

"Alek?"

"Go," he told Ivan again.

At least his younger brother remembered his manners. He shot off towards Evelyn, throwing back a few 'thank yous' and half explained apologies. Aleksandr was grateful. Rudeness had a way of sticking in someone's mind. The last thing they needed right now was to draw more unwanted attention. With a wave of what he hoped came across as gratitude, he lumbered after the others. His joints protested every step and he couldn't keep the pace he had before. Evelyn grabbed Ivan's hand when he was close enough, but she didn't move. Vlas was back on his feet. He pushed through the crowd without a word. The crush of bodies made it almost impossible to keep sight of him.

"Hey, maybe you shouldn't be walking," a stranger said as they grabbed Aleksandr's forearm.

The moment he turned, he saw the dark head once again. Looming just over the stranger's shoulder. Eyes impossibly wide and trained solely on him. Viciously jerking his arm back, Aleksandr took off in a sprint, feeling his hipbones clicking together as he moved.

Chapter 11

The roof of the Bellagio lobby was covered in a garden of glass flowers. They spilled out from a large rectangle gouged into the ceiling, each one a colossal petal catching the carefully positioned lights to make them shine. It was an eye-catching display. Even as Evelyn ran for her life, the colors drew her attention, making her glance at them more than once.

Nadya clutched Evelyn's shoulders as she rode on her back. The older woman could feel her bones bending under the constant pressure. Ivan ran alongside her. They both found it easier to move while not holding hands, but it left a gnawing feeling in Evelyn's gut that they were going to get separated. They paused under the display, where the lighting was its brightest, and turned back to the front doors. Aleksandr shouldered his way through one of the rotating doors while Vlas got an easier run, slipping in while someone was heading out. There was a marked limp in Aleksandr's stride. Evelyn didn't know if it was because of pain or panic, but he no longer seemed to care about drawing unwanted attention. At least, not when he bellowed across the barely populated lobby.

"Move! I'll catch up!"

"I don't even know where I'm going!" Evelyn shot back.

There hadn't been time for them to make a plan. All of her ideas of pitting the two forces against each other had crumbled into ruins. Now, they were stuck. Flee or die. And there didn't seem to be a safe place to run. His retort was lost under a barrage of fine cracking. Evelyn looked up in time to see the first of the flower petals fracture. The thick shard of glass crashed down towards them. Rushing forward, she scooped up Ivan, narrowly avoiding the crash. But it wasn't the first. With the crackle of live wires, the massive hunks of glass separated from the ceiling. Each one shattered as they hit the ground. Becoming a wave of shrapnel just as deadly as the original blow. A thousand tiny cuts were sliced into her bare skin as she raced across well-maintained carpeting, Nadya on her back and Ivan trapped awkwardly under one arm. The closest exit took her over a couch. She stomped her foot into the soft material, her muscle screaming at the extra weight of the two children, and hurled herself out into the open tiled area just as the final remains plummeted in a single strike.

It was a struggle to maintain her balance. Not just from the horrible landing, but because Ivan had started to slip from her weak grip. Nadya was choking her now, her small arms squeezing her neck, the grip slick with blood. A few more steps and she dropped heavily onto her knees.

"Are you guys okay?" she asked in panted breaths.

"Please don't walk on the furniture." The front desk receptionist spoke the words clearly but with an obvious edge of disinterest. It was undoubtedly something they had to repeat numerous times in one shift.

Evelyn twisted to look over her shoulder, not sure what she was going to say back. She never had the chance. The words died in her throat when she found that the lobby was gone. There now existed a fine line between realities. Everything in front of her was Las Vegas and the Bellagio hotel. Everything behind her was the dim stone basement from the ghost town. The two worlds butted up against each other with a razor-sharp transition. Humid, stale air pressed against her back while the air-conditioning of the Bellagio ravaged her front. Aleksandr was gone. Everyone was. There was just the array of torture instruments hanging from the bare walls and the heavy metal door before her.

A cold sweat covered her trembling skin as she stared at that door. She had only stepped into the room that lay beyond it once. Sure in the knowledge that she was not coming back out alive. If the Furies hadn't chosen that moment to strike, she wouldn't have. Even if she had won the fight, killed Aleksandr with her bare hands, Petya and Olga wouldn't have let her live. Beyond that door was the room she was supposed to have died in. Her breathing became shallow pants as she watched the door slowly creak open. It came with a rusted squeal and encroaching darkness. Hot air hovered her shoulders, crept down her arms. The old reality was fighting back the new. *I'm going to be stuck here.*

The thought imploded in her mind, demolished any thought or reason. Only instinct remained. And that told her to run. Reaching back with one arm, she shoved Nadya higher onto her back. The other arm looped around Ivan's waist as she darted forward. Fire burned within her exhausted muscles. Every tendon in her shoulders threatened to tear as she tucked the frail boy under her arm. It felt like she was buried under a thousand pounds. But none of it mattered. All that was real was the heated air threatening to swallow her entirely.

She sprinted down the first hallway she spotted. An extravagantly decorated straight path that sparkled in the welcoming light. Weaving their way through the minimal crowd, they passed a bar and at last came to a T-intersection.

"Right," Nadya said.

Evelyn's shoes squeaked over the tiles as she obeyed. It seemed they had hardly gone any distance at all before they came to the first and only off shoot.

"Left!"

Evelyn managed to round the corner and get on the new hallway just before the old reality claimed the path they had just left. The world swept out after them, somehow taking everything while remaining as that one room. Small and empty and with the metal door now wide open like a gaping mouth.

Adrenaline spurred Evelyn on. Dread knotted her stomach with barbed wire. *I can't outpace it forever,* she thought as some dark, cruel part of her mind began to taunt her. *You're going to have to go back there. The Furies are going to take you back.* She pushed the thoughts aside, letting the raging current of rising hysteria take them. All she needed to focus on was putting one foot in front of the other.

A circular space appeared before them, offering three pathways. Nadya pointed to the far right. The other world was pushing up behind them. Every time her heel flicked up, she could feel the crippling damp air. The unbearable heat. Light and shadow played in the corners of her eyes as she neared the end of the hallway. Then, in a sudden rush, the reality overtook them and Evelyn was left sprinting towards the open metal door. To the abyss that lay within that room that stank of bleach and blood. There was no time to stop. Nowhere else to go. She ran through the doorway. A loud clash of metal and the world was gone. Lost in impenetrable darkness.

"It's not real," Nadya repeated into Evelyn's ear, marking each word with a frantic slap. "It's not real. They're just trying to scare you."

Not real. The worlds held little weight. Seemed to be nothing more than an empty promise. But Evelyn could hold onto the other part. *They're just trying to scare you.* Evelyn stopped short and squeezed her eyes shut. *Like they did with my mother.* The flush of rage was met with a bright light against her eyelids. She blinked them open and glanced around. They were in a new corridor. One with a high ceiling made of glass and light fixtures that hung down like antique lanterns. Luxury brand stores lined the walls and the last strings of the dancing fountains drifted in from her left. She dropped Ivan. Luckily, the boy had the sense to be clutching her arm or he would have fallen face first onto the hard floor. Nadya slipped from Evelyn's back and hurried to her brother's side.

"What happened?" he asked. "Did it decide to go after Aleksandr instead?"

"Maybe we loosened its grip," Nadya said.

Evelyn didn't have the strength to look over to them as she answered. Her focus was on the man before them. The one with a wide grin and a familiar face.

"No. It led us right to where it wanted us."

"What?" Nadya asked. "Why?"

She motioned with her chin, "That's Radmiar, right?"

The twins glanced up. Instantly, they started to inch closer to Evelyn, making sure to be one pace behind. She couldn't decide if this was the act of scared children or if they were just trying to use her as a human shield. In the end, it didn't matter too much to her. Her body was running low on adrenaline. She didn't know how much longer she could go before she crashed.

Radmiar hadn't moved. He leaned one shoulder against the window of the Louis Vuitton store, ankles crossed and a cruel smile on his lips. Calm and confident, his body language screamed that they were exactly where he had wanted them to be. Like he had planned it all. Perhaps if she hadn't just been chased by a Fury, she would have found it intimidating. Now, it just came across as arrogant.

With one sweeping hand, she pushed the kids onto her left side, angling herself between them and their brother. They went easily enough but were hesitant to move forward.

"Just look straight ahead and keep walking," Evelyn said.

"You think he's just going to let us walk by?" Nadya almost squeaked.

"Yeah, it's worth a shot."

She ushered them forward, keeping Radmiar carefully in the corner of her eyes. The vast part of her had assumed that he would just fall into step behind them. Stalk them from a distance. But Radmiar wasn't Vlas. Far bolder, he stalked across the hallway to cut in front of Evelyn and waited for her to close the remaining distance between them. She wanted to hit the smirk right off of his face.

"Hello," Radmiar grinned. "You must be the infamous Evelyn. So nice to see you in the flesh."

There was something about the way he said 'flesh' that made it clear to Evelyn that he was longing to peel hers off her bones.

"Look, Raddy," she said with a smile. "Can we just not? Seriously, wait around a little longer and someone will be along to kill you."

Evelyn moved to step around him, only to be blocked. He snarled at her, barely able to hold onto his mask of civility.

"Do you know who I am?"

"Yeah, I just don't care."

Radmiar leaned closer, putting his face only an inch from hers, "I will gut you."

Evelyn couldn't help it. Didn't even try to. She laughed until her sides were sore and she was breathless. It clearly wasn't the response he had planned on eliciting. His arms quaked. A telltale rattle that Evelyn knew well. He was barely suppressing the urge to hit her.

"I'm sorry," Evelyn gasped, unable to stop her hysterical laughter. Growing up, she had often wondered why people used the phrase 'mentally unstable'. Now she knew. She could feel it. A rickety looseness around the edges of her mind. It made her laugh harder. "I'm sorry. It's not you, it's me. I'm just done."

"You're done?" he parroted.

"Yeah," she said. "Done. Look, I've had one hell of a night. I'm really too tired to pretend to be afraid of you."

"You won't need to pretend," he promised.

"Honey, I just got chased around my childhood home by a demented version of my mother. And that's after I almost got attacked by zombie sharks. You really think you can compete with that?"

Radmiar's eyes flicked down to his siblings before fixing them back onto Evelyn's.

"Are you insane?"

"Not right now. But check back with me before dawn."

The fountain show had come to an end, and the dispersing crowd slowly seeped into the hallway. The increased audience made Radmiar take a controlled breath.

"Do you take me for a joke?" he hissed through his teeth.

"Well, you're wearing a fedora. So ... yeah. Pretty much."

"You have no idea who you're talking to."

"No, I do," Evelyn snapped as rage rushed up inside her. It boiled her blood, scorched her bones. Destroyed every trace of thought and reason. Glaring, she stepped closer to Radmiar. Unprepared for the sudden movement, Radmiar wavered, barely willing to hold his ground. "You're the kind of creep that sneaks into girls' rooms while they're sleeping. What's wrong, Raddy? Can't take the risk of a girl fighting back? Well, I'm awake. I'm staring right at you. And I will knock you on your sorry ass."

"I've killed women for less," he snarled.

"Well, go on!" she screamed as she flung her arms out wide. The motions drew a bit of attention. Just enough to put Radmiar on edge. "I'm right here! Take your best shot and I'll take mine!"

Of all the people that passed them, the majority had clearly had a bit to drink. They didn't have the attention span left to care about the confrontation. Fury burned within Radmiar's eyes. Instead of quelling her own rage, the sight fed it. In the back of her mind, somewhere buried under the haze of emotion and fatigue, a voice told her that this might end in her death. That she was poking a predator, a killer. She felt like she was on fire. Burning alive. With only one chance to satisfy the gnawing beast inside her. She hit him.

Radmiar hadn't seen the blow coming. His nose crunched under her knuckles.

Blood gushed out to cover her skin as he staggered back. Shock held him still for a moment. Then he charged her with a wild, feral cry. They crashed together, each past the point of reason. There was no thought or effort in the strikes. No higher plan of attack and defense. Each one was fueled by the same unrelenting need to rip the other one apart. A few untamed strikes and Radmiar hunched forward, driving his shoulder into Evelyn's stomach. She latched her arms around his middle, using every bit of strength she had to throw him off balance. They slammed against the window of Louis Vuitton before staggering across the massive foyer. People shrieked. A shrill sound that Evelyn knew was supposed to be words. Consumed with rage, she couldn't understand a single one of them.

A sharp knee to Radmiar's gut and an elbow to his spine dislodged him. He clubbed her knee with his fist, his blow landing higher on her legs as she yanked him back up by his throat. Her nails were short, but her grip was tight enough to draw blood. The moment he was up, she jerked her hips and brought her fist up unto his nose again. They reeled back, through the doors of a Prada store and into a display. Bags and shoes fell around them, catching her feet and blurring her vision. Strong arms wrapped around her from behind. They pulled her clean off her feet and away from Radmiar.

People were yelling again. Somehow, amongst the chaos, she realized it was the store's security guard who was holding her, and that there was a threat of calling the police. Neither of those things stopped Evelyn from stomping her foot into Radmiar's face the second he was close enough. The first two strikes to his nose had done some damage. But now it was truly broken. The tip hooked to the side on a strange angle and blood rushed free, joining the trickle that bubbled from his split lip. Crimson droplets fell to stain expensive leather and thin carpet. With a sharp twist, Evelyn jerked free of the strong grip. She charged for Radmiar. In a split second, she realized that he had grabbed hold of one of the metal frames used for display. She had just enough time to register his face before he swung. The blunt end hit her temple and the world went black.

Chapter 12

The moment the twins had directed Evelyn down the first hallway, Aleksandr had decided to go backwards instead of pressing deeper into the Bellagio. He knew his kids. Knew how they thought and where they were headed. Back to the Polaris. To room 3622. The Bellagio hugged the lake. There was a second exit that would give them a straight shot to the bridge back home. Aleksandr had never let them come into contact with the man in room 3622, but they knew his reputation. Most importantly, as Alison had reminded them, he was currently on the orange list. Since he was the only man that was supposed to be working room service tonight, there would be very little risk of someone disturbing them once they were inside the hotel room. Getting entrance would be easy enough. Even at this time of night. They had Evelyn. And that man would open his door for any female. He knew, without doubt, that the twins planned to muscle their way inside and wait there for him to come and find them. He wasn't about to keep them waiting.

Vlas clearly didn't want to go back out into the night. To retrace their steps back to the lake. But without Vera to guide him, he seemed to lock onto the closest relative at hand. Aleksandr detested having Vlas so close. The situation only made bearable by the thought that at least it wasn't Radmiar he had clung to.

With the show over, the crowds had dispersed, allowing them to pick up a decent amount of speed. The lake was still, peaceful, and clear. A shallow little pool instead of the writhing hellscape it had been. Aleksandr pushed himself to go fast, still deciding to deal with Vlas once he had made it back to the Polaris. They took the stairs two at a time, pushed their way across the bridge, and slid down the bannisters on the other side, exploding back into the space-themed casino drenched with sweat and barely able to keep on their feet. Aleksandr staggered his way to the elevators, panting for air. Vlas followed.

"What?" It was all Vlas could get out.

"Furies," Aleksandr said with the same amount of difficulty.

"What?" It was more of a grunt than a real word.

"Greek myths," Aleksandr muttered before he stalked towards the elevator. It bothered him that his older brother followed.

"So, what? They just show up and attack random people?"

"Not random," Aleksandr said. "Vengeance."

They slipped into the first available elevator. It was both a blessing and a curse that they were alone. Aleksandr clenched and released his fists, waiting for his brother to make the first move, sure that the blade of a knife would cut into his flesh soon enough.

"Well that's just not fair," Vlas whined, catching his brother completely off guard.

"What?"

"Why come after me? What did I do?"

The numbers set above the door clicked, seeming to go at a far slower pace than normal as Aleksandr gaped at his brother.

"The murders, Vlas. I'd say they're coming after you because of all the murder."

"So, what, they just take the dead guys word over mine? Where's the due process in that? I have a right to a lawyer."

"I don't think creatures of ancient legend care about modern legal systems."

"Hypocrites," Vlas snorted.

He knew he was going to regret asking, but he had nothing to do for a few more floors, "How?"

"It's all fine and good for them to kill someone for vengeance and not me?" Vlas snapped.

"You hunt innocent people for fun."

"Hookers, junkies, and hobos," Vlas corrected. "If anything, I do a public service."

"It was all for your own amusement," Aleksandr muttered.

"Which is another reason they should thank me. Vera and I gave their pathetic lives some purpose before we put them out of their misery."

"This conversation is over."

Vlas barked a laugh. "You don't get to be all high and mighty when they're coming after you too."

"I never wanted to kill anyone."

"But you enjoyed it," Vlas smiled.

Aleksandr turned and held his brother's gaze, "Only once, Vlas. I only enjoyed it once."

It took a moment for Vlas to understand his meaning. Slowly, the color seeped from his face, washed away with his smile.

"Mom or dad?"

"Mom," Aleksandr said.

"How?"

"Slit her throat." The confession rushed from his mouth, the words themselves void of the chaos raging inside his skin.

Aleksandr had built his identity on the single basic fact; he wasn't a sadist. Unlike so many others of the Sokolovsky clan, he was born without that driving force. There was no joy in torture, no delight in death. Everything he knew about himself rested on that one single fact. And it had all threatened to crumble when he had stuck his knife into his mother's throat. Because he had finally understood what his family had been saying for so long. Killing his mother had been one of the most euphoric experiences of his life. *So what does that make me?*

"You wouldn't have dared," Vlas hissed, his jaw twitching and tears welling in his eyes.

"I did."

"Why?"

Aleksandr could only smile and give the answer Olga had offered him so many times before, "Why not?"

There wasn't that much space in the elevator but Vlas used every inch to his advantage. He hurled himself into Aleksandr, driving him back into the unforgiving wall. The carriage trembled with the force and the doors opened with a sharp ping. Bracing his forearm across his brother's neck, Aleksandr pushed Vlas back, just enough for him to get in a decent swing. The mangled knuckles of his fists struck Vlas on his temple and made him stagger to the side. He toppled out of the elevator and dropped onto the floor. It was only as he followed that Aleksandr noticed the change. They weren't in a hallway. But a forest.

The scents of pine and wet leaves filled Aleksandr's nose as he looked around. All the trunks were uniform in size and shape. Set in even rows that seemed to go on forever. The dirt under his feet was loose but even, squishing slightly as he took each step. Above them, the canopy wasn't made of pine needles, but balloons. Ribbons were attached to each, the colorful slips coiling down to bounce just above Aleksandr's head. He reached up to touch one. *Nothing's there. I'm in a hallway. Nothing's there.* A spike of fear shot through him as his fingertip tapped against the ribbon. It was solid. Real. He leaped back, crouching low to keep as far away from them as he could.

"What is this?" Vlas asked as he got to his feet.

"The Furies feed off of your emotions. The more they scare you, the stronger they become."

"And you're afraid of balloons?" Vlas laughed.

"I'm afraid of what comes with them," he corrected before it occurred to him. "How are you scared of the woods? You're a hunter."

"I'm not."

"Well, they aren't here for me."

Vlas didn't have to explain after the first arrow sliced through the air and embedded itself in the tree by Aleksandr's head. Laughter drifted from the thick cluster of trees. Light and breathy and completely deranged. The sound had been a near constant soundtrack to Aleksandr's childhood. It was the blissful giggle of Vera and Vlas on a hunt.

Both boys turned around, desperately searching for the elevator. For an exit. It was gone. Replaced by the perfectly spaced orchard. Aleksandr was careful not to lose his bearings and he broke into a run. He knew this hotel. *Keep a clear head. Judge by feel. They can mess with your mind, but your muscles remember.* He promised himself this on a constant loop. Still, his thoughts strayed, returning to the newest revelation as the arrows came ever closer to hitting their mark.

"You jackass!" he roared at Vlas.

His brother almost fell over as Aleksandr suddenly cut in front of him. *Down this hallway to the ballroom. Back through there to the staff exit.* He rattled off the directions even as he hurled obscenities at his brother.

"What are you talking about?" Vlas snapped.

Neither of them could see where the archer was, but their aim was getting better. The next one sliced through the sleeve of Aleksandr's shirt. Close enough to draw blood. Far enough to know the Furies were just messing with him. He clenched his teeth against the pain and ran faster, struggling to keep track of the steps.

"Your biggest fear is someone doing to you what you did to others," Aleksandr said between panted breaths as Vlas fell in pace beside them. "Do you have a functional soul?"

"Is that what you're supposed to do with fears?" Vlas shot back. "Confront them?"

"Not inflict them!"

"It was therapy!"

Vlas hissed the words over his shoulder. As if he truly believed that he could convince the Furies. That all of this was negotiable. He just needed to say the right thing, present the proper argument, and they would come to see the world his way. If Aleksandr had the spare breath in his lungs, he would have laughed.

Working by instinct, he jerked to the side, protected his head with his forearms as he cut across Vlas. The visual hallucination was seamless. It played across his other senses, trying to lure his brain into believing everything it was told. None of it was enough to stop the real world from existing. Aleksandr plowed into a tree and felt the double doors of the ballroom smash against his skin. With a resounding clash of metal, the doors flung open, leaving him to stumble through the tree and into the empty room.

Being in Vegas, no one stayed in a single room for too long. Eventually, the allure of a new novelty drew people away, and this party was no different. Without the pounding music and constant chatter, the room had fallen into a crushing silence. Everything of expense had been stored away for the night, but the decorations had been left for tomorrow. The brothers' hesitant footsteps echoed off of the walls and stirred the thick layer of confetti that covered the polished floor. The silver and gold balloons, having only been given a night's worth of helium, had already begun to drift down. They hovered at different points, some merely an inch off the floor while others were still beyond reach.

"Did they just forget to do this room, or did we lose it?" Vlas asked, naturally keeping his voice to a whisper.

Aleksandr didn't answer.

Vlas latched onto his brother's arm and yanked him around so they were face to face, "So, how do we do this?"

"Do what?"

"Kill them."

"We don't."

"They murdered Vera."

"So?"

"So I want revenge. And you should, too."

Aleksandr ripped his arm free and jogged towards the door without responding.

"She was your sister," Vlas snarled.

"She used to throw Molotov cocktails at me."

"That was just a prank," Vlas said. "How did you survive these things for two years being so damn sensitive?"

"They let us go."

"After they took mom and dad?"

"Yeah."

Aleksandr had his hand on the exit before he realized his mistake. Vlas would come to the same conclusion he and Evelyn had. *They're happy as long as they don't go home empty-handed.* Aleksandr dropped to the ground just as Vlas struck. The blow went high, the edge of his knife slicing the top of Aleksandr's head instead of driving into his back. Hot blood trickled through his hair as he rolled to the side. One foot braced against the ground for balance, and with his fist up, Aleksandr looked back at his brother.

"How did you get a knife past the metal detectors?"

Caught off guard by the question, Vlas blinked and kept his silence. It gave Aleksandr the time he needed to get back onto his feet.

"It's human bone," Vlas said, flipping the knife back and forth so Aleksandr could admire it. "Vera gave it to me for our birthday this year. You know, you still haven't given me anything."

"You're trying to kill me."

Vlas snorted, "You can't use that as an excuse. I've only just decided to murder you, and our birthday was *a month* ago. It really hurt our feelings that you didn't remember."

In the back of his head, Aleksandr wondered if they were truly alone. Or if, like before, this hall was filled with people that the Furies kept him from seeing. If the second option were true, there were two key problems. Someone could get in the way. And someone was going to call security.

"I could go to the gift shop right now." Aleksandr had hoped that prolonging the conversation would distract his brother from noticing that he was shifting into a better position, readying himself for the fight.

But Vlas saw. His eyes tracked every move of Aleksandr's limbs with an almost detached amusement. There wasn't a shadow of doubt on his features. Vlas believed that this fight was as good as over, and history was on his side. A lifetime of beatings and torment had proved to Aleksandr that he couldn't stand against Vera and Vlas. *But there's only Vlas now,* Aleksandr reminded himself. In that, there was hope. Vlas had only ever killed as part of a pack. A piece of a greater whole. Aleksandr had survived by watching his own back.

"Don't make this harder than it has to be, Alek. We both know you're not going to leave Vegas alive. Let me make sure that your death has some meaning."

Vlas didn't wait to hear a response. He rushed the distance that separated them, knife slashing through the air, each swipe closer than the one before it. Aleksandr reeled back. Twisted and turned. Always feeling the stirred air just above his skin. Vlas was faster than he had given him credit for. His movements bold. He didn't hesitate. Moved with instinct instead of planning.

The tip of the knife was as sharp as a scalpel. It barely touched Aleksandr's face but still cut a near surgical wound from his jaw to his temple. Swallowing the scream of pain pulling at his skin, opening the wound wider. Blood trickled down his neck as he lunged onto Vlas. Barely half an inch separated the tip of the knife from Aleksandr's chest when he managed to grab hold of his brother's wrist. Vlas dropped the knife, his free hand already moving to catch it. Aleksandr was faster. He snatched the knife from the air, half of his palm safely on the hilt while the remainder of his hand was sliced open by the blade. Still, he clenched tight and shoved up.

The blade hit Vlas in the tender skin under his jaw. It sunk in smoothly, barely offering any resistance, only stopping when Aleksandr's own fist blocked the way. Blood rushed through the opening. A wet gargling noise worked its way through the silence. When Vlas parted his lips, the slightest hint of the bone dagger could be spotted just behind his teeth. But none of this was why he had stopped fighting back. Aleksandr couldn't understand it until he heard the laughter again. Vera and Vlas, giggling with demonic glee. Vlas jerked. Blood and spit bubbled from his mouth. His eyes grew impossibly large. And then he was flung backwards.

Aleksandr watched in stunned silence as his brother was dragged across the floor by the arrow embedded into his back. They were large, metal contraptions. More like a harpoon than an arrow. Aleksandr recognized them instantly. It had been the first game Petya had taught Vera and Vlas, and one that had remained their stable favorite. Impale a victim on a harpoon. Attach the other end to a car and drive. See how long they could last. The memories played in Aleksandr's mind as he watched Vlas desperately claw at the carpet. It was dumb luck that he managed to latch onto the doorframe. The harpoons continued to pull, the hooked tips tearing flesh and bone as Vlas refused to relinquish his grip.

Aleksandr trembled back a step when he first caught sight of the approaching figures. The monstrosity of their appearance rooted him into place, keeping him still when he longed to flee. All three had female figures. But their skin was gone, sliced clean from the muscle, and large animal skulls had taken the place of their own heads. A jackal. A vulture. A crocodile. The sun-bleached bones were the only part of the bodies not slick with blood and rot. On all fours, they crawled towards Vlas. Their limbs squished and the metal chains rattled as they closed in. Not one of them was in any hurry. They knew Vlas had no hope of escaping them. *They're savoring the kill.*

The realization made something click in Aleksandr's head. Evelyn's theory that they could be sated. Olga's death. That first night when the Furies had let them flee into the desert. And now, as he stood here, forgotten, a spectator to his brother's death. *Death enthralls them. Distracts them. They enjoy it.*

Aleksandr's hip and knee burned with renewed vengeance as he spun. If his theory was correct, his time was running out. He wasn't going to waste the precious seconds just to see Vlas die. He forced himself to run and crashed into the hidden staff hallway. Pulling his phone from his pocket, he pressed speed dial and held it to his ear.

"They got Vlas. Where are you?"

"The hospital," Nadya replied.

"What?"

"We're fine," she assured. "Eve's unconscious. The police are here. I don't know what Radmiar's told them, but he's trying to slip into her room unnoticed. We don't know what to do."

If he could hail a cab, it was only an eleven-minute ride to the hospital. By foot, it was more than an hour. More than enough time for the Furies to finish with Vlas and be on the prowl once more.

"Get to the airport," Aleksandr said as he sprinted down the narrow hallway, heading for the staff elevator.

"We're leaving her?"

"I'll get Evelyn. If we don't meet you out front in forty-five minutes, get the hell out of town. Don't wait for us. You remember how to slip the safety checks?"

"Alek–"

"Yes or no?"

"Yes, I remember. I'll get tickets for all of us, don't worry."

"If we're not there, go."

"But–"

"Just do it, Nadya!" he snapped. Realizing that this could be the last time he ever spoke with her, he quickly added, "I love you both," and hung up.

Chapter 13

Evelyn could feel her heartbeat in her skull. Each pulse like the blow of a hammer. Only when she tried to blink did she realize that her eyes were closed. Her breath catching in her throat, she snapped her eyes open and jerked up. A tight band cut into her wrist, yanking her back down as she tried to climb to her feet. The room was a blur of sterile white and shifting curtains. She heaved each breath, but air never seemed to find its way into her lungs. The room lurched and spun. She could almost feel her brain sloshing about.

"Evelyn?" She whirled towards the voice and almost blacked out. "Evelyn, it's okay. You're safe in the Las Vegas hospital."

"What?"

Squinting, she managed to bring the uniformed police officer into focus. He was still talking, but the sound came a second too late, making him appear like a poorly dubbed movie. It was distracting, and when he paused, looking at her for a reply, she discovered that she hadn't understood a single word he had said. "What?" she repeated meekly.

"You're Evelyn, aren't you?" This time, the officer kept his voice solid and his words slow.

"Yes," she swallowed, vainly trying to wet her dry throat. "Evelyn Figueroa. How did you know?"

"Your father's been very worried about you."

She tried to get up again. Once more, a sharp bite to her wrist kept her in place on the bed. "I forgot to call him back. Is he okay?"

"He called the station and asked for us to keep an eye out for you," the officer said.

"What did you tell him?" She patted her chest and found that the phone was no longer in her bra. "Where's my phone? I need to call him."

"We already have. He knows that you're safe. It's okay." Still, he presented her with a plastic bag containing her belongings. She sagged with relief that she hadn't been carrying anything suspicious.

A gaping pit opened up in her chest. "You didn't tell him I was in the hospital, did you? He'll come here if you did. He can't come to Vegas!"

"We assured him that you were alright. That we had a few questions for you and that you'd call him back in an hour or so. We didn't want him to worry until we knew what we had."

The words soothed Evelyn's mind enough for her to notice more detail. Most notably, what kept her pinned in place.

"Why am I handcuffed to the bed?"

After a moment of hesitation, the officer proceeded in a much softer voice. "Do you remember the fight you were in?"

"That was self-defense," she said hurriedly.

"I'm sure it was. But we need to get all the facts."

"Is strapping me to the bed necessary?"

"We didn't want you hurting yourself or anyone else."

"What are you talking about?"

"Witnesses said you were acting strange before the confrontation. Running from something that wasn't there. Do you remember that?"

Evelyn swallowed again and kept her silence. *What happened to the twins? Should I ask? Why hasn't he mentioned them?* The memory of Radmiar swinging the metal bar for her head came back to her. She winced at the phantom pain. *Did they get away?*

"Your father told us a little bit about you," the officer said when it became clear she wasn't about to speak. "About what happened to you a few years back?"

Just spit it out, she hissed at him in her mind. "Olga and Petya Sokolovsky."

"Yeah. That kind of thing ... well, time doesn't always heal those sorts of wounds. Did you perhaps take something to help?"

She blinked. "You think I'm on drugs?"

"I think there's a lot you might want to forget."

"Did I test positive for anything?"

"Doctors are still running their tests," he said. "But it's best to tell us before we find out on our own."

"Why? I didn't do anything wrong."

"You attacked someone. Witnesses said you swung first."

"He was threatening me," Evelyn cut in.

"We'll look into that. But there's also the matter of some property damage."

"The handbags? I might have bled on a few. How much could that really cost?"

"The bill is in the thousands. They're still assessing."

"This is unbelievable," she muttered. *Running for my life from Furies and serial killers and I get caught up because of Prada.*

"Evelyn, I want you to know that you have a sympathetic ear here. We want to help you. But you have to be honest with us."

"I'm just really confused." She tried to make herself sound as innocent and scared as possible.

"I know. Everything will be okay."

"My wrist hurts," she said. "Can you please loosen these?"

The officer mulled it over. "You seem lucid. Touch the index finger of your right hand to your nose."

"I'm not drunk," she assured as she performed the task.

"You're in the emergency room. Do you know what that means?" The officer sat on the edge of her bed and held her gaze. "It means that there are a lot of sick people who are hurting, who don't need any more fear on top of their problems."

"Okay," Evelyn said slowly.

"You cause me or anyone else a moment of trouble, I'm putting them back on. Deal?"

"Yes, of course. Sir, I'm disorientated, not dangerous."

"I don't know. People were telling me you know how to throw a punch."

"Self-defense," she repeated. Because there really wasn't much else she could say.

"I'm going to get your doctor. Can I trust you to sit here?"

"Yes, officer."

The moment he stepped beyond the curtain, Evelyn was tugging at the tubes and monitors that were attached to her skin. She ripped open the bag with her teeth, shoved her wallet into her pocket, and had just wrapped her fingers around her phone when it began to buzz. Cursing and fumbling with the buttons, she kept her eyes on the curtain as she answered in a hushed whisper.

"Alek?"

"I'm picking you up at the front entrance. Get there now."

"How did you know where I was?" She scrambled off of the bed, grateful that they hadn't felt a need to remove her shoes.

The hospital was filled with noise. Beeps and machine whirls and a thousand conversations. None of which the paper-thin curtains stifled at all.

"From Nadya," he replied. "Why are you whispering?"

"Police," she said. "Where are you?"

"I'm in a cab."

Evelyn shook her head as she crept towards the gap in the curtain. For some reason, that just stuck her as incredibly odd.

"Vlas?" she asked.

"Gone. Look, I have a theory that we didn't get away the first time just because they let us go."

"Okay," she said slowly, carefully peering out the gap in the curtain.

There didn't seem to be anyone guarding her makeshift room.

"I think there's a window of opportunity. A time after they get what they want when they don't care about anything else."

Evelyn's brow furrowed. "You think we got away from the Furies because they were too busy doing a happy dance over killing someone?"

"Or they were playing." She could hear the strain in his voice as he carefully picked his words. It made her wonder if the cab driver was paying more attention to the conversation than Aleksandr was comfortable with. "Petya and Olga were the same way."

"Okay. How long?"

"A few minutes. Half an hour."

She paused in opening the curtain. "There's a big difference between those two."

"I don't have a stopwatch with me," Aleksandr hissed. "I'm almost there. Get out now."

"Radmiar?"

"We've got it covered," Aleksandr cut in. "But we need to get the timing right. If you're not out front when I pull up, I'm going to have to leave without you. So move."

It had only been a moment of hesitation, but it cost her dearly. The curtain was ripped from her loose grip, the plastic hangers releasing a gasping sound as they scraped across metal, and Radmiar slipped inside. Surprised to find her so close, he quickly placed one finger against his mouth, silently shushing her.

"Easy now," he whispered. "Don't do anything stupid."

"You mean like scream for help because a serial killer is stalking me? Are you sure that's stupid? Because it sounds like a pretty smart idea to me."

"Oh, Eve," he smiled. "You're delusional. There isn't a single shred of evidence that I'm anything other than a law-abiding citizen. It's your word against mine."

"Yeah, maybe. But I'd love to see you talk your way out of it," she said.

"You're cranky when you have a concussion."

"You're egotistical when you've got a broken nose," she shot back, finding a vast amount of joy in the midnight dark bruise that was steadily growing across his face.

A small glint of metal drew her eyes. His fingers toyed with something, his flesh keeping her from spotting him properly. A few rotations and she realized it was a syringe.

"What are you planning?" she asked, reluctant to retreat but desperately wanting to get out of striking range.

He let the syringe slip a little further into his grip. Just enough for her to see that the needle was empty.

"I think I've seen this on TV," she said. "Air bubble to the vein, right?"

"Simple enough death. Resembles a heart attack."

"Yeah, nothing suspicious about a nineteen-year-old athlete in good health dying of a heart attack."

His eyes narrowed and his lip curled with disgust. Evelyn didn't look away, challenging him with her own murderous glare. To close that last bit of distance between them. To take his chance. Radmiar finally shifted his torso and Evelyn tensed. Still in a crouch, she tried to calculate how long it would take her to get to an exit. *Scream. Draw attention. The officer can't be that far.* Radmiar positioned his fingers around the syringe. A smile broke out across his face, cruel and laced with ice. Still, he didn't strike. Intent on prolonging the moment. Stoking her fear into a blazing fire. Giving her all the time her panicked brain needed to understand exactly what was coming next. And everything that it meant.

In a movement of pure instinct, Evelyn reared back and drove her head into his face. The solid plane of her forehead crunched against his already damaged nose before he could turn away. Blinding pain exploded behind her eyes, rattling her brain against the innards of her skull. The only consolation was that it hurt him just as much. With a string of bellowed, half-muffled cries, Radmiar doubled over. She ran, twisting herself up in the curtains as she fought for her freedom. The needle might have been thin, but if felt like a dagger as it dug into the back of her leg. She kicked wildly, trying to dislodge his grip before he could push the plunger down. Her knee collided with something solid. The rollers popped free and the thin curtain tore in two, dropping her out into the hallway.

People were already coming to see what was going on. By the time she was back on her feet, the crowd was closing in on Radmiar, drawn in by the blood that was currently pouring from his nose. Evelyn ripped the syringe free from her leg and stabbed it as hard as she could into his back. His scream coaxed the nursing staff to break into a run. The world rippled across her vision. That, along with the cold sweat that covered her palm and the calls for security prevented her from pushing the plunger. She chose instead to run while she still could.

Getting through the first wave of people was the hardest. Everyone behind them was too confused to know that they should stop him. Shoving and panting, she weaved through the hallways, struggling to stay focused. Everything blended. The colors. The people. The walls seemed to come from nowhere and disappear just as quickly. She alternated between believing that the Furies had arrived and that her head injury was a lot worse than she had thought.

"Evelyn!"

She skidded to a stop as the officer from before blocked her path. He had one hand on the hilt of his gun. The other was stretched out before him to keep her back.

"Just stop right there, Evelyn. I don't want to have to hurt you."

Slowly, she backed up a step.

"Evelyn–"

The sentence was cut short when Aleksandr slipped up behind the officer. He moved like smoke, silent but swift. One hand held the gun in place while the other smacked the officer's head against the brick wall. The resounding crack made Evelyn flinch. Her breath caught as the officer slumped to the ground.

"I thought you were staying in the car," Evelyn mumbled in disorientated shock.

"There wasn't any traffic." Aleksandr kept his voice low and hurried her along with a wave of his hand. "Let's go."

Evelyn moved around the officer, her eyes flicking between the limp man and Aleksandr.

"He's not dead, is he?"

"What do you take me for?" Alek snapped. "He'll only be out for a few seconds."

"That can't be good for him."

"He's in a hospital. Hurry up or we'll miss our ride."

The world was still rolling around her and she had to lean against Aleksandr before they made it to the exit. He wrapped an arm around her waist, but his growing limp kept him from taking much of her weight. The dawn was starting to lighten the sky as they hurried out of the side door, barely able to keep ahead of the people hurrying to gain some control of the situation. She didn't know how they got out without someone stopping them. They lurched and stumbled across the parking lot as a deep growl started to roll out from behind them. Feral. Monstrous. Hungry.

They didn't look back as they piled into the waiting taxi. It said a lot about what happened in Las Vegas that the driver didn't even bat an eye over the whole situation. Evelyn leaned back against the seat, staring up at the ceiling when she could focus her vision enough to see anything. Every breath was a struggle. Exhaustion crept down into her marrow. She hoped that was why it was so hard to keep her eyes open. It didn't seem like there were many good alternatives.

The drive passed in a blur, and she was just regaining her senses as they staggered into the airport. Their attempt to look presentable was half-hearted at best. She wondered if people simply assumed that they were hung over because, again, no one seemed to mention it. An ocean of people and they were completely left to their own devices. Aleksandr took over when it came to the formalities. This time, he spoke with a French accent. Pretending to struggle to recall certain words really sold the illusion of him being a baffled tourist. Evelyn thanked everything in Heaven and Earth that she still had her I.D with her. She only got a glimpse at what Aleksandr pulled from his wallet, but she was sure it said his name was Etienne. The combination of confidence, a credit card, and lies already established by the twins before them got them all the way to the boarding gates. She had no idea where they were going. It didn't really matter. As long as it put some distance between them and what was coming.

"I'll be back," Aleksandr said abruptly. "Stay right here."

She snapped out of her daze. Looking around, she saw that 'here' was an open space right in front of their gate. No protection. Nowhere to hide.

"Where are you going?" she asked.

He licked his lip, glanced around, and sighed. "I need you to stand right where you are until I get back."

You can only get away from the Furies when they're busy, a voice in the back of her head whispered. *He wants you to be what keeps them busy.* Ice crept along her spine as she met his gaze.

"Why?"

"I just need you to trust me."

He's getting the twins away and leaving you to die, the voice whispered. She sucked in a deep breath. All the while, images of that day with her mother, or the pure terror she had felt, the longing for someone to help her, played in her mind. *They're so little. Suck it up, Eve. Let them do what they have to. Besides, an air marshal will probably shoot me before the Furies can have too much fun.*

"I'll be here."

The agreement startled him, but he recovered quickly. Squeezing her shoulder once, he disappeared into the gathering crowd. Evelyn didn't try to keep track of him; her focus was on breathing. On planning what to do next. Survival instinct told her to run but she locked her knees and worked the kinks out of her shoulders. A part of her was still back in that moment the Furies had shown her. She could almost feel the scratch of the blankets against her skin. The push of humid air against her face. And the ever-repeated melody played by a discarded music box. *Don't make it too easy for them,* she told herself. *Fight long enough to give the twins a chance.* Nothing that happened after that really mattered.

A chill curled up her spine and her gut gave a familiar squeeze. She was being watched. She knew it. Squaring her shoulders, Evelyn kept her eyes focused ahead, locked on her own reflection in the night drenched windows. Between one blink and the next, the world began to decay. The plastic chairs cracked and crumbled. Paint flecked off of the walls. The carpet became a squishy sludge beneath her feet. Human skin wasn't spared from the rot. Everyone who passed her began to fester. Flesh turned gray, faces bloated, eyes turned milky, and hair fell from their scalps. The sensation of being watched increased. All of her instincts screamed that a predator was closing in on her. Despite this, she wasn't ready for the hand that grabbed her forearm like a vice. It was as strong as iron but unmistakably human.

"The cops are looking for you," Radmiar hissed into her ear.

"Were you just waiting for Alek to get out of sight?" she asked. "Didn't know you were that afraid of him."

Radmiar growled but ignored her comment. "Assault and battery. Although, I think I heard some of them throwing around the term 'attempted murder'. Doesn't matter though. You're mine now."

Something hard rested against the soft skin of her back as he spoke. It pushed forward, not breaking skin but enough for her to know it was sharp.

"How did you get that through security?" she asked, eyes still locked on the world falling apart around her. Vaguely, she was aware of the last boarding call.

Although she couldn't be sure if that tether to reality was real or not.

"My dad taught me well." His breath was humid against her cheek as he whispered. "Be a good girl and come along."

"Don't you see this?"

"We'll be gone before–" The rest of his sentence was lost as a passing person carelessly bumped into Radmiar's back.

Evelyn tried to rock with the blow, avoiding the knife tip while surging forward. He didn't follow, didn't strike out or try to pull her back, and she moved to whip around and face him. Before she had time to blink, both of her hands were captured by tiny fingers. She was coaxed to walk forward, her legs obliging the pull while her mind struggled to understand what was going on.

The twins kept their grip on her hands, smoothly tugging her forward while never glancing behind. There was a slight clatter of metal against metal as the child on her right passed by a trash can. Evelyn was quick enough to catch a glimpse of a syringe as it toppled into the depths and out of sight.

"Don't look back," the one on her left said with a pleased smile. "Just keep moving."

The flooring was mush under her feet. In a split second, a small pocket of commotion broke out. Evelyn saw the moving corpses slip past her. A few voice speaking over each other. 'Are you okay' overlapping with 'get help' and a flurry of other questions.

Aleksandr arrived as they approached the putrid body taking the tickets. He handed them over and let the twins go on ahead. As they stepped into the tunnel leading to the plane, Evelyn couldn't resist a glance behind. Radmiar had slumped to the ground, gaping and sucking on air as a half dozen people ran around him.

"Air bubble," Aleksandr said. "Ivan's really good at hitting the vein in the inner thigh."

As she watched, Radmiar's body endured the same ravaging as the world around him. His eyes withered and shrank, reducing his eye sockets to bottomless black holes as his lower jaw cracked and drooped. Out of the mass of bodies swirling around him, Evelyn noticed three that stood unmoving. In a split second, the figures turned from shadows into skinned hunks of human flesh with bare animal skulls serving as their heads. She flinched back. Beside her, Aleksandr did the same.

"We should go," Aleksandr said.

Evelyn heard the words, but she could not stop staring at the Furies.

"Come on, let's hope the flight takes off before they get bored."

"Right," she mumbled. *We'll get away. They won't follow tonight.* She knew these two facts as surely as she knew her name. Faced with the demented world they had created, they seemed to be the only things that made any sense. Why she put such trust in them, she couldn't say.

But she knew. *They're satisfied.*

For now.

* * *

Scorched Earth
Wrath and Vengeance Series Book 3
Written by Sara Clancy

Chapter 1

There was never silence in a mental hospital.

Classical music drifted out of the overhead speakers, trying to cover the beep of monitors and a thousand murmured conversations. Everything was new and pristine, but that never stopped the gears of the wheelchairs from creaking.

Evelyn hated the sound. She cringed every time the nurses wheeled one of the patients down the long corridor, the tires squeaking against the highly polished tiles. The now familiar scent of disinfectant and lemons made her stomach churn, and the plastic of the chair carried the chill of the air conditioning.

Ten minutes. It taunted her. *Ten minutes. I only lasted ten damn minutes.* It was a failure she couldn't tolerate. A complication that lingered after her last encounter with the Furies. Before the creatures of ancient Greek legend had returned to her life, she had been able to tolerate her mother's presence for hours. Now, their visits were measured in minutes.

Evelyn raked her hands through her short hair, the crinkled curls coiling around her fingers. It didn't help to stop the memories. The Furies had only forced her to relive the single moment in time. A day when the chemicals in her mother's brain had shifted out of sync, turning the whispered voices into a screaming army. On that day, Ana Figueroa had been convinced that the only way to save her young daughter was to kill her before the demons could.

Evelyn couldn't breathe as memories played across her mind. She hunched forward, braced her elbows against her thighs, and clutched her hands together until the joints ached. The Furies had chosen that one forgotten moment in time, but it had broken a dam inside her, and Evelyn was drowning in everything she had suppressed.

I'm terrified of my mother. Guilt crushed against her lungs and forced her down a little more. She hung her head between her knees and sucked in deep breaths. It didn't help. Not in a place like this. Not with reminders of her greatest fear pressing down around her like floodwaters. Encountering Furies had taught her more about herself than she would have ever learned. She knew herself. Knew what she feared more than her mother or death or even the demonic forces themselves. The truest terror she had ever known was the idea that her mother's unidentified condition was hereditary. That one day she'd have a room here, all for herself.

As she sat there, head drooped between her legs, Evelyn focused on sucking air into her cold lungs. The simple, repetitive task was soothing. Her heart began to slow. Feeling better, she slumped back in her seat and rested her head against the wall, staring up at the sunroofs that spotted the ceiling. Gray clouds littered the winter sky, casting shadows down the length of the corridor as they drifted. It was peaceful and her mind turned quiet. Only one part of her memory remained. *Swan Lake.*

It was the tune her jewelry box had played. She had knocked it over while trying to hide from her mother, making it the honorary theme song for her mother's murder attempt. Clenching her jaw, she struggled to drown out the notes. Forget how the metallic cling of the jewelry box had slowed. How it had continued even as her mother had torn the room apart in search of her.

An icy chill crackled along her spine as she realized that the song wasn't playing in her head. Her eyes were drawn to the speaker system set high on the wall.

Swan Lake continued, each note the distinctive ping of a music box instead of a piano. Her eyes widened. *Swan Lake* grew louder. Turning from a soft melody to the pounding of drums. Louder. Louder. Drowning out her thundering heart and all the sounds of the hospital. Louder still. Then nothing. One blink and she was flung back into normality. Blinking her dry eyes rapidly, Evelyn glanced around. The music had changed to something she didn't know. Everyone was moving about as normal. People coming and going from the communal conservatory at the end of the hall.

Calm down, she commanded herself with an edge of bitterness. *Don't lose it here or they won't let you leave.* Sighing, she ran her hands over her face and smoothed down the hem of her dress. The squeak of a wheelchair made her wince, every repetition of the sound eroding her nerves a little more. She kept her eyes on the chessboard pattern tiles as the person drew closer. *Go on*, a mocking voice laughed in the back of her head. *Take a look. You'll be joining them soon enough.*

Her eyes stayed on the floor, tracing the lines of grout between the large white and black tiles. The wheelchair squeaked again. Followed by the slow, sucking slide of the rubber against ceramic. Squeak and slide. Lethargic and monotonous. The shiny plate of the footrest had just entered her vision when the patient began to whistle, the sound just as slow as they progressed.

Swan Lake.

Evelyn snapped her head up. A scream lodged in her throat when she met the dark, deranged eyes of Olga Sokolovsky.

"You're dead." The words croaked out of her throat as Olga latched onto Evelyn's forearm.

It's not real. No amount of reassurance could convince her that the sharp nails weren't digging into her flesh. Pain shot up her arm, intensifying as she tried to wrench free. Olga grinned. A savage baring of her teeth. The hot, humid puff of Olga's breath washed across Evelyn's face, playing across her senses, another layer of proof that it wasn't in her mind. Evelyn clenched her jaw, fighting back a tremble that threatened to shake her apart.

"I saw you die."

Olga giggled, tightening her nails as they sliced into Evelyn's forearm. Blood seeped down her skin and dripped onto the pristine floor.

"Welcome home, Eve!" Olga laughed.

Evelyn lunged to her feet. At the same moment, she yanked her captured arm back, rolling Olga closer as she struck out with her free hand. Cartilage crunched against Evelyn's knuckles. Warm blood and spit splashed across her fingers. The grip released, a startled cry breaking the uneasy silence as the chair rolled away.

"Mr. Birch!" The nurse's cry made Evelyn flinch. A flash of white, a familiar woman crouched down beside the elderly, frail man in the wheelchair. "It's okay, Mr. Birch, I'm here now. Let me look."

Evelyn swallowed thickly. All she could do was stare at the man, willing him to transform back. The thought of Olga being alive made her blood run cold. But, the idea that Evelyn had imagined it all was worse.

"What happened?" Another nurse asked as he came to stand beside her. *Trevor,* she thought. *His name's Trevor.*

Evelyn shook her head. The female nurse answered, barely looking up from Mr. Birch. "She hit him."

"I didn't mean to," Evelyn mumbled.

"I saw you," the nurse hissed. "There was nothing accidental about it."

The sound of her father calling her name made her sag with relief. She turned slightly as he slipped into the thin gap between her and Trevor.

"Are you okay, princess?"

Before she could say anything, the female nurse told the story again. Evelyn hunched her shoulders and endured it.

"I'm sorry. I didn't mean to."

"You keep saying that," the woman hissed.

"He grabbed my arm. I reacted."

"Someone touches you and your first thought is to attack them?"

Trevor cleared his throat sharply, the universal signal to keep quiet. The woman didn't take kindly to that, so he continued in a loud whisper.

"That's Evelyn Figueroa. You know," he jerked his head towards Evelyn and lowered his voice a little more. "The only survivor of the Red Death killers."

Evelyn's face twisted with disgust. *Red Death killers,* she thought. *Whoever came up with that probably thought they were being clever.*

She didn't know why, but almost every magazine and news source liked to go on about the dual meaning of it. Edgar Allen Poe's story, *The Mask of The Red Death*, was all about an unstoppable killer. Evelyn reluctantly admitted that this was an accurate way to describe Olga and Petya. They killed across countries for decades without drawing attention. *It took monsters from hell to take them down.* The 'red' part was almost a laughable nod to the couple's Russian heritage which, apparently, made them 'exotic', since America led the world in producing serial killers. Evelyn hadn't looked at anyone the same way since she had learned that little fact.

Recognition flicked across the nurse's face. Her hands stilled as she took in every inch of Evelyn's small form. Now twenty-one, Evelyn had given up hope for a growth spurt. Standing at just over five feet, she still cut an intimidating figure. She was a kickboxer before she was taken by Petya. She still was now. And had more muscular bulk than most men could brag about.

"Oh," the nurse said eventually as she stood up.

"I really didn't mean to hurt him. Is he okay?"

"He'll be fine," she assured with a pitying smile. "I'll take him to the infirmary."

Evelyn caught the man's gaze, a task made harder by the tissues now pressed under his nose. His eyes had the glazed, glassy look of someone heavily medicated, and his mouth moved restlessly, saying nothing.

"I'm very sorry." *I wonder if he can even hear me.*

Wrapping her hands around the handles of the wheelchair, the nurse paused.

"I'm really glad you were found not guilty," she said.

Evelyn clenched her jaw until her teeth ached to force a grin. "Thanks."

"I have no idea why the prosecutor even let it get that far," she said. "After all, they were the kids of The Red Death. They weren't stalking you to catch up. They were obviously out for revenge. I have to admit, though, I never thought that there was that much loyalty in serial killer families. Did you know they had kids?"

"Olga and Petya? They mentioned them in passing, I think."

The nurse shook her head. "I can't imagine escaping two killers only to have their children track you down."

And they weren't even the worst of it, Evelyn thought but said nothing.

"I think this is enough," Trevor said, still in a whisper.

"You've survived four serial killers." The expression she had was a mangled mix of horror, awe, and morbid fascination. It was a look Evelyn had seen a lot. "Or was it five?"

"Five," she muttered as she awkwardly shifted her weight.

"That's right. Olga and Petya. Vera, Vlas, and Radmiar."

"That's the lineup," Evelyn said.

"Maybe you should get Mr. Birch to the infirmary now," Trevor said sharply.

"Yes, of course." Still, she hesitated. "It's been four years, right?"

"Four since the first attack. Two since the second," Trevor snapped.

Evelyn smothered a groan. *He followed the case just as much as she did.*

"I'm just thinking," the nurse said as gently as she could. "Perhaps, if you're still this jumpy, you should think about therapy."

Evelyn's father gave her shoulders a slight squeeze, signaling that he had reached his limit. *Screw being polite or reserved. Let sarcasm and mockery reign.*

"Yeah, you know, that occurred to us, too," he said conversationally. "But, oddly enough, having random strangers constantly making small talk about the most traumatizing experiences of her life hasn't helped her to move on."

"Juan," Trevor began, looking beseechingly at Evelyn's father.

But Evelyn was already snorting in laughter and talking over him. "Isn't that just odd?"

"It's almost like triggering someone's PTSD isn't a good idea." Juan twisted his face up in an exaggerated baffled expression.

"Now, that doesn't seem like something an employee at a nut house would know," she countered.

Trevor swallowed uneasily, realizing that neither of them was going to stop. "You should take Mr. Birch down now."

The nurse nodded rapidly and began to wheel Mr. Birch away from the conservatory.

"And after that, change professions," Juan called after the nurse's retreating form. "Mental health isn't your strong suit."

Evelyn chuckled, her shoulders shaking under the arm Juan still had draped over her shoulders.

"I love you, dad," she grinned.

He squeezed her shoulders again. "Right back at you, princess."

"Juan," Trevor began again, nervously clearing his throat. "Please accept my apologies. She's new. I didn't have time to warn her about your daughter."

"*Warn* her?" Juan turned to face the nurse full on. "Evelyn isn't violent. I think anyone would freak out about a stranger grabbing them without warning."

"Yes, of course. But you have to admit, Evelyn's response was …" He sucked a breath in through his teeth before settling on, "Extreme."

"If you don't walk away right now, I'm going to show you an *extreme* response. Understand?"

"Juan, you have to admit that—"

"Walk away, Trevor." Juan's voice carried a razor-sharp edge that made it clear he wasn't going to admit anything. Right or wrong, he wasn't going to give an inch. Trevor nodded and stalked down the hallway, obviously seething. "He's not going to forget that," Evelyn noted.

"Yeah," Juan said. "But I've got to say, it was fun to be the one using that whole 'I pay your salary' thing."

Leaning against his side, she looked up at him. "I didn't think firefighters get that a lot. Seems more like a police thing."

"Don't contradict your elders," he dismissed.

They stood in silence for a moment, offering each other a one-armed hug and the reassurance that the other was there. From her first day of life, Evelyn had been a daddy's girl. And their bond had grown stronger when her mother's health had started to deteriorate. It had hurt both of them to realize just how much she had kept hidden from him in childhood. About the dozen close calls she hadn't spoken a whisper of. There was no mystery as to why she had kept silent. He wouldn't have been able to do anything. They had no other family. And at the time, no money or health insurance. Juan had been working hard to improve their situation. To care for Evelyn and get his wife the help she needed in a place that wasn't a complete hellhole. He couldn't do that with Evelyn on his hip. It was a choice with no perfect answer. And while they had made it through the storm to something better, guilt still lingered.

Juan kissed the top of her head and squeezed once more. "You okay, baby girl?"

"Yeah. It was nothing."

"You slugged a mentally ill elderly man."

"I am so sorry about that," she said. "I didn't think it was him."

Juan pulled back. Just far enough to study his daughter's face. "Who did you think he was?"

"It doesn't matter."

"It does to me," he pushed.

She stared at him for a while, trying to find the right words. "I was afraid. Just for a second but, well, logic doesn't hang around when fear comes to party."

Juan didn't return her smile and she sighed. While she knew he wasn't about to let it go, she wasn't prepared for what he asked.

"Was it the Furies?"

Biting her tongue, she kept her silence. It had never been her intention to tell him about everything that had happened in the ghost town. He didn't need to know what it had been like to be in a room, alone, with Petya and Olga. And trying to explain how the Furies created giant snakes and raised zombies wouldn't go over well. She had been convinced that he would think she was insane. Maybe he would have, if it hadn't been for Las Vegas. A few things were caught on film. Not the creatures themselves. *They're too smart for that*, she thought. But enough had been caught to make it clear that something wasn't right.

The easiest explanation, the one that almost landed her in jail, was that Evelyn had killed the others in a drug-induced haze. That couldn't stand up against the other evidence. Like the coroner's report stating that Vera had died from a shark attack. The surveillance tape said that she had died in a bone-dry room in the middle of a Las Vegas hotel. The marks on her body and the water in her lungs said she was attacked in the ocean by a great white shark. There was no doubt in her mind that if the victims hadn't been killers themselves, she would have been convicted. Proof or not.

It was on one of those nights when she was sure she was going to prison, that she had broken and told him everything. She had preferred that her father thought of her as ill rather than murderous. Evelyn had admitted to setting them up for the Furies to take, but she had never given the death blow herself. To both of their shock, he had believed her.

"Are you with me?" Juan asked, drawing her back from her thoughts.

"Yeah, of course." It took a lot of effort for Evelyn to force a smile. "It was nothing."

He arched an eyebrow. "Just so I know what kind of offended I should be right now, are you suggesting I'm gullible or just plain stupid?"

"What if I'm going for a fancy, classy kind of stupid?" She shrugged when he didn't crack a smile. "How about unobservant?"

"Me? Juan Figueroa? Master of the elements and soldier against infernos? Have you lost your mind, child?"

Evelyn shook her head. "Why can't you just say you're a firefighter like a normal person?"

"Because that doesn't make you laugh," he countered. "So, hurry up with the answer or I'm going to start with the dad jokes. The lame ones."

Evelyn heaved a sigh and forced out, "I thought he was Olga."

"Huh."

She stared at him, watching his brow furrow and his jaw go slack.

"Just for a second. The moment I hit him, he changed back. Not 'changed back'. I know he wasn't ever Olga. I'm not insane."

"Never crossed my mind," he said, mostly on reflex. "Just gathering information here, but does this feel like an 'I'm stressed and sleep deprived' kind of moment? Or is it more of a 'the Furies are here and we should run' scenario?"

"Stress."

"Is everything alright now?"

"Are you really you?"

He nodded. "Damn straight."

"Then I guess everything is what it should be," Evelyn replied.

"Yeah, I guess," he grinned.

"And here I don't have any confetti," she mumbled.

They lapsed into silence, neither knowing what else to say. Most of the awkwardness had lifted, however, and they felt sure enough to sink in the chairs rather than stand there hanging off each other.

"You don't have to go back in," he said at last. "You did well today, princess."

"Ten minutes," she said flatly.

"You're timing yourself?"

"Timing my failure," she muttered under her breath.

"Hey." He waited until she met his gaze before continuing. "She's your mother. All she's ever wanted was for you to be happy and safe. She understands this is hard for you."

"She does?" The words were out before she noticed the look on his face. "Oh, God. You told her, didn't you?"

"It seems like you want me to say no.

"Dad."

"Yeah, of course, I did," he said.

"Why would you do that?"

"You never said I couldn't."

"Because it went without saying!"

"Oh, good, yell. That won't draw attention."

She huffed a breath and shook her head. Both were signs that she was gearing up for a very long rant, so Juan cut in again before she could start.

"Honey, name one person who would understand demons more than her?" he challenged.

Taking a deep breath helped Evelyn push back her rush of resentment and focus on the logic. Ana Figueroa's disorder hadn't set in until her late twenties, but had quickly progressed from there. At first, she had been diagnosed as schizophrenic, but her thought patterns had proven to be too organized and structured. There was always one common theme. And she set about it with a twisted but solid kind of logic. *Demons were coming to take Evelyn away. They were going to make her daughter suffer. Mothers had to protect their children, even if the only way to do it was death.*

A dark chuckle escaped her lips. "I guess she was right."

Juan patted her knee, just enough pressure to draw her back into the conversation.

"When did you tell her?" she asked.

"Just then," Juan said.

Evelyn frowned. "How? It took me two years, two encounters, and a truckload of state's evidence to figure out a way to tell you without sounding crazy. How did you manage to get it all out in ..." she paused to check her watch, "fifteen minutes?"

"I'm offended that you underestimate just how incredible I am."

It was hard to stay mad when he looked so pleased with himself.

Valiantly fighting back her smile, she asked, "How did she take it?"

"She looked me square in the eyes and proceeded to make me admit that she was right. Repeatedly. There may or may not have been a victory dance in there, too." He chuckled. "My God, you two are similar."

Evelyn flinched. Logically, she knew that he had meant it as a compliment, but the comparison never felt like that. Not while her genetics was still a razor-sharp pendulum swinging over her head. *I'm twenty-one*, a voice whispered in the back of her head. *Mother was twenty-nine when the symptoms began.* She pushed the thought aside so she could summon a smile for her father. Just like before, he didn't buy it.

"Let's go home, yeah?" he offered. "We'll stop and get something for dinner. Whatever you want. You know, within reason."

"Actually," she swallowed thickly, not believing the words she was about to say. "I want to go back in and visit with mom again."

"Really?"

She arched an eyebrow at him. "Well, it seems like we have a lot to talk about now."

Juan chuckled, completely unrepentant. "I guess you do. You're welcome."

"Yeah, you're a saint."

"Alright," he patted her knee and stood up. "Let's get back in there."

Evelyn was slower to stand. "Well, I was thinking I'd go see her alone."

Evelyn had prepared herself for his scrutiny. She hadn't been alone with her mother since childhood. At first, it had been a matter of excuses and stalling tactics. Once she hit her teens, she gave up on the pretense. If Juan hadn't already been in the room, ready to serve as a buffer, Evelyn wouldn't have set a foot across the threshold.

"You're sure, princess?"

She nodded, smoothing the wrinkles out of her dress, and getting her hair under control. Anything to keep her hands in motion and prevent him from seeing that they were trembling.

"Yeah," she said. "I can do it."

Juan didn't look at all convinced, but he didn't call her on it. "I'll walk you, yeah?"

"You don't have to."

Rocking back on his heels, he shoved his hands into his pockets and looked around the hospital hallway.

"There's not really all that much for me to do out here, is there?"

Chapter 2

Nurses passed by, never really rushing, but walking with undeniable purpose. Not staring, but definitely looking Evelyn over more than once. *Guess the word's gotten around. That was fast.*

Evelyn kept close to her father's side as they started towards the end of the hallway. Behind them was the way to the exit. Before them, the conservatory. Here, the patients that required minimal attention were allowed to mill around. She could see them meandering by the threshold long before they were in the room themselves.

The communal conservatory was a spacious room, with both the walls and ceiling made of reinforced glass. The kind that couldn't be easily broken or used as a weapon. It gave the air an almost surreal honey glow. Comfortable sofa chairs and small tables were set out around the space. They passed by people playing kids' board games and others reading heavy volumes from the small but well-stocked library. A woman pampered a plastic doll as if it were a real child, while the people beside her chatted and laughed, as if they were in a cafe. Every effort had been taken to create a pleasant, soothing, and safe environment. Oddly enough, it was that determination that made Evelyn's skin crawl. The cultivated serenity had an edge of fakeness to it. A lie that everyone had just agreed to abide by.

She didn't know if he had noticed her discomfort or if it was just a habit at this point, but Juan began to rest an arm on the top of his daughter's head. Since Evelyn had inherited her mother's smaller stature, she was just the right height for him to be comfortable, and it had become a running joke between them. She endured the weight of his arm for a while before swatting it off. It made him laugh and she felt the tension ease in her chest.

Ana had a favorite chair, one nestled in the far corner, framed by glass walls and overlooking the well-maintained gardens. Sitting there, it was easy for someone to believe they were somewhere else. That they were free. The large winged chair made her mother look even smaller than she was. Fragile and slender. Her face was tilted up, eyes closed as she soaked up as much of the winter sun as she could. Evelyn looked to her dad, who nodded once and gradually started to fall behind. She knew he wouldn't be too far.

Sure of this, she studied her mother again. *She looks tired*, Evelyn thought. *She always looks exhausted.* Dark circles made Ana's deep-set eyes look bruised and sore. *Given how tawny her skin is, it would take a lot of sleepless nights to achieve that much of a haggard look.*

Ana was very good at looking serene. Almost blissfully unaware of her surroundings. She was always astute. Half of the room was still separating them when her eyes snapped open and her cool, deep eyes locked onto Evelyn's own. Surprise slipped over her face as quick as wildfire, soon replaced with a hesitant but welcoming smile. Evelyn rolled her shoulders as she approached, trying to work out the tension that was welling within them. She stopped in front of her mother, battling against the urge to check where her father had gone.

"Hey, sweetheart." Ana's voice was barely a whisper, but it chilled Evelyn's bone marrow. "I thought you were heading home."

Evelyn cleared her throat but couldn't trust her voice. So she just shrugged and sunk down into the chair she had evacuated moments ago. They were carefully arranged and bolted into the floor. Close enough for conversation but not to touch. Evelyn endured her mother's searching gaze. It was one of the things that bothered her the most. No matter what drugs they put her on, her eyes were always focused and piercing. Cutting her open like blades.

"I take it your father spilled the beans," she said with an attempt at humor.

"Yeah."

"Honestly, you brought this upon yourself," Ana said with a wave of her hand, her smile growing at Evelyn's confusion. "Well, what did you think would happen when you told a man a secret?"

Evelyn's brow furrowed. Her mother heaved a sigh and rested her bird-thin arms along the armrests. "A bitch don't snitch, honey."

Shock emerged from her chest in a short burst of laughter.

"Men are gossips," Ana continued, leaning forward as if sharing some grand knowledge of the universe.

"Yet they always say it's the other way around," Evelyn said.

"Yes, we should all trust the gender that is constantly going on about all the secrets they keep." Her mother brushed her hand out again. A loose gesture that meant nothing and everything. "We, my sweet darling, have the remarkable talent of talking for hours without ever letting a thing slip. Try to remember that in the future."

Evelyn rolled her shoulders. It felt like each muscle and tendon had been replaced with stone. She gave some thought to just how accurate her assertion was. True enough, there were a thousand secrets that hung between them. Horrors and mistakes that neither had confessed to Juan, as far as the other knew. Things that they would probably never say.

"You could have told me yourself," Ana said softly. "I would have listened. I would have believed you."

"It didn't seem like the sort of thing I should tell you. What with your condition and all."

"Evelyn, I'm on very close terms with the demons in my head. I can tell them from the real ones."

Evelyn nodded, not knowing what else to do. "You were right. Demons were out to get me. You just had the timing wrong."

"Maybe. In a way," Ana replied in a breathy voice. "I just always knew someone was going to try and take you from me. Admittedly, the Furies were a surprise."

"Why?"

"Why is it a surprise?" Ana asked.

"Why did you always think that I was in danger?"

Ana smiled, tightlipped and haunted. "Ask your father."

Her protest cut off in her throat. "Right. A bitch don't snitch."

"And I'm the queen of bitches." Ana said it boastfully, but there was sorrow in her eyes.

The silence that followed was far less tense than all those that had come before it. Ana waited, staring at her daughter, challenging her with her eyes to speak. To tell her why she had decided to return.

"I never asked you what it is that you see," Evelyn said at last.

"Are you worried that, all this time, I've been living with the Furies? I must admit, the Wi-Fi here is horrible, but I've managed to do a quick search. It's not them."

Why is my entire family more efficient than I am? Evelyn wondered.

"Are you sure?"

"If it is them, they've been really lazy. A few decades and they still haven't offed me. No, baby. If my demons exist beyond my head, they are a very different breed than the ones following you."

"It's been two years since I last saw them," Evelyn said. "That's how long they gave me the first time. Before they returned."

"Your father said that you thought they left you alone because taking Petya and Olga severed as a kind of sacrifice."

Evelyn nodded.

"But, when they returned, you offered up three lives, didn't you?"

"I wouldn't put it like that."

Ana snorted a laugh. "I'm not your father. I don't have his soft heart. And it's not like you care about what I think of you."

Evelyn nodded once and straightened her spine. "Vera, Vlas, and Radmiar wanted to kill me. They were murderers. Wasn't it better that the Furies took them instead of me?"

"Much," Ana agreed readily. "No shame in giving the people what they want. But you don't think that they brought you three years? Why?"

"It's just a feeling. An icy twinge in my gut."

"Trust it," Ana said without hesitation. "And get ready to do what you need to do."

It took a second for her to understand what her mother was implying. "You're suggesting I set up more people for them to take?"

"Juan told me that there are at least three other Sokolovskys bouncing around the place."

"Aleksandr and the twins, Nadya and Ivan. But they're not bad people. Not really. They were born into a bad situation. You can't blame them for surviving."

"I'm not suggesting blame. Just that you let the Furies kill them."

"No. I'm not going to do that."

Ana heaved a sigh. "You wouldn't be my daughter if you didn't pick the harder path, I suppose. So, what is your grand plan to kill these mythical creatures?"

"I don't need to kill them. I only have to stop them."

"I don't have to fly, I just have to survive the fall," Ana replied with a smile.

"That's not helpful."

"I'm afraid I can't be of much use, all things considered."

Ana was silent, her eyes roaming the room as she thought. At last, she leaned forward and beckoned Evelyn closer with a curl of a finger. Glancing around quickly to check that none of the nursing staff had gained an interest in their conversation, Evelyn scooted to the edge of the seat.

"Baby, listen to me very carefully," Ana whispered.

She returned to silence until Evelyn nodded that she was listening and shifted even closer. Only inches separated them now. It was the closest they had been for years, and the proximity made Evelyn's skin itch.

"When they drag you to hell," Ana pushed forward and whispered in Evelyn's ear. "Overthrow the devil ... and take his throne."

Ana's hands latched into Evelyn's hair. With a strength she shouldn't possess, the older woman hurled her onto the floor. The moment her back hit the floor, Evelyn pulled her knee to her chest and kicked out. Her foot slammed into her mother's chest and forced her back, her vice-like grip ripping Evelyn's hair from the roots. Trickles of blood oozed across her scalp as she easily pushed herself into a roll, flipping back over her shoulder and onto her feet. Reflex took over. She crouched slightly, arms up and hands balled into fists. Nurses rushed forward, swarming down onto Ana as she thrashed against the seat.

"Princess?" Juan asked as he appeared by Evelyn's side. "Are you okay?"

She nodded and let her father check for wounds. All the while, she stared at her mother. *Small and frail and still fighting like hell. Impressive.*

"Come on, we should leave," Juan said, gently pushing at Evelyn's shoulders.

There was no need for anything else. They had been through this before. The chemicals in Ana's head had shifted beyond her medications' ability to compensate. There was nothing to be done. The visions would come soon and it was best Evelyn wasn't around for them. That was when Ana would start listening to the voices.

"Thanks, mom," Evelyn said around the lump forming in her throat.

"Juan!" Ana screamed. "Juan, don't go!"

She struggled against the nurses trying to hold her down, her hand stretching beseechingly towards her husband.

"It's okay, dad," Evelyn said softly. "I'll meet you outside."

"Juan!"

He kissed his daughter's forehead before hurrying to his wife's side. Evelyn didn't stay to see how it all played out. Spinning on her heel, she almost sprinted to the door, trying to ignore the stares of the staff members. All things considered, she decided that this wasn't the worst way for their conversation to end. If the Furies took her tomorrow, if this was the last conversation they were to ever have, she'd be okay with that. Eyes burning, she threw herself out into the hallway.

The moment she crossed the threshold, the world darkened. A door that shouldn't exist slammed shut behind her, sealing her in with a thunderous crack. She looked over her shoulder to find nothing but a bottomless abyss. Carefully, she turned back to the front. No sunlight streamed through the skylights. The cheerfully painted walls had been replaced by a sheet of ebony. The light fixtures, now small circles rimmed in polished silver domes, swung slightly, making the shadows dance and roll like crashing waves.

She glanced behind her again, already knowing that she wouldn't find an escape. The Furies wouldn't make it that easy for her. Their illusions shrouded reality. Cocooned their victims in a world of terror. *Surrounded by people with no one to help you*, she thought as she focused forward again.

The hallway had narrowed in the split second she had looked away. Darkness played against the weak light. Even when her eyes failed, she knew they were there. The three nurses that stood at the far end of the corridor. Their uniforms were ancient. The kinds of things that belonged on the civil war battlefield, stained with eons of blood, sweat, and mud. They each stood, hands clasped before them, heads lowered. Evelyn backed away, as fear swelled her throat shut. Her breath became a rapid wheeze, a cold sweat glistening on her palms. Moving as one, the nurses began to stalk towards her.

Evelyn turned and sprinted back the way she came. Her eyes might not see the door, but reality demanded that it was there. Spurred on by this thought, she sprinted towards the wall. But couldn't keep from protecting her head with her arms at the point of contact. The shift of light she had been expecting didn't come. Panting hard, she lowered her arms to find herself within a darkened abyss, disrupted only by spotlights of stark white that didn't seem to have any source.

Shadows shrouded the walls, making it impossible to see anything beyond the circles of the overhead lights. The tiled floor had been replaced by a rough concrete that scraped against the soles of her sneakers. Her pace slowed as she looked around. There had to be people in the room. Logic told her as much. She strained her senses, trying to catch the faintest trace of life. There was nothing. She was alone.

A flash of movement made her turn. The three Furies materialized before her. Remaining in their mock nurse disguises, they stood in formation on the very rim of light. While they were looking at her now, their faces remained obscured. Inky shadows welled where their eyes should have been and reduced their mouths into deep pits. It was as if their faces had been peeled to the bone. Evelyn rolled her shoulders as she backed up a step. Survival instincts battled against her lizard brain. Run. Fight. Both options pulled at her, and she clenched her jaw as she waited to see which would win out. The weight of their gaze pushed down upon her like an icy spear burrowing into her chest. It was hard to breathe. Anxiety spread along her skin.

Moving once more in unison, the Furies lifted their right arms. They pointed to the side. Silently. Still as stone. Evelyn didn't want to look. She refused to. But a sudden crash made her jump and dragged her gaze to where they had pointed. There, illuminated by a distant spotlight, was the heavy metal door that haunted her dreams. It was the door in the Sokolovsky basement. The one that led to a bloodstained concrete room. The room she was supposed to die in. A crimson glow pulsed before her eyes as the copper, sickly scent of rancid blood filled her nose.

Evelyn's stomach heaved and she quickly swallowed, hoping to force the rising contents of her stomach back down. Snapping her eyes back onto the Furies, she locked her knees, trying to keep her ground. *They feed off of fear*, she told herself, clutching onto the thought for some measure of comfort. *Don't make them any stronger.*

It was easy to conjure the thought. Harder to take the advice. The room continued to pulse in time with her throbbing heartbeat. The Fury sisters stared at Evelyn with dead eyes as the doorframe swelled, growing closer, the screams of dozens of victims rising into a deafening roar. Fear flooded Evelyn's mind. It drowned out every thought, leaving only the sensation to fill her skin. With the last of her conscious mind, she resolved to one task. Don't look away. The Furies watched her for a moment and something in the air changed. She could feel their amusement. They enjoyed this. Savored it.

A hand fell on her shoulder. The scream she had been holding in ripped out of her throat, coming out so hard and fast that her lungs ached. On impulse, she whipped around, finding herself face to face with her father. The world rippled as the illusion faded. Sunlight blinded her and her ears rang with the sudden shift to muttered voices instead of blood-curdling screams. One glance at a passing nurse made her freeze. Reminded her to keep calm. *You don't want a room next to mom.*

Her father's brow furrowed as he studied her face. "They're here?"

"You didn't see anything?"

"No." He looked over his shoulder, a quick glance back at Ana. There were too many people swirling around her now to see exactly what was going on. But chaos alone promised that something was wrong. "We need to get out of here."

"Right," Evelyn swallowed a few times, waiting for her brain to start working again. "Should I say goodbye?"

"Not right now," he said.

Without thought, she clutched the sleeve of her father's jacket as he urged her towards the door. Every step closer was like walking on glass as her nerves threatened to shake her apart. It wasn't hard for Juan to notice, and he wrapped a protective arm around her shoulders. The weight of it made her relax a little, but she couldn't keep him from noticing that she was shaking.

She searched every inch of the hallways as they passed. Cold stone and blank walls. The air thickened. Her chest tightened. Every step rattled along her legs, almost as if the bones would shatter. Finally, the layers of glass doors that lead to the exit came into view. They had to pause at each, waiting for an attendant to unlock the reinforced barriers. Evelyn flinched at the shrill buzz and she left it to Juan to push them open. She barely managed to keep from sprinting forward in the last bit and forgot entirely to acknowledge any of the workers. Cool air slammed into her as she ran out onto the lush, sloping garden that attached the building to the street. Hunching forward, she braced her hands on her knees and sucked in deep breaths.

"Are you okay?" her father asked as he closed the distance between them.

She nodded but didn't look up.

"Is that the way it normally goes down?"

The tips of her hair smacked around her chilled cheeks as she violently shook her head.

"They were messing with me," she whispered, the knowledge suddenly hitting her.

"Why?"

"I don't know." Pulling herself up to full height, she met his gaze. "I need to call Aleksandr."

Chapter 3

Aleksandr was certain he was covered in a layer of ice as he trudged through the small arctic town towards his rental home. He had barely gotten out of the door from work before every inch of exposed skin had been ripped raw by the ferocious, winter wind. The whole world was ice and snow, too cold to breathe. The water of his eyes freezing into place and turning into crystals on his lashes. This close to the arctic wasn't exactly hospitable, no matter how prepared he thought he was. One step outside always proved him wrong. He probably wouldn't be warm again until spring.

And he loved it.

The twins hadn't been quite as excited about the idea of living where the winters were so harsh. Born and raised in the ghost town that Olga and Petya had used for a killing zone, the desert heat was all they had ever known. Even when they had escaped, they had only traded the stifling, crushing heat for Las Vegas, another desert town. After the Furies had destroyed that life for them, Aleksandr had craved a change. Leaving the United States had been the best decision. While they never said it out loud, Aleksandr knew his siblings well. They had hoped for somewhere near a beach. But they also knew, thanks to the Furies' torments, that their older brother was terrified of water. Snow had been a good consolation prize.

Blinking against the arctic winds, Aleksandr looked down at the twins. It was a vast improvement from where they had started. The first ten years of their lives had been malnutrition and starvation. Both things were hard to shake. Aleksandr had been left a good few feet shorter than he probably could have been. Four years of freedom at a critical age had helped them, but they were still lagging behind their age bracket. Thirteen years old and easily fitting into the weight range of a ten-year-old. They were gaining height though. Gone were the little kids that barely made it up to his hips, the little children that seemed never to grow up. Now, they reached his shoulder. It wouldn't be much longer before they were taller than he was.

"What?" Ivan yelled through layers of scarf now wrapped around his lower face.

"You're both growing like weeds," Aleksandr called back.

In unison, the twins rolled their eyes. It wasn't something they planned to do. Just the left-over traces of a defense mechanism. Women didn't last long in the Sokolovsky household. For Nadya's own protection, it had been best for her to hide in plain sight, mimicking her twin brother to the smallest detail. Ivan had helped by learning to be Nadya, allowing them to switch places and generally confusing everyone. Now that their parents and siblings were dead, it had become more of a comfort. They kept themselves identical now. Boy or girl, they didn't care. As long as no one could tell them apart.

Both of them shared the fear that puberty would tear them apart. Their slowed development worried Aleksandr more. Not just physically, but mentally. His attempts to keep them properly educated hadn't been a complete success, at least as far as standardized testing was concerned. That hadn't surprised Aleksandr. There was no doubt that they were bright, perceptive kids. But the only one they had to learn from was himself. And he was a twenty-four year old that still needed to silently mouth the words to read anything. Four years of a proper education from someone who knew what they were doing was quickly bridging the gap, but they still lagged behind their peers in a few subjects.

"Do you want to go camping this weekend?" Aleksandr asked.

"It's supposed to be negative four degrees this weekend. And a few inches of snow," Nadya said.

Ivan had to turn his entire torso to look at her. "So?"

"So, nothing. I'm just saying. I'm all for the trip."

Aleksandr smiled to himself as he let them take the lead up the small flight of stairs to their rental apartment. Small town hospitality had taken care of them. When they arrived, they had set up in a hotel room while he looked for work. Once their cover story made it through the gossip chain, that Aleksandr was the young father of pre-pubescent twins, an elderly couple had offered him a job at their restaurant. The twins put on their charm, and in only two weeks, had secured an invitation to sublet their cozy two-story home.

Huddling into the coatroom, they shook off the snow and ice that had clung to every inch of their outer layers. The twins stored their hockey gear away and neatly hung up their coats, scarves, and gloves. One thing that living with psychopaths taught them well was to take good care of what they wanted to keep. Apparently, this behavior was a big tip off to their new landlords that the twins weren't normal teens. Aleksandr cleared his throat and they remembered to leave a few things out of place. Not enough for a mess. Just enough to not look neurotic.

"I'll make the hot chocolate," Ivan shouted as he headed into the main house.

As stealthily as a ninja, Nadya pulled the bag of food from his hands and raced after her twin. Another bonus of working at a restaurant; he could always bring home dinner. The downside was that he always smelled like French Fries and barbeque ribs. He was starving, but his jacket zipper wasn't cooperating.

By the time he got it all in order, he was sure his younger siblings had eaten everything. He didn't get two steps before his cell phone buzzed. The moment he saw the caller ID, he yelled out for the twins to start and pushed back towards the door for a little privacy.

"Hey," he said as Evelyn's face filled the screen. Instantly, his gut twisted. "This isn't a social call, is it?"

"No. The Furies paid me a visit."

"Are you driving?"

"My dad is. Meet Juan. Dad, this is Alek," she turned the screen around to show a strong man who had begun to plump with age. The man had just enough time to flash a smile before the screen focused back on Evelyn. "Oh, don't worry, I told him everything."

"You didn't tell *me* that."

"Yeah, I did. I remember. It was around the time that they were threatening to put me up on murder charges for Radmiar's death. I said 'I really need my dad to know' and you said, 'Hold on, I've got to get this off the stove'. If that isn't unwavering support, what is?"

"Oh, right," Aleksandr muttered, tugging a hand through his short-cropped hair. After Vegas, he had to change things up, ridding him of the fringe he had been using as a shield for twenty odd years. He missed it now. He hated eye-contact.

"I would have liked a reminder later on," he said.

"It was on my to-do list," she said with an innocent expression. "And, you know, maybe that's not really what we should be focusing on right now. What with the monsters running around and all."

"Because that's out of our norm," he grumbled.

"Oh, great. Both of you have attitude. This is going to be fun."

The strange voice snapped Aleksandr out of his thoughts.

"Dad," Evelyn laughed. "We're trying to have a very important conversation. Serious and stuff."

"Oh, well, I didn't know that *stuff* was involved," her father said from somewhere off screen. "By all means, continue. I'll just stick to driving."

"You do that."

Aleksandr marveled at how easily the man shifted his daughter's mood. By all rights, she should have been stuck in a state of fear right now. Instead, she was laughing, acting as if there wasn't a single thing wrong in the world.

"Anyway," Evelyn said as she came back to the conversation, "we need to meet up and take care of this."

"How are you so calm?"

"Oh, I'm freaking out on the inside," she said with a tense, toothy grin. "But, I have a new life purpose. I've recently dedicated myself to a singular task. I'm going to kill the Furies. You in or out?"

"In," Aleksandr said instantly. "Do you have a plan?"

"Of course. And here it is; ask you what your plan is."

"The beauty is in the simplicity," her father said.

"Hey, I'm a big picture person," she countered. "And all of my research hasn't brought up anything that could be useful. It's like they don't exist."

"Ivan has been thinking about that," Aleksandr said.

It had never occurred to him that his little brother's obsession with the paranormal would ever become a necessity for survival.

"To him, it seems that they might not have been summoned by the man I ..."

There was a moment of awkward silence before Juan cleared his throat.

"I'm not about to judge you, young man."

Aleksandr barely kept from snorting. "So, you know I've killed people and you don't care?"

"I was told that you weren't a *willing* participant. That your parents forced you."

It couldn't be that easy. "Did Evelyn tell you that I almost killed her?"

"She said it was the other way around," Juan said after a moment of hesitation.

"It was," Evelyn insisted with a distinct note of offence. "He's got a solid jab but his footwork's a joke. I was totally going to win that fight."

Aleksandr wondered if she honestly believed that or if it was a story she convinced herself with over the years. She would have been his first female victim. Tossed into the canyon with all the others he had been forced to murder for Olga and Petya's amusement. Tension turned his muscles to stone. The pop and click of his mangled knuckles told him that he was subconsciously clenching his fists.

Years of beating people to death with bare hands had left the joints functional but permanently distorted.

"Aleksandr," Evelyn snapped. "Focus. What was Ivan thinking about the Furies?"

He sucked in a deep breath. "The man I killed. He told me that they were coming, in his dying breath. I always thought that this was what had called them, but Ivan thinks that it should be more complicated than that."

"So, he thinks someone else sent them after us?" Evelyn asked.

"Essentially."

She frowned in thought. "Like who?"

"His parents," Juan said as if it were obvious. "It's all about revenge, right? Well, they're the ones left standing who would want it."

Aleksandr pondered that. It was hard for him to believe that anyone would pass that kind of retaliation onto someone else. *Half of the satisfaction would be getting the kill yourself.* However, he had enough sense not to say it out loud. *It's not like I know what a normal response is to anything.*

"Okay," Evelyn said with a slight smile. "Yeah. I mean, logically, whoever called them would know how to kill them, right?"

"Or at least stop them," Juan added.

She shrugged. "Either way works."

"Right." Juan couldn't keep the hint of amusement from his voice. "So, our first step is track down this man's remaining family. We'll need his name."

"Right," Evelyn chirped.

Silence followed as she stared at Aleksandr through the screen. He stared back, not wanting to have to state the obvious out loud. Silence. Aleksandr leaned his back against the wall and skirted his eyes to the side.

"I don't know it."

"I'm sorry?" Juan said.

He must have been trying to catch sight of Aleksandr on the screen because there was the distinct sound of the car swerving.

"You killed a man without knowing his name?" Juan asked.

"There is a distinct note of judgment in your voice," Aleksandr replied.

"Sorry, but ... Nah, I'm not really sorry. How does that happen?"

"Dad," Evelyn hissed through her teeth.

"Why would I ask?" Aleksandr said at the same time. "It wasn't for enjoyment. It was necessity."

"Seems to me that you could have at least given them the respect of learning who they were."

Shock rattled through Aleksandr, making him bark out laughter before he could suppress it.

"Don't you feel guilty at all?" Juan asked.

"Dad. Stop."

"Not at all. I did what I had to," Aleksandr answered.

"Simple as that, huh, son?"

"If I died, my twins would have been alone with Olga and Petya. I never wanted to kill, but I would have slaughtered the world to keep that from happening."

"Right," Juan muttered. His next words came out with a stronger edge. "Look, I can't imagine being in your position. I get that. But, I have to ask, why didn't you just kill your parents?"

That caught Aleksandr off guard. "Didn't Evelyn explain Vegas to you?"

"All of his older siblings liked their parents," Evelyn whispered. "He didn't have any backup."

"Okay," Juan said repeatedly for an extended period of time. Eventually, he pulled over and leaned into the view of the phone's camera. "So, what do we do now? I don't suppose your parents kept a record or something."

"Videos," he said.

"We need those videos," Juan said.

"You want to break into the FBI and steal evidence?" Aleksandr said.

Apparently, Evelyn took after her father.

"Have you got a better way?" Juan shot back.

"The ghost town tour." Both men fell silent and waited for Evelyn to elaborate. "Some people bought the ghost town and turned it into a kind of murder tour. Like a psychotic Disneyland or something. You can go around and learn all about Petya and Olga. There'd have to be something about the victims. And you can't tell me that those sickos didn't tuck some souvenirs away somewhere."

"Princess," Juan said slowly.

"It's okay, dad. I can do this."

"The things that happened to you there—"

"Are nothing compared to the Furies," she cut in.

"I'll come with you," Aleksandr said, the words tasting like ash in his mouth.

"You don't have to. Just, point me in the right direction."

"Evelyn, I've got this," he assured. "It'll take a few hours for us to get there. Remember the hotel out of town? The one I was supposed to drop you off at? We'll meet there."

"I'm not sure that I like this plan," Juan said.

"It'll be fine, dad. We'll be in and out. You remember what he looks like, right Aleksandr?"

"Yeah."

"See?" Evelyn beamed to her father. "Easy peasy."

"You and I have different definitions of that," Juan noted.

"Dad, please, a little trust?"

"I trust you." The older man said the words as if they had personally offended them.

Even through the phone line, Aleksandr could sense the growing resentment of that surrender. For her part, Evelyn was enjoying herself. Four years of this and her reaction to impending death still made him uneasy. There was a precipice she reached, a moment when fear shifted into a challenge. And that was just dangling a steak in front of a rabid dog. It seemed like she was allergic to doing anything the easy way. *One day that's going to get her killed,* he thought.

"Okay, so we're all in agreement?" Evelyn amended at her father's scoff.

"Reluctant agreement?"

"I'll accept that," Juan said. "*Reluctantly.*"

"How long would it take for you to get back there?" Evelyn asked.

"All things going well, about eighteen hours, forty minutes."

She stared at him through the little screen, her dark eyes squinting slightly. "You just know that off the top of your head, huh?"

He didn't have to say it out loud for her to catch on. The ghost town would forever be the center point of his existence. Everything was compared to it. Everything existed around it. She offered him a slight, pitiful smile but didn't try to console him.

"We'll see you in a day or so," she said eventually. "Watch your back."

"You too." There was nothing left to say so he didn't bother to keep the call going.

Hanging up, he stalked into the main house. The twins had taken their meals into the small dining room set beyond the kitchen. There wasn't a whole lot of house to speak of, so he instantly spotted them at the table. It was still strange to see them with red hair instead of the natural dark brown. Even more than the odd times he caught a glimpse at his own reflection. But the dye and forced Irish accents worked as a great cover. Red hair, especially in town, was rare. It drew attention away from their faces.

"Bad news, guys." He stopped short when neither of them turned around.

Something cold and hard settled into the pit of his stomach. Shoving his phone into his pocket, he clenched his now free hands, hearing each of his knuckles crack. The twins still didn't turn. They sat silently. Still as stone. Staring at the far wall. While the twins had begun to embrace the concept of teen rebellion, they didn't ignore him. Aleksandr slowly reached behind him, pulling his pocket-knife out from his back pocket.

Slowly, he crept forward. One press of a button and the blade slipped free with a familiar hiss of sliding steel. It was small but strong. He flipped it around in his palm as his moved silently across the floor. Tiles gave way to wood boards and the twins still hadn't acknowledged him. He carefully watched for even the slightest trace of movement. There was nothing. Not even the slightest motion of breathing.

Aleksandr leaned forward and craned his neck. Even when he crossed beside them, obviously in their peripheral vision, the twins remained still. Messy, sweaty red hair gave way to the pale skin. His breath caught in his throat and his chest crushed tight. Their faces were gone, replaced by an unblemished blank slate.

In the same instant, they snapped their heads towards him. Aleksandr lunged back. Eyes wide, legs bashing into the low coffee table that worked to separate the space. It tripped him up and he fell hard. The chair legs scraped across the floorboards as the mockery of the twins stood. Aleksandr struggled to regain his footing, surging up, the blade held carefully and ready to strike with precision. But the monstrosities didn't come closer towards him. Even on his feet, they seemed to loom over him. Creatures far bigger than their skins allowed. *Where's the third?* His brain was thick and sluggish with fear, leaving the question to swirl without a hope of an answer.

The world went silent, lost beneath the rushing of blood through his veins. His fingers moved restlessly, squeezing and shifting across the handle of his pocket-knife. One of the twins stepped towards him. Pale, slender fingers reaching, stretched out and grasping. Aleksandr swung out. The knife met little resistance, slicing cleanly through the skin of its arm and releasing a wave of blood. A scream broke the silence. The noise sounded so much like Ivan that shock hit Aleksandr like a solid blow.

It only took a blink of an eye for reality to come rushing back into focus. Ivan now stood before him, gripping tightly to his forearm, the tight squeeze of his fingers doing little to stop the blood that flowed out onto the floor. Nadya had already retrieved the first-aid kit from the kitchen and was fastening a tourniquet. No one was screaming. There was no chaos. Simply a passing glimpse of understanding that crossed their eyes.

"Ivan," Aleksandr gasped. "I'm so sorry!"

"It's fine," Ivan said.

"Not that deep," Nadya added.

The reassurances didn't ease the inferno of guilt that threatened to char him to the bone. Rushing forward, he gently cupped his brother's arm, surprised when he was allowed to make contact.

"I didn't know it was you," he whispered, not trusting his voice to be any louder.

"Yeah, I figured that out myself," Ivan chuckled as Nadya continued to work.

She secured the ends of the bandage and slugged Aleksandr in the arm. "You didn't even hit an artery. You're losing your touch."

"We don't want him to hit an artery right now," Ivan snapped.

She rolled her eyes. "You know what I mean. Alek, was this a mental snap or have they found us?"

All he had to do was nod. Everything else was muscle memory. A routine that all knew well, leaving no need for discussion or debate. Nadya grabbed their 'go-bags', packs already filled with everything they would need to flee. Ivan cleaned up the more damning of the evidence, and Aleksandr secured their method of escape. It only took three minutes and they were out the door, never once glancing back. Each one unsettled that the attack had been so short lived. Aleksandr couldn't shake the feeling that they were being manipulated. *There had only been two of them. Where was the third? Had it stayed with Eve?*

A thought came to him as they piled into the car, and it left him cold.

They want all of us in the same place. We're heading into a trap.

Chapter 4

The motel was cheap, although it was trying hard not to look like it.

Everything was clean but worn. Sitting on the end of the bed, she restlessly ran her hands over the sheets, feeling the rough material scratch her palms. Her father wouldn't stop pacing. There wasn't a lot of space, so he kept passing in front of her every few seconds. It was putting her on edge. They hadn't spoken much since Aleksandr had hung up on them. It hadn't occurred to her, under the city that had given away to crimson soaked sand, how much she needed the distraction.

The desert wasn't that far from the city she had grown up in. Only a few hours at the most. But she had only ever been there once. When Petya had taken her. When the Furies had first come storming into her life. When she had fled, bloody and beaten, she had promised herself that she'd never be back. That there was nothing in Heaven or Earth that could force her to. But here she was. In a cramped room in the middle of nowhere, listening to a dying air-conditioner struggle to make a difference against the hellish heat.

Of all the things that had remained to haunt her, the heat was the worst. It was something she hadn't been able to breathe in. It had drained her, crushed her, and left part of her mind convinced that she hadn't survived the first attack. That she was already in hell.

"Dad, is there any chance I could get you to sit down for a bit? You're kind of putting me on edge."

"Right." He sat down on the other bed and patted his hands against his knees. This lasted about a minute before he was back to pacing. "Sorry, princess. I'm having a few issues dealing with this."

"Yeah, it's an awkward situation. Maybe I should have found a nicer way to tell you about all of this."

"What? No. Well, yes, there's that. Right now, however, I'm focusing on the fact that we're literally waiting in a cheap motel room for a serial killer to show up. I've seen this day time movie, honey, and it doesn't end well."

"Aleksandr won't hurt me."

Juan paused mid-stride and stared at her.

"Okay, yeah, he totally would. But only if I threatened the twins. And I love those kids. They're creepy as hell but they have their charm."

"And they've killed people, too?"

She shrugged. "Honestly, it never came up in conversation."

"Really?"

"It seemed rude to ask."

Juan shook his head, huffed a breath, and started to pace again. "How did this become your life?"

"Petya decided that I looked enough like a guy to ease Aleksandr into killing girls."

That made her father pause again. "I'll never get that. If you're not in boxing gear, you're in dresses."

A verbal response wasn't necessary. Instead, Evelyn just lifted her arm and flexed. In her father's eyes, she'd always be his tiny little Puerto Rican princess.

But kick-boxing wasn't really a sport that left one looking slight and delicate. Before the attacks, she had used the ring as an emotional outlet. There was just something so relaxing about beating the hell out of someone. After Petya and Olga, not to mention the Furies, the sport had gone from a hobby to an obsession. Consequently, she could now lift as much as some of his firefighter buddies. Juan studied her for a moment before he scoffed.

"Petya was an idiot."

"He also murdered people."

"Thank you for reminding me," Juan said sharply before resuming his pacing. "Could those things show up again?"

"Sure. But don't worry, they're like cats. They don't go in for the kill until they've fully terrorized their prey."

He didn't stop moving as he glared at her. "Never get a job as a counselor."

The sound of car tires crunching against the gravel parking lot drew their attention. Evelyn leaped at the chance to escape the conversation and hurried outside. The car had barely stopped moving before two gangly kids hurled themselves out and made a beeline for her.

"You're still alive," one of them declared.

"You're a red head," she said back.

Phone cameras didn't really do the dye job justice. A mix of relief and delirium rocked her, making her giggle happily as the twins collided into her chest.

"Damn, you kids have gotten strong," she said as they squeezed her tightly.

She wasn't going to mention that they were now as tall as she was. They hadn't lost their baby faces yet.

"How did the game go?" she asked. "You guys did get to finish it before you had to come here, right?"

They both started talking at the same time, Nadya explaining how she was the best goalie in existence while Ivan insisted they would have lost it if weren't for his shooting skills. Evelyn couldn't stop smiling. The second attack had put them securely into her life, and she felt a fear now she hadn't experienced before. She was terrified that the Furies would come for them. *They're just starting their life,* a voice in her head whispered. *They need to survive this.*

"What happened to your arm?" she asked.

The question never got an answer. Instead, they had noticed Juan and had gone to fuss over him as if he were a zoo exhibit. The noise they created was deafening. Watching them served as enough of a distraction that Aleksandr appearing next to her was a surprise. She didn't have time to catch her laughter before it was out.

"I'm sorry," she said. "Your hair. It's all gone. I can see your face."

"You saw me yesterday."

"On the phone. That doesn't count."

Their first encounter, from introduction to fleeing into the night, had all happened without her seeing two thirds of his face. How he had managed to see through the mattered tendrils of his fringe was a mystery she had never solved. Now he had a buzz cut. And wasn't covered head to toe in mud and sweat.

"I have to ask." She pointed at his hair. "Can I touch it?"

"No."

"You're no fun."

Aleksandr had taken to chewing on his thumbnail and didn't stop as he replied, "There's something wrong with you."

"We've been through this already," she said with a dramatic sigh. "There are things that scare me more than the Furies."

"Ending up like your mother."

Evelyn bit her tongue but couldn't keep from wincing. There was no chance that Aleksandr missed it. He was far more observant than he let on.

"How is she?"

"Well, she knows. So there's that."

That got his attention. "You told her?"

"Dad did."

He paused. "How did that go?"

"Surprisingly well."

Still gnawing on his nail, he studied her carefully. "Are you alright?"

She understood now why he hid his face so much. His eyes gave everything away. It stunned her to see the amount of sympathy he had for her situation.

"Yeah. You know, I'm starting to think that you're actually a big softy."

His eyes narrowed. "I'll leave you to die in a ditch."

"We'll see," she dismissed.

They couldn't avoid it any longer.

Aleksandr finally bit the bullet and stated of obvious.

"I think the Furies are setting us up."

"I got that impression, too," she said. "I've been trying to think of what they're planning, but I've got nothing. You?"

"All I can think is that they want us to die where it began."

This is a suicide trip. The thought made her sneer. "This is the easiest way to get the name. So, I'm going. If you have a problem, tell me now."

"Your dad shouldn't come with us."

"Well, duh. I can't talk him out of it, though. He's not hearing it. He's in that protective dad mode, you know?"

The words were out before it occurred to her how cutting that sentence might be. Holding her breath, she looked over to him, an apology ready on her lips. Instead of pain, she found a look of determination seeping into his eyes.

"Yeah, I do." Switching to Russian, he called out to the twins. Whatever he had said was enough to have them heading over to the rusted vending machines. Juan watched them go before tossing Aleksandr a questioning look. "We haven't properly met."

Juan took the hint and stalked closer. "You're right. We have a few things to discuss."

"Dad," Evelyn said, taking a slight step closer, subtly trying to put herself between them.

Aleksandr was shorter than her father. And his body was far more lopsided, carrying all of his strength in his upper body. But there wasn't a doubt in her mind that Aleksandr would slaughter him.

"He's a friend, remember?"

"We need to talk about your friends," Juan said.

"You really should have some standards," Aleksandr added.

"Thank you. It's good to have someone with common sense in the mix."

Evelyn looked between the two of them. "I feel like this was a bad idea."

"Can I have a second with your dad?" Aleksandr asked.

"Um, sure," she said slowly, eyes still flicking between them. "I'll just check my phone or something. Let the menfolk talk."

"You can stay if you have a kid you're worried about," Aleksandr said.

She made a dramatic show of rolling her eyes and pulling out her mobile, but she didn't move that far off, careful to remain in ear shot. By the time they had struggled through the awkward introductions, Evelyn was just about bored enough to wander off.

"You know you can't come," Aleksandr said, instantly seizing Evelyn's attention once more.

"I'm supposed to leave her with you?" Juan asked.

"Sir, with all due respect, this would break you."

"You don't know me very well."

"Yes, I do," Aleksandr said. "If you haven't caught on, I'm raising two kids with no concept of what it takes to be a good father. So I call Evelyn and I ask her what you would do. I know you, sir. But you don't know my family. You don't know what they're capable of."

"I did my research."

Aleksandr chuckled. "Concept and reality don't keep close company. Right now, you have a concept. A notion. Believe me, that's a lot easier to live with than the reality."

"They've made a sick theme park out of it."

"People with no connection to the victims, to the *reality*, have done that. Are you really ready to see the room they kept her in? See photos of the others they took? What they did to them? Learn just what they intended to do to your little girl? Concept and reality will clash. And you'll never be able to go back."

The silence that followed broke Evelyn's heart. She blinked slowly, feeling tears swell in her eyes.

"I can't leave her to face that alone," Juan said.

"She won't be."

"You want me to trust you with my only child."

"I'm hoping I can trust you with mine," Aleksandr said. "Ivan and Nadya are just starting to adjust. And they've done that by suppressing as much as they could. The rest, I spent my life trying to keep from them. Going back there now ... seeing it all again ... they won't survive it."

"Are you actually asking me to look after them?"

"They're just kids," Aleksandr said, his normally rough voice deepening slightly. "They can handle a lot. Run into hell with nothing but a smile and glint in their eyes. But not this. It's too much."

The muscles in Juan's neck jumped as he ground his teeth together. Instead of responding, however, he glanced over his shoulder, seeking out the twins. Evelyn quickly looked down at her phone, trying to be subtle. Her father didn't call her out for eavesdropping. His attention was fixed on the two gangly kids that were debating over which soda to get from the machine. It was impossible to make out what they were saying, but their voices were a soft murmur marked with bursts of laughter.

"They're not really your kids, are they?" Juan asked numbly.

"No. My parents never crossed that line," Aleksandr added as an afterthought. "Well, not with me or them. I made a point not to know what the rest of the family was up to."

"Is there any part of your life that isn't greatly disturbing?" Juan asked.

"I like going to planetariums," Aleksandr offered.

That made Juan chuckle and he finally turned back to face him. "You're the only parent those kids have ever known, aren't you?"

"Yes, sir."

"You're all they've got."

Aleksandr nodded once.

"I'm all Evelyn's got. It's always been her and me. I've failed her so many times. I can't do it again."

"I'll watch her back."

"And what about the emotional fallout?" Juan hissed. "Do you really think she's going to be fine? If you make her go back there—"

"With all due respect, I can help her with that more than you can. You can sympathize. But you can't possibly understand. And if you come along, she's going to be more concerned about your safety than anything else."

"Do I get a say in this?" Evelyn asked. "Or is this something menfolk need to sort out."

Juan sighed. "You listened to the whole thing?"

"Duh."

"Okay. What do you think?"

"You know me. I'm all for teamwork," Evelyn grinned.

Juan took a slow breath as he thought it over, weighing his options and anxiety.

"Here's the deal," he said abruptly. He jabbed a finger towards Aleksandr. "If you come back without her, I get to keep one of your kids as a replacement."

Aleksandr's hands balled and every muscle in his face pinched tight.

"God, kid, I'm joking. Breaking the tension. You really think I'm that much of a weirdo?" Juan shook his head and tossed a lost look towards his daughter. "I'm already regretting this."

Chapter 5

Aleksandr's knuckles clicked audibly as he tightened his grip on the steering wheel. The small town had shrunk out of sight of the review mirror, leaving only the scorched desert sand stretched out before them. Winter didn't seem to touch this place. Heat pulsed against the windows, struggling against the air-conditioning to reach them. Tension twisted up his gut and wrapped his muscles in barbed wire. Fine tremors rattled along his arms. He squeezed his hands tighter in an attempt to suppress it. It had to be visible, but Evelyn didn't comment. She hadn't said a word since they had left the motel. His hands were twitching with the urge to turn on the radio. Normally, he enjoyed silence. Right now, it hurt. A real solid ache in the center of his chest that made it hard to breathe.

A cluster of buildings rose up from the sand. Dark figures that the light didn't seem to touch. The air grew heavier as they neared. Sweat broke out across the back of his neck, chilling his skin as his heart began to thud, pounding like a drum against his bones. He swallowed thickly, trying to move the mound of dirt that had gathered in his throat.

"You feel that, too, right?" Evelyn said in a whisper. Turning to him, she mimicked his gulp, her eyes slightly widened. "It's not just me."

He nodded once.

"This is a really stupid idea, isn't it?" she asked.

Again, he opted for nodding rather than talking. He didn't trust his voice. Sinking back into her seat, Evelyn started to shift her shoulders, a clear sign that she was readying herself for a fight.

"So," she clicked her tongue a few times. "Did I just get us killed?"

"Too soon to tell."

"Right. Sorry 'bout that."

A small smile twitched the corner of his mouth. "I got here myself."

The buildings were taking shape and they were soon moving through the sand-drenched streets. It was as if he had never left. The new owners hadn't put any effort into cleaning up the place, most likely wanting to keep the aesthetics intact.

The winds shifted the sands, pushing them up against the sides of the buildings, and drifted across the streets. The broken remains of the windows caught the light, making them flash as they passed. Most of the buildings had stood unused even when his family had run the place. Olga and Petya had chosen structures at random to use as murder rooms. And even then, no attempt had been made to keep the buildings from falling into ruin. As they snaked around the building, climbing higher up onto one of the dunes, he spotted a few roofs that had caved in. The only other change he could pinpoint were the small signs that were affixed at the intersections, marking the path to the house that had last served as his home.

'Red Death Murder House' stood in large block letters before an almost cartoonish picture of a bloody knife pointing the way. That, more than anything else, made Aleksandr feel sick. He had prepared himself for a few people running about, clicking off photographs and sharing a cheap thrill. The reality that confronted him as he turned the last corner was a punch to the gut.

They were still a few blocks away from the main house. A barricade prevented them from going any further, leaving the visitors to park along the street. People filled the space, milling around in a cloud of color and noise. Stalls littered the footpath. A large sign posted over one announced it as the gathering point for the tours. Others sold food and drink. Speckled in-between were brightly decorated patches of souvenir stands. Aleksandr yanked the wheel, parking in front of a caravan, and killed the engine. He didn't move. Evelyn didn't, either.

In uncomfortable silence, they watched a group of friends stagger out to cross the road before them. In a haze of giggles, one of the women posed for a photograph, screaming in mock terror as her friend reared up behind her with a plastic knife. Bile rushed up Aleksandr's throat, burning the back of his mouth. He swallowed thickly to keep it down. Beside him, Evelyn squirmed in her seat. The muscles of her jaw clenched, the tendons of her throat bulging, a molten red swelling under her dark skin. Her rage was an almost tangible thing. Just when he was sure she was about to snap, the picture was taken and the group went on their way. Hidden behind sunglasses and tinted windows, they tracked the group back to their SUV. The group didn't notice the fury and disgust that was leveled towards them. Not even when they passed by.

"The perfect victims gushing over serial killers," Evelyn hissed out from between her teeth. "Is that what they mean by irony?"

He turned his head just enough to catch sight of her in the corner of his eyes. "Perfect victims?"

"No situational awareness. Not one of them moved like they could fight. No one protected their personal stuff. Even I could have stolen their wallets and found out exactly where they lived. Did you notice that they didn't even check the back seat before getting in? Yeah, there's a group of them, but a whole heap of people could hide in that trunk."

Her voice was monotonous, but her muscles hadn't stopped twitching with the tension building under her skin.

"You've been reading up on this?"

"It didn't even take Petya two minutes to kidnap me. A girl kind of takes that personally. I wanted to make sure it couldn't happen again."

He hesitated to tell her the truth of the matter. "You can't."

"Can't I?" Whipping around, he was suddenly faced with her full, wrathful focus.

"No. Not unless you're willing to obsess about it as much as they do. Serial killers," he clicked his tongue, struggling to find a way to express it. "It's *all* they think about. You can't compete with that."

"Yeah, well, I can make myself a harder target."

He nodded his agreement and scanned the area around them. The crowd was larger than he had anticipated and he growled. Living in a small town had taught him something about himself; he really hated people.

"Four years!" Evelyn declared in a sudden burst. She kicked at the dashboard before vainly trying to work her anger out. "I get that people are fascinated with killers and all, but come on! Four years is not enough to build up a Psycho Disneyland!"

"When the monsters die, everyone wants to dance on their graves."

"So? Respectable time limits should still exist."

"I heard that they did tours after Jack the Ripper went quiet," he said idly. "And the Manson Family ranch was a big draw."

"They didn't kill people on the ranch," she snapped, dragging her hands over her hair. "Don't they know that we have the internet now? They don't have to go this far to satisfy their morbid curiosity."

"If you say so," he mumbled before finally turning to look at her. "You're the optimist here."

"Oh, that can't be right."

He arched an eyebrow.

"Damn it." A small laugh bubbled up from her throat, breaking the static charge in the air. "That's just wrong. I never agreed to that."

"Well, get better friends," he dismissed with a shrug and a smirk.

It made her snort and she thumped the back of her head against the seat. "Okay, let's just get this over with." She sniffed the air. "I smell pizza. Do you think we'll have time to grab a slice before the Furies show up?"

"There's that sunny disposition."

"Oh, I will hit you in the face," she chuckled as they climbed out of the car.

Without the air-conditioning, the heat moved forward to roll over their flesh. The sudden change in temperature made him shiver as he jogged around the hood to meet her on the footpath.

"How long do you think it will take for someone to notice you look just like Radmiar?" she asked, her light tone not fully covering her concern. "I mean, red hair and sunglasses aren't exactly the most brilliant of disguises."

"Don't worry about it," he dismissed as they moved towards the check-in booth.

"Fine, but you're on your own if you're recognized."

They'll recognize you first, he thought. Pressing his lips, he kept himself from voicing it. She must have read it on his face because she stiffened and pushed her large sunglasses higher up on her nose. She obviously hadn't thought that part through.

They came to the booth and picked up the first pamphlet they could find, subtly trying to disrupt the view of their faces. The people before them were settled quickly and they stepped forward.

"Welcome to hell on earth," the worker said with a bubbly smile. "The first and original Red Death tour. Are you here for the tour?"

"Yes, thanks." Aleksandr masked his Russian accent with an Irish one. Perfecting accents had been an important lesson for the Sokolovsky household. It was surprisingly useful. "You take cash?"

"Of course. It's $24 for an adult ticket."

Aleksandr froze in place, only snapping out of his shock when he heard Evelyn's barely suppressed snort. *$24 for a death tour.* He forced a smile and handed over the cluster of bills.

"Hold onto your ticket stub so you can get a ten percent discount at the restaurant, the Masquerade."

"The what?" Evelyn asked.

"It's just a little inside joke," the woman said. "If you didn't know, their alias,

The Red Death, came from one of Poe's short stories. So does the masquerade reference. We feel that only he truly understood the true horror of their crimes."

"Well, him, and all the people they killed," Evelyn noted. "I'd say they'd have a fair idea."

Aleksandr cleared his throat, drawing the woman's attention away from Evelyn's wolfish grin. "Does the tour go inside of the building they used for their home?"

There were few things Aleksandr had witnessed that creeped him out as much as Evelyn's fixed, ecstatic smile. She beamed up at him and he struggled not to cringe.

"Yeah. We want to see where they slept. It's just so strange, to know people that evil did something as mundane as sleep."

"They were human, just like the rest of us," the worker said, head tilting and smile still in place. "We're the only species on the planet capable of cruelty."

"Never owned a cat, have you?" Evelyn replied.

Aleksandr began to chew on his thumbnail, keeping his silence as Evelyn smiled her plastic grin.

"I don't think a cat toying with a mouse is the same thing," the woman said, her smile faltering for the first time.

"Not to the mouse," Evelyn muttered under her breath.

The woman's eyes narrowed. "You have to admit that humans are the only creatures capable of true evil. We're the only ones that have war."

Evelyn's burst of laughter surprised them all. "War is just establishing a pecking order. Even chickens do that."

"They don't fight for oil."

"That's just a resource. Like water or food. Animals fight for that all the time. They have battles to the death for the right to mount the female. Now *that's* sick."

"What about genocide?"

"Do you know there's a species of bees that infiltrates another hive and then kills them all?"

Aleksandr, shifting his attention to the soft skin of his nail bed, tried to hide his smile as he plucked the tickets from the worker's stunned fingers.

"She means that evil's a part of the world order," he said with a casual shrug. "When is the next tour?"

Jumping on the chance to end the conversation, the woman pointed out a small bench a bit farther away, marked with a ghost mask fixed onto a pole. A golf cart was rattling towards the meeting place, dragging a long line of carriages behind it, filled with guests on their way back down.

"If you hurry, you can catch the next tour."

"Lucky us," Evelyn grinned, squeezing Aleksandr's shoulder like an excited child.

They thanked the woman and moved away. Evelyn couldn't stop rolling her eyes as they followed her gesture towards the collection point. It was clear even behind her sunglasses. Almost to the point that she staggered, slightly dizzy. He put an arm out behind her back, ready to catch her if she fell.

"A murder amusement park," she whispered to him. "I'm not sure I can put up with an hour of this."

Aleksandr checked the tickets. "The tour's an hour and a half."

"The Lord is testing me."

"Remember that we need to keep a low profile," he said as they neared the crowd gathering around the bench.

"I didn't do anything."

"People remember the annoying and obnoxious." Before she could say anything, he continued, "Pick your fights, Evelyn."

"I have enough anger to handle them all," she replied.

Grabbing her arm, he pulled her closer and whispered in a low voice, "If you have a problem, tell me now."

Her brow furrowed. "I'm good."

Silence lingered between them as the golf cart came closer.

"Alek, I've got this."

She tried to jerk her arm free, but he tightened his grip.

"There's a time pressure here."

"Nah, really?"

"I need to know that you have my back." He tried to keep the edge of panic from entering into his voice.

Paranoia had been bred into him. It always played on the edges of his mind. He could feel it now, digging into the fragile edges of his trust, eroding it away. It was possible to see the moment she figured it out. Her features softened and her shoulders slumped.

"I'm good." The words came out with far more conviction than they had the first time.

The low, heavy sound of mournful church bells played through the speaker system of the cart as it pulled to the curb. Neither one of them could resist rolling their eyes at the dramatics. Especially when they noticed the tour guide was dressed up like he was trying to channel Petya Sokolovsky. Paying as little attention as possible to the guide, Evelyn and Aleksandr took the back seat and kept to themselves. Flying under everyone's radar wasn't hard. All the other guests were captivated by the idea of finally getting to see what they came here for, and the guide, Brad, was eager to engage to stoke their expectations.

The trip up to the house was slow and bumpy, even as it stuck to the only cleaned road. Aleksandr didn't know where to look. The desert, the houses, the people, all of them sparked a grotesque, simmering nausea within him. It made it hard to successfully tune out everything Brad was saying. It was astounding how much they got wrong.

"Breathe," Evelyn whispered next to him.

Aleksandr sucked in a noisy breath. "Why do they have to romanticize them?"

"They're the new Bonnie and Clyde."

He tipped his head closer to her. "Bonnie was a necrophiliac and Clyde was gay."

"What?" Her stunned outburst drew the attention of the guide.

In the split-second pause, they both knew they had messed up. Slowly, they turned to see the realization crossing Brad's face.

"Twenty bucks he makes you first," Evelyn mumbled out of the corner of her mouth just before Brad spoke.

"Oh, wow. You're Evelyn, right? Evelyn Figueroa."

Every person on the tram turned instantly to look at her.

"Damn it," she groaned.

"No one told us you were on the tour," Brad grinned.

"Yeah, I was trying to keep a low profile," Evelyn said on reflex.

It seemed that she remembered her talk with Aleksandr the second after that, because she cast him an apologetic glance.

"Sorry—" Brad was cut off by one of the guest.

"Why on earth are you here? Why would you come back?"

"Therapy," Evelyn burst out, fleshing out the idea as she went. "They said coming back here and seeing it all will help me find closure."

"You look familiar," a woman before them said, eyeing Aleksandr carefully.

"Yeah," he said in his fake, thick accent. "I've got one of those faces."

"What's it like being back here?" someone asked. They barely had time to finish their question before another disembodied voice asked, "How did you make it across the desert on foot?" At the same moment, someone else on the other side of the crowd pressed, "What was it like being alone with them?" The questions started to bombard her from every direction, each one overlapping a dozen others. "Are you going down into the cage room?" "Did their kids really come after you?"

Evelyn bared her clenched teeth, her knuckles pressing like white peaks against her skin. But she held on. Kept her silence. Fighting with every ounce of control she had to keep her word to Aleksandr.

"Enough!" he snarled.

Seeing that she had permission, Evelyn took it from there.

"The last person who wanted an interview with me offered me $60,000. Meet it or shut the hell up."

"Right," Brad rushed to say. "Of course. We understand. It's just that, well, I don't think any of us expected you to be here. You have to anticipate that we might have a few questions. Really, you probably should have given us some warning."

Aleksandr pressed one of his knuckles into Evelyn's thigh. An uncomfortable point of contact to tell her that he, too, thought this guy was a moron. Also to remind her that they didn't have time for violence.

"Sorry about that," Evelyn said through clenched teeth, her cheeks pulling taut, forming that creepy smile. "How rude of me. Oh, look, we're here now. Let's get on with the tour and completely ignore all other factors."

Evelyn had already jumped out before the carriage had lurched to a stop, Aleksandr close on her heels. They were forced to linger as the others took their time. That left a few agonizing minutes with nothing to distract him from just where he was standing. The two-story building he had called home for years loomed beside him like a dark, consuming beast. Time had shredded the white paint from the outside, warping the wooden slats and breaking apart the shutters. There was new damage. There was something within the pattern of the damage that he found theatrical. He wondered if the new owners had a hand in it.

Aleksandr blinked and the world shifted. Like a projection played upon reality, the sky darkened and the ghostly figure of a car emerged beside the golf cart train. A dark, showy image of his father and mother stood beside the front of the car, intoxicated by each other's company, completely oblivious to the child and unconscious woman dumped only a few feet away. The moment in time lingered before him. Like a weak film projection, his memories began to unfold, the cast of ghostly players passing through the unsuspecting tourists. No one else saw them and Aleksandr could only watch in transfixed horror.

The touch of fingers made him whirl around. Nadya, years younger than she was now, stood beside him, small hand grasped onto his. Each finger a solid, real touch. Large eyes pleading and filled with terror.

"Alek."

Her voice was laced with another, both recognizable and distinct.

"Aleksandr," the dual voices pressed again.

"Nadya?" His voice was a whisper but loud enough to twist up his little sister's face.

Not her. Not real. The words echoed in his head. He turned back to the ghostly image of the car. To the still body that lay sprawled near the back wheel.

"Alek." The voice was sharp and joined by an equally violent tug on his arm.

In the time it took to turn back again, the memories evaporated. The images of his family dispersed like smoke in the breeze, leaving only the present moment. Clear and simple. He looked down, silently studying the fingers that were now wrapped tightly around his palm. Not Nadya's fingers. But still slender. Frail. Tiny next to his. Unmarred and darker. Evelyn pulled her hand away.

"Okay, no touching, I got it," Evelyn said, her voice now solely her own. "But do you wanna fill me in on what's going on?"

"I was just thinking." His voice was slack and slow.

Evelyn stepped closer and whispered sharply, "You called me Nadya."

"This is where I first saw you. You were right there. I was there," he pointed out the positions as discreetly as he could. "It seemed too insignificant at the time."

"Aw, I'm significant?" She was teasing him, trying to use annoyance to get him to focus.

"I don't think we would have made it out alive with anyone else," he said.

"Yeah. I guess I'm the best present he ever got you," she smirked.

Aleksandr couldn't help but smile at that. "Yes. You were."

"You know, when you agree with it, I start to take offence." The smirk on her face eroded any edge the words might have had.

"You're the only friend I've ever had."

After a moment of hesitation, she smiled slightly and took his hand again. "Wow. Emotional trauma makes you sappy." By now, the other tourists were starting to edge in closer. Near enough to overhear their conversation and force them to edit their words. "Was this a visit?"

Aleksandr could only shrug with one shoulder. It hadn't felt like the other times. Nothing had attacked him. *But they have tricked you into hurting Ivan.*

"Just stay close," he whispered. "I don't want to get confused."

The understanding that welled in her gaze told him they were on the same page, both worried about this change. They had survived twice. Now the Furies had changed the rules.

"Yeah, well, now you're putting up with this," Evelyn said as she took his hand again.

Physical touch. A tether to reality. Proof that the other was real. He noted each benefit in his head as they focused on the speech Brad was reciting by heart. Aleksandr winced at the dramatics. And couldn't resist leaning slightly closer to Evelyn and whispering, remembering just in time to put on his fake accent.

"He's really putting on a show for you."

"Shut up," Evelyn hissed back, but there was a chuckle in her voice that made him grin.

The Furies feed off of fear, Aleksandr told himself. *Let the bastards starve.* He didn't pay much attention to the inflated lies that Brad prattled on about. There were nuggets of truth, but they were never focused on for long and had been polished up with a sort of mythical radiance. Caught up in the frenzy of his story and the admiration of the crowd, Brad caught Evelyn's gaze.

"Is there anything you can add?"

Aleksandr grunted at the sudden pain that shot up his arm. Evelyn had a grip like a vice, almost crushing his fingers as she clenched his hand.

"Yeah, we're not going to communicate anymore," Evelyn said, her voice as cold as ice but as lively as wildfire. "From here on out, send all questions and comments through my friend here. We're done."

Brad's face flushed as he realized just how inappropriate the question was. Not everyone in the crowd seemed to be of the same opinion. Some of them bold enough to cast her dark glares and whisper about how rude she was being. That, more than anything, solidified to Aleksandr that none of this was really about Petya or Olga. All that mattered was the story. The legend. Not the reality. An arctic wind crawled across the earth, twisting around his feet and clawing up his legs.

We need to hurry, he decided. *Or reality is going to catch up with us.*

Chapter 6

Evelyn didn't want to go into the house. She gripped Aleksandr's hand with a bone crushing force, hoping that he would accept the stories her ego told her to tell. That it wasn't fear churning through her view. Only rage. Anger was easier to deal with. It was better than tears, terror, or the unrelenting knowledge that she was tiny, frail, and breakable. Anger was something she could clutch close to her chest and use as a shield.

She felt the alien chill creeping up her legs, making her shiver against the heated air. *The Furies are coming*. The fact taunted her and she squeezed Aleksandr's hand tighter to endure it. He didn't complain even as he winced. *It's not the worst pain he's experienced*. She wasn't sure how to take that thought. So she pushed it away and tried to refocus. They needed to get the name. Their time was running out.

Eventually, after a long speech that she didn't bother to listen to, they were taken inside. She and Aleksandr lingered at the back of the crowd as they funneled inside. There were still a few odd glances cast their way, but no one said anything. It was that awkward mix of attention that people like to give a car crash. When people thought that they were being subtle in their attention, when really they were just randomly gawking.

Aleksandr didn't say a word. Instead, he tapped his index finger against her knuckles. Over the years, she had started to understand the silent cues that Sokolovsky kids used to express a vast amount of information. Three taps to the knuckle. *We have to do this. I hate it, too. Give me the word and I'll set everything on fire*. It was surprising how many of their little habits had an offer of arson mixed in with reassurances. She returned the gesture as best she could, sure that she had gotten it wrong somehow.

"Where do we need to go?" she whispered as the last of the people slipped into the building.

"They had two main stashes. Basement and bedroom."

"Super." *Two places I'd never want to go*. "Sounds about right."

Three taps on her knuckles and it was time for them to cross the threshold. She took a deep breath and stepped inside. It was the normalcy that rattled her. No drastic changes of light or lingering chill. There was nothing. It was just an old, worn down building like any other. Common place. Calm. The horrors that had occurred covered with red velvet ropes and little plaques noting the different things of interest. It looked fake. Safe.

"Well, that was anticlimactic," she said even as she clutched onto Aleksandr's hand.

"Just wait for it," Aleksandr grunted.

A cold sweat broke out across her skin as she moved deeper into the house. As her flesh turned to ice, each breath felt like fire in her lungs. It burned her throat and made it hard to speak. There wasn't much need for words. Aleksandr's grip was solid even as sweat began to gather between their skin. It made it easier to move with him. If there was one thing the Sokolovsky kids knew, it was how to blend into a crowd. Like a tiger blending into long grass. Aleksandr picked his times perfectly. Flowed with the movements of the others, inched into the shadows. Evelyn had to admit that she found it impressive. Especially after they had drawn attention, it shouldn't have been so easy for him to slip away. But before she knew it, they were up the stairs and working their way down the hallway, with Aleksandr expertly avoiding every creaky floorboard.

Each of the doors was open, exposing the rooms that had been preserved like a museum exhibit. The rooms weren't in a pristine state, with random clothes and items scattered around the floor. She hesitated when she noticed the cans scattered in an arch around the doorway of one room. A quick glance at the other items made it clear that it had been Aleksandr's room. Curiosity drew her closer. It struck her then, how strange it was that she hadn't seen the other parts of the house. She had been destined to die between these walls and there was so much of it she had never laid eyes upon. Careful not to hit the velvet rope that crossed the doorway, she stepped into the room.

It played out in her head. How the opening door would have knocked the cans, effectively turning them into a makeshift security system. The sheets were twisted into a serpent coil, flopping off of the bed to pool on the floor. It looked like something had just gotten up. The cleared space on the wardrobe floor told a different story. It was a small area. Just enough to fit Aleksandr if he curled tightly into a fetal position. He would have slept there. Hidden away from his parents.

"Evelyn," Aleksandr hissed, suddenly appearing behind her. "Come on."

"Do you still sleep in the closet?"

He didn't need to say a word. The look on his face was enough. *It's the only place he feels safe.*

"Can we go?" he asked.

"Isn't there anything you want in here?" she replied. "All you took with you are the twins."

"They're the only ones that meant a damn thing," he whispered, constantly glancing back to the door.

"Yeah, but, what about momentous? Old birthday presents? Photos?"

She hadn't thought it was possible for his normally stoic face to twist into that much sheer disbelief. "Are you new?"

"Oh, right. Your family was horrible and your life was worse."

"Thanks." He angrily gestured to the door. "Can we go now?"

She nodded, and after a quick check of the hallway, they slipped back out. A rattle made them turn in time to see one of the empty cans slowly rolling through the threshold. They sprinted forward before it had time to reach the opposite wall, neither one looking back to see what had caused it. Aleksandr barreled into the room first and was already ready to slam the door shut by the time Evelyn caught up. Not caring about the noise, he threw the door closed and locked it. The world became silent again. Normal. Evelyn had long since stopped questioning if she was overreacting or not.

"They're not going to like that we're ignoring them," she whispered.

"So, let's get the hell out of here. Check the drawers."

"You check the drawers," she shot back, cringing at the very thought of what she might find in their bedside table. "I'll check the wardrobe."

Aleksandr decided against protesting the moment he opened his mouth. With a put-upon sigh, he stalked over the bedside drawers and started his search for hidden compartments. Evelyn tugged open the wardrobe and started to find it filled with clothes. *Hadn't they taken anything?* The hangers rattled, creating a small clatter and making the clothes sway. Nothing smelled musky or old. *They preserved this place. It's a monument.*

There wasn't time to dwell on the thoughts. Reaching out, she shoved the clothes aside, exposing the back of the wardrobe. Striking it a few times to make sure there wasn't a hidden trap door, she pushed up onto her toes and started to trace her fingers over the high ledge.

The soft tinkle of the clothes hangers made her freeze and she dropped back down onto the balls of her feet. The clothes swayed slightly, having returned to their original position, creating a curtain that blocked her view of the back of the wardrobe.

"Alek," she said, her voice hard and low.

Without hesitation, Aleksandr picked up one of the bedside tables and swung at the wall. It crashed through the thin drywall, dust and plaster raining down to fill the small gap between the inner and outer wall with a smoke-like haze. She didn't hesitate to jump through the opening, not caring if she was about to plummet into the basement. Protecting her head exposed her forearms to the rough wood slats. Splinters dug deep into her flesh as she fell. Each panted breath was choked with dust and plaster. It took an eternity and yet was over in a second. Pain shot like electricity through her joints as her feet collided with the bottom.

She went slack, dropping into a roll in the limited space, trying to disperse the impact. Gravity more than intent dumped her out of a slender hole. She scrambled across the floorboards, making room for Aleksandr. He appeared a heartbeat later, grabbing her arm and yanking her to her feet before she was able to wipe the dust from her face. Staggering at first, bumping into each other as Aleksandr dragged her down the hallway. A streak of color passed her blurred vision. By the sound of the startled, disgruntled protest, she assumed that it was Brad. Neither of them paused to talk to the guide, shoving past him instead. Aleksandr lead the way to the hallway, steering them towards the back door.

"We still need the name," Evelyn said.

Aleksandr growled and tightened his grip on her arm, drawing her closer to his side, as if he was worried she was going try and sprint away.

"They're playing with us," he hissed.

"Yeah, I'm not stupid."

The tour trip had gathered in the small area dividing the living room and kitchen, neither trying to stop them nor get out of the way, forcing Evelyn and Aleksandr to squeeze along the wall. Her shoulder smacked against the flaking paint. A flash crossed her vision. She realized too late that it was the door to the basement opening. Hands felt but unseen latched onto her and yanked her into the darkened room. The hard edges of the stairs hit her back, shoulder, face, and knees. Pain filled her skin as she tumbled down the seemingly endless flight of stairs.

One last, bone rattling thud, and she slammed down onto the sandy floor. Loose particles of dust filled her throat and made her choke. One staggered breath and Aleksandr's weight bore down onto her back. She cried out in broken pain as her face was pushed harder into the sand. Dirt filled her lungs and lined her throat. Agony consumed her, whiting out her mind and leaving her unable to do more than idly swat at him.

"Heavy," she rasped.

He recovered faster than she did and was able to roll off of her. *Bloody muscle,* her mind groaned. If he didn't have the upper body of a gorilla he wouldn't have weighed half as much. As she struggled up onto all fours, a hand patted her shoulder.

"Yeah, I'm fine. Nothing's broken," she groaned.

The grunt he gave in return wasn't the one she had expected. *He didn't ask.* Her insides turned to ice. Aleksandr hadn't asked and the hand was still on her shoulder. The basement door slammed shut, sealing them in complete darkness.

"Alek," she whispered the word out as the fingers on her shoulder clenched. The sand gave her nothing to hold onto as she was dragged across the floor. "Alek!"

Clawing at the air, she searched for him. For anything to hold onto. For any way to defend herself. There was nothing. Only heated sand and the humid abyss. She thrashed, trying to dislodge the hand still clasped onto her shoulder. The nails sharpened as she fought, slicing into her flesh, digging deeper until she could feel the tips scraping against her collarbone.

Her scream echoed off of the walls. A scurry of movement that she could only hope was Aleksandr rushed towards her. Before she could latch onto him, there was another solid pull and the world stilled. The hand left her. Deafening silence fell over her, a stifling, physical weight. Panting hard, Evelyn pushed herself up onto her knees. Blood seeped from a thousand different cuts. Her heartbeat pounded against her skin, a deep sting that promised bruises to come. Swallowing thickly, she glanced around, attempting to catch even a glimpse of difference. Light seeping under the door. A silhouette that could give her a hint of what was in the room with her. She might as well have had her eyes closed.

Straining her senses, she searched for a hint of sound. Movement over the sand. Aleksandr's breathing. *Don't be afraid,* she ordered herself. The command was easier to give than to follow. A sense of complete isolation settled inside her. She felt small and weak. And that brought a spark of anger that she could cling to like a life line. Anger was clean. Easy. *Raise hell.* Her mind cast back with those words, thinking over what her mother had told her. Balling her fists, she slowed her breathing and crept up onto her feet. *Why hasn't it struck yet?* Anticipation kept her on a razor's edge. She rolled her shoulders and crouched low.

"Aleksandr," she whispered.

There was no reply. Edging in the general direction of the exit, she kept her arms up, ready to protect her head.

"Aleksandr?"

Something stuck her from above, flattening her to the floor. Within seconds, walls snapped up, clicking into place with a metallic thud, locking her into the cold in which Petya and Olga had kept her. She raged against the walls, hurling herself against the bars, rocking her enclosure until it almost toppled from its rolling pedestal. Screaming and snarling like a beast, she fought until the skin of her arms had been shredded by the iron.

A light clicked on overhead. It was dim, barely more than the glow of a candle, and attacked her eyes like burning needles. Baring her teeth, she squinted into the blaze, catching sight of a shadowy figure.

"Couldn't stay away." Olga's laughter crushed something delicate inside of Evelyn. Something she couldn't put a name to but didn't think she could survive without. "It was always going to end here."

A spike snaked through the bars of her cage. A hiss of electricity and a blinding blaze of pain. *A cattle prod.* It was an agony that she would never mistake for another. The stench of burning flesh attacked her nose as she screamed. *It's not real. She's dead. This can't be real.*

"I outlived you!" Evelyn roared, spit flying from her lips as she lurched towards the pain.

"I'm back."

"Then I'll kill you myself!"

The prod crackled again. She snatched for it. But the moment she made contact, the world shattered like glass. Hot sand puffed up around her as she landed. Her fingers dug into the ground as she pushed up, spitting dirt and blood from her mouth. While the world changed, the sensation of being watched, hunted, didn't lift. Something was lurking out of sight. She could hear it breathing. A shudder ran down her spine as a breath of rancid air crossed her shoulders. Darting forward, she fell back onto her butt, scurrying backwards until she found a wall. She pressed it to her spine and searched as much of the room the muted light could show her.

It's not real.

They were even in the wrong building, but here it was. The murder room. A basement that was nothing more than a pit gouged out under the earth. Torture devices hung from the walls. Some with clear uses. Others showing Olga and Petya's creativity. *It can't be real.* As she repeated the words to herself, she found no comfort in them. *What are they waiting for?*

Each rapid breath came with the lingering scent of cooking meat. The searing pain in her stomach made the source undeniable. It was her. No matter how much she reminded herself that none of it had any basis in reality, she felt herself burning. She pressed shaky fingers against one of the marks, determined to prove to herself that the sensation was nothing more than a cheap illusion. Her body refused to cooperate. The slight touch made her double over and almost whimper.

A solid clack drew her eyes back up. She already knew what she was going to see. The Furies had taunted her with the sight enough times for her to recognize the sound. Across the room, situated where it couldn't possibly be, stood the metal door. Frozen in horror, she watched as it opened once more. The sight and sound were familiar by this point. Something lodged deep within her soul. But it affected her just as it had the first time.

Barely able to breathe, she pressed herself against the wall, her fingers clawing at the clumps of earth. It broke apart in her hands and lodged under her nails. Raw and real. The red glow of the room crawled along the floor as the door swung back. It flowed towards her like blood. Staining the uneven sand. Bubbling and curling while the room blazed. Evelyn clenched her teeth to keep herself from whimpering.

A heavy thud made her flinch. Shadows danced across the walls as a figure moved within the red room. A hand flopped into view. Slick with rot, the flesh split as the fingertips dug for purchase, exposing the bones. Each bone clicked together, the joints popping free as it dragged itself forward. Bit by bit, the decayed figure dragged itself through the threshold. A thin strip of skin kept the lower jaw from falling completely free. Its tongue was black, flopping about as it tried to speak. All that came out was a broken, gargled groan. The sound came to her again. Only from far closer. Above her.

Evelyn looked up. Another corpse clung to the wall above her head. Its eyes had long since decomposed, leaving liquefied skin and muscle to drip from the gaping sockets. The scream she had been holding back ripped from her throat as the creature reached towards her.

Chapter 7

Aleksandr opened his eyes to dirt and blood. With a solid shove, he pushed up and tucked his legs in, landing in a low crouch. The cut on his head oozed, dripping hot liquid into his eyes as he took in the basement. Just like all the other rooms, this one had remained mostly intact. A root cellar divided into sections by rows of thick wooden shelving. It was one of the few places that could hold onto a chill. Not cold or even tolerable, but a few degrees lower than the surrounding area. If they had proper preparation, it would make a functional storage cellar. The first owners had left only a few odd jars. Mostly jams and homemade pickles. Everything else had been his family's contributions.

He eyed the shelves. Mason jars full of ears placed next to tall narrow containers of eyes. Little souvenirs. Pickled, flavored, and sorted. Leftovers from the times that Olga had the notion to try cannibalism. Logic clicked in as he rose up to his feet, his eyes scanning the full rows. *They have to be fake,* he reasoned with himself. *No law enforcement agency would ever let a tourist company keep human remains for display. Especially when it's evidence.*

Fighting the urge to chew on his thumbnail, he looked around the space. His heartbeat was an earthquake within his skull. Each contraction made the world tilt and spasm. He blinked hard against it but couldn't force his vision to focus.

Concussion, he reasoned. *Not a severe one.* He'd had enough to tell by sensation alone how much trouble he was in. Assessing himself only took a second. After that, his mind cleared enough for one thought to push through. *Evelyn.* He searched the room again. She wasn't there. *She still could be. Another trick of the Furies.* The thought made his hands twitch and he balled them to try and maintain control.

"Evelyn," he whispered.

A sudden pounding on the basement door made him jump.

"Hey!" Brad screamed from the other side. "Open the door! This is not okay!"

"Brad," Aleksandr bolted up the stairs. When the guide refused to stop screaming at them long enough for him to listen, he smashed his balled fist against the door, hard enough to make it rattle. "Shut up, Brad! Is Evelyn out there with you?"

Aleksandr's first thought was that the sudden reprisal had stunned the man. It was only a heartbeat later that he realized he hadn't covered his Russian accent. A visual resemblance to Radmiar Sokolovsky was easy enough to dismiss when one can change their hair color. But when one had both his appearance and accent to work with, it didn't take a genius to put a few things together.

"You're a Sokolovsky," Brad all but whimpered.

Aleksandr tried the doorknob. He had known from the start that the door wouldn't open, not while the Furies were playing their games, but that didn't kill his hope that it would. Chaos swept through the kitchen. A dozen different voices mixing together in panic, confusion, and sick delight. *Couldn't have been passed out long if Brad hadn't cleared the room yet,* Aleksandr thought as he tried to regain their attention. His attempts only made the screams beyond the layer of wood louder. From the snippets he could gather, a few of them thought this was part of the tour. But through their groans and quips about obvious tricks, there was a growing unease. Distinct notes of fear began to thread through their words. Questions became sharper. Rejection turned into denial. Aleksandr knew it all by heart. He'd heard it a thousand times in these walls. *Being in a killer's house is all fun and games until there's a murderer with you,* Aleksandr thought bitterly.

"Oh, my God. You're a Sokolovsky! There were rumors that Radmiar had a twin!"

"Brad," Aleksandr forced himself to sound calm, reasonable, even as his frustration was building. "I need you to focus. Is she with you?"

"I'm calling the police!"

"Brad!" He kicked the door hard enough that the wood splintered. "Is Evelyn out there?!"

"I'm not going to fall for that. We all saw you shove her in there. Don't you dare hurt her! I'm calling the cops!"

Aleksandr barely managed to keep his composure. Grinding his teeth, he hissed out that crime doesn't stop just because someone made a phone call, assured that the words would be lost under the constant chatter of the crowd. Sucking in a breath, he slammed his hand against the door and bellowed for Evelyn.

"Leave her alone!"

Aleksandr would have lost that sentence amongst all the other words if they hadn't been repeated in chorus. *She's not out there,* he reasoned, turning around to search the root cellar once more. There wasn't a trace of her.

"I've called the police!" Brad cried out, drawing Aleksandr from his thoughts. "They'll be here in fifteen minutes!"

"You obviously have no idea what can happen in fifteen minutes," Aleksandr muttered.

Of course, it was then that the crowd had decided to have a lull in their accusations. A few of them must have heard him. Brad certainly did, if his renewed hammering on the door was any indication. Aleksandr noticed that the doorknob never moved. For all the ferocity the crowd possessed to want to save Evelyn, not one of them was actually trying to get inside.

Fifteen minutes, Aleksandr repeated to himself. If this was real, if he were truly having this conversation with a flesh and blood person, then a timer had been set. In the past, the Furies had shown either reluctance or an inability to spread their illusions over a mass number of people. They were focused predators, preferring to limit their torments to one or two people at a time. *When the cops show up, things would get too distracting for them to keep their games going. In theory, at least. But if I'm the one they're playing with, I'm talking to myself. No one's coming.* He shook his head and pushed it all away. *One thing at a time,* he told himself. *Find Evelyn.* Aleksandr wasn't going to leave without her.

Running back down the stairs, he didn't bother to call out for her. There wasn't any point to it. Either she would find him or she wouldn't hear him at all. The loose floor shifted under his feet as he crossed the room. With the shelves positioned as they were, it was impossible to see every part of the room at once. He'd have to check each aisle in turn. The passageways were narrow. All he would have to do was push out his elbows and he'd completely consume the space.

There was only one window. Years of dust and grime encrusted the thin glass, forcing the sunlight to battle against it. It darkened the room into twilight and allowed fledgling shadows to gather in the corners. He spared it a glance before moving into the stacks. It was too high for Evelyn to crawl out of on her own. Since none of the dust was disturbed, he could safely assume that she hadn't even attempted to get out that way. *So she's in here somewhere. But in what state? It had hardly taken them much effort to get me to attack the twins.* Fire crackled through his bone marrow at the thought. A potent mix of terror, remorse, and rage that left him breathless.

"Evelyn," he whispered as he slowly crept down the first hallway.

There was no response. The room darkened as he rounded the end and started up the next aisle.

"Evelyn."

Nothing stirred, but something shifted. The air. The sand. A shadow through the muted light. He couldn't place the physical source. It was more of a sensation. A primal instinct that made his skin spark and an icy sweat spread across the nape of his neck. He felt it and knew; he wasn't alone. There was something in the room with him. Dark and hungry. He could taste its barely shackled hostility. Feel the brewing storm of its madness. Every cell of his being felt the unseen presence and responded to it. A lifetime spent around evil people didn't prepare him for the sheer volatile contempt the Furies possessed.

Swallowing back bile, he entered the new aisle and stopped. The ground heaved. Slow and rhythmic. As if a colossal heart was pulsing under the surface. A central mound grew, the loose grains of sand toppling down the edges and tinkling against the low stored glass bottles. Instinct took over, sliding Aleksandr's feet back and lifting his arms, his body adopting a boxer's stance even though he knew he couldn't win this fight.

Blood bubbled out of the tip of the peak, trickling down the edges to well at the base. Aleksandr's body trembled as he watched fingers worm their way free. They pushed out of the mound, clawing it open, reducing it to tattered shreds and exposing more of the thrashing limbs. Propelled up by the movement, the flow of blood gushed up in torrents, drenching the surrounding jars and splattering the legs of his jeans. Aleksandr knew he should run, but a notion of familiarity held him back. Kept him enthralled. Groping. Mauling at the earth with blunt nails and short fingers. Breaking the mound apart until the arms could burst free.

The hands braced themselves on either side of the forming bit. The hole quickly swelled with crimson liquid, covering all but the fingers that gouged into the rim. In one sudden burst, Evelyn broke free. She choked on her screams, each cry making the liquid in her throat bubble and froth. With all the blood, it wasn't instantly noticeable that her eyes were missing. The skin around it shredded and darkened. *Ripped out.*

Impulse took over. He sprinted forward before dropping onto one knee. The sand kicked up like a wave before him as he slid. The moment he was close enough, he latched an arm around her waist and hurled her free. It was only once he had her flat on her back that the stupidity of the act hit him. *Not Evelyn. Run! Go!* The second the thought entered his head, Evelyn changed. Instead of a broken, shrieking figure, she had flipped over onto her stomach and was scurrying after him. Fast as a rattlesnake. Nimble as a tarantula. He could barely keep his limbs from her grasping hands.

She rotted as she moved. Skin decaying to drip from her bones. A putrid stench stained the air, radiating from her, spreading as blood flicked from her jerking limbs. A high-pitched scream broke her jaw. It fell to the ground with a dull thud. He slipped and fell. Knocked into the shelves. Broke the bottles in his panicked need to escape. Formaldehyde and decay made him gag. Glass cut into his palms. All the while, Evelyn drew closer. He couldn't keep the distance between them. Her hands grasped his ankles. One swift pull and he was thrown onto his back. A heavy weight kept him down. Pinned him in place. Her flesh was as cold as ice and just as unrelenting. Without her jaw, Evelyn's tongue dangled, flopping about as she moved higher up his body. Her body crushed him. The gaping pits where her eyes should have been bore into him like black holes. She lowered her face towards him and he swung.

His fist collided with something real and solid. Flesh and bone. But he couldn't shake the monstrosity off of him. The grotesque replica of Evelyn struggled to cover him. Consume him. He struck out, over and over, but it was a losing battle. Blood covered his knuckles. His arms started to tremble with the strain. The creature fought back. With a wild cry, Aleksandr rocked his hips, tossing her off and quickly rolling on top. He grasped for the nearest shard of broken glass. The broken edges cut into his palm, but he gripped it tighter still, clasping it like a lifeline as he swung towards the beast he now straddled. The tip dug into flesh, enticing a scream that was altogether too human. Too real. Too much like Evelyn.

The heavy thuds on the door. His own panted breath. The bellowing roar of the crowd beyond the door rushed back into focus with all the ferocity of a tsunami. The ferocity of it left him trembling and shell shocked. All of the broken fragments of reality melded back together. The veil had lifted. The Furies had released them. Little whimpers of pain echoed up from below him.

"Alek?" Evelyn groaned.

He felt like his skull was breaking apart. *It can't be real.* But as much as he said it, he was still holding the broken hunk of glass that was embedded in Evelyn's shoulder. Hot blood slicked his hand, but he couldn't tell which one of them it was coming from. Evelyn bore her teeth. The sounds that slipped out between them were a mix of pain and righteous indignation.

"Get. Off. Me," she groaned.

"Evelyn," he muttered.

It's not real. It's not real. It's not real.

"Yeah, it's me. Get off."

Aleksandr leaped to the side. All of his care wasn't enough to prevent some jostling. The glass wiggled in her shoulder and she sobbed. A weak, broken cry that made his chest clench.

"I'm sorry. I'm sorry," he whispered, his voice barely heard over the screams outside of the room.

She waved him off, hissing as he helped her sit up. The sound turned angry when he swatted her hand away from the glass.

"Leave it in until we have a first-aid kit. We can't risk you bleeding out."

"That would just be the highlight of my day."

He stripped off his shirt, shredding it into makeshift bandages. It wasn't clean, but it was the best they had. He packed some strips around the glass, his delicate touch making her hiss and whimper. The rest he wrapped around her, keeping the shard in place. She didn't fight him, letting him take most of her weight as she looked around.

"I thought you were a monster," she said.

"It's okay."

She snorted a laugh. "It wasn't an apology."

"I kicked your ass," he muttered back, just to keep her smiling. "I need you to get to your feet. We need to leave."

"Did you get the names?" she asked as they staggered up, each one leaning more on the other, each feeling their wounds anew.

"No."

"Can't leave."

"Do you not hear that? Sooner or later, mob mentality is going to make one of them bold enough to break down that door."

"So? Seems like they're angry at *you*. I'll be fine."

"Being stabbed makes you mean."

Their whole discussion took place as he moved them along the rows, heading towards the back corner. There, Aleksandr motioned for her to stand against the wall. Despite the wobble in her step, her gaze was as sharp as a hawk's. His own vision blurred, making the task of finding the hidden latch harder. Evelyn didn't seem surprised that there was a passageway cut into the wall. It was a small tunnel. One that would force them to crawl.

"Did you build that?" she asked as he moved the large chunk of drywall out of the way.

"No. Petya and Olga liked their escape routes."

"But you made the one upstairs?"

He paused. *A family habit.* There was time to linger on how grotesque that thought was. "Yes."

"How is this house still standing with all of you cutting into it?"

"Good point. Can we flee now? Angry mob, remember?"

"We still have time. They still have to find pitchforks," she said even as she followed his gestures to get moving. "That can't be easy in the desert."

He waited for her to arrange herself, attempting to find a way to slip through without putting any weight on her injured arm. In the end, she sat down and put her foot into Aleksandr's arms. Her legs were strong as she was able to use the foot hold to slide herself through the gap.

"There's a few in the shed," Aleksandr answered as he followed her.

"Why?" She scrunched her eyes closed. "No. Don't answer that. I don't want to know."

"That's a wise decision."

Aleksandr didn't want to hurry her. She was injured. Losing blood and in pain. But there wasn't much of a choice.

"Why do you think they let us go?" she asked as she hobbled alongside him.

"It's more fun this way."

"How do you figure that?"

"Signs of a struggle. Blood splatter. Brad figured out who I was."

"He did? Good for him. Brighter than I thought."

"The point is, those people are going to whip themselves into a frenzy and come after me."

She scoffed at the idea, leaning on him as they rounded the house.

"Do you know the Night Stalker? Richard Ramirez?" he asked in a hushed voice.

"Not personally."

"He was a serial killer with a death grip on California. He ruled over it with all of the ferocity and grandeur any killer could hope for. His end came when some random people on a bus recognized him. It started with them. Then it spread like wildfire. People on the streets chased him down. The cops actually had to pull citizens off of him. They almost beat him to death on the street. People love a chance to kill a monster."

They stilled, pressed their backs against the wall of the building as they carefully peaked around the corner.

"It's not often I hear fear in your voice," she noted.

"They taught us young to fear the power of the herd. Numbers made even sheep strong."

They darted forward. A short sprint to a nearby house down the slope. She had the decency to hold off until they were in their new hiding place to ask.

"So, what's the plan? We haven't gotten the names."

"The Furies are here."

"If you're right, they're sitting back and watching the show. We need the names."

"You have glass in your shoulder."

"And I'm high on adrenaline. Which is limited," she countered. Grabbing his arm, she hurled him around to look at her. "Just tell me where to look. I'll get it. You get the car. We meet up."

"Or we almost murder each other again."

"I just assumed that was always a risk in our friendship."

"I know what you're doing." Placing a hand on her stomach, he pushed her back slightly, hiding her from the sight of a few passing workers. "You're trying to disarm me with casual chatter and sassiness."

"It seems so wrong to hear you say 'sassy'."

"Stop."

Flattening his tone was enough to get her to take him seriously. But without their self-imposed distractions, the reality of the situation became a heavy weight on them. His body was shaking with the effort to keep upright. What had started as a splitting headache was progressively getting worse, bringing with it a wave of dizziness and the ever-increasing need to vomit.

"What's wrong with you?" Evelyn asked.

He squeezed his eyes shut, willing himself to keep control. *Just a little longer. Just until we're out of here.* His vision blurred, rippling and coiling like oil in water. As he blinked it away, phantom images settled over the world like a film. He saw himself being chased down by the crowd. A fevered pack. Crazed and wild. The ghostly masses swarmed him, forcing him to the ground. The air filled with his agonizing screams. The snapping of bones. Aleksandr watched with a growing sense of terror as the prophecy unfolded. Saw himself torn about. His limbs thrown and scattered amongst the dunes. His own scream cracked his skull apart.

"Alek?" Evelyn said, one arm grabbing his wrist tightly. "What is going on?"

He couldn't tear his eyes off of the scene before him. "I have a concussion."

"Oh. Great. Alright, new plan. I'll get the car, you get the names."

"We're not getting back in that house."

The distant sound of crushing wood and screams proved his point. *It won't take long for them to break the door down now,* he thought.

"We need to go. Now."

"Aleksandr."

A sudden rush of bile surged up in his throat. Hunching forward, he wretched, spilling the contents of his stomach over his shoes. It effectively cut off any further protest. Evelyn grabbed him by his shoulders and hurled him out of the shadows. A ringing entered his eyes as they hobbled towards the golf cart. It barely took him any effort to hotwire it, even with his decreasing balance and mounting confusion. Muscle memory guided him through it. The smaller electronic engine allowed them to make their escape before anyone could get out to stop them. Security was nonexistent and they managed to get to their car unimpeded.

It was the laughter that followed. The shrill, taunting cackle that didn't diminish with distance. The Furies were with them.

Chapter 8

Aleksandr tightened the muscles of his jaw, smothering a cry as Nadya's fingers prodded at the back of his head. The buzzing of the electric razor and the pull of his hair as they carefully shaved it off had combined to turn his headache into a migraine. *Or it could be because you bashed your head repeatedly on a flight of stairs,* a voice in his head noted. Aleksandr cringed. Even thinking hurt.

"Stop moving," Nadya said as she smacked his shoulder. "You'll mess up my work."

Aleksandr grunted, both in annoyance and agreement, and settled under her hands. Sokolovsky kids knew well the virtues of always having an extensively stocked first-aid kit on hand. And they all knew the human body well. After some prodding, Juan had let Ivan take control of Evelyn's care. He was better with arteries. And with Nadya taking care of Aleksandr's split open skull, the older man had little else to do but worry.

They had managed to cut off her shirt without disrupting the shard too much. But there was blood. Bubbling up around the glass and dripping down to stain the mattress she lay on. *We're going to have to flip that,* Aleksandr thought idly. He couldn't be bothered to decide what they should do with the sheets. The bed he was sitting on wouldn't fare much better.

The local anesthetic hadn't had time to take its full effect. Evelyn tried her best to keep silent. It wasn't working. Juan sat next to his daughter, half on the bed, vibrating with restless energy. He patted her hair, kissed her knuckles, whispered soft words of encouragement and praise as she endured Ivan's work. Aleksandr watched in fascination as Nadya threaded her needle.

"You have an oddly shaped skull," Nadya noted.

Aleksandr chuckled. It wasn't exactly holding his hand but the sentiment was the same.

"I was thinking that, too," Ivan said.

Even with a needle lacing through her skin, Evelyn wasn't about to pass up the opportunity to mock someone. "It's the hair. You couldn't see it when he had a rat's nest. There's nowhere to hide with a buzz cut."

Nadya hummed thoughtfully. Pushing Aleksandr's head forward, she prodded the tip of her needle along his scalp, never hard enough to break through the tender skin.

"It's going to be super hard to stitch you up without leaving a scar," she told him.

"You think you have it bad," Ivan muttered. "Evelyn's going to look like her arm was sown on no matter what I do."

"It's not a contest," Nadya snapped.

"Says the loser of said contest."

"Can we focus please?" Juan cut in. "We need to get this done before the police come looking for us."

"What would it matter if they did?" Nadya said. "It's not like they broke any laws. You know, apart from a short joy ride."

"And property damage," Ivan added.

"The property was already damaged. He just drew their attention to it. If anything, that's helpful," Nadya said.

"Don't know if they'll see it that way," Juan said.

"Guys!" Evelyn cut in. "Please, work on my shoulder. I'm getting light headed. And for the record, the official story is this; I freaked out, smashed some stuff, accidently hurt myself, we hurried to get first-aid."

"Sweetie." Juan soothed a hand over her hair. "I don't think that'll work. You said that the door locked. That doesn't exactly go with the story."

"It's an old house. It locked on its own. A freak accident." Her dismissive shrug ended with a sharp cry and a few barely suppressed swear words.

Ivan used one hand to hold her steady until her breathing evened out and she melted against the mattress. He never stopped stitching.

"You know what's going to be harder to explain?" Ivan said as he worked. "Why she's hanging out with you."

"Hey, Alek is a catch." Nadya gave his shoulder a pitying pat. The touch barely made him wobble but left Aleksandr convinced that his head was going to explode. "I've got your back, bro."

Ivan smirked at his twin. "My point is that he's the son of a couple that tried to kill her. And the brother of three people that also tried to kill her. Those two hanging out seems pretty messed up."

"Thank you," Juan muttered under his breath.

"Messed up isn't a crime. It's my God given right as an American to have as many twisted relationships as I want." Evelyn's words were pained but her tone was as solid as iron. "It's not what's important right now. The Furies let us go but we didn't get the names."

Juan frowned. "Is mercy something they normally do?"

"Nope," the twins said at once.

"So, what does this mean?"

"No idea," Aleksandr said.

The humor seeped from the room, replaced with tension and the near synchronized sound of needles puncturing skin. The slick and pull of thread sliding through flesh. There was a certain nostalgia to the task. It was an awkward kind of calm, one that Aleksandr could almost consider peaceful. He relaxed into the sensation, letting his sibling do her work, feeling the drugs pushing through his veins.

"How do we get the damn name?" Evelyn abruptly snapped to the ceiling, as if she were trying to force an epiphany by anger alone. "I'll think of something," she growled.

"Well, baby girl," Juan said with a suspicious chuckle. "Now, remember how you did something stupid, even though I told you not to? Remember that? How the two of you left me with the kids, spouting off about how I shouldn't worry?"

Evelyn lifted her head up to better stare at her father. "Dad, we've been through his. You're not funny."

"I'm a little funny," he countered. "But, to the point, I needed a fun game to keep the kids occupied."

"I had fun," Nadya chirped.

Ivan nodded. "And it was educational."

Seemingly resigned, she huffed out a sharp breath, wincing when the motion aggravated her wound.

"What game did you play, dad?" she asked.

"It's a little game called 'competence'," he said with a grin. "I called a friend on the police force."

"You have friends on the police force?" Aleksandr asked with a flash of anxiety.

"I'm a firefighter. First responders get to know each other pretty well. Anyway, the point is that I called in a few favors. And liberally played the very concerned father card."

"They're sending you the reports?" Evelyn asked.

"Oh, hell no," he laughed. "But they are emailing me some photographs of the victims they have managed to identify."

"Unbelievable," Aleksandr muttered.

"Yeah, maybe next time, you can remember that other people can be useful and not get my daughter stabbed."

"Dad," Evelyn whined.

"I'm not going to try and cut into your dance here, sweetheart. You know more about this than I do. I acknowledge that. But I *can* be a useful resource. I even got the kids to eat vegetables."

Ivan finished his work on Evelyn with a final snip of the cord. It was impossible to tell who moved first. Whatever the case, they soon were curled up together. It looked natural. Easy. A contact not born from fear or a need for comfort. *They're used to simple affection,* he thought. The twins noticed it, too. They cast little smiles to him, looking like they had just seen adorable kittens snuggling. It almost made him laugh.

"Here," Juan said as he passed over his mobile phone, the first image already filling the screen. "Scroll away."

Nadya rested her chin on Aleksandr's shoulder so she could see the screen. Not one to be left out, Ivan scrambled off the opposite bed to come and settle down next to Aleksandr.

"I don't suppose there's a way to separate them by gender," Aleksandr asked.

"No," Juan said. "I couldn't figure out a non-creepy way to ask for just the men."

Evelyn clicked her tongue. "Lack of creativity."

Aleksandr went back to studying the pictures, ignoring Juan's chuckle and the bickering conversation he proceeded to have with Evelyn. It seemed that father and daughter communicated mostly through sarcasm and playful taunts. Aleksandr found himself marveling at this survival skill. *They probably picked it up after her mother got sick,* Aleksandr reasoned. *Things aren't as scary when you make fun of them.*

"They all look different when they're smiling," Nadya said.

Ivan pressed closer and arched his neck, frowning at the constant precession of pictures taken, collected from yearbooks, drivers' licenses, and family photos. "I don't recognize any of them."

"Well, that's the one who broke Alek's nose," Nadya noted.

"Oh yeah. And didn't this one fracture his jaw?"

"No, that one broke his leg. You're thinking about the red-head, three photos back."

"Stop," Aleksandr said softly.

"We're being helpful," they said in unison.

He smirked at that but didn't comment. Swipe after swipe, he studied the seemingly endless array of faces.

"Must be daunting," Juan said after a long moment of silence. "Seeing them all one after the other like this. Makes you realize how many there were."

None of the Sokolovsky siblings looked up as they said, "This isn't all of them."

"No," Juan reprimanded as he lifted a finger. "No more talking all together like that. It makes me feel like I'm in a bad remake of *The Children of the Damned.*"

Ivan looked to his twin, then they both frowned. "We haven't seen that movie."

"And you won't for a few more years. It's got an R-rating."

"They've witnessed a lot worse," Evelyn said.

Aleksandr cut them off before he could have this conversation again. "They're my kids and they're going to have some boundaries."

"Damn straight," Juan said.

Having Juan agree with him only reassured Aleksandr that he was on the right track. A smile tipped his lips until he flicked his thumb and the image appeared.

"Him." He spun the phone in his palm and handed it back to Juan. "This guy. Good jab. Sloppy footwork."

Evelyn rushed to take the phone, fighting hard to keep herself from screaming as she pulled her stitches. Determination paid off, and she managed to snatch up the phone before her father did. He didn't try to take it off of her, but lingered close.

"This guy summoned the Furies?" she asked. "Huh. I was expecting something more ... flamboyant."

"Like a stereotypical gypsy?" Nadya said. "I'm pretty sure that's offensive."

"Sounds like it should be," Ivan noted.

Juan studied the photograph, searching for something remarkable. There was nothing. It was a face that could easily pass through a crowd unnoticed. "How did he do it?"

"No idea," Aleksandr said. "He just said that they were coming. That they'd make us suffer. Furies arrived the next day."

"What's his name?" Evelyn asked, finally handing the phone back to her father.

He fiddled with his device for a bit. Waited for a bit more. A small ding marked the reply. "Still waiting on next of kin, but his name was Dylan Cox."

"Again, I was expecting something more. Something ..." she paused, struggling to find the right words as she waved a hand around in the air. "Well, just *more.*"

"Wow, Eve. Judgmental, much?" Nadya said.

Juan chuckled, leaning forward with a hand outstretched for a high-five. The teenager looked immensely pleased with herself as she smacked his palm.

"He was teaching us 'normal kid sass' while you were gone," Ivan explained in a whisper.

"Just what I need," Aleksandr smirked.

Everyone fell silent at the next ping. They waited in silence as Juan read the message and groaned.

"Well, now I understand why the Furies let you go."

"What is it?" Evelyn asked.

He sighed. "The next of kin's name is Eunice. She lives in Australia."

Chapter 9

As Juan pointed out every fifteen minutes, all of the major airlines don't take 'vendetta' as a form of payment. They needed money. Aleksandr no longer had any. The trip back to the desert had drained his account. It was a point he made again when they had pulled into the diner outside of the airport. It had taken two hours to get out of the desert and into the city. So there was still enough morphine in his system to dull his irritation.

"We'll get some," Aleksandr said.

"You keep saying that," Juan replied. "But you never explain how."

From their perch on the bonnet of the car, the twins didn't stop devouring their hamburgers as they spoke in unison. "Don't worry about it."

"Don't speak with your mouths full," Juan said on parental reflex.

The twins pressed their lips into a smirk. For the first time since they had arrived, they looked up from their laptop and at their older brother. Aleksandr could only shrug. Their table manners didn't make the list of their bad habits that concerned him.

"It's illegal, isn't it?" Juan accused. "You're going to do something illegal."

"Don't worry about it," Aleksandr said.

"You're not thinking of killing anyone, are you?" Evelyn mumbled around a mouthful of greasy fries.

"Manners," Juan reminded.

"But my shoulder hurts."

"Killing is extreme," Aleksandr said to cut off Juan's response. It got him a smile from Evelyn.

"Stabbing isn't a group bonding exercise." Juan pinched the bridge of his nose and sighed.

"It is if you do it right," Ivan said under his breath.

The older man released a pained groan. "I'm going to need you to give me a bit of an answer here."

Aleksandr nodded to his sister's questioning look. After ripping off another mouthful of junk food, Nadya pulled a small box out of her bag and set it down in the middle of the table.

Juan remembered just in time to keep his voice down. "A credit card reader? That's your plan, Alek? Theft. What are you teaching your kids?"

"How to survive," Aleksandr growled.

"And darts," Nadya added. "We're really good at darts."

Juan narrowed his eyes. "So you can hustle."

"So," Nadya said thoughtfully, "we're not allowed to get money illegally or legally?"

Ivan shoveled the rest of his meal into his mouth. "It's almost like we're not allowed to *have* money."

"Try working for it."

"We're thirteen," the twins declared in unison.

"They have a point," Aleksandr said.

There was a little sober part of Aleksandr's mind that suggested it wasn't the best idea to antagonize the older man. The morphine buzz kept him from caring.

"If I'm only allowed to pay my way through respectable means," Aleksandr asked, "how do you propose we do this, Sir?"

Silence met his question. At least, as much silence as one could expect in an airport terminal. They had slipped in as far as to one of the diners set up to the side. It still filled him with warmth to see the twins with an appetite. It was something that Evelyn had encouraged. With that much muscle, she burned through calories fast, and always seemed to be ravenous. She was on her second burger, which the twins took as a challenge. It was scraping the bottom of Aleksandr's savings to provide it. *The food service pays surprisingly little. Maybe I should be a mechanic.*

"You know," Evelyn seemed more interested in her meal than the conversation. "It's only Aleksandr and I that need to go."

"The last time I left you two alone, he stabbed you."

"I've apologized for that. Repeatedly," Aleksandr said.

"And that makes it better?"

"Does it make it worse?" Aleksandr asked.

"More importantly," Evelyn cut in. "It wasn't his fault."

"Thank you."

Her smile was a little loose. Her eyelids drooped. *How much painkiller did Ivan give her?*

"I'm going to want a rematch," she said.

"I'll be happy to stab you again," he smirked.

Juan growled. "I'm standing right here."

"He's just got a dark sense of humor," Evelyn dismissed. "Also, according to my phone, it's almost boarding time. So, what are we doing? My call; you take the twins again and keep them someplace safe. Aleksandr and I go, kill these things, and catch up with you guys later for our victory dinner. Right now, I'm leaning towards pizza but I'm open to other suggestions."

The twins opened their mouths but Evelyn was already talking again. "And before you two begin, no, it's not because you're kids. It's because I'm petty. The Furies have been working hard to get us all into the same place at the same time. And, well, I'm just itching to mess with them." She rolled her shoulder and winced. "Return the favor a bit."

"You're willing to die for spite?" Juan asked.

"Yep," she chirped.

He stared at his daughter for a long moment before heaving a sigh. "You're just a damn clone of your mother."

"I'm starting to take that as a compliment."

"That's how it was always intended, honey," he said with a wistful smile.

Aleksandr wasn't sure if he should interrupt the moment they were having. He shuffled his feet and longed for his hair. It was always the perfect shield against the rest of the world.

"So, we're agreed?" he asked reluctantly.

"I have just enough money to cover both your tickets. Barely," Juan thought aloud. "I'm not liking this, though."

"Come on, dad. Is there anything that could happen right now that you'd be okay with?"

"No. But ..." His voice trailed off as he looked at the twins. "What do you guys think?"

They looked at each other; exhausted, worried, and still identical. Nothing more than a glance was needed for them to conduct a silent conversation. Everyone else waited impatiently to hear the twins' final decision.

"Even if we split up, there's no way to tell which one of us the Furies are going to go after," Ivan said.

"You think we should stick together?" Juan clarified.

"Hell no!" Ivan said with a snort.

"I don't think hell's spawn are above playing by war-crime rules," Nadya said. "If they decide to mess with Evelyn by going after her daddy, we need to be around to stop them." She looked Juan over. "You're very killable."

"I," Juan stuttered. "I don't know how to take that."

"That's fine," Nadya said while she refocused on the laptop.

Juan's brow furrowed. "So, you're saying you're behind Evelyn's plan?"

The twins looked at each other, their brother, then back at Juan. "Duh."

At Juan's grumble, Aleksandr shot them a small smirk. "Guys, remember what we talked about."

"No speaking in unison when people are already freaking out."

Aleksandr had to smother a laugh when, going right against the point, they said it at the same time, in matching chastised tone. They returned to clicking away while Juan begrudgingly pulled his phone out to purchase the airline tickets.

"Here's a question," Evelyn said while taking advantage of the kids' distraction to steal some of their fries. "When we get there, how do we find this Eunice? I mean, Australia's a big place, right?"

"Found her address," Nadya declared. Ivan was already sending it to Aleksandr's mobile.

"How?" was all Evelyn could ask.

"We're trained predators," Aleksandr dismissed. "We know how to hunt."

"And social media just makes everything easier," Nadya noted.

Ivan smirked. "I've been talking to her on Twitter for the last few hours. She's a night owl and really into peacocks."

"Yeah, what is with that?" Nadya asked.

"What? They're a cool bird," her twin smirked.

Aleksandr shifted closer to Juan's side, arching his neck slightly so he could read the phone screen. Preoccupied with watching the twins argue, Juan didn't seem to notice his presence. Eventually, he dipped his head to the side, and mumbled.

"They only had a country and a name."

"And their relative," Aleksandr added. "The press around a close relative's murder is surprisingly helpful. How long will the flight be?"

"So, they really have her address?" Juan asked absently.

"Yes."

He huffed lightly, half in awe, half in disbelief. "Should I be afraid of them?"

"Probably." Aleksandr didn't try to hide his pride at that notion. It was a strange position to be in. Loving that they can take care of themselves, but horrified about how they had learned it. "Don't worry, Juan. They've taking a liking to you. Now, the flight?"

"Oh, right," he shook his head, tried to refocus, and eventually settled for passing him the phone.

"Twenty-two hours," Aleksandr said.

"I think there are ones with fewer layovers."

"No, they're probably a good idea. It takes the Furies a while to track us down. I'd prefer to throw out a misdirection here and there."

"Right." Juan suddenly brought himself back into the conversation and turned to look at him. "How will Evelyn last a flight that long? She'll need more painkillers."

"I've got something that can knock her out for a while. When she comes to, I'll give her a dose of painkillers."

"And, how are you going to get that past customs?"

"You'll be surprised what I can smuggle onto a plane."

Juan skirted his eyes over to him. "Another lesson from your parents?"

"Dead but not forgotten."

***

"Wake up." The voice was a hushed whisper, echoing and crackling at once. "Evelyn. Wake up."

A drug haze forced her eyelids together. She longed to remain in the dark, cool world of sleep. To float within her skin. But the voice called again. She squirmed, burying her face against the harsh material that covered her plane seat. It scraped against her cheek as the voice continued to beckon, drawing her back, bringing the world with it. The constant drone of the engines. Jolts and rocks of turbulence. The soft clatter of unseen items clicking together.

"Evelyn." Her name came as a hiss. "Wake up."

She stirred but her eyes remained shut tight, too heavy to pry apart.

"Now!"

Her breath caught in her throat as she jerked awake. Still not fully alert, she sluggishly lifted her head, blinking heavily. The world heaved like ocean waves until her stomach lurched. Swallowing thickly, she pushed herself up in her seat. Disorientation lingered for a while, reducing her senses into a dull haze, keeping her from noticing little more than the fact that something was different. Wrong. Forcing herself to focus, she braced one hand on the side of the plane, grounding herself as she reached over to the seat next to her. Hard plastic. Corse fabric.

"Aleksandr?" she mumbled sleepily.

It took a few hard pats against the back of the chair to believe that it was empty. Being alone sobered her. While she still couldn't get her mind to function clearly, she was able to lurch up onto her feet. There wasn't much space separating her seat from the one in front. The hard backing knocked against her knees, forcing her to put a knee up on her seat or fall.

"Aleksandr?"

Her voice quavered but carried louder than it had before. Locking her joints, she steadied herself as best she could. It was then that she realized what had been playing against the edges of her awareness. The thing that was fundamentally wrong. She was alone, as far as the ebony darkness allowed her to see. Slender beams of stark white light carved out patches of reality. A few seats. Some scattered patches of the aisles. Half a dozen windows. That was all that remained. Everything else had been swallowed by the void. *Just like the hospital,* she recalled as dread crept into her bones. *It's too soon. They couldn't have found us already.* Her fevered thoughts clashed together, feeding her panic and the thought that this was what the Furies had been driving her towards all along. Isolated. Helpless. Trapped a thousand feet in the air.

You're not alone, she told herself sharply. *Don't play their game. Take control.* Drawing in a deep breath, she struggled to regain her footing and clear her mind enough to think. Truly think. A fine tremble worked its way through her veins. A building pressure driving her to take some form of action. The tangible world was where she was strong, comfortable, safe. Or, at the very least, it was where she could think of herself as such. *And that's what matters.* She dug her nails into the arm rest. The physical sensation an anchor to reality. *Don't be afraid. Don't cower. Let them starve.*

She pushed her way out into the aisle, barely able to keep herself upright. It was a wobbly shuffle during which her legs never brushed against anything. *If Aleksandr was sitting next to me, shouldn't I have run into him?* She pushed the thought aside for now and concentrated on securing her feet. The plane jostled and bucked. Reaching into the abyss beside her, fingers trembling and a cold sweat covering her palm, she blindly searched for the opposite seat. There was only empty space. She glanced down and watched her hand disappear into the void as cleanly as if it had been severed.

Breathing heavily, she twisted around, remaining upright only because of her crushing grip on the back of Aleksandr's chair. With every passing second, the plane rocked harder. The engines strained, gears grinding against each other, stuttering as they loosened. Bracing her feet, she crouched low to secure her balance. It was close enough to a boxer's stance that she felt herself comfortable.

That's when it changed.

The floor stilled. Silence engulfed her. Bit by bit, the world became pliable under her feet. Squirming under her weight. Sand poured out from the shadows, flowing like a rising tide. An orange light burned the air. She wasn't in a plane. The desert stretched out in every direction, sun blistered and barren. A hot wind whipped around her, hurling particles of dust against her bare skin. Using her forearm to shield her eyes, she inched back a pace, clutching her teeth against the scorching sting. The quiet returned, deafening in its intensity.

Between blinks, the world before her shifted. Darkness gathered and squirmed. There but not. Tangible and an illusion at once. A colossal figure of monstrous proportions, then something barely larger than the palm of her hand. She squinted at the specter, trying to force it to solidify. A tangled mass of limbs. Distorted. Twisted around themselves and the bulk of the body like gnarled roots. With the sick, wet crack of bones, the limbs unfurled, the motion both broken and swift. It never fully untwisted, but the batted pieces formed a recognizable whole. A human. Too mangled to be able to determine a gender.

The dark pit that served as its head twisted on its axis. Its face was a featureless mask, void of anything but the inky, intangible shadow that made up the rest of its body. Time stretched out. Seconds became hours as they stared at each other. A sharp burst, and it surged towards her as a soundless mass. Evelyn reeled back, her feet tripping over the uneven sand. She fell, her back slamming hard against the ground, the dust exploding up to attack her eyes. Scraping at her face didn't clear her vision.

The creature was on her. A heavy weight clawing its way along her body. Evelyn struggled and thrashed, but it moved too erratically for her to know where best to strike. In seconds, it had her pinned. Its face looked over her. Inches away but still void of any features. Still, she knew it was looking at her. That it was pleased.

Evelyn, its voice gargled within her skull. Inhuman but mocking.

Evelyn.

It lowered itself down. Unable to escape, she could only turn her face aside as she the monster began to nuzzle along her cheek. It vibrated. A grotesque purr.

Evelyn, welcome home.

Chapter 10

"Evelyn," Aleksandr spoke in a harsh whisper, careful not to draw the attention of other passengers.

They had pulled up to the gate fifteen minutes ago. The long trip had left the other passengers desperate to get out. Most of them had already exited. Those that remained didn't seem all that inclined to pay much attention to anything. Still, he wasn't about to risk stirring their interest, despite his growing desperation.

I didn't give her that much. He repeated the fact over and over as he subtly checked the pulse point of her throat. *There was no way she could have overdosed.* His whole body shook with relief when he felt the steady beat against his fingertips. Swallowing thickly, he tried to quiet his mind and think. To do the math. *She's so small,* he couldn't keep from thinking. *A miscalculation would be easy.* But she wasn't showing any obvious signs. If anything, she just appeared to be in a deep sleep. He shook her shoulders.

"Evelyn, wake up."

Her eyes remained closed. Her breathing deep and slow.

"Evelyn," he said harshly.

A shuffle made him look up. A few of the last stragglers had paused beside their seat. They eyed him curiously but said nothing. He waited for them to lose interest and move along before he tapped Evelyn's cheek.

"Wake up," he hissed.

Still, she remained as she was. Not even releasing a groan as he put more strength behind it. Her cheek reddened but she kept her eyes closed.

"Are you okay?"

Aleksandr jerked his head up to see a stewardess. *Get her out of here. Deal with the rest later.* He forced a smile and tried to look as innocent as possible.

"She's a heavy sleeper."

Not taking the time to see if his lie was believed, Aleksandr got to his feet, shoved his backpack on, and hurled Evelyn into his arms. Laced with hard muscle, she was a lot heavier than she looked. Especially as a dead weight. The limited space created quite a lot of jostling and the stewardess retreated to keep from getting hit.

"Do you need any help?" she asked.

"No. I've got her. Thanks."

He could feel the woman at his back, watching them carefully as they travelled down the aisle. *What are the odds that she alerts security?* he winced. *Probably about as good as no one questioning him carrying an unconscious woman through a crowded airport.* They still had a few hours of travel ahead of them and couldn't afford the delays.

Exiting the plane into the retractable tube, Aleksandr turned around, hoping that he had managed to look convincingly surprised to find the woman so close behind him.

"Hey, I don't suppose you have a wheelchair or something I could borrow. When she sleeps this deep, it's because she really needs it. I'd hate to wake her up if I don't have to."

"Of course," the stewardess said with a tightlipped smile.

Aleksandr watched her carefully, trying to determine what the woman was thinking. He had a growing unease that she was suspecting some kind of kidnapping.

"Come with me. We'll have some at the gate."

Remembering a moment later to thank her, he followed the woman through the tube. His mind whirled, trying to determine all the different ways this could unfold. *Come on, Evelyn, wake up,* he beseeched in his mind. *I can't get you out like this.* He reasoned that it might be for the best. The authorities would take her to a hospital. *It would be a lot easier to recollect her than keep a hold of her.*

Blood raced through his veins like liquid lead. Heaving and boiling. His muscles twitched as he arrived at the main area. It surprised him that the woman actually did supply him with a wheelchair. To keep with the story, Aleksandr made sure to fuss over Evelyn as he arranged her in the chair. She never gave any sign of coming around. Not so much as a flutter of her eyelids. The stewardess was still watching them. *Lie with enough confidence and people will question the facts.* Olga's voice echoed in Aleksandr's ears and he hated himself for using the advice.

"Shh, it's okay," Aleksandr said in a warm, hushed whisper. He shifted to the side, using his broad shoulders to obstruct the view of their witness. "Yeah, we're here. But you can sleep a little longer if you want."

Casting a look back, he smiled at the stewardess. "And just like that, she's out again."

Indecision lingered in her eyes. He saw the moment that Olga's words proved true.

"It happens more than you think. Some people just don't travel well. Come on, we'll go and get your bags."

"You don't need to come with us. I know you're busy."

The woman dismissed his protest with a wave. "I have to get the chair back anyway."

The only bag to their name was the carry on that Aleksandr had refused to relinquish for the whole of the flight. *Nothing suspicious about that.*

"Oh, no, our family is taking care of that," he said with a chuckle. "They get the bags, I have to lug this one to the resort. I got the worst end of that deal, didn't I?"

He succeeded enough in his illusion to have the woman's smile widen. The invitation turned to getting her to the front entrance. Tension coiled around his muscles like barbed wire as they progressed through customs and security. He couldn't take the crowd. Hundreds of people filled the space, creating a deafening roar that pressed against his nerves. It felt like all eyes were upon him. Endlessly scanning the crowd, Aleksandr never failed to make eye contact with a few people. Paranoia welled in the pit of his stomach. It was hard to keep a conversation going while he sought out the different exits.

Sunlight wafted in through the wall of glass that served as the entrance to the international airport. It carried with it the summer heat, creating golden bars of warmth that the air conditioning couldn't quell. The constant opening and closing of the doors allowed erratic gusts of fresh air to waft in. Aleksandr relished in them. In the promise of freedom. His eyelids fluttered closed as he tried to stifle a sigh, to keep his facade. *Just a few more feet.*

He stepped into the sunlight. It warmed his body, chasing away the artificial chill that had encased him for almost a day. Goosebumps rose up over his skin. *Almost.* The doors opened with a soft whoosh, allowing him to step out onto the wide footpath. His foot hit the ground and slipped. Gripping the arms of the wheelchair, he managed to keep it steady as he dropped onto one knee, landing with an audible splash. Tacky hot liquid seeped into his jeans as the rusted stench of blood filled his nose.

"Are you okay?"

The stewardess's question barely crossed the edges of his awareness. His attention was locked on the trail of blood. Droplets fell from the spokes of the wheels, adding to the thick puddle beneath the chair. Aleksandr pressed the tip of one finger into the blood by his knee. It was warm to the touch. Fresh but rotting. A quick glance was all he needed to know that Evelyn wasn't hurt. The path was made by drips and tires. He had dragged around enough corpses to know the pattern it created.

Life remained around him. People bustled past, eagerly clambering into the waiting cars, their shoes and luggage wheels smearing the bloody trail. The sun beat down upon his face. Announcements blared through the overhead speaker system. Conversations mingled with the rumble of engines. Horns interrupted laughter and provoked sharp words. Still, the blood remained.

"Sir?" The stewardess asked as she stepped closer. "Do you need help?"

Aleksandr's gaze traced the line of blood back to the entrance. Everything beyond the sliding glass doors was gone. All that remained was a sheet of complete darkness, as if the terminal had been swallowed by a black hole.

"Sir?"

Something stirred. Writhed. It bulged up from the floor, a glowing white against the abyss. Aleksandr never looked away as he steadily rose to his feet. Under the thin ivory veil of light, three bodies writhed, caught between clawing for freedom and twisting in agony. The light didn't illuminate the whole body at once. Limbs seemed to melt into the torso before reappearing. Their faces were distorted into eyes, screaming masks before they too rejoined the bulk of the body. With each push, they grew a little bigger. Became more visible.

"What's wrong?"

Aleksandr snapped around to the voice. It was only a second of distraction but, when he looked back, the terminal was just as it had been before. The blood on the ground was gone. The droplet on his finger remained.

"Sorry, I zoned out there for a bit." His forced smile failed him but his voice didn't waver.

"I guess you need some sleep, too."

The stewardess stepped closer to Evelyn, crouching as she did so.

"Hey, time to get up. Your car's waiting."

Her flesh peeled away from the bone like mist as she reached for Evelyn's shoulder. Aleksandr harshly yanked the chair away, preventing the contact and retreating a few steps.

"It's fine. I've got her."

His stammered explanation failed. The suspicion in her eyes shifted, giving way to something stronger. A heartbeat passed. Neither moved. Staring at the woman, Aleksandr witnessed the moment that the woman listened to the primitive part of her brain. The instant she felt the presence of the Furies. Her eyes widened. Her breath caught. But he was the one she could see.

The moment snapped and they both lunged forward. She latched onto the handles of the wheelchair and yanked. Aleksandr went for Evelyn, managing to pull her into his arms before the chair rolled back. He kicked, forcing it back harder than the stewardess had expected, throwing her off balance. The shock kept her silent for a second. Just long enough for Aleksandr to carry Evelyn to the nearest taxi. He hurled open the back door as the woman found her voice. Only after dumping the still unconscious Evelyn into the back seat did he bother to look at the driver.

"Hey! I already have a fair!"

"We need to get to the hospital," Aleksandr said. "Please, she's unconscious. We have to hurry."

He tried to speak over the shouts of the stewardess. Scrambling inside, he slammed the door shut, locking it just as the woman began to pound on the glass and scream for security.

"What's going on?" The driver asked.

"Hospital! Now!"

He reached between the side of the car and the passenger seat, managing to fumble the lock into place before the woman could try it.

"Hey, if–"

"My friend is dying! We can't wait around for an ambulance!"

The pretense was flimsy, but the desperation in Aleksandr's voice was real. The driver heard it and forced the car into gear. He cut out into traffic, leaving behind them the screaming woman and the blare of horns. Aleksandr only spared one glimpse behind. The stewardess stood on the road. She was screaming, her panic mangling her words and leaving those around her confused. There was an army of people at her disposal and no one knew enough to help. Guards and police were rushing towards her. It would be a moment before they would be able to calm her down enough to understand, he knew. *And a moment was all they needed.*

"Go faster," Aleksandr ordered as he spotted the three figures of ivory white standing in the middle of the chaos.

Still. Silent. Watching.

He waited until they were a few streets away from the hospital to attack, in hopes that it wouldn't take too long for them to be discovered. The man next to him had been easy. Half pinned under Evelyn's weight and caught off guard, he hadn't had a chance to fight back. Aleksandr had crushed his head against the metal rim of the car door. The driver had been harder to take care of. They swerved, bounced a curb, and rear-ended a parked car before coming to a stop. In a twist of luck, the street had been deserted as he dragged both unconscious men out of the car.

He headed north out of the city before switching cars. Whoever the owner of the station wagon was, he hoped that they weren't too put out. But Evelyn needed to be comfortable, and it had the space for her to lay down.

Eunice lived on an island situated a far distance down the coastline. The misdirection had cost them a few hours, and still she wasn't awake. His fear of her overdose had long since changed into something of a different breed. Darkness fell as he was driving down the highway. *A little longer. Find an empty parking lot. Check on her.* It was a list of priorities that he repeated endlessly to keep his focus. The moment he stopped, other thoughts entered. *They've got her. I can't get her back.*

***

It's just a dream! Evelyn knew it was. But no matter how much she screamed it in her mind, she couldn't drown out the cackling laughter of the Fury. It mocked her as she scurried away. *It's just a dream!* The laughter grew louder but it let her slip away. She pulled her legs up and kicked, catching the dark monstrosity in its jaw. Her heel passed through it as if it were made of mist. That infernal, maddening noise never stopped. The sand kicked up around her. Moving in piles under her, nails clawing into dry caked earth. It crunched under her weight. Making her drop. Slowing her pace. Allowing the disjointed creature to catch up. It took its time. A slow crawl that still consumed the distance between them.

"Wake up," Evelyn commanded herself.

There wasn't a trace of doubt within her that this was an illusion. A figment of her imagination. That didn't stop it from feeling real.

"Wake up. Wake up. Wake up."

Stay with me, the Fury whispered within her skull. *You belong with me.* It inched closer to her. Evelyn struck out blindly, her hands sliding through the creature even as it held her down.

"Wake up!" she screamed.

The creature began to melt, transforming from smoke to tar. Black and putrid, it rained down upon her. Filled her mouth. Burned her eyes. Made her skin blister and peel. Agony seared her flesh. Burned her down to her bones. Boiled her blood. As her flesh peeled away from her bones, the tar took its place. Drowning her. Setting her alight. Forging her into something new.

Chapter 11

A scream ripped from her throat as she finally managed to toss the monstrosity off of her. The world shattered like glass. She could feel each one slicing into her skin as they rained down upon her. Protecting her face with her arms left her no way to brace herself as the ground bucked under her. Something solid blocked her path, and she let out another scream. Pain exploded behind her eyes. Suddenly, everything jerked to a halt and she was tossed forward. Another impact. Another burst of agony.

"Evelyn!"

"Alek?" she groaned through clenched teeth. Steadily, her senses returned enough for her to take in her surroundings. "Why am I on the floor of a car?"

"You were on the seat," he countered apologetically.

"Until you hit the brakes."

"You screamed."

"I just woke up," she argued.

"You've been asleep for over a day."

Shock cleared the fog in her head. She looked up as Aleksandr slipped an arm between the two front seats. It was an awkward hold. She almost popped his shoulder out of its socket and came close to kicking him in the head, but eventually, she was in the front passenger seat. She wiped off her brow, heaved a breath, and twisted around to face him.

"What is this about a day?" she demanded.

"Do you remember getting on the second flight?"

"Of course, I do," she said. "There was that stupid delay. I must have fallen asleep on the tarmac."

"You were rendered unconscious from a dose of potent painkillers."

"I like my way better."

"My first thought was that you overdosed."

"No," she shook her head and blinked rapidly. "I think it was the Furies."

"That was my second thought," he acknowledged.

Drawing her knees up to her chest, she wrapped her arms around her legs. "It was like it was keeping me there."

"But you escaped."

"Maybe."

He bit down on his thumbnail. "Meaning they might have let you go?"

She hunched her shoulders. "I don't know. Maybe? Why doesn't that make me feel warm and fuzzy?"

"Because we're becoming the main form of entertainment for paranormal psychopaths," he huffed.

She couldn't help but smirk. "That's so different for you."

Pausing on chewing his nail, he narrowed his eyes.

"What? Making fun of you is my tension relief." When that didn't alleviate his scorn, she offered a weak smile. "Hey, I was just terrorized. Cut me some slack."

"What was it like?"

"Honestly? A nightmare I couldn't wake up from. Simple as that. Out of curiosity, what were you going to do? You know, to wake me up?"

He nipped at his thumb thoughtfully before muttering around it, "No idea."

Thinking that over, she could only come to one conclusion. "We can't sleep anymore."

"Maybe in short shifts. You only dream in R.E.M sleep. That's deep sleep. If we stick to quick bursts, we might be alright."

"How do you know that?"

"It was in the twins' homework a month or so back."

The sky outside darkened, making the overhead lights battle against the growing night. Without a word, Aleksandr turned the engine back on. There was no reason to ask where they were going. Evelyn already knew that.

"How far 'til we get there?" she asked.

"We're almost there." He shivered with disgust. "Just the worst part to go."

"Ah," she said as she fastened her seatbelt. "The boat ride."

The trip was far shorter than she had anticipated. Far too soon for Aleksandr. She could see it in the white knuckled grip he had on the steering wheel. The tendons of his neck twitched and strained against his skin. *If he doesn't calm down, he's going to have an aneurysm,* Evelyn thought with a hint of amusement. *At least he's not chewing his nail. That's when things get bad.* She had barely finished the thought when his right hand lifted to his mouth.

"I think you've developed a twitch," she said.

"Must be all this sunshine and fresh air."

He pulled up to the harbor. Evelyn couldn't help but think that it was a horrible spot for it. Perhaps the waterways were good. She didn't know much about boats, but it was hidden amongst warehouses and industrial roads. *It wouldn't have killed them to put up a few more signs,* Evelyn thought. Then, she supposed, that might have been the point. Only the people who knew where they were going could find it.

"So, this island is a resort. But it also has normal housing?" she asked, trying to find a way to distract him.

"That's what the twins said." His voice turned into a deep rumble as it escaped his clenched teeth.

"And Eunice lives in one of these houses?"

"You know this already, Tempest."

"Just trying to distract you."

"You're horrible at it," he said, still sounding on the verge of pain.

Lights on the horizon forced their hand. The ferry to the island was pulling in and they had to be there to meet it. Unbuckling her seatbelt, she offered him a quick smile.

"It's just a little boat ride."

"I understand."

"It'll all be safe and regulated. There will be life jackets."

He glared at her as they got out of the car. "It's not the threat of drowning that's the problem."

"Right. You're aquaphobic."

She ensured that the word didn't come out as an accusation. If anyone had a reason to be fearful of water, it was Aleksandr. She had never been able to get his confession out of her head. The tale of his little brother rotting into sludge in the family bathroom. She had nightmares for years. Dreams that she had been the one Olga and Petya had forced to bathe with the decaying remains of their sibling. It showed his sheer force of will that he was even able to set foot in a bathroom again. She must have failed in her attempt for the perfect tone because he ended up glaring at her.

"I can handle it."

"Fine," she said.

"Fine," he repeated in a petulant tone.

"Well then, we're in agreement."

"I suppose we are."

"Let's go then," she said.

His bravado faded in an instant and he was back to chewing on his quickly diminishing thumbnail.

"I'm right with you," she said.

"That's a comfort?"

"I resent that you make it sound like a question," she smirked.

He rolled his eyes, which she assumed was about as good as she was going to get. By now, the final boarding call was sounding and they had to jog to make it in time. Most of the seats were already taken by the time they paid the fare. They were forced to sit separately. She kept Aleksandr in the corner of her eyes. He appeared fine until the boat actually started moving. The first jolt had him clutching his cheap plastic seat. It got worse as they moved out of the harbor.

She wondered if it were easier or harder for him to make this trip at night. The ocean lay out before them like oil. Moonlight caught the tips of the waves, gilding them with silver. The air was laced with the scent of saltwater and the sea spray made it impossible to pretend they were anywhere else. For fifteen minutes or so, they crept along at a sluggish pace. Waves lapped against the side of the hull. Evelyn would have described it as a pleasant sound.

Aleksandr appeared to have a very different definition.

Caught between the desperate need to keep his grip and the neurotic urge to bite his nails. He kept his eyes locked on the water-slicked plastic that served as the walkway. *Look up,* she willed him. *That's just nothing but a reminder that you're on a boat, idiot.*

They passed a final cluster of lights. One turn and the driver pushed the throttle. The front of the boat reared up like a living beast. Evelyn was pushed back into her seat at the sudden burst of speed. Around her, people gave surprised gasps and released nervous little chuckles. That was soon disrupted by a hard thump and a few disgruntled murmurs. Aleksandr, never one to do something as normal as whimpering, had slammed his fist into a chair in front of him, hard enough to make it crack. Hunched forward, with one forearm braced on his thigh and the other still gripping the chair, he panted each breath through his bared teeth.

She hadn't realized how much he relied on his long hair until now. It was his eyes that gave him away. She'd seen them show his pain and fear. But now they glistened with rage. Pure, unrelenting, feral rage. A coping mechanism she used herself. *Fear's crippling. Terror leaves you weak and vulnerable. But anger.* She smirked at the thought. *Anger's useful.*

Resentment, fury, disgust; they were all emotions that could be transformed into purpose. Action. She had long since reconciled herself to the fact that she had survived this long not because of intelligence or luck. But spite. It drove her forward. The bitter disgust that something, human or otherwise, would try to reduce her to nothing more than a victim. *Not exactly noble. But effective.* Apparently, Aleksandr had come to a very similar conclusion. The dim light within the body caught the first droplets of sweat that beaded across his forehead. He looked fevered, near deranged. A wounded animal ready to strike.

"Hey," Evelyn said as she pushed past the man beside her. Reaching across the aisle, she tapped the person next to Aleksandr. She had to put some force into it to get them to tear their eyes away from the growling man beside him. "Yeah, hi. That's my friend. Wanna switch?"

The person nodded readily, and after some awkward shuffling, they managed to change places. Leaping over each other, the boat rattled and thumped. Evelyn dropped heavily into the seat beside Aleksandr, her shoulder slamming against his side. He didn't acknowledge her.

"You're scaring the locals," she whispered.

He growled.

"Not helping."

His eyes flicked to her. *He really needs his hair back,* she decided in that instant. From the first moment they had met, when Petya had joyously declared that she was to die by Aleksandr's hands, there had always been a vulnerability about him. Like a dog that had been kicked too often. Volatile but pitiful. Fear had stripped him bare. Returned him to a wounded beast that should have been put down long ago. Ice formed in her veins when she looked into his eyes.

"Alek?" Swallowing thickly, she pressed, "You're here with me, right?"

Body still as stone. Eyes screaming the fevered mania that swirled like a hurricane within his mind. Evelyn had seen this before. Not with Aleksandr. Nor Petya and Olga. It was the same look her mother gave her before wrapping her hands around her throat.

"Alek," she pressed, her voice weaker than she had intended.

Her hand trembled as she reached out to him. She hesitated twice before she was able to touch the hand he gripped the chair with. It was the slightest of contact, barely anything at all, and he still flinched as if her fingers were a branding iron. He blinked rapidly. Something shifted, but the bloodlust didn't fully fade away.

"You've got my back?" she asked.

He nodded slowly, as if the motion itself caused him pain.

"Anything you want to share?"

"I'm okay."

She eyed him carefully. It was still there. The sensation of a beast on the edge. Prepared to snap and take someone with them.

"You're with me?" she asked again, tightening her grip on his hand.

His lips peeled back from clenched teeth. "Yes."

"Hold onto that."

"For as long as I can."

Evelyn didn't ask what would happen if his grip slipped. Instead, she held his hand tight and kept her gaze focused on the lights of the island that emerged on the horizon.

Chapter 12

Aleksandr thought his fingers would break. It didn't stop him from squeezing harder. Vaguely, he was aware that he had garnished the attention of the other passengers. *You're drawing attention,* Petya's voice whispered in his ear. The sound of it put him on edge. It made him wonder if a part of his parents lived on inside him. *You'll never be free of us.* Both Olga and Petya had told him that a thousand times. It was their favorite taunt and shackle to put around his neck. Murder and madness tied him to his family. It was a bond that even death couldn't sever. The damage was done. The scars were too deep. Aleksandr knew he was tainted and there was no way to clean his soul of the stains. No matter what he did, a part of him would always be the monster they had intended him to be.

"Alek?"

He snapped around to Evelyn's voice. Fighting against the raging current of his thoughts, he worked his way back to the moment. To Evelyn. Ashamed of his display of weakness, it was a struggle to meet her gaze.

"Alek, look at me."

Clenching his jaw until his teeth ached, he forced himself to look up. The iron will in her gaze helped to steady his own nerves, and he swallowed thickly.

"We're here, Alek. Time to move."

Holding her gaze, he nodded. "Right."

"You have to get up," she stressed.

"Yes."

Her eyebrows crept up her forehead. "*Now,* Aleksandr."

The knowledge of having to move didn't mesh well with the reality of it. He couldn't move. No matter how hard he tried, his limbs remained heavy, his bones locked into place. The warmth of her fingers pried his palm loose from the chair.

"Just keep your eyes on me," she instructed.

She waited for him to nod before she began to pull. Getting his legs to work was a battle. At first, most of the work was on Evelyn. She took the task without debate or comment. With an unwavering strength, she steadily hurled him on his feet and took on his weight to keep him upright. It was then that he noticed they were the last ones still aboard. In his relief, he slumped against her a little more. Once again, she didn't complain. They shuffled along together to the opening that would release them onto the dock. At first, he had imagined that to be the point of his salvation. That illusion was shattered the moment his feet hit the bobbing wooden beam.

His knees buckled. Wrapping an arm around his waist, Evelyn kept him from hitting the dock. Her grip was as sure as iron, keeping one arm slung over her shoulders. They were just about the same height and they moved without knocking into each other. Still, he could only get a few feet before he had to pause for breath.

"We're almost there," she said.

He growled.

"Yeah, I know you don't like this," she smirked.

His glare only made her smile. She squeezed his wrist and jerked her head towards the end of the planks.

"Come on. It's just another walk through hell. Nothing we haven't done before."

"Hell's nice this time of year," he said, deep voice reduced to the whimpered crunch of gravel.

But it made her laugh. The sound released some of the tension in her chest and they started to move again. He kept his eyes locked on the resort entrance. Fairy lights lined the rising slope of the dock. It rose up a few feet up from the water to join onto a restaurant deck area. Just beyond that was a relatively normal hotel check-in area. Only more open to the elements. *A few more feet,* he told himself. *Just a few more feet.*

The array of scents wafting out from the restaurant helped more than it probably should have. It covered the scent of seawater and wet sand. As they neared, the chatter of the restaurant and nearby bar rose loud enough to cover the lapping of the water below them. *A few more feet.* Breathing became a little easier with every step.

"Oh, look," Evelyn said cheerfully. "There's karaoke on tonight."

"Stop," he groaned.

"I bet you have a lovely singing voice."

"I'm going to get you back."

"Can't wait," she beamed.

It kept him moving those last few steps and they reached the flat area. Aleksandr laughed. It came out as a strange kind of mewling sound that he instantly regretted. They crossed into the spacious reception area to find that the planks extended into this room as well. Aleksandr stopped dead when he heard the echo.

"There's nothing under us but a clear drop into water, is there?"

"I'm sure there are some pipes or something," she replied.

He heaved a sigh, straightened his spine, and took some of his own weight off of her shoulders. Not quite ready to let her go too far, he grabbed her hip and pressed her to his side.

"Aw. I didn't think you cared," she teased.

"If I end up killing anyone, it's going to be you."

"Tough words from a guy who lost our last fight."

"I stabbed you," he muttered out of the corner of his mouth.

"That wasn't a fight. That was a minor tiff. So, who's paying?"

"I took some cash off of a few people. It's in the front pocket of the bag. Damn it, the bag. We have to go back."

Evelyn shifted her torso to bump the backpack against his side. "I've got ya covered. Just keep breathing."

And then they were at the reception desk. They had already drawn the attention of the man behind the desk. Tall and slender, he towered over both of them as they neared.

"Not locals, I take it?" the man asked, a thick Australian accent playing over his words.

"Oh, this," Evelyn said.

Neither of them had thought to come up with a passable explanation for their current state.

"Don't worry about it," the man said. *Jim,* his nametag read. "This happens all the time when the water's choppy. Some people just shouldn't travel by boat."

Evelyn latched onto the excuse. "Yeah, he could get seasick in a bathtub."

Just the mention of a tub was enough to make Aleksandr's stomach lurch. A pathetic little groan worked its way out of his throat and his head flopped forward.

"Let's get you checked in before he throws up in my lobby, yeah?" Jim chuckled. "What's the name of your reservation?"

Out of the corner of his eyes, Aleksandr noticed Evelyn turning towards him.

"Thornton," he mumbled.

Jim was already tapping at the keyboard of his computer. "Alright, just give me one second."

"When did you make the reservations?" Evelyn whispered.

"Twins did while we were en route," he swallowed. "When are you going to catch on that we've done this sort of thing a lot?"

"Right."

She pulled him closer to the counter, letting it take his weight as she started digging through the backpack. It appeared to amuse her to find his fake ID and a few handfuls of brightly colored Australian cash. She handed it all over at Jim's request.

"Alright, Mr. Thornton."

"Richard."

Jim smiled as he handed back the ID. "Richard. We've got you with us for a week, is that right?"

"Yep," Evelyn answered for him. Aleksandr was incredibly grateful for it.

Jim took them swiftly through the necessary process of checking in. Their room keys and a general idea of the island layout. As an eco-lodge, it was a matter of pride that the environmental impact was kept to a minimum. A few standard resort rooms were clustered near the shoreline. The cabins, however, had each been designed to give the guest the impression they were alone on the island. A pioneer in untouched natural beauty. As such, a thick forest, filled with wallabies and snakes, separated the resort area from the residential one. There were a number of nature walks and bike paths. Most of the entertainment was outside. Tennis courts, swimming pools, natural lakes, and a variety of sporting grounds. On the far end of the island was a beach view restaurant and there was another one closer by. They received a map and a warning to keep to the lit walkways to avoid stepping on something they shouldn't.

He barely paid attention. Every lull in the conversation allowed him to hear the lapping waves under his feet. Evelyn thanked Jim, collected everything, and thumped Aleksandr on the shoulder.

"Ready to go?" she asked.

"God, yes," he groaned.

He still felt sick to his stomach but was able to carry his own weight again. Letting him set the pace, Evelyn kept close to his side, studying the map while they still had the light.

"Do you know where Eunice lives?" she asked.

"No. But she's a local. The restaurant staff would be able to give us a clue."

"I don't think they're just going to come out and give us that kind of information," she scoffed.

"We're not going to ask directly," he replied in a clipped tone. "It's called subtly."

"Well, I suggest we clean up a bit first then. No one will tell us anything looking like this."

He swept his eyes over her. Almost two days of travel and no chance to shower had taken its toll. *If Evelyn looks run down, I must look like a troll.* Aleksandr knew that he had harsh features. Coupled with his perpetual scowl, it didn't take much for him to appear untrustworthy or cold. Reluctantly, he nodded.

"Fine," he mumbled.

"Okay. We just have to cross the bridge."

"Bridge?"

They stepped out into the night and his stomach dropped. Before them was a giant ocean fed lake. There was an island in the middle, fitted with the promised restaurant and a pool. A narrow bridge connected it all together.

"I hate this place."

"We just have to cut across and you'll be surrounded by trees and poisonous reptiles."

"No one ever said they were poisonous," he muttered.

She kept the chatter up, keeping him distracted as they crossed the lit path. Having solid earth at the mid-point helped to get him through it. During the walk, he recalled once reading that exposure to a fear could help people overcome it. If there was any truth to it, it didn't come. He felt sick the entire time. And bitterly resented every second of it.

He kept his eyes fixed on the far bank. It was marked with one last bright light. Its brilliant glow highlighted a patch of pathway and the beginning of the tree line. The trees were thin and tall, like skeletal fingers clawing out from the earth. No light penetrated the gaps in between. It was impossible to see more than a few inches into the interlocking leaves. Ferns covered the ground, hip high and lush. *Petya would have loved it*, Aleksandr thought. *An army could hide in there, unseen.*

Finally, the planks of wood gave way to grass and gravel. Aleksandr closed his eyes as he dropped onto a knee, barely managing to brace a hand on the ground before he crumbled into a fetal position. Blades of grass tangled around his fingers and his nails dug into the rich earth. It was almost an intoxicating sensation. *Land. Solid earth.* Aleksandr didn't believe himself to be a spiritual man, although he steadfastly believed that hell was real. He couldn't stomach the idea that his family would go unpunished. So, he didn't really know which God he was thanking when he muttered a few prayers. *God wouldn't be on your side*, Olga's voice laughed in his ear.

"Do you need a minute?" Evelyn asked.

"I need a drink," he muttered.

"Sorry, all out. But I wouldn't mind another dose of painkillers if you've got 'em."

Opening his eyes, Aleksandr nodded. "We should clean your stitches, too."

"Also important."

Aleksandr rolled his eyes and resigned himself to the fact that they've reached that point. That threshold of stress that made it impossible to have a conversation devoid of sarcasm. Getting back to his feet, he didn't bother to brush the dirt off of his knees.

"Which way?" he asked.

She checked the map once more by the light of the lamppost. "All of the rooms look to be separate cabins." Pointing off to the left, she continued. "If we follow this, it should loop around past the tennis court and get us there."

"Why are you saying it so weird?"

"Because I don't want to go the fastest route."

He arched an eyebrow and she pointed to the woods. After his eyes adjusted, he noticed a slender path that was cut into the thick brush.

"I don't like snakes," she said.

"I didn't know that."

"Well, seeing the Furies turn into rattlesnakes the size of buildings left a lasting impression."

"Fair enough. Lead the way."

The sounds of the restaurant faded away with the light. A few solar powered lamp posts lighted the borders of the pathway. But they were far spaced and dull. Completely inadequate to deal with the darkness that gathered under the canopy. One twist in the path and they were severed from the rest of the world. Evelyn pulled out her phone and clicked on the flashlight. The addition did little. Unseen animals moved through the underbrush, rustling the ferns and crunching the dead leaves. They both snapped their head up when something flew overhead. The screeching of a bat joined the flutter of wings and the call of what he assumed was a bird.

"People come here to relax," Evelyn whispered.

"I'm sure it's a lot better in daylight."

They kept close to each other as they ventured on. The world steadily reduced down until nothing could be seen beyond Evelyn's flashlight. Aleksandr didn't let his gaze settle onto any one thing for two long, taking note of every trace of movement he could discover. Steadily, their speed dwindled until they were barely covering any distance. Evelyn gasped. He looked over to see her clutching her shoulder. *She's nervous.* He had long since noticed her habit of rolling her shoulders when she was preparing for a fight.

"Are you okay?" he asked.

She drew a harsh breath in through her nose and nodded.

"Give me the backpack."

It was a struggle to get it off her without further pain. His fingers brushed something tacky. Not wanting to concern her, he sniffed it instead of asking her to shine her light onto the fabric. *Blood. Did she pop a stitch?*

"Sit down," he instructed as he unzipped the bag.

"Here?"

She pointed her flashlight onto his face and squinted into the glare.

"Do you want to wait for the next dose?"

"Here is good," she said and plopped down without further hesitation.

Crouching down next to her, he blindly found the hidden compartment that had kept his stash from discovery. While he prepared the specially made needle, one that his parents had constructed for just such occasions, Evelyn continuously scanned the area with her phone. Sitting here, it was easy to believe that there wasn't another human being on the island. The forest smothered the light and muffled the noise, leaving only the chatter of the animals and the whisper of the wind through the trees. At any other time, the silence would have soothed Aleksandr.

Evelyn swiped her phone around them like a lighthouse. Each pass glistened off of the syringe tip. She left it to him to pull the neckline of her dress aside to expose the stitched-up wound.

"Light," he said softly.

She reluctantly focused the beam onto her shoulder, although she didn't relinquish her role as look out.

He rested the tip of the needle against her skin. "Ready?"

"Just don't give me enough to knock me out," she said.

As gently as possible, he broke the skin. She winced slightly but took it without complaint.

"What exactly are you giving me, anyway?" she asked.

"Don't worry about it."

"Alright," she shrugged with her good shoulder. "But, for the record, it seems like something that should concern me."

"Duly noted." He smiled softly and packed away the needle.

Along with the drug itself, there were the basics of a first aid kit. He retrieved a few antiseptic wipes and drew her phone closer. He carefully checked them over as he cleaned the sweat from her wound. Nothing had torn free from her flesh. Droplets of blood welled around her stitches, looking as black as tar when the shadows touched it. Brow furrowing, he pressed the cloth a little harder to the wound. She hissed.

"Sorry," he said.

Her hands balled, her teeth clenched, but she still responded with a strained, "I'm fine."

He pulled the antiseptic cloth away, but before he could look at it, a small voice crept out from the shadows. A shrill voice. One that cackled around each syllable and broke like glass.

"I see you."

Chapter 13

The solar lights that lined the path flicked off. Without them, the night rushed forward like a hungry beast ready to consume them. The thin beam of Evelyn's mobile phone was all that was left to see by. She snapped it around to direct it on the patch of forest the voice had come from. The beam weakened before it reached the other side of the path. As her eyes adjusted, she could make out shapes amongst the darkness. Branches and slender trunks. Shifting ferns that rustled both with winds and wildlife.

"Can you see anything?" Evelyn whispered.

"No."

Carefully, they rose to their feet. A twig snapped behind them. Both of them whipped around, the thin beam failing to highlight whatever had moved.

"*I see you,*" the voice whispered again.

Evelyn kept the light focused as it was and looked over her shoulder.

"You heard that, right?"

"Yes," Aleksandr's voice lowered to a growl as he whispered.

"Is that good or bad?"

"Take your pick."

She swallowed thickly and fought down the urge to roll her shoulders. It left an increasing tension inside of her with no outlet. It prickled across her skin and twisted up her gut. Her feet shuffled over the rough concrete of the path as she restlessly turned. There was no other source of light. Nothing stirred.

"Let's go," Aleksandr said as he grabbed her elbow.

"Harder to hit a moving target," she acknowledged with a nod. "Yeah. Alright."

Still, she didn't move until he pulled at her arm again. They stumbled for a few feet before adopting a stronger stride. With the still darkness, it felt like they never moved an inch. That they were simply walking in place. *No escape. Nowhere to go,* she thought. Aleksandr kept close. Tipping his head, he whispered into her ear.

"Can you run?"

"Faster than you," she smirked.

It was agreed without discussion that she would wait for him to make the call. He had more experience with monsters, and she trusted his instincts. Their footsteps and the soft wail of wind through the trees filled the humid night air. She forced her breathing to be even and slow, keeping it in time with the sway of her light.

"*I see you.*"

They paused.

"Did that sound closer?" Evelyn asked.

The question lingered unspoken between them; if the Fury was trying to herd them backwards, it was best to push on. By the same token, moving forward could be heading towards the beast. Aleksandr's hand found her elbow again and squeezed slightly. She balled her free hand. Her arm trembled as she tried to resist rolling her shoulders. The inability to move as she wished was like a shackle around her neck. She felt hindered and broken. Still, at Aleksandr's touch, she forced herself forward.

Their pace was slower now. Hesitant. Cautious. Another twist in the path and the dim light of her phone caught on some metal. She fixed the beam on the spot and brought a chain-link fence into view. A tennis court lay beyond. There were a few other items, perhaps an outdoor weight set, but she couldn't make out the finer details.

"We're halfway there," she told him.

A few feet more and the shadow of a short, wide building emerged from the inky darkness. At first, she thought it was just an illusion created as her eyes strained for a glimpse of light. When her suspicion grew, she nudged Aleksandr with her elbow and jerked her head towards the building. The grunt he gave made it clear that he saw the lights too. Soft, blurred, pulsing pin prinks of color. It lured them in closer. Their footsteps became silent as they closed in on the side of the building.

Hovering points of light suddenly burst into existence. Evelyn jumped back, crouching low, muscle memory pulling her body into a defensive stance. It was the sweeping movement of her hand that made her want to kick herself.

"It's glass," she whispered to Aleksandr.

He looked around his raised knuckles to throw her a quizzical look. In response, she slowly waved the phone back and forth. The floating lights followed the movement, illuminating the series of small sheets of glass that had been set like a checkerboard into the wall. Kept clean, it didn't take much for the building to reflect the light. Aleksandr thrust his hands down, more annoyed than relieved. The furrow of his brow made her turn back. Reflection explained the dancing white lights. Not the colored ones.

Aleksandr clicked his tongue to regain her attention. A jerk of his head indicated the door. The opening in the wall was covered with a metal gate. It was obviously not part of the original structure since there was a good few inches at the top and bottom of the threshold left unguarded. Moving as silent as ghosts, they crossed over to the door, each one picking a side of the solid wall to press against. The glass, warmed by the hot air, grabbed at Evelyn's sweaty shoulder as she carefully leaned towards the gap. Her phone preceded her, scanning the room. Old arcade games lined the walls. An air hockey table filled the middle and she glimpsed a door beyond it. *No lights,* she noticed. She arched an eyebrow at Aleksandr. The features of his face barely moved, but his expression still somehow screamed, 'no shit'.

She tipped her head. *Should we go in? Check it out?* There was a degree of madness to the thought. The gated door was the easiest way in and out. Not exactly a great situation if something was lurking in there. Despite all this, Evelyn wanted to go. Wanted to face it. To show the Furies that she wasn't playing their games anymore. She wasn't afraid.

Aleksandr's sharp gaze flicked across her face before surveilling the room once more. He nodded. It made her smile. It was in that moment that she realized just how much she craved a fight. She turned off her phone and shoved it into the pocket of her dress. As the light faded, Aleksandr crouched to hide the backpack under a few rocks by the door. A small rattle of metal told her that he had opted for climbing up the gate. Evelyn dropped to the ground and slid under it, grateful for once that she was small. The motion made her shoulder burn. Tears of pain pricked in the back of her eyes and she bit her tongue to keep herself from whimpering.

The rough concrete floor scraped at her palms and chest as she squeezed under the bar. Aleksandr dropped down next to her, inches from her fingers. It was a soft sound. *Boy can move like a cat when he wants to,* Evelyn noted with annoyance. She jumped up, a spike of pain almost making her crumble again. *Won't be long for the painkillers to kick in,* she told herself. It helped her to keep her silence. On her feet, the dark bars blocking her exit and the cavernous room before her, she realized just how stupid a plan this was.

Footsteps made her heart stutter. Slowly, calmly, they clicked over the stone floor. The sound echoed. It was impossible to pinpoint the source. All she could tell for sure was that the person was drawing closer. Evelyn slipped her left foot back and twisted her torso, taking on a boxer's stance, making her body a smaller target. The footsteps became louder. Heavy breaths joined the sound. Labored and stuttered and producing puffs of foul air. Aleksandr's hand touched her arm, silently coaxing her to the side, away from the limited moonlight that could slip through the bars. Working blind, she followed his taps, shoving her hand into her pocket to retrieve her phone. Her fingers only found material and stitching. *It fell out,* she realized, her heartbeat picking up. *Why are girls' pockets always so small?*

Her eyes adjusted and she spotted a small black square sitting just beyond the bars. Instinctively, she reached for it. Before she could make it a step, the moonlight was blocked. Not by the door. On the floor. A dark shadow of a woman clomped across the rectangle shredded moonbeams that lay upon the concrete. There was no source. No physical being by the doorway to cast the shadow. Only the shadow itself. Evelyn scurried back, knocking into Aleksandr as they pressed deeper into the darkness. Scraping footsteps marked the shadow's movements as it lumbered into a position in the center of the doorway. Then it turned. As if looking for them. Aleksandr and Evelyn froze, holding their breath, eyes focused on the dark shape. It didn't move. Evelyn's chest rattled with her heartbeat. Her lungs ached for air. Silence.

"*I see you.*"

Color exploded before her. A dozen blinding lights that burned her eyes. A carnival of noise and mechanical whirls. She ducked away, her hip hitting the air hockey table as she turned. Where she had been hiding was now lit up like a stage. An old game had been turned on. Little cartoon spiders poked up out of the holes in the base, moving in time to the music, taunting the passing players to hit them and earn their points. A plastic statue of a giant funnel web spider, fitted with a shawl and a toothy, welcoming grin, hung on the back of the machine. It tilted its head from side to side. Time had worn the gears, reducing what should have been a smooth motion into a broken jerk.

"*I see you,*" the machine declared before unleashing a cackle.

Gripping the side of the air hockey machine, Evelyn whirled back around, desperate to catch sight of the shadow again. The moonlight was unable to exist alongside the array of pulsing lights. Colors splashed and danced over the floor, unbroken or blocked.

"It's gone," Evelyn said.

Aleksandr's shoulders squared as he looked around the room. Neither of them believed the Fury had let them go so easily. It was lurking somewhere. Waiting. Bracing one hand on the side of the air hockey table, Aleksandr jumped up, using the vantage point to search the space. Adrenaline ran through Evelyn's veins like a livewire. The flickering lights made shadows grow and fade. They lingered in corners and in the cracks behind the machines. Danced over the walls. Gathered under the table. Each time she thought she spotted the creature, the lighting changed and it would disappear before her eyes. As if it had never been there. Clenching her fists, she stalked to the end of the table, randomly crouching low to check under it as she went.

"Alek?"

"I'm not sure," he admitted. "Retreat?"

"Bloody hell," she hissed by way of agreement.

"*I see you,*" the machine crackled again.

Its music began, distorted and slow, as if emitting its death throes. The simple tune wobbled and sputtered, reducing to a whining crawl.

"*I see you.*"

As if struck, the game bucked, rattling a few feet before slamming back onto the stone floor. The tune sped up, rushing to a fevered pace, the notes becoming shrill screams instead of a melody. The game lurched again and fell, crashing face down in a hailstorm of plastic and sparks. It blocked Evelyn's path back to the door.

"*I. See. You.*" Plastic ground against concrete as the machine shook.

The music stopped. The last of the sparks died. The lights gave one last brilliant pulse before flickering off. By the glow of the other machines, she could see something leaking out from under it. Bleeding from the machine's body.

"Do arcade games have oil?" Aleksandr asked.

Evelyn's eyes bulged as the black mass scattered and took shape. Not a pool of liquid but an ever-increasing swarm of spiders. She hopped up onto the table as the arachnids flooded out to cover the floor. Their bodies, slick and smooth, reflected the joyful lights of the games as the click of their exoskeletons rose above the blaring songs. Evelyn squirmed as she watched them, her skin crawling.

"Maybe the back door," she said as she pointed towards the back. "I think it was over there."

Aleksandr's eyes widened.

"You never told me you were afraid of spiders."

"This is a little different," he hissed.

The squeak of straining plastic silenced them. Hesitantly, they turned back to the fallen machine. With a thunderous crack, the large decorative spider tore one leg free from the backing. It scrambled and twisted, battling to free another limb. Then another. Leverage made the rest easy. It peeled itself away and scattered across the floor. Rearing back its front legs, the tips of them almost brushing the ceiling, it snapped its head up. Almost human. Undeniably rotting. Its lips pulled back in a grotesque snarl. Black venom dripped from its fangs like saliva and the hollow pits of its eyes glowed like red embers.

"*I see you.*"

Aleksandr and Evelyn flew off of the table and bolted for the door. Spiders crunched under their shoes. Their innards slicked the floor, quickly reducing their steps into wayward slides. Manic laughter filled the space as the spider launched itself towards them. It landed on the air hockey table, shattering it under its weight. Evelyn found the door tucked away in the far corner. As she grasped the handle, Aleksandr beside her, a blur streaked across the corner of her eyes. The wood splintered under the strike of spider leg. As thick as a human arm, the leg ripped a line through the door as it clawed free.

"Get the door open!" Aleksandr said.

He ducked from her sight and she grabbed the handle with both palms, finding it locked. Spiders crawled up her legs, under the hem of her dress, finding tender skin to sink their fangs into. Poison scorched her veins like acid. Her hands shook again as she gave up on the handle and instead threw her body against the already battered wood. The door rattled on its hinges. The cracks deepened. Spiders reached her wound. She couldn't stifle her screams of agony.

Throwing herself harder against the door, she caught sight of Aleksandr behind her. Straddling the enormous spider, he grabbed one of the creature's fangs with both hands and yanked back. The fang ripped free with a gush of poison and blood. Aleksandr instantly drove it back down, crushing the hard exoskeleton and releasing new waves of slop. He didn't hesitate to strike again. Rearing back, Evelyn kicked out with every ounce of strength she could summon, sending the small spiders flying in all directions. Her heel collided with the handle, snapping it in two. The door slammed open to reveal the darkened innards of a convenience store.

"Alek!"

She passed through the door, batting the spiders off of her skin, crushing them under her shoes. Aleksandr sprinted across the threshold and shoved her aside. Before she could hit the floor, the arms of the enormous spider surged through the doorway. They wrapped around him, hurled him off of his feet, dragging him back to its sole remaining fang. It sunk into the soft skin of his neck. Black sludge gushed up around the fang, mixing with the blood that poured free.

Evelyn jumped to her feet. Ignoring the spiders that were still attempting to burrow into her flesh, she raced to grab Aleksandr's outstretched hand. With a feral scream, Aleksandr drove the severed fang over his shoulder and into the spider's eye. Green blood oozed free, but it didn't let go. Grabbing his shoulder in one hand and bracing her other palm against the spider's face, Evelyn tore Aleksandr free. Bone snapped and skin ripped. Bellowing to the sky, Aleksandr dropped free. They both landed in a heap, an entwined sprawl of blood, flesh, and spiders. Rolling onto her side, Evelyn kicked the door closed. It swung shut as if something pulled it from the other side.

An echoing slam, and the world was silent once more.

Chapter 14

Aleksandr couldn't breathe. He could feel his lungs liquefying, drowning him from the inside. Each limb was as heavy as lead. It prevented him from rolling onto his side, from spitting the liquid out, eliminating any chance of drawing one last gasp.

"It's not real," Evelyn said as she hurried to his side. "Come on, snap out of it!"

He opened his mouth but could only force frothy bubbles past his lips. Evelyn's fist cracked against his jaw.

"Get a grip! We need to go!"

A dull ringing filled his ears and blurred her words. Squeezing his eyes shut, he gathered his senses, forcing reality back into place. His chest swelled as air poured into it. The force arched him off the floor like a physical blow. He dropped to the side, coughing and sputtering, and spitting onto the tiles.

"There you go," she said as she pressed a hand between his shoulder blades.

Gulping down breaths, he glared at her. "You hit me."

"You had it coming."

He shrugged, stunned to find that it didn't hurt. The wound wasn't there.

"It wasn't real," he mumbled.

"Well, the door damage was, though. And I'm pretty sure this place would have a silent alarm, so let's go."

She was already pulling him up, and he scrambled to be of some use.

"You could have killed me," he said. "You could have ripped my throat open."

"I took a risk."

"A risk?"

She dragged his arm over her shoulders and pulled him tight to her side. "Yeah. I gambled that the giant arcade game spider wasn't real."

They staggered past the counter. Aleksandr pulled away to grab a bottle of water, downing half of it before he met her scolding look.

"I'll leave a big tip," he muttered.

Thinking over that, she grabbed a handful of glow sticks from a display by the cash register.

"If something did have me, I would have bled out," he said after finishing the bottle. He grabbed a second one for her. She didn't hesitate to take it.

"I'll keep that in mind. Come on, help me out that window."

Jogging behind the counter, he crouched down and laced his fingers together. She used it as a stepping stool to reach the window latch. It moved easily but not far, leaving only a slight gap for them to wiggle through. She gripped the edge and threw herself head first through the gap. The muscles of his shoulders felt like stone, but the phantom pain had faded, dwindling to a point that he could jump and grab the ledge with manageable discomfort. There were a few twinges as he pulled himself up, steadily increasing as he squirmed through the gap. They failed him a second later and he dropped, barely managing to roll enough that his back took the impact instead of his head.

"You alright?" Evelyn asked.

"I hate this island," he groaned.

With a small crackle and a quick shake, a luminous purple halo grew out from one of the stolen glow sticks. By it, her smile came into view. He was caught between the desire to smack her and the urge to return the smirk. Taking her offered hand, he let her pull him up. The hum of the electric motor of a golf cart made them both pause. *Their response time is impressive,* Aleksandr thought as they broke into a run.

There was no destination in mind except for away. They charged through the undergrowth, breaking branches and trampling the gnarled roots that escaped the earth. Quickly, the moonlight was lost, leaving him with only the swinging light of Evelyn's glow stick to follow. It was barely anything, and he hit into more things than he avoided. The night itself seemed to become sharp. A thousand unseen obstacles sliced at his bare skin, tearing him open as his chest heaved. Fire started to well in his legs, but he pushed himself faster, struggling to keep up with Evelyn's breakneck pace.

They exploded out into a thin hiking trail. It gave him a clear view of Evelyn and she waved her hand fast enough to paint a streak of purple across the air. Drawing one more deep breath, he sprinted forward. She waited only long enough for him to catch up with her, then they fell into pace together. The ground was rocky and open, dropping out from under their feet in random pits. There was no way to tell just how deep each hole was until they stumbled into it. Battling to keep upright, they pressed forward, forcing themselves to keep in a sprint. A crossroads appeared and Evelyn broke to the right. Dirt gave way to sand then stone. They ran until their bodies forced them to stop. Hunching forward, Aleksandr braced his hands on his knees and tried to keep upright. A few feet away, Evelyn did the same, sweat dripping down her face.

"For the record," she said between pants. "I was faster than you."

"Why are you so competitive?"

She tilted her head to the side and swallowed thickly. "Only child."

A huffed breath escaped his throat and he shook his head. A murmur of voices made him jerk upright. Evelyn thrust her hand out, holding the glow stick high in an attempt to extend the field of its glow. It didn't do much good, but it didn't have to. Not when the solar lights stuttered back to life and revealed a paved street that lay only a few feet away. They shared a look and headed towards it, trying to look as casual as possible. Or, at the very least, not draw the attention of anyone who might be wandering the street.

It proved to be a needless concern. There wasn't another soul to be seen. A few cabins were speckled along the path, their windows shining as the muffled sounds of TVs and conversations drifted out. Evelyn swung the glow stick back and forth before heaving a sigh.

"I'm open to suggestions," she said.

"Do you have the map?"

"It's back at the game zone. Along with our room keys, your bag, and my phone. And that really sounds like something we should worry about. Oh, and the car."

"The car is in a company parking lot," Aleksandr said as they crossed the road. "That should buy us some time. The backpack is hidden. And we'll just say that you dropped your phone when you were startled by a snake."

She snorted. "It's adorable that you think anyone would believe that."

"They didn't have any security cameras."

"You had time in all of that to look for cameras?" Evelyn swatted his arm.

"Are you annoyed or impressed?"

She chose a shake of her head instead of any verbal answer, which clarified nothing. They turned the corner and Aleksandr thrust his hand out to stop her. Instantly, she was on high alert. It didn't take long for her to see what had caught his attention. A cabin with a little balcony stood to their left. Placed on the doormat, its screen still shining like a beacon, was a mobile phone.

"Is that mine?" Evelyn asked meekly.

"Why would it be there? That's not our room, is it?"

She checked the numbers painted on the side of the cabin. "No."

"Coincidence?"

She arched an eyebrow at him and he nodded. *Yeah, stupid idea.*

"This seems like a trap," she said.

"Are we going to walk into another one?" he grumbled.

Evelyn grinned up at him. Aleksandr knew that smile well. It was the one that always came right before she hit something.

"I've got nothing else planned for this evening."

"Evelyn," he hissed under his breath as she jogged up the path. "Damn it."

Checking that they hadn't been spotted, he followed her. She had already snatched up the phone when he jumped up the stairs.

"It is mine," she whispered.

"Couldn't wait until I had a knife?"

She didn't look up from her phone. "I assumed you always have one."

"Where would I have–" he cut off his own question when he saw her gaze flicking between her phone and the door. "What is it?"

Evelyn reached up a hand and knocked on the door. It opened almost instantly, as if they had been expected, pouring light out onto the deck. Aleksandr blinked against it, trying to focus on the woman now blocking the threshold. Staring at her, Aleksandr prepared himself for a blow. But it never came. He looked over the familiar arch of her nose, the curl of her ears, the shade of her hair. Each trait reminded him slightly of the man that had muttered his death sentence years ago. But he could also recognize a dozen others in her too. *It should hurt*, he knew. *Seeing the surviving family should destroy me.* Numb to his bones, he lowered his eyes to his feet.

"Hey. Sorry to bother. Eunice, is it?" Evelyn asked with only the slightest, surprise-induced stammer.

Eunice arched an eyebrow, her lips curling down with disgust as she looked at them each in turn. There wasn't a need for the woman herself to confirm it. The driver's license photograph the twins had found had already done that.

Evelyn held her smile. "This is awkward but, well, we really need to talk."

"We know that you don't know us–" The words choked off in his throat as her gaze turned razor sharp.

"I know *exactly* who you are," Eunice said, ice encrusting each word. "Why you're still breathing is the question."

Evelyn paused, her bravado slipping as she caught Aleksandr's eyes. It all clicked a second later. *Radmiar.* In his death, his twin had been linked back to

Olga and Petya. *And I look just like him.*

"I'm not Radmiar," he promised.

"Aleksandr Vaughn Sokolovsky," Eunice spat out before a short, bitter laugh.

His gaze snapped up to meet hers.

"*Aleksandr,*" she scoffed again. "Let me guess, they named you after Alexander the Great. A conqueror. A killer that's supposed to bring the world to its knees."

"Actually, it was my mother's childhood dog," he said.

Eunice smirked. "Oh, how sweet. For all her evils, she loved animals."

Indignation straightened Aleksandr's spine. "She drowned it when she was six. Something she liked to brag about during bath time."

"Hold up." Evelyn never could help herself, and this was no different. Turning to him, she lowered her voice as if it were possible for them to have a private conversation with Eunice standing right there. "Just to clarify. You're saying that when you were a kid and your mother was bathing you, she'd tell you about the time she murdered the dog she named you after?"

"Yes."

"That's messed up," she whispered.

Caught up in the moment, he leaned closer to her and joined her in whispers, "It worries me that you're so surprised."

"Can we focus on the current situation, please?"

"Right," Evelyn straightened, turned back to Eunice, and realized that she had no idea what to say. "Alek isn't going to hurt you, I promise. Sorry, I'm Evelyn."

"I know who you are. Did you really think I wouldn't keep a tab on both of you? You killed my boy."

"He wasn't your son," Aleksandr said.

Rage flared within her eyes, the lines of her face deepening with disgust. "He was the only family I had left. I raised him."

"I'm sorry for—"

Eunice stepped closer to Aleksandr, towering over him as she screamed, "Don't you dare say his name! He was good. And kind. And you murdered him."

"I didn't have a choice."

Her face lowered down until it was only an inch from his own. "Am I supposed to feel sorry for you? You knew what your parents were and you went along with it. All you ever had to do was pick up a phone and call the police. One call. Just the one and my boy would be alive."

"It's not that simple," Evelyn said as gently but firmly as she could. "He was born and raised in that environment. Years of mental and physical torture changes perspective."

"He wasn't a child when they took my boy. He was a man who chose to beat someone to death."

"He had the safety of two kids to think about."

"Evelyn," Aleksandr touched his fingers to Evelyn's wrist.

Her arm trembled lightly under his touch, but she took a deep breath and tried to calm down.

"Isn't this touching," Eunice said. "Killers sticking together."

"Ma'am," Evelyn rushed, struggling to keep her voice even. "I can't possibly understand what you're going through. And I'm sorry. Truly sorry. Neither of us want to cause you any further suffering. But this isn't about us. You've unleashed something that I don't think you know the true power of."

"The Furies." Slowly, she turned to Evelyn with a small, bitter smile. "They'll make you pay for what you've done."

"She didn't do anything. Evelyn's a victim. Just like your boy."

"She helped you and your family," Eunice snapped. "She deserves everything she gets."

"No. Evelyn never did. We worked together only for survival."

"Why do you think the Furies went after her? I'm not a fool and neither are my Furies. She had to have offered help."

"To protect two innocent children!" Aleksandr snarled.

"The twins?" Eunice smirked.

Aleksandr swallowed thickly and struggled to keep himself from swinging a punch. Hearing any mention of them coming out of this woman's mouth turned his stomach to ice.

"You're going to let her die because she helped a child?" Aleksandr asked. "That's your form of justice?"

"They were never children. They were demonic spawn."

Aleksandr bared his teeth in a feral growl. Squaring his shoulders and balling his fists, he crowded into her personal space.

"Oh, look at you. Your real nature comes out at last. You're a rabid dog, Aleksandr." Loosely gesturing to Evelyn, she continued. "You infected this one with your evil. It's best for everyone that you're put down. And my Furies will do just that."

It startled Aleksandr that, for all the ferociousness of the woman's glare, she was easily distracted. Without warning, she looked clear over his head and smiled.

"Well, this was pleasant, but it appears our time is up."

Dread hit him like a physical blow. Looking over his shoulder, he looked back down the path to the paved road. The solar lights were still on, glowing weakly against the clustering night, unable to touch the three figures that stood by the tree line. Each wore shadows like robes. Not one of them took a step. Instead, they glided forward, skimming across the earth while their bodies remained as still as corpses.

Evelyn shuffled on her feet. "Inside."

"What?" Eunice snapped.

Not waiting around for explanations. He charged forward, ducking down to drive his shoulder into Eunice's stomach. It was easy enough to hurl the larger frame onto his broad shoulder, carrying her as he charged into the cabin. Evelyn followed close behind. Slamming the door shut, she locked what she could as Aleksandr dumped the woman onto the floor.

"Call them off," he growled.

Sprawled across the floor, Eunice looked up at him with unbridled rage. "No."

He smirked. "Then get ready to die with us."

Chapter 15

Evelyn peeked out of the slender window beside the door as she flicked the locks into place. The Furies were in no rush. Moving as mist, they crossed the road, closing in on the house.

"Locks aren't going to keep them out," she said as she jogged the short distance to the others.

Eunice was still on the floor, half sitting up with her hands braced behind her. Chin high, she stared daggers into Aleksandr.

"Call them off," he said, his voice a rumbling growl.

"Why would I do that?" Eunice laughed. "They won't hurt me. I'm not a killer."

"Didn't stop them from coming after me," Evelyn said.

Eunice smiled, bitter and cold. "They'll come after anyone who helps any Sokolovsky."

"Oh God."

The words left Evelyn's lips on a whisper as memories consumed her. The first time she saw a Fury played across her mind's eye. She couldn't breathe. Trembling with fear and growing rage, she heard Eunice's laughter drifting across her awareness.

A red haze spread across her vision and she burst mindlessly into action. Surging across the limited space, she latched onto the older woman, one hand clutching a handful of hair while the other wrapped around Eunice's wrinkled throat. With this grip, she dragged the struggling woman through the house, bringing her into the kitchen before tossing her against the cabinets.

"Evelyn?" Aleksandr asked, watching her carefully but making no move to intervene.

"The first time I saw a Fury was on the night Petya took me," she hissed. "I walked to an empty parking lot and a crying child. All I did was offer to help. That was it. That's why you condemned me to this?" Evelyn paced the kitchen like a wild beast, sure that her fury would rip her apart if she stopped.

Eunice's mouth worked itself into a thin, tensed line as she stared at Evelyn.

"You helped them," she said at last.

Aleksandr made a choked nose. "That's the only instruction you gave the Furies?"

"I will not be judged by a killer."

"You are a killer!" Evelyn snapped. "You're killing us. Hell, your stupid-ass wording could get retail workers killed. They offer their help to a Sokolovsky, too."

"No," Eunice shook her head and fixed her eyes onto the far wall. "This is justice."

"My father is a good man," Evelyn said. Still pacing. Tears of rage burning her eyes. "He's kind and generous. The best man I have ever known. He's taking care of the twins."

"If he can stand to be in a room with a Sokolovsky, then he is a vile man." She smiled up at Evelyn. "He'll die screaming."

Evelyn didn't know she had moved until the moment her fist drove into the older woman's face. Blood spurted against her skin, the wet warmth soothing the animal gnawing in the pit of her stomach. Aleksandr took a step closer but did little else to stop her.

"Get them to back off or I swear to God I will kill you," Evelyn hissed.

Blood dripped from Eunice's nose as she narrowed her eyes. "Do you really think that I'm not willing to die to avenge my boy?"

"Let me tell you something about embracing death," Evelyn laughed bitterly. "I was born with a genetic gun to my head. Odds are good I'll develop an aggressive mental illness that's proven resistant to medication. My future will be nothing but experimental drugs, confinement, and a roller coaster ride into hell. Everything I am will be stripped away. I'll be reduced to nothing more than an emotional and financial drain on my father."

Crouching down before Eunice, she grinned broadly. "Sweetheart, I've been ready to die since childhood. Alek, what's your thinking on death?"

Evelyn looked over her shoulder. He was close by, every inch of his body ready for a fight, his face cold. Their eyes met as the first strikes began. Ghostly hands slammed against the windows, battered the outer walls, thundered against the roof like hail. The Furies had arrived and there was nowhere left to run.

"I should have died in infancy," Aleksandr said at last, his voice as emotionless as expression. "This has all just been an extra."

"So go and die," Eunice spat.

"And leave my dad unprotected?"

"And my twins," Aleksandr added over the growing noise of the Furies.

"If our only chance to save them is to kill you," Evelyn said. "We're going to take it."

"Not if they kill you first."

Evelyn looked to Aleksandr again, a silent question conveyed with a look. He nodded his agreement. Before Eunice could move, Evelyn grabbed the woman's ankle and yanked. The moment her leg flattened against the tiles, Aleksandr struck. One solid stomp onto the aging woman's knee shattered it. Clamping a hand over Eunice's mouth, Evelyn smothered the screams. Blood and tears slicked her skin. The walls rattled under the assault and the windows promised to shatter. Leaning down until her mouth was level with Eunice's ear, she whispered.

"You're murdering us. My father. Two innocent children. I'm going to make sure you die before I do."

"Evelyn," Aleksandr warned an instant before the windows shattered.

Dark arms snaked in through the newly formed gap. Clawed and twisted. Thrashing about like a pit of snakes. Faces formed in the writhing mass of flesh, appearing only to retreat again with the next movement.

He was already pulling out the kitchen drawers, searching for a weapon. Lunging up onto her feet, she took the knife he offered and stood to defend their position. Aleksandr took her place next to Eunice.

"You had called them. How?"

"Go to hell," Eunice sobbed in pain.

"Hell's coming to us," Evelyn smirked, adjusting and readjusting her grip on the handle.

"We don't have time for this." Aleksandr grabbed the woman's jaw, jerking her face around so he could stare into her eyes. "There has to be something. An object or book. Where is it?"

Creatures began to emerge from the tangled limbs. Full body monsters that crawled across the walls like insects, smearing blood on everything they touched.

"Alek," Evelyn warned.

Slender arms reached for Evelyn and she swiped out with knife. It pulled back, its very motion carrying amusement. There was no hope to keep them at bay forever.

"Alek?"

He tightened his grip of Eunice's jaw. "Where? Kitchen? Basement? Bedroom?"

Evelyn didn't see what it was in Eunice's face that betrayed her secrets. Whatever it was, Aleksandr trusted it enough to toss the older woman across his shoulders and order Evelyn to get moving. The kitchen had already filled with the creatures born from the writhing limbs, their numbers enough to turn the walls and floor the color of rotten flesh. They ran, Evelyn leading the way while Aleksandr carried Eunice behind her.

The rest of the house had fallen away. Gone was the cozy cabin with its bohemian decorations. The hallways now looked like the inside of something living. A red hue filled the air. Floor, ceiling, walls; it was all now formed of tacky, blood-soaked flesh. As they travelled down the short passageway, the walls rippled, like the pulsing of a heart. Blood thickened. Sloshing over their feet. Swelling to lap at their knees as they ran. Before them, the hallway stretched out into an endless tunnel. Behind them, the clawing, disembodied limbs blocked their only means of retreat.

"Where is your room?" Evelyn demanded.

"There! Right!" Eunice shouted.

Evelyn broke to the side and slammed the hidden door with her shoulder. The pain was worth the break of the wall. She staggered into the room. Grabbing the doorknob with one hand, she yanked Aleksandr into the room by the front of his shirt. Even with the help, the severed limbs had caught up to them before she had crossed the threshold. Evelyn braced her good shoulder against the door and threw her body weight against it. The soles of her shoes squeaked against the polished floor. Arms slipped through the small gap that she couldn't close. Fingers worked into her hair, groped at her skin, tore at her clothes in an attempt to pull her out. Aleksandr tossed the wounded woman on the bed and ran to help her.

The door jerked as he threw himself against it. The distance they gained was almost instantly lost again as the creatures continued to fight their way in. Evelyn couldn't contain her scream as the grasping limbs turned sharp. They slashed her open wounds. Blood gushed out, soaking her clothes and pooling around her feet. Aleksandr strained, bracing himself and shoving with all of his might, all of his efforts unable to work the door closed.

Living shadows slipped across the walls. Each one had the shape of a demon and moved like a rushing tide. The walls steadily grew brighter, making the shadows almost tangible. Between one breath and the next, the air began to boil. Sweat joined her blood. Evelyn's muscles began to tremble. Her head swam. She could feel her blood flow over her skin, steaming as it trailed down. The room became an oven. Her skin bristled and burned as the door became like a sheet of heated metal. One more combined thrust, and the door slammed shut.

The sudden victory jerked Evelyn forward. It slammed her against the scorching hot surface. Instantly, her skin blistered. The blinding pain made her feet slip. She landed hard on her knees. The impact coursed along her nerves like an electric shock. Her mind swam, her vision blurring around the edges when she saw the pool of her blood she sat in. It pulsed from her ripped flesh. As black as night. Sticky like tar.

"Evelyn," Aleksandr said, concern laying thick on her name.

She swallowed, the motion rocking her body, and turned to him. The severed limbs hadn't left him unscathed. Neither had Eunice. Claw marks left behind by fingernails crisscrossed his arms and neck. Barely upright, he looked in horror as black blood seeped from his wounds. Neither of them had time to fully take in the horror as Eunice screamed. They both whipped around to find that the bed the woman lay on had grown limbs.

Dozens of them sprung free from the mattress. Each one whipped around her, grasping at her flesh, pulling her down. Evelyn scrambled to her feet. She only managed to take a few steps before an invisible force slammed into her chest. It tossed her into the air, hurling her back into the wall with enough force to crack the plaster. The shadow demons were on her instantly. Grabbing her. Latching tight onto her limbs and keeping her pinned in place. Evelyn thrashed against the hold. Kicking herself free only for the dark masses to reach off of the wall like a physical being, reclaiming her and bringing her back to the scolding hot wall.

Continuing to fight, she could only watch as Aleksandr made it to the bed. He grabbed at the phantom arms, pulling them back and hacking them off with his kitchen knife. He glanced at her as he worked, his face twisted up in pain as she failed to contain her screams. She couldn't stop. The wall burned her like a branding iron, adding to her desperation for freedom. Aleksandr half turned to her as she wrenched her arm free.

"No! Help her!" she bellowed to him. "We need her!"

The shadowy demon figures pulled free from the walls, becoming near tangible witnesses. They stalked towards the bedside. Slowly. Each step shaking the room.

"Call them off!" Aleksandr bellowed as he hacked away the ever-growing limbs.

Evelyn fought a limb free, the battle keeping her from seeing the moment Aleksandr pried Eunice loose. His pained cry snapped her attention back to them. Eunice had slithered to the side and pressed her back to the headboard. Aleksandr had taken her place, his arms and legs locked against the mattress, the demonic shadows at his feet. They stood there. Watching. Frozen.

Evelyn screamed as figures stalked free of the wall behind her. Appearing as they had in the hospital, ancient nurses whose every facial feature had been replaced with dark, empty pits as they circled around her. The hands kept her still as they leaned close. They sniffed and smile and cooed, their voices echoing in both her ears and head.

One swiped a finger across the wounds on Evelyn's shoulder, gathering the tainted blood on her fingertip.

"*Black.*" The word sounded more like a death rattle than a voice.

Another leaned forward, sniffing along the curve of Evelyn's cheek. "*Rage.*"

"What are you waiting for?" Eunice snapped, chest heaving and words cracking with hysteria. "Kill them!"

Evelyn tried to jerk away as one of the Furies raised a finger. The ghostly hands held her in place. Over the rushing of her heartbeat, she heard Aleksandr screaming for her, his voice recognizable but the words lost in desperation. The fingertip pressed against her eye. Evelyn clenched her teeth, steadied her breath, strained against the intangible hands holding her. One sharp jab and the finger bore into her eye.

Sensation exploded inside her skull. None of them images. But knowledge. A sure, pure, surge of things that didn't belong to her. *Wrath. Vengeance. A pure rage that burned hotter and wilder than the entirety of hell. A lust for revenge. A hunger, insatiable and raw, for a bloody form of justice.* It reduced her mind to slush as she slumped, boneless and heavy, to the floor. Evelyn blinked heavily as the world bucked and swayed. Aleksandr's voice remained the one constant, bringing her back each time unconsciousness loomed. Eunice shrieked, each cry adding to Evelyn's disorientation.

She clutched to the end of the bed, dragging herself high enough to see over the edge. The Furies had joined at Aleksandr's feet. Eunice, still pressed as far away from the kill zone as she could, demanded his execution. Evelyn stabbed her knife into the mattress, using the hold to push herself up onto her feet. The heat of the room had gone from stifling to oppressive. Hovering dust particles sparked, creating flares that drifted down to ignite whatever it touched.

Small fires already crackled across the bed by the time Evelyn lurched forward. She swung. Her knife slipped through the body of the nearest Fury but found the flesh of Eunice's cheek. The woman screamed, rolled to the side, finally falling silent. Half slung over Aleksandr, Evelyn held the blade out, her body already failing her.

"We'll feed you," she cried in desperation.

The Furies stilled. The sensations they had given her rattled through her body, and it clicked.

"That's what you want, isn't it?" she asked, choking on the thickening smoke. "You can't kill unless you're called. And no one calls you anymore. That has to suck. Here, all you want is a good meal. But no one trusts in the ancient Greek mythological system of corporate punishment anymore."

The Furies didn't move, but she felt them. Felt their desire to kill her battling against their longing.

"You want a steady food source," she stammered. "I can do that. There's a world of killers out there. Serial and otherwise. I'll find them. I'll summon you to take them."

The silence that met her was full of anger and doubt. Heat and smoke pushed Evelyn to the verge of passing out. Her hand shook, her body swayed. Still, when Eunice tried to speak, she didn't hesitate to swing at her again.

"I swear, I'll slice your throat," she hissed. Sweat dripped down her face as the walls ignited. She turned back to the Furies. "That's what the blood was about, right? I'm rotting inside. Dad always told me that anger would do that to me."

"*Feed.*" The single word crackled in her head, buzzing like a thousand hornets.

"Yeah. I'll feed you," she said.

"*You.*"

The nearest Fury reached for Aleksandr's leg. Evelyn wrapped her arm around his thrashing shoulders, trying to yank him free. In retaliation, the ghostly hands wrapped tightly around his mouth and nose, smothering him.

"Us," Evelyn corrected. "We're a team."

Aleksandr's face paled and his body shook in a fight for air.

"Look what we did together. How quickly we tracked her down," she jerked her head to indicate Eunice. "Without him, you'll have to wait."

Time stretched out, the pause draining her. The air scorched her lungs with every breath.

"*You.*"

"Both or nothing," she said. "Starve!"

The hands moved from Aleksandr's mouth and he sucked in a deep breath, coughing and sputtering. He wrenched his arms free, tearing the burning mattress apart as he broke free. Evelyn helped to pull him back, both of them ignoring Eunice's harrowed screams. He leaned against Evelyn's shoulders, batting out the small licks of fire that had gathered on his clothes.

"And my father. The twins. What do you need to take them off of the menu?"

"*A soul for each.*"

Aleksandr hacked in an attempt to clear his throat. "Three?"

"*For each.*"

His brow furrowed. "For each of *my* victims?"

"*All.*"

Evelyn's knees almost buckled. "One meal for *every* Sokolovsky victim. That's got to be hundreds."

The Furies remained silent as the room burned.

"*Pay the debt.*"

"Okay," Evelyn agreed.

She and Aleksandr shrunk back as the last of the bed caught alight. The flames spewed heat and ash into the still sparking air. Eunice barely got off in time, but Evelyn didn't bother to check where she went.

"Let us go. You'll get the first payment in a month."

The Furies smiled as one. "*One for a month. Two, two weeks.*"

Evelyn didn't have the brain power left to make sense of it. As she struggled, Aleksandr pulled her back.

"You'll let us both live but we have only two weeks to find you a killer?"

"Deal," Evelyn said.

One heartbeat and the Furies were gone. They took the shadow creatures with them, but left the flames. The entire room was engulfed, the heat along burning their flesh and scorching their lungs.

Aleksandr pulled away from her, roughly grabbing Eunice's shoulders and hurling her up. It was Evelyn's job to find an exit. She peeled off her dress and wrapped it around her elbow. Left in her crop top and exercise shorts, there wasn't much left to protect her from the airborne embers. Charging against the window, she smashed her clad elbow into the glass. It shattered around her, the addition of cool air making the flames behind her lap and burst. A few of the shards shredded through the cloth but never sunk deep.

"Alek," she coughed, eyes watering from the smoke.

He emerged from the inferno, Eunice cradled in his arms. Letting Evelyn help him with the weight, they tossed the injured woman out of the window, neither caring about her pained screams upon landing. Aleksandr laced his fingers to give Evelyn a boost. She clambered through the window, shoved Eunice out of the way, and crouched down onto all fours. Barely a second had passed before Aleksandr gripped the top of the window and swung his legs out, using her bare back to shorten the drop, allowing him to hit the ground running. He grabbed Eunice and dragged her into the forest beyond the burning house. Evelyn followed, making it to the tree line just as the neighbors came out of their houses, each one running for their fire hoses in an almost practiced measure.

They ran until the bush and stone gave way to towering grass and sand. It was only once they dropped onto the sand, panting and exhausted, that they heard it. The steady, rolling sounds of waves.

"We've run across the island," Evelyn chuckled.

"You've made a deal with the devil," Eunice hissed.

Whatever else she was going to say was converted into a scream when Evelyn drove her fist into the woman's broken knee. Without looking, Aleksandr reached out, clamping his hand over Eunice's mouth until the worst of it had passed.

"Do you still think you're better than me," Eunice whimpered, jaw clenched and eyes blazing. "You killed my boy. Destroyed my home. Broke my leg."

"But we didn't send demonic creatures to torment and murder you and everyone you love. Which, by the way, can be classified as a war crime," Evelyn shrugged. "So, yeah. Me and the United Nations say we still have the higher ground."

Aleksandr chuckled and scraped a hand over his shaved head.

"Just kill me already," Eunice said after a moment of silence.

"Nah," Evelyn said. "I quite like the high ground as it is. I'll even call 911 for you."

"You mean triple zero! You're in Australia. We don't use the number 911," Eunice said.

"Good call."

The woman glared at each of them in turn, her mouth twisted up in fury. "I'm still going to try to kill you."

"That seems fair," Aleksandr said.

"But it does bring forth a question, Alek. What do we do now?"

"In order; I want to get the hell off of this island, call my kids, drink myself into a stupor, and maybe cry a little."

"Then a nap?" she asked with an amused smile.

"Nap is good."

"So," Evelyn forced herself up to her feet and held out a hand for him to take. "Tonight we party. Tomorrow we hunt."

A bright smile crossed his face as he took Evelyn's outstretched hand, letting her pull him up onto his feet.

Epilogue

Evelyn's shoulder carried a dull ache, her stitches itching like crazy as her skin healed around the thread. She scratched at it absently as she made her way through the shifting crowds of the airport, dragging her single carry-on bag behind her, only stopping to pull her buzzing phone out of her coat pocket.

"Hey, dad," she greeted with a smile.

"How's Paris, princess?"

"Well, since I have just landed three seconds ago, I haven't actually seen any of it. The airport is lovely though. There are a lot of people speaking French."

"How strange," he chuckled.

"I know, right? How's mom?"

"She misses you."

"I'll Skype with her tomorrow," Evelyn promised.

Making her way through the large open area, she headed lazily towards the taxi terminal.

"That'll make her really happy."

She tapped the edge of her phone against her lip as she smiled. Drawing it back to her ear, she tried not to sound like a sobbing mess. *Who knew that this was all it took to get on good terms with my mother?*

"It'll make me happy, too," she cleared her throat. "The twins got the result of their math test back today, right?"

"They passed. Nadya's doing better with it, which she is holding over her brother's head."

"Oh, I bet Ivan loves that."

"He gets his own back with biology," Juan chuckled.

Evelyn smiled. It had become obvious by this point that Juan loved having the twins under his roof. He was a natural father, loved the role, and relished the opportunity to have another go at it. For their part, the twins were flourishing. They missed Aleksandr, of course, but his absence had seemed to signal to them that they were truly free. That they could be normal. Quick to adapt, they had settled into life in Evelyn's family home, with Juan as their adopted father. For the first time in their lives, Aleksandr was simply their brother. The remaining Sokolovsky siblings had hated the idea at first. Each one sure that they would detest the situation. Evelyn found it amusing. It was nice to know she wasn't the only one who had to learn the hard way that Juan was always right.

"I don't know what time it would be in Paris," Juan continued, the phone muffling his voice slightly. "But we're heading over to visit your mom around 8pm our time. See if you can Skype around then. It will be great to have us all together."

"She's going to end up loving the twins more than me."

"Never," he laughed.

She scanned the area and spotted a familiar face in an ill-fitting shirt. "Oh, I think I see my boy. I have to go."

"Evelyn," he said cautiously.

"We'll be careful. They're not our first human traffickers."

"They're the first ones you've found, princess."

Evelyn bit her lips to keep her first comments at bay. Mostly remarks about how she was just as good at finding sacrifices as Aleksandr and the twins were. It wasn't quite true yet, as much as her pride hated to admit it.

"I've been taught well."

"Right ..." Juan let the word trail off.

"We've been through this before, dad," she sighed. "Human traffickers are notorious for hanging around airports. A lot of naive tourists in a country they don't know are easy pickings."

"I know."

"And I did my research. The twins got us into the airport surveillance system. This guy always arrives with no luggage, never takes a flight, and always leaves with a girl."

"Well, that does sound suspicious."

"And by looking through numerous websites for missing people, we managed to get a few matches. He leaves with girls and they're never heard from again. I don't think they all just really love Paris."

"No. But that could be a coincidence."

Evelyn drew the phone away so he wouldn't hear her growl under her breath. When she returned it, she decided that there wasn't enough time to argue the point.

"Aleksandr signed off on it."

Juan paused. "He did?"

"Yep."

While Juan still questioned Evelyn's judgment, he had no doubts that Aleksandr could spot a psychopath a mile off. The Sokolovsky upbringing had left the siblings with a sixth sense for deranged minds. It was in a look or a move or something undefinable. They always knew. And they were never wrong.

"Dad, I love you, but time is a factor."

"Could you at least not get in the car with them?"

That was a promise she and Aleksandr didn't have the time to keep. The Furies always knew where they were. Being in the company of their sacrifices was just easier. And, since they had taken some time off, they were under a time crunch.

"Aleksandr has my back."

"Princess."

She sighed. "I'll try my best. Promise, okay? Now, I really have to go. I don't want to spook him."

"Love you."

"Love you, dad. See you tonight."

She turned her phone off and shoved it in her pocket. Aleksandr's lessons in how to look like the perfect victim weren't wasted on her. Smoothing down her pretty dress, she adjusted her long jacket, making sure to disguise her bulk. It had been harder to perfect the air of innocent gullibility. Coming to stand next to their sacrifice, she pulled out a map and tried to look as lost as possible. It only took twenty minutes for him to look over to her.

"Do you need help?" his words purred around a thick accent.

"Oh, my gosh. You're French," she beamed.

"You are in France."

"Right," she shook her head, trying to look embarrassed. "I just mean that you're my first French conversation. Officially, anyway."

The sacrifice looked around. "Where are your friends?"

"I'm travelling on my own," Evelyn said.

It was hard to endure the man slowly raking his eyes over her. "Where are you heading?"

"Downtown. Can I catch a taxi out front?"

"They're all crooks. Come, I'll give you a ride."

"That's so nice," she grinned. "Thank you."

Evelyn let the sacrifice take her bag and lead the way. They passed Aleksandr as they headed out into the open air. She spared him a wink. He rolled his eyes but she knew he would fall into step behind them.

"So," Evelyn chirped as she looped her arm around the sacrifice's. "Have you ever heard of the legend of the Furies?"

* * *

The Sign of Ouroboros
Ouroboros Series Book 1
Written by David Longhorn

Prologue: Wychmere, England, Autumn 2016

Now this is what I call a nice house, thought Andrew Leadsom. *Should be some rich pickings here.*

He stopped his car outside the gates of Garlock House. The stone gateposts were topped by heraldic stone lions. The lions were badly weathered, but there was a new feature on one gatepost. A brass plate. Leadsom frowned. The plate bore no words, but was etched with an unfamiliar circular design. He leaned out of the car window to peer more closely at the image.

A snake eating its own tail? Weird. But the English aristocracy has always been a tad eccentric. They keep marrying their cousins, all that inbreeding sends them daft. Just look at some of the royals.

Leadsom glanced up the broad driveway to the large house, then turned and looked back down the road he had come. The village of Wychmere was a small, sleepy place, and after a few moments of thought, he had decided not to try his luck there. It did not seem especially wealthy, despite the number of tourists who came to see the prehistoric stone circle. The big house on the outskirts of the village seemed like a much better bet. It could prove an ideal target for a veteran con artist like Leadsom.

He got out and tried the wrought-iron gates. They were not locked, and he was soon driving his car up to the house's classical portico. He was just setting foot on the steps leading up to the front door when it opened and a statuesque, dark-haired woman appeared.

Well, today really is looking up, he thought. Nothing *like a curvaceous hottie on a cold day.*

The girl was an inch or so taller than Leadsom, who noticed that she was barefoot. She was also dressed quite skimpily for a chilly October afternoon, in a colorful silk wrap of some kind that was not very well secured. The house was well-heated. A wave of warm air washed over Leadsom as he tried not to stare down her cleavage. She smiled down at him as he reached the top of the steps.

"Yes? Are you expected?" she asked.

Her voice was surprisingly deep, a husky contralto. Her eyes were a wonderful golden-green and were large, almost freakishly so. Her mouth was wide and full-lipped.

This one just gets sexier by the second, he thought. *But let's not mix business with pleasure.*

"I'm afraid I don't have an appointment, no," he replied. "But I am here to do you a big favor, I hope. You see, I deal in antiques, and I'm sure an old place like this must have some hidden treasures that could raise quite a tidy sum."

Leadsom handed her his business card, a lavishly produced one, calculated to inspire consumer confidence. The card was embossed with a fake name, a useless email address, and the phone number of a Thai restaurant in Coventry he had selected at random. But the details, coupled with Leadsom's nice suit, professional but friendly demeanor, and shiny Lexus inspired confidence. Nobody had ever tried to check his background until it was much too late.

The girl smiled, showing impressively white teeth, as she took a step back. Leadsom stepped inside. As he passed close to her, he got a strong whiff of perfume. It was patchouli, rather stronger than he normally liked. There was an undertone of something else, a less pleasant odor that, for some reason, triggered childhood memories.

Maybe she just doesn't bathe too often, he thought. *Anyway, that's not important. Focus on the smell of money, Andy.*

"Nice to meet you, Mister Nuttall," she said, handing back the card. "I'm Olivia. You'd better come in and speak to Jonathan."

"Ah, Jonathan is your husband?" he asked. Then, when Olivia shook her head, "Your father?"

"No, he's the spokesperson of our group. We are a small spiritual community."

The words took a few moments to register, as the entrance hall was better than Leadsom could have hoped. Glancing around, being careful not to look even slightly impressed, he noticed a Louis Fourteenth clock and a fine Georgian table. If the rest of Garlock House contained similarly fine antiques, it could prove to be a very lucrative visit.

"Religious, you mean?" he asked, becoming wary. Conning any large organization was hazardous. It was always best to target individuals; the older and greedier, the better.

"Not in the conventional sense," said a new voice. "We are very broadminded in our attitudes."

A plump, bald man appeared from a side door and came up to shake Leadsom's hand. Leadsom noticed that the man was limping slightly and filed the fact away. Even the most trivial detail could come in handy when you were trying to win someone's trust.

"Mister Paul Nuttall, wandering antique dealer," said Olivia, "Meet Jonathan Clay, the Herald of Ouroboros."

Now that does sound barmy, thought Leadsom, smiling at Clay. *These people could be ideal marks.*

"Please, call me Jonathan, we don't need fancy titles," said Clay. "Come, join me for a cup of tea, and tell me what brings you to our little colony."

Clay led him into a splendid drawing room with wood-paneled walls and a huge fireplace.

"Excuse me while I help Olivia with the tea tray," said Clay, gesturing at a fine divan suite. "Can I offer you biscuits, or some of our home made Victoria sponge cake? No? Oh well, make yourself comfortable, Paul."

Free to act unobserved, Leadsom wasted no time in scrutinizing everything that looked valuable. As in the hall, he was impressed by several fine-looking antiques, calculating that there must be at least ten thousand pounds worth of loot in this one room. He was also struck by the presence of a number of odd statues in stone or clay. They varied widely in style, and he thought he recognized Indian, Aztec, and Babylonian artifacts. But he dismissed them as they were outside his field of interest.

Leadsom turned his attention to the paintings, hoping to strike gold again. But here he found nothing of obvious value, just a few mass-produced topographical prints. The only large picture was over the fireplace, and it was more grotesque than attractive. It was, he concluded, a scene from classical mythology, but Leadsom had no idea what the story behind it might be. Against the backdrop of a huge city on a plain by the sea, a horrific multiple killing was taking place. Three men were struggling in the coils of a huge serpent while aghast spectators looked on.

"Ah, I see you are admiring our rather graphic masterpiece," said Clay, appearing at the door with a silver tea tray. Olivia followed him in with a plate of biscuits.

"I don't recognize the story," said Leadsom. "But I assume those three angered the gods? That's usually the way of these things."

"Quite right," said Clay, limping across to stand by him. "Laocoon, the old man in the middle, warned his fellow Trojans not to take the wooden horse into their city. The gods, who wanted Troy to be destroyed, sent a serpent to kill him and his sons, the two lads on either side of him. The Trojans took the wooden horse inside the city, and the rest, I'm sure you know."

"But why kill his sons?" asked Leadsom, genuinely curious. "It seems so pointless and cruel."

"To put an end to his line, of course!" said Clay. "Even today, in much of the world, to be without sons is to be ranked not quite a man. But you have more pleasant things to discuss, I'm sure."

A few moments later, Leadsom was seated on a fine Edwardian sofa while Olivia handed him a cup of herbal tea. He pretended to be fascinated by all things spiritual, as he chatted with Clay about the latter's crackpot beliefs.

"So you see, Paul," Clay was saying, "we use the symbol of Ouroboros to signify recurrence, rebirth, regeneration. The story of Laocoon, taken literally, is grim indeed. But if one sees the serpent as symbolizing 'nature' it is simply a statement of the obvious, that nothing human endures, only life itself, and struggling against the inevitable merely leads to suffering."

"Fascinating," said Leadsom, cautiously taking a sip of the steaming tea. It was more pleasant than he expected, and he took a generous mouthful, almost scalding his tongue.

"Our tea is a mixture of herbs," said Clay. "Very refreshing, and a good way to alleviate stress. But you came here to discuss business, I believe?"

Leadsom set his half-empty cup down.

Now we get to the nitty gritty, he thought.

"Well, Jonathan," he said, "I've recently set up shop in Hereford, and I'm essentially familiarizing myself with the surrounding area. I specialize in less valuable antiques, the kind of things that people tend to just put in a cupboard or the attic and forget about. I have an international network of buyers and, with no false modesty, I can say I've managed to raise tidy sums for a lot of locals already."

"Fascinating work," exclaimed Clay, "isn't it, Olivia?"

"Yes," she said, topping up Leadsom's teacup from a silver pot that he valued at around six hundred pounds. He could think of at least three collectors who would snap it up.

"And very satisfying, to help all those little old ladies turn their knick-knacks into ready money," added the girl, settling herself next to Leadsom so her slim hip just touched his. "Why, you're quite the public benefactor, Paul!"

Is she taking the piss?

Something about the tone of the girl's voice bothered him. It wasn't the only thing that seemed off-kilter. There was a distant roaring noise, like a waterfall or waves breaking on a beach. And again, under the strong perfume, there was that other smell. Stale, vaguely feral.

"Are you feeling all right, Paul?" asked Clay. "Would you like to lay down?"

"No, I'm fine," said Leadsom. But the simple phrase did not come easily.

"Tell us, Paul," said Olivia, running a finger through his hair, "is there anything around here that takes your fancy?"

He guffawed stupidly, staring more blatantly down the front of her wrap. She laughed and tapped him on the end of his nose.

"Now you know I meant antiques!"

"Well," he said, "there's a ton of stuff here I could shift. This couch is worth a cool thousand. That little gilt clock in the hall, another two grand at least. Lovely item, that."

Leadsom babbled on, giving a completely honest assessment of the valuables he had seen. Part of him, the seasoned con man, looked on in horror as he continued to blurt out tricks of the trade. He even told them his real name.

"The best way to take in your classic little old lady," he babbled, "is to make her think she's put one over on you. Buy some piece of tat for way over the odds, then trick her out of something really valuable."

"You naughty, naughty boy!"

Olivia ran her hand down his cheek. Her flesh was cool despite the warm room, and slightly rough.

"You should wear rubber gloves when you do the washing up, darling," he said. "You've got dishpan hands."

The girl giggled, then got up just as Leadsom made a wobbling lunge at her. He ended up face first in a velvet cushion and dropped his teacup.

"Oh dear," said Clay, putting down his own cup, which was still full to the brim. "It seems we have a dishonest man on our hands."

"True," said Leadsom, as he struggled upright again. His mouth seemed to have a mind of its own, resisting his best efforts to control it, "I'm a total bastard who cons pensioners out of their family heirlooms. Pays them a pittance, and when they find out I lied, I'm long gone. Move on to a new area, start again."

Herbal tea, he thought desperately. *They drugged me. Jesus, I'm in trouble.*

Leadsom's first instinct was to make a run for it, but his effort to stand up merely led to him plunging face first into an Afghan rug.

"Oops a daisy," laughed Olivia, helping him to his feet.

"Bloody hell, you're very strong, even for a big girl," said Leadsom. "Must work out. I blame feminism. Ruining romance. Not natural."

The roaring in his ears was so loud now that he could barely make out what Clay was saying. The plump man was talking to the girl. Something about 'having a little lie down.'

"I'm fine, really," Leadsom insisted. "People will be wondering where I am. I must be going."

"I don't think you'll be able to drive in such a state," said Clay, looking closely into Leadsom's eyes. "Yes, pupil's dilated. But it's hard to calculate the dosage with these things. After all, everyone's different."

Clay took Leadsom's other arm. Between them, Clay and Olivia steered the befuddled con man out into the hall, then up two flights of stairs. Leadsom lost consciousness for a while. When he came to, his mind was still clouded by the 'herbal tea.' He was apparently on a bed in a dimly-lit room.

He could hear voices. Clay and the woman were out in the corridor, just out of sight. They seemed to be arguing. Clay said something about an 'unworthy subject,' but Olivia cut him off, sounding insistent. He made out the word 'sacrifice'.

Oh God, they really are some kind of insane cult, he thought. *They're going to kill me!*

He made a tremendous effort to move. His body resisted his urging and all he managed was a groan of despair.

The light from the doorway diminished as a slight figure entered. Again, he smelled patchouli, its cloying fragrance. And once more, he detected that undertone of something else, the odor that conjured up an image of a favorite aunt, ice cream, a day out at the zoo.

Olivia climbed onto the bed next to him. She was naked, her curvaceous body pale and sinuous. He felt her flesh brush against his limp hand and again felt that odd roughness, coldness. Her face, just a couple of inches away from his, looked subtly different somehow. As if her features had coarsened in some way. *Is her mouth larger, were her eyes that far apart?* Leadsom wondered if it was a trick of the half-light.

"You've told us so much about yourself, Andrew," she said. "You have no family, no close friends, and you always keep a low profile. The only people who'll wonder where you are have a strong aversion to contacting the police, isn't that right? You're the sort of man who can vanish easily, and never be missed."

Olivia's tongue flicked across her lips, then she opened her mouth. It gaped far wider than any human mouth had a right to. A pair of fangs protruded from her upper jaw. At the sight of them, he suddenly remembered where he had first encountered the stale, unpleasant smell that was not quite masked by the patchouli.

It was somewhere hot, and dark. The Reptile House at the Zoo!

Her mouth closed on his neck for a moment and he felt cold, sharp pinpricks penetrate his flesh. When Olivia pulled away, her face was barely human. Her eyes were a bright green now, displaced almost to the side of her head, their pupils turned to slits. Her mouth was opening again, wider than any human mouth, a glistening void that soon filled his entire field of vision.

Before her transformation was complete, the venom had done its merciful work.

Chapter 1: A Dream of Armageddon

In his dream, the world was coming to an end, and his daughter did not want to know him. It was hard for him to decide which was worse.

Brad Steiger saw the world from an astronaut's perspective, a beautiful blue and white orb lit by dazzling sunshine. Directly below him was the Atlantic, with the Americas in full daylight to his left, Europe and Africa emerging from darkness on the right. He got no pleasure from the vision, though, because he knew with the certainty of nightmare that something bad was coming.

The catastrophe began on the night side of the earth, where Brad could just make out the scattered light of cities in Asia and the Middle East. A brighter light appeared, very different from the blue-white of human settlements. This was an angry orange-red glare, and formed a sinuous line. More lines appeared, intersecting and spreading at terrifying speed. As they grew, the glow they emitted brightened.

The planet is cracking open, like an egg!

The lovely blue and white of the sunlit earth began to vanish, swamped by gouts of black and brown. Brad realized that smoke, volcanic ash, and steam were rushing out of the cracks in the world's crust. And the seismic eruptions had created vast tsunamis. He could see one now, a dirty-white wave of terrifying force heading for the eastern seaboard of the United States.

"Dad? You're not listening. Again."

Brad was sitting in a Starbucks with his daughter, Kelly. Outside, the world did not seem to be ending. As usual, she seemed disappointed with him. She reached out across the table littered with cups and sugar packets to take his hand. He saw that she had a tattoo on the back of her hand. It was an ornate circular pattern, the weird image of a snake apparently eating its own tail.

"You're not supposed to see that," Kelly said, reprovingly. "Just stay out of it, Dad. Listen to me for once."

Because it was a dream, she was not just the Kelly of today, but all the Kellys Brad had known. She was the young woman he struggled to understand, the little daughter he had loved more than life itself, the teenager who had so bitterly resented him for leaving her mother. And she was more. There was someone else looking out of her eyes, a stranger.

"Kelly, where did you go?" he asked. "I just want to know you're okay."

"It's a bit late for that," she said. "Seven years too late. I'm gone for good now. The world you knew is gone, too. Sorry, Dad. That's just how it is."

There were screams from outside, the sound of car horns and sirens, a huge crash that sounded like a building collapsing. The sky darkened. A great wall of glistening dark green appeared in the distance. There were more screams, people began to run. He grabbed his daughter's hand in both of his, determined never to let her go again.

"Kelly, we have to stay together, there's a tsunami coming! We might make it to high ground if we get to the car!"

She shook her head.

"That's not what's happening, Dad. It's just the same old cycle coming around again, like it always does. Rise and fall, birth and death, renewal."

Brad stared out of the window. She was right; it was not a great wave that was blocking out the sun. It was a vast wall of scaled flesh, gleaming dully in green and gold, higher than the tallest skyscrapers. It moved ponderously, growing ever closer, smashing down buildings in great explosive clouds of glass, dust, and rubble.

"Ouroboros," said Kelly, pulling her arm away from his grip. As she did, the tattoo on her hand became a living serpent, uncoiling and rearing up, growing at an impossible speed, becoming so vast as to blot out the sky, its huge jaws gaping as it lunged down to devour him.

"No!"

Brad woke up shouting, tangled in sweaty sheets. As always, the dream left him disoriented, and he only slowly came to realize that he was not at home. He groped for the bedside light, flicked it on, and saw a standard hotel room.

Okay, I'm in London, he thought. *Get a grip. Focus. Right, this is the Russell Hotel, so-called because it's in Russell Square. It's Monday morning. Everything's normal.*

It was just after four, and Brad was badly jet-lagged from the six-hour trans-Atlantic flight, but he knew better than to try and go to sleep again. He had been having the same apocalyptic nightmare about Kelly for nearly three months, ever since she had stopped replying to his calls and texts. At first, he had dismissed it as an inevitable symptom of fatherly concern. She had once been his little girl, but now she was a grown woman of twenty-one and living her own life. Making her own mistakes. Maybe taking big risks. Of course, he was worried. And of course, it seemed like the end of the world, because in a sense, it was.

But try as he might, Brad had been unable to rationalize the sheer scale of the disaster in the dream, and the way it was somehow linked to his daughter. And there was the recurrence of that word, Ouroboros. He had tried Googling it but ended up none the wiser. It seemed to be just one of many mystical symbols from ancient times. He wondered if he had he read about it, or maybe seen it in a TV documentary.

"Something must have planted it in my subconscious, that's all," he told the bathroom mirror. "And my God, Mister Steiger, you look like crap this fine morning."

His reflection showed a man just on the right side of fifty, with a full head of iron-gray hair, and what his mother had always insisted was a firm jawline, 'not a big chin.' He shaved, showered, and then went back into the bedroom to make himself some coffee. As he glanced across the room, he saw a form rearing up in the shadowed corner opposite. It seemed poised to strike. He flicked on the main light and the cobra-like being was revealed as a desk lamp.

"And that's getting really old," he muttered, pouring boiling water on instant coffee granules.

He had been glimpsing serpentine forms for weeks, now. It might be a laptop cable on the floor, or the hose of a vacuum cleaner curled up in a closet. Anything elongated and winding might suddenly take the form of a snake, and move like one.

Brad had not told anyone about the hallucinations, but was sure they were linked to Kelly. If he could find her, they would end and so would the nightmares.

He clung to that belief.

Now tidy yourself up, man, he thought. *You've got to come across as a solid citizen, and concerned father.*

***

Brad looked up dubiously at the block of apartments. Much of London's notorious East End had been regenerated, thanks to the 2012 Olympics. But there were pockets of squalor. This apartment building looked shabby and neglected, especially in the drizzle of a dull English April morning. As he stood watching the entrance, a couple of girls emerged, deep in conversation.

They look like students, he thought, *moving to intercept them. Maybe they can confirm I've got the right place.*

"Excuse me," he said, taking out a picture he'd found on Kelly's Facebook page, "I'm looking for someone who used to live here. Perhaps you knew her?"

They had known Kelly to talk to occasionally, but did not know where she had gone. Brad thanked them, went inside, and sought out the building supervisor. Doris, a middle-aged Nigerian woman in pink overalls, agreed to show him Kelly's room, as it was technically still hers. The dim-lit corridors were suffused with the smell of junk food and less pleasant odors.

"You say she was quiet, no trouble, Doris?" he asked the supervisor.

"No trouble at all," replied Doris, "not like some of these young rapscallions! Always in nice and early, Kelly, and she spent lots of time studying. A credit to you and her mother."

"But then she just disappeared?" he asked, looking around the bleak little room.

She slept in that bed, he thought. *Studied at that desk. But I get no sense of her identity in this place at all. It might as well be a hotel room.*

"Gone like a thief in the night," said Doris. "That happens a lot in a place like this. But her rent was paid up a month in advance. Now that's very unusual, believe me! Anyway, this is it."

Doris unlocked the door of an apartment and ushered Brad inside. It had a few posters on the wall, but not for singers or bands. Instead, they showed exotic locations in the Middle East and Asia.

"Did she travel a lot?" he asked, gesturing at the posters.

"No," replied Doris, "Kelly told me these were famous places in the science she was studying. Archaeology, I think."

"And she took all her personal belongings?" he said, opening the wardrobe to find nothing but clothes hangers.

"Yes, all her stuff was just gone one morning."

Doris shook her head.

"And you tell me you can't get in touch with her? That's a terrible thing. Family is the most important thing."

Brad could see nothing in the cramped little apartment that might help him find Kelly. All it told him was that she was no longer there. He felt a familiar despair start to well up as he looked through a chest of drawers, then the bedside cabinet. In the latter, he found a pamphlet. The front page bore an ornate circular symbol and a single word.

"Ouroboros," he said.

He stood staring at the black-and-gold cover. He was back in the nightmare, the world ending, his only child rejecting him.

How can I have dreamed this word? Maybe I read it somewhere, connected it to Kelly? Did it burrow into my subconscious?

"Beg pardon, sir?" asked Doris, coming over to look at the pamphlet. "Oh, those things. Disgraceful ungodly gibberish!"

"You've seen this before?" he asked, snapping out of his reverie and flipping through the glossy pages.

"Yes, somebody left one on the hall table. I threw it in the rubbish!"

Skimming the pamphlet, Brad could make little of it. It seemed to be promoting a bizarre, alternative view of history and spirituality, based on a rejection of Christianity and indeed, all Western culture. The tone struck Brad as less crazy than some religious propaganda he had read. The language was insidious and seductive, not ranting and judgmental. But the overall feel was still disturbing.

A cult, he thought. *Kelly has joined some kind of cult. Brainwashed. Oh Sweet Jesus.*

"Do you mind if I keep this?"

"No, take the evil thing away!" exclaimed Doris. "I'm only sorry I can't give you any more help."

Brad glanced around the bare room again, and shrugged.

"Not your fault," he said. "Thanks for letting me take a look around. Erm, do you mind if I use the bathroom? Had too much coffee at breakfast, I guess."

"No, not at all."

Brad felt slightly guilty, as he didn't need to pee. He just wanted to check and see if anything of Kelly's might have been left in the bathroom. It was a totally irrational impulse, and all the more powerful for that. All Brad wanted was some trivial object or item that would provide a sense of contact with her. But the cabinet over the sink was empty, though. He flushed the toilet and was about to open the door when he noticed a triangle of yellow material protruding from the plughole in the tub. He thought at first that it was a piece of plastic. But when he pulled it out with his thumb and forefinger, he found it was more like a parchment. It was dry, waxy in texture, with a natural curve to it. It reminded him unpleasantly of fingernails and calluses.

Old skin. Dried skin.

The sound from the cistern was dying away, so he put it into his pocket and rejoined Doris.

"Thanks for letting me see her room," he said.

"It's the least I can do, you poor man," said Doris. "I hope you find her. Come on, down to my room, I'll make you a cup of tea."

"Thank you, but I really need to keep looking," replied Brad. "And this afternoon, I have to meet a guy who's good at finding lost people. A professional."

"Good luck," called Doris after him as Brad left Trafalgar House. "And may the Lord go with you."

Let's hope he does, thought Brad. *I need all the help I can get.*

***

The Peninsular Agency was based on the third floor of an office building in Canary Wharf, a thriving business district right on the river Thames. As he got out of the elevator at the reception, Brad felt reassured by the professional feel of the business. It was nothing like the shabby office of the old-style Hollywood private eye.

These people look like they get things done, he thought. *I've done my best, let's see if the professionals can do better.*

A smart young PA showed Brad into a bright, spacious office. Matt Arnold, a senior partner in the firm, came around his desk to offer Brad a firm handshake. The detective was of average height, slender, and about thirty-five. He also looked kind of nondescript, the sort of guy you would not remember if you saw him in a bar or walking through the park.

"Can I ask why you got in touch with this particular agency?" asked Arnold, gesturing at Brad to take a seat. "No shortage of private detectives in London, after all."

"A colleague at my company recommended you," replied Brad. "He said you have a good reputation for getting the job done."

Matt shrugged slightly.

"That's in part because I pick cases I think I can solve," he said. "Missing persons can often lead to frustrating dead ends."

"But you have found people who've gone missing, been abducted, whatever?" demanded Brad.

"Sometimes," said Matt. "Quite often, in fact. But I prefer to be up front about this. Most of a private detective's time is spent on mundane stuff. Checking up to see if a husband or wife is cheating, or if a mild-mannered corporate accountant is spending a lot of money on, what you American call, boats 'n' hoes. That kind of thing."

"Not as exciting as I'd thought," commented Brad.

"It pays the bills," returned Matt. "But we didn't meet up to discuss my career choices. You hinted, rather strongly, that this is not a routine job."

"No," said Brad, "here's the problem."

He explained that Kelly, who had been studying archaeology at London University, had simply dropped off the radar a month earlier. At first, Brad had assumed she had been preoccupied with college work. But after she had failed to return calls and texts for over a week, he had flown to London to find out what was going on. He had found that Kelly was no longer at her apartment, had moved out weeks earlier, telling no one where she was going.

"But there was a clue, this group she was meeting up with?" asked the detective.

Brad nodded and took the Ouroboros pamphlet from his jacket pocket, handed it over. Arnold looked at it, and frowned.

"How do you pronounce that?" he asked.

"Not sure," admitted Brad. He considered mentioning his dream, decided not to. "I'd never heard of it before. But apparently, Kelly had cut her old friends out of her life and hooked up with these people."

"So where did you get this?" asked Arnold.

"From the student apartments where she lived," replied Brad. "It seems that these things had been spread around the campus recently."

Arnold frowned at the pamphlet.

"*The Earth doth like a snake renew,*" he read. "Very poetic. But if we're dealing with a cult, things could get very complicated."

"You mean legally?" asked Brad.

The detective nodded.

"Yes, because your daughter is an adult. So if she wants to join a bunch of nutters who dance naked in the woods on alternate Thursdays, there's nothing you can do to stop her, under English Law, that is."

"That's what the police told me when I called them from the States," said Brad, feeling increasingly frustrated. "Look, Matt, I'm not paying you to tell me what can't be done. I want to find her and …"

He hesitated, and Arnold nodded in sympathy.

"You want to save her from herself, and from these weirdos?"

"Yeah," said Brad, "she's still my little girl and I want to save her. That simple."

"I'll do my best," said Arnold. "And if you agree, I'd like to bring in an expert on cults and all things mystical? He charges reasonable rates."

Brad shrugged.

"Money's no object at this stage," he said. "I just want to know she's okay. And to talk to her."

Arnold paused for a moment, coolly appraising Brad before speaking.

"And if, when you talk to her, she tells you she's fine and to leave her alone?"

Brad took a deep breath.

"We'll cross that bridge when we come to it."

"And there's nothing else you can tell me?" asked Arnold. "No other data other than the raw facts about Kelly, her course, and so forth?"

Brad looked out of the broad office window and saw the curved trail of a jet climbing high over London. It transformed itself briefly into a serpent, writhing in the sky.

"No," he said, looking Arnold in the eye. "There's nothing else. Just those facts."

"Okay, first the good news," said the detective, "nobody can do much these days without leaving an electronic trail. If she's left the country, I have contacts who can find out where she's gone. If she's still in Britain, she must be registered with the National Health Service and other agencies. Again, there are ways to get that data."

"I don't care what it takes or how much it costs," said Brad. "Just find her."

"I'll keep you informed," Arnold assured him. "How long are you in London?"

Brad shrugged.

"My firm has given me a couple of weeks of unpaid leave. After that, we'll have to see. Are you sure there's nothing I can do?"

Arnold paused, and gave Brad an appraising look.

"I can't let you tag along on my investigation," he said, "but if I come across any situation that you can help with, rest assured I'll let you know at once. In the meantime, let me give you my card. You can call any time."

The detective took out a business card, then produced a second card and handed them both to Brad.

"Contact details for Marcus Valentine, the cult expert I mentioned," he explained. "He lives in London. I'm sure he'd be happy to talk to you about all this, maybe offer some advice on how to win Kelly over."

"I might just do that," said Brad. "Thanks."

He was about to leave when he remembered the odd substance he had found in Kelly's apartment.

"Do you have any idea what this is?" he asked.

Arnold took the parchment-like material and turned it over.

"Long time since I saw this stuff," he said, with slight distaste. "An old girlfriend of mine kept a Burmese python. Bloody thing ate live mice, gave me the creeps. Eventually, I gave her an ultimatum, said it was me or him, and she chose Monty."

The detective handed the fragment back to Brad with a grimace.

"Yeah, that's definitely shed snakeskin. Where did you get it?"

Chapter 2: Close to the Serpentine

Matt Arnold walked out of Hyde Park Corner Tube station and unfurled a map of London that he had just bought at a vending machine. He was dressed in smart but casual clothes, and looked around curiously like a tourist. It was a tried and tested way of looking like a borderline idiot, the sort of visitor to the capital that Londoners habitually ignore. At the same time, it allowed Matt to gaze at anything and anyone for longer than would normally be considered polite.

Across the street was Apsley House, residence of the first Duke of Wellington. He gave it a puzzled stare, referred to the map again, then took out his phone for a picture. He added a selfie of himself in front of the Underground station sign.

Right, that's more than enough camouflage for now.

He checked his phone for texts. Sure enough, there was another one from Kathy Hopkirk. Sensibly, she had agreed to meet in Hyde Park in mid-morning. It was a public place, but one covering hundreds of acres. This would allow them to talk well out of earshot of onlookers. He crossed the road and went through the gate heading for the Serpentine, the sinuous lake that wound along the eastern edge of the park.

Odd coincidence, picking that particular location, he thought. *Or maybe she has a weird sense of humor.*

***

Brad called Marcus Valentine after he got back to his hotel on Monday afternoon. The cult expert was keen to help in any way he could, so they arranged to meet up at Valentine's apartment the following day. After another uneasy night, Brad traveled via the London Underground to Camden, where Valentine lived in an apartment over a bookshop. He was buzzed in and was met on the landing by a man of about fifty who was almost a parody of the old-fashioned English gentleman. Valentine wore iron-framed glasses, a tweed suit, and a waistcoat with a watch-chain.

"Mister Steiger? Please, come in!"

"Thanks for seeing me so promptly, Mister Valentine," said Brad, looking around a small apartment that seemed to be entirely walled with bookshelves. A large ginger cat lay sleeping on the only armchair that wasn't covered in books, magazines, or computer printouts. A PC stood on a desk by the window. Valentine cleared a space on a sofa for Brad.

"Please call me Marcus. Can I offer you some tea?"

Brad smiled, and shook his head.

"Sorry, I'm a coffee kind of guy," he replied. "And call me Brad."

"Very well, let's get down to business," said Marcus. "Take a seat."

After talking for a few minutes, Brad felt sure that Marcus Valentine was a man he could trust. He opened up about his troubled relationship with Kelly.

"Pat and I split up when she was five," he explained. "I was away from home a lot; it put a big strain on the marriage. Then I had an affair, a dumb pointless affair that smashed up my family. And since then I've seen Kelly hundreds of times, but as the absent father. Deadbeat Dad. She called me that once. The fact that I work for an oil company doesn't help. Destroying the planet, all that stuff."

He paused, still feeling the hurt of uncounted blazing rows with his only child. Marcus gave a rueful smile.

"You know," he said, "I've often observed that it takes about five minutes for an American to reveal things that an Englishman might hint at after five years of friendship."

That got a laugh from Brad, and they moved on to the Ouroboros cult.

"Well, I might have a breakthrough there," offered Marcus. "But first, what do you know about this group?"

"Only what I read in this thing," said Brad, offering the pamphlet he had found at Trafalgar House.

Marcus glanced through the pamphlet, nodding.

"Yes, this is much the same sort of thing as their website."

"They have a website?" exclaimed Brad. "They advertise their craziness?"

Marcus looked at him for a moment, then asked, "Have you seen the internet lately? There are people proudly proclaiming their belief that the Earth is flat."

Good point, thought Brad. *Why wouldn't a cult use every means to lure in converts?*

"So what's the real deal about Ouroboros?" he asked. "How long has it been around?"

"Not long," replied Marcus. "It first appeared in the mid-Nineties as a fringe group in what was called the New Age movement. What's odd about it is that its founder, Jonathan Clay, does have some genuine academic credentials. A doctorate in archaeology, in fact."

"Kelly was studying archaeology," Brad pointed out. "Could there be a connection?"

Marcus shrugged.

"Could be. Like a lot of cults, Ouroboros seems to try and snare bright young people, especially students. Some of its adherents are highly qualified in various fields. One of Clay's own students, Olivia Ballard, was among the founding members."

"But what made this guy go off the rails?" asked Brad. "Assuming he wasn't wacko from the get-go, of course?"

"He was the obsessive type," said Marcus, "there are a few hints in his early work. You see, he was fixated by ophiolatry."

Seeing his guest's puzzlement, Marcus got up and gently dislodged the cat, who meowed in protest, looked at Brad accusingly, then stalked out of the room.

"Here it is," said Marcus, handing Brad a hefty volume. The title was *Snake Cults In The Ancient World.*

"People worshiped snakes?" said Brad. "That really is crazy."

"But common," said Marcus, perching on the edge of his desk. "The symbol of the Pharaohs was an Egyptian Cobra, for instance. The Aztecs worshiped Quetzalcoatl, the Feathered Serpent. The Minoan civilization of Crete venerated snakes. In India, there were snake-beings called Nagas, rather similar to the Lamias of ancient Greece. Putting together all these legends, Clay formed the theory that they represented some kind of deep, primal truth about our species. A kind of vague ancestral memory, if you like. There's much more to it than that, I'm sure. Every cult has a big secret, one only revealed to the highest initiates."

Brad flipped through the book, pausing at illustrations of various idols and demons.

"The only snake I know of that was linked to religion is the one that tempted Eve," he remarked. "So does that make Ouroboros a devil-worshipping cult?"

"Clay would deny it," smiled Marcus. "The Ouroboros is an ancient symbol that has no evil connotations. Clay claims that the story in Genesis is a hint at the way other deities displaced the old, worldwide snake-cult. Thus the Ouroboros, symbol of regeneration and recurrence, proclaims the need to return to the old way, become one with Nature again, all that New Age malarkey. He's one of those clever debaters who has an answer for everything. And he did have a point, it must be said. Turn to page one-three-five."

Brad found himself looking at a picture of a snake-woman, voluptuously human from the waist up, sinuous reptile from the waist down.

"Is that a Naga?" he said.

"No, but she may be a close relation. That's a medieval painting of Lilith. In the Hebrew Talmud, Lilith was Adam's first wife, but was banished when God created Eve. Predictably enough, she is said to have born sons and daughters to him, all nice and scaly."

Brad stared at the weird hybrid creature.

"I thought Lilith was Frasier's bitchy ex-wife in that TV show."

"The original one was even more formidable, and much more seductive," said Marcus. "The Victorian painter-poet Dante Gabriel Rossetti was very keen on the legend. 'Not a drop of her blood was human,' he wrote, 'but she was made like a soft, sweet woman.' Rossetti depicts Lilith as a rebel against God, seeking to recruit Adam for a kind of cosmic revolution."

"Fascinating," said Brad, closing the book. "But how did all this wild-eyed speculation turn into a cult that brainwashed my daughter?"

"Good question," said Marcus. "Something happened to send Clay over the edge. He was trying to prove that prehistoric stone circles were related to his universal snake-cult. He was excavating one in Ireland when he seems to have had a breakdown, or an epiphany, or something. Ouroboros emerged about a year later, and he turned his back on academia for good."

"Presumably he has some kind of headquarters?" said Brad. "Wouldn't that be a good place to start?"

"Ah, now that's interesting, because the original headquarters of Ouroboros in London was closed down last year after the group moved out. Where to, we're not sure."

"But you do have something? You said earlier," pointed out Brad.

"Ah, yes, I've just relayed an email to Matt Arnold about it," said Marcus, getting up and turning to his PC. "Come and look."

Brad watched Marcus log on to a site entitled *Cult Survivors*.

"It's mostly an opportunity for people who've escaped cults to share experiences in a safe online environment," Marcus explained. "Sometimes we're contacted by fugitives, people who are afraid of retribution. For instance, this person contacted me via a secure link."

The Englishman opened a window, and Brad saw a dialogue between Marcus and someone called Kathy Hopkirk. The last few exchanges concerned arranging a meeting.

"And Kathy is a fugitive from Ouroboros?" asked Brad.

"So she says," replied Marcus, carefully. "You'll note that she gives a mobile phone number. I passed that on to Matt first thing this morning to see if he can persuade Kathy, or whoever it is, to meet him in a public place. I prefer not to risk exposure, you see."

"Are they violent, the Ouroboros?" asked Brad.

"Other cults certainly are, I've had a few close shaves with unpleasant people. Matt is a bit more clued-up on security matters, though."

As they watched, another message appeared.

They hacked me it's not me don't go!'

Marcus and Brad looked at each other, then Marcus picked up a phone from the desk.

"With a bit of luck, we can head him off," he said. But his tone was not optimistic.

Jesus, thought Brad, hearing the fear in the man's voice as he tried to call the detective. *What have I gotten myself into? Who are these people?*

"It went to voice mail," said Marcus. "I'll keep trying."

"Try his office," suggested Brad. "Maybe they can help."

***

Matt Arnold passed the Diana Memorial Fountain, being careful to take yet another selfie, all the while looking around for a likely contact. After walking around the Serpentine for ten minutes, he had seen no young women on their own. Then, when he was wondering if he should give up, he saw a black-clad figure emerge from the dense woodland up ahead.

Could that be her?

The figure raised a hand in a distinctive gesture and his phone buzzed. Another text.

'I see you! Check your map. Old gazebo.'

When he looked up, the figure had vanished. He did as instructed and saw that the gazebo was inside the woods. It was just visible, in fact. But then he saw a red-striped warning sign. CLOSED! UNSAFE STRUCTURE. Beyond it was a partly-overgrown footpath.

Glancing around, Matt saw no one nearby, and simply dodged around the sign. As he did so, his phone vibrated. He quelled the urge to answer, let it go to voicemail.

No distractions permitted now.

It took him about ten minutes to reach the gazebo by the winding footpath, which stood in a small clearing. There was some scaffolding around the structure, but no sign of any workmen. The woman in black was waiting inside, leaning on one of the wooden pillars that held up a domed roof. Her face was in shadow. He had seen a poor-quality image of Kathy Hopkirk from her now-defunct Twitter account, and this young woman could be her. She had the same blonde hair and heart-shaped face. But something about the set-up made him uneasy.

"Hello!" called the woman, sounding friendly.

And maybe a bit too confident, he thought. *Not the kind of jittery state of mind you'd expect.*

He stopped about five yards away and asked, "Kathy?"

"Kathy couldn't come. Sorry! Will I do?"

The stranger stepped forward out of the shadows and Matt took an involuntary step back. Though she was only about five feet tall, he was suddenly very aware that he was alone with her. The meet-in-a-public-place rule had been for Kathy's benefit. But now he wished he had stuck to it for his *own* sake.

"Look, I don't know who you are," he said, as she came closer. "But I'm just going to walk away now, unless you can offer me useful information."

"I am known as Salome. And I can offer you more than boring information, Matt," she said, stepping close and looking up into his face. "I can offer you truth, peace, kinship. A place in a bright new future."

Her eyes, they're so green. Piercing. As if they're reflecting the sunlight.

"I'm here to put a proposition to you," she said, reaching up to touch the side of his face. He tried to disengage her hand, but struggled to move it.

"Don't struggle," she said. "Just listen. Listen to my voice."

Her words seemed to echo inside his head. He felt his will starting to ebb away.

"We'd like you to be on our side, Matt," she said, her voice silky, seductive. "Wouldn't you like to be on my side? Wouldn't it be so much easier?"

My God, she's trying to hypnotize me. Almost succeeding.

He made a huge effort and forced her hand away from his cheek.

Salome tilted her head to one side.

"My, you're quite a rarity, Matt. One in a million, perhaps. We've hardly ever found someone who can't be won over."

"Sorry to disappoint you," he said, trying not to sound as rattled as he felt. He backed away a few steps then turned to leave. He strode purposefully along the footpath, trying to ignore the itching sensation between his shoulder blades.

"Think again, Matt," said Salome. "You're running out of options."

Something about her voice had changed. It was not echoing in his mind now, but seemed oddly slurred, as if she had some sort of speech impediment. He paused and looked back, then started to run. What he had seen was impossible to his rational mind. But his instincts had taken over, and adrenaline was coursing through his system.

Can't be true, it's a trick, he thought. *Maybe more hypnosis, making me see things.*

He looked back again as he left the clearing and saw nothing except the heap of clothes on the ground by the gazebo steps.

She was stripping off her tee-shirt, he thought. *Her skin, her face, all changing.*

He stumbled over a tree root, recovered, and went back onto the path.

It was all a hallucination. Nobody can elongate their body, nobody can change the shape of their head.

Matt slowed, glanced back yet again, and saw no sign of pursuit.

Is she running around naked?

Confused, he slowed to a walk, starting to doubt everything that had just happened.

So I go back to Steiger and explain that, having failed to mesmerize me, a cultist did a shape-shift and left her jogging pants behind in the park. Then he'll pay my fee with a smile.

A swishing and rustling in the undergrowth to his left sent his heart racing in panic. He would withdraw, regroup, and maybe drop the case.

"I need a holiday," he said to himself. "A long vacation. Maybe a cruise."

There was a loud hiss that was a little like a humorless laugh. He looked down and saw huge, green eyes in a wedge-shaped head. The serpent reared up as Matt recoiled, screaming in primal fear, he tripped and fell flat on his backside. He reached behind him and felt a tube of scaly muscle writhing, tightening. Coils wrapped themselves around him as he struggled to stand. He tore at the huge reptile with frantic strength as it wrapped itself round his chest.

As the constriction began, the hideous face came close to his. As he blacked out, the last thing he was aware of was a forked tongue caressing his face.

***

After some discussion, Matt Arnold's PA informed Marcus Valentine that the detective's phone contained a tracker that could not be turned off. It was at the rendezvous point where he had been due to meet Kathy Hopkirk. And no, the PA could not contact her boss, but that was not strange when he was working a case.

Marcus ended the call and looked at Brad.

"We could call the police, I suppose," said the Englishman.

"And tell them what?" asked Brad. "That a private detective is doing his job? All we have is a bit of web traffic that might be a hoax."

"All right," said Marcus, scooping a bunch of car keys from his desk. "We can damn well go and check things out ourselves!"

"I like your style, Mister Valentine," grinned Brad as he got up, glad to be taking some kind of action.

It took them nearly an hour to get to Hyde Park from Camden, thanks to central London's notorious traffic. More time was wasted finding a parking space, and by the time they got to Hyde Park, it was nearly two hours since the ominous message. As they drew near the park's main gate, Marcus pointed out an ambulance parked by the Serpentine lake. People in uniforms, police and paramedics, seemed to be busy in the area.

"That's not a good sign," observed Brad.

When they arrived at the police cordon, they saw the paramedics carrying a covered body out of the woodland. Uniformed police were talking to a couple of teenagers.

"What could have done that to him?" the distraught girl was saying, while her boyfriend tried to comfort her.

"Three guesses as to who found the body," said Brad. "Should we make ourselves known?"

"We're honest citizens," said Marcus. "What choice do we have?"

Half an hour later, they were in an office at New Scotland Yard talking to

Detective Sergeant Declan Healy. Brad was initially skeptical about the officer, given his earlier experiences with the Metropolitan police. But Healy came across as warm and perceptive. It was a long, involved conversation but eventually they produced formal statements that Brad and Marcus signed.

"And now we've got the paperwork sorted," said Healy, "maybe we can have an informal discussion? Because I don't mind saying, this is a weird one."

"Anything we can do to help," said Marcus. "Though I realize you can't disclose too many details to us."

"True," said Healy, "but I don't mind disclosing stuff the papers will get by tomorrow anyway. Preliminary findings are that Mister Arnold was crushed to death."

"Crushed?" asked Brad. "Something fell on him, or he was run over by a vehicle?"

"That's what I thought," replied Healy, "especially as he was found near a building closed off because it was unsafe. But the poor bloke's ribcage was cracked by pressure from all around his body. Something literally squeezed the life out of him."

"Like a boa constrictor?"

Healy looked at Brad, clearly puzzled by the suggestion.

"I suppose so, but we don't get many of those running amok at this time of year."

"But you couldn't rule it out?" insisted Brad.

"We'll leave that to the forensic team," said Healy, turning to his computer screen. "Now, on to the issue of your daughter, Mister Steiger. I see you tried to report her as a missing person?"

This led to a discussion of Kelly's background, and her involvement with Ouroboros.

"New one on me," said Healy. "But these weird groups spring up like weeds in a city like London."

"Ouroboros is a low-key outfit," said Brad, "nobody seems to know much about it."

"But this Kathy Hopkirk promised to spill the beans, eh?" said Healy. "I think I can legitimately look into her background. She's involved in this case, perhaps a material witness. In the meantime, I will list your daughter as missing, Mister Steiger. I think in the circumstances, she could be at risk."

"What does that mean in practice?" demanded Brad. "That she's on some database with ten thousand other names?"

"I'll make it a national priority and involve Interpol, if my superior approves," promised Healy. "Will that do?"

Brad nodded, pleased that his initial impression of Healy was correct.

"In the meantime," the officer went on, "I have to ask, are either of you gentlemen at risk?"

"Yes, I'm afraid we may be," said Marcus. "Ouroboros may claim to be peace-loving, but I've had some near misses with fanatics over the years. I'd put nothing past them."

"Unfortunately, I can't allocate any officers to protect you," said Healy. "You won't be surprised to hear our budget simply won't stretch to that. But I would advise you both to be very careful in the future. And get out of London. Take a holiday, Mister Valentine. And you, Mister Steiger, would be well advised to go back to the States.”

“Sorry, but I think I have to stick around,” said Brad. “I can't just abandon my daughter.”

“And I can't just throw everything up and leave,” put in Marcus.

Healy sighed.

“Thought so. For what it's worth, you can contact me directly if you suspect you're being followed, or if you receive any threats. In the meantime, I'll try to keep you informed as far as I'm able.”

With that, the interview was over, and Healy was left alone to write up his own preliminary report. He made a point of mentioning Ouroboros in the Hyde Park case, and in his missing person file on Kelly Steiger. He then immersed himself in work on another one of his half dozen active cases. At five O' clock, he was interrupted by a junior officer bearing a cup of coffee.

“Just in time, the disgusting instant caffcinated brew that energizes the lonely sleuth,” said Healy.

“Yes, sir,” said Constable Knapton. “And a rumor from on high has it that the Deputy Commissioner wants your guts for garters.”

“Again?” asked Healy. “It's only Tuesday.”

“Yes, sir,” continued Knapton. “Apparently you've violated protocol and such like.”

“Aren't I the little reprobate,” returned Healy, blowing on the steaming coffee. “You couldn't manage a doughnut or a cupcake or something to go with this muck?”

“I'll do my best, sir,” said Knapton, but before he could leave, the Deputy Commissioner himself appeared, blocking the doorway.

“Don't get up, Healy,” began the senior officer. “Just a flying visit. About this missing person thing.”

The Deputy Commissioner barged past Knapton as if the latter did not exist.

“We can't squander resources on every American who decides she doesn't like her dad anymore. I've blocked your request to list the Steiger girl as missing.”

“Sir,” began Healy, “I felt that the cult involvement merited–”

The Deputy Commissioner silenced the detective with an impatient gesture.

“If the girl is in any kind trouble, that's a problem for the local force to deal with,” he barked. “Just leave it, it's not our concern. Focus on the actual evidence, not your usual speculation and touchy-feely stuff.”

Without waiting for Healy to respond, the senior officer left without bothering to close the office door.

“That's me told, eh?” said the detective.

“Yes, sir,” said Knapton, apparently unruffled.

“You want to get out of uniform one day, lad?” asked Healy.

“Yes, sir,” returned Knapton, now sounding wary.

“Well, put your keen intellect to work and tell me what was wrong with that conversation.”

“Don't get you, sir,” admitted the constable. “I think you just got the usual bollocking for overstepping the mark.”

Healy sighed, leaned back in his chair.

"You fail to bring me doughnuts, or elementary deductive powers. Think, what did the old bugger actually say?"

Knapton frowned, then enlightenment dawned.

"He said it was for the local force to deal with! But that means he knows she's not in London anymore."

"And almost certainly knows where she is," added Healy.

The two officers stared at each other for a few moments.

"Feel free to just walk out, closing the door behind you," said Healy, eventually.

Knapton walked to the door, closed it, and then leaned against it.

"I might not be the brightest, sir, but I don't like crooked coppers."

"Me neither," said Healy. "Let's see if we can find out exactly what this particular one is trying to hide."

Chapter 3: West of Ireland, May 1994

Jonathan Clay woke in a cramped bunk bed on a cold, damp morning. It was spring in Ireland, but since his team had arrived at the site, it had rained every day. It made work difficult and unpleasant. He looked out of the window of the trailer, and saw no break in the lowering ceiling of gray cloud.

But if you don't want to get your hands dirty and your socks wet, he thought, *don't be a professional archaeologist.*

Clay was sharing a trailer with Dermot Kavanagh, a student from Dublin University. A separate, smaller trailer was occupied by Olivia Ballard, his other student. They had been forced to rent the trailers to live at the site of their dig instead of taking accommodation in the nearby village of Ballymahan. Even though Clay had started hunting for rooms months in advance, the locals had claimed that all the B&Bs were booked. At the time, he had believed them. Now he was not so sure.

"Wakey, wakey, Sam," he said loudly. There was a groan from the upper bunk.

"What time did you get back from the pub, young man?" demanded Clay.

Dermot's round face appeared, bleary-eyed and unshaven.

"Let's just say it was late, boss," said Dermot. "Sorry."

Something about Dermot's expression told Clay that the student was concerned about something more than a hangover.

"What's wrong?" he asked. "Not more superstitious nonsense?"

Dermot swung his legs over the edge of the bunk, groaned, held his head in his hands. He was a gangling, red-headed young man who Clay often thought looked like a parody of an Irishman. The one exception to the stereotype was that the lad could not hold his drink.

"I'm afraid so, boss," Dermot said. "We've lost Kieran. He won't be coming up today. Or any day."

"What? But Kieran was our last volunteer!" protested Clay. "We'll never get the work done now!"

"I know," moaned Dermot. "It's a bloody disgrace. I reckon the priest got to him. And maybe some of the old biddies. He was ashamed of himself, I could tell. But it's hard to go against the grain when you live in a little village. I know that myself."

Clay grunted noncommittally. They had begun their excavation at Ballymahan's stone circle with no less than a dozen volunteers, mostly young men and women, a few kids, and a couple of keen retired folks. But one by one, they had dropped out. Some had apologized and offered fairly lame excuses, but most had simply stopped showing up.

Before he could question Dermot further, there was a loud banging on the trailer door.

"Morning, boys! If you're not decent, tough luck, I'm coming in anyway!"

Olivia climbed into the trailer, carrying her usual morning burden of fresh eggs and milk from the farmer whose land they were camped on.

"Why the long faces, chaps?" she asked when they greeted her with desultory Hellos.

Clay explained that they would be working without help.

"Bloody hell," she erupted. "What is wrong with these people? You'd think it was the Dark Ages, not the twentieth century."

Olivia was just a shade over five feet tall, but Clay often thought that she had enough energy for two full-grown men. He had had to effectively bar her from visiting the village pub because of her propensity to get into arguments with the locals about the Nine Sisters, as they called the standing stones near Ballymahan.

"There's no point in complaining," said Clay, trying to mollify her. "Let's just have breakfast and try to work out what we're going to do."

A few minutes later, they were sitting in the cramped 'living room' of the trailer eating scrambled eggs, washed down with mugs of coffee. The discussion of their plight had gone in circles. It seemed inevitable. The dig would have to be abandoned.

"It's just so bloody infuriating!" erupted Olivia. "We're so close to making a genuinely worthwhile discovery. It would put this place on the map, probably boost tourism. Don't these Irish yokels know a good thing when they see it?"

Clay noticed Dermot bridling slightly at the Englishwoman's remark about the villagers, and said, "Look, we don't know for sure that it's superstition. It might simply be that people have better things to do. Paid work on the farms around here, for a start."

"I suspect the real reason is approaching right now," said Olivia, looking out of the window at the dirt road to the village. Clay and Dermot half-stood to look past her. Heading up towards them was a battered Fiat that they all recognized at once.

"Father Quigley," Clay said, resignedly.

"Come to gloat, the arrogant bugger," fumed Olivia.

"I'd better talk to him, you two check those geophysical results for me."

The two students exchanged a glance but said nothing. It was obvious to them that Clay was creating make-work for them, keeping them busy to try and shore up morale. The archaeologist felt ashamed at the failure of this, his first big project, and a growing anger that the young people's careers should be blighted. He got up and went out to face the priest.

"Good morning, Doctor Clay," said Father Quigley, slamming his car door. He was a youngish man with thin, sandy hair and freckled features.

"Not really," replied Clay. "As I'm sure you're aware, we've lost our last volunteer. And I daresay no more will be forthcoming. You must be pleased."

The priest shook his head.

"You misjudge me, Jonathan," he said. "I don't bear you any ill-will. I merely speak for the community. People simply don't want you here."

Quigley gestured at the stone circle known as the Nine Sisters. Legend had it that the stones were evil witches who were petrified by Saint Patrick. As if on cue, a rent in the clouds permitted a shaft of sunlight to fall onto the ancient monument.

"Walk with me, Father," said Clay to the priest. "Come and meet the Sister and tell me just what you find so disturbing about archaeology."

"I've nothing against science," replied Quigley, falling in step beside Clay. "I just think there are other forms of knowledge, other paths to truth. And that scientists, like yourself, have uncovered some terrible truths that are better left alone. The events of this century prove that, I think."

"That didn't take long," said Clay, with a wry smile. "From folk stories about a Neolithic monument to Hiroshima in one giant leap."

Quigley laughed.

"I'm not suggesting some terrible catastrophe would arise if you excavated the Sisters," he said. "I'm just saying the locals don't like it and sometimes you have to go with the flow. There's genuine fear among these people. They come to me, and I see it in their faces, hear it in their voices. How can I ignore that?"

Frustrated, Clay pointed at the stones.

"We've done no damage, not even touched one of the Sisters!" he pointed out. "All we've done is put a trench across the center of the circle. We've found some pottery, arrowheads, the usual stuff."

"Yes," admitted Quigley, "but the legend says that digging anywhere around the circle is blasphemous."

"How can it be blasphemy to disturb a pagan monument?" protested Clay. "This circle pre-dates the arrival of Christianity in Ireland by at least a thousand years!"

They had just passed into the circle and Quigley stopped to look at the nearest stone. Like all the Sisters, it was about waist-height, an unremarkable lump of unworried granite. Irish stone circles tended to be much more modest than their British counterparts.

"Legends have their own logic," said the priest. "Locals believe that my namesake, Saint Patrick, drove all the snakes out of Ireland by overcoming the witches who worshiped the serpent. He turned them to stone, and their weight somehow pins down their great snake-deity that lies beneath our feet."

Clay looked down at the green Irish turf before he could stop himself, smiled at his response to such nonsense.

"There were no snakes in Ireland in the first place," he pointed out. "Not a shred of scientific evidence. Not a single skull, bone, or scrap of reptile skin has been found in any part of the Emerald Isle. You know that; you're an educated man."

"As I said," replied the priest patiently, "it is a legend. Not susceptible to scientific logic, but it conveys a truth of its own. Good conquered Evil, the Good Lord was victorious over the serpent."

"Do you want to hear my theory?" asked Clay. "Not the garbled version your parishioners might have got down the pub from Dermot and Olivia."

"As I understand it," said Quigley, in measured tones, "you think some kind of serpent cult lies behind ancient monuments? All across Europe and Asia, from India to Ireland?"

Clay nodded.

"Not just stone circles, but also the Stone Age obsession with spirals and circular labyrinths, which are found in hundreds of places. I think snake-worship was overthrown by new faiths, and its adherents condemned as evil. The story of the snake tempting Eve in the Garden of Eden is an echo of that conflict."

Quigley shook his head.

"That's just the sort of talk to get the locals riled up. And before you condemn them as ignorant peasants, let me tell you, I've seen some things out here. Nothing too definite, I admit. Could be it was just my imagination. But I would never go near the Nine Sisters by night."

Clay took a breath, then said, "Look, come and see what we're actually doing. Nothing remotely blasphemous. Nothing remotely interesting, either, to the average person. We're just digging up rocks and bones to test a theory about a culture that's three thousand years dead."

The two men walked over to the trench. It was some four feet deep, three feet wide, and about twelve feet long. A small excavator stood next to it.

"We had hoped to put in at least three more trenches and in around the circle," explained Clay. "But with just the three of us working it would be pointless."

Quigley looked puzzled, and glanced at the digger.

"We only use machinery," said Clay, "to go down a couple of feet. That's going back just a few hundred years, time-wise. If we used the digger to go deeper, we'd smash all the stuff we're looking for. Most finds are quite fragile."

Clay helped the priest down into the trench and then started indicating areas where finds had been unearthed. Quigley listened attentively and asked thoughtful questions. Not for the first time, Clay wished he could somehow recruit the priest as an ally, a respected figure in the community who could win the villagers over. He said as much, but Quigley shook his head.

"You don't understand, Jonathan," he said. "I'm on their side. In all conscience, I cannot help you."

Quigley seemed about to say more, but then he frowned and looked down into the mud at the bottom of the trench. Following the priest's gaze, Clay saw a buried object with a straight edge, the sure sign of an artifact.

"How in the name of God did we miss that?" he exclaimed, crouching down to gently ease the dirt away from the object.

"Maybe you didn't," said the priest, as if to himself.

"What do you mean?" asked the scientist, but Quigley said no more and simply looked on, frowning slightly. When Clay freed it from the soil, the object proved to be a flat stone, roughly worked, with some kind of engraving on it. It was hard to make out the badly-corroded pattern, but it was circular.

"What do you make of that, Father?" he asked, holding up the stone to the sunlight. "A circle in the circle, yes?"

Clay held out the plaque to Quigley, but the priest made no move to take it. Instead, he looked at the object with distaste.

"You've got it bad, haven't you?" said Clay.

"Why didn't you find it earlier?" asked Quigley. "Did it somehow work its way to the surface overnight?"

The question stumped Clay for a moment.

We were all in the trench yesterday, he thought. *None of us noticed it. But we did finish when it was already getting dark. We were tired. But still...*

A terrible suspicion began to form in his mind. He thought of notorious scientific hoaxes, such as the so-called Piltdown Man discovered in England before the First World War. In that case, someone had faked the bones of a supposed 'ape man' and planted them at an archaeological dig site.

"No," Clay said aloud, "none of us would plant evidence to back our theories.

But someone else might, to try and discredit us."

He stared accusingly at the priest, who shrugged.

"I'm accusing nobody of fraud, Doctor Clay," he said, starting to clamber out of the trench. "If only it was merely a matter of human perfidy. But if you won't listen to me, I will leave you to your work. I only hope you're right, and that there's nothing here to unearth but the works of dead men."

Clay stood and watched the priest making his way out of the circle.

"Oh, to hell with the lot of them," he said in disgust, and stared at the stone plaque. Then he examined the small hole from which he had removed it. Had the plaque been covering something, maybe protecting it? That would make sense. He squatted to examine the hole more closely, worked at the sides to enlarge it. There was something odd about the pattern of soil around the hole. But it did not suggest that someone had buried the plaque.

No, he thought, *it almost looks as if something had pushed the thing up from bellow, like Quigley said. But what could have done that?*

Clay heard a stir, a small amount of earth shifting. Something glistened in the darkness beneath him, and he stood up and took a step back. He was suddenly aware of being alone, and of the absence of birdsong.

Again, there was movement in the dark, then two bright objects appeared. They were golden-green orbs about six inches apart. Clay bent down to look more closely.

Clay felt an odd crawling sensation, as if something was slithering into his mind. It was repellent and seductive at the same time. He shuddered as a mind that was as cold and inhuman as it was powerful wrapped itself around him, caressed his very soul. A tiny part of him remained unaffected and began to panic. But his body remained frozen, crouching over the dark pit where the huge eyes gleamed.

'I am dying.'

The voice was gentle but insistent. When the words sounded in his head, they drove all other thoughts away.

'For so many seasons I have lain in the dark, a captive. How I longed to return to the world of warmth and light, and revel once more in the delights of all fleshly things.'

Clay felt the being's pain and frustration, its yearning for freedom. It was a huge, monstrous emotion. A single tear rolled down his cheek.

'I need a vessel to carry what remains of my power, to let my essence flourish in the world once more.'

"I will be your vessel," said Clay, possessed by a desire to be of use.

'No, you will not suffice. Be a loyal messenger instead, and send me another. The young female. She has great energy and will be a worthy avatar.'

Clay felt a pang of rejection at being found unworthy by such a great entity. But he understood his task. Never taking his eyes off the hole, he climbed out of the trench, and was just standing upright again when he felt a sharp stinging sensation in his left calf.

What just happened?

Confusion reigned for a moment in Clay's mind as he rolled up the leg of his jeans. Two small, angry red marks showed on his flesh. But there was no pain anymore, just a vague numbness in his calf.

There are no snakes in Ireland. Everybody knows that.

Trying to ignore the weird sensation in his leg, Clay set off towards the trailers clutching the plaque. His memory of what had just happened was vague, swathed in clouds of confusion. He recalled arguing with the priest. Then he had found the plaque, Quigley had gone away, and after that, Clay had climbed out of the trench.

Why do I get the feeling that there's something else? Something important?

Clay shrugged off the weird sensation. The plaque was the most important thing for him, an artifact that could make his name in archaeological circles. As he left the circle of the Nine Sisters, his heart rate slowed to something near normal, and he found the courage to laugh at himself.

Getting spooked by Quigley's stories. Probably just an insect of some kind. Best get it looked at by the doctor in the village, though.

He was so excited by his find that by the time he got back to their camp he had quite forgotten the insect bites, or whatever they were. The numbness in his leg was oddly comfortable, as if the limb were swaddled in warm cotton wool. And Dermot and Olivia were so excited by the find that he finally set aside his initial reservations about it.

"Ouroboros," said Olivia, cleaning soil away from the plaque's engraved side with a camel-hair brush. "See? The serpent with its tail in its mouth."

"No one has ever seen anything like that in Ireland," said Dermot, eyes wide. "Do you think it was imported, maybe by Phoenician traders?"

"Oh, don't talk bollocks!" snorted Olivia. "It's clearly more Celtic in style than anything else, look at the flowing lines."

"Let's not speculate too wildly, you two," cautioned Clay. "The important thing is to get some pictures of the site for provenance. You can do that now Olivia. And we need to inform the lab back in Dublin, tell them to prepare for a major job."

Olivia and Dermot continued to half-discuss, half-bicker over the plaque. But as he sat opposite the youngsters, Clay found himself increasingly unable to follow what they were saying. The numbness had spread from his leg to his whole lower body.

"I don't feel too well," he managed to say. His words were slurred, his mouth uncooperative.

"Oh, Jonathan," exclaimed Olivia. "You do look very pale and tired! All this stress has taken it out of you!"

"You'd better lie down," said Dermot, helping Clay over to the bottom bunk. "A good rest will see you right."

"I'll go down the village and call the lab," Dermot said to Olivia.

"Good idea," she said. "I'll go up to the Sisters and take a few pictures of the actual location."

No! Don't go up there, thought Clay, but the numbness had developed into an immense tiredness. He heard the two students leave the trailer just before he lapsed into unconsciousness. The sleep that followed was almost dreamless except for a sensation of being constricted. He felt himself wrapped in something like coils of rope but thicker. And alive.

"Jonathan? Can you hear me, Jonathan?"

Clay slowly surfaced into consciousness to see Olivia's smiling face looking down at him.

"Feeling better?" she asked.

"I found the Great One," she said. "Just as you did. The difference is that you were a little too old to be transformed. Or exalted, maybe that's the better term."

"Olivia?" he whispered, not understanding.

He tried to sit up, but she put a small hand on his chest and pushed him back onto the bunk.

"Rest," she said. "And listen up. The Great One is dead, now. She used the last of her strength to imbue us with her spirit. We found her just in time. It must have been fated from the start, don't you think?"

Memories of the being in the trench came flooding back.

The thing clouded my mind, somehow. Hypnotized me into doing its will unconsciously. Doing her will, rather.

"You were bitten, too?" Clay managed to say.

Olivia nodded.

"And the Great One's power, or what remained of it, passed on to me! Isn't that amazing?"

Clay shook his head, confused, still only half-believing what had happened. He noticed from the light streaming into the trailer that the sun had shifted. It was mid-afternoon.

"How long have I been out?" he asked. "Where's Dermot?"

Olivia smiled, shook her head.

"When he came back from the village, I offered him the chance to join us. He refused. Instead he threatened to reveal our secret."

She stood up and stepped away from the bed. Looking past Olivia, he saw Dermot's body on the floor. His face was contorted in death-agony and two angry red marks showed on his neck.

"When you feel a little better you can help me bury him in the circle. None of the locals will dare dig there. We can report him missing later. A little mystery, and our secret."

Again, Clay tried to rise. He was angry and afraid. Once more Olivia shoved him back, seemingly without effort. Then she leaned close, her face a few inches from his. Her tongue flickered along her lips.

"Don't fight it, Jonathan," she said. And now her words echoed in his mind in an insidious, seductive way that was all too familiar. "Just obey me without question. It's so much easier for both of us if you accept your fate."

"Your eyes," he managed to say. "They were brown?"

"And now they're green," she said. "Just one of several wonderful transformations! And there's so much still to come."

Chapter 4: Bite Marks

After their interview with Detective Sergeant Healy, Brad and Marcus returned to the latter's apartment in Camden. There they found more messages purportedly from Kathy Hopkirk. She claimed that she had thwarted the hacking attempt by Ouroboros and would like to meet up.

"I'm getting a little paranoid," admitted Brad. "I mean, you can never be sure of anyone's identity online, right?"

"True enough, so I think this time we should arrange to meet her together, and in a very crowded public place," said Marcus.

Wednesday morning they entered the huge complex of buildings that was the British Museum. Brad, who had only ever made brief working visits to London before, was surprised to find the original Victorian structure inside a futuristic dome. The original circular building with its famous reading room was in the center of a vast quadrangle with long galleries on all four sides.

"The enormous sci-fi roof protects the museum from our miserable London weather, not to mention the pollution," explained Marcus, as they threaded their way through the crowd. "Nice and public. Eye witnesses from the four corners of the earth."

"So where is this cafe we're meeting her at?" asked Brad.

Marcus gestured at a distant corner of the enclosure.

"It's between North America and the Enlightenment," he replied. "I'm sure there's a joke there somewhere."

The Court Cafe was thronged with people talking in half a dozen languages, and at first, they saw no one who might be Kathy Hopkirk. Then Marcus drew Brad's attention to a slim young woman standing near the entrance, looking around furtively.

"Could be her," Brad agreed, and took out the Ouroboros leaflet. He held it so that the cover was clearly visible as they walked over to the young woman. She gave them both a searching stare before she spoke.

"You Kelly's dad?" she asked Brad. "You look a bit like her. Around the eyes."

Introductions were made, then they debated where to go.

"I'd like to keep walking, where there's crowds," said Kathy. "Nowhere too quiet."

They settled for the North American gallery, and were soon ambling through a display of Aztec artifacts. The centerpiece was a beautifully-crafted double-headed serpent, made from turquoise. Seeing Brad looking at it, Kathy gave a thin smile.

"It's hard to get away from them, isn't it? Once you start seeing them, they're everywhere."

"You have nightmares, too?" asked Brad.

She nodded.

"End of the world stuff, the Earth cracking open? Like an egg hatching?"

"Yeah," said Brad, "but Kelly is in them, trying to reassure me, somehow."

Kathy shook her head.

"Mine involve nobody I know," she said. "Just global disaster. I feel a bit jealous."

Marcus looked puzzled by the exchange, so Brad explained as best he could the nature of his nightmares.

"I'm normally skeptical about this sort of thing," said the Englishman, dubiously.

Kathy gave a humorless laugh.

"They rely on that," she said. "If you don't believe something can happen, you've got no defenses prepared when it does."

"So what happened to you?" asked Brad.

Kathy looked around quickly. There was nobody nearby. She rolled a sleeve of her hooded jacket, revealing dozens of old scars on her arm before quickly covering them again.

"I never knew my dad. My mum couldn't cope, so I went through a long line of foster families. Nobody wanted me, I was too much trouble. I ended up in a care home. It's an old story. I got into trouble, self-harmed, did some drugs. Other things I'm not proud of to get drugs."

"And then someone offered you a new start in life?" said Marcus.

She looked at him, gave a mirthless smile. Brad could not help noticing that, even for a Brit, she had very bad teeth.

"Yeah," said Kathy, "Last spring I was living in a squat down in Whitechapel and trying to avoid some very brutal people when I met a girl my own age, or a bit older. Told me it was the system, exploitation, greed, cruelty. That there was a better way, and people who'd be a real family to me."

"And you joined Ouroboros?" asked Brad,

"No, I told her to sod off!" exclaimed Kathy, "I'm not a bloody idiot!"

Some people browsing the exhibition turned to look, and Kathy lowered her voice.

"Sorry," she said. "But it took them weeks to wear me down, they're so persistent. This girl, she called herself Salome, she acted like a big sis, kind of. Putting up with my lip, acting sensible, being kind, buying me burgers and stuff. So one day, when I'd not been fast enough and one of my customers had beaten me up quite badly, I went with her."

Kathy sniffled, wiped away a tear. Marcus offered a handkerchief.

"Thanks, you're a nice bloke," she said, blowing her nose. "I couldn't even pronounce Ouroboros then, didn't know anything about it except that it was a kind of religion. They gave me some First Aid, a proper meal, a place to sleep. It was in this nice house up the West End, Knightsbridge I think."

"Did you see this guy, Clay?" asked Brad.

"Yeah, the Herald, they called him. He was nice, not a perv or anything. Like a kindly old uncle to me and the other girls. But then it got weird. One morning, I found these."

Kathy fell silent, then she pulled down the top of her shirt. At the base of her neck, just above her collar bone, were two tiny red marks edged in white.

"Mark of the vampire, eh?" she said, with another grin. "But after that I got all confused. I mean, even more than before. I reckon I was hypnotized or something."

"Brainwashing can feel like hypnosis," said Marcus. "The principles are much the same. Repetition, loss of self-control."

Kathy shook her head.

"No, it was more than that. They had ceremonies and stuff, but it was the private meetings with Olivia that really did my head in. We all had to do those, all the novices."

"Olivia Ballard?" said Brad.

Kathy nodded.

"She's this tall, really beautiful woman, but she's so scary. The way she talks, like she's pretending to be friendly but really, she's mocking you. And her eyes. When I was with her, I never really remembered what she said. I just got all fuzzy."

"When did you meet Kelly?" asked Brad, unable to hold the question in.

"About a week before I did a runner," said Kathy. "I didn't talk to her much, but she seemed happy enough. I know the leaders were really excited about her. One of my duties was general cleaning. I wasn't much good at anything else, I suppose. I was outside Clay's office door when I overhead them talking about this new girl, how much potential she had."

"What sort of potential?" asked Brad. "What did they mean?"

Kathy shrugged.

"Dunno. Then they mentioned me. Olivia said I was too badly-damaged to be a true convert. Because of the drugs and stuff, I suppose she meant. Clay sounded upset by this, but the big bitch kept saying I had to be 'disposed of', that they couldn't let me go. I did a runner right then, just grabbed some cash, and went. I'd heard people talk like that before. Pimps, dealers."

"You really think they were going to kill you?" asked Marcus, sounding incredulous.

"They killed that bloke in Hyde Park," she shot back.

"Yes, but how?" asked Brad. "He was crushed to death."

Kathy shrugged.

"Maybe they've got a trained snake. That would explain those rats." Seeing the men's bafflement she went on, "Every week, they'd take a delivery of half a dozen white rats in a big cage. They'd be taken upstairs to Olivia's room. And every week, the empty cage would be sent back to the supply firm for another batch. So she must have been keeping one of them big snakes, right?"

***

"Piglets?" said Mickey Garvin, incredulously.

"Live piglets," corrected Bill Stroud.

"You're making this up," scoffed Garvin, the younger and more garrulous man.

They were in the bar room of the Lamb and Flag, the only public house in Wychmere. Talk, as it usually did, had turned to the financial problems faced by farmers. Garvin, the local handyman, had asked Stroud, the pig farmer, how things were going. The latter had then revealed his new sideline.

"So you take a piglet up to Garlock House every week," said Garvin, "and they pay you fifty quid for it?"

"That's right," said Stroud. "Cash on the nail. Not a word to the bloody Inland Revenue, either."

Garvin pondered this a minute, then asked, "But what do they do with them?"

"I don't bloody know!" replied Stroud. "Kill 'em and eat 'em, I suppose."

"Well, that's downright strange," mused Garvin. "But I suppose they are from London. Or foreigners, maybe?"

Stroud shrugged.

"I only see the bald bloke, Clay. I drive up in the van, drop off the piglet, he takes it and gives me the money."

"How many of them live up there, anyway?" asked the landlord, who had been eavesdropping from the other side of the bar.

"No idea," said Stroud. "I catch glimpses of faces at the windows now and again. And I did see this real peach of a girl a few weeks ago, waiting for Clay when he took the piglet inside. Fine big filly, she was."

To underline his point, Stroud outlined voluptuous curves in the air.

"Well," said Garvin, downing the last of his pint and climbing off his bar stool, "I'll soon find out. I'm going up there this afternoon."

"What for?" demanded the landlord.

"This Clay bloke rang me this morning, wants me to take a look at their central heating boiler," explained Garvin. "Hope he pays me in cash, too. See you later, fellas!"

"See if you can find out what they do with them piglets," called Stroud as the handyman left.

An hour later, Garvin was shaking his head as he replaced a panel on a boiler in the cellar of Garlock House.

"Sorry, Mister Clay," he said, "I can't find anything wrong with it. Apart from it being very old, of course, but I dare say, you don't want to replace it?"

Clay, who had looked on during Garvin's inspection, put his hands together as if in prayer.

"If we have to, we will," he said, "but perhaps the problem with the erratic heating lies not in the boiler but the pipework?"

"Could be," said Garvin. "Maybe an air lock. Did you drain the radiators?"

Clay looked puzzled.

"Ah, that's probably it," Garvin went on.

"Would that explain why one particular room is not heated adequately?" asked Clay.

"Yeah, sure," said Garvin, picking up his toolbox. "Just let me take a look at it. Probably a five minute job."

"Oh, good," responded Clay, "it's just upstairs. Let me show you."

Clay let the handyman back up into the hall, then up the impressive main staircase. Garvin took his jacket off and loosened his shirt collar.

Shouldn't have had that pint at lunchtime, he thought. *But bloody hell, they keep it hot in here. Must cost them a fortune.*

When they reached the top of the stairs, Clay ushered Garvin along a corridor to an oak-paneled door.

"This is the room," said Clay, and opened the door. A rush of hot air scented with a flowery odor came rushing out. The interior of the room was dark.

"Seems warm enough to me," said Garvin dubiously.

"Oh no, it's very erratic," said Clay. "Please, take a look."

Still Garvin hesitated, waiting for Clay to step inside. Then someone spoke from inside the room.

"Is that the handyman from the village?"

Now that, thought Garvin, *is a sexy voice.*

"Do go in," said Clay, "Olivia will show you what to do."

"My pleasure," said Garvin, and strode into the darkened room. "Do you mind if we have some light, though, miss? I need to see to work."

The door closed behind him, cutting off the light from the corridor.

"Of course," said the husky, feminine voice. "Just a moment."

A match flared and he saw a red candle being lit. He caught a glimpse of pale flesh, an arm, the curve of a breast. Then the woman retreated from the light. The candle cast just enough of a glow to show that it stood on a small table against the wall. Everything else was still in shadow.

"That's not nearly enough," Garvin said, "couldn't you just open the curtains?"

"I much prefer the dark," came the reply. "I have very sensitive eyes."

Garvin remembered everything he had heard about the outsiders who had taken Garlock House.

Bunch of weirdos, he thought. Best play along if I want my money.

"Do you mind if I use my torch?" he asked, already searching in his toolkit.

Instead of answering the question the unseen woman asked, "What's your name?"

"Mickey. Mickey Garvin."

"Mickey," purred the voice. "I'm Olivia. I understand you're here to examine my plumbing?"

Mickey tried not to laugh.

"Erm, yes, I'd like to look at your radiator, miss."

He switched on the torch and swept the beam around the room. It was big, as he'd guessed from the echo, and luxuriously furnished. There was a huge four-poster bed opposite the door, its diaphanous curtains half-open. And on the bed was a half-naked woman. She was unclothed from the waist up. Her lower half, so far as he could see, was encased in some sort of sleeping bag.

"Bloody hell!" exclaimed Garvin, staring.

"Don't be alarmed, Mickey," said Olivia. "I prefer to feel the air on my skin. Don't you?"

"I don't know what you're playing at," he said, "but I'm not here to play any kinky games."

"Oh, that's a pity," she pouted. "I so wanted us to get better acquainted."

Sod this, thought Garvin, *these people really are nutters.*

He reached behind him for the doorknob. It wouldn't budge. He was locked in. He began to feel panic on top of his confusion. He turned, dropping his torch, to try and move the knob with both hands. But it was obviously locked. He heard a surge of movement behind him.

"Surely you don't want to go so soon?" asked Olivia, from close behind him.

Garvin turned, and saw the looming figure of the woman. She was a good head taller than his six feet two inches. He flinched, felt his back press against the oak panels of the door.

How did she move so fast? And how come I didn't hear any footsteps?

He looked down and saw that she was still half-inside her sleeping bag. Then he realized that it was nothing of the sort; her human form ended at the waist, and below it was a tubular body, scaly and muscled.

"Don't be scared, Mickey," she said, leaning down. Her eyes were suddenly bright, glowing in the murk. Their pupils were slits.

She's a monster! And she's moved on from piglets!

"Leave me alone!" he shouted, striking out in fear. Olivia, moving with lightning speed, grabbed his hand in hers and made a soothing noise.

"It's all right, I won't hurt you. I just want to give you a present."

With her other hand she grabbed him and, as he wriggled in futile terror, pressed her mouth against his neck. The sting of her bite produced a strangled scream, then he felt something course through his veins, robbing him of will-power.

Again, she looked into his eyes, and this time he did not find her terrifying.

"I'm so beautiful, aren't I, Mickey?"

"Yes, so beautiful," he agreed.

"You want to be my friend, don't you? And help me and my friends?"

"Oh, yes please."

Mickey listened, smiling in numb delight, as Olivia explained his task to him.

***

"You can't remember anything else, any detail that might help?" asked Brad.

"It's a blur," said Kathy, shaking her head. "Like they fogged up my mind. Every time I try to focus on details I get confused."

"There is something we could try to reach suppressed memories," said Marcus. "But it's risky."

"You don't mean drugs or anything?" asked Kathy, her voice panicky.

"No, I mean hypnotic regression," explained the Englishman. "Just a kind of relaxation, really, letting your unconscious mind get at things your conscious mind can't access."

"Have you done it before?" asked Brad.

"Yes," replied Marcus. "A few times. It's a way of overcoming traumatic experiences as well as recovering memories. But there are no guarantees it will work."

Kathy looked from one man to the other.

"So two middle-aged blokes are asking me to come to their place so they can make me lose all self-control? Well, I've had worse offers."

Seeing their expressions, she laughed.

"Only joking, guys," she said. "Now, are you going to buy me lunch before you start poking around in my mind?"

An hour later, the three were in the Englishman's living room in his Camden apartment, preparing for the experiment. Kathy, nursing a cup of tea, sat in a comfortable armchair. Marcus closed the heavy curtains against the afternoon sunshine, so that the only light came from his desk lamp. A microphone stood on the desk, pointed at Kathy, its cable connected to the PC.

"You sure you want to go through with this?" asked Brad.

Kathy nodded. She looked tense but determined.

God, she's so thin and pale, thought Brad. *That lunch must have been the first proper meal she's had in days.*

"I want to know what happened to me," she said, "and I want to help you. Let's go for it. Just so long as my head doesn't spin all the way round or anything."

She handed her teacup to Marcus, then settled herself in the chair.

"What do I do?" she asked.

"Try to think of a happy place, like a tropical island, or somewhere nice from your childhood," suggested Marcus, tapping a key to start recording the session.

"Don't you dangle a watch in front of me or something?" she asked.

"Not quite," said Marcus, sitting down to face her. He took out a silver fountain pen and held it about six inches in front of the young woman's face.

"Focus on the light reflected from the pen," he said, his voice quiet, gentle. "Hear only my voice. And keep thinking of a good place, a safe place, the place where you're happy."

Marcus kept talking for about a minute, making the same suggestions over and over. Focus on the light, the happy place, his soothing voice. Brad had expected some sudden change in Kathy's expression, but she simply looked blank. Then Marcus paused in his monologue and put the pen back into his pocket.

"Can you still hear me, Kathy?"

"Yes," she replied in a flat voice.

Her voice is normal, thought Brad, slightly disappointed. *Like they're having a regular conversation. Nothing like the movies.*

"Cast your mind back to last year," said Marcus gently. "Do you remember your time with Ouroboros, Kathy?"

"Yes," came the reply, in the same emotionless tone.

"Do you remember them talking about their new home, the place they were going to relocate to?"

Kathy was silent for a moment, her face blank. Then she spoke again.

"Litch-weir. Hitch-mere. I can't hear it properly. They never mention it when I'm around. I just catch things, as I'm coming into the room, or passing by outside."

"Try, Kathy," urged Marcus. "You're doing very well."

The young woman's face contorted in terror. She gave a strangled cry.

"No!" she said, in a small voice. "They've found me! They can see me! And you!"

"What the hell?" asked Brad. "Maybe you should snap her out of it."

For the first time, Marcus looked uncertain.

"Kathy," he said, "speak to me."

Kathy's expression changed again. The fear vanished, replaced by a confident smile. She turned her head to look directly over at Brad, sitting in the shadows on the couch. Something about her expression seemed familiar to him.

"Hi, Dad," she said in what sounded like Kelly Steiger's voice, all trace of British accent gone. "How's it going?"

***

"You've got the flu?" asked Leanne. "In the middle of April?"

Mickey Garvin groaned, and turned over in bed.

"I just need to rest up for a bit," he said.

Leanne stood, hands on hips, in the doorway of the cottage bedroom. She was skeptical about her on and off boyfriend's condition.

"This isn't an alcohol-induced flu by any chance?" she demanded.

"No," Garvin moaned from under the duvet. "It came on sudden, like. After I did that job up at the big house."

"Well, that explains it," she sniffed. "Bunch of weirdos, they are. Come from all over the place. Foreigners bringing diseases into the country, I shouldn't wonder. I'll get you some chicken soup. You need to keep your strength up."

Leanne was in the small kitchen heating up the Heinz soup in a saucepan when her boyfriend emerged, wrapped in a threadbare dressing gown.

"Feeling better, love?" she asked, glancing round.

"Yes, I'm much better," Garvin replied, sitting down at the table.

Leanne was not so sure.

He looks like a ruddy zombie, she thought. *All pale and lifeless. Maybe he really is ill.*

She poured the soup into a bowl and set it on the table in front of him. He looked down at it, as if trying to work out what it was. Then he smiled, picked up his spoon, and began to eat.

"So how did it go up at the big house, anyway?" she asked, sitting down opposite him. "You get their boiler sorted?"

"It was fine," he said. "Very nice people. Paid me in cash. Wish they were all that straightforward."

Garvin looked up from his soup.

"They've got a job for you as well, darling," he said. "Regular work. Nice little earner."

Leanne, who ran a one-woman mobile hairdressing and manicure business, was surprised.

"I'd have thought those posh folk wouldn't want any dealings with me," she said. "Wouldn't they go into Hereford to get their hair done and that?"

"No," explained Garvin, "they really want to see you. I told them about you, see? And they said, yes, you send her up to us."

He smiled again, returned to his soup.

Well, she thought, *their money is as good as anybody else's.*

"All right," she said, "I'm going up that way tomorrow. I'll drop by and see what they want."

"Sooner the better," he commented. "There's one lady who's very eager to see you."

"How come they're so keen to meet the locals all of a sudden?" she asked. "They've been all standoffish for months. What did they say to you, exactly?"

Garvin looked confused, and with his free hand, he tugged absentmindedly at the collar of his pajama jacket. Leanne saw an angry red mark just above his collar bone. She looked more closely and saw a second mark just visible under the first.

"Here, is that a love bite?" she said, jokingly.

"No," he said, looking down again. "Not a love bite."

"I wouldn't be surprised if you had fleas, this place is so scruffy," she said.

She did not give the marks any more thought until it was too late, and she had acquired some of her own.

Chapter 5: Signs and Wonders

"Kelly?" said Brad, startled into responding.

Marcus made an impatient gesture. He had asked Brad not to speak during the session.

"Kathy?" said Marcus. "Listen to me. I want you to wake up."

"Forget it, Svengali," said Kelly's voice, "I'm catching up with my old man."

"What is this?" exclaimed Brad. "Some kind of trick?"

"No tricks, Dad! It's all for real. That's what I discovered. Once you're in the circle, everything becomes clear."Kathy's face was serious now.

"That's how I can see you now, Dad. We all do. Kathy left us, but we didn't leave her. The circle is unbroken. We can see through her eyes. And that's just *one* of our powers!"

"Kelly, why can't you just meet me face to face?" demanded Brad. "If it's all so wonderful, why won't they let you see me?"

"Like I said," replied Brad's daughter, "I see you now. I'm not a prisoner, Dad. For the first time in my life, I really belong. You should join us too!"

"I just want to see you, hon," said Brad, "I just want to meet you, in person, to be sure you're okay."

Kathy's expression changed again, her eyes narrowed. This time her voice was harsh, deeper, and had a cold, inhuman quality.

"If you value your lives, do not interfere."

"Kathy, if you can hear me, I'm going to count down from ten, and by the time I reach one, you'll be awake," said Marcus, firmly.

As Marcus began his count, Kathy's eyes rolled back into her head and she slumped to one side. A fleck of foam appeared at the corner of her mouth.

"She's having some kind of fit," said Marcus. "Help me, Brad, in case she swallows her tongue."

A minute later, a baffled Kathy was sipping from a small glass of Scotch. She remembered nothing after being told to focus on the fountain pen.

"Did I help you at all?" she asked Brad.

"Kind of," he said. "But you also raised some more questions."

Marcus had been quiet since Kathy had recovered from her seizure.

"You should get medical help," he said. "But I have a feeling you won't."

Kathy shook her head.

"Don't like hospitals," she said firmly. "Anything official, I'm keeping away from it."

She got up ready to leave.

"Got to be going, gents. Things to do, people to see. And even more people to avoid."

"You never told us where you're staying," said Brad.

Kathy gave a thin smile.

"That's right, I didn't. Let's just say it's not luxury accommodation, but it's rent free."

"You do know the police want to talk to you about Matt Arnold's death?" asked Marcus, getting up to open the door for her.

She shrugged.

"I don't want to talk to them," she replied.

"How will we get in touch with you?" asked Brad.

"I'll get in touch with you," she said. "Thanks for the tea and booze, Marcus."

Just as she was leaving, Kathy stopped, realization dawning on her pallid face.

"Bloody hell, there is something else," she said. "Maybe you did churn up a lost memory or something. It's a bit daft, but I should tell you. About that book."

"What book?" asked Brad.

"Clay's book," she said. "He wrote it years ago, he said. Anyway, we were all told that if we ever saw a copy, we had to buy it, and bring it back so they could destroy it. Stop it getting into the hands of unbelievers."

"What was it called?" asked Marcus.

"Some boring title, like a schoolbook," she said. "Something like *Theories About Stones And Circles*. Anyway, it's the only one Clay wrote, so it shouldn't be hard to find it. See you around, fellas!"

It took Marcus five minutes online to find that Clay's book was entitled *A New Theory of Stone Circles*. It had been published by a small academic press in 1993, when Clay was still a respected archaeologist. Copies were indeed rare, but Marcus found one on eBay and ordered it at once.

"This could be a major breakthrough," said Marcus. "Fingers crossed."

"Because Clay wanted them destroyed?" asked Brad.

Marcus nodded.

"If it wasn't important, why worry about the likes of us reading it? Clearly there's something in it, however marginal or obscure, that he wants to keep secret."

"It doesn't bring us any closer to Kelly, though," observed Brad. "What do you make of that performance, or whatever it was?"

Marcus shrugged.

"I've seen some strange things," he said. "But I'm going to reserve judgment on that. There was one thing Kathy said, though. A clue that might help us find Clay and his cult."

He turned to the computer again.

"Clay was obsessed with stone circles," explained Marcus. "And there are only so many of those. The name Kathy half-remembered might just coincide with one, or a place near to one."

"Worth a try," agreed Brad.

Marcus opened the audio file and found the phrases Kathy had recalled.

"Litch-weir," he said, "or Hitch-mere. Let's find a list of stone circles and compare the names."

"Sounds like a one man job," said Brad, standing up. "I really need to get some air and do some thinking."

"We've no reason to believe that was Kelly," Marcus pointed out. "Hypnosis isn't magic, and I don't believe it triggered some sort of telepathic link to the cult."

"You think it was just Kathy's subconscious being playful?" asked Brad.

Marcus nodded.

"That's the reasonable explanation. She's been through a lot. So-called multiple personalities, like we've just seen, are a kind of play-acting, the subconscious trying out different roles."

"I'd like to believe it," said Brad. "But my dreams keep telling me something weird is going on. And that voice, it really did sound like Kelly. The sassy way she usually talks to me. When she talks to me at all."

"I'm not saying you're wrong," said Marcus, obviously choosing his words carefully. "Let's just suspend judgment for now."

"Agreed," said Brad. "Let me know if you find anything."

A few moments later, Brad was in the bustle of Camden Market, surrounded by people of all ages, races, and degrees of wealth. He began half-heartedly browsing the various stalls while his mind raced.

Was that really Kelly? How could Kathy have faked her voice so well? Or was it all down to a convincing American accent plus wishful thinking on my part?

"Five-ninety-nine, that one dearie," said a female stallholder. "But if you don't want to buy it, don't muck it about."

Brad realized that he had picked up a tee-shirt decorated with a circular image. It was the Ouroboros, a snake eating its own tail.

"Do you sell a lot of these?" he asked.

The woman frowned.

"Doing a survey, are you? Yes, there's been a lot of demand for 'em lately. Question is, do you want that one?"

"No, no thanks," said Brad, putting the garment back. The woman turned away, muttering something about tourists.

He looked around at the other clothing stalls, then at the people thronging the market. In a matter of seconds, he saw a middle-aged woman wearing an Ouroboros tee-shirt. Then he noticed a girl in her teens with a bag bearing the same distinctive logo. After a few minutes of walking up and down the aisles between stalls, Brad had seen the circular image half a dozen times.

Just a fashion thing, he thought. *Surely, it can't be more significant than that?*

He could not quite convince himself.

Returning to his hotel on the Underground, he saw the sign of Ouroboros three more times. After a while, he tried not to look. Leaving the station at Russell Square, he glimpsed a crude graffiti image. It was too badly faded to be sure what it represented. But it was circular.

***

On Tuesday night, Brad's dream was even more bizarre and disturbing.

Again, he found himself face to face with Kelly in an ordinary coffee shop. This time, when he looked out the window, he saw the turning Earth below. Again, he watched cracks appear in the planet's crust. Great eruptions of smoke and flame obscure the familiar continents, tarnish the blue of the oceans.

"Kelly," he said, turning to his daughter. "You can't want this to happen. This is evil, insane."

"Dad," she sighed, with familiar exasperation, "don't be so damn literal. Maybe it's a metaphor? Maybe the old world needs to be destroyed to bring about something new, something better?"

The vista of the planet in chaos was replaced by a new horror. Outside the coffee shop, hordes of people were milling about, confused and afraid. Then they started pointing, screaming, running. A vast reptilian head appeared, its jaw gaping beneath huge slit-eyes. The colossal serpent writhed down the street, darting back and forth, grabbing individuals, and gulping them down whole. For every one it consumed, it must have crushed a dozen people. Brad heard faint cries of terror from the tiny fleeing humans before they vanished under the scaly coils.

"You call this something better?" Brad yelled at Kelly. "This monster? This carnage?"

She shook her head in pity.

"Metaphor again, Dad," she chided. "Death and rebirth. People fear change. They run away from it, rather than face it."

She reached out her hand for his, gripping his fingers with surprising strength. He tried to pull away but failed.

"Come on, Dad," said Kelly, in her most persuasive voice. "Come and join us. Don't be left behind when the big changes come."

Outside, the huge serpent cast its shadow over them, a great wall of scaly flesh hurtling through the wrecked city.

"No!" he shouted, looking back to see his daughter's face transformed by a snarl. Long fangs protruded below her upper lip. The table between them rocked and was overturned. A long, scaly body writhed from under it.

Brad woke to find himself tangled in sweaty sheets. What had become a familiar routine kicked in. He got up, made coffee, tried to work a little, then gave up. He checked his emails and ensured that things were okay with his company. Brad emailed his boss and asked if he might have another couple of weeks leave, unpaid. He was calling in a lot of favors. But he had the growing conviction that this was his one and only chance to find Kelly. He found a message from Marcus Valentine, sent late the previous evening, saying that he had located the most likely place for the cult's new base.

'That's great,' he typed back. 'Let's meet up at my hotel, lunch maybe?'

Brad sat back and pondered the new elements of his nightmare.

Would she really want me to come and join them? Am I in some kind of telepathic contact with her? Does that explain what happened when Kathy was hypnotized?

He gave up in frustration, accepting that he simply did not have enough data to draw any conclusions. To clear his head, he got dressed and went out for a walk, taking in the sights and sounds of London waking up to a new day. It was just after six, and Brad decided to have an early breakfast.

Brad chose a greasy spoon diner and ordered 'the full English,' a lavish breakfast of eggs, bacon, sausages, and other artery-hardening ingredients. The place was full of shift workers and the like. It reminded Brad of his days in the field as an oil geologist, and he felt himself relaxing as he sipped instant coffee.

"Look out, lads, we're being ogled."

The remark came from one of a group of truckers at the next table. Heads turned to face the window, and when Brad looked around, he saw a young woman gazing in, looking straight at him. As soon as he caught her eye, she smiled, turned, and walked off.

"Aw, I'd have offered her a nice bacon butty!" said the trucker, to general amusement.

Brad continued to stare after the woman had vanished from sight. There was something about the way she had moved that bothered him. She had been a little too sinuous, languid, self-consciously slinky. And her expression had been peculiar, as if she were taunting him to follow her.

In every movie I've seen where this happens, the guy jumps up and rushes after the mystery girl, Brad thought. *So screw that. I'm not playing anyone else's game.*

A few moments later, his breakfast arrived, a steaming carnivore's feast.

***

Later, on Wednesday morning at New Scotland Yard, Detective Sergeant Declan Healy opened his dossier on Deputy Commissioner Sir Nigel Faversham. It gave him a thrill to know that, if it were discovered, he would be in deep trouble. And yet the dossier had only one entry so far. It read, 'Links to Ouroboros? Kelly Steiger – knows whereabouts?' He added 'Arrogant bastard, treats subordinates like dirt,' then deleted it.

"Not exactly a cast iron case," he muttered to himself.

Healy looked at his phone lying on the desk. He was conflicted about the Arnold case. Preliminary findings from the medical examiner had confirmed that the private detective had died from constriction. The air had literally been squeezed out of his lungs. The best the expert could come up with as a murder weapon was 'some kind of mechanical device, possibly pneumatic in nature, involving a steel cable.'

Which tells us nothing while sounding impressive, thought Healy. *And surely, somebody would have noticed a gadget like that being carted around Hyde Park at lunchtime?*

What bothered him more than the odd nature of the crime, though, was Faversham's attitude. That stuck in Healy's craw. He picked up his phone and called Brad Steiger, offering to meet up.

"I'm sorry," he said, "I can't talk about this in detail over the phone. All I can say is I've not been permitted to list Kelly as a missing person. No, I agree Mister Steiger, and I'm going to find a workaround if I can. But let's talk about this face to face. Lunchtime? Sure. See you at your hotel, about one pm."

After hanging up, Healy rejigged the file on the Matt Arnold killing. He added Kelly Steiger as a possible witness. It was a deliberate abuse of procedure but one that would flag up her name on the national police computer. He would be informed if she were arrested, had hospital treatment, or otherwise came to the attention of the authorities.

Now for Ouroboros, he thought. *Let's see just how naughty they are.*

Faversham had not expressly forbidden Healy from investigating the cult. It took him a few minutes to find that there had been several complaints about the cult over the years. All were from relatives of converts. None had been followed up on. The reports stated that no evidence of coercion could be found. But the files did reveal an address for the cult's headquarters, albeit in a report that was two years old. It was a large town house in Berkeley Square, in the pricey Mayfair district.

Worth checking out. Well, why not? Let's see what these nutcases are up close, maybe put a scare into 'em.

Healy put on his jacket and summoned Knapton.

"Your lucky day, Constable," he said. "We're going to visit a fringe religious group that apparently worships reptiles."

"Yes, sir," said Knapton, unworried. "Looks like rain, I'll bring my brolly."

An hour later, Healy parked their unmarked car outside Number 50, Berkeley Square. After a moment's thought, Healy sent Knapton to talk to the neighbors on either side.

"What am I supposed to ask them, Sarge?"

"Tell them you've had a complaint about noise, or something like that," replied Healy, "if people have any complaints about the cult, it might give us some extra leverage. Also, you never know when a snippet of information might prove valuable."

"Okay. What are you going to do?" asked Knapton.

"I'm going to walk up to the front door and ring the bell," replied Healy. "It usually works."

In this case, though, it failed. There was no reply, and on closer examination, it seemed as if the house was not in use. Knapton confirmed this, returning from a chat with a neighbor.

"They say all the weird people left last autumn, Sarge."

"So the house is empty?" asked Healy.

"Seems so."

"Hard to believe," said Healy, looking up at the house's impressive frontage. "This is a posh neighborhood. Properties like this aren't just left empty."

"What do we do now, Sarge?" asked Knapton.

"We check doors and windows carefully," said Healy. "Just in case there's any evidence of burglary. Whoever owns this place would thank us for it, don't you think?"

Knapton followed his boss around the block and into the alleyway behind the luxurious town houses. The back door of Number 50 was secure. But a broken basement window caught Healy's eye.

"Now that's an obvious invitation to the criminal element," said Healy. "Wouldn't you say, Constable?"

Knapton sighed, knowing what was going to happen next.

"I feel we have grounds to investigate the premises," Healy went on, "just in case some hapless citizen is all trussed up while villains ransack the place."

"Yes, sir," said Knapton. "Do you want me to go first?"

"No," said Healy, "I've got this."

Wrapping his arm in his jacket Healy reached through the broken pane and opened the window. Then he managed to squeeze through the narrow gap to find himself in a basement room. It was full of old furniture and other junk. Healy caught his foot in the springs of an old mattress and managed to tear the cuff of his pants while freeing himself.

"Bloody hell, this place is a death trap! Go round the front and I'll let you in," ordered Healy.

The detective clambered over the junk and found the door unlocked. He made his way up a narrow stairway into a large kitchen. The place was clean but had an abandoned air. Checking cupboards, he found no food. The refrigerator was also empty. A large black garbage bag stood against the back door. He opened it to find a rolled up piece of fabric, light brown in color. It was like a roll of old wallpaper, but felt more like hardened skin to the touch. Grimacing in distaste, he closed the bag, dismissing the odd material as irrelevant.

Rubbish could have been there for weeks, anyway. Place is obviously not in use, he thought. *The crackpots have long since moved on.*

Healy left the kitchen and worked his way along a corridor, opening doors and checking rooms. The first two contained nothing but objects covered in dustsheets. In one, there was a circular design on the tiled floor. It had been nearly erased so that Healy could not quite make out what it represented. The third room was different. In one corner, there was a sleeping bag, a small heap of brightly-colored clothes, and some kind of cage. Entering, Healy went closer to the cage and saw it was occupied by half a dozen hamsters. The animals' small, pink muzzles pointed toward him, black button eyes shining with curiosity.

"Hello, fellas," he said, bending down to examine the cage. "What are you doing here? Claiming squatters' rights?"

Suddenly the little animals ran to the far side of the cage, squeaking in evident terror.

"I might ask you the same question," said voice behind him.

Healy turned around to see a woman's face looking through the door. She was young, with large dark eyes and an abundance of black hair. She had a dark complexion, or was deeply tanned.

"Sorry, miss," he said, reaching for his ID, "but I thought this property was abandoned."

"No," she said, "I'm the caretaker. Is that a police identity card?"

"Yes," he replied, walking toward her. "Please, take a closer look. Detective Sergeant Declan Healy, New Scotland Yard. And you are?"

The woman smiled.

"You can call me Cleo," she said, and walked into the room. He could see now that she was indeed dark all over because she was completely naked. Healy stopped, lost for words, then took a step backward. He was vaguely aware of the hamsters becoming even more agitated behind him.

"I'm afraid you caught me while I was changing," said Cleo, walking up to him. A powerful fragrance filled the air.

"Oh, erm, sorry," Healy stammered. "Look, miss, perhaps you'd better put some clothes on? This is hardly proper."

"I'm quite secure in my own skin," she replied, putting her hands on his shoulders. Her eyes were level with his. "How about you, Declan? Feeling uncomfortable? Try to relax."

Healy gulped, again lost for words. The woman's eyes seemed to be getting larger, expanding to overwhelm everything in his field of vision. Cleo was still talking, but her words were going deeper in his conscious mind, seeming to echo in his skull.

"Relax, let's get to know each other," she said, "I'm always keen to help our boys in blue. And I'm sure you can be a great help to me."

"Help," he said weakly, feeling his consciousness ebbing away. "Help."

A loud knocking noise broke in on her silky words. A distant voice shouted. He felt Cleo's concentration waver. Her eyes flickered uncertainly.

"You all right, boss?" A voice echoed along empty corridors. "Can you let me in?"

Knapton, Healy thought, focusing on his job, his duty. He summoned all his willpower and broke free of the woman, shoving her hands away as he staggered backward.

"Don't fight it, Declan," Cleo said, stepping forward, smiling. "This was meant to be."

He kept backing away, collided with the window sill, then dodged around her and headed for the door. He felt cool fingers brush his neck, heard a throaty giggle.

I'm running away from a naked woman, he thought. *They'll never believe this back at headquarters.*

He raced along the corridor and found himself in a large hall. Fists were hammering at the front door. Healy quickly unbolted the door and rushed out into the street, almost knocking down the startled Knapton.

"You okay, boss?" asked the young officer.

Healy took a moment to compose himself before replying.

"Just had an interesting experience, Constable," he said, hesitantly. "Keep it to yourself, but I may be going a bit bonkers."

"I see," said Knapton, looking into the hall. "Is there anyone in there?"

"Possibly a young woman," replied Healy. "I – I thought I saw someone inside. But let's go and check. Together, not splitting up."

"Yes, sir."

After twenty minutes, they had searched every room in the house, and found no living things other than the hamsters. The back door was still bolted from the inside.

"If there was someone here, where might they be hiding?" asked Knapton. "Unless this woman climbed out through that broken window."

And ran through the streets in her birthday suit, thought Healy. *Not very likely.*

They went down to check the cellar. It was clear that, while Healy had been able to scramble in, no normal person could have climbed up and out without a ladder.

"It's a mystery all right," said Healy.

His encounter with the enigmatic Cleo now seemed unreal, like a fading memory of an intense dream. And yet he could still smell the strong perfume she wore. Then he realized it was in the air again.

"Patchouli," he said. "Can you smell that, Knapton?"

The junior officer nodded, and walked around the cellar, sniffing.

"Seems to be strongest over here, sir," he said, pointing at a dark rectangle set low on the wall. "Some kind of ventilator grille."

The policemen examined the outlet. It was roughly eight inches high and a foot across.

"No way an adult human being could squeeze through a gap that small," said Knapton, decisively.

"No," agreed Healy. "I suppose not."

He crouched down to examine the grille more closely. It was evidently secured from the other side. Healy tugged at it, but it didn't budge. The scent of patchouli was strong, but now it masked another odor. An acrid smell, quite unpleasant. Peering through the wire mesh, he thought he saw a glimmer of yellow in the darkness.

I'm in too deep with this malarkey, thought Healy. *This is no ordinary case. I need to regroup, rethink the problem.*

"We've done everything we can here," he said, standing up. "I've got to get to Russell Square, have a word with that Steiger bloke. Oh, and call the Royal Society for the Prevention of Cruelty to Animals about those poor bloody hamsters."

As he left the cellar, Healy thought he heard a husky laugh echoing somewhere behind him.

Chapter 6: Connections

Marcus Valentine arrived at the Russell Hotel to find Brad Steiger waiting in the lunchroom. The Englishman ordered a light meal and a pot of Earl Grey tea before producing a file containing a sheaf of printouts.

"I've made some progress on the possible location of the cult's new base," he explained, spreading out some sheets on the table. "In fact, there's only one place in this country it could be."

Brad picked up one of the printouts, which showed a map of a rural area.

"Wychmere?" he said, raising an eyebrow. "They named a village after witches?"

"Nothing so exciting," replied Marcus, with a smile. "A 'mere' is a pond or small lake, and the first part of the name refers to a type of elm tree. You can see that the village is clustered around a body of water."

"Ah," said Brad, slightly disappointed. "But there is something special about this place?"

"Oh yes," said Marcus. "Look more closely."

Examining the map, Brad noticed an irregular dotted line forming a circle. The village, a few dozen homes, was mostly within the circle. A small legend indicated that the dots constituted a 'prehistoric structure'.

"One of those temples to their snake-god?" he asked, putting down the sheet.

Marcus shrugged, and passed over some more printouts.

"So it would seem. The thirteen stones of the circle are known as the Dancers, and they're quite famous in antiquarian circles. And the locals are quite fond of them, too, as you can see."

Brad looked at a sepia photo labeled 'Wychmere, May Day 1908'. It showed a smiling family in old-fashioned clothes standing under a great irregular slab of granite. The stone had been decorated with garlands of flowers.

"So they have a big celebration of some lumps of rock?" asked Brad.

"One of our many quaint British customs," said Marcus. "Harmless, in this case. May Day is an ancient festival celebrating the arrival of spring. And yet, when I made some discreet inquiries this morning, I found that Jonathan Clay's been trying to rent a large property in the area for over a year."

"I take it he's finally got one?" asked Brad.

Marcus nodded, handing over another sheet.

"Garlock House, a stately home, less than half a mile from the village."

Brad looked at the picture, read the brief history of the house.

Is this where Kelly is staying now? Brainwashed, maybe even held captive?

"We can't be sure she's there," said Marcus, as if reading Brad's mind. "But obviously you want to go and see for yourself."

Brad nodded.

"Will you come with me?" he asked Marcus. "I'd be willing to pay you for your trouble."

"No trouble," replied Marcus, "but there is someone I'd like to talk to first. A priest who's been at a Catholic retirement home in Sussex for a while now."

Before he could explain further, Detective Sergeant Healy arrived, ordered a large brandy, and sat down at their table after taking a large gulp.

"Difficult morning?" asked Marcus.

"You could say that," replied the detective. "And no, I don't normally drink while on duty. But I just had the strangest experience. I have a feeling you two might know something about it."

Healy described the abortive search at Berkeley Square.

"A naked woman tried to hypnotize you?" asked Brad.

"A naked woman with a cage of hamsters," Marcus pointed out. "Remember what Kathy said about rats being delivered to the cult."

"I don't like where this is going," said Healy.

"I wouldn't normally countenance tales of shape-shifting and the like," said Marcus in measured tones, "but there are some very well-attested cases."

"You're telling me this woman was some sort of were-snake?" demanded Healy.

Marcus shrugged.

"I don't quite believe it either," said Brad. "But it would explain Matt Arnold being crushed to death."

"But has anybody actually seen this happen?" asked Healy.

"Someone may have," said Marcus. "I was going to tell you about this, Brad. I dug up some old newspaper references to incidents involving Jonathan Clay. There's one name that crops up twice. An Irish priest named Quigley."

"He witnessed the cult's ceremonies, or whatever?" asked Brad.

"He seems," said Marcus, "to have been present when a ceremony went terribly wrong. Whatever he witnessed left him badly shocked, and he's still mentally fragile."

"Poor guy," said Brad. "Do you think he might talk to us?"

Marcus looked doubtful.

"He's in the care of an order of nuns. I called them up, asking about Father Quigley, and the lady I spoke to seemed reluctant to let me 'bother the poor man,' as she put it."

"I've an idea," said Healy. "This man could, at a stretch, be involved in my investigation of Arnold's death. So I could go along, give it an official veneer?"

They agreed this would be helpful. But Brad was also be eager to go to Wychmere straight away, to try and speak to Kelly.

"Suppose I get over there pronto while you guys follow up this lead?"

"Sounds like a plan," said Healy. "Normally, I wouldn't conduct an investigation like this, involving civilians. But what with this morning's weirdness and obstruction from my superiors, I feel justified."

"You could get into a hell of a lot of trouble," Marcus pointed out.

"True," said the detective. "But I resent being told not to do my job. Against that, I'd very much like to keep my job. It's a bit of a bind to be in. Which is why I'm going to have another brandy."

***

On Tuesday night, Kathy Hopkirk tossed and turned on a narrow bed in a Whitechapel hostel for the homeless. Her dreams, while often troubled, had never been so strange. She found herself walking through a big, expensive-looking house she had never seen before. It was nighttime, judging by the fact that the lights were all on. She entered a book-lined room and Jonathan Clay got up from a writing desk. As she got closer, Kathy had the odd sensation of looking down at him. She recalled that in life, he was half a head taller than she was. Now he looked like a little boy trying to behave like a grown-up.

He looks worried, she thought. *Or is he scared of me, whoever I am?*

"You wanted to see me?" said a voice. Kathy realized she was seeing things from the speaker's point of view.

"Killing the private detective was a mistake," Clay said. "And trying to convert a Scotland Yard officer! You must see how reckless that was?"

"Don't be silly, Jonathan," Kathy heard herself saying. "These people are mere nuisances."

"It's drawing too much attention!" protested Clay. "We are so close to our objective!"

"Don't weaken, Jonathan," she said. "This evocation must not fail, and nothing can stand in our way. Last time your nerve failed, remember, and it was bungled."

"That wasn't my fault," said Clay. "We chose the wrong place, the wrong time. Here there is a deep-rooted tradition, a spiritual energy we can exploit."

"I hope you're right," she said, moving closer to Clay, who flinched slightly. "We do not want any more failures."

Without waiting for a response, the speaker turned on her heel and walked out of the room. She entered a passageway and as she passed a mirror, she saw herself for the first time.

Olivia!

She was seeing the world through the woman's eyes. Olivia came to an entrance hall and went up a grand staircase to what was evidently her bedroom. Kathy realized that she was not just seeing through the big woman's eyes but also feeling some of her sensations. The house was cool, even a little chilly, and the lights a shade too bright. Olivia shut the bedroom door and at first total darkness engulfed her. Then Kathy found shapes forming in the blackness. One shape in particular, a small object that moved.

It's like one of those cameras they use to film wildlife at night, she thought.

Olivia crossed the room, and as she got closer to the glowing thing, it squealed. Kathy made out the shape of a piglet inside a small cage. Olivia stooped down and the animal became frantic, clearly sensing peril.

Oh God no, this can't be happening.

Olivia easily caught the wriggling piglet and lifted it out of the cage. Then she let it go, whereupon it ran under the nearby bed. Olivia laughed, and dropped on all fours.

No, not all fours. All threes. All zeros.

Kathy felt the body, in which her mind was a passenger, transform itself into a lithe tube of steel-taut muscle and sinew. Her night-vision became more intense, and her flickering black tongue was now an organ of taste and smell. The odor of the piglet was intoxicating to this transmuted body. She glided, limbless, towards her terrified prey, which tried to rush past her. She struck, sank fangs into the plump, quivering body. Then she withdrew for a moment, unhinged her jaw, and began to swallow her prey whole.

Oh God! I can't stand this.

Kathy awoke, staring at the dim-lit ceiling, still feeling a sickening mixture of pleasure and revulsion. She ran her tongue along her upper teeth, found no fangs. They had been so real a moment before.

That Marcus did a number on me, she thought. *He never said this might happen. I need him to put it right. If he can.*

It was not just the disgust and horror of being in Olivia's mind that disturbed her. In the fraction of a second, before the link had been broken she had felt something cold and inhuman brush against her thoughts. A reptilian mind had reached out and tried to catch her. Or sink its metaphorical fangs into her.

Did she know I was there? Could she find me? What might she do to me?

As she waited for the dawn to arrive, Kathy tried hard not to think about the piglet. Confused and afraid, she could not decide whether to contact Marcus Valentine again.

***

On Wednesday evening, Wychmere Parish Council held its weekly meeting at the church hall. Bill Stroud, the Chairman, noticed that some of the members seemed distracted.

Or drunk, he thought, uncharitably.

"Well, let's begin with the inevitable preparations for May Day and the dressing of the stones," he said.

There was a murmur of agreement. Stroud braced himself for controversy as he asked the customary question.

"Do we have any candidates for Queen of the May?"

The effect was startling. The other four members of the council all looked at him and smiled. It was an eerie effect, especially as Stroud was expecting a dispute.

"Now I know," he continued, "that this often causes friction between rival families and so on. There will always be differences of opinion over which young lady is suitable."

"Not this time," said the parish priest. "I think we have reached an ideal solution."

"Okay," said Stroud cautiously. "Let's hear it."

The priest looked round at the others, who nodded.

God, they look even more stupid than usual, thought Stroud. *What's gotten into them? Or been taken out?*

"In previous years," the priest said, "we have disagreed over which local lass should be crowned as May Queen and take pride of place at the center of the circle. This year, I think we can avoid all such controversy by having an honored guest as monarch for the day."

Puzzled, Stroud asked, "What honored guest? A celebrity, you mean, like a BBC weathergirl? Because it's far too late to start organizing something like that! These people are booked up months in advance."

The priest shook his head.

"No, not at all Mister Chairman," he said. "I mean one of our visitors currently residing at Garlock House."

"What?" exclaimed Stroud. "They're a bunch of crackpots, complete outsiders. They're not part of the community. We can't just throw our centuries-old traditions out of the window like that!"

"I think we all understand your reservations, Bill," said the priest, to murmurs of agreement from the other three councilmen. "But if you go up to the house and speak to Mister Clay about it, I'm sure you'll change your mind."

"I'm not changing my bloody mind!" declared Stroud. "And this matter is not settled! I'd rather put on a frock and do it myself."

The others exchanged glances that seemed more pitying than angry.

"We've all been won over by Mister Clay," said the priest. "I'm sure the American girl would make a fine May Queen."

"American?" exclaimed Stroud. "Not even British? Some shrieking moron with capped teeth and a fat arse? No, thank you. That's a big slap in the face for tradition."

The meeting broke up with the majority still blandly insisting on their choice. Stroud drove back to his pig farm seething with annoyance at the others bizarre fixation. He had seen his business arrangement with Clay as a good, if minor, source of tax-free income. Now he felt vaguely soiled by it, as if he had committed an act of treachery against the spirit of Wychmere. He took a stubborn pride in having rejected Clay's repeated invitations to go inside the house for a drink.

Sod them, he thought, as he got out of his Land Rover. *They can go elsewhere for their livestock.*

Stroud did his usual rounds of the small farm, ensuring that the pigs had plenty of feed. He had a whiskey as a nightcap and turned in early, as he usually did. But first, he went around the farmhouse and checked doors and windows. The out-of-kilter feel of the parish council meeting had unnerved him.

It was just before one in the morning when the squealing of the pigs woke Stroud. They were unlikely to make a fuss if a fox or badger was sniffing around. He looked out of the window towards the sheds where the pigs slept. There was nothing out of the ordinary. There had been a heavy shower that evening. Now a bright April moon was shining on the muddy farmyard. It was, as always, rutted with tire tracks.

There's something wrong, he thought. *What is it? I'll take a closer look.*

Stroud got dressed, picked up a baseball bat he kept by his bed, then went downstairs and out into the yard. The pigs had quieted down but when he went over to check on them they seemed nervous.

As if they sense a predator. But there are no large predators in England.

Again, he examined the tire tracks in the yard, wondering what was bugging him about them. Then he noticed the anomaly. The marks left by his Land Rover were clear enough, fresh. But there was another track crossing over them. A single trail over a foot across led along the yard towards the house.

Something being dragged, thought Stroud. *But if so, why no footprints?*

Stroud followed the trail to the wall of the house, then followed it around a corner. The mud gave way to concrete and the trail petered out. In front of him was the barn where some old machinery was stored. Stroud hesitated, then hefted his bat and went into the building. He groped for the light switch, flicked it on.

There was nothing out of the ordinary. He walked around the place, checking under tarpaulins, satisfying himself that the barn was empty.

I'm going barmy, he concluded, returning to the entrance. Just as he turned off the light, he heard a giggle. He spun round, turning the light back on, bat at the ready. Again, he saw nobody in front of him.

"Who's there?" he said, feeling foolish. "Play games with me, you'll regret it."

He raised the bat in a two-handed grip, advanced a step. Again, there was a giggle, and this time Stroud could tell where it was coming from. He looked up, heart racing, and a woman's face descended towards his. Her hair cascaded about his face as a strong hand grabbed the bat and easily plucked it away. Above her, he could make out muscular coils wrapped around a roof beam.

"Hello again, Mister Stroud," said Olivia. "I just thought I'd drop in and see if I could change your mind."

***

On Thursday morning, Brad set out for Wychmere, while a parcel arrived for Marcus Valentine. The parcel contained a battered hardback without a dust-jacket. *A New Theory of Stone Circles* by Jonathan Clay, Ph.D, Fellow of the Royal Society of Antiquaries. At first glance, it seemed dry and scholarly; hardly the work of a fanatic. But as Marcus skimmed through it, he noticed a subtle change come over the tone as well as the content.

The early chapters were couched in the sober, careful phrases of the professional academic. There were plenty of references to learned publications, nods to esteemed colleagues. But towards the middle of the book, the academic style gave way to a more insistent, almost crazed tone. What had been suggestions became assertions, and there *were no more scholarly references.* Clay had begun by proposing a hypothesis, but ended up asserting a belief.

And what a belief, thought Marcus.

According to Clay, all the stone circles in Britain and beyond had been temples to a universal snake-deity. Clay dubbed this hypothetical god 'Ouroboros' and seemed to believe that it represented some kind of primal force of nature. All subsequent gods, Clay asserted, were creations of human superstition and credulity. Only Ouroboros was real.

So why, wondered Marcus, *isn't the Snakey One still in charge?*

Here, Clay's theorizing became vague and contradictory. But one thing was clear. Clay believed that some kind of cosmic cycle was coming to its climax, and that this would herald the return of the 'Great Old One,' as he called Ouroboros. The book ended with an exhortation for all 'true believers' to prepare the way for the return of the world's true god.

"Crackers," said Marcus, slamming the book shut. "But obviously sincere."

In his years of investigating cults, he had encountered plenty of scam artists, eager to exploit their followers financially and sexually. Clay seemed to belong to a different category.

Declan Healy arrived just before midday to drive them to Sussex and the Catholic rest home. Marcus gave him a synopsis of the book, trying to sum up its peculiar blend of scholarship and mysticism.

"How useful is it to us, do you think?" asked Healy.

"You never know," replied Marcus. "Knowledge is power. I think Clay is sincere, which arguably makes him more dangerous than a mere charlatan. And the violent death of Matt Arnold is a fact, however it was done. We should tread carefully."

"Too right," said Healy. "I still can't quite remember what happened to me yesterday. I keep getting flashes of this naked woman."

Marcus tried to suppress a smile.

"Not nearly as pleasant as it sounds," said Healy. "Now, what's the best route to this rest home?"

An hour later, they arrived at the gates of Saint Benedict's Retreat for Retired Clergy. They were met by a formidable Irish nun who introduced herself as Sister Mary Assumpta. Healy, who had called ahead, introduced Marcus as 'an expert consultant,' and insisted that Father Quigley might have vital information in a murder inquiry. The nun looked skeptical, but led them into the rambling Victorian building, all the while warning them not to over-excite the priest.

"The poor man's had a few rough days lately," she explained, "what with the nightmares and all."

"Nightmares?" asked Marcus.

"Yes, he's been screaming about demons and pagans and the like," said the nun. "He has his good days, but they've been precious few lately. So don't expect him to be too coherent."

Sister Mary showed them into a wing of the house that had been converted into some self-contained apartments. They stopped outside a green door marked Father Patrick Quigley. The nun knocked and called, "Father? I have some visitors to see you."

There was a brief pause before a nervous, high-pitched voice said, "Who are they?"

"One is a policeman," she explained. "The other seems a nice enough gentleman. Are you decent, now? We don't want a repeat of the incident with the plumber, now do we?"

"Yes, woman, I'm fully dressed!" came the exasperated reply.

A chain rattled, the door was flung open, and a man of about sixty looked out. Father Quigley was dressed in clerical garb, but his hair was untidy and he hadn't shaved for several days.

"Men are all right," he said, staring at Marcus, then at Healy. "No strange females allowed in here, that's the rule."

"Yes, Father," sighed Sister Mary, waving the visitors past her.

Quigley slammed the door and chained it behind Marcus and Healy.

"Got to be careful," he said. "Security, you know! Now, let me put the kettle on."

The priest bustled into his tiny kitchen. Following, Healy introduced himself and explained that he was working on a case linked to Ouroboros. Marcus lingered in the living room, noting the bookshelves stacked two deep with books on a wide range of topics. Most seemed to be about religion, paganism, and related matters. Something else caught the Englishman's eye. He went over to the window to check. It was sealed shut with heavy masking tape. Then he noticed that the pleasant ornamental fireplace had been bricked up.

"Security," said Quigley, emerging from the kitchen. "You can't be too careful. They can wriggle in through the smallest crevice."

Healy looked thoughtful at that.

"I found your name in some old news reports, Father," said Marcus, deciding to get to the point. "I thought you might be able to enlighten us about Jonathan Clay and his followers?"

"Followers?" echoed the priest. "Ah, who's following who? I thought he was the leader, but now I'm not so sure. No, no, it's not so clear at all."

Further questioning produced a garbled account of the incident in Ireland.

"I was sure Clay had murdered that poor lad," said Quigley. "But I was wrong. It was worse than that. But I must get your tea."

When the priest was out of sight, Marcus and Healy discussed him in low tones.

"I've seen some unreliable witnesses in my time, but this one takes the biscuit," said the detective.

"I don't think he could stand up to cross-examination in a courtroom," agreed Marcus, "but we could still learn something useful."

Quigley returned with tea and biscuits, and before either visitor could speak, he had resumed his rambling narrative.

"You see, it took me years to track Clay down," he explained. "I was a parish priest, I had duties, and the church is not happy when a clergyman goes rogue, so to speak. I became an embarrassment. Started to lose my grip a little, I dare say."

Quigley paused, then looked at Marcus.

"You've seen something of evil."

The Englishman looked uncomfortable.

"When I was young, a student at Oxford, I dabbled in the occult. It was my way of rebelling. Things went wrong. Someone died."

Marcus looked over at Brad.

"That's why I try to help, I suppose. To make amends."

The priest nodded.

"I sought to do what was right. I sought them out after that dark business at Ballymahan. But I didn't realize quite how dangerous it was, not really."

With a little prompting from Marcus, Quigley began to tell them his story.

Chapter 7: Southern England, June 2005

"Oh yes," said the barman, "they're camped up on top of the earthwork. I saw their campfire last night. Been there for a few days now."

Father Patrick Quigley followed the man's pointing finger. Out of the wide front window of the pub he could make out the great prehistoric structure known as Hampton Round. This early in the morning the Sussex village of Lesser Hampton literally lay in the shadow of the grassy mound. The earthwork was a vast artificial hill, flat-topped, and surrounded by a deep ditch. Its purpose had been a mystery since the beginning of recorded history.

"And does anybody know what they're doing up there?" asked the priest.

The barman shrugged.

"I've heard they dance about at night, singing, doing some kind of ritual," he said. "But that's nothing new. All kinds of folk come down here. There are scientists, pagans, psychics, Wiccans, and ghost hunters. Their money's all equally good, as far as we're concerned. Got to make a living, after all."

"Do they come in here?" asked Quigley. "The people up there now?"

"They stopped off for a drink on the way," replied the barman. "Nice chap seemed to be a sort of leader. Had quite a harem of pretty, young ladies. Nice work if you can get it, leading these cults, eh?"

"Quite," said Quigley. "So they didn't tell you why they came here?"

"No," conceded the barman, "but he was very interested in the name of the pub."

"He asked about the Hampton Worm?" asked Quigley.

"Yes, very keen to know all the folklore. Of course, it's just a load of nonsense for the tourists, and I told him that. All that stuff about monsters, it's just for kids, isn't it?"

The barman gestured at a plaque on the wall behind him.

"Old folk song," he explained.

Quigley read the verses that referred to 'the Hampton Worm' that supposedly once terrorized the area. It had, according to the song, emerged from the prehistoric mound at the behest of a sorceress. The worm had possessed 'great big jaws and great big teeth, and great big goggly eyes.' Fortunately, after eating all the local sheep and cattle, plus quite a few peasants, the fearsome beast was slain by the brave Lord Hampton. Similar stories of enormous 'worms' were found throughout England. They were dismissed as folk legends by most experts. The priest was not so sure.

"If only real evil could be dealt with so simply," Quigley murmured.

The priest thanked the barman for his help, finished his beer, and left the pub. His rental car was parked in the one street of Lesser Hampton, which had only a few dozen residents.

I can't be sure it's them, Quigley thought. *So many years spent searching, so many false leads. But I have to know. And the legend of the worm is just the sort of thing to draw the cult.*

He drove out of the village and took the winding dirt track to Hampton Round. The earthwork grew more imposing as he neared it. The priest struggled to suppress a sense of looming evil about the mound.

It's just a great work of men long dead, he told himself. *Deluded men, denied the true faith. If they worshiped a false god, so much the worse for them. If anyone seeks to revive such worship, I have a duty to denounce it.*

The makeshift road petered out at a turning place where two cars were already parked. The whole area was overgrown with grass and wild flowers. Quigley saw that a winding track to Hampton Round had been made by people passing to and from the vehicles. It led to a rudimentary footbridge over the ditch, and then around the conical hill in a spiral path.

Sighing, Quigley set off to hike up the slope in the bright morning sun. By the time he reached the top, he was perspiring, jacket slung over his shoulder. Sure enough, when he breasted the rise at the top of the Mound, he saw a cluster of three tents. A half dozen people turned to look at him as he came into view. One he recognized at once.

Jonathan Clay, he thought. *Older and plumper, limping a little, but unmistakably the man. Found you at last!*

"Father Quigley!" said Clay, recognizing the priest at the same moment. "This is an unexpected pleasure. What brings you to this obscure little corner of Sussex?"

"I think you know," replied Quigley, walking up to Clay and studying the renegade scientist. "It's a matter of simple right and wrong."

"Ah, an ethical question," said Clay. He gestured at a path that circled the summit of the Hampton Round. "You can see the English Channel from here, on a clear day like this."

Quigley fell into step beside Clay, glanced at the distant glimmer of the sea.

"I'm not here for the view, Jonathan, and I don't think you are, either," he said. "I want to know what happened to your student. Young Dermot Kavanagh. His family have a right to know the truth."

"The local police concluded that he must have fallen into the bog," Clay pointed out. "A tragic accident. What more can I say?"

Quigley grabbed Clay by the arm and spun him round.

"In the name of all that's decent, man," he shouted. "What did you do to the poor lad? What part did he play in your unholy antics? And what are you planning to do here?"

Clay looked down at the priest's hand gripping him until Quigley let go.

"I don't mean to be inhospitable, Patrick," he said, all trace of friendliness gone. "But we have the landowner's permission to be here, and you do not."

"And that's another thing," said Quigley, "how come you've suddenly got all these rich and influential friends? Why are you so hard to find? What are you all up to, here?"

"We are pursuing our path to spiritual enlightenment," said a new voice. "It may not be yours, priest. But the days when your sort could suppress other faiths are long gone."

A woman had walked up behind Quigley. She was tall, nearly six feet, and seemed vaguely familiar. Her expression, while not hostile, was calculating. The priest felt he was being sized up and found wanting.

"No need for unpleasantness, Olivia," said Clay, with a touch of nervousness. "Father Quigley just dropped in to say hello."

"I'm sure he has someplace he has to be," said Olivia. "Very soon."

"Olivia?" said Quigley, staring at the woman. "The little student? That's impossible. You haven't aged a day in over ten years, and you've grown eight inches. More!"

Olivia laughed. Clay looked uncomfortable.

"You should be careful, Father," said the woman. "Go around talking like that and people might get the impression you're a trifle unhinged."

"What happened to Dermot Kavanagh?" demanded Quigley.

"His physical body is no more, his soul is united with Ouroboros," replied Olivia, in a matter-of-fact tone.

"That's a lot of nonsense!" shouted the priest.

"Whereas believing a god impregnated a virgin is rational?" asked the woman. "You're on rather thin ice, Father."

"You can blaspheme all you like," said Quigley. "But I will go on until the truth is told about your nasty little cabal."

"You are trespassing," said Olivia, in a condescending tone. "We could call the police to have you removed. It would probably feature in the local paper. Would that go down well with your bishop?"

The priest retreated in confusion, stumbling down the hill and back to his car. He sat for nearly half an hour, pondering the impossibility of an adult growing in stature by such a huge amount.

No normal human being could do that, he thought. *Something strange and blasphemous is at work here.*

Quigley drove back to Lesser Hampton to make a few more discreet inquiries. He learned from the village's sole shopkeeper that the Ouroboros cult had reserved the site until the following night.

"Apparently," his informant told him, "it's about this thing called the solar system."

Puzzled, Quigley went back to his accommodation at the pub. It took him several hours to work out what the woman had meant. Inspiration came around midnight, when he took out his diary. Sure enough, the following day was marked 'Summer Solstice'

The shortest night of the year, he thought. *A significant time for pagans. But what are they going to do?*

Lying on his bed, still fully dressed, Quigley went through his sparse collection of material published by Ouroboros. There was nothing about Hampton Round, but then there were only general references to circular prehistoric monuments. He fell into a fitful doze that lasted until morning.

As he ate breakfast in the dining room of the Hampton Worm, Father Quigley saw a steady stream of cars pass through the village. They were heading for the great artificial hill. The barman, doubling as waiter in the morning, noticed too.

"Never seen such a turnout for Midsummer Eve," he remarked. "Quite the festival they're going to have."

A thought struck Quigley.

"Will any locals be going up to the Round this evening?" he asked.

The barman hesitated, then laughed.

"Nobody round here's got any time for that nonsense," he said cheerfully.

I saw fear, if only for a moment, thought Quigley. *There is something about that earthwork, some lingering trace of pagan power. People here sense it, and know to avoid it on certain days.*

Quigley spent much of the day trying to contact his bishop. He had made a nuisance of himself with the church authorities for years, claiming that a murderous pagan cult was rising. He knew that he was considered a joke by some, an embarrassment by others, but not a serious figure. After his fourth attempt to contact his superior was rebuffed by an underling, he gave up.

No help from on high, he thought. *Or at least, not from any earthly power. No point in contacting the Sussex police. They'll file me under 'crackpot', just like they did in Ireland.*

After lunch, Quigley went up to his room and checked what he thought of as his Holy War kit. It consisted of a bag containing bottles of holy water, a large crucifix, and an old prayer book containing the rite of exorcism.

"I am acting like a lunatic," he said to himself. "But when reason and moderation fail, what else is there but madness of some sort? And someone should speak out against evil, at the very least. Perhaps even strike a blow for what is right."

The long June day eventually drew to a close. The setting sun was casting a blood-red shadow on Hampton Mound when Quigley set out. He drove to the parking spot, noted more than a dozen cars, and then slung his bag over his shoulder and set out for the earthwork. As he neared the lower slope, he heard chanting from above.

The sunset, he thought. *The dying of the Good Lord's daylight must mark the start of the ritual, the blasphemy.*

By the time he had hiked to the top of the hill, the chanting had become louder. And there was something in the air. Quigley felt the hairs on the back of his neck standing on end.

A static charge, he told himself. *Foreshadows an electrical storm. Summer lightning.*

The priest did not quite believe his own rationalization, but as he reached the top, the sight drove all other thoughts from his mind.

A large fire burned in the middle of the round space, and dozens of people were circling it, hands joined. Looking more closely, Quigley realized that there were two circles. The outermost consisted of around two dozen people of both sexes, all well-dressed and seemingly prosperous. The inner circle was composed of eight or nine young women, and they were all naked. As the priest watched, one broke free of the inner circle and jumped over the fire to general cheers.

Sky-clad witches, thought Quigley. *A stupid, pornographic fantasy of medieval paganism.*

At first, the priest could not make out the words that were being chanted, but as he crept closer he picked out a few phrases. 'Ouroboros will rise again' was repeated, as was 'the Great Old One' and something like 'the closing of the circle'.

More mystical mumbo-jumbo, he thought. *They can't even be bothered to chant it in Latin.*

But as he edged closer to the group, he felt the electric charge in the air intensify. There was an undeniable power about the ceremony, no matter how much contempt Quigley felt about Clay's beliefs. And, if he was right about the Kavanagh boy, these people would even stoop to murder.

The priest set down his bag and took out a large crucifix and the prayer book. He had memorized the ceremony of exorcism, anticipating near-total darkness. But the last light of the sun was still bright enough to make out the words. He began to intone the ancient ritual as loudly as he could, and heads turned as people in the outer circle heard him.

"Most glorious Prince of the Heavenly Armies," he chanted, "Saint Michael the Archangel, defend us in our battle against principalities and powers, against the rulers of this world of darkness, against the spirits of wickedness in the high places."

"Stop him!" shouted a voice that might have been Clay's.

Continuing the rite, Quigley raised up the cross. He heard angry voices, and mocking laughter. A couple of men were coming towards him, their faces angry. The priest had a sudden conviction that he was going to be thrown off the mound.

They would call it an accident, he thought, as he continued to intone the rite.

But before the men could get to him, there was a sudden rumbling noise, so deep that it was felt rather than heard. The ground seemed to shift under Quigley and he almost fell. There were exclamations of surprise, tinged with fear, from the circle of dancers. The last of the sun dipped below the horizon.

"Do not be afraid!"

It was Olivia's voice, loud and confident. Quigley saw her standing close by the fire, arms upraised, the flickering light playing over her naked form.

"Continue the ritual!" she commanded. "The Great Old One is starting to awaken!"

Clay rushed up to her, seemed to protest, gesturing at Quigley.

"Ignore the holy man," she said, her voice dripping with scorn. "Let him chant his magic spell. He will bear witness to the rebirth of a deity."

The group began to circle the fire again, hesitantly at first, then with more confidence. The chant was resumed. Then another earth tremor shook the summit. A glow began to form above the top of Hampton Round. It was like a sinuous cloud of luminous vapor, weaving in the air above the cultists. It formed a spiral, began to descend towards the summit.

"See!" cried Olivia. "The Great Old One, the child of Lilith, manifests herself!"

Quigley raised his cross like a shield and continued the rite of exorcism.

"I adjure you, ancient serpent, by the judge of the living and the dead–"

If the words were having any effect on the phenomenon, it was not apparent. The glowing cloud encircled them, and started to become more clearly defined. Greenish scales flashed, a great triangular head formed, huge red eyes gazed balefully on the tiny creatures within the creature's coils.

"It's going to eat us!" someone screamed.

"No, no, don't panic! We are here to pay homage!" shouted Clay. But his voice betrayed his fear.

This is not what he had in mind, thought Quigley.

"Surrender to her, to ancient Lilith, the first true mother!" cried Olivia, her voice triumphant now. "Let her consume your souls!"

Quigley almost laughed at the effect the woman's words had on the cultists.

He remembered a playful remark from one of his theology lecturers.

The last thing any pagan needs is for his god to actually turn up in person. It would be embarrassing, at the very least.

The priest reached down into his bag and took out the vials of holy water. Well aware that the gesture was a cliché, but lacking a better idea, he opened one small bottle and hurled it at the glowing serpent. There was a brief flash of greenish light as the liquid entered the nebulous being, and another subsonic roar shook the mound.

"That hurt didn't it, you big scaly bastard?" yelled Quigley. "Have another!"

He hurled two more vials at the serpent-being, then was shoved hard in the back and sprawled on the trodden grass. He twisted around to see Olivia standing over him, her face contorted with fury.

"She will consume your pious soul!"

In the uncertain light, Quigley could not be sure, but he thought he could see scales begin to form on Olivia's naked flesh. Her face seemed misshapen, her eyes grown huge with vertical slits for pupils. One of the people from the outer circle barged into Olivia and she fell, writhing.

Her legs, they're merging together, thought the priest. *A monstrous transmutation.*

The worshipers, or most of them, were fleeing. Quigley saw the huge spectral head of the glowing monster descend upon one elderly man. The man cowered, holding up his hands as if to fend off the serpent. Quigley groped for his last vial, threw it, splashing the holy water over the hapless cultist. There was another, much louder roar, so intense that the priest clamped his hands over his ears. He was buffeted and kicked by running figures. In the unearthly light from above, he caught a glimpse of Olivia, her lower body now pure serpent, raising her arms in supplication to the glowing behemoth.

"Fill me with your power, Great One!" she cried, voice rising above the screams of panic and dismay.

The huge serpent seemed to hesitate, gazing down at the snake-woman. Quigley unsteadily got to his feet, brandishing his cross and babbling what parts of the exorcism rite he could still remember.

"Go back to hell!" he shouted. "Get ye gone, old deceiver!"

Another fleeing cultist collided with him and knocked the crucifix out of his hand. He scrambled for it, wincing as another shadowy figure stepped on his fingers. He felt bones crack, wept tears of pain and fear. Looking up, he saw the baleful gaze of the false god, its huge fanged jaw opening to engulf him. A terrible pain shot through him as he clasped the crucifix, held it close to his chest. Darkness overwhelmed him.

The next thing he saw was a pulsing light. He was lying on his back, floating through space. A young, beautiful face appeared directly above him. The face was framed by golden hair and illuminated by blue flashes. A cool hand rested briefly on his forehead, brushed back his hair.

"Don't be afraid," said the face. "You're quite safe."

Lightning, he thought. *An angel of the lord appearing midst heavenly fire.*

He heard a different voice saying, "This one's alive, but he's been through the wringer."

Quigley realized he was being carried toward an ambulance on a stretcher. A plastic mask was put over his nose and mouth. He turned his head to look sideways at the scene where the ambulance was parked. There were police cars, too, and officers were apparently taking statements. There was also a body covered in a sheet.

"Could have been worse," said the young paramedic he had taken for an angel. "Only one dead."

"Heart failure, I reckon," said the second voice from near Quigley's feet. "God knows what they were doing up there."

He does indeed, thought Quigley.

A familiar face appeared in the crowd by the vehicles. It was Jonathan Clay, talking to a police officer. A senior officer, judging by the man's uniform. As the paramedics carried Quigley past them, the two glanced at the priest then resumed their discussion.

"I'm sure we can keep this discreet," Clay was saying. "Nobody wants a scandal."

Yes, we bloody well do, thought Quigley. He tried to shout but the oxygen mask silenced him.

"How is he?" said another familiar voice.

Olivia was bending over the stretcher, feigning concern.

"He'll be okay, but we'd better get him to the emergency unit," said the angelic young woman.

Quigley began to shake his head and protest loudly as Olivia reached out and patted his shoulder. She acted the part of the concerned friend with conviction, but her smile did not reach her eyes.

"Hang in there, Patrick," the big woman said, soothingly. Her tongue flickered along her lower lip. "You're in good hands. And when you're feeling better, we'll all come and visit you. That's a promise!"

After that, Quigley became so agitated that the paramedics had to sedate him.

Chapter 8: Westward

It took a while for Marcus and Declan to calm Father Quigley down.

"I'm sorry," said the priest. "I do get a bit worked up, you know? But it's not surprising."

He took Marcus by the arm with both hands and looked beseechingly into the Englishman's face.

"None of them will help me," said Quigley. "The church, the police, the government. I've written to them all, campaigned for years. The press is even worse, making me out to be a lunatic. Now I have to hide away here. I hear slithering in the night, stealthy noises in the loft, under the floorboards. I don't even know if the sounds are real or in my head."

Marcus made soothing noises. Healy, who had plenty of experience of fearful and disturbed individuals, intervened.

"Father," he said, "I can assure you that Scotland Yard will not rest until this case is solved. It's a murder inquiry, and I have no intention of letting it drop. You have my word."

Quigley looked back and forth between the two men, then shook his head in resignation. He sank back into his chair, staring blankly at the tea service on the table before him.

"They are too powerful and there are too many of them," he said. "You don't know what it feels like. The sidelong glances, the snatches of conversations overheard. Going into a room and knowing that everyone else is in on the secret, the conspiracy. Facing a brick wall of lies and equivocation at every turn."

"Father," asked Marcus, "have you ever heard of a place called Wychmere?"

The priest did not look up when he replied, "Yes, it was one of the places I thought Clay might be interested in. He wasn't there, of course."

"I think," said Healy, "we've taken up enough of your time, Father."

They discussed Quigley's incredible story on the drive back to London.

"How much of that can we believe?" asked Healy. "I mean, I was okay with it until he started talking about giant glowing snakes. I tend to see these things in terms of official reports, and there's no category for that one. But drug-induced hallucinations, that's another matter."

"I've no idea how accurate his account is," admitted Marcus. "He's clearly been under a lot of pressure. But there is one rather mundane point that I find believable. Most cults have hierarchies, and it seems Ouroboros is no exception."

Healy frowned, then asked, "You mean the inner and outer circles, during the ritual? So the naked ones leaping over the fire are the upper echelon?"

"Exactly," said Marcus. "It seems the inner circle is exclusively female, which raises another question. Is Jonathan Clay really in charge?"

Healy drove on without speaking for a few minutes, then said, "All that stuff about the woman turning into a snake, and the monster appearing. Hallucinations, right? Symptoms of mental illness?"

"I sincerely hope so," replied Marcus. "Because if even part of it is true, we really are up against something very powerful, and very dangerous. Oh, and I did check all the press reports of what happened back in June, 2005. And you may be interested to know that, for the first time in recorded history, on that night there was a small earthquake in the county of Sussex."

"Quite a coincidence, if that's what it was," agreed Healy. "When we get back to London, I'm going to do some digging in our files from around the time. If anything significant was covered up, there'll be traces. I'm an old hand at finding them."

"I'd be careful if I were you," warned Marcus. "Matt Arnold was killed."

"By a snake-woman?" asked Healy, raising an eyebrow.

"By someone or something," returned Marcus. "And he was lured into a trap."

"Point taken," said the detective. "Seductive reptilian ladies to be avoided at all costs."

***

Brad hired a car and set out for Herefordshire determined to speak to Kelly face to face. As he drove westward from London, he ran possible scenarios in his mind. Over and over again, he came to the same basic questions.

What if she won't talk to me? What if she does and it turns into another blazing row?

Brad had never ventured far from London before on his visits to England. He had never had to, as he had only ever been concerned with work matters. Now he found himself on a 'motorway,' as the British called their freeways. It was an unusual road, curving in great arcs left and right through verdant countryside. At first, he found this irritating. Then he recalled someone telling him that motorways were deliberately made that way so drivers did not fall asleep at the wheel. He had to admit that it worked.

It was when he was about an hour into his journey that he noticed the silver Lexus.

Brad's job in the oil industry had taken him to some dangerous places. He had received a lot of training in security matters. Apart from the threat of terrorism, foreigners were sometimes ideal kidnap targets. So he had been taught to recognize when he was being followed. He was not sure when the suspect car had first appeared, but he soon became suspicious of its pattern of behavior.

The silver Lexus was always two or three vehicles behind him, never right behind. He slowed down at one point to give following cars a reason to overtake. Two did, but the Lexus fell back and let a red Toyota tuck in behind Brad's rental BMW.

Could be a coincidence, he thought.

Brad decided to try another experiment. Every few miles there were 'motorway services,' essentially mini-malls with burger joints, coffee shops and the like. When the turnoff to the next one appeared, Brad took it, and waited to see if the Lexus followed. Sure enough, the silver car appeared in his rear-view mirror, still keeping its distance.

Okay guys, let's take a look at you.

Brad parked some distance from the entrance to the mini-mall and waited to see where the Lexus ended up. Sure enough, it slid into a parking slot some rows behind him. He waited, but no one got out of the silver car. In the April sunshine, he could not make out anything through the tinted window of the Lexus.

"Well, I could use a coffee," he said, and got out.

He did his best to saunter casually into the mall, wondering how fake he looked. He bought a coffee to go and a newspaper, then went back outside. There were plenty of people around, but none seemed to pay him any attention. He looked around for his car, and for a few moments struggled to find it among the dozens parked. That gave him an idea.

Yeah, he thought. *Dumb tourist just forgot where he parked his rental car. Gosh, I wonder where it might be?*

Brad put on what he hoped was a puzzled expression and set off across the car park towards the silver car. As he got within five yards of the Lexus, he could make out someone in the driver's seat.

Okay, genius, what's the plan now? Just saunter past it, I guess.

There was a sudden movement and the door of the silver car opened. A young woman got out, and for a second, Brad thought it was Kathy Hopkirk. The impression only lasted a second, as this young woman was healthier looking, less thin, and much more confident.

"Hi, Brad!" she said, smiling. "How's the coffee?"

"As bad as usual," he replied, for a moment off balance. "Why have you been following me?"

"Because you're headed in an interesting direction," said the woman, walking up to him. "I'm guessing Herefordshire?"

"I'm told it's a beautiful part of the world," said Brad. "And somebody I care about might be living there. Who are you, by the way?"

"Salome," she said, as if it were the most normal name in the world.

"As in the Bible?" he asked. "Girl who got a prophet's head cut off?"

She shrugged.

"I chose it when I converted. It's a way of saying, 'I'm starting a new life.'"

"Has Kelly changed her name?" he asked bluntly, hoping to catch her off balance.

"No," she said, "but she might do so soon. A lot of things are going to change. Now, if you'll excuse me, I think I'll get myself a cup of tea and a jam scone."

She walked away without looking back.

As if she had just had a nice chat with a casual acquaintance, he thought. *Whereas in fact she's informed me that they know exactly what I'm doing, and I don't scare them.*

He went back to his car and set off immediately. After about twenty minutes, the silver Lexus appeared, just visible, two cars behind.

***

Declan Healy dropped off Marcus at his Camden apartment. The cult expert was taking out his door-key when Kathy Hopkirk appeared out of the bookshop doorway.

"I need help, Mister Valentine," she said, gripping his sleeve. "I need you to stop them getting into my head. I'll go barmy if this goes on."

Five minutes later, she was sprawled on the sofa in Marcus' living room. He listened while she explained the way her dreams had become a conduit into the not-quite-human mind of Olivia Ballard.

"You have to put me under again, break the link somehow," she insisted. "I can't stand it much longer."

Marcus noted her red-rimmed eyes, her face even paler and more gaunt than before.

She's been through the wringer, he thought. *And I'm responsible as much as anyone.*

"I'll do anything I can to help," he said, "but there are no guarantees."

Kathy leaned forward, resting her face on her hands.

"If this goes on I'll do myself in," she mumbled from behind a screen of mousy hair.

"Okay," said Marcus. "I will hypnotize you again and try to block Ouroboros in some way. Would you like a cup of tea first?"

Kathy laughed, looked up.

"And they say there are no more English gentlemen. How about some more of that Scotch?"

"Maybe afterwards," he said. "And I'll probably join you."

Marcus made the same preparations as before, dimming the light and setting up a microphone. Kathy's tiredness made it easier than the first time. Soon she was sitting, eyes closed, responding to his every suggestion.

"Where are you now?" he asked.

"The big house," she said. "The big house in my dreams."

Marcus was about to ask another question when Kathy went on, "I'm in the village, at the shop. No, in the pub. No, I'm on a farm, working."

Kathy continued to describe a series of different people engaged in different tasks; dozens in all. Puzzled, Marcus sat back, wondering how to proceed.

Is she just fantasizing? he wondered. *Or could it be some kind of multiple personality disorder? Or something else?*

"What are you doing at this moment, Kathy?"

"Pulling pints," she replied, her voice expressionless. "Mucking out the pigs. Watching telly. Lots of things."

"You can't do all those things at once," Marcus said, then bit his lip. The trite words had come out before he could stop himself.

"We're in lots of places at once," she said, and for the first time she smiled. "All through the village, all across the parish. We are the people now."

Baffled, Marcus changed tack.

"Are you all in Wychmere?"

She nodded, her face, once more, expressionless.

"Why are you there? What are you planning to do? What is going to happen?"

Kathy tilted her head to one side, and seemed to ponder.

"We're going to bring the Old One back," she said, hesitantly, as if trying to recall something only half-remembered. "The lines, the lines that feed the circle will awaken her. Then she will be made flesh again, and all will be filled with wonder and awe."

"What lines?" asked Marcus. "How will the Old One be made flesh?"

Kathy's face suddenly twisted in pain.

"No, she's found me again! I can feel her in my mind! She's too strong."

"Kathy," said Marcus firmly, "wake up now. Open your eyes.

The young woman's eyes opened. Marcus reeled back in his chair, putting up a hand in instinctive revulsion. Kathy's eyes were yellow, the pupils vertical slits.

"Your second warning, Marcus," she said, in a voice far louder and deeper than before. "There won't be a third."

The young woman's back arched, her eyes closed again. Marcus rushed over as Kathy's body went limp and she began to slide off the sofa. He tried to make her comfortable and checked that she had not swallowed her tongue, then got his phone. But before he could make the call, she was awake again. This time her eyes were normal.

"Hey, I told you no doctors, no police, none of that," she said muzzily, trying to stand up.

"You need the kind of help I can't give you," he argued, hesitating. "At least think about it."

"What happened?" she asked. "And where's that booze you promised?"

Rather than risk her running out on him, Marcus put the phone down, then got a bottle of whiskey and two glasses.

"Come on, spill the beans," she said as he poured out the Scotch. "What did I say?"

Marcus replayed the digital recording of the session.

"Bloody hell," she said, after taking a gulp of Scotch. "I sound, well, bonkers."

Marcus realized she was putting a brave face on a disturbing experience.

"You did say one thing that might be very significant."

He stood up and, after searching for a few moments, took a book from an unsteady heap piled in the corner by his desk.

"I was re-reading this a while ago," said Marcus. He handed her a battered paperback with the title *The Old Straight Track*.

Kathy looked at the volume dubiously.

"A book about roads by a bloke called Watkins?"

"Not exactly," said Marcus. "It's a highly speculative work about prehistoric sites and the links between them. It dates from the 1920s. The author was condemned for his unscientific approach and is almost forgotten, but I've always felt he had a point."

"So what's it about, then?" she asked, flipping through the book, pausing to peer at illustrations.

"Ever heard of ley lines?" he asked. When Kathy shook her head he went on, "The idea is that mystical lines of paranormal energy run across country and converge at sacred sites."

"Like Stonehenge?" said Kathy.

"Among many other places, yes," explained Marcus. "Watkins thought our ancestors laid out a network across the whole island thousands of years ago. But traces were obscured when the old pagan religion died out."

"And Wychmere is part of this network?" she asked, flicking through the dog-eared pages.

"Not just part of it, but a very important focal point," said Marcus.

He turned to his computer and opened a file. It showed red lines spread out across England and Wales, intersecting at a few dozen places.

"Now, if we just look at the lines that intersect at Wychmere," said Marcus, clicking with the mouse.

Dozens of red lines radiated from a single point near the Welsh border.

"Okay, there are lots of these magic lines," said Kathy. "But what does it mean?"

Marcus shrugged.

"Maybe nothing, but 'the lines that feed the circle' is what you said. It could mean that energy, in some form, is being channeled into Wychmere and that the cult intend to tap it somehow."

"And revive this Old One? How?"

Marcus shrugged.

"I think they've already failed once, bungled the job at Hampton Round in Sussex. Not surprising, as they're trying to revive a spiritual power that's been dormant for thousands of years."

"So they hope it'll be second time lucky?" Kathy asked. "And then what? I never did understand that bit. Maybe I'm not very bright."

"Perhaps they don't know themselves," suggested Marcus. "It could be that they're all being used, Clay, Olivia, all of the cult. While they think they're manipulating others."

Kathy stared into her whiskey glass.

"Don't want to sound selfish or anything," she said, "but I'd be happy to forget all this stuff and try to get on with my life. But that's not an option, is it? They've got their hooks into me. Or their fangs."

Marcus felt uncomfortable, unsure how to respond.

"I think that if we can thwart their plans," he said, "there's a good chance whatever influence they have over you could disappear."

"A good chance, eh? Not very reassuring," Kathy laughed. "Is this a clever way to get me to fight the good fight?"

"You're the only person who's been part of Ouroboros and escaped, went your own way," he pointed out. "That means you beat them. And I need all the help I can get, as at the moment I've no idea how to do it."

Kathy shrugged.

"Okay, Mister Valentine," she said, "I'll think about it. Anything that keeps those bastards from crawling around in my brain is worth a try."

***

Declan Healy returned to his office at New Scotland Yard to find a backlog of internal emails and plenty of paperwork. He struggled to focus on normal police bureaucracy for the rest of the afternoon as he pondered what he had heard from the old priest. Eventually, he opened his file on Deputy Commissioner Faversham and added a few thoughts.

'Ouroboros – cultists capable of hypnosis? Questionable, never known it was used by criminals. Drugs? Father Q. - not reliable, mental issues. But could be core of truth somewhere.'

Healy thought back to the house in Berkeley Square, and the mysterious Cleo. He had no resources to put any kind of surveillance on the house. He had no surname or other details to try and identify Cleo.

"Probably not her real name," he said to himself.

On impulse, he called the RSPCA to find that the animal welfare charity had recovered the hamsters from the premises.

"We're looking for people to take them as pets, might you be interested?" asked a bright young volunteer.

"No thanks, we have a cat," replied Healy. "But when your people were at the house, did they find anything else? Signs of anyone living there, for instance?"

"No," replied the charity worker, "they said the place was deserted. Though it was strange that someone had been keeping the hamsters fed and watered. They had fresh lettuce, apparently."

There was a knock at the office door and Healy quickly thanked the woman and hung up.

"Come in!" he shouted, and Knapton entered, closing the door behind him.

"Oh, it's you," said Healy., "We need a special knock if we're going to do this cloak and dagger stuff."

"Yes, boss," said Knapton. "I just wanted to tell you I've been reassigned for a couple of days."

"What?" exclaimed Healy. "Why?"

"Some sort of training course," explained Knapton. "It's called 'Improving Community Awareness,' whatever that means."

Healy sighed, and rolled his eyes in resignation.

"We've never been so highly trained. It's amazing that any criminals can avoid capture, really."

"Yes, boss," said Knapton. "So I won't be back until Monday."

"I'll struggle to survive without your help, Constable," said Healy. "But we all have our crosses to bear. Is it time for coffee yet?"

"Always time for coffee, boss," came the response, as Knapton left, grinning.

Healy was about to return to routine form-filling, when a thought struck him. He logged on to the police intranet and checked training courses for his section. Sure enough, Knapton's course was listed and everything seemed above board.

But still, thought Healy. *Old Quigley said there was a conspiracy. Whispers in corridors and all that. What if this is part of it? Taking away my only ally?*

"Got some cupcakes, boss," said Knapton, returning with a tray. "One of the admin ladies has been baking again."

"Great," said Healy.

The detective picked up a cupcake, sniffed it. It was chocolate flavored, decorated with pink icing and multi-colored.

"Knapton," he went on, "suppose this apparently innocent cupcake was spiked with a powerful hallucinogenic drug that would make me putty in the hands of an evil conspiracy?"

"Not very likely, sir," replied Knapton. "I've had Mina's cakes before, she's quite traditional with ingredients."

Healy took a bite of the cake, and paused for a few moments.

"You're right," he said, "no ill effects. The point is, once you get paranoid you can't trust anyone or anything."

"Very true, sir," said Knapton, taking a bite of his own cake as he leaned on his superior's desk. "Of course, just because you're paranoid doesn't mean they're *not* out to get you."

"Exactly. So when you go for this training course," Healy said, "watch your back. And whatever you do, don't end up alone with a naked woman."

"I'll do my level best," replied Knapton, with a grin.

Chapter 9: Encounters and Deceptions

Brad arrived in the city of Hereford late on Thursday afternoon. After navigating the typical maze of confusing streets, he found his hotel and checked in. For the last few miles, he had lost sight of the silver Lexus. But he felt sure that she, and her fellow cultists, knew where he was staying.

He was in the middle of unpacking when his phone rang. He glanced at the screen, then stared. It was apparently a call from Kelly's number.

"Hello?" he said, not really believing his daughter wanted to speak to him.

"Dad?"

"Kelly? That really you?"

"Large as life. Look out the window."

Not understanding, he looked out at the roof-scape of the ancient city. Then he looked down and he saw Kelly, across the street. She had a phone in one hand while she waved up at him with the other. She looked like her usual self. She was even smiling.

"I'm coming over, meet you in the lobby," Kelly said, and ended the call.

Brad watched her looking for a gap in the traffic.

Don't just stand there, you idiot, he thought.

Brad was halfway down the stairs when he wondered if it might be some sort of trick. He slowed his descent, trying to work out how Kelly's presence could be used against him. Then he caught sight of her standing in the small lobby, talking to the receptionist.

"Here he is now," she said, nodding towards Brad.

Kelly walked over to Brad and hugged him as if they had been parted for a few days. He clutched her more fiercely than he had intended.

"Hey," she said, "easy on the ribs."

"I just can't believe you're here!" Brad exclaimed.

"Where else would I be? You came all the way to England to see me, after all."

Kelly glanced behind her at the receptionist, who was scrutinizing her computer screen.

"There's a cute little park near the cathedral," she said. "Let's go and take a walk there; it's a nice day."

She took his hand and led him out into the busy street. Pointing at the cathedral, she started to tell him about its long history, chatting as if they'd never been estranged. They crossed a bridge over the river.

"This is the Bishop's Green," explained Kelly, as they entered a small park. "Once it was fenced off so only the bishop and his guests could use it."

"God, this is so normal," said Brad, half to himself.

"No, Dad," said Kelly, looking up at him. "It's not. It's really weird, and I wish it could be different. But I had to come here and deliver one simple message."

"And what message is that?" said Brad, suspecting he already knew.

"Leave me alone," she said. "I'm a big girl now and I have my own life. You don't like my new friends? Well, that's nothing new. But I'm happy, and you're not the boss of me, are you?"

Brad felt a familiar frustration, and tried to hold it down.

Don't get angry, that's the way to lose her.

"Okay," he said, "I can't tell you what to do. That's a fact. But I can't stop caring about you. I love you, and you worry about people you love."

"I know, Dad," said Kelly. "But ask yourself who's being conned here?"

"What do you mean?" he asked.

"Your new friends," she said. "What do you really know about them?"

Brad was baffled for a moment, then retorted, "If you mean Marcus Valentine, he's an expert on cults like Ouroboros, so I don't imagine they like him very much. And Kathy ran away from them, so she's a traitor, right?"

Kelly shook her head.

"Dad, you're a rich man," she said. "Sure, you don't think of yourself as rich, but wealthy people rarely do. Has it ever occurred to you that when a rich man asks for help, fakers and con-artists start queuing around the block?"

"Marcus and Kathy are on the level," he declared. "Neither of them asked me for a single red cent."

"So far," replied Kelly. "I'm just saying, you've decided to believe a lot of stuff on zero evidence."

"I heard your voice come out of Kathy's mouth," Brad said. "Do you deny that happened?"

"No," she replied, "but doesn't that prove that Ouroboros taps into something real? That it's not the kind of cult Marcus claims?"

We're not going to agree, Brad thought. *But how can she be so obtuse about this? Has she been brainwashed?*

"So what's the solution?" he asked. "I just disappear out of your life?"

"It wouldn't be the first time," she shot back. Then, seeing his wounded expression, she went on, "Sorry, but you did kind of ask for that. Why not come and see for yourself? You trust your own judgment, right?"

"You want me to come and meet this Clay guy?" asked Brad. "Right now?"

"Anytime you like," said Kelly. "But why not now?"

"You do realize this sounds like a trap?" he asked.

"Why not meet on neutral ground?" returned Kelly. "At the village pub, for instance?"

Brad considered for a moment, then said, "Okay, but not straight away. I want some thinking time and I've got stuff to do. Make it tomorrow morning?"

"It's a date." Kelly surprised him by giving him a kiss on the cheek. "I'll see you around midday?"

Brad watched her walk out of the small park and cross the street, where she got into a silver Lexus. The car pulled out and he watched it weave its way into the small city's traffic until it disappeared from view. Then he took out his phone and called a number he had used several times that week.

"Yeah, it's me," he said. "I do need that stuff we talked about. Yes, carefully packaged. No, not a large amount. Standard seismic kit. No, not at the hotel. I'll meet you at this place, Bishop's Green. You won't have any trouble finding it, it's pretty central."

The conversation continued for another minute as Brad finalized some technical details and then authorized payment for the goods he needed. As he finished the call, he wondered what Kelly would make of his behavior.

She wouldn't be surprised by this at all, he thought. *Maybe she does understand me all too well.*

***

Sister Mary Assumpta brought Father Quigley his dinner at the usual time, and set the tray down outside the priest's door. She knocked. There was no response.

"I've got your evening meal, father," she said. "It's spaghetti Bolognese, your favorite!"

Again, Quigley did not reply. The nun sighed and was about to leave when she noticed that the door was not quite closed. She gave it a tentative push and it opened a few inches.

Not like the old fella, she thought, *to fail to lock his door.*

It suddenly occurred to her that the old man might be ill. Mary put her head through the door to see if Quigley was unconscious, or worse. But he was not there. She set off back to the main entrance of the retreat, only to meet another nun hurrying toward her.

"Sister Mary," said the breathless novice. "Somebody's been in the office and taken all the petty cash!"

"Lord, bless us and save us. The daft old bugger's only gone and run away!" exclaimed Mary. "Did that policeman leave his card?"

***

On Thursday afternoon, Declan Healy started to do some more digging on the Ouroboros affair. He had already identified some odd patterns of behavior among influential people linked to Deputy Commissioner Faversham. There was nothing especially damning about the data, not yet. But Healy, who never ignored his hunches, felt sure there was a hidden network. Perhaps a conspiracy reaching to the very top of the British establishment, and beyond.

Technically, he told himself, *I'm still looking into Matt Arnold's death. Just not in the way Faversham wants me to.*

He would have continued to build his file on Ouroboros, but a case he had been assigned a few months earlier intervened. A low-level drug dealer and pimp called Wayne Dotrice had knifed a social worker, then vanished. The suspect had been carefully avoiding his usual haunts and the case seemed to be going nowhere. But this morning, a report reached Healy that Dotrice was hiding in an old warehouse by the Thames. Wishing he could call on Knapton, Healy set off for London's East End to join up with two local beat officers, Higgins and Clark.

The red brick warehouse at Jamaica Wharf proved to be a huge building that had been almost converted into yuppie apartments before the money ran out. There were signs of vandalism, and it was an obvious place to hide out.

"A big place for just three of us to search," mused Healy. "How reliable is your informer, Constable?"

Clark, the older of the two uniforms, shrugged.

"Not too bad, but all they told me was that a nasty piece of work was living here, and he answers your description of Dotrice."

"Okay," said Healy. "It's a big place to search, just the three of us. Plenty of escape routes, probably. But we can give it a try."

Inside the Jamaica Wharf building was a labyrinth of hanging plastic sheeting and incomplete building work.

"Tell you what," said Higgins, "let's split up. We know Dotrice is a spineless toe-rag, and we've got our tasers."

"Yeah," added Clark, "it looks like a bust, anyway, and we don't want to waste hours on this."

Reluctantly, Healy agreed. He was the outsider, and did not want to appear timid in front of junior officers. While the two uniforms went upstairs, he began to work his way through the unfinished apartments on the ground floor. There was, he soon realized, no sign that anyone had been living there.

Clark's probably right, he thought. *If Dotrice was ever here, he's long gone now.*

Then he saw something that puzzled him. The bare floorboards were covered with a layer of plaster dust, and in it, he saw footprints. Healy put his own foot next to one and judged that it belonged to a flat-soled shoe worn by a woman or a smallish man. He followed them through a series of corridors, towards the back of the building. Then the prints seemed to stop in an area where the dust had been swept away.

This feels wrong, thought Healy. *The old Spider-sense is tingling.*

He spoke into his radio, asking Clark and Higgins if they had found anything upstairs. There was no reply. He heard stealthy movement, a plastic sheet being lifted. Before he could turn around, his right arm was gripped and twisted behind his back. Another arm locked across his windpipe, pulling his head back. His radio clattered onto the floor.

"We meet again," said Cleo, from behind him. "And this time, we won't be interrupted."

Healy felt her breath on his neck. He groped for his taser with his free hand as the woman nuzzled at his neck in a disturbing parody of affection. He felt a slight scratch as he found his weapon and jabbed with it blindly while pushing the button. The distinctive buzzing of the taser was almost drowned by the woman's shriek. Her hold relaxed and he broke free.

"You bastard!" she shouted, her face contorted with anger.

Fully clothed this time, he thought. *And not nearly so friendly.*

"Don't try anything," he warned, brandishing the taser. "You are under arrest. Turn around so I can put the cuffs on. Don't make this difficult."

Cleo lunged at him, trying to knock the taser out of his hand. She was fast, but he managed to jump back out of her grasp and then jabbed the weapon into her forearm. She screamed in rage, and Healy was taken off guard by the two prominent fangs in her upper jaw.

Plastic teeth? She must be barmy!

The tall woman spat at him, not emitting a gob of spittle, but two jets of dark fluid. Startled, Healy twisted his head, crouched, and put an arm across his face. A few droplets of the liquid hit bare skin on his hand and face and he felt a sharp, stinging sensation. Cleo sprang forward and grabbed his wrist. They struggled for the taser, and Healy felt himself losing. He tried to break free but lost his footing on some of the ubiquitous plastic sheeting and fell backwards.

The accident was a stroke of luck. Taken off balance, the woman hit her head on the door jamb. Healy recovered first and handcuffed the moaning Cleo just as Higgins and Clark appeared at the other end of the corridor.

"Did you get him?" shouted Clark.

"Yeah, only the him is a her," replied Healy. "She must have followed me here."

He expected questions from the uniforms but they said nothing as they advanced towards him.

Hang on, Healy thought. *Why would she follow me and then attack me with two other coppers nearby?*

He switched the taser to his left hand, took out his telescopic baton with his right.

"Don't come any closer, lads," he said to Higgins and Clark. "As you can see, your friend here didn't get me. Now suppose you tell me what this is about."

"Let me go!" shouted Cleo. Healy glanced around, saw her trying to struggle to her feet. When he looked back, he saw his brief moment of inattention had let Clark and Higgins split up. They had been shoulder to shoulder, now they were about three feet apart, and just out of reach of Healy's baton.

"Let's be reasonable, now," said Higgins.

"That's how we talk to criminals, mate," responded Healy, feinting with the baton. Higgins flinched. Predictably, Clark made a move, and Healy's taser connected with the man's overhanging beer gut. Clark crumpled, swearing.

"I thought you were the stupid one," said Healy, turning to hit the off-balance Higgins on the elbow. "I'm told that really hurts."

Healy secured both officers with their own handcuffs and felt pretty good about it.

"Came for one scumbag, got three," he said, bending over Clark. "Why did you do it? Faversham's orders? Part of his little conspiracy, are you?"

"Piss off," snarled Clark. "You've no idea how high this goes, you wanker."

"Tell me," said Healy, picking up his radio, "just how high? Because when I call this one in, a lot of people will be going down."

Healy paused, unsure exactly how to call in the arrest of two colleagues. He decided to play it straight and made a straightforward request for assistance. He was told to wait five to ten minutes for a unit to respond.

"Right," he said, squatting beside Higgins. "Let's try you. Is it money, sex, drugs? Do they have something on you?"

Higgins said nothing, did not even meet Healy's eye. Instead, he stared past Healy, eyes wide.

"You'll find out," whispered Higgins. "It's a great privilege. Don't struggle."

Suspecting a trick, Healy got up and stepped away from the two men. Then he heard an odd groaning noise behind him. It was coupled with a series of sharp cracking sounds, like someone snapping their fingers. Healy took a quick glance over his shoulder, then spun round, baton raised. The handcuffs were lying on the floor, still locked. The cuffs lay beside a small heap of clothes and a pair of shoes. The last vestiges of a woman's face disappeared as Healy looked on, immobilized by shock.

A huge golden-brown serpent, jaws agape, reared up until its head was in level with Healy's face. He started to back off, forgetting the bound men directly behind him. He tripped over Higgins and sprawled on the dusty floor just as the creature made its move. The scaly body landed on top of him, and its nightmare head spat black venom into his eyes, blinding him. Screaming in pain and fear, Healy jabbed the taser into the scaly flank of the monster.

***

Marcus Valentine and Kathy Hopkirk set out from London after lunch on Thursday. It had not taken either of them much time to pack. Marcus believed in traveling light, and all Kathy's possessions amounted to two bagfuls.

"You got a plan?" asked Kathy.

Marcus glanced over at the pale young woman. They had just left London's sprawling outer suburbs and were passing into rich farmland. Kathy was staring out at black-and-white dairy cattle. He wondered if she'd ever been out of the city before in her young life.

"I've got some ideas," he said. "All of them a bit vague. For a start, Clay's book offers a few clues."

"About what?" she asked.

"I think about Clay's conversion, whatever it was, took place when he was halfway through writing his book," Marcus explained. "He had obviously prepared a lot of scholarly notes and other material, but had only actually written the first few chapters. That's why it begins in such a reasonable tone."

"And then it goes a bit bonkers in the middle?" she suggested.

"Pretty much," laughed Marcus. "Towards the end of the book, he becomes obsessed with the idea of traditional festivals as the half-remembered rituals of Ouroboros. So to him, May Day, which is coming up, would qualify."

"But people have been doing these things for hundreds of years," Kathy objected. "May Day, Halloween, loads of others. None of them have raised up some ancient god. Not as far as I know, anyway."

"True," said Marcus, "but Clay's argument is that the rituals have degenerated. People don't focus on Ouroboros. Invoke the name and the concept. If they did, according to Clay, there's a chance the summoning would work."

"So why did it go wrong back in Sussex?" she asked. "Like that priest told you."

Marcus shrugged.

"Clay and his acolytes might have chosen the wrong place, or the wrong time. They went for Midsummer's Eve, the solstice. But if the core of the Ouroboros cult is a belief in renewal and regeneration, a spring festival might make more sense."

Kathy fell silent for a minute or so, then said, "So how do you stop them from doing this?"

"There are a few possibilities," said Marcus. "One is simply to get the police involved and say that an illegal gathering is taking place. I could throw in a claim that the cultists are vandalizing a historic site, the stone circle."

"You don't sound very sure," she said. "Will that copper you know help out?"

"Unfortunately, Detective Sergeant Healy seems to be incommunicado," he replied. Then, seeing her puzzlement, he added, "He's not answering his phone at the moment."

Kathy snorted. "Police. When you actually need 'em they're never around."

"As I said, there are other possibilities," Marcus pointed out. "Such as putting a spanner in the works during the actual ceremony."

"Wouldn't that just lead to a big fight? With us badly outnumbered?"

"Let's hope we can avoid any violence," he said.

Again, Kathy snorted.

"You're an optimist."

"From everything you've told me," Marcus went on, "there may be some kind of *gestalt* entity involved here."

"Try me in English, professor?" she said, irritably.

"*Gestalt* a German term for a kind of linked consciousness," he explained. "Your and Brad's dreams suggest some kind of telepathic linkage between cultists. It could be that one strong personality is dominating all the others in this way."

"You mean Olivia?" she asked.

Marcus made a noncommittal sound.

"It could be her," he conceded, "or it could be something working through her; Ouroboros itself, a being that is both one and many."

Kathy looked baffled.

"It's just a theory, of course," added Marcus.

Kathy did not reply, and they drove on in without speaking for half an hour. Then she said, "I can feel them."

"The cult? You sense their presence?" asked Marcus.

"Ahead of us, still some way off," she explained. "It's the same feeling I get in my nightmares. Being part of somebody else's mind, one piece in this bigger thing."

"If it gets unbearable, let me know and we'll stop. I can find you a hotel while I go on."

She looked at him, her eyes narrowed with anger.

"For a clever man, you can be a really stupid bastard," she said. "Don't you get it? I want to do them some damage. I want to get back at them! I can't do that in some random motel room."

Marcus struggled to think of something to say.

"I hate them so much," Kathy went on. "Don't you see? The one time in my life I was part of something, the only time I've ever belonged. And they rejected me. I wasn't good enough, I was a dirty junkie, a streetwalker. Just like all the others, all the people who've treated me like shit!"

Marcus started to protest but she cut him off.

"Yeah, I know they're probably killers and bonkers with it, but some of us can't be all cool and rational like you."

She was crying now, with anger and frustration. Marcus reached into the glove-box and handed her some tissues.

"Thanks," she said, after blowing her nose. "I needed that. Got to let it out sometimes. And I'm sorry I called you a stupid bastard. You're not. Well, not all the time."

"That's all right," he said. "I should have realized. Okay, we'll continue on to

Hereford and see how you feel then."

Kathy did not reply, and he glanced over to see her close her eyes. Her brow was furrowed with concentration. Perhaps, also, with pain.

Chapter 10: Plans and Observations

Brad met up with Marcus and Kathy for dinner that evening. He brought them up to speed about his encounter with Kelly.

"Well, at least you know she's in good health," said Marcus. "But I smell a trap."

"Could they grab me in broad daylight?" asked Brad. "We'll be in a public place."

Marcus agreed that it was unlikely.

"Besides," he added, "Clay might let something slip about their May Day games."

Brad noticed that, while Marcus was his usual buoyant self, Kathy seemed even more withdrawn and unhappy than before. Her eyes were red-rimmed, and her hands shook as she handled her cutlery. She saw his concern and explained that getting closer to the cultists was affecting her mind.

"You mean you can see into their minds?" Brad asked.

Kathy shook her head.

"It's not like that, not when I'm awake. It's like hearing somebody whispering all the time, only with thoughts instead of sounds."

"Any particular thoughts?" asked Marcus. "Any clue what they're planning?"

Kathy frowned, seemed to concentrate.

"It's all about May Day and the ring of stones," she said slowly. "I keep getting images of snakes, circles. There is something else, more of a flavor than a thought. An emotion, maybe. Hard to put it into words."

"Try," said Marcus, reaching out to put his hand on hers. "If you can."

Kathy closed her eyes, oblivious to stares from diners at nearby tables. She started to breathe heavily, rocking back and forth.

"Wake her up, she's going under!" said Brad urgently.

But before the men could react, Kathy opened her eyes and gave a crooked smile.

"No need to slap me, guys," she said. "But you won't like this."

She looked over at Brad.

"Especially you. This image, or feeling, I keep receiving. The nearest I can get to it in words is 'sacrifice.'"

Brad and Marcus stared at her.

"You're sure about this?" asked Brad.

Kathy nodded.

"It's all bound up with the idea of purity, loss, rebirth. But sacrifice is in there, somewhere."

"Perhaps it's a symbolic sacrifice," suggested Marcus.

"How likely is that?" asked Brad.

The Englishman pondered for a moment, then said, "It's a fact that lambs used to be sacrificed for May Day. And some think that it went further than that in ancient times."

"That's something you can tell the cops, surely?" asked Brad.

"I can try," agreed Marcus. "Unfortunately, Healy has gone quiet, I can't reach him at all. He's probably too busy with other matters, so I'll try the local police force. But they might just file me under 'crank.' It's happened before."

"I've been studying maps of this stone circle, the Dancers," said Brad. "And these so-called ley-lines. It's a bit like an electrical circuit, isn't it?"

Marcus looked surprised.

"I suppose so," he conceded. "But I don't see how that helps."

"Just that," said Brad, "whatever they're planning relies on a continuous flow of some sort of earth-energy?"

"Yes," said Marcus, "the stone circle collects and focuses it, that's the theory. Why do you ask?"

"Oh, just spit-balling," replied Brad. "Trying to get things clear in my mind." Brad turned to Kathy.

"The million dollar question," he said. "Do you really believe these people turn themselves into snakes or whatever? Or do they just believe they're shapeshifters?"

Kathy gazed levelly back across the table.

"They can do it. I'm sure. And I don't think that's all they can do. I can't put it into words, but in my gut, I just know that what they're planning at Wychmere is far stranger, and far more dangerous."

***

That night, Brad's dream of Kelly was very different to the ones that had haunted him for months.

He found himself lying in a forest glade, with small birds hopping close by. A gentle breeze rustled the wild grass and ferns, swayed the leaves of ancient oaks. It was an idyllic scene that reminded him of books he had read as a child, stories that always ended with the hero safe and sound after his adventures.

"Come on, Dad," said Kelly, kneeling beside him. She was wearing a white robe, sandals, with flowers in her hair. "Get up, sleepyhead!"

Brad stood up and let his daughter lead him through the forest, then out onto a sunlit plain. Rolling grasslands stretched in front of them, and a small village nestled by a stream. The village was inside a stone circle, and he felt sure that these were the Dancers of Wychmere.

"Come on, we'll be late!" urged Kelly, tugging at his hand. They set off towards the village. The scene had a timeless quality. As they got closer, he noticed that the fields were being worked not with machines, but by men, women, and children in homespun clothes. They came to a road that was not a tarmac highway but a cart track. The village, he could see now, consisted of white, half-timbered cottages. There was no sign of telephone poles, satellite dishes, or any modern technology.

"So," he said, "this is what happens after the really big god-snake smashes up the old world order? The survivors grow organic kale and sing folk songs by candlelight?"

"Isn't it peaceful?" said Kelly. "So beautiful and serene."

"A Golden Age," Brad said, "so long as you don't start thinking about stuff like clean water, antibiotics, and criminals appearing over the horizon. Oh, and high infant mortality, that'll help keep the population down."

"You're so cynical, Dad. Has it ever occurred to you that people can live simply, and in harmony with nature? That there needn't be criminals if everyone learns to just get along? And that most of the illnesses we suffer from are down to a crazy, artificial lifestyle?"

Brad looked at her, baffled by her obvious sincerity.

"There was a time you'd have called all this cheesy and boring," he said. "This isn't you, Kelly. You like traveling, loud music, a bit of booze, and quite a bit of other stuff I shouldn't know about. You'd go crazy living as some kind of hippie peasant in the middle of nowhere."

"Oh, Dad," said Kelly, shaking her head, "you don't really know me at all. But that can change. Now, though, let's listen in on your new friends."

"What do you mean?" he asked.

Kelly's reply was to put a finger to her lips and lead him to the nearest cottage. The window was shuttered but through the slats, Brad could see into Marcus Valentine's living room. The Englishman was sitting opposite Kathy Hopkirk. And another figure had their back to Brad.

That's me, he thought. *This is the hypnotism session.*

He heard Marcus begin the process, setting Kathy at ease and then putting her under. But then things departed from Brad's memory. Instead of questioning the girl, Marcus said, "Okay, you can stop pretending."

"Is he under?" asked Kathy, looking over at Brad on the couch.

"Oh yes, he's quite suggestible," replied Marcus. "Anything I tell him now he'll believe. But we'd better not go too far. Just soften him up a bit, so he'll follow my advice."

Kathy stood up, walked over to Brad on the couch.

"What do you reckon he's worth?" she asked.

"He might be good for a few hundred thousand," said Marcus, smiling. "But let's not be greedy. You've got to give the fish a bit of play on the line before reeling him in."

Brad pulled away from the shuttered window.

"That didn't happen!" he protested angrily. "It's just another bullshit mind trick!"

"How do you know?" asked Kelly. "You think I'm being manipulated, yes? Maybe it's you who's the real victim here."

"That's a load of crap!" Brad said. "You're being manipulated by a death cult, don't you realize that? Haven't they told you about the sacrifice?"

Again, she shook her head pityingly.

"These things are symbolic, Dad," she said. "But even if they weren't, I'd give my life to make a better world. Wouldn't you?"

Brad could not answer, and as he struggled to find the right reply, the sky darkened.

"Or would you like to stick with your world? Because we can do that?" said Kelly.

The spring sunshine was blotted out by clouds. The rolling rural landscape faded to be replaced by a gray wilderness, a dust-bowl. On the horizon, a line of black oil derricks topped by gas flares belched smoke. The quaint village and cultivated fields were gone, replaced by the ruins of a nameless city, a concrete hell of ruined and damaged buildings. People clad in ragged clothes picked their way through rubble while camouflage-clad men with assault rifles stood watch over them.

"What is this?" Brad demanded.

"This is the real great little world you want to keep," his daughter replied. "The world made by the practical men, businessmen, people like you. Driven by oil, and money, fear, and death."

As if on cue, sirens wailed and a squadron of military jets screamed over the horizon. Brad ducked instinctively as explosions erupted around them. Gunfire blazed across the leaden sky. Brad saw a screaming woman clutching a child to her breast as a wall collapsed onto them. All around, people ran for cover as a firestorm engulfed the area. Brad could almost feel the heat from the flames.

"Yeah, Dad," said Kelly, looking at the vista of misery and devastation, "we can just carry on pretending it's all great. Or we can do something about it. However crazy it might sound, Ouroboros is all about doing that something."

"This is horrific, but it can't ever be stopped, not really," he insisted. "You can't change human nature!"

Kelly looked him in the eye, unblinking.

"Wrong. Because that's exactly what we aim to do."

Brad woke in the dawn light, still tasting the smoke and dust of the bombed-out city.

I'm sure you're wrong, Kelly, he thought. *But God, I never could tell you that and not feel like a total asshole.*

It was just before six. Brad got up and splashed some water on his face, then got dressed. He would just have time for breakfast. He had an appointment with a courier at Bishop's Green at seven sharp. The kind of person Brad was dealing with did not like to be kept waiting.

After the deal was concluded, Brad put the package into the trunk of his car. Then he checked in with Marcus and explained that he was going to Wychmere to meet Clay. Brad felt a slight pang of guilt at not sharing everything he knew with the Englishman, but reasoned that the fewer people knew his plans, the better.

***

Brad's car crested the gentle rise to the east of the village. Though he had seen pictures of Wychmere online, he was still impressed by the ancient monument. The ring of thirteen stones known as the Dancers was about half a mile across, and surrounded by a large ditch about six feet wide and three feet deep. The village was small, picturesque, and sleepy in the warm April sunshine.

The stones give it a weird, timeless vibe, he thought. *But it looks harmless enough.*

The neat road passed over the ditch. Brad stopped his car and got out to walk over to one of the stones. It was a granite slab, about eight feet high. He put out a hand and after briefly hesitating, put his palm onto the moss-covered stone.

Nothing, he thought. *No weird jolt of energy, no visions of prehistoric times. Just a big lump of rock somebody brought here thousands of years ago.*

Then his hand encountered something different to the roughness of unworked stone. He stooped to look more closely at the granite. It was barely perceptible to the eye, but his fingertips traced out a circular pattern.

The Ouroboros. Must have cut it pretty deep for it to still be apparent today. Or they renew the design every few centuries.

Brad continued to walk around the stone, examining every square inch of rock. He found signs of weathering, some graffiti scratched in decades or centuries earlier. He began to wonder if he would have to move on to the next stone, and how much unwanted attention that might bring. But then he found what he was looking for.

Just above ground level, he thought, *and nice and deep. I could seal it up with turf and grass easily enough. Nobody would notice if they didn't know what they were looking for.*

Satisfied with his examination, Brad went back to his car and drove into Wychmere. The pub was not hard to find. The sign of the George and Dragon puzzled him, as it showed a knight on horseback slaying what was essentially a winged serpent. St. George was putting his lance through the dragon's neck. The creature was vainly trying to bite through the warrior's shield, which was decorated with a red cross.

As Brad gazed up at the sign, someone spoke behind him.

"It signifies the triumph of the new religion over the old."

A bald man, dressed in a sober business suit, walked over from the pub doorway. Brad recognized the face from old photos of Jonathan Clay, though the archaeologist had clearly put on some weight and lost what little hair he had had in the Nineties. Brad noticed the plump little man was limping slightly. It made Clay seem even more inoffensive, vulnerable. Hardly a conventional image of a cult leader.

"So Christianity defeated the serpent?" asked Brad. "And now you're planning a rematch?"

Clay smiled benignly.

"Christianity is all about progress from A to Z, from original sin to judgment day and the end of the world," he said. "It does not take cycles of recurrence into account. We see things differently."

"I know a bit about your beliefs," Brad cut in. "I agreed to talk to you. But you can't convert me, so don't bother trying."

"Walk with me a ways," said Clay. "Up this road."

Brad fell in beside the bald man. As they walked through the village, people smiled and greeted Clay as if he were an old friend. Clay, for his part, returned their hellos and engaged in a little village gossip. One theme kept recurring. Saturday was May Day, and a big celebration was being planned. Clay and his cultists seemed to be central to the big event.

"They seem to have taken you to their hearts," said Brad, sourly. "How did you do it?"

"No doubt Mister Valentine would say we brainwashed them all, very rapidly," smiled Clay. "An entire English village. Not very likely, is it?"

Brad did not reply.

He's right, he thought. *It's a crazy notion, like something out of a comic strip. But how else could the cult suddenly be so popular round here?*

"What we really did," Clay went on, "was reveal the truth about the May Day ceremony these people have performed for centuries. Their focus on the stones, the spring ritual of rebirth. They were in possession of half the truth. We brought the other half, the truth about the deity that lies sleeping here. And in many similar places."

"So what is Ouroboros, really?" demanded Brad. "An ancient god, or goddess? Some kind of primal force out of the earth? A kind of ancestral memory lurking in the subconscious?"

"Well done!" said Clay, without apparent sarcasm. "You've done some research. Ouroboros is all those things and more. Ouroboros is unity, a sense of oneness that we lost long ago and constantly seek to rediscover. And the day after tomorrow, with luck, we will."

By now, they had reached their destination. Clay gestured at two stones standing very close together. Both had been crudely fashioned into points.

"These are sometimes called the Fangs," said Clay. "For obvious reasons. Look more closely."

Brad examined the stones. On one, he noticed the circular Ouroboros symbol of the snake biting its tail. On the other, the snake was contorted into a figure eight.

"How old are these carvings?" he asked.

"About five thousand years, according to most authorities," replied Clay. "They are the oldest religious images in the British Isles."

Brad ran his fingers over the carvings. Again, he got no sense of any unusual power.

Just two big old rocks, he thought.

"You are apparently immune to their influence," said Clay, as if reading Brad's mind. "Most people get a jolt of spiritual energy from the Dancers."

"Why call them the Dancers?" asked Brad. "Seems to me thirteen lumps of rock couldn't be more static."

Clay smiled, and gestured at the broad arc of the stone circle.

"The stones have attracted all sorts of nicknames down the centuries, and they seem rather fanciful. The one at the entrance to the village, for instance, is the Warden. We have just passed Mother Grindle, said to resemble a stooped old lady. But to answer your question, some say pagan dancers were struck by the wrath of God and turned to stone," he explained. "Or is possible that a ritual dance was held here in prehistoric times."

"And you're going to recreate that dance?" asked Brad. "With Kelly playing the leading role?"

Clay wagged his finger in reproof.

"That would be telling," he said. "You'll have to wait and see."

"I won't let you put her at risk," warned Brad, moving closer to the plump little man. "Tell me what you're planning. Is it as risky as the stunt you pulled at Hampton Round?"

The barb struck home. Clay looked confused, as if struggling to remember something.

"No," he said, hesitantly, "nothing happened at Hampton Round."

"Someone died!" insisted Brad. "A priest was driven insane. There was an actual earthquake. That's not nothing!"

Clay put a hand to his forehead.

"No, nothing really happened," he said, his eyes oddly unfocused. "You're mistaken. It was a non-event. We simply timed it wrong. There was a silly accident, not my fault."

"That's enough. It's time for Jonathan to come home."

Brad turned to see a tall woman clad in black appear between the Fangs.

"You must be Olivia," he said. "Keeping an eye on the Herald of Ouroboros? Afraid he'll say the wrong thing?"

The woman ignored Brad, striding past him to take Clay by one arm. None too gently, she began to steer him back towards the village.

"Are you the high priestess?" Brad shouted after them. "The real leader of this crazy outfit?"

Olivia did not pause, but called back over her shoulder.

"There are no leaders, Mister Steiger. There will be no need for leaders ever again, when all are followers."

Brad could think of no answer to that. He watched the tall woman guide Clay to a car that then drove off.

Presumably to Garlock House, he thought. *Where Kelly is either a captive, in some sense, or a willing resident.*

Brad walked back to the center of the village and went into the pub. It was a small, snug place, evidently a centuries-old tavern. A sign by the door read 'Original Coaching Inn'. A sprinkling of patrons sat around on benches. A TV screen above the bar was showing a soccer match with the sound set low.

"What can I get you, sir?" said a friendly-looking barman.

Brad explained that he was driving and ordered a diet soda.

"Very sensible, sir," replied the barman, fetching a glass. "Are you here for the ceremony?"

"May Day, you mean?" asked Brad.

"Of course!" The barman grinned. "Our only claim to fame, apart from the Dancers. Looks like fine weather for May Day, too."

"So what happens on this big occasion, anyway?" asked Brad as he paid for his soda.

"Well, there's a parade," said the barman. "A bit of a sing song, with the parish brass band, and the May Queen is crowned."

"All to welcome in the spring?"

For a moment, the barman looked hesitant.

"Yes," he said, "it's a time of renewal. Everybody knows that."

"And Mister Clay and his friends, they're taking part?" asked Brad.

"Oh yes, they've been helping prepare things," agreed the man.

"Odd, isn't it, for so many outsiders to just roll up and take over a local event?"

The barman's broad smile faded, a hint of puzzlement crossed his face.

"No, sir, quite the opposite. We're all one now, after all. I thought everyone knew that."

Brad felt a slight but definite change in the atmosphere. He noticed that some of the other drinkers were no longer looking at the soccer match, but at him. It reminded him of a few similar occasions in less law-abiding countries. He downed his soda and left.

The time to get out of Dodge, he mused, *is well before anyone actually tells you to get out of Dodge.*

As Brad drove out of Wychmere, he looked at the village receding in his rear-view mirror. The old cottages still looked quaint and inviting. But now the dark stones loomed over the whitewashed homes like malign sentinels.

Brad took careful note of landmarks along the way, and found a good place where he could park his car that night. He concluded that he would have to approach Wychmere without headlights to ensure he was not seen. It would be touch-and-go.

But I need insurance, he thought. *Never go into a hazardous situation without a Plan B.*

Chapter 11: Flesh and Stone

Brad got back to the hotel to find Marcus and Kathy waiting for him. The Englishman had disappointing news.

"The local police were very skeptical, bordering on derisive," Marcus admitted. "It doesn't help that I couldn't really spell out what the danger to the public was."

"Did you tell them Kelly was listed as a missing person by Scotland Yard?" asked Brad.

"She isn't," said Marcus, bluntly. "It seems Detective Sergeant Healy is, to use the American phrase, full of it."

"You can never trust the filth," said Kathy.

"Maybe they got to him," pointed out Brad.

"Maybe," admitted Marcus, "but I had to think fast. So I suggested that the cultists might damage the stones in their ritual. A bit feeble, I know, but it might prompt them to send a car on Saturday morning. These ancient monuments have a complex legal status, it's quite fascinating."

Brad quickly changed the subject and told them about his encounter with Clay, Olivia, and the villagers.

"Sounds like they've got the place sewn up," commented Kathy. She raised a hand to the faded bite marks near her throat. "Small place like that, wouldn't be too difficult."

"But they can't hold an entire village in thrall indefinitely!" protested Marcus. "Outsiders would notice, for a start."

"They only need to be in control for a few days," Brad pointed out. "They probably left the takeover as late as possible."

Marcus thought that over.

"It would make sense to involve the villagers if they want to pervert the familiar May Day ritual to their ends. If only we knew exactly what they're planning."

"Sacrifice," said Brad. "That's all I need to know. If it's symbolic, fine. But if not, we need to be ready to grab Kelly and get her out of there. I know it's a rough and ready approach, but at least it's simple."

"I'm with you, of course," declared Marcus. "For what it's worth."

Yeah, you're on the level, but you're no action hero, Brad thought. *Which brings me to the tricky part.*

"Guys," he said, "I need your help tonight. I have to go to Garlock House. And I want you both to monitor Ouroboros, if you can. Make sure they don't spot me, maybe run some interference on my behalf."

"What are you going to do?" demanded Kathy.

"You're not going to try and snatch Kelly?" asked Marcus. "That would be most unwise for several reasons."

"I can't tell you," said Brad. "I'd like to, but the way I see it, if I did, I'd be doomed to fail from the get-go."

"You don't trust us?" said Kathy, accusingly.

"If I've got this right," said Brad, "you're linked to the rest of the cult, telepathically? So they could know what you know?"

Kathy reluctantly agreed.

"So your plan can't be shared with Kathy," said Marcus, slowly. "But what about me?"

"What if they take you over somehow between now and tomorrow morning?" asked Brad. "I don't like doing this, but I'm used to working alone and being self-reliant. Sorry, but if this is my show, it has to go by my rules."

Marcus shrugged, unwilling to argue further. There was a marked coolness as the three had lunch and then worked out what Brad needed. Kathy was unhappy about being put under by Marcus for the third time, but was eventually won over. It was agreed that the hypnotism session would take place at midnight, when Brad reckoned he would be arriving on the outskirts of the village. More than that, he refused to tell them.

***

"What do you think he's doing?" asked Kathy, as she settled back on the sofa. They were back at the hotel room where Marcus and Kathy were staying.

"Your guess is as good as mine," replied Marcus. "I only met him a few days ago. He's a bit of a dark horse, really."

"Plenty of money, I reckon," she said. "He hired a private detective, and you. And he paid for our rooms."

"He's not short of a few bob," agreed Marcus. "He works in the oil industry, some kind of geologist, I believe."

"Loads of money," murmured Kathy. "But she still hates him. That's a laugh, isn't it? Some people can have the whole world on a plate and they turn it away."

"I don't think his daughter hates him," objected Marcus, moving a chair to sit facing her a couple of feet away. "Most families have rough patches, especially with adolescent offspring. What cuts do is drive a wedge into a gap that might otherwise close up naturally."

Kathy looked bored by his theorizing.

"Is it time yet?"

"Nearly," said Marcus, checking his watch. "You know the drill by now."

With a thin smile, the young woman closed her eyes and Marcus began the process of suggestion. After a few minutes, Kathy's eyelids began to flicker, like those of a sleeper having troubling dreams.

"Can you see them?" asked Marcus. "Ouroboros, the villagers, are they there?"

"Some of us are asleep," she replied in a voice just above whisper. "You would find our dreams so strange. Beautiful, but strange. When the earth is cleared off, it will be wonderful. So clean and peaceful."

"Cleared off?" he asked.

"The detritus of a failed and decadent culture must be swept away," said a voice much clearer than Kathy's. "The process has to begin somewhere. The awakening of Nature's guardians will be the start."

"Who is this?" demanded Marcus.

"I think you know, Mister Valentine," came the reply. "Your little parlor tricks are becoming very wearisome."

Kathy's blank expression gave way to a condescending smile.

"Olivia Ballard?" asked Marcus.

"My human name, for now," said Olivia. "Soon we will move beyond such limitations as individuality."

"Then you'll lose your humanity!" exclaimed Marcus, almost forgetting the purpose of the session.

I must keep her talking, he thought.

"Being human is vastly overrated," said the condescending voice. "A pity you are so negative in your attitudes. You would have made a useful ally."

"Ally, or tool?" he asked. "You seem to leave converts no real choice in the matter."

"If you saw a child crawling towards an open fire you would snatch them away, regardless of their desire to play with the pretty flames," returned Olivia.

The verbal jousting went on for several minutes. But then Kathy's brow wrinkled in concentration.

"Why did you pester me tonight of all nights, Mister Valentine?"

The directness of the question threw Marcus off balance for a moment.

"We, that is, I, wanted to glean more information," he said. "You can't block us out, so don't bother trying!"

"No, that's not it!" said Olivia. "I'm sensing something else here, in this poor stupid girl's muddled mind. Secrets. Plans."

Damn, thought Marcus, *this is happening too quickly.*

"I'm going to bring you out of it, Kathy," he began.

"Too late, little man!" said Olivia's voice, sneering in triumph. "It seems Brad is trying to play the hero. Well, that will simplify things considerably. A touching reunion of father and daughter, all differences settled at last."

Kathy slumped forward, groaning. Drool trickled thinly onto her lap. Marcus did his best to make her comfortable then tried to phone Brad. It seemed the American was out of cell phone range. While he waited for Kathy to come to, he kept calling and texting. Eventually, sometime after one pm, he got a reply.

"For God's sake, man, what happened?"

"Nothing unpleasant," replied Brad. "It all went smoothly, thanks to you two."

"But they found out that you were trying to break in!" exclaimed Marcus.

"No, they found out that you both thought I was targeting Garlock House," said Brad.

It took a moment for the truth to sink in.

"You cunning bastard," said Marcus. "You guessed they'd probably read her mind so you lied to us. That was the distraction."

"Don't knock it, it worked," replied Brad. "Tell Kathy I'm sorry. And apologies to you, too."

"Not at all," said Marcus wryly, "it was textbook stuff. I just hope whatever you got up to was worth it."

***

The next morning, Kathy did not come down to breakfast. Marcus figured that she deserved some rest and could hardly be expected to come any closer to the cultists.

"When this is over," said Brad, "I'd like to try and do something for her. Is she still taking drugs?"

"I don't think so," replied Marcus. "I've seen none of the obvious signs. But she's still a lost soul."

"If I can get her some help, I will," Brad declared. "She's suffered a lot for my sake."

"Our sakes," corrected Marcus. "Ouroboros may be a threat to all of us. What I heard last night might have been grandiose propaganda. But if it were even partly true, the cult really does want to bring the whole of modern civilization crashing down."

Brad thought about his dreams of Kelly.

"Idealism can do even more harm than greed or cynicism, can't it?"

Marcus paused in buttering a slice of toast.

"All the most violent and destructive forces in history seem to be driven by pure ideals rather than everyday greed."

"And that's the problem," said Brad. "Kelly always was drawn to ideals, Utopias, clean and simple solutions to complex problems."

"It's a common fault of the young," agreed Marcus. "But let's look on the bright side. Ouroboros may simply fail again."

"That might be our best bet," said Brad. "Otherwise I'll just try to grab her and see how it goes."

It was about half an hour after dawn on May Day when they arrived at Wychmere. The village still looked quaintly picturesque, but was definitely not sleepy.

All the villagers were lined up along the edge of the great ditch. They looked zoned-out to Brad, who had walked up to the circle unnoticed. All the locals were facing inward with beatific smiles. All except a handful of younger children, who seemed confused and frightened. He wondered if children were impossible to control, or had simply been ignored as irrelevant by the cultists. People seemed to be in their Sunday best on this Saturday morning; women in print dresses, men in suits. There was even a brass band on a small platform beyond the Fangs. But Brad noticed that everyone from the village or neighborhood was outside the circle on his side of the ditch.

About a dozen followers of Ouroboros were walking slowly in a circle within the ring of Dancers. In white hooded robes with garlands of wildflowers around their necks, they did not look particularly sinister. In fact, the procession had a touch of Woodstock about it. Brad thought of barefoot Flower Children in the morning sunshine. Kelly, also in white and crowned with flowers, was at the head of the procession, flanked by Salome and Olivia. She looked happy, beautiful, utterly sure of herself.

At first, Brad couldn't see Clay, the so-called Herald of Ouroboros. Then he noticed a short, plump figure at the back of the procession. Brad made out Clay's face under the hood. The supposed leader looked out of place, as if his inclusion was an afterthought. Clay caught Brad's eye as he went past and his blank expression changed for a moment.

Is he panicking? He seems confused, maybe scared. This isn't what he signed up for, clearly. But he has no way of breaking free.

A hoarse voice broke in on Brad's thoughts. Father Quigley burst through the ring of villagers, stumbled down into the ditch, then clambered out. Disheveled and red-faced, his pants caked with mud and grass stains, the old man was wild-eyed and ranting.

"Whores of Babylon!" he cried. "Devotees of Satan, the Old Serpent!"

Some of the onlookers laughed, a few seemed annoyed by the interruption. But none of the villagers moved to interfere as Quigley ran forward, brandishing a crucifix. The priestesses did hesitate, but then Olivia gestured for them to continue. As they walked on, the tall woman interposed herself between Quigley and the cultists.

"You're making a fool of yourself, priest," she said. "And April Fool's Day has come and gone. This is a very different festival."

The old man stopped and looked up at Olivia's impassive features. Then he tried to push the cross into her face. She frowned in distaste and grabbed the priest's wrist, easily forcing the crucifix away. Quigley winced in pain and fell to his knees.

"No," he moaned. "Lord, give me strength!"

"There are no lords here, old man," said Olivia, raising her voice to reach the nearest villagers. "Only the great goddess. It is *her* time now."

Salome waved to someone and the brass band on the other side of the circle struck up a tune. The onlookers started to sing. The sheer normality of it took Brad by surprise. The tune was cheerful with a folksy feel, while the words seemed to be in archaic English. He made out 'summer is a-comin' in,' and a reference to a cuckoo. As the cheerful voices soared, Olivia wrenched the crucifix from Quigley's hand and pressed it to her forehead. Brad could not hear what she said to the priest then, but he could guess the tone from her scornful smile.

She's showing him how powerless he is, how little the symbols of his faith matter.

Something caught his eye, then, a brief flurry of movement near the rear of the procession. Brad could not make out what had happened, except that one of the white-clad women was slight apart from the rest. Clay was holding her by the arm, apparently in some kind of discussion. Nobody else was paying attention, though. Olivia was rounding off her impromptu drama by releasing Quigley and going back to rejoin Kelly, who was still smiling benignly.

She's under their influence, brainwashed, Brad told himself. But he still could not be sure.

The parade continued towards the Fangs. Brad shadowed it, moving behind the chain of singing onlookers. He wondered what would happen if he crossed the ditch. He had no idea what he could accomplish if he did. Tearing Kelly away from the cult by force was clearly a non-starter. He had tried talking to her. He felt impotent rage and despair at being reduced to a mere onlooker. The feeling was made worse by his uncertainty as to what was going to happen next. Brad had the sickening conviction that something very real and profoundly evil was about to happen.

The white-clad cultists were now spacing themselves out in a line along the ditch, leading away from the Fangs. Some kind of wooden seat covered in spring flowers had been set up between the pointed stones, and Kelly took her place on it.

Brad realized this was the enthroning of the May Queen; the ancient pagan ritual that Marcus had described. Kelly looked serene and happy. She glanced in her father's direction but gave no sign of having seen him. The singing died down. There was a sense of anticipation. Clay stepped forward, raised his arms. Brad could just make out what he was saying.

"For thousands of years, the Ancient One has slept, dreaming of the day when we would rediscover the eternal truth. That all Nature is one, and that we are one with Nature. And that this great oneness is Ouroboros, the eternal truth that is reborn today."

Brad expected some kind of response to what sounded like a prayer, but instead Clay shuffled off to one side. Olivia stepped forward, and raised her arms.

Now for the real leader, thought Brad. *Clay's just the warm-up man.*

"This is the time of transformation!" proclaimed Olivia. "Do not be afraid, brothers and sisters. For the first time in fifty centuries or more, Ouroboros will become flesh."

Brad expected Olivia to continue, but instead the woman simply turned and walked to the nearest stone. The other white-clad cultists did the same, and Brad realized that there was one follower per Dancer. No, he was wrong, there was one person left over, a smallish figure with her head bowed standing by the Fangs.

A spare wheel at the big party, thought Brad. *Do they keep one in reserve or something?*

He was distracted from such thoughts by Olivia removing her robe. There was a sharp intake of breath from some onlookers as they realized she was naked. The other cultists did the same. Brad saw one mother cover her small son's eyes, but other parents gazed on benignly.

"Yes, different levels of influence," said Marcus Valentine. "Some are simply less susceptible than others."

Brad had not noticed the Englishman sneaking up.

"I think most of them are well under control, though," Marcus continued.

"What kept you?" asked Brad.

"I had to rent a car. Kathy stole mine," replied Marcus. "Have you seen her?"

"No," said Brad.

Another wave of exclamations came from the crown, a mixture of awe and excitement. Brad looked back at the cultists. Olivia was writhing on the damp grass by the stone.

"Possibly having some sort of fit," said Marcus, uncertainly.

Then the woman's pale skin began to darken under the morning sunlight. It took on a greenish-gold tinge, and as it altered, her limbs began to change shape. Her arms grew shorter, shrank to tiny flippers, then disappeared entirely.

This can't be happening, Brad told himself. *It's a trick, some kind of mass hypnosis.*

Despite his strenuous attempt to deny it was real, Olivia's transformation continued. Her long, dark hair seemed to withdraw into her skull as her forehead shrank, while her nose and mouth merged to form a kind of muzzle. Even more extreme was the blending of her legs into one tapering mass of flesh. Soon all semblance of humanity was gone, and Olivia had become a snake, ten feet long.

"Oh my God," breathed Marcus. "It's not just a metaphor. They really are lamias, or shape-shifters!"

A gleaming serpent now reared up on its thick coils where Olivia had stood. Along the inner etch of the ditch, the other cultists had chucked off their robes and were changing, too. Someone screamed, and a young woman in a pink frock pulled away from the ring of onlookers. She began to run away across the field beyond the Fangs. Nobody tried to stop her.

Brad looked over at Kelly. Her face was astonished, awe-struck, but not horrified.

"I think she was expecting this," said Marcus, his voice breaking. "She's been prepared for these changes."

"But why, what comes next?" whispered Brad. "Or is this it?"

"No," said Marcus, "this is not what they mean by renewal, I think. Remarkable, though it is."

The huge serpents began to move sinuously around the circle of stones. Brad stared into the red, slit-eye of one monster and felt a very human intelligence looking back at him. Another scream from the crowd, and this time a middle-aged woman and a small child broke away. But, as before, the remaining villagers stared on, some smiling contentedly, others blank-faced as zombies.

"Come on," said Brad, not checking to see if Marcus was following. He set off to get round behind the Fangs. He had a vague idea that, if Kelly was threatened in some way, he would swoop in and save her. Details eluded him. As he ran past the crowd, he caught glimpses of the lamias. The snake-beings were now forming up in front of the Fangs, circling nose-to-tail in a kind of grotesque parade. Then the largest creature, the thing called Olivia in human form, opened her huge jaws and gripped the tail of the monster in front of her. The other lamias followed suit.

"Ouroboros!" gasped Marcus, catching up with Brad as they neared the Fangs. "A circle within the circle. Look at the ditch!"

Brad looked and saw what seemed to be coils of morning mist forming in the shadowed depression. But instead of drifting away, the vapor grew denser, began to form into a definite shape. He remembered what Quigley had told them at the first, failed ritual in Sussex. As he watched, the gray-white vapor lifted like a smoke ring and hovered for a few heartbeats. There was dead silence from everyone, crowd and cultists. Then the weird cloud shrank, growing even denser, and stopped a few feet above the ring of lamias.

"This is how it happens, the renewal," whispered Marcus. "The spirit of the Old Serpent entering new flesh."

As he spoke, the cloud descended, merged with the ring of monstrous beings. The reptilian bodies shuddered, then began to change again. Scaly flesh flowed like viscous liquid. It was even more bizarre than the first transformation, so strange that at first Brad was unsure what was happening.

Oh God, he realized. *They're merging into one.*

Head and tails flowed together, the cultists blending into one huge being. Only Olivia's head remained distinct, growing larger and releasing the tail from its jaws. All trace of the vapor had gone, now. The vast serpent writhed and then reared up, its gleaming eyes some twenty feet above the ground.

"Ouroboros!" gasped Marcus. "The ultimate merging of the deity with her followers. The union of mind is followed by that of the flesh."

It is awe-inspiring, thought Brad. *I can see how people could worship that thing. We're witnessing a kind of evil miracle.*

Brad saw Kelly stand up, and raise her arms towards the monster. Her face was ecstatic, radiant with joy. The huge jaws opened, revealing fangs over a foot long, as the vast serpent reared up over her white-clad form. A terrible certainty gripped him.

She is a sacrifice. She can't really want this!

Brad started to run forward, not knowing what to do, only that he had to somehow save Kelly from an appalling fate. He heard Marcus shout a warning. Brad had forgotten the ditch, and tumbled into it, wrenching his knee. He was scrambling frantically up the other side when a white-robed figure dashed forward, between Kelly and the serpent. There was a flash of metal, and a roaring sound so deep that he felt it in his bones.

It was Kathy Hopkirk. She held a large knife in both hands and was stabbing into the huge mass of scaly tissue. The serpent reacted predictably, rearing up and then descending, jaws agape. Brad had a sudden flashback to the time he'd seen a snake devour a mouse.

"No!" Kelly was standing up, shouting. "This is wrong, don't take her!"

It was too late. The monster, reacting with the instinct of a goaded predator, had already devoured Kathy. Brad saw a bulge moving down the creature's body. As he looked up, the creature seemed to see him for the first time, and opened its vast maw with a hiss.

That's it, he thought, reaching for the device in his pocket. *Game over.*

Brad took out a specialized radio transmitter, jabbed at a red button, listened for the explosion. Nothing happened. The small gelignite charge he had planted at the base of the Warden failed to detonate. Then he realized that, in his near-panic, he had failed to turn on the unit's power. He flicked the switch just as the shadow of Ouroboros fell across him. He pushed the red button again, and there was a loud crack followed by screams of shock and confusion.

Too damn late! Probably didn't even topple the goddamn stone. Too rough-and-ready, no finesse.

As he dropped the radio unit, the monster's jaw began to engulf Brad, a black forked tongue as thick as his arm wrapped itself around him. Cold slime covered his face. Fetid carrion breath filled his lungs and he started to choke. Far away, he heard Kelly's voice, desperate, pleading with her goddess.

Brad closed his eyes, bracing himself for a terrible death in the belly of the beast. He felt a sudden rush of energy like an electric shock, and blacked out.

Epilogue: Spring 2017

"Thought we'd lost you there," said Marcus, helping Brad limp away from the Fangs. "We'd better get out of here before the police arrive."

"Kelly?" asked Brad, barely able to utter the one word.

"I was a bit confused for a while back there," admitted Marcus, "like most people. When I got my bearings, she had gone. So had Clay. Probably to Garlock House to do some hasty packing."

"What about Ouroboros?" croaked Brad, trying to look over his shoulder.

"Not pleasant," said Marcus. "A horrific mish-mash of tissue, some of it recognizably human. Some not. God knows how the authorities will explain it. Or cover it up."

"Kathy's dead, then?"

Marcus did not reply. The two struggled over the uneven ground to where the Warden no longer stood, but lay diagonally across the road surrounded by rock fragments. Scorch marks around the base of the stone showed where Brad's charge had blasted a chunk out of it along a natural fault line, felling the Warden much as a lumberjack fells a sequoia.

"A very professional job, I'm sure," said Marcus, "but that means you're the only living person here who's actually committed a crime. Another reason to make ourselves scarce."

"Yeah," gasped Brad, head pounding, "but it sure did a number on their magic power system, didn't it?"

"Not denying that," said Marcus.

The Englishman was driving Brad away from Wychmere at a careful forty miles per hour when flashing blue lights appeared in the distance.

"Do you think they'll find her?" asked Brad.

"Kelly? I doubt it. She's rather good at staying lost," said Marcus.

"So we're back to square one?" Brad could hardly believe that he had done so much, risked so much, for nothing.

"Look at it this way," said Marcus. "If we can take Ouroboros at their word, you may have just saved the world from near-total obliteration. But I wouldn't put that on your resume just yet."

"What can I do?" Brad was thinking aloud now, but Marcus had a ready reply.

"You can dream," he said. "Because your dreams have linked you to Kelly since this started."

"How do we know that link will still be there?" asked Brad.

"I suppose we'll know tomorrow morning," said the Englishman.

***

Amid the chaos that followed the explosion, some villagers had come to their senses and called in the emergency services. Ambulances arrived to find what they initially thought was a vast heap of organic remains. Then one paramedic noticed that some parts of the bizarre corpse were still breathing. The police, equally baffled, decided to seal off the area near the Fangs and wait for what senior officers termed 'special contingency units.'

The units in question arrived in four unmarked helicopters that landed in a meadow half a mile from Wychmere. Soldiers wearing respirators pushed aside protesting police officers, dragged the remains of Ouroboros into the ditch, then proceeded to incinerate it. A few weak screams were heard from the ditch, but were soon lost amid the roar of the flames. As this process neared its end, a convoy of unmarked vehicles appeared and men in white biohazard suits emerged. The charred remnants of the snake-being were loaded into special containers and the ditch sprayed with a series of chemical agents. Senior police officers asked for more detailed information about the process, and were told nothing.

While the anomalous creature was being dealt with, men and women in medical coveralls went among the villagers administering what were termed vaccinations. After being vaccinated, each villager was taken aside for an 'interview' with a gentleman introduced as 'Mister Jones from the Home Office.' When discussing events of that May Day later, the people of Wychmere agreed that Mister Jones had made a very strong case for 'discretion about the whole unpleasant business.'

A press release from the Ministry of Health announced that a chemical leak had occurred in the village after a truck had taken a detour and collided with one of the ancient standing stones. This, said the officials, had caused widespread headaches, vomiting, and even some hallucinations. But there were no long-term problems.

Within twenty-four hours, a number of conspiracy theory websites were referring to the Wychmere Incident, variously linking it to UFOs, chemical trails, parallel universes, and a host of other paranormal phenomena. The man known as Mister Jones, who supervised such disinformation, was pleased to note that it never lost its effectiveness.

***

Constable Knapton arrived at New Scotland Yard on Monday morning. Most of the country was enjoying the May bank holiday, so traffic was light and he arrived earlier than usual. But he still found Detective Sergeant Healy in his office, apparently deep in thought.

"Morning, boss," said Knapton. "I'm back. Got you some coffee from that place over the road."

"Thanks," said Healy. "You enjoyed that, err, thing. A training course, wasn't it?"

"Yes," replied Knapton. "I wasn't tempted by any naked lovelies, worse luck."

Healy looked puzzled. To fill the awkward pause, Knapton went on, "I hear you nearly nabbed that bugger Dotrice while I was away, sir?"

Healy's face lost its confused look.

"Oh, that. Another wild goose chase, the little sod was long gone. If he was ever there."

"Well, he can't stay lost forever," remarked Knapton, taking the lid off his latte.

"I wouldn't bet on it," said Healy. "Some cases just don't get solved. Like this Matt Arnold thing. We're going nowhere fast with that."

Knapton was so surprised that it took him a moment to respond.

"I thought we had a sort of lead, sir?"

Healy shook his head decisively.

"Nah," he said, "I'm going try and pass it off onto someone else. Complete waste of time."

Knapton, who had been leaning on the side of Healy's desk, straightened up slowly.

"I see, sir. Well, that'll certainly reduce our caseload."

Later, after discussing their other cases, Knapton went to the washroom. After checking that the stalls were all empty, he made a phone call.

"Yes, you were right. Looks like they got him. Pity, he was a good man. Maybe he will be again. No, I don't think so; he seems to buy the whole training course thing."

The entry of two detectives loudly discussing their weekend exploits put an end to the call. The incomers ignored Knapton, a low-ranking uniformed officer. And that was fine with him.

***

"Would I have died, Jonathan?" asked Kelly, looking out over the stern of the fishing boat. "Would she have consumed me?"

The coast of England was almost out of sight, a black smear silhouetted against the setting sun.

Clay hesitated, torn between his own judgment and the persistent voice in his head.

We failed again, he thought. *But we must persist. What else is there? How can we turn back now?*

"I don't know," he said finally. "But I have always believed that there is something beyond death, something wonderful."

"Dying would be an awfully big adventure," murmured Kelly. "That's what Peter Pan said. I always loved that movie as a kid."

"Let's not be morbid," said Cleo, striding onto the after-deck. "We've got a long journey ahead of us. Lots to do. No point in dwelling on the past."

Kelly looked up at the dark woman, and for a moment, Clay feared that she was about to challenge Cleo for dominance. He had no idea which side he would take in the event of a struggle. Or whether his opinion would count for anything.

"Where are we going?" asked Kelly. "No one can overhear us now that Kathy is dead. Along with the rest."

"Olivia was over-confident," retorted Cleo. "She misjudged her enemies. I won't make that mistake."

"They won't give up," said Clay. "The American and that self-styled expert. They'll try to find us, no matter how many obstacles our allies put in their way."

Kelly nodded in agreement.

"Dad won't give up; he's not made that way. But I don't want him harmed, do you understand? There's been enough violence."

Cleo smiled, then.

"It's a big world," she said. "And Brad has no idea where we are going. By the time he finds out, if he does, Plan B will be underway."

Kelly looked uncertain, and asked, "Is it really worth all the suffering? The deaths?"

Cleo leaned on the stern rail of the boat, gazing out at the wake spreading over the dark water.

"You haven't slept for nearly two days, Kelly," she said. "Maybe you should go below and get some rest."

* * *

Fortress of Ghosts
Ouroboros Series Book 2
Written by David Longhorn

Prologue: Unit 774, Poland, 1968

"Why are we here at all?" demanded Captain Kuragin.

Colonel Shevchenko raised a bushy eyebrow.

"Quite a philosophical question for a junior officer," he rumbled.

"You know what I mean, sir," said Kuragin. "Why are we stuck in the middle of nowhere with a bunch of glorified witch-doctors? Surely these eggheads could do their experiments in Moscow."

The colonel arose ponderously from behind his desk, pointed at his subordinate with a half-smoked Havana cigar.

"It is not for you to question our mission, Captain," the big man said quietly. "It is for you to obey orders. If you cannot maintain discipline among your men, I will have you sent back to the Soviet Motherland to undertake less onerous tasks. Supervising penal activities in Siberia, how about that? Do you own plenty of thick woolly undergarments?"

Kuragin turned bright red, and his lips quivered, but he said nothing. He knew better than to challenge the colonel when Shevchenko was using his 'reasonable' voice. It was designed to be especially menacing, and it worked.

"What is the precise nature of the problem, Captain?"

The third man in the colonel's office was a small, thin civilian, wearing a tweed jacket with elbow patches. Professor Zamyatin of the Soviet Academy of Sciences was, in theory, in charge of the operation. In practice, however, Unit 774 was a military outpost and the colonel was never tired of asserting his authority.

Captain Kuragin waited until his commanding officer gave a curt nod, then turned to the scientist.

"The men say there are people in the woods," said Kuragin, reluctantly. "They say these people appear among the trees whenever you make a run with that, that contraption downstairs."

Zamyatin's small mouth twisted up in a smile.

"Are your men seeing ghosts, Captain?"

Kuragin colored again.

"They think they are enemy soldiers, perhaps Western infiltrators, or Polish traitors."

Zamyatin said nothing more, but took off his round glasses and began to wipe them. The colonel turned to a map of central Europe and placed a stubby finger on southern Poland.

"We are many miles from any help if we are attacked, Captain," he said. "I need your men to be alert, disciplined, and ready for anything. Not nervous or jumpy. See to it. Impose iron discipline. Treat any fools or cowards with the severity they deserve. Dismissed!"

Kuragin whipped his arm up in a salute, then exited without another glance at Zamyatin. Once the door had closed on the captain, Shevchenko looked hard at the scientist.

"Is this problem caused by your infernal machine?"

Zamyatin shrugged.

"Our experiments are radical in nature. It is not impossible that some psychic residue may be stirred up by the Transducer."

"Psychic residue?" growled the colonel. "You mean ghosts, yes?"

The professor shook his head emphatically.

"That is an obsolete superstition foisted on the masses by religious leaders," he said in his precise, dry fashion. "No true Marxist believes in the supernatural. I speak merely of after-images of dead men, a kind of recording. The fabric of a structure may retain psychic images of emotionally-charged events. The presence of a brain attuned to the right frequencies may trigger the recordings, that is all."

"That sounds like double-talk for ghosts to me!" objected the colonel.

"A shadow is not a man," retorted the scientist. "We are dealing with mirages, echoes, a mindless residuum. This castle has seen much bloodshed down the centuries, not least in the Great Patriotic War against the Nazis. But the after-images are more dangerous to your men than playing music from a gramophone. The dead are dead. You should prevent them from mixing with Polish villagers. They are reactionary Catholic peasants, not enlightened agrarian workers."

The colonel stood looking at the little man for a couple of seconds.

"I hope you're right," he said. "I am here to defend this installation from the living. Phantoms are above my pay grade. As for the Poles, if I didn't let the men buy moonshine vodka and fraternize with village girls, I'd have a mutiny on my hands."

After offering more reassurances, Zamyatin took his leave of the colonel and returned to the main laboratory. The lab was situated in the old wine cellars of Mista Venja castle. The location was ideal because the cool stone floor and walls reduced the risk of the experimental machinery overheating.

"Are we ready for another run?" Zamyatin called as he descended the steps to the underground chamber. Technicians confirmed that the generators were ready, and the subject in place. Zamyatin went among his subordinates scrutinizing dials, ensuring that checklists were complete, discussing minor changes to the procedure.

"This time we'll get it right, eh?" was his constant refrain.

After he had assured himself that all was ready, Zamyatin went to examine the Transducer itself. The machine was a bizarre-looking construction. At the heart of an array of cables was a sealed capsule that reminded the professor of a Soyuz capsule. Through a small, round window of thick glass he looked in at the test subject. A young woman in striped prison coveralls stared back. Her eyes were dull, unfocused, her jaw slack. Her shaved head was covered in electrical sensors. An intravenous drip ran into her arm.

I hope we did not overdo the drugs, Zamyatin thought. *We must have some kind of response. If she can't tell us what she sees, we achieve nothing. Suitable subjects are not easy to come by.*

Zamyatin went back to his position at the main switching panel. He took a deep breath, looked around at his team, and gave a curt nod to the chief technician. The man threw the main power switch. The lights flickered as energy surged through the machine. Zamyatin could just make out the woman's face through the glass panel. Her mouth was wide open now, but if she was screaming nobody outside could hear her.

"Take it up to full power," said Zamyatin, calmly. "Keep your eyes on your gauges. The only things we need to know about the subject will come down those wires."

***

Private Pavel Lermontov paused in his patrol of the perimeter fence to light a cigarette. It was nearly midnight, and the castle was an island of electric light surrounded by an ocean of darkness. That darkness was a dense forest broken only by a narrow cart track to the nearest village.

The perimeter lights flickered.

Those sneaky bastards, he thought. *What are they doing in there? These scientists gave us nerve gas and the H-bomb, who knows what they might cook up next?*

Pavel looked up at the castle. The soldier had heard the gossip in the canteen. He had done his share of staring into the woods, wondering if every movement was a 'ghost'. There were stories about the bloody battle for the castle in 1945, when the remnants of a Nazi regiment had been slaughtered by Russian troops. And there were older stories, the ones told by the Polish villagers, about the castle's dark, bloody history.

Pavel shuddered, took a deep draw on his cigarette. Then he hefted his rifle and set off again on his patrol.

Stories. Ghost stories. For old women and children. Nothing for a man to worry about.

The firing began away to his left, in the darkest part of the woods. At first, he heard single shots, interspersed with shouts. Then came bursts of automatic fire. He unslung his rifle and lay flat on the ground, peering into the night. All the shots sounding the same, he noticed. That meant all the guns firing were standard Red Army Kalashnikovs. Which left two possibilities.

Maybe the Americans use our weapons, he thought. *Dress in our uniforms. Special forces trick.*

The other possibility was no less worrying. It meant that Pavel's comrades were shooting at shadows.

Or at beings like shadows, he could not help thinking.

The firing died down as suddenly as it had started, but the shouting continued. Lermontov recognized several voices, including his corporal who was swearing profusely. The perimeter lights flickered again, then went out completely.

"Bugger!" hissed Pavel. "The silly sods have blown the fuses!"

He got to his feet and took out a flashlight, swept the beam around him. The weak light picked out tree trunks. Above were boughs heavy with spring foliage, below was the undergrowth. A thin figure was standing half-hidden by a tree. But as he swept the flashlight back, Lermontov saw that it was just a sapling.

A hand fell on his shoulder. He jumped, spun around, finger on the trigger of his rifle. His flashlight picked out the red star badge on the tunic of the newcomer.

"You bloody moron, I could have shot you!" said Lermontov.

He flicked the flashlight beam up to see which particular moron he was dealing with. The yellow light revealed a dead face, eye sockets sunken hollows, skin like parchment stretched taut over the skull, black lips pulled back from grinning teeth. Pavel staggered back, dropping his flashlight, as the dead soldier lunged forward. A dead face was pushed into a living one, and Private Lermontov felt a terrible coldness pierce his eyes, his heart, and his brain.

He heard the distant shouting turn to screams.

***

"Get the power back on!" shouted Zamyatin. "And remove the subject from the capsule."

In the gloom, it was hard for the professor to make out if his orders were being followed. Figures in lab coats rushed back and forth, some tinkering with equipment, others apparently fleeing the cellar.

"Anyone who abandons their post will be subject to extreme sanctions!" Zamyatin yelled, his voice hoarse. The coded threat of death by firing squad did not have the desired effect. He tried to make out who was running up the cellar steps. It was only then that he realized he should not be able to see anything. The cellar had no windows, and anyway it was pitch black outside. Yet a faint, bluish glow allowed Zamyatin to make out his colleagues and the sharp-edged forms of equipment.

Where's that light coming from? Some residual static charge, perhaps?

The scientist started groping slowly towards the Transducer core. As he did so, he heard distant shouts and the crackle of gunfire.

"Remain calm, comrades!" he said, but was dismayed to hear his voice sound less than resolute.

Zamyatin reached the sealed unit and peered into the window. The glow was coming from inside, which made no sense to him. He began to undo the lugs that secured the hatch. "Someone help me with this!" he shouted, but nobody came to his aid. Cursing, he bruised and bloodied his hands unlocking the capsule. The neural sensors were dangling from the roof of the metal cylinder, no longer attached to the test subject. The woman's overall was lying heaped on the floor.

Where is she?

Zamyatin leaned forward and put his head through the hatchway. The overall shifted and he realized, a split second too late, that it was not empty. A wedge-shaped head with glowing eyes reared up. The scientist tried to pull back but the creature fastened onto his face. Pain coursed through his body. The last words he would hear as a living man echoed through his mind, inhuman in their cold avidity.

"Feed me your soul!"

Chapter 1: Cries for Help

Ghosts.

In Brad Steiger's dreams, there were too many ghosts in the castle. A few were familiar. Most were strangers, figures in all kinds of historical costumes wandering the stone corridors of the strange fortress. There were Victorian gentlemen and ladies intermingled with dashing officers and silk-gowned beauties from the age of Napoleon. Renaissance lords and ladies wandered through a dim-lit banqueting hall. Brad even glimpsed what might have been a Roman soldier in an iron helmet and red cloak.

The ghosts of these strangers were merely a distraction, though. The familiar faces were more worrying. There was the private detective, Matt Arnold, killed by Ouroboros in London while working for Brad. He looked reproachful, puzzled.

"I'm sorry," Brad said as the investigator walked up to him, "I didn't know what we were getting into."

"You got me into death," replied Arnold. "Or something even worse. But hey, no hard feelings, pal."

The detective drifted away into the milling crowd of ghosts. Then, in the distance, at the far end of the great hall, Brad saw a young woman amid the throng. Brad half-recognized her, and at first hoped that it was his daughter, Kelly.

No, he thought, *let it not be her, because then she would be dead, too.*

The woman came closer, and he saw that the resemblance to Kelly was superficial. The face was too pale and pinched, the hair mousy and lank; a damaged person, someone who drew a bad hand in life and then died.

"Hello, Brad," said Kathy Hopkirk. "In case you were wondering, I'm still dead."

"I'm sorry," Brad said in his dream. "I couldn't save you."

Kathy smiled, and Brad tried to remember if he had seen her smile when she was alive. She had had little to be happy about.

"I'm not here for my health," she said, waving a slender hand at the assorted ghosts. "I'm supposed to deliver a message."

"A message? From whom?" he asked.

Kathy shrugged.

"They didn't show me any ID. It was all very informal. They just told me to tell you about the Place of the Serpent."

Brad was puzzled, but before he could speak, again the milling assembly of the dead bore Kathy away. He tried to get to her, but the ghosts of strangers held him back. As he tried to push through them they changed, fine clothes fading and turning to rags. Their flesh also grew ragged, bones breaking through the skin of cheek and knuckle. They overwhelmed Brad, yellow-nailed fingers tearing at him, reaching for his eyes.

"Save us!" they pleaded with black-tongued mouths, even as they tried to kill him, "Save us from the jaws of Old One!"

Brad awoke, he lay staring at the ceiling. He watched shifting patterns of shadow, cast by cars, passing in the street until he felt sure he was awake. He switched on his bedside lamp and reached for a notepad and pen. Brad had begun to write down the contents of his dreams at the suggestion of cult expert Marcus

Valentine. The experiment had not yielded much so far. After several weeks, he had scrawled a seemingly random set of words and phrases. Some were attempts to describe weird images or sensations, others were half-remembered snatches of conversation.

He wrote *Place of the Serpent. Kathy H. Castle. (British?) Ghosts of many eras.*

After a moment he added, *Nothing about Kelly. Again.*

Brad got up, showered, and checked his business email. He was officially in London again for work purposes. He had attempted to get a permanent assignment in the British capital but so far, it was no dice. As a result, he had spent the last couple of months liaising with Marcus from the US. The Englishman had done his best to locate Kelly, but the trail had gone cold.

As he attended to routine matters, Brad mused on the disaster in the village of Wychmere that had almost killed him and his daughter. The bizarre incident had instead destroyed most of the members of the Ouroboros cult. But at least one survivor, Jonathan Clay, had presumably escaped with Kelly. He was almost sure she had been brainwashed. Almost. But his only conversation with her since she joined Ouroboros had planted a seed of doubt.

She seemed so damn rational, he thought. *She really believed that damn snake cult could change the whole world for the better.*

Brad turned the TV on and caught the news. Wars, famines, terrorism, other horrific crimes, plus bigotry and stupidity in abundance. He could understand how a young idealist, like Kelly, could look at such a situation and think that the only solution is to tear it all down. But he was still coming to terms that his only child was not only committed to such a plan, but part of a group that might be able to achieve it.

***

Brad arrived at Marcus Valentine's Camden flat in time for lunch. The cult expert was his usual welcoming self. The two were soon chatting like old friends over a scratch meal in a book-lined living room.

And yet, thought Brad, *we only worked together for a few days. It feels like we went through a war together.*

"I wish I had more detailed information for you," explained Marcus, "but what remains of the Ouroboros cult seems to have dropped off the radar."

"I thought they had friends in high places?" said Brad. "Why would they need to hide?"

Marcus shrugged.

"I suspect that the disaster at Wychmere, with the loss of so many key members, left the rest of their network in chaos."

He got up and took a few computer printouts from his desk. Brad flicked through them, not quite seeing their relevance. Then he realized that all concerned sudden resignations, dismissals, or retirements were of influential people. The names listed were of bureaucrats, police officers, and the editor of a national newspaper.

"You think all of these people were working for Ouroboros?" he asked.

"It's a tentative hypothesis," admitted Marcus. "But look at it this way. The cultists did have the capacity to hypnotize or brainwash people. Call it what you like, they possessed some kind of effective mind control. This allowed them to avoid the scrutiny of the police, and the media. Yes?"

Brad nodded. One thing that had been apparent from the moment Kelly vanished was how little Ouroboros seemed to attract official interest.

"You'll notice," Marcus went on, "that all of these career-ending incidents happened in the first days of May. In some cases, people were admitted to hospitals suffering from mental breakdowns. That lends support to my theory that the cultists are linked, and what happens to one affects the rest. In this case, the death of a dozen members produced quite a mental shock-wave."

"Does this mean that Clay and Kelly are on the run?" asked Brad, handing back the printouts. "That they've got no support network anymore?"

Marcus shook his head, smiling.

"I suspect things are a little more complex than that," he said. "We've been assuming that all the leading cult members went to Wychmere to try and raise the Old One that was dormant under the stone circle, yes? But what if we're wrong? What if one of the lamias survived because she wasn't there in the first place?"

Brad pondered that idea. He still found it difficult to come to terms with the May Day ritual that had turned to carnage.

"Marcus," he said tentatively, "is it possible that most of what happened there was down to hallucinations? This mind control you mentioned, could it be a kind of mass hypnosis?"

"You mean did we really see what we both remember seeing?"

The Englishman got up and went to his desk, started searching for something on his computer. Brad stood at Marcus's shoulder and watched him open a video file.

"This was all over the internet last month," explained Marcus. "But it was quickly dismissed as a hoax. A lot of people think it's a trailer for one of those cheap found-footage horror movies."

Brad could see the logic of that last claim. The video was of very poor quality. It seemed to have been shot on a phone or a cheap camera from inside a car. It was so shaky and badly-focused that he could only just make out the stone circle at Wychmere in the middle distance. There was a soundtrack, too.

"We're approaching Wychmere to take a look at their traditional crowning of the May Queen," said a woman's voice. "Barry, slow down!"

Barry, evidently the driver, slowed a little and the footage became less shaky.

"There's certainly something going on. Quite a big event! Stop the car, Barry, we'll get out!"

The woman filming set off across a field towards the village. Brad could make out the circle of villagers around the outside of the stone circle. A procession of white-clad figures was making its way within the stones, and Brad caught his breath.

"This is a lot more elaborate than we were expecting isn't it, Barry?"

The amateur camerawoman continued to approach the ceremony, giving an inane running commentary, then suddenly stopped.

"Are they taking their clothes off? Oh my God! Don't look, Barry! Barry, stop *looking!"*

The inner circle of cultists, now naked, were starting to writhe on the grass in front of a smaller figure robed in white. The film, already jerky and grainy, began to flicker and freeze at intervals.

"That's Kelly!" exclaimed Brad.

"Yes," said Marcus, "and you can see us making our way around towards her."

Brad watched the bizarre events of May First played out from this new angle. He saw himself and Marcus running to get closer to Kelly as the cultists began to change form. The video quality deteriorated even further, but still offered glimpses of the transformation of humans into snakes.

"Barry, what's happening?"

Barry's reply was inaudible, but to Brad he surely sounded scared. The merging of the snake-beings' bodies to create one vast serpent was beginning, now, though barely visible due to electronic snow almost blanking out the screen. Marcus stopped the video and scrolled back and forth, trying to find a clear image.

"You see," he said, "this is interference of some sort. I think the energy that was focused by the circle was responsible."

Marcus let the video run on, and despite the terrible quality, Brad could still make out the huge serpent rearing up over Kelly. A second white-clad figure, tiny in proportion, rushed forward, stabbing at the monster.

"Kathy Hopkirk," he said. "Do we have to see this?"

Marcus stopped the video, closed the window.

"The rest of it is pretty much Barry telling his hapless missus to run away, and they obviously did leave the area before the clean-up squad arrived. Nobody believes it's real, of course. Apart from anything else, the villagers seem to have no memory of it."

"But there were still dead bodies," Brad pointed out.

"Which were quickly disposed of," returned Marcus. "The dead cultists, like Kathy, were people who'd gone missing years earlier. Dropped off society's radar. Several were homeless and a lot of them had changed their names on joining Ouroboros."

"This clean-up squad at Wychmere," asked Brad. "Any idea who they were?"

Marcus gestured at the bookshelves lining two walls of the cramped room.

"I can let you borrow any one of a dozen volumes with titles like 'The Secret State' or 'Who Really Runs the World?' But the truth is, I don't know for sure. Only that someone with power did notice Ouroboros, but didn't feel they could intervene until us, amateurs, had done all the dirty work."

"Great," Brad said, trying to keep his anger and frustration in check. "So we're back to square one? We have no idea where Kelly is or what Jonathan Clay is planning? And we can expect no help from anyone?"

"Ah, well that's not strictly true," said Marcus. "Because I've been calling in a few favors since we last worked together. And later today, I'm going to introduce you to someone who might be able to help. If she thinks it will benefit her."

"Great, someone else with an agenda," said Brad.

"There's something else, isn't there?" asked Marcus. "You told me you were dreaming about Kelly again. But you didn't say anything about the content of your dreams."

Brad gave Marcus a brief description of his nightmare.

"The Place of the Serpent?" mused the Englishman. "Could be a literal place name, in some language. Or it might be descriptive, like the stone circle at Wychmere. But why 'Save us', I wonder? Save them from what?"

"I'll take a wild guess," said Brad, "that whatever it is, it's long, wriggly, and has fangs."

***

"It is the Devil's work!" said the priest.

Officer Fabian Minkowski sighed.

The things I have to do just because I wear this uniform.

"It's just some kids messing around, Father," he said soothingly. "This is classic attention-seeking behavior. They want us to make a fuss, and you're just giving them the attention they crave."

Fabian had lived in the village of Goritza for three years since being reassigned from a larger town nearby. Goritza was a quiet place, the classic Polish rural community where most crimes consisted of drunkenness, motoring offenses, and petty vandalism. It was a case of the latter that had brought Fabian to the church this morning.

"Occult. Words. Written. In. Blood," said Father Jerzy, jabbing a long finger into the officer's vest to stress each word. "How can this be down to hooligans? Are you so blind?"

The policeman sighed again and took a step back, looking up at the church wall. Phrases, in foot-high letters, were scrawled across the ancient stonework. Minkowski did not believe for a moment that the messages were written in blood. He felt sure that the vandals had used red paint. But there was something else that bothered him.

"Do many kids around here know Russian?" he asked.

"Of course not!" spluttered Father Jerzy. "Why would they learn the language of their oppressors? We were well rid of those barbarians!"

"How about German? No, don't answer that," said Fabian. "Language of oppressors, got you."

He took out his phone and snapped a shot of the graffiti on the wall.

"I don't suppose you know what it says, Father?"

The priest shook his head.

"Satanic verses, perhaps! Some blasphemy or obscenity."

Fabian went up to the wall, stretched up to his full height, and reached for the graffiti. His fingertips just touched some of the trails that had dripped from the words. He examined the red marks on his fingertips, sniffed the supposed paint. It had an odd smell, a bit like rotten meat. Fabian was about to taste the stuff, then decided against it.

Christ, he thought, *maybe the little buggers did use blood. Perhaps they got it from the abattoir down the road?*

"Is there a ladder on the premises?" he asked.

The priest looked puzzled for a moment.

"Yes, but it's locked up in the shed. Come, look."

"No," replied Fabian, "I don't need to. See here? No trace a ladder was used."

The police officer gestured at the patch of grass by the church wall. It was a little overgrown, but any marks from a ladder would have left definite marks. The priest looked puzzled for a moment, then turned pale.

"Not again!" he said.

"What do you mean?" asked Fabian. "This has happened before?"

The priest ran a hand nervously through his close-cropped gray hair.

"It is nothing," he said. Then, more loudly, he went on, "I'm sure you are right, young man! Silly young fools trying to get a rise out of us. I will fetch the ladder and wash this muck away. No need to make a fuss."

The priest's apparent mood-shift caught Fabian by surprise. He could only stare as the priest stalked away without another word.

"You don't want to lodge an official complaint, then?" he said to Father Jerzy's retreating back. The only reply was a dismissive wave of the hand.

"Well, that simplifies my life."

Shrugging, Fabian climbed back into his car and returned to his police station. At lunch time, Fabian's wife, Katrina, appeared as usual with his lunch. As they shared their frugal meal in the tiny office, he told her about the odd call out to the church.

"So you don't know what this graffiti actually said, Fabian?" asked Katrina.

He shrugged.

"Probably the usual crap kids scrawl on buildings," he said. "Though I still can't figure out how the little bastards got so high up without a ladder. Maybe they formed a human pyramid or something."

They laughed at the image this conjured up, then Katrina asked if she could see his picture of the graffiti. She frowned as she studied the image on the small phone screen.

"Both messages are very short, and the writing is very messy," she said slowly, "but I think I know what some of the German words say. See here, *Rette uns*."

"What does that mean?" asked Fabian.

"Save us," replied Katrina. "Just that one phrase, repeated over and over. Save us. I wonder if the Russian words mean the same thing?"

"Maybe," agreed Fabian. "If I can get our lousy internet to dial up I can try and check. But it's a damn strange message for vandals to leave. Save who? And from what?"

"All good questions," said Katrina. "Maybe you could be a detective instead of just the village policeman, and find out?"

Fabian ate a couple of mouthfuls of his lunch without replying.

"It's the castle, isn't it?" asked his wife. "That's what this is really about."

"Oh, Katrina," he said, tossing his fork into the bowl. "These people are superstitious. Anything weird that happens is blamed on the castle. But it's just a tumbledown place that nobody goes to."

"Including you," she pointed out. "We've never been up that road since we came here. But isn't the castle on your turf? Shouldn't you have inspected it at least once?"

Fabian shook his head.

"It's officially off limits to anyone except Defense Ministry personnel. There are signs, barbed wire, the whole thing."

"Okay," said Katrina. "Maybe the graffiti is a one off, and we can just forget it. But if it isn't, what will you do?"

"I will report the situation to my superiors," replied Fabian instantly. "In accordance with proper procedure."

They both laughed. They knew the chances of getting any help from the authorities out here were close to zero.

***

Not suitable for children, or adults of a nervous disposition!

Andreas read the warning twice to be sure. It was the first time he had seen such a thing at a circus. But then, sideshows were traditionally stranger than the main acts performing under the big top. And this particular show was on the outskirts of Berlin, after all. The German capital had long been famed for its exotic entertainment, legal or otherwise. Andreas looked at the picture on the sign again. It was certainly unusual. He felt tempted to give it a try.

"What is it, honey?" asked Helga, his girlfriend, who had been powdering her nose. She looked at the sign outside the carnival tent and elbowed him sharply in the ribs. "So, I leave you alone for five minutes and you start ogling half-naked women!"

"Aw, darling, it's just a dumb sideshow," the young man protested. "I was looking around while I waited for you and I was intrigued by the name, that's all."

"Oh yeah, the name," said Helga, poking him in the ribs. "That's what stands out. Not the nearly naked boobs. You sleazeball!"

Fortunately, for Andreas, his girlfriend was giggling as she told him off. They both looked up at the sideshow facade again.

LILITH THE SEDUCTRESS!

Beneath the big title were a few words of what passed for description of the sideshow.

See the Serpent-Woman Who Tempted Adam!
Do You Believe in Shape-Shifters?
Dare you brave her mesmeric powers?

The words were nothing compared to the garish image in the center of the sign, though. It showed a beautiful, dark-skinned woman in a cage. Lilith the Seductress was snarling at the onlooker, revealing fangs so big they were almost ludicrous. She was wearing just a skimpy leopard skin bikini. Helga described the picture as 'both borderline racist and really tacky.'

"I agree, honey, it's ridiculous," said Andreas. "Come on, I'll win you a cuddly panda. Or you can win me one, in a spirit of gender equality."

He linked arms with Helga, preparing to walk on to the rifle range. But just as he did so, a man in a fancy red and gold tunic emerged from the sideshow tent and stood on the small platform outside. Andreas noticed that the man, who was short and bald, was also limping. This was unusual for a carnival barker, just another oddity about the whole Lilith sideshow.

The short man glanced down at the handful of people who were waiting to hear his spiel, gave a slightly nervous smile, and began.

"Roll up, roll up, ladies and gentlemen!" he said. "The show will begin in five minutes! A show that you will not believe! A show so strange that you will be stunned, not to say disturbed!"

Andreas noticed that the man's German was heavily accented. When he mentioned it to Helga, she said, "Yes, he's probably English. They are very weird people, especially the ones in showbiz. Perhaps this might be fun."

A small crowd had begun to gather as the barker continued to whip up interest. There was the usual carnival mixture of teenagers and more mature people, but also a few family groups. The latter were disappointed when the showman emphasized that children could not be admitted.

"Why not?" shouted a young man among a group of giggling student-types. "Is this some kind of a dirty show?"

"Dirty? No! It is a show that involves amazing stage effects that will take your breath away," returned the barker. "You will believe a beautiful woman can become a terrifying, venomous reptile!"

"Oh, how ridiculous," said Helga, searching in her purse. "Come on, it's only a couple of Euros each."

"Really?" asked Andreas. "I thought you said it was politically incorrect to show a brown-skinned woman in a cage?"

"It may well be racially insensitive," she said, taking out some change. "And if I am offended, I will denounce it quite ferociously on Twitter and Facebook. But I've got to see it first, yes? So come on!"

Andreas knew better than to argue with Helga, so he let her lead him up to the ticket booth. The bald showman greeted them with a big smile.

"Two young people, keen to experience something new! Believe me," he said, "you will not be disappointed."

Chapter 2: New Recruits

"There she is," said Marcus, leading Brad into a pub that stood just opposite the Englishman's apartment.

Denny Pollard was not what Brad had expected. When Marcus had described her as a freelance journalist, he had expected a sleek, well-dressed career woman. Instead, the person sitting at a corner table with a half of ale in front of her looked like a grad student down on her luck. She wore jeans, sneakers, a New York Dolls T-shirt, and seemed to have had no time to brush her hair that morning. He commented on this to Marcus as they made their way across to her.

"Protective camouflage," replied Marcus in a low voice. "She is sharp and very ambitious."

After they were introduced, Brad revised his opinion of Denny. While she seemed untidy and a bit of a ditz, she asked pertinent questions and seemed to have done her research.

"So why are you interested in Ouroboros?" he asked.

"Firstly," replied Denny, "because a lot of news and feature editors aren't interested. That's always interesting to me. Secondly, it's a human-interest story. A lost generation of kids, looking for answers, falling for crazy ideas, becoming enslaved by a mad cult. And thirdly, if I get a book out of it there might be rich pickings over film rights."

"At least you're up front about it," admitted Brad. "But why do journalists seem so cynical nowadays?"

Denny took a sip of her beer.

"I believe you work in the oil industry, Brad? I think we've both got a fair share of professional cynicism."

Marcus quickly put in, "Let's stay focused on what we can do for each other. We help you expose Ouroboros, you help us find Kelly Steiger."

Denny nodded.

"That's the deal. But it won't be easy. I've a few contacts in various security outfits, government, and private sector. From what I can glean, two people answering your descriptions of Clay and Kelly left the country by sea in early May."

"They went to Europe?" asked Brad.

"They sailed from Harwich, that's a port on our east coast, to Rotterdam in Holland, via fishing boat," Denny said. "And there, they vanished. Most of Western Europe has open borders now. So they could be in Germany, France, Spain, Italy. You name it."

"How do you know this?" asked Brad.

"I don't reveal my sources," said Denny. "Suffice to say, some people trafficking networks are allowed to stay in business, just so they can be monitored by certain departments."

"Like MI5?" asked Marcus.

"Let's get back to the facts," said the journalist, "because there's one inconsistency about the information I obtained for you."

"Let me guess," said Marcus. "There were more than two people in the party?"

"Correct!" replied Denny. "There was a third passenger. According to my sources, she seemed to be the one in charge."

"She?" asked Brad, exchanging a worried look with Marcus. The Englishman shook his head slightly.

"Yeah, there was a second woman," said Denny. "Is that especially significant? Ouroboros had a lot of female members, as I understand it. Sounds a bit kinky, like a harem."

"This woman," asked Marcus, "was she described as very tall? Physically imposing, perhaps?"

The journalist took out her phone and scrolled through some emails.

"About six feet, looked to be in her early twenties, Afro-Caribbean in appearance," she read. "Why, do you know her?"

"I doubt it," said Marcus. "We've no idea how many cult members survived Wychmere. This may be someone we've not seen before. An unknown quantity, if you like."

Denny leaned back in her seat.

"Suppose you tell me all the stuff you've been keeping back?" she asked. "Because if you don't give me all the facts, I can't help you. It's that simple."

"The trouble is," said Brad, "the facts, as we've experienced them, sound kind of crazy."

The journalist persisted, and over the course of the afternoon, Brad and Marcus gradually revealed everything they knew or suspected about Ouroboros. Predictably, Denny interrupted them when they described the lamias, or snake-beings.

"Oh, come on!" she exclaimed. "You're telling me these people are shape-shifters?"

The background noise in the pub dropped and people at nearby tables turned to look.

Denny leaned forward and lowered her voice.

"I'm trying to do a serious investigation, here," she hissed. "Are you serious?"

"We're dead serious," said Marcus. "But I understand if you want to walk away from this. It's dangerous, and it sounds insane."

The journalist stared at him for a moment, then broke into a smile.

"My two favorite things," she said. "Tell me more."

***

Andreas and Helga bought their tickets from the bald man and filed into the dimly-lit tent with a couple dozen others. The place was pretty much as Andreas had expected. The floor was just a layer of canvas, the seats were cheap plastic items, and the stage where the show would take place was a crude platform. At the center of the stage was a rectangular item covered in a white cloth.

"That must be the cage," whispered Helga.

Andreas stopped when they were halfway down the tent, but Helga urged him on.

"Let's sit near the front!" she said. "Then we might be able to see how they do the trick."

Reluctantly he complied, so that when the tent flap was closed and the show began they were the only people right at the front. The bald Englishman in the uniform climbed onto the stage, and Andreas noticed he was limping. He felt a sudden sympathy for the showman, perhaps forced to carry on earning a meager living this way despite failing health.

"Ladies and gentlemen," said the bald man. "Again, I must emphasize that this is not a show for the faint of heart, or the easily offended. What you are about to see is a mystery that dates back to the very dawn of time. A transformation so bizarre, so shocking, that onlookers have been known to faint!"

"Get on with it!" shouted a young man at the back of the tent. There was a general murmur of agreement.

The bald man looked as if he might continue, but then thought better of it. He took a step back, and made a sweeping gesture. The cloth covering the cage lifted with a whir of a pulley, and the cage was revealed. There were a few gasps, and then a wolf-whistle.

Lilith the Seductress was lying on a heap of shiny purple blankets in the middle of the cage. Golden manacles bound her ankles and wrists, but there was nothing slavish about the woman's demeanor. She gazed out at the crowd with extraordinarily forceful dark eyes. She looked straight at Andreas and smiled, and for the first time since his school days, he blushed and looked down.

"Wow," he mumbled. "It's just as tacky and inappropriate as you said."

"Yes," replied Helga, quietly. "But isn't she beautiful?"

Andreas looked round and saw his girlfriend staring, mouth half open, at the woman in the cage. For a second, he wondered if Helga was joking. Then the bald man started talking again.

"Ladies and gentlemen," he announced. "You see before you an immortal being, a goddess who was old when mighty Babylon was young; the serpent who tempted Adam in Eden."

"Lucky old Adam!" shouted the man who had heckled before. But this time the laughter was subdued.

She really has cast a kind of spell, thought Andreas, still looking at Helga's wide-eyed expression. *This is very strange.*

"Now," went on the bald man, "prepare yourselves for the most baffling and horrifying of transformations. For as we know, Adam was tempted by the serpent. But, as that young man just remarked, can you blame him when the serpent was Lilith the Seductress? In a moment, the cage will be covered again for just a few seconds. In that time, Lilith, using her occult powers, will transform into a creature of your worst nightmares, or perhaps your wildest dreams. Prepare yourselves!"

With another gesture, the showman brought the cloth down, and at the same time, a bright light came on behind the cage. This gave the audience a distorted view of Lilith's silhouette as the woman stood up. She began to perform a kind of dance to piped music that sounded vaguely Egyptian. Just as the audience started to become restless again, the silhouette fell to the floor and all the lights went out. A heartbeat later, the cloth lifted, a dim green glow illuminated the stage, and the audience leaned forward to peer into the cage.

At first, Andreas thought nothing had changed. There Lilith lay, still skimpily attired and staring boldly out at the crowd. But then Andreas noticed that her lower half was covered by the blankets, which were moving. Slowly what looked like a tentacle emerged from the heap of cloth. It was a dark, tapered cylinder that seemed to have a scaly surface. It moved back and forth, as if searching blindly, then slid out through the bars at the front of the cage.

Is that it? A fake tail? Some lame animatronic piece of crap?

Andreas felt disappointment, tinged with irritation at being conned out of three Euros for such an obvious trick. He felt tempted to simply get up and walk out. Then Lilith laughed, a throaty chuckle. She was looking straight at him, licking her lips. The tail began to weave its way towards him, more emerging from the blankets until the base of the appendage was over a foot thick. It was nearly six feet long.

"Oh my God," said a woman's voice behind Andreas.

"Ladies and gentlemen," said the bald man, "please do not move or make any loud noises. I cannot be held accountable for what may happen if Lilith becomes too excited."

The pointed tip of the golden-brown tail stopped an arm's length in front of the young couple. Again, it seemed to hesitate, swaying back and forth between Andreas and Helga. Then it darted forward and tapped Andreas on the nose. He gave a yell and jerked his head back, and there was a ripple of laughter and some applause at that.

Andreas reached out and took hold of the tail, expecting to feel plastic or foam rubber, and some kind of metal armature inside. Instead, what his fingers closed upon was warm and felt very much like scaly flesh. Again, the tail moved with lightning fast speed, pulling itself free of his grip, then darting back to wrap itself around his arm.

My God, it feels just like real muscle, he thought, confused. The tail began to tug gently but firmly, and Andreas got up and began to walk towards the stage. Lilith's eyes seemed to bore into his soul, and he began to feel slightly disoriented by her intense stare.

Can't look away, he thought. *Should look away.*

Andreas became aware of a perfume, patchouli, that masked a different odor, a smell like the reptile house at the zoo. Lilith opened her mouth to reveal fangs that, now that he could see them up close, did not seem at all fake to Andreas. Then Lilith reached out her arms and drew him up to the bars of her cage. He felt the muscular tail release his arm, then coil itself more strongly around his torso. Lilith's eyes were immense now, filling his entire world. Somehow, they had changed from deep brown to a fiery yellow.

Must be contact lenses, he thought. *Just another simple trick.*

He felt cool, soft lips pressed against his, felt a tongue flicker into his mouth. Then the questing lips moved down to his neck. Andreas heard a scream. It sounded like Helga.

***

"And all this is off the record?" asked Denny for the third or fourth time.

"For now," said Marcus, patiently. "Remember, I'm only involved in this because Brad asked me to help rescue his daughter."

"But if we save her, I can write a book, cash in big time?" demanded Denny.

"I don't care if you put in a book, or on a T-shirt, or project it onto the side of Buckingham Palace," said Brad. "If Kelly's safe, you get to say anything that isn't outright slanderous."

"Fine," said the journalist. "I'll carry on digging; see if I can find a trace of Ouroboros on the continent."

"They're unlikely to use that name publicly any more," Marcus pointed out. "Most likely, they'll pose as British tourists seeing the sights."

"Maybe," said Denny, but she looked dubious.

"What is it?" asked Brad. "You think they won't lie low?"

The journalist looked around the pub, then asked quietly, "I count about fifty customers. How many criminals are there in this pub at the moment? How many hookers? How many drug dealers? How many people in here, right now, could supply you with a handgun, no questions asked? Or at least have contacts that could?"

She leaned back and used her normal speaking voice again.

"My point is that lying low doesn't mean avoiding people. It can mean the opposite. And what you told me about the disaster at Wychmere gives me pause for thought."

"Go on," urged Marcus.

"All organizations suffer setbacks, whether they're armies or political parties or businesses. Cults are much the same. And there's a standard response, which is to try and make up your losses by recruitment."

"That makes sense," admitted Brad. "But how would they go about recruiting people without giving themselves away? Especially in foreign countries where they'd be more conspicuous than in England?"

Denny shrugged.

"That I can't say. Perhaps they've discovered a way to hide in plain sight?"

***

"Behold, ladies and gentlemen, how Adam was seduced in Eden!" said the bald man. "The ancient drama is re-enacted for your amazement and delectation."

Helga jumped to her feet and ran forward. She had been fascinated by the snake-woman, forgetting all her reservations. But now something was very wrong. The scaly body wrapped around her boyfriend felt all too real to the touch as she tried in vain to yank the coils away.

"Let him go!" she shouted, beating with her fists against the serpentine body. She knew that it must be fake, but part of her was still terrified.

"No need to be afraid, little sister," said Lilith, speaking in English. The beautiful woman smiled and let go of Andreas with her arms. He flopped backwards, only the coiled tail holding him upright.

"It's a stunt, those two clowns are obviously in on the act," said a man's voice from behind Helga. But he sounded uncertain.

"Do not be alarmed," shouted the showman, "the kiss of the timeless seductress often renders her victim unconscious with pagan ecstasy."

The tail unwound itself from Andreas and he fell backwards. At the same moment, the cloth descended over the cage, and the scaly tail withdrew coyly under it. Helga struggled to help her boyfriend back to their seats. Then, seemingly out of nowhere, a young woman appeared, smiling anxiously.

"Help me take him backstage," said the woman. She too spoke English, though with an American accent. "You understand?"

Helga nodded, and between them, they steered the stumbling Andreas around to the back of the stage and through a flap in the tent. The young woman guided Helga to a trailer, and inside they laid the semi-conscious young man on a bunk.

"It sometimes gets them like this," said the American. "It's kind of overpowering."

"What has happened to him?" asked Helga, finding the English words. "Should we find a doctor?"

"No, he'll be fine!" insisted the American. "He'll come to in a while. It's just that Cleo can be a bit intense."

"Cleo?" Helga was puzzled for a moment, then understood that she meant the woman in the cage. "How is that trick done?"

"Now that would be telling," said the bald man, stepping up into the trailer. "Is he all right, Kelly?"

"Yes," replied the American girl. "She overdid it, as usual."

"Overdid it?" demanded Helga. "I do not know this word, please?"

In German, the man said quickly, "Your boyfriend has fainted, but will soon come round."

Then he said something to Kelly too quickly for Helga to follow, but he sounded unhappy. Kelly replied and Helga heard the phrase 'guess she knows what she's doing.' Helga loosened Andreas' shirt, and noticed a couple of small marks at the base of his neck. They looked like mosquito bites, but she was sure they had not been there earlier that evening. Leaning closer, she touched the marks, and Andreas moaned.

"How's he doing?" said a husky voice in heavily-accented German.

Cleo stood over them, wrapped in a long dressing gown. Helga looked down to see a pair of shapely brown feet in sandals. She had half-expected the huge, muscular tail.

I'm going a bit crazy, she thought. *All that's happened is that Andreas fainted in that stuffy tent.*

"He is fine," Helga replied to Cleo. "All he needs is some fresh air. I will take him home now."

"No, don't go," said Cleo, putting a slender hand on Helga's shoulder. Behind the tall woman, Helga saw the bald Englishman and the American girl leave the trailer, closing the door behind them.

"We would like to leave now," said Helga, trying to sound firm.

"Just when we were getting acquainted?" replied Cleo, this time in English. "We've been looking for the right people, and now two come along on the same day."

Helga tried to stand up, but the tall woman held her down effortlessly.

"No," said Cleo, "this was meant to be."

There was a click from the direction of the door, and Helga realized that they were locked in.

"Don't be afraid," soothed Cleo. "For this young man, the change is very minor. For you, it will be far greater. You will become one of the chosen. You will shed your skin, grow stronger, and live on for centuries to see the new world arise. You will be like me."

"What do you mean?" cried Helga, now unable to conceal her fear and confusion. "I just want to leave!"

Cleo's smooth golden skin began to ripple and roughen. Scales formed as her jaw began to lengthen. The dressing gown fell away and the woman fell to the floor. Helga's mind struggled to come to terms with a transformation that she had already seen, but believed to be a trick. Cleo's legs merged to form a writhing tail as her arms shrank and merged with a scaly, tubular body. The woman's head lengthened, flattened, became a bony wedge. Fangs protruded from lip-less jaws, eyes that had been brown turned yellow, their pupils narrowing to slits.

Helga jumped up and ran to the door, screaming for help and pummeling on the metal. She could hear the noises of the circus outside, human and mechanical, and realized that any sound she could make would be inaudible just a few feet away. But she had to try.

Muscular coils wrapped themselves around Helga's legs, easily pulled her off her feet. She flailed at the serpent-creature as it reared up above her. Then, as the huge eyes grew closer, Helga felt all her will-power vanish. Just before she felt two needle-sharp fangs pierce her body, she heard a voice that was now barely human repeat a promise.

"You will be like me."

***

"Wake up, Fabian! It's that mad priest again."

Fabian tried to roll over but Katrina kept shaking him, so he got up. Now that he was almost awake, he could hear a loud banging on the door of their little house.

"Christ, what time is it?" he asked.

"Nearly seven," Katrina replied. "Old people don't need much sleep, you know."

"Yes, but policemen do," said Fabian, pulling on his trousers.

By the time they let Father Jerzy in, the priest was almost hyperventilating with outrage.

"You cannot simply ignore it this time!" he gasped. "The vileness is there for the whole village to see!"

Trying not to sigh too loudly, Fabian pulled on his boots while Katrina attempted to placate the cleric. Then the policeman allowed himself to be dragged out into the street, where a remarkable sight awaited him.

"See?" said Father Jerzy, gesturing dramatically. "The forces of evil, at your very door!"

Fabian was genuinely taken aback. Goritza's tiny police station stood opposite his home. The front of the station was daubed with the same graffiti that had defaced the church. The German phrase 'Rette uns' was very apparent.

"Cheeky little bastards!" Fabian breathed, striding across the village street. "If

I catch them, they'll be scrubbing this off, don't you worry."

"Darling," said Katrina from behind him. "It's not just the station."

The tone of her voice made Fabian look around, and he saw that the front of his own house was covered in the strange graffiti. He turned slowly, his bleary eyes adjusting to the morning sunlight. Every house and every shop front in sight bore the same blood-red words. Locals were milling around, some in animated discussion. Angry voices were raised. Fabian realized it could get ugly if someone tried to find a scapegoat.

"I'll go and get my bullhorn," he told his wife. "And call headquarters, for what it's worth."

"I told you it was happening again," said the priest.

"What are you talking about?" asked Katrina.

"It was long before you outsiders came here," replied Father Jerzy. "Back when the Berlin Wall came down, and the Soviets collapsed. Then the whole country was suddenly full of foreigners trying to make easy money."

"I don't need a history lesson," began Fabian.

But the old man had already begun his story.

Chapter 3: Goritza, 1991

"Seen one of these before?" asked Steve Patton. He held out a device that looked like an army walkie-talkie.

Father Jerzy took the gadget, turned it over curiously, handed it back.

"We have radios in Poland," he said politely. "We are not living in the Stone Age."

Patton laughed, a loud guffaw that prompted echoes of mirth from his two sidekicks. Father Jerzy decided then that he did not like this Englishman with his big car, his yes-men, and his 'personal assistant' who looked like a tart.

"It's what they call a cell phone, Father," said Patton. "A telephone, but one that works by radio. Without wires! State of the art Motorola. With one of these you can call anywhere in the world, from anywhere."

"I could call His Holiness in Rome?" asked the priest, so impressed that he forgot to dislike the foreigner for a moment.

"Well, not at this moment," admitted Patton, looking less pleased with himself. "This one-horse town of yours has no coverage. But mark my words, the day of global communications is here!"

"Yes," said the priest, wearily. "But what has that got to do with the castle?"

Patton smiled, and leaned forward, as if confiding a great secret to an old friend. Jerzy's initial dislike hardened. The Englishman's attitude was exactly like that of the corrupt officials and black marketeers who had flourished under communism. The pretense of doing you a favor, letting you in on a good deal. When in fact the intention was to hustle you.

"The castle is a wonderful opportunity just waiting for the right investor!" breathed Patton. He clicked a finger and one of his dark-suited minions handed him a folder. Patton took out some photographs and spread them on Father Jerzy's kitchen table.

The photos showed the castle of Mista Venja from various angles. They were all in black and white, and not very clear. Father Jerzy looked more closely at one and saw a date. 1942.

"Nobody goes to the castle," he said, simply.

"Why?" asked Patton. "The place looks great! Like something out of a Hammer film mixed up with a touch of Disney."

"Locals are superstitious," said the priest. "They think it is an unlucky place. It is certainly dangerous. People have died. A few years ago, they tell me, some foolish young men went hunting in the forest between Goritza and the castle. They went on a dare, apparently, despite warnings. They did not come home, so a search party was sent out. Only one hunter was found, and he was raving mad."

Patton waved away the priest's words as if they were annoying insects and stood up.

"I haven't got time for folk stories, padre! That castle is a godsend to anyone with the resources to renovate it. A luxury hotel and conference center for the new, capitalist, democratic Poland."

"Don't the Poles get some say in this?" asked Father Jerzy.

But the foreigners were already leaving, and probably did not hear him.

***

"Sheesh, communist roads are as crappy as their cars," said Patton.

The Soviet-built limousine they had hired in Warsaw was stuck in the rutted track leading to the castle.

"Honey," said Natalie the PA, climbing out of the clumsy vehicle, "maybe we'd better find a farmer with a tractor to pull us out?"

"That could take hours," snorted Patton. "And they'll try and rip us off. No, we can walk to the castle from here, take a look, then go back to the village. There's a garage there."

Patton's two yes-men looked at one another, but neither objected. Instead, they set off after their boss who was already striding away.

"I can't walk that far in these heels!" objected Natalie.

"Then stay in the car," shouted Patton over his shoulder. "Keep the wolves at bay."

Natalie looked around at the dense forest that cut off the view in all directions.

"Wolves?" she said in a small voice, then climbed into the limousine and locked the doors.

Time passed. Midday shadows lengthened and all Natalie heard through the car's open window was the sound of birds, and what she hoped were small, cute, harmless animals. She wished she had brought a book. She cursed Steve, and vowed to dump him and find a decent man. One who had plenty of money, of course, but with a good heart.

What if they don't come back?

The thought wormed its way into her mind. She tried to ignore it, but it kept coming back. And it brought a friend.

What story was that priest trying to tell us? What's so scary about this castle?

With no details at all, Natalie began to imagine all kinds of terrors that might lurk nearby. She imagined a homicidal madman watching her from the trees, a horror movie figure with a meat cleaver, face concealed in a ski mask. It was impossible to tell if someone was creeping up to the car, keeping low until he got close, then smashing the window, and dragging her half out of the window by her hair.

Natalie resolved to never watch another horror movie, and wound up the window. The June shadows were so long now that it must be very late. For the first time it occurred to her that she might be stuck out in the woods in the dark.

She began to whimper a little.

***

The castle was everything Patton had imagined. In fact, it was more spectacular than in the old photos. A small picture could not convey the scale and majesty of the high stone towers, the walls, the huge gate complete with portcullis. The whole thing might have been devised by a set designer for some Hollywood epic.

But there were obvious problems.

"Look at all that vegetation!" he said. "Nobody has cut back these trees for years, and that ivy on the walls is going to be a nightmare. It's blocking all of the windows!"

Patton's aides, Phil and Dave, agreed. They always did. It was why he hired them. Patton was a man so sure of his own opinions that he never bothered asking people for theirs. What he depended on was loyalty, plus accurate information. In this case, Patton had obtained the loyalty of a well-bribed Polish official who had told him of the one major castle in the country that was intact, uninhabited, and in legal limbo.

"Look at this, boss," said Phil, pointing to a square object almost hidden by tall weeds. Phil and Dave beat away some of the foliage to reveal something like a jeep. It was certainly a military vehicle, judging by the faded green paintwork and the Russian lettering on the side. For good measure, there was a big red star on the hood.

"Seems like the Russkies left a lot of their stuff behind," said Patton, leaning into the vehicle. A bird flew out, almost hitting him in the face.

"Reckon that's been there a long time, boss," said Phil. "Didn't they say this place had been empty since the Sixties?"

"That would explain the state of the road," agreed Dave. "But why would they leave it abandoned for so long?"

"Weird," said Phil. "Look, the tires on that thing, must have just rotted away. You'd think someone would have stolen them."

Patton felt irritated, as he always did when his yes-men started to think for themselves.

"That's enough chatter, boys," he declared. "Let's try and get inside, take a look-see at my new acquisition."

The three made their way up the overgrown road to the main gate, which was almost blocked by a big, rusted truck. Again, it was obvious that the thing had been abandoned in a hurry. They had to climb around it, getting dirt and rust on their expensive suits. Patton was sweaty and irritable when they finally got inside the courtyard.

"This place doesn't feel safe," said Phil, staring up at rows of blank windows.

"Don't be a wimp," said Patton. "I don't hold with that 'health and safety' nonsense. A bit of common sense is all you need to stay safe."

"I didn't mean it in that way," said Phil, hurrying to keep up with his boss. "I mean it's not right."

"Not right?" snorted Patton. "What are you, a little girl?"

"You'd think there'd be birds," said Dave, looking around the courtyard walls.

"Birds?" demanded his boss. "What, you mean an aviary?"

"He's right, boss," said Phil. "We're in an abandoned building in the middle of a forest. It's summer. Why are no birds singing?"

After a brief pause, Patton swore and ordered them to follow him to the inner doorway. Reluctantly, they obeyed.

***

"Father, you must stop them!"

The priest looked from one face to the other, puzzled by the anxiety among his flock. He had only arrived in Goritza three years ago, taking over from a long-lived and popular priest. He still did not fully understand these rural folk. Now they mobbed him at the very door of his church.

I should be flattered that they look to me for leadership, he thought. *But I'm not.*

"Why do you care what happens to greedy foreigners?" he asked. "I told them it was dangerous to go to the castle. They went. Whatever happens next is on them, yes?"

A chorus of protest arose, and then an old farmer stepped forward. The priest could tell from the man's expression that he was a reluctant spokesman for the villagers.

"You don't understand, Father," said the gray-bearded peasant. "That which dwells in that place must not be fed!"

"Fed?" Father Jerzy sensed some rural superstition above and beyond all the talk of ghosts. "What is this nonsense? Are you talking about a dragon or a werewolf?"

"All we know, Father," the farmer replied, "is that the Fortress of Ghosts has a terrible beast at its heart. That is why nobody goes there."

"What kind of beast, good people?" asked Jerzy. Nobody seemed willing to reply, or look him in the eye.

I should be denouncing superstition, he thought. *But I can't, these people are so fearful. I must work with them, somehow.*

"If you do not tell me, I cannot do anything," he said firmly.

"The beast has need of souls," said the old farmer. "The godless Russians raised the beast that slept for centuries. It sleeps more lightly, now. Go too near and it stirs."

The crowd nodded and muttered approval. The priest held up his hands.

"Very well, good people," he said. "I will go and try to bring the foreign idiots back. Which of you men will come with me?"

Again, nobody would look him in the eye.

***

Inside the castle was a mess. Dave and Phil stayed very quiet as Patton picked his way through broken furniture, old papers, piled of tinned rations. The fabric of the castle seemed solid enough, but the interior was grim. It would cost millions to bring it up to basic standards. To turn it into a luxury hotel would take much more.

"Why the hell did they just run away?" asked Patton, as they worked their way along an echoing corridor. "They left all their garbage behind. I thought it would be run down, maybe a little damp. But this is a junkyard."

Phil, who was right behind them, thought, *Why didn't you find this out before we came, you jerk?*

"Time's getting on, boss," said Dave tentatively. "Maybe we should think about getting back?"

Patton carried on looking into rooms, and Dave did not labor the point. Eventually, they reached an atrium that had two staircases. One led up, the other down.

"Okay, split up," said Patton, "you come upstairs with me, Dave, Phil take a quick look in the cellar."

While the other men climbed the stone staircase, Phil stood looking down into the darkness below. He had no flashlight. But he also knew he would have no job if he did not at least make some pretense of exploring the cellar. He began to pick his way carefully down the stairs, hoping that some vestige of natural light from above would let him see any hazards.

Phil reached the floor of the cellar without any problems, and stood for while to let his eyes adjust to the light. Dark blurs gradually formed into machinery, control panels, desks and chairs. Then Phil noticed that there were people standing back in the shadows, all around the walls. He tried to back up and tripped on the bottom stair, fell hard on his ass. Before he could get up, the figures emerged from the shadows. Some wore ragged white coats, others were in what remained of combat fatigues. As they got closer he saw that the flesh of their faces, like their garments, was rotten and in rags.

"No!" he shouted, holding up an arm to ward off clutching hands. It did no good. The ghosts took hold of him, and their touch was cold as ice on a midwinter night. They dragged him upright, and began to half-carry him towards the far end of the chamber. He heard whispers, snatches of words in a language he could not understand.

In his terror, Phil took a few moments to realize that the darkness had diminished a little. There was a faint, blue glow emanating from a dull metal cylinder. He saw a flash of movement inside, heard a faint hiss that might have been breath emitted from human lungs.

"Phil? Was that you yelling? What are you playing at?"

Patton's voice echoed in the distance, far too remote to offer hope of rescue. As the dead men lifted him up towards the hatch in the cylinder, one small consolation flickered briefly amid the terror. His arrogant boss would almost certainly be next in line.

***

Natalie began to panic in earnest when she heard, or thought she heard, a scream in the distance. She tried to tell herself it was some animal, cute or otherwise, but it had sounded all too human. After the distant sound had died away, she sat totally still for a minute, then made a decision.

"Sod it, I'm off," she said, climbing out of the limousine.

Natalie took off her designer shoes and began to pick her way along the muddy track, wincing as she stepped on sharp stones and rough branches. To try and quell her fear she imagined all the things she would say to Steve before dumping him. She had had plenty of other offers from nicer guys.

How did I end up in a Polish forest ruining my stockings? I'm just too nice and trusting, she thought, *that's the problem.*

Righteous anger kept her going until she misjudged a tricky obstacle and fell to her knees. As she tried to clean the muck off her skirt, Natalie's sense of danger kicked in. Something had changed in the forest. What was it?

The birds, she realized. *The birds aren't singing anymore.*

Natalie stood up and resumed her barefoot walk, then realized that she had dropped her shoes. She had a moment of agonizing indecision, then turned to retrieve them. She was bending to pick them up when a quiet voice spoke her name.

"Who's that?" she shouted. "Is that you, Steve?"

"Natalie."

The owner of the voice must be in the trees, but she could not work out which direction it was coming from. But it must, logically, be one of the boys. Nobody else around here knew her name.

"Phil? If that's you, mate, stop mucking around!"

"Natalie, you are beautiful."

Again, the sibilant words might have come from anywhere. It was puzzling.

"Dave? Don't be a perv!" she shouted. "I'm going, right? If you want to play silly buggers out here in the dark, be my guest."

"Don't go, Natalie!"

There was a rustling in the dense foliage above her head. Too late, she realized where the voice was coming from. Natalie looked up to see a face, pale and hairless and staring with mad yellow eyes. She dropped her shoes again as the creature descended upon her.

***

Father Jerzy plodded up the forest track, glad that he had taken the time to put on his old hiking boots. The castle was only a few kilometers away, but it was tough going. He kept up a brisk pace, telling himself this was common sense. He had to get home by nightfall. After all, nobody walked on an unlit road at night, if they could help it. It was nothing to do with fear of this absurd 'beast.'

I can't let these people's folk stories get to me, he thought. *But I'm letting them get to me if I make a point of defying them. Paradox.*

The priest expected to find the Englishman's limousine stuck in a pothole somewhere along the road. With luck, they would all be covered in mud and bickering as they tried to free their car. But the first sign of the foreigners was not the vehicle, but two red shoes. Father Jerzy bent to examine the shoes, noting that they had been dropped in the middle of the road. There were small footprints in the mud leading up to the spot.

"Hello?" he shouted, standing up and looking around.

Whatever he thought of wealthy outsiders corrupting Poland, he wouldn't want anyone to be hurt. Perhaps the young woman had wandered off the track? If she was lost in the woods, he would demand that the villagers send out a search party, regardless of superstition.

It's damn quiet, he thought. *When did the birds stop singing?*

The stillness was broken by a sound in the undergrowth. It sounded to Jerzy like a large animal moving stealthily nearby. He thought of the wild boar sometimes found in remote areas, and wished he'd brought a shotgun. Some branches shook a few meters off the track, and he caught a glimpse of pale skin, auburn hair.

"Oh, my lord!"

The young woman writhed and squirmed her way out of the brush, arms by her sides, face down. She was covered in mud and grass stains, her hair caked with dirt. Her expensive clothes, what was left of them, were filthy. Jerzy felt a frisson of terror at the sight.

This is madness, he thought. *I must not be afraid of the poor creature.*

The woman looked up at him, and she was smiling.

"What happened to you, my child?" he said in English, trying to sound kind and confident.

The woman laughed.

"Can't you tell?" she asked. "I'm a snake now. A big, scary snake! Careful so I don't bite you."

And she hissed, then giggled.

Chapter 4: In Plain Sight

"Wriggling along like a snake?" asked Katrina, eyes wide.

"That's what I saw," insisted the priest. "She was quite mad, this foreigner. But at least she was alive. The others, those men, they were never found."

Fabian pointed to the graffiti defacing the village street.

"What the hell has some nonsense from a year ago got to do with this?"

"The Fortress of Ghosts is a place of evil," said Father Jerzy. "These messages are from the souls of the damned who are trapped there. Look more carefully! See, I will show you."

The priest led Fabian and Katrina halfway up the street to the small village store, whose shutters were now covered with words; German and Russian phrases. Fabian could see nothing unusual, apart from the graffiti itself. But then Katrina gave a gasp.

"What is it, darling?" asked Fabian.

Katrina pointed to the upper right corner of the shutter.

"See?" she asked. "The words are small, but I can make them out."

Fabian squinted in the early morning sunshine, and understood what she meant.

SAVE US

The words were written in English.

"The souls of those foreigners were taken by the beast," said the priest. "Ask anyone. That is what it does. To live, it must consume souls not mere bodies."

"How does that account for the madwoman wriggling in the mud?" objected Fabian.

"That I cannot explain." admitted Father Jerzy. "If there is an explanation, it lies in the castle. And I for one will not seek it out."

***

The day after their first meeting, Denny Pollard called to say she might have something more for Brad and Marcus. They arranged to meet at Marcus's place.

"It might be too good to be true," she said, taking a seat on the overstuffed couch. "But could this be your daughter's new home?"

"Circus of the Bizarre?" asked Brad. "You mean an actual, real-life circus? With clowns and stuff?"

Denny Pollard handed a tablet computer over to Brad. The screen contained the website of the circus, and Brad saw that it was an arty, somewhat surreal outfit. The front page of the site emphasized that there were no animal acts, 'apart from humans'. There were clips of jugglers, high-wire acts, even a human cannonball.

"I don't see anything that might involve Kelly," Brad pointed out.

"Check out the Sideshow page," said Denny. "Lilith the Seductress. Anybody you know?"

The various sideshows got less information than the Big Top acts, and the Lilith act was described with only a series of superlatives. No performer names were given. But there were a couple of small pictures, and one showed a man in a fancy coat trying to drum up business.

"Could that be Jonathan Clay?" asked Brad, handing the tablet to Marcus.

"Same build and general appearance," agreed the Englishman. "But isn't this taking the whole 'hide in plain sight thing' too far?"

Denny shrugged.

"It was the only possible lead on Ouroboros I could find," she said, taking out a small notebook. "But I did hear some other things. Have you ever heard of a medieval castle in southern Poland called Mista Venja? My pronunciation may be a bit off, here I wrote it down."

Neither of the men were familiar with the name.

"Why do you ask?" asked Marcus.

"Because there's a lot of internet chatter about it. Not on the regular web, but on darker sites. Requests for information, that sort of thing."

"I'm sorry," said Brad, "but I don't see how that's relevant."

Denny smiled, clearly enjoying a cat-and-mouse game.

"What if I told you that the name translates as 'the place of the serpent'? And that, during the Cold War, there was a Soviet psychic research facility there?"

"Oh, bloody hell," said Marcus. "That does change things."

"Thought you'd like it," said Denny.

"I wish I understood any of this," put in Brad. "The Soviets didn't worship Ouroboros, surely?"

"No, but something bad happened at this research station," explained Denny. "Officially the place never existed. But some declassified documents show that a team of scientists and a military guard unit vanished. Overnight. And instead of investigating, the Soviets simply put the castle off limits."

"I've often wondered about Cold War research into the paranormal," said Marcus. "But so much nonsense is out there, digging through it is a daunting task."

Brad felt out of his depth all of a sudden, and asked what kind of 'nonsense' they were talking about.

"For instance, KGB allegedly tried to create psychic assassins," said Denny. "Though how much of their research was founded on fraud and wishful thinking, I don't know. Take a look at this."

Brad watched a grainy YouTube video showing a woman sitting at a table. She was flanked by men in white coats, presumably Soviet scientists. The woman was staring at a small animal that was fastened down in the middle of the table.

"This is supposedly authentic footage of secret research," said Denny. "The woman is Nina Kulagina and the creature she's concentrating on is, I believe, a hamster."

"She's trying to kill it?" asked Brad, incredulous. "With her mind?"

"The official version is that she attempted to slow the little chap's heart rate," explained Denny. "Supposedly she could do it."

The video showed some kind of monitoring device. The needle wavered, then fell back towards zero.

"It's quite possible that the whole film is a fake," Denny continued, "or that Kulagina fooled the scientists. A good conjurer can trick scientists, who are really not very good at unmasking deceit."

"I find that hard to believe," objected Brad. "Besides, we can be damn sure that some paranormal forces are real."

"True," said Marcus, standing up and walking to the sideboard, "but that's all the more reason for being aware of charlatans. Let me show you something."

At the Englishman's invitation, Brad sat at the coffee table while Marcus took some small objects from a drawer.

"Take a look at these," he said, handing them to Brad, who puzzled over the props. They consisted of an ordinary wine cork with a needle in one end, and a piece of paper folded into a kind of shallow ridged cone or parasol, about an inch across.

"No sign of any trickery?" asked Marcus, taking the objects back.

"Nothing apparent, anyway," returned Brad.

Marcus sat down opposite his guest and put the wine cork in the middle of the coffee table. Then he balanced the paper parasol on the needle. Placing his hands about a foot apart, Marcus said, "Now, let me show you some telekinesis."

The Englishman leaned forward, eyes narrowed, his brow furrowed with concentration. His hands did not move. The parasol wobbled slightly, then began to turn, slowly at first, then it sped up so that for a few seconds it became a blur. The piece of paper stopped spinning and Marcus leaned back.

"Phew!" he said, smiling. "I must rest now, my psychic energy reserve is almost totally drained."

Brad looked closely at the 'experiment', then picked up the parasol, unfolded it. It was just a store receipt torn into a circle and folded. The wine cork and needle were equally unremarkable.

"Okay," said Brad. "I give up. How did you do it? A really fine thread, I'm guessing, though how you'd pull it I can't figure out."

Marcus shook his head.

"It's a trick that fooled reputable scientists for years," he said. "But I know that if I explain it, you'll say 'Aw, that's so simple!' as I'd cheated you at cards."

Brad laughed.

"So now I'm playing Watson to your Sherlock Holmes?" he asked.

"If only," said Marcus. "Unfortunately, my problem solving abilities aren't on that level."

"Let me try," said Denny. After a few moments she, too, had the little parasol spinning on the needle.

"God, now I feel really dumb," said Brad, with a rueful laugh. "Put me out of my misery, please!"

"She's blowing it," said Marcus. "A gentle jet of air out of the side of the mouth. It's that simple."

"Oh for Chrissake," said Brad. "How could I miss that?"

"Most people aren't good at spotting fakery," said Denny, "Which is why I've always taken claims of paranormal powers with a large pinch of salt. Maybe Lilith the Seductress is pure fake and the guy working with her isn't Clay."

"I sense a 'but' coming," said Marcus.

Denny picked up her tablet computer again, and touched the screen. The itinerary of Circus of the Bizarre appeared. It led eastward from Paris through the Netherlands to Berlin.

"Next stop, Poland," said Denny.

"Isn't that jumping to conclusions?" asked Marcus. "We may end up on a wild goose chase. Kelly and Clay could be in America, Russia, Japan, pretty much anywhere."

"Well, we can either go with the information we have," retorted Denny, "or just sit back and spectate. What do you think, Brad?"

Brad paused before replying, choosing his words carefully.

"I'm very keen on finding Kelly," he said, "but I'm not convinced she's in this circus. The only way to find out for sure is to take a look for myself."

"Very diplomatic," conceded Marcus. "I'm outvoted. Let's hope you're right and that Lilith the Seductress is just a cheap sideshow act. It does seem an odd sort of camouflage."

Denny shook her head.

"It's brilliant, I want to believe it, from a journalistic point of view," she said. "Think of the colorful circus background. Also, it must be a great way to recruit new converts, yeah? From what you've told me, cultists have some sort of amazing hypnotic power. So why not incorporate that into an act? Then nobody will suspect foul play."

"Twisted logic," said Brad, "but no stranger than what we've already seen."

After some discussion of practicalities, it was decided that the O-Team, as Denny insisted on calling the trio, would go to Poland as soon as possible. They would make their way to 'The Place of the Serpent' and investigate. This made Brad feel more positive about the situation for a few minutes. Then Denny said, "Of course, we'll need to set aside a day or two in Warsaw, to get the relevant permits."

As part of her investigation, the journalist insisted on interviewing Brad about Kelly's disappearance and his search for her. He was guarded about some aspects of his story so far, trying to play down the supernatural elements of the case. It was impossible not to talk about psychic experiences, though, and he had to admit that his dreams played a major part in the story so far. Marcus, too, was reticent, especially about Wychmere. But between them, they provided the journalist with hours of interview material, despite leaving out some of the more bizarre facts.

***

"How are you feeling? A little fuzzy? Headache, maybe?"

Andreas opened his eyes with difficulty. Jonathan Clay looked down with sympathy.

"It can feel like the world's worst hangover," he said. "Don't try to move, my friend."

"Helga!" Andreas shouted, trying to sit up. The young man's eyes rolled up into his head as he lost consciousness again. A few minutes later, he awoke a second time.

"This dizziness will pass," said Clay. "Eventually."

Andreas looked up at the Englishman, suddenly remembered him.

"The carnival sideshow man!" he said. "What are you doing here?"

"I live here," replied Clay. "You are in my trailer, heading across the border.

We'll be in Poland shortly."

"Poland?" moaned Andreas. "I can't be in Poland, I have to get to work!"

The young German made another attempt to sit up, and again failed, though this time, he remained conscious.

"You can't kidnap me," he protested. "My boss, my mother, friends, they'll report me missing. The police will put out some kind of alert."

"Yes," admitted Clay, "they probably will, but not for a day or two. And by that time, you won't want to be found, Andreas. That is the real change. You will cease to be a solitary individual, driven by purely selfish impulses, and become one with Ouroboros."

"What?" Andreas stared at Clay, incredulous. "Please let me go! You are talking like a crazy person."

Clay nodded, and gave a sad smile.

"Yes," said the Englishman, "I'm afraid I am, by any reasonable standard. Let me tell you how it came about. It all started when I was an archaeologist, excavating a stone circle in Ireland. I had become convinced that there was one unifying spiritual force in ancient religions and was seeking evidence to support my theory. I got a lot more than I bargained for."

Clay talked on, trying not to sound too much like the lecturer he had once been. At first, Andreas seemed incredulous, but gradually the German began to look worried.

Not surprising, thought Clay. *He thinks he's trapped in a trailer with a maniac who might be dangerous. When, in fact, the situation is far stranger than that.*

"I just wanted to make a better world," said Jonathan. "I thought that if we went back to the true, old religion, things would be better. After all, it would be perfectly natural."

"I don't understand," moaned Andreas. "This makes no sense!"

"I'm not surprised," said Clay, soothingly. "In my idealism, I forgot that Nature is cruel, heartless, and often destructive. All the natural beauty we enjoy is built on ruthless competition for survival. Why should the gods of Nature be any different? When by chance I woke one, I learned the truth. But it was too late. I was already a slave of the Old Ones."

"Please?" said Andreas. "Where is Helga?"

"She is quite safe," replied Clay. "But she is no longer the person you knew. You will find her changed."

"Changed how?" demanded Andreas.

"She will be a stronger, more powerful being," said Clay. "She has been touched by an ancient divinity, albeit at second hand. This has transformed her into a being, both inhuman and superhuman. An incarnation of a Nature goddess, if you will."

Clay watched realization dawn on the young man's face.

"No!" cried Andreas. "Have you turned her into a monster like that creature in the cage?"

"Perhaps. But one man's monster," Clay replied, "is another man's deity. Try to hold that thought."

***

Over two frenetic days, Brad, Marcus, and Denny, prepared for their expedition to Eastern Europe. Each had their own work commitments to try and square with their project on Ouroboros. In his dreams, Brad still encountered Kathy in the haunted castle, and tried his best to recall details when he awoke.

The night before their flight to Warsaw, Marcus and Brad sat drinking brandy in the former's apartment. Marcus agreed that the castle in Brad's nightmare was probably the Place of the Serpent, but was at a loss to explain the throng of ghosts.

"But I think," the Englishman added, "that we know what they want you to save them from. Another Old One must be there."

"How many of these things are there?" asked Brad.

"Arguably, there's only one," replied Marcus. "If I'm right about Ouroboros being a kind of *gestalt* entity, all individuals are linked. It's an imperfect analogy, but think of all the individual bees in a hive. We see furry little insects buzzing around flowers, but each bee is just one component of a greater whole that outlives them."

"And Kelly has been part of this entity for months, now," said Brad.

"Perhaps, but Kathy Hopkirk asserted her independence, turned against Ouroboros."

Brad thought of Kathy's death at Wychmere, her sad, pale face in his nightmare.

"Sorry," said Marcus. "Not a good example. But the more we learn, the better our chance of saving Kelly and stopping the cult from doing more damage."

"That's what I have to believe," agreed Brad. "And, for the record, I appreciate everything you've done for me, Marcus. You didn't have to stick your neck out. All I asked you for was information and advice."

"Oh, don't mention it," said the Englishman, coloring slightly. "Anyone would have done the same."

"Okay, no more embarrassing stuff," Brad laughed. "But I had to say it."

After a moment's hesitation, he asked.

"What do you think of Denny? Can she be trusted?"

"I think so," replied Marcus. "Why do you ask?"

"I guess I just don't trust reporters," admitted Brad. "I've spent nearly twenty years in the oil industry, and you get very wary of the media."

Marcus shrugged, poured out more brandy.

"She's young and ambitious," he said. "And, of course, a woman. And here we are, two middle-aged blokes discussing her possible failings. Over booze."

Brad grinned.

"Yeah, we are a couple of sexist stereotypes, I guess," he said. "It's just that very ambitious people make me nervous. And, sure, maybe some of that is sexism in her case. If Kelly were here now, she'd be giving me grief for it, that's for sure."

"Changing the subject," said Marcus, "I've been wondering about the logic of Ouroboros. What they might be trying to achieve."

"Power, isn't that it?" asked Brad.

Marcus explained that he thought something more complex was going on. He pointed out that the cult was trying to tap into sources of occult power via sacred sites and so-called 'ley lines.'

"So the castle of Mista Venja is like the stone circles in England, a focal point for this energy?" asked Brad.

"Yes," agreed Marcus, "but the Soviet experiments carried out over there might also be crucial. I've found very little detailed info about them. I'll tell you what I know."

"I've got a feeling this is going to be unpleasant," said Brad, gulping down the last of his drink.

"Yes," said Marcus. "Unit 774 was a nasty operation by all accounts. The scientist in charge, Zamyatin, believed in boosting psychic powers by artificial means. That meant drugs, and perhaps some kind of electrical brain stimulation."

Marcus paused to pour them both some more brandy, then continued in a somber voice.

"You probably know that, under the communist system, anyone who didn't conform was classed as a mental patient. Gay people, members of religious groups, and of course political dissidents were all subjected to terrible psychiatric abuse. Prisoners were mistreated so that they became mentally ill. Zamyatin tapped into that system, it seems, for his experimental subjects."

"Oh, God," said Brad, realization dawning. "This Zamyatin tortured political prisoners? Sent them crazy, or experimented on those who'd already been driven crazy?"

"Yes," said Marcus. "I'm afraid that is what happened, according to some declassified documents."

Brad sat back, trying to grasp the possible implications. Eventually he said, "They tried to boost psychic powers in mentally disturbed people? And this was all going on at a site where one of the Old Ones, an aspect of Ouroboros, was dormant?"

Marcus nodded.

"If Ouroboros somehow possessed a person so tormented and confused, the results would certainly not be pretty. And it would explain why Unit 774 became a dirty secret they had to hide."

The men sat in silence for a while. Brad thought of Kelly, traveling across Europe for a rendezvous with an ancient, inhuman power that might be tainted with very human madness.

"There's another aspect to this whole affair," said Marcus. "One we've never really examined, just taken for granted."

"What is it?" asked Brad. "There's so much weird stuff it's hard to keep track sometimes."

"Your dreams," replied Marcus. "This psychic link to Kelly that seems to kick in when you sleep. You told me it started when she joined Ouroboros, yes? It never happened before?"

"That's right," said Brad, frowning. "At first, I thought it was just worry, my subconscious trying to work it all out. But now, I know it's something more."

"That might explain why Kelly is so important to Clay," said the Englishman. "As far as we know, she's not been bitten, not actually incorporated into Ouroboros, and why she was deemed a suitable sacrifice at Wychmere. Your daughter has some exceptional power or gift. The dreams are one manifestation of it."

"You think they might want to sacrifice her to the being at Mista Venja?" asked Brad.

Marcus gave a shrug.

"Or they need her for some other purpose. All I can suggest is that you keep looking for clues in your nightmares."

***

"How do you feel?" asked Kelly. "Kinda woozy?"

Helga stared blankly at the American girl, struggling to find the right English words. She lay in near-darkness on a bunk in Cleo's trailer. Her vision and hearing were clear enough, yet her memory was fuzzy. Recent events blurred together. The circus; deciding to see the sideshow; Andreas fainting. She became aware of engine noise, felt a slight bump. She was in a moving vehicle.

"How did I get here?" she asked. "Where am I? My parents will worry."

Kelly shook her head.

"We're you're family now, Helga. This is your home, for the time being."

Struggling to make sense of Kelly's words, Helga sat up and swung her legs off the bunk. A momentary dizziness quickly passed, and she stood up. She felt fit and well. In fact, she could not remember feeling better. Helga took a deep breath, flexed her arms, and found herself smiling.

"They tell me it's quite a rush," said Kelly. "Maybe one day I'll find out for myself."

Helga looked more closely at the American girl. There was something odd about her face. It was as if Kelly was glowing in a color that had no name. Kelly's face and hands were brightest, but her entire body seemed to be radiating a strange, unearthly radiance.

"How are you doing that?" asked Helga, wondering if it was another sideshow trick.

"I'm not doing anything," replied Kelly. "Your senses have changed."

Kelly got up and walked over to a small refrigerator, and opened it. She took a tray of ice cubes from a freezer compartment and brought it over to Helga. Puzzled, Helga stared down at the tray. The cubes seemed to be darker than normal, as if they were absorbing light.

"You can see heat, now," explained Kelly. "Or the lack of it. It takes time to adjust, I think. That's why I closed the blinds, in case the sunlight dazzled you."

"What are you talking about?" asked Helga, plucking a cube from the tray. She held the ice up to her eye, saw a weird darkness at the core of the cube. Again, she struggled and failed to find a name for the color. "People can't see heat," she pointed out.

"No, they can't," admitted Kelly. "But you're not exactly a person anymore."

"What about Andreas?" asked Helga. She felt slightly ashamed of not having thought of her boyfriend sooner.

"He's fine, and not far away," Kelly reassured her. "But he's changed too. It won't be easy to adjust at first. Give it time."

"Changed?" asked Helga. "In what way?"

"I guess you could say that he's your slave now," said Kelly. "What with you being a goddess and all."

Helga felt the urge to laugh. But somehow, for all the apparent absurdity of Kelly's statement, no laughter would come.

Chapter 5: Borderlands

Brad's next dream of the castle was different. This time he went beyond the mirrored ballroom, through labyrinthine corridors, and down into a cellar. The chamber was almost a caricature of the mad scientist's laboratory. Dials flickered on machines that threw off electrical sparks. Tangled cables converged on a strange cylinder that looked something like an old-fashioned diving bell, or maybe a Soviet space capsule. White-coated scientists with clipboards studied readouts, worked controls.

This is Zamyatin's experiment, he thought. *This is where they unwittingly raised Ouroboros.*

Kathy Hopkirk appeared again, but he did not recognize her at first. She was wearing striped pajamas and her head had been shaved. She was dragged to the central cylinder by attendants in surgical smocks. The men held her down and a doctor administered an injection, straight into a vein in her neck. The young woman stopped struggling and was shoved into the cylinder, none too gently. Sensor pads were fixed to her body and hairless scalp. As the heavy steel door was closed on her, Kathy looked directly at Brad for the first time and said,

"Save us."

The experiment began with commands barked out in Russian, the rising whine of a generator. Brad felt a sense of foreboding as he moved closer to the cylinder. There was a circular porthole in the door. Inside, he saw a shaven-headed figure jerking and writhing, while bolts of energy played around the interior of the machine. The woman lunged forward, pressing her face against the porthole. The glass was fogged with moisture, smeared. But something had happened to the face.

Kathy had become Kelly. He cried out, tried to open the cylinder, but his hands pawed uselessly at the cold metal. Then, with the crazy jump-cut of a true nightmare, he was sitting by Kelly's bedside in their old house, the first one he had owned. His daughter was still shaven-headed and wired up with electrodes, but otherwise looked like her five-year-old self. Brad was reading to her from her favorite book, and had reached the part she liked best, the Mad Hatter's Tea Party.

"How do you know I'm mad?" said Alice.
"You must be," said the Cat, "or you wouldn't have come here."

"Mad means crazy, doesn't it Daddy?" asked Kelly. "Not angry."

"That's right, honey," he replied. "They're all crazy."

"And so are you," said Kelly. "Crazy as a loon. You just don't realize it yet."

Brad felt a presence behind him in the bedroom, but could not turn around to see who or what it was. He heard stealthy movement, and Kelly looked past him, eyes wide.

"It's tainted with madness, now, Dad," she said, and he saw she was a grown woman now. "It's mad in both senses, crazy and full of rage. Best keep away."

He woke up, then followed his usual routine, writing down as much as he could remember. Later, on the flight to Warsaw, he told Marcus about the nightmare.

"I still don't really understand this connection you have to Kelly," the Englishman admitted. "But the nightmare seems clear about one thing. The force that Clay and the others want to tap into was affected by the Soviet experiments. It might prove to be even more dangerous than the one we encountered at Wychmere."

"The cultists must know how risky it is, surely?" said Brad.

"One would assume so," agreed Marcus, "but perhaps they think the risk is worth taking. And, as we've seen, they do tend to be over-confident. It's their biggest weakness."

***

It took the people of Goritza most of the day to scrub the graffiti from their village. As they did so, they discussed whether the strange messages had been written in red paint, which was the majority's verdict, or blood. A vociferous minority, led by Father Jerzy, held out for blood. People were also divided over whether the incident was down to human vandalism or supernatural forces. One thing was generally agreed upon, however. That if it happened again, something should be done. People tended to look at Fabian when they expressed that opinion.

"They're worried," said Katrina, holding the ladder while her husband cleaned the facade of the police post. "And you missed a bit, just under the leaves. No, to the left."

"If it happens again," said Fabian, "I think we should just leave all the graffiti and make it a tourist attraction. No, seriously, there are crazy people out there who love this kind of crap. Americans, mostly. They would come here to investigate the paranormal and spend money, all good. We could sell baseball caps, mugs, hoodies."

"Don't be silly, darling," said Katrina. "You need to compromise. We're still relatively newcomers here."

Fabian was about to broach the subject of moving back to Krakow when he heard the police phone ring. Glad for a break, he climbed down and went to answer it. A few minutes later, he emerged, looking puzzled. When his wife asked who had called, he replied, "Someone asking for permission to visit the castle."

"That's quite a coincidence," said Katrina.

"I wish I could believe that," replied Fabian.

"What did you tell them?" she asked.

"I said they need a government permit, as the place is officially under state ownership," Fabian replied. "Let's hope they don't get one."

As he climbed back up the ladder to scrub away the last of the blood-red letters, Fabian looked over his shoulder towards the forest. The ancient trees stretched away far to the south, towards the Slovakian border. From this height, he could just make out the upper turrets of the castle.

I've never been there, he thought. *A few kilometers away, but it might as well be on the Moon for most of these people.*

"I should go," he said. The thought surprised him, yet made sense.

"What did you say, darling?" shouted Katrina.

"I should go to the castle," he said. "These people will never respect me if I give in to their superstitions."

Later, Katrina tried to dissuade him, but Fabian was adamant.

"North, west, east, I'm a police officer," he pointed out, "but south I have no jurisdiction. What if some smugglers or terrorists were using that castle? What a damn fool I would look if it came out that I was responsible for it but never went there. And that graffiti bullshit. Whoever is doing it, don't you think they want to keep people away from that place for some reason?"

Katrina gave up trying to talk him out of it. Instead, she demanded to go with him, and that started a new, and much longer, argument.

***

"Where are we going?" asked Helga. "Why have you done this to me?"

"That's different versions of the same question," said Cleo, reaching across the small table to take the German girl's hands in hers. "We are going south, to a sacred place. I changed you because you were the right kind of person. Only some can endure being transfigured by Ouroboros."

"Why won't you let me see Andreas?"

"All in good time," replied Cleo. "First, you need to grow into your new self. You can already see more clearly than any mere mortal can. Your physical strength is growing, too. Soon you'll feel other powers developing. It might be unpleasant, even painful. But in the end, it will be worth it."

Helga thought back to Cleo's transformation in the cage. Like the rest of the audience, she had believed it was a simple trick. She tried to imagine how it might happen in reality, but failed. Part of her still refused to believe that the woman sitting opposite her was in some sense inhuman.

It's some kind of trick, she thought. *They hypnotized me. Maybe drugged me. Such monstrous things don't really happen.*

"Will I ever be able to go home again?" asked Helga.

Cleo shook her head.

"None of us can go back," she said. "My home was not a good place, and I do not miss it. I was saved by the power of Ouroboros, like many others. I am sorry if you miss the good things in your old life, but it is in the past now. The future is bright for us. Cling to that thought."

Helga started sobbing, but felt no tears come.

"Why can't I cry?" she wailed.

"Tears are for lesser beings," said Cleo, as if it were obvious. "We never weep."

The trailer came to a halt, and the tall woman stood up.

"Another town, another show," she said. "It will take a while to get to the Place of the Serpent. But when we do, you'll better understand what we're trying to achieve."

Cleo left the trailer. Helga sat on her bunk whimpering in the dark. Then a thought struck her. She got up and tried the trailer door. It was locked.

But she said I'm stronger than I was before, she thought.

Helga gripped the door handle in both hands and yanked hard. There was a metallic snap and the door opened a fraction. Helga quickly found her shoes and jacket, dressed, and climbed down. Looking around she saw that the trailer was parked in a field near a highway. About a dozen circus wagons were parked all around, and carnies were working to erect a great marquee. A couple of passersby glanced at Helga, but showed no interest. Everyone seemed busy.

Trying to look calm and confident, Helga started to walk in a straight line past the group that was putting up the big tent. She heard people talking in English, German, French, and other languages she could not identify. There seemed nothing sinister about the circus folk, and she wondered if they were even aware of what Cleo and Clay were doing. For a moment, she toyed with the idea of asking the nearest sympathetic-looking person for help. But it seemed too risky.

I'll ask the police, she thought. *They'll have to help me.*

The field where the circus was setting up camp was surrounded by a wooden fence. Helga made her way to the nearest gate and strode out. Nobody challenged her, and she saw that they were on the outskirts of a large town. She began to walk along the verge of the highway.

'You can't leave us now, Helga.'

The voice seemed to come from directly behind her, but when she spun around there was nobody there.

'I can see through your eyes.'

It was Cleo's voice, but Helga realized it was insinuating itself into her mind, not speaking normally at all.

'Once made, the link cannot be severed.'

"No!" Helga shouted. "Get out of my head! This is just another trick!"

'No tricks, no lies, no deceit. You are us, and we are you. All are united in Ouroboros.'

Helga started to run towards the town, but rogue images started to appear in front of her eyes. A reptile head with glowing eyes, scaly bodies coiling in darkness, almost blotted out the pleasant summer's day. And there were feelings. She felt the inhuman impulses of cold-blooded creatures, including the urge to strike and kill warm-blooded prey. She fell awkwardly, sprawled by the roadside.

'Don't fight it, Helga. Who can reject the primal goddess? Cease to be one mortal being, and join the great whole.'

"No!" Helga shouted, covering her ears as if that could stop the voice in her head.

A terrible agony shot through her legs and arms. Through the teeming visions of reptiles, she saw the flesh of her hands changing, the fingers growing shorter as the skin turned green. Scales began to form. She felt her face grow distorted as fangs emerged from her upper jaw. A feeling of joy, of liberation, started to submerge her initial horror. She began to wriggle out of her clothes, felt a powerful urge to dart into the tall grass by the roadside.

Helga heard a vehicle draw up, felt its shadow fall across her. A door opened and she heard Cleo's voice.

"Quick, help me get her inside!"

Another voice she recognized as that of the bald man.

"It was reckless to push her so hard."

"We need her to be ready!" hissed Cleo.

Helga felt hands lift her new, strange body. She tried to speak, but found it impossible to form words with her new mouth.

***

The day after he made his resolution, Fabian got up early and put on his old hunting gear. After a moment's thought he strapped on his police-issue pistol, and made sure his two-way radio was fully charged.

"I need you to stay here," he explained to Katrina.

"Who am I going to call for help? That crazy priest?" Katrina asked.

"If anything happens you can call regional headquarters and they will send in a search team."

"Why risk it?" Katrina demanded. "You won't change people's minds. This is the sort of stubbornness that got you assigned here in the first place."

"We weren't going to talk about that," Fabian reminded her, lacing up his boots. Katrina followed him out into the street, still protesting, but then kissed him goodbye.

"I know it's just a stupid old castle," she said. "But please take care. I don't want to lose you because of some stupid accident."

"I'll be careful," he assured her.

It was still early and only a few villagers were around. A few greeted him as he set off out of town. Most just stared.

Yes, I'm going to challenge the forces of evil, he thought. *Because I'm a big city boy and I don't believe in ghosts.*

He was soon at the margins of the woodland and after a few minutes among the trees, he had lost sight of Goritza. The sun was now well above the horizon, and Fabian was glad of the shade provided by the ancient trees. He was less happy about the road, which was badly rutted. He had been wise not to bring his car.

Besides, he thought, I need the exercise. Katrina might like my love-handles, but a cop should be fit.

At first, he did not recognize the limousine as a car at all. The undergrowth had almost erased the road, and layers of leaf mold had covered the old, Russian limo. Fabian took a few minutes to examine the vehicle, recalling Father Jerzy's story about the foreigners who had vanished. There was no sign of any bodies, though.

Maybe they just dumped the car and left some other way, he thought. *Or maybe their bodies are up ahead.*

He carried on up the vague outline of a road. Just as he thought the track would vanish completely, it became slightly clearer. He was nearing the edge of the forest and remains of an old tarmac road were just perceptible. Then he saw the castle looming ahead, a huge structure of gray stone. He took out his radio and called Katrina. She was anxious, but relieved to hear he had made it unscathed.

Right, let's do this.

Emerging from the woods, Fabian stared up at the so-called Place of the Serpent. He had read a little of the castle's history, and knew it was steeped in blood. A fortress since ancient times, it had been besieged, sacked, captured, and recaptured many times. During World War 2, a German regiment had made a last stand against the Red Army, and dozens of troops had died on both sides as they fought through the stone corridors.

If ghosts are unquiet spirits, he thought, *this place would logically be full of them.*

Having arrived at the castle without incident, Fabian was unsure what to do next. It was one thing to claim a place was haunted and point to evidence. But how could he prove the castle was just an old building?

By looking around it, I guess. Then making it back home intact.

He set off to walk around the outside of the castle, but was soon stopped by dense bushes that grew right up against the walls. He checked out the entrance, but it too was blocked by vegetation and the rusting remains of an old truck.

Fabian took out his phone and filmed himself standing outside the main gate.

"Well, folks," he said, "as you can see, there's nobody here, living or dead. It's just me and the local wildlife."

Fabian swept the phone around to get a panoramic view of the scene. The video would look amateurish, of course. But after he went home and showed it to the priest, none of the locals would be able to claim he had not been here. And that would break a taboo.

"Nobody goes to the castle!" he said, derisively. "What century are we living in?"

He sat down on a fallen tree trunk and replayed the video, noting that it had the shakiness of authenticity. The camera swept away from his face to cover the forest.

There were men among the trees.

Fabian was so startled that he looked up, expecting to see the dark figures standing in front of him. There was nobody there, just the rippling patterns of sunlight under the trees.

He looked down at his phone again. The video had stopped playing, so he started it again, fast-forwarded to the bit where he panned the camera round. There were no figures, just the view he had before him now. His mind, he concluded, was playing tricks.

Too much talk of ghosts, he thought. *No matter how skeptical you are, that sort of thing gets to you.*

The first gunshot was so loud that he almost fell off his improvised seat. The sound echoed off the high walls, and had just died away when a volley of gunfire followed it. The noise was coming from the woods right in front of him, not just shots but shouting, now. Men's voices. Fabian could not make out what they were saying, but he could tell they were excited and afraid. A ricochet screamed off the wall just a few feet behind him, passing over his head. He could still see nobody in the forest, but the sound of the bullet decided for him; *I can't just sit here and be shot at. Need to find cover!*

Fabian looked around for somewhere to hide. The scrubby vegetation might hide him, but it wouldn't stop a bullet. Crouching low, he scuttled towards the castle gateway. It would be a tight squeeze, but stonewalls would provide hard cover. Drawing his pistol, he began to squeeze between the stalled truck and the wall, forcing his way through overgrown weeds that raked his skin with brambles.

Behind him, the din of battle grew louder, closer.

***

The O-Team arrived at Warsaw airport to find a hire car awaiting them, plus two Polish people with their own transport.

"Are these the local guides?" said Marcus. "They've come a hell of a long way to meet us, then."

Denny looked slightly uncomfortable.

"Something you'd like to share?" asked Brad.

"To be honest," she said, "I couldn't find anyone from the area near the castle who was interested in helping. They really do think the place is cursed or something. The best I could do was find a couple who've spent a lot of time in the general area. They've done some blogging, been interviewed, that sort of thing. A Polish agency reporter I know said they're okay."

"Are they historians, or archaeologists?" asked Brad.

"Kind of," said Denny. "They're treasure hunters. After the end of the Cold War, there were lots of rumors about hidden Nazi gold, Soviet gold, just gold in general. The wilder regions of Poland have seen a lot of surreptitious digging."

Brad and Marcus exchanged a look.

"These guys know we're not after any kind of treasure?" asked Brad.

"Yes, I've told them the basic facts," insisted Denny. "Members of a weird cult, brainwashed daughter, going to this castle for unspecified reasons. I could see that last part didn't make much sense to them, but what could I do?"

"Well, let's meet them," said Marcus, with a heartiness that didn't mask his uncertainty. Pavel and Lenka presented an interesting contrast. He was tall, red-haired, and taciturn. She was small, dark, and talkative. They were dressed in outdoor gear and seemed competent enough. Their vehicle was an old, Russian military truck. Brad had seen plenty in the Middle East and knew it was a tough, reliable ride, if uncomfortable.

After introductions were made, they set off in convoy, with Pavel and Lenka leading the way while the rest followed in Denny's hire car. She dropped Brad and Marcus off at their hotel, then went on with the 'treasure hunters' to the Polish interior ministry.

"With luck, we might get the permits tomorrow," she said brightly before leaving.

"Or next week," observed Marcus, watching the little convoy drive away. "Bureaucratic time works differently to the normal kind."

"What do you think of the new guys?" asked Brad, as they carried their luggage into the hotel foyer.

"My granddad would have called them rough diamonds," said Marcus. "He was a colonial police officer in the last days of the Empire. Met a lot of people out to make their fortunes. Most of them were harmless, he said, if somewhat naive."

"I hope you're right," said Brad. "But I've met a lot of guys like them, in the oil business. And sometimes there's too much rough and not enough diamond."

They checked in and a couple of hours later held what Denny called 'a council of war' in her hotel room. Pavel spread out a map and proceeded to point out their route. It was clear that Mista Venja was well off the beaten track. The nearest village was a tiny dot, with a broken line indicating some kind of route to the castle. Marcus asked what kind of place Goritza was.

"Is very silly place, full of idiots," said the excitable Lenka, "ignorant bumpkins, as you English say!"

"We drive straight through that shithole," added Pavel. "Buy plenty of supplies in Krakow."

"Well, that's nice and clear," admitted Marcus.

"What about the castle itself?" asked Brad. "Is it accessible?"

The Poles exchanged a look.

"You've never actually been there, have you?" Brad demanded.

"No reason go there!" insisted Lenka. "Is old place, bits falling down. Road very bad, overgrown."

"Let's focus on the main issue," said Denny, after an awkward pause. "We want to get to the castle before Ouroboros. But we haven't settled on what we'll do if and when they arrive."

It was Brad's turn to fall silent for a moment. Then he said, "If they're going to try and conduct some kind of ritual, we have to stop them. It's that simple."

He could tell from the faces of his companions that none of them thought it was simple at all.

***

Fabian spent a few minutes in the castle courtyard, listening to the shots and yelling from outside. He saw no sign of movement, only the restless stirring of leaves in the breeze.

Phantom soldiers, he thought. *Fighting old battles over and over again.*

He pondered whether the ghosts could actually hurt him if he simply went out and boldly returned to Goritza. In theory, ghost bullets could do no harm to the living.

In theory.

Fabian took out his radio and tried to reach Katrina. Her signal came in weak, distorted, at times almost obscured by static. He guessed the thick stonewalls around him were causing the interference.

"I've arrived safely," he shouted. "Everything's fine."

No need to scare her, not because of a few noises.

Katrina's reply was almost lost amid crackles. He made out the phrase 'come back.'

"I'll be back before nightfall," he yelled, trying to sound optimistic. The static was even worse this time. Then a voice came through clearly, chillingly, for a split-second.

"Rette uns."

Fabian stared at the radio, trying to convince himself that it was a joke by someone listening in to his conversation. Then a burst of gunfire sounded very close to the gateway, and again he heard shots passing overhead. He retreated across the weed-grown courtyard and ran up a flight of stairs into an open doorway. Pressed against the wall he tried to contact Katrina again, but this time the radio produced nothing but the hiss of dead air.

If I can find another exit, maybe I can work my way back to the road.

Without a map, Fabian could stumble around for hours before finding another way out. Then he recalled something he had once been told about old-time fortresses. A drinking buddy in Krakow had told him that they often had tunnels and other concealed exits so that defenders could escape, or launch surprise raids on besiegers.

All fine in theory, he thought. *But where would they be?*

Looking around the entrance hall, he mentally crossed the staircase off his list. Going up made no sense. Trying to move stealthily, he checked two other doorways. Both led to unlit corridors. The final doorway led to a cellar. Holstering his sidearm, Fabian took out a flashlight and shone it down into the gloom.

Okay, a cellar might lead onto a tunnel, he reasoned. But it could well be blocked.

The sounds of battle outside were coming closer. It occurred to him that, if the ghosts were endlessly re-enacting the capture of the castle in World War Two, the Russian attackers would logically end up inside. Then he would find out if ghost bullets could hurt him. Or he could try and find an escape route inside an old and possibly dangerous building.

"Lesser of two evils," he muttered, as he began to pick his way down the litter-strewn staircase. The beam of his flashlight picked out papers, old wooden crates, and the looming shapes of what might be electrical equipment. A rustling noise made him hesitate. He thought of rats, then wondered if they were to be found where there were no people. Shrugging, he decided that any rodents would likely keep away from him. He made his way down to the cellar floor and swept the flashlight beam around more carefully.

The electrical machinery nearby was old, metal panels flecked with rust. Heavy-duty cables snaked across the floor. Lettering was in Cyrillic characters, and some crates bore a familiar red star. Fabian picked up a few sheets of paper from the floor. So far as he could make out, they were circuit diagrams, blueprints for some kind of device.

So, it was a Soviet facility of some kind, he thought. *I wonder what they were trying to do.*

Curiosity led him on. He weaved through the assorted debris to see where the cables converged. The flashlight beam played on a tarnished metal surface, curved, riveted. Fabian thought of an iron lung or some other old-time medical apparatus. But as he got closer, he realized that the steel cylinder was more like a space capsule.

This thing was built during the Space Race. Were they training astronauts?

The door was stuck, perhaps rusted shut. No matter how hard he pulled on the handle, it would not budge. Dismissing the puzzle of the experiment, for now, he moved past the cylinder and started to examine the far wall of the cellar. The area was cluttered with equipment. There was also a heap of old clothes. The clothes looked oddly out of place, as they consisted of a business suit and a pair of what had once been expensive loafers.

Fabian took a few steps closer, then stopped. The suit was still occupied. A corpse, wrinkled skin drawn tightly over bones, lay gazing up at him. It seemed to have been mummified. He moved gingerly to stand over the body, reached down to search for identification. There was a bulky gadget in the suit's inside pocket, which at first, Fabian thought was a military radio. Then he saw the trademark and realized it was a primitive cell phone.

The foreigners Father Jerzy talked about, he thought. *Or one of them, at least. Wonder what killed him.*

A screeching noise echoed around the cellar. It was the sound of metal protesting as a door that had been shut for a long time was wrenched open. Fabian was on the opposite side of the cylinder from the door. He drew his pistol and began to work his way around the cellar wall, trying to get a look at what was happening without going too close.

The door he had not been able to budge was now open, and still swaying slightly on its hinges. As Fabian sidled along, a thin form clad in pale rags emerged from the cylinder and fell to the floor.

My God, there was someone trapped in there!

Fabian's first instinct was to try and help. He had already started forward when it occurred to him that nobody could have survived in the castle for that long. No normal person, at least. The thin figure crawled on all fours from under the metal door toward him. It was hairless, and almost devoid of flesh. Huge, dark eyes looked up at him from a pale face. Fabian saw a terrible yearning in those eyes.

Yearning for what?

He did not want to find out. He darted sideways, trying to work around the crawling creature and get to the staircase. Then he heard the rattle of gunfire above, so loud that it must be inside the courtyard. Or perhaps even closer. Unable to retreat the way he had come, he went past the staircase as the crawling creature followed him. It was not moving fast, but he would soon run out of room.

Fabian raised his pistol, took aim at the pale, hairless head.

"Don't come any closer!" he warned.

The creature giggled, drool falling from its mouth. It reached out with a clawed hand and grabbed at his leg, then began to crawl up his body. Fabian fired once, twice. The shots were deafening in the stone cellar.

Chapter 6: Convergence

Denny managed to sort out their paperwork within twenty-four hours. During the same period, Brad used his shadier business contacts to obtain a gun. He told Marcus, but not Denny, that he had purchased a lightweight, semi-automatic pistol.

"I suppose it's a step down from high explosives," observed Marcus. "This is because you don't trust our treasure hunters, right?"

"Right," replied Brad. "They seem okay, but I'll bet they're packing too. I know you wouldn't carry a gun, and Denny trusts them, so that leaves me."

"We've no idea whether guns would be effective against those lamias, snake-beings, call them what you like," Marcus pointed out.

"True," said Brad. "But we don't know they'd be ineffective. And to be honest, I've carried guns in so many dangerous places that it would seem wrong to go unarmed now."

The next morning, the team met up outside the hotel. Denny had swapped her airport rental car for a SUV, and took the first turn at driving. As before, Pavel and Lenka led the way through the heart of Warsaw in their big ex-army truck. Soon they were heading out of the medieval city into pleasant countryside. Brad noticed small Catholic shrines by the roadside, small roofed structures with images of the Virgin Mary. Many were decorated with offerings of flowers.

"A very spiritual country," Brad remarked over his shoulder to Marcus. "Religion goes deep here."

"True," replied the Englishman, looking up from research materials scattered on the back seat. "The Catholic Church was a strong opponent of the communist regime. I did think of asking for their help, but they're not really keen on me. I've had a few disputes with them about certain issues. Exorcism, mostly."

Brad realized that there was a lot he did not know about Marcus Valentine. The amiable, bookish expert had devoted hundreds of hours to helping him search for Kelly. But Brad had been so wrapped up in his quest that he'd had no time for anything else. He didn't know if Marcus had any family, for instance. Brad resolved that, when they achieved their goal, he would get to know the man who had helped him the most.

Assuming, he could not help thinking, *we both get out of this alive.*

"I think there might be a separate feature in your cult-busting activities, Mister Valentine," said Denny. "If you're agreeable, that is."

"Let's not count our chickens," replied Marcus. "I'll happily give you my life story once I'm back in London, safe and sound."

"How's the research going?" asked Brad.

"Oh, wonderfully," said Marcus, his eyes lighting up with enthusiasm. "The fortress of Mista Venja seems to have been a lively place down the centuries. If by lively, one means 'drenched in blood.'"

"Well, doesn't that happen to castles a lot?" asked Denny. "They weren't built as tourist attractions."

"True," replied Marcus. "But Mista Venja seems to have been on the route of every army to cross Eastern Europe, from the time of Attila the Hun down to Stalin. Bloody sieges and battles took place there at least once a generation. It's been a fortified place since Roman times, at least. And some old archaeological surveys from the nineteenth-century suggest it was originally a sacred site for the ancient snake cult. Hence the name, Place of the Serpent. It was a bit like Wychmere, but it seems the original megalithic monument was destroyed to make way for the castle."

"But if the sacred site was erased," objected Brad, "wouldn't that tend to diminish whatever power was contained there?"

"Logical thinking," agreed Marcus. "But I have a theory. I think that the carnage, all that bloodshed, acted as a kind of sacrifice to the Old One that lies beneath."

Marcus waved a couple of sheets of printout.

"There are numerous stories of ghosts haunting battlefields," he said. "Gettysburg is the best known example, but there are many others. Now, suppose what we'll call the psychic energy of all those dead soldiers could be somehow exploited by the aspect of Ouroboros at Mista Venja?"

"You think regular slaughter kept some pagan god's battery charged?" exclaimed Denny. "Wow. That's such a good line to take. We'll definitely use that."

Brad thought about the idea for a while, then asked, "But there have been no battles there lately. Does that mean the being is dormant?"

"Again, a logical assumption," said Marcus. "Of course, we don't know how much energy it has left, or whether it has been able to tap into any more living energy in recent years."

"What does 'tap into' mean?" asked Denny. "Is it like a vampire or what? You said hypnosis is involved. Aren't vampires supposed to be able to enslave some mortals? Like James Mason in *Salem's Lot*?"

Marcus admitted he had no idea.

"The last time we encountered Ouroboros, it arose from dormancy thanks to an ancient ritual. But that was when the cult had dozens of members, lots of energy to draw upon."

The Englishman fell silent.

"You're thinking of Zamyatin's machine?" asked Brad.

"Yes," admitted Marcus. "After centuries of bloodshed priming the pump, so to speak, the archetypal mad scientist comes along and awakes the snake-deity."

"Put like that," said Denny, "it sounds like more of a movie pitch than a news feature."

*****

Katrina stood at the edge of the village, staring anxiously down the road to Mista Venja. She ignored the small gaggle of locals standing just out of earshot, gossiping about the crazy policeman and his equally crazy wife.

"My child, he should not have gone to that place."

She looked round to see Father Jerzy standing at her shoulder.

"He said he was all right," she pointed out. "He will be coming back shortly. He told me on the radio. You wait and see."

The priest shook his head.

"Nobody who has gone there has come back, not in my time. The thing that dwells there—"

The old man stopped, his mouth half-open, eyes wide. Katrina turned to look down the forest road again. A figure had emerged from the tree line. It was too far off to make out the face. But Katrina could see that it was wearing the same sort of clothes that Fabian had put on that morning.

"He's coming!" she screamed, and was about to run to meet her husband when the priest caught hold of her arm.

"No, wait, you can't be sure!" said Father Jerzy. "If he has been released, there is a reason."

"Because he's a sensible man, that's why!" Katrina shouted, struggling to break the old man's surprisingly strong grip. Freeing herself, she set off to meet Fabian.

Silly old fool, she thought as she ran. *Filling people's heads with superstitious nonsense. But that's the last time I let my man go off by himself like that.*

As she drew closer to the camouflaged figure, she had a moment of doubt. She had expected Fabian to shout, wave, perhaps even run to her. But he just kept plodding up the track, looking straight ahead, face expressionless. Then she was near enough to see his eyes, and his slightly crooked smile.

All's well, she told herself. *He's just a bit subdued. I wonder what happened.*

"Are you okay, honey?" she asked. "I was so worried when I couldn't reach you earlier!"

Fabian looked down at his wife, as if seeing a stranger for the first time. Then Katrina saw a dim light of recognition dawn in his eyes.

"Ah, yes," he said, tilting his head slightly. "I am sorry. I was inside the castle, where there is no radio signal."

"Inside? What did you see?" she asked.

Again, Fabian tilted his head.

"I saw nothing except empty rooms, rubbish, and rusted equipment. There is nothing there. It is just an old building."

The words should have been reassuring, but Katrina felt conflicted. She was pleased to have him back, but puzzled by the diffident way he was speaking.

"You must be tired after that walk," she said, starting to lead him back towards the village. "I've made lunch. Your favorite."

The small crowd of locals scattered as the couple approached, but Father Jerzy stood waiting. The priest was clutching a crucifix and mouthing inaudible words, presumably saying a prayer. As they passed him, the old man made the sign of the cross.

"See Father?" Katrina could not help saying, "A person can visit the castle and return. So much for your talk of ghosts and monsters."

She expected the priest to respond sharply. But instead, after a hard look at Fabian, he learned close to Katrina and said, "If you need my help, you know where I am."

During the exchange, Fabian seemed oblivious to the priest. Katrina began to wonder if her husband was in shock. She led him back to their house, chattering nervously, hoping he would become more talkative. But he only spoke when she asked a direct question, and each time with that odd tilt of the head.

It's almost as if, she thought, *he's listening to someone prompt him every time he has to reply.*

Katrina tried to rationalize the situation and decided that he must be ill. Perhaps he had caught a chill, despite the warm day. Fabian did not argue when she suggested that he take his boots off and lie down for a while.

"You can eat later," she said. "It will keep."

Fabian fell into a deep sleep almost immediately. She watched over him as he lay atop the covers. Then she noticed a red mark at the base of Fabian's neck. It looked like a bad insect bite. She reached down to move his collar to get a closer look. Suddenly Fabian's eyes opened and his hand reached up to grasp her wrist.

"It's nothing," he said. "Give it no mind."

Katrina retreated from the bedroom, wondering if she should call the doctor in the next village.

But what could I tell him? My husband went to the haunted castle and now he seems strange? That makes me sound like the crazy one.

***

"I think I can sense a victim, in the castle or very nearby," said Cleo. Still alive. A convert. The first she's made, perhaps. Interesting development."

Clay looked startled. He searched his own mind, trying to find some psychic trace of their quarry. But nothing presented itself.

"We didn't know the Insane One could do that!" he blurted out. "What other powers might she have?"

Cleo shrugged, looked over to the bunk where Kelly was tending to the being that had been Helga.

"Even if she recruits one or two locals we still have the advantage," Cleo declared. "In terms of numbers, knowledge, and of course in self-control."

That's a matter of opinion, thought Clay.

Cleo detected the skepticism immediately and said, "Ouroboros demands loyalty, Jonathan. She is greater than all of us, than all humanity. What we must do is unpleasant, but there's really no other way. The Insane One is a damaged vessel. Normally, we would simply leave her to her madness. But we need the secret she guards. At the very least, we can't risk anyone else getting it."

Clay passed a nervous hand over his face.

"The nearer we get, the more disruptive she becomes," he complained. "You can sense her now. She haunts my nightmares and Kelly's of course. Soon she will be whispering her madness into all our minds while we're awake."

"Some things must be endured for the greater good," said Cleo. "If we are to bring about a new age of Ouroboros, we need more power. And that power lies in Mista Venja, according to you, Jonathan."

The tall woman stood up.

"We need to tell the management we're leaving after the circus gets to Krakow," she said. "The cover won't be needed anyway. The only person that matters knows we're coming."

Reluctantly, Clay stood and followed her to the door of the trailer.

"What if Steiger and this Valentine person get there before us?" he asked. "According to Kelly her father knows about the castle."

Cleo smiled as she opened the door to admit the sounds of the circus folk striking camp.

"If they get there first, they might defeat the Insane One and save us the trouble," she said. "But I wouldn't bank on it."

***

The O-Team drove for six hours and reached the southern Polish city of Krakow in mid-afternoon. They stopped to eat, and Denny found an internet cafe where she and Marcus tried to track the circus. The web page for the traveling show suggested it was heading for Warsaw. Brad felt a momentary pang of doubt, wondering if they should turn back and confront the cultists.

"Websites don't necessarily give up to date information," Denny pointed out.

"Besides," Marcus added, "if we get to the castle first, we might be able to forestall whatever they're planning. Remember, at Wychmere it was last-minute improvisation. A lucky guess on your part. We might not be so lucky a second time."

Reluctantly, Brad agreed to stick to the original plan, as nebulous as it was. After they had eaten, they set off again. Brad took his turn at the wheel of the SUV, while Denny rode in the truck with Pavel and Lenka.

"Now we can speak freely," said Marcus, as they left the city, "perhaps I can put forward a few way-out ideas?"

"Fire away," replied Brad.

"I've been thinking about the ultimate aim of Ouroboros," Marcus continued. "Sometimes cults are just massive ego trips for their leaders, an opportunity for an elite to exploit the followers. But this clearly isn't the case. They do have an ultimate purpose."

"I've never doubted that," put in Brad. "The first dreams I had were apocalyptic, the world cracking open. They've changed, but I still get that feeling of some strange plan working itself out."

"Quite," said Marcus. "Ouroboros is idealistic in the worst sense of the term, quite prepared to sacrifice any number of lives to some supposedly noble aim. Their propaganda talked vaguely about abandoning modern materialism, bringing down the existing order. But how could they do that?"

Brad shrugged. Looking out at the traffic on the highway, the existing order seemed secure enough. But he had traveled widely enough to see how impermanent such order could be. Whatever plan for disruption Ouroboros might have, Brad did not want to see it given a chance to work.

***

"Strangers are coming," said Fabian, getting up from the kitchen table. "Foreigners. I must be ready to meet them."

He left his dinner half-finished, put on his uniform jacket, and left without another word. Katrina stared after her husband. Since he had returned from Mista Venja, he had been remote, as if sedated. Or hypnotized.

He has changed, she thought. *Something happened to him in that place. The priest was right. The graffiti was more than a prank.*

At first, she had meant to follow Fabian as he set off across the road to the village police station. Then she changed her mind and ran up the road to the church. Father Jerzy had never seemed warm or understanding to Katrina. But now, confronted by what seemed to be some kind of supernatural evil, she felt the need for a man of God to help make sense of things.

The priest was holding his evening Mass, and it seemed to Katrina that the entire village was there. Other people clearly felt the need for spiritual strength. She waited in line, took part in the ritual, then lingered while the priest dealt with the rest of the congregation. After Mass, Father Jerzy seemed to hesitate. Then, looking at Katrina, the old man broke routine and said, "Let us say prayer for all of those going through great tribulation."

After the service was over, Katrina pushed forward and asked to speak privately to the priest. He agreed at once, and looked as if he had been expecting the request. In his spartan residence by the church, Father Jerzy made Katrina strong, black coffee and listened to her troubles.

"In olden days," he said, when she had finished, "it would be said that our policeman has been possessed by an evil spirit."

"Yes," said Katrina, "it is as if something has drained away part of his character, so that he is no longer the man I married."

"Some demons prey on the soul, I have heard," mused Father Jerzy. "It is not fashionable to talk so plainly of evil beings in the modern church, however. My bishop would not approve."

"But you will try to help us?" pleaded Katrina.

The priest sighed.

"I will try. You say Fabian expects strangers to arrive? That may herald more evil. We must be prepared."

Father Jerzy studied Katrina for a moment.

"Will you do something for me? A test?"

She agreed, and the priest got up and took down a plain wooden box from a high shelf. Opening it, she saw that it was half-full of communion wafers.

"It is believed that evil beings cannot bear to be touched by anything that has been blessed," said the priest. "I am unsure of their efficacy, but take one. See if it has any effect."

Katrina looked at the white disc with its impression of a crucifix.

"What if it doesn't work?" she asked.

"Then we will try something else," said the old man, smiling for the first time. "Never despair, my child. If God is on our side, who can stand against us?"

Katrina still looked dubious. The priest patted her hand, stood up, and put a battered, leather-bound prayer book in his pocket.

"Come, I will go with you. You will not struggle with evil alone."

***

Helga lay on her bunk in the darkened trailer. Her heightened senses bombarded her with impressions of the world outside the vehicle. She could feel not only what kind of road it was traveling on, but also how heavy the traffic was.

It was obvious whether they were in the countryside or the town. The blaring of car horns, the noise of sirens, the roar of low-flying aircraft, all struck her like blows.

After Helga had been recaptured at the roadside, Kelly had explained that extreme sensitivity to sound and vibration was part of the transformation. Helga had at first taken some solace in the fact that she could close her eyes. But then, when she reverted to her human form, strange images had started to appear in her mind.

"Describe them to me," Kelly said, stroking Helga's brow. "It might help. I could interpret them."

Helga moaned in fear and discomfort.

"I see the world," she said. "It is like an egg, waiting to hatch out. There are cracks, great flaws in the crust of the planet."

"Yes," said Kelly. "That is a vision of Ouroboros."

"The world is breaking open!" exclaimed Helga.

She saw orange flame erupt from the cracks in the earth's surface, billowing smoke and dust thrown up to darken the air. The eruptions blotted out the green of the land, the blue of the oceans. From the roiling tumult of destruction, something began to emerge. It uncoiled, scales flashing in the sun, huge eyes opening, vast jaws agape. It was at once beautiful and terrifying, something utterly natural yet supernatural. Helga felt the mind of the leviathan, sensed an alien awareness that transcended all human concepts of right and wrong.

"The terrible serpent at the heart of the world!" moaned Helga. "It is waking up!"

"That is a prophetic vision," said Kelly, admiringly. "You're fortunate. Not everyone gets those. Not at first, anyhow."

The intensity of the vision was like a stabbing migraine behind Helga's tightly-shut eyelids. She would have done anything to banish the monstrous Ouroboros, to return to the normal life she led with her family, her friends, and Andreas. She gasped her boyfriend's name, yearning to hear his voice, feel the touch of his skin.

Suddenly, Andreas was there. She saw him, lying on a bunk like hers, with Jonathan Clay sitting by him. The Englishman was feeding Andreas some soup.

He looks so pale, so weak, Helga thought, and felt a surge of compassion.

"What are you doing?" asked Kelly, speaking more sharply than before.

Ignoring Kelly, Helga used her new-found power to move closer to Andreas, and tried to reach out for him with her mind. It was a strange, new sensation, and she was clumsy. But after a few moments, she felt a sensation like a static electric shock, mild but very clear. At the same time, Andreas, in her vision, gave a jerk. Clay's spoon was knocked aside, and soup fell onto Andreas's shirt.

"Helga?" said her boyfriend, clearly puzzled. He looked around as if someone else in his trailer had spoken.

"Stop that!" warned Kelly, grabbing her by the arm. "Come out of it, Helga, open your eyes!"

"Andreas!" cried Helga, trying to focus all her concentration on him. A link was developing, she was sure. She was sensing, albeit very tenuously, Andreas's feelings.

Oh, this is wonderful, she thought. *My love, I can share your mind!*

425

"Helga!" repeated Andreas, this time sounding amazed.

Then the sensations she was experiencing changed. There was a wave of confusion, then outright panic, quickly followed by revulsion, disgust, and fear. It was as if she had taken a drink of cool, clear water, only to find raw sewage at the bottom of the cup.

"Oh my God!" cried Andreas, putting his hands to his head. "Oh Christ, what is this? Foul, foul!"

Helga recoiled from the connection, feeling nausea. The mental image of Andreas vanished. She opened her eyes to see Kelly looking down at her.

"I'm told it's a real bad trip the first time," said the American girl. "Don't worry, it gets better, and a lot easier, according to Cleo."

"But why?" asked Helga, still trying to understand what had happened. "Why was it so horrible? That is not how I feel about Andreas! Or how he feels about me!"

Kelly stroked Helga's forehead again.

"The upside of becoming a lamia is that you have all these great mental and physical powers," she said. "The downside is you're not a human being anymore. And Andreas is still human. You can control him with your mind, but human love is beneath you now."

Helga covered her eyes with her hands, sobbing. As before, no tears came.

"How did you stand this?" she wailed. "How can anyone?"

Kelly gave a humorless laugh.

"Oh, I haven't changed at all," she said. "Sometimes I wish I had. But I have a higher purpose, and so I have to remain a mere human. Sometimes it's a downer."

"What is this higher purpose?" asked Helga, looking up at her companion.

"To become the first willing sacrifice to Ouroboros in three thousand years," said Kelly. "Without that, nothing else can happen. No new world can come into being. So I guess I'm kind of important. In an expendable way."

"I don't understand!" wailed Helga. Then her empty stomach growled. "Oh God, I'm so hungry. Can I have some soup, too?"

"Oh, honey," said Kelly. "You'll have to wait a while. Soup isn't going to get the job done, I'm afraid. We'll need to find you something a bit more ... lively."

Chapter 7: The Place of the Serpent

The O-Team's small convoy reached Goritza in the early evening.

"Not even a one *Starbucks* town," commented Brad, as they followed Pavel's truck down the narrow main street.

"Looks like Denny is going to present her credentials to the local law enforcement," said Marcus, as the truck pulled over next to a small police post.

"This could be fun," said Brad grimly. "I know we're in Europe, but I find provincial cops to be damn nuisances wherever you go. The lower the status, the more they want to throw their weight around."

"I suppose all we can do is keep our fingers crossed," said Marcus, as they pulled in behind the truck.

Denny, Pavel, and Lenka met a young, uniformed officer at the doorway to the police post. As Brad and Marcus got out to stretch their legs, they watched a conversation begin, with Denny trying to show the officer documents. He seemed reluctant to even look at the permits from the interior ministry in Warsaw. The situation was complicated by both Pavel and Lenka trying to translate back and forth. The result was a lot of jabbering in Polish and English, but no real sense of what the problem might be.

"Does not bode well," said Marcus. "Seems like you were right."

Brad was about to make another acerbic comment when two people appeared around the truck. One was an elderly Catholic priest, tall and thin, with sharp features. The other was a young woman who seemed upset, looking up at the priest for reassurance. The two stopped when they saw the group at the police station and conferred, then the woman walked over to Brad and Marcus.

"Good morning," she said, in heavily-accented English. "You go to the castle, yes?"

"Yes," said Marcus, surprised. "But we might have some trouble with the police officer."

"My husband," said the woman. "His name is Fabian. He is a good man. But something is wrong."

While Denny and the treasure hunters continued to argue with the officer, Katrina introduced herself, and Father Jerzy. The priest, who spoke no English, seemed dubious about the foreigners. He took her aside and spoke in low tones to Katrina.

"What's going on, do you think?" Brad asked Marcus.

"I've no idea," admitted the Englishman. "But I'll bet the Holy Father is not keen on us going to the castle."

"I thought we were just going to drive straight through this place," said Brad.

"I think Denny wants to do everything by the book," suggested Marcus. "Unlike our treasure hunters. She may regret her virtuous impulse, though."

The discussion over the paperwork had reached an apparent impasse, but then something odd happened. The police officer, who had been obdurately repeating the same phrase for a couple of minutes, suddenly fell silent. At the same time, he tilted his head as if listening to someone.

Like a dog hearing one of those ultrasonic whistles, thought Brad. *Weird.*

Then the officer took the papers from Denny, glanced at them, and spoke a few words in Polish. Lenka began gabbling excitedly, apparently thanking him, while Pavel simply turned and went back to his truck. Denny took back her permits from the cop and walked over to Brad and Marcus, looking bemused.

"Well, that was distinctly odd," she said. "One minute he was all for refusing us permission to go up the forest road, the next he's nice as pie. What does that suggest to you?"

"Mind-control," said Brad, without thinking.

"Ouroboros," concurred Marcus. "He has that slightly out-of-it expression."

Denny looked from one man to the other, then said, "So the mysterious creature lurking up at the castle has decided to let us in? Why?"

"Come into my parlor, said the spider to the fly," replied Marcus. "It isn't scared of us, and might well want to exploit us in some way."

Denny stared at Marcus.

"You could turn back," said Brad. "If it's just started to dawn on you that Ouroboros is real, and dangerous."

"No way," Denny exclaimed. "If this thing is half as powerful as you claim, it will make a brilliant story. Come on!"

She turned and walked over to the treasure hunters' truck, where Lenka was almost jumping up and down with impatience.

"Come, come!" she shouted over the noise as the big diesel engine coughed and roared into life. "We all go in truck; it can manage crappy country roads real good!"

Brad and Marcus climbed into the back of the truck and tried to make themselves comfortable amid a cargo of assorted equipment. As the truck rumbled out of Goritza, they looked back to see the priest and Katrina approaching Fabian. The old man held up a book, while the wife seemed to pleading with her husband.

"What do you think happened to him?" asked Brad.

"I think the being that lurks beneath Mista Venja got him," replied Marcus. "It's still active. But the fact that others in the village are free, suggests its power is not that great."

"Putting an optimistic spin on our situation," said Brad. "Thanks!"

"All part of the service," said Marcus, with a wry grin.

***

"Why did you let them go on?" demanded Father Jerzy.

Instead of replying, Fabian turned to go back inside the police post. Katrina rushed forward and grabbed her husband's arm.

"What happened, Fabian?" she pleaded. "Tell us and we can help you."

Fabian looked down at his wife, and tried to break free. But she clung to him with one hand while fumbling for the communion wafer with the other.

"Nothing is wrong, darling," said Fabian. "I merely had to confirm that they had the correct documents, that is all. Please let go, I have work to do."

Katrina pulled out the wafer and pressed it against the back of Fabian's hand. He jerked his arm away as if he had been stung. The wafer fell onto the road as Father Jerzy stepped forward and took Fabian by the wrist.

"See?" bellowed the priest. "It is as if he has been burned."

Katrina looked down to see a round, red mark on her husband's flesh. Now, for the first time since his return from the castle, Fabian's face took on a lively expression. It was one of amusement, bordering on contempt.

"Priest!" he sneered. "You are as big a fool as Zamyatin and his scientists, as deluded as those Russian soldiers. All liars, all fools, no good to me at all."

The voice emerging from Fabian's mouth was both his and not-his, to Katrina. It was shaped by her husband's mouth and larynx, but it sounded wrong. High-pitched and shrilled, it might have been that of a child on the verge of hysterics.

A child, or a woman.

"Fabian," said Katrina, "let us help you!"

"Leave me alone, you bitch!" spat the strange voice. "Or I will split you open and drink your soul!"

Fabian's eyes were bulging, his mouth flecked with spittle, as he tried to break free. Father Jerzy took out his prayer book and began chanting in Latin, making the sign of the cross as he did so.

"Stop your nonsense!" screeched Fabian. The policeman pressed his hands over his ears and staggered sideways, then sat down heavily. "I was a Christian, once, it did me no good! They tormented me, put me in a padded cell, stole my mind with their drugs and electric shocks!"

A mental patient, thought Katrina. *Can he be possessed by the spirit of some poor lunatic who died at the castle?*

Villagers were gathering to watch the extraordinary scene. Some were crossing themselves. Katrina ignored them, kneeling by her husband and trying to comfort him as he writhed and sobbed.

"I was the mad girl, then I was the immortal snake!" he shouted, his shrill voice almost drowning out the priest's prayers. "So many dead, all the blood seeping down onto me, so many thousand years of blood."

"Somebody, call the doctor!" shouted Katrina. "And help me get him inside!"

Two brothers, local farm laborers, came forward and they carried Fabian across the street into the house. All the while he talked what Katrina told herself must be nonsense.

Yet there is a kind of wild logic to it, she thought as the farmhands put the still wriggling Fabian onto the couch.

"Oh, when the great wars came I slept so lightly!" Fabian screeched. "So many souls to suck dry, yes! But it was that infernal machine that gave me life, the life of the starved and withered flesh, the life of the mind damaged and tormented!"

Suddenly Fabian's expression changed again, and Katrina found herself looking into the face of the man she loved. He was scared, and took her hand to pull her closer.

"Don't let them go!" he said. "She wants more souls, so she can live and grow! The serpent-goddess is insane, she can only destroy!"

Then Fabian let go of her and slumped back. The mad smile appeared again, and he chuckled. Then he hissed, running his tongue along his lips.

"Oh, I'll wrap them in my coils and gulp them down, and then digest them slowly!"

Father Jerzy took out a small bottle marked with a cross, opened it, and splashed a few drops on Fabian's face. Red marks appeared where the liquid struck, and the possessed man howled in protest, almost falling off the couch as he convulsed. The priest turned to the laborers, who stood gawping in the doorway.

"If you have the stomach for this, help us hold him down. This will take a long time, I fear."

***

"Are you getting anything from your father?" asked Clay. "Any idea of how far ahead of us he is?"

Kelly shook her head.

"I only connect with him when I sleep," she said. "We're together in dreams, though he probably sees them as nightmares. That's ironic, that when we're miles apart we're closer than we ever were before."

Clay did not speak for a while, keeping his eyes on a police car that was overtaking them. He was taking a shift driving their sole trailer. Now that they had left the circus, they'd removed the garish posters from the side of the vehicle. Their new cover was simply that of a group of tourists seeing the sights.

After the police car had passed, Clay asked, "How is Helga? Andreas is reacting badly to recruitment, I suspect he won't be much use against the Insane One."

"Helga is upset, but they always are," replied Kelly. "She seems strong in her powers, though, maybe because she's so young and smart. Has anyone ever changed so quickly?"

"Cleo did," replied Clay. "She obviously recognized the same potential in Helga. If only she hadn't decided to use Andreas to lure the girl in. That was unnecessary."

"But smart," Kelly pointed out. "Take one and the other would report it. Take them both and people will assume they've run off together."

Clay glanced sideways at the American girl.

"You take it all in your stride, don't you," he commented. "Nothing fazes you at all."

Kelly shrugged, checked her hair in the driving mirror.

"You stumbled into this," she said. "You were looking for truth, but you found more than you bargained for. I always felt something like this would happen. For as long as I can remember, I knew the world was all wrong. It didn't have to be this way, with pollution and famine and war. And when I found Ouroboros, or Ouroboros found me, I just knew this was the way I could make a difference. Change things forever."

Clay did not reply.

"Deep down, you can't believe we'll make a better world this way, can you?" she challenged. "Part of you is still the rational scientist, the objective seeker after facts. Even after all the things you've seen, all the things we've done."

They drove on in silence until they reached a medium-sized town where they parked in a retail district.

"What's Polish for pet store?" asked Kelly, unfastening her seat-belt and taking out her phone.

"No idea," admitted Clay. "I suppose you could Google it."

"I'll need your help when I find one," said Kelly, as she opened the passenger door. "And when we've bought the food, we'll still have to persuade Helga to eat. I don't think she'll be too keen."

"Maybe we should start her with mice," suggested Clay. "Then work up to white rats?"

***

Brad worked his way forward over the truck's cargo until he was looking through a slit into the driver's cab. He could make out the top of Lenka's head and the road ahead. From what he could see, the track through the forest was rutted, badly overgrown, and getting worse the farther they went from the village.

We're going to get stuck, he thought. *Pavel is putting too much faith in this old heap.*

Sure enough, after about ten minutes there was a particularly vicious bump followed by a metallic crunching sound and a clashing of gears. The truck started to rock forward and backward while the treasure hunters had a loud discussion in Polish. Eventually, Pavel turned off the engine and got out. The others followed suit, and were soon standing around the remains of a car. Pavel had tried to shove it aside but the old wreck had proved hard to shift. Examining the car more closely Brad saw it was entangled in vegetation, literally rooted to the spot.

"Pavel not drive round," said Lenka, gesticulating excitedly. "Truck gets stuck if go off road. We need carry gear to castle. Is not far!"

The Poles began unloading stuff from the back of the vehicle, and the others helped as best they could. There were backpacks for all, and plenty to put in them, including rations and camping gear. Brad noticed that Pavel's pack had a metal detector and a shovel strapped onto it.

"They still think they're going to find some kind of Nazi hoard?" he asked Denny quietly as they prepared for their march.

She nodded.

"My Polish is terrible, but I know the words for gold and hidden. You can't blame them, though. Buried treasure makes more sense than some obscure stuff about experiments and sacred sites. I've given up trying to explain all that and just said we're interested in the castle's history."

"True enough," put in Marcus, as he slung a backpack over his shoulders. "Well, this isn't the first time I've gone hiking in Europe."

"Let's go!" shouted Lenka, cheerfully. "We get there before dark, yes?"

"Yes!" replied Marcus.

I just hope these guys are philosophical about it when we find precisely zilch in the way of valuables, thought Brad as they set off. *Lenka seems nice enough, but Pavel seems like the kind of guy who could turn nasty if things don't go his way.*

Denny was frowning at her phone.

"No signal," she said. "I shouldn't be surprised, but I rely on this damn thing so much, whenever it fails it's like I've gone back in time. Or into some parallel universe."

"Both true, in a way," said Marcus, half to himself. "We're heading for a place

431

where the normal rules don't apply."

"Yeah, lets us three keep that in mind," added Brad, "even if those two don't get it."

"If only there was some way we could warn them of the real danger," said Marcus. "Okay, they may be greedy and foolish, but you see my point?"

"They'd never believe us," said Brad bluntly. "And if I were in their position, I'd never believe us either."

They trudged on for about twenty minutes, with the Polish couple pulling ahead until they were almost lost to view.

"Slow down, you guys!" shouted Denny, to no avail. "Christ, are they planning to lose us in the woods?"

"Gold fever, maybe," suggested Brad. "Some people just get obsessed with the striking it rich, it's all they live for. Anyway, we can't get lost so long as we follow what's left of this road."

"Amazing how quickly Nature erases things," mused Marcus as he stepped over a fallen bough. "A few decades and a road is half-gone. A few centuries and virtually anything we build will be destroyed if we don't strive to preserve it. And yet we think we achieve so much. Such is the vainglory of mankind."

"Less of the sexist language," said Denny, smiling. "How do you know womankind didn't make this road? There were plenty of strapping female comrades laying tarmac under communism."

"He's right about Nature being remorseless, though," said Brad. "Until Ouroboros, I thought Nature was blind, mindless, driven by forces science can't understand. That's how I was trained to think. Now I know Nature has some very clever allies."

"You really think Ouroboros is a force of Nature," said Marcus, "determined to stop Man, sorry Denny, humans from wrecking the planet?"

"It's as good an explanation as any," replied Brad. "Is it a coincidence that this has happened when we're doing more harm to the environment than ever before? When there are simply so many us, swarming everywhere like locusts?"

"Sounds like you sympathize with your daughter," said Denny. "Isn't that very like her point of view?

"It is," admitted Brad. "She's been saying it for a long time. I wish I'd talked to her more instead of dismissing all her fears. She was passionate about saving the whales, saving the rain-forests, stopping climate change. And I was so damn condescending, pointing out that the oil business put food on the table and paid her way through college."

"It's hardly your fault that she was recruited by a cult," pointed out Marcus. "As I said when we first met, they always target bright young people. The discontented idealist is easiest to con."

"But was she conned?" asked Brad. "Or did she just find exactly what she'd been looking for all along? I don't know for sure anymore."

"Hey, they've stopped!" exclaimed Denny.

Pavel and Lenka were standing still, looking up at a structure that was largely obscured by the dense foliage. As the three English-speakers drew nearer, they saw the castle gradually take shape.

"God, it's enormous," said Marcus. "We could spend days searching the place."

They were so close that Mista Venja was impossible to take in, as they could only see part of the fortress. A stonewall towered above the young trees that had struggled to grow in the castle's shadow. There were turrets and battlements, plus slit-like windows and a tall, square central tower. Most of the fortress was overgrown with creeping ivy, so that the castle looked as if it were part-organic.

"At least the gate is open," said Denny, in a low voice. "Though it seems to be blocked with junk."

A sharp snapping sound from behind made all of them turn around. There was nothing to be seen.

"Somebody stepping on a branch, maybe?" suggested Brad. "Maybe we were followed."

Pavel muttered something in Polish to Lenka, who moved closer to him.

The same sharp sound came again, and this time it seemed to be off to the right. Then a series of staccato cracking noises.

"That's a sub-machine gun!" said Brad. "Get under cover!"

Pavel and Lenka were already running toward the castle gateway. Brad was close behind, followed by Denny, with Marcus struggling to keep up. The Englishman had been flagging during the hike through the woods, but Brad had deliberately slowed to stay with him. Ahead of them, the Poles were taking off their backpacks to squeeze past a rusted truck blocking the castle entrance. Brad started to do the same, and as he loosened his straps, he heard Marcus give a shout of pain. He stopped and saw that the Englishman had fallen.

Dropping his pack Brad went back to help his friend, who was waving him away.

"Go on!" shouted Marcus, "I'll keep down and crawl."

Brad felt a sharp tug at his jacket. At the same time, the sound of a ricochet came from the wall behind him.

They've got eyes on us, he thought, dropping on all fours. *And firing from cover, they've got a big advantage.*

"Got me in the leg," said Marcus, worming his way towards Brad.

"Drop your pack," hissed Brad. "It's too conspicuous."

He helped Marcus get rid of the backpack, then checked for a wound.

"I can't see any blood," he said, puzzled. "Maybe it just grazed you."

Marcus grimaced.

"It felt like a direct hit, believe me!"

The sound of gunfire was accompanied by shouting, now. The language was harsh, guttural, single words or short phrases being rapped out. And the shouts were coming from several directions.

"That's German, isn't it?" Marcus asked. "What would German soldiers be doing here?"

Brad saw the realization dawn on the Englishman's face.

"Yeah," he said, "the last big battle in these parts. Seems like we're getting a replay."

They began to crawl towards the castle gate, Brad dragging the packs. He could see Denny crouching by the abandoned truck but the Poles were gone.

Off to seek their fortunes, I'll bet. Probably think a rival outfit is shooting 'em up.

Denny, to her credit, had a First Aid kit ready when they got to cover. But when they examined the spot where Marcus said he was hit, they could see nothing but a red circular mark, like a bad bruise.

"Hit by a ghost bullet," said Marcus. "I should take a picture for the family album. Unfortunately, it still hurts like hell. I think I'll be limping for a fortnight."

"You think those are ghosts out there?" asked Denny, peering out into the forest. "Pull the other one!"

"What happened to our native guides?" asked Brad.

"They went inside," said Denny. "And by the way, Pavel's got a gun."

"I knew it," said Brad. "Well, so have I. Though I can't imagine it'd be much good against a bunch of dead Germans." He and Marcus tried to explain that Mista Venja was a haunted place, but it was obvious that Denny was not convinced.

"Why rerun some old battle?" she asked. "What's the point?"

"Well, it ensured we'd come running in here," Marcus pointed out. "And it also split us up for good measure."

Chapter 8: The Castle

After what seemed like hours of writhing and shouting, Fabian lay in an uneasy sleep. Father Jerzy's voice was hoarse after reciting the old Latin ceremony of exorcism again and again. Katrina, herself almost exhausted, knelt by the couch, holding her husband's hand and wiping his brow with a damp cloth. The local doctor had arrived halfway through the prolonged ritual, pronounced it a case of severe mental illness, and left. The farmhand brothers had left, too, but unlike the doctor, they had offered to return if called for.

We're on our own, Katrina thought. *But we will get through this. Together we can defeat this evil. These villagers are good people. I'm sorry I sneered at them.*

Fabian started to mumble in his sleep, and Katrina leaned close to try and hear. He was speaking in more than one language. She heard Russian and German, but also occasional lucid phrases in clear Polish.

"The others are coming," he repeated. "They desire the secret in the citadel of madness, the power to break the world."

"Who are these others?" croaked the priest.

"Don't trouble him further!" protested Katrina.

"This is not just a matter for you!" retorted Father Jerzy. "Who are the others who are coming, Fabian?"

The police officer moaned, "The monstrous cabal, the cult. Beasts in human form, and their slaves. The one in the castle fears them, hates them. You will see them soon enough."

The priest, grim-faced, gathered up his prayer book and holy water.

"Look after him, Katrina," he said, "the crisis seems to be past. See? The marks are almost gone."

He was right. The red marks that resembled insect bites on Fabian's throat were now pale, barely visible.

"Thank you, Father," she said wearily. "I don't know what we would have done without you."

"Thank God," the old man replied. "Be thankful that in this world there is a force for good to balance out that which is evil. I pray that in this struggle, evil will be vanquished. But nothing is certain. Watch over him."

The priest left, and Fabian's muttering died away as the young man fell into a deep-sleep. Katrina dozed, her head resting on his arm. The summer evening had turned to night when she awoke to a rumbling sound. She stood and looked out in time to see an SUV pulling a big trailer pass the police post. The clumsy vehicle seemed out of place so far off the beaten tourist track.

Tourists, she thought. *I should go and stop them. They're heading towards the castle.*

Then it occurred to her that the trailer would never get up the forest road. Besides, she had responsibilities at home. Stooping over Fabian she whispered, "Come back to me, my darling."

He mumbled something that might have been a reply, but she could not make out any of the words.

***

"It'll be dark soon," said Brad. "If we lose the daylight, we'd better be somewhere safe. Safer, anyhow."

"Define safer, in this context?" said Denny.

"More easily defended, I guess," replied Brad. "We stay in this courtyard. One of those guys out there might just throw in a grenade."

He took out his pistol, showed it to the journalist, put it back inside his jacket. Denny gave a low whistle.

"You're full of surprises," she said. "I suppose you know Pavel has a gun, too? I saw him take it out of the cab of the truck when we abandoned it. Oh, and he has some sort of chart, but when I asked him about it he pretended not to understand."

"Figures."

Brad looked out of the gateway again, keeping his head down. The sounds of the phantom battle were growing nearer, but he could still see no actual combatants. The lengthening shadows made the forest even more menacing.

You could hide a small army in those trees, Brad thought. *No way can we go out until those ghosts are gone.*

"We're being herded inside," he concluded. "But we have no real choice. Can you walk, Marcus?"

The Englishman was busy with his backpack. He took out a telescopic walking stick and stood upright.

"With this, I should be all right," he said. "Often use it when I'm hiking the Mendips."

"I've no idea what those are, but well done for thinking ahead," said Brad. "Now let's get inside."

"Okay," said Denny, shouldering her pack. "But what's the actual plan now?"

"Find this machine, the Zamyatin device. Destroy it so the cult can't get it," said Brad as they set off across the courtyard.

"And any blueprints," Marcus said. "Otherwise they might just build a new one."

"And this gadget, do we know what it looks like?" asked Denny.

"Not a clue," admitted Brad.

"Me neither," said Marcus. "I found nothing online except vague references. It could be the size of a house or small enough to fit in a footlocker."

Denny thought for a moment, then said, "So we could be looking right at it and not realize what it is?"

"Yes," said Marcus brightly. "But that's all part of the fun, isn't it?"

They climbed the stone steps to the entrance and found themselves inside a high-ceilinged entrance hall with two corridors leading off. There was also a staircase and what looked like a cellar doorway. The walls were bare except for what looked like faded old pictures. Brad and Denny took out flashlights, as the windows were small and dimmed by dirt.

"Look."

Brad swept his flashlight beam across the floor, showing where dust and some fallen plaster had been disturbed. The trail led to the cellar door, which stood open.

"Somebody went downstairs very recently," said Marcus. "Pavel and Lenka, maybe?"

"Do we follow them?" asked Denny, sounding dubious. "And risk being shot at by the living as well as the dead?"

After a brief discussion, they decided to take one of the corridors instead. But before they left the entrance hall, Brad stopped to look at one of the pictures.

Pavel had some sort of chart, he thought. *Which means he somehow found a copy of an old chart, surely?*

"Hang on guys, this might be useful."

Brad began to rub the dust off the glass with his sleeve. Denny shone her flashlight on the picture. As the picture emerged from beneath the grime, it showed that it was not art but a diagram of some kind.

"A plan of the castle?" asked Marcus, joining them.

"Makes sense," Brad said, then pointed to the lower part of the picture. "Yes, see, this looks like a 'You Are Here' marker. At least, I assume that's what the legend says in Russian."

"Great, so where's the laboratory?" asked Denny. "I guess that's where the experiment took place."

Marcus peered at the diagram while the others held their flashlights on it. But eventually the Englishman shook his head.

"Either the lab's not marked or my Russian simply is not up to the job," he admitted.

"I don't understand what these dotted lines are," said Denny, tracing them out with her finger.

"They're not labeled at all," said Marcus. "But judging from the way they run out under the walls, they could be tunnels."

"So that's one potential escape route. Is there a generator room marked? Anything to do with power, that kind of thing?" asked Brad.

"Why, yes," said Marcus, slightly puzzled. He indicated a room near the center of the building. "See these little lightning bolts?"

"Looks defensible," said Brad. "And I have an idea that might help us. But I could be wrong. Anybody not want to give it a try?"

The cacophony of battle outside grew louder, and Denny had to raise her voice when she said, "I vote we go for it." Marcus gave a wry thumbs up.

"Okay," said Brad. "Just step back while I confiscate this map."

He smashed the glass with the rubber-coated end of his heavy flashlight and carefully removed the diagram of the castle from its frame.

First bit of plunder taken from the fortress, he thought, as he folded and pocketed the yellowed paper. *Score one to the bold invaders.*

***

Beneath the castle, the creature waited.

Born of fear and torment, the Insane One was a bizarre hybrid of paranormal entity and insane human being. The two aspects of its nature had never quite merged, but instead worked together or clashed as chance dictated. The serpent-deity and the abused political prisoner, neither comprehending the other, occupied one body. It could not even decide on its own name. Sometimes it was Ouroboros, sometimes merely Olga Volkova, a dissident and experimental subject.

The Insane One spent long periods almost inert, fretting over its pain. Then it sought diversion in manipulating the spirits that thronged Mista Venja, playing games with its retinue of ghosts. It believed itself immortal, yet eternal life offered only eternal loneliness. It longed to leave the cold stone fortress, but feared what it might find beyond the forest.

Then it sensed a change in the wider world. Something had happened in a faraway land. The nameless creature became aware of others like itself, and rejoiced. It learned that it was something called a lamia, part of a family, not a solitary freak. It tried to call out to the Others, hoping to find understanding, to finally belong. But instead, its questing mind found puzzlement, then revulsion. Minds that were cold, hard, and determined probed its memories, examined its madness, before the creature could withdraw its psychic feelers.

The Insane One faced a horrifying truth. That it was a monster even in the eyes of other monsters. The shock of that encounter with the cult had driven it to a frenzy of indecision. The Others knew where it was, so it could not simply hide. It was outnumbered, so it could not hope to win if they came for it. It sank into despair, cowering in the tunnels beneath the castle, consumed by fatalism.

But then a miracle occurred. The power of the Others was suddenly negated by some catastrophe. A great triumph became a terrible defeat at a place called Wychmere. A frightened pariah awaiting its fate was granted a sudden, joyous reprieve. Its enemies had been laid low.

They cannot harm me now, it thought.

The relief did not last. Soon the Insane One sensed that at least one of the Others had survived. This enemy was strong, clever, and determined. The enemy was coming to the castle with a group of followers to slay the Insane One and take the machine, the thing Zamyatin had made.

The Insane One might not be able to defeat the cultists. But there was another factor, occasional psychic glimpses of a rival group that was determined to thwart the enemy. This could prove useful. From somewhere in the depths of a fragmented human mind came a useful phrase.

My enemy's enemy is my friend.

With manic energy, struggling to think clearly and driven by desperation, the Insane One set about making its haphazard preparations. When the first group of intruders appeared, it had formulated a plan, of sorts. But it depended on the group staying together. When they split up almost at once the Insane One grew angry, confused, and even more dangerous.

***

"This is as far as we go," said Cleo as the trailer drew to a bumpy halt. "From now on, we approach on foot."

The tall woman looked over at Helga.

"Unless you would prefer to crawl, honey?"

Helga shuddered at the attempted humor. During the long journey across

Poland, she had gradually become accustomed to her new powers. The serpentine transformation that had come upon her unbidden had been painful, terrifying. And yet at the same time some part of her had exulted in the revelation that she was no longer exactly human.

If only Andreas could be like me, she kept thinking. *Then we could be together forever.*

"Bad idea," said Cleo. Seeing Helga's reaction, she raised her eyebrows. "We are linked now, little sister. Have been for a couple of days. What you feel, think, do, is part of me. Like a constant murmuring in the background, subliminal unless I focus on it. But always there. And you can read me, too. You just don't know how, yet."

Cleo came over and sat by Helga on the small bunk. The German girl tried not flinch, as she had done at first when Cleo came close. There was a sense of immense animal strength about the tall woman that frightened her. But it was also fascinating.

"Give me your hand," said Cleo.

Helga hesitated, and Cleo reached over and gently took the girl's hand in hers. A tingling sensation ran through Helga's flesh. It was pleasant, somehow felt right. And as the feeling grew, so did Helga's consciousness. She felt herself merging with a greater mind. She suddenly saw herself, small and pale, through Cleo's eyes. It was a shocking vision, totally unlike seeing herself in a mirror. Then the two women's shared consciousness expanded to embrace Jonathan Clay and Andreas.

Helga struggled to understand what she was perceiving. The two men seemed weak, feeble, not radiating the primal energy that flowed from Cleo. Or from Helga herself.

Why do they seem different? What is wrong?

The other woman's lips did not move, but Cleo's voice sounded clearly in her mind.

'Men cannot be like us. That is the decree of Ouroboros, which some call the Mother Goddess, others Lilith, the true Serpent of Eden.'

Helga wanted to reject the idea, but the evidence of her new, god-like senses was clear enough. She and Andreas had once been a loving couple. Now they were parts of a great whole, and very unequal parts at that. Some vestige of her former human self rebelled at the idea, again yearning for the old limitations and weaknesses of mere humanity.

'Be brave, my sister.' Cleo's mind was cool, strong, insistent. *'You are fortunate, in a way, to have had a human life to regret.'*

Suddenly Helga was bombarded with thoughts that at first made no sense to her. She was tiny, afraid, cowering in the corner of a dim-lit room as a man towered over her. His face was in shadow, his hands immense as they reached down for her. Now she was running up an alleyway, hearing a gang in pursuit, screaming in panic as a bottle smashed against a dumpster. She dodged, escaped. Now another fragment, the pastor of a church talking of God's love, but with the eyes of a predator. Again, hands reached out for her. Suffering, escape, more pain, exploitation, rejection, followed in a cascade of misery. And then Helga understood that this was what Cleo had been. A symbol appeared, the snake biting its own tail, Ouroboros. The skinny, frightened girl was welcomed by a tall, beautiful woman with strange golden eyes.

'Olivia. She was the first true lamia for many centuries.'

The beautiful woman took the skinny child into her arms. There was a brief stinging sensation, for a moment the lost girl feared yet another betrayal. But then the transformation began. "One day you will be the strongest of us all," Olivia had said to young Cleo. And she had been right.

The fragmentary images were gone as suddenly as they had appeared. Now the collective mind of Ouroboros expanded, reached out into the shadowy world of spiritual forces.

'Hold on tight, Helga. We're going for a little ride.'

They swept upwards, leaving the trailer behind. The world looked very different to the ancient eye of Ouroboros. All living things, the forests, plains, and seas, glowed with intense life. But most of these living regions were disfigured by blotches of darkness, as if some disease had spread across the face of the planet. Helga sensed that this was the work of mankind, destroying Nature or at best enslaving her.

The Earth was being maimed and plundered by short-sighted greed. She had always paid lip service to the idea, but now it was part of her, as essential as breathing. Compared to this, her love for Andreas, the plans they had made, evaporated like dew in sunshine. The individual was nothing compared to the whole, the *gestalt*.

Ouroboros resented the encroachment of tiny, ephemeral, swarming human beings. It longed to smash the sprawling cities, swat the swarming planes like flies, sink filth-belching ships. For thousands of years, it had been powerless to check their advance, because it lacked worshipers. But now, Helga felt, things were about to change.

'It's time for a reckoning. The tide must be turned. And what we're doing here is part of a greater scheme to achieve just that.'

Helga was sitting on the bunk again, and the tall woman was letting go of her hand.

"Do you understand a little better, now?" said Cleo.

Helga nodded.

"I understand. But what must I do?"

Cleo took Helga by the shoulders. Again came the rush of perception, but this time it was focused on one place. The castle. Mista Venja lay before Helga like a child's toy fortress. A toy made of glass, as she could see inside. Three small glowing points moved through the corridors, and Helga understood that these were rivals, seeking to thwart Ouroboros. Two more glowing specks, fainter than the first, were also moving, but underground. And there was something else, a dark blur that Helga could not focus upon.

'The Insane One.'

Cleo's thought was full of revulsion, outrage at such a perversion of the sacred power of Ouroboros. It was a thought tinged with fear of madness, of the unpredictable. But beneath it all, lay steely determination.

'If necessary, we will kill it.'

***

The O-Team moved slowly due to Marcus's injured leg. He insisted that Brad and Denny should go ahead and he would catch up. The two vetoed that idea, and instead spent time examining the rooms leading off from the corridor. The first few were empty, but then they came across a door that had obviously been smashed in.

"I think the sign says it's the Guard Room," said Marcus, hobbling up to the doorway.

"They tried to barricade themselves in," remarked Brad, shining his flashlight on a haphazard array of chairs and tables piled just inside the room. He flicked the beam at the far wall, and they all gasped. Beyond the makeshift barricade was a heap of bodies. Rifles and pistols lay among the corpses, the guns long since rusted to the floor.

"Military uniforms," said Denny, picking her way over the debris to look more closely. "And overalls, I think. Technicians for the lab, perhaps?"

"Could be," agreed Brad, following her inside. Marcus stayed in the doorway. *She's a cool customer,* he thought. *Obviously seen death before.*

"There are bullet holes in the door, and the walls," Denny pointed out. Her flashlight beam picked out patches on the walls where shots had gouged out chips of stone.

"They put up a fight," said Brad. "At this range they must have hit whatever it was. Didn't stop it."

"One of your lamias?" asked Denny, bending over the nearest corpse. "I can't see any signs of injury on this guy, though to be fair there's practically little left beyond the skeleton."

"The life was sucked out of him," said Marcus. "Or perhaps his soul, if there's any real difference. The creature that they unwittingly created came after them and destroyed them. It was probably berserk, out for revenge, attacking anyone and everyone."

"This one's been badly mangled," Brad pointed out, playing the beam of his flashlight over another uniformed figure. The skull was deformed, smashed in, or crushed by tremendous pressure. The jaw had been torn off, and one arm was twisted into an impossible position behind the victim's back.

"All this must have happened in the minutes immediately after Zamyatin fired up his machine, for the last time," said Denny. "But why did they take refuge in here? Couldn't they have simply ran outside and driven off? They had at least one vehicle, we know that."

"You're forgetting the ghost battle in the woods," said Marcus. "This is a blood-soaked place, and Zamyatin didn't just raise Ouroboros. He also raised an army of ghosts. The soldiers and scientists must have been terrified, convinced they were under siege while a monster ran amok."

Brad turned away from the huddled bodies.

"Well, now we know guns are useless against a lamia," he said. "But we always suspected that."

"Bad news for our treasure hunters," observed Denny.

As if on cue, they heard a distant scream, followed by two shots. Everyone froze, then Denny asked, "Was that Lenka?"

"Could've been a man," replied Marcus.

"Let's get going," said Brad determinedly, and they set off again after consulting the chart of the castle. They found several more rooms where Soviet personnel had been killed, but did not stop to examine the remains.

The generator room was cramped thanks to an array of bulky machinery, all badly rusted. The cobwebs they had to brush aside to get in suggested that no one had visited the place in years.

"I've seen this kind of thing before," said Brad, looking around. "With luck there'll be a kit of specialist tools. Help me look?"

"Okay," said Denny, "but what exactly are you trying to do?"

"That big metal box with the Cyrillic lettering? That's the emergency diesel generator. It's standard in any old-style Soviet installation. The machinery is preserved in layers of grease so it should run okay, even after decades. Hell, it could probably still run after a hundred years. There's a sealed fuel tank that works. Soviet engineering. Heavy duty, not flashy, but it works."

It took them a few minutes of searching to find the tool kit. Brad was in his element for once, handling a practical problem he understood. He had soon opened up the small generator and, with Marcus's help, figured out the basics of its operation.

"You're assuming the emergency lights will still work?"

Brad, now filthy from removing decades-old grease from components, shrugged.

"I don't see why not. If the cables are intact. Rats could have chewed them all to hell, I guess. But I get the feeling rats wouldn't survive long around here."

Marcus gave a humorless laugh.

"No, they'd just be a light snack for the current occupant."

It took Brad half an hour of tinkering and a few false starts, but eventually the generator stuttered into life. It ran smoothly, and its roar and exhaust fumes were oddly reassuring for Brad. Again, the familiar gave him confidence.

"Look!" said Marcus, turning off the flashlight.

Dim lights flickered into life, dispelling some of the gloom.

"Better than nothing, I guess," said Brad. "At least it offsets our snakey friends' heat vision."

"We still don't know where the laboratory is," pointed out Denny.

"But we can accurately determine where it definitely isn't," replied Brad, taking out the chart and laying it on a small table.

"Ah, a process of elimination," said Marcus, hobbling up to pore over the diagram.

It took them a couple of minutes, but eventually they had eliminated all of the rooms marked. All were either clearly designated for some other purpose, or simply too small to be used for much other than storage. This left the possibility that the lab was, in Marcus's words, 'high above or down below,' in the cellar or one of the castle's towers.

"Apart from Baron Frankenstein, of course, who actually does scientific research in a medieval turret?" asked Denny.

"Quite so," agreed Marcus. "I'm afraid the cellar is the only logical option."

"And if I had to pick a good place for a scaly monster to have its lair, that would be it," said Brad grimly. He started to search around the generator room. "We need something to give us an edge. Something that will hurt one of those things."

"If guns don't work, what will?" asked Denny.

"Something more traditional, perhaps. That joke about Baron Frankenstein gives me an idea. Most living things have an instinctive fear of fire," said Brad. "We can make torches. Let's break off some chair legs, wrap the ends in plenty of cloth, and add a splash of oil. Does anyone have a match? I can't see any here, but I guess we can go back and search the corpses."

"I've got a lighter," admitted Denny, rummaging in her pocket. "Been trying to quit smoking for a couple of months now. Not going too well."

After a few minutes, Brad had created four makeshift torches. He explained that each team member would carry one, with a spare in his backpack. The others looked at the makeshift torches dubiously, but when Brad lit his, the flame shone impressively. It also filled the room with black, choking fumes.

"Let's get moving before we suffocate ourselves," said Brad. "If we encounter trouble, light yours from mine. Thrust it at the creature's face, the eyes. Try to blind it."

"The creature was a human being," said Marcus, quietly. "It didn't choose its fate."

"And we can't afford to let it choose ours," retorted Brad, leading the way.

Chapter 9: The Zamyatin Device

Roughly two out of three emergency lights were working as they went back along the corridor to the main hall. The flickering torch in Brad's hand continued to smoke, leading to coughing and streaming eyes.

"It's never like this in the movies," complained Marcus, still limping along with his stick. "The angry mob never seems to splutter its way up to the castle."

"Truth is messier than fiction," agreed Denny. "One reason why I prefer it."

A shot rang out in the distance. The three stopped, listening, but there was no follow up.

"Hey, what happened to the phantom soldiers?" asked Denny. "That was the first shot I've heard in a while."

"Battle seems to be over," said Brad. "I think that was Pavel. It was a pistol shot, not a rifle."

"You can tell from the sound?" asked Marcus, peering back the way they had come.

"Yeah," said Brad. "Pistols use different ammunition, as a rule. That sounded like a nine millimeter round."

"I'll take your word for it," said Denny. "But what do we do?"

Brad shrugged.

"Carry on, we can't help them."

They reached the hall without further incident, then stood looking down into the murk of the cellar. The emergency lighting there was even weaker than on the ground floor. Brad led the way down the steps, flaming torch in his left hand, pistol in the right.

Guns might not be much use, he thought, *but holding one is still damn comforting.*

"This looks like the place," said Denny, shining her flashlight around the large chamber. Gray-painted metal boxes were arrayed around a central cylinder. Brad made out power cables, control panels, dials, and meters. It was obviously decades old, but he had worked with almost equally obsolete systems in his time.

I understand this well enough to wreck it, he thought. *That's all we need.*

They reached the floor of the cellar and, after establishing that nothing of any size could be hiding in the shadows, began to look around. They found bodies in various stages of disintegration heaped anyhow against the back wall. As in the guard room, some were badly mangled, others showed no obvious signs of injury.

"Doctor Zamyatin and his team, I presume," said Marcus, looking down at a heap of corpses in what had been white coats. "Scientific hubris meeting some horrific occult nemesis."

"That's a great phrase," said Denny admiringly, "can I use that?"

"You can write an epic poem about it, but only if we get out of here alive," cautioned Brad. "Marcus, try to find the blueprints and other documents, so we can burn them. You can at least read some Russian. We'd just be guessing, we might end up destroying the cleaning schedule."

"So what do we do?" asked Denny.

"Find something big and heavy," said Brad simply, "and smash up all this gear."

Marcus began the unpleasant task of searching the dead scientists for any likely documents. But wrecking the machines proved a more challenging task than Brad had expected. There were no available tools, such as hammers or wrenches that could have been used. And as Brad examined the cables, he realized that, as was typical of Russian engineering, the whole setup was extremely robust.

"I'll get the toolbox from the generator room," said Brad. "You two stay here. Keep a torch to hand, and that lighter, Denny."

***

Marcus managed to piece together some of the technical data from the brittle, yellowed sheets of paper. But, as he explained to Denny, all he had were the instructions to operate the device. The blueprints that would allow another to be made were not in the cellar.

"Probably in a filing cabinet in Zamyatin's office, somewhere upstairs," suggested the reporter.

"That makes sense," agreed Marcus. "We could go and search for them after Brad gets back."

"Or we could burn the castle down," said Denny.

Marcus looked at her, mouth open, for a moment.

Surely, the woman's joking?

"Seriously," she went on, "why not just torch the place? The floors above ground level are all wood, they'll go up easily enough. And if there are blueprints somewhere, they'll be destroyed."

"You can't just destroy a historic building in a foreign country!" exclaimed Marcus. "Apart from the legal aspect, it's outright vandalism!"

"It's obvious that nobody in Poland gives a damn about the place. We'd be doing them a favor. And I thought the world was in peril? Something like that, anyhow," returned Denny. "So the less time we spend dicking around here, the better. Wouldn't it be better to burn it down than risk getting killed running around a maze of corridors?"

Marcus still felt unhappy, but returned to the Russian documents.

"Well, Brad's in charge, let's see what he thinks," he said diplomatically.

"So now you know how to turn this thing on?" asked Denny. "You could, in theory, fire it up?"

Marcus looked suspiciously at her.

"Yes, it seems straightforward," he said, "but obviously I'm not going to."

"Pity," said Denny. "It would be nice to get a few pictures of the thing in action. Control panels lit up. And maybe that thing in the middle glows, throws off sparks, that kind of thing."

"I very much doubt–" Marcus began, but was interrupted by a scream. It was loud, obviously from nearby. They both looked up to see Lenka appear at the top of the stairs. She began babbling in Polish as Denny ran up to catch her before she fell. After a few seconds, Lenka calmed down enough to convey that she and Pavel had been attacked in the tunnels.

"I lose him, I lose him!" she kept repeating. "The white thing, it attack, and I run, and I think he with me, but when I climb out he not there."

"Was this white thing like a big snake?" asked Marcus.

Lenka nodded, eyes wide with terror.

"But it also have head, face, arms like a person!" she insisted. "Please, you must help me find Pavel!"

Denny and Marcus exchanged a look. This time they were on the same wavelength.

"We can't go into the tunnels," Denny explained, "we have work to do here."

Lenka became frantic again, and broke away from Denny.

"You come, you help, please!" shouted the Polish girl. "Please! You good people, you not let him die!"

After a moment, Marcus said, "Go with her, Denny. I'll be okay here. Brad will be back any minute."

Denny protested but eventually gave in, leaving the Englishman in the cellar. It was only after she had gone that it occurred to Marcus that she had taken her lighter. He looked at his makeshift torch lying on the floor by his pack.

Well, he thought, *I can always use it to hit any troublesome monsters on the head.*

***

The Insane One was enjoying itself, despite its initial frustration at the behavior of the intruders. If they insisted on splitting up, well, that meant it could pick them off at its leisure. Currently it was making its way through the tunnels beneath Mista Venja, possessed by the thrill of the chase. Two people, a large male and a much smaller female, had come into its domain. The creature's psychic sense allowed it to feel out their rough location, then its night vision revealed them as they entered the underground labyrinth.

The instincts of the predator combined with the mercurial impulses of the lunatic. The Insane One was unsure whether to kill and consume the intruders or seek to convert them. It would be nice to have a companion, another lamia to share its realm. But what if the young woman, when converted, proved a rival, not a friend? Best kill her and convert the man into a slave, especially since the holy man in the village had somehow stolen away the policeman.

But no, a slave is of little worth, it thought. *Another lamia might be a valuable ally. Yet I can trust a slave, he would be in my thrall as no lamia could be.*

These confused thoughts chased one another around the Insane One's mind just as its serpentine body pursued the frightened humans. At one point, it showed itself, leaped forward into the bream of the man's flashlight. He managed to fire a shot that buried itself in the creature's torso. The sting of pain was slight, almost pleasurable. The bloodshed gave flavor to the hunt. And it was satisfying to see the humans cry out in panic, and flee.

They are fleeing a monster, came the unwelcome thought from its own human nature. *Why did I become this foul freak?*

And the Insane One raged against fate that had given it so much power, and such a long life, knowing that it could never truly be content. It shook off the troublesome image of itself as an abomination, and returned to the chase.

Live in the moment, it told itself. *Let's see what happens next.*

***

"Ugly place," remarked Clay. "Apt setting for an ugly experiment."

"No room for doubt, Jonathan," warned Cleo. "We need you on the ball. This could be messy."

The five followers of Ouroboros stood outside the main gate of Mista Venja. Kelly could sense the tension between the two leaders, Clay the originator of the cult, Cleo the forceful commander.

"Where do we go first?" Kelly asked, pointedly directing the question at Cleo.

"We have the map," said the tall woman. "We know Zamyatin's office is on the second floor. We go straight there, get all the paperwork, and leave."

"What about my Dad and the others?"

"If we encounter them," put in Clay, "we should give them the option to withdraw."

"Or surrender," added Cleo. "How about that, Kelly? Would your father make a good convert?"

Kelly knew Cleo was testing her faith. She had often thought that her father would be happier if he could be forcibly shown the truth of Ouroboros. But part of her revolted against the idea. What was more, she knew Cleo could sense this.

"You are the only one of us who has retained any family ties," Cleo went on. "And yours is exceptional, a psychic link. You're an extraordinary person. Maybe your father is, too. Should he waste his life, as he has been, on material gain? Should he be allowed to sabotage our efforts to improve the world?"

"No, of course not," said Kelly, uncomfortably. "But I'm convinced that he will come around one day. If only he'd put aside all his prejudices."

Cleo laughed shortly.

"Fat chance of that," she said. Then, dismissing the subject, she gave instructions to the team. They would first go to the office to collect the blueprints of the Zamyatin Device. If they encountered the Insane One, Cleo and Helga would try to kill her, or at least drive her off. If they ran into mere humans, they would overpower them, without causing permanent harm.

"And without converting them," added Cleo, "to salve Kelly's conscience."

The team crossed the courtyard and entered the main hall, where Clay noticed the broken picture frame. He deduced that it had contained a chart of Mista Venja.

"Why are the lights on?" asked Helga, looking down into the cellar. "Surely the Insane One could not do this?"

"They started the generator somehow," said Kelly. "It's probably Dad, he knows that kind of stuff."

"Maybe they're planning to start the machine?" suggested Clay. "That could be disastrous. It might even increase the power of the Insane One."

"It also undercuts the advantage of heat vision," said Cleo, thoughtfully. "A neat trick."

"Did you hear something?" asked Helga. "It sounded like metal scraping."

The German girl gestured toward the cellar entrance. Without hesitation, Cleo strode over to the dark doorway and looked down into the old laboratory.

"No sign of anyone," she said, returning to the group. "Sounds can be deceptive in these places."

The tall woman thought for a moment, then issued new instructions.

"Jonathan, you and I will take Andreas upstairs to the office. Getting the blueprints is the first priority. Kelly, take Helga and go to the generator room. If there's nobody there, turn the power off. If there is, use your discretion. But cut the power."

"Is this a test of my loyalty, Cleo?" asked Kelly. The tall woman shook her head.

"It shouldn't be, should it?"

Kelly simply nodded and set off along the corridor Cleo had indicated, accompanied by Helga.

***

Brad found his way back to the generator room and quickly selected a heavy hammer from the tool kit. After a moment's thought, he also picked up some small screwdrivers. He reasoned that he might need to partially dismantle some lab equipment in order to wreck it more effectively.

All those years improvising in the middle of nowhere, he thought. *How I used to bitch about that back at the head office.*

He had not heard any sounds other than those he was making. So it came as a shock when he walked out into the corridor to be confronted by two people. One was a stranger, a fair-haired young woman. The other was his daughter.

"Hi, Dad," said Kelly. "Got time to chat? Or you just gonna shoot me?"

Brad lowered the gun he had raised instinctively.

"Kelly," he said, "if you don't want to come with me, stay the hell out of my way."

Kelly frowned in puzzlement. She started to speak, then checked herself. The stranger looked from daughter to father, clearly waiting for some kind of cue.

"Surprised I'm not pleading with you?" asked Brad. "You've joined up with a gang of killers. People have actually died, thanks to your pals. Now you're trying to exploit some sick experiment that should never have happened."

The tirade had the desired effect. Brad saw the familiar anger in his daughter's face.

"You're in no position to lecture me about morals!"

He raised the gun again, but this time aimed it at the stranger's face.

"I'm in no mood for lectures, yours or mine," Brad retorted, "and if you don't want me to shoot your friend in the kneecap you'll get out of my way."

"He wouldn't do it, Helga," said Kelly to the young woman. "Stand your ground."

Brad took careful aim and fired past Helga's head. It had the desired effect, making both girls step back.

"Next one goes in her kneecap," warned Brad. "I may not be a killer, but I'm less squeamish about maiming."

The two fell back as Brad advanced along the corridor, Kelly began pleading with him to leave the cultists alone.

"Dad, it doesn't have to be this way! If you don't co-operate I can't be responsible for what happens."

"What?" he asked, trying to rein in his own anger, "So you're just obeying orders, now? Is that your defense?"

Helga stopped suddenly, and her gaze shifted from Brad. Kelly stopped too, and her jaw dropped. She, too, was looking over Brad's shoulder.

"Look out!" she shouted.

"Aw, come on–" he began to reply, but a tremendous blow between the shoulders knocked him down. He lost his grip on the pistol, which went skittering across the stones, but managed to hang onto the guttering torch. His right hand hit the floor hard and he swore at a crack, followed by piercing pain. Something pale and sinuous slithered past. Kelly screamed while Helga shouted something in German.

As Brad raised himself on his left hand, he saw a white serpentine creature wrapping itself around Helga. A face that might once have been human appeared behind the young woman's head. Human shoulders and torso emerged next, attached to a reptilian tail about eight feet long. The pale creature's expression was exultant, full of demonic pleasure. The bleached lamia reminded Brad of the colorless creatures that spend their entire lives in caves. He felt revulsion as well as fear.

"Help her!" shouted Kelly.

Brad scrambled upright and shoved the torch into the scaly body. The thing screamed and seemed to spasm. Helga echoed the creature's scream and Brad heard ribs breaking. He lunged again, this time aiming for the monster's face. It reared back out of reach and spat at him, jets of black liquid spraying across his face and chest. His right eye began to sting and his vision blurred.

Three shots rang out in rapid succession. Brad could just make out bullet holes appear in the lamia's torso. The creature screamed again, and this time its muscular coils relaxed. Lightning-fast it released the limp Helga, and turned on Kelly.

"Shoot it in the head," shouted Brad, but before he could complete the sentence the monster had knocked Kelly to the floor. Brad rushed forward, holding out the torch, which chose that moment to go out. He raised the charred table leg and smashed it down onto the lamia's head, feeling a satisfying crunch. The monster flung out a muscular arm and sent him reeling backwards. The distraction had been enough, though, and Kelly raised the pistol and shot it in the face.

Screeching and spitting black venom the monster put its hands over its damaged face. Brad brought his makeshift club down again, twice more. The white creature gave a gurgling cry and moved like a flash, heading towards the entrance hall. Kelly aimed Brad's gun after it but the lamia was gone before she could fire again.

"You okay?" said Brad, taking the pistol from her with his left hand. His right wrist was throbbing painfully, and his vision was still defective. Kelly looked at him as if she was struggling to remember who he was.

She's in shock, he thought.

"Snap out of it, Kelly!" he said harshly, which seemed to have some effect.

Helga groaned, and Brad hesitated.

"Look," he said. "You get Helga here to safety while I go after that thing. Maybe we'll have time for a heart to heart later. If both of us are still alive."

Brad looked down at the German girl, and then reeled back in shock and disgust. Helga had wriggled out of her pants and was transforming into a lamia. The process was fascinating, horrifying. The young woman's legs merged into an extended, scaly tail, like the white creature's. But this time the process went further. Helga's arms shrank, the metamorphosis of human flesh into scale continued up her body, and her head lost its human shape. In just a few seconds what had been a woman of about Kelly's age had become an eight-foot serpent.

The creature reared up, black tongue flickering over its lip-less jaws, and regarded Brad with golden eyes. They were oddly beautiful, for all their reptilian strangeness, and he remembered the hypnotic powers of Ouroboros. He looked down, and the serpent sprang into movement, going after the pale monster at lightning speed.

"Amazing, isn't it?" said Kelly.

"Hard to believe, even when you see it," he admitted. "But it doesn't change anything."

"You're right, I'm wrong, huh?" Kelly put her hands on her hips, fear forgotten, defiant again.

God, Brad thought, *she hasn't changed that much.*

"No time to argue," he said. "I've got to get back to my friends."

Kelly stood aside and made a sarcastic 'after you' gesture. Brad stopped, as a thought occurred to him.

"Just a minute, why were you in this part of the castle at all?"

Kelly shrugged.

"Just taking in the history, Dad."

"You're not turning the power off," he declared, reaching out to grab her. She dodged away.

"You can't put energy into that thing in the basement!" she said. "You don't know what you're dealing with."

Before Brad could reply, the lights, already dim, flickered off, then slowly came back up again. He turned and went into the generator room, examined the auxiliary power plant. There was no evidence that it was failing. The output was steady.

"Something must be drawing off the energy," he admitted. "Odds are it's the device."

Crap, he thought, *either Marcus turned it on or someone else is down there.*

"Turn it off, Dad!" cried Kelly, trying to push past him to get at the controls. Before she could reach the switch, he flicked it himself.

"There," he said. "Most of the castle's in total darkness, or very nearly. Your slippery pals have a huge advantage over us mere mortals. Satisfied?"

***

The Insane One was furious, raging against the fate that had not only robbed it of a good hunt, but severely wounded it as well. Its recuperative powers were such that it would recover in a few minutes, but only if it was safe from attack by other lamias. Once the castle had been its own lair, a safe warren of corridors, rooms, tunnels. Now its enemies might emerge from any doorway and wrap it in killing coils.

It skulked in a small chamber, one easily overlooked, struggling to come to terms with its perilous situation. It saw a golden serpent rush past, felt a momentary relief. But from the speed and size of the other lamia, it knew its chances of winning a fair fight were poor.

I must have more power!

The words were almost an echo of something buried in the creature's fractured memory. Something about power, energy, words that heralded the moment of creation.

'Take it up to full power!'

The last order given by Soviet Academician Yevgeny Zamyatin, the Insane One's unwitting creator. It had enjoyed absorbing the scientist's soul. It had taken the very essence of its first victim into itself in a moment of perfect predation. Zamyatin's fear and confusion when his life essence had been drained away was still a delicious recollection.

But why remember this now?

Then the Insane One noticed the lights. For the first time, energy was coursing through the wires that threaded the ancient fortress. This meant something important, if only it could remember what. Then revelation came. The Zamyatin Device would be operable again. And the Insane One had all of the memories of the machine's designer at its beck and call. It uncoiled itself, ready to spring forth and slink its way to the cellar by hidden routes, secret tunnels it had discovered in its decades of demented isolation.

And when I get there, I will be born again.

***

When Marcus heard the voices from the hall, he panicked. They were unfamiliar, and speaking English, so they must be the cultists. He looked around the cellar, searching for some hiding place, however unlikely. There were no cupboards, no large items of furniture. The bulky equipment in the lab was mostly ranged around the walls. There was only one place to hide, and that was the metal capsule in the center of the room. The cylinder was roughly six feet high by four feet across.

If someone just glances down here they won't see me if I'm inside it, he told himself. *Better than nothing.*

The sound of rusty hinges seemed very loud as Marcus climbed in, and then closed the thick steel hatch. There was no handle on the inside. The cylinder had not been designed for volunteers. There was a metal chair that was in clear sight of the porthole in the hatch, but it was far too small to hide behind.

But maybe I could squeeze myself up against the metal, to one side of the door? Then I'd be out of sight. Probably.

It was better than nothing. Marcus contorted himself into a curved shape, despite the pain from his wounded leg. In the claustrophobic darkness of the cylinder, he tried to breathe silently, despite knowing nobody could hear him through the steel casing. He began to wonder if the machine was airtight, and whether he would suffocate.

No, he thought, *there must be an air vent of some kind, I just didn't notice it earlier.*

Time passed. He began to feel hotter, and the small porthole in the hatch misted up. His breathing became faster, shallower, though he was unsure whether this was down to mounting fear or a shortage of oxygen.

Why can't it be both?

He began to feel panic again, the pounding of his heart filling his head. He wanted desperately to open the heavy door and fling himself out onto the cool stone floor of the cellar. Yet he had a vision of the cultists waiting for just such a move, of their sadistic glee as they killed him.

Or worse, they might convert me to become another drone.

A small light flickered on above Marcus's head. It was so unexpected that he jumped, gave a little shriek. There was also a humming sound. It seemed to be coming from the wall of the steel cylinder. It took him a moment to realize what was happening.

Oh Christ, they've turned it on!

Now panic did possess him, and he clumsily shifted around to push the hatch open. But before he could get a purchase on it, the hatch swung outwards. Marcus flinched, pressed himself against the far side of the steel container. A face from a nightmare appeared in the hatchway. Hairless, disfigured by wounds, and stained with black blood, the Insane One hurled itself into the metal womb where it had been created.

The last thing Marcus remembered before the creature wrapped itself around him was the look of deranged glee on its face.

Chapter 10: Showdown

The Insane One felt the power of the device surging through its damaged body, enhancing the power of Ouroboros. The human it had found cowering inside the cylinder was a wonderful surprise. It would suck out his soul, drain his psychic energy to boost its own ability to fight. It knew it would not have much time. It had left a trail of blood from the scene of its first ever defeat.

The power of the Device allowed the creature to raise up the phantoms of all the dead who had perished in the castle. They would, it hoped, provide a distraction and buy it time to recuperate. What's more, it reunited some of the dead with their former bodies. The ones that it had killed and drained of life in the initial massacre, just after its transformation, became the walking dead. They could only walk for a while, but again it was a useful ploy. The Insane One sensed the confusion it had sown among its foes.

I can still win! I will survive!

The Insane One exulted in its own cunning, the way it had responded to its greatest challenge. But then something strange happened, a bizarre event even by the weird standards of the Insane One's world. To fully exploit its human captive, to feed on the man's very soul, it had to connect with the essence of his being. Inevitably, this involved some exchange of thoughts and feelings. Normally, all that it sensed from its prey was fear, sometimes anger. It took some pleasure in these intense emotions. They added seasoning to the feast. But with this man, there was something else. It was a feeling that at first felt so alien, so unexpected, that the Insane One paused in its feeding to wonder at the sensation.

'Poor girl. So wrong.'

The words made no sense, but there they were. The man pitied the monster that was destroying him. Yes, he was afraid, and in pain from the scaly coils that held him captive. But the Insane One also sensed a deep well of compassion in the mind of the feeble human. It realized that this was because a few scraps of its oldest memories had somehow passed over to the man and been understood.

A face appeared in its mind's eye, conjured up by its subconscious. It was the face of a woman, a thin face with dark, deep-set eyes, a firm mouth, and a snub nose. It looked maddeningly familiar, and yet the Insane One could not recall ever killing such a woman. Then a terrible realization dawned.

'It was my face when I was human, my face when I could walk in the sunshine and laugh and love and didn't have to wriggle in the darkness like some foul worm.'

Again came the wave of compassion from the man, this prey animal it now knew was called Marcus. He, too, had a name. And he, too, had suffered. Fragments of his memories became jumbled with those of the Insane One, and it relaxed its grip, physically and mentally.

'They say your life flashes in front of you when you're dying.'

The Insane One saw the man's greatest regret, the death of a long ago friend. It was a tragedy he had failed to prevent. She felt the intensity of his emotions, the resolution he had made to help others, the path he had chosen. That path had led inevitably to his fate in this grim cellar, so very far from home.

'So unfair!'

Was that Olga's thought, or that of the good man, Marcus? The Insane One could no longer tell. Baffled, it withdrew from his mind, leaving him half-alive, not wholly consumed. The whole incident, from discovery of the prey to realization that the prey contained a great mental sea of compassion, had taken very few heartbeats.

There was a wrenching sound and the door of the cylinder was jerked open. A golden serpent lunged at the Insane One, at Olga, at the confused monster. The two creatures grappled, white and gold coiling and lunging, each trying to crush or bite the other. There was no room for confusion now as the Insane One fought for its life.

***

"We'll never find him stumbling around in the dark," said Denny.

Beside her, Lenka was becoming ever more frantic. Denny suspected the Polish girl was lost, too, as Pavel had had the map of the castle. Denny had followed Lenka into a well-concealed tunnel entrance not far from the entrance hall. The situation was made worse by the fact that, as a precaution, Denny had lit her makeshift torch. In the confined tunnel, the smoke was almost blinding and choking them.

"We find him, he could be dying," said Lenka, before doubling over in a coughing fit.

"This is absurd," said Denny. "We could wander around here for days."

Lenka looked up at her pleadingly and began to beg again. But Denny didn't hear her, as she was staring at the people who had appeared up ahead.

More than one, she thought. *Maybe the cultists.*

"Let's go back," she said to Lenka, gesturing at the newcomers. "They might be hostile."

The mysterious strangers were barely visible in the flickering torchlight. But as they got closer, Denny saw that they were in some sort of uniform. Their clothing seemed threadbare, incomplete. There was something wrong with their faces, too. She moved the torch so that it was behind her, and the smoke cleared a little.

"Oh my God!"

The nearest man's face was even more damaged than his uniform. It was mostly skin and bone, with no eyes, nose, or lips. A few strands of lank hair fell over a bony forehead. Yellowed teeth were fixed in a permanent grin. The dead soldier shambled forward on twisted legs, arms outstretched. Behind it other long-dead warriors advanced, all moving jerkily like puppets.

"Run, Lenka!" shouted Denny, and hurled her torch at the oncoming phantoms. She had had half-expected expected it to pass through them. Instead, the ancient uniform of the leader caught fire. But he kept on coming, a walking inferno. Another attacker blundered into the first, and caught fire as well.

A burning mob, thought Denny, repressing the urge to giggle. If she did, she might lose it completely.

The two women ran back along the tunnel. When they came to a T-junction, Lenka tried to drag Denny off to the left. Denny was sure the way back was to the right, and after a brief tug-of-war she broke away.

"Follow me!" she shouted, but didn't wait to see if the girl was following. She stumbled in the darkness, fell, got up only to run into some unseen obstacle and almost fell again. Behind her, she heard the shuffle of footsteps in the dust. Around her, the walls were lit with the flickering redness of flames. Even as it burned away to ash, the reanimated horde was on her trail.

***

Suddenly the castle was full of ghosts. As Brad and Kelly ran towards the entrance hall, phantoms appeared, seemingly at random. Some showed no sign of seeing the living father and daughter. Others responded to their presence with surprise, fear, or hostility. One even looked amused. Just as varied as their reactions was the appearance of the phantoms. Some were dressed in military uniforms. Brad recognized Russian and German troops from World War 2. But there were also ghosts from earlier eras, dating back many centuries, in both military and civilian garb.

"What's happening?" asked Kelly, flinching away from a grimacing figure in a top hat. "Where did they come from?"

"I guess the device helped conjure them up," suggested Brad. "It's supposed to generate some kind of psychic field."

"Can they hurt us?" she asked, clutching her father's arm. "Or touch us at all?"

"Let's not find out," he suggested.

A terrible screech caused them both to freeze. It came from the cellar. Brad dashed over to the entrance and was about to run down the steps when he saw something pale and sinuous rushing up to meet him. He jumped aside as the lamia hurtled past him, stopped himself from falling with his right hand. Pain shot through his arm from his injured wrist. Kelly screamed as the monster flung itself at her and knocked her down, but instead of continuing its attack, it fled out of the castle.

"I'm fine," said Kelly. "See to your friends."

Brad raced down the stairs into the cellar, then stopped halfway. He could just make out a serpentine shape lying on the laboratory floor. It was half-hidden among the smashed metal cabinets that had housed Zamyatin's equipment. He raised the gun and approached the creature cautiously, but it did not move.

"Oh my God!" said Kelly, from the top of the stairs. She ran down past him and bent over the lamia, wailing, "I think she's dead!"

Brad took out his flashlight and shone it onto the mangled body. It was in the process of changing back from golden-scaled serpent to human being. He watched, fascinated, as the transformation reversed itself, until Kelly was weeping over the broken and torn body of Helga. When the reversion to human form was complete, it became apparent that the girl's head had been twisted around so far that her neck must have been snapped.

Brad stepped over the pathetic corpses, playing the beam of the flashlight around the lab. He saw no sign of Marcus, but then heard a low sobbing noise. It came from inside the central cylinder. The hatchway and exterior of the capsule was stained with black splashes. Looking inside, he saw the Englishman curled into a ball by the metal chair. His back was heaving as he wept.

"Marcus?" he said gently. "It's me, Brad. You can come out now."

The sobbing figure did not move, but continued sobbing gently. Brad reached out to touch Marcus on the shoulder, and his friend froze and grew silent. When Brad took his hand away, the crying continued.

"Marcus, you can't stay here buddy, we have to go. You have to get back to England."

This time Marcus did look round, and Brad almost recoiled from shock. The Englishman's face was contorted with misery, wet with tears. It was also badly bruised. Brad noticed belatedly that his friend's clothes seem to be soaked in the same black blood that had started to congeal on the metal floor.

"She's so lonely," said Marcus. "So much pain. I can't bear it."

He curled up again, and Brad backed out of the hatchway.

"Who is it?" asked Kelly.

"Someone who's probably safer in there than out here, for now," he replied. "Where is the rest of your team? Keeping out of the danger zone?"

"Not all, Mister Steiger," said a familiar voice. "As you can see, we're right at the heart of things. As usual."

***

Denny came to what seemed like a dead end. She crashed into a wooden door, bounced off, and reeled back. She was bruised, exhausted, terrified. But she was still able to think. The door had yielded. She had heard a cracking sound. For a moment, she thought her shoulder had broken.

No, she thought, *after so long any wood must be rotten.*

Denny hurled herself at the door, shoulder charging what she hoped was rotten wood. There was another cracking sound and she felt the wood give some more. She realized that she could see the door now, and glanced round. A flaming corpse was closing in, the stench of its burning flesh now reaching her nostrils.

Gagging at the stench Denny made a final, desperate charge and crashed through the barrier, stumbling onto the bottom of a stone stairway. At the top of the stairs was a square of light, almost dazzling after the murk of the tunnels. Nails clawed at her back as Denny scrambled up the stairs, using her hands to stop herself from collapsing. There was no obstacle above, just an opening into a small chamber. The room was lit by a single high window. It was full of junk, mostly old furniture, and Denny emerged behind what looked like a bookcase. She shoved it and clambered over it. There was a closed door ahead of her.

If it's locked, I'm dead.

It was not locked, but it took her a few tense seconds to open the heavy, long-disused door. She looked around again and saw a smoking, flailing figure emerge from the stairway. The walking corpse was almost eaten away by the fire; little left of it but bone and charred cartilage. A few scraps of cloth and flesh still clung to it. The skull, scorched almost black, grimaced at her. Then the long-dead soldier fell forward onto the fallen bookcase. The head came off and rolled away, still smoking, until it was stopped by a pile of books.

Denny paused, hoping all her pursuers had been destroyed. But then a smoking head emerged from the tunnel entrance, and this corpse was still moving purposefully. She wrenched the door open a few inches, squeezed through, then tried to close it. It wouldn't shift. A hand, half covered in flesh, nails like brown talons, appeared around the door. It clawed feebly at her, and was easily dodged.

Denny ran, hoping that the direction she had chosen would lead her out of Mista Venja, and into the daylight. She looked back again before turning the corner. Smoke was starting to billow through the gap in the door.

***

Brad looked up to see Jonathan Clay standing at the top of the cellar stairs. Beside him was a woman who was tall, strikingly attractive, with dark bronze skin.

"I assume you're not actually called Lilith?" said Brad.

The woman laughed.

"Just a stage name, Brad. I see you cut the power, Kelly," said the woman. "And took a prisoner. Well done."

"I'm nobody's prisoner," said Brad. "And your friend, Helga, didn't make it, in case you cared. Which I suspect you don't."

"I can see that for myself," replied the woman. "A pity. Perhaps with more time she would have been ready for the fray."

Clay and the woman started down the stairs, and a third person appeared, a young man carrying several cardboard box files. Brad started to back away, then remembered Marcus. He stopped beside the cylinder hatchway and raised his pistol pointing it at the tall woman. He tried to remember how many shots he had left, and failed.

"If I have to make a last stand I'll make it one to remember," he warned. The three cultists paused in their descent, then Cleo carried on down. After a brief hesitation, the two men followed.

"Cleo," said Kelly. "If you've got the information, we can just leave."

Cleo looked from daughter to father and back, then shook her head.

"This link between you and him, it's more than a nuisance," she said. "Remember the slaughter he perpetrated at Wychmere. Look at the trouble he's causing now. He has to join us, or die. Try to persuade him–"

Brad switched his gun to his right hand and fired a shot into Cleo's left kneecap, wincing at the recoil. The woman gave a hiss of pain as her leg buckled under her. Steeling himself, he fired two more shots into Cleo's torso. The woman's body writhed but did not begin its transformation.

I guessed right, he thought. *If the human form is too badly hurt, it lacks the energy to turn snakey.*

"You bastard!" Kelly ran forward, belatedly putting herself between Brad and his target as she bent over the tall woman.

"I'm guessing she'll recover soon enough," said Brad. "Just get her out of here. But you," he said to the young man, "you leave those blueprints behind."

"No!" shouted Cleo. "You'll have to kill us all, Steiger."

"That includes me!" shouted Kelly over her shoulder. Her face was contorted with hate, far more intense that anything Brad recalled from their earlier life as a family.

457

He slumped against the cylinder, let the barrel of the gun drop.

"Have it your way," he said, feeling sudden exhaustion. "Get out before I change my mind. And if you run into the crazy albino snake lady, give her my regards."

Kelly and Clay carried Cleo up the stairs. At the top, Cleo looked down at Brad and blew him a kiss.

"I know we'll meet again, as the song goes," she said weakly as she vanished from sight. "Remember whose side Kelly chose. It's the side she always chooses."

The side I'm not on, he thought. *You don't need to read minds to get that.*

Brad turned back to the cylinder to try and help Marcus. For a second he thought his friend had climbed out of the metal box himself. But the man was stumbling towards him, arms outstretched, and he was wearing a suit. As Brad stopped in bafflement, another figure arose from the debris at the far end of the cellar. This second animate corpse seemed to be clutching an antiquated cell phone.

Zombies? That's all I need.

Brad raised his gun again and, holding his injured wrist with his other hand, shot the nearest one in the head. It seemed to work. He had, after calculating, two shots left. He leveled the barrel of the pistol at the second walking corpse just as a third stood upright. Then a fourth, and a fifth. Bodies in decayed white coats tried to stand upright, or simply began to crawl towards him on hands and knees.

"Okay," said Brad, let's do this.

He shot the first two and then looked around for an improvised weapon. Marcus's wooden torch, unused, lay by the cylinder. Brad could not light it but it would make a good club.

Reckon those skulls must be a bit fragile, he thought, hefting the broken table leg. *After all these years.*

***

The Insane One was badly wounded after its battle with the golden enemy. It had won, but at a terrible cost. It had to regenerate, and that meant lying low. It writhed rapidly through the labyrinthine ways of Mista Venja, trying to get as far as possible from any pursuers. It assumed that its enemies would try to finish it off. Only after a couple of long minutes of dodging and doubling back did it realize that it was not being chased.

They have withdrawn in dismay and confusion! I destroyed their champion!

The sense of triumph did not last. It had killed one worthy foe, and before that, it had enslaved a mere human. Reaching out with its mind, it found that another intruder had been killed by its slaves. Three down, then, but how many left? Its paranormal senses were inefficient due to pain and weakness, but it could detect several strong minds in the heart of the castle. Its lair, where it had lurked for decades, was still not safe.

Curled up in a bare tower room, the Insane One fretted over its limited options. It was used to roaming freely through the castle, enjoying the sense of ownership. It thought of itself as a great monarch in its domain, but now it was a fugitive. After years of security, its world had been turned upside down in a matter of minutes.

On top of its confusion and pain, it was still haunted by its contact with the man, Marcus. If it had not been so distracted by his thoughts and feelings, it might not have fared so poorly in the fight. But no matter how hard the Insane One tried to push away the memory of his compassion, the unaccustomed feeling returned. It yearned to be human, to go among people, to experience life.

I'm a monster, a freak, I can't ever leave here!

Inner turmoil was displaced by an outer concern. A smell of smoke was in the air. It thought of the flaming torch carried by the man who had attacked it, and hissed in displeasure. It scanned its immediate surroundings, reaching out telepathic feelers, but sensed no human presence. Yet the odor of burning grew stronger, more insistent. And it was accompanied by a crackling noise.

Fire, it thought. *The castle is on fire.*

Panic goaded the Insane One to flee again, but this time it had a specific direction in mind. It would go into the tunnels and recover. It writhed as fast as it could toward the nearest escape route only to find a wall of smoke ahead. Changing course it worked around towards a second escape route, only to find a wall of flames barring the way. As well as the crackle of flames, it could hear crashing sounds as ancient wooden beams gave way.

Its home was burning down around it.

Eventually the creature reached a tunnel entrance and plunged into the cool, damp darkness. As the Insane One coiled up on the dirt floor it felt despair for the first time in its inhuman life. Even if it recovered its full strength, the Insane One would have no realm to reign over, merely a heap of blackened ruins. For a moment, it toyed with the idea of remaining in the tunnels, perhaps luring more people into the ruins to enslave them. But then another unaccustomed thought sprang to mind.

For how long? Forever? Am I to be a white worm, wriggling in the darkness, until the end of time?

Again, despair surged up from the depths of its fractured mind. The human part of its nature, so long submerged, revolted against such a bleak future. Again, it searched its fragmented thoughts for a solution, at the same time reaching out with its mind. This time it touched something new, the human it had taken control of earlier. The man was coming round from the effects of the bite. His mind was crude, easily understood, a good slave. Probing his thoughts the Insane One found a discarded series of facts, images, and impulses. Then it lingered over one fact, a simple human attachment. A name.

The Insane One had an idea. A way of squaring its human desires with its serpentine nature. It was audacious, risky, but it offered almost infinite possibilities. It ordered its new slave to rendezvous with it and began to wriggle towards a place where it could obtain fresh human garments, and other useful items. It giggled, despite its pain. It would recuperate for a day or so, then execute its cunning plan.

It's crazy. But it might work.

***

After neutralizing the undead, Brad half-carried Marcus up the stairs into the entrance hall. He noticed a strong smell of smoke, and guessed that Denny's matches were to blame somehow.

No way can I look for her and stay with Marcus, he thought. *One thing at a time.*

Brad took the Englishman out of the castle to the gateway and set him down next to the old truck.

"Marcus?" he said, shaking his friend gently by the shoulder, "can you understand me, buddy?"

Marcus looked up, gave a lopsided smile.

"Understand?" he said. "Oh yes, I understand perfectly. It will crack open like an egg."

Dismayed, Brad crouched down and looked into Marcus's eyes. They were unfocused. In his time, Brad had seen similar reactions from men in shock after accidents, or terrorist attacks. But he had no idea what extra mental harm a lamia might have done.

Damn it, where's Denny?

He stood up and looked around. Smoke was billowing from a slit-shaped window in a nearby tower. He heard a splintering crash as something big collapse.

"Okay, buddy," he said, helping Marcus up again. "Safety One-O-One. You can never get too far from a burning building."

By the time he reached the woods, the castle was well ablaze. Brad wondered if the Insane One was somewhere inside, or whether the monster would lurk in the tunnels. He consoled himself with the thought that the creature might already have died from its wounds.

"Wait for me!"

Denny was half-jogging towards him around the outer wall of Mista Venja. Brad paused for her to catch up. The reporter was limping, her clothes were filthy, and her face was a mass of scratches.

"I got out somewhere around the back," she explained. "Had to battle through the forest. Needs pruning. What happened to Marcus?"

Brad explained the situation as Denny took the Englishman's other arm. The remains of the O-Team slowly made their way along the forest path to find their SUV still intact. Brad had feared the cultists would sabotage it in some way. Denny got the car started while Brad propped Marcus in the back and fastened his seatbelt.

"Look," said Denny, pointing back towards Mista Venja. A column of black smoke rose vertically into the still summer air.

"So much for the Place of the Serpent," remarked Brad sourly. "Let's get out of here."

"Place of the Serpent. Day of the Serpent," said Marcus, apparently to himself. "A place you can just leave behind. A day dawns for us all."

Epilogue: After the Fire

"How is he?" asked Brad.

The young doctor smiled as she led him along the hospital hallway.

"He is no better, but no worse," she explained. "He is calm most of the time, rather popular with the nurses. So polite. But sometimes he becomes agitated and it helps if he is given writing and drawing materials. That seems to provide him with an outlet."

They came to a half-open door.

"I can just go in?" he asked.

The doctor nodded.

"Push the buzzer if you need help, but otherwise visiting time ends at seven."

The room was pleasant, lit by the evening sun. Marcus was sitting at a small table by the window, his back to the door. At first, Brad had hoped that his friend would improve under professional care, but as the weeks passed, he had resigned himself to a long wait.

If he ever recovers, he thought. *If he's like this for the rest of his life, it's on me.*

"Marcus," he said, stepping into the room. "How are you, buddy?"

The Englishman gave no sign that he had heard. Brad walked over and stopped a few paces away from his friend, not wanting to startle him. He walked around to the side to try and get within Marcus's field of vision.

Still the same scribble, he thought, looking the sheets of paper scattered on the desk. Brad picked up the nearest. It was covered in apparently random jottings. Words in various languages were set out of in columns. Brad recognized one list. Cotopaxi, Etna, St Helens, Stromboli.

"Volcanoes?" he exclaimed. "Why are you so interested in geology all of a sudden, Marcus?"

The Englishman stopped working and looked up at Brad, as if seeing him for the first time.

"You're here! So glad you could make it, old chap," said Marcus. "How's that lovely daughter of yours?"

Brad felt a sinking sensation in his gut but tried to smile.

"Kelly's fine, as far as I know," he said. "I haven't seen her in a while."

"Off gallivanting about with her trendy friends, eh?" said Marcus, with a mock grimace. "Young people today, eh? But what can you do? I sowed a few wild oats myself, so I can't criticize."

"What does all this mean, Marcus?" asked Brad, gesturing at the papers that covered the small table. "What exactly are you working on?"

"Ouroboros, of course!" replied the Englishman. "We have so much to do. What their plans might be I can't say of course. Keeping those very close to their scaly chests, ha! But there are hints, plenty of hints. See?"

Marcus held up a sketch that seemed to be a rough map of the world, complete with slightly wobbly lines of latitude and longitude. The continents were mapped out with blue crayon. Yet across and between them were bolder lines done in red. It took Brad a moment to remember his basic science. The pattern, though very sketchy, was one he had seen many times before.

"Plate tectonics?" he said, tentatively. "There are fault lines, right?"

"Exactly!" responded Marcus, like a teacher helping slow students. "Fault lines, that's what it's all about. Snaking around the globe like an intertwined mass of serpents, the fiery driving force of Ouroboros itself. Oh yes, that's the essence of the power. I feel sure of it."

Brad looked at the crude drawing.

"I don't see the connection," he admitted. "Are you saying that they get their power from the earth, that it's stronger where the planet's crust is cracked?"

"Crust?"

Marcus peered at the diagram as Brad put it down in front of him.

"Never look under the crust, Brad," he went on. "Don't look too deep. See too much. Feel too much. And she's always there, waiting. Waiting to wrap herself around you, waiting to share all the pain, the madness."

Marcus started looking around the room, then jumped up to peer under the bed.

"There's nobody else here, buddy," said Brad. "Nothing can hurt you. You're safe now."

But the Englishman had already shuffled on his backside into a corner, and put his hands over his head. Brad went to sit by him, put a tentative hand on his friend's shoulder. Marcus was mumbling something he could just make out.

"Nobody's safe now, nobody's safe now," Marcus repeated.

Brad said nothing more, but got up and left. Outside he met Denny, who asked how Marcus was.

"No real change," replied Brad, as they walked over to her car. "Moments of clarity, then he goes back into his shell. I wish I could explain what really happened to him."

"They'd check you into that place if you told the truth," she said. "Best to stick to the story about an accident, post traumatic shock."

"You should go in and see him."

Denny shook her head.

"Hospitals give me the creeps, and mental hospitals are the worst," she replied. "Besides, I feel guilty about facing him. I left him in that cellar."

"You did what you felt you had to," said Brad, not wanting to run through events at the castle again. "And you couldn't have helped him. Besides, if it hadn't been for your connections we might still be stuck in Poland arguing with bureaucrats."

"What's that you've got there?" asked Denny.

Brad held up the drawing of the world, explained what it represented.

"I'll take your word for it," said Denny. "Thought with that grid of squares it looks a bit like Snakes and Ladders."

Seeing Brad's puzzlement, she went on, "It's a kids' game, one where you race up the board a row at a time. If you arrive at the bottom of a ladder you go up one row or more, if you land on the head of a snake you slide down."

"Sounds like a game we called Chutes and Ladders," said Brad. "No doubt Ouroboros would design a version where the snakes raise you up."

"But you think this is about earthquakes and volcanoes?" said Denny, studying the crude map. "How does that fit with the Zamyatin Device?"

"Maybe it doesn't," admitted Brad. "But what if using such a device on a fault line could tap into more power than Ouroboros has harnessed up to now? Imagine the damage they could do."

"Too pessimistic," said Denny, unlocking her car. "We don't know if this Cleo you mentioned even survived. And even if they did, they'd need technical expertise, plenty of money, a safe place to work. No more wandering sideshow stuff. That means they'll be easier to find."

"Even easier if I still had some link to Kelly," Brad pointed out.

Denny steered them onto the highway for London.

"I know it bothers you," she said. "But maybe it's a good thing you don't literally share her dreams any more. How often does she have to tell you to piss off before you take the hint?"

"She's my child," he said simply. "I have to try and help her regardless."

Denny shrugged.

"As a professional journalist, I'm delighted by your monomaniacal obsession. As a human being, I think you're setting yourself up for another big disappointment."

Brad laughed.

"Kids today," he said. "What can you do?"

***

The day after the castle caught fire, two strangers came out of the woods. One, a big man, was bruised, limping, and carrying a girl who was in even worse shape. Father Jerzy and Katrina took the strangers to the priest's home, where the man fell unconscious. The girl drifted in and out of lucidity, and seemed to be running a fever. Again, a doctor was summoned, and again he failed to diagnose anything remarkable.

"Superficial injuries, cuts and bruises, plus exhaustion," he said, handing over some painkillers, "though the young man seems to have a cracked rib. Probably from a fall. What they both need is rest."

Katrina was not convinced. The man had taken a battering that might have left a less robust individual at death's door. The girl had not been so badly hurt. Katrina spent an anxious minute examining each of her patients for wounds like those inflicted on Fabian. But there was no trace of the ominous red puncture marks on either of the strangers' throats, as she told Father Jerzy.

Fabian, although he was still feeling weak, insisted on trying to do his duty as a police officer. As he could not question them, he searched their clothes. From credit cards, he learned that the strangers' names were Pavel and Lenka. Pavel had been carrying a chart of Mista Venja. The chart was marked out with particular emphasis on what seemed to be tunnels. Other papers suggested that the pair had been searching for valuables supposedly hidden under the fortress.

"Fools," responded Father Jerzy to this news. "Seeking earthly riches they found only evil, fear, and suffering. A lesson for us all."

Pavel was put in the priest's spare room, while Lenka was given a bed at the police house. On the morning of the second day, the girl seemed to recover her senses. Katrina had been trying to persuade Fabian to take the couple to a hospital in Krakow, just in case. She had little confidence in the doctor, who was said to like the booze too much. But when she went to check on Lenka, she found the girl sitting up, and smiling.

She's so pretty, despite being so pale, thought Katrina. *She must be very strong to be so resilient.*

"Hello!" said Lenka brightly. She seemed completely recovered and talked as if they were meeting at some pleasant social gathering. "What a pretty room! How did I get here?"

Katrina told her what she knew, skirting around the question of why the couple had been at Mista Venja in the first place. Instead, the girl raised it herself.

"Burned down?" said Lenka. "Oh, then poor Pavel will never find his treasure. If it ever existed."

"Is that really what you went there for?" asked Katrina. "I've never heard that the castle had any hidden treasure."

Lenka nodded, smiling.

"No, I never really believed it either. But my man was kind of obsessed, and when you love someone, you humor them, don't you?"

"I guess so," admitted Katrina, thinking of Fabian's trip to the castle. "But what will you do now?"

Before replying, Lenka threw back the covers and got out of bed. She seemed very sprightly for someone who had been so ill just a day before.

"Are you well enough to get up?" asked Katrina, worried that her patient might collapse from over-exertion. "You've had nothing to eat for at least a day."

"Oh, I'll be fine," said Lenka. "Where's Pavel?"

Katrina got Lenka some spare clothes first, then showed the girl to the priest's house. A surprised Father Jerzy showed them in.

"She is well," he muttered to Katrina, frowning. "A very healthy young lady."

"I am very well," said Lenka, "I must see my Pavel, he was so brave."

The big man was lying on a sofa in the front room. His face was disfigured by purple bruises, and Katrina had done her best to put some strapping on his cracked rib. When Pavel saw Lenka, he gave a grunt of recognition.

Strong, silent type, thought Katrina.

"How are you, honey?" said Lenka, sitting on the bed and running a small, delicate hand through the man's untidy hair.

"I'll be fine, my darling," Pavel replied.

Katrina wondered if that was true. Pavel's expression was almost blank. He had not smiled once at seeing his girlfriend safe. He also had such a low blink-rate that Katrina felt her own eyes starting to water.

"My man will soon be well enough to travel," said Lenka, looking up brightly at Katrina. "I am so grateful to you both for looking after us."

"Don't mention it," said Katrina. "But don't you think he should go to a hospital?"

Lenka shook her head.

"No, he's had worse injuries, you know! He's a tough customer, my Pavel. Aren't you, dear?"

She ruffled her boyfriend's shaggy mop of hair again. He managed to produce a weak smile.

"If you want to go, I will go," he said slowly. "I live only for you, my love."

The words should have sounded romantic, but when she heard them, a chill went up Katrina's spine. There was something about Pavel's manner that suggested he was drugged. But then, he had been given some strong painkillers.

"Do you have transport?" Katrina asked. "If not, I could drive you to the nearest railroad station."

The girl looked at Katrina as if she had suggested something remarkable.

"A railroad station?" she said. "Trains! I would love to ride a train."

"Where is your home, my child?" asked Father Jerzy. The old priest was standing in the doorway. His expression was neutral, but the tone of his voice expressed concern.

"I used to live near here," replied Lenka. "But now, Pavel and I are going to spend some time traveling. We want to see the world, don't we, sweetheart?"

"Yes, my dear," said Pavel in the same robotic way.

"Let's leave these two young people and I will make some tea," said the priest.

As she closed the bedroom door, Katrina smiled up at the old man.

"That was surprisingly tactful of you, Father," she said. "They may not even be married, you know."

Father Jerzy did not reply at once, but instead placed a finger on his lips, then led Katrina downstairs to his kitchen.

"I don't want to be overheard," he explained. "Don't you think there is something odd about that couple?"

"Yes," admitted Katrina. "But if I had narrowly escaped a burning building, as she said, then I might not behave normally."

The priest shook his head.

"There's more to it than that," he insisted. "He does not seem all there, as if he has suffered some injury to his brain. Or something worse."

"You think he might be possessed by evil, as Fabian was?" asked Katrina, taking the teapot out of a cupboard. "No, there were no marks."

The priest nodded distractedly as he filled a kettle at the sink.

"Perhaps it is not so, then. Certainly the young woman seems normal enough, despite her appearance."

"She is very pale," admitted Katrina. "But perhaps she avoids the sun. Many do. And having starved for a while does make one anemic."

The priest switched on the kettle and stood looking out at the forest. Smoke from the blaze was still rising, albeit in faint wisps. All that could be burned must have been consumed.

Later that day, Lenka insisted on leaving with Pavel, and Katrina agreed to drive them to the railroad terminus. They had no luggage and only the donated clothes they stood up in. Yet Lenka seemed downright joyful as she led her boyfriend to Katrina's Skoda. During the journey, the girl peered excitedly at almost everything they passed, as if being given a lift was a huge novelty.

It's like she's never experienced modern life at all, thought Katrina. *She's surprised by so many things, it's as if she's a visitor from another world.*

"Well, here we are, you guys," exclaimed Katrina as she pulled up outside the station. It was a public holiday, and the place was thronged with travelers. She got out to show the couple the way to the booking office.

"Thank you so much for all your help," said Lenka, holding Pavel's hand. "I'm sure we can manage now."

"Well, take care," replied Katrina. "And come and see us if you're ever in town."

Lenka laughed so loudly at that that Katrina wondered if the girl was wholly sane. People nearby turned to look.

"Sorry," said Lenka, making an obvious effort to speak normally, "I just don't think we will be back. It's a big world, after all. And there's so much fun to be had!"

The girl turned and led the big man towards the ticket windows. Katrina saw that Fabian's old T-shirt was too small on Pavel, and left a couple of inches of waistline showing. Katrina smiled at the incongruous sight, then did a double take. But before she could look more closely at the exposed band of flesh, the strangers had been lost in the crowd.

As she drove back to Goritza, Katrina kept asking herself what she had seen.

Probably just minor injuries, she thought. *Like the doctor said, bumps and bruises.*

But no matter how she tried to reassure herself, the worrying notion would not go away. It seemed to Katrina that she had glimpsed two small red marks a few inches apart, just to the left of Pavel's spine.

* * *

Day of the Serpent
Ouroboros Series Book 3
Written by David Longhorn

Prologue: Scotland, 1913

"Someone called you the wickedest man in the world," said the journalist, pencil poised above her notebook. "Another was a little more restrained and described you as merely the most evil man in Britain. I believe you have referred to yourself as the Great Beast? Or sometimes simply as Six Six Six?"

Aleister Crowley picked up a teapot and poured out a cup for his guest.

"I hope you don't mind, Miss Burns," he said, "all I have is plain old Assam tea. And my housekeeping arrangements are so primitive that I have no sort of cake to offer you at all."

Leaning back on an old, worn out sofa, Crowley adopted a slight frown of concentration as he went on, "Now, as to my magical names; Megatherion, or Great Beast, is certainly one of them. And the triple-six is another. But the latter is not nearly as disturbing as one might think. In numerology, it refers to the sun. You may, if you like, call me Little Sunshine."

Catherine Burns could not help smiling. She had come to this remote house in the Scottish Highlands expecting to meet a monster. Instead, she found a witty, intelligent man, albeit one who dressed very unconventionally. Aleister Crowley was handsome, and if his eyes had not been so penetrating, Catherine might even have found him attractive. He had, after all, consented to be interviewed by a female journalist who simply turned up at his door unannounced. There were many upstanding Christians, of both sexes, who would not have treated her with such consideration.

But, while polite and articulate, nobody would mistake Aleister Crowley for a typical English gentleman. At the moment, Crowley wore a plain white robe that the reporter felt might have originally been a nightdress. And there was something else about him, a troubling reminder of another scandalous figure. Catherine had never seen Oscar Wilde in the flesh, but Crowley slightly resembled photographs she had seen of the disgraced writer.

"You seem to be trying to pierce my very soul with those wonderful dark eyes of yours, Miss Burns."

Catherine flushed, embarrassed to have been caught gawking like a silly girl. Crowley smiled.

No, she thought, *definitely not attractive. And not a gentleman, either.*

"Aren't you joining me?" she asked, gesturing at her solitary teacup.

"No, I regret that I am approaching the end of a prolonged period of ritual cleansing," he explained. "No stimulants, not even tea, can pollute my metabolism. Unfortunate, but sacrifices must be made."

"Why did you come all the way here from London?" she asked, as she jotted down Crowley's words. "Does this place have some mystical significance?"

"At last, a sensible question!" Crowley clapped his hands with child-like pleasure. "I have come to Boleskine House because it is so far from London. Here, I can work without fear of being pestered by silly, small people with their trivial questions. Can you foretell the future? Do you worship Satan? Can you put curses on people? I grew weary of such nonsense."

Crowley shook his head in dismay.

"Those things you mention are hardly trivial matters," said Catherine, "certainly not for God-fearing people."

"Certainly not for your esteemed Presbyterian readership of the *Inverness Gazette*," returned Crowley with a superior smile. "I was surprised to find that I had not outdistanced the press. Who would have thought newspapers existed out here in the wilds of Caledonia?"

Catherine felt color rise to her cheeks. She was sensitive about her birthplace, and took her professional status seriously.

"Inverness is a city, sir, often called the capital of the Highlands," she said, "and has an erudite and well-informed population. And since you raise certain matters, perhaps you can answer those questions you mentioned?"

The so-called *magician* raised an elegant eyebrow.

"The answers are as follows. Sometimes I can foresee future events, albeit in a glass darkly, to quote scripture. No, I do not worship Satan, though I've often wondered if he is quite as bad a fellow as he is painted by some."

"And can you put curses on people who offend you in some way?" asked Catherine.

Crowley looked at her for a long moment, as if scrutinizing a bug under the microscope.

"No comment," he said, finally.

Catherine felt a slight chill, despite her thick woolen clothing. She remembered that she was alone at Boleskine House with a man often said to be depraved. Crowley supposedly enjoyed himself in ways that would be unmentionable in polite society.

"What about the Order of the Golden Dawn?" she asked. "It is the best-known occult society in the world. Is it true that you've quarreled with all its leading members?"

"It is more correctly termed *The Hermetic Order*," Crowley corrected her, "and I have had disagreements with a few individuals. I am still a member, I believe. Rather like the priesthood, one cannot be thrown out by a mere vote. One must be ritually expelled, and nobody has dared try that on me."

"Can you explain the purpose of the ritual you mentioned?" she asked. "In terms my readers will understand, of course."

Crowley got up and went to a bookcase. The volume he took down was old, small, and bulky. It reminded Catherine of the Burns family Bible, but she guessed that this was nothing of the kind.

"The Book of Abramelin," said Crowley, sitting down again and opening the text. "It is a grimoire. You are familiar with the term?"

"An ancient book of black magic," she said, again feeling a chill.

Crowley shook his head, again gave that superior smile.

How I would like to slap you, she thought. *With your smug London manners and your fancy talk.*

"Really, Miss Burns," said Crowley, eyes wide with feigned astonishment, "physical violence is the last resort of the ignorant. And I might just slap you back."

"How did you know–" she began, then caught herself. Again, she blushed, and Crowley laughed.

"You did not ask about mind reading, which I can do in a limited way.

Powerful emotions, for instance."

He set the book down on the low table between them and opened it.

"A grimoire is not a book of black magic," he said, adopting a school-masterly tone. "It merely conveys certain mystical truths. This text, dating back to the late Middle Ages, offers different means to summon various supernatural beings. To perform what is termed the Abramelin Operation, it is necessary to remain celibate and abstain from most worldly pleasures for six months. It is also necessary to have a house with a north-facing door, located on a site sacred to certain beings."

"This is a sacred site?" Catherine asked, surprised. "I thought it was just an old hunting lodge."

"Really," Crowley said, "you should have done your research. Boleskine House was built in the 18th century on the site of an old church. It burned down. With the congregation inside."

"What a terrible accident!" exclaimed Catherine.

"Or a rather obvious message from those *beings* I mentioned," returned Crowley. "Now, let me tell you a little more. My purpose is to summon my Guardian Angel. You smile! But we are all born with such beings assigned to us, and if we can actually contact them directly we might acquire great wisdom, perhaps even immortality. Unfortunately, the route to such spiritual treasure is long and hazardous."

Catherine scribbled frantically as Crowley delivered an impromptu lecture on his bizarre and disturbing beliefs.

***

Fergus Mackay was fishing.

His job as caretaker and general servant at the Lodge was not especially onerous. As he had often remarked to drinking buddies, Mister Crowley may be a strange man, and an Englishman at that, but he was a fair employer. What's more, the Master employed a fine, buxom widow as his housekeeper. The good lady, Jean Brash, was bound to give way to Fergus's advances at some point.

The only problem was the salmon. Or rather, the lack of them.

Loch Ness was famous for its salmon, and Fergus enjoyed fishing in his spare time. This happened to be the ideal fishing season, so there ought to be plenty of gullible young salmon thronging the loch's waters. The trouble was that, try as he might, Fergus had landed nothing for days. When he had commented on this in the pub, others had said the same.

"They're not biting," muttered the old man.

Fergus looked up and down the long, narrow expanse of Loch Ness. A small pleasure steamer was just visible, far to the north, but otherwise nothing broke the surface.

So why do I get the feeling I'm being watched?

He turned to look around through three hundred and sixty degrees, taking in the whole sweep of the loch and its shores. As far as he could see, he was the only living thing in sight. Normally, one might expect to see ducks or geese on the water, or deer drinking at the waterline. But now there was nothing.

Almost as if, he thought, *the wildlife are in hiding. As if there's something near that they're avoiding. Something evil.*

***

"And out here," said Crowley, leading the reporter out of the house, "is my lodge."

Catherine's head was reeling. Her notebook was crammed with a shorthand account of his bizarre beliefs and practices. Crowley had founded his own religion called "Thelema." The sacred text had been dictated to him by an Egyptian god as he spent the first evening of his honeymoon inside the Great Pyramid at Giza. The only commandment of his new faith was 'Do what thou wilt shall be the whole of the law.' Part of Catherine was revolted by the blasphemy of it all. But the professional side of her was exulting at the thought that it would make a wonderful story.

"I still don't understand," she admitted, as she walked onto a pathway made from fine sand. The building in front of them was a small gazebo, evidently new judging by the brightness of the paintwork.

"To summon one's Holy Guardian Angel," Crowley explained, enunciating slowly, "it is necessary to exit a north-facing doorway, follow a pathway of sand, and enter a place of mirrors. The Victorian spiritualists called it a psychomanteum. Come, I will show you."

He led her into the windowless gazebo, which was indeed lined with mirrors. A divan upholstered in red leather stood in the center. A book, a jug of water, and a cup stood on a small table. A series of black candles were arranged in a circle around the divan.

"Disappointed?" asked Crowley, seeing Catherine's expression. "As I said, I do not indulge in satanic rituals, black magic, or any of that nonsense."

"But what do you do?" she asked.

"As I said," Crowley replied, somewhat testily, "I seek to invoke my Holy Guardian Angel. But you want a demonstration, no doubt?"

Crowley took a box of matches from the table and walked around the small gazebo, lighting candles. Then he closed the door, shutting out the daylight. In the dim, flickering light, he sat cross-legged on the divan, closed his eyes, and lifted his hands until both were palm-outward. He began to mumble something.

An incantation, thought Catherine, noting it down. She began to contemplate headlines. *'I Met The Wickedest Man in Britain.'* Or perhaps *'The Black Magician of Loch Ness!'*

But despite the blasphemous nature of Crowley's beliefs, Catherine was starting to find him more amusing than offensive. He seemed more like a showman than a sorcerer. The candles reflected seemed infinite in number, but it was a cheap effect, reminiscent of carnival sideshows. Catherine began to wonder if gentle mockery, rather than moral outrage, might be the best line to take.

'The Fraudulent Messiah,' that might do, she thought. *Or perhaps simply 'Charlatan Rents House in Neighbourhood.'*

Crowley's eyes opened. For a moment, she began to wonder if he really could read her mind. But then she saw the confusion and panic in his face. He composed himself quickly, but there was no doubt.

Something has rattled our black magician, she thought.

Crowley stood up and declared abruptly, "The ritual cannot be performed. Something is disturbing the ether."

"Wrong angel, Mister Crowley?" she asked, raising a quizzical eyebrow.

"Don't mock forces you don't understand!" he shouted, and again she saw fear in his eyes. Then he composed himself and went on, "We must leave, Miss Burns. Now."

Catherine was about to ask why when she noticed movement in the mirrors. The candles guttered, almost plunging the psychomanteum into darkness, despite the lack of any breeze.

"What's this?" she asked, peering into the reflected darkness. "An optical illusion you've cooked up for me?"

How can a thing have a reflection yet not be here in the room? Especially something so large?

The shape in the mirrors moved closer, circling them. Crowley looked into Catherine's face then stared into the glass.

"What can you see?" he asked. "What is coming? I can sense it, but I can't see it! This is wrong."

"You can't see it?" she said, wonderingly. "But it's so beautiful. Its scales shine so brightly."

***

Fergus laughed, albeit nervously, at the thought of some unknown creature frightening away the fish. He had been raised on folk-tales of ghosts, monsters, and strange water-beasts that supposedly inhabited every loch. And Loch Ness was no different. There was the legend that, in ancient times, some great serpent had risen from the depths, terrifying the local populace, only to be banished by Saint Columba. But, in this age of airplanes, motorcars, and telephones, Fergus was inclined to be skeptical about such things.

"One thing's for sure, the fishing's lousy," he said resignedly, and turned away from the shore to pack up his gear.

As he did so, he heard a quiet splash behind him. He turned, but saw nothing except a spreading ring of ripples about thirty yards off the shingle beach. The turbulence quickly dissipated, leaving the blue-gray surface of the loch as featureless as before.

Probably just young salmon at play, he thought. *Taunting me, little buggers.*

Fergus turned once more, and once again there was a splash. This one was a little louder than the first. He turned quickly, trying to catch a glimpse of whatever had broken the surface. But again, all he saw was a spreading circle of ripples, now much closer to the shore.

Could be a seal, he thought. Seals sometimes got into the loch via the canals that linked it to the open sea at either end.

Harmless beasts, but with a ravenous appetite for fish. Of course! A seal would have spoiled the fishing.

Then a creature that was quite obviously not a seal broke the surface just a stone's throw away from Fergus. Huge, serpentine, and scaly, it looked at him with great golden eyes. Its mouth opened to reveal a dark, gaping maw. The creature's vicious fangs seemed to Fergus as long as his forearm. It ran a black, forked tongue around its lipless mouth, as he stood there, frozen in wonder that was rapidly turning to terror. Then it lunged forward, its sinuous body driving it through the dark waters towards the shore.

***

"Go!" Crowley replied, grabbing her roughly by the arm and pushing her towards the door. She was about to protest when he did something extraordinary. He threw his free arm over his eyes, as if afraid to even glimpse at what was forming in the mirrors. "Don't look! Don't meet its gaze!"

But it's so beautiful, she thought, resisting Crowley so that she could gaze at the mysterious form. Two bright golden points appeared, and grew to become eyes that looked deep into her mind. *So wonderful, so graceful, so immense,* she thought.

I could look forever.

The marvelous being from the mirror world was closer now, so close she could almost reach out and touch it. Catherine was vaguely aware that Crowley had let go of her arm and was rushing back towards the divan.

'I am Ouroboros. See my beauty. Look deep into my eyes. Become one with me.'

The words, silky sweet, seductive, echoed in her mind. All thought of proper Christian conduct was swamped by the eyes, the words, the overwhelming desire to become one with the wonderful creature that was now coiling its glittering body around them. Each flickering candle had become a shining scale.

"Oh yes," she gasped. "Let me be yours."

A tremendous crash shattered her reverie. The little three-legged table was now two-legged, and smashed like the mirror which Crowley had hurled into it. The beautiful, fascinating eyes were gone.

Crowley yanked the door open, and the sane light of day flooded into the circular room. Catherine saw herself reflected in the shattered glass, a staring pale-faced, young woman, slack-jawed.

I look like an idiot, she thought, closing her mouth. Crowley grabbed her and this time she allowed him to pull her out into the fresh air. She could hear the magician's quick, shallow breaths. For a few moments, neither of them could talk. Then Crowley took her by the shoulders and said, "You must never speak of this to anyone, Miss Burns."

"What was it?" she managed to say.

"Not an angel, I think that much was apparent," he replied, with a trace of his old humor. "No, I was grievously in error to come here at all. I have heard rumors of such beings from other adepts, but never really believed that they still existed."

"But what was it?" she said, dismayed to hear her voice was high-pitched, like that of a frightened child. "What did I see?"

"Something even older than the angels, I suspect," he said, releasing her and walking back into Boleskine House. "Now, let me call you a taxi back to Inverness.

In fact, we can share it. Just give me half an hour to pack a few things."

"What?" asked Catherine. "What do you mean?"

"I'm leaving this place," replied Crowley, tersely. "I have no intention of ever coming back. And if I were you, I'd try to find a job as far away from here as possible."

***

Jean Brash was making her way back to Boleskine House with milk from a nearby farm when she saw Fergus Mackay running up the road towards her. She set down the milk can and smiled, expecting him to offer to carry her burden. But as he grew closer, her smile faded. Fergus was disheveled, red in the face, and kept looking over his shoulder.

What on Earth could have possessed the man? He's running as if the Devil himself is chasing him!

Jean peered past Fergus along the side-road that led to the loch shore. She could see no sign of anything that might have alarmed him. Then she thought of the number of times she had shared some malt whiskey in the kitchen of an evening. Unlike Jean, the man never stopped at just the one. Fergus was notorious for the amount of time he spent in the pub, too. As a good Christian, Jean knew where over-indulgence could lead.

It's delirium tremens, she thought. *He's gone barmy. Perhaps he's seeing pink elephants!*

"Run!" shouted Fergus, finally seeming to recognize her. He was wheezing, barely able to get the words out. "It's coming!"

Jean glanced along the road again. Fergus was so clearly terrified that she half-expected a rampaging pink elephant to appear. But there was nothing except the familiar expanse of water, shining in the sunlight. Fergus, seeing her confusion, slowed down to a jog.

"Now you keep your distance, Fergus Mackay!" warned Jean. "This is God's punishment for all that tippling!"

"Nonsense, woman!" he gasped. But he stopped a few yards away. He was almost bent double with exhaustion before standing up and turning to face the water.

"Where is it?" she heard him say. "Something that big can't just vanish."

A few minutes later, Jean had satisfied herself with the fact that Fergus was not drunk. He insisted that a huge water-beast 'with eyes as big as coach lamps' had emerged from the loch and chased him up the shingle beach. Jean, now suspecting some kind of prank on the old man by local lads, insisted on them going back to the scene of the supposed attack. When Fergus seemed unwilling, she questioned his manly courage. And so he squared his shoulders and led the way.

"There," she said, as they crested a low ridge and looked down at the shore. "Nothing to be seen except your fishing gear."

They made their way down to the waterline, feet crunching on shingle. As they approached the spot where Fergus always fished, Jean grew uncertain. The fishing rod, instead of being upright on its wooden stand, was smashed. The broken rod lay in a trench that wound across the shingle, leading from the water almost to the edge of the beach.

Almost, she thought. *But it just stops. As if something huge was dragged – or dragged itself – up the beach for ten yards or so, then simply stopped.*

"Don't go near the water!" warned Fergus, taking her arm. He was still wide-eyed, scanning the surface of the loch. His fear was infectious, and Jean laid her hand on his.

"What was it?" she whispered.

The caretaker shook his head.

"I canna say," he replied, his Highland accent much broader than usual. "All I know is that my grandma told me stories of strange beasts in the lochs. Things that lay sleeping for ages, so that they're almost forgotten. And then they rise, and–"

He stopped, shaking his head again.

"We should go, woman!"

He quickly gathered up the broken pieces of his rod, along with his crushed haversack, and set off back up to the road. Jean hesitated, then caught up with him. They said nothing while walking back to Boleskine House. As they were nearing the house, a motor taxi from Inverness clattered by.

"That'll be for the lady reporter," remarked Jean. "Just think, if she'd been on that beach with you, she'd have got herself a far better story than anything that Englishman could tell her."

When they arrived at Boleskine a couple of minutes later, they were surprised to find their employer putting luggage into the taxi. Crowley saw the servants approaching and paused briefly to shout, "Lock up the house. I will return in due course. When I do, I will bring your back pay."

They never saw him again.

Jean Brash and Fergus Mackay married soon after, and enjoyed a happy marriage despite his love of Scotch. When he died, Mrs. Mackay settled into respectable widowhood, and was known to her neighbors as a calm, good-natured woman. Only on one occasion did she show unseemly excitement, and that was over something most locals saw as nonsense.

In the summer of 1933, Mrs. Mackay was at the corner store and, as usual, along with her groceries, she bought a copy of the *Inverness Courier*. She was in the middle of a pleasant chat with the assistant who was packing her purchases, when suddenly the widow stopped in mid-sentence. She turned pale and bystanders noticed that the hand holding the newspaper quivered.

"Are you all right, ma'am?" asked the sales girl.

"What?" asked Mrs. Mackay, in confusion. Then she put the *Courier* on the counter.

"Quite all right," she went on, "I just don't see the point in newspapers. They'll print any old rubbish."

Without another word, she gathered up her bags and left.

The assistant, who took little interest in the news, looked in puzzlement at the front page of the paper. It was dominated by a blurred photograph of a black object apparently rising from the water of the loch.

They call it the silly season, the girl thought. *I mean, why would anybody be upset by such foolishness? Even the headline is silly.*

The girl folded the paper carefully and put it in the rack next to all the other copies, each repeating the question that had set the whole of Scotland, and the wider world, talking.

IS THIS THE LOCH NESS MONSTER?

Chapter 1: Innocent Bystanders

Brad Steiger arrived at the North London Psychiatric Hospital for the evening visiting hour. It had been two months since he had last seen his friend, Marcus Valentine. Brad's job had made heavy demands upon his time following the incident at Mista Venja in Poland. The clash with dark forces had left Marcus mentally shattered, and Brad demoralized. Without the scholarly Englishman's expertise, Brad felt powerless to pursue Ouroboros, the cult that had brainwashed his daughter, Kelly.

As Brad got out of his rental car, he saw the British reporter, Denny Pollard, waiting at the entrance to the hospital. She had kept him up to speed about her investigations while he had been busy elsewhere. Unfortunately, as she had admitted in their last Skype session, she had found precious little of use since their return from Eastern Europe.

"Hi, Denny," he said, giving her a hug. "How's it going?"

She gave a grimace of annoyance.

"I think we've completely lost the trail of Ouroboros," she said. "I've put out feelers to contacts all over the world. Nothing. They're in hiding, and they're obviously very good at it."

"Which means they could be building their own version of the Zamyatin Device," said Brad. "And we would never know until they fired up the damn thing."

Denny nodded.

"God knows what that would do," she said. "I wish Marcus was more coherent. You only realize how vital someone is when you lose them. Well, let's see how he's doing. You never know, people have recovered from worse traumas."

They went inside and checked with the nurse at the reception.

"Hello again," said the nurse brightly. "You're here to see Mister Valentine?"

Brad remembered her, vaguely, from his last visit. Her name badge read Anita Sharma. He had visited many times in the immediate aftermath of what they had called Marcus's 'accident.' They had claimed that Marcus had almost been killed in the burning castle of Mista Venja, which was true so far as it went.

We could hardly tell professional psychiatrists that he was attacked by a deranged snake-woman created by a mad Soviet experiment, he thought. *That would just get us checked into the same wing as Marcus.*

"That's right," replied Denny. "How has he been?"

"He's been quite chipper," replied the nurse. "Such a nice gentleman! Always very polite. But he was a little agitated this morning after his daughter dropped in."

"Oh, I didn't know–" Brad began, but Denny touched him lightly on the arm, and he realized he should shut up. Then Denny asked, "Oh, his daughter visited? I didn't know."

"Yes, yes," said Anita. "She's been here a few times lately, always in the mornings. She's very nice, but I think seeing her upsets him a bit."

"I've never met Debbie Valentine," Denny went on. "I think he said she was living in America. Or was it Canada?"

The nurse frowned.

"No, her name's not Debbie, it's Lisa, and her accent was more like Russian or something," she said. "She certainly didn't sound American. I assume she grew up abroad with her mother."

As Anita was speaking, her previously cheerful expression faded, and she started to look confused.

"Ah, yes, that's right," said Denny, still improvising. "I'm thinking of someone totally different! Duh! Did Lisa leave any contact details? Only because we couldn't get in touch with her when Marcus fell ill. What with her living abroad."

"I'll just check."

Anita took her computer mouse and clicked a few times, then looked up from the screen with a puzzled expression.

"That's weird," she said, "I've only got yourself and Mister Steiger registered as visitors for Mister Valentine. That can't be right."

"Maybe it's a glitch in the system," said Denny gently. "You know how computers are."

"Yes," said the nurse, vaguely, "that must be it."

But the young woman still looked confused.

"We'll just sign in," said Brad, impatient to talk to Denny in private.

Nurse Sharma produced the visitor's book. As he signed, Brad checked the other visitors' names for that morning. He noticed a printed LISA VALENTINE next to a scrawl that might have passed for a signature. The handwriting seemed unformed, as if it was the work of a small child.

Or an adult who's learning to write? Or who's almost forgotten how?

They thanked the nurse, and were buzzed through to the long-term care wing of the hospital. As soon as nobody could overhear them, they stopped and had a hasty discussion.

"Who the hell is this Lisa?" asked Brad. "One of the Ouroboros gang?"

Denny shrugged.

"Might be," she said, "but as far as we know, they consist of just four people. Cleo, the lamia, Clay the founder of the cult, plus Kelly of course, and that young German, Andreas. I suppose Kelly might have put on a fake accent, but why?"

Brad thought for a moment, then said, "Do you think that accent she mentioned might be Polish? We never found out what happened to Lenka, that treasure hunter's girlfriend."

"Perhaps," admitted Denny, "but there's something niggling at the back of my mind. A Russian link. Professor Zamyatin was Russian, so was his whole team at Mista Venja. Maybe the Russians want their psychic gizmo back."

"After decades of not giving a damn?" asked Brad. "They just left the thing in a derelict building. No, I don't buy it. Let's keep it simple and just ask Marcus who she is. Hell, maybe he does have a grown-up daughter in Russia. When he was young he might have, how do you say it? Put himself out a bit?"

"True," conceded Denny, "he never talked much about his private life. And I can quite see this young Marcus as a bit of a Romeo. The intellectual ones, in my experience, are the ones to watch out for."

They carried on to their friend's room and found him, as usual, sitting at a desk by the window. The room was lit by the evening sun. The Englishman looked up as they came in then gave a hesitant smile.

A good sign, thought Brad. *Sometimes he doesn't notice we're there at all.*

"Hey, Marcus!" said Denny, "look who's here! The man himself!"

Fake cheerful, thought Brad. *God, we all sound the same when we visit someone in a hospital. Hearty and bogus.*

"Brad," said Marcus. "Good to see you. How's Kelly?"

"You always ask me that," said Brad, ruefully.

Marcus frowned.

"Do I? I'm so sorry, old chap. I think my memory isn't what it was."

"Hey," said Brad, sitting on the bed, "none of us is getting any younger. And in answer to your question, I haven't seen Kelly for a couple of months now."

"Not since Poland," put in Denny. "Not since the fire at the castle."

Marcus looked even more puzzled, then his face cleared.

"Ah yes, the Place of the Serpent! They tell me I was hurt. I can't really remember much. Except I seemed to have a very long, involved conversation with a very strange person–"

Marcus stopped, clearly struggling with errant memories.

"Hey," said Brad, "the nurse on duty said your daughter came over. You never said you had kids."

"Oh yes," said Marcus, nodding seriously, "she's my only child. Rather late in life, I must admit. But all the more precious, I feel."

Brad and Denny exchanged a glance, then waited for Marcus to continue. But he said nothing more.

"So tell us more about Lisa," prompted Denny, sitting next to Brad.

"Well," said Marcus, "she's not had an easy time. A bit like Kelly, in fact. She got into dangerous company and had all sorts of problems. I'm afraid she did a few bad things, too. But she's good at heart, I know. I like to feel everyone is essentially good, or at least that most of us are. Don't you agree?"

Brad didn't, but he gave a sympathetic nod before asking, "So where does she live? Does she have a job?"

Marcus looked as if he were struggling to recall something, and gave a hesitant smile.

"I don't think she has either, Brad," he said, hesitantly. "She's been struggling to come to terms with life. It's not given to many of us to be born three times."

Brad and Denny exchanged a glance, then Brad asked, "Three times? What does that mean?"

"I mean she was born three times!" exclaimed Marcus. "First, she was born in the usual way, then she was reborn against her will, and finally she became my daughter, my only child. Isn't that wonderful? Thrice born, a miracle of sorts!"

The Englishman's voice had risen, and his eyes were shining with a fanatical glee. Denny put her hand on Brad's arm.

"Hey, this isn't an interrogation," she turned to Marcus. "I think we both want to know, when do we get to meet Lisa?"

"I'm sure she'd love to meet you," Marcus replied, calming down noticeably at the commonplace question. "But my Lisa is rather secretive, and she goes her own way. She's been traveling, you know. Like a student on a gap year. Only–"

The Englishman paused again, inclined his head as if listening to some noise Brad could not hear.

"She says there's something she needs to do. A problem that needs solving. And you two will play a big part in her plans!"

Marcus smiled.

"Isn't that nice?"

Oh yeah, thought Brad. *Nice as pie.*

***

The dining room of the Rabbie Burns Hotel in Fort Augustus offered a splendid view up the length of Loch Ness. As Paul Meroney had grumpily remarked, they probably added fifty pounds to the bill as a result. But Paul's wife, Julie, loved dining at the table by the picture window. The only downside was that the sight of the loch prompted their daughter Cressida to chatter incessantly. With the obsessiveness of a five-year-old, she had had just one topic of conversation during the entire holiday.

"I saw a mermaid today," said Cressida, a spoonful of pasta poised halfway to her mouth.

The news did not surprise Julie, given that Cressida had mermaid plush toys, mermaid pajamas, a mermaid duvet cover, a mermaid night-light, and mermaid socks.

"No, you didn't," said her brother Will, a nine-year-old rationalist. "There's no such thing as mermaids."

"I did see a mermaid!" retorted Cressida, with a hint of outrage. The girl's tone set off alarm bells in Julie's brain. Cressida turned to her mother and went on, "The mermaid said 'hello' to me and asked me to come into the lake for a swim, but I said 'no,' because I know you should never go with strangers."

"Well, that was very sensible of you, darling," said Julie. "Now, eat your dinner before it gets cold."

"Anyway, if there were mermaids, they'd live in the sea, not a lake in Scotland," grumbled Will, before shoving a forkful of ravioli into his mouth.

"It's a loch, not a lake," said Paul wearily. "Loch Ness. It's famous. But for big long-necked monsters, not mermaids."

"She wasn't a monster," insisted Cressida, "she was very pretty. In fact, she looked a bit like Beyoncé, but she wasn't like the mermaids in books or films, or the one on my night-light."

"Beyoncé?" asked Paul, showing genuine interest in his daughter's conversation for the first time in days.

Cressida, sensing a more receptive audience, turned to her dad.

"Yes, she was pretty with long hair. And she had nothing on so I could see her boobies."

The little girl had a voice that carried extremely well. There was a lull in the general hum of conversation in the dining room. A man at the next table spat soup, spluttered, and quickly wiped his face with a napkin. Paul said nothing but tried to catch his wife's eye. She avoided looking at him, trying to suppress a giggle.

"Now, dear," she said to Cressida, "don't be so loud. And if it was a lady having a swim with no clothes on she'll just get into trouble with the police."

"Where did you see this mermaid, petal?" asked Paul, with an air of detached curiosity that did not fool Julie.

"On the little shingle beach this afternoon," said Cressida. "You were asleep and Mummy had taken Will for a poo in the forest."

"We don't use that word at the table if we want some sticky toffee pudding!" said Julie sharply. "Finish your food, dear, we're all waiting for you."

Cressida shoveled another mouthful in with a sulky abruptness.

"I did see her," she added. "And I took a picture of her with daddy's phone."

"Of course, dear," said Julie, glad to have defused the incident. Other diners were returning to their meals and conversations, now that there was no prospect of Cressida having a meltdown.

Later, when he and Julie were undressing for bed, Paul complained that his wife over-indulged their daughter's mermaid fantasies.

"It's just a harmless phase," said Julie. "Anyway, you're obsessed with Will playing for Manchester United, even though he hates football. I'm not living out my dreams through my children."

"Now that's totally unfair–" began Paul, but then stopped as his phone beeped.

"We made a solemn vow to answer no work emails," warned Julie, climbing into bed. She patted the covers next to her. "We promised to have some together time. Extra special time. Make the most of it, big boy."

"Okay," sighed Paul, "I'll just turn it off after I've made sure it's not an emergency, because remember what happened last ... Good grief!"

"What is it?" asked Julie.

Without speaking, he handed his phone to her. Julie looked at the photo, then at Paul.

"Did someone from work send you this? You should report them. It's that Alan, isn't it? He's a sexist dinosaur, that bloke. Talking to him is like meeting a grubby time traveler from the Seventies."

Paul shook his head.

"It's not from Alan, it's not an email at all," he said. "Look at the time stamp. That's a photo taken this afternoon. Don't you recognize the beach? Not to mention the mountains in the background."

Julie stared at the beach and the mountains. They did look very familiar, but she found it hard to concentrate on the background. The figure in the foreground drew the eye.

"Well, she has got undeniably big boobies," she admitted. "Not sure about the Beyoncé thing, though. Rather a hard face. Calculating. Not a good look on a mermaid."

"Topless bathing's strictly forbidden," Paul said, taking the phone back. "I'll keep this as evidence."

"Oh yeah, it's evidence of something," mocked Julie. "Just delete it."

Her husband paused, sitting on the bed staring at the cell screen.

"Paul? Are you perving over another woman rather than getting into bed with me?"

He held up the screen to her.

"What do you make of that behind her?" he asked. "That curved thing in the water?"

Julie laughed.

"Are you suggesting she's actually got a tail? It's just a wave or something. Delete the pic and come to bed."

"Okay," he said. "Your wish is my command."

***

Lisa Valentine, she thought, studying herself in the mirror of the hotel bathroom. *I was Olga Volkova. Then the very clever, very stupid, very bad men made me The Insane One. And then a good man gave me so much of his humanity that I became a person again. And so I chose to become his only child.*

"I am someone again," she said to herself, and smiled. "I am moving among people, doing human things. I wear nice clothes, and shoes, and make up. I have a nice daddy, who's been very ill, so I go and visit him. I even take him fruit and puzzles! And I even have a handsome boyfriend who loves me. I am living the dream!"

Lisa went back into the bedroom and leaped onto the bed next to Pavel. He was staring at a movie on the television. She watched along with him for a few minutes, but found much of the dialogue baffling, the plot incomprehensible. Besides, the movie was about men with guns fighting monsters in some kind of labyrinth. She had had quite enough of that sort of thing. She picked up the remote and switched channels until she found a cartoon about a family of amiable pigs.

"Are you happy, darling?" she asked in Polish, snuggling up beside Pavel.

"Yes, darling," he replied. "I am the luckiest man in the world."

Lisa gave a slight frown. His voice was flat, expressionless. He said whatever she wanted, as a real lover should. But his robotic delivery was off-putting.

"Oh, honey," Lisa said, sighing, "perhaps a bit too deeply when I made you my slave. If only you had more – more, what's that word?"

She looked up into Pavel's blank face, not expecting him to reply.

"Freedom," he said, surprising her.

"Yes," she said, "freedom. Just enough to think for yourself, while remaining true to me of course. But when I was insane, I tended to overdo things, didn't I? Oh well."

She watched the animated pigs have a cozy adventure for a few more minutes, then the show ended and the evening news began. Lisa found news almost as distasteful as the film about men with guns, and for similar reasons. But she forced herself to keep up with current affairs, just in case bulletins offered some clue as to the location of her enemies.

"Why are people so stupid?" she asked, as reports of a man-made disaster followed an update on a terrorist atrocity. "They have a wonderful world, and they spoil it in so many ways. Why don't they all just wake up and ..."

She groped for a suitable phrase. Again, Pavel surprised her.

"Wake up and smell the coffee."

"Yes!" she cried. "Wake up and smell the coffee, hear the birds, feel the heat of the sun. Laugh and love and leave out lying, cheating, killing."

"I think you'll find this world a bit more complicated than that," said Pavel, in the same robotic voice.

Lisa laughed.

"Maybe you have got enough freedom, to think at least," she said, approvingly. "Or maybe my bite is wearing off?"

She was pondering whether she would have to renew her influence over Pavel, when suddenly an image flashed onto the screen. The announcer adopted an arch tone, one Lisa had learned that people use when they are feeling clever and superior.

'And finally, is this Nessie or the Not-So-Little Mermaid? As you can see, we've had to pixilate this photo. An Australian tourist claims he took it from the passenger seat of a car driving along the shores of Loch Ness this morning. The image, which has been viewed millions of times online, seems to show a half-woman, half something else. The prevailing view is that it's a hoax, possibly created as a viral marketing campaign for a new superhero movie. And now a look at tomorrow's weather for us mere mortals ...'

Lisa sat bolt upright.

"It's her! The bitch who would have killed me."

Pavel gave a stifled yelp and she realized she was almost crushing his hand in hers.

"I'm sorry, my darling," she said, patting his shoulder. "I'll kiss it better. Then we will find out where this place is, and we will go there, and I will slaughter our enemies and possibly bathe in their blood and entrails. If circumstances permit, of course."

She smiled up at Pavel's impassive face.

"After all," she added, "we've got a world to save."

***

"You were seen!" said Jonathan Clay. "You attracted attention! We were supposed to be laying low."

Cleo stretched her naked body luxuriously, hands and feet pushing against the walls of the small cabin. She was over six feet tall, and the old pleasure boat they had hired felt cramped even for Clay, who was shorter than average.

"I had to get out, take the air," she said languorously. "And nobody believes I'm real when I'm half-transformed."

She's becoming reckless, unpredictable, Clay thought. *Ever since Steiger shot her, she's been acting erratically.*

Cleo smiled, and sat up on her makeshift bed. Reaching up, she cupped Clay's face in one elegant, strong hand.

"Jonathan, I may not be able to read your thoughts precisely, but I don't need telepathy to know you're pissed off. But you're a clever man. You should know there's a method to my madness. Stop questioning me."

"What's going on?" asked Kelly, climbing down into the cabin via a metal ladder. "You two bickering again? That's gotten really old."

Cleo released Clay and got up, crouching to avoid hitting her head on the low roof.

"Why do you think I gave a few tourists a thrill, Kelly?" she asked the American girl.

Kelly shrugged. "To attract attention, but not from the authorities. If you Brits have some kind of government department that deals with the paranormal they'd have come at us before now. So, logically, you wanted to get someone else's attention, right?"

"Bingo!" said Cleo. "But who?"

"Not my dad, I'm guessing," replied Kelly. "Not since he shot you."

Cleo's smile faded. She ran her fingers over the scars left by bullet wounds on her body.

"If he wasn't your father, I'd have killed him for that," she said. "And if he interferes again I won't hesitate to finish him. This is too important for any kind of family loyalty. But as it happens, I have a distraction in mind for daddy dearest. Chances are, you won't see him again. How do you feel about that?"

Kelly shrugged.

"I see the big picture," said the girl. "What I don't understand is why you want the Insane One to come here."

Clay gasped.

"What good would it serve, bringing that monster to us? She killed poor Helga."

Cleo leaned forward until her face was close to his. A pink tongue flicked around her full lips.

"She is a rogue, an unknown quantity. While she lives, Ouroboros is divided, its spirit weakened. I sense it, I sense her. She's not far away. She wants a showdown as much as I do. Remember, she killed one of us. A reckoning is due."

"Does it have to be about blood and revenge?" pleaded Clay. "Can't we just go ahead and complete the device? Once we activate it, all this hatred and spite will be irrelevant."

Cleo gave a snort of laughter.

"Easy to say if you're a world-weary old man," she sneered. Then, in a kindlier tone, "Jonathan, without you, none of this would be possible. You rediscovered Ouroboros. Without you, I would have led a miserable, short life. But you fail to see the big picture that Kelly grasps so firmly. Random elements like the Insane One cannot be permitted to exist in our new order."

She's almost talking like a politician, now, thought Clay, then hastily tried to suppress the idea. But Cleo was not focused on him, he realized. She had lain back down and was starting to writhe on her worn mattress. Her mocha-colored skin began to grow scaly, and her legs started to merge into a great muscular tail. She moaned and they heard sickening cracks as bones and cartilages re-configured.

"Again?" whispered Kelly to Clay. "It's getting more frequent."

Clay shook his head, unable to offer an opinion. This was something new. Cleo was barely able to retain fully human form for more than a few hours a day. Even Olivia, the first lamia created in centuries and former leader of the cult, had been in control of her metamorphosis right to the end. In Cleo, the human element had been almost overwhelmed by the serpent-goddess.

"Send Andreas down," lisped Cleo. The tongue that flicked over her lips was black, now, and forked.

Clay looked into the lamia's golden-yellow eyes and saw fathomless, inhuman lust. This, too, was new and disturbing. But he dared not demur. He followed Kelly up onto the deck of the *Talisman* and spoke to the young German at the wheel.

"She wants to see you."

Andreas looked at Clay, then at Kelly, who smiled and nodded.

"It'll be okay," she said. "She just needs to take the edge off."

Andreas made a familiar, unconscious gesture, running his fingers over the now nearly invisible scars on his neck. Cleo's bite had made him her slave.

Part of him must be revolted by this, thought Clay. *Some locked away fragment of the ordinary man he was.*

Andreas let go of the wheel and went down the cabin ladder. The young man closed the hatchway behind him. But not before Clay had heard a moan of anticipation from below that turned into a spine-chilling hiss of anticipation.

Chapter 2: Sketches and Charges

For a few days after the clash with Ouroboros in Poland, Brad's nightmares had eased off. At the time, he felt that the confrontation had provided some catharsis. But it had been a temporary respite, because he knew that nothing had been resolved. Brad had not persuaded Kelly to leave Ouroboros. He had not prevented them from taking the plans for Zamyatin's psychic amplification device. Above all, he had left his greatest ally, Marcus, to the mercies of a monster, and the creature had mutilated his mind.

"*True,*" said Kelly, as he enumerated these failures, as he did almost every night. "But nobody said life is a bowl of cherries."

In this dream, father and daughter were sitting in a boat, a small wooden skiff. Kelly was dressed in old-fashioned ladies' clothes, all white silk and taffeta, complete with a pink-ribbon bonnet and high buttoned boots. Brad was wearing a light-colored suit, and a panama hat. He was rowing them across a lake. The problem was they seemed to get no nearer to the shore. He kept glancing over his shoulder, but the dark hills that surrounded the expanse of blue-gray water stayed remote, seemingly unattainable.

Brad was puzzled by this, but also by Kelly's comment.

"*I thought that's exactly what the old song said? That life is a bowl of cherries. Isn't that how the lyrics go?*"

"*Well, we can easily find out!*" exclaimed Kelly, with a winsome smile. She picked up an old-style record and put it onto a wind-up gramophone, then began cranking up the clockwork. The record began slowly, then sped up. The lyrics became comprehensible.

"*There,*" said Brad. "*Life is indeed a bowl of cherries. It's in a popular song, must be true. Why aren't we moving? I'm rowing as hard as I can.*"

"*You're not going to the island, that's why,*" said Kelly. "*If you don't row us to the right place we can't smash the rotten, corrupt system. And you know how much you want to do that.*"

"*I don't—*" he began, then realized what he was saying. Kelly laughed.

"*Fooled ya! When I was little, you told me that most people are good and the world is a good place, basically. Don't you ever feel ashamed of the way you lied?*"

"*You were just a kid,*" he protested, easing up and leaning on the oars. "*Anyhow, there are lots of good people out there. And, you know how it is, I didn't want to tell you about wars and famines.*"

"*No, you let me find out for myself,*" she retorted. "*Through the one simple trick of not being there most of the time. Gee, thanks, Dad!*"

Brad shook his head, was about to argue that she was being unfair. But then the boat heaved, pitched, and lifted almost out of the water before splashing down again.

"*Oops,*" said Kelly. "*Don't know my own strength. Or our own strength. Sometimes it's hard to tell.*"

The dark gray water parted a few yards to one side in an eruption of foam. A golden serpent appeared, magnificent and terrifying. It looked down at Brad with golden eyes, and smiled. Then it opened its mouth and descended upon him, taking his head between its vast jaws.

And that was when he woke up, as usual. He followed his customary routine, turning on the bedside lamp and reaching for pen and notepad. If he didn't write down the dream's contents at once, it tended to fade, and blur into earlier nightmares. Within minutes, all he would be left with was the familiar, depressing sensation of failing to communicate with his daughter.

Kelly. Monster. Lake. Boat. Not moving. Old song about ...

He paused.

Damn. Some kind of fruit? Strawberries?

"Crap," he said to the functional, charmless hotel room. "Missed it again."

It was just before dawn on an August morning in London. Knowing it was pointless to try and get back to sleep, Brad got up and did a couple hours work on his laptop. He was now officially based in England for work purposes, though his assignment would only last for six months. He was supposed to be looking for rented accommodation but had made little progress. London's housing situation was even crazier than in big-city America. He was also taking more unpaid leave days than was good for his reputation in the company, but there was nothing he could do about that.

After dealing with a few emails, Brad went back to his notepad, hoping that his subconscious would dredge up some more details. Instead, he became frustrated and eventually found himself reciting the names of fruit out loud.

"Apple. Orange. Raspberry. Blueberry. Boysenberry. Roddenberry, goddamit! I sound like a crazy person."

He stopped doodling, realizing that as he had struggled to recall the elusive fruit, his pen had traced a familiar circular pattern. It was the symbol of the ancient Ouroboros, the snake eating its own tail.

Life. Death, Rebirth. The eternal cycle.

Dismissing the nightmare, he shaved, showered, and dressed. Then he looked through some more of Marcus's writings and drawings. Every time he visited his friend, the Englishman handed over sheets of paper he had covered in words and images. They were clearly of great significance, but Marcus could never explain in plain English what their meaning might be. The problem was made worse by the scholar's poor handwriting, which often degenerated into a baffling scrawl.

Brad sighed as he looked over lists of seemingly random words, sketches of places that might be purely imaginary. One recurring image was of a long, diagonal shape. It reminded Brad a little of a rough slash in a piece of fabric. There was also a dot at one end of the slash. Two words next to the dot might have read Chilly Island.

Brad gave a grunt of displeasure and looked at the next page. This needed no interpretation. It was yet another of Marcus's crude renditions of something most people would never recognize. At first glance, it seemed to be a rough circle covered with cracks, like an egg about to hatch. Thanks to his training in geology, Brad knew that it showed the Earth. Instead of continents and oceans, Marcus had sketched out the tectonic plates lying miles beneath the surface. The cracks were the places where these plates collided as they drifted over the planet's molten core. The jagged lines, therefore, showed where volcanic eruptions and earthquakes occurred.

Brad picked up a folder of earlier sketches, compared the latest to its predecessors. Sure enough, Marcus had repeated his earlier perspective, showing the Earth from directly above Western Europe.

Ominous as hell, thought Brad. *But what does it mean? The Zamyatin device can't cause earthquakes, can it? The sheer energy involved would be immense.*

Brad tried to visualize some means of triggering a major seismic event that didn't involve deep holes and big nuclear bombs. His reverie ended when his phone chimed, and he set the drawings aside. The call, he saw, was from Detective Sergeant Declan Healy of Scotland Yard. Healy had been assigned the case of Matt Arnold, the private investigator Brad had hired to find Kelly. Pursuing a lead, Arnold had been killed in Hyde Park, apparently by constriction. Brad recalled the police detective as a decent kind of guy, albeit one who had seemed a little out of his depth with the Ouroboros cult.

"Hi," he said, "what can I do for you?"

Healy explained that there had been some new developments in the case and would like to meet up.

"I can be at your hotel by nine," he added.

"Great," said Brad. "See you there."

After he had hung up, Brad called Denny, inviting the reporter along to the meeting.

***

Detective Constable Knapton of Scotland Yard took off all his clothes, folded them neatly, and stood in front of an array of closed circuit TV cameras. The cameras meant he was visible from four angles through fish-eye lenses. He was in a small, tiled room with two doors. He had just come in from an underground car park through the entrance door, using a key card. A woman's voice spoke from a grille over the inner door, which had no handle. *'Turn around, slowly.'*

Knapton did as he was told. *'Not bad. You have a very charming blush reflex.'*

The voice was mildly amused.

"Curse you and your paranoid security nonsense, Melissa," said Knapton. "Am I clear or not? I don't recall anyone biting me lately, but then I did spend Saturday night in an Irish pub." *'Tsk tsk. We'd better have another little twirl, just to make sure.'*

"Remind me not to sign your birthday card," muttered Knapton, attempting a pirouette. "There, have you had enough eye candy?"

In reply, there was a buzz, a click, and the inner door swung open a couple of inches. Knapton put his clothes back on and entered the complex. It was, at first glance, a normal office building. But none of the doors had names, only numbers, and there were security checkpoints at the end of every corridor. After he had been scanned, patted down, and bantered with by three sets of armed guards, Knapton finally reached his destination.

"Take a seat," said the white-haired man known only as the Director. "We've got some catching up to do."

On their first meeting, Knapton had pointed out that, as a detective, he might easily find out the Director's real name. The Director had spelled out why that would be a bad idea for both of them, and Knapton had dropped the idea. But he felt sure the Director was a bureaucrat in some seemingly innocuous role.

Deputy Under-Secretary of State for Ancient Buildings, he thought. He was making a mental list of possible titles. Knapton would never be so foolish as to write the list down.

"How is our mutual friend?" asked the Director. "Still looking a bit seedy? Distracted? Off his game?"

"Yes, and not just at work. His wife left him," explained Knapton. "Took the kids. Said he wasn't the man she married, allegedly. Which he isn't, I suppose."

"No, quite. Sad situation."

"Can't we do anything to help him?" asked Knapton. "It's not easy, working with a man who, you know, is ..."

The police officer struggled to find the right words.

"Enchanted?" suggested the Director. "Mesmerized? Whatever you call it, we can't cure it. We could of course confine him for his own safety, but that would involve legal procedures. A police officer can't just vanish. Too many people would notice."

"Is that why you can't do anything?" demanded Knapton. "Or is it because it would risk making your secret outfit a little less secret?"

The white-haired man smiled.

"The Prime Minster, and not to mention the Queen, know nothing about this unit," said the Director. "It's been around for a long time precisely because only sixty-six people in the world know it exists. And you're quite right; this leads to the paradox that hampers all covert organizations. The more we actually do, the less secret we can be. So we prefer to operate at a certain distance from the action. In this case, the Ouroboros problem. We need to tackle it urgently, so we are doing as little as humanly possible about it ourselves."

"That's a bit barmy, sir, with all due respect," said Knapton. "I prefer to go straight at a problem, get it sorted out."

"It's in the nature of government to be somewhat barmy, as you put it," said the Director. "Or schizophrenic, if you want a fancier term. The modern state tells its citizens, over and over, that we're in a state of crisis. There is always some imminent disaster, some deadly peril. Yet at the same time, the state tells them that everything will be fine, just trust us to do our jobs, it's no big deal really. Conflicting messages all the time, about the economy, crime, terrorism. It's not surprising that ordinary people get disillusioned. Living with a government can feel a lot like sharing a padded cell with a lunatic."

Knapton nodded slowly.

"Fair enough," he said, "but that doesn't tell me why we can't simply neutralize Ouroboros rather than providing discreet nudges to amateur monster hunters."

"Because we don't know two key facts," shot back the Director. "One, how far does their reach extend? Most of them died at Wychmere, when Steiger managed to mess up their May Day ritual. We know at least one recruit was killed in Poland, again thanks to Steiger's intervention, or so we suspect. The Poles are even cagier about this stuff than we are."

"So their numbers are depleted," said Knapton, "and they've been beaten back twice. Why not make it a hat-trick?"

The Director waved a dismissive hand.

"The other factor," he said, "is what they plan to do with the Zamyatin device? It may be almost useless, or more dangerous to its users than anyone else. Remember, this was a technology that the Soviets abandoned. If we suspect it's a real threat, we would move instantly. As we did with the cleanup at Wychmere."

"So, in brief," said Knapton, "we can sit back and watch a right bloody mess develop in the hope that everyone we don't like will obliterate themselves? And if a few innocent people get killed along the way, that's just tough luck on them?"

"That's not how I would phrase it in an official report," said the Director, slowly. "But you have summed up our approach rather neatly."

"So if we let Steiger carry on his personal crusade and he shoots a few more of them you'd be happy?" asked Knapton, incredulously. "Because at Scotland Yard that might be considered a tad negligent."

The Director waved a hand in gentle dismissal.

"I'm sure it would," he said. "But we are above minor matters like the law."

A bit less of the 'we,' thought Knapton. *If you don't mind.*

***

"You're joking, surely?" asked Brad.

He was sitting in the lobby of his hotel looking at a photo on page three of a British tabloid. Like all such newspapers, it was a slightly crazy mish-mash of editorial outrage, celebrity gossip, facts about sports that Brad did not really understand, and general weirdness. In the latter category was the picture of the so-called 'Loch Ness Mermaid'.

"Well, it is what we call the silly season," conceded Denny. "But think about the location."

"Loch Ness?" said Brad. "I thought that was just some dumb hoax about a plesiosaurus. What's the connection?"

Denny shrugged.

"Maybe no link at all," she admitted. "It's not a good picture. I just thought you might recognize her."

Brad took out a pocket magnifier and scrutinized the grainy color picture more closely. The face of the so-called mermaid was turned away, but there was something familiar about the head and neck.

"You think this is the one who was at the circus sideshow?"

Denny nodded.

"Lilith, who deceived Adam, according to her publicity," she said. "Though I believe you said her real name was Cleo?"

"That's what Kelly called her," said Brad. "Clearly a few bullets didn't slow her down much. Any normal woman would have died, bled out on that cellar floor."

Denny looked at him approvingly.

"Was it the first time you shot someone?"

Brad shrugged.

"First time I hit someone I shot at," he said, standing up as a familiar figure walked into the lobby. "Let's leave it there. Here's the man from Scotland Yard."

Brad started to introduce Denny to Detective Sergeant Healy, but was cut off before he could finish. The police officer barely glanced at the reporter then said to Brad, "Mister Steiger, sorry, but I must ask you to accompany me to the Yard for questioning. You are free to refuse of course, but if you do I will feel compelled to seek an arrest warrant."

Brad was dumbfounded. Healy's cold, abrupt manner was as surprising as his demand. When they had first met, Healy had been helpful, witty, clearly a good cop. Now Brad felt the need to be defensive. He noticed a uniformed policeman standing just outside the hotel entrance.

"Ms. Pollard was just leaving anyway," he said, with a significant glance at Denny.

No need for two of us to get tangled up in this, he thought. Clearly, she was of the same mind.

"Right," she said, gathering up her bag and the newspaper. "Okay, I'll be in touch about – well, I'll be in touch."

"Let's go," said Brad, leading Healy out of the hotel. "Can you tell me what this is about?"

"The death of Matt Arnold," said Healy, hurrying to keep up. "Plus the death of Kathy Hopkirk in Wychmere, which the local police asked us to look into."

The uniformed officer ushered Brad to a car. He expected to be handcuffed, then recalled that he was not actually under arrest. On the ride to Scotland Yard, he kept quiet for a few minutes and observed Healy and his colleague. The latter seemed normal enough, if taciturn. But the detective was distinctly odd-seeming. His skin was pale, his hair untidy, and at times he gave a characteristic tilt of the head.

As if he's listening to someone talking to him through an earpiece, thought Brad. *Except he's not wearing one.*

Brad had seen that mannerism before often enough to know its significance. He decided to attempt a simple test.

"When were you turned?" he said.

Healy's head snapped round, his eyes wide.

"What?" asked the detective. "What did you say?"

Brad smiled, his suspicion confirmed.

"I said I thought we should have taken a turn back there," he said. "But I guess you guys know your way around London."

Healy stared at him for a second longer before turning back to face front. The rest of the journey was uneventful, and Brad was shown to an interview room in London's riverside police headquarters. He felt reasonably sure of himself. If things turned unpleasant, he planned to protest, politely at first, then make a hell of a fuss. But he suspected that Healy was trying to intimidate him, or simply wasting his time.

Chapter 3: Control Freaks

Brad's interview with Healy was conducted in the usual way, in a stark, windowless room with a table and two chairs. There was a closed-circuit TV camera in one corner of the room, and a couple of microphones stood on the desk. A second plain-clothes officer was waiting. He was introduced as Detective Constable Knapton.

"I guess you must be playing nice cop?" Brad asked him, but Knapton just smiled.

Brad had seen variants on the method in dozens of movies and TV shows, but had managed to avoid such interrogations in real life. Until now. While Knapton stood back, observing, Healy began by naming the people present, then began to question Brad about Matt Arnold and Kathy Hopkirk.

"Two people you were involved with ended up dead," said Healy. "And in Miss Hopkirk's case, it was shortly after some kind of bomb was detonated in a public place."

And you can't tie that to me, thought Brad. *I was too careful.*

"As I understand it," he said carefully, "the explosion destroyed a stone monolith and harmed nobody. Of course, the damage to your country's cultural heritage is lamentable. But I was there, and what killed Kathy was not a bomb. It was ..."

Brad hesitated. He had been about to try and get a strong reaction from Healy. He was going to state bluntly that Ouroboros, an ancient snake-deity, had been invoked and killed Kathy in a rage when Brad had wrecked the ceremony. But Knapton, who was standing behind and to the left of Healy, had given Brad a clear instruction. The junior officer made the throat-cutting gesture familiar from media interviews that Brad had given a few times.

"What was it, Mister Steiger?" asked Healy, leaning forward. The detective's eyes were a little brighter now. Suddenly he seemed less robotic, eager to press home some kind of attack.

"I don't know, for sure," continued Brad, weakly. He looked questioningly at Knapton, who gave a quick nod, before continuing, "A lot of weird stuff happened. Last time we met, you were going to look into Ouroboros. What happened?"

"It's an ongoing investigation, Mister Steiger," replied Healy. "Our inquiries into the cult have been hampered by the fact that most of its members are now deceased. Perhaps it no longer exists, have you thought of that?"

"It still existed a couple of months back, in Poland," retorted Brad. "Do you know what a lamia is?"

The question was intended to have some shock effect, but Healy simply smiled.

"Lamia? I'm afraid I don't, Mister Steiger. Perhaps you would care to explain it to me?"

Again, Knapton made the 'cut' gesture, but this time Healy, turning his head, almost caught him. Knapton improvised a fake-sounding cough and covered his mouth with his hand. Meanwhile, Brad realized the point of Healy's questions. It was not intimidation, but ridicule that was being attempted. If Brad went on official record as believing in shape-shifting serpent-women the recording could be conveniently leaked. If it reached his employers, he would be through. And without a job, he certainly could not afford to spend time chasing Kelly around Europe.

"Look it up on Wikipedia," said Brad, leaning back and folding his arms.

"Did you obtain an illegal firearm in Poland?" snapped Healy. "And did you shoot someone with it?"

"I have never shot a human being in my life," replied Brad, choosing his words carefully. "Shot a few animals though. Vermin, poisonous snakes, that sort of thing."

At that, Healy's expression contorted into genuine anger, then reverted to its familiar impassivity. Brad had a sudden intuition that he was not being questioned by the man sitting in front of him.

"What's the matter, Cleo?" he asked in a snide voice. "Still licking your wounds?"

Healy jumped up out of his chair and seemed about to fling himself over the table at Brad. But what was even more unusual was the strange hiss Healy emitted before Knapton leaned and grabbed his colleague by the shoulder.

"Careful, you'll damage your puppet," said Brad, knowing he had guessed right. Behind Healy's eyes was the lamia he had wounded at Mista Venja. She was acting as a kind of puppeteer, projecting herself into Healy's mind.

"You will regret that Steiger!" said Healy in a voice that was incongruously feminine and husky rather than his normal tone. Then the detective seemed to fold up and collapse into his chair. Knapton went from restraining Healy to trying to stop him from falling sideways to the floor.

Having propped Healy up, Knapton reached for a switch next to the nearest mic and, before flicking it, said, "Interview interrupted due to Detective Sergeant Healy becoming indisposed. Recording stopped at nine forty-three."

"Can I go now?" asked Brad. "Seems to me you have no reason to detain me here other than a desire to annoy a US citizen."

"No!" moaned Healy feebly. His pale, sweaty face and vacant expression suggested a man in the throes of fever.

God, thought Brad as he stood up, *what must it be like to have one of those creatures controlling your mind?*

"I think the American consul might take an interest in what some might call harassment. Or are you actually going to charge me with something?"

Knapton gave a quick, almost imperceptible shake of the head.

Glad he's on my side, thought Brad. *Or at least, not on the side of Ouroboros.*

"Do I need to sign a form or something?" he asked. "If not, I'll just go."

"Be careful, sir," said Knapton, helping Healy to his feet. "Maybe you should get some air."

"How long has he been – like this?" asked Brad, hesitating at the door.

"Happened a few days after you first met him," said Knapton, speaking fast and low. "Now go, sir, please."

Brad did not need urging and within a couple of minutes was outside Scotland Yard looking for a cab. He caught sight of Denny waving from her car. She was illegally parked outside the national police headquarters, so he got in as quickly as he could.

"What was that about?" she asked, as she drove confidently into London's chaotic traffic.

"Healy, the detective? He's under their control," he replied, and gave a quick account of the bizarre interrogation.

"Well, we know Cleo survived and is not your number one fan," she commented. "But it doesn't take us any nearer to Kelly and her merry band of rascals. Which is why we're on our way to see a man about a magician. One of the network of experts Marcus used in his battles to rescue cult victims."

"What?" Brad was puzzled. "Did this guy get in touch with you?"

"Not exactly," replied Denny. "Let's just say he sent Marcus a few emails, and I happen to have our friend's phone. And I know a man who can hack into accounts, that kind of thing."

"You British journalists really do sail pretty close to the wind," he remarked.

Denny laughed.

"You'd be amazed at the stuff some of my colleagues get up to," she said. "Believe me, a bit of phone hacking is trivial by comparison. Anyway, this bloke is called Professor James Norton, and he's some kind of lecturer here in London. We're meeting him for lunch. He sounds like a hoot."

Brad gave her a quizzical glance.

"I meant," she said, "he's just the sort of old-school academic you'd expect Marcus to know."

They drove in silence for a while, then Brad said, "It wasn't your fault. It was mine. I left you, I split the party. The one thing you don't do and I did it."

"Yes," she said, "but then I left him behind to try and rescue someone who was probably dead already."

"We both screwed up, big time, and equally," he insisted. "And the best we can do now is finish the job. For Marcus."

***

Knapton walked Healy around Scotland Yard's inner courtyard for a few minutes. Healy seemed confused, disoriented. Holding Healy upright, Knapton could feel how thin he had become. His ribs, once well-padded thanks to fast-food lunches, were all too evident.

He's almost starving, thought Knapton. *Who or whatever is controlling him doesn't care about his health. Steiger was right, this man's a puppet.*

"You should take a few weeks' leave, boss," said Knapton. "Get away from it all, maybe go abroad. I hear there are some good deals for holidays in Cyprus."

Healy nodded, but his vague expression make Knapton wonder if he was being understood. He sat Healy down on a bench and stood over him, wanting to question him about Ouroboros.

"I'll be fine, mate," said Healy, eyes still unfocused. "Just leave me to it. I'll be back in the office after lunch."

"Can I get you anything, boss?" asked Knapton. "How about a pastry, or we could push the boat out and have fish and chips?"

Healy looked Knapton in the eye, and grinned. It was a mirthless grin, so out of character that Knapton took a step back.

"Let's stop playing games, Sherlock," hissed Healy in the strange, feminine voice. "We both know I'm the third wheel in this relationship."

"Who are you?" asked the detective.

"Wrong question," sneered the voice. "*What* am I? Something you will never comprehend. Something that will soon engulf your worn-out, rotten world, with its uniforms and laws and petty concerns. I am the Alpha and Omega, Mister Policeman. I am the storm that will blow all your kind away."

Healy's face went blank, his eyes rolled up showing their whites, and he fell forward. Reaching out to catch him again, Knapton wondered if the entity was still playing games. But then he heard Healy's voice, his real voice, and was in no doubt that the possessor had gone for now.

"Help me," croaked Healy. "Help me before she comes back."

Knapton felt exasperated, all too aware he was out of his depth.

"What can I do?" he demanded. Healy replied with one word.

"Valentine!"

"What?" asked Knapton. "You mean the guy who was injured? In Poland?"

"I can't ... I can't−" repeated Healy, clearly struggling to retain control of his own faculties. He began to spasm violently, and Knapton realized his boss was having a fit. Struggling to stop Healy from swallowing his tongue, he heard one more word before the detective passed out. It was a simple word, but in the circumstances he found it ominous.

"Bite!"

***

Lunch took place in a pub near one of London University's many campuses. Professor James Norton proved to be a thin, precise man. Brad guessed Norton was in his early sixties, wearing a tweed suit that looked to be in its mid-thirties.

"Denny tells me you're an expert in folklore, magic, and all related areas," said Brad, after they had ordered. "How well do you know Marcus Valentine?"

"Not very well at all," replied Norton. He had a dry, precise manner. "He attended some of my lectures three years ago, then asked me for help on occasion. Ouroboros was by far the most interesting case. I was unable to provide much information, though. And I understand that now Marcus has become a bit of a cropper. Very foolish to tangle with such people, in my humble opinion."

Brad found himself resenting Norton's tone on behalf of his friend. But he was careful to disguise his annoyance.

"On the way here, Denny mentioned a magician," he said. "Who might that be?"

Norton gave a slightly smug smile.

"Have you ever heard of Aleister Crowley?"

Brad shook his head, prompting a sigh from Norton.

"How quickly notoriety fades," said the professor. "He did try so very hard to be famous."

"This Crowley, he has some link to Ouroboros?" asked Brad.

"Indirectly," said Norton, shifting his gaze to Denny. "If this strange story of a bare-bosomed mermaid in Loch Ness is to be credited."

"According to my sources, the picture is genuine," she said. "It's not a standard hoax, or viral advertising. But I don't see how Crowley fits in. Wasn't he just some kind of nutcase back in the nineteen hundreds?"

"An understatement, Miss Pollard," replied Norton, as if talking to a student at a seminar. "Crowley was, depending on who you ask, the supreme nutcase of the early twentieth century. He called himself a magician."

"Let me guess," put Brad, "he didn't pull rabbits out of hats or make girls in spangled costumes disappear?"

"No," said Norton. "He invoked what he claimed were guardian angels. Others said they were demons. But the point is that he lived in a place called Boleskine House on the shores of Loch Ness."

"Crowley was a member of the famous Order of the Golden Dawn," put in Denny, "which was supposedly all about spirituality and improving the world. A lot of famous people were members, including famous writers and aristocrats."

Norton looked peeved at the interruption.

"That's partly true," he said. "In fact, Crowley belonged to a splinter group that was less interested in spiritual purity and more into sex and power. Crowley formed a cult and performed rituals that were rumored to be fairly debauched and cruel. Hard to say where truth ends and myth begins."

The waitress arrived with their food and Norton paused his mini-lecture until she left.

"What we do know is that, in 1913, Crowley suddenly left Boleskine House after spending months trying to raise some powerful entity. He went to Paris, supposedly for some kind of showdown with the Golden Dawn. But it's a fact that he never went back to Loch Ness, even though he lived to a ripe old age. And a few years later, the legendary creature in the loch started to be seen more frequently. Just before World War 2, sightings came in thick and fast. Then they gradually tapered off."

Brad pondered the idea. It seemed tenuous, but not quite flimsy enough to be dismissed.

"You think Crowley stirred up some archetype of Ouroboros?" he asked. "And that it somehow manifested itself as a monster in the loch? That's quite a reach."

Norton shrugged.

"Unlike Marcus, my activities are purely academic," he pointed out. "I advance suggestions, hypotheses, guesses, if you like. But it seems quite a coincidence that Crowley should lead to Nessie, and then your cult gravitates to the same area."

"Which just happens to be on a major fault line," added Brad. Norton, he was pleased to see, seemed baffled by that. He told Norton about Marcus's drawings, and the first dreams he had shared with Kelly.

"You saw the world end in a dream?" said Norton. "I am impressed. That's what you Americans call old-school visionary material. Biblical, in fact. Clearly, we are in possession of a number of puzzle pieces. I wonder what links them together."

"The Zamyatin device," said Denny. "That must be it."

Again, Norton looked puzzled. This time it was Denny's turn to explain.

***

"Okay, honey, you wait here and I'll be back in half an hour," said Lisa, giving Pavel a peck on the cheek. He nodded, not speaking.

"I do wish we could talk some more, Pavel," she said in Polish as she unbuckled her seat-belt. "Have little chats. I remember, a long time ago, when I was Olga and human, I enjoyed little chats. It was one of those things that make you feel warm and safe."

She gave a pout, ruffled Pavel's hair. He returned a faint smile, like a man concussed or heavily sedated.

"Ah, if I could give you your freedom, would you love me?" she said.

No, she thought, *mostly because I killed your girlfriend. Poor Lenka. We could have been friends, and I went and did that. I am terrible sometimes.*

She got out of the car and went into the hospital, beaming at a group of nurses having a smoke around by the bins.

"Those things will kill you!" she shouted cheerfully.

"Up yours!" replied one of the smokers.

English sense of humor is the best in the world, she thought. *I wonder what Scotland is like? I know there must be bagpipes, played by men in those skirts with strange furry pockets at the front. But what else? So much to learn!*

Nurse Sharma was at the reception, as usual, which was a break. Lisa had timed her visits to coincide with the shifts of the nurse she controlled. Anita Sharma had been happy to help when Lisa had pretended to sprain her ankle outside the foyer. After helping Lisa to the car, it had taken just a couple of minutes to get her under control. With access to Anita's mind, Lisa could time her visits according to the nurse's shifts.

"Hello, Lisa," said the nurse, "your dad's had a good day. He's been listening to music and he ate all his lunch."

"That is truly good news," replied Lisa, choosing the English words carefully. "If he is enjoying hospital food then he must be in a very optimistic frame of mind."

The conversation was for the benefit of bystanders, both staff and members of the public. Anita buzzed Lisa through into the ward, and the thrice-born daughter was soon with her spiritual father again. As usual, Marcus seemed alarmed to see her, and his smile had a nervous look about it. But Lisa had convinced herself that he loved her as she loved him.

"You are looking a little better, I think," she said, sitting down on the bed.

Marcus, seated at his desk by the window, ran a nervous hand through his hair.

"I am in good health, I think," he said, "but my mind is not behaving itself. It is as if fragments of my memories are swirling in a maelstrom, spiraling ..."

He stopped. Lisa nodded, reaching out to touch his wounded mind with hers. The American and the journalist had been asking about her, as expected. But Marcus and Anita knew nothing of importance.

Besides, she thought, *they are Marcus's friends. Therefore, they are my friends. They just don't know it yet.*

She tended to skim the surface of Marcus's mind because the depths of his being had been wounded and left in disarray by her attack. Every visit was an act of repentance, an attempt to make amends.

"I brought you some grapes," she said, "I almost forgot! And more CDs. Bach, and Monterverdi, and Chopin, of course, a great Polish composer. You have such good taste!"

"Thank you," said Marcus, "you're very kind."

"But you are still afraid of me," she said, sadly. She felt tears start to come. "These talks are so upsetting for both of us!"

On impulse, she jumped up and went over to him, hugging him even as he flinched.

"I'm sorry, I'm so sorry, please forgive me!"

Tentatively, Marcus patted her on the back. She might have felt better about this had it not been for the way their close contact enhanced the psychic link. Lisa received a jolt as the deep-rooted trauma she had inflicted was replayed, like an old wound being opened. What made it worse was how well she remembered the pleasure of attacking Marcus, the defenseless man trapped like a cornered animal.

But there was something else, a rogue memory that she almost missed as it swirled past. She glimpsed a face, some questions, a stranger standing in this room, examining Marcus's drawings.

"You've had another visitor!" she exclaimed, leaning back to hold her adopted father at arm's length.

"It was just a policeman asking some routine questions," he replied. "I don't think I was much help. So many things I know I shouldn't tell him, and others I can't remember."

Lisa nodded, uncertain. Marcus had failed to retain even the memory of the officer's name. All she got was the impression of a face, quite young and handsome, and a kindly manner.

"Well, he can interrogate me any time," she said. "Quite a hottie, eh?"

Marcus joined in her laughter, sounding nervous.

"I am going now, Daddy," she said, releasing him. "I have to go and deal with the baddies. A super-heroine's work is never done! But when I get back we can–"

Lisa's enhanced senses told her a third person had entered the room and she was already turning when something struck her in the back. A tremendous jolt of energy shot through her, and she dropped to the floor.

Lightning, the weapon of gods and magicians.

Nausea, panic, anger welled up as she tried to reach around and pull the darts out of her shirt. Her arms would not obey her. The face that she had just seen in Marcus's mind appeared, upside down, as she writhed on the floor.

"Sorry about that," said the face. "But I thought it best if we discussed this matter on roughly equal terms. And as you could crush me to death without really trying, this is my equalizer."

He held up a black plastic gun. It looked like a toy. But when he pushed a button on the side, the lightning shot through her again.

Chapter 4: Strong Spirits

Mike Carlton was annoyed. His phone had not stopped ringing for at least twenty-four hours. As leader of the Loch Ness Cryptozoologists' Network, Carlton took his self-appointed task seriously. It was his job to collect and collate data on the unidentified creature called 'Nessie' by the popular press. He did not appreciate being asked about mermaids.

"No, I have not seen her," he was saying to a Japanese reporter whose English was not equal to her enthusiasm. "That's because she is a hoax. Hoax. No, a hoax. It means something made up. No, she wasn't wearing make-up, that's not–"

Another call came in, and Carlton used it as an opportunity to put Ms. Tanaka on hold. Unfortunately, the other call was from a local newspaper reporter in Colorado asking if he had seen the latest Bigfoot video.

"No," said Carlton in an icily polite tone. "But I hope the zipper on the guy's costume isn't quite so conspicuous in this one."

That got rid of one nuisance but more kept calling. After a few more minutes, he did the unthinkable and turned off his phone. The silence in his small office was oddly disturbing. Gradually, though, the sounds of the Scottish Highlands began to assert themselves through the half-open window. The wind over the loch, distant bird-calls, the sounds of children playing on the shore.

"Sanity," Carlton sighed. "I should switch off more often."

He stood up and, after a momentary hesitation, left his phone on the desk. Today he would go to the pub for lunch without his link to the silly, shallow outside world. He was just closing the door to his office – a small wooden cabin – when someone waylaid him.

"Mister Carlton?"

Turning, he saw a young woman toting a substantial camera. Behind her, parked on the loch-side road, was a bright orange car bearing a spiky logo and some kind of dish antenna. A small group of onlookers were gathered by the vehicle. He recognized a couple of people. One shouted something inaudible in a jocular tone.

"Katie Fox, Midland News Network," the woman explained. "Can I ask you–"

"No!" Carlton snapped and turned to walk off. Unfortunately, he was flustered by Fox and found himself stalking towards the loch. The pub was in the opposite direction.

If I turn around and walk the other way, I'll look like a proper clown, he thought, and continued down to the shore. The reporter followed him, repeatedly asking for an interview.

"You are the recognized authority on the Loch Ness Monster," she wheedled. "Just a few words?"

Carlton sighed and turned to look into the lens of the camera.

"The term 'Loch Ness Monster' is one I find most objectionable," he said, adjusting his anorak and resettling his glasses on his nose.

"And why is that?" asked Fox. "Because it's not real?"

"No!" he replied. "Because it assumes that any creature in the loch must be somehow unnatural. Whereas I, and other researchers, consider the so-called monster to be merely a large, unidentified animal."

"Like a dinosaur, you mean?" asked the reporter.

Carlton suppressed another sigh.

"You are no doubt referring to the plesiosaurs, which do indeed bear some resemblance to the creatures spotted and photographed hereabouts," he began. "But they became extinct some sixty-five million years ago. It seems impossible that a breeding colony of large reptiles might have survived in this one, relatively small–"

Carlton, now well into his standard lecture on the subject, took a few moments to notice that the lens of the camera was now pointing at his midriff. Katie Fox had let the eyepiece fall away and was staring, apparently at Carlton.

"What on earth are you doing?" he asked. Then, looking past her, he saw the small crowd on the road pointing and holding up phones. He turned to look out over the loch just in time to see a huge, terrifying head vanish beneath the dark waves. Carlton stood looking at the water for a while, then became aware that his mouth was open.

"What do you think of that, Mike?" asked Katie Fox, now standing beside him, camera back on her shoulder and focused on his face.

Carlton closed his mouth and said, "Well, I'll be buggered!"

There was a sudden tremor, and again the camera slewed away. Screams came from the onlookers, this time more urgent than before. A great rumbling sound echoed between the hills that flanked the loch.

***

"Our first test, and it went well," said Cleo, turning the small truck onto the highway out of Inverness. Kelly sat beside her in the passenger seat. The two men were in the back with the bulky device. The latter, a mass of old-fashioned valves and dials, was powered by hefty batteries that left little room for Clay and Andreas.

The cult members were listening to an interview on the local radio news. A talk show host was talking to someone who had witnessed the 'latest manifestation of Nessie.'

"So," asked the presenter, "was it another buxom mermaid?"

Cleo laughed.

"No," said the eyewitness, "it was more like, you know, Nessie."

"Well," persisted the host, "what did it look like?"

"Something between a Chinese dragon and a sea serpent," was the reply. "I filmed it on my phone, anyway. So did lots of people and–"

"Yeah," the host butted in, "and it did coincide with this earthquake, first we've had in a long while. You think Nessie might have tummy trouble, Angus? Maybe eaten a shepherd that didn't agree with her?"

Cleo flicked off the radio.

"Mockery. Disrespect. But at least some of them saw one of the Old Ones."

"One of the oldest aspects of Ouroboros," Kelly agreed. "I felt her, albeit for a fleeting moment. Felt her need to be reborn. She wants to rise again and claim her inheritance."

"It was still very reckless," said Clay, crouching in the back of the truck. "Somebody could have been killed! And now there are witnesses."

Andreas looked puzzled, staring from Clay to Cleo and back.

"You're upsetting him, Jonathan," Kelly admonished Clay. "The whole point is to attract attention, remember? It creates a sense of wonder, of myth becoming reality."

"Yes," chimed in Cleo, "it all helps prepare people mentally for the Big Event. And if the Insane One comes as a result of our actions, so much the better. She has to be destroyed, or she could derail the whole process."

"But why do we have to go to Culloden Moor?" demanded Clay. "We know it works."

"We know it worked once," Kelly replied. "We need another test, and the loch is too close to home, right Cleo?"

"You read my mind, honey," smiled the big woman. "We'll be there in half an hour. Then we see if that thing raises the dead."

"I still think we should have built up our numbers," muttered Clay. "Followed the old ways."

"The old ways got most of us killed at Wychmere," snapped Cleo.

There was a long silence. Kelly reached out to Cleo with her mind.

He means well, she said. *He just can't grasp the essence of what we're trying to do.*

I know, Cleo replied. *He was the first to understand the Old Faith. I should be more patient.*

Kelly felt Cleo's irritation start to melt away, only for it to surge up again when a red sports car cut in front of her.

"You stupid bastard!" Cleo shouted.

Kelly received a sudden, shocking image of Cleo's lamia-body wrapped around a flabby, screaming, pathetic man. The victim was clad in an expensive suit, patent leather shoes, every inch the corporate type. He was also being slowly crushed in Cleo's golden coils, blood bursting from mouth, nostrils, eyeballs. Kelly realized that this stood for all the men who had abused Cleo. A generic Powerful Man who would soon be powerless, begging for a mercy that would not be forthcoming.

"Sorry," said Cleo, seeing Kelly's face. "I really need to rein it in. But oh baby, there's gonna be a reckoning with all those arseholes. I can hardly wait for the glorious day to come."

***

"This is boring," moaned Will. "I thought there'd be soldiers and stuff."

"Shh, dear," said Julie, smiling apologetically at the small group of tourists. Nobody smiled back. The bleakness of the tourists' expressions mirrored the weather. It might still be summer back in England, but up on Culloden Moor it was damp, with a thick mist getting denser by the minute.

Miserable old sods, thought Julie. *Why did Paul want to drag the kids to a battlefield? Anybody can see that when the battle's finished, it's just a field.*

"There's a film, with lots of explosions," said the young tourist guide, in an optimistic tone. "And we do have some re-enactors coming later to demonstrate how to fire a cannon. It makes a tremendous noise."

For a moment Julie thought Will was going to ask, in his usual bellicose tone, exactly how many explosions were on offer. But instead, her son fell silent. His expression remained eloquent, though. He was still convinced the battlefield of Culloden was boring. Cressida, clutching her plush mermaid, looked equally unimpressed. But to openly agree with her older brother would have been unthinkable. Instead, Cressida stood staring up at the guide, a disconcerting habit Julie hadn't been able to break.

"Anyway," the guide went on, "let me fill you in on a few details. Culloden was the last pitched battle fought on British soil, and took place in 1746. The forces of King George II clashed with those of the Young Pretender, Charles Edward Stuart. Charles, or Bonnie Prince Charlie, who was considered the legitimate king by his followers, of course."

"And still is by some of us," said a severe looking old man.

"Quite so," responded the guide, "but it was here at Culloden on that fateful day that the last attempt to win the throne by force ended in a welter of bloodshed. Lots of blood," he added, looking at Will. Will remained impassive.

"Now," the guide went on, "if you will come inside the Visitor Center we will view the award-winning film, 'Culloden,' which combines historical re-enactment with modern reportage to bring the many and varied characters involved to life."

People began to follow the guide inside, but then the group hesitated in confusion. The children heard it first.

"What's that noise, Daddy?" asked Will.

Paul was baffled initially but then he, too, heard the remote, eerie wail.

"I think," said the guide hesitantly, "that it might just be someone playing the bagpipes. You do get the odd lone piper around here. It's a place of pilgrimage for some."

"That's more than one piper, laddie," said the severe old man. "Sounds like a dozen or more."

"Are those the reactors, Mummy?" asked Cressida, pointing into the mist.

Julie squinted at the fleecy haze. There were figures in the mist, showing up dark gray against silver gray.

"Perhaps we should go inside, now," said the guide. He sounded nervous.

"Why?" asked Paul. "Isn't this the re-enactment?"

Before the guide could answer, there was a tremendous bang. Julie gave an involuntary scream. She heard something pass swiftly over the Visitor Center, caught a glimpse of a hurtling gray sphere. In the mist, there was a red and orange flash, then the boom of a second explosion. Ripples spread through the mist, jerked it aside for a moment. A line of men briefly came into view. There were dozens.

Nobody can afford that many re-enactors, thought Julie.

"Are they making a movie or something?" asked an American voice, without much conviction.

A series of loud bangs came from the other side of the Visitor Center. More shells passed over the tourists and tore the mist apart. And not just the mist. Cries of agony and rage came from the half-hidden men. And now booming sounds came from their direction as the artillery barrage began in earnest.

"Everybody please get inside, now!" shouted the guide. The words combined with the panic in the young man's voice unfroze the crowd, and they started to crowd into the small doorway. Julie grabbed Cressida as Paul tried to shield Will.

"Let the kids in first!" the guide pleaded, but only a couple of people moved aside. The rest continued to block the entrance in their panic. Now Julie could hear voices from the mist, voices shouting in a language that certainly wasn't English. She glanced over her shoulder, weeping in anguish, and saw an uneven line of men running straight at them.

The Highlanders would have looked quaint in their tartan kilts and headgear, had it not been for the blood-lust in their faces, and the huge swords in their hands. They charged towards the Visitor Center. The rage in their battle cries made Cressida cling tightly to Julie.

"Don't be scared, don't be scared," Julie whispered urgently. But she could hear the terror in her own voice.

***

"Zamyatin?" said James Norton finally, after mulling over their account for half a minute. "New one on me, I must admit. But then the Cold War is a little outside my sphere of interest. I tend to favor Victorian and early twentieth century occultism."

"But what do you think?" asked Denny, pushing away her plate. "Could this device somehow end the world, or at least bring down civilization as we know it?"

"What do I think? If you weren't friends of Marcus, I would dismiss you as arrant impostors," said the professor. "But as he took you seriously, I suppose I must do so as well. If this device can tap into some kind of primal energy, perhaps it will wreck this so-called civilization. And many might argue that that would not be an entirely bad thing."

Brad felt frustrated. He had hoped, he now realized, that Norton would prove to be a kind of substitute for Marcus. But instead, they seemed to have found a sedentary academic when they needed a man of action. Still, Norton was the real deal when it came to occult knowledge.

That's something, Brad thought. *But can he suggest anything useful?*

Denny must have had the same thought.

"What about Ouroboros, though?" she asked. "From what we've told you, is there any way to stop whatever they're planning?"

"Surely you have more practical knowledge than I?" Norton parried with a thin smile as he toyed with his last chicken wing. "But I will look into it. Perhaps the library archives will have something of interest. At the very least I may find the basis for an interesting paper on snake worship."

"Better hope the world doesn't end," put in Brad. "Otherwise, there'll be no academic journals to publish it in."

Norton picked up his glass of a single malt Scotch.

"Well, let's drink to that noble sentiment!"

Why not? I'm paying, thought Brad.

"Do you think the cultists might have moved into Aleister Crowley's old house?" he asked Norton.

"No," said Denny, before the professor could reply. "Boleskine House burned down a couple of years back."

"I see you've done your research," said Norton, looking a little peeved. "Yes, it is just a ruin now. Before the fire, it was owned by some kind of pop star who bought it for the ambiance. Apparently it features on a famous album cover."

"So we've got no idea where they might be?" asked Brad, rhetorically. "Still, it can't be that big an area, can it?"

"Loch Ness is one of the biggest lakes in Europe," Denny pointed out. "It's about fifteen miles long. And it's surrounded by mountainous country with lots of small towns and villages."

"But those are places where newcomers would stand out, surely?" queried Norton.

"Yeah, but the cultists have a way of controlling people," said Brad, and explained what happened to the people of Wychmere.

"Good lord, how extraordinary," said Norton, looking as if he only half-believed Brad's account. "So they could be anywhere in the region?"

"But they must have gone there because of something specific," said Denny. "A precise location. Perhaps if we–"

She stopped talking as the waitress arrived with their desserts.

"Who ordered the cherry cheesecake?" she asked.

"Mine, I think," replied Denny. At the same moment Brad looked up at the cheesecake and began to speak, then stopped himself.

"Is it yours, sir?" asked the waitress, confused.

"No, no sorry," said Brad, "I just wish I'd ordered a dessert."

Denny gave a puzzled smile.

"Share mine if you like," she offered. "I'm trying to lose a few pounds."

Brad shook his head, waited until the waitress had gone, then explained, "Something about cherries. It almost came to me. I think I dreamed it. Might there be a link to the loch?"

Denny and Norton looked baffled, but then the academic nodded hesitantly.

"You know, there might be. I can't imagine why, but perhaps I could look it up."

"Hang on," said Denny, taking out her phone.

"Oh," protested Norton, "of course you can't credit things you find on Wikipedia and such."

Denny smiled into the screen, then turned it around to show a small picture. To Brad, it seemed to show a featureless round blob in an expanse of blue-gray.

"Really?" she asked Norton as she handed the phone back to Brad. "Take a look. There's your connection."

Brad stared at the screen, looked up at the reporter.

"That's weird enough to be right," he said. "Worth a try, anyway."

"What on earth is this about?" asked Norton.

Brad tried to explain.

***

"This is wrong, this is wrong, so very wrong," Anita Sharma kept repeating.

"It's by far the lesser of two evils, that's how it pans out sometimes. Now please shut up, go outside, and keep watch," ordered Knapton.

The nurse hesitated, staring at the young woman tightly bound up in tape on the floor of the empty hospital room. Knapton grabbed Anita by the arm, leaned close to her.

"You've broken half a dozen rules to allow a non-relative to visit a vulnerable patient. Your job is on the line. I know you feel some weird compulsion to defend this creature–"

He nudged Lisa with one booted toe. She writhed and started shouting through her tape-gag. Knapton brandished the Taser Gun again and Lisa stopped moving, became quiet.

"But I reckon you're a good person, Anita," he went on. "You know you were used, hypnotized, whatever. Don't you remember?"

The nurse hesitated, frowning. Then she shook her head and went outside, closing the door behind her.

"I think we're alone now, as the song has it," said Knapton, bending over Lisa and pulling the tape from her mouth. She spat at him, then snarled a series of words in a foreign language.

"And I agree," he said, "you do have grounds for complaint. But consider my position. And remember who's in charge."

He brandished the Taser again.

"I need your help, and I'm breaking a lot of rules to ask for it. Out in the car park is a friend of mine, a good man. Unfortunately, he was bitten by one of your cohorts and now he's a puppet. Not really a man at all."

"How sad!" sneered Lisa. "I am heartbroken."

"Sarcasm is the lowest form of wit," replied Knapton. "The point is, he suggested to me that there is a solution to his problems. And you are it."

"How did you know what I am?" she shouted. She started to writhe again but, Knapton noted that she showed no sign of losing her human appearance.

"What if I said it was Mister Valentine?" suggested Knapton.

Lisa froze, then snarled again.

"No! He would never betray me!"

"As I understand it, you put him in here," returned Knapton. "Nearly killed him. Not nice behavior. In his place, I might be inclined to hit back."

"He is a good man!" Lisa yelled. "Not cruel! Not like you, fascist bastard!"

Knapton hunkered down beside her and patted her on a tape-wrapped shoulder.

"I'm trying to help a friend," he said. "And I'm going to release you in a moment so that you can help me help him."

Lisa smiled, all trace of her rage gone.

"You're thinking about killing me, of course," said the police officer, producing a clasp-knife. "I've seen that look on the faces of regular humans a few times. Well, you could do that. But then you'd never have your revenge on Cleo, would you?"

The smile vanished, and Lisa snarled. For a moment, Knapton thought he saw fangs appear. Then the smile was back and the girl said, "Tell me more, Mister Policeman. And you're right. When it comes to that bitch, my enemy's enemy is my friend. That is the right saying, yes?"

"Oh yes," said Knapton, cutting her free. "Very old saying. Now Miss Valentine, all you have to do is pretend to be a normal person while we walk out of here and go to see my friend. Do you think you can do that?"

Lisa wriggled impatiently as the knife sliced through the tape.

"I am a normal person!" she protested. "In fact, I got one better. I am *two* normal people, and both of me are fun-loving girls with oodles of charm!"

Seeing Knapton's expression she went on, "Okay, two fun-loving girls plus one scary monster from the dawn of time. But nobody is perfect, right?"

Chapter 5. A Second Bite

"You share dreams with your daughter?" said Norton, after Brad had finished. "What she dreams, you dream? And this only began when she fell in with Ouroboros?"

"That's about the size of it," admitted Brad. "But why, I don't know."

The academic pondered his empty whiskey glass.

"I've heard of such psychic connections before, but there must be a reason why this happened so suddenly. Perhaps that's the key to the whole business?" suggested Norton. "It might explain why Kelly is so important to the cult. And why they haven't killed you."

For a moment Brad stared at the professor, dumbfounded by the idea.

"We assumed that was because Kelly didn't want her dad crushed to death," put in Denny.

Norton made an impatient gesture, as if family ties were a minor point.

"Sentiment is all well and good," he said, "but this is a cult dedicated to power. You say in one dream she showed you a vision of some of kind of rural Utopia, presided over by the benevolent spirit of Ouroboros."

"That's right," said Brad. "It struck me as kind of absurd, fake. You know, a sort of Disney-world paradise."

"The kind of place you'd like to visit but you'd go crazy if you had to live in?" asked Denny.

Brad nodded.

"Exactly that," he said. "A world devoid of conflicts, suffering, inequality, all presided over by some supernatural being. People living like that wouldn't really be human, would they?"

Norton gave a humorless bark of laughter.

"What you describe would be paradise for millions of less fortunate folk alive today," he pointed out. "But I take your point. They want to remake the world and remake humanity in the process. And their ideal world is one with very few people in it, all living in little villages, yes?"

"Which implies a lot of death and destruction to get to that ideal," said Denny. "Big heaps of corpses and cities in flames."

"And how does that tie in to Loch Ness, exactly?" asked Norton.

Brad tried to describe his dreams of the earth cracking along the fault lines in its crust.

"And I think," he went on, "that they're in Scotland because it's where the nearest fault line is. It runs straight down the middle of Loch Ness, through what they call the Great Glen."

Brad noticed that Denny was not giving her full attention, and looked over his shoulder to see the television screen. The volume was turned low, but he could make out an amateurish-looking video clip.

"Oh my God," he said.

"Is that what you saw in Wychmere?" asked Denny, eyes wide.

Norton, too, was staring. Others in the pub were scornfully dismissing the footage as a hoax, part of the same 'viral campaign' that had produced the mermaid. Only Brad and his companions kept straight faces.

"Yes," he said. "That's what we saw in the stone circle. Only I think that one is way bigger."

The TV news moved on to the day's sports highlights. Clearly the Loch Ness item had been the piece of fun that drew a line under the 'real news.'

"At least that settles it," said Denny, sounding subdued. "We're going to Scotland. Care to join us, Professor Norton?"

Norton looked nonplussed.

"A sane man would stay well away from murderous cultists trying to raise a giant monster from the dawn of time," he mused. "But my students all think I'm a mad old coot, so why not? I'm on sabbatical anyway. And if I get myself killed, my colleagues will probably heave a sigh of relief, because everyone else will get promoted."

For the first time Brad felt himself getting to like James Norton.

***

"What is this place?" asked Lisa Valentine as Knapton closed the door behind her.

"Safe house," said the detective. Then, seeing her puzzlement, Knapton added, "It's a place where we put witnesses who are in danger before they give evidence."

Lisa stood, looking up at him, and for a moment Knapton forgot what she was. He made himself remember that this young woman was not a pretty, slightly ditzy Polish tourist adrift in England.

She's so naïve about the real world, he thought. *But that's not so surprising, given that the real world doesn't acknowledge things like her exist.*

"It does not look very safe," said Lisa, dubiously. "Also, the curtains and the furniture are tacky."

"We're not here to discuss the décor," Knapton said. "He's upstairs. I had to sedate him."

He led her up to the main bedroom where Detective Sergeant Healy lay on the bed, fully clothed except for his jacket and shoes. He was looking toward them as they walked in, but his eyes did not quite focus.

"This man, he is slave to that bitch, yes?" asked Lisa, looking down at Healy's unshaven face.

"Right," said Knapton. "And the only time he got free of her, just for a moment—"

"I know, you tell me a million times!" she interrupted, waving him aside. "I never tried this before. My gut tells me it might work, but I don't know why."

Without another word, Lisa started to undress, kicking off her shoes then removing her oversized football shirt and jogging pants. When she got down to her bra and panties, she stopped and arched an eyebrow.

"You always stand there watching while a girl changes?"

"Not this kind of change," Knapton muttered, turning his back. But in the mirror on the door of the wardrobe he could still catch glimpses of the girl as she finished unclothing and stood for a moment, taking deep breaths.

"Okay," said Lisa, "here we go!"

At first, Knapton saw and heard nothing unusual. But then Lisa's breathing became labored and there was a sickening crunch. Knapton imagined cartilage and bone being wrenched apart. He resisted the temptation to turn around as the girl vanished from his field of view.

"No!" shouted Healy. "Not again, no!"

He's forgotten what he told me, thought Knapton. *Maybe because he's just bloody terrified, which is hardly surprising.*

"It will not hurt much," said a voice that was still just recognizable as Lisa's. "I promise."

Healy shouted some more and Knapton heard a thrashing on the bed, then a crash. He recalled a cheap lamp on the bedside table. Then there was a cry of panic and despair from Healy. He sounded half-smothered.

"What are you doing?" Knapton shouted, turning only to freeze.

He saw a flailing mass of limbs, hair, and clothing roll off the bed onto the floor at his feet. Lisa's body from the waist down was a pale silver, shining with smooth scales. It was wound around Healy's legs. She had her arms around him, pinning him down while she bit into his neck. Her face was contorted, no longer fully human. Her expression spoke of desire, a kind of lust that Knapton had never seen before. Her fangs were deep in the folds of flesh. There was a spot of blood on one of her scaly cheeks.

"Get off him you bitch!" shouted a voice that was familiar, but not Healy's. It was the voice of the woman from the interview, the one Steiger had called Cleo. The woman's voice cursed at Lisa, who seemed to be chuckling between bites. After what seemed an eternity, the shouting ceased and Healy stopped fighting.

"That's enough!" Knapton shouted, groping for the Taser. But before he could draw the weapon, the lamia uncoiled itself, releasing Healy, and wriggled into the far corner of the room. Knapton bent over his boss, his friend, checking for a pulse. Healy was alive, but seemed paralyzed.

"If you've killed him," he began.

The lamia reared up and, too late, Knapton realized he had strayed too close. The creature wrapped its arms around him, pinning the Taser at his side. The immense snake-tail coiled around his legs. Lisa's face rose until she was gazing into his eyes. He saw himself reflected in bright green irises with pupils that were vertical slits.

"You would be such a useful little friend," she said. "A nice English policeman who would keep me informed about all sorts of things."

She opened her mouth, and he stared at the inch-long fangs protruding from her upper jaw.

"No!" he shouted. "That wasn't the deal."

Even as he protested he realized he sounded like a prize idiot. As if this monster, this grotesque hybrid of serpent and woman, would keep her word. Lisa giggled and dipped her head in a parody of nuzzling his neck. He felt the coldness of her fangs on his neck, and tried to brace himself.

But she did not break the skin. Instead, Lisa leaned back, smiled, and then gave Knapton a long, sensuous kiss. He felt her tongue flicker around his lips. Her grip on him grew tighter and he gasped as the air was forced out of his lungs. The forked tongue darted to the back of his mouth. Then the pressure was gone and Knapton fell to his knees as Lisa uncoiled, withdrew.

"A deal's a deal, Constable," she said. "But remember, I am not someone you can push around. Don't make that mistake again."

Knapton could not reply, as he was still gulping great lungfuls of air. He doubled over, and out of the corner of one eye saw Lisa start to transform again. By the time he could stand up again, she was pulling on her shoes.

"He'll be fine, I think," she said, looking down at Healy. "I get no sense of anyone in control, you know? Well, apart from him."

"Boss?" said Knapton, kneeling beside Healy and gently slapping his face.

"Maybe you should call an ambulance?" suggested Lisa as she stepped around the men. "Tell them some story. Sort of lie people tell you all the time, yes?"

"Yes," said Knapton numbly, taking out his phone. By the time he'd made the call, the girl was gone. It was only then that it occurred to Knapton that he was alone in a half-wrecked bedroom.

Alone with a man who had what might well appear to be love bites on his neck.

"They'll be here in five minutes, boss," he said to Knapton's impassive face. "By then I'll have worked out a brilliant cover story. Just you wait."

Knapton started to rack his brains, but by the time the paramedics had arrived he still had not come up with a good explanation.

"We were checking the place out and he just had a fit," he lied, adding. "He's been feeling unwell for a few days now."

At least that last bit is kind of true, he thought.

***

"She neutralized him," snarled Cleo. She punched the jamb of the door to the cabin. Wood splintered. The big woman kept pacing back and forth like a caged beast until Kelly put a hand on Cleo's arm.

"I don't get it," said Kelly. "Why should one bite cancel out another?"

"Interference," said Clay, who was sitting in the corner of the boat's cabin, as far away from Cleo as the limited space permitted. "It's like two people trying to control a model airplane with radio signals on the same frequency. The plane crashes. Or, in this case, goes catatonic."

"A true follower of Ouroboros would never do such a thing!" shouted Cleo. Then, in a lower voice. "We have to kill her."

"She's certainly a loose cannon," said Kelly, in a conciliatory tone, "but she's just one person. And she's crazy. How much harm can she really do?"

"Perhaps we should stay focused on the greater task," put in Clay.

Cleo looked from girl to man and back.

"You still don't get it, do you? She could ruin it all for us. If she barges into the middle of the raising process, she could run just the kind of interference she did with Healy. Only to a far worse effect. No, first that creature dies. Then we raise Ouroboros in all its forms."

Clay looked as if he might continue to argue, but Kelly said quickly, "Time for the news, let's see if there's anything about Culloden."

Again the story was relegated to what Clay derisively called 'the skateboarding duck slot' after business and politics had been covered. This time the interview was with a woman clutching a little girl, who was in her turn clutching a plush mermaid doll. The caption read, *Julie Finnegan, Tourist.* The backdrop was a low building in front of which a bemused-looking policeman was talking to some agitated people.

"I really thought we were going to be killed," said Julie. "At first, they looked like historical re-enactors, but then cannonballs started flying overhead and these men came charging out of the mist. We were all terrified!"

"What did you think, Cressida?" asked the interviewer off camera. The microphone was pointed at the little girl, who looked at it dubiously before speaking.

"I was scared," said Cressida. "I don't like ghosts very much. I liked the mermaid better."

"Well," laughed the interviewer, "that's one way of looking at it. Now back to Kirsty in the studio."

Kelly killed the broadcast and tossed the remote onto Cleo's couch.

"Still not taking us seriously," she said. "I guess that's a good thing?"

"The media doesn't know what to make of it," agreed Clay. "But that doesn't mean the government isn't sniffing around."

"I sensed nothing from Healy, in all those weeks," Cleo pointed out. "He wasn't very senior, true, but he had connections. Called in favors. Nothing official."

"So who cleared up the mess at Wychmere?" countered Clay. Cleo snorted but did not reply.

"Someone knows more about us than we'd like," Clay went on. "And they know about Kelly's father. Maybe he's being used as a decoy, a way of drawing us out into the open. Giving us the chance to make a mistake."

"Dad's no threat," said Kelly. Then added hastily, "I mean he can't stop us without risking hurting me."

"He shot me," said Cleo. "More than once."

"And stopped when I stood between you," Kelly pointed out. "We've been over this. If he comes, I'll deal with it."

"You'd better," warned Cleo. "Because if you don't, well, I have unfinished business with Brad."

Cleo threw herself down onto her improvised bed and pulled her knees up. It was her sign that the others were dismissed. Clay stood up.

"I'll go and check if Andreas is finished," said Clay. "His English is a bit shaky. We want to look irrelevant, not stupid."

"I wrote it out for him clearly enough," Kelly pointed out, following him up the ladder onto the deck of the *Talisman.*

"I think Cleo has taken a lot out of Andreas," said Clay quietly as they paused in the hatchway. "He's looking pretty washed out."

"Do you really think they can – you know?" asked Kelly. They were both speaking more freely than usual because they no longer felt Cleo's watchful presence in their minds. As usual she had gone to sleep almost immediately.

"I have no idea," replied Clay. "But I can't say the idea fills me with joy. This was not what I expected when I began all this."

Andreas was standing on the little pier of the village of Invercraig, paintbrush in hand. A small crowd of locals, mostly children, were standing around him surveying his handiwork. Kelly and Clay stepped off the boat and went to stand by Andreas to get a clear look at the new lettering on the cabin of the *Talisman*. In foot-high letters, it read LOCH NESS MONSTER SURVEY.

"A bit amateurish, but clear enough," commented Clay.

Kelly agreed, adding, "It makes it clear what we're about, anyhow."

Clay glanced around at the villagers.

"Yes, at least people will know why we're sailing up and down the loch at all hours."

Hiding in plain sight, he thought, taking some pride in his idea. *Nobody takes monster hunters seriously.*

"Hey mister!" shouted a little boy, one of a group of smirking friends. "Do you really think there's a monster out there?"

Clay looked at the kids without smiling.

"Oh yes," he said. "I'm quite sure of it."

***

"That was my good deed for today," said Lisa, watching the paramedics carry Healy out of the safe house. Knapton followed his boss into the ambulance.

"Good deed," said Pavel, staring blankly as the ambulance sped away, lights flashing, siren wailing. Other vehicles gave way, pulling over to the curb. Soon the ambulance had vanished and London traffic was restored to its customary ill-tempered chaos.

"You see how they obey the rules, Pavel?" said Lisa. "Even the selfish bastards, even the bad guys. Sometimes they work together. But not most of the time, and not very well."

"Work together," said Pavel. He turned to look into Lisa's eyes. "Like you and me."

Surprised, it took her a moment to find words.

"Yes, like you and me," she repeated, running her fingers around his cheek. "Oh God, you're still there, aren't you? The big guy I took. And I killed your girlfriend, your Lenka, and took her clothes, passport, all of it."

"Lenka," said Pavel. A tear appeared at the corner of his left eye and rolled down his cheek. Lisa brushed it away, sucked the salt from her fingertip.

"I'm sorry," she said. "It was before I was reborn. Before Marcus. Before I became human again. Kind of."

A sudden thought struck her with the impact of a blow. She sat bolt upright, then started the ignition.

"My God, it's so obvious!" she cried. "I can save you. I can beat that bitch and save the world and give you your life back."

"Lenka," repeated Pavel, staring ahead of them as Lisa pulled out. Soon horns were blaring and Lisa was giving outraged road users the finger.

"Yeah, you too buddy," she shouted joyfully. "I'm a woman on a mission, asshole!"

Chapter 6: Heads, Hearts, and Eyes

That night, Brad's dream was even stranger than before.

Again, he was in a small boat with Kelly, but this time they were not in old-time costumes. Instead, they wore ragged clothes, torn and scorched. Around them the shores of the dream-lake showed signs of devastation. Smoke rose in columns from dozens of fires, and Brad could make out wrecked houses and cars.

"*It's pretty awful, isn't it?*" Kelly said. "*But people tend to sow what they reap.*"

"*Nobody wanted this,*" Brad replied, scanning the banks for signs of life. He saw no movement other than the pillars of smoke, the odd flicker of flame from a ruined building. The silence was eerie. He was not rowing, just leaning on the oars as the boat drifted. After all, there seemed to be nowhere to go.

"*Millions voted for this,*" Kelly countered. "*They voted with their wallets, buying into every kind of cruelty and exploitation. They voted with their remotes, flicking away from the documentaries and onto the mindless pap. They voted for it every time they filled up at the gas station. And they just plain voted for it by electing assholes, plausible liars offering short-term bullshit gimmicks. So they wanted it in every way except by saying outright, 'Hey, let's wreck the world!'*"

Brad recalled a hundred arguments that had begun in just this way.

"*Ordinary people just want what's best for themselves and the people they love,*" he said. "*They make mistakes, sure. But they're not evil, not destructive.*"

"*Collectively that's just what ordinary people are,*" she shot back. "*And shouldn't you be rowing? We'll never get to the island at this rate.*"

"*You'll have to navigate,*" he said. "*Just like every vacation.*"

"*Yeah,*" she laughed. "*You'd always get lost and wouldn't ask anyone the way, so I'd have to go on at you 'till you let me ask. Good times.*"

Kelly stood up in her seat and pointed over the bow of the boat.

"*You can just make out the eye,*" she said.

Brad turned to look ahead. A small, round patch of green on the water was just visible.

"*That's an eye?*" he asked.

Kelly nodded.

"*The eye that's got to be opened, for the first time in thousands of years,*" she said. "*So that she can see what we've done to the world. She'll be kinda pissed, but that's what happens when you mess up someone else's property.*"

"*You think the world belongs to Ouroboros?*" he asked, pulling on the oars. The sound of the wooden blades cutting the water seemed unnaturally loud on the silent lake.

"*Who else does the world belong to if not the gods of nature?*" asked Kelly.

"*Can't help feeling we should've sent you to Sunday school,*" said Brad.

Kelly laughed, then peered past Brad ahead of them.

"*Nearly there,*" she said cheerfully. She reached forward and opened the old wind-up gramophone. With typical dream-logic it was undamaged. Kelly took a record from its sleeve and placed it carefully on the turntable, lowered the needle. A tinny, old-fashioned orchestra began to play.

"*Got anything by the Ramones?*" asked Brad. "*Or Tom Petty, maybe?*"

"Oh, Dad." Kelly shook her head. *"That world had to go."*
The song began.

'The eyes are the windows of the soul
But it's the heart that beats with love for you
Lips can tell lies and hands can be cruel
It's the heart that's bound to be true'

The record stuck and kept repeating the last line until Kelly lifted the needle.
"They don't write 'em like that anymore," said Brad. *"For which we can be truly thankful."*
"Here we are, you old cynic!" cried Kelly, jumping up. The boat bumped ashore and Brad shipped the oars. He turned to see they had run around on a moss-grown circle of stone about five yards across. It seemed an almost perfect circle, and must have been artificial.
"If this is the lady's eye, I'd say she had a pretty bad infection," he commented, running his hand over the moss. Then he jerked back as the surface of the island rippled under his fingers.
"We need to open her eyes, Dad," said Kelly. She nodded to a group of people who had suddenly appeared. Brad recognized Jonathan Clay dressed in a monkish robe, and next to him Cleo formed, smiling broadly as her muscular tail writhed over the moss. There was also a young man, fair complexioned and looking zoned out. Brad remembered Andreas, the young German that Cleo had enslaved.
"This your family now?" he asked. *"And yeah, that's a rhetorical question."*
"They can be yours too, Dad," said Kelly, climbing out of the boat onto the island.
"At least one of them would gladly kill me," he said, following her cautiously.
"Nothing personal, Brad," said Cleo, wriggling closer. *"Besides, don't all families have their little disputes?"*
The dark woman came closer, and Brad tried not to flinch as she towered over him.
"We could be kissing cousins," breathed Cleo, leaning down to look into his eyes.
"No time for distractions," said Clay. *"We must awaken the Great Old One."*
"Yes," said Kelly, going to stand by Clay and Andreas. *"This is the moment."*
"Come on, Brad," said Cleo, taking his hand and leading him to the water's edge. *"This is a great day for you."*
"The end of the world?" he asked.
Cleo shook her head, eyes wide with disbelief.
"You mean she still hasn't told you? Naughty Kelly. Oh well, you'll soon see for yourself."
Before Brad could ask any more, the island split down the middle, the mossy surface rolling back. A huge eye appeared, its iris golden green, with a slit pupil. Shocked, Brad reeled back and fell into the water. But even as he struck the surface, the vast head of Ouroboros rose up. As the dream ended in noise and turmoil, he could just make out the entire surface of the lake erupting, and a scaly, shining body vaster than a city arose under the bleak gray sky.

Crap, that was more ominous than usual, he thought as he groped for his phone.

It was just before five in the morning. He had set his news alert app to search for key words and phrases. 'Loch Ness Monster' cropped up several stories. One contained a name he had flagged.

Jonathan Clay. My God, the guy's on the radar again. After all these years.

It was a short piece on the site of a British tabloid, under the heading, *Weird News*. There were a couple of paragraphs about a group of 'scientists' who had outfitted an old boat with unspecified equipment to 'hunt for Nessie.' The team was shown standing on a jetty in front of a rusty old pleasure cruiser. Brad was looking at the people from his dream, except that Cleo had a pair of very human legs in denims. She was also, he noted, wearing large sunglasses.

In case somebody recognizes the Loch Ness mermaid. Wow.

Between Clay and Cleo stood Kelly, smiling at the camera and giving a 'peace' sign.

"That's my girl, mastering the irony," he muttered, getting up to ready himself for a long journey.

He met Denny for breakfast at a nearby fast food joint. The place had just opened and they were the first customers.

"I got a kind of weird look when I ordered," said Brad, setting the tray down.

Denny looked over at the young servers, and laughed.

"They probably think we spent a night of passion together," she said. "We make a slightly odd couple, after all."

Brad looked down at his smart-casual jacket, then over at Denny's fashionable Bohemian chic get up.

"They think you're my – what's that British expression, a bit up the side?"

"It's a bit on the side," she corrected him. "A bit up the side sounds downright perverted. But yes, the age difference might suggest it, don't you think?"

Brad shrugged, taking a bite of his breakfast muffin.

"You're not actually seeing anyone?" asked Denny.

"Not for a while now," he said. "A few relationships since I broke up with Kelly's mom, but I travel a lot, so it's always understood that the job comes first."

"So you're used to living in hotels, I guess?"

"Oh yeah," he replied, "I just don't like it. Wish I could find somewhere in London, but the property scene, it's just crazy. I mean, New York crazy and then some."

"You need an apartment? Well, there may be one going in London's fashionable Camden area. Just by the market where Lily Allen used to get all her gear."

Laughing at Brad's puzzlement, Denny produced a bunch of keys and dangled them.

"As well as Marcus's phone, I sort of relieved him of these too."

"I can't just move into someone's home without—" began Brad.

"Their permission?" finished Denny. "What do you think Marcus would say?"

"He'd be fine with it, I guess," he admitted. "And it would at least mean the place wasn't empty."

"Okay," she said. "When this is over it's an option, at least. Maybe I could come over? Help you move in?"

"Sure," he replied, not sure where the conversation was going.

She glanced at the counter staff again, then smiled at Brad.

"After all, you're an engineer," said Denny. "Big oil man, out in the wilderness?"

Puzzled, he nodded, took a sip of coffee.

"So," she went on, "you must know that vital equipment needs regular servicing. Otherwise it gets rusty."

Brad nearly choked on his coffee and felt his face flush. Denny laughed and gave an odd shuffle in her seat. He felt movement under the table, a small foot in a sock running up his leg.

"If people are going to assume these things anyway," she said, and left the rest unspoken.

***

"This will be the last time, Anita," said Lisa as Nurse Sharma ushered her through the security doors onto Marcus Valentine's ward.

"Thank you," replied the nurse. "I've done my best to oblige."

"I know," said Lisa.

She put a hand on Anita's arm and, after checking that they were alone, looked into the nurse's eyes.

"Don't be scared," said Lisa. "Look into my eyes. Hear only my voice."

She felt an ancient, inhuman power coursing through her, focusing on Anita, molding her to Lisa's will. It was intoxicating.

And that's why it has to stop, Lisa thought. *No more of this. I will be more human.*

"This is the last time you will obey me, Anita," she said. "When I leave this time you will remember me as a strange young woman who came to see poor Marcus. If we ever meet again, I will be just someone you met through work. Nothing more. Do you understand? You are free now, Anita."

For a moment, the nurse looked puzzled, then she nodded and walked back to her desk without another word. Satisfied, Lisa went to Marcus's room, trying to work out what she would say to him. She found him lying on his bed dozing, a book fallen open on his lap.

Just like daddy when he came home from work, she thought, standing in the doorway. Jarring, conflicting memories vied in her mind. Was she remembering the father of Olga, the tortured dissident, or Lenka the treasure hunter? It was so hard to sort through the jumble of lives she had lived, or half-lived.

Shaking her head to try and clear it, Lisa padded softly over to the bed and sat by Marcus. She reached out a slender hand towards his, but then flinched back when he stirred.

"Who is it?" he mumbled. Then his eyes opened wide in panic. Lisa saw him suppress his fear, but imperfectly.

"You don't need to be scared anymore," she said softly. "I'm going away. I don't think you'll see me again."

Lisa struggled to think of a way to make him believe her. Something from the memories she had plundered from him rose to the surface of her mind.

"I am going to fight the good fight," she said. Then she got up and sat next to him, and again the dark, ancient power welled up inside her. She reached out to his mind, touched his fear, and saw it in all its starkness. For every moment of every waking hour, and much of his time asleep, Marcus was trapped in the Zamyatin Device with the Insane One. She had tried to heal this pain so many times.

It had never worked. The Insane One had half-consumed the soul of Marcus Valentine, recoiling when it encountered his deep compassion, his love of humanity. The encounter had created the near-human being that was Lisa, but left Marcus's mind permanently disfigured. He had looked into the soul of a monster. Lisa could not figure out how to un-mix their beings and restore the man's sanity.

One last time, she thought. *I must put it right. If not this way, then perhaps* ...

"No, no," she whispered, stroking his cheek, "I won't hurt you again."

But she could not help him either. No matter how deeply she delved she could not find the essence of his pain and confusion.

Because it is in me, she thought. *All the evil and madness is shared out, but much too unevenly. I can't help him here.*

Lisa stood up, then bent over and kissed Marcus on the forehead.

"I'm going to Scotland, now!" she said. "I will send you a nice postcard."

She did not add 'Daddy,' but it took an effort.

***

"Nobody takes monster hunters seriously!" complained Mike Carlton.

I hope I don't sound too whiny, he thought. *I can come across as an overgrown teenager. People will think I still live with my mother.*

"Why do you think that is, Mike?" asked Katie Fox.

Carlton shifted awkwardly in his seat, then remembered about the sensitive clip-on microphone and froze. Despite being at his own office desk, he felt exposed, nervous.

"Well," he said, "even though you captured evidence of a creature's existence, Katie, people are claiming it's a hoax. Despite eyewitnesses, I'm seeing lots of internet chatter about it being part of the same viral marketing campaign that produced the mermaid. And those ghosts at Culloden."

"You don't believe in ghosts, then?" asked Katie.

"Of course not!" he snorted. "The point is that a large, unknown creature could exist in the loch. As far back as the 1930's, serious investigators found abundant evidence of a marine life-form that could have entered Loch Ness via the canals that link it to the sea."

"I understand one of those early investigators claimed Nessie might be a giant newt?" said Katie.

Sensing a trap, Carlton tried to head her off.

"That was Commodore Gould, a notorious eccentric without any formal qualifications in marine biology," he pointed out. "And what you filmed wasn't a newt, was it?"

"No," Katie agreed, "but it wasn't much like a dinosaur either. So what do you think it was?"

"Well," Carlton took a deep breath. "It looked remarkably like what Victorians called a sea serpent. Elongated creatures were reported by the captains of many ships in the nineteenth century. But gradually reports tapered off. At the same time, in the early twentieth century, people started seeing Nessie more often."

"But that suggests Gould was partly right," Katie pointed out. "A sea serpent might have migrated into the loch."

Carlton had managed to confuse himself.

"No," he objected, "Gould rejected ancient folk tales that report a frightening beast in the loch. These date back to the Dark Ages. Saint Columba is said to have driven the monster back when it tried to eat a peasant."

"If the monster is afraid of a holy man's power," said Katie, "doesn't that mean these people in the new Loch Ness Survey have a point?"

Carlton frowned. Katie had not mentioned taking this angle when they had chatted before the interview.

"I don't accept their argument that the phenomenon is paranormal," he said. "As for the so-called survey, well, you can paint anything on the side of a boat. I can wear a Superman costume, it doesn't mean I can fly."

"But the leader of the survey is a professional archaeologist, Jonathan Clay," Katie rejoined. "He has a Ph.D. Do you?"

Carlton squirmed again, forgetting the mic.

"No, but I have had years of experience hunting cryptids," he insisted. "Those are legendary creatures that might be real. And as far as I can tell, Doctor Clay has done no new research in decades."

"It so happens that I've arranged to interview him tomorrow," said Katie. "Would you be willing to participate in a debate about the monster? Just so we can hear both sides of the argument?"

Ambushed, his mind a blank, Carlton stammered out a reply.

"Of – of course," he said. "Happy to!"

Katie swung the camera around on its stand to sign off, then said, "Well, I think that's a wrap."

"I don't think that was very fair–" began Carlton, but Katie cut in.

"Don't worry about Jonathan," she said brightly. "He's a sweetie and so is his team. Nice young people, really hospitable. I'm sure you'll find lots of common ground."

"It's not the ground, it's the dark waters that worry me," muttered Carlton, but as she was busy packing away her gear, Katie gave no sign of having heard him.

***

"Wow, I'll bet that guy lives in his mom's basement," remarked Brad after Denny showed him the interview. "I mean, check out that cardigan."

They were talking in the lounge of his hotel, waiting for James Norton to turn up. Brad was impatient to set off for Scotland, but the academic was proving less than reliable in regards to timekeeping.

"But doesn't it strike you as odd?" asked Denny. "Not the guy's knitwear, though it is horrendous. I mean the way Clay's willing to be mentioned on television? I mean, until now he kept a low profile."

"It does seem peculiar," said Brad. "But I think I get what he's doing."

"Is it hiding in plain sight again?" asked Denny. "Like Cleo in that circus sideshow?"

Brad nodded.

"Exactly. I think that's it. After all, now they're part of a silly season news trend and we can't very well claim they're a murderous cult. And if we added, 'Oh yeah, and that tall black girl? She can turn into a snake, either totally or just from the waist down, hence the mermaid thing.' Well, what would the local DA say?"

"So as usual the authorities can't help," said Denny. "Oh well, this is like one of those movies where the crusading journalist and the macho hero beat the bad guys on their own. Oh, and it's not the DA. In Scotland, it's the Procurator Fiscal."

"Sounds like a skin disease," replied Brad.

Norton finally appeared, and after perfunctory greetings, they set off for the airport.

"A couple of hours from now we'll be in Glasgow," she explained. "Then it will be a long drive through very winding roads into the Highlands."

"Across the Highland Line," added Norton from the back seat. "Where according to the old saying, the Law of Man ends and the Law of the Sword begins."

"If only we could kill Ouroboros with a sword," said Brad.

"A magical sword like Excalibur," returned Norton. "That would be ideal for slaying monsters."

"Is a lady liable to rise out of the loch and hand me a magic sword?" asked Brad.

Denny laughed and shook her head.

"Wrong country, wrong legend," she said.

"And the wrong guy," added Brad.

Denny gave him an appraising look.

"Maybe you're the right guy," she said. "I think James is right. Your paranormal link with Kelly proves you're somehow at the heart of all this, just as she is. If we can figure out why before the showdown, maybe we'll have a chance."

There was a pause, then Norton put in, "In many tales of chivalry, the hero has no real idea what he's doing, but he wins through regardless – slays the monster, rescues the maiden, all that sort of thing."

It was Brad's turn to laugh.

"What if the monster's big enough to crack open the earth, and the maiden doesn't want saving?"

They drove on in silence for a while after that.

Chapter 7: Consumption

The debate went better than Mike Carlton expected. Katie insisted on conducting it on the quayside in Invercraig, with a bemused but good-natured crowd of locals looking on. She was now supported by an actual cameraman so that she could act as mediator. Clay and Carlton stood in front of the *Talisman*, so that the words LOCH NESS MONSTER SURVEY were in shot. Carlton nearly complained that this was bias in favor of the interlopers, but held his tongue in case he seemed like a whiner.

Besides, he had thought, *that rusty old boat hardly inspires confidence.*

When the actual debate began, though, it turned out to be pleasant enough, at first. Far from being an arrogant crackpot, Jonathan Clay came across as erudite and good-humored. The archaeologist seemed to have some far-out theories, true. But Carlton had been ridiculed for his ideas so often that he found himself warming to the scientist.

"Well, Doctor Clay," Katie Fox was saying, "we've heard Mike's view that Nessie is some kind of prehistoric reptile, and that there's probably a family of them in the loch. What do you think?"

"It's a fascinating argument, Katie," said Clay. "I'm very impressed by the time and effort Mike has put into researching sightings."

Clay paused, and the reporter interjected, "I'm sensing a But."

"Yes," Clay resumed. "The problem is that if a colony of giant marine creatures have been living in the loch since time immemorial, wouldn't there be a lot of hard physical evidence? Such as skeletons brought up in fishing nets, decayed carcasses washed up on the shore, that sort of thing. And of course, reptiles lay their eggs on land. So a reptilian Nessie would be clearly visible, heaving herself ashore in the mating season, every year."

Carlton suddenly felt as if the ground had fallen away beneath him. His normal ripostes to these arguments seemed hollow now.

"Wow," said Katie, genuinely taken aback. "It sounds like you're actually dismissing your own project, though? You can't hunt monsters that aren't there."

"Not at all," Clay responded. "While I would question the term 'monster,' as what we're dealing with here is a being of a different order of reality."

"Which means what exactly?"

Yeah, thought Carlton, *what on earth does he mean?*

"What you and Mike call Nessie," said Clay, "myself and my colleagues call Ouroboros."

Katie frowned prettily.

"Now that's a familiar word, but I just can't place it."

"It's a word a lot of people will be hearing in the future, believe me," said Clay. "You see, many years ago, my research convinced me that in prehistoric times people were genuinely connected to nature. They did not feel the supposed dichotomy between the living world and our one, over-mighty species."

"That's hardly a radical view–" began Carlton, only to be shushed by Katie.

"I think Jonathan's earned the right to speak without interruptions."

And so Jonathan did, talking of Ouroboros, the female principle of nature that had been suppressed by a patriarchal culture. Turning our back on nature to find civilization had led, in Clay's version of events, to a planet plagued with greed and violence. The Iron Age, according to the archaeologist, had marked the beginning of this decline. A reliance on technology and an obsession with ever-more advanced weapons had led mankind down a disastrous path.

Carlton, in spite of himself, found Clay's fervor impressive. And while some of the onlookers scoffed, others were nodding sagely.

He's making converts, thought Carlton ruefully. *Something I've never done.*

"I don't quite see how this connects with Nessie, though," put in the reporter.

"I was coming to that," returned Clay. "We believe that Ouroboros, once rejected by Man, essentially went to sleep, or into hibernation. Visions of Nessie or the sea serpents seen by the Victorians reveal Ouroboros stirring in her sleep, so to speak. What we intend to do is wake her up properly."

"And how do you intend to do that?" asked Katie.

"Dangle a large haddock under her nose?" put in Carlton, but the laugh he had hoped for did not materialize.

Clay shook his head.

"We hope to invoke Ouroboros by the power of prayer on an ancient site of worship, when the time is right."

"And what will happen then?" asked Katie.

Clay paused again, looked at the camera.

"The old world will pass away, giving way to the new," he said.

For a moment, Carlton felt a chill run down his spine.

Absurd, he thought. *The man's a crank after all. A very committed one, though. I wonder if that applies to his whole team?*

As Katie signed off, Carlton turned to scan the deck of the boat behind them. Nobody was visible. But then he saw a curtain twitch in a cabin window and a woman's face appeared for a moment. She winked and was gone almost before Carlton realized that he had seen her somewhere before.

"The mermaid!" he said, forgetting his microphone.

Katie looked slightly annoyed, then asked the cameraman, "We can cut that, can't we Gavin? Good."

"No, but it was the mermaid, she's on his boat!" spluttered Carlton. "The hoax, it was he – or they – all along! I saw her!"

"Why would a mermaid need a boat, Mike?" asked Clay. "Somewhat redundant, don't you think?"

"She's obviously not a real mermaid, you know what I mean!" Carlton protested.

"Debate's over, guys," said Katie. "If you want to carry on, be my guests, but I'm off to talk to a Presbyterian minister who thinks Nessie might be the Beast of Revelation."

The television team began packing up and the small crowd started to disperse. A few children stayed on, pointing and giggling. Carlton looked from Clay to the boat and back.

"I thought," he said, drawing himself up to his full five feet seven inches, "that you were a man of principle. Now I see you're just another vulgar charlatan. I don't know who's paying you for this scam but–"

Clay held up a hand to silence him.

"Really, Mike," said the archaeologist, "I have better things to do than argue."

Ignoring Carlton's further protests, Clay turned to board the *Talisman*. But then he stopped, and his head tilted to one side as if listening to a voice inaudible to Carlton. For a moment, Carlton thought the man must be wearing some kind of earpiece given to him by Katie. But he saw no sign of any such gadget.

"I'm sorry," said Clay, pausing to speak over his shoulder. "I shouldn't have been so rude. You are of course entitled to an explanation."

"Oh," replied Carlton, slightly taken aback by the change of mood. "That's more like it."

"Yes," said Clay, half-turning and staring past Carlton. Again he seemed to be listening to some prompter. "Please come by the boat later this evening when things have settled down. Everything ... will be made ... clear then."

The invitation sounded unnatural, forced.

As if he's struggling to get his words out, thought Carlton. *Or being pressured into saying them?*

But he could hardly turn the offer down.

"Of course," he said. "What time?"

"We will expect you at dusk," said Clay in a monotone voice, then climbed aboard the *Talisman* and was gone.

The thought bothered Carlton as he drove back up the loch side to his headquarters. But by the time he had reached his office, he had forgotten the odd incident. He was going to get at the truth about what must be some kind of publicity campaign. That made sense, so he clung to the idea despite his instincts telling him not to go back.

***

"You need to go and check the installations," said Cleo. "We don't want any last-minute failures due to meddling. Do we? So make sure the truck is fueled up. You can take Andreas. I'm done with him for now."

Kelly started to leave the cabin, but Clay hesitated.

"It's a bit early, isn't it?" he asked. "Shouldn't we wait until dark?"

As the big woman's gaze turned to him, Clay felt Cleo's mind pressing into his own. It was a sensation that had grown more unpleasant in recent months as she had grown appreciably less human. For weeks, she had spent most of her time in lamia form. Even now, though Cleo looked like a remarkably tall woman, closer examination showed traces of golden-bronze scales on her neck and arms.

Olivia never went this far, he thought. *And she was the first of the true lamias.*

"Olivia was killed by Steiger before she had a chance to reach her full potential," snapped Cleo. "I don't intend for that to happen to me. And if for some reason I don't survive, well, at least we have an insurance policy now."

She passed a slender hand across her midriff. A rippling motion moved across her skin. Clay was almost sure it was down to muscles.

"Keep telling yourself that, Jonathan," Cleo smiled.

She looked down at Andreas. The young German lay sprawled on the stained and disheveled mattress, his body marked by a spiral of darkening bruises.

"At least you didn't kill the poor lad," said Clay. "What did he do to deserve such treatment?"

"Same as millions of others. He was born, he lives among us," Cleo retorted. "That's enough to guarantee lifelong misery and untimely death to millions in your man-made world. Cry for all the victims, not just one so-called victim."

She leaned over and caressed the young German's shoulder. He twitched, gave a moan that might have come from fear or desire.

Probably a bit of both, thought Clay.

"Indeed," said Cleo. "Now prepare to check the devices, as I said. I'll get Andreas dressed and ready for the journey. It will probably be getting dark by the time the poor moppet is fit to walk."

"I know why you made me invite that fool," said Clay. "I don't approve, you must know that."

"Then you know that the sacrifice is necessary," purred Cleo, standing upright again and putting her hands on her hips. "Or are you trying to give me orders? This was never really your cult, old man. You're just a convenient figurehead. If you cease to be that ..."

Cleo did not finish the sentence. Instead, she looked down, and again the odd spasm rippled the flesh of her torso.

"Come on, Jonathan," said Kelly from the deck hatchway. "We need to get gas."

Just over an hour later, Cleo's three minions set out from Invercraig. As they drove out of the village onto the highway, they passed Carlton returning.

"Where are we going to eat tonight, anyhow?" asked Kelly.

Clay looked at her with an appalled expression.

"Sometimes," he muttered, as he turned his eyes back to the road, "I feel I don't know you at all."

***

Brad, Denny and Professor Norton took a break for lunch in Glasgow before picking up their rental car. They ate at a pub with the usual television on. As was usual in Britain, the TV was tuned to international soccer with the occasional news bulletin. It was during the latter that they saw the brief debate between Jonathan Clay and Mike Carlton. Amid the hubbub of the drinkers and diners, it was hard to make out everything that was said. But it was clear to all of them that, in Denny's words, Clay had 'gone full crackpot in public.'

"Let's check it again," suggested Denny, taking out her phone. They crowded around and watched the interview with the volume turned up to maximum, despite disapproving stares from a couple of nearby patrons.

"Yes, it's clever," agreed Norton. "He's telling the truth in such a way that nobody will take him seriously. And yet, he has just planted the seeds of his cult in hundreds of thousands, perhaps millions, of unsuspecting viewers."

"They know the name of Ouroboros now," agreed Brad. "The internet will be burning up with people searching for it."

"In any number of strange spellings," added Norton, pedantically. "But they'll get there. The idea is in their heads."

"They really believe it will be their world soon," mused Denny. "But can the Zamyatin device really work as they expect? It's got a patchy record, to say the least."

"From a technical viewpoint," said Brad, "a lot has changed since the Sixties. Modern technology means that kind of equipment can be produced more easily, and made more compact. It's a kind of electromagnetic transducer somehow wired into the brain of a subject. Or victim. That sounds like a variation on brain scanners that already exist. Off-the-shelf components are available to make them."

For a second, Denny looked puzzled, then she realized what Brad was implying.

"You mean they could make a lot of devices that are far more powerful than the original?"

"Why not?"

Brad took out a map of the Scottish Highlands.

"Look at the size of the loch. If the being they're hoping to raise is of comparable size, one gizmo won't cut it. All my engineering instincts tell me they'll produce some kind of field generated in a lot of places along the two shores. But I'm convinced that there is a central point."

"This mysterious bowl of cherries in your nightmare?" asked Norton.

"Which points to a specific location," said Brad. "That's where they'll be for the main event. Last night's dream might as well have spelled it out in mile high letters."

"Okay, so that means we're going to Fort Augustus, which is here."

Denny prodded the map before continuing.

"Since they've got a boat, do you think we should rent one?"

"Reckon so," said Brad. "If we have to confront them, that would be essential. But we could also use it as a mobile detector."

"I sense a burst of technobabble coming," sighed Norton.

"Nothing too complicated," said Brad. "Some oil guys I know in Scotland should have a powerful magnetometer waiting for us. That means we'll pick up any unusual fields generated in the area. It should lead us to the Zamyatin device, or more likely devices, they're using."

"And if we just smash them, that's game over for Ouroboros?" said Denny.

"We could just turn them off, but yes, that is my crude plan," admitted Brad. "And if they do have a network of devices, they can't guard all of them. So if we detect a surge of energy we track down the source and neutralize it."

"With a large hammer if necessary," added Denny. "Speaking as a journalist, it just sounds better."

"Call me an old cynic," said Norton, pausing in an attempt to eat a cheeseburger with a knife and fork, "but is it possible that they will have planted more of these devices than they actually need? By way of insurance?"

Brad sat back, pondering the question.

Norton's no fool, he said. *If Ouroboros still has plenty of cash, they might well have saturated the area with Zamyatin devices. And we could never disable enough of them to make a difference.*

"I guess we'll know soon enough just how they propose to play it," he said finally. "But you're right, James. We need a plan B in case A is a bust."

"Direct confrontation?" said Denny, dubiously. "In Poland that was very messy. And they got away."

She's right, Brad thought. *If I try strong-arm tactics, Cleo would try to kill me. And judging by the size of her in that picture, she's even more powerful than before.*

"You're right," he said, frustrated. "If only we had allies, someone with real clout. Doing this on our own seems crazy when you look at it objectively."

"It is quite obviously crazy," said Norton. "But sometimes doing the crazy thing is your only option."

"You sure hit the nail on the head," admitted Brad.

"Yes, I," Norton paused, hesitating, then said, "could I watch that clip again, Denny? I think there was something rather odd about what that Clay chap said. I mean, odd even in the context of the rest."

"Okay," said Denny, "but use my earphones this time. You don't want to antagonize people in a Glasgow pub."

After Norton had re-watched the debate, he took the earphones out and said, "Yes, I thought so. Clay seems to have a personal grudge against the Iron Age. Look at the moment when he mentions it. The expression on his face."

Denny quickly found the sequence.

"You're right," she said, showing Brad. "He looks like he's sucking a lemon. Is that significant?"

"Surely it just means they hate what we call civilization," put in Brad. "We already knew that."

"Yes," agreed Norton, "but civilization began long before the Iron Age. The pyramids were built with wood and stone technology. So why single out iron?"

"Something to do with magnetic fields?" Denny hazarded.

"Iron, cold iron, is master of them all," said Norton. "Iron in folklore is the Devil's enemy. Hence the practice of putting an iron horseshoe over one's door for luck."

"I'm guessing that's a quotation?" asked Brad. "The first part, I mean?"

Norton gave his familiar, superior smile.

"Hardly anyone reads Kipling nowadays, but he knew a thing or two."

***

"Your action was not only unauthorized, it was counter to the entire spirit of the organization," said the Director. "You may not have done your friend any good, either."

The gray-haired man gestured at Healy, lying in bed connected to a bewildering array of monitors that beeped and buzzed quietly to themselves.

Knapton shook his head.

"Somebody once said that if he had to choose between betraying his country or his friends, he hoped he'd have the courage to betray his country."

"A bad attitude," said the Director. "Think what kind of a world we'd be living in if we all thought that way."

"Not very different from the one we've got," returned Knapton.

A young female doctor appeared carrying a tablet computer. She gave both men an appraising look.

"I don't suppose there's any point in asking what really happened to him?" she asked. After a moment's silence she walked past them to start checking Healy's condition.

"Any change, doctor?" asked Knapton.

"No, he's still comatose, still showing signs of some kind of toxic shock syndrome. I've consulted colleagues in Africa, Australia, and the Americas about what venom he might have been exposed to. It's like no kind of snakebite they've seen."

She looked at the Director.

"But if I were a gambler I'd bet good money you've seen it before. Am I right?"

The older man ignored her and spoke to Knapton.

"We'll have a formal hearing, of course. I'll be in touch."

"You should do something to stop this!" said Knapton, but the Director left without another word.

"I take it that old bastard works for one of the dirtier bits of our glorious government?" said the doctor, going back to her checklist.

Knapton thought for a moment, then a useful phrase came to him.

"You may think that, I couldn't possibly comment."

The doctor gave a short laugh.

"Very tactful. And I wasn't being wholly honest while that old bugger was here."

"He's improving?" asked Knapton.

The doctor shrugged.

"He's been verbalizing, as we call it, which is a fancy way of saying talking in your sleep."

The woman reached into her coat and took out a digital voice recorder.

"Make of this what you will," she said, handing it over. "I probably shouldn't have recorded him but it was creeping the nurses out, so I thought it should be on the record somewhere. You can drop it off at the main desk for me when you're done. Now, if you'll excuse me, visiting time is over and I have a lot of other patients."

For the next five minutes, Knapton sat in the reception area, headphones on, listening to what Healy had said. It made little sense.

Fragments from a ruined mind, he thought. *Some trace of the boss I knew. Not much, though. Too badly damaged.*

He realized he was crying and blew his nose before leaving the hospital to sit in his parked car to get himself together. Then he returned the digital recorder and set off back to Scotland Yard. As he wove through the traffic, Healy's chaotic mumblings swirled in his head. But one phrase kept returning.

'With the chaos will come the breeding.'

***

Dusk had almost fallen as Carlton parked his Fiat carefully alongside the jetty and got out. There were a few locals standing around talking, a couple of kids fishing. Again, he felt an odd sense of trepidation despite the commonplace scene.

Get a grip, man, he told himself. *This is your chance to blow the lid off a conspiracy, or at least a hoax.*

The old pleasure cruiser seemed deserted, though.

What if they're simply not there? Maybe it's all a joke at my expense. They might be up to something elsewhere on the loch, and needed me out of the way.

Trying to push his doubts to the back of his mind, Carlton walked up to the *Talisman* and stood hesitating.

"Hello?" he said.

"Hello," came the reply. The voice was husky, unmistakably feminine, oddly thrilling. But Carlton could not see the speaker. Then he saw a brief movement at the cabin hatchway.

"I'm here to see Doctor Clay?" he called.

"I'm afraid Jonathan had to go ashore for a while," said the hidden woman. "Perhaps I can help? Do come aboard, Mike, we can talk more privately inside."

Carlton scrambled onto the boat and went to the hatchway, looked down. There was a dim, flickering light, evidently from a candle. It revealed only the wooden planking of the cabin floor. Then a striking face appeared, smiling up at him.

"Come on down! It's nearly time to eat."

Climbing clumsily down the ladder, his back to the woman, Carlton said, "Oh, I already ate, but thanks for the offer."

"Well," she said, "I hope you don't mind if I have a rather large meal."

"Not at all, feel free," he began, but stopped as he turned around to find her towering over him. In the faint light of a candle on a small table she seemed even more prodigious, a being of myth rather than mundane reality. She reached up above his head and closed the cabin hatch.

My God, he thought, *she must be nearly seven feet tall.*

"Before I dine," she said, smiling down at him, "let's settle this silly dispute once and for all."

"Of course, Miss – erm," Carlton struggled to remember if Clay had mentioned any of his team.

"Call me Cleo," she said, taking him by the arm and leading him to a small fold-out table and chair. "Take a seat."

She sat on the floor next to him, and her eyes were still level with his.

"Well, Cleo," he began, trying to keep his tone light, "I have to say you made a very good mermaid. Is your tail anywhere around here?"

Her eyes widened and she gave a throaty laugh.

"Really, Mike, you just meet a girl and straightaway you're asking to see her tail?"

Carlton felt himself blush, and stammered, "I meant the prop, the fake – you know what I mean, it looked very professional."

"Thanks!"

She leaned forward and before he could react, she had taken his chin in one sinewy hand. Her flesh seemed remarkably cool, and he got a whiff of intense perfume.

"But I can't show you my tail until you understand why you're here. Why I need a man of just your size."

"Size?" Carlton said, distressed to hear that his voice had gone up an octave.

"Oh yes, size is very important to me," she breathed.

Carlton smelled something strange now, an undertone almost smothered by the flowery scent Cleo wore.

The reptile house at the zoo, he thought.

"Size, and the fact that you won't be missed for a good while. Poor, lonely little man."

"That's not true," he protested.

Cleo pulled him closer to her, so that her eyes were inches away from his. Now he could smell the odd reptilian odor more clearly. It seemed to be growing more intense. He raised both hands to try and break free, but this prompted her to put her other hand behind his head. It felt like he was in a vice. And, as he struggled futilely with her, he felt her cool skin roughen beneath his fingers.

"Don't struggle, Mike," she breathed. "Look into my eyes."

He wanted to close his eyes or look away, but he had to obey her.

Were her eyes that color before, that golden yellow? And the pupils – could they be contacts?

A few moments later and his mind stopped trying to rationalize what was happening. Instead, he became fascinated by a writhing form that appeared in the depths of her amber-tinted gaze. It grew clearer, larger, and suddenly stopped moving. It seemed to become aware of him, Carlton. He felt himself scrutinized by an intellect ancient, cold, and utterly inhuman. It was pure in a way no human mind could be. Pure in its desire, its fixation on consuming prey. He saw himself as a tiny creature while the glowing, sinuous entity circled, coiled, pounced.

"No!" he shouted, jerking backward. He realized that he was free of Cleo's grip just as he banged the back of his head against the hull. Cursing and rubbing his bruised scalp, he looked around but could only make out vague, dark forms.

Bloody hell, he thought. *How long have I been under?*

The candle had gone out, or been snuffed. Only the faint gray light of the dying day illuminated the cabin as Carlton tried to struggle upright.

"You can't go, Mike," said Cleo. "You must stay for dinner."

Her voice seemed even deeper, and there was an odd lisp to it. With a great stir of movement on the opposite side of the cabin he saw Cleo's head and shoulders rise up in silhouette. There was something not quite right about the way she moved. It was too smooth, as if she were being lifted by some kind of machine. Then he felt a hard object touch his calf. He reached down and felt scales, living flesh, steely muscles.

"Jesus, there's a snake in here!" he shouted, and tried to rush to the hatchway ladder. His ankles were caught in muscly coils and he crashed onto the planks. Winded, he sensed swift movement and heard a cracking, stretching sound. Cleo's head and shoulders changed shape, elongating until there were no shoulders at all, only a wedge-shaped head atop a column of shadowed flesh.

"Help!" shouted Carlton, thinking of the people on the jetty. Then he remembered the closed hatch.

"You are helping," said a voice that was now barely recognizable as Cleo's. "You've heard of eating for two? I'm eating for many more than that."

He began to punch and kick, and his fist connected with something sharp. He grabbed hold of what must be a mouth, though it was vast. As he tried in vain to push the creature away, the mouth opened wider still. Carlton remembered a wildlife documentary in which a snake ate a rabbit almost as large as itself. He remembered the sickening snap as the reptile's lower jaw unhinged.

The sound this time, when it came a few seconds later, was far louder.

Chapter 8: The Crannog

"How do I pronounce any of these names? Apart from Fort Augustus."

Brad was supposedly navigating as Denny drove them north from Glasgow. He had never entirely trusted GPS and similar gadgets, hence his purchase of an actual paper map. Unfortunately, whenever Denny asked for advice about an upcoming junction, Brad struggled to make sense of Highland names. Among the ones baffling him now were Dunlichity, Errogie, Beauly, and Drumnadrochit.

"Do what I do with unfamiliar words," she advised, "just take a good run at them and hope for the best."

Brad had to smile, despite the grimness of his mood. The closer they got to Loch Ness, the worse their situation would be. He looked out at the mountains that hemmed in the winding road. As a geologist, he knew they were many millions of years old, formed by the violent upheavals of the planet's fiery youth. The valleys in them had been gouged by glaciers comparatively recently, a mere thousands of years ago.

And we're up against something just as ancient, just as impervious to human desires.

"Penny for your thoughts?" said Denny.

"If we can't find and destroy the Zamyatin devices, we need a solid Plan B," he replied. "And I'd feel a lot happier devising one if I had a gun."

"A gun?"

In the driving mirror, Brad saw James Norton sit bolt upright. The folklore expert had been dozing off since their departure from the city. But the word 'gun' had galvanized him.

"Yeah," Brad went on, "I had a semi-automatic pistol when we took them on in Poland. It gave me an edge, kind of."

"I won't be party to actual crime," said Norton, his voice once more that of the prissy English professor. "Well, not violent crime, and certainly not of that sort."

Brad sighed.

"I know guns and firearms are illegal in England."

"Pistols are illegal," put in Denny, "you can get a license for shotguns or sporting rifles."

"But even if I could get a license," protested Brad, "I can't go around waving a twelve gauge! A pistol is what I need!"

"You'd have to buy it illegally," Denny put in. "And that's not something I can be associated with. I couldn't pass that off as research."

"Jesus Christ!" Brad exploded. He had never understood the British fixation on curbing gun ownership. "The world might be coming to an end and you're worried about one little handgun? It's not like I was planning to order an H-bomb!"

There was an awkward silence, then Denny went on, "As I was about to point out, there's a good chance the police would catch you if you tried to get a black market handgun. They're very hot on that kind of thing. And where would we be then?"

Brad let out a sigh, but he could not contradict her. He would be no use to anyone if he got arrested. And he had no desire to spend what might be the last days of Western civilization cooling his heels in a police cell.

"Well, if not a gun, then some sort of weapon," he said. "And no, James, don't tell me I need a hero's sword. If Ouroboros is summoned from the deep, it'll take more than a bit of sharpened iron to deal with it."

He saw Norton's reflection grow pensive and asked, "What is it?"

"Probably nothing," said the Englishman. "For a second there, I almost had an epiphany. A vision, if you like. Very unscientific of me. I'm sure it will pass."

Denny smiled slyly at Brad.

"Okay," she said, "we need to get our plans sorted. But instead of Plan A with B as a fallback, how about launching a sort of pincer movement?"

"What do you mean?" asked Norton.

"I mean," said Denny, "that the cultists are going to have their hands full when they finally get round to their summoning. So anything we can do to throw a spanner in the works would be good, right?"

"Okay," said Brad, starting to grasp her line of thought. "You think we should attack the Zamyatin devices and Cleo's gang at the same time?"

Denny nodded.

"If we mess up their stolen Soviet technology they'll know it, and come after us anyway," she said. "So why not confront them when they start their ritual, or whatever?"

Brad mulled this over. It would make sense for Norton, and perhaps Denny, to keep away from the cultists. Especially from Cleo, who was a killer. He could confront Kelly and her friends while Denny and Norton went along the shores of the loch, wrecking the devices. But to find them in the first place would require some expertise with the magnetometer. The detector was in the trunk of the rental car, and he doubted if he could train either of his companions to use it in less than a day. He explained his doubts to the others.

"It's a bit patronizing to assume I can't learn stuff quickly," said Denny. "Also, I don't need to do a mineral survey with the damn thing, just find a few things that are producing really powerful energy fields. How hard can that be?"

"When put like that, shouldn't be too hard," admitted Brad.

"What I find much more questionable," said Norton, "is that you propose to fight these people on your own. It's not *High Noon*, you know."

"Yeah, in that movie he had a gun," Brad replied sourly.

"You're hoping blood is thicker than venom, aren't you?" Denny asked.

The phrase was shocking, but Brad had to admit the journalist was right. He was still hoping that, when it came to choosing between creating her brave new world and her own father, Kelly would change sides. But he did not dare say it aloud, in case it came out sounding even more naive, or desperate.

"She's had plenty of chances to leave them," Denny said quietly. "She's never wavered. I know we want to believe in people we love. But sometimes they're … well, they're not the people we think they are."

They drove in silence for another half hour or so. Finally, they rounded a hillside and saw a town spread out below them. Fort Augustus was neat and compact, its buildings clustered around the tapering southern end of Loch Ness. And in the small bay just off the quayside of the town was the circular island that had featured in Brad's dream.

"Cherry Island," Denny said. "That's a cute name, considering ..."

It is, thought Brad, peering at the brown oval in the blue-gray water. *Like something out of a children's book. Hard to believe it's the place where a global disaster could be triggered.*

"A crannog," put in Norton, leaning forward to see as they wound their way towards the edge of town. "A stone age artificial island, essentially a stone platform just offshore. Purpose unknown."

"I read that some people believe crannogs were built over the water for defense," said Denny. "Like the Lake Town in *The Hobbit*?"

"Tolkien may have been aware of that theory," conceded Norton. "Though I think Venice was his model for that particular flight of fancy."

"The Eye of Ouroboros," said Brad. "That's what it is. A center for ritual worship of the deity. A forgotten purpose, for thousands of years."

"Until clever Doctor Clay figured it out," added Denny.

"Or Cleo got some kind of psychic message from her goddess," returned Brad.

"You're sure that's where they're going?" asked Denny. "I mean, it's just a round platform, no structure to hide in. And you can't just land there without permission. It's a registered national monument. The police would send out a boat."

"What if they go at night?" asked Norton, leaning back as they lost the view of the island and entered Fort Augustus.

"Exactly," said Brad. "If they don't show much light they won't be challenged for hours, maybe."

"That means they could raise Ouroboros tonight?" asked Denny, a trace of alarm in her voice.

Brad pondered, trying to remember the feel of his last dream.

"I don't think so," he said. "I think we might have a couple of days."

"On what evidence do you base that reassuring conclusion, Mister Steiger?" demanded Norton, reverting to full professor mode.

"I got the sense they were waiting, planning, but not ready to act," he said. "I know it's not much, a feeling. But there it is."

"Vague plans and feelings, evil conspirators, snake-women who can crush you to death, and the end of the world is imminent," grumbled Norton. "This is not how I envisioned spending my sabbatical."

Denny snorted with laughter.

"You think you've got problems?" she asked. "The more I actually find out, the more convinced I am that no editor in his right mind will ever buy the story."

She followed the GPS directions, which took them down to the quayside and their hotel. As Cherry Island came into view, again they saw a white cabin cruiser passing it, heading into the town's small marina.

"Is that what I think it is?" asked Brad.

Denny nodded.

"The enemy's flagship," she said. "Well, at least we know exactly where they are."

"Did you have any luck trying to hire a local boatman?" asked Norton.

"Yeah," said Denny. "I asked somebody at the local paper. They suggested a bloke called Angus. On the phone, he sounds like the quintessential Scots fisherman. Gruff to the point of rudeness, but probably got a heart of gold."

"Oh yeah," said Brad, with a smile. "The rude ones are always the best."

"Sarcasm," put in Norton, "remains the lowest form of wit."

Brad and Denny shared a sigh.

***

Katie Fox waited impatiently on the quayside for the *Talisman* to dock. She became even more frustrated when the boat, instead of mooring by the shore, dropped anchor in the bay about fifty yards out.

"Bugger!" she exclaimed, taking out her phone. For the hundredth time that morning, she tried to phone Jonathan Clay, but the scientist was not picking up. She only had one number for the Loch Ness Monster Survey, his. She went back to her car and poured some coffee from a flask. She had spent the morning shadowing the *Talisman* down the loch from Invercraig, impatient to talk to Clay. She was a persistent journalist.

"Come on then, you have to get off your boat sometime," she muttered. She stared out at the cruiser, willing Clay or one of his team to appear. But the boat might as well have been abandoned, showing no signs of life.

"Sod this," she grunted, and got out again.

It took Katie five minutes to find a local fisherman willing to row her out to the boat. It took her nearly fifteen minutes to haggle with him down to a price that her production company expense account would cover. She clambered into the small boat and the fisherman, Angus, started the outboard motor. As they puttered away from the quay in a cloud of blue smoke, he asked, "Are you that woman off the telly, then?"

"Probably," she replied cheerfully. "I'm doing a series of interviews on the monster."

Angus looked her up and down and then spat into the bay.

"What's the matter?" she asked. "Nessie eating all the salmon?"

"Oh, it's a load of nonsense," he rumbled. "I've fished on the loch, man and boy, for nearly fifty years. I've seen nothing stranger than daft English tourists sitting around all day waiting to see a monster that isn't there."

"I'm guessing you're a tad skeptical," said Katie.

Angus looked at her sourly.

"Sarcasm is all very well, young lady, but harping on the legend makes us all look like ignorant peasants. And we can't all make a living selling bloody T-shirts and cuddly Nessies."

"So you don't like these monster hunters?"

"Not that lot!" rumbled the fisherman, jerking his head at the Talisman. "Buggers dumping their stuff in the loch, nearly ran me down. Fouled my nets, no apologies, just motored away!"

"They dumped garbage?" asked Katie, looking dubiously at the boat.

Perhaps I should ask them about that?

"Nobody takes that much trouble over garbage, young lady!" snorted Angus. "They were using weighted containers of some kind, they sank like stones. All wired together, that's what buggered my nets. Typical bloody English."

533

"Actually I think one of them was American."

His snort told her what he thought of that information. Katie was glad that the conversation was cut short by Angus needing to tie up his boat to the *Talisman.*

"Ahoy!" she shouted at the cruiser. "Anybody aboard? Coming alongside, here."

Katie thought she saw a curtain twitch at the cabin window, but could not be sure. She felt a sudden urge to ask Angus to turn around and take her back to Fort Augustus, and the familiarity of her car. The quietness of the boat seemed not so much frustrating as sinister, now.

Rubbish, she thought. *Get a grip, they're probably having a tense committee meeting or something. These fringe groups lose all sense of reality.*

"You're going aboard?" rumbled Angus. "Or did we just come out here to stare at the side of a bloody boat?"

"Yes, give us a hand," she replied, grasping the rail of the *Talisman.* Angus assisted her on board. In doing so, he placed one of his large hands firmly underneath her left buttock.

"Hey! I'd report you if I knew who to report you to, you old perv!" Katie gasped, almost falling into the bigger boat.

"Ugh, you can find your own way back, ye wee nuisance!" Angus replied, and she heard the outboard motor start up again.

"You shifty old bugger, I paid for a two-way trip!" she shouted at his departing back. Angus's only response was a traditional two-fingered gesture, casually flipped over his shoulder.

"I'll report you to our consumer affairs correspondent!" Katie shouted, adding to herself, "And I suppose that's a pretty feeble threat when you think about it."

"Please?" said an unfamiliar voice.

Katie turned to see a young man looking up at her through a half-open hatchway.

"Oh, sorry!"

She recognized one of the members of Clay's team, a slender, fair young man.

"Please, it is important to be quiet."

Katie noted a trace of accent in the stranger's voice.

German? Maybe Dutch or Swedish. And he looks ill.

As she walked the few paces from the boat's stern to the hatchway, she was surprised by how unhealthy he looked. The young man's paleness was coupled with redness around the eyes. He was wearing a short-sleeved shirt, and she noticed welts or bruises on his arms. She had seen pictures of prisoners with similar marks from cruel restraints.

What kind of games are these people getting up to? You read things about cults.

"Sorry," she repeated. "I was looking for Doctor Clay? I'm Katie, you remember? The interview, yesterday?"

The young man nodded dubiously.

"Jonathan is not here. He is on an ... an errand with Kelly."

"Oh, dear," she said. "Well, who is here?"

"Only me," replied the man, too quickly. Katie had not been a journalist for long but she was already well attuned to lies. As if to confirm her judgment, there was a groan from somewhere below.

There was a pause as the two looked at one another.

"Sounds like someone is a bit seasick," said Katie.

"It is Cleo," said the man. "She must rest. She needs the rest, she is absorbing energy."

"Cleo is the tall, black girl?" asked Katie. "Or the short American?"

"I don't think you should be here," said the man, ignoring her question. He folded his arms. He was still blocking the hatchway.

"Well," said Katie, choosing her words carefully, "I can't really go now, can I? Unless you give me a lift, of course. Erm, what's your name by the way?"

For a moment, she thought he would not reply, but then he tilted his head as if hearing a sound inaudible to Katie.

"I am called Andreas," he said.

"Pleased to meet you, Andreas!" she said, reaching out for a handshake. He complied hesitantly. His palm was cold, moist, his grip surprisingly flaccid for such a young, well-built person.

"Since I'm here, maybe I can talk to you and Cleo?" she said, raising her voice slightly. She hoped she was being heard in the cabin, as women were generally more amenable to being interviewed than men.

Again, she thought Andreas would not answer. There was an unnatural pause as he again seemed to listen.

"Cleo is resting," he said. "She says ... she says I cannot give interviews. You are welcome to come back tomorrow."

Andreas then twisted the corners of his mouth up into the most painfully insincere smile Katie had ever seen. And she had interviewed a large number of politicians.

"Oh," she said. "I was hoping to round off my interviews about the monster with a few comments from Jonathan and Mike. You haven't seen Mike, by the way?"

Andreas shook his head briefly.

"That's odd," Katie said, half to herself. "I thought I saw him driving back towards Invecraig yesterday evening. You were still moored at the village jetty then, weren't you? I assumed he was going to have a word with Jonathan. Did he come here?"

Andreas's eyes widened in apparent alarm. Again, he tilted his head and gave the mechanical smile. At the same time, he took hold of the ladder and started to climb down.

"Cleo thinks she could talk to you, but just for a moment," he said.

"Oh, that's great!" said Katie. She was already descending into the darkness of the cabin when it occurred to her that she had not heard Cleo speak. Then another oddity demanded her attention. The cabin was dark thanks to curtained windows, and smelled peculiar. There was a cloying odor of incense, but beneath it something altogether less pleasant.

"You're looking for Mister Carlton?" said a deep voice from a corner of the cramped compartment.

"Yes," replied Katie, peering into the gloom. The new voice emanated from what seemed to be a large heap of bedclothes along one side of the cabin. "Cleo, is it?"

"Yes," came the reply. "Sorry I can't get up very easily in my current condition. I'm feeling a little delicate."

Condition? Katie suddenly realized what Cleo was implying.

"Oh, God," she said, "you mean you're pregnant?"

"Yes," said Cleo. The heap of blankets moved ponderously, and a head appeared. Katie could not make out the woman's features in the semi-darkness. Then two green-gold eyes gleamed, almost like a cat's. The feeling of something sinister returned, and Katie took a step backwards. She bumped into Andreas, who put his hands lightly around her waist.

"Hey, now," she protested, pulling away and turning to face the young man. "No funny business. People know I'm here!"

"We'll soon find out," said Cleo. Katie heard a stirring behind her and what seemed to be a slithering. She spun round to see a huge body emerge from the heaped blankets. It had a human head, plus arms and a torso, but below the waist, it was a huge bloated sac of tissue. The skin of the thing glistened faintly in the gloom.

"By the way," said Cleo, as Andreas gripped Katie more firmly, "you're quite right. Mister Carlton did come here last night. As a matter of fact he never left."

The monster ran a hand down its swollen form.

This is some kind of gag, she thought. *Nothing this weird can be real.*

"Okay, joke over, where's the camera?" she demanded, just as Andreas grabbed her arms. This time his grip was much firmer. Then Cleo squirmed ponderously across the cabin as Katie struggled to break free. The wriggling lower body made gurgling sounds.

"No cameras here," chuckled the monster. "Just us girls, and my lovely boyfriend of course. He's the father. He's why I needed poor Mike. Lots of energy required for a multiple birth."

Andreas forced Katie forward and the creature rose up to grasp her head in its hands. Katie wanted to close her eyes as the bright gaze pierced her mind, her soul. But before she could act upon the impulse, and all her other thoughts, belonged to the lamia.

***

"Close, but not too close," said Lisa. "Inverness is just a short drive from the bad guys' base! We are within striking distance."

"Close," repeated Pavel. He stood in the doorway of their hotel room, burdened by half a dozen bags. Most of them contained Lisa's shoes and clothes.

"Put them on the bed, silly!" she chided him. "Oh how I wish you still had a mind of your own."

But there's only one way that could happen. And I'm not letting that evil creature bite him, that's for sure.

As she watched Pavel put their bags down, a troubling thought arose and lingered at the edge of her mind.

Maybe there is another way.

But the idea was too disturbing, and she pushed it away. Instead, she started to unpack, which mostly consisted of closely supervising Pavel. When they had finished, she kicked off her shoes and flung herself onto the bed. Pavel obediently lay beside her when she patted the covers.

"Okay, baby, let's check out the news," Lisa said, picking up her phone from the bedside table. As she scrolled through various media reports, she reflected, not for the first time, on how baffling all this new technology had been when she left her lair in the wilds of Poland. Now, being part of the internet culture was second nature to her.

"So much to see, so much going on!" she said, checking rumors about her favorite boy band. "Whoa, they're breaking up? Bullshit! I call bullshit, Pavel."

"Bullshit," he repeated, with a vague smile.

Lisa brushed a strand of hair away from her slave's forehead. She would have to order him to get a haircut soon. She had tried doing it herself, but the results had been more comical than stylish.

Being a hot chick with superpowers doesn't mean you can manage the small stuff, she thought.

"Hot chick," said Pavel, looking into her eyes. He seemed puzzled, as he often did when she touched his mind with hers.

"Sorry, honey, I know it's confusing," she soothed, kissing him on the tip of his nose. "I'll kiss it better all over while we have a shower, how about that?"

But before she could carry out her plan, a call came through. She frowned at the unfamiliar number, touched Accept. It was Knapton.

"What do you want, Mister Policeman? Your friend, did he get better?"

"It's still touch and go," replied the officer. "But Healy did become lucid for a moment. That's why I'm calling."

"To thank me, maybe?"

She heard a tiny bark of humorless laughter.

"To warn you," he said. "And maybe help. I've got two bits of information."

"About Cleo?" she asked.

"I assume so," he said. "What the boss said was 'With the chaos comes the breeding.' Does that mean anything?"

Lisa frowned.

"No," she admitted. "Is that all he said?"

"Yes," said Knapton. "I think it came via his link to Cleo, which was badly damaged but not entirely broken. Is that possible?"

"Yeah, why not?" she said impatiently. Lisa had never thought deeply about the nature of her or Cleo's powers. Ouroboros was a source of energy that she tapped, but at the same time, she did her best to block the collective consciousness behind that primal force. It had driven her insane once before, she did not intend to let it have untrammeled access to wreck her mind again. She knew she was far from stable.

"You said there were two things?" she went on. "But he only said one?"

"The other is just old-style detective work," he said. "Same as the kind that got me your number. It's about the American girl, Steiger's daughter. She seems central to the cult, yes?"

"Yes, yes," said Lisa impatiently. "I don't know why, but they need her. Without her, they cannot succeed."

Suddenly it occurred to her that killing Kelly Steiger would be so much easier than taking on Cleo, and probably just as effective. She smiled sweetly at Pavel, who smiled back. The revelation meant she lost track of what Knapton was saying.

"What do you mean?" she asked, interrupting him. "You say she has a bad credit card?"

"No!" sighed Knapton. "Not that kind of visa. The point is that if someone were to tell the local police they could, in theory, arrest her."

"Why don't you tell them?" she asked.

"I'm under orders not to contact law enforcement, or Steiger, or any of his friends," said Knapton sourly.

Lisa giggled at the thought of anyone obeying orders they did not agree with. *Silly little men, and to think this is how they run the world.*

"So you told me?"

"Right, oddly enough my other boss, the one I can't afford to disobey, did not mention telling crazy half-human killers about my findings."

"Hey, less of the crazy, fella!" she protested.

"Sorry," said Knapton. "You may be a very sensible half-human killer, I suppose. I don't have much experience of the type."

"That's better," she said dubiously. The British habit of inserting irony and sarcasm into almost any situation was still confusing her. "But I don't want to talk to the police!"

"Well, tell Steiger," Knapton suggested. "She's his girl, after all."

Before she could object that Steiger might shoot her if he knew she was still alive, the policeman had ended the call.

"Bugger!" she said. It was one of her favorite British words.

"Bugger," repeated Pavel.

Lisa turned on the television and checked for more news of the monster or other strange phenomena. There was nothing, so she found a show about American teenagers with perfect looks enduring very complicated personal lives. The show was new to her. It looked promising. She provisionally added it to her list of favorite things.

"And this is the world those idiots want to destroy!" she said, snuggling up to Pavel. "It's all so amazing!"

"Destroy," Pavel breathed.

Chapter 9: Blood and Iron

Clay and Kelly returned to the *Talisman* in the cruiser's small dinghy to find Katie Fox waiting for them. Already aware of what had happened, Clay helped her into the smaller boat then took her ashore without speaking. Only when they landed did he engage in some inane conversation for the sake of appearances. When he returned to the *Talisman*, he asked Kelly if she knew why Cleo had taken control of the journalist.

"You don't know already?" Kelly asked, as she worked on a meal in the vessel's tiny galley.

"You know I don't," he replied impatiently. His link to Cleo, while strong, was largely one way. She monitored him, issued orders, saw through his eyes. With Kelly, it was very different. Clay knew the girl was Cleo's confidante, their psychic link much stronger and more intimate. He had tried to stifle his jealousy and frustration at being 'out of the loop' but it was not easy.

"I think the plan is just to throw dad and his pals off the trail," she explained. "That's the impression I get. Simple, right? But there could be more to it. Cleo's become harder to read due to her ... well, her condition. And when she's sleeping, I get practically nothing from her, when shared dreams used to be a regular thing. And she's asleep most of the time now."

"She's also become more unpredictable," he complained. "None of this was part of the original plan."

"The people who made that plan are mostly dead," Kelly pointed out, stirring a saucepan of organic rice. "We survived Wychmere through luck, and Cleo wasn't there. You left her in London, didn't you?"

Because she was deemed too unpredictable to take part, thought Clay. But that was a fact he had never spoken aloud, and he hoped Cleo was unaware of it.

"Anyway," Kelly continued, "if Katie can throw dad off the trail, it must be a good thing, right?"

Clay was dubious. There was still so much he did not understand about Ouroboros and the way Kelly and her father fitted into the scheme of things. The connection between father and daughter was unique, so far as he knew. For one to be part of the cult's 'hive mind' while the other was not might simply be a fluke. But Clay suspected that it was far more than that.

He tried, not for the first time, to probe Kelly about her relationship with Brad.

"There was nothing special about my childhood," she interrupted. "My dad spent a lot of time away working, and then mom found a guy who was around all the time and they split up."

"But there was no hint of any paranormal connection until you joined us?" Clay persisted.

Kelly took plates from a cupboard, slammed the latter shut in irritation.

"I had this real boring, very normal childhood in the Midwest," she sighed. "Nothing happened in Wisconsin, believe me. Every day, nothing happened."

But she did not meet Clay's eye.

There is something, he thought. *Perhaps something she has suppressed.*

"Knowing the nature of the link might be important," he said in a gentler tone.

"It might endanger the whole project. Is it worth taking the risk?"

Kelly stood for a moment staring into the steaming pan. Then she took it off the stove and began spooning out the rice.

"There was one thing," she said. "Just one thing that happened that was out of the ordinary. But I don't see how it could make a big difference."

"Tell me," said Clay. "I have been known to guess rightly in the past."

Kelly laughed.

"Yeah, okay Mister 'I Revived Ouroboros That Time,' I guess it can't hurt to tell."

***

"That's definitely their boat," said Denny, squinting through the viewfinder of a lightweight video camera. "My sources told me they were moored at some village a few miles up the loch. Invercraig, it's called."

The three companions were standing at the large window of Brad's hotel room, which looked out over the small harbor of Fort Augustus.

"Evidently they decided to move closer to Cherry Island," said Norton. "Which I must confess is a little ominous."

"Yeah," agreed Brad. "It suggests their plans are further advanced than we'd hoped. They may even be ready to go tonight."

Denny lowered the camera to look at Brad.

"Maybe you'd better get that magnetic gizmo out and teach me how to use it, then."

Norton gave a snort of laughter.

"Not even the pretense that I could learn, then?" he asked.

"I think, on balance, that you'd better remain here at base," said Brad. "After all, these are violent people."

He was surprised to see Norton look disappointed.

My God, thought Brad, *was he looking forward to a scrap?*

"I agree," put in Denny, "if only because we need someone who knows what we're up to. Someone to write the story. If we don't come back."

Norton looked suitably sober at that thought, gave a curt nod.

"I only wish I had been more help," he said, sitting down on the small sofa by the television. "There is something I'm missing, I'm sure. Something maddeningly obvious."

"To do with Clay's remarks in that interview?" asked Brad.

"Yes," confirmed Norton. "I can't help thinking that iron is the key. After all, it's a ferrous metal, isn't it?"

Brad paused, wondering if the academic had something.

"Could be," he said. "If they're using electromagnetism in some way, then any ferrous metal would disrupt the field."

"But it must be a really big field," objected Denny, raising the camera to her eyes again. "You'd need a huge lump of iron. And where exactly would you put it?"

Brad was stumped, and admitted it.

"Whoa," said Denny, "I can see them. Well, Clay and your daughter, Brad. They're on the deck, the bit at the back. Anyway, looks like they're eating. All very

540

relaxed."

She passed the camera to Brad and he studied the scene aboard the *Talisman*. Denny was right.

"It is them," he said. "They're taking it easy. Don't look like people planning to destroy civilization, anyhow."

"How exactly do people look when they're planning to do great evil?"

Norton's question shocked Brad. It was the first time he had heard anyone call Kelly evil. He almost retorted that his daughter was misguided, but could not bring himself to say the words.

I can't really believe that, he thought. *Not after all I've seen. I just don't know what to make of her anymore.*

An awkward silence was broken when Denny's phone chimed. She checked the number and frowned.

"No idea who that might be," she said, "but better answer it."

After a few moments of conversation, Denny raised her eyebrows at Brad, then covered the phone to speak urgently.

"It's Katie Fox, the Midland News reporter? She got my number through contacts back in London, apparently. Anyway, she wants to interview you."

Brad took the phone and asked, "How did you even know I was here?"

"Your daughter told me," said Fox. "She said you're involved in some kind of family feud over Ouroboros. I thought it might make for an interesting human angle on this whole monster thing, and–"

"I'm not interested," snapped Brad and gave Denny her phone back.

"Just a minute, Katie," said Denny, putting the other reporter on hold. "Brad, think about it," she went on, "you could turn this against them somehow."

"How, exactly?" Brad demanded. "This woman just wants 'human interest,' that usually means making people look like cranks, or at best, idiots."

"She's got a decent reputation," insisted Denny. "I think she'll play fair. Why not tell the truth, or at least some of it? Your daughter was drawn into a doomsday cult. That might lead the authorities to pay some attention. I can give you some tips on how to hint at some of their serious crimes without stepping over the line."

"It seems like an excellent idea," put in Norton, surprising Brad. "The power of the media, one must use it or be used by it."

"Okay," Brad conceded. "I'll do a brief interview. And when my boss sees it, I'll be out of a job, in all likelihood. I just hope it's worth it."

"Tell her how worried you are about Kelly, and how much you love her," suggested Denny. "Show the viewers the decent man you are. Draw a lot more media attention to Ouroboros, and make it harder for them to operate. It's worth a try, yes?"

"I just hope she doesn't edit it to make me look like an asshole," said Brad. "No offense, but sometimes you can't trust reporters."

***

Clay and Kelly sat on the small deck of the *Talisman*, eating under the summer sky while looking out over the loch.

"I was twelve," Kelly said. "That was when it happened. The only real something in the middle of all that nothingness. There was an accident. I was fooling around with this boy, who I really liked, which shows how stupid I was then. I mean, he was a jerk. We were playing some dumb game on his family's farm and I fell. I can remember this old harvester, all rusted up, and we were climbing over it pretending we were in some sci-fi movie, I think. And I fell off onto the blades. I can still see them coming up at me, all the rust. And one was broken, and it went into my side and cut an artery. There's not much of a scar, now, considering."

"That must have been terrifying," said Clay, to fill a pause.

After gazing out over the water for a few moments, Kelly continued.

"Thing is, I lost a lot of blood. By the time they got me to the local hospital, which was over twenty miles away, I found out later that I needed transfusions. And it turned out I'm this rare blood group, and they didn't have enough of the red stuff. So I was gonna die. Except I didn't. Obviously."

Clay realized what was coming next.

"Your father gave blood to save you?"

Kelly nodded.

"It was touch and go, but he insisted on giving more and more. They put out a call for donors, of course, but none arrived until later on when I was over the worst of it. But his blood was mixed with mine. Do you think that accounts for the link?"

Clay shrugged.

"One thing I do know is that, in ancient times they had no blood transfusions. Lots of blood rituals, certainly, but nothing like our modern techniques. So who knows how that mixing might affect your powers? Such as they are."

They sat in silence for a while, Clay finishing his meal while Kelly absentmindedly stirred a fork in what was left of hers.

"I should have died," she said. "That was my destiny."

"Why?" he asked. "It was just an accident. Kids take risks, and it was hardly your fault some piece of agricultural equipment was just left–"

"No," she interrupted, "I mean that dad was never at home, or it seemed like it anyways. That's your freak occurrence, your wild card – him actually being at home with his family. The odds were stacked against it."

"Perhaps it was ordained that it should be so," Clay suggested. "As part of a wider plan."

Kelly looked at him for the first time since she had started her story.

"That sounds like the bullshit the Lutheran minister came out with, when he visited me," she sneered. "And all I could think of was, if I had died because dad was away working for some global corporation, would that have been God's plan, too?"

For the first time, Clay understood the foundation of Kelly's attitude to her father.

"That was when you really started to resent him?" he asked.

"No," she replied. "It was when I stopped giving a damn about him and the world he's part of. It was when I started to question everything, began wanting to know why there was all this misery, pain, injustice. It was when I stopped being his little girl. Ironic, huh?"

She picked up their plates and went back down the hatchway, leaving Clay to contemplate the loch, its shores, and the bustling town. He peered at the front of the hotel where he knew Steiger and his team were staying, but could see no sign of anyone looking back.

***

"Someone here would like to talk to you," said Denny. She had phoned Brad with an urgent request to come to the hotel bar, where she had met someone 'we both remember.'

Brad looked past her to a young couple who were sitting at the bar drinking sodas. One was very familiar, a sturdily-built man of about thirty with a mop of untidy dark hair. Seeing him brought Brad's dark, violent memories of Mista Venja castle flooding back.

"Pavel!" he exclaimed, taking a few steps towards the couple. "My God, I thought you'd been killed. What happened to you? Did Lenka get away?"

The treasure hunter looked at Brad in apparent confusion.

"And how is–" he began and then stopped in confusion.

Brad looked down at the woman beside Pavel. She, too, rang a bell, but it was an alarm bell. She was petite and pretty. Her clothes were fashionable, though she seemed to be wearing too few of them for the Scottish climate. Her eyes and hair were dark, but her skin was startlingly pale, as if she had spent years away from sunlight.

For a moment, he had thought that she was Pavel's girlfriend Lenka, albeit much altered. Then it clicked. He had seen that face before, but it had not been smiling up at him as it was now. Her features had been contorted in bestial rage. She certainly was not Lenka.

Holy crap, it's her, he thought. *The Insane One.*

"Denny, get over here beside me," he said urgently, retreating. "These are not friends."

"Oh!" pouted the pale girl in a strong East European accent. "I am hurt! I am the daughter of your good friend Marcus, so we are friends too, yes?"

"You're Lisa Valentine?" said Denny, moving to stand next to Brad.

"The very same!" replied Lisa. "And I am here to offer the olive branch of peace, and all that nice stuff."

"Did you offer it to him first?" asked Brad, pointing at Pavel. "You got your fangs into the poor bastard after you killed his girlfriend, right?"

Lisa's smile faded, then returned.

"I was not feeling very well then, I am much better now," she insisted. "Besides, he is very happy in his own way."

She pressed herself to Pavel's side like a teenager with a new boyfriend. Brad felt nauseous.

"Who are these people?" asked Norton, ambling into the bar behind Brad. "That poor chap looks drugged, and the girl's tricked out like some sort of Balkan tart."

"You, I do not like!" snarled Lisa. "Careful what you say or I will go away and leave you without my help!"

"And what help is that?" Brad demanded. "The kind you gave Marcus,

543

maybe?"

At that, Lisa looked genuinely ashamed, looked down at the floor, and mumbled something inaudible.

Maybe she is more human than not, thought Brad. *Or she can fake a human reaction perfectly.*

"Please, give her a chance," pleaded Denny. "We're not exactly spoiled for choice when it comes to allies."

"Okay, we've got nothing to lose by listening," Brad sighed. "But not here."

The barman and a couple of early drinkers were pointedly not looking at the confrontation, but they could obviously hear every word.

"We can go up to your room, maybe?" suggested Lisa.

"You're joking, of course?" replied Brad. "No way I'm sharing a confined space with one of your kind. And whatever your proposal is, we all need to hear it, so don't buy a drink just yet, James."

A few minutes later, the five were walking through a small park. This allowed them to keep far enough from evening strollers to have a private discussion while still being in a public place. Lisa, after some playful evasions, finally got to the point.

"Your little girl is in this country illegally. Just like me!"

"Shit!" exclaimed Brad as the realization struck him. "Why didn't I think of that? It's so goddamn obvious."

"What is?" asked Denny.

"Kelly's an illegal alien," explained Brad. "She must be. She was here studying archaeology at London U. on a student visa, right? But she hasn't been to classes for over six months. They must have thrown her out of the course by now."

Understanding dawned in Denny's eyes. Norton looked from one to the other and chuckled.

"I'd had thought it was obvious she was in the country illegally," said the academic. "We're always having problems with that. Bloody students, always going AWOL."

"Then why didn't you mention it?" demanded Brad in exasperation.

"I didn't think it mattered," said Norton huffily. "Besides, it's obvious. I assumed you knew."

A reasonable assumption, thought Brad. *I just wish the guy wasn't so damn snooty about it.*

"But don't you see, James?" said Denny. "This means we can disrupt their activities by reporting Kelly to the police."

"Not that simple," replied Norton, shaking his head. "It has to go through the Home Office. They handle visas. It might take days for them to contact the local police. The fact that Scotland has slightly different laws on such matters is another complication."

"Oh, Jesus Christ," groaned Brad. "British bureaucracy again! I can't get a gun, I can't call the cops. If only we'd known about the visa weeks ago! Now it's probably too late."

"But knowing Kelly has been reported might force them to show their hand before they're fully prepared," said Denny in a soothing voice. "Why not give it a try? Do it, then tell her."

"This is all very exciting," remarked Lisa sourly. "Just like a James Bond movie, only without the action. Or a car that is also a submarine."

"I suppose you favor something a bit more violent?" asked Denny.

Lisa nodded.

"I would be killing Cleo now if it wasn't for Pavel," she said, clutching the tall man's arm. "Without me, he would be lost."

"Lost," said Pavel, looking down at her blankly.

He's like a man child, thought Brad. *Most of what made him a human being has been erased. Or is it simply suppressed?*

"Or perhaps your young man would be free," said Norton, giving the foreign couple a calculating stare. "And able to live his own life again?"

Lisa shot the academic a venomous look. Her mouth opened and there was a distinct hiss.

"Well, I think that confirms my hypothesis," Norton went on, sounding smug, as if he had just proven some obscure point in a college seminar. "In folklore, if a witch or enchanter dies, the harm they have done often dies with them."

"That's it, isn't it?" asked Brad. "Your power over individuals can be reversed by death. And that goes for all the lamias."

Lisa nodded.

"Andreas, the German boy who Cleo keeps, he will be free when I kill her," she said sulkily. "But maybe I take him for myself. As a prize."

"When are you planning this big showdown?" demanded Denny. "Because it sounds to me like you're just talking a good fight."

"You insult me again, I will not tell you the other thing!" exclaimed Lisa.

"What other thing?" scoffed Brad. "Is Clay driving without a license?"

"No," sneered Lisa. "Cleo is ... how you say? Ready to pop."

Chapter 10: Waking Nightmares

"I don't believe it," said Brad flatly. "I think she's lying. Lying as well as stone crazy."

They were sitting in his hotel room again, having left Lisa and Pavel in the park at twilight. It was now near midnight, but in this high latitude, it never grew fully dark. They had been discussing Lisa's warning for hours, Denny at the window observing the *Talisman*, Norton in his corner chair. Brad paced, full of nervous energy, trying to collate what he had been told about Cleo.

"Is it possible?" asked Denny. "Can those *things* reproduce?"

"Why not?" asked Norton. "Living things can, it's one of the things that defines life. But what worries me is exactly how many offspring this Cleo might produce."

Brad stopped pacing and looked down at the Englishman.

"Yeah," he said. "Don't snakes lay dozens of eggs or something?"

"I doubt that we can use nature as our guide here," warned Norton. "Mythical creatures, such as lamias, are traditionally exempt from normal restrictions. Indeed, one of the most common features of monsters in folklore is their extraordinary fecundity."

Denny looked over, a horrified expression on her face.

"You're saying Cleo could spawn more than a few dozen little horrors?"

"She might produce hundreds or even thousands of offspring," pointed out Norton. "The snake is a near-universal fertility symbol, after all. If she is 'ready to pop,' as that pale creature put it, we could be knee deep in hungry little monsters. And I suppose the loch in high summer would make an ideal spawning ground."

"It must be linked to the raising of Ouroboros," declared Brad, starting to pace again. "Another reason to stop it."

"Look, we've got stuff to do," said Denny, putting down her camera. "Like learning to use your magnetic gizmo, Brad. No sign of movement from the enemy, so we've got tonight at least."

"Right," he said. "You both up for this?"

Norton and Denny were keen to complete their training. Brad led them down to the rental car, where they retrieved the magnetometer. The device looked like a metal detector, but was much more advanced.

"What we really need," said Brad, fastening the power pack around Denny's waist, "is some kind of magnetic field so as to calibrate it."

"Power lines?" suggested Denny.

"Or a cell phone mast?" put in Norton.

Brad shook his head as he switched on the device.

"All main electricity is underground here," he pointed out. "And phone masts radiate microwaves, totally different signal. Best we can do is—"

He stopped, staring at the small indicator screen.

"What is it?" asked Denny, looking at the same reading without comprehension.

"There's a powerful field nearby," said Brad. "Fluctuating, but strong."

"Maybe their Zamyatin devices are already in operation?" suggested Norton, looking out towards the *Talisman*.

"Crap," said Brad.

It had never occurred to him that the cultists might have equipped their field generators with long-lasting batteries. But it made sense. Rather than rush around the loch-side switching them on, or risking that some kind of signal would fail, their energy field would be in place for days.

"They could start their rite any time they liked," he said, thinking aloud. "Still, at least this means we can find the devices and disable them."

"No time like the present," suggested Denny, offering Brad the car keys.

"Nope," he said, starting to unstrap the magnetometer from her. "You drive, I'll work this detector. It'll be quicker."

"And what will I do?" asked Norton.

"Provide any extra muscle we might need," said Brad, keeping a straight face as he climbed into the car.

They set off along the loch-side and within ten minutes, Brad had zeroed in on the first field generator. The Zamyatin device, a metal box the size of a small suitcase, was hidden in some bushes by the roadside.

"Not very well hidden," Norton remarked as he and Denny heaved the device onto the grass verge. "Some curious soul would have found it quite soon, one would think."

Brad grunted in agreement.

"Suggests they're on a tight schedule," he said.

"We are approaching the autumn equinox," said Norton. "Traditionally a time when the powers of light and dark are in delicate balance."

"That might be it," agreed Brad, getting a toolkit out of the trunk. "But whatever the reason, this component in their plan is about to be removed."

While his companions held the box steady, Brad pried it open with a large screwdriver. He removed the lid of the casing to be confronted with a powerful industrial battery connected to a magnetic coil. The important part of the device, an array of circuit boards, looked impressive. But Brad had no time to puzzle over the complexities of Zamyatin's invention. He selected a set of pliers and tore out vital connections, rendering the machine inert.

"Let's get it good and wet," he suggested, "nothing like old-fashioned water to screw up fancy gizmos."

"It's that simple?" asked Denny, sounding slightly disappointed as she helped Brad carry the device to the waterline and throw it in.

"You'd rather it had blown up in our faces?" asked Brad, packing up his tools.

"My God, I never thought that it might be booby-trapped!" exclaimed Norton. "You could have gotten us all killed!"

"Nah," Brad said, "buying explosives would be as risky as buying a gun, right? Draw too much attention."

Norton looked unconvinced, but said nothing more. They found a second box within half an hour, and went through the same routine. By three in the morning, they had almost circumnavigated Loch Ness, and destroyed five identical devices. The sixth they found as they were driving back into Fort Augustus. It was hidden amid a heap of trash behind a bus stop.

"Let's keep this one," suggested Brad, after disconnecting the battery. "I'd like to tinker, find out more about it."

"Isn't that what led to the creation of our friend, Lisa?" asked Denny.

"I swear on a stack of Bibles that I won't conduct any unethical experiments," he replied, putting his hand on his heart.

The conversation continued in a slightly silly vein as they drove back to the hotel. The sense of relief was palpable, all three of them expressing surprise at having thwarted Ouroboros so easily.

"They can still make a lot of mischief," Norton pointed out. "And they, too, probably have a Plan B."

"Don't be such a grumpy old man!" said Denny, giving the eminent professor a shove as they went up the hotel steps. "We've won this round."

"Yeah, every one you walk away from," said Brad, carrying the last Zamyatin device.

Except that it was kind of easy, he thought. *Sure, they might not have expected us to go looking for their gear. But still, how hard would it have been to hide it more professionally?*

He said his goodnights and put the device in the wardrobe of his room. While he longed to investigate the mechanism, he was having trouble staying awake. He checked his phone for the first time since dusk and found a message from Katie Hopkins confirming the time of their interview tomorrow.

No, Brad thought, as he undressed. *Not tomorrow. Today.*

He lay awake thinking about what he would say to the reporter. Eventually he gave up trying to work it out. He also resolved to ask for a list of questions beforehand. He was beginning to drift off to sleep when there was a knock at the door. He got up and opened it to Denny. Without speaking, he led her to the bed.

"I couldn't sleep either, and I just thought," she said, "we might not get another chance."

"There's a lot to be said for the direct approach," he said.

***

"This is the time," said Cleo. Her voice was deeper than before, and she spoke slowly.

"How can you be sure?" asked Clay. He could barely make out Cleo's face in the gloom of the cabin. From what he could see of it, she was now unable to return to truly human form.

Even after the birthing, he thought, *she may not revert.*

"It's no big deal, Jonathan," said Kelly. "And in the end, it's my choice. I've been yearning for this ever since the start."

She knelt down beside Cleo and pushed her hair back, exposing her neck. Clay, though he had seen this several times, still looked away. There were a few moments of silence, then he heard Kelly standing up.

"Are you all right?" he asked, going up to offer her support.

The American girl looked round. In the gloom, he saw a glimmer of golden-green in her eyes.

"I'm fine," she said. "I'm part of it all now, really part—"

The gleam faded rapidly and she fell forward, collapsing so quickly that Clay almost missed the catch. As he helped her across to the cabin's only chair, Cleo began to groan.

"That might have triggered it," she said. "I need to be outside. Quickly! I can feel their minds clearly now, they're impatient."

"Andreas!" shouted Clay, but the young man – summoned by means more powerful than any vocal command – was already clambering down the hatchway ladder. Clay put Kelly in the chair, then helped Andreas get Cleo's hugely swollen form up on the small deck. For a moment, Clay was afraid the creature would get stuck in the hatchway, but her own strength and gritty determination got her topside. She lay panting, a woman-like head and torso attached to a bloated snake body. Cleo gave another, louder groan, and her body jerked.

There was a tearing sound that made Clay feel sick to his stomach, and the scaly belly split open lengthwise. Clay and Andreas both stepped away instinctively as dozens of dark, wriggling forms surged out on a tide of bloody fluid. So far as Clay could see, they were like regular snakes, each about six inches long. They moved swiftly, and with purpose, heading for the boat's rail and plopping overboard into the dark water.

Cleo heaved a sigh and her body began to heal with astonishing speed.

I had expected something a bit more grandiose, thought Clay. *Not this business-like spawning.*

"Oh, Jonathan," said Cleo, and this time her words were much clearer. "Would it have been better if we'd had a marching band? This is just the first of many birthings. It will be a routine matter soon enough."

"But why do you need to give birth at all?" he asked. "Surely conversion–"

"Conversion would be too slow without extra lamias," said Kelly, appearing at the hatchway. This time her eyes were shining brightly in the moonlight. As she got closer, Clay could make out her slit pupils. He had gotten to know her well during the previous months, and understood her intense devotion to the cause. She was far more committed than he had even been. But part of the conventional man he had once been still recoiled from Kelly's decision.

It's one thing to join with Ouroboros, he thought. *But to do it for this reason.*

"What's the matter, Jonathan?" asked Kelly. "You think I'm betraying someone I should care about? Isn't it a little late for that, considering what we're doing here?"

Clay did not trust himself to speak. Cleo stood upright, her human form restored. She was once more a tall, striking woman. Or so Clay thought at first. As she walked over to join them, he saw metallic gleams in the faint moonlight. He realized that she was still covered in fine, golden-bronze scales.

"Yes," said Cleo, looking down at her body. "I think this is the true form all women will one day assume. All those who survive, that is."

***

In his hotel room, James Norton lay awake on his bed, fully clothed. He never slept well away from his room in college. His life had, until this point, been that of the book-loving thinker, moving from child to student to professor without much effort.

I am not a man of action, he thought. *And yet I have spent my entire life studying and teaching folklore – old stories about brave heroes battling monsters.*

He got up, abandoning the pretense of trying to rest, and went to the window. His room looked out onto the streets of Fort Augustus. A few cars and trucks were moving, and as he watched, someone walked around a corner. It was a teenage girl, dressed for a night out, picking her way barefoot with her shoes in her hand. She almost collided with a lamppost before going out of sight.

Slightly drunk, he thought. *Probably get an earful from her mother when she gets home. I daresay she feels it's worth that minor annoyance.*

The commonplace sight made him choke up, suddenly. It was part of a world he had never been part of, merely observed, a world of love, families, children. Tears came as he felt an almost painful regret for the life he might have had, if he had been braver, more honest, when the opportunity presented itself.

But she married someone else, someone who was a lot more fun of course, and that was that.

Norton was about to turn from the window when he noticed a dimming of the more distant streetlights. At first, he thought his vision was blurred and dabbed at his eyes with a handkerchief. But it had no effect, and he realized what was really happening. A chill ran through him. The town was being blotted out before his eyes. It was deeply unsettling.

"Oh my God," he said. "This must be it."

***

"It's a fake," said Brad.

Denny sat up to see him sitting at the window, bits of the Zamyatin device scattered on the desk in front of him.

"What?" she asked, still bleary from a deep sleep. "What do you mean? How long have you been awake?"

"About half an hour," he said, turning off the desk lamp. Now the window was admitting a dim, gray pre-dawn light. "The device, it's a fake. It was never intended to work. The circuit boards don't do anything, as far as I can see. The field generator is real, but it's just a dumb, un-modulated magnetic field. If that was enough to raise Ouroboros, the world would be knee-deep in lamias."

"You're sure?" asked Denny, getting up and clutching a sheet around her. "It's not just something unusual, maybe something you've never seen before?"

Brad shrugged.

"I could be wrong, I'm not an electrical engineer. But I've tinkered with enough gadgets in my time to know that this looks fake as hell."

She went over to stand by him and looked at the haphazard array of components.

"But why go to so much trouble?"

"To make us go away, or keep us busy, bit of both," he sighed. "We certainly wasted time and energy last night. Fool your enemy into doing something pointless, it's an old tactic."

"But if that's true," she pointed out, leaning on the desk, "it means they have their real system set up. So they could go ahead any time."

"Yeah," he agreed, looking up at her. "But I still don't get it. I mean, Cherry Island is much closer to the town than I thought, and a lot smaller. So how can they expect to go there and perform their ritual without being seen?"

"Maybe their ritual only takes a few minutes," she suggested, twisting around to look out over the harbor. "Or maybe–"

Denny froze, and Brad stood up. At first, he could not see what might have shocked her. There was something wrong with the view. It was misty, a thin haze lying on the water and blurring their view of the quayside.

Well, the sun will soon burn that off, he thought.

But then he realized what was wrong with the view. Yesterday he could see almost the whole length of Loch Ness, just over twenty miles. Now the view was truncated. A wall of white, seemingly as dense as cotton wool, was rolling down the loch towards Fort Augustus. He leaned closer to the window to see if it was just on the loch.

"It's closing in on all sides," said Denny. "A fog that dense. In August."

"No way it's natural," he agreed. "And when it arrives they'll go to the crannog, and raise the serpent."

"What can we do?" she said, almost too quietly for him to hear.

Brad grabbed a pad and pencil and started to write down a list of items.

"Go shopping, first thing. Take James to help – no, scratch that, let the poor bastard sleep, he's done his best, and it's not much to carry. Buy this stuff, I'm not sure what the British names are for some of the products, but they're all regular household chemicals. Bring 'em back here. I'll be waiting. I can use some of this decoy to make a remote detonator, rig it to my phone. We'll trigger it with a message from your cell."

Denny looked dazed as he tore off the page and handed her the list.

"You mean you're going to make a bomb?"

"Got any better ideas?" he asked. "We've got no superpowers to fight them, but we've got brains. We know bullets can hurt them but not kill them. Let's see if blowing them apart can do the job better."

Denny looked from the list to Brad, open-mouthed.

"Hey," he said, kissing her quickly on the tip of the nose, "don't crack. Tough investigative reporters get the job done, right?"

"Right," she said, trying to smile as she stood up. "I'll go and see if the all-night supermarket has some of these."

"Maybe put some clothes on first?" he suggested. "Our decadent civilization is still around for now."

At that, she did manage a brief smile. She dressed, kissed him again, and left. He watched her leave the hotel. The fog was now so dense that she vanished from view after less than ten yards.

Can I make a bomb? And how the hell can I use it on the crannog without blowing myself up?

"I can try," he said to the empty room. "Maybe I can blackmail them with it, make them stop."

He threw himself into his new task and tried not to think about how desperate his improved half-plan was. Denny had been gone an hour and Brad was tinkering with what he hoped would be a trigger mechanism when his phone rang. It was

Katie Fox. He had totally forgotten their interview, which now seemed utterly irrelevant.

"Sorry," he said brusquely. "I have to bail. Something much more important has come up and—"

"Oh, that's a pity," said the reporter. "I have someone here who really would like to discuss things with you."

Brad was about to end the call when a familiar voice said, "Hi, Dad! Whatcha doin'?"

Chapter 11: The Day of the Serpent

"What is it, Cressida?" asked Julie, trying to keep the worry out of her voice.

Ever since their experience at Culloden, the family had been trying to get back to normal and enjoy their holiday. Julie thought things had more or less returned to normal until this morning, when they had woken to find Inverness wreathed in dense fog. Paul had at first played up the spookiness of this until Julie had given him one of her special looks. Now he was trying to cheer up Will and Cressida with a promise of a trip to a castle, then to McDonald's. But, while Will was already spelling out just what burger he wanted, Cressida was gazing vacantly out of the breakfast room window.

"It's just fog, darling," Julie said. "Nothing to be scared of."

"I'm not scared," said the little girl, still looking towards the loch. "I'm waiting."

"Waiting for a mermaid," jeered Will.

"We've talked about that, son," put in Paul quickly. "It's all in the past. We move on."

Cressida shook her head.

"No, it's in the future," she said softly.

Julie leaned closer to her daughter, tidied her hair.

"What do you mean?" she asked, keeping her voice low.

"The mermaids," said Cressida. "They're coming. Which sounds nice when you say it like that. But I'm not sure I want them to come. It feels ... funny."

Julie was wondering if a stricter approach might work when she saw a child's face reflected in the window. It was a little boy at the table behind them. He, too, was looking out at nothing. Looking around the guests at other tables, Julie saw three more young children also staring intently into the cotton-wool wall of fog.

"Eat something, dear," Julie urged, touching Cressida lightly on her arm. The girl turned round and looked into her mother's eyes.

"All right," said Cressida. "I'll have some toast."

When they finished breakfast, Julie corralled her children and took them upstairs to put on their coats. The weather, she explained, was unseasonable. She then had to explain the word to Will. Cressida was still distracted, and Julie began to wonder if her daughter was suffering post-traumatic shock.

Then she, too, started to feel the influence emanating from the loch.

At first, it was vague, slightly irritating, the sensation of something that needed attending to. Julie even looked down to see if she had a trailing shoelace. But then she realized that it was something like a call, a kind of mental dog-whistle that could not be ignored. She found herself standing beside Cressida at the window, gazing into the silver-gray murk.

"Who is coming? What is coming?" she murmured.

"You all right, love?" asked Paul, coming to stand beside her. "Bloody hell," he went on, "it's a real pea-souper, as my old dad used to say. Still, that's the Highlands for you. At least it's not bucketing down with rain, eh?"

"No," said Julie, only half-hearing him.

"We ready for the off?" Paul asked. "This museum opens at ten. I hear there's some kind of animatronic dinosaur."

"Yay!" shouted Will, his loud enthusiasm piercing Julie's reverie. She blinked, shook her head.

"Yeah, right," she said, smiling at Paul. "All ready to go. Today's adventure may begin!"

***

Denny had managed to find every item on Brad's list, after searching for British brand names online. It had taken her just over an hour and she was on her way back to the hotel when an obvious point occurred to her. She stopped dead in the street.

How is he going to plant this bomb on a flat stone platform surrounded by water?

None of the possible answers were reassuring. She set off again, walking just as fast, but now confused and conflicted. The thought of Brad going on a suicide mission was abhorrent to her. Her feelings for him had grown, ripened, over the last few months.

But if the world's in peril, the feeling of two people doesn't amount to a hill of beans.

She was so preoccupied that it took her a few minutes to notice how oddly people around her were behaving. A steady stream of pedestrians was emerging from the fog, passing by, and disappearing again. What was strange about this was that almost all of them were heading in the same direction. They were heading for the quayside.

'So should you.'

Denny stopped again, looking around. Of course, there was nobody close enough to whisper in her ear. But the insidious voice came again, more insistent this time.

'Come follow the crowd.'

Denny felt a pressure, now, an almost physical force trying to turn her towards the lochside. It grew, and at the same time, the whispering voice grew louder, and started to overwhelm her own thoughts. It began to repeat a kind of mantra, and the hypnotic rhythm of the phrase threatened to send her into a trance.

'Hurry, hurry to the water, come and greet the Great Old One!'

"No!" she shouted, and a couple of elderly passersby looked at her in alarm. Denny dropped her purchases and put her hands over her ears, but this did nothing to block out the command. It was not just powerful, but seductive. It promised wonderful things. Denny's mind began to fill with images of writhing forms. At first, these images were as insubstantial as the fog around her, but they rapidly grew clearer. They were terrifying at first, but then she felt some inner barrier, a final bastion of self-hood, collapse. And in through the gap rushed the spirit of Ouroboros.

***

"Almost ready, now," said Clay. "The field is reaching full strength."

Cleo gave no sign that she had heard. Instead, she continued to gaze out of the harbor, towards the crannog. Cherry Island was invisible thanks to the fog. But Clay, too, could feel the mesmeric pull of the Eye of Ouroboros. He had to struggle to go through the checks that would set the Talisman in motion on what would probably be the old boat's last voyage.

"Don't be so pessimistic, Jonathan," said Cleo. "I think you'll live through this. The Great Old One will spare you. After all, you made it all possible."

"By accident," Clay could not help replying.

"You uncovered the truth," said Cleo, turning from the aft rail to look down at him. "You wanted to know what came before the blight that was civilization, this shopworn machine-world, this Age of Iron. And now you know."

"I never really believed that there were gods on earth," he blurted out. "I was simply doing research, trying to make a name for myself."

"And you still struggle with the implications," she chided, reaching out to grasp his shoulders and shake him gently. "That what scientists call the laws of nature are provisional – that there are older laws. Laws that have been revived, along with the beings that employ them. Ironic, isn't it, that we exploit science only to abolish it?"

Clay said nothing, but looked at the throng on the quayside. More people were still crowding into the area. As expected, most were girls and young women, but there was also a number of young men.

"Yes," said Cleo, now reading his thoughts as easily as she could hear his words, "the world will soon be a much younger place. The old are superfluous, after all, when all wisdom can be obtained directly from the gods."

There was a sudden shock, and some people on the quayside cried out in alarm. Most, however, continued to stare past the *Talisman* into the great eye that had opened in their minds. An alarm started to sound, then another.

"The first tremor," said Clay. "Sooner than I expected."

"The Great Old One has slept for thousands of years," Cleo retorted, then stretched out her arms towards the hidden expanse of the loch. "She is refreshed, renewed, and yearning to take her pleasure with the world."

Somewhere in the fog-shrouded town, sirens began to wail.

***

James Norton awoke from a light doze, sure that something had happened, baffled as to what it was. Then he felt a slight vibration and saw the glass of water by his bedside start to move across the bureau. He reached out to stop it falling to the floor, but by then the tremor had passed.

Norton recalled everything that Brad had told him about his prophetic nightmares. He thought of the earth splitting open along lines of geological weakness, of earthquakes paralyzing global civilization.

It's started, he thought. *We didn't beat them at all. They fooled us. It seemed too easy because it was.*

Norton got up and rushed to the window. The fog was so dense that he could barely make out the crowds moving along the street, but he could see enough. The composition of the silent, expectant mass of humanity was clear.

"New disciples, my God!"

As he watched, a police car, lights flashing, swerved into the hotel's street and plowed into a group of walkers. One girl was flung into the air like a rag doll, another went under the wheels. But none of the advancing multitude stopped or even turned to look. The victim who had been hurled clear by the impact stood up with painful slowness, and started limping towards the quayside. The girl who had been run over lay still.

Norton gazed in horror as the car door opened and a uniformed officer fell out onto the sidewalk, hands pressed to the sides of his head. The academic could just make out another policeman, apparently unconscious, in the driver's seat. He studied the crowd again and now saw one or two people who were also in apparent agony. A stocky tattooed man was staggering blindly into the oblivious walkers, who ricocheted off him and kept going. An elderly woman in a shop-worker's overall was kneeling in the middle of the road. She, too, was clutching the sides of her head.

Some kind of psychic field, he thought. *It harms those it doesn't control. Am I immune?*

Norton was aware of a slight tingling sensation, a vague nausea, but nothing more.

"Evidently I am immune," he said.

Which means others must be too. Free minds, undamaged brains. I wonder if the others are affected?

Norton felt a sudden unexpected concern for Brad and Denny. He looked around the room, wondering if there was anything he might need to face the end of the world as he knew it. He saw his phone, his watch, a hip flask of Scotch. He took the flask and left.

***

"What the hell is going on?" demanded Brad. "When you said let's meet up here I didn't realize the whole town would be coming too."

The quayside was thronged with people, most of them standing quietly at the water's edge staring blankly. Katie Fox was standing on the edge of the crowd, camera in hand, though she was not filming at the moment.

"Something is happening, that's for sure," said the reporter. "Maybe we should move away before it gets too crowded."

"Where's Kelly?" he asked, following her as she wove her way past another surge of newcomers. Most of them were young women, he noticed. And they all had the same vacant expression, except for a few who seemed puzzled, as if trying to work out why they had come here.

The ideal age range for recruits, he thought. *All the lamias started off as teens and people in their twenties.*

"Where's Kelly?" he asked again. "She is coming, right?"

"Yes," replied Katie over her shoulder. "She is very keen to meet you. There, see? Over by the lifeboat station."

Brad looked over the heads of the crowd and saw his daughter leaning against the side of a boat-shed. When she caught sight of him, she stood upright and gave a wave. Her movements were languid, confident, seemingly uninfluenced by the strange atmosphere.

She knew this was coming, he thought. *It's part of the plan, like the fog. They were ahead of us every step of the way.*

He felt despair, and a sudden stab of pain struck between his eyes. Flinching, he collided with a group of girls, almost knocking one down.

"Sorry," he said. "My bad."

The girl he had collided with looked at him blankly then walked on. Again the stabbing pain came.

This must be caused by the energy field too, he thought. *It's like catnip to the right people, migraine to the wrong ones. Those who are past their sell-by date.*

"You okay, Dad?" asked Kelly, coming up to him. She looked up into his eyes.

"It gets some people like that," she went on. "It's usually because they're too old, their minds are no longer flexible enough to accept Ouroboros. And you've been against us from the start, so the Great Old One is not pleased with you. She knows her enemies, so you're getting the full treatment. But we can fix that."

She took his arm and led him over to a bench. He could barely see, now, and she had to guide him when he sat down. He was vaguely aware of Katie Fox standing by, camera still dangling from her hand.

"No way can I do that interview," he managed to say.

"That was never the idea, Dad," said Kelly. "This is about the link we have. It's time to fix it in place. Time for you to stop fighting us."

"We need people like you," put in the journalist. "You understand the old system, and how to dismantle it effectively. We'll need that expertise for a while."

"And besides, we're still family," added Kelly brightly. "How could I leave my old dad behind while we build our brave new world?"

She came closer, and hugged Brad close as she had not done since she was a little girl. Her embrace was stronger than he expected, so tight that he couldn't have broken free even if the pain in his head wasn't almost crippling. He twisted his head around to look into her eyes, but they were not the eyes he remembered at all. She dipped her head and he felt a cold, stinging pain at the base of his throat. It was over as soon as it had begun, and with it went the pain in his head.

And suddenly Kelly's mind was in his mind, along with those of Cleo, Katie, Clay, and Andreas. All the cultists were merged in the greater whole that was Ouroboros. Some individuality persisted but as a trivial thing, a minor detail of a vast oneness that had existed for so long that it had forgotten its origins. Ouroboros was literally as old as the hills, if not older, and yet perpetually striving for renewal. Brad finally understood. He was almost converted to the cult in the first wave of shared perception. For the first time he saw Kelly's belief as something exhilarating, miraculous. But he also saw something else, and it stopped him from becoming submerged in Ouroboros. He recoiled from a truth that now, as he faced it, should have been apparent from the start. It was the true nature of his daughter's soul.

Everything that had gone before, all the dream revelations had been filtered through the prism of his love for her. Now there was no filter, and he could see that she did not love him at all. Kelly's soul burned with a flame of idealism that she would happily see consume the world. No sacrifice could be too great if it ushered in the new Age of Ouroboros.

She's never loved anyone at all, he thought coolly. His emotions had almost been burned away by the power of the gestalt. *She likes me, maybe. Tolerates me, certainly. But there's no love here in this wilderness.*

Brad wandered in a timeless no-place, lost in the colorless void of his only child's bleak idealism. He could find no direction home, nowhere to go at all.

"Come on, Dad," he heard a familiar voice saying. Kelly seemed to be speaking from a vast distance, yet her words were very clear. He stood up, knowing that that was what Ouroboros wanted, and began to walk back to the quayside between the two women.

***

Lisa Valentine stood on the shore near Inverness, surrounded by panicking and confused people. There had been at least two tremors, and people were complaining that phones and computers had stopped working. There was a confusion, an edge in voices that suggested full-blown panic could break out at any moment.

"It has begun," said Lisa in Polish, turning to Pavel. "And I have to go."

She saw confusion in the big man's face as he struggled with the idea of separation. They had been together for every moment since she had enslaved him.

"Go?" he said, tentatively.

"Yes," she replied, reaching up to touch his cheek. "I am sorry," she went on. "I did many bad things. I will do a good thing now."

Lisa stood on tiptoe to kiss him, then turned away to walk down the shingle towards the fog-bound water. As she went, she started to shed her clothes, first kicking off her shoes, then stripping off her clothes with polished ease. Someone wolf-whistled, there were catcalls.

"Yeah, enjoy it while it lasts, guys," she shouted, wading into the shallows. The water was icy and she shivered. Then she leaned forward and started to swim. As she began to move through the water, her form changed. She powered forward, porpoising through the dark waves far faster than any mere human.

"Did you see that?" someone asked Pavel. "She grew a tail! What's going on?"

Pavel looked at the man talking to him.

"That was my girl," he said. "She left me. I have no one now."

The stranger looked at Pavel for a moment, then gave an uncertain laugh and walked off up the beach. There was another tremor, greeted by a chorus of screams. Pavel continued to stare after Lisa, watching her white wake vanish.

"What's happening now?" shouted someone.

Pavel frowned, half-understanding what he was seeing. The fog above the loch was starting to clear a little. Or rather, he realized, it was clumping together, losing its even blankness. A shape began to form, a vast form many miles long and hundreds of feet high.

"Snake," said Pavel in Polish, pointing down the loch. But nobody who heard him understood.

Chapter 12: Gods and Monsters

Norton had found both Denny and Brad gone. Of the hotel guests and staff, all the young had already gone, while the old were paralyzed with pain. Norton at first tried to help the afflicted, but it soon became apparent that there was nothing worthwhile he could do. So long as the field endured, it would inflict agony on those deemed worthless by Ouroboros.

The academic was in the hotel lobby when it occurred to him to turn around and set off back up the stairs. He was not in good condition and it made for a hard climb, but he would not risk the elevator. The lights were flickering and the computer screens at the reception were blank. Eventually he reached the exit to the flat room, which was luckily unfastened.

"Let's get some perspective on this," he muttered.

Looking up Loch Ness, he saw a great sea of fog. He was just above it here, and the fog had begun to retreat. Or maybe regroup. It was no longer the featureless shroud of silver-white that had enveloped the town at dawn. Now, nearly an hour later, it had begun to clump into denser clouds and thin out elsewhere. It was hard to get a clear impression of what was happening, but a coherent form was definitely starting to appear. The shape was so vast it was hard to take it all in, but it reminded him of something. A diagram, or perhaps something from a school textbook.

Of course, he thought. *Internal organs, a skeletal structure, sensory apparatus. All cohering out of air and water.*

Norton recalled one of his colleagues, a biologist, explaining in the pub that all living beings are made of a handful common elements plus traces of a dozen others. "We're all just air and water, plus energy and very detailed organization," the scientist had said. The truth of that was now being demonstrated in front of Norton as a being twenty miles long created a body for itself. He made out the shadowy forms of a vast, tapering skull, beyond it a spinal column snaking up the loch towards Inverness. Below the slowly cohering backbone were masses. One, dimly-red and vastly pulsing, must be a heart the size of a mountain.

"No," he said, unable to take it all in.

Nothing that size could live, breathe, move.

Then Norton thought of the nightmares Brad had described, of a mile-high wall of scaly flesh smashing down the puny skyscrapers of London. No natural being so immense could function, but this was the supernatural at work. Another quake shook the building and he almost tumbled into the street below. A crack appeared between his feet. From somewhere below in the fog there was a crash, a tinkle of falling glass, a scream cut short with horrible suddenness.

Nothing could stop that, once it starts to move.

Despair almost overwhelmed Norton. But he forced himself to think. Ouroboros had not become flesh yet, and judging by the slow rate at which the fog was cohering, it might take another hour at least. The sheer scale of the process was in his favor if he could just think of something.

Internal organs, energy fields, iron is the Devil's enemy.

An idea formed in his mind with lightning swiftness, a notion so crazy that it might have sprung from the pages of the ballads and sagas he knew so well.

Day of the Serpent

Heroes of legend had slain monsters in many ways. This one was probably the most extreme.

"Why not?" he asked himself. "Nothing to lose. A world to save."

He was already running back to the stairway, clinging to the slimmest of slender hopes. A line from a television show he had been urged to watch by a younger colleague kept running through his mind.

'Time for some thrilling heroics!'

***

Brad sat beside Kelly in the stern of the *Talisman*, watching as the crannog came into view. Andreas was at the wheel, with Cleo and Clay standing at the bow of the boat. Around them the vast reptilian head of Ouroboros was becoming clearer, the boat tiny as it sailed beneath shimmering fangs of mist.

"You were almost right, Dad, seeing Cherry Island as the eye of the Great Old One," said Kelly. "But you didn't really think big enough."

Brad tried to speak, but was unable to form words.

"You're keeping him on too tight a leash, honey," shouted Cleo, before jumping gracefully onto the crannog. "You've got to ease up a little."

"I'll get the hang of it eventually," Kelly called back cheerfully.

Brad felt the pressure on his mind ease a little. He was still unable to move his limbs, but when he tried to speak, he formed words.

"Not – too – late."

"Is that it?" asked Kelly, standing up and looking down at her father. "The last minute plea for the bad guys to have a change of heart?"

She bent down until her yellow slit eyes were inches from Brad's.

"We're not the bad guys. That's something you'll never get. We're saving the world. Saving if from people like you, the regular guys who let everything slide because it was good for business, let the forests and oceans start to die. Now come on."

Kelly took him by the arm and guided him along the boat rail so that they could join the others on the artificial island. Cleo, Andreas, and Clay were standing in a rough triangle round the edge of the crannog. Kelly stood Brad near the water facing inwards, then took her place a few yards away. Cleo began to chant in her deep, resonant voice.

'From out of the mist and the water, from out of the air and the earth, comes our one true mother, goddess of death and birth ...'

It went on, mystical and strange, but oddly compelling. Without being told, Brad knew that this was a modern rendition of an ancient chant. The gestalt he had been forced to join showed him the minds of the cultist, diverse within the greater whole. He sensed Clay's intellectual pride in having unearthed the ritual, Cleo's steely determination to remake the world in her image, and Andreas's hopeless devotion to the queen lamia.

And above them all, forming a mind as it formed a body, the enormous serpent was gradually awakening. Brad understood, too late for it to be any use to him, that all the previous sightings of the so-called monster had been pale foreshadowing of this moment. After Crowley unwisely called to it, the Great Old One had stirred in its centuries-long sleep. People had glimpsed its shadow, its pale reflection. But now the true beast was emerging into the world in all its prodigious power. This final ritual, the uniting of five followers, would complete the final union of deity and followers. The Great Old One would be incarnate, blending with its followers. After the vast serpent head solidified around them, worshippers and worshipped would be of one mind in a literal sense.

And I'm necessary to that, he thought. *Cleo embodies the power, Kelly the idealism, Clay the knowledge, Andreas the obedience, so my role is that of the defeated rebel. All human life is here.*

Suddenly, Cleo's chanting stopped. There was a splash like an explosion and a white shape hurled itself onto the big woman. Pale coils wrapped around golden-bronze scales. Cleo, screaming in fury, fell backwards onto the crannog's stony surface. The lamia that had tackled her was familiar to Brad.

"The Insane One!" gasped Kelly, running past the fighters towards the boat. "Keep clear, Dad, there's a machete in the cabin."

Brad found himself free to move as Kelly's concentration dissipated, but he could think of nothing to do. Clay, too, looked on as the lamias grappled and bit. Cleo, Brad realized, might be at a disadvantage because she was still in human form. She could hardly transform in battle. But Lisa Valentine was by far the smaller of the two, and the outcome seemed uncertain. Then Andreas lunged forward and tried to tear the pale attacker from his mistress, only to be hurled aside by a whiplash tail-flick.

Brad felt another tremor shake the island, sensed a disturbance in the field of energy around them. There was uncertainty and mounting anger in the Great Old One's mind.

This is screwing it up, he thought. *She might be insane, but she's got the right idea.*

Andreas, having almost been hurled into the loch by Lisa, picked himself up to rejoin the fray. Brad leaped forward and swung at the German, but Andreas was younger and faster. He punched Brad on the side of the head, stunning him temporarily, and then turned to help Cleo again. Brad jumped onto Andreas's back, bearing him down and hearing a satisfying crack as the young man's skull struck rock.

"Dad!"

Kelly's furious yell coincided with a sudden paralysis, and Brad sprawled onto his back. The mental agony he had felt when the fog closed in returned, but this time it was ten times worse. The wrath of Ouroboros focused on him, and beneath that onslaught he was a like a worm under a burning glass. Andreas got up, gave Brad a perfunctory kick in the ribs, and started to pummel Lisa with his fists. Kelly circled the embattled lamias, a hefty machete in her hand, afraid to hack at Lisa in case she harmed Cleo.

What a fucking mess, thought Brad as his vision began to darken. He was being killed by a torrent of inhuman hatred, and could do nothing about it.

***

"Denny? Denny!"

Norton grabbed the young reporter, spun her around, but she showed no sign of recognition.

"Denny, what are you doing here?"

But he already knew the answer. She was within the age range, and the right sex, to become one of the slaves of Ouroboros. When he had arrived on the quayside, Norton had tried asking for help from the assembled youngsters, but none had responded with more than a vacuous smile. Seeing Denny, he had foolishly jumped to the conclusion that she was still on his side.

Perhaps she still could be.

"Denny, Ms. Pollard, think!" he urged. "Remember who you are! You are a freelance reporter, a career woman, your own woman, beholden to no one! You are free!"

"Free?" she said, sounding puzzled, as if the word was unfamiliar.

"Yes, free!" He shook her by the shoulders. "Think, I need your help! I need a boat! Do you remember you hired a boat? From Angus?"

"Angus?" Again the child-like enunciation.

Moaning in despair, Norton let go of Denny and looked around desperately. There were several boats tied up at the quayside, but he needed one of reasonable size for what he planned. He began to push through the crowd so he could get a clearer look at what was available.

Do boats have ignition keys like cars? If so, I won't be able to steal one. If only there was a sane person I could talk to.

"What in the name of God is happening?"

The speaker was a huge old Scotsman in fisherman's garb. He was clambering onto the quayside from a battered boat.

That fishing boat's far too small, thought Norton, *but he must be immune or he couldn't be complaining like that.*

"Hey there, I need help!" he shouted, then gestured at the vessels moored nearby. "Do you know how to drive one of those big boats?"

Five minutes later, Angus was on board with Norton's plan, figuratively speaking. It had not been difficult to persuade the Scotsman that desperate measures were needed. Not with the malign mass of Ouroboros growing more substantial by the minute.

"But I'm buggered if I'm going to stay to the bitter end," Angus rumbled, as he helped the Englishman onto a large trawler. "I'll take my chances in the loch."

"What will you do, then?" asked Norton, stumbling over nets and bright-painted marker buoys.

"Life jacket," replied Angus simply. "I'll jump overboard before you start your kamikaze run."

"I think we might find a more optimistic term for my plan," began Norton, but Angus had already opened the cabin door and was gesturing to the boat's bow.

"Untie the bloody thing, man, or we'll never get anywhere."

The trawler was tied to a bollard on the quayside, and Norton had to stretch to untie the line.

"Let me help, James."

Denny appeared, hunkered down, and began to unwind the heavy mooring rope.

"You're all right?" asked Norton, startled by the new turn of events.

"Yeah, it took a minute, but what you said sunk in," she said, throwing the line onto the boat. Then she jumped down with surprising agility, before Norton could even think of helping her aboard.

"What can I do?" she asked.

"Perhaps help me steer for the last mile or so," said Norton, and explained his plan as Angus started the boat's diesels and reversed her slowly out of the harbor. Once on the loch, they swung wide around Cherry Island, steering as close to the shore as possible to avoid going inside the serpentine cloud.

"You really think you can do it?" asked Denny when Norton had finished.

"I've no idea," he admitted. "But it makes sense. The whole cult of Ouroboros thrived when there was no technology more advanced than fire, woodworking, and flint tools. Such beings must have some vulnerabilities, after all. They're not really gods."

Denny said nothing, but continued to stare into the vast spectral form.

"What's happening on the crannog? I can't see from that foul murk," asked Norton.

"Conflict," said Denny. "The rite has been interrupted."

"That's a stroke of luck!" exclaimed the professor. Then he noticed that Denny's expression, which had been lively, was reverting to unnatural vacancy.

"Come inside the cabin with me," he said, taking her arm. "We might even be insulated from the thing in there."

"Who's this wee baggage?" grunted Angus.

"A friend," said Norton shortly, closing the door behind him. "Can't this thing go any faster?"

***

There is no death.

The words rang in Brad's mind, tolling like a great bell. He believed them. It was a self-evident fact that nobody could die in Ouroboros. And that, he understood, was the key to the old religion that had dominated the earth for uncounted millenniums.

Was this where people got their belief in an afterlife, in immortality?

"Of course."

The pain and darkness vanished, and Brad was in a forest glade, lit by beams of vertical sunlight. A woman sat on the moss-covered trunk of a fallen tree. She was naked, beautiful, with a heart-shaped face, a wide, humorous mouth. She looked something like Kelly, with a little of Cleo, and a hint of something else. He sensed that this being was ancient, yet permanently young, capable of renewing herself in perpetuity.

"There can be no death where nothing is lost," she said. "Imagine that, if you can. A world where the memories of your ancestors, back to the dawn of time, are preserved. And you can speak to them, know them as you might know you neighbors."

"And you provide that link?" he asked.

The woman smiled, and stood up.

"In all my facets, all my forms, I did. And will again. If you help me."

Brad gestured at their surroundings, taking in the wild flowers underfoot and the blue sky above the dense foliage.

"This is an illusion. What you want is death and destruction. You are Ouroboros, with what looks like a fake ID. Is the burlesque thing supposed to win me over?"

The woman shook her head.

"I am your conception of what I might be, if I were bound by time and matter, as your kind is. You think of me as a nature goddess, so I am."

She bent down and picked up a small branch that bore a few bright leaves.

"On this little world," she said, turning the branch before her eyes, "empires might rise and fall. Ants and spiders and beetles, and creatures even small, all locked in their struggle for survival."

"People are not bugs!" Brad pointed out.

"But they are mayflies to me," she said. "So ephemeral, so fragile, so easily hurt. Which is why, when I found this world, I chose to help a stumbling, frightened being that was little more than a glorified ape. And I did, for so many years."

"So what went wrong?" he asked. "That's the sixty-four thousand dollar question."

Ouroboros frowned, dropping the branch. She looked past Brad, her eyes focused on a time unimaginably remote.

"There are greater seasons, cosmic cycles, that means my power ebbs and flows. I was weakened for a time, and distracted from human affairs. I admit, I took your kind for granted. And I paid a heavy price."

She reached out a slim tanned hand and he flinched, then made himself be still. Smiling, she touched his forehead, and he saw a vision.

Tribes migrating across great plains against a backdrop of snow-capped mountains.

A priestess decked out in feathers and bright body paint denouncing a young man who stood proud, aloof, defiant. Around the antagonists, tribesmen and women stood, uncertain what to do. Some began to gather behind the young man, who raised a knife of gleaming bronze.

Worshipers of Ouroboros danced within a stone circle by night, their orgiastic worship illuminated by bonfires. Suddenly, out of the darkness, armed men appeared wielding gleaming swords and steel-tipped spears. The disciples fled only to be cut down by cavalry sweeping around their flank.

The pace of events accelerated. Great cities arose, blackening the skies with smoke. Forests were felled or burned, rivers poisoned, great fleets set forth to conquer the oceans. The world grew senile, sick with the blight of civilization. Nature withered. Far beneath the surface of the world, a thwarted deity writhed, its powers depleted, almost forgotten. But then Ouroboros was rediscovered. Brad saw Jonathan Clay exploring a prehistoric site in Ireland, discovering a dormant Old One. Brad witnessed the transformation of Clay's student, Olivia, into the first of the new breed of lamia.

Brad was back in the dream-glade, and Ouroboros was smiling again.

"It cannot endure, this machine-world you have made. If it must end, why not today?"

"No!" he said. *"What you offer is sterile perfection, an unchanging world. All those thousands of years worshipping you, achieving nothing, going nowhere."*

"People were happy," she insisted, her expression hardening.

"People were zombies, slaves, just pets!" he shouted. *"And when you got bored with your pets, they escaped. It happens."*

"Remember all those little bugs, Brad," she said, all her former sweetness gone. *"I don't require their worship because I cannot help them. They do not fear death as your kind does."*

The sunlight faded, shadows spread. At the same time, Ouroboros grew until she towered over Brad. Looking down at him, she raised a vast leg and made to step on him as he ran for the edge of the clearing.

***

"Stop it! Stop it!" shouted Kelly as she circled the combatants, trying to focus on the battle between Lisa and Cleo. Kelly's mind was awash with confused, violent images as the joint entity that was Ouroboros reacted to the combined attack upon it. Several times, she tried to slash at the Insane One with her machete, only to be confused by a surge of emotion from the great being that enveloped them.

Everything's falling into chaos, she thought in despair. *They're ruining it all!*

Andreas was trying to grabble with Lisa, now, only to be brutally knocked aside by Cleo. In a fit of rage, the larger of the lamias had become obsessed with killing Lisa herself and would brook no interference. Lisa, for her part, seemed to be enjoying the fight, even though her snake-body was oozing blood from bites, and one arm hung limp. Despite her efforts to block Lisa out, Kelly was almost overwhelmed by the creature's wild enthusiasm.

"You should be on our side!" she screamed, taking another swing at Lisa. The machete connected with the stone surface of the crannog and sent a jarring shock up Kelly's arm. She retreated, looking over to where her father lay writhing at the edge of the round platform. For a moment, she considered using the machete on him, removing one more complication from an over-complex problem.

I should kill him, for the greater good.

"Here," said Andreas, "give it to me. I will kill the mad beast!"

Kelly let the German take the weapon as her mental turmoil grew greater. She sat down heavily, clutching her head, as the battle between Ouroboros and her puny mortal enemies grew more intense.

***

Brad looked up. He had instinctively curled into a fetal ball when Ouroboros made to tread on him, but the crushing impact had not come.

Where did she go?

He realized he was looking up into the sky when his antagonist was down near ground level again. The giantess had shrunk to almost human size. Ouroboros was frowning, her eyes no longer focused on Brad. She gave a jerk of the head, like a nervous tic, and ran a slender hand through her hair.

"Got problems?" he asked, standing up. "Are things not going according to plan?"

Brad had no idea why he had been spared, but clearly, something was wrong. It made sense to distract this facet of the monster as much as possible. He started to run toward Ouroboros, arms outstretched, ready to make a flying tackle.

"You try my patience!" she said, but her voice did not have the same confidence as before. "I will deal with you later!"

The sunlit glade, the trees, the blue summer sky all began to fade.

She's switching off her virtual paradise, he thought. *But what if I keep her in it?*

He hurled himself at Ouroboros, felt what seemed like the very real flesh and bone of a human body as they collided. She even gave a realistic cry of dismay, which confirmed Brad's suspicion. If they were entangled in this fantasy world, it would keep her from business elsewhere.

"Let me go!" she yelled, all composure gone. She was still taller and stronger than Brad, and she began to pummel his back with her fists. The blows were brutal, and all he could do was try to hang on, wincing from the pain.

Her world, her rules, he thought. *But if time is the critical factor, I must keep her occupied.*

"True," she said, suddenly growing still beneath him. "I have much to do. And one of your friends is proving a little troublesome. But it is no great matter."

Brad opened his eyes, himself looking into the face of Ouroboros just a few inches away from his own. She smiled, and her hands began to caress him.

"I can be a benevolent deity, Brad," she whispered. "Just give me a chance to show you."

"Somebody really has got you worried," he replied. "Must be Denny, right?"

Ouroboros smiled, tightening her embrace.

"She is young, passionate, full of noble ideals," said the goddess. "A natural follower. No, let us rest here a while and I will deal with a few minor problems."

And if I can't move I can't bother her, he thought.

Brad tried to wriggle free but realized that she was too strong for him.

"Hush, stay quiet while I deal with this," she said, patting him like a mother trying to calm a fractious toddler.

Well, this little boy's gonna have one hell of a tantrum.

Brad began to grope in the foliage around them, wondering just how realistic this fantasy was. He touched something hard, rough – a tree branch. Acting swiftly so that she could not read his intentions before the deed was done, he aimed a clumsy blow at his captor's head. The beautiful face contorted with rage, her grip relaxed momentarily, and Brad broke free. Ouroboros snarled, and began to transform, eyes turning golden-green, naked legs fusing into a scaly tail.

"Oh, shit," he said, hefting his improvised weapon and slowly retreating. The lamia sprang toward him, jaws agape. He swung the branch again, but she easily deflected it with one hand, then bore him to the ground.

"This," she said as her muscular coils entrapped him, "is a privilege. You will be the first heretic to be sacrificed to me."

Ouroboros began to grow again, and as she did so, she lost all human characteristics. Brad struggled vainly as the vast maw of the serpent opened and began to engulf his head. Visions of the world transformed again, flooded his mind. He saw cities devastated by earthquakes, tsunamis, and volcanic eruptions. He saw the vast body Ouroboros was creating for itself in the loch.

Then he saw something else, a tiny shape like an arrowhead of silver and blue. It was moving with painful slowness, heading into the flank of the miles-long monster.

"They've still got a chance!" he exclaimed. "They're coming for you!"

Brad felt himself being swallowed by the ancient serpent. Determined not to go gently, he began to kick and punch the quivering innards of the beast.

***

"There it is!" said Angus.

It was a superfluous remark. They had hugged the coast for a third of the way up the loch, and now they were opposite Invercraig. Between them and the village, the fog had almost cleared, to be replaced by a huge, complex structure. The first hints of gleaming scales could be seen as Ouroboros continued to cohere. But the inner workings of the gargantuan body were still visible. Most conspicuous was the heart, a slowly pulsating mass like an iceberg, half submerged.

"This can't work," said Denny. "You should turn back, you'll only get us killed."

"What?" demanded Norton. "No, we've come this far."

Denny turned away from the view of the monstrous heart and grasped Norton by the arms. Her strength startled him.

"No, James," she said, "Brad will pull it off at the last moment, like he always does. Turn back, Angus."

"Denny, let go–" Norton began, but then he saw the first gleam of golden-yellow in her eyes.

"Angus! Help me, she's still one of them," he shouted, struggling impotently to free himself. His arms were pinned to his sides so he tried to kick Denny in the knees, but he might as well have been kicking the boat's steel hull. The young woman threw Norton backwards against the back wall of the small cabin, then turned to the Scotsman. Angus let go of the wheel and swung a clumsy punch at Denny, who dodged most of the force but was still knocked sideways. She kicked out at Angus's groin and he doubled up. Then with his head down, he charged at her so that the two of them smashed through the door out and over the rail of the trawler.

Norton stared after them, hearing the splash but taking several long seconds to grasp what had just happened. Then he saw that the boat was in a hard turn and grabbed the wheel to steer back towards the heart of the beast.

"Not quite a silver bullet," he said wryly as the crimson mountain grew nearer. "But it will have to do."

The timing had been good. The tissue was just dense enough to tear apart as the bows of the boat ripped into the heart. There was a silent blast of energy as the trawler was flung up and backwards, and Norton felt himself suspended weightless for a moment in the tiny cabin. The line from Kipling's poem ran through his head.

Iron, cold iron, is master of them all.

A scream rang out, not just in the air around Norton, but also in the depths of his mind. It was a cry of rage, pain, and despair from a being that had lived so long that it had forgotten that it could perish.

Even gods can know hubris, thought Norton. *Pride cometh before a fall.*

There was a moment of terrible pain, then merciful nothingness.

***

Brad woke to find himself lying on the edge of the crannog, one arm trailing in the loch's cold water. His head was throbbing, but only with the pain of a regular headache. He sat up and saw Andreas hacking with the machete at a pale shape that was now criss-crossed with gaping red welts. Brad staggered upright and ran over, shoving the young man clumsily aside. The machete clattered across the stone platform then plopped over the side. The effort needed to make his attack exhausted Brad and he fell down on all fours. But Andreas, too, was in no state to fight on.

Cleo was dead. She, too, had reverted to humanity, and her body was a pathetic sight, broken and twisted. Kelly was sitting by her former leader, rocking back and forth. Jonathan Clay lay on the other side of Cleo, gasping painfully. Brad crawled over to him. The man's chest had been crushed by a blow requiring more than human strength.

"I tried to stop them, in the end," said Clay. "I was wrong. Too much has changed in the world. The time of the old gods is long past. We need to be free, to grow–"

He coughed up a gout of blood, speckling Brad's face. Clay's eyes rolled up and he slumped back.

"He's no longer in pain," whispered Lisa. "I think we might have been friends. He reminds me of Marcus."

They were her last words.

"Kelly?" said Brad, moving painfully over to his daughter.

She looked at him with her old eyes, the eyes of childhood, wonderfully brown and full of reproach.

"Oh, Daddy," she said. "You and your dumb friends. You ruined everything."

A trickle of drool ran down her chin.

Epilogue: The Heart of the World

"They haven't found James's body," said Denny. "Just the remains of the boat. The fuel tank exploded, they said. But according to my sources that doesn't explain the way the hull was melted. It's as if about a million volts had gone through it."

"Do you remember anything about it?" asked Brad gently.

Denny shook her head.

"I just remember almost drowning, and that Angus fellow holding my head above water. He tried to explain to me what had happened. I didn't believe him at first."

"I'm not surprised," said Brad. "It sounds crazy. But everything about this was crazy from the start."

They walked in silence for a few minutes, crossing the park that lay opposite the North London Psychiatric Hospital. They had two patients to visit now, though one, Marcus Valentine, was showing signs of improvement since the so-called 'Loch Ness Incident.' Kelly, by contrast, had been almost totally unresponsive since a police boat had taken her and Brad off Cherry Island.

"Why do you think James did it?" asked Denny finally. "I mean, he wasn't exactly a man of action, was he?"

"You don't have to be macho to do the right thing," Brad pointed out. "And in James's case, it was really his brain that mattered. He grasped a pattern that we missed."

"And he saw a powerful weapon in a rusty old fishing boat," added Denny. "That was his magic sword, his Excalibur."

"In the end, the expert on legendary heroes turned out to be one," said Brad. "Kind of makes sense. I misjudged the guy, that's for sure. I screw up, he saves the day. And nobody would believe it if you told them."

"He might not have planned on a suicide attack," said Denny gently, putting a hand on his arm. "Perhaps that was my fault."

"None of it was your fault," retorted Brad. "I know what it feels like to be a slave, too. James saved the world and nobody will ever know, right? Instead they're just making all sorts of shit up, I suppose."

"Take your pick of crazy theories," said Denny, with a wry smile. "Officially, people went a bit crazy during an unprecedented earthquake, and all the clips of weird stuff online are fake. Unofficially, it's even more ridiculous. One conspiracy theory blames the Russians."

"Well, that's half right," he pointed out.

"Another claims it was a CIA mind-control experiment," Denny want on. "And then there's the ever-popular 'I'm not saying it's aliens–"

"But it's aliens," completed Brad. They both managed to smile at that.

"Scientists have talked about a quantum singularity at the earth's core," Denny added. "That super-dense object that breaks known physical laws."

"Again, half right."

"Are they going to deport her over her visa?" asked Denny.

"No," said Brad. "They told me they'll hold off on that as air travel would be difficult. Kind of civilized of them. Besides, these bureaucrats have got a lot on their plates now."

"What was it like for you?" Denny blurted out. "I can only vaguely remember. Like a dream."

"Same here," he lied. "Best forget it. Sooner the better."

He could not tell her the truth because he hoped it would soon stop being true. Since his encounter with the woman in the clearing, he had had flashes of perception, sudden visions that he hoped were merely symptoms of mental disorder. He saw a world beyond and beneath this world.

The Great Old One, for all its titanic size, was a mere reflection of Ouroboros. The one true, original being had become dormant again, and slept fitfully. It had sustained a temporary setback, no great defeat for an immortal. Vast beyond comprehension and a thousand miles deep, Brad saw Ouroboros lying coiled around the heart of the world.

That was not all. For a split second, just after he looked into Kelly's eyes, he had shared her mind again, for the last time.

Did I imagine it?

Brad could not be sure. Perhaps he would never know. But he wanted desperately to believe it. Just when he had almost lost hope, had he seen a tiny flicker of love for him, like a faint star just visible on a winter's night. He clung to the conviction that it had been real, that remote glow so briefly glimpsed.

It would have to be enough.

***

"I still don't think we should have come back here," said Paul quietly.

"The therapist said it would be cathartic for them," retorted Julie. "Besides, it's been a whole year. And look at them, they're having a whale of a time."

Paul could not disagree. Cressida was splashing about in the shallows and Will was searching the beach for fossils, his latest obsession. Other families were scattered about, and the sails of small boats dotted the loch. The B&B in Invercraig was pleasant and the locals were keen to revitalize the tourist trade.

So why do I feel this is a big mistake?

Suddenly there was a piercing, childish shriek, and Cressida came splashing ashore.

"Daddy, daddy!" she shouted.

Paul felt his heart leap to his mouth as he and Julie ran down the beach. The little girl was emerging from the water, obviously upset, but at least she did not appear to be in danger. Paul scooped Cressida up in his arms.

"What's wrong, sweetheart?" he asked. She did not seem to be quivering with fear, which was something. He and Julie had had to cope with many nightmares that had left his children screaming in terror, rigid with fright.

"It bit me!" said Cressida, holding up her left arm. "I just wanted to play with it and it bit me."

"Let me see," said Julie, examining her daughter's left arm. "Well, that doesn't look too bad, but we'd better put something on it."

"Let's go to the car," said Paul, putting Cressida down, "and we'll dab some disinfectant on it, all right?"

"What was it anyway?" asked Julie as they led their daughter up the beach.

"Great white shark? Rogue lobster?"

"I thought she was an eel at first," replied Cressida. "Because she was all brown and wriggly. Then it looked up at me and I saw it was a little mermaid. But she wasn't as nice as the one I saw last time. Maybe they're not so nice when they're little."

Paul stopped, letting go off Cressida's hand to look back, out over the dark waters of Loch Ness.

"Means nothing," said Julie under her breath. "There are all sorts of things out there She might just have grazed her arm on a rock or something."

"Yeah," said Paul, glancing back at the dark waters of Loch Ness. "Let's get you some First Aid, princess."

As he dabbed at his daughter's arm, Paul looked closely at the two small pinpricks in the girl's tanned flesh.

"Julie," he said, "go and make sure Will keeps well clear of the water, will you?"

Without a word, Julie did as she was asked.

* * *

Blood Carousel

Written by A. I. Nasser

Prologue

There was very little in this world that could wake up Steve Rum. As a child, his mother was quick to embarrass him in front of their guests, telling and retelling stories of how she would practically have to set a marching band loose in his room just to stir him from his slumber. As he grew older, the habit never really changed much; he lost count of how many classes he had missed during his college days and how many dates he had screwed over just because he couldn't wake up on time.

When he married, his mother had told Alison that she was in for a lifetime of hellish mornings; his new bride had politely smiled and shrugged it off. It would be a constant topic of argument during the next fifteen years of their marriage, especially when he was jumping from one job to another because he couldn't make it to work on time. Even when he was late for his court meeting, blowing away any chance he had to win custody over the twins, Alison had just smirked and shook her head in frustration. To the judge, he was the man who couldn't care enough to wake up early for the sake of his children.

That's why the night shift in Gambler's Park was a blessing. He had answered an advertisement in the classifieds, looking for a graveyard shift groundskeeper who could keep the horny teenagers and the druggies out of the park at night. They had hired him on the spot, and Steve couldn't have asked for a better opportunity.

Usually, the park was empty, and it was rare that he would bump into any trouble on his regular rounds. He had a lot more time on his hands now, enough to read and brush up on his French, and definitely didn't have to worry about sleeping in. There was no denying just how much of a night person he was, and strolling through the empty park after midnight, feeling the cool air against his skin, was enough to lighten his mood every time.

Of course, there were many other perks, too. The bi-annual concerts that were held in the field behind the duck pond were always something to look forward to. The crashing of the music and the crowd of drunken freshmen was something he would probably never get used to, but he reveled in the energy of those nights. The lights, the laughter, the simple joy of being *alive*. It made him feel less lonely, like he was part of a secret group of people who truly understood the value of the night.

And, of course, there was always the carnival.

Steve sat on one of the many park benches dotted across the open field and watched the carnival staff set up.

What did they call themselves? Carnies?

He smiled as he took a long sip from his coffee cup and let his eyes wander over the bright lights and the flashing colors.

"They're here for a week," his supervisor had told him earlier, "and they're donating a hell of a lot of money from their proceeds. Make 'em happy, Rum."

Steve intended to do just that. Not because of the donations, or the threat of being fired, but because he always enjoyed the traveling carnivals he had experienced as a child. He could still remember the first time his parents had taken him to one, back when he was only six. The food stands, the games, the

573

rides. And of course, the attractions. There were always attractions.

Not to mention the crowds of guests that strolled back and forth between the stands, laughing and joking, voices rising up into the night and filling the air with merriment. There was a peculiar charm to it, a welcoming that made him feel like this was exactly where he belonged.

Steve wondered if the carnivals of today had lost that charm.

Another sip from his coffee, and he was on his feet, stretching. A light drizzle had started, and he pondered walking over to where the carnival was setting up and offering his help.

"Quite a sight, isn't it?"

Steve jumped, his heart slamming into his throat, his hand instinctively reaching for the mace he kept in his pocket. A man sat on the bench he had just occupied, tall and slim in a dark suit, legs crossed and hands folded on top of one knee. His top hat hung low, covering his eyes, and a narrow nose peeked out from under the brim. A cane leaned lazily against his thigh, and Steve could barely make out the man's strange smile that seemed to extend from one ear to the other.

"It will be even more majestic once it's operational," the man continued, looking up at Steve. The red, green, and yellow lights from the fields beyond reflected in the man's dark eyes, and Steve felt a slight chill race down his spine.

"You shouldn't be out here," Steve managed to stutter, keeping his grip tight on the bottle of mace in his pocket while trying his best not to seem too threatening. For all he knew, the man was just another friend of the night who had come to watch the carnival being set up. Harmless.

Of course, there was still the matter of how he had suddenly appeared out of nowhere, but Steve felt that he could let that slide for now.

"My apologies, friend," the man's smile widened even further. "I must have startled you."

The man stood up, his tall frame easily towering over Steve, and despite the slim figure, he seemed to block out all lights around him in a shroud of eternal darkness. Steve watched the man grab his cane and swing it between his fingers effortlessly.

"My name is Ebenezer Cage," the man introduced himself, "and I run the establishment you were just admiring."

Of course.

Steve relaxed a bit, his hand sliding out of his pocket as he ran it across his forehead and wiped the few drops of sweat that had gathered beneath his brow. "Sorry, Mr. Cage, I didn't mean to offend," Steve stammered.

With his free hand, Ebenezer waved the apology away. "No need, friend," he said with a soft chuckle, a raspy sound that seemed a lot more guttural than anything. "It's always nice to meet a fan of the carnival."

Steve ventured a slight smile, still uneasy as he tried to appear less uncomfortable. "It seems like it's going to be fun."

Ebenezer raised a slender finger and shook it slowly, his cane never stopping its spin. "Ah, that is where you are mistaken," he said. "It is an attraction like no other. I assure you, many have come to be deeply enamored with our little band of nomads, and it is often that I have had to close my doors to those wishing to join the life of the carnival."

Ebenezer stopped spinning the cane and brought it down in front of him, leaning his weight against it as his eyes bore into Steve's.

"However, I have quite the talent for spotting those who desire more than they can hope to find, and the carnival always delivers."

Steve returned the man's smile and looked around him uneasily. The sounds of the night he had grown accustomed to were now gone. There was no chirping, no croaking, and no ruffling of leaves in the gentle breeze. It was almost as if the world had come to a complete stop except for them.

"Tell me, friend," Ebenezer's voice deepened as his eyes flickered different shades of red. "What is it that you desire the most?"

Steve frowned, unable to answer the question while at the same time a bit taken back by it. He was suddenly transported to the carnivals of his childhood, sitting beside his mother in a small tent where an old woman waved her hands across a crystal globe and promised the ability to foresee the future. Steve felt a sudden familiarity here, except the old woman was replaced by a tall man that looked as though he had just stepped out of Victorian England.

"I'm not quite sure," Steve replied. "I never really thought of it before."

Ebenezer's shoulders bobbed as he chuckled and shook his head. "That can't be right," he said. "There is always *something*."

Steve shrugged. "I guess, the night."

Ebenezer's head cocked to one side as he frowned at Steve, the smile on his face unfaltering. "The night?"

"Yeah," Steve shrugged again. "I've always loved the night. Never really liked the daytime. You know, the constant noise, the crowds, all that stuff. Always felt comfortable at night."

Ebenezer stared at Steve for a long moment before breaking into a fit of laughter.

"Is something wrong?" Steve asked.

"No, no, of course not, friend," Ebenezer replied. "If eternal night is what you desire, then I am sure the carnival can make that happen for you."

"How?"

Ebenezer stood upright, folding out into his complete height and holding the cane in both hands. "The carnival always finds a way."

Steve was about to reply when a hand burst out of the ground below his feet and latched onto him. He felt a sudden burning sensation race up his leg and spread through him, coursing through his veins until it enveloped him in scorching pain. The hand around his ankle tightened as Steve opened his mouth to scream, but no sound came out.

Ebenezer's hand was clasped tightly against his mouth, and Steve's eyes widened in horror as the man's eyes burst into a bright glowing red. A deep stench of rot erupted from Ebenezer's mouth, filling Steve with an odor of death and decay. The world around them blurred, and suddenly nothing was visible except for a heavy sheet of darkness that quickly enveloped them within it.

"All you desire," Ebenezer's voice echoed inside his mind, scratching like sandpaper against the inside of his skull. "All for a price."

Steve felt the darkness close in and push against him, pulsating as if it were alive. It washed over his body in waves, wrapping him in its shroud, suffocating him within its vacuum. The hand around his ankle tightened then pulled, and as Steve began to fall into an abyss of nothingness, all that was left were the twin flames of Ebenezer's eyes and the echoes of raspy, manic laughter.

Chapter 1

Jack Heldon *knew* books.

Ever since he was a toddler, his parents had told him stories about how he had sat completely still in his father's study, staring up at the multitude of shelves filled with books. At one point, his father had found it a little disturbing, and just to make sure that his son wasn't autistic, took a book down from the top shelf and handed it to Jack.

From that day on, Jack's world consisted of nothing else outside the pages of a book. Sure, he would go to school, and there was no tearing him away from his friends and their adventures. But, when a book was handy, when the pages were open and the words jumped up from the sheets of paper to dance, sing, and laugh along with him, Jack Heldon was a completely different person. His father joked about it to his friends, smoking his pipe and waving at his son as if he were a specimen to be studied and admired.

And it wasn't too far from the truth. By the time Jack was five, he was reading the small collection of Hardy Boys mysteries his father had stored on the lower shelves where Jack could reach them at will. At eight, he had graduated to abridged versions of classics while testing his skills with larger volumes of Clancy and Archer. By his tenth birthday, he was reciting Shakespeare. All to the merriment of his father and the mild worry of his mother, who believed Jack's nose was stuck in a book longer than was healthy for a child his age.

Jack never blamed her for that observation, though. He knew that it was hard for anyone to truly understand how he felt when he was immersed in a book. The adventures, the love, the merriment, the fictional world of another person's mind ultimately much more comfortable than the real one. No one understood that, not really, and Jack never minded. He was too busy flying with Peter and Wendy, falling down the rabbit hole with Lily, and bouncing up and down with Mr. Toad.

Majoring in English Literature had been a must, an expected outcome everyone foresaw. He had been labeled 'most likely to die with a book in his hand' during high school, and it only made sense that he would make those words true. By then, his father had died of cancer and his mother had no one else, and Lensfield College was known for its Humanities Department. He never had to be more than a five-minute walk away from home.

And through it all, Jack had his books.

That was why he didn't hear the chimes above the Lensfield Books door as it swung open and allowed a much-needed breeze of fresh air to rush through the store. Jack was half-buried in a box of new deliveries, eyes wide and hands shaking in excitement as he emptied his treasure trove and marveled at the books, one by one. He loved the smell of a new book, the feel of its cover before the spine broke, and the way the pages fluttered before some idiot dog-eared them. It was like this every Friday, and Jack never failed to feel like a father welcoming his newborn to the world.

They're your lifeline, his girlfriend, Faith, always said with a shake of her head and a half-smile. *If the house were burning down, you'd save your books before me.*

Jack always told her that she was being ridiculous, but deep down, he had a feeling she was right.

"Jack?"

It took Jack a second to register that someone else was in the store besides him. Lensfield was a small town, and the regulars were few. Jack knew them all, their schedules, and their visits to the store almost like clockwork. Mrs. Stevens on Saturday, early, ready to go through the batch of new arrivals before anyone else got the chance to. Mr. Gold on Monday, who always seemed to find the books no one else took notice of, the ones that kind of fell through the cracks and apparently waited for no one but him. And of course Jennifer Timm, college journalist with an eye for the non-fiction, every Wednesday evening just before he closed, her parcel of ordered books packed and ready for her by the door.

The other visitors were usually college students, and those never came in on Fridays. By then, most were already on their way back home.

"Jack Heldon."

Jack looked up at the tall man standing just inside the door to the bookstore, glasses riding high on a long, almost beak-like nose, the hair on his head greased and combed to one side. Jack took in the expensive suit, the shiny shoes, and the leather briefcase quickly before looking back at the face of a man he hadn't seen in five years.

"Danny Bufano," Jack smiled.

Danny's smile widened. "I'm home!"

***

The guttural, thunderous sound of the Harley broke through the calm, afternoon air with a loud retort. It roared down the interstate like royalty, king of the road as its heartbeat-rumble reached out across the fields. Michael Cooper was astride it, leading his girl off the interstate and onto Route 35, straight towards Lensfield.

Michael loved his hog. The rumble, the smell of the gasoline fumes, the heat from the engine mixed with the breeze all around him. He could ride his girl all the way across the country and never think twice about stopping. In the past few years, it was all that had kept him sane as he waited to return to Lensfield.

Ahead of him, he caught sight of the top of the gas station just outside the town limits, the structure growing more and more as he neared it. Michael closed his eyes for a second against the flashes of childhood memories that burst through his head as he took in the first landmark of the place he had once called home. He sniffed, shook his head, and slowed his hog down, angling slightly to the right and onto a wide dirt road that cut across the green fields.

To his left, Michael could see the roofs of the first line of Lensfield houses, his eyes darting back and forth between them as he tried to single out his own home. His bike threw a cloud of dust behind him as he roared north, closer to Lensfield Brook. In the distance, the old Barton farm stood out like a sore thumb, the charred remains of what had once been the biggest pig farm on this side of the state. Michael felt a tingle race through him, the memory of the fire still fresh in his mind even after all this time.

Ten years, he thought to himself. *Ten years and the place still gives me the creeps.*

The dirt road led straight to the farm, the main house built at an angle that allowed it to face the town and the open green acreage where Lensfield College now stood. Michael contemplated stopping at the Barton's and venturing a quick look inside, just for old time's sake, but quickly decided against it. There was nothing there that he was nostalgic for anyway.

Michael turned his hog off the dirt road and onto the fields, racing through the tall grass and maneuvering his ride with expertise to the top of the small hill just beyond the farm. He wondered if anyone was watching the hill and fields, keeping an eye on the abandoned relics of the once rich and proud Barton family. He doubted it, though. He doubted anyone wanted to remember what had happened ten years ago.

At the top of the hill, Michael turned off the engine, already missing the soothing sounds of its rumbling, kicked down the kickstand and reluctantly got off his bike. He stood tall, his leather jacket keeping the strong winds at bay, his long hair flying about his head as he looked out upon Lensfield.

His eyes made their way past the college and to the fields north of it, just past the brook, across Gambler's Bridge. He smiled to himself as he remembered the old tales his grandmother used to tell him, the warnings of what happened to children who crossed the bridge and strayed onto the fields beyond. 'It was unholy land', she had said. Land that was better left alone.

Land that the town council had turned into a park. Gambler's Park.

And the carnival was in town.

Michael's smile faded quickly. He gazed out at the tents and the booths set up, the rides being tested, the dots of carnies walking back and forth as they went about their business. From here he could see the vastness of it, and a shiver burst through him as he noticed how much larger it had grown since the last time it had come to Lensfield.

Wonder what'll burn this time, Michael thought as he gazed out onto Gambler's Park. He pulled out a pack of Lucky's from his breast pocket, flipped open his Zippo and lit himself a cigarette. He looked back at the Barton farm, let his eyes wash over the entirety of it, and gave it a mock salute.

Michael Cooper was home.

***

"It tastes like garbage, but it does the trick."

Jack Heldon placed the cup of coffee in front of his old friend with a smile before balancing his own mug and settling into the opposite couch. The two men sat in the small back office; a crammed space that was of barely any use except for the times when Jack needed a little shut eye in the middle of the day. If not for that, he would have probably turned it into more shelf space.

"Anything other than the sludge I've been drinking on my way here," Danny chuckled, nestling his mug between his hands as he took a tentative sip. "You're right, it's awful."

Jack laughed. "Danny Bufano," he mused. "Man, how long has it been?"

"Almost ten years," Danny replied, taking another sip from his mug and trying not to wince. "Give or take."

"That long?" Jack asked. "Wow, it's like I was just saying goodbye to you yesterday."

Jack remembered the day Danny had jumped into his father's station wagon right behind the moving truck, how the entire gang had been there to see their friend off. It had been an emotional time, and Jack wondered how he could have forgotten how far back it was. Then again, everyone was leaving Lensfield back then. The band had played its last tour together and the members were going their separate ways.

Danny laughed. "Come on, it took you a while to recognize me," he said.

"Well, you look a hell of a lot different," Jack replied, gesturing to where Danny's belly had been. He remembered the other kids at school teasing Danny, calling him things like 'medicine ball' and 'Mr. Potato head'. Jack shook his head at the memory of the timid boy who had always hid behind his friends and just did whatever everyone else was doing. He wondered if that little boy were still inside the more confident version of a man sitting opposite him now.

"I'd like to say it's a combination of watching my daily intake and exercise," Danny laughed, patting his stomach. "Truth is, had the old grinder stapled."

Jack raised his coffee in a toast. "Well, here's to modern medicine," he said.

"Indeed," Danny raised his own and chuckled.

"So what brings you back to Lensfield?" Jack asked, placing his cup back down without drinking, amused that Danny was still trying to be polite while sipping his own.

"The carnival," Danny gulped, adjusting his glasses and pushing them up the bridge of his nose.

Jack's hand stopped mid-air for a brief moment before he replaced his cup on the table. "The carnival?" he asked.

Danny nodded and smiled. "I'm writing a piece about traveling carnivals and the people that make it what it is," he said, his eyes wide in excitement. "Ebenezer's Carnival is one of the more famous ones. You remember it, right?"

Jack sat back and gazed at his friend. "Sure, I do," he said. "It's setting up out at Gambler's Park right now."

"Yes, it is," Danny nodded. "Ten years on the dot. Never early, never late."

"Excuse me?"

"Oh surely you must have known about that little tidbit," Danny went on. "Ebenezer never stays for more than a week in any one place, then moves onto the next stop, only to return ten years later. It's like a ritual."

"A ritual?"

Danny nodded excitedly. "Really good stuff, buddy," he said. "I've been following it since Maine, but never really took the time to actually visit it. Always too far from New York for my liking. But when I realized it was coming back to Lensfield, I knew I couldn't let the chance pass me by."

"You're back for the carnival?" Jack raised an eyebrow.

Danny froze for a beat before venturing a weak smile. "Life, buddy," he said, his tone giving away that he was not at all convinced with what he was about to say. "I would have stayed in touch, really, but things got a bit complicated after, well, you know."

"Life got complicated for all of us, Danny," Jack said, the smile on his face now more of a mask to cover the little bit of anger he was beginning to feel. "You're not the only one who left, you know? And the rest of us who stayed had to pick up the pieces left behind."

Danny sighed, adjusted his glasses again, this time with a finger that shook slightly, and looked at his friend solemnly. "We were too young to understand what happened."

"We were fifteen," Jack replied.

"What do you want me to say?" Danny asked.

Jack sighed and shook his head, waving his hand in dismissal. "Don't worry about it," he smiled. "My fault. High expectations and all."

"My whole family picked up and left, Jack," Danny continued. "You know I had nothing left to come back to."

"You had us," Jack said.

Danny was about to say something when he thought better of it and reached for his mug.

"It's crap," Jack said, suddenly frustrated. "Stop pretending to like it."

Danny winced at his friend's outburst, and Jack raised a hand in apology, mentally slapping himself for losing his cool. He hadn't seen Danny Bufano for almost a decade, and here he was getting angry over something as silly as losing touch. He had to remind himself that phone calls went both ways, after all, and he hadn't really been much of a friend, either. It was hard growing up in Lensfield after the Barton incident, and it was even harder to think that the world outside was moving on while the people in town were still hanging onto the tragedy of '96.

And it's all because of that damned carnival.

It was absurd, of course, to blame the carnival for what had happened. The logical explanation, the one the entire nation had come to accept as true, was that old Ted Barton had lost a few screws up in that head of his and had killed those children in cold blood. There was nothing supernatural going on, despite what he and his friends had tried to tell the police. Still, Jack had nightmares of the fire, of the man in the flames with the red eyes and the fanged smile. Nightmares that woke him up in the middle of the night screaming, his sheets covered in sweat, his heart hammering away in his chest like a locomotive.

"I'm sorry," Jack said. "It's just, you brought up the carnival, and I kinda lost it a bit."

Danny opened his mouth to reply, then closed it again. Jack could see the doubt in the other man's eyes, the pity that radiated from him in waves, as if Danny were trying to tell him that whatever he thought had happened ten years ago, it was all just the imaginative minds of kids. Only, Jack really hoped Danny wouldn't say that, because he didn't know how he'd respond to it. Of all people, Danny should have known better. Danny had been there. He had seen what all of them had.

"It's just an article," Danny said. "I'm not trying to stir up memories."

"The carnival is stirring them up all on its own," Jack chuckled. He looked at his friend for a minute before saying, "I did miss you, Bufano. I really did."

Danny smiled and relaxed. "Me too," he said. "Any word from the rest of the Bionic Six?"

Jack laughed at the mention of their old code name for the gang. "The last I've heard of Michael was a few months after he left. Since then, nothing."

"I actually bumped into Philip Tucker a few months ago," Danny said. "Recently graduated, looks like hell."

"Little Tuck?" Jack laughed, his eyes wide in surprise. "Are you kidding me?"

"Nah, I'm serious," Danny smiled. "I swear to you, he was on something. Had the jitters, always looking over his shoulder all paranoid-like. It would have been sad if I hadn't been so happy to see him. Went on and on about his roommate and this town called Melington, apparently near here?"

"Yeah," Jack nodded. "About an hour from here."

Danny dismissed it with a wave. "Never mind, it was nothing. And the girls?"

"Amanda's still Amanda," Jack smiled. "Runs Huck's coffee shop like a pro."

Danny nodded, hesitant for a moment before asking, "And Faith?"

Jack paused. He remembered Danny's childhood infatuation with Faith Stone, always willing to go the extra mile for her, always eager to impress. From the way Danny asked about her, Jack didn't think the infatuation had completely worn off, even after all this time.

"Head Librarian," Jack finally said, opting to not tell his friend that he and Faith were living together now. "Doing well for herself."

The smile on Danny's face made Jack feel even worse about not telling him. "That's great! I'll have to stop by and see her."

"If you'd like, we usually hang out at the bar by Huck's," Jack said. "We're going there tonight, actually. Where are you staying?"

"At the motel," Danny replied. "The Possum? I'm not sure, some animal or another."

"The Badger," Jack laughed. "I can pick you up later. I'm sure everyone'll be thrilled to see you."

Danny clapped his hands together and stood up. "Sounds like a plan," he said with a smile. "Anyway, I better get back to the article. Carnival's opening tomorrow, and I actually want to make the most out of it."

Jack nodded and walked his friend out of the office and to the front of the store. "Listen, tonight, try not to bring up the carnival, okay?" Jack said, opening the door. "It's still a pretty sore subject for Faith."

Danny raised his hands and nodded. "No worries," he said. "Consider my lips sealed. However, I'm not going there alone, so you better be ready to join me when the doors open and the music begins."

Jack smiled and shook his head. "I wouldn't be caught dead over there."

***

Jacqueline Stevens almost had a heart attack when she turned around and saw the tall man in the top hat smiling down at her. She had been closing up shop, locking the front door, whistling a tune to herself, and hadn't noticed the stranger creeping up behind her. She was taken aback by how tall he stood, almost as if hanging over her, the top hat adding to his figure and the cane in his hand glinting in the sunlight.

"I apologize wholeheartedly, madam," the man smiled, his eyes never leaving hers. "I didn't mean to startle you."

Jacqueline let out a long sigh and smiled uncomfortably. Her eyes quickly scanned the street for any other pedestrian, but she was alone with the stranger, and that in itself struck her as odd. Main Street was usually a lot busier this time of the day.

"I was just marveling at the gamut of breathtaking dolls lining the shelves of your store," the man said, his eyes shifting to the large window display by the door.

Jacqueline looked back at her store. She was flattered that someone took notice of her dolls, their different sizes and colors lining the store shelves snuggly, her life's work on display for those who appreciated it. It was frustrating that business was slow, that people refused to see the value of what she had to offer, but deep down inside she was a little relieved. Over the years, the dolls had become more like her children, and on the occasional days when she actually made a sale, it was like selling her own flesh and blood. It didn't help when the brat buying the doll didn't understand what they were holding.

Jacqueline turned back and jumped again, the stranger much closer now and bending down so that their eyes were level. "Your children must have a wonderful childhood," the man said. Even though he stood a few feet away, his voice seemed to be coming from deep inside her head, as if he were whispering directly in her ear.

"I don't have children," Jacqueline replied with a forced smile. *Why did I just tell him that?*

The man stood tall and frowned, what seemed like genuine concern on his face. "No children?" he repeated. "What cruel irony. A woman such as yourself, with an impeccable talent that can make millions of children happy, has none of her own?"

"I really doubt I make millions of children happy," Jacqueline said. "I don't sell a lot of them."

Again, too much information. You don't know this man!

Yet, opening up to him did not seem or *feel* wrong.

The man shook his head and reached out a hand, long, slender fingers looking more like bones than flesh. "My name is Ebenezer Cage," he said, and she took his hand hesitantly. "I run the carnival out in the fields yonder."

"At Gamble's Park?" Jacqueline asked. She had only lived in Lensfield for a few years now, but she knew about the carnival.

"Precisely," the man smiled. "It would bring me great joy to see you there when we open our doors tomorrow, and maybe we can help you find what your heart desires."

Jacqueline smiled incredulously, trying her best to be polite. "Are we selling wishes, Mr. Cage?"

Ebenezer Cage chuckled, a deep, raspy sound more like a cough than laughter. "My dear, the carnival always finds a way."

And with that he tipped his hat to her, smiled, and walked away.

Chapter 2

Faith Stone loved closing time.

The Lensfield Public Library was a magnificent structure, a feat of architectural genius that very few people appreciated and even less truly understood. Nestled within three acres of land, surrounded by the large branches of red maples, its brick walls camouflaged it within the background during the fall season. The library spanned almost half an acre, and rose three stories high. On the eastern and western sides, large windows rose to allow light in from all sides throughout the day, and the large chandeliers hanging down from the ceiling gave the establishment a Hogwarts quality that was beautifully mesmerizing.

Students from Lensfield College usually filled the large areas lined with study tables and desktop computers. The library allowed for both physical as well as digital research. Despite its size and the fact that it was usually full to the brink during the daytime hours, there was a constant tranquility that was rarely broken except for the occasional cough or whispered conversation that only added to the charm.

Faith loved the library. It was her second home, and when Jack was acting like a complete idiot, sometimes her first. She spent hours going through the rows of books, cataloguing and monitoring, making sure that her kingdom was always in top-notch condition. Rarely did she ever have to clean up after the students that frequented the building, most with enough common sense to return the books to their proper place. All in all, Faith couldn't have asked for a better job.

But closing time, now that was something else.

When the evening settled in, the sun low enough for the skies to turn into a kaleidoscope of red and orange, the light coming in through the windows cast a brilliant glow across the entirety of the library. Often, Faith would find herself sitting at the large front desk, chin in her hands, gazing lovingly as the colors reflected off the wooden shelves and table tops, creating a secret calm that she would have liked to imagine was hers alone.

She remembered the last time Jack had picked her up a little earlier than usual. She remembered his wide eyes and the stark look of amazement on his face when he witnessed what she had hoped would remain hidden from the rest of the world. His expression was enough to confirm that if anyone else knew about closing time, if the students found out how the light seemed to dance across the books and walls, it would quickly turn into an attraction. Faith wasn't willing to share it with the rest of the world just yet. For now, it was her little piece of magic, and hers alone.

And this evening was no different.

Faith sat comfortably in her chair, watching as the red and orange rays of the sun pierced through the windows and made the wooden surfaces around her glow. The colors mixed together in bubbles of light that shifted, turned, and swirled. She watched it with her usual awe, her mouth slightly open, her breath caught in her chest as she marveled at the sight before her. She stayed in that position for almost an hour, when the daylight disappeared completely and the chandeliers had to be turned on lest she be immersed in complete darkness.

Faith sighed as the chandeliers burst into life, filling the library with enough artificial light to make it seem like it were still afternoon. She grabbed her pad from the top drawer and flipped the pages to the correct date, the checklist she had created staring back at her in anticipation. This was one of the reasons why she had been promoted to Head Librarian quickly. No one could argue how meticulous she was.

Faith began her rounds on the third floor. She quickly checked that the windows were latched shut, the discarded books had been returned to their appropriate places, all the computers had been shut down, and no one was still lingering behind after hours in the bathrooms. Once the tasks were all ticked on her pad, she switched off the fluorescents and made her way down to the second floor to do it all over again.

Her mind drifted as she worked, the motions more second nature than actual chores. Often, she had pondered allowing the senior assigned to as her assistant to complete these tasks for her, but Faith knew that in the end, she would probably go over it all herself, just to be sure. Besides, she wasn't willing to share closing time with anyone yet.

On the ground floor, Faith went back to the main desk and sat down heavily, running a hand through her hair as she took off her glasses and pinched the bridge of her nose. The ground floor was a lot larger than the floors above, and it housed the audio-visual center as well as the three large project halls. It was never easy going through it all at once.

Faith looked at her watch, realized that she had almost an hour left before Jack picked her up, and pushed herself to her feet. She ruffled her hair and scratched the back of her head, the fatigue of the day slowly beginning to set in. Luckily, she had the weekend to look forward to, and she completely intended to capitalize on every hour of sleep offered. Jack would probably wake her up early before he went to the bookstore, and she slowly began to come up with a multitude of excuses to give him when he tried to drag her out of bed.

A loud bang brought an involuntary scream from her mouth, and her heart jumped into her throat. Above her, a large flash of light illuminated the dark skies, and the clapping of thunder boomed again. As if the heavens had been given the proper introduction, they opened in a rush of rain that fell in bullet-like torrents against the large windows. The tapping intensified, and as if on cue, thunder boomed again, quickly followed by bright white lights.

Faith waited for her heartbeat to slow before shaking her head at her complete lack of self-control. One day she was going to give herself a heart attack. Worried Jack might be caught in the storm, she pulled her cellphone out of her pocket and dialed his number, balancing the phone between her ear and shoulder as she checked her pad for the project hall checklist.

"Let me guess," Jack answered after the second ring. "The storm caught you by surprise."

"I'm never going to get used to how it just starts like that," Faith replied, making her way through the shelves of books towards the back of the library.

"Well, if it's any consolation, I'm dead center in it," Jack said.

"That doesn't make me feel any better," Faith replied. "How long before you get here?"

"I'm going to make a small detour at the Badger, then I'll come pick you up."

Faith frowned. "The Badger?"

"You will never believe who walked into my store today," Jack laughed. "Danny Bufano."

Faith stopped mid-stride, lowered her pad, and held her phone in her hand. "No."

"Yes," Jack assured. "I'm picking him up right now."

"Danny Bufano?" Faith asked with a smile. "Are you sure?"

Jack laughed again, and the sound of thunder almost drowned it out. "I was just as surprised as you are," he said, his voice breaking up. "He walked...store...nothing like you'd imagine..."

Faith frowned and walked towards one of the large windows. "Jack, you're breaking up."

"Is...better?"

"Jack?"

"The storm...coverage...minutes..."

The line died, and Faith cursed as she tried to redial his number. When she got a busy signal, she stuck her phone back in her pocket and walked towards the project halls.

That was when the chandelier lights went out.

***

Danny Bufano flinched at the first sound of thunder.

He sat on the motel bed, cross-legged and dressed only in his jeans. He briefly looked at his watch, made sure he still had some time before Jack picked him up, and went back to the open files strewn across his bed. He frowned in concentration as he read through one of the several newer reports that had been faxed to him by his office in New York.

Danny scratched at the scars on his abdomen from the laparoscopic procedure that had stapled his stomach. He hadn't felt an itch there since the procedure, but over time, it had become a habitual scratching that accompanied deep thinking. And right now, Danny was engrossed in what he was reading.

His research had taken him almost three years to compile, ever since he had received the package that had started it all; anonymously sent to his New York office and placed dead center on his desk for him to find. The mailroom hadn't had a clue as to where the package had come from, but once opened, Danny's world had been turned upside down.

Thunder crackled outside again, and Danny felt the window of his motel room shake with the force of the storm. He wondered if Jack would be coming anyway, the torrents outside enough to make any sane man think twice about leaving the shelter of the indoors. Danny rubbed the nape of his neck and continued reading.

When he had gone to his editor with his theory on Ebenezer's Carnival, he had come dangerously close to losing his job. It had been a heated discussion, with his editor ordering him to stop wasting time with theories and actually do some proper investigative work. It hadn't mattered what Danny said; there was no concrete proof that any of the deaths and missing person's reports that followed the traveling carnival across the nation had anything to do with the establishment itself. The world was striking it off as coincidence, but Danny knew better.

Knowing that the paper wouldn't support his quest for the truth, Danny had begun calling on favors to get what he wanted, and always made sure his editor remained in the dark. What he got was enough to warrant a return to Lensfield and a deeper investigation into the carnival itself.

Danny hated lying to Jack, but truth be told, he knew how his friend would react if faced with the evidence he had been collecting over the years. Danny remembered the fire well. He could never forget the crazed look on Ted Barton's face before the house was engulfed in flames.

And the eyes. Those red, blazing eyes.

They had all lost a chunk of their innocence that night, each and every one of the 'Bionic Six'. Danny would never admit it, though, would never give it the power to shock him back into the vegetative state he had been in when the flames had begun to lick at him and burn his skin. He remembered Faith's screams, and the paralyzing fear that had stopped him from helping her when she needed it the most. If not for Jack and Michael, there would have been two more charred bodies to find in the wreckage of the Barton farm.

Danny's fist clenched as he read the report in his hands, the page crumbling in his grip before he quickly calmed himself down and let it drop back onto the file in his lap. Ten years. The carnival had traveled around the country for ten years, and in every town where it had stopped, disaster struck. Now it was back in Lensfield, starting the cycle again, and Danny was determined to put an end to its reign of terror once and for all.

A loud knock sounded at his door. Danny quickly gathered his research, tucked the files into his briefcase, and opened to let Jack in.

***

It took Faith a few minutes to collect herself. Although it was not uncommon for the lights to go out during a storm, this one just happened to coincide with a burst of thunder that sounded dangerously close. The immediate flash of lightning through the windows sent long shadows across the walls and between the rows of bookshelves, a stark difference to the charm of the setting sun.

She reached for her phone again and switched on the flashlight, casting the narrow beam right and left as she stared out into the vast darkness. She waited for the emergency lights to come on, their sickly red light always giving her headaches when she looked at them for too long.

Nothing happened, though, and Faith found herself contemplating between checking the project halls anyway, or just calling it a day and dealing with whatever mess was inside later. She bit her lip, knowing that her OCD would definitely get the best of her. Faith knew she would ultimately end up waking early tomorrow morning just to have Jack drive her back so she could finish her rounds.

Thunder sounded above her head, and she instantly gave up on the idea of feeling about through the dark. Besides, it wasn't like Jack was actually going to let her sleep in anyway. Faith turned on her heels, kept the flashlight aimed in front of her and made her way back to the main desk. To her right, the large glass windows rattled against their frames, the strong winds from outside pushing against them and trying to force its way inside. Faith shone her light to make sure the latches held, and her light fell on a lone chair pushed against the far wall.

Faith froze when she saw eyes staring back at her

Sitting on the chair was a little girl, her hair long and flowing over her shoulders to her seat. She couldn't have been older than five or six, her legs hanging above the ground as she swung them back and forth playfully. The light from Faith's phone barely illuminated her, the girl's face hidden by shadows and strands of loose hair.

Faith felt like a cold finger had touched her nape and was gently sliding down her back, sending shivers of fear radiating throughout her entire body.

"Hello?"

The girl giggled in glee and rocked her legs harder, gently pouncing on her seat and waving to Faith. "Hi!" came the short reply, a soft hiss of a whisper that seemed to have been spoken directly into Faith's ear.

Faith felt like she recognized the voice, the chirpiness in it, but the raspy undertone was enough to force her a few steps back. The light fell on and off the little girl, Faith's hands shaking uncontrollably as she tried to make sense of what she was seeing.

She had made sure no one was still in the library, and even though she had yet to check the bathrooms and projects halls on the ground floor, she was sure no sane person could have forgotten a little girl behind. And of course, there was the girl's inexplicable happiness; the simultaneous darkness and booming storm should have had the opposite effect on a child her age.

"Mom said I could stay with you tonight," the girl said, that underlying raspy touch to her voice like knives against the inside of Faith's head. Still, she could have sworn she knew the girl from somewhere, although she couldn't quite put a finger on it.

"What's wrong, Faithy? Aren't you happy to see me?"

Faith almost dropped the phone in her hand. All of a sudden, everything rushed to her in a horrific wave of understanding. Of course she knew the girl. How could she not?

"Lily?"

The little girl giggled and rocked harder in her chair. "Let's play hide-and-go-seek!" she blurted out suddenly. "You hide and I have to find you."

Faith took another step back, her hand still shaking as she desperately kept the light shining on the girl. She felt that imaginary cold finger on her back transform into a hand that reached inside her, grabbed her by the spine, and squeezed. Her mind shifted into overdrive, and she could feel her knees giving out. But she kept the light on the girl. She didn't dare do otherwise.

"Don't you want to play, Faithy?"

Thunder bellowed from the outside, the winds picking up enough so that the windows were fully shaking against its force, and when lightning flashed and illuminated the library, Faith saw the girl pull something out from between the folds of her dress. The knife glinted in the light of the storm, then disappeared once the flashes were gone.

"The tall man told me that you wanted to play, Faithy," the girl said, her voice deepening a bit, yet the chirpiness was still there. "He said that if I win, you get to come with me to the carousel. You're going to love it, Faithy. It's so big!"

"Lily," Faith whispered, and the girl broke into menacing laughter that echoed throughout the library.

The phone's narrow beam of light fell squarely on the girl's face, and in the darkness, the red glow of her eyes made the blood in faith's veins freeze. Lily's lips curled into a horrible smile, and she slowly slid off the chair and held the knife up for Faith to see.

"Hide, Faithy," Lily growled. "Hide wherever you want. And when I find you, you'll come with me to the carousel."

Faith dropped the phone and screamed, turning and racing away from Lily, deeper into the darkness. Behind her, the giggling rose to a deafening boom of laughter, followed by a scurry of little bare feet against the hardwood floors. Faith had no idea where she was going, and felt a sharp pain in her thigh when she hit the main desk and fell with a crash to the floor.

"I found you, Faithy!" Lily giggled, too close for comfort, as if she were standing directly above her. Faith tried to push herself to her feet again, but hands grabbed her by the shoulders.

Faith screamed, and the lights of the chandeliers burst into life with such suddenness, it was blinding. She punched out, fighting to break free of her captor's hold, screaming at the top of her lungs.

"Faith!" Jack yelled above the screaming, shaking her forcefully.

Faith stopped fighting and opened her eyes. Jack's hands were firm on her shoulders, his eyes filled with concern, and Faith quickly turned around to the library behind her.

Lily was gone.

Chapter 3

Amanda Brians recognized Michael Cooper the minute she set foot in the bar.

The day had taken its toll on her, the end of the week always a busy time at Huck's coffee shop. Between the multitude of students pouring in from the college campus and the rush of employees from the surrounding businesses, Amanda hadn't been able to take a single breather. What she wanted more than anything right now was a couple of drinks and a few minutes of chain-smoking bliss.

That was why the weekly meets at the adjacent bar were a ritual she rarely passed on. Even when she was sick, bedridden with a fever, she always found a way to drag herself out of her apartment and make the short trek to the bar for drinks. To her, it was almost blasphemous to suggest doing anything else on a Friday night, and she made sure Jack and Faith knew that.

Sometimes, Amanda could sense their unwillingness to keep up with the ritual. Often, she would notice the dark rings under Jack's eyes and the stifled yawns from Faith. Moving in together had made them soft, and she knew that if it were up to them, they'd be huddled up on the couch in their living room watching Seinfeld reruns and drinking hot cocoa.

Amanda would not have it, though. Even on nights like tonight, with the rain coming down in blinding torrents and the winds threatening to throw her off her feet, she made sure to send them both a warning message. Not showing up tonight would come with severe consequences, and she wanted to believe that after all their years together, they took her threats seriously. Besides, there was no logical reason why they couldn't relinquish a few hours of playing house and spend Friday night entertaining her. Little made her happy these days anyway.

Seeing Michael Cooper, though, changed all of that.

Usually, Amanda never gave bikers a second glance. She never found herself attracted to the leather, tattoos and the misogynistic attitude, and in a small town like Lensfield, they usually spelled trouble. Still, her eyes had quickly caught the long hair falling over the leather jacket, and even with the beard and dangling cigarette, Michael Cooper's eyes immediately gave him away.

The guitar-playing teenager from her childhood sat alone at the bar, his eyes fixated on the pool table and his hand wrapped around a beer mug as he puffed circles of smoke from his mouth. She felt a small smile form on her lips, and when he looked her way, his eyes locked on hers, her smile widened in response to the look of recognition on his face.

She made a beeline towards him, her steps quick, and he barely had enough time to climb down from his stool when she threw her arms around his neck and hugged him tight. Michael wrapped his arms around her waist, lifted her off her feet, and laughed.

"Brians!" he hollered, briefly grabbing the attention of the small crowd around them as he squeezed her to him.

When he set her down, Amanda immediately punched his chest with her fist and kicked at his shin playfully. "You bastard!" she laughed.

"Hey!" Michael feigned hurt. "What the hell was that for?"

"Ten friggin' years, Cooper, that's what!" Amanda yelled over the music that suddenly burst out from the jukebox. "What the hell, Michael?"

Michael laughed and leaned back against the bar. "Would you believe me if I told you I tried to reach you before coming back?"

"No," Amanda squinted at him.

"I tried your house phone, honest," Michael chuckled as he raised his hand to ward off another attack.

"It's 2006, Cooper," Amanda said. "We have cellphones now."

"Right, right," Michael nodded. "And I bet you have one of those Blackberry's, right? Instant messaging and all that."

Amanda shook her head in amazement. "You're still an asshole," she remarked.

"Always," Michael raised his beer in salute. "What are you drinking?"

"Right now, anything would be good," Amanda said, pushing herself onto the adjacent stool and folding the straps of her purse onto each other as she placed it on the bar. "I'm waiting on Jack and Faith, but in this storm, they could be a while."

"No way!" Michael raised his eyebrows as he took a deep drag from his cigarette. "I was actually hoping to pass by Jack's place tonight, but the storm kinda stranded me here."

"Well, it's a good thing you didn't go," Amanda said. "The old place was sold years ago. He and Faith are renting an apartment in the new buildings up by the hospital."

Michael broke into a laughing fit, coughing on his smoke and taking a sip from his beer. "Those two together? Really?"

"Who would've thought, huh?"

Michael shook his head with a smile. "And how have you been doing, Brians? I see Huck bought the run-down coffee shop next door."

"That run-down coffee shop keeps him busy," Amanda smiled. "Well, at least every now and then when my brother actually comes in and checks on the place."

"Has you running it?"

"The more reliable of the Brians siblings," Amanda rolled her hand and bowed.

Michael laughed and took another swig from his beer.

Amanda watched him for a second, taking him in. Nobody would have believed that the bulky man in the biker jacket and rings was the same class clown from ten years ago. Amanda remembered the scrawny teenager with the Slipknot t-shirts and the faded jeans, black hair always cut awkwardly because his mother refused to let anyone besides her cut it for him. She remembered how hyperactive he had been, always quick with a joke, the boy who never wanted to go home. He had been the one to call their group the Bionic Six, in honor of his favorite cartoon.

And of course she remembered how in love she had been with him. She had only been thirteen, had no idea what love was or what it was she was feeling, but Michael Cooper had always occupied her thoughts and mind. She had picked up the guitar because he liked to play. She had learned about cars because he would not shut up about them. At one point, she had even tried convincing her mother to dye her hair black to match his.

Now, sitting next to him at the bar, ten years after losing touch with him completely, she felt all those emotions rush back. Michael looked at her, frowned, and smiled.

"What's wrong, Brians?" he chuckled.

"Nothing," Amanda smiled and shook her head quickly, hoping her face didn't give her away. "It's just really good to see you, Cooper."

Michael winked at her and gestured for the bartender, and as he turned back to her, his eyes shifted to the door and did a double-take. "Well, I'll be damned."

Amanda turned around to where he was looking. Jack and Faith had walked into the bar, and beside them stood Danny Bufano.

***

Samuel J. Gold sat in his favorite chair in the study on the second floor of his house, gazing out the window at the falling rain. In his hands, he nestled a freshly poured cup of tea, full to the brim, strands of steam rising up from its surface like fingers. The warmth spread through the glass and into his hands, soothing them and calming the pain in his joints. A slight shaking threatened to spill some of the tea into his lap, the cup gently rattling against the saucer it sat on, but Samuel didn't notice. Over the years, he had grown comfortably accustomed to his ailments, and he rarely registered what had once frustrated him and made him hate old age.

It had been easier with Nancy. She had always made things better.

Samuel closed his eyes and sighed, slowly raising the cup to his lips and sipping slowly. The sting of the tea on his tongue refreshed him, and the drowsiness he had been feeling earlier slowly began to slip away. He gazed back out the window, looking through the storm at the bright lights coming from Gambler's Park. The carnival was in town, and Samuel thought it was just right that the heavens would be crying tonight.

"Wash away that garbage, I say," Samuel mumbled to himself as he took another sip of tea.

He had been one of the first firefighters at the Barton farm ten years ago, and the sight of the house and barn burning still haunted him. It was as if the flames had had a life of their own, and no matter how much he and his crew had tried to stop it, it raged on through the night, fueled by an unearthly force. The children had been saved, the four idiots who had somehow found themselves inside when Ted Barton decided to light the fuse and set his home on fire. The same couldn't be said for Ted.

"Good riddance," Samuel sneered, talking to no one in particular. "Should have burned sooner."

His doorbell rang, and Samuel frowned in confusion, unable to comprehend why anyone would visit him at this hour, in this weather. He continued to stare out the window and grunted, comfortable in letting whoever was at his door suffer in the storm, and ultimately leave him alone. When the doorbell rang a second and third time, Samuel angrily placed the cup and saucer on the small desk to his right and heaved himself out of his chair.

"Shut up, ya damn fool!" Samuel yelled as he trudged down the stairs and the doorbell rang again. He deliberately took his time, slowly walking down the small hallway until he was able to look out the side window and see who was bothering him.

The tall man standing on his porch smiled at him and tipped his hat.

"Whaddaya want?" Samuel yelled through the glass, making it clear that he wasn't about to open the door for the man and ease his suffering. Only, the visitor didn't seem at all fazed by the storm, and even though the rain hammered at him, he maintained his smile and comfortable posture.

"I beg your pardon, kind sir," the man said, his voice half-muffled by the glass. "On such a night, I find it quite rude of me to disturb what I could only assume was a comfortable seat by the fireplace and a hot cup of tea. However, I find myself in the most unfortunate position of having to disrupt your peace of mind and ask for your assistance."

Samuel frowned in irritation and squinted at the tall man. "Mister, I have no idea what you're blabbering about, so take your funny looking hat and get off my property."

The tall man's smile widened. "My name is Ebenezer Cage, owner of the delightful establishment at Gambler's Park, which I am sure you can see from your second floor window. The storm has, unfortunately, stranded me during my return and I would be in your debt forever if you would be so kind as to allow me the use of your phone."

Samuel felt a pang of anger at the mention of the carnival, and his frown quickly turned into a deep scowl. "Listen, top hat, I don't care if you have to walk all the way back to that freak show of yours. Personally, I hope the storm gives you pneumonia and you die slowly and painfully. No carnival freak is coming into this house! Now git!"

Samuel turned away from the window and cursed under his breath, slowly walking away from the door and back to the staircase. He realized that his fists were balled and shaking by his sides, and he quickly began rubbing them together to ease the tension there.

"I apologize for the disturbance, Mr. Gold," Ebenezer's voice came through the door, inexplicably louder, as if he were standing inside the house. "Give my love to Nancy."

Samuel froze at the mention of his dead wife's name, and the blood in his veins immediately began to boil. He turned back and raced towards the door, his muscles, and joints screaming in protest, and grabbed the baseball bat from on top of the umbrella rack. He threw the door open and stepped outside, raising the bat above his head with both hands and ready to go to town on the tall man.

No one was there. Samuel gazed out into the storm, the rain slapping against his face and the wind finding its way into his clothes and chilling him. He waited for a few more seconds, breathing heavily, his knuckles white as he gripped the bat angrily, his face flushed in fury. When he was certain the man was gone, he lowered his weapon, spat into the falling storm, and walked back into the house.

***

"So what happened back there?"

The bar had quickly filled up in the past hour, more and more people escaping the storm and opting for the company of friends rather than the solitude of home.

The cigarette smoke formed a thick fog in the air, and every now and then a window would be cracked open enough to let some air in without the accompanying rain.

Jack sat beside Faith in a corner booth as they both cradled their drinks and watched the others by the pool table. The reunion was bittersweet, and Jack found it difficult to be overly thrilled at the return of both Danny and Michael to Lensfield. The fact that they had come home at the same time as the carnival made the feeling of impending doom even stronger. Still, he couldn't deny that it felt good to be around old friends again, even if they had become completely new and almost unrecognizable versions of their previous selves.

"What do you mean?" Faith asked, smiling at Amanda's attempt to play a game she knew very little about. When Jack touched her, she flinched.

"That," he said. "The library. The screaming. What happened?"

Faith met his gaze for a beat before turning away and sipping from her beer. "Nothing," she said. "The jitters, that's all. The whole storm and blackout combined."

"You ran into me," Jack pushed.

"I didn't see you."

"The emergency lights were on."

"No, they weren't."

"Faith."

"Stop it," Faith snapped, looking at him angrily. Jack raised his eyebrows in surprise, and Faith quickly turned away and took another sip from her beer. "Sorry."

Jack decided to let it go. If there was one thing his relationship with Faith had taught him, it was that she didn't like being pushed. In their five years together, nothing good ever came from his incessant questioning, and it had taken a few nasty fights for him to finally come to terms with the fact that sometimes she just needed to be left alone when she wasn't feeling well. However, it never failed to bother him, and he always felt incredibly helpless in these situations, a feeling he detested.

"So the Bionic Six are back together," Jack said, changing subject.

Faith smiled. "I can't believe you still remember that," she said.

"Danny reminded me."

"Well, Philip isn't here," Faith pointed out. "So, it's really the Bionic Five right now."

"I don't think there ever was a Bionic Five."

"Shut up, Jack," Faith laughed. She leaned in against him and allowed his arm to wrap around her shoulder.

In the back of her mind, she could still hear Lily's manic laughter, could still see her disturbing smile and bright red eyes, the way the light reflected across the knife in the little girl's hands. It sent a shiver down her spine, and everywhere she looked, she imagined Lily standing in the shadows, staring at her, watching her, waiting for her. Hide-and-go-seek; Faith had hated that game.

Faith shook the feeling away and relaxed in Jack's arms. It felt good being here, surrounded by friends and strangers alike. She couldn't imagine going home right now, sitting alone in the bedroom while Jack went about his nightly routine of washing the dishes and making sure the door and windows were locked. She feared that even those few minutes alone might be enough for Lily to come for her, that she would be completely vulnerable even inside her own home.

For the first time in a while, Faith was actually happy to be at the bar, despite her exhaustion. Over the past few months, she had toyed with the idea of convincing Amanda to change their Friday ritual, feeling that they had grown a bit too old for the bar, but now she was glad she had never gone through with that. The loud music, the noise of the crowd, they all helped ease away the dread she was feeling.

Besides, it had been almost a decade since she had seen either Michael or Danny, and catching up was already proving interesting. And of course, not having to worry about Amanda feeling like a third wheel was a welcomed reprieve. Faith glanced over at the pool table where the trio was making a raucous over whose turn it was, and immediately saw the look on Amanda's face every time she glanced over at Michael when he wasn't looking.

"Amanda's still not over her crush," Faith mumbled.

"What?" Jack asked, looking down at her.

Faith gestured to the trio. "She's still infatuated with Michael, even with the long hair and leather jacket."

Jack laughed. "Some things never change, I guess."

Faith nodded, silent for a second, before saying, "Do you think they remember?"

Jack didn't reply right away. "Danny definitely does."

"How so?"

"It's why he came back," Jack said. "He's doing a piece on the carnival."

Faith frowned. "Why would he want to do that?"

She felt him shrug. "I have no idea," Jack said. "Then again, I'm assuming Michael's back for the same reason."

"I didn't get a chance to ask him about his brother," Faith sipped from her bottle.

"I wouldn't," Jack replied. "No reason to. Some things are too painful to bring up."

Faith didn't reply, only watched her friends go about their game in merriment. The crowd had slowly become thicker, and a few people were crowding around the pool table and impeding the fun. Faith was finding it harder to breathe, the cigarette smoke hanging in the air like a deathly blanket, the oxygen in the bar diminishing. Someone was eventually going to have to crack open another window.

"I miss Lily," Faith said suddenly, and despite the night she was having, she felt tears well up in her eyes.

Jack was taken aback by the sudden mention of Faith's dead sister, and instead of probing, pulled her closer to him and kissed the top of her head. Faith took another drag from her beer, closed her eyes, and let the exhaustion slip her away.

***

"So journalism, huh?" Michael Cooper looked across the pool table as Danny bent down and took aim, steadying his hand in front of the white ball and picking out his next target.

"Ink and paper," Danny said, letting the white ball fly. It shot across the table, hit a solid ball, and ricocheted into a second. Both found their respective pockets, much to Michael's dismay. "Or in this time and age, the world wide web."

"Never trusted the internet," Michael leaned against his stick as Danny moved around the table and took position for his next shot. "A lot of garbage flying around there."

"You fail to see the value of the digital world," Danny smiled. "Besides, in a few more years, print will probably be dead. It only makes sense to start thinking of alternative options."

"Yeah, right," Amanda scoffed. "Maybe we'll be getting our news off of that Facebook thing that's been going around instead of the newspapers."

Danny let the white ball fly and dropped another solid into a pocket. He stood up and adjusted his glasses before chalking his cue. "It seems the trend's going in that direction."

"Couple of years, and you're going to have people playing pool on their computers instead of the regular way," Michael winked at Amanda.

"Why the carnival?' Amanda asked, lighting a cigarette and taking a sip of her beer.

Danny stood up and leaned on his cue stick, gazing at the remaining solid balls strewn across the table. "Infatuation, I guess," he said dismissively. Amanda and Michael shared a quick look and waited for him to continue. "There's this kind of mystery surrounding carnivals. They're like a family, a closed circle that rarely lets anyone in."

"Apparently not rare enough," Michael said, and Danny winced. He had forgotten about Michael's brother.

"So it's the enigma of it that interests you?" Amanda asked, quickly changing subjects.

Danny looked at her with gratitude. "I guess it is," he said. "But that's just me. Not everyone sees the carnival that way. For most it's pure entertainment."

"So you're going?" Michael asked, looking at Danny intently.

Danny nodded, took his position, and dropped another solid into a pocket.

"So that makes two of us," Michael said.

Danny looked up at his friend to see whether he was joking or not. Michael gazed back at him seriously. "The more the merrier," Danny said. "I doubt Jack will come, although I did ask him to."

"Do you blame him?" Amanda asked.

Danny shook his head, then turned to Michael. "Are you sure, Cooper?"

Michael gave him a quick smile, one that couldn't be less honest if he tried. "Of course," he said. "I'm going to need the distraction after visiting the old lady."

Amanda was about to reply when someone bumped into her and sent her flying into the pool table. She turned around and gazed angrily at the man occupying the space where she had just stood.

"Watch it," Amanda snapped.

"It's a full house," the man replied curtly. "Stand in a corner if you don't want anyone bumping into you."

"What did you say?" Michael asked, coming up beside Amanda and staring the man in the eye. Michael stood at least a foot taller than the drunk, and the way he held his cue stick should have been enough to stop any quarrel.

"I said, make room, or leave," the man replied.

Michael smiled and walked up to the man so that their faces were only inches apart. "I suggest you apologize to the lady," Michael hissed.

The man was unfazed. He stuck a finger in Michael's chest and returned his gaze. "Get back on your bike and go find some zoo to play gorilla in," the man retorted. "No one's afraid of you here."

Michael's hands rolled into fists, and he barely registered Amanda's hand on his arm. "Let it go, Cooper," she was saying. "He's not worth it."

"Shut up, bitch," the man said, and before he could turn back, Michael slammed his fist into the man's face and sent him sprawling to the floor.

The bar immediately fell silent, the crowd backing away as Michael brought his cue stick up and slammed it down the man's back. It broke with a loud crack that was deafening, and before anyone could react, Michael pulled a switchblade from his back pocket and bent over the man, pushing the cold steel against his neck.

"Cooper!" Amanda cried from behind him.

"I said apologize," Michael spat, the man's eyes wide as he stared back at him, his nose bloody. "Do it!"

"Cooper!"

Michael felt a hand grab his arm, and he pushed at it forcefully, turning around and aiming his knife at his next victim. Jack stepped back and raised his hands in surrender. "Michael, what are you doing?"

Michael's eyes darted across the bar. All eyes were on him, frozen faces watching in horror, everyone staring at the angry biker with the knife. He could almost feel the judgment in their eyes, the stereotypical labeling, and it only made him angrier. He looked over his shoulder at Amanda, and the look of shock on her face was enough to make him hate himself for not being able to control his anger.

Every time, he thought. *No matter how hard I try, the same thing happens every time.*

Michael reached out a finger and pressed the top of his weapon, folding the blade back and pocketing it. He stood up, glanced briefly at his friends, then at the rest of the guests, and made for the door. People backed out of his way, and Michael slammed his fist against the door as he stormed out into the falling rain.

He went straight for his bike, oblivious to the storm around him, cursing under his breath. He straddled the hog, pulled on his helmet and stared out across the crowded lot as he strapped it in place. His eyes caught sight of a lone figure standing at the edge of the parking lot, leaning against a tree and watching him through the torrents of rain.

Michael froze as he recognized the man.

"Josh?" he whispered in disbelief.

Thunder boomed above him, and when the lightning followed, briefly illuminating the parking lot, his brother was gone.

Chapter 4

Faith Stone woke up with a terrible headache.

She rolled over slowly, groaning as she reached up and massaged her temples, resting her other hand on the empty space where Jack should have been. She sighed, slowly registering the sound of the shower from behind the closed bathroom door.

The blinds had been left closed, and the rays of sunlight escaping into the room reminded her of her cellphone's flashlight, and suddenly, last night rushed back in agonizing, pounding waves. She sat up slowly, wincing at the rush of blood to her head that left her dazed.

That's it, my drinking days are over.

Faith leaned her head back against the headboard, eyes closed as she waited for the dizziness to subside. She listened to the creaking sound of the shower being turned off followed by the sliding of the bath curtain, and waited as Jack stepped out of the bathroom with a towel wrapped around his waist.

"Morning," he said in surprise. "I thought you were going to sleep in today."

"Couldn't if I wanted to," Faith squeezed her eyes shut. "Can I play the girlfriend card and have breakfast in bed?"

"How about coffee first?"

"I knew I moved in with you for a reason."

Jack laughed and grabbed his clothes off the chair by the window. He dressed quickly, then made his way into the kitchen and switched the coffee machine on. Almost as if on autopilot, he turned on the laptop he left on the kitchen table and waited for it to load as he reached for a bowl and cereal. He logged in his password, then went back to the coffee machine, pouring Faith a mug and taking it back to her.

"Better than breakfast?" he asked, handing her the mug.

Faith nodded as she cradled the hot coffee close to her chest, shivering slightly. The weather had begun to cool, but she was still adamant on sleeping in nothing more than a top and panties. In a few weeks, she was going to come down with a nasty flu, as she usually did, and Jack was going to fight the urge to use the I-told-you-so speech, as *he* usually did.

"Could you wait for me?" Faith asked, taking a sip from her coffee.

Jack shrugged. "Sure," he said. "You're especially active for a Saturday morning."

"I need to check up on the library," she replied. "I never got through the entire round."

"You sure you're okay going back there?"

"What am I going to do, never go to work again?"

"Not what I meant," Jack said. "Maybe just avoid it today. Relax and read or something, maybe go out for a jog. If you're up for it, we can go to the carnival later."

Faith almost dropped her mug and looked up at him in surprise. "The carnival?"

Jack didn't reply, only looked at her silently.

"You're not serious, right?" Faith asked, gently placing her mug on the nightstand.

Jack shrugged. "I'm not entirely thrilled about it, but Danny was saying he wanted us with him, and I mulled it over."

"When?" Faith asked, her voice rising. "When you were drunk?"

"Faith—"

"Don't Faith me," she snapped, suddenly furious. "Are you out of your mind? If Danny's forgotten what happened, I certainly haven't. And until just now I was sure you hadn't either."

"I haven't," Jack said. "And neither has Danny. He's writing an article on the place, and wanted extra hands on deck."

"Then tell him to find other hands," Faith retorted. "What's wrong with you?"

"Nothing," Jack sighed. "I guess he just made me a little curious, that's all."

"Whatever," Faith threw her hands into the air, getting out of bed and storming past him to the bathroom. "Do whatever you want." She slammed the door behind her.

Jack sighed heavily, then went back to the kitchen, shaking his head in frustration. It was going to be a long day.

***

Ebenezer's Carnival opened its doors to the public around midday. Despite its history, the queue reached all the way to Gambler Park's entrance. Families edged forward step-by-step, laughter and cheerful chatter filling the air, the faint sound of music from inside diffusing across the park like a piper's call, rallying all towards it.

Since it had last set up in Lensfield, the town had changed drastically. The establishment of Lensfield College brought in a magnitude of business, and a lot of real estate construction to match. With new homes came new blood, and although the natives of the town still remembered the tragedy that had accompanied the carnival's last arrival, most of the current inhabitants were completely oblivious to its dark history.

Either that, or they simply shrugged it off as local lore.

For Cindy Kale, the carnival was just another reason why she couldn't spend the weekend in the comfort of her home, watching television and sipping on iced tea while she relaxed after a grueling week of work. Nothing would have given her more pleasure than finding out that the protests in front of town hall, going on since eight in the morning, had been successful and the carnival was being forced to pack up and leave.

She stood a few feet away from the large entrance, her sunglasses hiding the black bags under her eyes and her two children pulling and pushing at her excitedly. They had been bombarding her with questions about the carnival ever since the fliers had popped up all around town, and her husband had even gone a bit further and helped them create a calendar to count down the days until 'mommy would take them to see the rides'.

She hated Phil for that, and even more when he woke up this morning and told her that he wouldn't be able to come with them.

Cindy wrapped her hand around her elder son's arm and yanked him back to her side, barely looking at him when he cried out in protest. Her daughter laughed at her brother's pain, and that eventually led to a small squabble that Cindy had to half-heartedly break up. A part of her actually wanted to leave them at it. She could sit back and watch the two of them tear at each other's throats, and maybe, just maybe, she'd finally have some peace.

The line moved a few more feet, then stopped.

Cindy sighed, pushing to her toes and looking out across the queue to the entrance. Only a few more feet and she could finally get this over with. She didn't intend to spend too much time inside, just long enough to satisfy her children's curiosity. A few rides, one or two games, a hotdog maybe, and then it was back to the car and the promise of a few relaxing hours on the couch while Phil took them out for ice cream.

The line edged closer to the carnival entrance, and Cindy spotted a tall man standing to one side, clad in a black suit, top hat and cane. He smiled at the train of eager guests, his lips drawn up in a ridiculous angle that made him look more sinister than welcoming. Cindy immediately grasped both her children as she neared the man, and she felt a shiver break out through her body despite the afternoon heat.

"What lovely children," Ebenezer Cage smiled towards Cindy. He bent down, his tall frame casting a long shadow across the queue, and lifted his hat up in greeting. Cindy watched one slender hand reach into a pocket, and when it returned, Ebenezer held out two pieces of candy. "The carnival always welcomes its younger guests with a treat or two."

"Thank you," Cindy said, quickly pulling her children back. "That's very kind, but I usually limit their sugar intake."

Ebenezer looked up at her, and although his face was jovial, his eyes were dark and devoid of any emotion. It made Cindy feel even more uneasy.

"What a wise decision," Ebenezer said and returned the candy to his pocket. "I must say, a mother with your perseverance will result in the upbringing of two productive and significant members of our future society. I salute you, madam."

Cindy smiled in spite of herself. "Not so sure about productive and significant," she replied.

"Come on, mom!" Her son pulled at her hand, and Cindy shook out of his grip in frustration. "See what I mean?"

"Children will be children," Ebenezer cooed. "You are a lucky woman."

"If you say so," Cindy joked. "You can have them if you want. You'd be doing me a favor."

Ebenezer chuckled, a laugh that sounded more like crumbling rocks than anything else. "Enjoy your stay," he gestured towards the entrance. "You might just find the peace you desire within."

If only, Cindy thought, smiling and nodding at the man before pushing her children forward and towards the ticket booth.

Ebenezer watched her for a few seconds, and his smiled widened. "The carnival always finds a way," he whispered, then turned back to welcome the other guests in the queue.

***

Jacqueline Stevens sat back in her chair and took off her glasses. She ran a finger back and forth across her brow, closed her eyes, and tried to squeeze away the multiple colored spots that danced behind her closed lids. She had been staring at the doll on her table for a few hours now, the only light in the room coming from the circular fluorescent around her workstation's magnifying glass. The strain in her eyes was blinding, and it was enough to let her know that the day's work was done.

She glanced at the digital watch across her worktable, grimacing at the time. By now, the sun had probably begun to set outside, and she had hoped to make it to the carnival before dusk. She never felt very comfortable in Gambler's Park at night, although she knew there was rarely anything to worry about, especially in a small town like Lensfield. She had grown up in the Bronx, after all, an inner city girl who understood what danger really was, and she doubted anything in Lensfield could come close. Still, there was something eerie about the park, and after her visit there, she had made up her mind to only set foot across the bridge during the daytime.

So much for an afternoon's rest.

She looked down at the doll that had taken up her entire afternoon, and Jacqueline felt her heart flutter. The little thing looked beautiful, blonde locks under a white cap, the pink dress surrounding it in folds. She smiled at it, proud of her latest work of art, and ran a hand across the doll's dress, twisting the fabric around as she pondered whether or not to add a sash to it.

Let it go.

Jacqueline sighed and pushed back her chair, standing up slowly and stretching. The day was over, and the idea of a nice hot cup of coffee and a book was tantalizing. She picked the doll up, switched off the lamp, and walked out of her workroom and into the dimly lit outer store.

It was getting darker, the streetlights illuminating the world outside in patches of orange light. Jacqueline contemplated turning the store lights on, then decided against it, content with the hue coming in through the large display window. She wasn't going to be long anyway, and she doubted she would be getting any last minute shoppers at this hour. Besides, Saturdays were never the busiest of times along Main Street, most of Lensfield crowded into the cafes and bars around the college.

Or at the carnival.

Jacqueline placed her new doll on the center shelf, right in front of the door where it could be seen with ease by anyone walking in. She remembered Ebenezer Cage's words from the day before, and she felt a sudden pang in her chest. She had never thought twice about children, and she found it odd that his bringing it up would awaken some dormant maternal instinct inside her she hadn't known existed before now. Her mother usually berated her about it, most calls these days were about Jacqueline's life choices and the lack of grandchildren, but it hadn't been until the carnival owner brought it up that she gave it a second thought. She suddenly felt a rush of emotion course through her, a wave of feelings that was simultaneously warm and uncomfortable.

Jacqueline shook it off. She didn't need children. She had her dolls.

"I might as well give you all names," she said as she looked about the shelves lined with her handiwork. The dolls gazed back with their fixed smiles and lifeless eyes. "I'll call you Beatrice," Jacqueline chuckled, smoothed the pink dress of her newest creation, and gazed into its beady eyes.

And now you're talking to yourself. Add a few cats, and you'll fit the stereotype perfectly.

Jacqueline sighed and turned away from the row of dolls, walking towards the front of the store as she rummaged in her purse for her keys. She found them and pushed at the door, crashing into it when it didn't slide open with its usual smoothness. She cursed under her breath, her forehead throbbing, and tried again.

The door didn't budge.

That's weird, I never lock it.

"Mama!"

Jacqueline froze when she heard the soft sound of a child's voice behind her. A sudden chill enveloped her completely, and the temperature in the store felt like it had dropped a few dozen degrees.

"Mama!"

This time, the voice was different and seemed to come from a different part of the store. Jacqueline clutched the keys tight in her hand, their teeth digging into her palm. She turned around, slowly, and looked back into the darkness. The light from outside filled parts of the store with its orange hue, casting long shadows in the places it didn't reach, and her eyes darted back and forth as she tried to make out where the voices had come from.

"Mama!"

Jacqueline's eyes snapped to the center shelf where Beatrice sat, the doll's smile frozen in place, its eyes staring out into nothingness. She could have sworn the voice had come from that direction, but nothing was out of the ordinary.

"Mama!"

Jacqueline looked back at Beatrice, the doll's white cap slightly askew, the pink dress a ruffle of dark cloth hidden by the shadows. She stared at the doll for a few more seconds, and as she began to turn back to the door, she stopped.

Beatrice's head shifted and turned so that its beady eyes were staring directly at Jacqueline. Jacqueline felt her heart jump to her throat as the doll's carefully stitched mouth shifted into a smile, and the black eyes burned a bright red.

"Mama!"

Jacqueline shifted her attention to the shelves on her left, and she felt the terror well up inside her as one doll after the other shifted its head and smiled at her. She reached behind her, slowly, and tried to open the door again, but it didn't move.

"Where are you going, Mama?" Beatrice's mouth opened and closed as she spoke, the cute smile turning into a horrible grin as the doll began to move. It stood up slowly on the shelf and held its arms out to Jacqueline. "Take me with you."

The other dolls began to move as well, and from behind the counter, three of them stepped out of the shadows and trudged towards her, arms wide, mouths opening and closing like fish out of water. Jacqueline turned around quickly, fumbling with her keys as she rushed to unlock the door, pushing and pulling at it in frustration. The urgency racing through her made her clumsy, and her hands were numb with terror. She tried to slide one into the keyhole but couldn't control the shaking of her hand, and she cried out when the keys fell out of her hand and crashed onto the ground.

Beatrice had climbed down from her shelf along with a dozen more dolls, and they all wobbled towards her, eyes burning red and smiles wide. Jacqueline tried to back away, the door stopping her retreat as she pressed up against it as if somehow she would be able to just slip through and escape.

"Mama!"

The first doll touched her leg, and its fingers dug into her flesh like miniature knives.

Beatrice came up behind the other dolls, and the darkness behind the doll's mouth seemed like a deep abyss of nothingness that promised an eternity of solitude.

"The carnival always finds a way," Beatrice giggled.

And as the dolls crowded around Jacqueline, digging their nails into her flesh and climbing up her legs, she screamed.

Chapter 5

"And you let him go?"

Faith sat snuggly on the oversized couch in Amanda's living room, a blanket thrown over her legs and the low tunes of REM playing in the background. Amanda was on her laptop, glasses at the end of her nose, her blonde hair tied in a high ponytail and a pencil stuck behind her ear. Clad in a top and shorts, her fingers danced away on the laptop keyboard as changing colors from the screen reflected across her glasses.

"It didn't sound like he was taking permission," Faith replied. "Can you believe it, though? I mean, just mentioning the damn place made my stomach turn. I have no idea how he could go."

"Boys will be boys," Amanda said, her eyes fixated on the screen as she worked.

Faith sighed. It didn't surprise her that Amanda couldn't understand how much the situation bothered her. She and Philip hadn't been at the Barton farm when the place went up in flames, and the whole incident had never been easy to explain. There were so many details that Faith had blocked out, so many missing pieces that she didn't want to be reminded of, but the incident had left a lingering feeling of dread inside her.

She knew Jack felt it, too. She was fully aware of his nightmares, how he would wake up sweaty and gasping in the middle of the night and then toss and turn for a good hour before falling asleep again. It was one of the reasons why she couldn't comprehend his desire to go to the carnival. For years now, they had been on the same page about what had happened. They both knew what was to blame, even if it could all be chalked up to the imaginations of children.

But I didn't imagine the fire. And I definitely didn't imagine those eyes.

"Maybe you're reading too much into this," Amanda said, pulling Faith away from her thoughts. "At the end of the day, it's just a carnival."

"It's not *just* a carnival, Amanda," Faith returned. "That place is pure evil."

Amanda sighed and looked up from her laptop. "We've been through this, sweetie," she said calmly. "The carnival had nothing to do with Barton, and it definitely had nothing to do with, well, you know."

Faith didn't reply, only gazed at her friend for a moment before shaking her head and looking away.

"Have you visited her lately?" Amanda asked.

Faith shook her head.

"Maybe you should," Amanda suggested. "It might bring some closure."

"If it could, then I would have gotten closure ten years ago," Faith replied, reaching over to the coffee table and picking up her pad and notes. She unclasped the pen from its place and began to flip through the pages of her work. Amanda sighed and the tapping of keys continued.

Faith tried to concentrate, the paperwork in her hand a quick task that wouldn't have taken longer than an hour to complete on any regular day. Tonight, though, her mind was elsewhere, and no matter how much she tried, she couldn't seem to get through a page without drifting off.

Jack had escorted her to the library, and despite her protests, joined her inside to keep her company. Faith finished what remained of the tasks from the night before quickly, avoiding the windows where she had imagined seeing Lily, and rounded up her work for the weekend. All in less than an hour. Even Jack had been surprised, and although he had tried to make small talk to lighten the mood, she had given him the cold shoulder until he dropped her off at Huck's. She hated doing that, but she had been fuming, and despite her usual capability of easily letting him off the hook, she couldn't bring herself to do it this time.

The coffee shop didn't help take her mind off of the carnival, and neither did Amanda's suggestion that they spend the evening together working. She tried talking, venting, but that did little good, and all she was getting in return was a dismissal of her worries. Sometimes she wished that Amanda had been at the Barton Farm with them just so she could have someone other than Jack to talk to about it.

Faith looked up at her friend as the other woman tapped away and mumbled under her breath, focused on whatever it was she was doing. She envied Amanda's ability to just shrug things off and get on with her life, looking ahead and forgetting the past, sometimes even the present. It was admirable at times, and at others, Faith just wanted to grab the woman by her collar and shake some sense into her.

Then again, the whole issue of the carnival wasn't bothering Amanda in the least bit, and Faith began to wonder if maybe she were the one who needed some sense shaken into her.

***

The first thing that Jack registered as he walked into Gambler's Park and made his way to the gates of the carnival were the lights.

It had been years since he had last set foot in any carnival, let alone Ebenezer's. But, the one thing he remembered clearly was, despite the brightly illuminated rides and stands, there had been enough dark corners to make him constantly question what could be hiding in the shadows. That had all changed apparently, and as he neared the ringing music and faint screams of joy of the carnival, he felt almost as if he were being blinded by the flashing green, red, and yellow lights. There was nothing dark and mysterious about the carnival anymore, and even from a distance away, the entirety of Gambler's Park seemed to be alight with colors and noise.

Jack felt a small smile form on his lips, although he had convinced himself that the only reason for his coming here was to assist Danny with his article. Still, a part of him, some deep inner child, seemed to jump up and down in excitement the closer he came to the gates.

From across the makeshift rails, he could see the giant Ferris wheel, turning slowly with its blinking lights, its mesmerizing motion only interrupted by the tossing and turning of a second ride he did not recognize from the last time he had visited Ebenezer's. The tops of dozens of food stands and game booths lined the main path beyond the entrance, and through the crowds, he could see entertainers juggling and spitting fire much to the amusement of the carnival's guests. In the background, chimed the familiar music he had learned to hate over the years, a haunting tune that always made him shiver, yet now seemed to only add to the charm of the magical playground beyond.

He found Danny and Michael standing by the ticket booth, deep in conversation, with equal smiles on their faces. For the briefest of moments, Jack remembered the first time they had visited Ebenezer's Carnival. They had all had that same look on their faces, just an innocent group of kids going through another adventure they would one day tell their children and grandchildren about. They had no idea what would happen to them over the span of that week, and Jack felt a chill course through him at the thought of reliving that nightmarish experience.

"Wipe that smile off your face, Heldon," Michael said, trying to deepen his voice but unable to stop smiling himself.

"I get the feeling we're a little too old to be this happy about the carnival," Jack replied, taking the ticket that Danny held out to him and looked at it. The name 'Ebenezer's Carnival' was etched in gold, and from some dark, twisted corner of Jack's mind, he could hear the Oompa-Loompas chanting.

"Has it always had this many rides?" Danny was saying, digging his hands into his coat pockets and bracing himself against the cold wind that had begun picking up. For some reason, I remember it a lot smaller."

"And darker," Michael chimed in, looking up at the large sign hanging over the entrance. Its lights made the space in front of the entrance seem like mid-day in comparison to the rest of the park.

"Hey, do any of you remember that rhyme they used to tell us about Gambler's Park?" Danny asked, leading the small group towards the carnival's mouth and handing his ticket to the scantily dressed girl by the door. "Something like, 'Watch your windows, watch your doors', something, something?"

"No idea, man," Jack shook his head.

"Keep your children in sight," Michael continued. He handed the girl his ticket and winked at her, and Danny turned to him in surprise.

"You know it?" he asked with a smile.

Michael nodded. "My grandmother used to croak it out every time she got the chance. She hated the park."

Jack laughed. "Urban legends?"

"Depends," Michael said, his eyes darting about as he took in the booths and stands and rides. "Ten years ago, I might have agreed."

"How did the rest go?" Danny asked.

"Watch your windows, watch your doors, keep your children in sight. For somewhere across the Gambler's bridge, evil lurks through the night."

Jack suddenly remembered the old rhyme, and as he gazed upon the carnival, he could sense the words seething through the air and into the ground, filling the cheerful atmosphere with a kind of impending doom. It made him shiver, and he pulled his coat closed and pulled the collar up around his neck.

He followed his friends into the carnival.

***

Matt Steel sipped loudly on his soda pop and belched. To his right, a woman turned to look at him in disgust before shaking her head and pulling her daughter away and towards the other side of the children's rides. Matt watched her leave and chuckled, grabbing a handful of popcorn from his bucket, tossing them into his mouth and crunching down.

He was alone, sitting idly on the backrest with his feet planted firmly onto the bench, gazing out into the crowd. He looked as though he were staring into space, his eyes fixated on nothing in particular as he slurped his drink and ate his popcorn, but that was far from the truth. In reality, Matt couldn't care less about the carnival, and on any other day, would have probably not even bothered coming.

But Hailey Astern was here, and wherever she went, Matt followed.

He threw another fistful of popcorn into his mouth and washed it down with the soda. Leaning on his knees, he kept his eyes focused on the beautiful brunette giggling near the shooting range, surrounded by her friends. Matt smiled to himself, observing the high school cheerleaders from afar. His eyes focused on Hailey as she aimed her gun and missed the target completely. The other girls giggled along with her.

Matt watched as the man running the booth talked to the girls, obviously cajoling them into playing one more round, probably promising them that this time they might win something. Matt could tell a bullshitter from a mile away. His father was one, and Matt had learned to master the art from the old bastard. He would never be tricked into playing the carnival's rigged games, but he wasn't surprised when he saw Hailey shrug, pull cash out of her pocket, and take the gun in her hands again.

The things I'd let her do with those hands, Matt thought to himself, and smiled.

His eyes traced Hailey's body as she took aim. Despite the cold, the girl wasn't fazed by Lensfield's autumn chill, and her long legs stuck out seductively from under her shorts. Matt began to undress her with his eyes, something he was accustomed to doing every time he laid eyes upon her. It had become a frequent thing since he had memorized her schedule and took the same route she did home. And every time, his imagination went to places he rarely wanted to return from.

"The affection of the young."

Matt almost fell from his seat in surprise, and his head snapped angrily to the tall man sitting on the bench beside him.

Who the hell wears top hats these days?

"Forgive me, young man, but I do believe the girl is what you commonly refer to as 'out of your league'," Ebenezer Cage said with a smile.

"What do you know about my league, gramps?" Matt shot back, already furious that his daydreaming had been interrupted.

"I notice things," Ebenezer responded. "It helps me judge the people before me, and it has served me quite well so far."

"Yeah?"

"Indeed," Ebenezer nodded, and turned to look at Matt. "For instance, your clothes are faded, your shoes worn, and your hair has not seen a scissor in months. Your fingernails are dingy, there is a scar above your right eye which I believe is the result of a trauma, and the stench of oil radiating from your body is quite pungent. I would like to add that the very fact you are sitting here and salivating over that young woman over there is enough for one to draw an accurate conclusion about your persona."

Matt stared at the man in a mix of shock and anger. "Who the hell are you?"

"My name is Ebenezer Cage, and I run this mighty establishment that brings both the innocent and the perverted together in one place."

"Say something like that again, gramps, and I'll punch your friggin' teeth out," Matt snarled.

Ebenezer let out a soft hearty chuckle, and Matt could feel the laugh dig into his head and scratch at the insides of his mind. "I believe you just might, young man," Ebenezer said. "However, I am not here to aggravate you, nor do I mean to insult. I merely state the obvious, and believe that you may be in need of some assistance."

Matt frowned and cocked his head to one side. "You want to help me?"

"Indeed, my astute friend, I want to *help* you."

"What makes you think I need help?"

"Ah, the question of the hour," Ebenezer chuckled. "I am of the opinion that what you lack in domestic adoration, you seek in the embrace of our female companion over there."

"Talk in English, Shakespeare," Matt snapped.

"The irony of your comparison is hardly mind-boggling," Ebenezer smiled, "but I will accommodate your wishes. In plain speech, I know what you want."

Matt felt taken aback as the man's voice changed, deepening into a hollow rumble that seemed to echo all around him.

Ebenezer leaned in closer, a glimmer of red reflected in his pupils. "I can see it in your eyes, your perverted mind at work, imagining that girl's legs wrapped around you as you screw the hell out of her," he said. "I can see every imaginable, disgusting, pornographic image in your head, and I am here to tell you that you can have it all. All you need to do is ask."

Matt opened his mouth to reply, then closed it again.

"My dear boy," Ebenezer cooed, his voice returning to its original tone. "There is no harm in speaking of that which we desire. I beg of you, make use of this opportunity. It does not happen often."

"I want Hailey," Matt said immediately. "I want her to want me as much as I do, more than I do!" He looked over at Hailey hungrily.

Ebenezer nodded. "Definitely uplifting, isn't it?"

"But how?" Matt asked.

Ebenezer's smile widened, and between the open lips, Matt could have sworn he saw fangs. "Young man," Ebenezer said, "the carnival always finds a way."

***

There was a healthy crowd about the carnival grounds, and the laughter of children seemed to echo from every corner. Between the ringing of rides either starting or stopping, and the calls coming from the various concessions, it was easy to lose yourself in the surrounding energy. At the back end, the crowd seemed to grow considerably in number, the bigger attractions and concessions flashing their lights and drawing more and more people down the middle towards them.

Michael had broken away from his friends, leaving them behind at a hotdog stand while he searched for a lavatory. When he was younger, it had been a dare to try and find some dark corner in the carnival where he could let fly and hope no one saw him. Now it seemed that everywhere he went, even more people gathered, and it was impossible to find where one path started and the other ended. The arrows marking the bathrooms confused him even more, and by the time he had finally found them, he was ready to give up completely and just hold it in.

An overweight man sat half-asleep on a lawn chair, hands folded over his protruding belly, snorting as his eyes closed and fluttered open again. When he saw Michael approach, he adjusted himself in his seat, and Michael winced at the sound the chair made under the big man's weight.

"Dollar for the donniker," the man coughed.

"Donniker?"

"The small room," the man said, irritated. "The closet. Whatever you townies wanna call it."

Michael smiled and pulled out his wallet, drawing a dollar from within and placing it squarely in the big hand reaching out and waiting. "Didn't know you had to pay to take a leak," he said.

"Everything's gotta be paid," the man replied and leaned back in his lawn chair, closing his eyes immediately and snoring again.

Michael shook his head in merry disbelief and made his way to the stalls. He replaced his wallet in his back pocket and looked back towards the crowd, and stopped.

From across the midway, he caught sight of a man in front of the Hall of Mirrors, a figure that stood out from the crowd and was watching him intently. Michael recognized the flannel shirt and faded jeans, as well as the oversized beige coat his brother had been wearing the day he disappeared. The figure stood completely still, the crowd of carnival guests walking past him without a second look, yet at the same time keeping a well-enough distance away.

Michael didn't need to second-guess what he was seeing.

It was Josh.

It was his brother.

Michael forgot about the bathroom and his need for relief, and immediately made his way back onto the midway and towards the Hall of Mirrors. He walked quickly, urgently, unwilling to let Josh slip away again like the night before. When his brother broke his stance and walked through the doors of the attraction, Michael picked up the pace and half-jogged after him.

He didn't remember the hall from the last time he had been to Ebenezer's, and being one of the more common attractions at carnivals, he half-expected to find the place crowded with fun seekers. But as he barged through the double doors, he was immediately taken aback by how dark and empty the hall was. In front of him was a second set of doors, and to his right a small window lit in red, the word 'Tickets' flashing on and off above it. Michael walked over to it and knocked on the glass barrier, waking up the young man behind it.

"Did you see a man walk into here, my height, maybe an inch or two taller, long hair?" he asked.

The boy yawned, stretched, and sniffed, squinting as he took a closer look at

Michael. "Nobody's been in here for hours."

"That's impossible," Michael replied, feeling the frustration inside him grow. "I just saw him come in here."

The boy leaned closer to the glass and searched the small vestibule Michael was standing in, shaking his head. "Sorry," he said. "Can't see no one."

"Probably walked right in while you were sleeping," Michael snapped, the anger in his voice startling him.

The boy sniffed again and shook his head slowly. "Can't get in without me buzzing you," he said. "Are you here to talk or are you actually going inside."

Michael pulled out his wallet, looked at the sign by the booth that advertised the attraction for two dollars, and threw the cash into the concave tray beneath the glass. The boy lazily took the money, pulled a ticket out of the slot beside him and tossed it back. Michael grabbed the ticket, hastily made his way to the second set of doors and pushed through them just as he heard the buzzing sound.

A flash of light burst and instantly blinded him, and as the doors slammed behind him, he blinked repeatedly and tried to adjust to the dimly lit maze of mirrors. Splotches of color filled his vision, and he leaned against one mirror to try and steady himself. He began to wonder how many people suffered severe epileptic shocks just by walking here.

Michael squeezed his eyes shut for a few seconds, and when he opened them, looked at the elongated reflection of himself in the mirror. On any other day, he would have found the reflection amusing, but right now he was more concerned with finding Josh than admiring the intricate maze of mirrors.

He began to make his way through the maze, briefly looking as the Michael Cooper in each mirror shifted and changed in shape and size. He imagined guests walking through the maze and laughing at their odd reflections, taking pictures and making fun of each other. However, he couldn't help but feel an odd heaviness in the air around him, as if the attraction itself were pushing against him and preventing him from moving deeper into its maze. The temperature inside was also significantly colder, and Michael zipped his jacket closed as he guessed his way along the rows of mirrors.

A loud crash echoed through the hall, and from somewhere to his right he heard the familiar buzzing of the doors. The lights above his head flashed again, and he quickly closed his eyes to avoid being momentarily blinded. Someone cursed, and a girl giggled.

Michael continued his search through the maze, holding his breath as he rounded every corner, each time confident that he would find his brother waiting just beyond the next row of shifting reflections. And every time, he was disappointed. He made his way deeper into the center of the hall, casting his eyes up to the rafters every few seconds and following their course along. He doubted anyone ever really got lost in the hall, but he hated closed places, and the claustrophobia was already gnawing at him.

"Why did you come back?"

Michael froze, the voice coming from directly behind him. He shifted his gaze to his left where his reflection stared back at him, albeit longer and much thinner, and nothing else.

"Why are you here?"

The source had shifted its position, a little further into the darkness, a hissing whisper came from around the next bend. Michael rushed forward and turned the corner, but no one was there. He was surrounded on all sides by mirrors, his body altered in each one.

"There's nothing for you here."

From behind each of his reflections, twin eyes appeared within a haggard face, black as the night. Michael turned around quickly and found himself alone. From further back, the girl giggled again.

"Where are you?" Michael hissed, his anger boiling. "Stop hiding, dammit!"

"Leave Lensfield," the voice whispered in his ear and a cold hand touched the back of his neck.

Michael lashed out, but his fist only slammed against one of the mirrors and it rocked on its stand. He turned around again, and when he saw nothing, stormed through the maze angrily in search of his brother.

"No one can protect you, Michael," the voice came from all around him. "No one can help you."

Michael turned another corner and came face to face with another oblong reflection of himself. In the dim light, even his eyes seemed darker than usual, and his hair seemed to float around his head. The haggard face appeared behind him again, and before Michael could turn, a hand grasped him by the neck and slammed him against the mirror.

"Go back," Josh hissed in his ear. In the mirror, his brother looked like a shell of his former self. The dark eyes were smoky, the skin folded in crevices around his mouth and sagged under his eyes. There was a gaunt look to his face and a grayish, pasty white hue that made him look like he had just crawled out of his grave. The hair on his head was brittle and thin, and when he opened his mouth to speak, a rush of rancid breath came out.

"I came for you, Josh," Michael said, his voice a croak against the firm grasp around his neck. "I came to get you."

"Josh is dead," his brother chuckled. "There is no Josh here."

Michael tried to break free of his brother's grasp, but to no avail. The grip was vice-like, and Josh was slowly choking him. "Josh," he stammered.

"Go back," Josh hissed. "Go to the girl you left behind. Go to your child. Leave here now and never return."

"I'm not leaving without you," Michael retorted.

His brother leaned in, his lips inches from Michael's ear. When he spoke, Michael felt his heart jump as his brother's familiar voice echoed inside his head. "They know you're here, Michael. They know why you've come back. Go home."

"I'm taking you with me," Michael replied stubbornly.

"Leave!"

Josh's sudden anger burst in resonance throughout the entire hall, and the mirrors around Michael exploded into a million pieces. From the other end of the hall, the girl screamed at the menacing rumble, and the entire attraction seemed to shiver with the force of Josh's rage.

The hand loosened from around Michael's neck, and when he turned, Josh was gone.

Chapter 6

"Do you want me to get you anything?"

Faith shook her head and didn't reply. She heard Jack sigh, and continued to stare aimlessly out of her window as he opened his car door and stepped out. She briefly watched him race across the small parking lot, pulling the collar of his jacket up against the wind as he made for the gas station store, and bit her lower lip in frustration.

She had spent most of the drive quiet, only breaking the awkward silence to talk to Danny so he wouldn't feel too uncomfortable as they drove him to his motel. Faith didn't know if she was angrier at the fact that they seemed a bit too jolly after their escapade to the carnival, or the fact that Jack had ignored her feelings and had gone anyway. Either way, she knew Danny wasn't to blame, and if she was going to take her frustration out on anyone, it was going to be Jack.

She was, however, bothered by the look on Michael's face when they had returned. Whereas Danny and Jack seemed to be smiling like two idiots who had just taken pictures with Mickey Mouse, Michael looked awful. There was a darkness in his eyes the minute he walked into Amanda's house, a look that was too disturbing for comfort. Amanda had tried a little small talk, had even directed some of her polite questions towards Michael, but the man was unresponsive. Whatever was bothering him, it definitely had something to do with the carnival, and Faith was furious that Jack couldn't see it.

What the hell does he need to get that the place is bad news?

Faith lifted her legs up onto the seat and frowned in anger. Ever since they had dropped Danny off at the Badger, Jack had tried to talk to her. Snippets of conversation, questions about her day, anything to get a better response out of her other than single syllable replies and grunts. Faith felt bad for him, but every time she remembered that he had gone to the carnival-had actually ignored her wishes and gone-her anger spiked and disappointment blinded her. Thankfully he had refrained from saying anything about the carnival to her, had steered clear of trying to make her feel better about what he had done, and for that, she felt he deserved at least some credit.

Faith sniffed and ran a tired hand across her brow, shifting her gaze to the gas station store as she waited for him to return. The winds had picked up, and if she concentrated, she could hear a gentle whistle coming through the back window that Danny had failed to shut all the way. Cars idled past her and stopped at the pumps, the drivers stepping out and bracing themselves against the weather as they tried to refuel for the night. Faith leaned her head against the backrest and closed her eyes.

"I found you, Faithy."

Lily's voice from the backseat startled Faith, and she automatically snapped her head back and stared into the grinning face of her dead sister. Lily's hair was matted against her head, as if she had just stepped out of a shower, and her skin was gray against the lights of the gas station. In her hand, she held the same knife from the night before, and her eyes danced in their sockets as if someone else were controlling them.

Faith wanted to scream, but her voice caught in her throat as her sister giggled with glee. She lifted the knife up for Faith to see and waved it about.

"The tall man promised you would come with me," Lily said, her voice raspier. "He said you would love the carousel, too."

Lily giggled again, and the car was suddenly filled with a tear-jerking stench that made Faith gag. She reached for the handle of her door, quickly pushing it open and jumping out into the night. The door slammed behind her, the wind crashing it back with such force that Faith had to pull back her hand from being caught in it.

Lily jumped at the closed window of the back seat, pressing her face against the glass with her mouth open and her tongue stuck to the cold surface. The breath coming from her fogged the glass, but it didn't stop Faith from seeing those cold eyes staring at her. Lily slammed the hilt of the knife against the window and screamed at Faith, the sound muffled within, but loud inside Faith's mind nevertheless. It was as if Lily had found a way to telepathically convey her fury directly to her older sister, and Faith instinctively covered her ears and pressed her hands against them. She wanted to squeeze the screaming out from inside her, and when the sound became so deafening, so painstakingly agonizing, Faith screamed as well.

The sound of a woman screaming in the middle of the gas station parking lot brought everyone running, and Faith was soon surrounded by the faces and hands of strangers trying to calm her down and figure out what was happening. Someone pushed up against her and wrapped her in his arms, and it took her a few seconds to realize it was Jack.

"Faith, oh my God, Faith!" he stammered.

Faith rocked back and forth in his arms, shivering uncontrollably, her eyes squeezed shut and not daring to look back at the car. "Lily!" Faith screamed. "Lily!"

"What's wrong with her?" someone said, and Jack quickly waved his hand to shut the crowd up. He pressed Faith tighter to him and joined her in her rocking, rubbing her arms and trying to soothe her.

"It's okay," he whispered in her ear. "I'm here. It's okay."

"Lily," Faith called out, crying freely now, her shoulders shaking as she sobbed. "She's coming for me, Jack. She's coming for me."

"No one's coming for you," Jack tried to calm her down. "It's okay, I'm here. No one's going to hurt you."

Faith clutched his shirt in her fists and buried her face in his chest. "The car," she said, her words muffled.

Jack looked up at the car, squinting to make out what had scared her, but the vehicle was empty.

"There's nothing there, sweetie," he said.

Faith shook her head and cried harder. The crowd backed up and gave them some room, and Jack nodded at the few who looked at him questioningly, assuring them that he had the situation under control.

Soon, they sat alone beside their car, rocking back and forth as the wind blew against them, carrying with it the faint tunes of the carnival.

***

"There are other rooms in the house, you know," Amanda said with a soft smile, placing a mug of coffee in front of Michael.

Michael looked up at her, returned her smile and thanked her weakly. He shivered, still feeling the chill coursing through his veins, starting from his neck where his brother had choked him a few hours before. He couldn't shake the feeling away, and he wrapped his hands around the steaming drink in hopes that it would somehow remedy his situation.

"Are you sure you don't want me to make one for you?" Amanda asked, sitting on the coffee table in front of him, frowning in obvious concern.

"I'm okay, really," Michael tried to give her his best reassuring smile. Only, it didn't feel genuine, and from the look on her face, it was clear she didn't believe it either. "Just a long day, that's all."

"You were at the carnival, Cooper," she said. "Big biker boy like you, playing fifteen-year-old all over again."

Michael scoffed. "That was definitely not the carnival I remember."

"Was it scarier?" Amanda mocked, widening her eyes in a mock expression of fear.

Michael tried his best to maintain his poker face. "Bigger," he said, "and definitely a lot brighter and louder. If it weren't for the name, I would have never believed it was the same carnival."

"Ten years are enough for something to change drastically."

"I know," Michael replied, sipping from his drink, an image of his brother's haggard face flashing before his eyes.

"Well, if you're real scared, you can sleep in my room," Amanda joked. "I can tuck you in and everything, maybe make you a warm cup of milk and sing you a lullaby."

"Shut up, Brians," Michael smiled. "Besides, I wouldn't want to deal with the wrath of Huck Brians seeing me in his little sister's bed."

Amanda raised an eyebrow. "I've missed you, Cooper, but not that much."

Michael almost spilled his drink laughing. Faith switched from her seat on the coffee table to the couch beside him. "So what happened at the carnival?" she asked, her tone a bit more serious.

"Nothing much," Michael shrugged. "Checked out the games, ate a hotdog that I'm pretty sure will kill me if I don't get it out of my system, and had a little kid puke on my shoes."

"That's not what I meant," Amanda said, but smiled nevertheless.

"What did you mean?"

"The others walked in as if they had just visited Willy Wonka's factory, but you look like you had a little dance with the ghost of Christmas future."

Michael looked at her for a second before returning to the coffee and sipping it slowly.

"The silence is deafening," Amanda continued.

"You're pushing, Brians," Michael returned.

"And you're avoiding."

Michael sighed, dropped his head, and shook it slowly. "You're friggin' persistent."

"One of my better qualities."

"Not one I remember."

"I said it before," Amanda winked at him. "A lot changes in ten years."

Michael gazed at her for a few seconds longer than considered comfortable, taking her in, lost for a moment in the blue eyes gazing back at him. He broke the gaze and ran a hand through his hair, then leaned back into the couch.

"Did you know I run a tech company?" he asked.

Amanda's eyes widened and she chuckled. "You're serious?"

"Well, not alone, obviously. A couple of pals of mine decided to create music software to run on Macintosh. It sold before we even finished it, and we kind of just kicked off from there."

Amanda grinned. "A brain behind the leather."

"I'm a software engineer, Brians," Michael said. "I'm not all bikes and tattoos."

"I run a coffee shop," Amanda pitched in, "and design book covers after hours."

Michael frowned.

"I thought we were sharing," Amanda shrugged.

"Okay," Michael laughed.

"Oh, there's a point behind your listing of credentials?"

Michael laughed harder, and put his mug down, worried he might spill his drink on the couch. "The whole thing started in college. My roommate, one of his friends and my girlfriend."

Amanda felt a sharp pain in her chest, disappointment washing over her like a tidal wave.

"Well, ex-girlfriend," Michael said, and Amanda was glad he couldn't see the look of relief on her face. "We were serious, moved in together even." He reached into his back pocket, pulled out his wallet, and rummaged through it. He took out a photograph and handed it to Amanda.

In the picture, Michael was hugging a beautiful brunette and smiling at the camera, a child in between them.

"That's my son," Michael said. "Jimmy."

Amanda felt her heart melt as she stared at the boy smiling in his mother's arms. He definitely had Michael's eyes, and within them, she saw something gentle and loving. For a split second, she wanted to reach into the picture and hug him. It was the strangest feeling she had ever felt, and it made her hand shake slightly as she returned the picture to Michael.

Michael took it from her and looked at it for a few seconds before returning it into his wallet.

"You look happy," Amanda said, her voice weak.

"We were," Michael replied.

"Did something happen to them?"

"I left," Michael said after a second of hesitation. "I packed my things, told them I was going to Lensfield, and that I probably wasn't coming back."

Amanda frowned in confusion. "Why would you do that?"

"Ten years ago, when that carnival came to town, my brother disappeared with it," Michael said. "We all know the story, the letter he left in his bedroom the night before that damned freak show disappeared. It broke my mother's heart, and my father, who I thought couldn't be any more of an ass, grew even more violent."

Amanda nodded. She remembered the night Michael's father had been arrested, and the entire week after that when she had visited him and his mother in the hospital. It had been so close to the Barton incident, people had started believing the town had become cursed. And of course, everyone blamed the carnival. It never made any sense to her, but over the years, she had come to learn that people had an affinity to blame anything other than the obvious for their problems.

"We left," Michael continued, "but I never stopped looking. I needed to find that carnival, find my brother, ask him why he left us, beg him to come back and fix it. But I never found it."

Michael ran a hand through his hair and took a sip of his coffee.

"My mother never got over it," he continued. "Soon her heart gave up, and I had to make do with whatever I could."

"I'm sorry," Amanda said. "I didn't know."

"No one does," Michael smiled at her uncomfortably. "It's alright, I made it through alright."

"So when you heard the carnival was in town—"

"I jumped on my bike, said good bye to my son and drove all the way here," Michael nodded. "I needed to find my brother."

"And did you?" Amanda asked.

Michael shook his head slowly. "I found someone. I found something. But whatever that thing was, it was definitely not Josh."

***

Samuel Gold woke up to a crashing sound from downstairs.

His eyes fluttered open, and it took him a while for his eyes to adjust to the dim lights of his study. Through the window, flashing red, green, and yellow lights all the way from Gambler's Park reflected off the books behind him, and he grunted as he turned in his seat. The cup balanced on his leg fell and crashed to the floor, the carpet cushioning its fall and preventing it from shattering. The tea spilled and formed a dark stain around the cup.

Samuel cursed under his breath and tried to push himself out of his seat, his joints aching, and his back protesting. He had no idea how long he had been sleeping in his chair, but from the way his muscles twisted and shot bolts of pain up and down his body, he assumed it had been a while.

One day, I'm going to die in that damn chair, he thought bitterly.

He made his way across the study, slowly, every step more painful than the one before and only serving to darken his mood. Whatever it was that had caused the crash downstairs, he had half the mind to finish the job himself.

Once he was on the second floor landing, the stench hit him hard. It rushed into his nose and filled his sinuses with enough foulness to make him sneeze and his eyes water. He quickly covered his mouth and nose with one hand and with the other tried to find the lights. When he switched them on, the bulb above his head exploded and showered him with broken glass.

"Dammit!" he called out through his hand.

Needing to use both hands, he pulled his shirt up over his nose and felt around until he reached the bathroom, flicking on the lights inside and illuminating the landing with a harsh fluorescent glow that threw shadows across the wall. It wasn't great, but it was enough to help guide him to the staircase.

The stench grew stronger as he moved, and a second crash echoed through the ground floor hallway.

I must have left the back door open, he thought as he made his way downstairs. *Damn raccoon's probably messing about in the kitchen.*

He flipped on the lights above the staircase and felt a little better in the soft glow of the overhead lamp. Downstairs, a shadow moved, large and slow, and Samuel stopped midway down the stairs. It didn't look like the shadow of a raccoon. Someone was in the house.

Samuel weighed his options carefully. At his age, there was very little fight left in him, and he doubted he would be quick enough to reach his bat before whoever was down there would get to him first. He looked back up, contemplating returning to the study and calling the police instead. He had lost the element of surprise the minute he had turned on the lights, so there was the off chance that he had spooked his intruder.

Another crash, and fury suddenly welled up inside Samuel.

This is my house, dammit. I'm not going to let some lowlife rob me while I cower upstairs.

With newfound resolution, he attempted to quicken his pace, and as soon as his feet touched the bottom floor, he turned and made his way to the umbrella rack by the door. He grabbed his bat with both hands and turned around, half expecting the intruder to be racing towards him by now, but the hallway was empty.

A light shone inside the kitchen, and the large shadow from before moved again. The intruder coughed, a sharp and raspy sound that made Samuel cringe. He tightened his hands around the bat and slowly moved towards the kitchen, his anger greater now.

Damn fool doesn't even have the good sense to hide it.

Samuel wondered what kind of idiot would break into another man's house and be this confident.

An idiot with a death wish, for sure. I'm going to bash his head in and they could peel him off the kitchen floor.

Another crash. Another cough. And the anger inside Samuel grew dangerously. A few feet away from the kitchen, he dropped all attempts at caution and stormed the rest of the way in. His lips were pulled back in an angry snarl, and he announced his presence with a loud cry of rage, the baseball bat held high above his head.

And he froze.

Nancy Gold stood with her back to him, rummaging through the cabinets, and dropping their contents all across the kitchen counter. A bowl fell from her hand and joined the rest of the broken china on the floor, the crash deafening now that he was this close to it. She was still wearing the same blue dress he had buried her in, her favorite Sunday attire that he had always loved. It made the color of her eyes pop.

Only, her dress was caked in mud, torn to shreds in parts and hanging loosely over her bony body. Her arms stopped moving, and he could see the skin hanging in flaps from her bones. Her hair was frighteningly thin, her scalp mirroring the kitchen's fluorescent light through the threads of white that still hung from it. She wore only one of her shoes, and the second bare foot was missing two of its toes.

Nancy coughed again and spat what Samuel could only hope was not clotted blood. Her breath came in shallow gasps, raspy, sounding like sand being rubbed against each other. She stood completely still, and then began to laugh. She dug her nails into the cabinet wood and brought them down, the scratching sound sending painful shivers through Samuel's bones.

When she turned around, Samuel felt all the strength inside him escape, and the bat dropped onto the linoleum floor with a clatter.

"You ate all the good chocolate," Nancy said, staring directly at her husband.

Samuel took a step back, eyes wide in shock. Nancy's mouth opened and closed with loud smacks, the teeth gone and the gums blackened. One side of her face had decayed completely, and through a hole so large he could stick his hand through it, he could see the soft bones beneath. Her right eye was missing, and in its place, something white was moving, sliding across the cavity, and disappearing into her skull.

"You should have left some for me," Nancy smiled, and as she did, the skin at the corner of her mouth cracked and revealed the pink flesh beneath.

Samuel turned and ran, fighting through the pain in his joints and muscles as he raced back along the hallway and towards the staircase. From behind him, Nancy laughed again and followed, her pursuit marked by a click of her single shoe followed by the sick slap of her bare foot. The front door of the house was slightly open, and Samuel immediately gave up the idea of escaping to his study and made a run for it.

His foot caught on the first step where the wood struck out, and he fell sprawling onto the floor. His crash sent jolts of pain throughout his body, and he cried out in pain. Nancy laughed harder, and before he could get back up, a cold hand grasped his ankle and squeezed hard. Samuel cried out again, feeling his dead wife's nails dig into his skin as she tightened her grip. He turned and looked up at her, fighting to break free, trying helplessly to kick at her with his other leg.

Nancy cackled in glee, and with her vice-like grip, turned and started pulling him back to the kitchen.

"You should be happy to see me, Samuel," Nancy croaked. "After all, you've been wishing for my return since the moment you buried me."

Samuel tried to grab onto anything, his hands curling around the legs of chairs and tables as she pulled him along. Every time he thought he had a hold of something, Nancy would heave and pull him away, continuing their retreat. She dragged him on, through the back door, out into the cold night, his nails breaking and bleeding as he scratched at the ground, and tried to break free.

"I thought it was beautiful that you respected my wishes, honey," Nancy chuckled. "Right beside the old maple. A perfect place for both of us."

Samuel continued clawing at the earth, and when he found the courage to look at where his wife was dragging him to, when he saw the mounds of earth where he had buried her earlier that year, he began to scream.

"Together forever, isn't that what you wanted?' Nancy laughed over his screaming. "Don't worry, Samuel honey, the carnival always finds a way!"

Chapter 7

Jeffrey Morgan parked his Mercedes in front of the old Barton barn and looked at his watch. The afternoon sun hung directly over his head, but the autumn winds had begun picking up, and he had his windows closed against the mild chill it brought along with it. Sheriff Don Gibson sat in the passenger seat beside him, hat pulled down over his eyes and head tossed back as he gently snored, shifting only slightly for a more comfortable position.

Jeff gazed out through the windshield at the remains of the Barton barn, a skeleton of the majestic structure it had once been. The East side had collapsed completely, and the remaining walls had been eaten away by the weather, the remaining planks still branding their scars from the fire all those years ago. Various wild animals had made their homes within, and the entirety of the barn was covered in fireweed and ivy as nature sought to recolonize what had once belonged to it.

Jeff snorted. He had been fairly young when Ted Barton had gone mad, kidnapping and killing children, hiding in his farm just outside town where no one would have suspected him. It was always the quiet ones that turned out to be the craziest, and it was a wonder how no one had suspected him sooner. Luckily for all of them, Ted's reign of terror had only lasted a week before he burned his farm down along with himself and the corpses of three children.

Back then, Jeff had only been a member of the council for a few years, and it was a surprise to all that he was voted in as Head of the Council when his predecessor had failed to deal with the situation quicker. No one understood how it happened, how young councilman Jeffrey Dean could quickly gain such popularity, but the town had been too busy dealing with the tragedy to really make a big deal out of it.

Jeff, though, knew exactly why he had become Head of Lensfield's town council.

It was, after all, part of the deal.

Don Gibson snorted again and sat up straight in his seat, quickly brushing his hat back and looking about the car as if perplexed by his being there in the first place. When his eyes caught sight of Jeff, he smiled and relaxed, exhaling forcefully and wiping his brow.

"Can't crank down the windows just a bit?" the Sheriff asked.

"No," Jeff replied, still staring at the barn.

"Smells like something crawled in here and died," Don pointed out.

"We have your flatulence to thank for that, Sheriff."

Don looked at Jeff for a second before looking out at the barn as well. "Still not here?" he asked.

"The man takes his time," Jeff grumbled. "Besides, we're the ones who want to talk to him, and not the other way around."

Don scoffed and folded his hands over the massive belly he had let grow over the years. "Bad news, if you ask me," he said. "The town's rounding up for more protests today because of that freak and his carnival. We should have him arrested and sent them on their way."

Jeff looked at Don with disgust. "Nobody's asking you, Don," he shot, "and if I remember correctly, we both had a little bit to benefit because of that *freak*. Let the town deal with their urban legends any way they want."

Don frowned in frustration. "I bet when they find out their urban legends are more real than they know, they'll do the kicking themselves."

Jeff lashed out and grabbed the Sheriff by the collar, pulling him close enough that their noses almost touched. "You listen to me, you overgrown pile of shit," Jeff hissed. "The only reason you have a star on your chest is because of my good graces. God knows you didn't actually earn your way up, so I'd pay better attention at which direction I'm throwing threats if I were you."

"I am paying attention," Don replied, angrily. "I think you're the one who's forgetting. You struck the deal with the devil, not me. The way I see it, you're the one who's in over his head." Don grabbed Jeff's hands and yanked them away. "And the next time you touch me, I'll have you arrested for assaulting an officer."

Jeff stared at the Sheriff, his cheeks flushed in anger, and then smiled. The portly idiot had obviously gotten a little too comfortable in his position, a position Jeff had put him in, and was already dealing the wrong cards. Don Gibson's time would come, Jeff knew this for a fact, and when it did, he would be there to piss all over his grave.

But for now, he needed the Sheriff.

"Your girlfriend is here, Mr. Morgan," the Sheriff said.

Jeff looked to his left and found Ebenezer Cage leaning against one side of the barn, his suit and top hat as black as night, swinging his cane around in lazy circles. He was watching them from the shadows and smiling, and it made Jeff shudder. He stepped out of his car, thought of telling the Sheriff to stay put and decided against it, then walked to where Ebenezer waited.

"A fine day, gentlemen," Ebenezer welcomed them, stabbing the end of his cane into the earth between his feet. Jeff half-expected the ground to crack open and the flames of hell to leap out at them, and was filled with a mix of relief and disappointment when nothing happened. To him, Ebenezer was the embodiment of all that was wrong with the world, maybe even the devil himself, and he put nothing past the man after what he had seen him do ten years ago.

"Mr. Cage," Jeff greeted.

Ebenezer clucked his tongue and shook his head slowly, maintaining his devilish grin. "Ebenezer, please. I have come to a conclusion I am most comfortable with, that we would be past all these formalities."

"Ebenezer," Don Gibson said, coming up right behind Jeff.

Ebenezer looked over at the Sheriff and cocked his head to one side. "You, on the other hand, can count yourself unlucky and maintain the title before my last name."

"What?" Don frowned in confusion, looking from Jeff to Ebenezer, then back again.

"Indeed," Ebenezer said with a hint of disgust in his tone. He turned his attention back to Jeff. "Now, I do believe you have requested a rendezvous pertaining to our previous agreement, have you not?"

"I have," Jeff replied, unsure as whether to smile or not. He enjoyed seeing the Sheriff ridiculed, even if Don didn't understand what was happening.

"Pray, do tell, are you not satisfied with your current employment?" Ebenezer asked. "Is there more that your heart desires?"

"There is always more," Jeff finally smiled.

Ebenezer chuckled, and from within the darkness of his eyes, a red glow flashed and disappeared quickly. "A man after my own heart, if I had one."

"To maintain my position, I need to keep Lensfield growing," Jeff explained. "New projects, new jobs, happy people."

"I would say your efforts have proven quite fruitful in recent years," Ebenezer said, leaning in on his cane. Jeff marveled at how much taller the man seemed to grow with every word he said. "The college is quite the tourist trap. I would be envious of the acreage it occupies if I did not lead a nomadic life myself."

"Unfortunately, the college isn't enough anymore," Jeff hurried on. "We need to attract business, and currently, our neighbors are beating us at that. I need to even the odds."

Ebenezer leaned back and squinted at Jeff, his smile faltering for a second before returning. "Your neighbors?"

"Specifically, Melington," Jeff nodded. "Chairman Daniel Cole has been able to round up quite a lot of interest in the town recently, and people are flocking there by the hundreds. We're losing ground against them, and it's not good for my image."

Ebenezer's face seemed to darken at the mention of the town, and he inhaled deeply before asking his next question. "Melington?"

Jeff nodded. "I need you to work your magic again," he said. "I need a new deal, anything you want. I need to switch interest to Lensfield instead."

Ebenezer looked at Jeff for a few seconds before turning to the Sheriff. "And what do you think, Sheriff Gibson."

"Whatever the Chairman wants," Don replied.

"I am quite impressed at your ability to attach strings to your puppet, Chairman," Ebenezer said, turning his attention back to Jeff. "However, I am afraid I cannot help in that respect."

"What do you mean, you can't help?" Jeff asked.

"There are rules," Ebenezer said. "Ones that cannot be broken."

"What rules?"

Ebenezer tapped his long fingers against his cane. "Such things cannot be explained. However, rest assured, if there were a way, I would not have hesitated. I have quite enjoyed our arrangements so far."

Jeff felt his anger begin to stir and tried his best to control his temper. "Arrangements which I can change if we don't reach an agreement right now."

"Actually," Ebenezer said, raising a long finger and waving it in the air. "That is not up to you or me. I have upheld my side of the bargain, as must you. Changing our arrangement would neither benefit you nor Lensfield, I assure you."

"I don't like being threatened, Mr. Cage," Jeff replied, and from the corner of his eye, he saw Don take a few steps forward and ready himself for a confrontation. He could see Ebenezer notice as well, and the tall man smiled at the gesture. Jeff knew that Don was not as threatening as the man probably believed he was, and Ebenezer was definitely unfazed by him.

"Ah, the formalities," Ebenezer chuckled. "It is quite humorous how a simple disagreement can lead to a change of heart in a matter of seconds. Please, tell your dog to settle down, if he knows what's best for him."

Don took another step forward, his face red, and his eyes shooting daggers at the tall man. "Say that again, and I'll shoot you right here, right now."

"Of course, Sheriff," Ebenezer said, his grin widening. "Then again, how that eventually plays out would be quite the entertainment."

Jeff held the Sheriff's arm and pulled him back. "Your final word, Mr. Cage," Jeff said firmly.

"No," Ebenezer replied. "There are rules."

"Then I expect you to round up your traveling caravan tonight and be out of Gambler's Park by tomorrow morning," Jeff said. "This is not a request."

"You would break our agreement?" Ebenezer asked, cocking his head and raising an eyebrow in amusement.

"As far as I'm concerned, Mr. Cage, you're the one breaking it," Jeff replied. "If you're not out by the morning, I'll have the Sheriff arrest you."

Jeff turned around and pulled the Sheriff along with him, walking quickly back to his car. He could feel Ebenezer's eyes boring into his back, and he smiled, proud that he had finally stood up to the man and shown him who was in charge.

Ebenezer watched the Chairman and Sheriff walk away, and as he stepped back into the shadows, began to chuckle.

***

Jack placed the coffee mug on the coaster in front of Faith and sat down at the opposite side of the kitchen table with his own. His body was numb, and he would have given anything for a few more hours of uninterrupted sleep. Ever since coming home the night before, he was on constant alert. Even after they had gone to bed, he had slept with one eye open, listening to her breathing, quick to react when she woke up screaming, trying as best as he could to comfort her.

In the end, neither of them had really gotten any proper sleep, and he was lucky that they both didn't have to go to work today. From the way Faith looked, hair disheveled, eyes red and puffed, he doubted she was in any condition to do anything more than lay back and relax.

Jack sipped from his coffee and then set his mug down carefully, his eyes watching Faith as she just stared into the rising steam from her own drink. She looked at him and sighed.

"Stop that," she whispered.

Jack lowered his gaze to his hands as he clasped them together and rolled his fingers over one another. The hands of the clock above their head were loud in the dreadfully silent kitchen, and with every ticking of a second that passed, Jack felt more and more anxious. He hadn't wanted to push last night, but the truth was, this was the second time he had to comfort his screaming girlfriend, and he needed to know exactly what was happening if he wanted to help. Besides, the mention of Faith's dead sister was not something he could easily let slide.

"Stop that, please," Faith whispered again, running a hand across her face and yawning into the palm.

"I didn't do anything," Jack protested.

"You're thinking," Faith murmured. "I can hear the gears inside your head turning."

"Do you blame me?" Jack asked.

Faith shook her head, looking at him through tired eyes. "It's just annoying."

"Do you want to talk about it?" Jack asked.

Faith shook her head slowly, and finally picked up her mug of coffee and drank. She winced and set it back down. "No sugar?"

"Thought you might want it strong, since you hardly got any sleep last night."

Faith grunted, closed her eyes, and took another sip. Jack smiled a little when she shuddered, and then leaned in to hold her hand. She barely noticed his touch, and only when he began massaging her hand with his thumb did she look down at it and then up at him with a soft smile. She held his hand firmly in her own, held it up to her lips, and kissed it.

"I'm sorry," she said.

"You shouldn't be," Jack replied. "Besides, I'm the one who's sorry."

Faith frowned. "What for?"

"For going to the carnival."

"I was being ridiculous," Faith admitted, although deep down, his words did warm her. She still felt uneasy about the whole ordeal.

"No, you weren't," Jack countered. "I should have been a little more empathic. I knew it bothered you and I went anyway."

Faith smiled again. "What were you going to do? Tell the boys no?"

"In retrospect, they should have known better," Jack said.

Faith raised a questioning eyebrow to him.

"I never forgot, Faith," Jack said. "Not really. The whole Barton incident isn't a distant memory. I still dream about it every now and then."

Faith nodded. "I know," she muttered. "But can we not talk about dreams right now?"

"I hate feeling helpless, that's all," Jack said. "I don't understand what happened to even begin to find a way to fix it."

Faith took another sip from her coffee, slowly getting used to the bitterness of it. "It's probably just an overworked mind, that's all," she said, her tone far from convincing. "I was just imagining things."

"Lily?"

The mention of her sister's name made Faith shudder, and she quickly wrapped her arms around herself and dropped her eyes to the floor.

"Faith, please," Jack pushed. "Were you thinking of Lily?"

"It's that damn carnival," Faith spat, her sudden anger surprising her. "It just brought up memories, and for some reason, I'm seeing her everywhere."

"The car?"

Faith nodded. "And the library. I swear, Jack, I'm too scared to even walk into the bathroom without leaving the door open. It's like she's everywhere."

Jack leaned back and ruffled in his chair. He had expected as much, especially with Faith's constant screaming of the girl's name, last night and during her nightmares. Jack wondered how similar Faith's bad dreams were to his own, whether she remembered everything as clearly as he did or not. He wondered if she could see the eyes.

He held her hand again. "She can't hurt you, you know that, right?"

Faith shook her head slowly. "No, I don't," she whispered. "It's too real. Far too real."

"You said it yourself, it's just your imagination playing tricks on you."

"I feel like it's more than that," Faith said, a shiver rushing through her again. "It's like she's come back for me. Her ghost's come back from the dead to haunt me." Faith felt tears well up in her eyes. "And I'm not so sure that I don't deserve it."

"Don't say that," Jack tried to comfort her.

"I can't," Faith stammered, tears rolling down her cheeks and her lower lip trembling. "This was my fault."

She pulled her hand away and began to cry, covering her face. Jack quickly got up and knelt down in front of her, grabbing both of her hands and holding them in his.

"You couldn't stop it," Jack said. "She was already dead, Faith. You didn't kill her."

"I did!" Faith gasped. "I killed my little sister!"

Jack pulled her to him and hugged her tight, his inability to comfort her only frustrating him more. "Barton killed her. He killed all of them. This isn't on you."

"It is, Jack, it is!"

"Faith, stop."

"I wished it!" she yelled, pulling away from him and standing up suddenly, rushing to the sink. "He did this to her because I wished it." Faith leaned against the sink and gasped for air, her head low as she felt her stomach turn. She gagged, her tears flowing freely now, he entire body shaking.

"What?" Jack stood up and looked at her, frowning.

Faith sniffed loudly and inhaled, trying to calm herself, her eyes stinging with tears. She took a few more breaths, her hands clenching the edge of the kitchen counter tight.

"Faith?"

"I wanted attention," Faith said, her voice low. "Lily was sick, and my parents were all over her. I felt left out. I felt like they didn't even care whether or not I existed. I was scared and confused, and no one seemed to notice. I wanted their attention." She turned around and looked at Jack through bloodshot eyes. She had stopped crying, but her body still shook as she spoke. "In the carnival, when the Tall Man asked me what I wanted most, I told him I wanted my parents to notice me again."

Jack felt the world around him begin to spin. He remembered the first night they had gone to the carnival, when their parents had finally given in and allowed them to go on their own. He remembered Ebenezer towering over them with his top hat and twirling cane, holding out his candy and wishing them a wonderful experience. He remembered how the man's eyes had bored into his, the chill he had felt from that look, the uneasiness that had followed. Everywhere they went, the man was there, watching, smiling, waving. Always from the shadows.

The Tall Man, Jack thought. *We called him the Tall Man.*

Ebenezer had scared the hell out of him, and Jack never forgot those eyes. They never went back to the carnival after that night. The kidnapping of Faith's sister and the other two children had followed the next day, and the entire town had been in uproar. Everyone blamed the carnival, and they had every right to. It had seemed like too much of a coincidence to believe otherwise.

Jack remembered the only other time he had met Ebenezer after that. At Gambler's Bridge. When the Tall Man had told him about Barton and the children and the farm.

And the eyes. Those red, flaming eyes. The same eyes he had seen in the fire, when he had realized just how sinister the carnival really was.

Lensfield never forgot Ted Barton, and Jack never forgot Ebenezer Cage. He hadn't told Faith, but it was the main reason why he had joined Danny and Michael in the first place. A part of him wanted to see Ebenezer again, to prove to himself that he wasn't crazy, that what he had seen ten years ago was not a figment of his imagination but an actual projection of the evil that lurked across Gambler's Bridge.

"Why haven't you told me this before?' Jack asked, finally finding his voice.

Faith shrugged and sniffed, her eyes downcast. "I blocked it, I guess. I never really believed it. I didn't want to believe it."

"We've talked about the carnival before, Faith," Jack shot at her. "You never thought to bring this up?"

"And what would it have changed?" Faith shot back, looking up furiously. "No one believed us when we told them about the fire. They thought we were crazy, Jack!"

"I would have believed you!" Jack shouted. "Me! Just me! That's all that matters, remember? For years, I thought that I was the only one who knew there was some connection between the carnival and what happened at the farm. You let me go about doubting my own sanity, and now you tell me about Lily?"

"I never called you crazy or doubted your story," Faith said. "I always told you I believed you."

"Because you actually *knew* there was something to it!"

"I saw those eyes in the fire, too!" Faith began to cry again.

"And you knew why they were there!" Jack fired. "You knew, and you never told me!"

"I'm sorry, okay?" Faith shouted, crying harder. "Talking about it would have made it real!"

Jack threw his hands up in the air, "You're unbelievable, you know that?" he scoffed. "You let me go back there, knowing well that I was right about the carnival."

"I told you not to go."

"You knew about Ebenezer, and you let me go anyway."

"I told you not to–"

"You *knew*!" Jack bellowed, and the rage in his voice made her flinch.

Jack stared at her for a few seconds before shaking his head and storming out of the kitchen. "I've got to get out of here."

"Where are you going?" Faith followed, her voice shaking. She picked up the pace when she saw him grab his coat and make for the front door. "Jack? Jack! Don't leave me alone!"

Jack didn't answer, didn't even look back at her, and she watched in dismay as he opened the door, stepped out and slammed it closed behind him.

Chapter 8

Danny Bufano sat back in his chair, pulled off his glasses, and rubbed his eyes with the heel of both hands. For the past few hours, he had been glued to the computer screen, unaware of the time and only now feeling the strain caused by the continuous stress. He took in a deep breath, and scrolled up and down the page he was on aimlessly.

He needed to get out more, but with only six days left before the carnival picked up and disappeared again, he knew he couldn't do that.

Danny looked about the small office space of the Lensfield Times. Scarcely furnished and a stark difference from his own workplace, he was alone except for the intern who had graciously allowed him access to the logs. Danny knew he was lucky to even find anyone in the office on a Sunday, and he wondered if he would cause the pretty redhead any problems just by being here. Then again, she had been a little too eager to please a reporter from New York, and Danny knew how to capitalize on his status.

He saw her standing by the copy machine, watching him intently, and he smiled and waved at her. She quickly waved back and returned to her own work, and Danny couldn't help but smile at her uneasiness. It wasn't every day that he was the focus of attention, and he felt like he could really get used to it.

He returned to the page in front of him and continued reading. He had compiled a hefty amount of history and information in regards to the carnival and Lensfield in general. Every time he came across something related to what he was looking for, he instantly printed the page out and slipped it into the manila folder by his side. Over the years, he had learned to quickly categorize and file everything he heard and saw into files inside his head, but experience had taught him that it was always useful to have the sources handy.

He leaned onto the palm of his hand as his eyes skimmed through the current article he was reading. He had been able to find his way all the way back to the early fifties, when the first signs of a carnival coming to town had been just a few caravans and tents with one or two attractions. There wasn't much there, and the old pictures seemed to portray a much darker and sinister venue of entertainment. Then again, he doubted there was much reason for the carnival to be any more attractive, After all, Lensfield barely had a few hundred people back then.

'Carnival Comes to Lensfield' the title boasted, but the grim faces of the people in the photo barely reflected the jovial sentiment.

Ebenezer definitely commercialized it when he took over, he thought to himself.

Danny clicked on the print icon and immediately opened the next file. This one dated back to 1946, just after the Second World War. The picture showed a burnt carousel surrounded by the police and a few onlookers, with the title 'Man Dies of Electric Fire'. Danny squinted as he tried to make out the faces, hoping to stumble across anyone familiar, but the picture was too hazy. He cursed under his breath, contemplated whether or not to print the article, unsure of its worth in the midst of the rest of his research. He sat back and pulled the freshly printed sheet from the tray, and as he slid it into the manila file with the rest of the slowly growing stack, his eye caught something in the picture.

Danny frowned, wondering if maybe he was just seeing things, and brought the freshly printed page up to his line of vision. He scanned the darker areas of the photo, his eyes searching the shadows cast between the tents of the old carnival, and when he found what he was looking for, his mouth dropped.

He looked back at the computer screen and the article he had almost ignored, and quickly clicked on the print icon. Before it had completely slid out onto the print tray, he snatched it, stuck it into his folder, and raced for the door.

He needed to find the others.

***

Amanda watched Michael sleep.

The light coming in through the drapes threw lines across his body as his shoulders rose and fell with his gentle breathing. From across the room, her legs curled under her with her coffee in her hands, she thought back to what he had told her the night before.

The mystery that hung like a dark shroud over the carnival was beginning to annoy her, and a part of her envied the bond Amanda's friends shared as a result of the tragedy ten years ago. She knew it was a horrible thought, that no person in his or her right mind could possibly wish that kind of horror upon him or herself. Still, she couldn't help but feel left out, and for some strange reason she wished she had actually been at the farm with the rest of them. Maybe she could finally understand what their obsession with the carnival was really all about.

Faith had told her stories, of course. Growing up, the two women had been inseparable, but Amanda found most of what her friend said hard to believe. That, and of course her parents' explanations of post-traumatic stress disorder, helped shape Amanda's true opinions of what was going through Faith's mind.

It was all in her head, Amanda had constantly told herself. *Whatever it was she had seen, it had all been her imagination.*

Of course, she had tried hard not to raise the subject around Faith or Jack, had never voiced her opinions to either of them, feeling she owed it to her friends to keep that kind of thinking to herself. Yet, Michael and Danny's return to Lensfield threw a wrench into what she had spent years telling herself was the truth. Now, watching Michael sleep and replaying his words in her head, she began to wonder if she had judged them all wrong.

Why couldn't Philip have come back? Then there would be two of us.

Michael grunted and turned around slowly, stretching his arms over his head as he readjusted his position on the couch. His eyes fluttered open, and she could see how he tried to make out where he was before finally recognizing his surroundings. When he looked over in her direction, she smiled at him.

"That's not creepy at all," Michael said, his voice still hoarse and his words heavy.

"Good morning, sunshine," Amanda countered.

Michael grunted again and coughed, pushing himself up onto one elbow and rubbing his eyes. "At least tell me you made one of those for me," he said, gesturing to the mug in her hands.

"Best drunk hot," she shook her head.

"With the headache I'm having, anything would be fine," Michael mumbled as he pushed up further to a sitting position and proceeded to massage his temples. "What time is it anyway?"

"A bit past twelve," Amanda replied.

"Shouldn't you be at work?"

"Told Huck I'd be late," she smiled. "Besides, who was going to stick around and wait for you to wake up?"

"Yeah, that was thoughtful," Michael scoffed. "Open your eyes to find someone staring at you from the shadows across the room. Couldn't think of a better way to greet the day."

Amanda pouted, feigning hurt. "Now you're just being rude," she joked.

"Get me some damn coffee," Michael grinned.

Amanda laughed, stood up, and crossed the room, placing her own cup in front of him. "I'll make two more," she said. "You drink this for the headache."

"Thanks," Michael said, and as she turned around, he grabbed her hand. "And thanks for letting me crash here."

Amanda felt the heat rise to her cheeks. "Of course."

She squeezed his hand, and then hurried out and toward the kitchen, a light skip in her step as she moved. Her emotions were running haywire through her, and despite knowing that somewhere far away, Michael had another woman and a son waiting for him, she couldn't help herself. A part of her was certain that once the whole carnival issue was over, Michael would be back on his bike and driving home to his girlfriend and son. She wasn't going to deceive herself into thinking that he would stay for her, that he would forget about the family he left behind and start fresh. Besides, she couldn't live with herself if he did. Still, being around him made her feel good, and she was going to capitalize on it as much as she could before she said her goodbyes and watched him leave again.

She heard the sound of his cellphone ring as she poured two fresh cups of coffee. She couldn't make out what he was saying, but when she walked back into the living room, he had his phone balanced between his shoulder and ear and was pulling on his jacket.

"What's wrong?" she frowned, gently placing the mugs down as he hung up and slid his phone into his back pocket.

"That was Danny," Michael said. "He says to meet him at the bookstore."

"Now?"

Michael shrugged. "He sounded pretty worked up." Michael smiled at the look of obvious disappointment on her face. "Tell me, Brians, ever been on a Hog before?"

***

Faith shook like a leaf as she stood in Gambler's Park and stared up at the sign above the carnival's entrance. The autumn winds had never bothered her before, and despite wearing her windbreaker, it did little to stop the chill that scurried up and down her spine and spread throughout her body. The park was filled with the gentle laughter of children mixed with the eerie sounds of carnival music permeating from behind the closed gates in front of her.

Faith looked down at the ticket booth where a couple stood merrily and chatted, waiting for the woman inside to hand them their tickets before they trickled away. Faith watched them leave, the excitement on their faces both endearing and frightening. She wondered how they would feel if they knew what horrors lie behind those closed doors.

Or maybe there's nothing there, a voice inside her head chirped. *Maybe you're just seeing things again, like at the farm.*

Faith shook her head quickly, pushing the voice back into the dark corner of her mind from whence it had come. She was not imagining anything. Everything she had experienced was real. The fire had been real. Those eyes were real.

Lily was real.

Faith made her way towards the ticket booth, her eyes downcast. She hadn't been able to stay in the apartment alone. Overwhelmed by guilt and unable to come to terms with the fact that she had probably driven a large wedge into her relationship with Jack, she had quickly made up her mind to leave. She needed to be out in the open, amongst people, where Lily wouldn't dare come for her. Or at least Faith hoped she wouldn't.

Why she had come to the carnival, though, was completely beyond her. She had left the apartment without a specific goal in mind, allowing her legs to carry her through the quiet streets of Lensfield, aimlessly turning left and right, and barely paying attention to her whereabouts. It was only when she was at Gambler's Park did she come to realize her bearings, and in her half-dazed state she had looked up to see the carnival.

It scared her to think that maybe the place had called her, had brought her here on purpose to finish what it had started all those years ago. She was certain that once inside, Lily would reappear and finally catch her, somewhere in the shadows and away from the eyes of any witnesses. She was sure that the carnival would find a way to swallow her in and never let her leave.

At the ticket booth, she stole a glance through the closed gates at the carnival's interior. With the afternoon sun above her head, it was hard to believe that anything remotely bad, let alone sinisterly evil, could be lurking about inside. She didn't let it delude her, though, and she turned her attention to the woman behind the glass.

"One ticket, please," she found herself saying.

The woman gazed at her for a moment, sizing her up before finally shrugging and pulling a ticket out from the drawer of her desk. She pushed it towards Faith and mumbled, "That's fifteen dollars, honey."

Faith paid her and held the ticket firmly in both hands, briefly looking towards the carnival gates.

"Doesn't open for a few more hours," the woman said.

"Actually, I wasn't thinking of going in," Faith replied.

The woman frowned and leaned against her desk. "Then why'd you buy a ticket?" she asked.

"Because she has questions," a voice said from behind Faith, and for a second she could feel the temperature around her drop tremendously. "She believes she can find the answers here."

Faith felt her heart jump into overdrive, and her breath caught in her chest.

When a hand rested on her shoulder, long fingers curling over her joint and clasping onto her tightly, goose bumps broke out across her arms and the blood in her veins froze.

"Faith Stone," Ebenezer hissed, his words followed by a hearty chuckle that sounded like knives in her ears. "Oh, how I have missed you."

Chapter 9

The chimes above the door of the bookstore rang as Michael and Amanda shuffled in. Despite the cloudless skies and the sun beating down on them, the wind had begun to pick up and gave the afternoon a slight chill neither of them had anticipated. Amanda rubbed her hands together in an attempt to stay warm as she followed Michael inside, wishing she had worn more than just a simple t-shirt before leaving the house.

Danny looked up from a makeshift table in the center of the store's front vestibule, the small shelves that had formed parallel aisles before, now pushed to a side to make for more space. He smiled and waved them over, returning his attention to the printed articles, notes, and reports that covered the tabletop. Amanda frowned as her eyes vaguely caught the titles of a few of the articles, the name 'Ebenezer's Carnival' standing out like a sore thumb.

"Jack's in the back trying to reach Faith," Danny explained and gestured to the chairs next to the table.

Amanda sat down heavily, rubbing her hands together even faster and balling up in her seat. It had been a while since she had visited the bookstore, and she made a mental note to remind Jack that winter was just around the corner and he would have to turn up the heat in here. She watched Michael walk up to the table, a deep frown on his face as he shuffled through some of the sheets.

"What is all this?" he asked.

"I'll get to that in a bit," Danny said quickly, a hint of excitement in his voice. "I just want to make sure everyone's here when I do."

Michael turned one sheet around and began skimming the contents of the article. "Are these all about the carnival?"

Danny nodded and grinned. "Years of research," he said.

"I thought you were working on an article," Michael looked at him in confusion. "This seems like you're working up a case."

"Well, I haven't really been all too honest about my intentions," Danny said, "but yeah, you're not too far off."

Michael raised his eyebrows as his eyes darted back and forth across the tapestry of information laid out before him. "This is intense, man."

"Still going to voice mail." Jack walked in from the back, shaking his head in frustration as he slid his phone into his pocket and nodded at Michael and Amanda.

"Did you leave her a message?" Danny asked, clearly disappointed. "This is kinda important."

"Yeah," Jack sighed and pulled up a chair, turning it around so that when he sat, his arms were resting on the back. "We had a bit of an argument today, so she's probably just avoiding me."

"What happened?" Amanda asked.

Jack waved and shook his head. "Relationship crap," he lied. "I'll try again in a bit."

Danny sighed and looked down at his display, then shrugged. "Well, we might as well start, and if you do reach her, then you're going to have to bring her up to speed with all this."

Jack leaned over and gazed at the reports in front of him. "What *is* all this?"

"This, my friends, is everything I could gather on Ebenezer's Carnival," Danny said with a smile, spreading his arms out dramatically.

The others looked at him for a few seconds before Amanda waved to him to continue.

"We all remember the last time Ebenezer was in town," Danny began, looking at each of his friends in turn and lingering when his eyes met Jack's. "The kidnappings, the killings, and of course, the fire."

He stopped, and Amanda threw her hands up in exasperation. "Seriously, enough with the dramatic pauses. Will you just spill?"

"Fine, fine," Danny said quickly, frowning at her. "Ever since my family left, what happened here ten years ago has always haunted me, and I'm assuming it's haunted each and every one of you as well. Something like that can't easily be forgotten. But I tried. I really did. It was one of the reasons why I never came back and why I just kind of lost touch with you all. I didn't want to remember any of it. I wanted to shut it all out."

Danny looked down at his hands as he rested them on the tabletop, and Jack could see his lids flutter. A part of him wanted to speak up and tell him that he understood, but unlike Danny, Jack didn't have the luxury of escape. For the past ten years, he had had to drive past the relics of the Barton farm almost every day and relive the past. Every night, the nightmares were there, taunting him, reminding him, taking away any chance of reprieve.

"Three years ago, a package arrived at my office," Danny said, closing his eyes for the briefest of moments before looking up at his friends. Gone was the excitement, replaced by a dead seriousness that made Jack shiver. "Inside the package were reports, photographs, and hand-written notes, all about Ebenezer's Carnival."

Danny pointed at a few pages to his right that were neatly stacked side by side, as if separate from the rest of the sheets on the table. Michael reached out and began to sift through them.

"Someone's been following that carnival for a good while," Danny continued, "and it all starts here, at Lensfield. The oldest report in there is about the Barton fire, and there are even pictures of us mixed in between, with special interest on you, Jack."

Jack frowned in confusion, stood up and walked to where Michael was standing. The other man pulled out a few photographs and handed them to him. Jack's eyes widened as he looked at his fifteen-year-old self. Some of the pictures were wide shots, obviously taken from a distance, while others had him staring right into the camera and smiling. One picture was taken of him standing at Gambler's Bridge, his back to the camera, his hands pointing away. Although he was alone in the picture, it looked as if he were talking to someone; Jack knew exactly who that someone was.

"The rest of the stuff in there is intense, pictures and reports of the carnival in other towns across the nation. The package was well-organized, sorted by location and date, and whoever put it together really went to great lengths to get his information right."

Amanda was standing now as well, looking over Michael's shoulder at what

Danny was referring to. "Who did all this?" she asked, looking at Danny with genuine concern in her eyes. There had been a picture of her with her brother outside the cafeteria that would one day be theirs.

Danny shrugged and shook his head. "I never found out," he replied. "All I know is that the man or woman who put this together was meticulous, and for some reason couldn't continue what he or she was doing. I felt like it was my responsibility to carry the torch and finish the job."

"These are terrible," Jack whispered, standing a few feet away from the table with a file in his hand, sifting through the pictures and articles within.

Danny sighed and sat down. "You remember that feeling you had when we were kids, Jack?" he asked. "When we were at the carnival and you said that something didn't feel right?" Jack nodded. "Well, something really isn't right with Ebenezer's Carnival."

"This is like reading through a murder case," Michael mumbled. Amanda gasped when he turned a page and the photograph of a mutilated girl flashed in front of their eyes.

"Death, chaos, mayhem," Danny said. "That's what happens in every single town that carnival passes through. It's like a moving carriage of pestilence, carrying its disease with it wherever it goes, spreading it to the local populace. Loved ones kill each other, freak accidents happen, sane and respectable people go mad–"

"And pig farmers become killers," Jack continued, losing the file in his hands and looking at Danny.

Danny slipped his glasses off and proceeded to clean them with the hem of his shirt, staring intently at what he was doing as if it required his full attention.

"What does it all mean, though?" Amanda broke the sudden silence. "Can't you take this to the police?"

Before Danny could answer, Michael chimed in, "This isn't evidence. All of this is just speculation." He looked at Danny. "That's why he's here. That's why he wanted to go to the carnival. He's trying to find evidence."

"Initially, yes, that was the idea," Danny said, "until I came across something at the Lensfield Times." He reached out and plucked two sheets of paper from the midst of the others and held them out to Michael. "Ebenezer's Carnival first came to Lensfield in 1956, but at that time it was just a moving caravan of hippies with a few attractions and rides. Nothing as great as what we see today. It wasn't even called Ebenezer's then."

"What am I looking at, man?" Michael asked.

"The first page is an article about a man named Gilliard Haselton," Danny explained. "He owned a small carousel, barely three meters in diameter, which he towed around the state and earned a meager living off, according to the article. A nomad, nobody knows where he came from, but very popular with the kids. One night, for some strange reason, Gilliard operates his carousel and dies in an electrical fire."

"That's terrible," Amanda whispered as Michael handed her the article.

"It is," Danny says. "The second article is about the carnival's first appearance in Lensfield, led by a woman named Sara Deer. It was a small attraction, like I said, and although it wasn't very well known, it became very famous when it came to Lensfield."

"Why?" Jack asked.

"Because three men died on the carousel when it went up in flames," Danny replied. "Electrical malfunction."

Amanda took a step back from the others, as if somehow being near the articles could hurt her, and Jack stared at Danny with an open mouth of surprise. The only one who didn't seem fazed by what Danny said was Michael, who was still staring at the page in his hands.

"Danny? Am I seeing this right?" Michael asked, and it was only then that Danny realized how the other man's face had drained completely of blood.

Danny knew exactly what he was talking about, and was a bit surprised at how fast Michael had noticed. He didn't reply.

"Danny?" Michael asked again, looking up at his friend. "Tell me I'm not seeing what I think I'm seeing."

Danny opened his mouth, then closed it again. He took a deep breath and let it out slowly, and that was all the answer Michael needed. Jack looked from one man to the other in anticipation, and then reached out and snatched the second article from Michael's hands. He gazed at the picture for a few seconds, frowning and shaking his head in frustration, unable to see what his friend was talking about. Michael reached out and tapped at a dark spot between two tents.

Jack felt his heart stop.

In the shadows, hidden where no one would happen to come across it, was Gilliard Haselton's carousel. It was a striking image of the burnt carousel from the first article, resting on its side, the charred face of one of the horses hanging upside down.

"Sara Deer lost everything, and Ebenezer Cage bought the carnival for less than ten dollars," Danny continued. "Since then, it's been moving around, wreaking havoc, and growing. A real hub of entertainment."

"You think Gilliard's haunting the carnival?" Michael asked, finally sitting down while he took in everything he was hearing.

Danny shook his head. "No," he replied. "I don't. But there's definitely something wrong with that carnival."

Amanda cleared her throat and walked up behind Michael, resting a hand on his shoulder. "Was there a carousel when you guys went there last night?" she asked.

"I don't think so," Michael replied, frowning as he tried to remember.

"There wasn't," Danny said. "Ebenezer's Carnival has never had a carousel. Maybe they're trying not to bring up memories."

Jack looked back at the table and the sheets displayed on it, his eyes scanning the documents Danny had collected over the years. A part of him wanted to strangle the man for knowing so much, yet never sharing the information with any of them. He knew that most of it was just research and conspiracy theories to the naked eye, but if their experience were to be put in the middle of it all, if what happened to them were to be taken into account, it sure as hell made a lot of things clearer.

Danny stood up slowly, scratching the back of his head as he wrestled with the next thing he had to say.

"There's more, isn't there?" Amanda asked, reading the man's body language.

Danny looked at her, his lips pressed together. "I've looked at all the notes, and all the pictures," he finally said. "I've read every report, checked every victim's background, and made every possible connection I could. There's no link between them, no history that ties them together, nothing. Only one thing stands out, and it makes absolutely no sense."

Jack felt a chill race through him. He had a feeling that he might just know what Danny was talking about. In front of him, the picture of a younger Jack Heldon standing on Gambler's Bridge stuck out from between the rest of the research lying around it.

"They've all talked to Ebenezer Cage," Jack said.

Danny's head shot up, a look of confusion plastered on his face. He frowned, unable to comprehend how his friend could have known, and nodded.

"I need to call Faith," Jack said, and raced into the back.

**

Jack pulled up in front of his apartment building with a screech and jumped out of his car. Forgetting to close the car door behind him, he raced towards the double glass doors and slammed through, cursing as he ran. He stopped at the elevators, clicked on the button several times, and waited impatiently as the lights above the doors blinked with the elevator's descent.

He pulled his phone out and dialed Faith's number again, and when he was immediately sent to voicemail, slammed his fist against the elevator's doors and raced for the stairs. He took them by twos, his breaths coming in toiled gasps and his muscles burning with the strain. There was a deep-seated fear inside him, a feeling of impending doom, and as the light outside began to fade with the setting sun, his urgency to reach Faith only intensified.

He hadn't waited for the others to bully an explanation out of him, to ask him what he had been doing at Gambler's Bridge all those years ago. He could see the confusion in Danny's eyes and the look of worry and fear in Amanda's. The only thing that troubled him was how calm Michael had seemed, how collected his friend was in the face of everything he was hearing.

Almost as if he had heard it all before.

But that couldn't be. Jack knew Michael Cooper well, and if there was one thing he could count on, it was that Michael was terrible at keeping secrets. There was no way in hell the man could have known all this and not spilled his guts to them back at the carnival. The only thing Jack could think of was that Michael had been worried about his brother and the elder Cooper's place in all this.

Jack reached his floor and stormed through the staircase door. He raced across the landing, pulling his keys out of his pocket just as he reached his apartment door and slammed his free fist against it.

"Faith!" he called out from the hall as he sifted through the keys on his keychain. He quickly slid the right one in, unlocked the door, and burst inside.

The apartment was drenched in shadows, the blinds in the living room half-drawn, and the dim glow of orange light from outside barely providing any illumination. Jack raced through the apartment, glancing into the kitchen before making his way down the hall to the bedroom.

"Faith!" he called out, already knowing that he wouldn't find her there. The bedroom was empty, the sheets unmade, and the windows latched closed. Jack cursed under his breath and raced back into the living room, pulling his cellphone out again and dialing Faith's number. He leaned against the kitchen door, and slammed his fist hard against the frame.

"She isn't here."

Jack swirled around, dropping his phone on the floor as his eyes settled on the figure of a little girl sitting cross-legged in his favorite seat by the window. Her hair was matted to her head, and the strands fell across her face and covered it, allowing only a single eye to gaze back at him above lips curled into a smile.

Jack recognized Lily immediately.

"The Tall Man took her," Lily said, and her smile widened. The skin on her chin peeled and fell away, floating down onto her lap where her fingers curled around a large kitchen knife.

Jack felt the scream inside him stop in his throat, and the cold fear he had been feeling as he had driven all the way back from the bookstore took complete control over him, paralyzing him. He took a tentative step back, and Lily cocked her head to a side and raised a finger at him, shaking it from side to side.

"Watch your windows, watch your doors," she said, the rest of the skin on her face beginning to peel off as well, "keep your children in sight."

Lily's voice deepened, and she unfurled her legs and slid off the seat, standing stoically across the room from Jack, staring at him intently. The knife in her hand reflected the orange glow of the setting sun.

"For somewhere across the Gambler's bridge, evil lurks through the night."

Lily began to laugh, and as she did, her voice deepened further and took on a raspier tone. When she stopped, her eyes had turned a bright red and the skin of her face lay in shreds by her bare feet. The flesh beneath pulsated, and she took a step forward, raising the knife in her hand.

"Run, little boy," she said, but it wasn't Lily that was speaking anymore. Jack felt the blood in his veins freeze as he heard Ted Barton's voice escape from her lips. "I really love a good chase!"

Jack ran, and as he raced out of his apartment and down the hallway, Barton's manic laughter followed.

Chapter 10

The smell of gasoline was overwhelming.

It hit Cindy Kale the second she opened the door to her house, balancing grocery bags in both arms and fumbling with the keys as she pushed her way inside. She had already prepared a long speech for Phil that she fully intended to deliver the moment she saw him. For a man who had decided that he didn't want to go shopping with her, the least he could have done was come out to help her. She hated how he could ignore her while she had spent the past ten minutes blaring her horn for him to notice she was home.

Cindy immediately forgot her speech and dropped the grocery bags onto the floor in front of the door, trying not to gag as the stench of the gasoline filled her nostrils and went straight to her head. She swayed for a moment, then balanced herself against the door and blinked repeatedly.

"Phil!" she called out, staggering through the house as she made her way to the kitchen, worried that maybe there was a gas leak coming from the stove. "Phil!"

Maybe he's outside with the kids.

Cindy hoped that was true. She couldn't imagine her family being in the house and not noticing the smell of gas.

Or maybe they're asleep. Asphyxiated. Didn't notice and just drifted away.

The thought brought a wave of panic that washed over Cindy, and before she even made it into the kitchen, she turned and raced up the stairs to the second floor. She had left them for only a couple of hours, and she couldn't remember the last time her kids went to sleep this early on a Sunday. Usually she was forced into a shouting match just to get them into bed, let alone make sure they weren't fooling around once the lights were off.

On the second floor, a second smell mixed with that of the gasoline, an almost metallic scent that was a lot stronger. Cindy frowned as she made her way to the room her children shared, her mind throwing up red flags. She knew that smell; somewhere in the back of her mind was a memory of where she had experienced it before, back when she was a child, at her parents' farm.

When she opened the bedroom door, the smell intensified, and her eyes flew open as her gaze fell upon its source. A scream came rushing out and stopped in her throat, choking her as she felt the world around her spin dangerously, and she fell heavily against the frame of the door.

Both children lay completely still on their respective beds, covers drawn up to their waists and their arms by their sides. Their eyes stared up at the ceiling, lifeless, and the blood that had escaped from their slit throats had turned the sheets a deep crimson color. Cindy stared at her dead children for what seemed like an eternity, her mind shattering at the scene before her, the images imprinting inside her head in a place where they would always return to haunt her. She raced towards them, shaking their lifeless bodies as she cried out their names, almost as if expecting them to wake up, as if the entire scene were an elaborate and sick prank. She gazed in horror at her blood stained hands, the realization slowly sinking in, and she staggered backwards until she slammed against the wall. She clawed at her throat as she tried to breathe, and the arteries in her temples were pounding away hard enough to burst.

A hand fell on her shoulder, and Cindy finally found the strength to scream. Her voice was shrill in the otherwise silent house, and she squeezed her eyes closed as a second hand grabbed her and pulled her out of the room. She kicked and screamed, and even with her eyes closed, she could still see her dead children on their beds, their lifeless eyes glazed over. She was going mad, she knew it, and there was nothing she could do to stop it.

"Cindy, honey, stop!"

Cindy's eyes flew open and she stared into her husband's eyes. Phil looked terrible, his hair disheveled and his eyes sunken, and she threw her arms around him as she shook uncontrollably. "Phil!" she cried out in his shoulder. "They're ... they're both ... how ... I can't–"

"Shh," Phil soothed, holding her tight and running his hand through her hair, pulling her further away from the room. "I know, honey, I know."

Cindy barely registered his words, crying hysterically as she shook in his arms, her entire body numbing as she felt a darkness envelope her. She could feel herself slipping away, and as her body grew limp, Phil struggled to keep her on her feet.

"Honey, we need to get out of the house," he said. "I called the police. They're coming."

Cindy didn't reply. Her entire world had come crashing down around her the minute she opened that door. She felt Phil lift her into his arms and carry her down the stairs, and a part of her wanted to tell him to stop. She wanted him to leave her upstairs with her children, to lock her in the room with them where she could gaze into their lifeless faces and slowly lose her mind. All of a sudden, nothing seemed to matter anymore, not even the inexplicably strong smell of gasoline; all she wanted was to close her eyes and float away.

The cold air hit her like a slap to the face, and now that she was outside, away from the intoxicating fumes, she could feel her mind work again and try to reconnect with the world around her. She wanted to stop it from doing that, to tell it to just let go, because coming back meant dealing with the horrors she had just seen. And she didn't want to do that.

The images of her children flashed before her eyes as Phil set her down on the front lawn, and her entire body began to shake again. Her mind spun relentlessly, and a sudden deep and puncturing ache burnt up inside her chest. She opened her mouth and gasped for air, croaking as she began to cry again, clawing at Phil when he pulled away from her.

"The kids!" her scream came out as a hoarse cough.

"I know, honey, I know," Phil said, his voice receding as he walked away from her and back to the house.

Cindy rolled onto her side and drew her knees up to her chin, her cries mixing with hoarse screams as she wrapped herself into a fetal position. In her head, she could hear her children shouting and crying, begging for some more TV time, fighting over who got to eat the last bowl of cereal. In her head, she could see herself yelling at both of them, wishing they would just shut up, and the image only made the pain in her chest even worse.

Phil came back and sat down on the grass beside her, one hand resting on her back as he rubbed it. "It's okay, honey," he whispered. "It's over."

Cindy could barely make out the cackle of flames over her own cries of pain and loss, her mind numb to the world around her, even as the fire spread through the house.

"It's okay," Phil said. "The Tall Man told me that this would be best for us, that we would be free and happy now." The flames reflected in Phil's eyes as he descended into madness, and a smile spread on his face. "He told me it was what you wanted. He told me it would make you happy."

Cindy turned her head slowly to her husband, staring at him in horror as she began to register what he was saying.

Phil looked at her, and his smiled widened.

"And all I want to do is make you happy, Cindy."

***

Jack Heldon walked right up to the carnival ticket booth and slammed his money down. The woman behind the glass barely flinched, only stared at him, and chewed her gum slowly. She smiled when Jack tapped the cash with one finger impatiently, and then leaned in close so he could hear her whisper.

"Sweetheart, you don't need a ticket, tonight," she said as she smiled and showed her crooked and yellowing teeth. "He's already waiting for you."

Jack crumbled the money into his fist and slammed it against the glass, but the woman didn't budge. She continued smiling at him and chewing, then she blew him a kiss, and leaned back in her chair, laughing.

Jack turned and made his way to the gate.

He had made it all the way to his car before he realized that no one was following him. In his head, the laughter had continued, though, and Jack had expected at any moment to look up in the rearview mirror and find someone in the backseat with him. Lily, or Ted Barton, or someone else completely. Either way, Jack knew exactly where he needed to go, and without his cellphone to call for backup, he was going to have to do it alone.

Wherever that monster was keeping Faith, Jack fully intended to get her back.

The large, hulk of a man standing guard at the carnival entrance, stopped him and asked for his ticket. Jack looked up at him menacingly and hissed, "Let me through."

The man eyed him for a second, and then looked over to the woman at the ticket booth. When she nodded, he moved to one side and let Jack pass.

The carnival felt different tonight. The mix of laughter and carnival music had a deeper, more sinister feel to it, and Jack could sense something darker beneath the surface of the merriment and flashing lights. He knew this feeling had a lot to do with what he had learned about the carnival from Danny, and of course his run-in with a girl who had been dead for ten years. Still, there was definitely more to it than just that.

Jack felt like he was in a sort of bubble. For the briefest of instances, he could almost see a glimmer in the air around him, a brief bending of the light as if it were passing through a prism instead of just waves in the air. The sound of the carnival also seemed to alter, muffled in parts and louder in others, almost as if he were walking from one pocket of vacuum into another. He moved his jaw around in an effort to relieve the pressure behind his ear drums, feeling the familiar pop before the sounds of the carnival returned to their regular volume.

Jack pushed on through the crowds, walking in no particular direction, allowing his feet to carry him to his destination. He had no idea where he would find Ebenezer, but he had a feeling that it had to be somewhere near the back end. Probably beyond the Ferris wheel, where ten years ago, Jack had sensed the same feeling of dread he was feeling now. He felt someone watching him, and when he turned to his left and looked past the crowd at the Hall of Mirrors, a familiar face appeared and disappeared almost instantly.

Jack stopped, squinting through the blinding lights and trying to make out who was standing near the dark attraction, but no one was there. He began to walk towards it, pushing through the crowd, and apologizing when he elbowed someone a bit too roughly, and finally walked up the few steps in front of the Hall of Mirrors and went inside.

The attraction had seemed much larger from the outside in comparison to the small room Jack found himself in. The dim red light strained his eyes and made them water, pulsating, as if alive, and forcing Jack to blink repeatedly. He could barely make out the room's furnishing, a few couches here and there, large framed pictures on the wall, and a large chandelier that hung dangerously low from the ceiling.

"It's quite remarkable, isn't it?" a voice greeted, and when Jack was able to see clearly, his eyes fell on Ebenezer Cage. The man was leaning back in his chair, his legs propped up on a large desk. His top hat rested beside him and his cane was swirling between his fingers as he smiled at Jack.

"You see, it is nearly impossible to know who can and cannot walk through that door," Ebenezer explained. "It never fails to surprise me."

Jack felt his anger soar and his hands curl into tight fists. "Where is she?"

"Who?" Ebenezer asked. Jack wanted to beat the grin off his face.

"You know who," Jack spat. "Faith. Where is she?"

"Ah, the child who wanted attention," Ebenezer nodded, striking the tip of the cane down onto the floor beside him. The sound of it echoed through the room and pierced Jack's ears painfully. "We must all pay our dues, Mr. Heldon. What we desire comes at a price. I find it hard to believe that you would not appreciate that."

Jack walked up to the desk and slammed his fist down hard. "If you hurt her–"

"My dear boy, why would I hurt her?" Ebenezer frowned, shaking his head at Jack in confusion. "On the contrary, she is worth more than you can fathom."

"Where. Is. She?" Jack could feel his body shake with fury, and it took all his self-control to stop himself from reaching over the desk and strangling the man sitting across from him.

Ebenezer's eyes flashed a bright red, and his smile widened. "I strongly suggest you take a few steps back, Mr. Heldon," he said. "The courtesy I showed you back at Gambler's Bridge is not one I care to repeat, and at the moment, it would bring me much joy to wrap my hands around *your* neck and watch your life slowly slip away."

"I'm warning you, Ebenezer," Jack hissed.

"You do not warn me, boy!" Ebenezer yelled, his voice dropping to a deep baritone coated in a snake-like hiss that dug into Jack's mind and pulled at the strands of his sanity. Jack felt his head implode, and he cried out in pain as his hands flew to his temples and he staggered away from Ebenezer.

Then the pain was gone.

"You see, Mr. Heldon, our lives are intertwined, you and I," Ebenezer said, standing up and walking around the desk, his cane jumping from one hand to the other. "You are what we like to call a catalyst. Your actions are based purely on emotion, and logic is as foreign to you as the concept of time. What is to be achieved here in Lensfield can only be done with your assistance."

"What are you talking about?" Jack asked, shaking his head and trying to stop the ringing in his ear.

Ebenezer chuckled, a raspy sound that was the complete opposite of jovial. "You have a gift, boy," he said, pulling up a small table with a case on top of it. "A rare gift that is often hidden to its owner unless prompted. That is where I come in." Ebenezer looked up at Jack and smiled. "Do you play chess, Mr. Heldon?"

Jack opened his mouth to answer, and then closed it again. Ebenezer was playing with his head, stalling for one reason or another, and Jack knew that playing along would not be in his greatest benefit.

Ebenezer pulled up a chair and sat down at the table, opening the box to reveal a chess set. He gestured to the opposite chair. "Please," he invited. "It has been so long since I have played this game."

Jack looked at Ebenezer for a few seconds, trying to figure out what was going on, and when he failed to read him, grudgingly sat down. The pieces were already lined up on the board in front of him, and he kept his eyes on Ebenezer as the man moved one pawn forward.

Jack moved one of his own.

"You know, Jack," Ebenezer said, and then looked up from the board. "Will you permit me to call you Jack?"

Jack didn't reply.

"I'll take that as a confirmation of your approval," Ebenezer continued, and moved another piece. "You know, I have not always been the fortunate owner of a successful carnival. Before I bought this carnival, I was only in possession of a small carousel."

Jack only stared at the man, then moved another pawn. "Gilliard Haselton."

"Ah," Ebenezer chuckled and sat back, folding his hands on his lap. "A name I have not heard in decades."

"That was you, wasn't it?" Jack asked. "The man who burned with his carousel."

"It is incredible how similar the times are," Ebenezer replied, his tone softer, yet a hint of anger mixed in there somewhere. "Even then, violence was commonplace. You would expect that after a war as great as the one led by the Germans, people here would be more appreciative of peace and tranquility."

Ebenezer leaned forward again, and moved his knight. "Alas, that was not the case. Gilliard Haselton did indeed die in an electrical fire. However, he died, strapped to a horse on his own carousel."

Jack's hand hung in mid-air, his queen shaking in his hand. "You were killed?"

Ebenezer's eyes flashed a bright red that quickly disappeared, and his eyes bore into Jack's. "Do not worry about old tales, Jack," he said. "What happened was merely the result of a joke gone terribly wrong, although the perpetrators did meet similar fates later."

"The fire at Sara Deer's carnival," Jack muttered.

Ebenezer nodded and gestured for Jack to continue playing. "Although I must admit, that carousel had been quite spectacular. It became the blueprint for my future building endeavors."

"Your carnival doesn't have a carousel," Jack pointed out.

Ebenezer smiled, a grin that sent chills up and down Jack's spine. "Oh, but you are quite mistaken, Jack," he said softly. "I have a wonderful carousel. Only, it isn't open to the public."

Jack frowned, and Ebenezer laughed. "You see, Jack, I have come to the realization that people are obsessed with their desires. Their wants and their needs. What they *must* have. Only, they rarely think of the consequences of these desires. When those boys tied Gilliard Haselton to his carousel, they wanted him to beg. They wanted him to cry and beg to be released, and when the carousel burned, when *I* burned, I gave them what they wanted."

Ebenezer's eyes darkened, and Jack could feel the entire room around him close in on them, the air thickening and pressing down like a heavy weight on his shoulders. The red glow of the lights pulsated at a quicker pace, and Jack began to breathe faster, as if the oxygen in the room were being sucked out.

"I begged, and I screamed, and I burned," Ebenezer said, a film of black smoke covering his eyes and his voice taking on a raspy undertone. "Tied to my carousel, Jack, I burned. And ten years later, I made sure those boys burned just like me!"

Jack felt that same pressure inside his head, as if a hand had reached within and was squeezing his brain between its fingers. He felt the pressure rise until it threatened to explode, and he fell to the ground on his knees, his arms around his head in an attempt to keep it from bursting. Jack heard the scraping of chair legs against the floor, and Ebenezer's cane came into view beside him. A hand grabbed him by the nape of his neck and lifted him to his feet effortlessly.

"Let me show you my carousel, Jack," Ebenezer hissed in his ear, and with his words came a strong smell of burning flesh. "Let me show you what you came to see."

Jack cried out as the pain inside his head grew to unbearable levels, squeezing his eyes shut against it, and he suddenly felt himself being propelled forward through the darkness. He felt everything around him swish by at incredible speeds, the wind slamming against his face and suffocating him, the darkness pressing down on him from every angle. The hand around his neck never left, and a sudden burning sensation came from where it held him, as if the hand itself were on fire as it gripped him tight.

There was a sudden popping sound, like a small, distant explosion, and Jack found himself falling to the ground again, landing on his hands and knees before rolling over to his side. He waited for the pain to subside, the throbbing in his head slowly fading and the burning sensation around his neck cooling in the gush of wind around him. When he finally opened his eyes, he was outside, lying in a large field, surrounded by the familiar Connecticut maples. The sky above him was blank, devoid of stars, and the darkness around him felt like a heavy blanket of emptiness, like something out of a nightmare.

The only light he could see came from somewhere between the trees. Jack stood up slowly, looking around him for Ebenezer, and when he couldn't find the man, he made his way forward and towards the light. The foliage was dense, the branches hanging down like hands reaching for him, curling around him, threatening to lock him in their embrace. The sound of leaves crunching beneath his feet echoed through the night, and only then did he notice how silent the woods were.

The lights ahead grew brighter as Jack approached them, and when he stepped out from between the trees and into the clearing, his eyes widened in surprise.

In front of him was a large carousel, easily the size of a basketball court, spinning slowly to the eerie sound of carnival music coming out of a small caravan beside it. Horses rose and fell, lions moved back and forth, carriages flashed with green, red, and yellow colors.

And they were all occupied.

Jack stared in horror at the lifeless faces of men, women, and children, holding onto the poles of their ride and gazing blankly ahead, locked in the carousel's eternal spinning. So many that Jack could not even begin to guess their number. The young and the old, some in bell-bottoms and others in flowery dresses, all from different times and places.

And as the carousel spun, as his eyes darted back and forth between the multitudes of faces, Jack caught sight of Faith, wearing the same clothes he had left her in this morning and straddling a white and brown horse with lips drawn back in a menacing smile. A large man sat on a carriage in front of her, and she was staring fixedly at the back of his head, unmoving except for the gentle rise and fall of her horse.

Jack made for the carousel, overcome with desperation and the need to reach Faith now, right now, before Ebenezer reappeared from the darkness to stop him. He raced forward, his feet pounding against the grass, the wind blowing strong against him as if trying to push him back. Then, just a few yards away from the carousel, just as he had started to believe that he could reach Faith and they could both get out of here, a hand grabbed him by the collar of his shirt and pulled him back.

Jack felt his legs fly out from underneath him, and he fell hard to the ground, his head slamming against the earth and bright spots flashing before his eyes. It took him a few seconds to regain his composure, and when his vision finally cleared, he stared up into the face of Josh Cooper.

"The carousel is not open for the public," Josh hissed, and his eyes blazed red as he reached down and pulled Jack up. He turned Jack around, and brought him close, their faces inches apart where Jack could see the black curls of smoke in his eyes and smell the stench of rot on his breath.

"Faith," Jack croaked.

Josh cocked his head and glanced over Jack's shoulder, and he smiled. "She is quite happy, it seems," the elder Cooper said, then turned his attention back to

Jack. "Forget about her. She is no longer yours."

Jack was about to reply when Josh suddenly lifted him off his feet and slammed him against the caravan. Jack's head connected with the hard, metallic side of the mobile home, and he slumped onto the ground, the world around him darkening quickly. The last thing he registered before his eyes closed was Josh grabbing him by the ankle and dragging him up the wooden steps and into the caravan.

***

"Hey!"

Jack's eyes fluttered open.

"Hey, wake up!"

Jack squinted, wincing at the sudden sound of ringing in his head, and forced his eyes open. He rolled onto his right side and gagged, then broke into a series of coughs. From somewhere far away, the sound of carnival music filled the night, and Jack could hear the screams of joy seekers on their rides.

He looked up into the stern face of Sheriff Don Gibson.

"Where am I?" Jack asked.

"In Gambler's Park," Gibson replied, grabbing Jack by the arm and forcing him up painfully.

"Hey, watch it," Jack hissed.

Gibson turned him around and pushed him down onto a park bench, twisting one arm around his back and snapping something cold around his wrist. Jack only realized what was happening when the cuffs snapped around his other wrist as well, and Gibson pulled him back up.

"What are you doing?" Jack yelled, his head still spinning and his back screaming in pain.

"Got a complaint from Mr. Cage," Gibson said. "Apparently, you were harassing his guests and attacked him in his office."

"What?"

"You heard me," Gibson said. "You're being arrested for misdemeanor and battery."

"That's absurd!"

Gibson pushed Jack forward, leading him out of the park, and began to read him his rights.

Chapter 11

"Rise and shine!"

Jack groaned as he opened his eyes, the throbbing in his head just as bad as when he had laid himself down the night before. He pushed himself up, swinging his legs over the edge of his cot and massaging his temples, squinting across his cell at Sheriff Gibson standing on the other side of the bars.

The Sheriff was smiling, sipping at his coffee, and raising his mug in a salute. "Slept through the drinks?" he asked, chuckling.

Jack rolled his eyes and massaged the back of his head, feeling the swelling where his skull had made contact with Ebenezer's caravan from hell. He tried to stand up, swayed a bit, and stretched his legs.

"How long are you keeping me in here?" he asked the Sheriff.

"Well, you know, battery's quite an offense," Gibson replied.

"Come on, Don," Jack sighed. "You know damn well I didn't do anything."

"That's Sheriff Don, Heldon," Gibson replied. "And I really don't know anything. All I have is Ebenezer Cage's complaint against your drunken ass word."

"I wasn't drunk," Jack sighed. "We settled that last night when you tested me."

"Which makes the battery a lot worse," Gibson smiled, "since, you know, you were fully aware of what you were doing."

Jack walked up to the bars and looked Gibson straight in the eye. "This is ridiculous, *Don*," he said.

Gibson pointed an angry finger at him and was about to reply, when a cough interrupted them. Jack looked over the Sheriff's shoulder just as Chairman Jeffrey Morgan walked into the holding area.

"I think that's enough, Sheriff," Jeff said.

Gibson turned around and frowned at the Chairman. "Mr. Morgan," he greeted. "What brings you here?"

Jeff walked up to the Sheriff and nodded to Jack. "I wanted a word with Mr. Heldon here, and of course, when we're done, he'll be leaving with me."

The Sheriff laughed. "No, he won't."

"Yes, he will, Sheriff," the Chairman looked at Gibson seriously. "I've already made sure that your report doesn't get filed, and as far as I'm concerned, Mr. Heldon here has never been arrested." The two men stared at each other for a few seconds, and Jack watched in amusement as the Sheriff's face turned a bright red.

"This isn't right," Gibson said, his voice barely a whisper.

"You can leave us alone now, Sheriff," Jeff gestured to the door and waited.

Gibson looked at Jack, then back at the Chairman. He opened his mouth to say something, then grunted and walked out.

"Thank you," Jack said, turning to the Chairman after he was sure the Sheriff was out of earshot. "This is all a misunderstanding."

"I'm sure," Jeff said, pulling up a chair from against the wall and setting it in front of Jack's cell. He sat down, adjusted his suit, and crossed his legs. "I don't usually free criminals, Mr. Heldon."

"I'm not a criminal," Jack replied.

Jeff waved off the remark and inspected his nails. "What I'm really interested in is what exactly happened at the carnival that led to your arrest in the first place."

Jack leaned against the bars of his cell, his arms hanging outside, and squinted at the Chairman. His mind was finally starting to clear, and the question of how Jeffrey Morgan knew he had been arrested in the first place began popping up.

"Am I being followed, Chairman?"

Jeff smiled. "No, Mr. Heldon," he said, "but Ebenezer Cage is what we call a person of interest."

"Why is that?"

Jeff gazed at Jack for a moment before saying, "We're looking into what happened at the Barton farm ten years ago. We believe Ebenezer Cage is involved."

"We?"

"The Council," Jeff explained.

"So not the Sheriff?"

Jeff shook his head. "This is not a public investigation, Mr. Heldon. We're not looking to alarm Ebenezer Cage before we can gather enough evidence against him."

Good luck doing that, Jack wanted to say, but kept his mouth shut.

"So?"

"He kidnapped Faith Stone," Jack admitted, watching closely for the Chairman's reaction. When there wasn't any, he immediately grew suspicious.

"And your proof?" Jeff asked.

"None."

"That's not something that I can work with."

"It's all I have."

Jeff raised an eyebrow, obviously not believing the lie.

What does he want me to say? That I saw Faith on a ghost carousel?

"Mr. Heldon, your cooperation would be greatly appreciated," Jeff pushed for more.

Jack shrugged and shook his head. "I'm afraid that's all I have."

"And how long has Miss Stone been missing?"

"Since yesterday afternoon."

"And you're sure she's not staying at a friend's house?" Jeff asked.

Jack smiled and shook his head in disbelief. The man was fishing, and Jack had nothing to give him that wouldn't make him seem like a nutcase. "Mr. Morgan, I assure you, that's all I know."

"So you went to the carnival and attacked Ebenezer Cage based on a hunch?"

"I didn't–"

"Yes, yes," Jeff interrupted, raising a hand to stop Jack. The Chairman stood up and adjusted his suit, his eyes fixated on Jack's. "I have the power to make sure Ebenezer's Carnival never returns to Lensfield, Mr. Heldon," he said slowly. "Keep that in mind while you try to remember why you were there last night."

Jack watched in silence as the Chairman turned and walked out.

***

"And you're sure it was Josh?"

Michael Cooper was rocking in his seat, his hands clenched together over his mouth as he stared directly at Jack. The four of them were in Amanda's house, occupying opposite couches in her living room, everyone shocked into silence after hearing what Jack had to say.

He had shared it all. Lily, the carnival, his meeting with Ebenezer and, of course, the carousel. Amanda had immediately walked out once he was done, obviously too shaken by what she had heard to stick around for any further discussions. Jack had seen the look of horror on her face, how her eyes had reflected the feeling of terror coursing through her after she had fully taken in his story. He could hear her crying in the kitchen, and although a part of him wanted to go check on her, he knew that anything he would say would be useless right now.

Danny stood up and walked to the large window facing the backyard, his arms crossed over his chest as he stared out pensively. Of all of them, he seemed the only one truly capable of making any sense of what had been said, and Jack could almost hear the wheels in the man's head spinning as he processed the information.

Michael, on the other hand, was in a mess.

"Josh was there?" he asked, snapping his fingers to get Jack's attention.

Jack nodded, shuddering at the memory of being lifted in the air and catapulted against the caravan. Whatever Josh Cooper had become, he wasn't someone Jack would want to run into again.

"So where's this carousel?" Michael asked.

Jack shook his head. "I have no idea," he admitted. "One minute I was in Ebenezer's office, and the next I was out in the woods. I don't understand it."

"So you have no idea how to get there again?"

"I think the real question is why the Chairman is interested in the carnival," Danny pointed out, his back still turned to them, rocking on his heels.

"Screw the Chairman!" Michael snapped. "I don't give a crap about that weasel. I'm here for Josh."

"And now Faith," Danny replied, looking over his shoulder at them. "I'm not saying that finding the carousel isn't important, but there are apparently other players in this game."

"This isn't a game, Bufano!" Michael burst, his fists shaking in rage. "This is my brother we're talking about. And that bastard has Faith, too."

"Calm down, Michael," Danny frowned.

"You calm down!" Michael screamed. "What are you doing? Playing Sherlock Holmes? Who the hell cares about some damned Chairman and his friggin' Council? We should be storming the carnival and looking for that carousel."

"We don't know where it is!" Danny shot back, his glasses slipping a bit on his nose as his face shook in anger. "We don't even know if it's in the carnival. Think, you idiot! Did you see any woods there when we last visited?"

Michael stood up and walked up to Danny, pressing his face up close to his as he snarled at him. "Watch it, Bufano, or you'll be eating your food through a straw when I'm done with you."

"Michael–" Jack got up quickly.

"Shut up, Jack!" Michael yelled at him angrily.

"Stop it!"

The three men turned to look at Amanda standing across the room and hugging herself, shaking in fear and anger.

"Stop it, both of you!"

Michael turned away, grabbed his coat and stormed out of the living room, slamming his fist against the wall as he left. Amanda flinched when the front door opened and closed, then collapsed onto the floor in tears. Jack rushed to her, kneeling down beside her and taking her in his arms.

"My God, Jack!" she sobbed, clenching his shirt as she cried into his shoulder. "Faith! He has Faith!"

"We're going to get her back, I promise you," Jack tried to calm her down, and he looked up at Danny in hopes that the man had any ideas as to what their next move would be. But Danny only shook his head and slumped down onto the couch, rubbing his brow with shaking fingers, feeling more and more like they were all in way over their heads.

***

Michael Cooper sped down Lensfield Road and turned left on College Drive. He ignored the stop signs and wail of horns from annoyed drivers, pushing his Hog forward as the wind blew through his hair.

He was high on adrenaline, his heart pumping like a jackhammer in his chest as he replayed everything Jack had told him. He now knew just how bad his brother's situation was, and that he had to do everything in his power to get him away from the carnival. Images of his brother's face in the Hall of Mirrors flashed before Michael's eyes, the graying skin, the brittle hair, the dark eyes. It didn't help that Jack had only confirmed the horrors that had befallen Josh, and the menacing aggression was just a stark reminder that Michael's brother was not the same person who had run away with the carnival ten years ago.

He was different. The carnival had changed him, and if Michael wanted his brother back, if he wanted to wash away the filth that was poisoning Josh's heart, then he would have to find a way to get him away from Ebenezer and that damned carousel.

Michael continued down College Drive. To his right, the distant remains of Barton's farm struck out in skeletal silence against the afternoon sky. The road weaved between the expanse of fields, between the farm and the college, until it reached Lensfield Brook and the bridge that crossed it. Michael knew there was a dirt road just across the brook, one that led into the East side of Gambler's Park to where the carnival was set up. It was the only road large enough for an attraction of that size to find its way in, and over the years, it had been used by multiple traveling shows that sought an audience in Lensfield. Beyond the dirt road was the highway, heading south.

Back home, Michael thought.

A part of his mind toyed with the idea of just driving on, past the dirt road and the carnival, but he quickly pushed the thought away and focused on saving his brother. Once the bridge was in sight, Michael gunned the engine and accelerated, his urgency spiking as he came closer to his destination.

He caught sight of a solitary figure standing on the walkway, leaning against the bridge railing, hair flailing in the wind. Michael squinted as he sped closer, then pressed down on the breaks and skidded to a stop. Josh stood completely still, watching as Michael quickly jumped off his Hog and rushed towards him.

"Josh!" Michael called out, unzipping his jacket.

Josh didn't reply, and the wind immediately picked up as Michael neared him. In the afternoon light, his brother looked nothing like the embodiment of horror that had attacked him at the Hall of Mirrors. If anything, Josh looked more alive than ever, despite the pale skin and dead stare. A sudden relief washed over Michael, knowing that he wouldn't have to break into the carnival after all to find his brother. It was almost as if Josh had been waiting for him, ready to join him and ride off into the sunset.

"Josh, thank God," Michael said, then immediately slowed down to a stop when he noticed the film of black clouds that swirled within Josh's eyes.

For a moment, they were mesmerizing, freezing Michael in place as he felt invisible hands reach out and dig into his head, groping about within his mind and scratching at the inside of his skull. A sudden excruciating pain erupted within him, and his hands flew up and grasped the sides of his head, as if to squeeze the pain out. A shrill ringing began in his ears, and Michael cried out in pain, falling helplessly to his knees as the slender fingers of hell cut through his mind like knives.

Josh pushed away from the railing and walked slowly towards his fallen brother, his eyes glowing a bright red beneath the swirls of black smoke. He reached down and grabbed Michael by the back of the head, his fingers curling within the long strands of hair, and pulled his brother to his feet. Their faces were inches from each other, and although Michael's eyes were squeezed shut against the pain, the smell of rotting skin coming from Josh perforated his senses.

"I told you to never come back," Josh hissed, the sound of his voice eliciting a sharper pain inside Michael's head that made him cry out again. "I told you to go home."

"Josh," Michael pleaded through clenched teeth, grabbing his brother's arm and squeezing. "Josh, please, stop."

"You were supposed to stay away," Josh said, sounding as if more than one person were talking at the same time, the bright red of his eyes now flames of fury that overwhelmed the black smoke. "Now we're all doomed. Now it's all over."

Michael slammed a fist against Josh's arm, and when that didn't loosen the man's grip, he punched out and struck his face. Josh was unfazed by the meager assault and began to drag Michael to the bridge railing, slowly. Michael fought harder, but still couldn't break free.

Josh brought his brother up to the railing, turned him around, and wrapped an arm around his neck, choking him. Michael tried to pull the arm away, tried to fight back, but he was losing the battle, his eyes clouding over as he gazed down at the running waters of the brook. He tried to call his brother's name again in hopes of reaching any remaining part of him that still had a soul, but all that came out was a croak and a gasp for air. Josh's arm tightened around Michael's neck.

"I warned you, brother," Josh hissed in his ear.

Michael's struggles weakened as the air in his lungs ran out. All he could do with the last bit of energy he had left was try and free himself from the arm that was suffocating him.

"You shouldn't have come back," Josh whispered.

The arm around Michael's neck loosened, and he barely had enough time to gasp for air before one hand grabbed him by the jaw and another the back of his head. The grip was strong, and it took less than a second for Michael to understand what was happening.

"The carnival always finds a way," Josh whispered.

Michael's head twisted forcefully and the sound of his neck snapping was deafening across the empty bridge. Josh let his brother go, took a step back and watched Michael's body fall over the railing and into the brook below.

***

Matt Steel woke up with a start, bolting upright in bed as the lingering dream of the man in the top hat reached out into the waking world and threatened to choke him. He was breathing heavily, his heart thumping wildly in his chest, the sheets thrown to one side of the bed in a tangled heap. He jumped when his bedroom window slammed closed, the glass rattling in its frame, and then creaked open again.

Matt ran a hand across his brow, wiping the sweat from it as he slowly rolled out of bed and latched the window closed. He leaned against it, waiting for his heartbeat to slow and his breathing to calm, shaking his head in an effort to rid himself of the nightmare he had awoken from.

"Matt?"

Matt jumped, spinning around and pressing up against the wall as he looked back into the darkness and at his bed. Someone else was in his bed, and the figure gently rolled to one side and turned on the night lamp. The room was washed in the dim glow of the lamp, and Matt stared at Hailey's naked body lying under his sheets.

She turned around again and smiled at him. "What's wrong?" she asked.

Matt's eyes grew wide as he stared at the cheerleader, his mind racing in an attempt to figure out how she had ended up in his bed, why she was naked, and how the hell he couldn't remember anything about it.

"Are you okay?" she asked.

"How ...?" Matt began, his voice barely a croak. He licked his lips and swallowed. "How did you–?"

Hailey sat up, and despite the fact that her breasts were on full display, he didn't seem to notice. She crawled off the bed and walked up to him, gently placing her hands on his chest then wrapping her arms around his neck.

"Matt, you're scaring me," she whispered in his ear.

Matt closed his eyes to her touch. "I'm sorry," he whispered. "I just don't understand how I can't remember you being here."

"Then let me help you remember," she whispered, and their lips locked.

Matt felt himself soar, her body pressed up against his, her fingers intertwined in his hair. The kiss was soft at first, then grew more intense, and Matt winced when he felt her scratch the back of his neck.

"Ouch."

"I'm sorry," Hailey mumbled as she continued kissing him. He placed his hands on her hips, and then pulled away when she bit down hard on his lower lip, enough to draw blood.

"Hey, easy," he said.

Hailey pushed him against the wall, her strength surprising him, her hands running across his face as she continued her assault. "But I really want you," she said between kisses. "So much, Matt."

"Do you have to hurt me?"

Hailey's nails scratched his face, digging into his skin and drawing blood.

"Hailey!"

Matt tried to push her back, but she was pressed up against him and he couldn't move. He struggled a bit, easy at first, then more seriously when he realized he couldn't break free of her. She continued going at him, her nails scratching his neck, her teeth digging into his ear.

"Hailey, you're hurting me!" Matt cried out.

"But I want you, Matt," Hailey continued, and he heard a nail break as she scratched the nape of his neck, warm blood trickling down his back. "I want you so much."

Matt began to forcefully push her back, even lifting his knee against her, but it was like he was fighting a wall. She still came for him, and when she bit down on his neck, he screamed in pain as he felt flesh being ripped from him. Matt's hand shot up to stop the blood rushing out.

"I want you so bad," Hailey muttered, kissing him and smearing his face with his own blood. Her hand pushed against his head, and as it came down, it ripped at his skin. One finger pushed forcefully into his eye, and blinding pain shot through him.

"So bad."

Matt began to scream.

Chapter 12

The cemetery was empty except for the few people standing around the bright, mahogany coffin. Jack stared at the closed casket in silence, barely listening to the priest, his mind trying to make sense of the world that was quickly crumbling apart around him. A few feet to his left, Danny stood in equal shock, his arm around Amanda who hadn't stopped crying since they had gotten the news of Michael's death.

The call had come at night, when Jack had finally gotten Amanda to sleep and Danny had given up on reaching Michael completely. They had spent only a couple of hours weighing their options, trying to figure out what to do and decide on whether or not the Chairman could be trusted, when the call to Jack's phone had come. He had listened to the Sheriff explain the situation in frozen silence, his mind drawing blanks with every word, and had hung up without acknowledging that he had understood what he'd been told.

Too much, he thought, the shades across his eyes hiding the redness of a sleepless night. *Too much happening at the same time.*

Jack looked across the casket where his friend lay and gazed at Chairman Jeffrey Morgan, flanked by his bodyguards and watching Jack intently. There was no doubt as to why the man was here, a silent reminder that he had warned them about Ebenezer and the carnival, that their friend's death should have been the nail in the coffin that would make them cooperate. Jack could see it in the man's eyes, the silent I-told-you-so look that bordered on sniggering pretentiousness. Jack wanted to beat him with his bare hands just for being here in the first place.

"Jack?"

Jack turned to Danny. The man looked down at Amanda and then gestured towards the cars parked behind them. The priest had finished and was shaking hands with the few mourners who had just shown up. Jack nodded to Danny and let him lead Amanda away, then waited as the Chairman walked around the coffin and made his way towards him. The man stood beside Jack in silence as they watched Michael's coffin being lowered into the ground.

"Do you still not remember why you were at the carnival, Mr. Heldon?" the Chairman asked.

"My best friend has just been murdered, Chairman," Jack replied through clenched teeth. "Fished out of the brook with a broken neck. And my girlfriend is still *missing.* So I really don't understand what this infatuation with my presence at the carnival is all about, but if you have something you want to do, then do it." Jack turned to the Chairman and took off his sunglasses, staring him directly in the eye. "If not, then stay the hell away from me and let me handle my problems on my own."

Jack turned away and stopped when the Chairman grabbed his arm. "I think we can both agree that it wouldn't be wise for either of us to go up against Ebenezer Cage alone."

Jack smiled, a fake grin that left his lips trembling. "Trust me, Chairman," he said. "I've had my fair share of experiences with the carnival. I know exactly what would or wouldn't be wise."

Jack pulled his arm and walked away, leaving the Chairman to stare after him in anger. He didn't look back, replaced his shades and made his way to where his car was parked. Danny was leaning against it, arms folded, looking over his friend's shoulder at the small crowd beyond.

"He seems happy," Danny said angrily, and Jack could see the fury all over the other man's face. It was clear that the Chairman's presence annoyed both of them equally.

"Where's Amanda?" Jack asked.

"She wanted to be alone," Danny replied, sighing as he took off his glasses and rubbed his eyes. "I called Huck and told him to give us a call when she got home."

Jack nodded and leaned against his car as well, sniffing loudly.

"What now?' Danny asked.

"I'm not sure," Jack replied solemnly, crossing his arms over his chest and gazing at the small crowd of mourners as they slowly dispersed.

"We need to find that carousel," Danny pointed out.

"I know."

"But we can't go to the carnival."

"I know that too."

Danny sighed and balled his fists in anger, slamming one of them against the car. "I'm going to kill Ebenezer Cage myself."

Jack continued staring ahead, watching as the Chairman made his way towards his own car. "I don't think the carousel's in the carnival," Jack said pensively.

"You said–"

"I know what I said," Jack interrupted. "It's just, there's something else I'm missing. Something Ebenezer told me when I walked into his office."

Danny looked at his friend and raised an eyebrow questioningly.

"It's nearly impossible to tell who can and cannot walk through that door," Jack recited, frowning.

"What does that mean?"

"I have no idea," Jack shook his head in frustration. "The only other thing in that field besides the carousel was the caravan, the one Josh pulled me into before I blacked out and woke up in the park. I have a feeling there's something there, but I just can't put my finger on it."

"Well, there's definitely nothing natural about anything you told us," Danny said. "Maybe that caravan is the key?"

"Maybe," Jack said. "A door that leads to the field?" Jack shook his head again and rubbed his brow. "It makes no sense."

"Did you see a caravan in the park?"

"There's maybe a dozen in the carnival," Jack replied, "but not in the park, no."

Danny pushed away from the car and scratched the back of his head, trying to think of anything that might help them figure this out. He began to pace back and forth, then stopped and looked at Jack.

"Why were you at Gambler's Bridge?"

The question took Jack by surprise. "What?"

"In that photo I showed you," Danny continued, "when we were kids. You were at Gambler's Bridge. Why?"

Jack hesitated for a moment before saying, "I went to see Ebenezer."

Danny's eyes widened, and Jack sighed at the look his friend was giving him. "The fight I had with Faith," he explained. "It was about Lily."

"What about Lily?"

Jack looked down at his feet, struggling with what he was about to say. "Ten years ago, Faith struck a deal with Ebenezer. She felt neglected, and wanted her parents to pay a little more attention to her. The next day, Lily was gone."

Danny's face looked almost comical as the information he was receiving sunk in. He opened his mouth, closed it, and then opened it again, but said nothing.

"We both remember how hard Faith had taken it, and even back then, I always had a soft spot for her," Jack continued. "So I went to Ebenezer. I met him at Gambler's Bridge, and asked him to tell me where Lily was."

"How did you know he would have that information?"

"I didn't," Jack said, "but he told us to ask for anything, and he would deliver. Remember that? It was the only thing I could think of."

"So Ebenezer told you about Barton, and we all followed you there," Danny said, a hint of anger in his voice. "You basically led us into the monster's lair."

"I had no idea," Jack replied, too tired to be defensive and more than willing to face his friend's wrath. "It didn't matter, though. Lily and those other kids were dead, and Barton had been expecting us."

Danny shook in frustration, but held his tongue. This wasn't the time for reprimanding, although a part of him wanted to punch Jack in the face.

"I'm sorry," Jack stammered. "I know I should have said something sooner, but I didn't really think it mattered."

"We almost died, Jack!" Danny shot, unable to stop himself. "I still have the burn marks on my arm from that fire."

"And you think it's been a walk in the park for me?" Jack shot back. "I still have nightmares, Danny. I can still see Barton. I can still feel the fear of having to hide in that closet while he stomped about outside looking for us. I can still see those eyes staring at me from the dark, and the smoke, and the fire. It's been just as hard for me, and I didn't have the luxury of leaving Lensfield."

"What did you say?"

"You and Michael left. I had to live with the memories of that place right in front of my eyes every day!"

"No, not that," Danny waved angrily. "Before it."

"The eyes?"

Danny nodded. "Where did you see the eyes?"

"When I was in the closet," Jack replied.

Danny rushed to him and grabbed him by the shoulders, squeezing tight. "You stupid, stupid man." Danny rushed around the car to the driver's side, beckoning Jack to get in.

"What are you doing?" Jack asked.

"We need to hurry back to the motel," Danny said. "I need to get a few things."

"Why?"

Danny climbed into the car. "Because I think I know where we can find the carousel."

***

The sound of carnival music pierced through Gambler's Park, the front gates swinging open and the eager line of guests laughing as they made their way forward. Although it had been three days, the carnival was still bringing in a crowd. It didn't matter that the rides hadn't changed, or that some people had even memorized the dialogue between actors in the small side shows. At the end of the day, there wasn't much that could be done in Lensfield, and the carnival brought with it a much-needed change from the norm.

Amanda's feet felt heavy as the crowd practically carried her forward and through the carnival gates. She was in a daze, her mind lost in thought and flashing images of Michael Cooper. She had little recollection of what had happened between her decision to find Ebenezer Cage and her current presence between the cheerful crowd that surrounded her. Her eyes fluttered briefly, and with the setting sun behind her, the neon sign of Ebenezer's Carnival flashed bright. It was joined by a multitude of colored lights from the rides, booths, and stands as the guests hurried down the midway to their favorite attractions, the air a mix of laughter and glee.

Amanda broke away from the crowd as soon as an opening presented itself, and despite her initial resolution to come here, she quickly made to one side and leaned against the side of a food stand, gasping for air. Her heart was beating much faster now, and she felt her stomach turn.

Michael! she cried out in silent agony.

She tried to control her breathing, feeling that her hyperventilation was going to throw her over the edge and into complete panic, and it took her a few more seconds of painful moans and eyes shut tight before she felt she could get a hold of herself. She stood up slightly, her hand on her chest, willing her heart to slow down, and she quickly wiped a tear away as it rolled down her cheek.

She needed to be strong. To get through this in one piece. For Michael. Amanda turned and walked back onto the midway, turning towards the back end and making her way through the carnival. To her far left was the Ferris wheel, and for the briefest of seconds she felt like she was being transported back in time, looking out at the large wheel as she and her friends walked up to it for the first time ten years ago. She remembered staring at Michael, admiring him in the dim light with his wide smile and bravado, making a joke about wheels that she just couldn't remember. She remembered the frown on Jack's face, the way he had told them that something felt wrong, and how they had all waved when they went on the ride without him.

Amanda made her way to the Ferris wheel, her eyes fixated on the large ride as carts rose and fell in their circular motion. The line was inexplicably short, despite this being one of the more prominent attractions in the carnival, but Amanda shrugged it off. She walked up to the man working the controls and tapped him on the shoulder. She flinched when he turned around, a large scar etched across his face, and closing one of his eyes, the other covered by a faint film of white.

"Whatcha want?" the man growled. "Git in line if ya wanna ride."

"I'm looking for Ebenezer Cage," Amanda said, her voice barely audible over the loud music and screams of children.

"Ah said git!"

Amanda quickly stepped back and walked up to the small gate that separated the line from the Ferris wheel landing dock. She looked up at the carts, rising and falling, disappearing into the night and then reappearing a few seconds later. Every few turns, the wheel would stop so the top cart could enjoy the view from above, and then it would start all over again. Amanda watched the cycle intently, for a minute forgetting why she had come to the carnival in the first place, mesmerized by the slow motion of the wheel.

A bell sounded, and her eyes dropped to the cart in front of her as the gate clicked open to allow her through. She froze in her place, the smiling face of Ebenezer Cage staring out at her from where he sat in the cart. He gestured to the seat in front of him with his cane, and before Amanda knew what she was doing, she walked through the gate and climbed into the cart with him.

The Ferris wheel began to turn again.

***

"Are you sure about this?"

Jack drummed his fingers against the steering wheel, staring out at the charred remains of the Barton farm. The sun had set, and the wind was already whistling through the small cracks he had left open in the windows to allow for some fresh air in. It chilled the inside of the car, and Jack blamed his sudden consistent shivering on the fact that he had forgotten to bring a jacket with him, instead of the real reason.

He looked over at Danny, and even in the dark, he could see the other man's pale face. It was clear that neither of them wanted to be here, but Jack was running along with his friend's theory, and if there was any chance it would get Faith back, he was going to take it. Still, it didn't shake off the fact that the old farm terrified him, especially after his recent run-in with Lily.

"As sure as I'll ever be," Danny said. "Besides, you have any better ideas?"

Jack shook his head and reached into the back seat, turning around slowly and carefully, fearful that he would find Lily sitting there with that horrific smile on her face and the kitchen knife in her hand. They were alone in the car, though, and he quickly grabbed the backpack and brought it into the front.

He unzipped the bag and rummaged through its contents. "Are we going to need all this?" he looked up at Danny questioningly.

Danny pulled the flaps open further and reached inside, pulling out twin flashlights and handing one to Jack. "Maybe not," he said, "but better safe than sorry." He dug inside again and pulled out a small case, placing it on the dashboard and opening it to reveal a 9mm and a box of bullets. He quickly slid the chamber out, checked to make sure it was loaded, and then pushed it back in.

Jack raised an eyebrow at him.

"Better safe than sorry," Danny repeated, and they stepped out of the car.

The wind slapped at them relentlessly, screaming in their ears as if trying to push away unwelcome guests. The Barton farm was a shell of its former self, the house having had collapsed on itself and the barn barely standing in the storm. It had always confused Jack how the place had been able to withstand the harsh New England winters all these years, and why no one had thought of tearing it completely down and ridding the town of the horrid memories it bore.

They made their way towards the house carefully, flashlights on and Danny in the lead. Jack could feel the house watching them approach, lying in shambles, and laughing as they made their way towards it, welcoming them back. He could almost hear it whispering to him, its words carried loudly by the strong wind and stinging in his ears.

Hello boys! Welcome back! It's been so long! I mean, yeah, I understand why you'd want to steer clear all these years, but come on! We have history! *If everything had gone as planned, you'd all be buried underneath me right now. Can you imagine that?*

Jack shuddered and quickened his pace, keeping close to Danny as they scurried through the night. The barn rose high to their right, and Jack fought the urge to look over there, to where Barton had cut the children up and tossed them to his pigs. He could imagine their screaming as the madman butchered them, and the squealing of the pigs at the taste of fresh meat.

The front face of the Barton house still stood, and although the door was missing from its hinges, the frame was still intact. All of a sudden, he could see Ted Barton dragging Michael across the threshold as the young boy thrashed, screamed, and scratched to stop their retreat. He remembered being inside the house, and the spine-tingling sound of nails across the wood as his friend was dragged about the first floor hallway, Barton laughing hysterically all the while.

I hid in the closet, Jack remembered, suddenly disgusted at his cowardice. *They were all going through hell and I just hid in the closet.*

Jack felt a rush of anger race through him at the memory, and he wished he could turn back time and knock some sense into his fifteen-year-old self.

The inside of the house was in complete shambles. The second floor had collapsed upon itself during the fire, and most of the hallway and rooms beyond were buried under piles of burnt wood and moss. Nature had weaved its fingers of ivy through the remains, and across the pile of rubble, the fields behind the house could be seen spreading out into the night.

Only the living room remained, the furniture within cracked and weathered, roots sticking out from under the floorboards and wrapping around the legs of whatever was still standing. The hallway was littered with fallen planks, but just beyond the maze of burnt wood and broken furniture, stood the closed door to the closet.

The beam of light flickered with the shaking of Jack's hand as he gazed at the door, remembering the cold and the darkness, and the eyes. He tapped Danny on the shoulder and gestured towards the closet.

"Time to test your theory," Jack whispered.

Danny nodded, and as he swept his beam across the rest of the house, something moved in the darkness. He brought his light back to where the movement had come from, and froze. Jack felt his friend's body stiffen beside him and angled his own light to the same place.

Lily stood completely still in the corner of the living room, her hair falling over her face, her eyes blazing red.

"You came!" she smiled at them, and before the two men could react, she bolted towards them.

Chapter 13

Amanda flipped through the channels on her television as she nervously bit her nails, trying to keep her mind busy with anything other than her meeting with Ebenezer. The wind outside had picked up tremendously since she had returned home, and the distant clap of thunder made her flinch. The lights above her head flickered, and she toyed with the idea of waking Huck up just to keep her company.

No, she thought quickly. *You can't do that. Not if Ebenezer keeps his word. Huck will never understand.*

He brother's gentle snoring washed down from his room upstairs, and the sound of thunder boomed again, this time a bit louder, a bit closer. She almost smiled, thinking that if the storm were inside the house, Huck would probably be able to sleep through it anyway. He would only be annoyed at her for waking him up, especially since he had been taking over her shifts at the café for the past two days.

The lights flickered again, and Amanda quickly got to her feet and made her way towards the kitchen. She needed coffee, or anything stronger, to cool her nerves. She had no idea what to expect now, and she was still feeling shudders of dread race through her since her spin on the Ferris wheel. Ebenezer had oozed darkness, and if what Jack had told them was true, there was no telling what their deal would result in.

It doesn't matter, she tried to convince herself. *All that matters is Michael. All I want is Michael.*

Amanda reached for the kitchen lights and switched them on, and as the fluorescents flickered to life, she let out a small scream.

Across the kitchen, just inside the backdoor that swung open and closed with the wind, Michael stood stoically, his eyes fixated on her. His hair fell in curls to his shoulders, thick and dripping water onto the linoleum floor, and his face was a pale shade of blue. His mouth hung open, his gums as black as night, and the bones in his neck cracked as he cocked his head a bit to one side and watched her with his lifeless eyes.

"Michael?" Amanda stammered, her eyes wide in shock at the sight of the man she had just watched lowered into his grave this morning.

Michael didn't reply, his chest rising and falling slowly as he watched her, his hands clenching into fists and then releasing again. His lips curled into an angry snarl, and she could see his skin crack and begin to bleed around the edges.

"Oh my God," Amanda gasped, her hand flying to her mouth.

Michael took a step forward, swayed a bit on his feet and then took another. "What have you done?" he croaked, his voice a gurgled cough, water erupting from his mouth and splattering on the floor at his feet. His scowl darkened. "You went to him."

Amanda nodded, fighting the urge to run and throw her arms around him, unsure as to whom Ebenezer had brought back from the dead. The look in Michael's eyes was one of menace that bordered on insanity, the soft glow of kindness that had once been there now gone. She hadn't wanted to believe it, she couldn't fathom just how terrible a deal with the devil could be, but there was living proof of it right in front of her, staring at her furiously.

"I had to," Amanda replied. "You weren't supposed to die."

Michael took another step forward, his fists shaking in fury as his eyes began to darken, black smoke filling the whites and covering his pupils in their veil. "You traded me for my brother!" he yelled at her, his voice booming through the kitchen. "Josh is lost forever because of you!"

"I wanted you back!" Amanda cried out, inching away from him and back into the hallway, her eyes never leaving his in fear that if she did lose sight, he would be on her within seconds.

Michael growled and slammed his fist down on the island counter, the cups on top of it shaking dangerously. "You have no idea what you've done!" he yelled. "To me! To Josh!"

"Michael, please, listen to me," Amanda pleaded as she backed into the hall, suddenly aware that he was much more stable on his feet and had come a lot closer than she had expected. He was already towering over her, just a foot or two away, with one hand reaching for her.

Amanda turned and ran, screaming as she raced down the hallway. She made for the stairs, hoping that she could wake Huck in time, but a hand wrapped around her hair and yanked her back hard. Amanda slipped and fell on her back, her head slamming against the hardwood floor as the world around her spun.

Michael dragged her into the living room by the hair as she screamed in pain, the thunder outside booming in reply and quickly followed by flashes of lightning. He let go of her, trudging towards the desk by the window that she used as a workplace. She rolled over, watching in horror as he opened a drawer and pulled out a pair of scissors, then turned back to her.

Amanda jumped to her feet and raced towards the makeshift fireplace just as Michael lunged for her. She felt the sharp pain of the scissors cutting across her shoulder blade, but the adrenaline kept her from screaming as she wrapped her hands around the fire iron and swung it around with all the strength left in her.

The curled end of the iron found its mark just below Michael's jaw, and he staggered back, eyes wide, hands wrapped around the weapon lodged in his neck. There was no blood, only a sickening, gurgling sound as he toppled over the coffee table and fell onto the couch. Amanda fell to her knees, her mouth open in a silent scream as she fought through the pain in her shoulder and the realization of what she had just done. She gazed at Michael through tears as he writhed about on the couch, the black clouds in his eyes dispersing slowly, the sounds of his choking like nails across a blackboard.

And then he stopped.

Thunder bellowed just outside her window, and Amanda finally found her voice, crying out as she let herself fall to the floor, the warm blood from her wound soaking into the carpet and spreading around her.

From the darkness, she watched in horror as Ebenezer Cage stepped out and gazed down at her, his smile wide.

"All you desire," he said, his voice raspy and his eyes blazing. "All for a price."

And as he reached for her, his face shifted and cracked, and Amanda screamed.

***

"Where the hell is she?"

The skies had opened up, and the rain fell in sheets around Jack and Danny as they hid behind the car. Lily had taken them by surprise, and both men had been too slow against her first attack. Danny was cradling his wounded arm where Lily had struck at him with her knife, his shirtsleeve soaked in his own blood as he winced in pain with every movement.

Lily had disappeared into the darkness again, only reappearing with the first flash of lightning to strike at Jack. She had missed him, but her screams of rage were enough to shock him into near paralysis if not for Danny pulling him out of the house and towards the car.

The storm hit them hard, thunder echoing through the night sky and mixing with the manic laughter of the little girl that seemed to be coming from everywhere. She was playing with them, and Jack was finding it harder and harder to think through the storm and her taunts. Sometimes he would feel she was whispering directly in his ear, other times he would see something move from the corner of his eyes. He felt like a prey being slowly pushed to the edges of sheer panic, and Lily was just waiting for the right moment to strike and end it once and for all.

And she was having fun doing it.

"She's just a kid," Danny hissed through the pain in his arm.

"She's not even alive," Jack said, his eyes darting back and forth in the darkness, their flashlights dropped and forgotten inside the house.

Danny shifted and cried out in pain, grasping Jack's arm tightly. Jack could see the dark stain on his arm growing.

"We need to get you to a hospital," Jack said.

Danny quickly shook his head. "It's now or never," he replied. "You have to get to that closet."

"And what if that isn't the door we're looking for?" Jack shot back, shivering against the rain and wind. "What if I open it and all I find is an empty closet?"

"Yeah, because that's why *she's* here, right?" Danny replied. "She's just really fond of this place. You know, good times and all that."

"Not a time for dark humor," Jack cursed, looking over the car hood at the house, his eyes searching the surrounding fields and the barn. There was no sign of Lily, but the sudden burst of giggling let him know she was waiting.

"One chance, Jack," Danny said. "That's all we got. I'll distract her. You make for that door."

"I'm not leaving you with her," Jack shook his head in anger. *Not again. I'm not running away again.*

"Faith is what matters," Danny said. "And getting rid of that damned carousel." Danny grabbed him by the collar and pulled him closer. "Burn the bastard, Heldon. Burn him back to whatever hell he came from."

Jack was about to reply when Danny pushed to his feet and raced out from the shelter of the car. He held his gun in his good hand, and he was yelling out for Lily, drawing her out. Jack watched him, and from the darkness beyond came the glint of light reflecting of metal.

Lily seemed to materialize from thin air, and her scream of rage pierced through the night like the cry of banshee, her knife held high as she raced towards Danny. Jack seized the opportunity, jumped to his feet and sprinted across the yard, making for the house. He heard the sound of gunfire behind him, but didn't dare look back, even when Lily screamed again and Danny cried out in a spine-tingling shriek of pain.

Jack burst across the threshold, immediately racing towards the hallway and jumping through the maze of fallen planks. He slipped and fell hard, pain shooting up his leg from where his knee connected with the floorboards, but he willed himself up to his feet and kept moving. Another burst of gunfire sounded behind him, and then a third, and Lily's screams were suddenly much louder, almost as if from right behind him. He felt something sharp scrape the back of his neck, and with a cry of fury, Jack threw himself against the closet door.

And then there was darkness. And nothing else.

Pain erupted in his shoulder where he had broken through the door, and he felt himself falling, slowly, through a murky nothingness that engulfed him completely and suffocated him. He gasped for air, his arms flailing about as if under water, and there was a sudden tug that drew him downwards.

He hit the ground hard, the wind knocked out of him and his head throbbing. He curled his hands on the grass beneath him, his fingers digging into dirt, and he slowly pushed himself onto his hands and knees.

When he looked up, his breath caught in his throat.

Danny was right.

Jack slowly got to his feet as the bright lights and music of the carousel washed over him.

***

Chairman Jeffrey Morgan knew that his time had come when the lights in his study flickered and went out. He carefully recapped the pen in his hand and set it down next to the papers he had been looking over, then sat up straight in his chair.

The study instantly filled with the familiar stench of burnt skin, and he could feel the heavy breath of his worst nightmare on the nape of his neck.

"I am very disappointed, Chairman," Ebenezer's raspy voice came from behind him.

Jeff felt a hand rest on his shoulders, soft at first, then tighter. Sharp nails dug into his flesh, and it took all of Jeff's power not to scream out in pain. He shook as he tried to maintain his calm, refusing to give Ebenezer the satisfaction of seeing him squirm.

"I thought we had an agreement," Ebenezer chuckled. "Especially since I held my end of the bargain."

Jeff shook his head in anger, clenching his teeth as he fought the pain. A sudden burning sensation began to race through him. "I refuse to be a puppet in your game," he said as his teeth clattered together.

"That is quite a shame, Mr. Morgan," Ebenezer said. "It is a fine game I am playing, one of patience and perseverance. You might even say I'm in it for the long haul."

"People know about you," Jeff said, the burning sensation inside him intensifying, and small flames began to flicker on the sleeves of his arm. "You won't last long."

"On the contrary, Chairman," Ebenezer whispered. "The pawns are moving exactly as I wish. In the end, the carnival always finds a way."

The flames grew, and the flesh underneath began to burn. Jeffrey Morgan, cried out in pain as he smelled the sizzling skin, and he desperately tried to break free. The hand on his shoulder kept him in his place.

"You're going straight to hell, Cage, you hear me!" Jeff screamed as flames erupted across his body and engulfed him.

Ebenezer smiled. "And what a place that must be."

***

Danny opened the car door and rolled into the passenger seat, the pain in his arm numbing. The wind slammed the door closed, and for a few seconds, he felt at peace, reveling in the warmth inside the car and trying to control his breathing.

He had panicked when Lily had veered away from him and went after Jack. Although he had gotten a shot out, it had missed its target completely, and he had been forced to chase after her. The girl was quick, though, and it had taken three more shots to finally bring her down. He closed his eyes, his ears ringing with her shrill screams, but he couldn't help the smile that came to his lips.

Jack had made it through. The girl had come close to stopping him, but he had made it through.

Now all Danny had to do was wait. And pray Jack would be able to find his way back.

Chapter 14

The night was darker here. Much darker. Almost as if it were enveloped in a black canopy, suffocating everything inside and bearing down like a heavy weight. There were no stars in the sky, no moon with its pale bluish glow. The trees hung like hunched men, branches reaching down to the earth, webbing out like a multitude of fingers that were trying to stop the trunks from toppling over. There were no night sounds escaping from the surrounding woods, no hoots of owls or chirping crickets.

The only life came from the carousel. It turned slowly, its lights illuminating the small field where it spun forever, the carnival music on an annoying loop that threatened to drive anyone mad. The riders sat lifeless on their horses and carriages, all staring straight ahead, all motionless as their mounts moved in monotonous ups and downs.

Jack gazed upon the clearing, hesitant to move from his place, half expecting Josh to appear from the darkness and come to end what he had started. If he had been merciful enough the first time around, Jack doubted he would be again.

But no one came. He was alone in the field with the carousel and its occupants, the caravan dark and forlorn behind him, the trees bending towards him as if in prayer. He took a tentative step forward, and then another, and when nothing happened, he rushed towards the carousel.

His eyes darted back and forth between the riders, searching for Faith amongst them, desperately trying to find her before his luck ran out, and he was forced to face whatever monster lingered in this no-man's land in wait for easy prey. His eyes fell upon familiar faces this time around, faces he hadn't know he had missed until now.

Jacqueline Stevens sat on a carriage, her legs crossed, her eyes staring straight ahead, as she cradled a doll in her arms. Jack did a double take, almost certain the doll had blinked and smiled at him. Behind her by a few unknown riders was Samuel Gold, riding his own brown steed, his fingernails bleeding and his hair muddy. There were scratches across his face, and his mouth was fixed in an open, silent scream.

And then there was Ted Barton.

Jack stared in horror at his childhood nightmare, the large man straddling what looked like a mix between a lion and a mermaid, his eyes squinting in concentration and a wide smile on his face. Jack took a few steps back, scared that if somehow he fell into the man's line of vision, it would break his trance, and Ted Barton would come after him again.

Where are you, boy? Come out, come out, wherever you are!

Barton's voice rang in Jack's ear, and he waited patiently while the carousel turned and Barton was out of sight. Jack felt his knees buckle, and from between the trees, a gust of wind broke loose and slammed into him, forcing him to sway. He shook his head and tried to stop the massive throbbing in his head as he diverted his attention to looking for Faith.

She came up a few seconds later, riding her horse, her hands clenching her pole tight and her eyes glazed. She had a deep frown on her face, as if she somehow understood where she was and was trying to force herself out of whatever trance she currently found herself in. Jack rushed forward, jumped on the carousel and grabbed onto a woman's arm to maintain his balance.

The woman's head turned slightly, her eyes facing him yet staring straight through him, and he quickly let go of her and staggered back, hitting his hip painfully against a carriage. The woman's line of vision followed him, and her mouth opened slightly. A low hum escaped from between her lips, and Jack could almost hear the word 'help' being forcefully voiced out.

Jack pushed away from her, ignoring the fact that her head turned to follow him, and he made his way through the riders towards Faith.

"Faith," he whispered, grabbing her by the arm and shaking lightly.

She didn't reply, staring straight ahead, oblivious to his being there.

"Faith," he repeated, and slowly he began to unclench her hands from the pole.

Faith let out a cry of pain and wrapped her arms around the pole completely, holding on for dear life, making it even harder for Jack to break her free. He wrestled with her arms, but her grip was strong, and he could see her muscles flexed as she fought to keep her position on the horse.

"Faith!" Jack yelled.

Faith's head snapped towards him, her eyes a black cloud of darkness. "Faith is not here right now!" she screamed at him.

Jack felt something reach into his head and squeeze, forcing a loud ringing in his ears, and the blood in his temples began a rhythmic thumping that threatened to explode. He grabbed onto Faith's horse as he tried to stop himself from toppling over, and a rough hand grabbed him by the shoulder.

"You cannot escape the carousel!" a voice hissed from behind him.

Jack turned and stared into the dark eyes of a young boy, no older than twelve, his lips drawn back in an angry snarl. Jack pulled away from him quickly, looking about at the other riders around him as they all stared at him angrily from atop their mounts.

"You turn and turn forever," another man said from his right, and a second hand pulled at his sleeve.

"You cannot leave!"

Jack fought the hands away and turned back to Faith, flinching when he came face to face with her dark eyes. He fought through the dread that raced through him and grabbed both her arms, yanking forcefully and pulling her off her horse.

Faith screamed and kicked, her hands scratching at his face as he fought to keep her in his arms and shuffled back. More hands reached for him, tried to stop him, and he used Faith's struggling body to lash out at them and force them away. When he finally reached the edge of the carousel, he stopped struggling and let himself fall over and onto the grass, Faith's body flying out of his arms as she landed with a thump beside him, still screaming and kicking.

"Faith!" he screamed, rolling towards her to stop her from scratching her eyes out. She continued to struggle, and it took every ounce of strength he had to pin her down. "Faith, it's me, Jack!"

"You cannot escape the carousel!" she boomed, her voice like a thousand razor blades inside his ears. "You cannot escape the carousel!"

"Faith!" Jack slapped her, hard, and winced when she suddenly fell silent in his arms.

Jack looked back at the carousel, half-expecting the others to have gotten off their mounts and come for him, but it was as if nothing had happened. They sat in the same position, staring straight ahead, lifeless with their dead stares. Jack sighed, feeling his face for the trickles of blood from where Faith had scratched him, then pushed his arms under her limp body and lifted her up. Balancing her in his arms, he turned towards the caravan, and stopped.

Amanda stood at the foot of the wooden stairs. Even in the dim light, he could see the black clouds in her eyes and the lifeless expression on her face. She stared at him, watching him standing in front of the carousel with Faith in his arms, and cocked a head to one side.

"They're right," Amanda said, only the voice that came from her was nothing like her own. This was raspier, deeper, darker, and coated with anger and resentment.

Jack could feel the world around him grow darker, the air thicken as he struggled to find his breath. "Amanda?"

"There is no Amanda," she replied, taking slow steps towards him, her fingers spreading out and then clenching into fists. "There is only the carousel, and you cannot escape the carousel."

"Amanda, what are you doing?" Jack took a few steps back, briefly looking over his shoulder in fear that he might fall onto the spinning carousel behind him and into the hands of the lifeless souls trapped in it.

"You shouldn't be here," Amanda said, coming closer, the clouds in her eyes shifting and a red glow growing from within. "She belongs to the carousel."

"She belongs with me," Jack said. A sudden burst of bravado washed over him, and he stood his ground, resolute in fighting his way out the same way he had fought his way in.

"She belongs here," Amanda said, the sternness in her voice echoing inside his head as invisible fingers raced through his mind and threatened to break him.

Jack frowned in anger, holding Faith tight to him as Amanda approached, ready to face the consequences of fighting back. He would leave this place with Faith, or die trying. Amanda's eyes blazed a fiery red, and she reached out for him.

"Leave him!"

Amanda stopped suddenly, her feet planted firmly in place, her hand inches from Jack's throat. The fire in her eyes dwindled almost immediately and was replaced by the smoky clouds from before.

Jack turned to where the sound had come from, and from between the low hanging branches of the bent trees, Ebenezer Cage stepped out into the field.

The Tall Man was smiling, the cane in his hand twirling, his top hat glinting in the lights of the carousel. He walked only a few paces into the clearing before he stopped, almost blending into the night if not for the twin flames in his eyes. The same eyes that had looked out at Jack in the darkness of the closet and from within the fires that finally engulfed it.

"You impress me, Mr. Heldon," Ebenezer said, his voice barely a whisper yet strangely audible across the distance between them. Behind Jack, the carousel stopped spinning and the music stopped. "Although I must admit, there is some predictability in your actions."

Jack didn't reply, his eye shifting between Amanda and Ebenezer, trying to figure out what to do next.

"Oh, please, I have no intention of harming you," Ebenezer laughed, a raspy sound that sent shivers up and down Jack's spine. "I told you before, you are worth more than you fathom."

"You said that about Faith," Jack replied.

"Did I?" Ebenezer frowned, and then a smile spread across his face. "I must have misspoken, then."

Jack took a few steps away from Amanda and slowly walked around her, keeping his eyes fixated on her as she turned and matched his gaze. He could see the anger all over her face at having been interrupted, and he hoped that Ebenezer's hold on her lasted long enough for him to escape with Faith.

"You do not have to worry about our dear Miss Brians," Ebenezer said, as if reading his mind. "We have a deal. She will not hurt you unless I want her to."

"What did you do to her?"

Ebenezer began to laugh, striking his cane down into the earth and leaning on it as his eyes flared. "My dear boy, you must choose your battles," he said. "You cannot save everyone."

"We'll see about that," Jack shot back, edging closer to the caravan.

"Indeed, we will," Ebenezer chuckled. "As for now, you are free to go. I cannot for the life of me bring it upon myself to come between you and such well-earned success."

Jack froze, a part of him dreading the catch that came with Ebenezer's words.

"There is no catch, Mr. Heldon," Ebenezer smiled. "Although I will ask that you do come back and visit. We have yet to complete our game."

Jack looked up at the caravan, then back at Ebenezer, then held Faith tighter as he moved towards the stairs.

"Just remember, Mr. Heldon," Ebenezer raised a finger to stop him. "Not all doors will be open to you forever."

Jack frowned, then quickly raced up the few steps and barged through the caravan door.

***

Danny's eyes flew open at the sound of thunder booming above his head.

He squeezed his eyes shut and opened them again, wincing in pain as he moved in his seat and shifted into a more comfortable position. The rain hammered against the car roof like pellets, threatening to break through and find their way inside. Danny glanced at the digital watch, noticed that Jack had now been gone for almost two hours, and leaned back in his seat to continue waiting.

Lightning flashed overhead, and in the brief illumination, Danny caught movement at the Barton house. He sat up quickly, reaching for his gun, groaning at the thought of having to deal with Lily again. Thunder clapped, closely followed by lighting, and in the flash of light, Danny caught sight of a larger figure racing through the rain towards him carrying something heavy in its arms. The figure came closer, and through the sheets of rain, he recognized Jack immediately, carrying Faith in his arms.

Danny quickly jumped out of the car, ignoring the screaming pain in his arm and raced out to help.

Chapter 15

Jack's eyes were fixated on the television screen hanging from the ceiling in front of him, watching as the news cameras filmed the outside of Chairman Jeffrey Morgan's house. There had been a massive fire, and the Chairman was being wheeled out in a body bag as the newscaster spoke into the camera and pointed to the scene behind him.

It was recorded footage from the night before, and Jack had a feeling he knew who had started the fire that had taken the Chairman's life.

Jack turned off the television, laid his head back on his chair and sighed. The sound of beeping monitors all around him had become a monotonous electrical lullaby, and he was finding harder and harder to stay awake. He looked over to the hospital bed where Faith slept, hooked to the machines that were monitoring her vitals, and reached out to grab her hand.

Jack hadn't bothered driving them to Lensfield Hospital, opting instead to speed through the night and the rain to the nearby town of Halem where he practically parked the car inside the emergency room. The doctors had been efficient, dividing their attention between Danny and Faith, simultaneously taking care of both while they made sure he was okay and then led him off to sign the paperwork. It had been a long night, and although Faith had woken up in the middle of it all, screaming and thrashing, forcing the doctors to inject her with something to calm her down, Jack was just happy that they had made it out of Lensfield in one piece.

He sat by Faith's bed all night, barely sleeping. Every time he closed his eyes, he would see the carousel and the faces of the riders, their eyes black, their hands grabbing for him. He would see Amanda coming for him, hands outstretched, ready to finish what Josh had started.

And, of course, Ebenezer, with his top hat and cane and smile. And the eyes.

They would haunt him forever.

The door to the hospital room opened and Jack quickly adjusted himself in his seat, relaxing immediately when Danny shuffled in. His friend had fared a lot better, although his wounds had obviously needed stitches. Physically, he was free to go, but the doctors wanted to keep him overnight for observation, which suited Danny just fine.

"How is she?" he asked, standing at the foot of Faith's bed and looking at her.

"Stable," Jack replied. "Although I'm not really sure what that means anymore."

Danny smiled and nodded. "And you?"

"What about me?"

"How are you holding up?"

Jack hesitated, then answered, "Shaken, confused, scared. A lot of things, really. I don't know, to be honest."

"I think that's a good thing."

"Do you?" Jack chuckled. "Thank you, Dr. Phil."

Danny laughed and sat down at the foot of the bed carefully, wincing. "You're probably going to have to talk about it, sooner or later."

"I'd rather not," Jack sighed.

"I never said it was a choice," Danny eyed him carefully.

Jack returned his friend's gaze, then shook his head and looked over at Faith. "How about we just wait until she wakes up, and then see what happens."

Danny nodded and adjusted his glasses. "Tomorrow's day seven," he said, almost to himself.

Jack glanced at him briefly before turning his attention back to Faith. "I know."

"And?"

Jack shrugged and didn't reply.

***

The carnival was gone.

Jack sat in silence on the same bench where he had been previously arrested and gazed out at the empty field the carnival had occupied. Groundsmen were walking about, working on restoring it, and Jack felt like he could hear the lingering sounds of carnival music in the air. Although Gambler's Park was not as alive as it had been during the past week, there were still enough people around to make him feel that there was still some normalcy in the world that was as yet unaffected by the darkness that had built its home here for seven days.

He had left Faith back at Halem after making sure Danny would drive her to her aunt's over in Hartford. She hadn't been entirely pleased with his decision to come back so soon after what had happened, but he assured her that he would catch up with them in a few days. There were things here he had to attend to. The world was oblivious to the truth about the carnival, and it wasn't going to stop for him or anyone else.

The show must go on. He felt the dryness of the joke linger in his mind.

He had said goodbye to Danny, though, promising to visit him in New York sooner rather than later, but both of them knew well that would be a while before they could go out for beers and act like nothing had happened. Again.

Jack frowned as he watched the families around him, walking about without a care in the world, probably talking about the carnival and how much fun they had had in it. Jack had picked up the Lensfield Times and was surprised that no one had noticed how much had happened during those same seven days. Phil Kale arrested for killing his children and burning down his house. Jacqueline Stevens dying of a heart attack in her own store. Samuel Gold found dead of hypothermia in his backyard. Matt Steel attacked and killed by Hailey Astern in his own room. The only incident that had merited any real attention was the death of Chairman Morgan, and that was written off as a gas leak.

Jack hated that he was the only one who could see the connections.

"Hey, mister!"

Jack turned to his left and gazed at a young boy, no older than twelve, smiling through his braces and holding an envelope.

"Are you Jack Hilton?"

"Heldon," Jack corrected with a smile.

The boy held out the envelope. "Then this is for you."

Jack frowned, reaching out and taking the envelope from the boy. "What is it?"

The boy shrugged. "No idea," he said. "The tall man told me to give it to you."

Jack froze. "What did you say?"

"The tall man," the boy grinned. "He had this strange hat and was wearing all black. He said you would be here and that I should give you that."

Jack looked at the envelope, then back at the boy. "Thank you," he whispered.

The boy nodded and ran back to his friends, calling out to them as he darted across the field to where they had set up for what looked like a baseball game. Jack watched him go, then looked down at the envelope. His hands began to shake, and a voice inside his head told him to just throw it away.

Nothing good could come out of it. Better yet, burn it!

Jack opened the envelope and pulled out the single sheet of paper inside, unfolding it slowly. He began to read the slanted handwriting.

> *My Dear Jack,*
>
> *I will not lie, this has definitely been a most exciting experience. I am jubilant that we were able to relive the past in our own special way. I was serious when I said our lives were interlocked, you and I, and I am most confident that there will be a day when our paths will cross again. Until then, the chessboard will be waiting, and we will complete our game.*
>
> *Ebenezer Cage*

Jack looked up at the field where the carnival had stood, and slowly folded the letter back into its envelope. He got up, pushed it into his back pocket, and let his eyes wander over Gambler's Park.

"I'll look forward to it, Mr. Cage," he said to no one in particular, then turned around and walked back to his car.

Epilogue

Ebenezer Cage stood with his back to the caravan, leaning heavily on his cane with his hands clamped over each other. In front of him was the carousel, unmoving, dark, silent. He wore a small smile on his face as he watched Amanda lead Lily and Michael out from the woods and towards the carousel, their faces blank and their eyes lifeless.

Amanda stepped onto the carousel and waited for the other two to do the same. Slowly, Lily walked between the frozen riders and climbed onto the small princess carriage she had previously occupied, settling in comfortably with her hands folded in her lap and her eyes staring straight ahead. Amanda guided Michael a bit further away, then waited patiently as he straddled his horse and settled in. Her eyes darted between him and Josh occupying the adjacent steed, both brothers side by side, at last.

Amanda walked off the carousel and made her way to Ebenezer. She stood stoically beside him, gazing back at the carousel. It instantly burst into life with its carnival music and flashing lights, and slowly began to spin.

"You let him go," she said to Ebenezer, finally finding the courage to speak up.

Ebenezer's smile widened. "I did."

"Why?"

"There is so much left for you to understand, my dear," Ebenezer chuckled, turning to look at her, his eyes blazing. "There is a much bigger game in progression, and at the moment, the next hand belongs to Jack Heldon."

"Then why take Faith?"

"How else was Mr. Heldon to learn that he can walk through doors?" Ebenezer replied softly. "It takes great emotional conviction to accept that kind of knowledge, and I must say, he handled himself quite well."

"I don't understand this game," Amanda said.

"You will," Ebenezer chuckled, returning his attention to the spinning carnival, his eyes burning brighter. "You will."

* * *

Blood Contract
Written by Ron Ripley

Prelude: Ignorance is No Excuse

"Then the motion carries," Alderman Williams said, fairly glowing with his pleasure at the board's decision.

Hollis Blood took his hat off of his knee and stood faster than his old body was used to. He thumped loudly on the chamber's floor with his cane until the cheerful prattle of the alderman stopped. They all looked at him with undisguised displeasure and unease.

Hollis pointed his cane at them. "This, Aldermen, is a poor decision. You've violated the agreement that my family had with the town."

No one responded. And why should they, Hollis thought. They've already made their decision.

"Hollis," Alderman Nadeau started, then stopped, swallowing nervously. "Um, Mr. Blood, the agreement was made with the belief that there would never be a need for Thorne to expand."

"I've no issue with expansion," Hollis snapped. "The town needs it. I have issue with you choosing my family lands." Without waiting for another response, Hollis put his hat on his head and left the small aldermanic chamber.

He navigated the long granite steps, ignoring the newly installed handicap ramp. All about him were signs of the town of Thorne moving steadily into the future -- or at least playing catch up with the present.

His cane thumped loudly on the old brick sidewalk and the early autumn sun set behind the small, wooden First Congregationalist Church. Hollis moved at a surprisingly fast pace for someone of his age and physical ability, and kept it up until he was well outside of town and came to his own driveway.

The drive was of dirt, the trees heavy around the borders of the property. They were tall and old and angry. Hollis slowed his pace as he walked up the drive, the trees' boughs interlocking a scarce fifteen feet above his head. A long, dark tunnel formed before him, curving slowly up and to the left.

Soon he came to a narrow path, hardly visible even to him.

It had been a long time since Hollis had found it necessary to travel to this part of the family land.

The path ran at a sharp angle from the drive. Beneath the leaf litter Hollis's cane thumped loudly upon cobblestones which had been set in place by his grandfather's father.

Hollis pushed through thin branches, ignoring the occasional sting of an insect and the cold air that thickened around him.

In a moment, he stood before the wrought iron gate to the family graveyard.

The gate was pure black, untouched by rust or age. The matching hinges were set into a tall granite post, the lock for the gate set into the post's mate standing opposite. A large fieldstone wall, nearly six feet in height, wrapped around the entire graveyard, making a perfect box.

Hollis put his hand on the lock, felt a short, powerful surge, and the lock clicked open. The gate swung in silently.

Hollis walked into the graveyard.

The grass was neat, not rising more than four inches above the ground. The headstones were laid out in even rows, one close to the other. The Blood dead were orderly even in their final repose.

Seventy-one family graves.

Five rows of twelve, one row of eleven.

At the end of the last row, on the far right, was a marker with his name and birth date carved into it. The terminal date had not been set -- or if it had, the information had not been shared with him.

Hollis looked at the graves for a moment.

"They've broken the contract," he said simply.

And with that he turned and walked out of the graveyard, leaving the gate open to the coming night.

Chapter 1: Playing Security Guard

Mike and Tom walked among the various pieces of equipment, checking the fuel tanks and the hydraulic reservoirs on everything from the JCB mini-loader to the CAT excavator. It took them nearly twenty minutes to check every piece and to make sure keys weren't in the ignitions.

"Looks good," Tom said, walking with the foreman back to the office trailer that had been set up on the side of Blood Road.

"It does," Mike agreed.

"Do I really have to pull this shift?" Tom asked as they walked into the trailer, the small heater warming up the interior and feeding off of the propane tank outside.

"We've been over this shit," Mike sighed, walking around his desk. He sat down in his chair, pulled a pint of whiskey out of a drawer and uncapped it. Mike took a long pull from it and didn't offer any to Tom.

Tom had been sober for three years, and Mike knew it.

Still, the sight of it made Tom's throat dry.

Mike saw the look, capped the pint and slipped it into the inner pocket of his jacket. "Sorry Tommy," Mike said.

"No problem, Bossman," Tom said, dropping into a beat-up recliner set against the wall.

"I don't know who's screwing with the equipment," Mike said, "but I can't have another morning of dry hydraulic tanks. Somebody managed to pump all of that shit out. I don't see why they'd have to steal hydraulic oil in the first place, but if it's someone who's just screwing around with us, they may decide to move on to bigger and better things."

Tom nodded.

They'd wasted nearly an hour of the work day just filling the tanks and checking out the rest of the rigs before starting them up. Then it was another forty-five minutes before the hydraulic oil was warm enough for the equipment to actually be usable -- nearly two hours down the shitter.

"We can't afford another day like today," Mike said.

Tom nodded.

"Winter's coming fast this year," Mike continued.

"I know, Mike," Tom sighed, taking his hat off and rolling the brim for a minute. "I know that another day will screw us on the schedule. I just don't want to have to sit here until, what, eleven?"

"Yeah," Mike said apologetically. "Eleven. That's when the hired security guard is going to come in. I'm paying you time and a half on this, Tom. Eight hours."

"And I appreciate that," Tom said, putting his hat back on his head, "but I want to be home."

Mike nodded.

Tom sighed.

Standing up, Mike put on his own hat and looked at Tom. "Just keep an eye out, kid. And an ear. Let's hope that this was just a one-time deal."

"Yeah," Tom said, "I will."

Mike nodded and left the trailer. A minute later, Tom heard Mike's diesel start, and a moment after that, the big red Dodge went rumbling out of the lot.

Tom was alone.

He dug his phone out of his pocket, checked his emails, his Facebook page, and played a couple of rounds of Candy Crush.

It was four o'clock.

"You've got to be shitting me," he groaned, dropping his phone to his lap. "Seven more goddamn hours."

His stomach rumbled, and Tom suddenly realized that he didn't have anything to eat. He had finished his lunch later than usual, but they had a hell of a time ripping out a stand of pine trees right near the day's end and he was hungry as hell now.

"This sucks," he groaned.

Picking up his phone again, he brought up Google and started searching for any place that would deliver. Thorne, New Hampshire wasn't exactly a hot place to be.

Hell, they had only just had a Dunkin Donuts move into the town and that was because there was going to be construction going on for the next year and a half with all the new developments that were about to be built.

Shaking his head at his miserable situation, Tom scrolled down until he found a pizza place in a nearby town called Monson.

He tapped on the number and hit call.

"Conroy's Pizza," a young girl said, "is this pick-up or delivery?"

"Delivery, I hope," Tom said.

The girl paused for a moment, "Um, what do you mean?"

"Well," he said, straightening up in the chair, "do you guys deliver out to Thorne?"

"Yup," she said.

"There's a new worksite out here, do you know it?"

"Yeah," she answered. "It's on Blood Road."

"Yes," Tom said. "I'm working here. I drive a blue Chevy extended cab, and it's parked right next to the trailer. I can't leave, but if I pay over the phone can you guys send a large pepperoni and a two-liter bottle of Coke out to me?"

"Yeah," the girl said, "that's not a problem. Should the delivery guy go to your truck or the trailer?"

"The trailer, please," Tom answered.

"Okay, that'll be sixteen even then," she said.

"Fantastic," Tom grinned to himself. He read off his debit card information to her, and a moment later he was up and out of the chair, plugging his phone into the extension cord so it could charge.

Beyond the thin walls of the trailer the day was getting darker and the air colder. He pulled his gloves out of his jacket's pockets and put them on.

Need to start the generator for the lights, he thought, opening the door and stepping out into the cold. He walked to the where the generator was chained to the back of the excavator for the night. Tom double checked the fuel, hit the ignition and fired up the generator.

The lights which were suspended from tall, temporary, steel frames flickered into life. Cones of bright, harsh light appeared around the gathered pieces of equipment and Tom nodded to himself. He turned and started to walk back to the trailer and then stopped.

What the hell? He thought, turning back towards the generator.

Standing just inside the tree line, just inside the very edge of the light was a young boy. Maybe six or seven, no older than Tom's youngest brother.

The boy's skin was pale and seemed sickly. He had short, black hair, and he wore a black suit and a white shirt with a black tie. On his feet were battered canvas All-Stars. The suit coat that he wore hung strangely, as if it was too wide in the back, or torn up the center.

Tom took a cautious step towards the boy.

They were out in the middle of nowhere, as far as Tom was concerned, and the only person that he knew of living in the area was the old man who lived up the dirt drive. And that was half a mile farther up the road.

"Are you okay?" Tom asked.

The boy nodded.

A little bit of relief slipped into Tom -- but only a little.

"Are you lost?"

The boy shook his head.

"Are you with someone else?" Tom asked.

Again the boy shook his head.

"Are you cold?"

The boy nodded.

"Well," Tom said, "do you have a phone?"

The boy nodded.

"Did you call anyone?"

The boy looked at him, confused for a moment, then shook his head.

Maybe it's not charged, Tom thought, or bad reception.

"I've got a phone inside if you want to use it," Tom said, "or I can grab you a blanket out of my truck if you want to wrap up in it. I've got pizza on the way, and I can call someone for you too."

The boy looked at him, hardly blinking.

"Um," Tom said, rubbing the back of his head. "Do you want to come inside and warm up and use the phone?"

The boy smiled and nodded.

"Cool," Tom said, relieved. He didn't want the kid to think that he was some kind of pervert or anything, but he didn't want the kid out in the cold either. Tom would sit at Mike's desk and let the kid sit in the recliner. Then Tom could call the police. That is, if Thorne even had a police department.

He shook his head and then stumbled back.

The boy was right beside him.

"Jesus Christ!" Tom said, his heart thundering in his chest. "I never even heard you!"

The boy smiled happily.

Yeah, Tom thought, shaking his head. This kid is exactly Matthew. Must be the age, he thought, remembering some of the shit that his youngest brother liked to do.

"Okay, kid," Tom said, "come on with me. I'm Tom, by the way," he said, extending his hand.

The boy shook the offered hand, the boy's own small hand was deathly cold to the touch. "I'm Morgan," he said.

"Nice to meet you, Morgan," Tom said, letting go of the boy's hand quickly. He led the boy to the trailer and up the three steps that took them inside.

The boy smiled and walked over to the heater, holding his hands out to it. Tom sat down at Mike's desk and saw that Morgan's suit coat was indeed ripped up to nearly the center of his shoulder blades.

"Does someone know where you are?" Tom asked, reaching for his phone.

"Yes," Morgan answered.

Tom disconnected his phone and saw that the battery was nearly dead. What the hell?

Shaking his head, Tom plugged the phone back in. Sitting back in Mike's chair, he looked up and saw Morgan standing in front of the desk.

Tom's heart leaped.

Christ! This kid is way too quiet. He must drive his parents nuts.

"What's up?" Tom asked.

Morgan looked confused, glancing up at the ceiling then back down at Tom.

"Ah, well," Tom said. "I mean, do you have a question?"

"Yes," Morgan said.

"What's your question?" Tom said.

"Why are you tearing down these trees?"

The boy had hazel eyes, Tom realized, and they were fixed steadily on Tom.

"It's my job," Tom answered. "The company I work for was hired to clear the land for houses."

"This is your job?" Morgan asked.

"Yup," Tom answered.

"This is your job," Morgan said again, then he added, "Do you live in Thorne, too?"

"Yes," Tom said again, wondering if something was actually wrong with the kid's head.

"Then I am sorry."

"Why?" Tom asked, genuinely confused.

Yet Morgan said nothing. He simply stared at Tom.

"Why are you sorry?"

And as the last syllable left Tom's mouth, Morgan leaned over the desk, grabbed Tom by the head with both hands and dragged him out of the chair.

For a moment, Tom was stunned, and then he felt how cold the boy's hands were. There was immense strength in that small frame. At first Tom shouted, then he screamed, flailing at the boy with his fists, trying to get to his feet, yet Morgan jerked him off balance.

Morgan pulled Tom towards the door, which flew open of its own accord as they neared it, and a heartbeat later Morgan was dragging him down the steel stairs and into the yard.

There, just a few feet away was a large hole. One that hadn't been there before.

Morgan moved confidently towards it.

Tom saw the hole, and he knew what was coming.

He shrieked and tried to wrench his head away, but the boy tightened his grip, stars of pain exploding around Tom's vision.

Tom punched at the boy, clawed at Morgan's hands, pulled at the boy's clothes, but nothing stopped the quiet child's steady approach toward the hole. Then Tom was in the hole, Morgan holding him down, looking calm as the dirt started to fall into the opening.

Tom continued to fight, but soon the earth had his legs buried, and then his waist and his chest. One arm became pinned beside him, the other upraised to strike when Morgan settled back, letting go.

"I'm sorry," Morgan said as the earth swept over and around Tom's head, leaving him gasping and in darkness. "It won't be quick."

And it wasn't.

Chapter 2: Checking on the Pizza Man

Jim Petrov was standing in the new Dunkin Donuts in Thorne when dispatch called him.

"Two-Nine do you copy?" Maggie said.

Jim paid for his medium hot regular and stepped off to the side with his coffee, keying the mic on his shoulder strap. "This is Two-Nine, dispatch, go."

"Missing driver from Conroy's," Maggie said.

He looked at his watch. Five o'clock.

"How long, dispatch?"

"Forty-five. And it was just the one."

Jim frowned. "Destination, dispatch?"

"The worksite on Blood Road in Thorne."

"Copy, dispatch. I'm on my way now."

Jim waved to the girls behind the counter and stepped out the backdoor to his Charger. He climbed in, settled into the seat, and pulled the belt on before starting the car. He didn't bother with the siren. Who knew what was going on? The kid could have pulled over for a quickie with his girlfriend, stopped to chat with a couple of buddies, or any number of things that kids did. However, Conroy usually hired kids who stuck to the job and didn't screw around that often, and if Cliff Conroy was worried about this kid, it meant that the kid really wasn't one to drift off.

Jim put a little weight on the gas pedal.

He took a sip of his hot coffee, saw the cars in front of him slow down with the cop-panic setting in. Sighing, he threw the lights on and increased his speed again as the cars happily got out of his way.

Keeping the lights on, he raced along Route 122 and turned onto Blood Road. Up ahead in the darkness he caught sight of work lights glaring down on the worksite. Jim could see a trailer and a small Mazda Miata parked beside a big old Chevy. The Mazda had its lights on, exhaust billowing out of the tailpipe.

The driver's side door was open, and it was empty.

Jim swung into the yard and his headlights splashed across a young man sitting on the ground, a red warming bag on his lap. In front of the young man, sitting on the steps of the trailer, was a boy, perhaps seven or eight. He wore a black suit with a matching tie over a white dress shirt.

Jim put the Charger into park and keyed his mic. "Dispatch this is Two-Nine. I am on scene. I have the delivery driver and a young boy. Something's not right. Send a local from Monson and a bus from Hollis, please."

"Copy Two-Nine," Maggie said.

Jim left the lights on but shut off the car before getting out.

"Hello," he called out cheerfully, stepping around the front of his cruiser.

"Hello," the young man said without looking back. His voice was thick with fear.

The boy on the steps smiled and waved.

Jim returned the wave as he walked closer. He finally stood beside the driver and looked down at the young man.

A look of abject terror was frozen on his face as he stared at something in front of him. Jim thought that it was the little boy on the steps, but as he followed the young man's line of sight he saw something else. Something which caused his spine to ripple with concern.

A hand protruded from the earth nearly halfway between them. It looked almost like a Halloween gag, but Jim knew that it wasn't. The fingers were slightly curled, the wrist slightly exposed, but the forearm vanishing into the dirt.

"It was still moving when I got here," the delivery driver said, staring at the hand. "It was still moving."

"The hand?" Jim asked gently.

The driver nodded, finally tearing his eyes away and looking up at Jim. "The hand was still moving when I got here, sir. I couldn't help. He wouldn't let me."

"Who's he?" Jim asked.

The driver pointed to the young boy.

"Hello," Jim said to the boy.

The boy waved again. He smiled happily at Jim.

"He asked me if I lived in Thorne," the driver said, staring at the boy. "But I don't. He said that was good."

"Do you live in Thorne?" Jim asked the boy on the stairs.

The boy smiled broadly as he nodded.

"Do you?" the boy asked, and his voice was low and happy and raised the hair on the back of Jim's neck.

"No," Jim said evenly, "I don't."

"That's good," the little boy said, standing up.

"Why is it good?" Jim asked.

"Because you won't end up like him," the boy said simply and started walking away.

"Son, you can't walk away from me," Jim said, taking a step forward.

The boy paused to look over his shoulder. He smiled again and said, "Yes I can."

The boy walked towards the tree line hidden just outside the range of the worklights.

Jim started walking after him, stepping around the hand. "Son, don't walk away from me."

The boy didn't answer. He simply slipped away into the darkness. Jim walked quickly after him, slipping his small LED flashlight out of its case and turning it on as he walked into the woods. He stopped and scanned the trees.

He couldn't see anything.

Faintly Jim heard the sound of sirens. It sounded like one of the Monson PD.

Frowning, he turned around, turning his flashlight off as he walked back into the yard. He started following his footprints back towards the trailer when he stopped suddenly and stared at the ground.

Jim could clearly see his own footprints in the dirt.

But his were the only prints there.

No sign of the young boy's footprints at all.

Chapter 3: Hollis and Coffee

Hollis sat on his porch, smoking his pipe and sipping at his coffee. From his chair he could look down through the thinning woods and see the flashes of police lights and the lights of an ambulance. The stark light of the worksite's lights polluted the night sky as well.

Hollis took the pipe stem out of his mouth, exhaled through his nose and took a drink.

In the slim light of the half moon Hollis caught sight of a small shape walking up the drive, staying in the center of the dirt. A soft, happy whistling was carried along the autumn breeze and brought a sigh to Hollis' lips.

He put the coffee down and returned the pipe stem to his mouth.

In silence, he watched the small shape move ever closer until he recognized the young boy -- not that he hadn't known who it was from the moment he'd seen the walk. and heard his brother's favorite piece from Schubert being whistled.

Morgan walked up the long, winding cobblestone path that their mother had their father install in 1933, a year before pneumonia would claim Morgan's young life. Hollis's brother wore his burial suit, hopping up each granite step cheerfully.

When Morgan's shoes rang out on the broad, wooden steps, Morgan waved at Hollis as he finally stepped onto the porch.

Hollis let out another sigh and waved back.

"Hello Morgan," Hollis said around the pipe stem. "I should have known that you would be the first."

Morgan laughed, a sweet and pure sound that Hollis had forgotten completely, and which brought tears to his eyes.

"I'm so glad to see you, Morgan," Hollis sighed, wiping his eyes before taking the pipe out of his mouth. "I've missed you."

"I've watched you grow," Morgan said, sitting down in the old rocker that their mother had favored. She had never allowed Morgan or Hollis to use it, afraid that they would tip over in it. "I'm very proud of you."

"Thank you," Hollis said, taking a sip of his coffee.

"You're welcome." Morgan looked at him, grinning. "You learned to fly a plane!"

Hollis smiled. "I did. A P-38 Lightning."

"You had a picture of you and me together when you flew," Morgan said, his grin turning into a giant smile.

"I always thought you were flying with me."

Morgan nodded happily. "I was."

Hollis returned the pipe to his mouth, and he smoked cheerfully for a few minutes as they sat in silence. The lights continued to flash down at the worksite and occasionally the sound of a two-way radio could faintly be heard as it echoed off of the trees.

Finally Hollis asked, "What happened down there?"

Morgan glanced over his shoulder, back down the way he had come. "That?"

"Yes," Hollis said, "that."

"I happened."

Morgan's tone was flat. The cheerfulness gone.

"May I ask?"

Morgan looked at him and shook his head. "We've decided that it is best that you don't know what we do. At least not from the family. We don't want you being held accountable for any of it."

Hollis nodded.

His brother stood up and put a cold, but gentle hand on Hollis's shoulder. "Someone will be up here soon, Hollis. A State Policeman. He was nice to me. Tell him to stay away. Some of the others won't care who is from Thorne and who isn't."

Hollis nodded. He looked at Morgan, wishing that they were still little boys, still hunting salamanders under the rocks by Hassell Brook, still picking apples in the family's orchard.

Morgan smiled at him. "I will see you soon enough, Hollis."

Once more Hollis nodded, closing his eyes and listening to the footsteps of his brother fade away.

Chapter 4: Jim Petrov and the Blood Road Worksite

Much to Jim's surprise, his coffee was still relatively warm.

He stood beside Brian Ricard's Monson PT cruiser while the EMTs treated the delivery boy from Conroy's for shock.

Jim and Brian had taped off the area around the hand protruding from the ground, and they had put a call in to the supervisor for the worksite, Mike Pinkham with the Deutsche Development Corporation. The Chevy at the site was registered to a Thomas Pelto, previous arrests for DUI, but that had been three years ago.

Jim had a suspicion that Thomas Pelto's hand was the one sticking up and out of the ground.

According to Cliff Conroy, his daughter had taken an order for a large pepperoni and a two-liter bottle of coke to be delivered out to a Tom at the worksite. Richard MacDonald, the delivery boy, had brought it out to the site.

All they could currently get out of Richard was that the boy whom Jim had tried to follow hadn't allowed Richard to try to save Tom.

The most frightening part of the whole deal -- aside from the little boy disappearing into the woods -- was that it didn't look like the dirt was even disturbed around the hand.

"It looks like the damned thing just grew out of it," Jim said outloud.

"What's that?" Brian asked.

"The hand," Jim said, taking a drink of his coffee and nodding towards the hand. "It looks like someone planted a seed, and the hand just grew out of the damned ground."

"Yeah," Brian agreed. "Kind of messed up. But what about that other kid?"

"I don't know," Jim said, shaking his head.

One of the EMTs came over, peeling off a pair of nitrate gloves. "We're going to transport him down to Nashua if that's alright," the young woman said.

"Sounds good to me," Jim said.

Brian nodded.

"He says there was another kid?" she asked.

Jim and Brian both nodded.

"Did you guys find him?"

"No," Jim said. "I tried to follow him, but he disappeared into the woods -- vanished actually."

"Did you check up at the Blood House?"

"The what house?" Brian asked.

The young woman smiled. "The Blood House. I grew up in Thorne. The Bloods had their main house right up off of the road here. I think the driveway is just a little ways up on the left."

"Didn't even know about that," Jim said.

"Let me know," the young woman said. "My name's Mary."

"Nice to meet you, Mary," Jim said.

She smiled at him, waved goodbye to Brian, and walked back to the ambulance. Just as the ambulance was pulling out, another pair of State cruisers and the crime scene truck arrived.

Jim saw Sergeant Ward step out of the first cruiser and nodded to the man.

The sergeant looked down at the hand, shook his head and walked over to Jim and Brian.

"Hello Pat," Jim said.

"Jim, Brian," Pat said, glancing back at the hand once more. "That's pretty."

"It is," Brian agreed.

"Did you find the other boy?" Pat asked.

"No," Jim said. "One of the EMTs said that there's a house up a little ways on the left. I'd like to go check on that."

"Sounds good," Pat said. "Brian, I hate to ask, but could you run some cones out for me and keep an eye out for the supervisor, please?"

"Sure thing," Brian said. "Things are pretty quiet back in Monson. I'll cover you on this."

Jim gave a wave to both men, walked back to his cruiser and climbed in. He finished his coffee, put the cup down in the holder and started the car. He pulled out of the yard, turned left up Blood Road and in a couple of minutes saw a dirt driveway break the monotony of the tree-lined road.

Signaling, Jim turned the car into the driveway and flipped on his spotlight, guiding it with his left hand and steering the car with his right. The driveway was long and winding, rising up ever so slightly as it continued.

Soon though, the drive turned a little to the left, and a large, grand New England farmhouse stood before him. A few lights shined inside, and a lit lantern hung near the door, illuminating the front steps and the beginnings of a wide, wrap-around porch.

Jim parked the car and keyed the mic. "Two-Nine to dispatch."

"Go ahead, Two-Nine," Maggie responded.

"Dispatch I am at the Blood House, Sergeant Ward is on scene and aware."

"Good copy, Two-Nine."

Once more Jim climbed out of the car, yet he loosened his service weapon in its holster before walking around the car. He moved steadily towards the house, stepping onto a neatly kept stonework path that led unerringly to the wooden steps. He climbed the stairs at a casual pace and almost didn't notice that there was someone sitting in a chair to the left of the main door.

"Hello," Jim said, stepping back down onto the top step.

"Hello," a man replied. Something red glowed in front of the man's face for a moment, and the wind shifted sharply, bringing to Jim the strong scent of pipe tobacco.

"I'm Trooper Petrov, and I was wondering if I could speak with you," Jim said.

"Please," the man said, "come up and have a seat."

Jim did so and as he sat down in the cold rocking chair set at a slight angle from the speaker, Jim saw that the speaker was an old man -- an extremely old man. He was probably pushing late eighties or early nineties. The man was smoking an old briar churchwarden's pipe and wrapped in a thick quilt with a knit cap snugly on his head. On a small table beside him there was a cup of half-finished black coffee.

"I don't get many visitors," the old man said politely. "And I do believe, sir, that you are the first State Police officer to ever visit."

Jim smiled, took his hat off and placed it on his knee. "I'm pleased to be the first, sir. However, I'm afraid that I don't know your name."

"Ah," the man said, removing his right hand from the quilt and extending it. "Hollis Blood."

Jim leaned forward and shook the hand. It was old, and it was thin, but the hand was strong. "That's a good New England name," Jim said as he let go of Hollis's hand.

Hollis chuckled. "It is indeed. You should have been here seventy years ago, Trooper, there were still Coffins amongst the Bloods in Thorne and Monson -- Halls and Copps, too. The old names. There are a few Halls about," he continued, "but I'm the last of the Bloods here in Thorne. The Coffins have died out -- the Copps too. I believe that I'm the only bench owning member still in the Congregationalist Church in town.

"I suppose, though," Hollis said, "that you're not here for a lesson in the family lines of Thorne. What can I do for you, Trooper Petrov?"

"Well," Jim said, "I noticed that you can see the lights down on Blood Road."

"I can," Hollis said. "Do you mind if I ask what happened?"

"Not at all," Jim replied. "However, I really don't know. The reason that I'm up here is that when I arrived on the scene there was a little boy, perhaps about eight years old. He slipped away into the forest, and I couldn't follow him. I was hoping that maybe he had come up this way, perhaps to your house."

Hollis Blood smoked his pipe for a moment, letting out a slim stream of smoke from his nostrils before responding. "Trooper Petrov," Hollis said carefully, "I don't think that you'd believe me if I told you what I saw."

Jim smiled. "I might, sir. Could you try?"

Hollis nodded. "I believe that you said that you saw a boy about eight years old?"

"I did." Jim leaned forward. Hollis's voice had gotten a little lower.

"I don't suppose that this boy was pale?" Hollis asked.

"Very," Jim said.

"Black hair and wearing a black suit?"

"Yes."

"And the jacket, it was unsewn up the back?"

"I thought it was torn," Jim said. Then he looked at Hollis. "You saw him."

"I did."

"Did you see where he went?" Jim asked. "Do you know who he is?"

"I did not see where he went," Hollis said, "and I do know who he is."

Jim waited a moment for Hollis to speak and when he didn't, Jim asked, "Will you tell me?"

"Yes," Hollis said, looking away. "His name is Morgan Blood."

Sitting back, Jim looked at Hollis. "I thought you said that you were the last."

"I am," Hollis said. He folded back the quilt and stood up. "Please follow me, Trooper Petrov."

Jim stood and walked behind Hollis as the man led him to the front door.

"Who is Morgan, Hollis?" Jim asked as Hollis opened the door and warm light washed over them.

"My brother," Hollis answered, motioning for Jim to follow him in.

Jim stepped into a long hallway that smelled pleasantly of pipe tobacco and a well-used fireplace. Wallpaper that had probably been hanging for at least a century covered the walls and family portraits in thick frames and clear glass hung upon the walls as well.

"Hollis," Jim said calmly, "are you feeling alright?"

"Quite," Hollis answered. He put the pipe stem back into his mouth and stopped in the middle of the hallway and turned to face the left wall.

"Hollis," Jim said.

Hollis let out a bit of smoke, took the pipe out of his mouth, and pointed politely at the wall. "Please," the man said, "simply look at the photographs, Trooper Petrov."

Jim turned and looked at the photographs.

He dropped his hat to the floor as he looked at the black and white photograph of the boy he had seen at the worksite. The boy was smiling at the camera -- an old leather baseball glove and ball in his hands.

"Morgan Blood," Hollis said, putting the pipe back into his mouth. "My brother died of pneumonia when he was eight. I don't know what he did down at the edge of the road. He told me that you were nice, Trooper Petrov and that you should be careful."

"Why should I be careful?" Jim asked.

"My relations are angry," Hollis said simply.

"About what?" Jim asked, a sense of the surreal replacing reality.

"Old contracts that have been broken," Hollis said.

"And I should be careful because of that?"

"Yes," Hollis said.

"But why?" Jim asked, looking at Hollis.

"Because," Hollis said, returning his look evenly, "not all of my relatives will be as gentle as my brother."

Chapter 5: Alderman Nadeau and his morning paper

Emil Nadeau watched the paper get delivered by a raggedy looking middle-aged man throwing The Telegraph from the driver's side window. The man was driving on the wrong side of the street and, not surprisingly, he had Massachusetts plates.

Frowning, Emil waited until the man had moved down to the McCalls' house before leaving his own for the paper. The Telegraph, wrapped in a protective sleeve of orange plastic, was light, as usual. Swinging the paper from one hand, Emil looked at his rose bushes and the rose of Sharon growing along the left side of the driveway. Everything had grown in well this year in spite of Daniel moving out.

Well, Emil thought, I'll certainly be able to find someone to replace Daniel, even if they won't necessarily have his green thumb.

Their two-year relationship had ended badly, but thankfully the man hadn't gone to the town about their living arrangements. The rest of the country might have been opening up to the idea of homosexual unions, but little towns like Thorne tended to be behind the learning curve.

Emil put the thought out of his mind as he opened the side door and walked back into the kitchen. He closed and locked the door behind him, tossing the paper onto the table before turning to put on a fresh pot of coffee.

He froze and stared at a tall, elderly man, whose back was to Emil. The man played quite happily with a burner on the stove. He turned the front left burner on, then off, seeming to enjoy the ticking sound of the ignition switch before the gas caught flame.

Emil took a deep breath and tried to settle his nerves.

The man looked at Emil, and Emil screamed.

The man's eyes were white as if dipped into a milky cloud. At the sound of Emil's scream the man smiled, revealing old and yellowed teeth.

"Sit, Alderman," the man said, his voice thick and cold. "Sit."

Emil simply screamed again.

Leaving a flame burning, the man took one long stride over to Emil, grabbed him by his throat, and thrust him into a chair.

Emil stopped screaming and stared at the man.

The man smiled again, let go of Emil's throat, and sat down on the table.

The man looked at Emil and Emil stopped screaming.

"Very good, Alderman," the man said. "Well done. How are you feeling?"

Emil blinked and found that he couldn't answer the man. He simply couldn't.

"Ah well," the man sighed. "I would introduce myself, but I think that you would find little use in that. Although, I must ask you a question. Is that alright?"

Emil stared at him.

"Is it?"

Finally, Emil nodded.

"Excellent," the man said. "Do you understand the phrase contractual obligations?"

Emil nodded.

"I'm surprised," the man said coldly. He looked hard with his milky white eyes at Emil. "When the town of Thorne was signed over in seventeen seventy-seven," the man said, "the town of Thorne agreed to honor the wishes of the Blood family should they render them assistance and protection from raiders drifting down from French Canada. My family held true to their bond."

The man stood, walked over to the stove, and lit another burner. With that done, he turned to face Emil. "As you can so easily testify, Alderman Nadeau," the man sneered, "the town of Thorne did not."

Emil finally found his voice.

"Who are you?" Emil demanded, his voice shaking. "How did you get into my house?"

"You left the door open, you bumbling frog," the old man said, turning another burner on. "And truly, do you wish to know my name?"

"Yes," Emil said, straightening up, "I need to know for when I have a warrant filled out for your arrest."

The man chuckled.

It was a distinctly disturbing and unpleasant sound.

"Well then, Alderman Nadeau, my name is Obadiah Blood," the man said, turning on the last burner. All four of the burners were blazing steadily.

"Obadiah Blood," Emil began angrily, and then he stopped. He looked closely at the tall, old man. "Obadiah Blood," he repeated in a low voice.

"Indeed," Obadiah said.

Emil's heart stutter-stepped and he managed to say, "You can't be."

"But I am."

"Obadiah Blood is dead."

"I am," Obadiah agreed. "In fact I have been for over a hundred years."

"They killed you," Emil managed. "They killed you for murdering the migrant boys. I read that. I read that you were a murderer."

"Oh, yes," Obadiah said, "I've killed in my day. But never boys. Always men. It was a Gauthier, in fact, who killed those boys. But they wrapped those murders around my neck and lynched me in the town center -- a blind man."

"They said that you didn't even defend yourself," Emil said.

"No," Obadiah corrected. "I remained silent. They were in a frenzy, led by Gauthier. It was my wish that I could return and gain vengeance upon him through his relatives, but the task of their deaths has been given to another -- you," Obadiah grinned, "you, Emil Nadeau, you are my given task." He turned away from Emil for a moment and took one of the decorative towels Emil and Daniel had purchased in York together from its place in front of the sink.

"What are you doing?" Emil asked, standing up.

The old man's head snapped around, and Obadiah snarled, "Sit."

Something pushed Emil back into the chair with enough force to make the chair rock on its back legs. As Emil tried to regain his balance he caught sight of Obadiah holding the towel over one of the burners. It took only a moment for the cloth to catch fire.

"What are you doing?!" Emil shouted.

Holding the burning towel carelessly, Obadiah turned to face Emil. The old man smiled happily.

"Did any of you bother to read the actual contract which the town agreed to?" Obadiah asked.

Emil couldn't answer, staring instead at the slowly burning reminder of a pleasant weekend in Maine.

Obadiah chuckled and stepped forward.

Emil's happy memory was shattered. He suddenly found himself unable to breathe, Obadiah's thick hand gripping his throat. Emil opened his mouth, gasping for air and Obadiah quickly stuffed the end of the towel into it.

Emil gagged, the flames licking at his pajama shirt, slowly setting it alight. Emil tried to breathe, but he could only do so by inhaling as he struggled against Obadiah.

The old man held him firmly, his strength atrocious.

"Now, now, Alderman," Obadiah said softly, "accept your death, as painful as it's going to be."

Emil tried to scream, but he couldn't. He felt his shirt catch fire, and his flesh started to burn. In his nose he could smell it, a stench reminiscent of a pig skin burning. Part of him recognized the fact that he was smelling his own skin burning, part of him wished that Daniel would roll over in bed and wake him from the nightmare.

Emil wouldn't wake up, though, for all of it was true. He was awake.

And finally, Emil found that he could scream.

Chapter 6: Jim Petrov at the Monson PD

"How many months has it been since the divorce, Jim?" Brian asked, handing Jim a cup of coffee.

"Four," Jim answered, nodding his thanks. "Four."

"You know," Brian said, sitting down on the edge of his desk, "you're not going to find your next date in here."

"You never know, Brian," Jim said, taking a sip of his coffee. "You guys just might pull in some extremely attractive DUI one day."

"Have you ever seen an extremely attractive DUI come through Monson?" Brian asked, chuckling. "Hell, have you seen a semi-attractive DUI ever?"

Jim shook his head, laughing. "Now that you mention it, no. No, I have not."

Before Brian could say anything else, the scanner burst into life and Harry, the day dispatcher for Monson, lifted his head up from his Sudoku puzzle.

"Monson Fire and Rescue, all hands, fire at eleven Stark Street," an unknown dispatcher said from the State's emergency call center.

The emergency phone by Harry rang sharply, and the man quickly hit the answer button. "Monson Police Department, Harry speaking," he said, typing rapidly into his computer. A second later he flashed a look at Brian that Jim had seen before. It was Harry's 'You Better Pay Attention' look, and both Jim and Brian waited, listening.

"Eleven Stark Street. Yes, we know there's a fire...you saw someone leave the building as it was burning? What's your address, Ma'am? Ten Stark Street? Phone number? Six Zero Three, Eight Nine One, Zero One Nine Five. Excellent, we'll have a cruiser there in a few minutes."

Brian and Jim put their coffees down, Jim grabbing his jacket off of a wall peg as he hurried out the door behind Brian. He followed Brian to the man's cruiser, got into the passenger seat, and closed the door, buckling his seatbelt.

Jim was off duty. It was officially a day off.

But there was a fire and a man who had walked away from the building.

Brian threw on his lights and siren and took off for Stark Street.

"Did you hear about last night yet?" Brian asked.

"Thomas Pelto?"

"Yeah."

"No, what?"

"He was buried alive. I saw the initial report this morning when I came in," Brian said. "No one can figure out how it was done. One of the crime techs is an archeology student, and he said that when they were digging Pelto out it looked like the dirt had never been disturbed by digging before."

"But he was alive?" Jim asked, thinking about the strange conversation he'd had with Hollis Blood the night before.

"Yeah," Brian nodded, turning sharply on Ridge Road. "No official cause yet, not until the autopsy is complete, but the medical examiner said that he suffocated."

"That's a suck way to go," Jim said.

"Yup."

The sign for Stark Street appeared on the left and Brian turned hard onto it. Ahead of them, Monson's pump truck and Thorne's fire engine were already on the scene. Brian jerked the cruiser over to block most of the road, leaving room for any additional trucks that might arrive.

Volunteer firefighters from both towns were racing up in their own vehicles as Jim and Brian climbed out of the car. People were coming out of their houses and watching as flames devoured the left side of the house, working their way up the side and into the roof.

A blue Prius with the vanity plate 'NADEAU' sat in the driveway.

"Shit," Brian muttered. "That's Emil Nadeau's house."

Jim wracked his brain for a minute until he found the bit of information that told him that Emil Nadeau was one of Thorne's aldermen. The man was a pain in the ass for both Thorne and Monson. He lived in Thorne but ran an insurance agency out of Monson.

"This'll be more than Thorne and Monson can handle," Jim said.

Brian only nodded. "I've got to speak with number ten."

"Want to pop the trunk?" Jim asked. "I'll grab a vest and make sure no one gets too close."

"Yeah," Brian said, leaning back into the cruiser and hitting the trunk's button.

As the trunk popped open, Brian walked off towards house number ten, and Jim went to the back of the car. He pulled a neon green safety vest with reflective strips out of the back and put the vest on before closing the trunk.

Jim walked away from the cruiser, back towards the intersection with Ridge Road.

An older man, wearing a dark suit and an old fedora, approached Jim slowly, leaning heavily on a well-used cane. The man's eyes, Jim saw, were milky white, and Jim wondered how the man could see at all.

The man stopped a few feet from Jim saying, "Excuse me, but I seem to smell a fire."

"Yes sir," Jim said, glancing around the man to make sure that no vehicles were coming. In the far distance, he heard the sound of more emergency vehicles approaching. Jim looked at the man. "Do you need to get to a particular house, sir?"

"No, no," the man replied. "Could you tell me what house it is?"

"Number eleven, sir," Jim answered.

"Jim!"

Jim turned away from the man to look back, and he saw Brian gesturing to him.

"Thank you, Trooper Petrov," the older man said behind Jim.

"You're welcome," Jim said over his shoulder.

Brian started jogging towards him, yelling, "Stop him!"

The old man? Jim thought.

And then he realized what the old man had said.

Thank you, Trooper Petrov.

Jim whipped around, and the older man was just disappearing around the garage of a nearby house.

Jim ran after him, turning around the corner of the same garage and coming to a stop just in time to avoid running headlong into a tall, chain-link fence. He stood there and looked along the fence's length, through the backyard and past the agitated German shepherd walking the perimeter with its ears back and its tail down. Jim could hear the dog's nervous whines above the noise of more fire trucks arriving.

In a moment, Brian was beside him, breathing heavily. "Where the hell did he go?" Brian asked.

"I don't know," Jim replied, scanning the tree line, which was thin and wide. There were no trees large enough for a man to hide behind, the land itself rolling upwards slightly at a gentle grade for at least a hundred yards.

The man should not have been able to vanish even if he was in the best of health, but he had been old and nearly blind.

"Where the hell did he go?" Brian said again, and the dog let out a long howl.

Chapter 7: At Alderman Nadeau's House

Jim stood with Brian and Travis Hope, the fire inspector out of Nashua. It had taken fire crews from Monson, Thorne, Hollis, Nashua, and the Pepperell, Massachusetts to get the blaze under control.

"The fire started in the kitchen," Travis said, smoking a cigarette and looking at the remnants of the house. A few crews worked around the house, picking apart anything that looked like it might spark and jump to the dry woods around the property. The coroner's van was already gone, taking the body of Alderman Emil Nadeau away.

"How?" Jim asked.

"With the Alderman," Travis said.

"I didn't think he smoked," Brian said.

"He didn't," Travis answered, taking a long drag off of his cigarette. "The medical examiner will have to confirm, but it looked like somebody stuffed a hand-towel down his throat and lit the goddamn man on fire."

"Jesus Christ," Brian muttered, looking away.

"Whoever it was had all the burners on as well. Whoever had the Alderman try and eat the towel also threw the morning paper on the stove. Really set it all going. Place burned quickly, though," Travis added. "Real quickly."

The fire inspector finished his cigarette, put it out, and flicked the butt towards the charred house. "I've got to write this up. See you at the next one, boys."

Jim and Brian watched him go.

"You ready to go?" Brian asked.

"Give me a minute, will you?" Jim asked. Brian nodded, and Jim walked up to the house. He looked at the remnants of the house.

Something was going on, and Jim wasn't quite sure what.

Hollis knows, Jim thought. Hollis knows.

Jim turned and walked back to Brian. "I'm ready."

Together they got into Brian's cruiser, and Brian turned off the lights before maneuvering the car around the Thorne fire truck, the only one which remained at the scene.

"Hell of a way to spend your day off," Brian said after a few minutes.

"Well," Jim said, looking out the window, "I don't have much else to do."

"You need a hobby."

"I had a wife," Jim answered.

Brian chuckled. "They may feel like the same some days, Jim, but you know that they're not."

"I know."

"Where are you headed to after we get back to the station?" Brian asked.

Jim shrugged. "I'm not sure. I'll figure it out, though."

A few more minutes passed by before they were back in Monson and Brian was pulling into an angled parking space in front of the station. They both climbed out, and Jim gave his friend a wave goodbye before walking half a block down Main Street to where his Dodge was parked in front of the diner.

Jim opened the door and got into the cab and sat there for a moment before buckling his seatbelt. He rubbed at his chin and looked out the windshield at nothing in particular.

Yesterday afternoon a man was buried alive at a worksite by the supposed ghost of a little boy.

Today a man was burned to death in a house fire. Jim had seen an older man, who was nearly blind, vanish as the boy had from the night before.

And the man had known Jim's name.

Someone had told Hollis Blood about Jim.

There was a connection, somewhere, between the murder at the worksite, the death of Emil Nadeau and Hollis Blood.

Jim started the truck's engines, checked his mirrors and pulled out onto Main Street.

He needed to find out what the connection was.

Chapter 8: The Thorne Historical Society

Jim rang the bell at the small white Victorian that served as the town of Thorne's historical society.

A few moments later, he heard the sound of someone's feet on stairs and then the door was being opened by a middle-aged woman. She had mousy brown hair pulled back into a bun and a pair of reading glasses. She looked over the tops of the glasses at him. "May I help you?"

"Yes please," Jim said. "I was wondering if you could help me with some research on the Blood family."

Her eyes widened a little. "Has something happened to Mr. Blood?"

"To Hollis?" Jim asked. "Oh no. I spoke with him, and I'm just curious about his family's history in Thorne."

"He let you call him Hollis?" she asked in a low voice.

"He did."

She smiled. "Come in, come in. I'm sorry. I didn't mean to grill you on the doorstep like that. There's simply been so much going on with the Blood lands these past few weeks."

Jim stepped in and waited until she closed the door. "Do you mind if I ask what's going on with the Blood lands?"

"You're not from Thorne?" she asked, leading him along a narrow hallway to a large room off to the right.

"No," Jim answered. "I'm a State Trooper, and I spoke with Hollis the other night and he was telling me that his family had been in Thorne for a long time."

The woman laughed pleasantly. "That's an understatement. Thorne is named after Hawthorne Blood, who originally was granted the land for extraordinary service in the French and Indian War. He eventually sold off small lots, or rather they were small when New Hampshire was still young, and eventually he incorporated a town. He made a contract with the other residents when he did, though. Hawthorne Blood told them the town would be theirs so long as the Blood lands were left alone.

"No one knew why, mind you," the woman said, gesturing to a small, Victorian loveseat in the room. The piece of furniture was set just beneath a large window, and Jim settled comfortably in it. "The land which Hawthorne Blood set aside for his own was not the finest by far. In fact, most of the land is unplowable, riddled with small streams as well as Hassell Brook, which tends to jump its bed every decade or so. No," she said, shaking her head, "it's one of those mysteries that New England towns thrive upon.

"Rumors sprang up, of course," she continued as she walked to an old wooden filing cabinet.

"Rumors of what?" Jim asked.

"Treasure stolen from the French. Treasure stolen from the British during the Revolution. Treasure stolen from the Confederates during the Civil War," she pulled a drawer open and glanced over at him, smiling. "Do you get the gist of it all?"

Jim nodded, smiling. "I do."

"I actually have a copy of the contract here as it was drawn up," the woman continued. "The original is at town hall, of course."

"Of course," Jim grinned. "I'm sorry," he said, "but I didn't get your name."

"Groff," the woman said, pulling a file out of the drawer. "Janine Groff." Closing the door, she walked over to Jim and handed him the file. After he had taken it, she went and sat in a high-backed chair standing by the room's door.

"A pleasure, Janine," Jim said, opening the file. "Is this a full-time job for you?"

"It is, but it's unpaid," she said.

"I'm sorry to hear that," he said, looking up at her. "You're extremely knowledgeable about this."

"Well thank you," Janine said, smiling proudly. "I'm a trained archivist, but my husband decided that he didn't want to live in the city, well, in Boston anymore. We moved up here to Thorne, and he works at home, telecommuting. The historical society was looking for help and, well," she laughed, "this also keeps us out of each others' hair."

Jim nodded. "That's completely understandable." He glanced down at the open folder and saw that there were two sets of pages within. One was a photocopy of an old document. The words were cut off on the bottom but continued on the following page. The other set of pages was typed out and looked to be a readable copy of the contract.

Taking the typed pages out, Jim closed the file and set it beside him on the loveseat.

"Be it known that on this Day, the Twenty Third of July, in the Year 1778, the Towne of Thorne in the Free Colony of New Hampshire and Hawthorne Blood enter into this Contract.

"Hawthorne Blood, the Founder of the Town of Thorne, wishes it to be known that all of His Property, extending from the Border of Monson to the Border of Hollis, and down to the Border of Pepperell in the Free Colony of Massachusetts, shall be given to the Towne of Thorne and the Residents therein for the profit and wellbeing of the Community.

"The only Land which the Towne of Thorne shall not dispose of shall be that which currently surrounds the Blood House. This Land shall consist of Four Hundred Acres and the Measurements of the Land shall begin at one hundreds of Rods from the Front Door of the Blood House and two hundreds of Rods on either side of the Blood House. The remainder of the Acres shall continue to the North East until the border of Cannae. These Acres shall forever be the Property of the Blood Family.

"They shall forever be the Property of the Blood Family, and if the Blood Family shall be no more than the Last Will and Testament of the Last Blood shall inform the Town of what is to be done.

"This Contract is never to be Violated, never to be Discarded. The Towne of Thorne with this signing agrees to this and knows that It shall suffer the Wrath of all of the Bloods in Thorne should the Contract be Broken."

Below this text, Jim saw the typed names of those who had signed and agreed to the contract.

Hawthorne Blood, Malachi Coffin, Jebediah Coffin, Alpheus Hall, Richard

Arnold, Elbridge Copp, and Harold Lee.

Jim looked up at Janine. She smiled at him, and he returned the smile. "Four hundred acres?"

She nodded. "He was, for that time, keeping an extremely small amount for his family. The other signers were said to have known this, and thus readily agreed to it, and, as you can see, for over two hundred years the town has held to that contract."

"It changed?" Jim asked.

"Just last week," Janine said.

"How so?"

"The board of Aldermen voted to take some of the Blood land through eminent domain after Hollis refused to sell."

"Why would they do that?" Jim asked.

"They're widening Blood Road, and they're going to erect two private developments -- one on either side of the Blood House and well into the Blood land," Janine answered. "Hollis is fighting it, of course, but a state judge has decided that the clearing of the land can continue before the appeal is heard."

"So they broke the contract," Jim said softly.

Janine nodded. "And Hollis Blood was none too happy about it."

"No," Jim said, looking down at the contract, "no I don't suppose that any of them were."

Chapter 9: Alderman Williams Working Late

Dean Williams logged out of his Ashley Madison account, shut down the incognito window, and powered down his laptop. With that done, he unplugged it and put everything away.

Dean had been carrying on a series of affairs for over twenty years, all whilst being married, and he had been able to do that by being careful. He put that concept into practice when it came to his legal practice and his investment methods. He wasn't a rich man, but he was a happy one, with a happy wife who had never suspected that her husband had ever strayed.

Or that he continued to stray.

Dean put that out of his mind -- another trick to keeping the various aspects of his life separated -- and stood up, stretching slightly. It was after eleven o'clock, and the crickets were singing loudly in the darkness. Smiling, Dean walked out of his office and up the stairs to the bedroom.

The light on his side of the king-size mattress cast a soft glow about the room. He started to unbutton his dress shirt when he realized that Lydia was sitting up at her vanity.

"Lydia?" he asked, turning to face her, and when he did he saw that the woman at the vanity wasn't his wife. His wife lay peacefully asleep on her side of the bed, a Danielle Steel novel open, spine up.

The woman at the vanity was much younger than his wife, perhaps no more than twenty, and she wore a nightgown that Lydia would have referred to as matronly. The woman was pale, her face narrow and had most of her deep brown hair tucked up beneath an old-fashioned nightcap.

Dean slipped his hand into his pants for his phone, and then he remembered that it was still in the kitchen on a charger. His gun safe was under his side of the bed and the only other phone was Lydia's, which more than likely had no charge, or was buried in her purse -- or both.

"Who are you?" Dean asked softly.

"My name is Elizabeth Blood," the woman said, and her voice was cold and harsh.

Dean bristled at the name. "Blood? Did Hollis Blood send you in here to harass me about the developments?"

"No," Elizabeth answered. "You did."

"What?"

"You did," she repeated. "You broke the contract."

Dean frowned, trying to figure out what the hell she was saying and then said, "That contract doesn't have any bearing on the eminent domain issue. Hollis was offered fair market value, and he refused."

"Of course he did," Elizabeth said, hate filling her eyes. "He was trying to save you. All of you. That's all any of us have ever done, and this is the repayment."

"You need to leave my house," Dean said, thinking: She's crazy.

From the folds of her nightgown, she lifted her hands. She was holding his .22 caliber target pistol. Even from where Dean stood he could see the rounds in the cylinder. The safety was off, and her hands were steady.

"On your knees," Elizabeth said simply.

Dean froze. "Please," he said, swallowing nervously, "the decision is out of my hands now."

"On your knees," Elizabeth repeated.

Shaking, Dean did so, looking at the woman as she stood up. "I didn't --"

She cocked the hammer back, and he went silent, staring at the small, deadly hole in the pistol's barrel. Elizabeth took a step towards him, and he closed his eyes.

The pistol barked, and something thumped softly to the floor, the sound nearly drowned out by Dean's own frightened yell.

When he didn't feel any pain, though, he opened his eyes carefully.

Elizabeth was standing in the same spot. Lydia's book was on the floor, and there was a tiny, neat hole in the side of Lydia's head. A trickle of blood seeped out, tracing the curve of his wife's cheek, gravity pulling the blood down to where it would stain the soft white sheets.

"Lydia?" Dean asked softly.

And then Elizabeth was beside him, the hot barrel of the pistol against his temple, the sound of the weapon being cocked loud in his ears.

Chapter 10: Mike Pinkham and the Mechanic

Damn cold out, Mike bitched to himself. He stamped his feet and clapped his gloved hands together. Way too cold this early in the season, he thought.

He walked through the beams of his truck's headlights to the generator and started it up again. The security guard they'd hired since Tom's death had disappeared in the night. Mike was pretty sure the son of a bitch had gone off and gotten drunk somewhere. The guy's car wasn't even in the yard.

Of course, considering the condition of the guy's Camry he'd have to be drunk to get in it willingly.

Mike stepped back, blinking as the worklights exploded into life. A moment later, the yard and all of the equipment was in sharp definition and --

Mike stopped. He shook his head and tried to figure out what it was that he was seeing.

A moment later, he realized that someone had taken the dozer and driven it over the security guard's Camry. Mike realized, too, that the man's arm was hanging out of the driver's side window, at least what was left of it.

"These new machines are impressive," a voice said behind Mike.

He jerked around and saw a tall, thick man standing with his arms crossed over a broad chest.

"I was surprised," the man continued, "that it could climb up that auto like that."

"You did that?" Mike asked softly. "You, you drove over that guy?"

The man nodded. "Squealed just like a suckling, too. No shame in it, though," the man said after a moment. "No shame in it at all. Terrible way to die."

Mike blinked, confused. "Why?"

"Why did I kill him?" the man asked.

Mike nodded.

"He was here," the man said simply. "He shouldn't have been."

Mike looked back at the arm.

"Why?" he asked.

The man smiled. "This is Blood land that you're on," the man said, "and you don't have the right to be here. None of us have given you approval. Hollis fought it for as long as he could. Now though, now you've left us no choice," the man said, his smile fading away. "Now we have to make sure that you don't come any further onto the land."

"Hell," Mike said, "I'll just get in my truck and go. I've no cause to be here. I don't even live in Thorne, man. I live down in Hudson."

"It matters not," the man said simply. "You're a warning now. A lesson to be learned." The man snapped his fingers, and the excavator roared into life, thick white diesel exhaust belching into the early morning sky.

Mike turned and looked at the excavator, the machine's giant boom unfolding and stretching out, the bucket swinging out and pulling in.

"When I used to work on autos, and the big caterpillars," the man said, smiling at the machine, "I never thought that I would see something as grand as this."

Mike was only half listening. He was watching the bucket at the end of the boom, the hydraulic lines shifting slightly in their harnesses as the machine worked hard in the cold.

"They really are impressive," the man said again. "And they listen so well."

Mike silently watched the boom rise up, the bucket curl in, and then it came crashing down towards him.

Chapter 11: Jim Petrov and Morgan Blood

Jim started his shift hearing about the death of Mike Pinkham, the foreman at the Blood Road job site, and the death of a security guard that had been hired.

The detectives were tight-lipped about it, and the local news agencies were crawling around asking everyone if they had seen or heard anything. The reporters didn't understand that when you lived off the beaten path you usually didn't see or hear anything unless it was at your door. There was also word that there may have been a murder-suicide as well, but that scene was sealed up tightly.

No one was gaining access to that road, though, although there was plenty of speculation that the dead were Alderman Dean Williams and his wife, Lydia.

By the end of his shift Jim had learned that most of the information out there on the State Police grapevine was true. There were two dead at the worksite, and it looked like Dean Williams had shot his wife and then himself although no one knew why.

After Jim got home, changed out of his uniform and put on his .38 revolver in its shoulder holster, Jim climbed into his truck and headed off the long way to Blood Road. He wanted to avoid the reporters and crime scene techs that were sure to be swarming over the worksite.

The drive took fifteen minutes longer than usual, but Jim avoided the mess on the far side of the driveway and turned right into the driveway. His lights cut a bright path up to the house, and within a moment he had the lights off and had turned off the truck. He hooked the keys to a belt loop and hurried up the stairs to knock on the front door.

The door opened a heartbeat later.

It was the small boy, Morgan Blood. Anger filled the boy's face.

"Jim," Morgan said. "My brother's dead."

"How?" Jim asked.

"Age. He was old." Morgan looked past Jim towards the lights. "He could have stopped this, had they listened to him. He wanted to stop this. He was the best of us."

Jim felt the hair on the back of his neck stand up and his balls shrivel into his stomach. Slowly he turned around and looked down at his truck. Dozens of people stood around it.

And they were silent.

Terribly silent.

Most of them were old. A few were middle-aged with several children mixed in amongst them as well. They wore clothes that ranged from those that Jim remembered seeing in paintings of the first colonists to the suits and dresses of the last century.

All of them were Bloods, of that Jim was certain. Thus all of them were dead.

"My kith and my kin," Morgan said grimly.

Jim shook his head, confused as he turned back to face the small boy. "What's going on? Why is everyone being killed?"

"They broke the contract," Morgan said sternly. "Hollis warned them not to."

"How many have to die because of the contract?" Jim asked.

"Whoever doesn't leave is going to die, Jim," Morgan said. "If not by our hands, then by another's."

"Who?"

"There's a darkness in our forest, Jim," Morgan said, "and we've kept the town safe from it for centuries. All of the old families knew of it. Whoever stays in Thorne, well, they're going to know about it too."

The porch trembled beneath Jim's feet. He looked around to see the trees shaking, although there was no wind to speak of. Then the porch trembled again as a large crack ripped through the night air.

"Oh yes," Morgan said softly, looking out into the forest. "They'll know about the darkness soon enough."

Chapter 12: Jim Petrov, Alone with the Dead

Jim sat inside of the Blood house.

Specifically he sat in the kitchen, at an old dining set that served as the kitchen table. It had evidently been where Hollis had taken his meals.

It had most certainly been where Hollis had taken his last meal, for the dead man sat in his chair, an empty plate before him. The fork and the knife were neatly placed at an angle upon the plate and the water glass beside it was half empty. The old man's churchwarden pipe was unlit and on its side. Fresh tobacco spilled across the scarred top of the table.

A book lay closed on the table. The golden title on the green cloth of the cover read: "Gaius Julius Caesar's Gallic Wars." Jim had already opened the book and seen that the writing inside was done in Latin. The book, Jim saw, was well read.

Hollis sat almost perfectly upright in his chair. His expression was slack, his eyes open and seeing nothing. There was no smile on his lips, no hint of pleasure.

Death came in, collected Hollis, and left as quietly as it had come.

Jim reached out, picked up Hollis's water glass and drank the rest of it down.

"Thataboy!" Morgan said gleefully.

Jim put the glass down and looked at the ghost.

"What am I doing?" Jim asked out loud, shaking his head. "I need to call this in."

"There's no time for that now, Jim," Morgan said in a low voice.

Jim looked up at him. "What do you mean there's no time for that now? What the hell am I supposed to do?"

"You have to bury Hollis," Morgan said.

Jim shook his head. "I can't do that, Morgan. I need to call it in and get this ball rolling. There's a lot of shit --"

"Jim," Morgan said gently.

Jim looked uneasily at the ghost. "Yes?"

"Did you feel the tremors earlier?"

"I did," Jim said hesitantly.

"And the cracking trees?"

Jim nodded.

"Well," Morgan said, looking out into the darkness, "I can tell you that if they get closer to us you're definitely going to wish that you were a Blood."

"What made that sound?" Jim asked.

Morgan shook his head. "Simply pray that you never meet them, Jim. Now please, if we're going to carry out our task with any success, we need to get Hollis down to the graveyard."

"You want me to help you bury him?" Jim asked, unable to keep the surprise out of his voice.

"Yes," Morgan nodded. "That is exactly what I want. Once Hollis is buried he will be able to return to us, to help us with the makers of the noise that you heard."

"What are they?" Jim asked.

"It is truly better not to ask," Morgan said. "Speaking their names only perks up their ears and brings them closer to you than you truly want them to be."

Jim rubbed his temples, sitting back in the chair. "I don't know. I don't.

Christ, I'm sitting with a dead man talking to a ghost. I have to go back to work tomorrow." He closed his eyes and pinched the bridge of his nose.

"No," Morgan said softly, "you can't go back to work tomorrow. We've too much to do."

"Why?" Jim asked.

Morgan opened his mouth to answer, but the answer came from someone who entered the kitchen.

"Tomorrow will be a terrible day," said the man. He stood tall in the doorway, wearing an elegant three-piece black suit. His hair was trimmed short with just a small forelock hanging over his forehead.

Morgan nodded.

"May I ask who you are?" Jim asked.

"Of course," the man said, coming in and sitting down opposite Morgan. "I am Morgan's grandfather, Ambrose Blood. You will, I trust, forgive my grandson for not knowing exactly what to say."

Jim could only nod.

Ambrose seemed to understand. "I will tell you what I know, and while it is much more than most of my family, it is still less than what is truly out there. Do you understand?"

"Yes," Jim said.

"Excellent," Ambrose said. He looked at Morgan, "Could you start some coffee, please, Morgan?"

"Yes, Grandfather," Morgan said. The boy stood up, walked to the percolator, and went about getting the coffee ready.

"You drink coffee?" Jim asked.

Ambrose smiled at him. "No, Jim, this coffee is for you."

"Oh," Jim said.

Ambrose nodded.

They sat in total silence until the coffee was ready, and Jim could only look at Hollis Blood. All three of the Blood family members were dead, but at least two were actually buried down the driveway in the family graveyard.

Those two wanted Jim to put the third in the ground himself.

I'm a cop, Jim thought. What the hell am I doing?

A few minutes later, Morgan put a ceramic cup of fresh black coffee in front of Jim.

"Thank you," Jim said, reaching out and picking up the cup. "I really don't know what I'm doing here."

"You're listening," Ambrose said, polite but firm, "simply listening."

"Okay," Jim said, looking at Ambrose, "okay."

Ambrose nodded. "When the family arrived in the colonies, they did so with indentured servants. These were men and women who had bound themselves to the families that could pay for their transport and passage to the New World. Some of these servants were English. Others were from Wales or Scotch. Several, however, were Irish, and these Irish brought some of the Old World with them.

"When the Blood family came to what would eventually be Thorne village, they had a pair of Irish maids. The Coffins came as well, as did the Copps. It wasn't long before the two families had the Halls, the Lees, and the Arnolds as neighbors.

One of the Blood maids fell passionately in love with one of the Lee sons, yet even though Hawthorne Blood released the maid from her contract of indenture, the Lee father would not give his son permission to marry.

"The young man, I am afraid," Ambrose said as Jim drank his coffee, "had a flair for the dramatic. He threatened to kill himself if his father did not grant him permission to marry the girl, and the tale is told that he had a loaded pistol up to the side of his head. The father refused, and as the boy began to lower the pistol, it accidentally fired.

"The boy was killed."

Jim finished his coffee, the caffeine slowly working its way through him. With disturbing silence Morgan took the cup, filled it, and brought it back. Jim nodded his thanks. "What happened to the girl?" Jim asked.

Ambrose gave a small, sad smile. "Unfortunately, she was not nearly as dramatic as the boy. With her freedom, she chose to leave the Blood house and the protection of the small neighbors. She moved deep into the center of the Blood lands, and there she built a small home. Nothing more than a single room house of field stones, but it stands still, close to the Goblins' Keep.

"It was there that she took out what she had brought from Ireland and opened the small lead-lined box she'd carried across the seas from the Old World to the New."

"What happened when she opened the box?" Jim asked. His confusion at what was going on was superseded by his fascination with the story. He didn't even mind the presence of the three dead men.

He just wanted to know the ending of the story.

"Ah," Ambrose said, sighing, "that was truly a calamitous day. When she opened that box, she briefly opened a door between the worlds. A door between our world and that of the fae in Ireland. Soon, there were a number of creatures in New Hampshire that should not have been. There were ogres, trolls, giants, goblins, faery folk of all kinds, banshees and watermen, too many, and by the time the box burst from serving as a doorway, the Old World was with the new."

Jim looked at Ambrose. "What are you saying?" he asked after a moment. "Are you seriously telling me that there are faeries and all of that? You're saying they're real and that they're here? How can that be?"

"Mr. Petrov," Ambrose said gently, "to whom are you speaking?"

Jim opened his mouth and then closed it. He looked at Ambrose, at Morgan standing by the corpse of Hollis Blood, and Jim nodded. "You're right. Either this is all real, or I have slipped the sultry bonds of sanity."

"There is more, though," Ambrose said.

"Of course there is," Jim agreed. "There has to be a reason for the contract. A reason why the Blood lands were protected and cordoned off."

Ambrose nodded. "Exactly. The release of the faery folk did not go unnoticed. In fact, it was the remaining Blood maid who saw the first faery ring and suspected what it was that her countrywoman had done. It is fortunate that Hawthorne was not only a literate man but a rational one as well. When the maid informed him of the ring and pointed out other signs, he could only accept it as fact.

"He released that woman from her bond as well, yet she stayed in the service of the Bloods and helped them to form the barrier that would stretch around the entire perimeter of the Blood lands. So long as those lands remained whole, and so long as at least one direct descendant of the families who signed the contract lived, the village of Thorne would be safe from the dangers of the faery folk."

"But they broke the contract," Jim said softly, looking down into the cold coffee. "Why are you killing them?"

"To scare them," Ambrose said simply. "We're trying to scare the others into leaving."

Jim thought about that for a moment. He wanted to argue that they could simply haunt the residents, but that wouldn't work. Some would leave. Others would simply call in priests or paranormal investigators.

Whatever was deep in the Blood forest would have time to reach them.

"When will the faery folk start slipping out?" Jim asked.

"Soon," Ambrose answered. "They know that there's a breach, down here by the house. They'll be nervous, but they've also been forced to stay in one place for far longer than they would have liked."

"What can be done?" Jim asked.

"An excellent question," Ambrose said. "I doubt there is much that can be done. A certain amount of vengeance is being taken upon those who broke the contract, although I am afraid that there shall be innocents who suffer as well. We can only hope that through terror we can drive the living out of Thorne. A few dead would thus be acceptable.

"If we don't drive them out, Mr. Petrov," Ambrose said, "then they risk slavery, torture, and death at the hands of the faery folk."

Jim looked down at his coffee once more and then he sighed tiredly. Looking back up to Ambrose he said simply, "Well, shit."

Ambrose nodded, and Jim took a drink of the coffee, wondering what the hell could be done.

After a short time, Ambrose stood up and said, "Please, follow me."

Jim did so, and Morgan followed him in return. They left Hollis's corpse alone in the kitchen.

Ambrose led the way down the long hallway to a closed door on the right. He reached out and touched the doorknob. A lock clicked, and the door swung inward silently. The lights came on, and Ambrose stepped into the room. Old books and gathered papers filled most of the shelves of the thin bookcases that lined the walls. On several shelves, however, were weapons.

One was a sword, still in its scabbard, looking ancient. Beside it was a long barreled Colt revolver -- one that you'd see in an old spaghetti western. The holster and belt for it were wrapped up and lay under it. A wicked looking knife, with a long blade and brass knuckles with spikes for a hand guard, lay on another shelf.

"This room," Ambrose said, looking around, "holds all of the history of those that protected the town of Thorne from the faery folk. These are the records of those who fought, what or who they fought, and those who died while fighting. Those weapons are the few that the families have found to work on the faeries and their ilk. Others exist, of course, but they were with the families.

"Most of the families, though, they themselves have ceased to exist."

Jim walked into the room and looked around. Most of the shelves were covered with a fine layer of dust, yet one near the door was not. Upon that shelf was a black and white composition book.

"Even until recently," Ambrose said, "Hollis was keeping the faeries at bay. He recorded his experiences there."

"Do I need to read those?" Jim asked, looking at Ambrose.

"No, Trooper Petrov," Ambrose said, "you need to arm yourself with those weapons."

Jim looked at the three weapons and the holster with its belt. He realized that the belt was designed to allow the scabbard of the sword and the knife to attach. There was no ammunition in the loops of the belt and none in the pistol.

"There's no ammunition," Jim said, glancing at the shelves.

"It isn't necessary," Morgan said from behind him.

Frowning, Jim looked at Ambrose, and Ambrose nodded.

"Morgan is correct," Ambrose said. "It never needs to be loaded when the faery folk are in its sights."

Jim was about to question that statement when he once again remembered he was speaking to the dead.

Wordlessly, he strapped on the belt, tied the holster down to his leg as he'd seen in so many westerns, and attached the sword to the left and the knife to the right. He picked up the pistol, which was heavy and felt beautiful in his hand, and slid it into the holster.

"Where did they come from?" Jim asked.

"The sword came from Hawthorne Blood himself," Ambrose said. "The pistol was used by a Copp throughout the entirety of the Civil War, and the knife," the man said, "my son used it in France during the Great War. As I said, there are other weapons, but they are lost to us, scattered amongst relatives on the wrong side of the family trees."

With everything in place, the belt was heavy, and Jim realized that he liked the weight.

"Good," Ambrose said. "Come now, we have the grave ready for our Hollis, but we need you to carry him down. Then we can hunt down any faery folk who seek to slip through the gap this evening."

"Fair enough," Jim said, loosening the pistol in its holster, "let's get Hollis home."

Chapter 13: Cold and Calm upon the Gauthiers

Ben Gauthier sat alone in the den watching the Raiders getting their asses kicked again. Angrily, Ben finished his Budweiser and put the empty can on the coffee table.

"Susie!" he yelled.

A moment later, his wife came into the room, popping the tab on the fresh can as she handed it to him.

"Thanks, Hon" he said.

"You're already through a six pack, Ben," she said, wiping her hands on a dish towel she had thrown over her shoulder. "We've still got to pick up Mary from the airport at midnight."

"I'll be fine," he said, taking a pull from the can. "It's only Bud."

"Don't be stupid, Ben," she said, "whether it's Bud or Natty, if you're over the limit you're screwed."

"I'll be fine," he said again and swore as the Bengals ran another touchdown straight up the middle.

Susie shook her head and walked out of the room.

The phone rang as a commercial started, so Ben picked up the phone out of the cradle and looked at the caller id.

"Hey Ryan," he said as he answered the call.

"Hi Dad," Ryan replied. "Can I stay over at Bobby's tonight?"

"It's Thursday," Ben said. "You guys have school tomorrow."

"I'll get to school," Ryan said.

"What does he want?" Susie called from the kitchen.

"To sleep over at Bobby's," Ben answered.

"Bullshit."

"Your mom says no, kid," Ben told Ryan.

Ryan groaned. "Come on, we're playing the new Call of Duty."

"You can go over tomorrow after football and play it, but I want you home by ten," Ben said. "Your mom and I have to pick up Mary and I can't worry about you jackassing around after ten. Too much weird shit is going on lately."

"Fine," Ryan grumbled. "I'll be home at ten."

"Bye, kid."

"Bye, Dad."

Ben ended the call and managed to catch sight of the Bengals intercepting a pass. "Oh what the hell," Ben spat.

The doorbell rang.

Ben looked at the clock.

It was nine.

Susie walked into the den as the doorbell rang again.

"Who the hell could that be?" she asked.

"I don't know," Ben answered. He stood up, still holding his beer, and walked to the front door. He flipped on the exterior light switch and said through the door: "Hello?"

"Hello" came a young voice, "do you happen to have a phone I could borrow for a moment? My car's broken down a little ways up the road, and your house was the closest one."

Ben glanced over at Susie, who shook her head.

"No," Ben said, "but why don't you go wait with your car and I'll call the police for you."

"Oh thank you," the voice said, sounding relieved. "I'm just up the street. It's a black Ford."

"You're welcome," Ben replied, smiling. He looked back to Susie and saw that she was smiling too, and then he watched the smile disappear in order to be replaced by an expression of horror as she opened her mouth to scream.

Ben turned around just in time to catch sight of a pale arm reaching through the door, seeming to grow out of it, before the fingers found and grabbed his sweatshirt.

A brutal cold spread out across his chest, and he wondered for the briefest of moments if he was having a heart attack, but that thought was literally driven out of his head as the arm and hand jerked backward through the door, smashing his head against the wood. Again and again the owner of the arm did it. The beer fell from his hands, and Ben felt his legs loosen, his head rolling on his neck. Susie was still screaming. Ben felt Susie's hands on his arms, then around his waist, trying to pull him free.

Then Ben felt himself falling, blood spilling down the door and onto the tiles of the front hall.

Suddenly, Susie was beside him, and all was quiet. He felt the beating of his heart, erratic and shuddering.

He closed his eyes and felt something striking him. The blows were hard, and then they were weaker and weaker.

Ben felt his heart slowing, air more difficult to breathe in. He managed to open his eyes once more, and he saw the back of Susie's head in front of him. Dully he realized that just beyond the tangled, bloody mess of her blond hair, he could see the gray mass of her brain.

They really are gray, Ben thought, and he closed his eyes once more.

***

Judy pulled up in front of Ryan's house.

"Thanks, Mrs. Showalter," Ryan said, opening the passenger door.

"You're welcome, Ryan. And we'll see you tomorrow?" she asked.

"Yeah," he grinned. "We'll beat the game tomorrow."

"I'm sure that you will," she smiled.

"Thanks again," he waved and closed the door.

Fourteen years old or not, Judy kept the car running at the curb and waited as Ryan walked up the driveway to the side door. She watched him open the screen and try the door.

It was locked.

She saw him knock and ring the bell.

There was no movement inside the house although the shades were up and the lights on.

Ryan knocked on the door again, and she could hear it through the windows. Judy rolled the windows down and turned off the car, leaving the lights on. Ryan took his cell phone out of his pocket and dialed a number. Faintly she could hear the house phone ringing. A moment later the ringing stopped.

Judy watched as Ryan dialed again, hung up after a moment, and then dialed a third time. Shaking his head he put his phone away, walked over to the side of the porch, grabbed a recycling bin, and brought it over to a side window. He climbed up, looked inside, and then stumbled back off of the recycling bin.

Twisting and turning, he finally managed to get to his hands and knees and started crawling towards her car.

Judy had been a parent long enough to know when something was really wrong.

Before she realized what she was doing, Judy was out of the car and running to Ryan as he managed to get to his feet.

"What's wrong, Ryan?" she asked, looking into his horrified expression.

"They're dead," he whispered, focusing on her. "They're both dead."

Judy looked at the house.

She'd never been exactly friendly with either Ben or Susie -- a little too much football and beer for her, but she couldn't leave someone injured if that was the case.

"How do you know, Ryan?" she asked.

"I saw my mom's brains on the floor."

Before she could say anything, Judy heard a rustling sound and something large and brown came out of a forsythia near the front door. She glanced at it then focused on Ryan --

Judy slowly turned her head to look back at the thing.

It couldn't have been taller than three feet, and it wore ragged leather clothing. It had ears that were sharp and tall, standing well past its bald head. A long, thin nose protruded from its face and it had large, black leather boots on its feet. In its left hand it held a wicked looking knife, the blade curved and winking in the light spilling out of the house's windows.

Perhaps the most disturbing thing was the pure black eyes set deep within the gray flesh of the thing's face.

A smile spread and revealed jagged yellow teeth.

More rustling sounded, and more of the things appeared. They varied in shape and size, yet all wore the same clothes and boots and carried either knives or axes.

In a moment, there were a dozen of them spreading out to encircle both Judy and Ryan, the latter of whose shock at losing his parents was quickly being dampened by the horror occurring.

"The boy, woman," one with an ax said, its voice surprisingly deep. "The boy, and you'll meet your maker quickly. Deny us and I'll take a century to kill you."

The air seemed to fill with the sound of her own breathing. She could smell them, a foul, stale smell that curled her nose and set her mind to racing.

"Too slow," one to the right chuckled, "let's take them back to the Keep. It's been far too long since we had one to play with."

The others laughed, and they moved in, laughing and chattering to one another even as Judy wrapped her arms around Ryan and pulled him into her. She closed her eyes, and a large explosion shook her.

Chapter 14: Jim, the Colt, and the Goblins

The loud report of the pistol nearly shook Jim's brains out of his head even as the invisible slug ripped through the jaw of one of the goblins in front of Ben Gauthier's house.

There was a ring of the things -- which Jim could only assume were goblins because of the way they looked -- around a woman and a teenager. The goblins had been closing in on the pair until Jim had killed one of them.

Now the things were staring at him, nervous glances flickering from one to the other.

"You're not a Blood," one of them said, his nostrils flaring. "Or a Coffin."

"Neither an Arnold nor a Lee," said a second.

'And definitely no Hall," said a third.

"Yet you bear some of their weapons," the first said. "Yes, you do."

Morgan was suddenly beside him. "They're crafty, and false, Jim," the boy said. "Kill them all and don't hesitate. They have every mind to force the boy to be a slave for eternity and to eat the woman."

Before Morgan finished the last word, Jim was firing.

His aim was perfect, the weapon impeccable. Even as the goblins tried to flee, he cut them down. In a matter of moments, there were a dozen corpses littering the front yard of Ben Gauthier's house.

He'd known Ben since high school, and Jim had a suspicion that Ben and Susie were inside and much worse for the wear.

Jim holstered the pistol and walked over to the teenager and the woman, both of whom were looking at him. He didn't know who the woman was, but the boy was Ryan, the Gauthier's' son.

"Ryan," Jim said.

The boy looked at him but didn't recognize him.

Jim didn't push it.

"What were those?" the woman asked, looking around at the bodies.

"Goblins," Jim answered. "Don't ask anything else. Get in your car, get to your house, get your family, and get the hell out of Thorne. Do you understand?"

The woman blinked several times, confused, but she still nodded.

"Good," Jim said. "Go."

He helped her get Ryan over to the car and into it. She hurried into the driver's side and got the car started. In a heartbeat, she was laying a track of rubber down the street.

"Why did you tell them?" Morgan asked, appearing again.

"They need to know," Jim said, watching the car disappear around a corner. "Even if they don't believe it, they need to know."

Morgan tilted his head slightly and then he said, "There's something coming, Jim. Something bigger."

Chapter 15: Fred O'Dierno and War

Fred had fought in Vietnam. He had more time in that country than he cared to remember, and he'd not only killed men for his own country's sake, but he'd trained men to kill in the name of Freedom.

War had shaped Fred O'Dierno and the way that he looked at the world.

When he heard a gunshot, he knew it for what it was.

When he heard a dozen of them halfway down the street, he knew that something was wrong.

Fred took his reading glasses off and put them down on the coffee table along with the copy of *Harry Potter and the Deathly Hallows* that he was reading. He stood up, walked over to his gun cabinet and took out the M14 that was waiting amongst his other rifles.

From the drawer of the bureau beside it, Fred took a handful of preloaded clips, slipped one into the rifle and the others into the pockets of his shirt.

Walking to his front door, Fred turned off his lights and kept away from the windows. The door was made of heavy oak and thick enough to stop most rounds if need be. Fred found himself breathing smoothly, the rifle a warm comfort in his hands. The weapon had been a yard sale find shortly after he'd gotten back to Thorne from Vietnam. The rifle had been worth its weight in gold in Southeast Asia after the introduction of the M16 -- that sorry excuse for a rifle which seemed to jam every time Fred was in a firefight.

Fred cleared his mind, though, pushing angry memories back and easing himself to a window where he could look out on the street beyond.

As he did so, the floor shook beneath his feet, the trees swaying haphazardly.

From behind the Gauthier's house, a pair of elm trees came crashing down onto the roof, branches snapping and shingles flying into the night sky. Then it was there.

It stood twenty feet tall, easily, and it was a rough copy of a man. The facial features were blunt, the red hair a tangled, unwashed mass. Thick red hair covered this giant's chest, and a blue, frayed tarp served as a rough skirt around his waist. In the giant's hands, he held a piece of metal that looked like it was ripped off of an excavator or earth mover of some kind.

It was advancing on a man standing on the Gauthier's driveway. The man wore a sword and a pistol and stood still, simply looking at the giant.

Fred pushed the unreality of the situation out of his mind and opened the door, stepping out onto his front step and chambering a round.

***

Jim stood frozen in place on the driveway. Fear and shock rolled over him in waves that sent adrenaline through him, yet he couldn't move.

The giant that had come out of the forest was huge and grinning down at Jim.

"Fresh manmeat," the giant chuckled. "Oh, sweetmeat, I've missed the likes of you these long years."

A rifle cracked out from somewhere nearby, and the giant howled in rage, a sound that both hurt Jim's ears and shocked him into motion.

Jim drew the pistol and backed up, firing as he went, both hands on the pistol as it barked and jumped in his hands. Blood exploded from wounds on the giant's chest as he took a step towards Jim.

"Damnable, man!" the giant howled, and Jim put another four rounds into the giant's chest.

The unknown rifleman continued to fire as well, and Jim watched as the shots from the rifle moved up from the chest to the head, and Jim understood.

Dropping to a knee, Jim steadied himself and fired shot after shot into the giant's head as the rifleman did the same.

The giant's screams of rage ceased as it let go of the metal, collapsed first to his knees, then fell to the left, smashing a blue minivan in the driveway, the windows exploding outwards and showering Jim with glass. Jim struggled to keep his footing as the world seemed to rattle and shake with the falling of the giant.

Carefully, Jim stood up, holstering the pistol once more and brushing the glass off of himself and out of his hair.

"Hello," a voice said calmly.

Jim turned around and looked at a man standing in the center of the street. The man looked to be in his late sixties. He wore a flannel shirt and jeans with a pair of sneakers. His white hair was cut short, and he carried a bolt action rifle with an ease that showed that he had a familiarity with weapons.

"Hello," Jim answered.

"What the hell is going on?" the man asked, perfectly calm.

"Well, that's a long goddamned story," Jim replied.

The man nodded.

"That's Nathan Coffin's rifle," Morgan said, suddenly standing beside Jim.

Both Jim and the stranger jumped.

"Sweet Jesus Christ," the stranger said, "where the hell did you come from?" The man squinted slightly, and then in a lower voice he said, "Oh. You're dead."

Jim looked at Morgan and saw that the ghost-child was smiling.

"Yes," Morgan said. "How did you know?"

"I've seen a lot of death," the man said, "and I know the walking dead when I see them. Now, what did you say about my rifle?"

"It belonged to Nathan Coffin," Morgan said. "He survived the Chosin Reservoir in Korea, where he carried that rifle the entire time. He brought that rifle home," Morgan said, "It's full of his will to survive."

The man frowned.

"Not all weapons work," Jim explained.

"Ah," the man said, nodding.

"You seem to be handling this really well," Jim said, looking at the man.

"I'll freak the hell out about it later on," the man said calmly. "Right now I can't. So I won't."

Jim nodded. He walked to the man and extended his hand. "I'm Jim Petrov, a trooper with the State Police."

"Fred O'Dierno," Fred said. "Retired history teacher, and a United States Marine."

"Well, Fred," Jim said, "care to take a walk with me back to the Blood house?"

"You'll tell me what's going on?" Fred asked.

"I'm going to try," Jim replied.

"Okay," Fred said, "let me grab some more ammunition and I'll be ready to go."

"Sure," Jim said, and he watched the man walk steadily to what was obviously his home.

"He's strong," Morgan said. "We'll need him."

Jim nodded his agreement.

Chapter 16: Scott Ricard and the Dullahan

"Brian," Scott said into the phone, "I don't care what's going on out there. I've got my shotgun and there's no way in hell that I'm going to leave the house or let anyone in."

"Scott," his brother said angrily, "there's something screwed up going on in Thorne tonight. You need to get your ass out."

"I'm fine here," Scott said.

"Then at least send the kids and Marie out. Send them down to Nashua to stay the night with her mom."

"They already left," Scott said, pissed. "She got a call from Judy who said that the Gauthier's' were dead."

"Shit," Brian snapped.

"Exactly," Scott said. "I don't know if it's true or not but Marie took the Jeep and my truck's in the shop. I'm going to have to telecommute tomorrow, and I hate that."

"No, you dumbass," Brian snarled. "Get the hell out of the house. Call a cab. Damn it, if I can get away I'll shoot over and grab you, but we've got multiple fires along the edge of the Monson and Thorne border."

"I'm fine," Scott said. "Talk to you later."

He hung up the phone before Brian could say anything else.

The house was quiet with Marie and the kids gone.

Shaking his head, Scott walked over to the charger and put the phone back on it. He took his shotgun down from the hearth and dug the shells out of their place atop the TV cabinet.

Walking back to his chair, he put on the Raiders game and watched as he loaded the gun. He didn't care about either one of the teams. The Patriots weren't playing until Sunday, but he needed to watch something. With the shotgun across his lap, Scott watched the game, yawned a few times, and felt sleep pulling at his eyes.

Too much chicken pie, he thought, and closed his eyes as the game shifted to commercial with the calling of a timeout by the Raiders.

Scott opened his eyes and saw that the game was over.

Long over.

He hit the 'guide' button on the remote and found out it was two thirty, and he was watching 'Westworld.'

"No, I'm not," he grumbled to himself, turning off the television.

Holding the shotgun, he stood up, stretched, and yawned.

There was a low rumbling sound that grew louder, coming from the street beyond. Frowning, Scott went to the window and looked outside. He couldn't see anything, but he definitely heard it getting closer. In fact, it almost sounded as if something had turned into his driveway.

"What the hell," Scott grumbled, walking to the front door and flipping the light switch before he opened the door and walked outside with the shotgun. The door clicked shut behind him, and Scott made sure that the safety was off on the gun.

He walked down the stairs and looked up and down his street.

Something was coming towards him. A black carriage drawn by a pair of black horses moved steadily down the street, the wheels loud and harsh upon the asphalt.

The horseman was headless, a wooden pail beside him on the seat.

Scott was fascinated. He couldn't tear his eyes away from the sight, and as the carriage drew abreast of him, it slowed down. The driver let the reins fall to his lap, and then he took up the pail.

A moment later, Scott was stumbling back, screaming and swearing as fresh, hot blood drenched him. His foot caught on a paving stone, and he fell to his knees, the bones cracking and the shotgun skittering away on the walkway.

The rich, sickening scent of iron filled his nose and brought bile up into his mouth. Scott spat it out onto the ground and tried to wipe the blood out of his eyes, his knees sending sharp, piercing pain into his mind. He managed to get into a sitting position, used the bottom of his tee shirt to clean the blood away, and looked out into the street.

The carriage was gone, but the blood remained.

Painfully, Scott got to his feet and turned around, looking for his shotgun.

The driver of the carriage was holding it, the twin barrels pointed at Scott. The driver was still headless.

The shotgun fired, and Scott felt the slugs tear into his chest as the sound of the blast reached his ears. He closed his eyes but never felt the ground when it rushed up to meet him.

Chapter 17: Jim, Fred and Hollis Blood

The air was cold as dawn painted the sky a deep red.

Jim and Fred sat on the porch drinking hot coffee brought to them by a child who had passed in 1933. The two men had weapons that could kill faery folk, and they listened to a gentle rumbling in the distance. Both men, unbeknownst to the other, were wondering if the rumbling came from yet another giant.

From the curve of the road a man appeared, walking upright and easily with a cane. He wore a button down shirt, suspenders and a pair of slacks with well-made shoes.

Hollis Blood.

"This place is full of the dead," Fred said before blowing on his coffee and taking a drink.

"That it is," Jim agreed.

Hollis climbed the steps of the porch and leaned against his cane, smiling at the two men. "Well," Hollis said, "it looks as though things have truly gone to the pot, haven't they, gentlemen?"

"You seem fairly pleased about it," Fred said evenly.

"I'm only pleased that I was right," Hollis said, the smile dropping away. "I have to say that I am upset about the unnecessary deaths. Those, however, I lay at the feet of the men who decided to break the contract which has kept this town safe for centuries."

"Well," Jim said, "what do we do now, Hollis?"

"My suggestion is that you finish your coffee," Hollis said, "then go inside and into the archives, which is where you got the weapons, Jim. In there, I'll show you the document you need to look at. It will tell you of a place where you can ride out the next few hours safely. You'll be able to rest and prepare for the later afternoon and evening."

"We shouldn't do anything now?" Jim asked.

Hollis shook his head. "You not only shouldn't," the dead man said, "but it would be dangerous for you if you did. My family and I are going to do our best to drive out the rest of the town, but the border needs to be mended, and we're not sure how that's going to be done yet."

"So," Fred said, "we hole up somewhere?"

Hollis nodded.

"Will you tell us when to come out?"

"Yes," Hollis answered.

"Sounds good to me," Fred said. "Come on, Jim," he said as he stood, finishing his coffee. "The sooner we're safe, the better I'll feel."

"What about the rest of the town?" Jim asked, standing.

"They'll either get out or they won't," Hollis said. "I can put it no simpler than that. You will serve everyone better by preparing for later on, Trooper Petrov."

After a moment, Jim nodded. "Alright," he said, and he followed Hollis as the ghost led the way back into the house in which he had so recently lived.

Chapter 18: Brian Ricard in Thorne

Brian didn't understand the call that came over the radio.

"What do you mean there's a roadblock set up?" he asked, pulling over on the side of Route 122. "Who the hell put it there?"

"Don't know, Brian," Jane answered. "We just got the call that there's a roadblock at 122 where it crosses over from Monson into Thorne. Can you check it out?"

"Yeah," Brian said, shaking his head. "I'll check it out."

He put the cruiser back into gear and checked the mirrors before flipping on the lights and pulling out onto Route 122. He was exhausted. He'd spent most of the night helping to take care of the fires that had sprung up along the border between the two towns. He'd managed to grab a few hours of sleep in one of the cells, but he was exhausted, and his bladder was full.

The road was absent of other cars and through the vent system of the car, he could smell fresh smoke from somewhere. Brian felt bad for the firefighters. More than likely, there were crews from other towns helping now.

What the hell is going on, he thought tiredly, the road curving slightly ahead of him. Then he stomped on the brakes, leaving rubber on the asphalt.

Ahead of him, dozens of trees had been felled and dragged across the road. It would take a crew with chainsaws and a front-loader at least half the day to clear it, and it wasn't even six o'clock in the morning.

"Damn it," Brian said aloud, throwing the car into park and getting out. He let out a sigh and stared at the mess. "Damn it," he said again. Leaning back into the car to grab the microphone, he stopped.

Something had moved in the corner of his eye.

Slowly, dropping his hand to the butt of his pistol, he backed out of the car and straightened up. He looked at the blockade from left to right, right to left, and up and down.

Nothing.

He waited another moment before he looked at it again.

Still nothing.

Brian closed his eyes and opened them.

Then he saw them.

Small, sharp faces among the gaps in the trees. Their skin was dark, almost gray.

When they realized that he saw them, they straightened up and climbed onto the trees. The things were small, wiry and wearing an odd assortment of what looked to be children's clothes, though they seemed to have paid no attention at all to what gender's clothing they were wearing, if that even mattered.

What mattered was that they had axes and knives, cudgels, and small bows. They looked at Brian with some interest and chattered back and forth in a language that sounded nothing like anything Brian had ever heard before.

Although, that wasn't true. He had heard something like it before. His daughter loved a movie in which the kids spoke Irish, and that was exactly what the words sounded like.

The strange creatures were speaking Irish, or Gaelic, or whatever it was called.

Brian didn't find himself feeling comforted by that information, or by the way the things started looking at him. They didn't seem to have any desire to leave the safety of the blockade, and that was working out just fine for Brian as well.

"They're goblins," a voice suddenly said from beside him, and Brian screamed.

Several of the goblins screamed as well, and when Brian regained some modicum of self-control he was pleased to see that some of them had left.

"They're not exceptionally bright," the voice said again, "but they are wicked creatures."

Brian looked around, and he saw a young woman standing slightly off to the right, looking at him.

There was something peculiar about the woman, or the old-fashioned black dress that she was wearing. Her deep brown hair hung in curls past her shoulders and her hands disappeared into a dark red, fur muff held properly in front of her stomach.

One of the Goblins called out to her in something that sounded like German, and the young woman responded with kind words. The tone of her voice, though, was vicious, and the goblin, who had spoken, cringed.

She turned her attention back to Brian. "I'm afraid that the only advice which I could offer you, sir, is that of staying away. No matter what you do, you will not be able to stop them. Your weapon is useless, and they will not take kindly to you trying to cross."

"How do you know?" Brian asked.

"Look at what they've done to those on the other side of the barricade," she said, nodding towards the goblins.

Brian looked back and saw the goblins placing aluminum poles in the barricade so that the poles stood up easily. Atop those poles were freshly severed heads, blood still leaking from the necks.

They were heads of men and women of a variety of ages.

The goblins put up perhaps half a dozen, and when they finished, they looked over and saw Brian looking at them. Cheerfully, they waved.

Out of pure reaction, Brian waved back, and then he threw up on the asphalt.

The laughter of the goblins filled his ears, and he tried to block out the image in his mind.

"Go back to Monson," the young woman said kindly. "They won't follow you."

"How do you know?" Brian asked, straightening up and wiping his mouth off with the back of his hand. He looked at her and asked again, "How do you know?"

She smiled at him reassuringly. "They're not the ones who built it."

"But what about the other people?" Brian asked.

"Who?"

"The people on the other side of the blockade," he said.

A cold expression settled on her face. "They don't matter," she said. "They broke the contract."

Brian looked back at the goblins and swore as something wet and soft struck him in the face. The goblins let out peals of high-pitched laughter, and Brian angrily wiped his face, and his hand came away wet with blood. He looked down at the pavement to see what he had been hit with and stumbled, slipping in his own vomit.

Lying on the pavement between the open door and the car's frame was an eyeball, part of the optic nerve still attached -- the blue iris still looking surprisingly alive.

Chapter 19: A Place of Safety

Hollis Blood opened the door to the small room that Jim had entered before with Ambrose. With the light turned on, Hollis pointed to a shelf on the far wall.

"On the second shelf," the dead man said, "you'll find a small letter. It's sealed, but you'll need to break it."

Jim walked into the room and walked to the shelf that Hollis had pointed out. Fred stayed in the hallway drinking his coffee and standing between Morgan and Hollis Blood, who watched Jim silently.

On the shelf, Jim found half a dozen leather-bound books, a pair of similarly bound leather journals and dozens of letters. He took the letters down and started going through them. They all seemed to be opened, and it took him a few minutes to find the one that wasn't.

The letter was indeed small, and it was heavy as well. Beneath the thick parchment paper, Jim could feel something small and hard. He returned the other letters back to the shelf and walked out of the room. He turned off the light and closed the door behind him absently, simply staring at the letter.

The paper was old and yellowed. The seal upon the letter was done with green wax and the shape of an oriental dragon.

"That's it," Hollis said.

"It is indeed," said another voice, and Fred snapped the rifle up to his shoulder instantly.

Then the man lowered it, for Ambrose Blood stood beside Hollis.

"That," Fred said, "is an uncomfortable habit that you gentlemen have."

Neither of the dead men responded.

"What's in the letter?" Jim asked.

"Only Hawthorne Blood knows that," Ambrose answered, "and he's quite busy at this time. Open it, please," Ambrose said, "it's time, and time is what we have very little of."

Jim nodded, broke the seal on the letter, and opened it carefully, unfolding each corner of the thick paper. Within, he found a small, old, iron key. Just a simple skeleton key that he'd seen reproductions of at crafts stores when he'd go shopping with his wife, but this wasn't a reproduction key.

He took the key and found it warm to the touch, as if it had been in someone's pocket rather than in the envelope. Still holding the key, Jim read the letter aloud.

"You who have opened this letter fully understand the significance of what has occurred here. For some reason, the barrier is down, the contract broken, and the faery folk rampaging as only the faery folk can. You will need a place of safety while you prepare yourselves for the difficult decisions ahead.

"I have no doubt that few of the residents of Thorne have fled at the first signs of the faery folk. We New Englanders are, by nature, a stubborn breed. In this case, however, stubbornness will cost them their lives.

"Go to Hassell Brook and follow it down as it makes its way to the Nashua River. There is a small pool off of the brook and in and around this pool are great boulders. Here, by the boulders closest to banks, you will find a door. This key will unlock it, and you'll be able to prepare.

"Beware of the pool, though. There is a washer-woman and a korrigan. Beware of them both."

The letter was unsigned.

Jim looked at the others.

Fred shook his head, and the two dead men looked confused.

"We do not know," Ambrose said. "None of us were schooled in faery lore."

"I was," a small voice said, and Jim turned quickly around to see a young woman standing shyly in a doorway. She wore a nightcap and a long, off-white nightgown.

"Mary?" Hollis asked, surprised.

She nodded. "I read everything that I could when I was a little girl, Hollis. That's why, after I heard you and your father talking about the land, I had to go and see if it was true."

"How did you die, Mary?" Fred asked simply.

"The Korrigan, down by the pool with the washer-woman wailing. I heard the washer-woman and went down anyway. When I arrived in the pool, the Korrigan cursed me, and I died at the bottom of the stairs, as you know."

Wordlessly Hollis nodded.

"Both the Korrigan and the washer-woman are still there," Mary said to all of them. "They have no desire to leave the pool. That does not mean, though, that they'll let you pass through without a care."

"Well," Fred said, "I don't see how we have much of a choice."

"No," Hollis said, "there's none."

"We'll be able to guide you to Hassell Brook," Ambrose said, "but you'll need to go the rest of the way yourselves. We have too much work to do while you learn what it is we need to do."

"What work?" Fred asked, looking over to Jim.

Jim shook his head.

Fred looked back to the dead men.

"What work?" he asked of them.

Hollis sighed. "You would know it as scorched earth."

Fred was quiet for a moment. "Stupid assholes," he said, shaking his head. "Alright, gentlemen, show us where this damnable brook is."

Chapter 20: Fires along the Roads

On Friday at six o'clock in the morning, Tom woke not to the alarm he had set for seven, but to the sound of a fire truck and the stench of smoke.

Sitting up in bed, he looked around, expecting to see smoke curling around the ceiling, but there was nothing. Vicki lay asleep on the bed oblivious to the sound and the smell. Tom got out of the bed and walked to the window where he pulled the curtain aside a little to look out on the street.

The fire truck was parked haphazardly on the road, the left front wheel up on the sidewalk. The siren continued to wail, and the lights continued to flash in the early morning light while the Wilsons' house burned brightly. In front of the house, standing on Bill Wilson's prized Kentucky bluegrass was a tall man with a sword. A huge sword, just like the ones that Tom had seen in the movie *Braveheart*.

The man wasn't wearing a kilt, though. He had an outfit on that looked like the man could have stepped straight out of the Revolutionary War. Hell, he even had a cape and a three-cornered hat on.

Tom shook his head. The guy was too tall to be Bill, but he could certainly be one of Bill's buddies still drunk from going out last night. The five volunteer firefighters that had come with the truck were trying to get the man away from the house so they could get at the fire.

Tom grinned, trying to think what the hell they would --

The grin dropped from Tom's face as the man with sword brought the weapon back and with a single, massive swing cut a firefighter's head off.

Tom watched, confused, as the head bounced and rolled, the body falling limply as the other firefighters stumbled back and away from the swordsman. Tom was sure that someone was screaming. Maybe even all of them.

But no one was going to go near that swordsman.

The swordsman, however, was going to go near them.

The man started walking forward, the sword held easily in both hands. Bill's sprinkler system kicked in, the sprinkler heads rising up out of the ground to care for the lawn. As one did, a firefighter tripped and fell, trying to twist away and catch himself.

Then the swordsman was on him, driving the sword through the firefighter's chest and twisting the blade before pulling it out. The firefighter, Tom knew, was dead.

A shape came staggering out of the front door of Bill's flaming house.

"Shit," Tom said.

"What?" Vicki asked sleepily.

"Shit," Tom said again.

A moment later, she was beside him. "Oh my God, Tom," she said.

Even as the words left her mouth, Tom saw the swordsman turn around as if he had sensed Bill's presence. With two long strides, the swordsman was upon Bill, driving the long blade up to the hilt into the soft white flesh of Bill's stomach.

Vicki screamed -- a loud, piercing scream that made Tom's ears ring and his head ache.

The swordsman looked up at them in the window.

"Oh no," Tom said. "Oh please no."

Vicki was still screaming as he grabbed her by the wrist and nearly dragged her away from the window and out of the bedroom. She finally stopped when they were in the hallway and by the time that they reached the stairs he didn't have to hold onto her wrist.

When they reached the kitchen, she grabbed her purse from the counter and his wallet from the top of the microwave while he removed the keys from their hook and stepped into his beat-up sneakers. He opened the door, a wave of smoke rolling into the kitchen and a wall of heat waiting for them as Vicki slipped into her flipflops. Even as Tom hit the 'unlock' button on the key, he glanced over at Bill's house.

The swordsman was killing the last of the firefighters, parrying a clumsy ax swing from the man before severing the firefighter's head partially from his neck.

"Oh Jesus," Vicki said. "Oh, Jesus, oh Jesus, oh *Jesus*, Tom. Where are Janet and the boys?"

"Get in the car," Tom said, turning his head away as he saw a small shape run by one of the upper windows of Bill's house. "Just get into the car, Vicki."

They both got in and for a moment, Tom almost laughed hysterically, wondering if he was going to drop the keys as he tried to get the key into the ignition, but the key went in smoothly, and the engine turned over as he slammed the car into 'reverse', backing up as fast as he could.

Then he lost control.

The car slammed into the back corner of the fire truck so hard that it got stuck part way under it. Cursing and swearing, Tom shifted into drive, but the car wouldn't budge.

Then, Vicki's window was smashed in. A pale hand reached inside, grabbed her by her blonde hair as she screamed, and dragged her out through the broken window. Tom watched in horror as the swordsman wrapped a massive hand around her neck and squeezed.

The breaking of her neck and the sudden, final gasp of breath set Tom to vomiting.

"Coward!" the swordsman snarled.

Out of the corner of his eye, Tom saw the sword driving in towards him.

Chapter 21: Elizabeth O'Grady and the Brownie

Elizabeth O'Grady slept little, if at all, most nights, and this past Thursday had been par for the course. She didn't hear particularly well anymore -- one of the sad truths of aging.

She sat at her dressing table and finished the last bits of a ritual that had lasted for decades. She put on her black dress, pinned her hair back into a bun, and made sure that the plain gold wedding band that Murphy had given her was still properly on her finger.

Lastly, she put her crucifix around her neck. The chain was of small, silver links, and the crucifix was of the same, each detail of Christ's suffering exquisitely wrought in the metal. Finishing with her ritual, she offered up a prayer to the blessed Virgin and took her cane off of the dressing table's edge. Using it carefully, she rose to her feet and made her way around her small bed to the hallway.

She traveled along the hall and realized that something wasn't the same.

The hall was spotless.

Not a single particle of dust. The floor was swept, the wooden wainscoting polished. Even the glass shades of the sconces had been washed. When she reached the kitchen, she found that it too had been scrubbed. The metal fixtures positively gleamed, and the few pots and pans which had been from last night's dinner were washed and put away. Fresh vegetables and fruit were in bowls upon the table.

The doors, Elizabeth saw, were still locked, as were the windows.

Elizabeth pulled one of the two chairs out from under the table and sat down. She picked a peach out of one of the bowls and looked at it for a long time.

Finally, she put the fruit back and stood up. She made her way to the refrigerator and took out a small container of cream. From a cabinet over the toaster, she removed a demitasse cup and saucer. She carried all three to the table, set the cup on the saucer, and poured cream into the saucer. With that finished, she returned the cream to the refrigerator, retrieved a paring knife and small plate from their respective places, and took her seat at the table once more.

After taking the peach out again, she carefully cut it in half, removed the pit, and cut the halves in half again. She placed one slice on the saucer beside the demitasse cup.

Elizabeth ate a wedge of peach, wiped her mouth with a napkin, dried her hand and said in a soft voice, "Thank you. Will you join me?"

She sat in silence for several minutes before a creak sounded near the back door. A small creature appeared from a shadow, a small hat held in his hands. He wore a neat pair of knickers and a white peasant shirt with a corduroy. His feet were large and bare, his arms and legs gangly. His hands, like his feet, were large, the fingers gnarled. He stood no more than two feet tall, and when he approached the table he climbed up the other chair deftly, standing politely on the table.

He looked her in the eye and gave her a smile of crooked, yellow teeth. He smelled of smoke and cleanliness.

"Please sit," Elizabeth said.

He nodded and sat down.

"The cream and the peach are for you."

"For me, Ma'am?" he asked, and his small but deep voice was thick with an Irish brogue.

"Yes," Elizabeth said, "in appreciation of the fine work that you did."

He smiled broadly and put the hat down on the table before picking up the demitasse cup daintily. He took a noisy sip and sighed happily. "It is a pleasure, Ma'am," he said, "to find a Mistress who is well bred."

Elizabeth nodded her thanks.

He picked up the peach and tucked the piece fully into his mouth. He chewed and hummed to himself, swallowed, and took another sip.

"You've met no others who know?" Elizabeth asked.

"I tried only one other before you, Ma'am," he said.

"And may I ask who?"

"Your neighbor," he said, "the one across the street in the yellow house."

"The Labries?" Elizabeth asked.

"French, were they?"

"Yes," Elizabeth said.

"Ah," he said, "that would explain it then."

"They were not pleased?"

"Not at all," he answered. "She ignored what I did, assumed it was some other. Not a word of thanks."

"What happened then?" Elizabeth asked.

"I burned their house down," he said simply, finishing his cream, "with them in it."

Elizabeth twisted in her seat slowly and finally could look out the front window. Not much remained of the house. It had burned almost to the foundation.

The place smoldered still, and the Labries' cars remained in the driveway, covered in ash and debris.

No one had tried to put out the fire. That was clear.

"What's your name?" she asked, turning back to him.

"Leabhar," he smiled.

"Leabhar," she repeated.

"Yes, Ma'am," he said. He looked longingly at another wedge of peach.

Smiling she picked one up and handed it to him.

He ate it quickly but politely. When he finished, he smiled at her. "Ma'am, I saw that your woodbox was empty, and winter's coming on. Would you like me to fill the wood box?"

She thought of him with the wood and near the fire.

Elizabeth smiled and nodded. "Please, Leabhar."

As he got off of the table and climbed down the chair, putting his small hat back upon his head, Elizabeth looked out the window.

A pity, she thought. Here's hoping that it was the smoke that killed them, and not the flames.

Elizabeth offered up a prayer to the blessed Virgin and smiled as Leabhar made his way outside.

Chapter 22: Down by the Pool

Somewhere, a fire truck, whose siren had been screaming for nearly an hour, suddenly went silent.

Jim looked over his shoulder toward where the sound had been coming from. In the early morning light, columns of smoke were rising up and staining the sky.

"Just keep moving," Fred said, patting Jim on the shoulder. "There's nothing that can be done right now."

Jim nodded and turned his attention back to the narrow path that ran along Hassell Brook. They had cut across the brook nearly half an hour before, and they were keeping a steady pace. The woods were strangely quiet around them. None of the bird or animal sounds were familiar in this part of New Hampshire.

Ahead of them, Jim caught sight of large weeping willow trees filling the spaces between the old trees. Boulders and large rocks started cropping up amongst the trees as well. The sound of water slapping against rocks reached his ears. Jim drew his pistol.

"Take it slow," Fred said softly, "nice and slow."

Jim only nodded.

He moved at a slow pace forward, listening.

Yet he heard only the water, nothing else.

The path they followed curved down slightly, and there before them appeared a trio of large boulders, looking almost like monstrous eggs. A little beyond them grew a massive weeping willow tree. The path led directly to the stones, cutting in amongst them.

Jim walked down, following the path directly to the stones. He passed through a curtain of willow branches, Fred right behind him, nearly bumping into him as Jim came to a complete stop.

In the trunk of the tree was a tall, broad door. There was no window, but there was a doorknob of cut crystal set into a brass plate with a keyhole.

"Well, damn," Fred said.

"You said it," Jim sighed. He put his left hand into his pants pocket and took the key out. Stepping up to the door, he put the key into the keyhole and unlocked the door before grasping the knob and turning it. With a grunt, he pushed the door open.

Within the depths of the living tree, a room spread out before them. It was far larger than the outside of the tree, and thick carpets were laid across a stone floor. A hearth with a small fire occupied the far wall, and torches were set in brackets along walls of smooth stones. Draperies hung from the tall ceiling down to the floor, and a single bed stood off to one side. A writing desk stood opposite of the bed and had a scattering of books and papers upon it.

"What the hell do we do with this?" Jim asked.

In the distance something roared -- a terrible sound that weakened Jim's knees.

"We go inside," Fred said.

Jim nodded, took the key out of the lock, and went into the room. Together he and Fred pushed the door closed and found iron mounts on the back for thick boards to be dropped into. Without speaking, both of the men did just that before stepping away from the door.

Whatever they had heard outside roared again, yet it was louder and closer than it had been. Faintly, they heard a splashing sound, and then the sound of two male voices arguing. The voices were incredibly deep, and Jim had a suspicion that giants were the owners of the sounds being made. A third voice suddenly joined the first two and there was a great deal of howling and yelling that arose.

Jim winced, put his pistol back into the holster, and covered his ears. It did little to help the raucous hurting his ears and causing his head to throb with pain. Soon came the sounds of blows. A glance at Fred showed the man to be standing impassively in the center of a rug, his rifle cradled in his arms.

Shortly, the battle being fought rolled away from the pool and silence returned, filled by the small noises of the fire burning in the hearth.

"Let's see if there's any coffee in this place," Fred said. "I've a thirst now."

They found the coffee in a clay jar by the fire, and behind one of the draperies they discovered a hand-pump and some cooking-ware as well. It took a minute to get the water but when it came, the water was cold and sweet. They filled a cast iron kettle and Fred set it on an iron hook before swinging it out over the flame. Jim carried a pair of clay mugs out of the small room and placed them near the hearth.

The two of them sat down on the floor a few feet from the fire and waited for the water to boil.

"So," Fred said, "this has been a hell of a day."

"Yeah," Jim agreed.

That sat silently for a short time.

"I keep wondering," Jim said, breaking the silence, "if any of this is real."

"That's to be expected," Fred said. "It's never easy to face these things."

"All of the killing?" Jim asked.

"That too," Fred said, "but I was talking about the dead and the faery folk."

Jim looked at Fred, surprised.

"What are you saying?" Jim asked. "Have you seen the faery folk before?"

"Not exactly," Fred said. "Not that we're seeing now. I did three tours in Vietnam, you see, and the supernatural is active there. Sometimes we were fighting the Vietcong, some days the NVA, and some days we were fighting things that could be seen but couldn't be defined." Fred looked over at Jim with a wry smile on his face. "Hell, Jim, I even saw a dragon over there. It was really a hell of a thing."

"Jesus," Jim muttered.

"Yeah," Fred said, "we called on Him a hell of a lot."

The two of them lapsed back into silence, waiting for the coffee to boil. When it started to boil, Fred got up, found a poker to pull the iron swing arm out from the flames, and took a rag off of the floor. Using the rag, he took hold of the kettle and carefully poured the steaming coffee into the mugs.

The smell was soothing as Fred handed him a mug, and Jim realized just how tired and worn out he was. All around them, the town of Thorn was being torn down and even though he was a State Trooper, Jim wasn't able to do a thing. He stopped a few creatures.

Hell, he even killed a giant with Fred, but they were losing the town.

The town would be lost.

Jim looked over to the writing desk and drank a little of his coffee.

"I suppose," Jim said after a minute, "that the information we want is over there somewhere?"

"Yes," Fred answered, glancing at the desk. "It probably is."

They both drank their coffee.

Jim watched the fire eat away at the neatly stacked logs before finishing the mug and standing up. Fred did the same a moment later. They walked over to the desk together, and Fred leaned his weapon against the wall.

From what they could tell, the papers on the desk were letters from a professor in England to one Thomas Blood. Jim and Fred scanned through them.

"Here," Fred said, holding up a letter.

"*18th April 1866,*

"*My dear Captain Blood,*

"*I have received your letter and have, as promised, scoured the literature on the question that you asked regarding the binding of a tract of land. Usually, these bindings are made to protect a home and not, as you are seeking, to bind the faery folk in. I have read of only one instance of such a use, and that is in your own state of New Hampshire, though the records do not tell me who or why or when such an event occurred.*

"*With that being said, sir, I have located the name of a book with purports to offer up the applicable information. The title of this book is Iussitut Ligatis Pedibus Mediocris. The book was published anonymously in the last years of the last century, and there are many who believe it is simply a satirical endeavor. There are few, if any, copies to be found for sale.*

"*If you wish to purchase the book, please let me know and I will put out a request for further information. Until that time, sir, I have been pleased to assist you, and I do hope to hear from you again.*

"*Sincerely Yours,*

"*Professor Archibald E. H. Wellington.*"

Fred put the letter down and pointed at the pile of books.

There, on the top, was a small leather bound book with gold lettering stamped into it: *Iussitut Ligatis Pedibus Mediocris.*

"Can you read Latin?" Jim asked, looking at Fred.

Grimly, Fred nodded. "As a matter of fact, Jim, I can."

With the fire crackling behind them, Fred reached out and picked up the book.

* * *

Chapter 23: Fred O'Dierno and the Book

It had been a long time since Fred O'Dierno had read any Latin other than those found on school mottos and for military units, but he hadn't forgotten what the Brothers of the Sacred Heart had taught him nearly fifty years earlier. It just took a few minutes to get back into the groove of it.

He sat on the bed, the M14 on his lap and the book in his hands. Jim lay stretched out on the rugs in front of the hearth, passed out from the stresses of the past few days. Fred understood that completely.

Fred turned his attention to the book in his hands and looked at the chapter on clearing the area to be bound.

"It is best if only the faery folk are in the area which you are to bind together. Any men, women, and especially children who are caught there will be at the utter mercy of the faery folk. These people, like the faeries, shall be unable to slip free of the bound area."

"Anything?" Jim asked.

Fred looked up at the younger man who had sat up and was rubbing his eyes. "Yes," Fred said, "yes."

"Anything good?"

"That really does depend on our definition of good," Fred sighed, closing the book. He rubbed the back of his head and sighed.

"Well," Jim said, "what's our definition of good then?"

"Our definition of good is that for us to establish the ring around the lands is going to definitely be a possibility."

"What are the negatives on that one?"

"A few," Fred said grimly. "We'll need to have at least seven signers, and it's very specific about that, but we'll need seven people to agree to take up the signing of the contract to bind the lands and keep them protected. That means that you and I have to find five other living individuals to sign the contract. I don't know if there are going to be five people left in the town of Thorne by the time that we get out of here."

Jim nodded his agreement.

"Okay," Jim said, "what about our definition of bad?"

"One of those seven signers is going to need to be inside the ring that'll be set up around the lands," Fred said. "They need to be inside in order to finish the last of the ritual to close the ring up."

"How is that going to be bad?" Jim asked.

"Because once the ring is set up," Fred said, "then anyone in the ring at the time of the final casting will be bound within. That's why it's so effective against the faery folk. The original ring was far from the town's original few roads. And as the town expanded, the ring's distance grew shorter and shorter until it was literally just the Blood lands that the faery folk were bound in. From what I read, it helped that the older families patrolled the original ring. The faery folk couldn't get out, but they sure as hell could be seen.

"The elder families, you see," Fred continued, "didn't want anyone entering the ring and putting themselves at risk, or seeing a giant or a goblin and putting the word out that something strange was living on the Blood lands. That's why the elder families patrolled. They kept the faery folk away from the edges so that no one would see them, and made sure the townspeople knew that no trespassing was permitted.

"But," Fred sighed, "If we can get those seven signers and a new barrier put up, we should be okay. We'll need to patrol the damn thing just like the elder families did. But once the barrier is up, it should work. It'll piss the little bastards off, since they live just about forever. It means that they can't get out."

"But whoever finishes the casting will be trapped as well?" Jim asked.

Fred nodded.

"With a bunch of pissed off faery folk."

Again Fred nodded.

"Wow," Jim said, "that really does suck."

"Yes," Fred agreed. "Here's another part that's a little disagreeable for most folks. The binding is only good so long as there are direct blood descendants in the town of Thorne *and* the ring remains unbroken."

"This was why Hollis was so concerned about the breaking of the contract."

"Yes."

"So," Jim said, "we need to find seven willing participants to sign a contract stating that they and their descendants are never going to move away from Thorn."

"Correct."

"One of them is going to have to be on the inside of the ring and risk almost certain death. And more than likely an unpleasant death."

"Correct."

"And if the ring is broken, like with a development, then the whole deal is going to essentially be null and void anyway."

"Correct."

"Yeah," Jim said, shaking his head, "this is pretty much a miserable situation."

"That too," Fred sighed, "would be correct."

Chapter 24: Brian Ricard and Gilson Road

Brian sat on the hood of his cruiser and looked down the length of Gilson Road, one of the few roads that traveled from Monson into Thorne. At seven o'clock in the morning, someone attempting to get home to Thorne by way of Gilson had discovered that the road was blocked.

For all intents and purposes, it looked as though someone had scraped up an acre of old growth trees and thrown them across the road. In fact, as far as Brian could see through the trees, there was deadfall and the like forming a barrier that curved off to either side.

Downed electrical wires skidded and surged across the pavement. Miraculously, they had ignited nothing in their whip-like passage from one side of the road to the next. The lines were part of the grid that connected Monson, Hollis, Brookline, Pepperell, and Tyngsborough with Thorne. Understandably, the electric company was nervous to cut power to those sections. Granted, there weren't a lot of residents, but schools, businesses, and farms would all be shut down for an unpredictable amount of time.

New Englanders could understand a power outage after a thunderstorm. They would deal with a power outage after a heavy wind, and, well, a snow storm was a guaranteed loss of electricity.

However, they would not abide a loss of power for no apparent reason whatsoever. Those people unfortunate enough to be trapped within the curious circle which had been made around Thorne, well, they would simply have to remain where they were until the electric company got everything up and running properly.

A few calls had come in on the state's 911 line, but they hadn't made any sense to the State troopers in the area. More than a few of them had joked over the radio about a gas leak somewhere being responsible for the callers' odd comments and descriptions.

Brian knew that the calls weren't jokes, though.

People were calling in giants, goblins, hell, somebody had even called in a troll, and all Brian could think of was Matthew running around the house after having watched the first Harry Potter movie yelling, "There's a troll in the dungeon!"

This wasn't the movies, though.

Brian took his hat off, checked the brim for the twentieth time, and put the hat back on his head. He looked at the barrier. He didn't have to trick his eyes anymore. He could easily see the goblins guarding the barrier.

"They're afraid to come out," a voice said suddenly from Brian's right.

"Jesus!" Brian yelled, nearly sliding off the hood with the way he reacted. With his heart thundering in his chest, he looked over and saw a young, pale boy standing by the car. The boy wore a black suit, the back of it torn up the middle. The boy smiled at Brian.

Brian gave a nervous smile back. "What are you doing out here?"

The boy looked at him, confused.

Brian put on his policeman voice. "Shouldn't you be at school?"

"I'm dead," the boy said simply, still smiling as he turned his attention to the barrier once more, "and even if I weren't, I would be old enough to be your grandfather."

The policeman's tone died in Brian's throat.

"What's going on here?" Brian managed to ask after a minute.

"Too much," the boy said sadly.

"What do you mean?" Brian asked.

"We've had to erect a barrier around the town of Thorne," the boy explained, "that doesn't keep them in, but it makes them cautious."

"Who?" Brian asked, shaking his head. "I mean, I saw some things earlier, but I don't know what they were."

"Goblins," the boy said simply. "The faery folk have had a long time to think about how they've been ill-used. From what we can tell, many of them are actually working together. The goblins, as you can see, are at the barrier. Further in, the giants are preparing to storm a section of the barrier that they think is the weakest, and somewhere, we're not sure where exactly, we can hear the hounds of the hunt."

"Oh," Brian said. He really couldn't think of anything else to say.

The little boy was next to him for a minute before asking, "Since you're a sheriff, do you know Trooper Jim Petrov?"

"I do," Brian said, suddenly worried. "Is something wrong?"

"No," the boy said. "Nothing's wrong. He's inside of the barrier. I think that he'll be fine. He's with a man named Fred."

"Fred?" Brian asked.

"Yes, Fred," the boy nodded.

Brian thought about that for a moment, and then he smiled. "Mr. O'Dierno, I had him for history in high school. He's a good man."

"Yes," the boy agreed. "They both are. I hope they can save you."

Chapter 25: John Kenyon and the Little Red School House

John had the longest driveway on Indian Rock Road. It stretched for almost a quarter of a mile up into his land. Yes, it was a pain in the ass to plow in the winter, but the seclusion was well worth it. Few political supporters found their way to his door. This was an exceptionally good thing since New Hampshire served as the first in the nation for the presidential primary.

Too much political grandstanding and stumping as far as he was concerned.

John climbed into his beat-up pickup, started the engine and started driving down the long driveway. Faintly, he could smell smoke. It wasn't the good, sweet smoke of autumn and winter.

This was the smell of a house fire.

John stepped on the gas and sped up to the end of the driveway.

Looking left, he saw one of the new houses that had been built a few years earlier. It was burning brightly in the morning sun. Looking over to his right, he saw a car racing towards him.

It had once been a Lexus, although the grille was smashed, and the headlights as well.

And a giant was chasing it -- a great, blonde-haired thing perhaps ten feet in height and grinning from ear to ear. The Giant was having a hell of a good time, the ground shaking as it kept after the car, although it was evidently not trying to catch it.

As the Lexus drove by, something screeching in the bearings, John saw a frantic woman behind the wheel. Packed into the car were children of all ages crying.

When the giant started to pass by, John put his foot down hard on the accelerator and blasted out of his driveway, smashing fully into the giant.

The seatbelt stopped John from bouncing his head off of the steering wheel as the truck came to a sudden stop. The giant collapsed as its left knee buckled in the wrong way, howling with pain. John tried to back up the truck, but he heard only the grinding of gears and smelled the sickly sweet scent of anti-freeze.

The truck was dead.

John left his keys in the ignition and unbuckled his seatbelt. He forced open the door and took off running down Indian Rock Road towards Hollis, New Hampshire. He needed to get out. That thing looked like a secret government project gone wrong.

As John ran up the road, the Giant rose slightly. By the time John reached the top, he could see down the road where the town line was. There was a barrier there -- a great mess of trees that blocked the road and spread out into the forest on either side.

The Lexus was there, parked at a haphazard angle in front of the little red schoolhouse. The children were running to the school house door where one boy, of perhaps ten or eleven, was desperately trying to unlock the door. The woman, who had driven them, was standing behind the last child looking out. She had an extremely large handgun.

Finally, the boy got the door open, and the children flooded into the school house. The woman followed slowly, looking left and right and then stumbling.

An arrow was lodged deep in her left thigh.

There was another in her right arm.

They were small arrows, John saw as he got closer, but they were arrows nonetheless.

A third arrow zipped in the air and drove into the unknown woman's head.

She collapsed just as John reached the school door. He whipped the door closed behind him as he heard what could only be an arrow striking the building where he had been just a moment before.

John turned around and saw seven children in the room. All of them were young. Not one could have been older than the boy who had opened the door. John glanced around the room at the tall windows. Locking the door behind him, John hurried to the windows, making sure to stay on one side or the other as he drew the blinds. Then he looked to the children, who in turn were looking at him in complete silence.

"Can anyone tell me what's going on?" John asked.

The key boy raised his hand.

"Yes," John said.

"Fairy tales are killing people."

One of the little boys started to cry quietly.

If John hadn't rammed a giant with his pickup, he would have laughed at the boy, but he didn't.

"Were you trying to leave?" John asked.

The boy nodded. "Weren't you?"

"No," John said, shaking his head, "I was just trying to get to work, although that doesn't exactly seem like it's going to happen today."

He looked at the children and forced a smile. "Why don't all of you go ahead and sit down on the floor. You can even lie down if you want to. Someone will come to help us soon, I know that."

A few of the children smiled at him, and all of them sat down.

John walked back to the door and sat on its right side. He crossed his legs Indian-style and adjusted his glasses. God only knew if someone was actually going to be able to come and help them, but he wasn't going to say that and freak them all out.

A gentle knock came at the door.

"Hello in there," a soft, feminine voice said, her voice carrying a gentle Irish accent.

John waited just a moment before saying, "Hello out there."

"We've come to negotiate with you, man," she said pleasantly.

"Negotiate?" Paul asked. "I don't have anything to negotiate with."

"Yes, we want to negotiate," she said. "For the children, you see."

John laughed and shook his head. "Oh. Well, you see, that's not an option. Not an option at all."

"We've simple enough terms," she continued.

"I don't need to hear your terms," John said. "I'm not negotiating with you about the children."

"Oh but you already are, man," she said sweetly. "As I said. We have simple enough terms. Your life for the children."

John sat and smiled at the children who were staring at him in horror and shock.

"No," John said to her. "No. My life is nothing."

"True," she said, her voice carrying a sad note. "But I'll say this for you, there's not many of your kind who would offer up their life to save the lives of children they don't know. I'm sorry that we'll have to kill you."

A moment later, the windows and the door blew inwards, and small, armored creatures came rushing in. All five were slim, with narrow faces and long brown and dark green hair. Their armor shined, and each of them carried an ax.

The children screamed, huddling together as John launched himself to his feet. Two of the creatures came at him, and he managed to avoid the swing of the first ax, but the second caught him in the stomach. He folded over the weapon, gasping as he reached out and caught the thing by the neck. He started to throttle the creature, the thing's bright green eyes growing larger as John squeezed.

Then there was another one screaming at him in some language, breaking his fingers to get them off of the thing's neck.

Next, one blow and then another slammed into his back, driving him to the floor. John watched his blood collect in dark pools around him. He raised his head and saw the children being carried out by the things when John realized that he couldn't hear anything.

He pushed himself to his knees and grabbed one of the creatures passing him. It yelled in surprise, turning on him with the ax. John managed to catch the weapon as it swung down towards him, but another creature had appeared. Even as John wrenched the ax free, the second creature brought its ax crashing down.

John lay on the floor, his face in his own blood. One of his feet twitched spasmodically, and he watched his blood slip away.

Chapter 26: Gerald and the Draugr

Gerald Greene had a scanner -- one that he had purchased off of the Dark Net so he could monitor the police. He didn't want to be caught completely unaware when the police eventually came for him.

He knew someone somewhere would talk.

They always did.

He had listened to the scanner all night. He knew that there were fires burning uncontrollably in Thorne. He knew that there were lines down and the state was arguing with the electric company about getting everything back up and running.

He had heard that there was some sort of barrier around the town. A sheriff from Monson had called in two roads that were blocked, and one of the Hollis PD had done the same.

Essentially, Gerald was trapped in his home, which he didn't mind. He had everything he could want. He was, if necessary, completely ready to live off of the grid. He had solar panels, backup batteries, freeze-dried food --the whole deal. Everything.

Bring on the end of the world. Gerald Greene was ready for it.

Except, he had left his laptop in his car. Gerald had moved it earlier that morning to let his roommate drive out for work.

That meant Gerald was going to have to go out to the car and get it. Going out to the car would require him to get off of the couch, use the bathroom, get dressed in somewhat acceptable clothing, and walk the twenty yards to his car. He didn't want to do it, but he knew that he had to do it. If it really was the end of the world, or just a major cluster for some reason, then he wanted to make sure that no one stole his laptop.

It held too much incriminating evidence. There were several police departments that wouldn't be too happy to know how much he knew, and not only about daily operations and such, but interpersonal issues as well.

Oh no, he needed to get that laptop.

Grumbling to himself, Gerald got up off of the couch and wandered into the bathroom where he relieved himself. He washed his hands, went into his small bedroom, and got dressed in his usual fare -- sweats and sneakers. Grabbing his keys, he headed towards the side door.

When he stepped outside, he felt the cool air and smiled. Gerald, being as big as he was, had a distinct dislike for heat. Autumn in New Hampshire was a blessing, and being able to sleep with the windows open until February was fantastic.

Gerald paused.

The street was abnormally silent.

He looked around and saw that there were a few people out, walking in a sort of daze as if they weren't quite there. They looked like extras in a mass casualty exercise for some tyrannical police force like the LAPD or the NYPD.

Funny, Gerald thought. I don't remember hearing anything about a mass casualty exercise. Shrugging he went to the car. He unlocked the passenger door and bent over to pick up his laptop, which he had hidden under a large, stained white towel. Straightening up, he winced at the pain in his back, tucked the laptop between his large arm and larger breast, and closed the door.

Turning around, he found himself confronted by one of the mass casualty actors.

The man looked spectacular. The torn flesh hanging from the man's face looked so realistic that Gerald had to turn away. The man stared at Gerald with dull eyes that set Gerald's teeth on edge. Something was wrong.

Gerald eased his way around the man, and the man turned to watch Gerald hurriedly walk to the side door, but there were more mass casualty actors between him and the door.

In his path stood trio of teenagers, one of whom had a terrible injury, the lower portion of his right arm having been cut off at the elbow.

All of it looked too real.

"Excuse me," Gerald said, "but I need to get inside of my home."

The three looked at him.

Movement caught his eye, and he turned his head slightly, just enough to see more of the mass casualties appearing on the road, coming out of open doors in his small suburban neighborhood. Gerald looked back to the teenagers and licked his lips nervously. He took a step back and screamed as he bumped into something. Turning around he realized that it was the first man that he'd seen.

The man was staring at him.

What is going on here? Gerald thought, twisting around. He took a few steps away, and all four of the mass casualty actors took a step towards him.

Am I in a movie and no one told me? Seriously, he thought backing towards his car. What is going here?

He turned once more to go to his car and found more of the actors around the car. They were all silent. None of them speaking. All of them staring. Each movement they made was rough as if they were marionettes controlled by a poorly trained puppeteer.

"They're interesting to watch, aren't they?" a voice asked from off to the side.

Gerald looked over and saw a small creature sitting on a tree branch. It looked like a miniature woman, her face pulled backward to form an elongated skull. Her eyes were wide and dark blue, the entirety of the orb colored and pulling his gaze back to them. Her hair was short and spiked, a dark brown that was nearly black. She was incredibly thin, almost sickly so, and she smiled a wicked smile at Gerald, her blazing white teeth flashing at him.

"What?" Gerald asked.

"The draugr," she said. "The walking dead. For that's what they are. Dead and walking. Walking and dead." She smiled.

"Zombies?" Gerald asked, twisting around. Seriously, he thought, am I high? Is there a gas leak somewhere?

She looked at him, confused. "I don't know the word, but they're more troublesome than anything else. Although they have been known to frighten people to death."

Gerald stood against his car as the draugr pressed closer to him.

"Yes," she chuckled, "they can be so frightening."

Gerald fumbled for the door handle on the car but couldn't find it, at least not before the walking dead were on him, arms reaching out and cold, freezing dead hands grasping him. The cold bit through his clothes and his heart started pounding erratically in his chest.

His breath came in great, terrible racks, his whole frame shaking as he squeezed his eyes closed.

Gerald's heart stopped as a hand reached out and cupped his chin.

Chapter 27: Jim and Fred and Walking Back

Jim checked the laces on his boots one more time and straightened up.

Fred was at the door, waiting quietly.

Both of the men had enjoyed another cup of coffee. They left the fire burning.

"Ready?" Fred asked.

"Ready," Jim answered, holding the key in his left hand and the Colt in his right.

Fred nodded and opened the door.

They stepped out into afternoon light, and Jim quickly closed and locked the door. He put the key in his pocket and moved up to stand beside Fred.

"I'll lead," Fred said. The older man started walking along the thin trail that led back the way from which they had come. The forest was silent, disturbingly so, and there was the distinct feeling that they were being watched, which, Jim realized, they probably were.

Fred set a steady pace that moved them along as the autumn sun rose and reached its zenith before they found the place from where they had started the day before. Neither Ambrose nor Hollis Blood were there. Fred continued on though, not stopping, and that was fine with Jim.

The air stank of smoke and fire. Faintly, Jim could hear the sound of trees crashing down. Soon, the Blood house appeared in the confines of the forest in front of them. There was no sign of anyone either living or dead around the home. Jim could only imagine what was going on in what remained of Thorne.

When they reached the house, Fred said, "Let's stop for a bit, Jim."

Jim nodded and went to the porch, climbing the stairs tiredly. His stomach grumbled loudly, and Fred chuckled.

"Mine, too," Fred said, trying the doorknob. It turned easily, and Jim followed the man into the quiet house. There was no ambient electrical noise. The power had been lost, and more than likely, that had been recent.

They walked to the kitchen and prowled around for a few minutes, digging out dry goods and getting water from the tap. Evidently, the well ran on its own source of power -- something Jim was exceptionally happy about.

With several boxes of crackers, a pair of knives, some peanut butter and a few glasses of water, the two men sat down at the table. Fred leaned his rifle against the table, and Jim put the Colt on it, the barrel pointed at the sink instead of himself or Fred. Silently they started eating, doing so quickly.

Thorne was waiting for them and whatever survivors were still around.

"Where do you think we should look?" Jim asked after taking a long drink of water.

"Town Hall," Fred said simply. "That'll be the most likely place. They may not be able to fight back, but the place is stocked and ready for a hard winter. People would figure that it would be the best place to hole up -- wait for the cavalry to arrive."

Jim chuckled.

"What?" Fred asked.

"Cavalry," Jim said, shaking his head. "Maybe we should find a couple of donkeys to ride in on."

Fred chuckled as well. "Yes, that would be appropriate for Thorne, wouldn't it?"

The front door to the house opened, and both men grabbed their weapons.

Ghosts didn't need to open doors.

Fred dropped to one knee and brought his rifle up to his shoulder.

Jim stood behind the man, the Colt up and pointed, held firmly in both hands.

A shape came stumbling towards them.

A young woman came into view, a baby swaddled and held to her breast with one arm. She was bloodied and pale. Her red hair was torn in some places, having been ripped from her head. In her free hand, she held a large meat cleaver, the kitchen tool stained dark with blood.

When her tired eyes focused on Jim and Fred, she came to a stop and brought the cleaver up, angling her body so that the child was protected.

"We're not faeries," Jim said gently, holstering his Colt. Fred stood up, pointing his rifle at the ceiling.

"Neither am I," she said in a raspy voice. Her eyes flicked around the kitchen and stopped on the food at the table.

"Come on," Jim said.

"Yes, there's plenty here," Fred added.

The woman came forward, then staggered to the table. Jim and Fred each caught one of her arms and helped her to sit down. The baby against her breast was sleeping peacefully, although the child's red hair was splattered with dark drops of blood. The woman let the meat cleaver fall to the floor and Fred sat down across from her, putting peanut butter on crackers for her as Jim filled a glass of water and put it down in front of her.

"Thank you," she whispered, taking a drink of water. "Thank you."

The baby grumbled but didn't wake up.

The woman continued to eat. She finished dozens of crackers and possibly half of the jar of peanut butter before she stopped.

Jim handed her a cloth napkin from on the counter, and she smiled at him, wiping her mouth. "Thank you both so much," she said after a minute. She looked down at her baby and kissed the top of the child's head.

"You're welcome," Jim said.

"I didn't think that anyone else was still around," she said. "Everywhere I went, there were dead people, houses burning, and damned faeries everywhere I looked."

Jim looked over at Fred.

"You know that they're faeries?" Fred asked.

She nodded angrily. "My mother was fresh off the boat from Ireland. I cut my teeth on the old faery tales. None of this garbage passed off on kids today. No, I knew what was going on as soon as I saw the faeries. I just didn't think that we would have any here, especially not in Thorne. The town's not exactly a Mecca for Irish Americans."

"True," Fred chuckled, "very true."

"Did that work for you?" Jim asked, nodding towards the cleaver on the table.

"Yes," she said grimly. "I was surprised. It's not an old iron weapon."

"Where did you get it?" Fred asked.

"It was in the house when we bought it," she answered. "My husband and I bought this old farmhouse up on Washington Road. When we were cleaning out the kitchen, I found this in the back of the pantry. I thought it would be an interesting thing to hang over the counter. It was the first thing that came to hand when a goblin came in."

"Is your husband alive?" Jim asked gently.

The woman nodded. "He's on a business trip to New York City this week. It's just Gwen and myself."

"I'm Jim," Jim said, extending his hand. As she shook it, he added, "State Trooper, New Hampshire State Police."

"Rose Mary," she said, letting go of Jim's hand and reaching over to shake Fred's.

"Fred O'Dierno," Fred said, "plain old retiree."

"How did you find this place?" Jim asked.

"A little boy," Rose Mary said. "He was down on the construction site, and he told me that there was a house up the road a bit. He told me that I'd be able to find food here and that I'd be safe.

"What about you?" she asked. "How do you two know about it?"

"That," Fred said, "is a fairly long story."

Chapter 28: Thorne Town Hall, 11:00 AM

Philip Delyani stood at a second story window in the town administrator's small office. From his vantage point, he could look down on the scene below and nothing he saw made him feel any better about life -- or rekindle his personal faith in God, for that matter.

Sighing, he pulled his deer rifle in closer to his shoulder, lined up his shot, and carefully squeezed off a round.

The sound of the weapon in the confines of the room was loud and painful, even through the shooter's ear protection that he snuggly wore.

"Shit," he said simply. He lowered his weapon, ejected the spent brass and put a fresh cartridge in before slipping on the safety and taking off his ear protection.

"Anything?" Chris asked.

"Nope," Philip said. "Same as usual. Beautiful head shot and the thing falls to the ground, gets up, shakes its ass at me and keeps on dancing." He put his rifle down on the desk and picked up the board that had been over that part of the window before and replaced it. Philip held it in place as Chris stepped up with a cordless drill and secured the board once more to the window's casing.

With Chris carrying the drill and Philip carrying his rifle, the two men started back towards the basement, where the few survivors were staying as safe as they could from the bizarre storm raging just beyond the walls of the town hall.

Philip waved to the two men standing guard at the front door. Each had a wooden baseball bat, which was proving only slightly more effective than Philip's rifle. The two men waved back, and Philip led Chris into the basement. Nearly fifty people huddled in the basement. Someone had gone into the storage closets and broken out the blankets and the Red Cross emergency cots as well as some of the tastier freeze-dried foods.

Although, Philip couldn't tell if that was an oxymoronic statement or not.

Reverend Schwerdt of the local Lutheran Church had brought a hand cranked radio. The Reverend, along with several others, was listening to the broadcast intensely.

"And now our update regarding the problem in Thorne, New Hampshire. Authorities are stating that a microburst seemed to have touched down at some point in the night and damaged power lines, causing delays in getting to the sites of multiple fires. There is no word as to when this situation might be resolved."

"Microburst my ass," Chris grumbled.

"I know," Philip said. "Keep it low, though."

Chris simply nodded and walked with Philip into the large kitchen. The heat and hot water of the kitchen were simple. They were attached to the main circuit panel and that, in turn, was connected to the generator outside of the town hall, kept safe in its own covering.

How long that might continue to last though, well, John really had no idea.

Some blessed saint had started a large, twelve-cup coffee maker.

"Do you want a cup?" Philip asked.

"No thanks," Chris said, shaking his head. "I'm all set right now."

Philip nodded, took down a paper cup, and poured himself some coffee.

Always appreciate the little things, he reminded himself.

He leaned against the countertop, enjoyed the coffee, and closed his eyes, listening to nothing whatsoever.

"Philip!" someone yelled.

Never lasts, Philip thought.

"What is it?" Chris called back.

"We've got someone trying to make it to us."

"Wave'em off," Philip yelled, straightening up and walking towards the doorway. "They'll never make it."

"We've tried," Jeff Parker said, coming down the stairs. "We've tried. I even threw a couple of bottles at him."

"Where's he coming from?" Philip asked, heading back up the stairs towards the front door.

"South end," Jeff said.

By peering through a slit between two boards, Philip could see down the road. A stumbling man was weaving between the faery folk. Many of the faery folk laughed at the man, and he could see why.

The stumbling man was naked and nearly dead. It wouldn't matter if the man reached them or not. He was a dead man walking, but he didn't know that.

Even as Philip watched, a faery tripped the man and he went sprawling, getting back to his feet a moment later. Fresh cuts and scrapes on both knees and hands bled freely, but the man paid them no heed.

"Free the door, please, Chris," Philip said softly. Chris moved forward, undid the screws connecting the board binding the door to the frame. "Jeff, door, please. About an inch should be fine."

Jeff stepped forward, pushing the door open just the slightest bit.

Getting down into a kneeling position Philip brought his rifle up and switched the safety off. He watched the man for a moment, watched the way he stumbled and could almost hear the man's labored breathing from where he knelt in the town hall. Philip took long, slow breaths, and started to take up second pressure on the trigger.

A moment later, the rifle shot cracked out into the air, and the naked man collapsed, his brains blown out in the morning sky.

Philip ejected the casing, put in a fresh round, and straightened up.

"Chris," he said.

"Yes?" Chris asked.

"Please secure the door."

With the sound of the drill in the background Philip returned to the kitchen to drink his coffee.

Chapter 29: Hearing the Hounds, 11:00 AM, the Blood Lands

Evan brought up the rear of his group of friends as they walked their way out of the Blood lands and back towards town. Ever since the town had grabbed a good deal of the property, people had been going in to hunt, and Evan had been one of them. It'd been a while since he'd shot at anything other than people.

Getting fresh venison would be fantastic.

"Would" was the key word, though.

They'd seen nothing and they had been out there since four in the morning, set up on a well-trod game trail. They had seen absolutely nothing. The line stopped, and Paul looked back, a confused expression on his face. He tilted his head slightly, trying to listen better.

Then, Evan heard it too.

The sound of dogs barking. Yipping at one another.

The sound continued to grow louder, and the men started looking at each other, frightened. Evan simply made sure that the safety was off his rifle and that a round was still chambered.

I don't care if it's a poodle or a Great Dane, Evan thought, it's going to die.

A heartbeat later, the dogs were howling, bursting into their line of sight.

The dogs were huge -- monstrous creatures that Evan had never seen before. They were like pit-bulls the size of Great Danes.

Evan brought the rifle up to his shoulder, squeezed off a shot and smiled as the beast he had hit stumbled, but his smile was erased as the beast got back to its feet and started to run with his siblings once more. Evan turned to tell his friends to run, but they had already done so.

Miserable bastards, Evan thought. With that thought in his mind, he started running northwest, and he kept running, for the hounds seemed to be searching for them all. A short time later, he found a good place to hide and did so, pulling ferns down onto him and settling in just under a thick, rotted dead tree. It definitely wasn't the best there, but it would certainly work for his needs. A few hours of silence and he'd be ready to go.

For two hours, Evan kept silent, watching and listening.

His breathing was slow and regular, his finger loose on the trigger. He had the area in front of him covered from his position, and he knew that he'd have to wait until later before he could move out and head towards town.

So he waited.

And he waited.

Then he heard the noise of the dogs -- a combination of barking and baying that set his teeth on edge and urged him to flee as quickly as he could. However, Evan steeled himself and kept his cool, concentrating on his breathing, watching and waiting.

In three minutes, the dogs were there, fifty yards out. They were chasing Mitch.

Mitch staggered and bounced off of a tree. His face was bloody, eyes wide and white in a mask of blood. Mitch bore an expression of pure fear.

The dogs howled joyfully.

They were going to eat Mitch alive.

Evan started to squeeze the trigger --

Mitch fell, and the dogs were upon him.

Evan sighed, relaxed his finger. He watched the dogs devour Mitch, whose agonized screams lasted only a few minutes.

And Evan waited.

Chapter 30: Erin and Klaus at the Bus Stop

Erin Harper had a delayed schedule at the Hollis Co-Operational High School, which meant that she could do her online studying for her advanced college classes in the morning. Unfortunately, her little Volkswagen bug had died over the summer, and they hadn't been able to fix it, so now she had to take a bus to school.

She waited at the end of her driveway, which was shared with her family and the Totenbuch family. The Totenbuch family had a son named Klaus, who also had a delayed schedule. He was a quiet, unassuming boy with round glasses and shaggy black hair. He looked like a tall, German version of Harry Potter, although without the magical ability -- or any social skills.

Klaus would say hello to her, and goodbye, but only if Erin initiated it. He always wore a white button down shirt, some sort of vest since the cold weather had started, and jeans with Dr. Martens. His backpack was large and seemed to pull at him. He also stank of pipe tobacco.

Erin knew that he didn't smoke -- Klaus's father never seemed to stop smoking, however -- but evidently no one in the house noticed the smell.

Other kids at school did, and Klaus had been christened with the unfortunate nickname of 'The Stinky German,' a name which did nothing for him, especially since he was a live action role-player too. No, the boy was a total reject on all levels of the social spectrum at the high school.

The bus, though, was supposed to pick them up at 10:30 AM.

The bus was late.

Erin couldn't call her mother because she worked in Nashua and left the house at five-thirty each morning. Since her parents were divorced, her father lived in Manchester and saw her on the weekends. That is, he did when he could be bothered to. Klaus' parents had left for Germany for a week. Erin had learned that from her mother, who had been asked by Christiana, Klaus's mother, to check up on him while they were away.

Thankfully, Erin didn't have to accompany her mother on the excursions over to Deutschland.

"The bus isn't coming," Klaus said suddenly, breaking the silence.

Erin took one of her ear buds out of her ear. "It doesn't seem like it."

"Something's wrong," Klaus said.

"How do you know?" she asked, trying to keep the dismissal out of her voice.

Klaus pointed, and Erin looked.

Towards the center of town, the air was filled with gray and black smoke.

"We should go inside," Klaus said. "This will not end for us well if we do not."

"Okay," Erin said, nodding, "yeah. Let me call my mom." She took her phone out of her back pocket and went to dial. There were no bars on the phone.

That was ridiculous, Thorne had one of the best reception areas out there. Erin tried to dial, but she didn't even get a dial tone on the phone. Frowning, she put the phone away.

"It is as I thought," Klaus nodded. "You are welcome to come to my home, Fraulein Harper."

She smiled, thinking, oh hell no. "No thanks," Erin said aloud, "but thank you."

He gave her a short bow. "If you need me, please call. I believe that your mother has our telephone number."

Erin smiled again and turned away, putting the ear bud back in. Taylor Swift came in full volume, and Erin walked up the driveway, not focused on anything other than getting back inside. She could do more homework on her college classes, which was great, but she was going to miss out on her Latin and history classes, both of which were taught by Dr. Kendall, and which she actually enjoyed.

Plus, she was going to have to try and call her mother from the landline and hope that it was working. She had little faith in the landline and couldn't figure out why her mother always wanted one in the house. The cell phone was usually far more reliable than the landline, especially in the winter when the snow would knock the telephone and power lines down every couple of weeks.

Erin turned up the walkway and then around the side of the house. She took her key out, unlocked the door, and went inside. She dumped her bag on the kitchen table and walked over to the old yellow rotary phone attached to the wall by the fridge. Why her mother kept the thing around, Erin would never understand. It was annoying to use and sounded terrible when it rang.

She picked up the heavy receiver and held it to her ear.

Nothing. No dial tone.

Sighing, she hung up the phone and noticed suddenly that the fridge was quiet. She pulled the fridge door open and saw that it was dark inside.

Fantastic, she sighed, quickly closing the door.

No service, no landline, no power, she thought. This is going to be a great day at home, she thought sarcastically.

Groaning, she walked back to her bag, dug out, *The Moon is Down* by John Steinbeck, which Dr. Kendall was having them read for history, and made her way into the den. The room was gently lit by the sun, and Erin settled in on the couch. The cat came in, meowed at her once, and then he wandered away.

Erin shook her head and opened the book to the first page.

Something banged heavily on the front door, scaring Erin into a sitting position.

Maybe it's Klaus, she thought.

Something banged on the door again, and she could see the door shake in its frame.

That's not Klaus.

Slowly, she got off of the couch and started walking out of the room, when the glass in the back door shattered. Erin screamed, and pleased laughter came out of the kitchen. The front door came crashing in, knocked free of its hinges. The steel door bounced off of the wall and slammed onto the floor.

They came in, one from the front door's gaping doorway, the other from the kitchen.

They were tall and thin, faces vaguely human in shape, but their eyes looked like cats' eyes. They wore loose robes with mottled colors of the forest, greens and browns that would have hidden them easily. Their hair was long and brown, twigs and leaves woven into them. The skin of these things looked like the bark of trees, and as they laughed, Erin saw that their mouths were barren of both teeth and tongues.

Erin held back a scream and stepped back towards the wall. She kept her head -- which she suddenly realized was one of Kipling's key points in the poem 'If' -- and wondered if she had time to unlock the window that she was approaching. Before she could formulate an idea as to whether or not she could, a shape came hurtling into the house through the front doorway.

It was Klaus.

Klaus with a sword.

A *sword*.

It was an old sword, and Klaus used it like it was a part of him, as cheesy as it sounded. He was phenomenal with the weapon, and within seconds, Klaus had literally hacked the thing to pieces, a black ichor spraying out of the thing's body, arms cut off and falling to floor before the thing itself did.

Then he and the second thing fell upon each other, Klaus roaring, literally roaring at the thing in German.

The thing stumbled back, howling in German and raising its arms up in defense, an action which only served to allow Klaus to cut off the left arm before driving the point of the sword home into the thing's breast.

Silently it died, and Klaus used his free hand to push it off.

"KommenSie, Fraulein Harper," Klaus said, looking at her and extending his hand. "We need to leave. Quickly. There are more coming. We must leave."

"What are they?" Erin asked, hurrying over to him and taking his hand.

"Holzmenschen," Klaus said, leading her to the front door. "Wood people. They have no love for us. We must find a place of safety."

"Town hall," Erin said, "if we can make it there. There's food. Water. Lots of supplies."

"Sehr gut, sehr gut," Klaus said nodding. Still holding hands they raced down the walkway to the driveway.

"Not the road," Erin said, pulling him towards a slim path that stretched off to the right before the driveway intersected with the road. "We'll keep to the woods. They're probably setting the houses on fire."

Klaus nodded his agreement, letting go of her hand so she could lead the way.

"Where did you find the sword?" she asked over her shoulder.

"My father's collection," Klaus answered.

"What does your father do?" Erin asked. She had known at one point but could no longer remember.

"He is a professor of classics," Klaus answered. "He collects them as well."

"What type of sword is it?"

"A gladius," Klaus replied.

"Gladius? Isn't that a Latin word?"

"It is," Klaus said. "And this is a Roman sword. One of those which helped to conquer the world."

"I can believe that," Erin said. "I can certainly believe that."

She led them deeper into the woods.

Chapter 31: At the Blood House

"It's getting close to the time," Morgan said, and nearly scared Jim to death. "Sorry," Morgan said.

"That's alright," Jim said, trying to catch his breath. Fred came in from the kitchen with a trio of coffee mugs.

"Hello Morgan," Fred said.

"Hello Fred," Morgan said cheerfully, sitting down on the stairs that led up to the second floor.

Fred handed Jim a cup of coffee, which he gratefully accepted. The older man then walked over to where Rose Mary sat, asleep in a wing-back chair with Gwen sleeping in her arms. The cleaver was on the coffee table in front of her. Fred set the mug down on a coaster in front of the woman before going to a second wing-back chair and sitting down in it. His rifle lay on the floor beside him.

The smell of the coffee alone awakened Rose Mary, and she looked around, confused for a moment. She blinked, stifled a yawn, and smiled at the coffee. With a skill only mothers seemed to have, she reached out with one hand, cradled Gwen and brought the coffee to her own lips.

The young mother sighed audibly and nodded her thanks to Fred.

"It's you!" she said cheerfully to Morgan.

He smiled, "It is."

Neither Jim nor Fred had had a chance to tell her the story of Morgan.

"Did the faeries tear your jacket?" she asked before blowing on her coffee.

"No," Morgan laughed. "This is my funeral jacket."

She took a sip of coffee, and it seemed to take a moment for that statement to sink in. When it did, her eyes widened, and she returned the coffee mug to the table. "Your funeral jacket?"

Morgan nodded happily.

"You're dead, aren't you?"

There was no question implied. Merely a stated fact.

Again Morgan nodded happily.

"And are there more ghosts out there?" she asked him.

"Seventy-one others," he nodded.

"Of course there are," she sighed.

"But," Morgan said, looking over to Jim, "we're getting close to the time."

"What time?" Jim asked him.

"When the faery folk will be able to leave. We're hoping that they won't be able to," Morgan continued, "that you'll have found something in that room."

"We did," Fred said. "We need five more people willing to sign a new contract in order to bind the faery folk within a ring."

"And of the seven of us," Jim said, "one of them will have to cast the rest of the spell from within the ring."

"But that will bind them in as well," Morgan said, looking upset. "They'd be stuck here with the faery folk."

"Yes," Jim said. "That's exactly what would happen."

"What are you talking about?" Rose Mary asked.

Fred briefly explained to her what it was that he had read in the book by the pool.

"Oh," she said afterward. "Wow."

Jim nodded.

"I'll sign," she said after a moment.

"You will?" Morgan asked her.

Rose Mary nodded. "Of course I will. I don't want this to spread."

"That's three of us," Fred said. He reached into his shirt pocket and took out a small folded piece of paper. "I wrote this down earlier," he said, handing it to Jim.

Opening the paper, Jim saw that it was a nearly identical copy of the Blood Contract. Where the names of the town's founders should have been, however, there was only Fred's. Glancing around, Jim saw a pen on the coffee table. He reached out, took up the pen, and put the paper on the table, signing it. He looked at Rose Mary, and she nodded, taking the pen from him and leaning over slightly to sign it.

"Now we only need four more," Jim said, holding the paper out to Fred.

Fred shook his head. "I lose everything. You hold onto it."

"You should go to the town hall," Morgan said as Jim folded the paper in his own pocket. "There are people there. But a great many of the faery folk are gathering around there as well."

Jim stood up and adjusted the knife and the sword on the gun belt. Fear and worry gnawed at him. The trip to the center of town wouldn't be more than two miles. But it would be two miles of faery-infested land that they would have to survive. He bent over and picked up his coffee from a side-table. Quietly, he finished it off and looked at Fred and Rose Mary. "Ready?"

Fred nodded, picking up his rifle and standing up.

"I just need a blanket to wrap Gwen in," Rose Mary said, standing as well, "then I'll be ready to go."

Chapter 32: 4:00 PM, Evan in the Forest

Evan carefully brought himself to a sitting position, and then he sat still for five minutes, listening intensely to the forest.

He heard nothing, which was both relaxing and frightening, the feelings twisting him into a knot. He hadn't heard the dogs for hours, and he liked it that way. However, Evan also feared that it meant the dogs had gotten to his friends.

With a slow, deliberate pace, he picked off the ferns before easing himself up to his feet. His body ached from the forced stillness, but it was better to be sore than to be dead, of that Evan was certain. He flipped the safety on for the rifle and slung it over his shoulder. There's no use carrying a weapon that wouldn't do anything against the dogs that had been, pardon the pun, hounding him and his friends.

The air had gotten remarkably colder, and he had to think about something other than the cold. He knew that he was only ten minutes out from Blood Road, but that wouldn't make the trip into town any easier, or any less stressful for that matter.

No, Evan just wanted to get it done and get into town -- preferably before anything tried to eat him.

Evan stepped off smoothly and quietly, moving quickly through the darkening forest. He soon found himself along the edge of the woods and scenes of destruction. Seemingly no house was left untouched, some of them still burning. There were bodies on the ground, on manicured lawns and on asphalt roads. Cars and trucks were stopped, some still idling long after their occupants had fled or been butchered. Some of the vehicles were on their sides, half crushed, as if some giant thing had battered them around.

The sights were terrible, but Evan kept to the tree line, skirting through backyards and thin stretches of open ground that would send his heart racing.

And as he neared Main Street, he could hear them.

The dogs were howling, as were other things. He crept up slowly, having reached the last house before the pharmacy, and he managed to find a position where he could look upon Thorne's downtown and Town Hall.

Evan grit his teeth at the horror laid out before him.

Chapter 33: Town Hall, 4:30 PM

Philip sat by himself on the first floor, looking out the town clerk's window.

The scene on Main Street was horrifying.

A large fire had been built in front of the firehouse, and a spit had been set up over the fire itself. A giant, perhaps ten or twelve feet high, was slowly turning the spit while a trio of gutted men was bound to it. A female giant, her great breasts swinging with each step, stood close to the fire, mashing up something in a dumpster.

Off to the left, in front of Franceur's Bakery, goblins had gathered, dozens of them. They were keeping themselves entertained by eating baked goods as well as banging on a variety of musical instruments taken from Alex's Music Shop, and let's not forget, by forcing a couple of people to dance endlessly.

Crying started on the far right and Philip shifted his gaze to there.

Faeries were crossing the road. Small things, no bigger than three feet. They were wearing bright clothing that they had found somewhere -- probably in the same houses from where they had stolen the children.

The faeries were carrying children, some under a year, some as old as four or five. Some of the children cried, but others simply walked along, stunned.

The wind shifted slightly, carrying to him the smell of the flesh roasting on the spit. He turned his head away and closed his eyes for a moment. The flesh smelled exactly like a pot roast slowly basting in its own juices.

With a sigh, Philip stood up and left the room, his stomach rumbling. He needed to find something to eat.

Walking down into the basement he looked around at the few survivors. Chris stood with the reverend, several women of various ages whom he didn't know, and the two men who had been guarding the door earlier. But guarding the door didn't seem to matter anymore. They all knew that the faeries out there would certainly come in whenever they wanted to.

Philip stopped by the boxes of bottled water and took one out, cracking open the top and taking a long drink. He'd have a meal shortly, but for now, just the water.

Although, he'd be happy with a few shots of vodka as well.

He went to an ancient-looking wooden folding chair and sat down, grunting as he settled in, taking another drink. The sun would be setting in another hour, hour and a half at max.

Night would come.

What would the faery folk do?

What would he do? Could they slip away, all of them at once? Would they have to leave singly or in pairs? Would someone panic and give the whole thing away? Would someone refuse to leave, try to stay behind and wait it out?

Philip shook his head.

It was one of those days when he really wished he'd made it to work at the garage so he could wrench on cars all day.

But that wouldn't have stopped what had happened -- probably wouldn't even have slowed it down.

Chris came over, took out a chair, and sat down across from him. "How are you doing?"

Philip looked at the man. Chris was a psychiatrist or therapist or life coach or something in Nashua and Philip really didn't want any therapy or New Age bullshit, but hell, he could at least talk to the man.

"Tired," Philip said honestly. "Worried too. I'm worried about what's going to happen tonight."

"Tonight?" Chris asked.

"Tonight," Philip said again, nodding. "We need to try and figure out what we're going to be doing. Are we staying? Are we going?"

"Why tonight?" Chris asked, genuinely confused.

"Too easy for them not to. Perfect opportunity for them to take care of us."

"Oh," Chris said, rubbing the back of his neck nervously. "Oh."

Philip finished the bottle of water, crushed it loudly and put the cap back on. "I'll be right back," he said, standing up.

"What's that smell out there?" Chris asked. "It's driving me crazy. Smells, like they're, have a great big pot roast. I'm so damned hungry for a roast now."

"Well," Philip said, turning away from Chris, "don't eat that one."

"Why not?"

"Because that's the smell of people being cooked for someone's dinner."

Chapter 34: Erin and Klaus in the Pharmacy, 4:30 PM

Erin led Klaus around the back of the pharmacy, when suddenly, he stopped her.

She stopped immediately, looking back at him. Silently, he pointed forward, and Erin saw, in the growing shadows, the shape of a man lying down on the ground. Beyond him were Main Street and a nightmare that numbed her mind.

Then Klaus's lips were close to her ear.

"My friend," he said in a low whisper, "we mustn't be afraid. That man waits and so shall we, with him. We must crawl, though, yes?"

Erin nodded, and together the two of them got on the ground and started crawling towards the stranger. She nearly jumped as Klaus put his hand on her behind and pressed down. It took her a moment to realize that she was moving with her rear nearly straight up in the air, and that he wasn't beinginappropriate.

She forced her hips to hug the earth. By the time they reached the shadow where the man was, the stranger had rolled silently to his side.

"Does that work?" the man whispered, nodding to the sword that Klaus carried.

"Ja," Klaus whispered back.

"He's great with it," Erin said softly.

The stranger smiled. "Good. Name's Evan."

"Erin," Erin said, "and this is Klaus."

"Sind SieDeutschlander?" Evan asked.

Klaus grinned, a great big grin and he nodded happily at Evan.

"Are we waiting for night?" Erin asked.

"That's what I wanted to do," Evan stated, "but I'm not sure now."

"No?"

Evan shook his head. "The situation is looking worse. I'm wondering if someone might try to make a run for it. I think that tonight is going to be bad for whoever is in there."

"Yes," Klaus said. "They will move in tonight. They'll try to flush the people within out. They will send in the giants, around three sides, you see, and force the people out through the front and into the arms of the goblins. The people will feel that they have a better chance against the goblins. It will be a rationale of fear."

Evan nodded. "That sounds dead on."

"So," Erin said, looking out once more, "we'll need to open a path through the goblins for them."

"Das istsehr gut, Fraulein Harper," Klaus said. "Very good indeed."

"Well," Evan said, focusing on the street again, "let's try to think of what we can do."

Then the three of them grew silent, listening to the horror of the street beyond and thinking of what it was they might be able to do.

Chapter 35: Jim, Fred, Rose Mary, and Gwen at the Cottage

"Look," Fred said softly, pointing across the street at the pharmacy.

Jim caught the faintest hint of two people moving, and then they disappeared, dropping down and out of sight.

"Definitely not faeries," Rose Mary said. Gwen was against Rose Mary's chest, swaddled and held in place by a blanket. Gwen had a pacifier in her mouth and was looking up happily at her mother.

"No," Jim agreed. "Definitely not."

The four of them were in the front yard of a modest little New England cottage, sitting behind a row of short hedges with an angled view of downtown. They could see the town hall, Main Street, and the pharmacy. The goblins had stopped tormenting the people they had captured, and Jim wasn't sure if the people were dead or simply exhausted.

The giants, in turn, were fighting over their rather disturbing rotisserie, and the sound of bones tearing out of joints actually reached the front yard. Regardless of the sound, the smell was disturbingly good.

Jim tried not to think about it.

"What do you think we should do?" Rose Mary asked.

"We should wait," Fred said, his eyes never leaving Main Street. "Those three by the pharmacy have the right idea."

"Three?" Jim asked, looking over to Fred.

Fred nodded. "I saw the glint of light off of gun metal. There's no mistaking it. Someone else is there, and the three of them have decided to wait."

"For what?" Rose Mary asked.

"The people in the town hall to make a decision," Fred answered.

"I didn't see any people," she said.

Neither did I, Jim thought, looking back at the building. Boards had been nailed up over the inside of the windows, and he suspected that the front door was barred from the inside, but that hadn't meant that anyone was still alive in there.

"Every once in a while a shape will pass by a window, specifically the one to the left of the door on the first floor," Fred said. "Add to that the smoke that occasionally comes out of the vent pipe on the roof. That means someone's in there to monitor the heat. And, finally, the door's closed. The few houses that we saw where the faeries had been through, well, they hadn't bothered to close the doors."

"True," Jim said, shaking his head. "Hell, I'm supposed to be a cop, and I didn't notice any of that."

"So," Rose Mary said, "what do you think they're waiting for?"

"I think the people in town hall are waiting for night. They'll think it's the best time to make a run for it. Pretty sure, though," Fred continued, "that the faeries will think that it's a grand time to force them out. Either way, something'll happen -- more than likely right after night falls."

"Well," Jim sighed, looking at the darkening sky, "we shouldn't have to wait too long then."

Chapter 36: Brian and the Dead

Brian zipped up and walked back to his cruiser. Around him, the Blood dead were gathering, dozens of them of all ages. They stood in silence, adding a deep chill to the air as the sun continued its descent.

"It won't be long now," Hollis Blood said. He stood by the cruiser, hands folded neatly over the top of his cane.

"No?" Brian asked.

"No," Hollis answered. "When they come, we will take care of the exit."

Brian looked over at him, wanting to ask what the hell the ghost meant, but then he didn't. The man was dead. Brian was literally speaking with a dead man. He could cut himself some slack in regards to questioning current events.

"We need you to be prepared to help those that come through," Hollis continued. "Morgan told us that the key is to have another contract drawn up. We will have to protect them while it is written and signed. Will you be able to help, Sheriff Ricard?"

"Yes," Brian said simply. He looked out at the barricade of trees. "Yes."

Chapter 37: Night Falls

With the coming of night, all hell broke loose in Thorne, New Hampshire.

***

"You have to leave," Philip said to those gathered around him in the basement of the town hall. He tried to keep the anger out of his voice, but as he buttoned his flannel jacket, his shaking hands betrayed him.

"We can't," the Reverend said. "We just can't. It's safe here. The National Guard will be here soon."

"Soon isn't going to come soon enough for us," Philip snapped, his patience gone. "Anyone who stays here is going to die."

Philip looked at Chris, but the man looked away.

"Jesus Christ," Philip spat, "listen --"

And the walls of town hall started shaking, deep, terrible voices howled, and Philip knew that the giants were attacking the building, seeking a way in.

"We have to go!" he screamed.

The rest of them, though, fled further back into the basement.

Philip dropped his rifle and ran up the stairs towards the front door.

There was nothing banging at the front door, and he knew instantly that it was a trap, all of it. He didn't have a choice, though.

He had no choice at all.

Bending down, he picked up the drill and started taking the screws out of the barrier.

***

"It's happening," Erin said softly.

Klaus and Evan rolled over and looked out at Main Street.

The giants ran, the ground shaking as they surrounded the sides and the back of the house. The great beasts started hammering away at the walls, yelling so loudly that Erin's ears hurt. Goblins gathered around the front of town hall, forming a semicircle around the stairs.

"It is time," Klaus said, standing up, rolling his shoulders back and forth, and swinging the sword with ease. "It is time."

The German teenager looked down at them both. "Be ready to help whoever comes out, yes?"

Erin nodded.

"Sehr gut," Klaus said, and he started walking towards the goblins, the noise of his approach drowned out by the howling of the giants.

***

"Someone's moving," Fred said.

Jim and Rose Mary looked out. In the light of the bonfire, they saw someone approaching the gathered goblins from behind as the door to Town Hall opened. A howl of joy rose up from the goblins, and they started jumping up and down happily.

"Move down to the pharmacy," Fred said, and it was an order, polite but firm. The man stretched out on the ground, his clips on a clean patch of grass, his rifle aimed downtown.

Jim and Rose Mary got to their feet, Rose Mary double checking that Gwen was still sleeping, and then they hurried towards the pharmacy as a goblin shrieked.

***

Klaus killed the first two goblins with ease, the beasts never seeing him as he managed to strike from behind, yet as the door to the town hall opened and a man came leaping down the stairs, Klaus's third target turned at the wrong moment. Klaus killed the thing, but it was a messy kill, and the thing managed to shriek before dying, which alerted its foul brethren to Klaus's presence.

The goblins were shocked, their weapons sheathed or set aside in anticipation of grabbing hold of those who would escape. Klaus killed the next pair neatly and efficiently.

Then the goblins near him turned on him completely, even as the others surged towards the sole runner.

A rifle cracked in the distance, and Klaus was surprised but pleased when a goblin's chest burst open directly in front of him. The goblins faced towards the sound of the gunshot as more broke through the violence of the night, and Klaus raised his blade and began killing once more.

***

Philip didn't know who was shooting, or how the shooter's rifle was effective against the damn things, but he didn't care.

He was running straight towards the teenager with the sword.

The kid was sprayed with dark blood, and he looked absolutely thrilled to be butchering the little goblin bastards, and Philip thought that was a great thing.

But it was time to leave.

"Run!" Philip screamed. "I'm the only one!"

The teenager gave him a curt nod, finished off another goblin, then turned and started sprinting towards the pharmacy. The tempo of the rifle fire increased, but Philip didn't look back.

He simply raced after the teen.

***

"Hey," Jim said as he and Rose Mary approached the pharmacy from the back. A teenage girl and a man in his twenties whipped around to face them.

"Who the hell is shooting?" the young man asked. "And how is the weapon working? My rifle didn't do anything."

"Too long to tell," Jim said, drawing the knife and stepping close to hand it to him. "You can use this?"

"Definitely," the young man said, shucking his rifle and dropping it.

Jim turned to the teenager. "Don't suppose you can use a sword can you?"

She grinned, "Three years of fencing."

A moment later, she had the sword in her hand and was checking the swing. "Beautiful," she sighed happily.

"Run!" someone yelled from the street, "I'm the only one!"

Jim and the others turned to look. The man with the sword killed another goblin, then turned and started running, another man close behind him. Fred's rifle fire increased, his accuracy remaining the same.

There was only the slightest of pauses, and then the firing resumed.

Jim drew his pistol as the teenager with the sword and the other man went running by, and started firing at the goblins racing after them.

Each shot found its mark and as goblins closed in, the others started fighting as well. Someone started yelling in German, and beyond the pharmacy, the windows of the town hall started shattering as boards fell to the pavement.

Within moments it was done.

Jim, panting, looked around. No one was hurt, but the ground was littered with goblin corpses.

"The giants," the boy with the sword said with a German accent, "they will be after us soon."

"Not what I'm worried about, kid," the man with the knife said, "the dogs."

Jim was about to ask what dogs when he heard them, great barking things whose cries echoed off of the buildings.

Then Morgan was there, his pale face serious.

"Run," he said, "run for Gilson Road."

***

Fred heard the dogs and held his fire. He had twenty rounds left overall. Not nearly as much as he'd like, but enough to do some more damage.

He could still remember the drill instructors on Parris Island hammering home the importance of shooting properly, and Fred did remember. Every shot he fired was a killing shot, but now he had to wait for the dogs.

The others wouldn't be able to outrun the dogs, especially not dogs of a supernatural nature.

So he waited.

The wait wasn't long.

Half a dozen of the creatures came streaming out from between the music shop and an insurance office. They were followed by what looked like an English gentleman riding on the back of a disturbingly large goat.

Fred ignored the frightening absurdity of it all, sighted on the galloping Englishman and shot him out of the saddle. The goat peeled off, and as Fred had hoped, the dogs were ignorant of their master's death. Working from the rear of the pack, Fred killed four more, and as he was reloading, the last two dogs stopped, suddenly realizing that the rest of their pack was missing.

As the dogs trotted back to examine the dead, Fred killed them both.

Screams rose up from Town Hall as the giants broke through.

Fred stood, gathered the remainder of his ammunition and headed back the way he had come.

***

Brian watched in silent amazement as the ghosts disassembled the section of the barricade which covered Gilson Road.

"They'll be here soon," Hollis said from beside him.

"Who?"

"The survivors."

How many? Brian asked himself silently. And would Jim Petrov be among them? Would Scott?

Brian held no hope for either of them. He didn't know how anyone could survive if even a tenth of the phone calls had been true, but of course, they had to be true. He was standing here with the dead.

Soon, the ghosts had cleared the road, leaving open both lanes for the fleeing survivors.

Brian walked towards the opening and folded his arms across his chest and waited.

***

How any of them made that final run, Jim didn't think that he would ever know. How Rose Mary made the run, with Gwen crying against her chest and a meat cleaver in her hand, he would never know.

Soon, though, they were nearing the town line, and the barricade of trees had been moved. The blue flashing lights of a cruiser lit up the night, and Jim could make out the shape of a man.

Brian. Brian Ricard.

Brian was running towards them, helping Rose Mary to the cruiser while the rest of them stumbled into the shifting, twisting arc of illumination cast by the lights.

"We need four people to sign this," Jim gasped at Brian, pulling the folded contract out of his pocket.

Brian took a pen out of his pocket as he opened the page. A boy with a sword stood up, having heard Jim.

"Here," the teenager said, "I will sign."

Brian brought the paper and the pen to the boy as a teenage girl stepped up beside him. The boy moved slightly so the girl could read the paper as well, and then the boy and the girl each signed it in turn.

An unarmed man wearing a battered flannel jacket walked up, looked at the paper, and held his hand out wordlessly to the girl. She handed him the pen and as he signed, the last man, carrying a wicked-looking knife came up, accepted the pen from the other man and signed as well.

"Where's Fred?" Jim asked.

Brian looked over at him. "Who?"

"Fred?"

***

Fred stood near the pool, in front of the door, which was open. The key which he had stolen from Jim was in the lock, and Fred held the book that he had read only hours earlier.

A whisper came rippling through the forest and the dead boy Morgan was there.

"The last of them has signed," Morgan said.

Fred nodded, opened the book, and with the light of the stars he read: "*Et ego erudivieostevinctossic ego.*"

The world shifted and far beyond, in the center of Thorne, Fred heard the faeries scream out their outrage.

Morgan smiled at Fred, and Fred smiled at Morgan.

Closing the book, Fred turned and walked into the curious cave, removing the key from the lock and closing the door behind him.

Epilogue: One Year Later

Scientists were still trying to figure out what had happened to the town of Thorne. No one could understand what had caused trees to be uprooted and to form a strange barrier around the town. Some people had attempted to push the State and Federal governments to investigate, but both governments had refused. At least two independent investigative news teams had attempted to discover what had happened to the three hundred and forty-seven missing residents of Thorne.

Neither of the teams, which had slipped over the jersey barriers placed across the sole remaining road into Thorne, had been heard from again.

There were, of course, rumors of a government experiment gone wrong, which caused the death of the residents and poisoned the town, making it unfit for human inhabitation. Others believed that this was the case, and that the news teams were killed for trying to find out what had happened.

A State sanctioned search party went in after each team, yet nothing was found of the reporters and their crews. There was no secret memory card or tape found containing the reasons why -- no last video journals.

The news teams -- eight men and three women -- had simply vanished. Eventually, their cars were towed away.

Theirs were not the only cars, however.

Others came seeking the mystery behind the destruction and abandonment of Thorne. Some never returned, although others did make it into the town and came back. Those that did return said that their various electronic devices were rendered useless during their time in the mysterious circle of trees.

What they had seen in the town had changed them.

Few of the buildings were still standing, and on Main Street they found the remains of large bonfires and the gnawed and broken bones of people. They also reported that the trees lining Gilson Road had human skulls nailed to them.

Jim Petrov and the other five signers of the contract knew all of this. Jim and Evan and Philip had actually been the ones to nail the skulls to the trees. Rose Mary had built dozens of disrupters, which Erin and Klaus had placed in the barrier around the entire perimeter, each connected to a solar-powered battery. These simple devices ensured that no recording equipment or cell phones would work properly within the faery confinement area. None of the signers of the contract were responsible for the deaths, however.

The faeries took care of that.

On the one-year anniversary of their escape from Thorne, the six of them sat in Jim Petrov's new house on the edge of the perimeter on Gilson Road. Brian Ricard was there as well, having full knowledge as to what had occurred. All of them were gathered in Jim's den with after-dinner coffees, yet this wasn't a mere social gathering.

"Have you spoken with Fred?" Jim asked Klaus.

"Yes," the young man said. His voice still had a hint of a German accent. Klaus adjusted his arm slightly, Erin slipping in closer to him. "Erin and I spoke with him on Saturday. We made it all the way to the pool and found him. He was pleased that the note he had thrown over the barrier on the road had been found. Thus, we brought to him those things which he had requested, the books and ammunition."

"Good," Jim said. "What's the word with rumor control, Phil?"

Philip grinned. "Good. The garage is a great place to spread information. Lots of tourists have the bright idea of trying to go through Thorne. I dissuade most of them, but a few get through," he said, the grin fading. "Those I feel pretty bad about. I wish that I could get all of them to stop."

"I know," Jim said, nodding. "Try not to worry too much about it, Phil, we can't stop them all. Rose Mary, what about any new electronics? I know that you were looking for a way to shut down onboard computers for the newer cars."

"I'm still looking," she said, sighing. "The tech's out there, but the Feds have most of it watched. I've got feelers out, but I have to wait until someone contacts me."

"Evan?" Jim said, looking at the man.

"Still patrolling the perimeter at night," Evan said, stifling a yawn. "Every once in a while I'll get a goblin troop that comes a little too close, but a few rounds from the Colt usually settle that business. Most of them are too afraid to come to the barrier now. With Phil spreading the bad news about the barrier and the faery folk kept away from it, well," Evan grinned, "I think that we'll keep accidental sightings to a minimum."

"Good," Jim said. He looked over at Brian. "And politics?"

"Politics is politics," Brian said simply. "We were fortunate that the few descendants of the original signers have as much political pull as they do. Without them, we'd never have been able to shut the world out. As of last week, Senator Copp from Massachusetts managed to get Thorne designated a National site, and Governor Hall of New Hampshire is going to have Thorne listed as a permanent monument. Judge Coffin has also managed to deny the release of any information on Thorne by way of Homeland Security."

"So we're covered," Jim said, "all the way around for now."

"What about the giants?" Evan asked. "What's going on with them? I know that they're kept back by the barrier, but we don't need someone sneaking around the perimeter and spotting one."

"Don't worry too much about them," Jim said. He put his coffee down on the coffee table and stood up. He walked across the den to the bookcases lining the far wall. He moved a small clock and pressed a switch. As he pulled his arm back, the wall started sliding to the right.

"Fred's been busy," Jim said, smiling grimly, "very, very busy."

Revealed by the moving wall was a large trophy case made of dark mahogany and museum-quality glass. Warm lights spilled down from recesses in the ceiling upon six massive, roughly human-looking skulls which had been boiled white. The skulls of the giants stared emptily out from the case with their death's head grins, a bullet hole in the center of the head.

"Damn," Evan said softly as the others murmured, "I guess Fred really has been busy."

* * *

Bonus Scene Prologue: Darkness in New England

There is an old and seemingly eternal darkness that resides and infects New England. You can find it anywhere, tucked into the culverts of brooks, amongst the apple trees, and even in the clear and quiet glens of the forest.

Ancient in their ways, we are less than nothing to these things, and indeed at times we are nothing more than a convenient meal which has walked into their kitchen.

All we can do is take heed of those who know better, and caution our children to do the same.

Bonus Scene Chapter 1: Old Man Copp in the Orchard, 1976

"What the hell is wrong with these trees?" Peter asked.

Dan shrugged, backing the car onto the dirt drive that branched off of Farley Road. The sun was just beginning to set, the Ford's engine running rough at idle as Dan put it into park.

"Hey," Peter said, looking at Dan. "Those trees don't even have any apples on them."

"I know, I know," Dan said, pulling the latch for the trunk so that it popped open. "I'm telling you, though, the best apples in Cross are from the Blood family's orchard."

"I don't know," Peter said, looking at the barren, twisted trees lining the drive, "these trees look like shit, man. And that's not really getting my hopes up for any good apples."

"Shut up and get out of the damn car," Dan sighed. He left the car idling and the door open as he walked around to the back. Peter met him there, and they each pulled a surplus Army duffel bag out of the cluttered trunk.

"You ought to clean this," Peter said.

"You should shut up," Dan replied.

Peter shook his head. "So, just windfall?"

"Yup," Dan nodded. "I'll pick the fresh stuff. Just make sure you fill that bag. I want to get as much for hard cider as we can."

"Me too," Peter said.

Dan led the way into the orchard with Peter following. They passed by rows of truly ancient apple trees. The boughs were heavy with age and absent of fruit, each aged branch hanging low, caressing the grass with each breeze. Gnarled branches and twisted trunks took on sinister appearances as the sun set. Peter felt a growing sense of unease, as though the trees were watching him. He kept close to Dan as they moved further in.

The old trees were quickly replaced though with younger ones, and soon the sweet smell of McIntosh apples was filling the cool, autumn air. Most of these trees, Peter saw, had been picked bare, and the windfall had long since been gathered up early on in the season.

Dan, Peter noticed with relief, kept on a straight track as they walked deeper into what was easily the largest orchard that he'd ever been in.

"Hey, what about the Old Man?" Peter asked suddenly, glancing behind him.

"What? Old Man Copp?" Dan asked, looking back at Peter.

Peter nodded. "I heard he's a son of a bitch. That the Bloods pay him to run off anyone that even comes near to the orchard."

"Nothing to worry about," Dan grinned, turning his attention back to the trees. "Guy's like sixty or seventy, or something. Pretty sure he's not patrolling the orchard with a shotgun or anything. Besides, I don't think he's going to be too upset about a couple of bags of apples, so don't be such a bitch."

"I don't know, man," Peter said. "Some of the farmers in Massachusetts get pretty upset if you're caught stealing apples."

"New Hampshire isn't that uptight," Dan chuckled. "And besides, things are pretty low key in Thorne. I've been doing field work for the Gauthiers out on Ridge Road since sixty-five. Things are pretty mellow."

Peter looked back again over his shoulder. Something didn't feel right, no matter what Dan said.

Soon they passed a gap in the trees. There were large, dark holes in the earth where trees had once stood.

"Careful," Dan said, giving the holes a wide berth.

"Thanks."

They walked for a good five minutes, the sky getting darker when Peter stopped and said, "Dan."

"What?" Dan asked, turning around and stopping.

"Did you bring a flashlight?"

"Why would I need a --" Dan's voice trailed off as he looked up at the sky, swearing.

It was a moonless night, and it would be pitch black in the orchard.

"Yeah," Peter said.

"Don't sweat it," Dan said after a moment. "We'll have enough starlight to get back."

Dan set off again and with a shrug Peter followed. They walked for a few more minutes before coming to trees with fruit on the lower branches. Reaching up Dan plucked an apple and tossed it to Peter.

"Take a bite of that," Dan said, opening his duffel bag and putting it on the ground.

Peter caught the apple easily, giving it a quick wipe on his sweatshirt. He took a big bite and tasted the sweetest McIntosh he'd ever had. "Wow," he said as he chewed.

"Right?" Dan laughed, picking apples as quickly as he could.

"Damn right," Peter said. He finished the apple in a few bites, tossing the core into the distance and smacking his lips. Grinning at the taste which lingered on his tongue Peter opened his own bag and began gathering up windfall.

"Hey," Peter said after a minute.

"Yeah."

"Have you ever made Apple Jack before?"

"No. Don't think I've even had it," Dan answered.

"It's good," Peter said. "Takes a while to make it, though. It's got to sit for a long time."

"Yeah?"

"Yeah. I've had it, just never made it," Peter said. "Don't like waiting."

"Right." Dan moved to another nearby tree, dragging the nearly full bag with him. "How are you doing?"

"About there," Peter said.

"Me too."

"Maybe we can hit the Indian Leap on the way back into town?"

Dan laughed.

"What?" Peter asked, stuffing in the last apple and zipping up the bag.

"You."

"What about me?

Dan zipped up his bag. "You're sweet on the bartender."

"So?"

"Nothing," Dan grinned, "it's just funny to watch."

"Let's go," Peter snapped, picking up his bag.

"Don't get --"

A loud click cut Dan off.

Peter turned around slowly and saw an old man standing in the fading twilight. He held an obscenely large double-barrel shotgun, both of the hammer's cocked. In his lips, the old man held the stem of a straight briar pipe, smoking casually as he watched them.

"Boys," the old man said softly, "this ain't loaded with rock salt."

Peter looked nervously to Dan.

"Look," Dan said.

The old man shook his head, his long white beard twitching. "Don't really want to look at a couple of thieves."

"They're just apples," Dan said.

"They're just Hollis Blood's apples," the old man corrected.

"How about we just put the bags down, and we'll call it even?" Dan asked.

"Not quite," the old man said. "But you will put the bags down."

Peter and Dan dropped the bags simultaneously, the thuds ringing out loudly.

"Walk," the old man said.

"Which way?" Dan asked, his voice cracking.

"The way you came."

Peter's heart hammered in his chest as they walked, his skin crawling at the realization that there was a loaded shotgun pointed at his back. He had no doubt that the old man would use it. The old man might be in his sixties, but he didn't move or act like it. He'd crept right up on them, right through the orchard --

"Stop," the old man said.

Peter and Dan stopped instantly.

Looking around nervously Peter saw the trees bending in the wind -- Peter shook his head.

There is no wind, he thought. How the hell are they moving? He looked around and saw that he was standing by the holes they had passed earlier and that young apple trees were moving towards them.

The ground rippled like water, roots appearing and disappearing in the earth which frothed and rolled around the trees as they came steadily on. Peter felt his eyes widen, unable to look away from the sight of the moving trees. They were small, no fruit on their branches, just thin leaves.

"Get into a hole," the old man said.

"No way," Dan said, turning around.

One of the barrels of the shotgun seemed to explode, the muzzle flash lighting up the gathering trees.

Dan let out a scream, his right leg a bloody mess from the knee down as he fell to the grass. Keeping the shotgun trained on Peter the old man walked over to Dan and kicked him into the nearest hole, where he landed with a wheezing sob and a crash.

The old man turned his attention fully to Peter.

"In," he said.

Peter jumped into the nearest hole, which was almost six feet deep. The old man came to the edge and looked down. Dan's sobs were suddenly muffled, then silenced altogether. As Peter stood in the hole, he smelled the old man's pipe tobacco and apples. Peter wanted to ask what the hell was going on, but the old man's grim look and the dull sheen of the shotgun's barrels in the starlight kept him quiet.

Something rustled behind him, and Peter turned to see tree roots snaking out of the hole's earthen walls. Dirt started cascading down from the sides, quickly burying Peter up to his thighs as thicker, and longer roots appeared. Within a matter of moments, Peter could see one of the young apple trees as it pulled itself into the hole, earth and roots crashing onto him.

The weight was unbearable, blackness plummeting down around him. Peter struggled against it but found that he was trapped. While the dirt continued falling between the roots, Peter heard the old man.

"This is the best way to feed them, you know," the old man said. "The reason why Hollis' macs taste the best."

Peter heard the old man chuckle once before the dirt filled his ears, packing his mouth as he tried to scream.

Bonus Scene Chapter 2: Kayaking in Hassell Brook, 2010

"How far into New Hampshire do you think we are?" Ken asked, slowing his kayak down to glide beside Tim.

"A few miles at least. Maybe even five," Tim answered. The two of them kept a steady, leisurely pace, moving along with the current of the Nashua River. The banks were higher than usual, the water level low after such a dry summer. Fall wasn't looking to be any wetter. Birds and squirrels called out from the banks as Ken and Tim kept to the river's center, wary of trees and snags.

"Do you want to pull up soon?" Tim asked. "Figure out how far we are from Hassell Brook?"

"That sounds good," Ken said, scanning the banks for a good spot. "What time are we supposed to meet your cousin again?"

"Eleven o'clock," Tim answered. "She said to just give her a call, and she'd pick us up."

"Cool." Ken smiled at the scenery slipping past. The current was fast but not unmanageable. He and Tim had navigated worse. He kept his eyes open for a grassy spot to pull up. Everything was choked with swamp grasses and deadfall, though, and he didn't want a rough landing if he could help it.

"River's pretty quiet for a Saturday," Tim said.

"Well, it is a little cold today."

"Not that bad," Tim laughed. "You're out here."

"True," Ken grinned. "But soccer season's started, too."

"I keep forgetting," Tim said. "Both girls playing this year?"

"Yup," Ken nodded. "Brenda moved up to U-14, but Sam's still in U-12."

"Do they have games today?"

"Yeah," Ken said. "The ex is there this weekend. We split the games."

"Still tough?"

Ken nodded. "How are you and Melissa?"

Tim shrugged. "I think it's almost done. She's getting a little psychotic."

"How so?"

"Little things," Tim said. "I'll tell you more later. I think I found our spot," he said, pointing.

Ken looked and saw a narrow path through the swamp grass. The path of still water ran along to the bank where it widened into Hassell Brook, curled around a turn and vanished into the tree line.

"Does it look good?" Tim asked.

"That it does," Ken grinned. Dipping his oar into the water Ken guided the kayak into the path. Tim dropped into place behind him, the two of them moving cautiously forward. As they neared the mouth of the brook, Ken felt a slight current, and he smiled, pushing the oar a little deeper into the water.

The brook wound its way lazily into a forest, young trees growing on the banks, branches stiffening with the steady push of fall in the air. The leaves had already begun to change their colors, and as the wind blew a few of them drifted down to rest upon the surface of the water. The leaves drifted past Ken and Tim as they continued on, some of the leaves caught along the banks or made their way steadily towards the river.

Ken steered the kayak around a large branch and hooked to the left, where the young trees sharply and suddenly gave way to ancient oaks and elms. Giant weeping willows clung to the banks, the long branches moving gently with the breeze and rasping against the chain-link fence which crossed from bank to bank and disappeared into either side of the forest. A large 'No Trespassing' sign hung directly above the stream on the fence, and there was barely enough clearance for Ken to get under the fence without rolling the kayak.

He came to a stop, and Tim came up beside him.

"What do you think?" Ken asked.

"Hold on," Tim answered. He set his oar across his kayak, unzipped a pocket on his jacket and took a plastic bag with his phone in it out. Within a moment, he had the phone free of the bag, and he was pulling up his GPS. "Well," he said, "if we go about two hundred meters in it's only a quarter mile to Blackfoot Road in Thorne. I'm pretty sure that Anne can pick us up there."

"Sounds good to me," Ken said.

"Okay," Tim said. He secured his phone and put it away before taking up his oar again. "Lead the way, my friend."

Ken nodded and headed towards the fence. He kept to the left bank, where the fence was a little higher, and he bent low over the kayak, pulling himself ahead with careful strokes. Once he was clear, he paddled ahead to give Tim room to come through.

Around them, the forest sounded and felt different, as though it was older than they could know.

"This place is great," Tim said softly after a minute.

Ken could only nod his agreement. Taking a deep breath he sighed and said, "So, two hundred meters?"

"Yes, yes."

"Okay," Ken said. "Let's go."

The brook remained wide enough for them to paddle side by side. Just before they hit the two hundred meter mark, the brook took a sharp turn to the right, opening into a large pool dominated by a weeping willow. Shadows covered most of the pool, the sounds of fish hunting water bugs on the surface were loud in the stillness. Somewhere a turtle dropped noisily into the water as Ken and Tim steered the kayaks to a sandy patch of banking just beyond the weeping willow.

"Wow," Tim said as they climbed out of the kayaks, hauling them up onto the sand.

"I know," Ken said, looking around. "We need to remember this place," he said, looking over at Tim. "This would be a great place to camp."

Tim nodded.

"Want to --" a whimper cut Ken off.

Ken looked at Tim, who shook his head.

The whimper came again, followed by a splash.

Ken turned, trying to pinpoint the sound.

More splashing and a deep, sorrowful moan.

"I think it came from the tree," Tim said.

Ken nodded, cautiously walking along the banking towards the willow. The splashing took on an odd rhythm while the voice settled into a steady, plaintive cry. When he reached the willow, Ken pushed through the curtain of leaves and whip-like branches. The pool opened up even more around a cluster of water-worn boulders, and Ken's breath caught in his throat as Tim came through the willow's veil behind him.

Standing waist deep in the water was a pale woman. Her back was too thin, and she wore a faded gray dress, shapeless, torn and ragged. Thin, wispy hair hung in wet clumps to her back while stick-thin arms slammed something wet and limp against one of the boulders. The steady cry came from her, the sound pushing itself deep within Ken's chest.

Tim let out a low curse, and the woman heard him.

She turned slowly to face them. Her face was sunken, her eyes a pale white and her teeth a milky green. Her mouth hung slightly open, the cry steadily slipping out. She held her arms out in front of her, a soaking wet jacket clutched in each narrow hand.

"Jesus Christ," Tim said softly, "are those ours?"

Ken looked hard at the blue jacket in the woman's left hand and saw a tear. A small, inch-long tear he'd put in the jacket when they'd taken the kayaks off of the BMW earlier in the morning. Ken glanced down and saw that he was still wearing the jacket, the tear plain to see on the left arm.

"You have got to be kidding me," Ken whispered. His stomach twisted itself into a nasty little knot and bile rose to the back of his throat. "Tim," he said, not taking his eyes off of the woman, "we should probably get out of here."

Tim nodded, and the two of them started backing away. The woman turned back to the rocks, her cries becoming louder as she began slapping the jackets against the boulders once more. Passing through the branches Ken and Tim quickly turned back, walking hurriedly to the kayaks. The horrific noises of the woman convinced Ken that he hadn't imagined it. That and the pale, frightened expression on Tim's face.

"We need to get out of here," Ken said.

Tim only nodded his agreement.

Wordlessly the two of them climbed into their kayaks, quickly pushing off and moving with the current back towards the river. As they rounded the sharp turn which had opened to the pool, there was a loud crack, and Ken snapped his head up in time to see a great oak crashing towards them.

The tree smashed into both kayaks simultaneously, driving them under water and into the soft, sandy bed of the brook. Ken found himself trapped in the kayak, holding his breath as he tried to work his legs free. His face was just inches below the surface, and he could reach his wet hands into the crisp fall air to claw at the bark of the tree.

Growing frantic he looked around for Tim.

Tim sat limply in his kayak, head and hair moving gracefully with the current. Blackness edged Ken's vision, and his lungs screamed for air. He looked to the left for --

Ken screamed the last of his air into the cold water as the woman from the pool settled down on the brook's bed beside him. With an expression of great sympathy, she watched him take in great gulps of water, her long hands gently brushing the hair out of his eyes as she waited for him to drown.

Bonus Scene Chapter 3: Meeting the Baker, 2014

Joel put his truck into park and killed the lights before turning off the ignition. He stifled a yawn and stretched in the confines of the cab, looking at the horizon as dawn started to break. Unbuckling the seat-belt he opened the door and stepped out into the chill morning air, breathing in the deep scent of fall. The noises of the Chevy's engine cooling sounded loud in the morning's stillness.

Smiling, Joel took the keys to the back of the truck, tucking them into a small niche he'd made just for that purpose. From the bed of the truck, he picked up his hiking pack and pulled it on. He adjusted the straps, clipping them into place before he put on his knit cap and leather gloves. Flexing his fingers to loosen the leather he walked over to his toolbox and took out a pair of heavy-duty wirecutters.

With the tool in hand, he left the side of his truck and walked to the chain-link fence which ran the length of woods that he'd heard about from friends down in Massachusetts. The fence, which was surprisingly well kept, surrounded the hundreds of acres of old-growth forest in New Hampshire. Joel had heard that the land belonged to a family, although he didn't know them and didn't care to either.

As far as he was concerned, Joel thought as he stepped up to the fence, no state, and definitely no single family, should be allowed to keep that much of the environment locked away for themselves. It was disgusting, and a prime example as to how the rich had come so far from understanding anyone other than themselves.

Locking the old growth forest away was a crime against the people. And not only should it be illegal, but the people who did such things should be prosecuted for locking away the beauty of Mother Nature the way that they did.

Shaking his head and sighing Joel ignored the 'Warning' and 'No Trespassing' signs bolted to the fence. Whistling he started cutting the fencing along one of the posts, starting at the bottom. In a few minutes, he had the fence cut three-quarters of the way up, and he rolled it back before putting the cutters back in the truck. With a spring in his step Joel walked back to the fence, slipped through without the pack catching, and soon was standing up, rolling the fencing back into place.

Just to be on the safe side Joel took a couple of black zipties out of his back pocket and secured the fencing back to the post in a couple of places. He'd be able to cut through them easily when he was done with his weekend.

Taking a deep breath Joel double checked the straps on his pack, making sure that they were just right. Satisfied he glanced at the trees and saw a small game trail between a pair of elms. Nodding to himself Joel headed out along the trail.

His long legs moved him quickly along the path, which became wider the deeper he moved into the forest. The undergrowth fell away, the forest dark and barely touched by the rising sun. Boulders appeared, and birdsong filled the air. Acorns occasionally settled down, thrown by squirrels from massive oaks. The feeling of serenity and the soft sounds of nature settled over Joel, and he felt great as he moved, the burdens and worries of life falling away as he walked.

Soon Joel passed through a small clearing, the tree's branches forming a thick canopy above. Joel didn't stop, though. He wanted to be further in before setting up camp for the night.

Joel hiked for several more hours before finding the perfect site.

The forest fell away from a small brook, the water whispering around a trio of boulders nearly as tall as the trees. The earth around the near side of the brook was beaten down, and the remains of a tremendous bonfire occupied the center. Amongst the ashes were the charred and broken bits of deer bones.

The site was old and looked as though it hadn't been used in months. Safe enough for a single night.

Jack shucked his pack and gloves, rubbing his shoulders. The sun shined brightly above him, moving steadily towards noon. Leaving his gear near the ashes, Joel started wandering around the brook and boulders. He picked up deadfall and branches, carrying several loads to his gear and stacking them neatly. Within a short time, he had a good supply stocked. Turning his attention to his pack, Joel took out his one-man tent.

He put the tent up and sat down beside it. Pulling his pack close, Joel took out his food, some water and his copy of *The Woman in Black*. Joel tore open an energy bar and ate it slowly, washing every few bites down with some water. When he finished the bar he tucked the wrapper into his pack before stretching out on the ground. He read slowly, eventually taking off his cap and sweatshirt, balling them together to serve as a pillow while the day continued to warm up.

By the time, four o'clock rolled around a definite chill had settled into the air. Putting the book down, and the sweatshirt and cap back on, Joel started preparing the wood for the fire. Disgusted he pushed the deer bones to the edges of the pit, shaking his head at the deep gouge marks in the bone.

Savages, he thought. Whoever the hell did this, that's all they are. Just savages. And evidently he wasn't the only one who had ignored the fence. Joel just wished that it hadn't been hunters. The deer had enough problems with the coyotes coming down from Canada and the mountain lions creeping back up through the Berkshires.

Joel pushed those thoughts out of his mind and kindled the fire. He smiled as the flames grew, creeping up around the pyramid of wood. Heat slipped around him as evening came on steadily. Joel took out his dinner, a prepackaged vegetarian meal, and added wood to the fire, building it up. It wasn't nearly as large as the remains of the old fire, but it was bigger than most he'd built. He was deep in the forest, far from the road he'd parked his truck off of.

By the time the sun set, Joel had finished both his meal and the book. He rolled a joint, lit it off of a branch from the fire, and lay back, watching as the stars started populating the sky. His eyes grew tired from the heat of the fire and the grass. With one last pull, he flicked the roach into the flames and let the smoke out slowly.

Too bad Karen couldn't make this one, he thought with a sigh, closing his eyes.

The earth trembled slightly beneath him, and Joel's eyes opened.

The earth trembled again.

An earthquake? he thought, sitting up. He glanced nervously at the giant trees and stones bathed in flickering light.

Again the tremble, and something in the forest fell.

Joel tried to shake away his self-induced haze, forcing himself to think as another tremble rippled through.

That's no earthquake, he thought. That's got a rhythm.

He climbed to his feet. What the hell is that?

And his answer stepped out of the forest by the brook and came to a stop.

A giant stood opposite him, a man probably a dozen feet tall standing naked in the firelight. He carried a massive wooden cudgel, and coarse, dark hair covered his body. Black hair hung in dreadlocks to his chest and a braided beard reached nearly to his waist. His face was broad, the features thick and he broke into a smile when he saw Joel, his nostrils flaring.

The giant took a step forward, a tremor rippling through the ground.

Joel took a nervous step back, glancing left to right.

The giant chuckled.

"There is nowhere to run, little one," the giant said, his voice deep. "This is Jack's parcel of Blood's Forest, and none knows it better than Jack."

Jack advanced another step, and Joel retreated one as well. Jack swung his cudgel casually. "Which way shall you run, hmm, little one?" he asked. "Back the way you came? Or shall you run right, to the Goblins' Keep?"

Joel licked his lips nervously, his heart beating faster.

"Is it left then, little one, behind the Stones of Coffin's Stand to Blood's dark orchard?" Jack raised an eyebrow. "Or perhaps you shall run by me, into the forest's dark heart where things worse than old Jack await the sweet taste of man?"

"What are you?" Joel blurted out.

"What am I?" Jack chuckled. "I'm Jack, a humble baker."

"A baker?" Joel asked, his blood pounding in his ears.

"Yes, yes. A baker," Jack grinned. "You've not heard the rhyme then, little one?"

Joel shook his head, confused.

Jack laughed, broad yellow teeth catching the firelight. "I'm sure that you have, and you've just forgotten." In a singsong voice Jack called out softly, "Be he live or be he dead, I'll grind his bones to make my bread."

Joel stiffened the full horror of the situation rushing through him.

"See there, little one," Jack winked. "Now you remember. Old Jack's a baker."

Joel bolted.

He ran towards the giant, leaping the brook and cutting hard to the right to stay --

The cudgel caught him in the stomach. Joel folded over it, the breath rushing out of him as ribs cracked. He felt himself flying backward and in a moment he splashed into the brook. He struggled to stand, but Jack was there, plucking him out of the water. Pain ripped through Joel as Jack carried him to the fire. The giant dropped his cudgel to the ground. He started to casually peel Joel's clothes off of him.

Pain wracked Joel's body, but he couldn't move. He was terrified.

Jack made a neat pile of Joel's sopping wet clothes, and then he stood and held Joel at arm's length, examining him. Joel was limp in Jack's grasp, unable to bring himself to do anything.

Jack nodded and set Joel down, turning his attention to the fire. Pain spiked in Joel's ribs, and he shuddered, the pain jarring his mind out of shock.

Jack turned away to throw more wood on the fire, and Joel scrambled to his feet and ran.

He sprinted past the giant, aiming himself towards the game trail which he'd followed in the morning. In spite of the pain in his ribs, he rushed towards the tree line.

And something struck him in the back of the knee, sending him rolling onto the hard forest floor. He struggled to get up, but Jack was there. The giant picked him up easily off of the ground, shaking his head as he brushed Joel off with a huge, calloused hand.

"Don't run, little one," Jack said, carrying Joel gently to the roaring fire. "You will only die tired."

* * *

FREE Bonus Novel!

Wow, we hope you enjoyed this book as much as we did writing it! If you enjoyed the book, please leave a review. Your reviews inspire us to continue writing about the world of spooky and untold horrors!

Don't forget to download your free bonus novel! Sign up for the mailing list below to download your full length horror novel, get free short stories, and receive future discounts: www.ScareStreet.com

See you in the shadows,
Team Scare Street

CPSIA information can be obtained
at www.ICGtesting.com
Printed in the USA
LVHW010932011122
732058LV00022B/462